THE  ENCYCLOPEDIA OF

SEVENTIES MUSIC

COLIN LARKIN

IN ASSOCIATION WITH MUZE INC.

Dedicated To Randy California

First published in Great Britain in 1997 by
VIRGIN BOOKS
an imprint of Virgin Publishing Ltd
332 Ladbroke Grove, London W10 5AH

A catalogue record for this book is available from the British Library

ISBN 0 7535 0154 6

Written, edited and produced by
MUZE UK Ltd
to whom all editorial enquiries should be sent
Iron Bridge House, 3 Bridge Approach, Chalk Farm, London NW1 8BD

Editor In Chief: Colin Larkin
Production Editor: Susan Pipe
Editorial and Research Assistant: Nic Oliver
Copy Editor: Sarah Lavelle
Typographic Design Consultant: Roger Kohn
Special thanks to Trev Huxley, Anthony Patterson and Paul Zullo of Muze Inc.,
and to Rob Shreeve of Virgin Publishing.
Typeset by War Of The Worlds Studio
Printed and bound in Great Britain by Butler & Tanner Ltd, Frome and London

INTRODUCTION

Elements of 70s music have recently been revived, not so much because of its' quality, but more because of the fashion connection. The disco interest of the early 90s prompted much Village People, Sister Sledge and KC And The Sunshine Band being played at nightclubs. It is surprising just how many people view this decade as being split into three camps: the aforementioned disco era, the 1973/4 glam rock segment and the 1977 punk rising. Too much has been linked to flares, tank tops, stack boots, safety pins, combat trousers and ripped fishnet stockings, and little credibility has been given to what was a time of extraordinary musical growth. Many 60s musicians and bands had fragmented, but some metamorphosized into something greater. Prog rock had its' heyday and the singer-songwriter had a blue period. Give an encore to the Doobie Brothers, Little Feat, Steely Dan, Roxy Music, the Faces, James Taylor, Joni Mitchell and Cat Stevens, and reappraise the beautiful soul music that came out of Philadelphia in 1973 via Harold Melvin and the O'Jays.

Magazines such as *Melody Maker* and *Rolling Stone* experienced record circulations as the thirst for serious rock journalism grew. Some of the biggest-selling albums of all time were released in the 70s; *Dark Side Of The Moon*, *Rumours*, and *Hotel California*. This fuelled the notion that those who survived the 60s with their brain cells functioning came of age in the 70s.

ACKNOWLEDGEMENTS

We lost John Bauldie (*the* Dylanologist), who tragically died in a helicopter crash in 1996. Love and respect to him wherever he is. His contribution to our appreciation of Bob Dylan is immeasurable. To Johnny Rogan, who continues to be a rational ear and sounding board. He was the first person to hear of my proposal for the original Encyclopedia and agree to be involved. His great attention to detail shaped the original editorial stylesheet. John Burton continues to send his never-ending supply of newspaper obituaries.

Our in-house editorial team is even smaller than before, such is our super-efficiency. The Database is now a fully grown child and needs only regular food, attention and love. Thanks to Susan Pipe; reliable and trustworthy as ever. Nic Oliver 'the new boy' is shaping up pretty well, and Sarah Lavelle is our brand new quality controller.

Our outside contributors are further reduced in number, as we now write and amend all our existing text. However, we could not function without the continuing efforts and dedication of Big John Martland, Bruce Crowther and Alex Ogg. Brian Hogg, Hugh T. Wilson, Spencer Leigh and Robert Pruter continue to supply their specialist knowledge. We also received some entries from our newer contributors; Salsri Nyah, Tim Footman, Christen Thomsen, Essi Berilian and Jamie Renton, while Lloyd Peasley sent some important corrections free of charge.

Other past contributors' work may appear in this volume and I acknowledge once again; Simon Adams, David Ades, Mike Atherton, Gavin Badderley, Alan Balfour, Michael Barnett, Steve Barrow, John Bauldie, Lol Bell-Brown, Johnny Black, Chris Blackford, Pamela Boniface, Keith Briggs, Michael Ian Burgess, Paul M. Brown, Tony Burke, John Child, Linton Chiswick, Rick Christian, Alan Clayson, Tom Collier, Paul Cross, Bill Dahl, Norman Darwen, Roy Davenport, Peter Doggett, Kevin Eden, John Eley, Lars Fahlin, John Fordham, Per Gardin, Ian Garlinge, Mike Gavin, Andy Hamilton, Harry Hawk, Mark Hodkinson, Mike Hughes, Arthur Jackson, Mark Jones, Max Jones, Simon Jones, Ian Kenyon, Dave Laing, Steve Lake, Paul Lewis, Graham Lock, John Masouri, Bernd Matheja, Chris May, Dave McAleer, Ian McCann, David McDonald, York Membery, Toru Mitsui, Greg Moffitt, Nick Morgan, Michael Newman, Pete Nickols, Lyndon Noon, Zbigniew Nowara, James Nye, Ken Orton, Ian Peel, Dave Penny, Alan Plater, Barry Ralph, John Reed, Emma Rees, Lionel Robinson, Johnny Rogan, Alan Rowett, Jean Scrivener, Roy Sheridan, Dave Sissons, Neil Slaven, Chris Smith, Steve Smith, Mitch Solomons, Christopher Spencer, Jon Staines, Mike Stephenson, Sam Sutherland, Jeff Tamarkin, Ray Templeton, Liz Thompson, Gerard Tierney, John Tobler, Adrian T'Vell, Pete Wadeson, Frank Warren, Ben Watson, Pete Watson, Simon Williams, Val Wilmer, Dave Wilson and Barry Witherden.

Record company press offices are often bombarded with my requests for biogs and review copies. Theirs is a thankless task, but thanks anyway, especially to Alan Robinson of Demon, Sue and Dave Williams at Frontier, Tones Sansom at Creation, Trisha Coogan at Essential,

Mal Smith at Delta, Darren Crisp of Science Friction, Julia Honeywell at Ace, Murray Chalmers and Laura at Parlophone, Pat Naylor and Nicola Powell at Ryko/Hannibal, and Dave Bedford at This Way Up.

Press offices in general at: 4AD (Colleen), A&M, All Saints, Alligator, Almo, American Recordings (Louise), Arista, Beggars Banquet, BGO (Andy Gray), Big Cat (Sharon), Blue Note, Che Recordings, Chrysalis (Iona), City Slang (Wyndham Wallace), Coalition, Cooking Vinyl, Deceptive, Dedicated (Paula), Domino, Duophonic, East West, Echo, EMI, Epitaph, Fire, Fontana (Tina Mawjee), Geffen, Grapevine (Jane), Greentrax, Gut, Carol Hayes, Hightone, Hit Label, Hollywood, Dorothy Howe, HTD, Hut, Indigo, Indolent, Infectious, Island (Deborah), Jet, Jive, Junior Boys Own, Koch (Pat), London, MCA (Ted Cummings), Mercury, Mushroom, New Note, No. 9, Nude (Ellie), One Little Indian, Park, Pinnacle, Poole Edwards, Poppy, Qwest, RCA (Sharon), Savage And Best, Silvertone, Sire, Strange Fruit (Jo), Sub Pop, Superior Quality, Telarc, Tommy Boy, Transatlantic, Trauma, Virgin, Warp, all at Richard Wooton's office, and Zoo.

I wish the press offices at Columbia, Epic, Polydor and Warners would take us more seriously; phew, talk about blood out of a stone.

Thanks for the enthusiasm and co-operation of all our new colleagues at Virgin Publishing under the guidance of Rob Shreeve, in particular to Roz Scott who is always reassuringly efficient. To our new owners at Muze Inc., who oil the smooth running of the UK operation and are the business partners I always knew I wanted but never knew where to find them. In particular to the immaculate Tony Patterson, the beautifully attired Paul Zullo, Steve Figard, Bill Mullar, Marc Miller and the effortless giant Trev Huxley. And lastly to my tin lids; don't follow leaders and watch your pawking meters.

ENTRY STYLE

Albums, EPs (extended play 45s), newspapers, magazines, television programmes, films and stage musicals are referred to in italics. All song titles appear in single quotes. We spell rock 'n' roll like this. There are two main reasons for spelling rock 'n' roll with 'n' as opposed to 'n'. First, historical precedent: when the term was first coined in the 50s, the popular spelling was 'n'. Second, the 'n' is not simply an abbreviation of 'and' (in which case 'n' would apply) but as a phonetic representation of n as a sound. The ' ', therefore, serve as inverted commas rather than as apostrophes. The further reading section at the end of each entry has been expanded to give the reader a much wider choice of available books. These are not necessarily recommended titles but we have attempted to leave out any publication that has little or no merit.

We have also started to add videos at the end of the entries. Again, this is an area that is expanding faster than we can easily cope with, but there are many items in the videography and further items in the filmography, which is another new section we have decided to include. Release dates in keeping with albums attempt to show the release date in the country of origin. We have also tried to include both US and UK titles in the case of a title change.

ALBUM RATING

Due to many requests from our readers we have now decided to rate all albums. All new releases are reviewed either by myself or by our team of contributors. We also take into consideration the review ratings of the leading music journals and critics' opinions.

Our system is slightly different to most 5 Star ratings in that we rate according to the artist in question's work. Therefore, a 4 star album from the Beatles may have the overall edge over a 4 star album by Des O'Connor. Sorry Des.

Our ratings are carefully made, and consequently you will find we are very sparing with 5 Star and 1 Star albums.

★★★★★ Outstanding in every way. A classic and therefore strongly recommended. No comprehensive record collection should be without this album.

★★★★ Excellent. A high standard album from this artist and therefore highly recommended.

★★★ Good. By the artist's usual standards and therefore recommended.

★★ Disappointing. Flawed or lacking in some way.

★ Poor. An album to avoid unless you are a completist.

PLAGIARISM

In maintaining the largest text database of popular music in the world we are naturally protective of its content. We license to approved licensees only. It is both flattering and irritating to see our work reproduced without credit. Time and time again over the past few years I have read an obituary, when suddenly: hang on, I wrote that line. Secondly, it has come to our notice that other companies attempting to produce their own rock or pop encyclopedias use our material as a core. Flattering this might also be, but highly illegal. We have therefore dropped a few more textual 'depth charges' in addition to the original ones. Be warned.

Colin Larkin, July 1997

ABBA

The acronym Abba, coined in 1973, represented the coming together of four leading figures in Swedish pop. Agnetha Faltskog (b. 5 April 1950) had achieved pop success in her country with the 1968 hit 'I Was So In Love'; Bjorn Ulvaeus (b. 25 April 1945) had previously appeared with the folk-influenced Hootenanny Singers (originally known as the Westbay Singers). They also recorded and released a few records overseas as Northern Lights., before teaming up with Benny Andersson (b. 16 December 1946) appearing occasionally with his popular beat group, the Hep Stars. The one non-Swede in the line-up was the solo singer Anni-Frid Lyngstad (b. 15 November 1945, Narvik, Norway). Under the guidance of Scandinavian svengali Stig Anderson, and following the break-up of the Hep Stars in 1969, Bjorn and Benny joined forces for one album, *Lycka*. After its release in 1970 the duo started working as house producers at Anderson's Polar record company. Meanwhile Ulvaeus continued to work with the Hootenanny Singers in the studio only. The marriage of Bjorn and Agnetha, followed later by that of Benny and Anni-Frid, had laid the romantic and musical foundations of the Abba concept. The Eurovision Song Contest served as a backdrop to their international ambitions and after Anni-Frid's tentative entry in the qualifying Swedish heats as a soloist in 1971, the quartet, now known as Bjorn & Benny, Agnetha & Anni-Frid, attempted to represent their country with the infectious 'Ring Ring' in 1973. They succeeded the following year as Abba, with the more polished and bouncy 'Waterloo', which not only won the contest, but topped the UK charts and, amazingly, for a Eurovision entry, infiltrated the US Top 10.

The middling success of the re-released 'Ring Ring' and singalong 'I Do I Do I Do I Do I Do' provided little indication of the chart domination that was to follow. In September 1975, Abba returned with the worldwide hit 'SOS', a powerhouse pop production highlighted by immaculately executed counter harmonies and an infectiously melodic arrangement. These classic ingredients of the Abba sound were ably evinced on their first trilogy of consecutive UK chart-toppers, 'Mamma Mia', 'Fernando' and 'Dancing Queen', which also found favour in Australia and Germany, and just about every other country in the world. The last also brought them their only US number 1 and precipitated their rise to pop superstardom with sales unmatched since the golden age of the Beatles. Firmly in control of their des-

tinies, both on the artistic and commercial fronts, the group undertook a tour of Europe and Australia in 1977, most remarkable for its extravagant use of costume, sets and orchestration. That same year they celebrated a second trilogy of UK chart-toppers ('Knowing Me Knowing You', 'The Name Of The Game' and 'Take A Chance On Me'), whose haunting grace was enhanced by some of the finest promotional videos of the period. Although *Abba: The Movie*, directed by Koln Lakkin, proved less memorable, there was no doubting their commercial acumen. With international stardom assured, they began the 80s with two more UK number 1s, 'The Winner Takes It All' and 'Super Trouper', taking their UK chart-topping tally to an impressive nine in a little over six years. Although the dissolution of both marriages in the group threatened their unity, they maintained a high profile, not least on the international business circuit where they eclipsed the car manufacturers Volvo as Sweden's largest earners of foreign currency during 1982. With little left to achieve within their chosen genre, they elected to rest the group that same year. Agnetha Faltskog and Anni-Frid (Frida) subsequently went solo, but found chart success elusive. Ulvaeus and Andersson, meanwhile, concentrated on composing, and enjoyed a productive relationship with Tim Rice, culminating in London's West End musical *Chess*. In 1990 the Australian band Bjorn Again enjoyed some success touring with a set composed entirely of faithful Abba covers. In 1992 a well publicized 70s fashion and music boom gave fuel to countless rumours of an Abba reformation.

●ALBUMS: *Ring Ring* (Epic 1973)★★, *Waterloo* (Epic 1974)★★, *Abba* (Epic 1975)★★★, *Arrival* (Epic 1976)★★★, *The Album* (Epic 1977)★★★, *Voulez-Vous* (Epic 1979)★★★, *Super Trouper* (Epic 1980)★★★, *Gracias Por La Musica* (Epic 1980)★★, *The Visitors* (Epic 1981)★★★, *Thank You For The Music* (Epic 1983)★★★, *Abba Live* (Polydor 1986)★★. Solo: Agnetha Faltskog *Agnetha* (Embassy 1974)★★, *Wrap Your Arms Around Me* (Epic 1983)★★, *Eyes Of A Woman* (Epic 1985)★★, *I Stand Alone* (Warners 1988)★★. Frida *Something's Going On* (Epic 1982)★★★, *Shine* (Epic 1984)★★.

●COMPILATIONS: *Greatest Hits* (Epic 1976)★★★★, *Greatest Hits, Volume 2* (Epic 1979)★★★, *The Singles - The First Ten Years* (Epic 1982)★★★★, *Energhighs* (Epic 1983)★★, *The Abba Special* (Epic 1983)★★★, *I Love Abba* (1984), *The Best Of Abba* 5-LP box set (Readers Digest 1986)★★★, *Abba - The Hits* (Pickwick 1987)★★★, *Abba - The Hits 2* (Pickwick 1988)★★, *Abba - The Hits 3* (Pickwick 1988)★★, *The Collection* (Castle 1988)★★★, *Absolute Abba* (Telstar 1988)★★★, *The Love Songs* (Pickwick 1989)★★, *Gold: The Greatest Hits* (Polydor 1992)★★★★, *More Abba Gold - More Abba Hits* (Polydor 1993)★★★, *The Music Still Goes On* (Spectrum 1996)★★★.

●VIDEOS: *Story Of Abba* (MGM 1986), *Video Biography 1974-1982* (Virgin Vision 1987), *Abba - The Movie* (MGM/UA 1988), *Abba: The Video Hits* (Screen Legends

1988), *More Video Hits Of Abba* (Screen Legends 1988). ●FILMS: *Abba -T he Movie.*

ACE

Formed in the UK during December 1972 and originally called Ace Flash And The Dynamos - quickly abbreviated after a couple of gigs - Ace comprised Paul Carrack (b. 22 April 1951, Sheffield, Yorkshire, England; keyboards/vocals), Alan 'Bam' King (b. 18 September 1946, Kentish Town, London, England; guitar/vocals), Phil Harris (b. 18 July 1948, Muswell Hill, London, England; guitar/vocals), Terry 'Tex' Comer (b. 23 February 1949, Burnley, Lancashire, England; bass) and Steve Witherington (b. 26 December 1953, Enfield, Middlesex, England; drums). All members were assembled from known bands and were all solid musicians. Carrack, Witherington and Comer came from Warm Dust and King and Harris arrived via Mighty Baby, whose antecedents were the highly regarded 60s group, the Action. Ace became one of the darlings of the UK pub rock circuit with their polished funky pop music. Before the recording of their first album, ex-Bees Make Honey drummer Fran Byrne (b. 17 March 1948, Dublin, Ireland) had replaced Witherington. The album, *Five-A-Side*, was a creditable debut. The single 'How Long', culled from this record, gave them an enormous hit that they were never able to repeat. It was a perfectly crafted song with a hypnotic bass introduction directly 'borrowed' from 'Travelling Song' by Pentangle, followed by Carrack's sweet electric piano. The simple tale of infidelity captured people's attention and it became a Top 20 hit in the UK and reached the Top 3 in the USA. They eventually moved to America but disbanded in July 1977 when most of the remaining members joined Frankie Miller's band. Paul Carrack has enjoyed most success having played in Eric Clapton's band, been a member of Squeeze and is now part of Mike And The Mechanics. Carrack re-recorded 'How Long' which became a hit again in 1996.
●ALBUMS: *Five-A-Side* (Anchor 1974)★★★, *Time For Another* (Anchor 1975)★★, *No Strings* (Anchor 1977)★★.
●COMPILATIONS: *The Best Of Ace* (See For Miles 1987)★★★, *How Long: The Best Of Ace* (Music Club 1993)★★★.

ADDRISI BROTHERS

Don (b. 14 December 1938, Winthrop, Massachusetts, USA, d. 13 November 1984) and Dick Addrisi (b. 4 July 1941, Winthrop, Massachusetts, USA) were a Californian-based pop duo who recorded for over two decades, but are best remembered as songwriters for their gentle ballad, 'Never My Love', which was a US number 2 in 1967 for the Association. As singers, they first charted in the US in 1959 with 'Cherrystone' on Del-Fi, the west coast label that also recorded Ritchie Valens. They later recorded without success for various labels, and it was not until 1972, signed to Columbia Records, that they reappeared in the US chart and had

their first Top 30 hit with 'We've Got To Get It On Again'. Five years later, at the height of the disco craze, they enjoyed their third and biggest hit with 'Slow Dancin' Don't Turn Me On' on Buddah Records, the label on which they also had a minor hit with their own version of their classic composition 'Never My Love'. They also recorded less successfully on Bell, Private Stock, Elektra and Scotti Brothers. Many of their singles were released in the UK but only one achieved chart status; 'Ghost Dance' made number 57 in October 1979. Don Addrisi died from cancer in 1984 aged 45.
●ALBUMS: *We've Got To Get It On Again* (Columbia 1972)★★, *Addrisi Brothers* (Buddah 1977)★★.

ADVERTS

The Adverts first came to prominence in 1976 at the celebrated London punk venue, the Roxy Club. Fronted by vocalist Tim 'TV' Smith and Gaye Advert (vocals/bass), the line-up was completed with Howard Pickup (guitar) and Laurie Driver (drums). Damned guitarist Brian James was so impressed by their performance that he offered them a support slot, as well as introducing them to the hip new wave label, Stiff Records. On tour they were initially promoted with the witty poster: 'The Adverts can play one chord, the Damned can play three. Come and see all four at . . .' Their debut single, the self-effacingly titled 'One Chord Wonders', was well received, but it was their second outing that attracted controversy and chart fame. 'Gary Gilmore's Eyes', a song based on the death-row criminal who had requested permission to donate his eyes to science, was a macabre but euphoric slice of punk/pop that catapulted the Adverts into the UK Top 20. One of the first punk groups to enjoy commercial success, the quartet also boasted the first female punk star in Gaye Advert. Despite some tabloid newspaper publicity, the next single, 'Safety In Numbers', failed to chart, although its successor, 'No Time To Be 21', reached number 38. The group barely had time to record their debut album, *Crossing The Red Sea With The Adverts*, before Laurie Driver was ousted and replaced by former Chelsea/Generation X drummer John Towe, who himself left shortly afterwards, succeeded by Rod Latter. Changing record labels, personnel problems and unsuitable production dogged their progress while *Cast Of Thousands* was largely ignored. On 27 October 1979, with a line-up comprising Smith, Dave Sinclair (drums), Mel Weston (keyboards), Eric Russell (guitar) and former Doctors Of Madness bassist, Colin Stoner, the Adverts gave their last performance at Slough College of Art. Smith went on to record with TV Smith's Explorers, then Cheap, and finally solo through a contract with Cooking Vinyl Records.
●ALBUMS: *Crossing The Red Sea With The Adverts* (Bright 1978)★★★, *Cast Of Thousands* (RCA 1979)★★, *Live At The Roxy Club* (Receiver 1990)★★.

AEROSMITH

One of the USA's most popular hard-rock acts, Aerosmith was formed in 1970 when vocalist Steven Tyler (b. Steven Victor Tallarico, 26 March 1948, New York, USA; vocals) met Joe Perry (b. Anthony Joseph Perry, 10 September 1950, Boston, Massachusetts, USA; guitar) while the latter was working in a Sunapee, New Hampshire, ice cream parlour, the Anchorage. Tyler was in the area visiting the family-owned holiday resort, Trow-Rico. Perry, then playing in the Jam Band, invited Tyler (who had previously released one single with his own band Chain Reaction, 'When I Needed You', and another, 'You Should Have Been Here Yesterday', with William Proud And The Strangeurs) to join him in a Cream-styled rock combo. Together with fellow Jam Band member Tom Hamilton (b. 31 December 1951, Colorado Springs, Colorado, USA; bass) and new recruits Joey Kramer (b. 21 June 1950, New York, USA; drums) and Ray Tabano (guitar), the group's original line-up was now complete. However, Tabanao was quickly replaced by former member of Justin Tyme, Earth Inc., Teapot Dome and Cymbals Of Resistance, Brad Whitford (b. 23 February 1952, Winchester, Massachusetts, USA). After playing their first gig at the Nipmuc Regional High School the band took the name Aerosmith (rejecting other early monikers including 'Hookers'). Their popularity throughout the Boston area grew rapidly, and a triumphant gig at Max's Kansas City witnessed by Clive Davis led to a recording deal with Columbia/CBS Records. In 1973 Aerosmith secured a minor chart placing with their self-titled debut album. Although its attendant single, 'Dream On', initially peaked at number 59, it became a Top 10 hit in March 1976. *Get Your Wings* introduced a fruitful working relationship with producer Jack Douglas. Nationwide tours established the quintet as a major attraction, a position consolidated by the highly successful *Toys In The Attic*, which has now sold in excess of six million copies worldwide. A fourth album, *Rocks*, achieved platinum status within months of its release. Aerosmith maintained their pre-eminent position with *Draw The Line* and the powerful *Live! Bootleg*, but despite popular acclaim, failed to gain the approbation of many critics who dubbed the group 'derivative', particularly of Led Zeppelin. Tyler's physical resemblance to Mick Jagger, and his foil-like relationship with guitarist Perry, also inspired comparisons with the Rolling Stones, with whom they shared several musical reference points. In 1978 Aerosmith undertook a US tour of smaller, more intimate venues in an attempt to decelerate their rigorous schedule. They appeared in the ill-fated *Sgt. Pepper's Lonely Hearts Club Band* film (as the Future Villain band), and although their rousing version of 'Come Together' reached the US Top 30, tension between Tyler and Perry proved irreconcilable. The guitarist left the group following the release of the disappointing *Night In The Ruts* and subsequently founded the Joe Perry Project. Jimmy Crespo joined Aerosmith in 1980, but the following year Brad Whitford left to pursue a new career with former Ted Nugent band member, Derek St Holmes. Newcomer Rick Dufay debuted on *Rock In A Hard Place*, but this lacklustre set failed to capture the fire of the group's classic recordings. Contact between the group and Perry and Whitford was re-established during a 1984 tour. Antagonisms were set aside, and the following year, the quintet's most enduring line-up was performing together again. *Done With Mirrors* was a tentative first step, after which Tyler and Perry underwent a successful rehabilitation programme to rid themselves of drug and alcohol dependencies, synonymous with the group's hedonistic lifestyle. In 1986 they accompanied rappers Run DMC on 'Walk This Way', an Aerosmith song from *Toys In The Attic* and a former US Top 10 entry in its own right. The collaboration was an international hit, rekindling interest in Aerosmith's career. *Permanent Vacation* became one of their best-selling albums, and the first to make an impression in the UK, while the highly-acclaimed *Pump* and *Get A Grip* emphasized their revitalization. Feted by a new generation of acts, including Guns N'Roses, the quintet are now seen as elder statesmen, but recent recordings show them leading by example. Those wishing to immerse themselves in this extraordinary band should invest in the impressive 13-CD box set *Box Of Fire*; it comes complete with rare bonus tracks and a free, ready to strike match! *Big Ones* was a well chosen compilation, satisfying long-term fans, but more importantly it introduced a younger audience to one dinosaur band that still sounds fresh and exciting, who has refused to compromise and has not 'gone soft'. The band returned to Columbia Records in the mid-90s and spent an age recording *Nine Lives*. In Tyler's words: 'this album has taken me as far as I've ever wanted to go and gotten me back again'. It was worth the wait, with all the usual trademarks - yet sounding strangely fresh. The hit single 'Falling In Love (Is Hard On The Knees)' preceded its release in February 1997. As Tyler approaches his half-century he seems ageless onstage, even Jagger and Bruce Springsteen seem jaded compared to this rock 'n' roll ballet-dancer, still seemingly in his prime.

●ALBUMS: *Aerosmith* (Columbia 1973)★★★, *Get Your Wings* (Columbia 1974)★★★, *Toys In The Attic* (Columbia 1975)★★★★, *Rocks* (Columbia 1976)★★★★, *Draw The Line* (Columbia 1977)★★★, *Live! Bootleg* (Columbia 1978)★★★, *Night In The Ruts* (Columbia 1979)★★, *Rock In A Hard Place* (Columbia 1982)★★, *Done With Mirrors* (Geffen 1985)★★★, *Permanent Vacation* (Geffen 1987)★★★, *Pump* (Geffen 1989)★★★★, *Get A Grip* (Geffen 1993)★★★★, *Nine Lives* (Columbia 1997)★★★★.

●COMPILATIONS: *Greatest Hits* (Columbia 1980)★★★★, *Classics Live* (Columbia 1986)★★, *Classics Live II* (Columbia 1987)★★★, *Gems* (Columbia

1988)★★★, *Anthology* (Raw Power/Castle 1988)★★, *Pandora's Box* (Columbia 1991)★★★, *Big Ones* (Geffen 1994)★★★★, *Box Of Fire* 13-CD box set (Columbia 1994)★★★★.

●VIDEOS: *Video Scrapbook* (Hendring Video 1988), *Live Texas Jam '78* (CMV Enterprises 1989), *Things That Go Pump In The Night* (Warner Music Video 1990), *The Making Of Pump* (Sony Music Video 1991), *Big Ones You Can Look At* (1994).

●FURTHER READING: *The Fall And Rise Of Aerosmith*, Mark Putterford. *Toys In The Attic: The Rise, Fall And Rise Of Aerosmith*, Martin Huxley.

AFTER THE FIRE

After The Fire were formed in the UK in 1972 by keyboard player Peter Banks, Andy Piercy (guitar/bass), Ivor Twidell (drums) and John Russell (guitar). The market was responsive to UK adult orientated rock during the early 70s but the band's mixture of 'pomp Christian pop' was slow to break through. They eventually secured a contract following the release of their debut album on their own label. CBS Records invested in them and they were rewarded with a UK Top 40 hit, 'One Rule For You', in 1979. The accompanying album, although polished, sold only to the converted. The band's subsequent recordings were minor hits until the unexpected major success of 'Der Kommissar'. Originally recorded by Falco in his native Germany, the After The Fire version went on to sell over a million copies worldwide, and made the US Top 5. However, by the time it charted the group had already broken up, frustrated by record company indecision and the Christian ethos which 'made things worse, as we couldn't have a good old swearing and slanging match.' Banks built his own studio before becoming managing director of Maldon Computer Company, a software and networking enterprise. Twidell released three Christian rock solo albums after leaving the group following its debut album - *Waiting For The Sun* (1981), *Secret Service* (1981) and *Duel* (1983). He then became a member of the Bedfordshire police force. Russell was last sighted working in a hi-fi shop. Piercy retained the rights to the name, although it was now abbreviated to ATF. Still a practising Christian, after submitting an unreleased solo album for CBS he went on to do production work for the Truth, T'Pau (when they were known as Talking America) and Gary Numan. He recently recorded an album with the Holy Trinity Church, Brompton, *Praise God From Whom All Blessings Flow*.

●ALBUMS: *Laser Love* (Rapid 1979)★★, *80F* (Columbia 1980)★★, *Batteries Not Included* (Columbia 1982)★★.

●COMPILATIONS: *Der Kommissar* (Columbia 1982)★★.

AIRFORCE

Formed in 1970 by drummer Ginger Baker, this ensemble included Steve Winwood (keyboards) and Ric Grech (bass), ex-colleagues from the 'supergroup' Blind Faith. The initial Airforce line-up also featured two of Baker's early mentors, Graham Bond (saxophone/keyboards/vocals) and Phil Seaman (drums), as well as Denny Laine (guitar/vocals), Chris Wood (saxophone), Harold McNair (flute), Bud Beadle (horns), Remi Kabaka (percussion) and Diane Stewart (Bond's wife; backing vocals). Although *Airforce* included the unit's promising, if ragged, interpretation of the Peter Yarrow and Paul Stookey song, 'Man Of Constant Sorrow', the set was marked by the leader's predilection for lengthy percussive interludes. Bond's guttural jazz-rock was another influential factor in a largely self-indulgent approach which precluded commercial success. The departures of Winwood, Wood, McNair, Kabaka and Seaman undermined an already unstable act and although the remainder of the band was augmented by eight new members, *Airforce 2* was a largely undistinguished collection. Having dissolved the band, Baker moved to Lagos to study African drumming, while Bond and Stewart pursued elements of the Airforce sound in a new venture, Holy Magick.

●ALBUMS: *Ginger Baker's Airforce* (Polydor 1970)★★, *Airforce 2* (Polydor 1970)★★.

ALBERT, MORRIS

b. Morris Albert Kaisermann, 1951, Brazil. Although Albert was born in Brazil, most listeners to his one and only hit assumed that he was French. The musically gifted Morris wrote 'Feelings', a slow ballad in the romantic style of Sacha Distel and Julio Iglesias which became a major worldwide hit in 1975, reaching number 4 in the UK charts. The song was later used as the theme music to an Italian tragi-romantic film. The subsequent album found similar success, but since then his career faded into anonymity. A decade after the song was first released, Albert found himself losing a case of plagiarism. It was established that the now notorious 'Feelings' was taken from 'Pour Toi', by French composer Louis Gaste. Not only did Morris lose the case, but he parted with £250,000 as a settlement. He is still actively performing in Brazil, but is reluctant to release new songs.

●ALBUMS: *Feelings* (Decca 1975)★★, *Morris Albert* (Decca 1976)★★.

ALBERTO Y LOST TRIOS PARANOIAS

This Manchester-based rock comedy troupe in the vein of the Bonzo Dog Doo-Dah Band and National Lampoon, was formed in 1973 by two former members of Greasy Bear; Chris 'C.P.' Lee (vocals/guitar) and Bruce Mitchell (drums), with Les Prior (vocals), Jimmy Hibbert (vocals/bass), Bob Harding (vocals/guitar/bass), Simon White (steel guitar/guitar), Tony Bowers (bass/guitar) and Ray 'Mighty Mongo' Hughes (second drummer). The group mercilessly parodied the major rock names of the 70s - 'Anadin' was a reworking of Lou Reed's 'Heroin'/'Sweet Jane'. As with many comedy ensembles, the Albertos belied their comic aspirations by their exemplary musicianship, but by the time it came to committing to record their finely honed act, the artists they had pilloried had ceased to become valid targets and the album flopped. The follow-up in 1977, *Italians From Outer Space*, went some way to re-establishing the Albertos' reputation, but once more the majority of songs were more miss than hit. That same year, the easy targets of the early 70s were put aside with the ascent of punk rock and the Albertos' highly acclaimed stage performance of C.P. Lee's rock play, *Sleak* at London's Royal Court Theatre, presented the story of the manipulation of an innocent, Norman Sleak, into giving the ultimate in rock performance - onstage suicide. This concept gave birth to 'Snuff Rock'. The play's run was punctuated by the comic disc jockey role of Les Prior, quite possibly his finest performance. The accompanying EP, *Snuff Rock*, released on Stiff Records, poked fun at the punk rock phenomenon, targeting the Sex Pistols ('Gobbing On Life'), the Damned ('Kill') and the Clash ('Snuffin' Like That') as well as a myriad of reggae bands in 'Snuffin' In A Babylon'. For once the Albertos act was successfully transferred to vinyl. They hit the UK Top 50 with the Status Quo spoof, 'Heads Down No Nonsense Mindless Boogie' in 1978. Chas Jankel and Roger Ruskin Spear assisted the Albertos on their last album, *Skite*. The group soldiered on into the 80s taking *Sleak* to the Squat Theater off-Broadway as well as producing a less successful stage production, entitled *Never Mind The Bullocks*. The death of Les Prior on 31 January 1980 from leukaemia left a large gap in the group, and although his illness had limited him to rare performances in his final years, his comic inspirations were sorely missed. On folding, Hibbert made an unsuccessful attempt to launch a heavy metal career with *Heavy Duty* (1980), but later found success as the writer and voiced character on the children's television cartoon, *Count Duckula*. Lee made a successful stage appearance portraying the hip-beat poet Lord Buckley, as well as releasing, on cassette only, under the title C.P. Lee Mystery Guild, *Radio Sweat* (1981) - on commercial radio stations. Bowers joined Durutti Column, and later Simply Red. There was a brief, but unsuccessful reformation, as the Mothmen.

●ALBUMS: *Alberto Y Lost Trios Paranoias* (Transatlantic 1976)★★, *Italians From Outer Space* (Transatlantic 1977)★★, *Skite* (Logo 1978)★★.

●COMPILATIONS: *The Best Of The Albertos* (Demon 1991)★★★.

●FURTHER READING: *Alberto's Umper Ook Of Fun*, Alberto Y Lost Trios Paranoias.

ALBION COUNTRY BAND

This volatile traditional folk ensemble was founded in April 1972 by defecting Steeleye Span bassist Ashley Hutchings (b. 26 January 1945, Southgate, Middlesex, England). Royston Wood (b. 1935; vocals), Sue Draheim (b. August 1949, Oakland, California, USA; fiddle) and Steve Ashley (guitar) completed the new venture alongside Simon Nicol (b. 13 October 1950, Muswell Hill, London, England; guitar) and Dave Mattacks (b. 13 March 1948, Edgware, Middlesex, England; drums), two of Hutchings' former colleagues from Fairport Convention. The Albion moniker had already been used by Hutchings to back an album by his wife, Shirley Collins, in 1971. The early line-up disintegrated six months after its inception and a caretaker unit, which included Richard Thompson, fulfilled all outstanding obligations. Hutchings, Nicol and new drummer Roger Swallow then pieced together a second Country Band with folk acolytes, Martin Carthy, Sue Harris and John Kirkpatrick, but this innovative sextet was also doomed to a premature demise. Their lone album, *Battle Of The Field*, recorded in 1973, was withheld until 1976, and only issued following public demand. Hutchings, Nicol and Mattacks were reunited in the Etchingham Steam Band, a part-time group formed to support Shirley Collins. The group subsequently evolved into the Albion Dance Band, a large-scale, highly flexible unit which recorded a series of collections evocative of 'merrie England' and enjoyed considerable acclaim for their contributions to several theatrical productions. *Lark Rise To Candleford* was a typical project, an adaptation of Flora Thompson's novel set to music.

The group entered the 80s as the Albion Band, retaining a mixture of traditional and original material, and always remaining open to experimentation; thus, *The Wild Side Of Town*, a collaboration with TV presenter and naturalist Chris Baines. Musicians continued to arrive and depart with alarming regularity, and by the end of the 80s the personnel tally easily exceeded one hundred. On one occasion in 1980, the entire band quit *en masse*, forming the critically acclaimed Home Service. Throughout, Ashley Hutchings has remained at the helm, ensuring their dogged individuality. He has also released over a dozen solo albums. The line-up for *Acousticity* comprised Hutchings, Nicol, vocalist Christine White and violinist Ashley Reed, White too having dabbled with a solo career. Julie Matthews appears on *Albion Heart*.

●ALBUMS: As the Albion Country Band with Shirley Collins *No Roses* (Pegasus 1971). As the Albion Country Band *Battle Of The Field* (Island 1976). As the Albion Dance Band *The Prospect Before Us* (Harvest 1977). As the Albion Band *Rise Up Like The Sun* (Harvest 1978)★★★, *Albion River Hymn March* (1979)★★★, *Lark Rise To Candleford (A Country Tapestry)* (Charisma 1980)★★, *Light Shining* (Albino 1982)★★★, *Shuffle Off* (Making Waves 1983)★★★, *Under The Rose* (Spindsrift 1984)★★★, *A Christmas Present From The Albion Band* (Fun 1985)★★, *Stella Maria* (Making Waves 1987)★★★, *The Wild Side Of Town* (Celtic Music 1987)★★, *I Got New Shoes* (Celtic Music 1987)★★★, *Give Me A Saddle And I'll Trade You A Car* (Topic 1989)★★★, *1990* (Topic 1990)★★★, *BBC Radio Live In Concert* (Windsong 1993)★★★, *Acousticity* (HTD 1994)★★★, *Albion Heart* (HTD 1995)★★★★.

●COMPILATIONS: *Songs From The Shows Vol. 1* (Road Goes On Forever 1992)★★★, *Songs From The Shows Vol. 2* (Road Goes On Forever 1992)★★★.

ALCAPONE, DENNIS

b. Dennis Smith, 6 August 1947, Clarendon, Jamaica, West Indies. Initially inspired by U Roy, Alcapone began DJing for El Paso Hi-Fi in 1969. He was the first DJ to enjoy success on record after U Roy, and likewise the first to challenge his dominance. His initial records were made for youth producer and sometime ghetto dentist Keith Hudson, with titles including 'Shades Of Hudson' (1970), 'Spanish Omega' (1970), 'Revelation Version' (1970), 'Maca Version' (1970) and 'The Sky's The Limit' (1970). From 1970 to 1972 Dennis had big hits with Duke Reid, toasting his witty, half-sung, half-spoken lyrics over classic Treasure Isle rhythms and coasting to the top of the Jamaican chart with regularity. Tunes like 'Number One Station' (1971), 'Mosquito One' (1971), 'Rock To The Beat' (1972), 'Love Is Not A Gamble' (1972), 'Wake Up Jamaica' (1972), 'The Great Woggie' (1972), 'Teach The Children' (1972) and 'Musical Alphabet' (1972), all of which were recorded at Treasure Isle, and 'Ripe Cherry' (1971) and 'Alcapone Guns Don't Argue' (1971) for producer Bunny Lee, put Alcapone in the front rank of Jamaican DJs.

In the period from 1970 until he left for the UK in 1973, Alcapone's services were continually in demand. He made over 100 singles in this time and released three albums, in the process working with such producers as Coxsone Dodd, Lee Perry, Sir JJ, Winston Riley, Joe Gibbs, Prince Buster, Randy's and others. He toured Guyana in 1970 and the UK in 1972 and 1973, after having won the cup presented to the best DJ by *Swing* magazine in Jamaica. He also began production work, issuing music by himself, Dennis Brown, Augustus Pablo and Delroy Wilson. Since the mid-70s he has been less active, still finding time to record albums for Sidney Crooks, Bunny Lee and Count Shelly. In the late 80s he returned to live performance, appearing at the WOMAD festival in Cornwall and Helsinki in 1989. In 1990 he made more club appearances in the UK. Later in the year he returned to Jamaica for three months and recorded over digital rhythms for Bunny Lee. Alcapone remains the classic Jamaican toaster, on his best form capable of transforming and adding to any song he DJs, in the great toasting tradition pioneered in Jamaican dancehalls.

●ALBUMS: *Forever Version* (Studio One 1971)★★★, *Guns Don't Argue* (Attack/Trojan 1971)★★★, *King Of The Track* (Magnet 1974)★★★★, *Belch It Off* (Attack 1974)★★★★, *Dread Capone* (Third World 1976)★★★, *Investigator Rock* (Third World 1977)★★★, *Six Million Dollar Man* (Third World 1977)★★★. With Lizzy: *Soul To Soul DJ's Choice* (Treasure Isle/Trojan 1972)★★★.

●COMPILATIONS: *My Voice Is Insured For Half A Million Dollars* (Trojan 1989)★★★, *Universal Rockers* (RAS 1992)★★★.

ALESSI

Formerly members of Barnaby Bye along with ex-Blues Magoos singer Peppy Castro, American brothers Billy and Bobby Alessi (b. 1954, West Hempstead, Long Island, New York, USA) sprang to fame in 1977 with the UK Top 10 and major European hit single, 'Oh Lori' (it failed in their homeland). This sumptuous slice of harmony pop evoked the carefree, summertime atmosphere of a more innocent era. Although subsequent releases continued in a similar vein, they lacked the charm of that initial success. The duo were signed to producer Quincy Jones' Qwest label in 1982, but this made little difference to Alessi's subsequent commercial fortunes.

●ALBUMS: *Alessi* (A&M 1977)★★, *All For A Reason* (A&M 1977)★★, *Driftin'* (A&M 1978)★★, *Words And Music* (A&M 1979)★★, *Long Time Friends* (Qwest 1982)★★.

ALICE COOPER

b. Vincent Damon Furnier, 4 February 1948, Detroit, Michigan, USA. Alice Cooper became known as the 'master of shock rock' during the 70s and remained a popular hard-rock artist into the 90s. The Furnier family moved to Phoenix, Arizona, where Vincent began writing songs while in junior high school. Inspired by a dream to become as famous as the Beatles and Rolling Stones, Furnier formed a group in the early 60s called the Earwigs. By 1965 their name had changed to the Spiders and then the Nazz (no relation to Todd Rundgren's band of the same name). Both the Spiders and Nazz played at local dances and recorded singles that were moderately popular regionally. In 1968, the Nazz, which also included Mike Bruce (21 November 1948, California, USA; lead guitar), Dennis Dunaway (b. 15 March 1946, California, USA; bass), Glen Buxton (b. 17 June 1947, Washington DC, USA; guitar) and Neal Smith (10 January 1946, Washington, USA; drums), changed its name to Alice Cooper, reportedly due to Furnier's belief that he was the reincarnation of a 17th century witch by that name. The name Alice Cooper was also attached to Furnier, who invented an androgynous, outrageously attired character to attract attention. The band played deliberately abrasive rock music with the intention of shocking and even alienating those attending its concerts. In 1969 the Alice Cooper band found a kindred spirit in Frank Zappa, who signed them to his new Straight Records label. The group recorded two albums, *Pretties For You* and *Easy Action*, before switching to Straight's parent label Warner Brothers Records in 1970. By that time Cooper had taken on more extreme tactics in his live performances, using a guillotine and electric chair as stage props and a live snake as part of his wardrobe. The finishing touch was the thick black eye make-up which dripped down his face, affording him his trademark demonic appearance. As the group and its singer built a reputation as a bizarre live act, their records began to sell in greater quantities. In 1971 'Eighteen' was the first single to reach the US charts, at number 21. Cooper's commercial breakthrough came the following year with the rebellious 'School's Out' single and album, both of which made the US Top 10 as well as topping the UK chart. A streak of best-selling albums followed: the number 1 *Billion Dollar Babies*, then *Muscle Of Love*, *Alice Cooper's Greatest Hits* and *Welcome To My Nightmare*, all of which reached the US Top 10. The last was his first true solo album as the band fractured and Cooper officially adopted the Alice Cooper name as his own.

In contrast to his professional image, the offstage Cooper became a Hollywood celebrity, playing golf and appearing on television talk shows, as well as developing a strong friendship with Groucho Marx, with whom he planned a television series. In tribute to the legendary comedian he purchased one of the 'O's from the famous Hollywood sign and dedicated it to his memory. The late 70s saw him appearing in films such as *Sextette* and *Sgt. Pepper's Lonely Hearts Club Band*. In 1978 Cooper admitted chronic alcoholism and entered a New York hospital for treatment. *From The Inside*, with songs co-written by Bernie Taupin, reflected on the experience. His band continued touring, and between 1979 and 1982 featured ex-Iron Butterfly lead guitarist Mike Pinera. Cooper continued recording into the early 80s with diminishing results. In 1986, after a four-year recording absence, he signed to MCA Records, but none of his albums for that label reached the US charts. A 1989 set, *Trash*, his first for Epic Records, returned him to the Top 40 and yielded a Top 10 single, 'Poison', his first in 12 years. *Hey Stoopid* found him accompanied by Joe Satriani, Steve Vai and Slash and Axl from Guns N'Roses, while his 90s tours saw Cooper drawing a new, younger audience who considered him a heavy metal pioneer. This impression was immortalized by Cooper's appearance in *Wayne's World*, wherein the haphazard protagonists kneel before their idol and insist they are 'not worthy'. In recent times Neal Smith is a property agent; Bruce is still a songwriter but bitter about the past. He became an author with the publication of *No More Mr Nice Guy*. Buxton lives in Iowa and has been plagued by ill health while Dunaway runs a craft shop with his wife in Connecticut.

● ALBUMS: *Pretties For You* (Straight 1969)★★, *Easy Action* (Straight 1970)★★, *Love It To Death* (Warners 1971)★★★★, *Killer* (Warners 1971)★★★, *School's Out* (Warners 1972)★★★, *Billion Dollar Babies* (Warners 1973)★★★, *Muscle Of Love* (Warners 1973)★★, *Welcome To My Nightmare* (Anchor 1975)★★, *Alice Cooper Goes To Hell* (Warners 1976)★★, *Lace And Whiskey* (Warners 1977)★, *The Alice Cooper Show* (Warners 1977)★★, *From The Inside* (Warners 1978)★, *Flush The Fashion* (Warners 1980)★, *Special Forces* (Warners 1981)★, *Zipper Catches Skin* (Warners 1982)★, *Dada* (Warners 1983)★, *Live In Toronto* (Breakaway 1984)★, *Constrictor* (MCA 1986)★, *Raise Your Fist And Yell* (MCA 1987)★★, *Trash* (Epic

1989)★★, *Hey Stoopid* (Epic 1991)★★, *Live 1968* (Edsel 1992)★★, *Live At The Whiskey A Go Go* (Edsel 1992)★★, *The Last Temptation* (Epic 1994)★★, *A Fistful Of Alice* (1997)★★.

● COMPILATIONS: *School Days* (Warners 1973)★★★, *Alice Cooper's Greatest Hits* (Warners 1974)★★★★, *Freak Out Song* (Castle 1986) ★★★, *Beast Of* (Warners 1989)★★★, *Classicks* (Epic 1995)★★★.

● VIDEOS: *The Nightmare Returns* (Hendring Video 1987), *Welcome To My Nightmare* (Hendring Video 1988), *Alice Cooper Trashes The World* (CMV Enterprises 1990), *Box Set* (Hendring Video 1990), *Prime Cuts* (Castle Music Pictures 1991).

● FURTHER READING: *Alice Cooper*, Steve Demorest. *Me: Alice: The Autobiography Of Alice Cooper*, Alice Cooper with Steven Gaines. *Rolling Stone Scrapbook: Alice Cooper*, Rolling Stone.

ALLEY CATS (USA)

The Alley Cats consisted of Dianne Chai (vocals/bass), John McCarthy (drums), and Chai's husband, Randy Stodola (vocals/ guitar, ex-Hubcaps) and they were formed in Los Angeles, California, USA, in the late 70s. They had a longer history than most of their peers on the venerated Dangerhouse Records label, having played around Los Angeles since the early 70s as a surf band. That influence was easily detectable in their good-humoured pop punk, comprising driving songs with surreal narratives. Among their major early bookings were the San Francisco Art Festival, before going on to support the UK's Vapors on their American tour in 1981. Ostensibly closer to what would become 'new wave' than punk or hardcore, they nevertheless represented one of the best examples of 'wigged out West Coast rock', as one critic described them. However, the perceptions and branding were limiting, as Chai confirmed: 'People would say our songs are too simple or too fast, and then punk started and people said we were too sophisticated.' 'Too Much Junk', something of a punk classic of the time, was a particularly incisive comment on such fashion-consciousness in the Los Angeles scene. However, neither of their two studio albums, the first for an independent label, the second for MCA Records, captured this vitality. They broke up shortly afterwards before reconvening as the Zarkons to limited interest.

● ALBUMS: *Nightmare City* (Faulty 1981)★★, *Escape From The Planet Earth* (MCA 1982)★★.

ALLMAN BROTHERS BAND

Formed in Macon, Georgia, USA, in 1969 by guitarist Duane Allman (b. 20 November 1946, Nashville, Tennessee, USA, d. 29 October 1971, Macon, Georgia, USA), the band included brother Gregg Allman (b. 8 December 1947, Nashville, Tennessee, USA; keyboards/vocals), Forrest Richard 'Dickey' Betts (b. 12 December 1943, West Palm Beach, Florida, USA; guitar), Raymond Berry Oakley (b. 4 April 1948,

Chicago, Illinois, USA, d. 11 November 1972; bass), Butch Trucks (b. Claude Hudson Trucks Jnr., Jacksonville, Florida, USA; drums) and Jai 'Jaimoe' Johanny Johanson (b. John Lee Johnson, 8 July 1944, Ocean Springs, Mississippi, USA; drums). The above line-up was the culmination of several southern-based aspirants, of which the Hour Glass was the most prolific. This pop/soul ensemble featured Duane and Gregg Allman, but broke up when demo tapes for a projected third album were rejected by their record company. Duane then found employment at the Fame studio where he participated in several sessions, including those for Aretha Franklin, Wilson Pickett and King Curtis, prior to instigating this new sextet. The Allman Brothers established themselves as a popular live attraction and their first two albums, *The Allman Brothers Band* and *Idlewild South*, were marked by strong blues-based roots and an exciting rhythmic drive. Nevertheless, it was a sensational two-album set, *Live At The Fillmore East*, that showcased the group's emotional fire. 'Whipping Post', a 22 minute *tour de force*, remains one of rock music's definitive improvisational performances. The set brought the band to the brink of stardom, while Duane's reputation as an outstanding slide guitarist was further enhanced by his contribution to *Layla*, the seminal Derek And The Dominos album. Unfortunately, tragedy struck on 29 October 1971 when this gifted musician was killed in a motorcycle accident. The remaining members completed *Eat A Peach*, which consisted of live and studio material, before embarking on a mellower direction with *Brothers And Sisters*, a style best exemplified by the album's hit single, 'Ramblin' Man'. A second pianist, Chuck Leavell (b. Tuscaloosa, Alabama, USA), was added to the line-up, but just as the group recovered its momentum, Berry Oakley was killed in an accident chillingly similar to that of his former colleague on 11 November 1972. Not surprisingly, the Allman Brothers now seemed deflated, and subsequent releases failed to match the fire of those first recordings. Their power was further diminished by several off-shoot projects. Gregg Allman (who later married Cher twice) and Dickie Betts embarked on solo careers while Leavell, Johanson and new bassist Lamar Williams (b. 1947, Hansboro, Mississippi, USA, d. 25 January 1983 from cancer) formed Sea Level. The Allmans broke up acrimoniously in 1976 following a notorious drugs trial in which Gregg testified against a former road manager. Although the other members vowed never to work with the vocalist again, a reconstituted 1978 line-up included Allman, Betts and Trucks. *Enlightened Rogues* was a commercial success, but subsequent albums fared less well and in 1982 the Allman Brothers Band split for a second time. A new incarnation appeared in 1989 with a line-up of Greg Allman (vocals/organ), Betts (vocals/lead guitar), Warren Haynes (vocals/slide and lead guitar), Allen Woody (bass), Johnny Neel (keyboards), Trucks (drums) and Mark Quinones (percussion). This much

heralded reunion spawned a credible release: *Seven Turns*. Neel left the band and the remaining sextet made *Shades Of Two Worlds*. Mark Quinones (congas and percussion) joined for *An Evening With The Allman Brothers Band* in 1992. Their 1994 album, *Where It All Begins*, was recorded effectively live in the studio, with production once more by Allman Brothers veteran Tom Dowd. Nevertheless, it is the work displayed on their first five albums that remains among the finest recorded during the late 60s and early 70s, in particular for the skilful interplay between two gifted, imaginative guitarists.

●ALBUMS: *The Allman Brothers Band* (Capricorn 1969)★★★★, *Idlewild South* (Capricorn 1970)★★★★, *Live At The Fillmore East* double album (Capricorn 1971)★★★★, *Eat A Peach* double album (Capricorn 1972)★★★, *Brothers And Sisters* (Capricorn 1973)★★★, *Win, Lose Or Draw* (Capricorn 1975)★★★, *Wipe The Windows, Check The Oil, Dollar Gas* (Capricorn 1976)★, *Enlightened Rogues* (Capricorn 1979)★★★, *Reach For The Sky* (Arista 1980)★★, *Brothers Of The Road* (Arista 1981)★★, *Live At Ludlow Garage 1970* (Polygram 1990)★★★, *Seven Turns* (Epic 1990)★★★, *Shades Of Two Worlds* (Epic 1991)★★★, *An Evening With The Allman Brothers Band* (Epic 1992)★★★, *The Fillmore Concerts* (Polydor 1993)★★★★, *Where It All Begins* (Epic 1994)★★★, *2nd Set* (Epic 1995)★★, *Twenty* (SPV 1997).

●COMPILATIONS: *The Road Goes On Forever* (Capricorn 1975)★★★, *The Best Of The Allman Brothers Band* (Polydor 1981)★★★, *Dreams* 4-CD box set (Polydor 1989)★★★★, *A Decade Of Hits 1969-1979* (Polygram 1991)★★★.

●VIDEOS: *Brothers Of The Road* (RCA/Columbia 1988), *Live At Great Woods* (1993).

●FURTHER READING: *The Allman Brothers: A Biography In Words And Pictures*, Tom Nolan. *Midnight Riders: The Story Of The Allman Brothers Band*, Scott Freeman.

ALLMAN, DUANE

b. Howard Duane Allman, 20 November 1946, Nashville, Tennessee, USA, d. 29 October 1971, Macon, Georgia, USA. One of rock's most inventive and respected guitarists, Allman initially garnered attention as a member of the Allman Joys. This promising group was succeeded by the Hour Glass who recorded two albums prior to their demise when their record company rejected their final recordings. However, Allman's playing had impressed Rick Hall, owner of the renowned Fame studio, who booked the young musician for a forthcoming session with soul singer Wilson Pickett. The resultant album, *Hey Jude* (1968), was both a commercial and artistic success, and Allman was invited to join the studio's in-house team. The guitarist made several distinctive appearances over the ensuing months. He was featured on releases by Aretha Franklin, King Curtis, Clarence Carter, Otis Rush and Boz Scaggs, but grew frustrated with this limiting role. During one of his periodic visits back home to Florida, he joined a group of local musicians which became the Allman Brothers Band with the addition of Gregg Allman, Duane's younger brother. Despite the deserved success this unit achieved, Duane Allman continued his cameo appearances, the most exceptional of which was his contribution to the Derek And The Dominos classic, *Layla And Other Assorted Love Songs*. Here he displayed a joyous empathy playing slide guitar alongside fellow guitarist Eric Clapton, which resulted in one of rock's truly essential sets. Yet despite the offer of a permanent slot, Allman preferred to remain with his own group. In the summer of 1971, the Allman Brothers began work on their fourth album, *Eat A Peach*, but tired from constant touring, they took a break mid-way though the sessions. On 29 October, in an effort to avoid a collision with a truck, Allman crashed his motor-cycle and died following three hours of intensive surgery. This tragic accident robbed music of one of its exceptional talents whose all-too-brief legacy reveals an individual of rare skill and humility.

●COMPILATIONS: *Duane Allman: An Anthology* (Capricorn 1972)★★★★, *Duane Allman: An Anthology Volume II* (Capricorn 1974)★★★★, *Best Of Duane Allman* (Capricorn 1979)★★★.

ALLMAN, GREGG

b. Gregory Lenoir Allman, 8 December 1947, Nashville, Tennessee, USA. A founder member of the Allman Brothers Band, he embarked on a solo career in 1973. *Laid Back*, highlighted the singer's measured, bluesy approach and featured a version of 'Midnight Rider', a staple part of the early Allmans repertoire. A double set, *The Gregg Allman Tour*, documented the in-concert work of his band, while *Playin' Up A Storm* consolidated the artist's identity outside the parent group. Relations had been severed in 1976 during a drug trial when, under a promise of immunity, Allman had testified against a former road manager. His highly publicized marriages to Cher resulted in the couple's *Two The Hard Way* album, but the relationship was short-lived. For the next few years Allman struggled against various chemical dependencies but a reconstituted Allman Brothers temporarily stabilized his personal life. When the group broke up in 1982, the singer established a new Gregg Allman Band but a continuing battle with alcoholism hampered its progress. Gregg re-emerged in 1986 with *I'm No Angel*, determined to revive his career. This made the US top 30 and Gregg's own Allman Brothers Band had further success with *Just Before The Bullets Fly* in 1988 prior to the full scale reunion of the original band.

●ALBUMS: *Laid Back* (Capricorn 1973)★★★, *The Gregg Allman Tour* (Capricorn 1974)★★★, *Playin' Up A Storm* (Capricorn 1977)★★★, with Cher as Allman And Woman *Two The Hard Way* (Warners 1977)★, *I'm No Angel* (Epic 1987)★★, *Just Before The Bullets Fly* (Epic 1988)★★.

●COMPILATIONS: *Dreams* 4-CD box set (Polygram 1989)★★★★.

●VIDEOS: *One Way Out* (Hendring Video 1990), *This Country's Rockin'* (1993).

ALMOND, JOHNNY

b. 20 July 1946, Enfield, Middlesex, England. This accomplished saxophonist and flautist rose to prominence during the mid-60s as a member of London R&B group Tony Knight's Chessmen. In 1965 he replaced Clive Burrows in Zoot Money's Big Roll Band and two years later joined the successful Alan Price Set. This group became known as the Paul Williams Set following the original leader's departure and the same unit also formed the basis for a 1969 venture, Johnny Almond's Music Machine. Williams (vocals), Jimmy Crawford (guitar), Geoff Condon (trumpet), John Wiggins (keyboards), Roger Sutton (bass) and Alan White (drums) were featured on *Patent Pending*, a propulsive set drawing inspiration from both jazz and blues, but Almond subsequently disbanded the line-up, and a second album, *Hollywood Blues*, was completed with the aid of American musicians. A session musician on albums by Fleetwood Mac (*Mr. Wonderful*) and John Mayall (*Bluesbreakers With Eric Clapton*), the saxophonist joined the latter in 1969 in a pioneering 'drummer-less' unit captured on *The Turning Point* and *Empty Rooms*. Here Almond forged a partnership with guitarist Jon Mark, which resulted in the formation of a breakaway act, Mark-Almond in 1971. This imaginative ensemble completed a series of albums during the 70s and although less prolific, continued their partnership into the subsequent decade.

●ALBUMS: *Patent Pending* (Deram 1969)★★★, *Hollywood Blues* (Deram 1970)★★★, *Enchanted* (Parlophone 1970)★★★.

●COMPILATIONS: as Mark-Almond *The Best Of Mark-Almond* (1993)★★★.

ALOMAR, CARLOS

This guitarist became known principally as a rhythm player after an apprenticeship in James Brown's employ qualified him for the house band at the trend-setting Sigma Sound complex, from which emanated Philadelphia's feathery soul style in the 70s. Nevertheless, as well as backing the likes of the Stylistics and the Three Degrees, he served David Bowie, an irregular Sigma client, who was sufficiently impressed by Alomar's urgent precision and inventiveness on 1975's *Young Americans* to retain him as a full-time accompanist and sometime bandleader on tour and on disc. During one *Young Americans* session, he, Bowie and John Lennon composed its infectious hit single ('Fame'), but more typical of Alomar's years with Bowie (and later, Iggy Pop) was his terse chord and ostinato picking beneath the soloing of Earl Slick, Robert Fripp and Stevie Ray Vaughan. This had become something of a trademark when Alomar returned to well-paid studio work in the mid-80s.

ALTERNATIVE TV

Formed in 1977, ATV was the brainchild of Mark Perry (b. *c*.1957, London, England), the editor of Britain's seminal punk fanzine, *Sniffin' Glue*. The original line-up featured Perry (vocals), Alex Fergusson (b. 16 December 1952, Glasgow, Scotland; guitar), Micky Smith (bass) and John Towe (drums, ex-Generation X), but this unstable group later underwent several changes. Although ATV completed numerous albums during their career, they are best remembered for a series of uncompromising singles, including their self-effacing debut, 'Love Lies Limp' (free with *Sniffin' Glue*) and the declamatory 'How Much Longer?'. A disillusioned Perry abandoned the group in 1979 in favour of the Good Missionaries and subsequent projects, namely the Door And The Window and the Reflections. He returned to recording under the ATV banner in 1981 and continued to do so sporadically throughout the 80s. Fergusson went on to join Psychic TV, up until 1986, subsequently turning his hand to producing Gaye Bykers On Acid and the Popguns. With residual interest in Alternative TV still strong, Perry was stated to be working with Fergusson once more in 1995.

●ALBUMS: *The Image Has Cracked* (Deptford Fun City 1978)★★, *Vibing Up The Senile Man Part One* (Deptford Fun City 1979)★★, *Live At The Rat Club 'ß77* (Crystal Red 1979)★, *Strange Kicks* (IRS 1981)★★, *Peep Show* (Anagram 1987)★★, *Dragon Love* (Chapter 22 1990)★★, *Live 1978* (Overground/Feel Good All Over 1992)★, *My Life As A Child Star* (Overground 1994)★★. With Here And Now: *What You See ... Is What You Are* (Deptford Fun City 1978)★★.

●COMPILATIONS: *Action Time Vision* (Deptford Fun City 1980)★★, *Splitting In Two* (Anagram 1989)★★★, *Vibing Up The Senile Man - The Second ATV Collection* (Anagram 1996)★★.

ALTHEA AND DONNA

Jamaican schoolgirls Althea Forest and Donna Reid were 17 and 18 years old respectively when their irritatingly catchy novelty hit 'Uptown Top Ranking', hit the top of the charts in their home country. Their producer Joe Gibbs had supplied the tune for his own label (Lightning in the UK) and the girls were responsible for the patois lyrics, complete with girlish yelps in the background. The infectious tune and lyrics caught the attention of the British record buying public in 1978 and the record went to number 1. A highly unusual event, made doubly so by the fact that 'Uptown Top Ranking' was actually an answer record to Trinity's 'Three Piece Suit'. Despite the backing of major record company Virgin, the duo found it impossible to produce an equally effective follow-up and went into the annals of pop history as chart-topping one-hit-wonders.

●ALBUMS: *Uptown Top Ranking* (Front Line 1978)★★★.

AMAZING BLONDEL

Formed in 1969 by John Gladwin (vocals/guitar/woodwind) and Terry Wincott (vocals/guitar/percussion), former members of Lincolnshire rock group, Methuselah. The duo completed their debut album with the assistance of session guitarist 'Big' Jim Sullivan, before switching labels from Bell Records to Island. Edward Baird (guitar/lute) joined the group in April 1970 as they honed a peculiarly English direction, embracing the music of the Elizabethan and Tudor periods. *Evensong* and *Fantasia Lindum* reflected this interest, although the trio also acquired an unsavoury reputation for a stage act that offset their scholarly music with 'off-colour' jokes. Gladwin left the group following the release of *England 72*, and the 'Amazing' prefix was then dropped from their name. Wincott and Baird continued to record throughout the 70s, augmented by a series of well-known musicians including Steve Winwood, Mick Ralphs and several members of Free, a group that had proved instrumental in introducing Blondel to Island. William Murray (drums) and Mick Feat (guitar) joined the duo for *Mulgrave Street*, their first release for DJM Records, but the unit's popularity withered in the wake of this rockier perspective. Wincott was the sole remaining original member to appear on *Live In Tokyo*, after which Blondel was dissolved.

●ALBUMS: *The Amazing Blondel And A Few Faces* (Bell 1970)★★★, *Evensong* (Island 1970)★★★, *Fantasia Lindum* (Island 1971)★★★, *England 72* (Island 1972)★★★, *Blondel* (Island 1973)★★★, *Mulgrave Street* (DJM 1974)★★★, *Inspiration* (DJM 1975)★★, *Bad Dreams* (DJM 1976)★★, *Live In Tokyo* (DJM 1977)★★, *Live Abroad* (HTD 1996)★★, *Restoration* (HTD 1997)★★★.

●COMPILATIONS: *The Amazing Blondel And A Few Faces* (Edsel 1995)★★★.

AMAZING RHYTHM ACES

Formed in 1972, the Amazing Rhythm Aces were a US sextet consisting of Howard Russell Smith (b. Lafayette, Tennessee, USA; guitar/vocals), Barry Burton (guitar/mandolin/dobro), James Hooker (b. Tennessee, USA; keyboards/vocals), Billy Earhart III (b. Tennessee, USA; keyboards), Jeff Davis (b. Tennessee, USA; bass) and Butch McDade (drums). Davis and McDade had previously backed singer Jesse Winchester. The group was a country/rock outfit that also incorporated elements of R&B and gospel into its sound. They recorded their debut, *Stacked Deck*, in Memphis in 1975, from which the single, 'Third Rate Romance', was culled. It reached the Top 20 on both the pop and country charts in the USA. The band later found success only in the country area, where its second single, 'Amazing Grace (Used To Be Her Favorite Song)', was a Top 10 entry. They disbanded in 1980. Smith went solo and Earhart joined Hank Williams Jnr.'s group, the Bama Band.

●ALBUMS: *Stacked Deck* (ABC 1975)★★★, *Too Stuffed To Jump* (ABC 1976)★★★, *Toucan Do It, Too* (ABC 1977)★★★, *Burning The Ballroom Down* (ABC 1978)★★, *The Amazing Rhythm Aces* (ABC 1979)★★, *How The Hell Do You Spell Rhythm?* (ABC 1980)★★.

●COMPILATIONS: *The Best Of 4 LP's* (ABC 1981)★★★, *Full House - Aces High* (ABC 1982)★★★.

AMERICA

Formed in the late 60s by the offspring of American service personnel stationed in the UK, America comprised Dewey Bunnell (b. 19 January 1951, Harrogate, Yorkshire, England), Dan Peek (b. 1 November 1950, Panama City, Florida, USA) and Gerry Beckley (b. 12 September 1952, USA). Heavily influenced by Crosby, Stills & Nash, they employed similarly strong counter-harmonies backed by acoustic guitar. The first single, 'A Horse With No Name', proved a massive UK hit, ironically outselling any single by CS&N and sounding more like Neil Young. With backing by Warner Brothers Records, and management by former UK 'underground' disc jockey Jeff Dexter, the single went to the top of the US charts, immediately establishing the group as a top draw act. The debut album *America* fitted perfectly into the soft rock style of the period and paved the way for a series of further hits including 'I Need You', 'Ventura Highway', 'Tin Man' and 'Lonely People'. David Geffen stepped in and took over the running of their affairs as Dexter was involuntarily pushed aside.

Working with former Beatles producer George Martin between 1974 and 1977, the trio maintained their popularity in the USA, even returning to number 1 with the melodic 'Sister Golden Hair'. In 1977, they received a serious setback when Dan Peek left the trio (to concentrate on more spiritual material after his conversion to born-again Christianity). America continued as a duo, and returned to form in 1982 with the Russ Ballard-produced *View From The Ground*, which included the hit single 'You Can Do Magic'. Since then they have maintained a low commercial profile. They returned (still as a duo) with *Hourglass* in 1994, a smooth and gentle affair although ultimately dull, it no doubt pleased existing fans but it failed to make any new converts to what remains essentially dated mid-70s west coast rock.

●ALBUMS: *America* (Warners 1972)★★★, *Homecoming* (Warners 1972)★★★, *Hat Trick* (Warners 1973)★★, *Holiday* (Warners 1974)★★★, *Hearts* (Warners 1975)★★★, *Hideaway* (Warners 1976)★★★, *Harbor* (Warners 1976)★★, *America/Live* (Warners 1977)★, *Silent Letter* (Capitol 1979)★★, *Alibi* (Capitol 1980)★★, *View From The Ground* (Capitol 1982)★★, *Your Move* (Capitol 1983)★★, *Perspective* (Capitol 1984)★★, *In Concert* (Capitol 1985)★★, *The Last Unicorn* (Virgin 1988)★, *Hourglass* (American Gramophone 1994)★★.

●COMPILATIONS: *History* (Warners 1975)★★★, *Encore! More Greatest Hits* (Rhino 1990)★★, *The Best Of ...* (EMI 1997)★★★.

●VIDEOS: *Live In Central Park* (PMI 1986).

AMERICAN FLYER

This acoustic rock group formed in 1976 and featured Craig Fuller (guitar), Eric Kaz (b. Eric Justin Kaz, 1947, Brooklyn, New York, USA; guitar), Steve Katz (b. 9 May 1945; guitar) and Doug Yule (bass). Kaz, who had previously been a member of the Blues Magoos, formed American Flyer after the former group disbanded. He had already become a noted songwriter, producing songs such as 'I'm Blowin' Away' and 'Love Has No Pride' (co-written with Libby Titus) for Bonnie Raitt and Linda Ronstadt. Kaz's solo work was not successful; *If You're Lonely*, and *Cul-De-Sac* were both commercial and artistic failures. Steve Katz had been a member of Blood Sweat And Tears and had added some lively guitar to their excellent debut album, although by the time of their second his role had diminished as brass took over. Craig Fuller had formerly been with Pure Prairie League, while Yule had worked with the Velvet Underground. The group's 1976 debut, *American Flyer*, was produced by George Martin. Despite the pedigree of the group members, and the ample talent on the session, including Larry Carlton and Joe Sample, the album failed to achieve commercial success. A change of producer and backing personnel for the follow-up did little to change the fortunes of the group. Fuller and Kaz subsequently combined to release *Craig Fuller/Eric Kaz* in 1978 on Columbia. Fuller was more recently a member of Little Feat.

●ALBUMS: *American Flyer* (United Artists 1976)★★, *Spirit Of A Woman* (United Artists 1977)★★.

AMERICAN GRAFFITI

Released in 1973 and written by George Lucas and produced by Francis Ford Coppola, *American Graffiti* was a haunting, affectionate paean to small-town America during the early 60s. The sense of innocence and loss it evoked was enhanced by an extensive soundtrack, the bulk of which featured songs drawn from the previous decade. The cast was thus already imbued with a sense of nostalgia, capturing to perfection the uncertainty of the post-Elvis Presley, pre-Beatles era. The accompanying album is a joy from beginning to end, collecting classic songs by Buddy Holly, Chuck Berry, the Beach Boys, Del Shannon and many more. It is highly satisfying in its own right, but takes on an extra resonance when combined with one of the finest 'rock' films of any era.

AMERICAN SPRING

Sisters Marilyn and Diane Rovell first attracted attention during the early 60s. As members of the Honeys they enjoyed a fruitful association with Beach Boys leader Brian Wilson, who produced the bulk of their output and invited the unit to add backing voices on several of his own group's releases. Wilson married Marilyn and although their marriage has now ended, they produced two daughters, Wendy and Carnie, who were better known as two-thirds of Wilson Phillips, the short-lived trio that also featured China Phillips. The Rovell sisters, however, were initially known as Spring, and they recorded two low-key singles before completing their self-titled album, which included John Guerin (drums) and Larry Carlton (guitar). This evocative set captured the essence of their previous work, yet remained refreshingly contemporary, balancing crafted rearrangements of established material - 'Tennessee Waltz', and 'Everybody' - with several exquisite originals from the Beach Boys family. Brian Wilson provided notable contributions as producer and arranger, but the collection was not a commercial success, and Spring was dissolved following the release of their 'Shyin' Away' single. Nevertheless their legacy was rekindled during the 80s when Marilyn and Diane joined Ginger Blake in a revamped Honeys.

●ALBUMS: *Spring* UK title *American Spring* (1972)★★★.
●FURTHER READING: *The Nearest Faraway Place*, Timothy White.

AMON DUUL II

This inventive act evolved out of a commune based in Munich, Germany. The collective split into two factions in 1968 following an appearance at the Essen Song Days Festival where they supported the Mothers Of Invention and the Fugs. The political wing, known as Amon Duul, did record four albums, but Amon Duul II was recognized as the musical faction. Drawing inspiration from radical US west coast groups and the early Pink Floyd, the troupe's *modus operandi* mixed lysergic lyricism, open-ended improvisation and piercing riffs, which during live shows were bathed in an awe-inspiring lightshow. Renate Knaup-Krotenschwanz (vocals/percussion), John Weinzierl (guitar/bass), Falk Rogner (organ), Dave Anderson (bass), Dieter Serfas (drums), Peter Leopold (drums) and Shart (percussion) completed *Phallus Dei* in 1969 with the aid of Christian Burchard (vibes) and Holger Trulzsh (percussion). The first of several albums released in the UK on Liberty/United Artists, it immediately established Amon Duul II as an inventive, exciting attraction. A double set, *Yeti* proved more popular still, combining space-rock with free-form styles, although its release was presaged by the first of many personnel changes. Serfas, Shrat and Anderson quit, and the latter joined Hawkwind before forming his own group, Amon Din. Lothar Meid from jazz/rock collective Utopia, left and rejoined Amon Duul II on several occasions while producer Olaf Kubler often augmented live performances on saxophone.

Chris Karrer (guitar/violin) was alongside Weinzierl and Renate at the helm of another two-album package, *Dance Of The Lemmings*, which featured shorter pieces linked together into suites as well as the now-accustomed improvisation. The melodic *Carnival In Babylon* was succeeded by *Wolf City*, arguably Amon Duul II's most popular release. By that point they were at the

vanguard of German rock, alongside Can, Faust and Tangerine Dream. The group continued to tour extensively, but given the spontaneous nature of their music, Amon Duul II could be either inspired or shambolic. Indeed, *Vive La Trance* was a marked disappointment and the group's tenure at United Artists ended with the budget-priced *Live In London*, recorded during their halcyon 1972 tour. *Lemmingmania* compiled various singles recorded between 1970 and 1975.

Hijack and *Made In Germany* showed a group of dwindling power. Four members, including Renate and Falk, left on the latter's release, undermining the line-up further. The distinctive vocalist later worked with Popol Vu. Weinzierl quit the line-up following *Almost Alive*, leaving Karrer to lead the ensemble through *Only Human*. Amon Duul II was officially dissolved in 1980 although within a year several founding musicians regrouped for the disappointing *Vortex*. Weinzierl kept the name afloat upon moving to Wales where, with Dave Anderson, he completed *Hawk Meets Penguin* and *Meeting With The Man Machine* which were credited to Amon Duul (UK) following objections from original members. Further poor releases ensued although Karrer, Renate, Weinzierl and Leopold reunited to play at Calvert's memorial concert at London's Brixton Hall in 1989. The above quartet reconvened three years later in order to protect the rights to the Amon Duul II name. They then commenced recording again with Lothar Meid. Recent judicious live material from the band's golden era, released on *BBC Concert Plus*, is a timely reminder of a group at the peak of its creative powers.

●ALBUMS: *Phallus Dei* (Liberty 1969)★★★, *Yeti* (Liberty 1970)★★★★, *Dance Of The Lemmings* (United Artists 1971)★★★★, *Wolf City* (United Artists 1972)★★★, *Carnival In Babylon* (United Artists 1972)★★★, *Vive La Trance* (United Artists 1973)★★, *Live In London* (United Artists 1973)★★, *Hijack* (Nova 1974)★★, *Made In Germany* (Nova 1975)★★, *Pyragony X* (Nova 1976)★★, *Almost Alive* (Nova 1977)★★, *Only Human* (Strand 1978)★★, *Vortex* (Telefunken 1981)★★, *Hawk Meets Penguin* (Illuminated 1982)★★, *Nada Moonshine* (Mystic 1996)★★, *Live In Tokyo* (Mystic 1997)★★. As Amon Duul (UK): *Meeting With Men Machines* (Illuminated 1984)★★, *Airs On A Shoestring* (Thunderbolt 1987)★★, *Full Moon* (Demi-Monde 1989)★★, with Robert Calvert *Die Losung* (Demi-Monde 1989)★★, *Psychedelic Underground* (Captain Trip 1995)★★★.
●COMPILATIONS: *Classic German Rock Scene* (United Artists 1975)★★★, *Lemmingmania* (United Artists 1975)★★★, *Rock In Germany - 5 Years* (Strand 1980)★★, *Rock In Deutchland - Volume 1* (Strand 1981)★★, *Anthology* (Raw Power 1987)★★★, *BBC In Concert Plus* (Windsong 1992)★★★, *The Best Of 1969-1974* (Cleopatra 1997)★★★.

ANDERSON, MILLER

b. 12 April 1945, Johnston, Renfrewshire, Scotland. Songwriter, vocalist and guitarist Anderson first came to

promenance in the late 60s as a member of the jazz/rock unit the Keef Hartley Band. Anderson grew in stature while a member of that band and was present for five albums. He was signed as a solo artist and released one credible album, *Bright City*, in 1971. Many of his former Hartley sidemen were present on the album including record producer Neil Slaven. Junior Campbell arranged some exquisite strings for the title track and there is beautiful flute from Lynn Dobson on 'Shadows 'Cross My Wall'. Following this album Anderson formed Hemlock with James Leverton (bass) and Eric Dillon (drums) who made one (unreleased) album with Deram. Anderson teamed up with Hartley in 1974 as Dog Soldier and also had spells with Savoy Brown, Canned Heat and T. Rex. Anderson continues to perform regularly in the UK and Europe and in the mid-90s the re-release of his album on CD, together with a reissued Hartley catalogue indicated his star was in the ascendant. His present solo act features an excellent version of Bob Dylan's 'Copper Kettle', but his finest moment is a blistering acoustic version of 'Don't Let Me Be Misunderstood'; his voice on this track can strip wallpaper and break lightbulbs. In 1997 Anderson was touring with a revamped version of the Spencer Davis Group.
●ALBUMS: *Bright City* (Deram 1971)★★★.

ANDERSON, MOIRA

b. 5 June 1940, Kirkintilloch, Scotland. A popular singer with a beautiful soprano voice, Moira Anderson studied at the Royal Scottish Academy of Music, learning to play several instruments. While still in her teens, she had her first break in an Andy Stewart show at the Gaiety Theatre in Ayr, which lead to feature billing in the following Popplewell Gaiety winter production, and further work on the variety circuit. She reached a wider audience after appearing on the popular television programme *The White Heather Club*, beginning in 1960. Shortly afterwards she was given her own series, and also appeared in popular programmes such as *Eric Robinson's Melodies*, at the London Palladium, in *Royal Variety Performances*, and numerous other theatres throughout the land. Her recordings have consisted mainly of popular standards and light opera, notably those of Gilbert And Sullivan, but the songs of her homeland remain her real forté. Anderson has made regular appearances on religious programmes, and was awarded an OBE for her services to the music industry. In 1991 she was appearing in Scotland in shows such as *The Pride Of The Clyde*, and a year later presented *Moira's Music* on BBC Radio 2, accompanied by the City of Glasgow Philharmonic Orchestra.
●ALBUMS: *Moira Anderson's Scotland* (Decca 1968)★★★, *Moira Anderson Sings* (Decca 1969)★★★, *These Are My Songs* (Decca 1970)★★★, *This Is Moira Anderson* (Decca 1971)★★★, *A Rosebud By My Early Walk* (Decca 1973)★★★, *At The End Of The Day* (EMI 1974)★★★, *The Auld Scotch Songs* (EMI 1975)★★, *Moira

Anderson Sings The Ivor Novello Songbook* (EMI 1976)★★★, *Someone Wonderful* (MFP 1978)★★★, *A Star For Sunday* (MFP 1979)★★, *Favourite Scottish Songs* (Waverley Glen 1980)★★★, with Harry Secombe *Golden Memories* (Warwick 1981)★★★, *Moira Anderson Sings Operetta* (Flashback 1985)★★, *The Love Of God* (Word 1986)★★, *Moira - In Love* (Dulcima 1987)★★★, *My Scotland - A Land For All Seasons* (Lismor 1988)★★★, *20 Scottish Favourites* (Lismor 1990)★★★.
●COMPILATIONS: *The World Of Moira Anderson Volume 1* (Decca 1974)★★★, *The World Of Moira Anderson Volume 2* (Decca 1974)★★★, *The World Of Moira Anderson Volume 3* (Decca 1975)★★★, *The World Of Moira Anderson Volume 4* (Decca 1976)★★★, *The World Of Moira Anderson Volume 5* (Decca 1976)★★★, *Focus On Moira Anderson* (Decca 1978)★★★, *Sunday Songs* (Eclipse 1978)★★★.

ANNIE

The events surrounding the chequered history of the making of *Annie*, the fourth biggest Broadway hit musical of the 70s, and its 90s sequel, *Annie Warbucks*, could probably form the basis of a dramatic production capable of winning a Pulitzer Prize. The lyricist and director, Martin Charnin, is credited with the idea of producing a musical show based on the famous US comic strip, *Little Orphan Annie*. That was in 1971, but it was over five years later, on 21 April 1977, before *Annie* opened at the Alvin Theatre on Broadway. As his composer and librettist, Charnin recruited Charles Strouse and Thomas Meehan. The basic concept of the show did not immediately appeal to producers or financiers, and so it was not until it was presented at the Goodspeed Opera House, Connecticut, in the summer of 1976 (at which point producer Mike Nicolls got on board) that the *Annie* bandwagon began to roll, and a Broadway opening became a feasible proposition. The story, set in 1933, concerns the orphan Annie (Andrea McCardle) and her dog Sandy. She is trying desperately to find her parents, so that she can escape the clutches of Miss Hannigan (Dorothy Loudon), the orphanage's hard-hearted matron. In line with the show's 'greasepaint sentimentality' and 'unabashed corniness', Annie is eventually adopted by the millionaire industrialist Oliver 'Daddy' Warbucks (Reid Shelton), partly through the good offices of his friend, President Roosevelt (Raymond Thorne), whom Annie serenades with the perhaps over-optimistic 'Tomorrow', a song that apparently helps the President work out his economic policy, and also ensures 'A New Deal For Christmas'. The other numbers, which contributed to an enormous Broadway hit, and a run of 2377 performances, included 'I Don't Need Anything But You', 'I Think I'm Gonna Like It Here', 'It's A Hard-Knock Life', 'Little Girls', 'You're Never Fully Dressed Without A Smile', 'Easy Street' and 'Maybe'. It all ended happily, if a little confusingly: Annie can finally be adopted because her parents are 'no longer with us', and the conniving Miss Hannigan is arrested for fraud. The show won several Tony Awards, including best score and best musical. In 1978, the prominent UK television actor, Stratford Johns, played Daddy Warbucks in a successful London production, and there was a West End revival in 1982. In the same year a film version of *Annie* was released, with Albert Finney as Warbucks and Aileen Quinn as Annie.

In January 1990, a sequel to *Annie*, entitled *Annie 2: Miss Hannigan's Revenge*, opened at the Kennedy Center Opera House in Washington, DC. During the next three years, with the constant and passionate co-operation of producer Karen Walter Goodwin, Charnin, Strouse and Meehan undertook extensive rewrites, and, with a revised title, *Annie Warbucks*, spent some time in Chicago, and toured theatres in Texas and west coast cities such as Los Angeles, Pasadena, and San Diego. A Broadway opening was set for December 1992, postponed until March, and then April. Finally, with new producers on board, the show was slimmed down from a $5.5 million Broadway high-risk operation, to an adventurous $1 million production which opened - with its third Annie in three years - off Broadway at the Variety Arts Theatre on 9 August 1993. (A weary Martin Charnin said: 'This is the ninth time I have put this mother into rehearsal.') Onstage, the time is Christmas morning, and the woman from the welfare, Commissioner Harriet Doyle (Arlene Robertson), is insisting that Daddy Warbucks (Harve Presnell) find a wife within 60 days or it's back to the orphanage for Annie (Kathryn Zaremba). The ideal candidate seems to be Daddy's Chinese secretary, Grace (Marguerite MacIntyre) ('That's The Kind Of Woman'), but he thinks that she is far too young, and favours the more mature Sheila Kelly (Donna McKechnie) ('A Younger Man'), who, we all know some time before the predictable ending, does not even stand a chance. The rest of the score included 'Annie Ain't Just Annie Any More', 'The Other Woman', 'Above The Law', 'I Got Me', 'Changes', 'Love', the jivey 'All Dolled Up', a touching tale of unrequited love, 'It Would Have Been Wonderful', and 'I Always Knew' (which was really 'Tomorrow' Mark II). The show will never be another *Annie*, but even so, as one critic pointed out, 'Charnin, Strouse, and Meehan can now get on with the rest of their lives.'

APHRODITE'S CHILD

Formed in Greece during the mid-60s, Aphrodite's Child consisted of Demis Roussos (b. 15 June 1947, Alexandria, Egypt; vocals), Vangelis Papathanassiou (b. Evangalos, Odyssey Papathanassiou, 29 March 1943, Valos, Greece; keyboards) and Lucas Sideras (b. 5 December 1944, Athens, Greece; drums). In 1968 the trio enjoyed a massive European hit with 'Rain And Tears', a haunting ballad memorable for Roussos's nasal, almost sobbing, falsetto. Although the single made little impression in Britain, the group did court a cultish popularity, particularly in the wake of a second album, *It's Five O'Clock*. It was their 1972 release, *666*,

that marked an artistic peak and this apocalyptical concept album, a double set, was applauded for its ambition and execution. However, this was their final recording. 'Break' from the album almost became a hit that year. Roussos subsequently found international fame as a purveyor of sweet, MOR material while Papathanassiou achieved notable solo success under the name of Vangelis. His instrumental and compositional dexterity reached its zenith with the soundtrack to the Oscar-winning British film *Chariots Of Fire*.

●ALBUMS: *Aphrodite's Child - Rain And Tears* (Impact 1968)★★, *It's Five O'Clock* (Impact 1970)★★, *666 - The Apocalypse Of St. John* (Vertigo 1972)★★★.

●COMPILATIONS: *Rain And Tears: The Best Of* (Philips International 1970)★★★, *The Best Of Aphrodite's Child* (Mercury 1975)★★★, *Greatest Hits* (Mercury 1981)★★★.

APRIL WINE

Formed in 1969 in Montreal, Quebec, this hard rock group became an immediate success, going on to make inroads in the American market after establishing itself as a platinum act in Canada. Through fluctuating line-ups they arrived at steady membership by the late 70s, including original lead singer Myles Goodwyn (b. 23 June 1948, Halifax, Nova Scotia, Canada), Brian Greenway (b. 1 October 1951; guitar), Gary Moffet (b. 22 June 1949; guitar), Steve Lang (b. 24 March 1949; bass) and Jerry Mercer (b. 27 April 1939; drums). Among their first admirers were former Rascals members Dino Dinelli and Gene Cornish, who produced early material for the group. The line-up for their first album had featured Goodwyn on guitar and vocals, David Henman on guitar, Jim Clench on bass and Richie Henman on drums. *Electric Jewels* saw the line-up switch with Gary Moffet coming in on guitar, and Jerry Mercer on drums to replace the Henman brothers. Clench was replaced on *The Whole World's Going' Crazy* by Steve Lang, with Greenaway added as third guitarist in time for *First Glance*. Despite uneven album performances, April Wine placed three Top 40 singles and five albums in the US charts, their greatest commercial successes coming with the gold album *Harder .. Faster* and the platinum *The Nature Of The Beast*. The group broke up in the mid-80s but re-formed at the turn of the new decade.

●ALBUMS: *April Wine* (Aquarius 1972)★★, *On Record* (Aquarius 1973)★★, *Electric Jewels* (Aquarius 1974)★★, *Live* (Aquarius 1975)★★, *Stand Back* (Aquarius 1975)★★, *The Whole World's Goin' Crazy* (London 1976)★★★, *Live At The El Mocambo* (London 1977)★★, *First Glance* (Capitol 1978)★★, *Harder ... Faster* (Capitol 1979)★★★, *The Nature Of The Beast* (Capitol 1981)★★★, *Power Play* (Capitol 1982)★★, *Animal Grace* (Capitol 1984)★★, *Walking Through Fire* (Capitol 1985)★★.

●VIDEOS: *Live In London* (PMI 1986).

ARGENT

When the 60s pop group the Zombies finally disintegrated, keyboardist Rod Argent (b. 14 June 1945, St

Albans, Hertfordshire, England) wasted no time in forming a band that would enable his dexterity as pianist and songwriter to flourish. The assembled unit also included Russ Ballard (b. 31 October 1947, Waltham Cross, Hertfordshire, England; guitar/vocals), Bob Henrit (b. 2 May 1944, Broxbourne, Hertfordshire, England; drums) and Jim Rodford (b. 7 July 1941, St. Albans, Hertfordshire, England; bass). Their critically acclaimed debut contained Ballard's 'Liar', a song that became one of their concert regulars and was also a US Top 10 hit for Three Dog Night in 1971. *All Together Now* contained the exhilarating 'Hold Your Head Up' which became a Top 5 hit on both sides of the Atlantic. Likewise, *In Deep* produced another memorable hit, 'God Gave Rock 'N' Roll To You' (a hit in 1992 for Kiss). Ballard, who by now had developed into an outstanding pop songwriter, left in 1974 to pursue a solo career and his place within the group was taken by two new members, John Verity (b. 3 July 1949, Bradford, Yorkshire, England; guitar/bass/vocals) and John Grimaldi (b. 25 May 1955, St. Albans, Hertfordshire, England; cello/mandolin/violin). From this point onward, the band became lost in an atrophy of improvisational solos. Argent disbanded in 1976, Rodford eventually joined the Kinks while Rod Argent opened keyboard shops and continued as a successful record producer and session player. He explored his jazz roots working with Barbara Thompson, showing an ability he had first demonstrated almost 30 years earlier, during the piano solo on the Zombies' superlative 'She's Not There'. He has now become established as a respected record producer, with recent major success with Tanita Tikaram.

● ALBUMS: *Argent* (Columbia 1970)★★★, *Ring Of Hands* (Columbia 1971)★★★, *All Together Now* (Epic 1972)★★★, *In Deep* (Epic 1973)★★, *Nexus* (Epic 1974)★★, *Encore - Live In Concert* (Epic 1974)★, *Circus* (Epic 1975)★, *Counterpoint* (RCA 1975)★★, *In Concert* (Windsong 1995)★★★.

● COMPILATIONS: *Anthology* (Epic 1984)★★★, *Music From The Spheres* (Elite 1991)★★★.

ARMATRADING, JOAN

b. 9 December 1950, Basseterre, St Kitts, West Indies. Joan Armatrading was the first black woman singer-songwriter based in Britain to compete on equal terms with white women. While Madeleine Bell and P.P. Arnold pre-dated Armatrading's success, the latter has remained consistent for 20 years. Although she has been inaccurately compared with Tracy Chapman, the two women have little in common other than the colour of their skin and the fact that they are both guitar playing singer-songwriters. The Armatrading family moved to Birmingham, England, in 1958, and Joan taught herself to play piano and guitar, before meeting Pam Nestor, also a West Indian immigrant (b. Berbice, Guyana, 28 April 1948). Both were working in a touring cast of the celebrated hippie musical, *Hair*. Armatrading and Nestor worked as a team, writing songs together,

but Armatrading was given the major role on *Whatever's For Us*, her 1972 debut album produced by Gus Dudgeon (who was also working with Elton John at the time, hence the participation of musicians such as guitarist Davey Johnstone and percussionist Ray Cooper). Released in the UK on Cube Records, the album was a greater critical than commercial success, and was licensed for North America by A&M Records. Armatrading and Nestor dissolved their partnership after the album; Nestor made an excellent one-off single for Chrysalis in the late 70s, but seems not to have recorded since.

By 1975, Armatrading was signed to A&M worldwide, working with producer Pete Gage (husband of Elkie Brooks). The album that resulted, *Back To The Night*, featured instrumentalists such as Andy Summers (later of the Police) and keyboard player Jean Roussal, but again failed to trouble the chart compilers. 1976 brought the album that first thrust Armatrading into the limelight. The first of four consecutive albums produced by Glyn Johns, *Joan Armatrading* made the Top 20 of the UK album chart, and includes her only UK Top 10 hit (and her best known song) 'Love And Affection'. 1977's *Show Some Emotion* became the first album to reach the UK Top 10 and 1978's *To The Limit* made the UK Top 20, although neither album included a hit single. In 1979, her partnership with Johns ended with *Steppin' Out*, a live album recorded in the USA, which did not chart on either side of the Atlantic. 1980 brought a change of producer for her seventh album, after a brief working alliance with Henry Dewy had provided a minor hit single, 'Rosie', which was included on a mini album, *How Cruel*, released in the USA and continental Europe but strangely not in the UK. Richard Gottehrer (once part of the Strangeloves and the producer of Blondie's first album) was obviously a good choice, as *Me Myself I*, released in 1980, became Armatrading's first album to reach the US Top 40 and returned her to the UK Top 10, while it included two minor UK hit singles, in the title track and 'All The Way From America'. *Walk Under Ladders*, Armatrading's 1981 album, was produced by Steve Lillywhite, and among the musicians who contributed to it were the celebrated Jamaican rhythm section of Sly Dunbar and Robbie Shakespeare, plus Andy Partridge of XTC and Thomas Dolby. The album, which reached the UK Top 10, but peaked somewhat lower in the US chart, included two more minor UK chart singles, 'I'm Lucky' and 'No Love'. Her 1983 album, *The Key*, was mainly produced by Lillywhite again, but with two tracks, 'Drop The Pilot' (which was her second biggest UK hit single, almost reaching the Top 10) and 'What Do Boys Dream' produced by Val Garay. The album largely restored Armatrading to international commercial prominence, peaking just outside the US Top 30 and reaching the UK Top 10. Later that year, a 'Best Of' album, *Track Record*, made the UK Top 20. By this point in her career, Armatrading appeared to have a solid core of fans who would buy every album, but who were too few to provide first division status. 1985's *Secret Secrets* was produced by Mike Howlett with musicians including bass player Pino Palladino (of Paul Young fame) and Joe Jackson, who was the only other musician involved on the track 'Love By You'. 'Temptation', another track from the album, was a minor UK hit single, and while the album once again made the Top 20 of the UK chart, it was not a major US success, despite a sleeve shot taken by celebrated New York photographer Robert Mapplethorpe. *Sleight Of Hand* was Armatrading's first self-produced album, which she recorded in her own quaintly named Bumpkin studio, and which was remixed by Steve Lillywhite. This was her least successful album in commercial terms since her debut, stalling outside the Top 30 of the UK chart and considerably lower in the USA, even despite the fact that this time the sleeve photographer was Lord Snowdon.

1988's *The Shouting Stage* was her most impressive album in some time but failed to reach the height achieved by many of its predecessors, despite featuring Mark Knopfler and Mark Brzezicks of Big Country as guests. *Hearts And Flowers* again demonstrated that even though the quality of Armatrading's output was seldom less than exemplary, it rarely achieved its commercial desserts. 1991 brought a further compilation album, which largely updated the earlier *Track Record*, and included a remix (by Hugh Padgham) of 'Love And Affection' which was released as a single. Armatrading seems to have reached a plateau in her career which is slightly below the top echelon in commercial terms, but which will enable her to continue recording with reasonable success (especially in critical terms) for as long as she desires. She has also contributed her services to a number of charitable concerts, such as the Prince's Trust, the 1988 Nelson Mandela Concert and Amnesty International. She is to be applauded for remaining unpretentious, and is also in the enviable position of being able to choose her own touring and recording timetable. In 1994 she signed to RCA Records after many years with A&M and released *What's Inside*.

●ALBUMS: *Whatever's For Us* (A&M 1972)★★★, *Back To The Night* (A&M 1975)★★★, *Joan Armatrading* (A&M 1976)★★★★, *Show Some Emotion* (A&M 1977)★★★, *To The Limit* (A&M 1978)★★★, *Steppin' Out* (A&M 1978)★★, *Me Myself I* (A&M 1980)★★★★, *Walk Under Ladders* (A&M 1981)★★★, *The Key* (A&M 1983)★★★, *Secret Secrets* (A&M 1985)★★★, *Sleight Of Hand* (A&M 1986)★★★, *The Shouting Stage* (A&M 1988)★★★★, *Hearts And Flowers* (A&M 1990)★★★, *Square The Circle* (A&M 1992)★★★, *What's Inside* (RCA 1995)★★★.

●COMPILATIONS: *Track Record* (A&M 1983)★★★★, *The Very Best Of Joan Armatrading* (A&M 1991)★★★★.

●VIDEOS: *Track Record* (A&M Sound Pictures 1989), *Very Best Of Joan Armatrading* (A&M Sound Pictures 1991).

●FURTHER READING: *Joan Armatrading: A Biography*, Sean Mayes.

ARRIVAL

This late 60s Liverpool group came together when former NEMS employee Dyan Birch (b. 25 January 1949), teamed up with Paddie McHugh (b. 28 August 1946) and Frank Collins (b. 25 October 1947) of local group the Excels. A second Merseyside girl, vocalist Carroll Carter (b. 10 June 1948) was added, along with Lloyd Courtney (b. 20 December 1947, Cheshire, England), Don Hume (b. 31 March 1950, Watford, Hertfordshire, England) and Tony O'Malley (b. 15 July 1948). The septet sent a tape to Decca Records' A&R representative Tony Hall, who was so impressed by the group's sound that he decided to record and manage them. Their early 70s Top 20 UK hits, 'Friends' and 'I Will Survive' were urgent performances with some excellent vocal work. Although their professed ambition was for 'Arrival to become a household name', the seven-piece band proved unwieldy and eventually split, with Birch, Collins, O'Malley and McHugh re-emerging in Kokomo.

●ALBUMS: *Arrival* i (Decca 1970)★★★, *Arrival* ii (Columbia 1972)★★★.

ARROWS

Formed in 1973, the Arrows - Jake Hooker (b. 3 May 1952, New York, USA; guitar/saxophone), Alan Merrill (b. 19 February 1951, New York, USA; bass/piano/harmonica) and Paul Varley (b. 24 May 1952, Preston, Lancashire, England; drums/piano) - were one of several groups associated with the glam-rock/bubblegum team of songwriters Chinn And Chapman. Merrill interrupted his solo career in Japan at the behest of old friend Hooker to form the Arrows along with Varley. Their debut release, 'A Touch Too Much', was a UK Top 10 hit in May 1974, but despite securing their own television series, the group's only other success came the following year with 'My Last Night With You', which peaked at number 25. This 50s-styled performance contrasted with the perky pop of its predecessors, but the Arrows were unable to shake off the teenybop tag which they had once studiously courted. The trio broke up when their mentor's own commercial grasp faltered. Hooker and Merrill's song, 'I Love Rock 'N' Roll' later provided Joan Jett And The Blackhearts with a US number 1 in 1982.

●ALBUMS: *First Hit* (Rak 1976)★★.

●FURTHER READING: *Arrows: The Official Story*, Bill Harry.

ASHER, PETER

b. 22 June 1944, London, England. Following the demise of the singing duo Peter And Gordon in 1968, Asher continued his growing interest in record production. His first outside work was with ex-Manfred Mann lead singer Paul Jones. It was, however, on being appointed head of A&R at the newly formed Apple Records that Asher had the big opportunity to prove himself. He signed James Taylor and produced his first album; it was Asher, and not Apple, who saw the potential of Taylor. Shortly after his resignation, Asher took Taylor and moved to the USA where he has lived ever since. His involvement with Taylor has lasted for over 20 years as both manager and producer. Additionally, he has skilfully and successfully overseen the careers of many other artists including Linda Ronstadt, Bonnie Raitt, J.D. Souther, Andrew Gold, John Stewart and latterly Joni Mitchell. Asher won a Grammy in 1978 and 1990 for producer of the year. His other notable production credits include two albums by 10,000 Maniacs.

ASHFORD AND SIMPSON

Nickolas 'Nick' Ashford (b. 4 May 1942, Fairfield, South Carolina, USA) and Valerie Simpson (b. 26 August 1946, The Bronx, New York, USA). This performing and songwriting team met in the choir of Harlem's White Rock Baptist Church. Having recorded, unsuccessfully, as a duo, they joined another aspirant, Jo 'Joshie' Armstead, at the Scepter/Wand label where their compositions were recorded by Ronnie Milsap ('Never Had It So Good'), Maxine Brown ('One Step At A Time'), the Shirelles and Chuck Jackson. Another of the trio's songs, 'Let's Go Get Stoned', gave Ray Charles a number 1 US R&B hit in 1966. Ashford and Simpson then joined Holland/Dozier/Holland at Motown Records where their best-known songs included 'Ain't No Mountain High Enough', 'You're All I Need To Get By', 'Reach Out And Touch Somebody's Hand' and 'Remember Me'. Simpson also began 'ghosting' for Tammi Terrell when the latter became too ill to continue her partnership with Marvin Gaye, and she sang on part of the duo's *Easy* album. In 1971 Simpson embarked on a solo career, but two years later she and Nickolas were recording together for Warner Brothers Records. A series of critically welcomed, if sentimental, releases followed, but despite appearing on the soul chart, few crossed over into pop. However, by the end of the decade, the couple achieved their commercial reward with the success of 'It Seems To Hang On' (1978) and 'Found A Cure' (1979). At the same time their production work for Diana Ross (*The Boss*) and Gladys Knight (*The Touch*) enhanced their reputation. Their status as imaginative performers and songwriters was further assured in 1984 when 'Solid' became an international hit single. Ashford and Simpson, who were married in 1974, remain one of soul's quintessential partnerships.
●ALBUMS: *Gimme Something Real* (Warners 1973)★★, *I Wanna Be Selfish* (Warners 1974)★★, *Come As You Are* (Warners 1976)★★, *So, So Satisfied* (Warners 1977)★★★, *Send It* (Warners 1977)★★★, *Is It Still Good To Ya?* (Warners 1978)★★★, *Stay Free* (Warners 1979)★★★, *A Musical Affair* (Warners 1980)★★★, *Performance* (Warners 1981)★★★, *Street Opera* (Capitol 1982)★★★, *High-Rise* (Capitol 1983)★★★, *Solid* (Capitol 1984)★★★, *Real Love* (Capitol 1986)★★★, *Love Or Physical* (Capitol 1989)★★. Solo: Valerie Simpson *Exposed!* (Tamla 1971)★★, *Valerie Simpson* (Tamla 1972)★★.
●COMPILATIONS: *The Best Of* (1993)★★★★.
●VIDEOS: *The Ashford And Simpson Video* (EMI 1982).
●FILMS: *Body Rock* (1984).

ASHTON, GARDNER AND DYKE

This short-lived but popular UK rock group consisted of two ex-members of the Remo Four, Tony Ashton (b. 1 March 1946, Blackburn, Lancashire, England; vocals/keyboards) and Roy Dyke (drums), plus bassist Kim Gardner (b. 27 January 1946, Dulwich, London, England), formerly of Creation. Having served briefly in one of singer P.P. Arnold's backing groups, alongside Steve Howe, the trio embarked on an independent career in 1968. Their albums featured a light, jazz-rock style similar to that of the Brian Auger Trinity. The three-piece proved equally adept at pop and scored a UK Top 3 hit in 1971 with 'Resurrection Shuffle', in which Ashton's throaty delivery was matched by a rasping brass section comprising Dave Caswell (trumpet) and Lyle Jenkins (saxophone) with additional guitarwork from Mick Lieber. Its success, however, was not sustained and the group broke up in 1972 without fulfilling its obvious potential. Dyke later became a founder member of Badger, where he was latterly joined by Gardner, while Ashton replaced 'Poli' Palmer in Family.
●ALBUMS: *Ashton, Gardner And Dyke* (Polydor 1969)★★★, *The Worst Of Ashton, Gardner And Dyke* (Capitol 1971)★★, *What A Bloody Long Day It's Been* (Capitol 1972)★★.

ASHTON, MARK

Ashton began his career as the original lead vocalist for the early 70s UK progressive group Rare Bird (best known for their 'Sympathy' hit). In 1974 he left that band to form Headstone, but when success with that group proved more elusive he elected to pursue a solo career. Little fanfare surrounded the release of his two solo albums for 20th Century and Arista Records in the late 70s - with new wave dominating the charts there was little commercial respite for an artist with designs as grand as those of Ashton. *Modern Pilgrims*, an unexpected 1988 release for new label RCA Records, included futuristic imagery in addition to bombastic hard rock with elaborate arrangements. Though it gained strong critical reviews its sales profile was minimal.
●ALBUMS: *Mark Ashton* (20th Century 1978)★★★, *Solo* (Arista 1979)★★★, *Modern Pilgrims* (RCA 1988)★★★.

ASLEEP AT THE WHEEL

Ray Benson (b. 16 March 1951, Philadelphia, Pennsylvania, USA; guitar/vocals), Christine O'Connell (b. 21 March 1953, Williamsport, Maryland, USA; vocals), Lucky Oceans (b. Reuben Gosfield, 22 April 1951, Philadelphia, Pennsylvania, USA; steel guitar), Floyd Domino (piano) and Leroy Preston (rhythm guitar/drums) formed the core of this protean western swing-styled unit. Although initially based in West Virginia, the group later moved to Austin, Texas, where they found a more receptive audience in the wake of their infectious debut album. They had a US Top 10 single in 1973 with 'The Letter That Johnny Walker Read' and won a Grammy for their version of Count Basie's 'One O'Clock Jump'. However, despite an undoubted live appeal and an appearance in the rock film *Roadie,* the group's anachronistic style has hampered a more widespread success.

●ALBUMS: *Comin' Right At Ya* (Sunset 1973)★★★, *Asleep At The Wheel* (1974)★★★, *Texas Gold* (Capitol 1975)★★★★, *Wheelin' And Dealin'* (Capitol 1976)★★★, with various artists *Texas Country* (1976)★★, *The Wheel* (Capitol 1977)★★★★, *Collision Course* (Capitol 1978)★★★, *Served Live* (Capitol 1979)★★★, *Framed* (MCA 1980)★★★, *Pasture Prime* (Demon 1985)★★★, *Jumpin' At The Woodside* (Edsel 1986)★★★, *Ten* (Epic 1987)★★★, *Asleep At The Wheel* (Epic 1987)★★★, *Western Standard Time* (Epic 1988)★★★, *Tribute To The Music Of Bob Wills And The Texas Playboys* (1993)★★★, *The Wheel Keeps On Rollin'* (Capitol 1995)★★★.

●COMPILATIONS: *The Very Best Of Asleep At The Wheel* (See For Miles 1987)★★★, *Greatest Hits - Live & Kickin'* (1992)★★★.

ASWAD

Formed in west London, England, in 1975, this premier UK reggae group featured Brinsley Forde (b. 1952, Guyana; vocals/guitar), George Oban (bass), Angus Gaye (b. 1959, London; drums) and Donald Griffiths (b. 1954, Jamaica, West Indies; vocals). Additional musicians include Vin Gordon, Courtney Hemmings, Bongo Levi, Karl Pitterson and Mike Rose. Taking their name from the Arabic word for black, they attempted a fusion of Rastafarianism with social issues more pertinent to their London climate. Their self-titled debut was well received, and highlighted the plight of the immigrant Jamaican in an unfamiliar and often hostile environment. A more ethnic approach was evident on the superior follow-up, *Hulet,* which placed the group squarely in the roots tradition only partially visited on their debut. Their instrumentation impressed, with imaginative song structures filled out by a dextrous horn section. The departure of Oban, who was replaced by Tony 'Gad' Robinson (the former keyboard player) did little to diminish their fortunes. Forde, meanwhile, was featured in the film *Babylon,* with Aswad's 'Warrior Charge' on its soundtrack.

A brief change of label saw them record two albums for CBS before they returned to Island Records for *Live And Direct,* recorded at London's Notting Hill Carnival in 1982. By early 1984 they were at last making a small impression on the UK charts with 'Chasing The Breeze', and a cover of Toots Hibbert's '54-46 (Was My Number)'. *To The Top* in 1986 represented arguably the definitive Aswad studio album, replete with a strength of compo-

sition which was by now of considerable power. While they consolidated their reputation as a live act, they used *Distant Thunder* as the launching pad for a significant stylistic overhaul. The shift to lightweight funk and soul, although their music maintained a strong reggae undertow, made them national chart stars. The album bore a 1988 UK number 1 hit in 'Don't Turn Around'. Since then, Aswad have remained a major draw in concert, although their attempts to plot a crossover path have come unstuck in more recent times, despite the appearance of artists such as Shabba Ranks on their 1990 set, *Too Wicked.* Although they have not always appealed to the purists, Aswad are one of the most successful reggae-influenced groups operating in the UK, thoroughly earning all the accolades that have come their way, particuarly with their riveting live act.

●ALBUMS: *Aswad* (Mango/Island 1975)★★★, *Hulet* (Grove Music 1978)★★★★, *New Chapter* (Columbia 1981)★★★, *Not Satisfied* (Columbia 1982)★★★, *A New Chapter Of Dub* (Mango/Island 1982)★★★, *Live And Direct* (Mango/Island 1983)★★★, *Rebel Souls* (Mango/Island 1984)★★★, *Jah Shaka Meets Aswad In Addis Ababa Studio* (Jah Shaka 1985)★★★, *To The Top* (Simba 1986)★★★★, *Distant Thunder* (Mango/Island 1988)★★★, *Too Wicked* (Mango/Island 1990)★★, *Rise And Shine* (Bubblin 1994)★★.

●COMPILATIONS: *Showcase* (Grove Music 1981)★★★, *Renaissance* (Stylus 1988)★★★, *Crucial Tracks - The Best Of Aswad* (Mango/Island 1989)★★★★, *Don't Turn Around* (Mango/Island 1993)★★★, *Firesticks* (Mango/Island 1993)★★★.

●VIDEOS: *Distant Thunder Concert* (Island Visual Arts 1989), *Always Wicked* (Island Visual Arts 1990).

ATLANTA RHYTHM SECTION

The cream of the studio musicians from Atlanta, Georgia, USA, the Atlanta Rhythm Section (actually from nearby Doraville, Georgia) came together in 1970 after working at a Roy Orbison recording session. Dean Daughtry (b. 8 September 1946, Kinston, Alabama, USA; keyboards) and drummer Robert Nix had been members of Orbison's backing group, the Candymen, and both Daughtry and J.R. Cobb (b. 5 February 1944, Birmingham, Alabama, USA; guitar) had been members of the Top 40 hitmakers Classic IV. Rounding out the line-up were vocalist Rodney Justo (replaced after the first album by Ronnie Hammond), Barry Bailey (b. 12 June 1948, Decatur, Georgia, USA; guitar), and Paul Goddard (b. 23 June 1945, Rome, Georgia, USA; bass). The group recorded two albums for Decca Records in 1972, neither of which made an impact, before signing to Polydor Records in 1974. Their first album for that company, *Third Annual Pipe Dream,* only reached number 74 in the US and the next two albums fared worse. Finally, in 1977, the single 'So Into You' became the band's breakthrough, reaching the US Top 10, as did the album from which it came, *A Rock And Roll Alternative.* Their follow-up album, *Champagne Jam,* went to the Top 10 in 1978, together with the single 'Imaginary Lover', after which Nix left, to be replaced by Roy Yeager (b. 4 February 1946, Greenwood, Mississippi, USA). The group's last hit on Polydor was a 1979 remake of 'Spooky', a song with which Cobb and Daughtry had been involved when they were with Classics IV. A switch to Columbia Records in 1981 gave the group one last chart album, *Quinella*, and a US Top 30 single, 'Alien', after which they faded from the national scene.

●ALBUMS: *The Atlanta Rhythm Section* (Decca 1972)★★★, *Back Up Against The Wall* (Decca 1973)★★★, *Third Annual Pipe Dream* (Polydor 1974)★★★, *Dog Days* (Polydor 1975)★★, *Red Tape* (Polydor 1976)★★★, *A Rock And Roll Alternative* (Polydor 1977)★★★★, *Champagne Jam* (Polydor 1978)★★★, *Underdog* (Polydor 1979)★★★, *Are You Ready!* (Polydor 1979)★★★, *The Boys From Doraville* (Polydor 1980)★★, *Quinella* (Columbia 1981)★★.

●COMPILATIONS: *The Best Of The Atlanta Rhythm Section* (Polydor 1982)★★★★.

ATOMIC ROOSTER

Formed in 1969 at the height of the UK progressive rock boom, the original Rooster line-up comprised Vincent Crane (b. 1945, d. February 1989; organ), Nick Graham (bass) and Carl Palmer (b. 20 March 1951, Birmingham, England; drums). Crane and Palmer had just departed from the chart-topping Crazy World Of Arthur Brown and it was assumed that their new group would achieve sustained success. After only one album, however, the unit fragmented with Graham joining Skin Alley and Palmer founding Emerson, Lake And Palmer. Crane soldiered on with new members John Cann (guitar/vocals) and Paul Hammond (drums), drafted in from Andromeda, who were featured on the album *Death Walks Behind You*. Their excursions into hard rock produced two riff-laden yet catchy UK hit singles in 1971: 'Tomorrow Night' and 'The Devil's Answer', as Crane adopted the Ray Manzarek (Doors) style of using keyboards to record bass parts. With assistance from Pete French of Cactus the trio recorded their third album *In Hearing Of*, but just when they seemed settled, they split. Cann and Hammond joined Bullet, then Hardstuff; French formed Leafhound. The irrepressible Crane refused to concede defeat and recruited new members, guitarist Steve Bolton, bassist Bill Smith and drummer Rick Parnell (son of the orchestra leader, Jack Parnell). The new line-up was completed by the famed singer Chris Farlowe. A dramatic musical shift towards blue-eyed soul won few new fans, however, and Crane finally dissolved the band in 1974. Thereafter, he collaborated with former colleague Arthur Brown, but could not resist reviving the fossilized Rooster in 1979 (the same year he teamed up with Crane once more for the 'Don't Be A Dummy' Lee Cooper jeans advertisement, backed by members of Gillan and Status Quo). After two anti-climactic albums with new drummer

Preston Hayman then a returning Hammond, Crane finally killed off his creation. The final Atomic Rooster studio album had included guest stints from Dave Gilmour (Pink Floyd), Bernie Torme (Gillan) and John Mazarolli on guitars in place of Cann. In 1983 Crane accepted an invitation to record and tour with Dexys Midnight Runners and appeared on their album *Don't Stand Me Down*. For some time he had been suffering from depression and he took his own life in 1989.

●ALBUMS: *Atomic Rooster* (B&C 1970)★★, *Death Walks Behind You* (B&C 1970)★★, *In Hearing Of* (Pegasus 1971)★★★, *Made In England* (Dawn 1972)★★, *Nice 'N' Greasy* (Dawn 1973)★, *Atomic Rooster* (EMI 1980)★, *Headline News* (Towerbell 1983)★.

●COMPILATIONS: *Assortment* (B&C 1974)★★, *Home To Roost* double album (Mooncrest 1977)★★, *The Devil Hits Back* (Demi Monde 1989)★★, *BBC In Concert* (Windsong 1994)★★.

AUDIENCE

This London-based act - Howard Werth (vocals/guitar), Keith Gemmell (saxophone), Trevor Williams (bass/vocals) and Tony Connor (drums) - made its recording debut in 1969 with *Audience*. A commercial flop, the album has since become one of the era's most sought-after artefacts of the art rock genre. The quartet was then signed by the fledgling Charisma Records, where *Friends Friends Friends* and *House On The Hill*, both produced by Gus Dudgeon, confirmed their quirky, quintessentially English style of rock. A US tour in support of the Faces followed, but internal friction resulted in Gemmell's departure. Patrick Neubergh (saxophone) and Nick Judd (keyboards) joined for *Lunch*, on which Bobby Keyes (saxophone) and Jim Price (trumpet) also participated, but the group was dissolved following its release.

●ALBUMS: *Audience* (Polydor 1969)★★, *Friends Friends Friends* (Charisma 1970)★★★, *Bronco Bullfrog* (soundtrack 1970)★★, *House On The Hill* (Charisma 1971)★★★, *Lunch* (Charisma 1972)★★.

●COMPILATIONS: *You Can't Beat Them* (1973)★★★, *Unchained* (1992)★★★.

AUGER, BRIAN

b. 18 July 1939, Bihar, India. This respected jazz rock organist rose to prominence in 1962 leading the Brian Auger Trio. Rick Laird (bass) and Phil Kinorra (drums) completed an act which, within two years, had evolved into the Brian Auger Trinity with the addition of John McLaughlin (guitar) and Glen Hughes (saxophone). An unsettled period ensued, but by the end of 1964 the leader emerged fronting a new line-up completed by Vic Briggs (guitar), Rickie Brown (bass) and Mickey Waller (drums). The revamped Trinity completed several singles, notably 'Fool Killer' and 'Green Onions '65' before being absorbed into the revue-styled Steampacket. A third Trinity - Auger, Dave Ambrose (bass) and Clive Thacker (drums) - emerged in 1966 to pursue a successful career with vocalist Julie Driscoll, which ran concurrently with the trio's own jazz-influenced desires. This direction was maintained with a 70s aggregation, Oblivion Express, which included guitarist Jim Mullen and drummer Robbie McIntosh, later of the Average White Band. Although UK success was not forthcoming, the unit was a popular attraction in the USA and Europe, but an unstable line-up hampered progress. Auger subsequently began a solo career but, despite embracing a dance-funk style on *Here And Now*, was unable to recapture the high profile he once enjoyed.

●ALBUMS: *Definitely What* (Marmalade 1968)★★, *Befour* (RCA 1970)★★★, *Oblivion Express* (RCA 1971)★★, *A Better Land* (Polydor 1971)★★★, *Second Wind* (Polydor 1972)★★, *Closer To It* (RCA 1973)★★, *Straight Ahead* (RCA 1974)★★★, *Live Oblivion Volume 1* (RCA 1974)★★, *Live Oblivion Volume 2* (RCA 1974)★, *Reinforcements* (RCA 1975)★★★, *Jam Sessions* (Charly 1975)★★, *Happiness Heartaches* (Warners 1977)★★, with Julie Tippetts *Encore* (Warners 1978)★★, *Here And Now* (Polydor 1984)★★.

●COMPILATIONS: with Julie Driscoll *Open* (1967)★★, *Streetnoise* (Polydor 1968)★★, *Jools/Brian* (EMI 1968)★★, with Sonny Boy 'Rice Miller' Williamson and Jimmy Page *Don't Send Me No Flowers* (Marmalade 1969)★★★, *The Best Of Brian Auger And The Trinity* (1970)★★★, *Genesis* (1975)★★, *The Best Of Brian Auger* (RCA 1975)★★★, *London 1964-1967* (Charly 1977)★★★, *The Road To Vauxhall 1967-1969* (1989)★★★.

AVERAGE WHITE BAND

This sextet was the natural culmination of several soul-influenced Scottish beat groups. The line-up featured Alan Gorrie (b. 19 July 1946, Perth, Scotland; bass/vocals), Mike Rosen (trumpet/guitar, ex-Eclection), replaced by Hamish Stuart (b. 8 October 1949, Glasgow, Scotland; guitar/vocals), Owen 'Onnie' McIntyre (b. 25 September 1945, Lennoxtown, Scotland; guitar), Malcolm 'Mollie' Duncan (b. 24 August 1945, Montrose, Scotland; saxophone), Roger Ball (b. 4 June 1944, Broughty Ferry, Scotland; saxophone, keyboards) and Robbie McIntosh (b. 6 May 1950, Dundee, Scotland, d. 23 September 1974, Hollywood, USA; drums). Although their 1973 debut album, *Show Your Hand*, showed promise, it was not until the band was signed to Atlantic Records that its true potential blossomed. *AWB*, also known as the 'White Album' in deference to its cover art, was a superb collection and paired the group's dynamism with Arif Mardin's complementary production. The highlights included a spellbinding version of the Isley Brothers' 'Work To Do', and the rhythmic original instrumental, 'Pick Up The Pieces', a worthy US number 1/UK Top 10 single. *AWB* also topped the US album charts but this euphoric period was abruptly halted in 1974 by the tragic death of Robbie McIntosh following a fatal ingestion of heroin at a Hollywood party. He was replaced by Steve Ferrone

(b. 25 April 1950, Brighton, England), a former member of Bloodstone. The group secured further success with 'Cut The Cake', the title song to a third album, but subsequent releases, despite an obvious quality, betrayed a creeping reliance on a proven formula. However, a pairing with singer Ben E. King (*Benny And Us*) seemed to galvanize a newfound confidence and two later recordings, 'Walk On By' and 'Let's Go Round Again', reclaimed the group's erstwhile inventiveness. The Average White Band retired during much of the 80s as the members pursued individual projects, the most surprising of which was Ferrone's work with Duran Duran. Hamish Stuart later surfaced in Paul McCartney's *Flowers In The Dirt* touring group, and was sadly unavailable when the AWB re-formed in 1989. The resultant album, *After Shock*, featured original members Gorrie, Ball and McIntyre alongside Alex Ligertwood, a fellow-Scot and former vocalist with Santana.

●ALBUMS: *Show Your Hand* (MCA 1973)★★, *AWB* (Atlantic 1974)★★★★, *Cut The Cake* (Atlantic 1975)★★★, *Soul Searchin'* (Atlantic 1976)★★, *Person To Person* (Atlantic 1977)★★★, with Ben E. King *Benny And Us* (Atlantic 1977)★★★, *Warmer Communications* (RCA 1978)★★, *Volume VIII* (RCA 1979)★★, *Feel No Fret* (RCA 1979)★★★, *Shine* (RCA 1980)★★, *Cupid's In Fashion* (RCA 1982)★★, *After Shock* (Polydor 1989)★★★, *Soul Tattoo* (Artful 1997)★★★. Solo: Alan Gorrie *Sleepless Nights* (1985)★★.

●COMPILATIONS: *Best Of The Average White Band* (RCA 1984)★★★.

AYERS, KEVIN

b. 16 August 1945, Herne Bay, Kent, England. Ayers spent much of his childhood in Malaya. A founder member of Soft Machine, this talented singer and songwriter abandoned the group in 1968 following an arduous US tour. Ayers' debut album, *Joy Of A Toy*, nonetheless bore a debt to his former colleagues, all of whom contributed to this innovative collection. Its charm and eccentricity set a pattern for much of the artist's later work, while the haunting, languid ballads, including 'Lady Rachel' and 'Girl On A Swing', stand among his finest compositions. In 1970 Ayers formed the Whole World, a unit that featured saxophonist Lol Coxhill, guitarist Mike Oldfield and pianist/arranger David Bedford. This impressive group was featured on *Shooting At The Moon*, a radical, experimental release which offered moments of rare beauty ('May I') and others of enchanting outlandishness ('Pisser Dans Un Violin', 'Colores Para Dolores'). The results were breathtaking and this ambitious collection is a landmark in British progressive rock. Coxhill left the Whole World soon after the album's completion and his departure precipitated their ultimate demise. Oldfield and Bedford did, however, contribute to *Whatevershebringswesing*, wherein Ayers withdrew from explicit experimentation, although the lugubrious 'Song From The Bottom Of A Well' maintained his ability to challenge. However, the artist never quite fulfilled his undoubted potential and while a fourth collection, *Bananamour*, offered moments of inspiration, an ambivalent attitude towards commercial practices undermined Ayer's career. A high profile appearance at London's Rainbow Theatre resulted in *June 1 1974*, on which Ayers was joined by John Cale, Nico and Brian Eno (as ACNE). Unfortunately, later inconsistent albums such as, *Sweet Deceiver*, *Yes We Have No Mañanas* and *Rainbow Takeaway*, were interspersed by prolonged holidays in the singer's beloved Ibiza. Despite this reduced public profile, Kevin Ayers retains a committed cult following and continued to follow his highly personal path throughout the 80s and into the 90s with a well-received album *Still Life With Guitar*.

●ALBUMS: *Joy Of A Toy* (Harvest 1969)★★★★, *Shooting At The Moon* (Harvest 1970)★★★★, *Whatevershebringswesing* (Harvest 1971)★★★, *Bananamour* (Harvest 1973)★★★, *The Confessions Of Doctor Dream* (Island 1974)★★★, with John Cale, Brian Eno, Nico *June 1 1974* (Island 1974)★★, *Sweet Deceiver* (Island 1975)★★★, *Yes We Have No Mañanas* (Harvest 1976)★★★, *Rainbow Takeaway* (Harvest 1978)★★, *That's What You Get Babe* (Harvest 1980)★★, *Diamond Jack And The Queen Of Pain* (Charly 1983)★★, *As Close As You Think* (Illuminated 1986)★★, *Falling Up* (Virgin 1988)★★★, *Still Life With Guitar* (Permanent 1992)★★★, *BBC Radio One Live In Concert* (Windsong 1992)★★★.

●COMPILATIONS: *Odd Ditties* (Harvest 1976)★★★, *The Kevin Ayers Collection* (See For Miles 1983)★★★, *Banana Productions - The Best Of Kevin Ayers* (Harvest 1989)★★★★, *Document Series Presents* (Connoisseur 1992)★★★, *Singing The Bruise* (Strange Fruit 1996)★★★.

AZTEC TWO-STEP

This folk-influenced duo from the USA, comprising Neal Shulman (vocals/guitar) and Rex Fowler (guitar/vocals), made its recording debut on Elektra Records in 1972. *Aztec Two-Step* showcased their informal style and featured admirable support from several exemplary associates, including Spanky McFarlane, John Seiter (both ex-Spanky And Our Gang), John Sebastian, Doug Dillard and Jerry Yester, the latter of whom also produced the set. Shulman and Fowler moved to RCA Records for their subsequent releases which, while accomplished, featured a less interesting supporting cast and lacked the charm of that first set.

●ALBUMS: *Aztec Two-Step* (Elektra 1972)★★★, *Second Step* (RCA 1975)★★, *Two's Company* (RCA 1976)★★, *Adjoining Suites* (RCA 1977)★★, *Living In America* (Reflex 1986)★★, *See It Was Like This...* (Flying Fish 1989)★★★, *Of Age* (1993)★★.

B.B. BLUNDER

Formed in 1971, the innovative UK rock group B.B. Blunder comprised Brian Godding (vocals/guitar/keyboards), Brian Belshaw (bass/vocals) and Kevin Westlake (drums/vocals), all ex-members of Blossom Toes. The trio's sole album, *Workers' Playtime*, displayed an appreciably heavy sound, but this power was combined with a penchant for quirky melody, notably on the loose 'Rocky Ragbag' the choral 'New Day' and the gritty 'Put Your Money Where Your Mouth Is'. The set featured sterling support from Brian Auger, Julie Driscoll and Mick Taylor, but is equally renowned for an imaginative sleeve design which was a typographical spoof copy of the BBC publication *Radio Times*, both on the front and inside. B.B. Blunder also supported ex-Action singer Reg King during his brief solo career but, unable to translate its cult appeal into wider success, the group was dissolved in 1972. Godding subsequently joined Centipede, a jazz-rock collective, which included Julie Driscoll and her husband Keith Tippett.

●ALBUMS: *Workers' Playtime* (United Artists 1971)★★★.

B.T. EXPRESS

Originally formed as the King Davis House Rockers in 1972, this Brooklyn-based septet underwent several name changes, including the Madison Street Express and the Brothers Trucking. Bill Risbrook (saxophone/vocals), his brother Louis (bass/organ), Carlos Ward (saxophone/woodwind), Richard Thompson (lead guitar/vocals), Dennis Rowe (congas), Terrell Woods (drums) and Barbara Joyce Lomas (vocals), had two gold discs with their first hits, 'Do It ('Til You're Satisfied)' (1974) and 'Express' (1975). Although the group continued to enjoy consistent chart success, they suffered from the facelessness that bedevilled many funk and disco outfits. Despite personnel changes, their later releases achieved little, musically.

●ALBUMS: *Do It 'Til You're Satisfied* (Roadshow 1974)★★, *Non-Stop* (Roadshow 1975)★★, *Energy To Burn* (Columbia 1976)★★, *Function At The Junction* (Columbia 1977)★★, *Shout It Out!* (Columbia 1978)★★, *B.T. Express 1980* (Columbia 1980)★★.

●COMPILATIONS: *Old Gold Future Gold* (Excaliber 1981)★★.

BABE RUTH

Formed in Hatfield, Hertfordshire, England, in 1971, this engaging progressive rock group was originally named Shacklock after founding guitarist Alan Shacklock. Janita 'Jenny' Haan (vocals), Chris Holmes (keyboards and organ), Dave Punshon (piano), Dave Hewitt (bass) and Dick Powell (drums) completed the initial line-up, which took its new name from the legendary American baseball player. *First Base*, which included 'Wells Fargo', a popular stage favourite, enhanced the quintet's growing reputation, much of which rested on Haan's raw delivery. However, despite enjoying commercial success in the USA and Canada, where *Amar Cabalero* achieved a gold disc, the group was plagued by personnel problems. Ed Spevock (drums) and Steve Gurl (piano, ex-Wild Turkey) replaced Powell and Punshon, but the departure of Shacklock following the release of *Babe Ruth* proved pivotal. A second Wild Turkey refugee, Bernie Marsden, was added for *Stealin' Home*, but in 1976 the line-up was again undermined by the loss of Haan and Hewitt. Ellie Hope (vocals) and Ray Knott (bass) joined for *Kid's Stuff*, but the group was now bereft of direction and split up. Marsden later surfaced in Paice, Ashton And Lord and Whitesnake while Spevock switched to Pete Brown's Piblokto!

●ALBUMS: *First Base* (Harvest 1972)★★★, *Amar Cabalero* (Harvest 1973)★★★, *Babe Ruth* (Harvest 1975)★★★, *Stealin' Home* (Capitol 1975)★★, *Kid's Stuff* (Capitol 1976)★.

●COMPILATIONS: *Grand Slam The Best Of Babe Ruth* (EMI 1994)★★★.

BABYS

Considerable attention attended the launch of this much-touted British rock group. John Waite (b. 4 July 1955, London, England; vocals/bass), Mike Corby (b. 3 July 1955, London, England; guitar/keyboards), Walter 'Wally' Stocker (b. 27 March 1954, London, England; guitar) and Tony Brock (b. 31 March 1954, Bournemouth, Dorset, England; drums, ex-Spontaneous Combustion and Strider) were promoted as the most promising newcomers of 1976, but while *The Babys* offered a competent blend of pop and rock, similar to that of the Raspberries, it lacked an identifiable sound and image. Obscured by the punk explosion, the quartet looked to the USA for commercial succour over the ensuing years. Jonathan Cain replaced Corby following the release of *Head First*, but although the Babys did achieve considerable US success, including two Top 20 singles with 'Isn't It Time' and 'Every Time I Think Of You', they remained in the shadow of AOR stalwarts Fleetwood Mac, Foreigner and Journey. Ricky Phillips joined as bass player for their final two albums. Waite subsequently embarked on a high-profile solo career.

●ALBUMS: *The Babys* (Chrysalis 1976)★★★, *Broken Heart* (Chrysalis 1977)★★★, *Head First* (Chrysalis 1978)★★★, *Union Jacks* (Chrysalis 1980)★★, *On The Edge* (Chrysalis 1980)★★.

●COMPILATIONS: *Anthology* (Chrysalis 1981)★★★, *Unofficial Babys* (NEMS 1982)★★.

BACCARA

This Spanish girl duo had a UK number 1 in 1977 with the disco orientated 'Yes Sir, I Can Boogie'. Sung by Maria Mendiola and Mayte Mateus, it was written and produced by the German team of Frank Dostal (ex-lead singer of the Rattles) and Rolf Soja, backed by studio musicians. There was a UK Top 10 follow-up 'Sorry I'm A Lady', but after this the group faded from view as they were unable to progress or change with the advent of new wave. Their particular brand of discopop soon appeared jaded and dated.

●ALBUMS: *Baccara* (RCA 1978)★, *Colours* (RCA19 80)★.

BACHMAN-TURNER OVERDRIVE

Formed in Vancouver, British Columbia, Canada, in 1972, Bachman-Turner Overdrive was a hard-rock group featuring former Guess Who member Randy Bachman (b. 27 September 1943, Winnipeg, Manitoba, Canada; guitar/lead vocals). Randy Bachman had left the Guess Who in 1970, recorded a solo album *Axe*, and, due to a bout of illness, had to cancel a projected collaboration with former Nice keyboardist Keith Emerson. Bachman subsequently formed Brave Belt with his brother Robbie Bachman (b. 18 February 1943, Winnipeg, Manitoba, Canada; drums), C.F. 'Fred' Turner (b. 16 October 1943, Winnipeg, Manitoba, Canada; bass/vocals) and Chad Allan, who had been a member of an early incarnation of Guess Who called Chad Allan and the Expressions. Brave Belt recorded two unsuccessful albums for Reprise Records in 1971-72, after which Allan was replaced by another Bachman brother, Tim. In 1972 the new band took its new name, the word Overdrive being borrowed from a trade magazine for truck drivers. They signed to Mercury Records in 1973 and released a self-titled first album which made a minor impact in the USA and at home in Canada. Tim Bachman departed at that point, replaced by Blair Thornton (b. 23 July 1950). After constant touring in the USA, BTO's second album, *Bachman-Turner Overdrive II*, provided their breakthrough, reaching number 4 in the US and yielding the number 12 hit 'Takin' Care Of Business'. The third album, *Not Fragile*, released in the summer of 1974, topped the US album charts and provided the US number 1/UK number 2 hit single 'You Ain't Seen Nothing Yet', sung with a dramatized stutter by Randy Bachman. *Four Wheel Drive*, the group's 1975 album, was its last Top 10 recording, although the group continued to release singles and albums until the end of the 70s. Randy Bachman departed from the group in 1977 and formed a band called Ironhorse as well as recording solo. He was replaced by Jim Clench, who appeared on the album *Freeways*. The following year the band officially changed its name to BTO but could not revive its earlier fortunes. In 1984, Randy Bachman, Tim Bachman and C.F. Turner regrouped and released a second self-titled album, this time for Compleat

Records, which barely dented the US charts. The group was still touring in the early 90s but had not released any further albums.

●ALBUMS: as Brave Belt *Brave Belt* (Reprise 1971)★★, as Brave Belt *Brave Belt II* (Reprise 1972)★★, *Bachman-Turner Overdrive* (Mercury 1973)★★, *Bachman-Turner Overdrive II* (Mercury 1974)★★★, *Not Fragile* (Mercury 1974)★★★★, *Four Wheel Drive* (Mercury 1975)★★★, *Head On* (Mercury 1975)★★, *Freeways* (Mercury 1977)★★, *Street Action* (Mercury 1978)★, *Rock 'N' Roll Nights* (Mercury 1979)★, *Bachman-Turner Overdrive* (Compleat 1984)★★.

●COMPILATIONS: *Best Of BTO (So Far)* (Mercury 1976)★★★, *Greatest Hits* (Mercury 1981)★★★.

●FURTHER READING: *Bachman Turner Overdrive: Rock Is My Life, This Is My Song: The Authorized Biography*, Martin Melhuish.

BACK DOOR

This jazz-rock trio from Blakey, Yorkshire, comprised Colin Hodgkinson (bass, vocals), Ron Aspery (saxophone, keyboards, flute, clarinet) and Tony Hicks (drums). This trio attracted much interest due to Hodgkinson's unique, adept full-chording bass technique. Their critically acclaimed first album, recorded in 1972, was initially released on the independent Blakey label. The praise and attention generated by the album resulted in the band signing to Warner Brothers Records who later reissued the set. Subsequent releases, which included production work from Felix Pappalardi and Carl Palmer of Emerson, Lake And Palmer, failed to capture the spirit of the debut set or the fire of their live performances. By the time of the fourth album, *Activate*, in 1976, Hicks had departed (replaced by Adrian Tilbrook), before the group split the following year. Aspery went on to work with the Icelandic jazz rock group Mezzoforte, while Hodgkinson guested with various artists including Alexis Korner, Jan Hammer and Brian Auger.

●ALBUMS: *Back Door* (Warners 1972)★★★, *8th Street Blues* (Warners 1974)★★★, *Another Mine Mess* (Warners 1975)★★★, *Activate* (Warners 1976)★★.

BACK STREET CRAWLER

Formed in England during 1975, Back Street Crawler took its name from founder Paul Kossoff's solo album. The ex-Free guitarist was joined by Terry Wilson-Slessor (vocals), Michael Montgomery (keyboards), Terry Wilson (bass) and Tony Braunagel (drums), but concerts in support of *The Band Played On* were cancelled when the group's leader was hospitalized after a drugs-related seizure. An American tour offered newfound hope, but such optimism was shattered on 19 March 1976 when Kossoff died in his sleep. The band truncated its name to Crawler following the release of *Second Street*. Geoff Whitehorn, formerly of If and Maggie Bell's group, was added on guitar, while John 'Rabbit' Bundrick, another ex-member of Free, replaced

Montgomery. Despite minor US chart success, the quintet was unable to escape the heritage of its founder and split up following *Snake, Rattle And Roll*.

●ALBUMS: *The Band Plays On* (Atlantic 1975)★★★, *Second Street* (Atlantic 1976)★★★, as Crawler *Crawler* (Epic 1977)★★★, as Crawler *Snake, Rattle And Roll* (Epic 1978)★★.

BAD BOY

The origins of this Milwaukee, USA, rock band date back to the mid-70s, when Steve Grimm (guitar/vocals) teamed up with John Marcelli (bass). The first incarnation of Bad Boy had included Lars Hanson (drums) and Joe Luchessie (guitar/keyboards/vocals). The band chemistry was wrong, though, and their debut album was a disappointing, half-hearted affair. Things improved with their second release, as the band moved in a heavier direction and made greater use of an up-front guitar sound, including Earl Slick (ex-David Bowie). Following a period of inactivity between 1978-82, the band hit back with a revamped line-up that saw Xeno (keyboards) and Billy Johnson (drums) alongside Grimm and Marcelli. Unfortunately, they switched back to a melodic pop-rock style once more. Both albums sold poorly and the band split up as a result.

●ALBUMS: *The Band That Made Milwaukee Famous* (United Artists 1977)★★, *Back To Back* (United Artists 1978)★★★, *Private Party* (Indie 1982)★★, *Electric Eyes* (Indie 1984)★★.

BAD COMPANY

This solid, highly acclaimed UK heavy rock group formed in 1973 with a line-up comprising Paul Rodgers (b. 17 December 1949, Middlesbrough, England; vocals), Simon Kirke (b. 27 August 1949, Wales; vocals/drums), Mick Ralphs (b. 31 May 1944, Hertfordshire, England; vocals/guitar) and Boz Burrell (b. Raymond Burrell, 1946, Lincolnshire, England; bass guitar). With Ralphs (ex-Mott The Hoople) and Rodgers and Kirke (both ex-Free), Bad Company were akin to a blues-based supergroup, with much of their style derived from the traditions established by Free, not least because of Paul Rodgers' distinct vocals. Their bestselling debut established their sound - strong vocals placed beside tough melody lines and hard riffing. A string of albums through the mid to late 70s brought them chart success on both sides of the Atlantic while a series of arduous stadium tours maintained their reputation as an exemplary live act. They achieved singles success with a number of powerful songs (notably 'Can't Get Enough Of Your Love' and 'Feel Like Makin' Love'), well produced and faultlessly played, although lyrically they were often pedestrian. A three-year hiatus ended with the release of *Rough Diamonds*, which provided another UK Top 20 album success (US number 26). After nearly a decade of extensive gigging and regularly released albums, they finally dissolved in 1983. A new version of the group with former Ted Nugent vocalist Brian Howe replacing Rodgers came together in 1986 for the reunion album, *Fame And Fortune*. The band's subsequent releases have been mediocre, a pale shadow of their first two albums. The late 80s/early 90s Bad Company model revolved around surviving original members Mick Ralphs and Simon Kirke. Rodgers' 1993 album, *Muddy Water Blues*, included three vintage Bad Company tracks. In 1994 Bad Company's legacy was remastered by G.M. and re-released.

●ALBUMS: *Bad Company* (Island 1974)★★★★, *Straight Shooter* (Island 1975)★★★, *Run With The Pack* (Island 1976)★★, *Burnin' Sky* (Island 1977)★★, *Desolation Angels* (Island 1979)★★★, *Rough Diamonds* (Swan Song 1982)★★, *Fame And Fortune* (Atlantic 1986)★★, *Dangerous Age* (Atlantic 1988)★★, *Holy Water* (Atlantic 1990)★★, *Here Comes Trouble* (Atlantic 1992)★★, *Company Of Strangers* (Atlantic 1995)★★.

●COMPILATIONS: *10 From 6* (Atlantic 1986)★★★★, *The Best Of Bad Company Live ... What You Hear Is What You Get* (Atco 1993)★★★, *Stories Old And New* (Atlantic 1996)★★★.

BADFINGER

Originally an all-Welsh group, they played the legendary Cavern Club in the mid-60s with a line-up comprising Pete Ham (b. 27 April 1947, d. 23 April 1975; vocals), Mike Gibbons (b. 1949; drums), David Jenkins (guitar) and Ron Griffiths (bass), using the name the Iveys. Not surprisingly, for a group who had taken their name in imitation of the Hollies, they were vocally tight and very melodic. During 1967, they became backing group to operatic pop singer David Garrick before leaving him to try their luck on the Beatles' enterprising new label Apple. By this time, Jenkins had been replaced by Liverpudlian Tom Evans, who wrote their debut for the label, 'Maybe Tomorrow', produced by Tony Visconti. The single passed unnoticed, as did the UK follow-up, 'Walls Ice Cream', so the group decided to bury the Iveys and reinvent themselves as Badfinger. By the time their next record was completed their original bassist left and was replaced by Joey Molland. The new line-up enjoyed an immediate hit on both sides of the Atlantic with 'Come And Get It', written by their label boss Paul McCartney. In order to increase their public profile, the group were invited to contribute to the soundtrack of the movie *The Magic Christian*, which starred Peter Sellers and Ringo Starr. The Beatles' patronage, which the press were quick to latch on to, was reinforced by the group's sound, which had strong traces of the Fab Four influence, particularly on the vocals. 'No Matter What', another transatlantic Top 10 hit, compounded the Beatles comparisons, though it was a fine pop record in its own right. By the beginning of the 70s, Badfinger were something of an Apple house band and even appeared on three solo Beatle recordings (*All Things Must Pass*, 'It Don't Come Easy' and *Imagine*) as well as appearing at George Harrison's Bangla Desh benefit concert.

The obvious songwriting talent that existed in the group was not fully revealed until 1972 when Nilsson enjoyed a huge transatlantic chart topper with the Ham/Evans ballad, 'Without You'. From that point onwards, however, the group failed to exploit their potential to the full. By the time of their final Apple recording, *Ass*, Molland was writing over half of their songs, but he chose to leave soon after, clearly weary of the financial and business wranglings that were now dominating proceedings. Worse was to follow the next year when Pete Ham hanged himself, after a long period of personal and professional worries. At that point the band split. Nearly four years later, Joey Molland and Tom Evans reformed the group, changing the subsidiary members frequently over the next few years. Commercial success proved elusive and in November 1983, history repeated itself in the most bizarre scenario possible when Tom Evans committed suicide at his Surrey home. Like Pete Ham he had been suffering from depression and financial worries. The Badfinger story is uniquely tragic and among its greater ironies is the now morbid chorus of the song with which Pete Ham and Tom Evans are best associated: 'I can't live, I can't live anymore' ('Without You'). Following the discovery of some home recorded tapes these were finally issued as a complete album by Ryko in 1997. Although the quality is poor and the performance naïve they indicate a great songwriter with a marvellous grasp of pop melody. This album in addition to the best of his Badfinger work is highly recommended.

●ALBUMS: *Magic Christian Music* (Apple 1970)★★★, *No Dice* (Apple 1970)★★★★, *The Magic Christian* soundtrack (Pye 1970)★★, *Straight Up* (Apple 1972)★★★★, *Ass* (Apple 1974)★★, *Badfinger* (Warners 1974)★★, *Wish You Were Here* (Warners 1974)★★★, *Airwaves* (Elektra 1979)★★, *Say No More* (Radio 1981)★★. Pete Ham solo *7 Park Avenue* (Ryko 1997)★★★★.

●COMPILATIONS: *Come And Get It: The Best Of Badfinger* (Capitol 1994)★★★★.

BAILEY, DEREK

b. 29 January 1932, Sheffield, Yorkshire, England. Bailey is one of the few jazz guitarists who can accurately be described as unique and entirely original, in that there are no real precedents for his style. His father and grandfather were professional musicians and Bailey studied music and guitar formally from 1941-52. From 1952-65, he undertook all types of commercial work, including as a session man in recording studios and as a member of pit orchestras: one celebrated engagement involved accompanying Gracie Fields. In 1963, he encountered Tony Oxley and Gavin Bryars, and the interplay of ideas within this trio set off a severe evaluation of his direction which resulted in a fearsomely austere and abstract music and a long-standing commitment to *total* improvisation. Bailey's music is difficult to decipher, and listeners lacking a taste for stern rhetoric subverted by unpredictable flashes of mordant humour will get little out of it. Critics claim that his playing sounds merely random, but anyone who thinks this is the case should be invited to try to mimic it: his mastery of the guitar involves extreme precision, used to examine material in microscopic detail, and that material never rests on conventional melody, chords or rhythm. He strives to exclude repetition and memory. He frequently plays solo, but on the occasions when he works with other musicians (he has played with both the Spontaneous Music Ensemble and the Globe Unity Orchestra, as well as in numerous duos with musicians such as Anthony Braxton, Evan Parker and Han Bennink) it is as if he tries to avoid hearing them, playing with his head bent down over the guitar, until he suddenly produces some sharp and apposite interjection. If he has done little to attract the general jazz public he has earned enormous respect from other musicians in the field of free jazz and improvised music. He has also contributed much to the survival of the genre, co-founding the Incus label in 1970 and running the Company festival which, surviving since 1976 against all the odds, facilitates jam sessions of both obscure toilers in the free and improvised fields and superstars like Parker and Peter Kowald. He has recorded over 60 albums, including several with various Company line-ups, and written an influential book, *Improvisation - Its Nature And Practice In Music* (1980), which was used as the basis for the four-part television series *On The Edge*, filmed in 1990-91 and first transmitted in February 1992.

●ALBUMS: *Derek Bailey/Han Bennink* (1969)★★★, with others *Instant Composers Pool* (1970)★★★, with Instant Composers Pool *Groupcomposing* (1970)★★★, *Music Improvisation Company 1968/70* (1970)★★★, with Evan Parker, Han Bennink *Topography Of The Lungs* (1970)★★★, *The Music Improvisation Company 1968-71* (1971)★★★, *Solo Guitar Vol. 1* (Incus 1971)★★★★, with Dave Holland *Improvisation For Cello And Guitar* (1971)★★★, with Bennink *At Verity's Palace* (1972)★★★, *Derek Bailey* (1973)★★★, *Concert In Milwaukee* (1973)★★★, *One Music Ensemble* (1973)★★★, *Lot 74 - Solo Improvisations* (1974)★★★★, *Improvisation* (1975)★★★, with Parker *London Concert* (1975)★★★, *Domestic And Public Pieces* (1976)★★★, with Tristan Honsinger *Duo* (1976)★★★, with Andrea Centazzo *Drops* (1977)★★★, with Anthony Braxton *Duo 1 & 2* rec. 1974, reissued as *Live At Wigmore* (1977)★★★★, with others *Company 1* (1977)★★★, with Braxton, Parker *Company 2* (1977)★★★, with Bennink *Company 3* (1977)★★★, with Steve Lacy *Company 4* (1977)★★★, *New Sights - Old Sounds* (1978)★★★, with others *Duo And Trio Improvisations* (1978)★★★, with others *Company, Vols. 5-7* (1978)★★★, with Company *Fictions* (1978)★★★, with Tony Coe *Time* (Incus 1979)★★★, *Aida* (1980)★★★, with Company *Fables* (1980)★★★, with Christine Jeffrey *Views From Six Windows* (1980)★★★, with Jamie Muir *Dart Drug* (Incus 1981)★★★, with Company *Epiphany* (1982)★★★★, with

George Lewis, John Zorn *Yankees* (1983)★★★★, with Braxton *Royal, Volume One* rec. 1974 (1984)★★★★, *Notes.* (1985)★★★, with Parker *Compatibles* (Incus 1986)★★★, with Company *Trios* rec. 1983 (1986)★★★, with Braxton *Moment Précieux* (1987)★★★, with Cyro Baptista *Cyro* rec. 1982 (Incus 1988)★★★, with Bennink *Han* rec. 1986 (Incus 1988)★★★★, with Company *Once* (1988)★★★, *In Whose Tradition* rec. 1971-87 (1988)★★★, with Cecil Taylor *Pleistozaen Mit Wasser* (1989)★★★, with Barre Phillips *Figuring* (Incus 1989)★★★, with Louis Moholo, Thebe Lipere *Village Life* (Incus 1992)★★★, *Solo Guitar Volume 2* (Incus 1992)★★★, *Playing* (Incus 1992)★★★, with Henry Kaiser *Wireforks* (Shanachie 1995)★★★★.

●FURTHER READING: *Improvisation - Its Nature And Practice In Music*, Derek Bailey.

BAKER GURVITZ ARMY

Former Gun and Three Man Army members, Paul and Adrian Gurvitz, joined forces with ex-Cream and Airforce drummer Ginger Baker to form this tempestuous UK trio. Their self-titled debut featured a powerful blend of heavy rock laced with Baker's unmistakable drumming. The lengthy 'Mad Jack' was the album's outstanding track. This autobiographical tale masquerading as a novelty lyric from Baker, told the story of his exploits through the African desert in his Land-Rover. The band enlisted the help of Snips from Sharks and ex-Seventh Wave member, Peter Lemer. The two following albums contained similar material, but the combination of a lack of success in America and personality clashes between the members, led them to retreat back to solo careers.

●ALBUMS: *Baker Gurvitz Army* (Vertigo 1974)★★★, *Elysian Encounter* (Vertigo 1975)★★, *Hearts On Fire* (Vertigo 1976)★★.

BAKER, GEORGE, SELECTION

Led by vocalist George Bouens - who assumed the stage surname 'Baker' - this MOR Dutch quintet scaled charts throughout Europe and then North America in 1970 with a debut single 'Little Green Bag' - composed by Bouens and group member, Jan Visser. Bouens alone wrote his Selection's next major hit, 'Una Paloma Blanca', which caught a holiday mood during the summer of 1975. Despite a cover by Jonathan King, it reached the UK and Australasian Top 10 charts and sold a million in Germany alone. There were no further international smashes but, despite a brisk turnover of personnel, the band continued as domestic chart contenders until the 80s.

●ALBUMS: *Little Green Bag* (Penny Farthing 1970)★★, *Paloma Blanca* (Warners 1975)★★, *River Song* (Warners 1976)★★, *Summer Melody* (Warners 1977)★★.

●COMPILATIONS: *The Best Of Baker* (Warners 1978)★★.

BALLARD, RUSS

b. 31 October 1945, Waltham Cross, Hertfordshire, England. Ballard attended the same secondary modern school as Cliff Richard before joining the Daybreakers, the backing group to Buster Meakle, another local singer (and future mainstay of Unit Four Plus Two). By 1963, with Daybreaker drummer Robert Henrit, Ballard was a member of Adam Faith's Roulettes in which he played keyboards before transferring to guitar. Among tracks recorded by the quartet alone were a handful of Ballard numbers - including its last a-side, 1967's 'Help Me Help Myself'. While briefly one of the latter-day Unit Four Plus Two members, Ballard also co-wrote that group's final single, 1969's psychedelic '3.30', before he and Henrit joined Argent. Ballard's compositions complemented those of leader Rod Argent and his confidence was boosted when his 'God Gave Rock And Roll To You' was among the group's hits. Three Dog Night reached the US Top 10 with a version of Ballad's 'Liar' in 1972.

After this lucrative syndication, Ballard remained with Argent for a further two years before showing his hand as a soloist. However, as neither *Russ Ballard* nor *Winning* attracted sufficient attention, he elected to concentrate on writing adult-orientated material. He was especially favoured by America whom he serviced well into the 80s with accessible catchy compositions. Other notable beneficiaries of his efforts were Hot Chocolate ('So You Win Again'), who had a UK number 1, and Rainbow ('Since You've Been Gone' and 'I Surrender'). Ringo Starr recorded another Ballard composition 'As Far As You Go' on his 1983 album, *Old Wave*. Ballard was also active as a session player for both old associates such as Faith (and his protégé Leo Sayer) and Rainbow's Graham Bonnet as well as newer acquaintances such as Lea Nicholson, Starry Eyed And Laughing and Phoenix. By 1979, he returned to the fray as a recording artist with *At The Third Stroke* (with its 'You Can Do Voodoo' single) which, like its *Barnet Dogs* and *Into The Fire* follow-ups, was a likeable collection that sold enough to make further Ballard product a worthwhile exercise. The second album called *Russ Ballard* was issued in 1984. Its singles and those on its successor, *Fire Still Burns*, were promoted on video with the artist still wearing the sunglasses that have been his visual trademark since treading the boards with Meakle's Daybreakers. A belated rise to a qualified prominence in his own right is not out of the question, but Ballard's fame in the early 90s rests on interpretations of his material by others. In recent times, the Little Angels, Magnum and Kiss have recorded his songs. Kiss had a hit in 1992 with 'God Gave Rock 'N' Roll To You' after Ballard had been commissioned to compose the soundtrack to the 1991 movie, *Bill And Ted's Bogus Journey*.

●ALBUMS: *Russ Ballard* (Epic 1975)★★★, *Winning* (Epic 1976)★★★, *At The Third Stroke* (Epic 1979)★★★, *Barnet Dogs* (Epic 1980)★★★, *Into The Fire* (Epic 1981)★★★, *Russ Ballard* (EMI 1984)★★★, *Fire Still Burns* (EMI 1986)★★★, *The Seer* (Bullet Proof 1994)★★★.

BALLS

Although this short-lived UK rock group barely managed a year of existence after being formed in February 1969, they are worthy of documentation as they were one of the first true 'supergroups', before that much-abused term was invented. The line-up of ex-Moody Blues Denny Laine (vocals/guitar), and ex-Move Trevor Burton and Steve Gibbons (vocals), was augmented at various times by ex-Plastic Ono Band member Alan White (drums), Jackie Lomax, Richard Tandy (ELO), Mike Kelly (Spooky Tooth), Keith Smart (drums) and Dave Morgan (bass). They released one single in January 1971, financially backed by their creator/manager Tony Secunda. 'Fight For My Country' failed, although it was heavily plugged by the UK pirate radio station, Geronimo.

BAND

When the Band emerged in 1968 with *Music From Big Pink*, they were already a seasoned and cohesive unit. Four of the group, Robbie Robertson (b. Jaime Robbie Robertson, 5 July 1943, Toronto, Ontario, Canada; guitar/vocals), Richard Manuel (b. 3 April 1943, Stratford, Canada, d. 4 March 1986; piano/drums/vocals), Garth Hudson (b. Eric Hudson, 2 August 1937, London, Ontario, Canada; organ) and Rick Danko (b. 9 December 1943, Simcoe, Canada; bass/vocals), had embraced rock 'n' roll during its first flush of success. One by one they joined the Hawks, a backing group formed by rockabilly singer Ronnie Hawkins, which included Levon Helm (b. Mark Levon Helm, 26 May 1942, Marvell, Arkansas, USA; drums/vocals). A minor figure in the US, by the late 50s Hawkins had moved to Toronto where he pursued a career consisting mostly of rabble-house cover versions. 'Bo Diddley' (1963) was a major hit in Canada, but the musicians later flexed their independence during sessions for the *Mojo Man* on 'She's 19' and 'Farther Up The Road' with Helm taking the vocal. The quintet left Hawkins later that year and toured America's small-town bars, performing for 'pimps, whores, rounders and flakeouts', as Hudson later recalled. Billed as the Canadian Squires or Levon And The Hawks, they developed a loud, brash repertoire, drawn from R&B, soul and gospel styles, while the rural life left a trail of impressions and images. The group completed 'Leave Me Alone', under the former appellation, before settling in New York where 'Go Go Liza Jane' and 'The Stones I Throw' were recorded as Levon And The Hawks.

The quintet enjoyed the approbation of the city's famed Red Bird label. Robertson, Helm and Hudson supported blues singer John Hammond Jnr. on his debut single, 'I Wish You Would' (1964), while Levon's pacey composition, 'You Cheated, You Lied', was recorded by the

Shangri-Las. The trio maintained their link with Hammond on the latter's fiery *So Many Roads* (1965), through which they were introduced to Bob Dylan. In August 1965 Robertson and Helm accompanied the singer for his Forest Hills concert and although the drummer reneged on further involvement, within months the remaining Hawks were at the fulcrum of Dylan's most impassioned music. They supported him on his 'electric' 1966 world tour and followed him to his Woodstock retreat where, reunited with Helm, they recorded the famous *Basement Tapes*, whose lyrical, pastoral performances anticipated the style the quintet later adopted. *Music From Big Pink* restated traditional American music in an environment of acid-rock and psychedelia. Natural in the face of technocratic artifice, its woven, wailing harmonies suggested the fervour of sanctified soul, while the instrumental pulse drew inspiration from carnivals, country and R&B. The Band's deceptive simplicity was their very strength, binding lyrics of historical and biblical metaphor to sinuous, memorable melodies. The set included three Dylan songs, but is best recalled for 'The Weight' which, if lyrically obtuse, was the subject of several cover versions, notably from Jackie DeShannon, Aretha Franklin, Diana Ross (with the Supremes and the Temptations) and Spooky Tooth.

The Band confirmed the quintet's unique qualities. Robertson had emerged as their principle songwriter, yet the panoramic view remained intact, and by invoking Americana past and present, the group reflected the pastoral desires of a restless generation. It contained several telling compositions - 'Across The Great Divide', 'The Unfaithful Servant' and 'The Night They Drove Old Dixie Down' - as well as 'Rag Mama Rag', an ebullient UK Top 20 hit. The Band then resumed touring, the perils of which were chronicled on *Stage Fright*. By openly embracing contemporary concerns, the quintet lacked their erstwhile perspective, but in 'The Rumour' they created one of the era's most telling portraits. Yet the group's once seamless sound had grown increasingly formal, a dilemma that increased on *Cahoots*. Melodramatic rather than emotional, the set offered few highlights, although Van Morrison's cameo on '4% Pantomime' suggested a *bonhomie* distinctly absent elsewhere. It was followed by a warm in-concert set, *Rock Of Ages*, arranged by Allan Toussaint, and *Moondog Matinee*, a wonderful selection of favourite cover versions. It served as a spotlight for Richard Manuel, whose emotional, haunting voice wrought new meaning from 'Share Your Love' and 'The Great Pretender'.

In 1974 the Band backed Bob Dylan on his acclaimed *Planet Waves* album and undertook the extensive tour documented on *Before The Flood*. The experience inspired a renewed creativity and *Northern Lights Southern Cross*, their strongest set since *The Band*, included 'Acadian Driftwood', one of Robertson's most evocative compositions. However, the individual members had decided to dissolve the group and their partnership was sundered the following year with a gala performance at San Francisco's Winterland ballroom. The event, *The Last Waltz*, featured many guest contributions, including those by Dylan, Eric Clapton, Muddy Waters, Van Morrison, Neil Young, Joni Mitchell and Paul Butterfield, and was the subject of Martin Scorsese's film of the same name and a commemorative triple album. The Band also completed their contractual obligations with *Islands*, a somewhat tepid set notable only for 'Knockin' Lost John', which featured a rare lead vocal from Robertson. Levon Helm then pursued a dual career as a performer and actor, Rick Danko recorded an intermittently interesting solo album, while Hudson saved his talent for session appearances. Robbie Robertson scored soundtracks to several more Scorsese films, but kept a relatively low profile, refusing to join the ill-fated Band reunions of 1984 and 1985. A third tour ended in tragedy when, on 7 March 1986, Richard Manuel hanged himself in a motel room. His death inspired 'Fallen Angel' on Robertson's outstanding 'comeback' album, but despite the presence of Hudson and Danko elsewhere on the record, the guitarist refused to join his colleagues when they regrouped again in 1991. Their first studio album in 17 years was released in 1993, but *Jericho* and the 1996 *High On The Hog* both suffered from lacklustre songs and the lack of Robertson's powerful presence. Altogether different was the legendary 1973 concert recorded at Watkins Glen Racetrack, which was finally released in 1995 and captures the band at a musical peak. The Band smelt of Americana (or Canadiana) like no other before or since. This is the flavour of Barney Hoskyns' compelling biography, which argues with conviction and evidence that they are North America's greatest ever rock 'n' roll band.

●ALBUMS: *Music From Big Pink* (Capitol 1968)★★★★, *The Band* (Capitol 1969)★★★★, *Stage Fright* (Capitol 1970)★★★★, *Cahoots* (Capitol 1971)★★★, *Rock Of Ages* (Capitol 1972)★★★★, *Moondog Matinee* (Capitol 1973)★★★, *Northern Lights - Southern Cross* (Capitol 1975)★★★, *Islands* (Capitol 1977)★★, with various artists *The Last Waltz* (Warners 1977)★★★, *Jericho* (Pyramid 1993)★★, *Live At Watkins Glen* (Capitol 1995)★★★★, *High On The Hog* (Transatlantic 1996)★. Solo: Rick Danko *Rick Danko* (Arista 1977)★★★.

●COMPILATIONS: *The Best Of The Band* (Capitol 1976)★★, *Anthology Volume 1* (Capitol 1978)★★★, *Anthology Volume 2* (Capitol 1980)★★★, *To Kingdom Come* (Capitol 1989)★★★, *Across The Great Divide* 3-CD box set (Capitol 1995)★★★★, *The Collection* (EMI 1997)★★.

●VIDEOS: *The Last Waltz* (Warner Home Video 1988), *The Authorized Video Biography* (ABC 1995).

●FURTHER READING: *Across The Great Divide: The Band And America*, Barney Hoskyns. *This Wheel's On Fire: Levon Helm And The Story Of The Band*, Levon Helm with Stephen Davis. *Mystery Train: Images Of America In

Rock And Roll Music, Greil Marcus. *Invisible Republic: Bob Dylan's Basement Tapes*, Greil Marcus.

BANGS, LESTER

b. 14 December 1948, Escondido, California, USA, d. 30 April 1982. One of America's most original and distinctive rock critics, Bangs' first major review appeared in *Rolling Stone* in 1969. His declamatory attack on the MC5's *Kick Out The Jams* was later recanted, but although Bangs then praised the album as fulsomely as he had savaged it, this *volte-face* was typical of the writer's emotional approach. A passionate, almost naïve, love of music ensured his position as one of the paper's most virulent voices, promoting acts that concurred with his 'trash aesthetic' while denigrating work perceived as pompous or pretentious. Bangs was banned from its pages in 1973 for showing 'disrespect towards musicians', but his stream-of-consciousness articles had already become the mainstay of another publication, the Detroit-based *Creem*. His articles praised personal avatars - 60s garage-bands, John Coltrane, Captain Beefheart, Black Sabbath, Patti Smith, Lou Reed - and mauled hypocrisy, the singer-songwriter genre and work smacking of indolence in a writing style that set benchmarks for several disciples, notably those at a newly invigorated *New Musical Express*. With the advent of punk Bangs discovered equally irreverent musicians, but although welcoming the rise of the Ramones, Sex Pistols and Clash, he did so with a more measured prose. His work for New York's *Village Voice* was the subject of several redrafts, rather than the amphetamine-charged impressions marking earlier material. He also led his own group, Lester Bangs And The Delinquents, which completed a single, 'Let It Blurt'/'Live' in 1979, and *Juke Savages On The Brazos* two years later. Bangs' writing, however, continued unabated, particularly when he undertook a rigorous detoxification regime, eschewing almost all alcohol and drugs. Bangs' accidental death in April 1982 was due to respiratory failure during a bout of influenza. Part of his effusive work was compiled posthumously in the uneven *Psychotic Reactions And Carburetor Dung*, in which editor Greil Marcus paid tribute thus - 'This book demands a willingness to accept that the best writer in America could write almost nothing but record reviews.'

●ALBUMS: *Juke Savages On The Brazos* (1981)★★.
●FURTHER READING: *Blondie*, Lester Bangs. *Rod Stewart*, Paul Nelson and Lester Bangs. *Psychotic Reactions And Carburetor Dung*, Lester Bangs, edited by Greil Marcus.

BARCLAY JAMES HARVEST

Formed in Oldham, England, the band comprised: Stewart 'Woolly' Wolstenholme (b. 15 April 1947, Oldham, Lancashire, England; keyboards/vocals), John Lees (b. 13 January 1947, Oldham, Lancashire, England; guitar/vocals), Les Holroyd (b. 12 March 1948, Bolton, Lancashire, England; bass/vocals) and Mel Pritchard (b. 20 January 1948, Oldham, Lancashire, England; drums). This quartet was made up of musicians from two Lancashire bands, Heart And Soul, and the Wickeds/Blues Keepers. As members of the former, Wolstenholme and Lees were invited to join the rival Wickeds, briefly making a sextet. After two original members departed, this left them with the unit that became Barclay James Harvest. Following their inauspicious debut on EMI's Parlophone label, the band became one of the first signings to the aptly named Harvest outlet. The band were perfectly suited to the marketing aims of that label: progressive, symphonic and occasionally improvisational. Their blend of melodic 'underground' music was initially acclaimed, although commercial success in the charts eluded them for many years. Their early albums heavily featured the mellotron, although they were able to combine earthy guitar with superb harmony vocals. 'Mockingbird' from *Once Again* became their unwanted 'Damocles' sword', the orchestrated classical style left them wide open to sniping critics. The unfair press they often received was itself perplexing. This musically excellent band was writing perfect material for the time, yet they failed to increase their following. Fortunes looked set to change when they left Harvest and signed with Polydor Records in 1974, releasing *Everyone Is Everybody Else*. Why it failed to chart is one of rock's minor mysteries, for it contained many outstanding songs. The beautiful harmonies of 'Poor Boy Blues' set against their *tour de force*, 'For No One', featuring a blistering example of wah-wah guitar, were two reasons alone why the album should have been a major success. It was in 1976 that their first chart success came, with *Octoberon*. 'Rock 'n' Roll Star 'and 'Suicide' were two of the outstanding tracks. Although they were unable to make any impression in the USA, their appeal in Europe kept them busy. *Gone To Earth*, again with a special sleeve, this time a cut-out, was a massive-selling record in Germany. Their own subtle 'Poor Man's Moody Blues' sniped back at critics, while the beautiful Christian anthem 'Hymn' became a regular encore. After *XII* Wolstenholme left the band, the first to leave in 13 years, and released a solo album *Maestoso*. Barclay James Harvest's live *Concert For The People*, recorded in Berlin, became their most commercially successful record in the UK. In Germany the band are major artists, while in Britain their loyal followers are able to view, with a degree of satisfaction, that Barclay James Harvest rode out the criticism, stayed on their chosen musical path without compromise and produced some of the finest 'art rock'.

●ALBUMS: *Barclay James Harvest* (Harvest 1970)★★, *Once Again* (Harvest 1971)★★★, *Short Stories* (Harvest 1971)★★★, *Early Morning Onwards* (Harvest 1972)★★★, *Baby James Harvest* (Harvest 1972)★★★, *Everyone Is Everybody Else* (Polydor 1974)★★★★, *Barclay James Harvest Live* (Polydor 1974)★★, *Time Honoured Ghosts* (Polydor 1975)★★★, *Octoberon* (Polydor 1976)★★★,

Gone To Earth (Polydor 1977)★★★, *XII* (Polydor 1978)★★, *Live Tapes* (Polydor 1978)★★, *Eyes Of The Universe* (Polydor 1979)★★, *Turn Of The Tide* (Polydor 1981)★★★, *A Concert For The People (Berlin)* (Polydor 1982)★★, *Ring Of Changes* (Polydor 1983)★★★, *Victims Of Circumstance* (Polydor 1984)★★★, *Face To Face* (Polydor 1987)★★, *Glasnost* (Polydor 1988)★★, *Welcome To The Show* (1990)★★★, *Caught In The Light* (1993)★★★, *River Of Dreams* (Polydor 1997)★★. Solo: John Lees *A Major Fancy* (Harvest 1977)★★. Woolly Wolstenholme *Maestoso* (Polydor 1980)★★, *Too Late* (Swallowtail 1989)★★, *Songs From The Black Block* (Voiceprint 1994)★★.

●COMPILATIONS: *Best Of Volume 1* (Harvest 1977)★★★, *Best Of Volume 2* (Harvest 1979)★★★, *Best Of Volume 3* (Harvest 1981)★★, *Another Arable Parable* (Harvest 1987)★★★, *Alone We Fly* (Connoisseur 1990)★★★, *The Harvest Years* (Harvest 1991)★★★, *The Best Of ...* (EMI 1997)★★★.

●VIDEOS: *Berlin A Concert For The People* (Channel 5 1982), *Victims Of Circumstance* (1985), *Glasnost* (Channel 5 1988), *The Best Of BJH Live* (Virgin Vision 1992).

BARDENS, PETER

b. 19 June 1945, Westminster, London, England. An accomplished organist, Bardens was a founder-member of the Cheynes, prior to a brief spell in Them. By 1966 he was fronting a club-based act, the Peter B's, which included drummer Mick Fleetwood and guitarist Peter Green. The unit recorded a single, 'If You Wanna Be Happy', but was then absorbed into the Shotgun Express, a soul-inspired revue that featured Rod Stewart. Bardens later formed the short-lived Village, before releasing his first solo album, *The Answer*, in 1970. This informal selection featured several telling contributions by Peter Green, masquerading under an 'Andy Gee' pseudonym, but an undisciplined approach undermined its obvious potential. A second collection, *Peter Bardens*, was more focused and showcased the artist's touring group, which included the multi-faceted Victor Brox, a former member of the Aynsley Dunbar Retaliation. In 1972 Bardens formed a new band, Camel. He remained with this successful unit for the next six years before resuming his solo career with *Heart To Heart*. He has since divided his time between session work and crafted 80s rock, exemplified on a 1987 release, *Seen One Earth*.

●ALBUMS: *The Answer* (Transatlantic 1970)★★, *Peter Bardens* (Transatlantic 19712)★★★, *Heart To Heart* (Arista 1980)★★, *Seen One Earth* (Capitol 1987)★★★, *Speed Of Light* (Capitol 1988)★★, *Water Colors* (1993)★★, *Big Sky* (HTD 1994)★★★.

●COMPILATIONS: *Vintage '69* (Transatlantic 1976)★★.

BATT, MIKE

b. 6 February 1950. Beginning his career as an in-house music publisher and songwriter, Batt swiftly moved into production, working on albums by Hapshash And The

Coloured Coat (which reputedly featured Brian Jones of the Rolling Stones) and the Groundhogs. However, Batt's early success came through the medium of television advertisement jingles, rather than progressive rock. By 1973, he discovered a new hit-making machine courtesy of the Wombles, a children's television programme that spawned a number of hit singles. He continued to produce for other artists, including the Kursaal Flyers, Steeleye Span and Linda Lewis. Like those 60s producers, Andrew Loog Oldham and Larry Page, he also released some eponymous orchestral albums, including portraits of the Rolling Stones, Bob Dylan, Simon And Garfunkel, George Harrison, Elton John and Cat Stevens. Although Batt attempted to forge a career on his own as an artist, and hit number 4 with 'Summertime City' in 1975, his subsequent album forays failed to win mass appeal. Ultimately, it was as a songwriter that he took top honours, when Art Garfunkel took his 'Bright Eyes' to number 1 in 1979. Since then, Batt has continued to write for films and musicals, scoring again with David Essex's reading of 'A Winter's Tale' (lyric by Tim Rice) which narrowly failed to reach the top of the UK chart in 1982. His ambitious stage musical, *The Hunting Of The Snark*, opened in London on 21 October 1991, and closed seven weeks later. Batt had been immersed in the project for several years. The 1986 concept album featured such diverse talents as Sir John Gielgud, Roger Daltrey, Julian Lennon, and Cliff Richard, accompanied by the London Symphony Orchestra.

●ALBUMS: *Portrait Of Bob Dylan* (DJM 1969)★, *Schizophonic* (Epic 1979)★★, *Tarot Suite* (Epic 1979)★★, *Waves* (Epic 1980)★★, *6 Days In Berlin* (Epic 1981)★★, *Zero Zero* (Epic 1983)★★, *Children Of The Sky* (Epic 1986)★★, *The Hunting Of The Snark* (1986)★★★.

BAY CITY ROLLERS

Originally formed during 1967 in Edinburgh, the Rollers were a Beatles cover group based round two brothers, Derek Longmuir (b. 19 March 1955, Edinburgh, Scotland; drums) and Alan Longmuir (b. 20 June 1953, Edinburgh, Scotland; bass). After falling into the hands of entrepreneur Tam Paton, they played consistently on the Scottish circuit until their big break in 1971. A posse of record company talent spotters, including Bell Records' president Dick Leahy, producer Tony Calder and agent David Apps witnessed their live performance and within months the group were in the UK Top 10. The hit, a revival of the Gentrys' 'Keep On Dancing', produced by Jonathan King, proved a one-off and for the next couple of years the group struggled. Names like Nobby Clark and John Devine came and went until they finally found a relatively stable line-up with the Edinburgh-born trio of Les McKeown (b. 12 November 1955; vocals), Stuart 'Woody' Wood (b. 25 February 1957; guitar) and Eric Faulkner (b. 21 October 1955; guitar). With the songwriting assistance of Phil Coulter and Bill Martin, they enjoyed a steady run of teen-orientated hits, including 'Remember (Sha La La)', 'Shang-A-Lang', 'Summerlove Sensation' and 'All Of Me Loves All Of You'. Paton remained firmly in control of their visual image (all fresh faces clad in tartan scarves and trousers) which struck a chord with young teenagers and pre-pubescent fans in search of pin-up pop stars. 1975 proved the watershed year with two consecutive UK number 1 hits, 'Bye Bye Baby' (a Four Seasons cover) and 'Give A Little Love'. That same year they topped the US charts with 'Saturday Night'. Further line-up changes followed with the arrival of Ian Mitchell and Billy Lyall but these did not detract from the group's following. Rollermania was triumphant. Inevitably, there was a backlash as the press determined to expose the group's virginal, teetotal image. During the next three years, disaster was heaped upon disaster. McKeown was charged with reckless driving after hitting and killing a 75-year-old widow, Eric Faulkner and Alan Longmuir attempted suicide, Paton was jailed for committing indecent acts with underage teenagers, Ian Mitchell starred in a pornographic movie and Billy Lyall died from an AIDS-related illness in 1989. It was a tawdry conclusion to one of the most famous teenybop acts in British pop history.

●ALBUMS: *Rollin'* (Bell 1974)★★★, *Once Upon A Star* (Bell 1975)★★★, *Wouldn't You Like It* (Bell 1975)★★★, *Dedication* (Bell 1976)★★, *It's A Game* (Arista 1977)★★, *Strangers In The Wind* (Arista 1978)★★, as the Rollers *Richocet* (Epic 1981)★★★.

●VIDEOS: *Shang-A-Lang: The Very Best Of...* (1993).

●FURTHER READING: *The Bay City Rollers Scrapbook*, David Golumb. *Bay City Rollers*, Elkis Allen. *The Bay City Rollers*, Tam Paton.

BE-BOP DELUXE

During the comparatively barren times for progressive music during the early 70s, guitarist Bill Nelson (b. 18 December 1948, Wakefield, Yorkshire, England) recorded the limited edition *Northern Dream*. Tapes of this collector's item were played by the pioneering disc jockey John Peel on his legendary BBC Radio programme, *Top Gear*. The line-up of Nelson, Nick Chatterton-Dew (drums), Robert Bryan (bass) and Ian Parkin (guitar) recorded *Axe Victim* as Be-Bop Deluxe. Nelson soon disbanded the group, and following a tour supporting Cockney Rebel he formed a new band, taking members from that fragmented unit. This short-lived combo also broke up. With the addition of New Zealander Charlie Tumahai (d. 21 December 1995) and Simon Fox, Nelson released *Futurama* and *Sunburst Finish*. The latter contained a surprise hit single, 'Ships In The Night'. Nelson's undeniable talent as a guitarist began to dominate the band and as his technical virtuosity grew, the songs became weaker. Nelson abandoned the name in 1978 for the more radical Red Noise, retaining Andrew Clarke from the old band, although he now records under his own name. During their peak, Be-Bop Deluxe were an exciting and refreshing group who were ultimately unable to find a musical niche that suited their varied styles.

●ALBUMS: *Axe Victim* (Harvest 1974)★★, *Futurama* (Harvestv 1975)★★, *Sunburst Finish* (Harvest 1976)★★★, *Modern Music* (Harvest 1976)★★★, *Live! In The Air Age* (Harvest 1977)★★★, *Drastic Plastic* (Harvest 1978)★★.

●COMPILATIONS: *The Best Of ... And The Rest Of Be Bop Deluxe* (Harvest 1978)★★★★, *Raiding The Divine Archive: The Best Of Be-Bop Deluxe* (Harvest 1990)★★★★.

BEACH BOYS

The seminal line-up comprised: Brian Wilson (b. 20 June 1942), Carl Wilson (b. 21 December 1946), Dennis Wilson (b. 4 December 1944, Hawthorne, California, USA, d. 28 December 1983), Al Jardine (b. 3 September 1942, Lima, Ohio, USA) and Mike Love (b. 15 March 1941, Baldwin Hills, California, USA). When the aforementioned three brothers, one cousin and a school-friend formed a casual singing group in 1961, they unconsciously created one of the longest-running, compulsively fascinating and bitterly tragic sagas in popular music. As Carl And The Passions, the Pendletones and Kenny And The Cadets, they rehearsed and played high school hops while the elder brother Brian began to demonstrate his songwriting ability. He was already obsessed with harmonics and melody, and would listen for hours to close harmony groups, especially the Four Freshmen and the Hi-Lo's. One of his earliest songs, 'Surfin'' (written at the suggestion of keen surfing brother Dennis), was released on a local label and the topical name, Beach Boys, was innocently adopted. The domineering father of the brothers, Murray Wilson, immediately seized on their potential and appointed himself as manager, publicist and producer. After his own abortive attempts at a career in music, he began to live his frustrated career dreams through his sons. 'Surfin', with Murray's efforts, became a sizeable local hit, and made the *Billboard* Hot 100 (number 75). His continuing efforts gained them a recording contract with Capitol Records during the summer of 1962. In addition to the developing group's conflicts, Nik Venet (the producer at Capitol) became embroiled immediately with Murray, and their ideas clashed. Over the next 18 months the Beach Boys had 10 US hits and released four albums of surfing and hot-rod songs (each cover showed the photograph of neighbourhood friend, David Marks, who had temporarily replaced Al Jardine while he attended dentistry college). The Beach Boys' punishing workload began to affect the main songwriter Brian, who was additionally writing similar material for fellow surf/hot-rodders Jan And Dean. In 1963 the Beach Boys phenomenon reached the UK in the shape of the single 'Surfin' USA', which mildly interrupted the Merseybeat domination. The predominantly working-class image of the British beat group scene was at odds with the clean and wholesome west coast perception blessed with permanent sunshine, fun and beautiful girls. During 1964 a further four albums were released, culminating in the *Christmas Album*. This represented a staggering eight albums in just over two years, six of which were arranged and produced by Brian, in addition to his having written 63 out of a total of 84 songs. In America, the Beatles had begun their unmatched domination of the charts, and in their wake came dozens of groups as the British invasion took place. The Beach Boys, more especially Brian, could only stand back in amazement. He felt so threatened that it drove him to compete against the Beatles. Eventually Brian gained some pyrrhic revenge, when in 1966 the Beach Boys were voted number 1 group in the world by the UK music press, pushing the Fab Four into second place.

Wilson's maturity as a composer was developing at a staggering pace with classic hits like 'I Get Around', 'California Girls' and 'God Only Knows'. The overall quality of albums such as *Summer Days And Summer Nights!!* and *Today* was extremely high. Many of Wilson's songs portrayed his own insecurity as an adolescent. Songs such as 'In My Room', 'Wouldn't It Be Nice' and 'Girl Don't Tell Me' found a receptive audience who could immediately relate to the lyrics. While their instrumental prowess was average, the immaculate combination of the members' voices, delivered a sound that was unmistakable. Both Carl and Brian had perfect pitch, even though Brian was deaf in one ear (reputedly caused through his father's beatings). In private the 'musical genius' was working on what was to be his self-intended masterpiece, *Pet Sounds*. Released in August 1966, the high profile pre-publicity proved deserved and the reviews were outstanding. The music was also outstanding, but for some inexplicable reason, sales were not. It was later reported that Brian was devastated by the comparative commercial failure of *Pet Sounds* in his own country (US number 10), and mortified a year later when the Beatles' *Sgt Peppers Lonely Hearts Club Band* was released. It was not widely known that Brian had already experienced two nervous breakdowns, retired from performing with the group and had begun to depend on barbiturates. Even less public was the breakdown of his relationship with his father and the festering tension within the band. The brief recruitment of Glen Campbell, followed by Bruce Johnston, filled Brian's place in public. Through all this turmoil the Beach Boys rose to their peak at the end of 1966 with arguably their greatest achievement, 'Good Vibrations'. This glorious collage of musical pattern with its changes of tempo, unusual lyrics and incredible dynamics earned Brian and the band the respect of every musician. The group embarked on a major tour of Europe with a new single, 'Heroes And Villains', another innovative excursion with more intriguing lyrics by Van Dyke Parks. Brian meanwhile attempted a counter attack on the Beatles, with a project to be known as 'Smile'. This became the band's albatross, although it was never officially released. The painstaking hours spent on this project is now one of pop's legendary tales. Parts of the material surfaced on their next three albums, and further tracks appeared on other collections up until 1971.

The conflict between Wilson and the band was surfacing more regularly. Mike Love in particular wanted the other Beach Boys to continue with their immaculate pop music, and argued that Brian was getting too 'far out'. Indeed, Brian's reclusive nature, fast-increasing weight and growing dependence on drugs added fuel to Love's argument. Observers felt that the band could not raise themselves to the musical level visualized in Brian's present state of mind. Many students of the Beach Boys saga feel, retrospectively, that at that point Brian should have completely broken away to concentrate on his symphonic ideas, and made his own records. The band, meanwhile, could have continued along the route that their fans loved. *Smiley Smile* in 1967 and *Wild Honey* the following year were comparative failures in the charts by previous Beach Boys standards. Their music had lost its cohesiveness and their mentor and guiding light had by now retreated to his bed, where he stayed for many years. In Europe the group were still having hits, and even had a surprise UK chart topper in 1968 with 'Do It Again', with Mike Love's nasal vocals taking the lead on a song harping back to better times. Love had now become a devotee of the Maharishi Mahesh Yogi, while Dennis Wilson, who was emerging as a talented songwriter, became involved with Charles Manson, later to become notorious as a murderer. Dennis's naïvety allowed him to be drained of money, parted from his home and ultimately threatened with his life. Manson and Wilson collaborated on a number of songs, notably 'Never Learn Not To Love', which, although a Beach Boys b-side, had the ironic distinction of putting Charles Manson in the charts. To highlight their discontent, three of their next four singles were extraneous compositions, namely 'Bluebirds Over The Mountain', and a competent version of Lead Belly's 'Cottonfields'. The third non-original was the Phil Spector/Jeff Barry/Ellie Greenwich opus 'I Can Hear Music', featuring a passionate lead vocal from Carl, confirming his status as acting leader. He struggled to maintain this role for many years to come.

In April 1969 the Beach Boys left Capitol in a blaze of litigation. No new product surfaced until August the following year, apart from 'Add Some Music To Your Day' in March 1970. They had the ignominy of having an album rejected prior to that. *Sunflower* was an artistic triumph but a commercial disaster, on which Dennis contributed four songs including the sublime 'Forever'. Throughout the following 12 months they set about rebuilding their credibility in the USA, having lost much ground to the new wave bands from San Francisco. They started to tour constantly, even appearing with unlikely compatriots the Grateful Dead. Through determination and hard work they did the seemingly impossible and allied themselves with the hip *cognoscenti*.

The arrival of *Surf's Up* in July 1971 completed their remarkable renaissance. The title track, with surreal lyrics by Van Dyke Parks, was another masterpiece, while on the rest of the album it was Carl's turn to put in strong contributions the beautiful 'Feel Flows' and 'Long Promised Road'. The record's strong ecological stance was years ahead of its time, and the critics were unanimous in favourably reassessing them. As Dennis co-starred with James Taylor in the cult road movie *Two-Lane Blacktop*, so Brian's life was deteriorating into mental instability. Miraculously the band were able to maintain their career which at times included only one Wilson, Carl, and no longer had the presence of the long-serving Bruce Johnston. The addition of Ricky Fataar, Blondie Chaplin and Daryl Dragon nevertheless gave the depleted band a fuller sound. One further album appeared before the outstanding *Holland* came in 1973. For this project the entire Beach Boys organization, including wives and children, moved to Holland for eight months of recording. Thankfully, even Brian was cajoled into going, because his composition 'Sail On Sailor' was a high point of the record. Murray Wilson died of a heart attack in June 1973, but Brian and Dennis declined to attend the funeral; they were greatly affected by his passing. At the same time the group's fortunes were once again in the descendent as a double live album was badly received. A year later an astonishing thing happened: a compilation, *Endless Summer*, put together by Mike Love, unexpectedly rocketed to the top of the US charts. It spent 71 weeks on the lists, disappeared and returned again the following year to a high position staying for a further 78 weeks. This unparalleled success reinforced Love and Jardine's theory that all anybody wanted of the Beach Boys was surfing and car songs. With the addition of James William Guercio, formerly of Chicago and ex-producer of Blood Sweat And Tears, the band enjoyed extraordinary concert tour success, and ended 1974 being voted 'Band of the Year' by the influential magazine *Rolling Stone*. *Spirit Of America* (1975), another compilation of earlier tracks, enjoyed enormous success staying on the American charts for almost a year. Meanwhile, Brian's condition had further deteriorated and he was now under the treatment of therapist Eugene Landy. The album *15 Big Ones* in July 1976 gave them a big hit with Chuck Berry's 'Rock And Roll Music'. The publicity centred on a tasteless 'Brian Is Back' campaign, the now obese Wilson being unwillingly pushed into the spotlight. It seemed obvious to all that Brian was not back; here was a sick, confused and nervous man being used as a financial tool.

Subsequent albums, *The Beach Boys Love You* and *M.I.U. Album*, attempted to maintain Brian's high profile as producer, but close observers were well aware that this was a complete sham. The material was of average quality, although the former showed strong glimpses of Wilson's fascination for childlike innocence. In 1977 they signed a recording contract with CBS reputedly worth $8,000,000, on the terms that Brian Wilson contributed at least four new songs and a total of 70 per cent of all the material for each album. The first album under this contract was the patchy *LA (Light Album)*, with Bruce Johnston recalled, to bail them out on production duties. The album did manage to produce a sizeable hit with Al Jardine's 'Lady Lynda'. The most controversial track, however, was a remake of 'Here Comes the Night'; this previously innocuous R&B song from *Wild Honey* was turned into an 11-minute extended disco extravaganza. This track alone cost $50,000 to produce. By now Dennis had a serious cocaine habit which hampered the recording of his own solo album *Pacific Ocean Blue*. It was released to excellent reviews, and was an album into which Dennis put his heart, using a host of musicians and singers, with the notable absence of the Beach Boys. Dennis now openly verbally abused the other members of the band except for Brian, whom he defended resolutely. When Carl fell victim to cocaine and alcohol, the fragmentation of the group was at its height.

The next official work was *Keeping The Summer Alive*, a poor album (with an even poorer cover), without the presence of Dennis who had left the group. He was now living with Christine McVie of Fleetwood Mac. During 1980 only Love and Jardine were present from the original group. Carl delivered his first solo album, a beautifully sung, well-produced record that flopped. One track, 'Heaven', later became a regular part of the Beach Boys' repertoire and was dedicated to Dennis during the 80s. In 1982, Brian Wilson was officially dismissed, and was admitted to hospital for detoxification, weighing a massive 320 pounds. In December 1983, Dennis Wilson tragically drowned while diving from his boat. Ironically, his death reportedly snapped Brian out of his stupor, and he gradually re-emerged to participate onstage. A clean and healthy-looking band graced the back of the 1985 Steve Levine-produced, *The Beach Boys*. Following this collection they found themselves without a recording contract, and decided to concentrate purely on being a major concert attraction, travelling the world. While no new albums appeared, they concentrated on singles, including an energetic, well-produced 'Rock And Roll To The Rescue', followed by their version of the Mamas And The Papas' classic 'California Dreaming', with Roger McGuinn featured on 12-string guitar. In 1987, they teamed up with rap act the Fat Boys for a remake of the Surfaris' 'Wipe Out'.

In 1988, a phoenix-like Brian Wilson returned with the solo album for which his fans had waited over 20 years. The much-publicized record showed a slim, healthy-looking man. The critics and fans loved it, but the general public did not respond and the album sold only moderately well. At the same time the Beach Boys released 'Kokomo', which was included in the film *Cocktail*. They found themselves unexpectedly at the top of the US charts, for many weeks. In May 1990, the Beach Boys took Brian Wilson to court in an alleged attempt to wrest his $80 million fortune from him. They maintained that he was insane and unable to look after himself. His medical condition was confirmed (extreme introversion, pathological shyness and manic depression). Wilson defended the case but eventually reluctantly accepted a settlement by which he severed his links with the controversial Landy. Wilson was then officially sacked/resigned and proceeded to get back monies which had been pouring in from his back catalogue. Murray Wilson had sold his son's company Sea Of Tunes to another publisher in 1969. During this latest court case Wilson testified that he was mentally ill and a casualty of drug abuse at the time. Wilson won the case and received substantial back royalties. No sooner had the dust settled when Mike Love issued a writ to Brian Wilson claiming he co-wrote 79 songs with him, including 'California Girls', 'I Get Around' and 'Surfin' USA' (the latter was 'borrowed' from Chuck Berry). In 1993 the band continued to tour, although their show was merely an oldies package. During 1994 mutterings were heard that the pending lawsuit would be settled, as Love and Brian were at least speaking to each other. Late that year it was announced that a substantial settlement had been made to Love, effectively confirming all his claims. In February 1995 a thin, handsome, recently remarried Wilson and a neat sprite-looking Love met at the latter's home. Not only had they mended the rift but they were writing songs together. Early reports indicate both enthusiasm and a desire to make up for many years of wasted time. Carl Wilson underwent treatment for cancer in 1997. Much has been written about the band, and to those wishing to study the band, David Leaf's book is highly recommended. Timothy White's recent book adds information that had previously never surfaced and is a well-written documentary of California life. Their career has been rolling, like the tide their great songs evoked, constantly in and out, reaching incredible highs and extraordinary troughs. Through all these appalling experiences, however, they still reign supreme as the most successful American group in pop history.

●ALBUMS: Surfin' Safari (Capitol 1962)★★, Surfin' USA (Capitol 1963)★★★, Surfer Girl (Capitol 1963)★★★, Little Deuce Coupe (Capitol 1963)★★★, Shut Down Vol. 2 (Capitol 1964)★★★★, All Summer Long (Capitol 1964)★★★★, Beach Boys Concert (Capitol 1964)★★★, The Beach Boys' Christmas Album (Capitol 1964)★★★, The Beach Boys Today! (Capitol 1965)★★★★, Summer Days (And Summer Nights!!) (Capitol 1965)★★★★, The Beach Boys' Party! (Capitol 1965)★★, Pet Sounds (Capitol 1966)★★★★★, Smiley Smile (Capitol 1967)★★★★, Wild Honey (Capitol 1967)★★★, Friends (Capitol 1968)★★★★, Stack-O-Tracks (Capitol 1968)★★, 20/20 (Capitol 1969)★★★, Live In London (Capitol 1970)★★, Sunflower (Brother 1970)★★★★★, Surf's Up (Brother 1971)★★★★★, Carl And The Passions-So Tough (Brother

1972)★★★, Holland (Brother 1973)★★★★, The Beach Boys In Concert (Brother 1973)★★, 15 Big Ones (Brother 1976)★★★, The Beach Boys Love You (Brother 1977)★★★, M.I.U. Album (Brother 1978)★, LA (Light Album) (Caribou 1979)★★★, Keepin' The Summer Alive (Caribou 1980)★, Rarities (1983)★★★, The Beach Boys (Caribou 1985)★★★, Still Cruisin' (Capitol 1989)★, Summer In Paradise (1993)★, Stars And Stripes Vol. 1 (River North 1996)★.

●COMPILATIONS: Endless Summer (Capitol 1974)★★★★★, Spirit Of America (Capitol 1975)★★★★, 20 Golden Greats (Capitol 1976)★★★★, Sunshine Dream (Capitol 1982)★★★, The Very Best Of The Beach Boys (Capitol 1983)★★★, Made In The USA (Capitol 1986)★★★★, Summer Dreams (Capitol 1990)★★★★, Good Vibrations: Thirty Years Of... 5-CD box set (Capitol 1993)★★★★★.

●VIDEOS: Beach Boys: An American Band (Vestron Music Video 1988), Summer Dreams (Polygram Music Video 1991).

●FURTHER READING: The Beach Boys, John Tobler. The Beach Boys And The California Myth, David Leaf. The Beach Boys: The Authorized Illustrated Biography, Byron Preiss. The Beach Boys: Silver Anniversary, John Millward. Look! Listen! Vibrate! SMILE, Dominic Priore. Denny Remembered, Edward Wincentsen. Wouldn't It Be Nice: My Own Story, Brian Wilson and Todd Gold. In Their Own Words, Nick Wise (compiled). The Nearest Faraway Place: Brian Wilson, The Beach Boys & The Southern California, Timothy White.

●FILMS: Girls On The Beach (1965), Americation (1979).

BEAVER AND KRAUSE

Paul Beaver (b. 1925, d. 16 January 1975) and Bernie Krause (b. Detroit, Michigan, USA) were early exponents of electronic music. Beaver played in several jazz groups prior to exploring synthesized instrumentation, and later contributed sound effects to various film soundtracks (Rosemary's Baby (1968), Catch 22 (1970), Performance (1970)). Krause came from a folk background as a member of the Weavers and was later employed at Motown Records in studio production. Moving on to Elektra Records, it was as a staff producer that he met Paul Beaver. Working together, their use of spoken word, acoustic instruments, tape loops and improvisation pushed back the boundaries of rock and, as session men, their work graced albums by the Beatles, Beach Boys, Rolling Stones, Simon And Garfunkel, Neil Young and many more. Gandharva, recorded live in San Francisco's Grace Cathedral, proved the most popular of their own releases, and featured additional contributions from guitarist Mike Bloomfield and saxophonist Gerry Mulligan. Paul Beaver completed a solo album, Perchance To Dream, prior to his death from a heart attack in 1975. Krause has meanwhile pursued a career in electronic music.

●ALBUMS: Ragnarock (Limelight 1969)★★★, In A Wild Sanctuary (Warners 1970)★★★, Gandharva (Warners

1971)★★★, *All Good Men* (Warners 1972)★★★, *A Guide To Electronic Music* (Nonesuch 1975)★★★.

BECK, BOGERT AND APPICE

The plan for guitar virtuoso Jeff Beck (b. 24 June 1944, Surrey, England) to form a power trio with the ex-Vanilla Fudge rhythm section was first mooted in 1969. Both drummer, Carmine Appice (b. 15 December 1946, New York, USA), and bassist, Tim Bogert (b. 27 August 1944, Richfield, New Jersey, USA), were dissatisfied with their present band. The plans were spoiled when Beck was involved in a serious car crash that put him out of action. Meanwhile, Bogert and Appice formed the heavy rock band Cactus, until in 1972 their paths again crossed with Beck and they put together the heavy rock unit Beck, Bogert And Appice. The self-titled commercially successful debut was instrumentally superb, but suffered from a lack of songwriting ability and strained vocals. Twenty years later the album sounds ponderous and is justifiably disowned by its members.

●ALBUMS: *Beck, Bogert And Appice* (Epic 1973)★★, *Live In Japan* (Epic/Sony 1975)★★.

BECK, JEFF

b. 24 June 1944, Wallington, Surrey, England. As a former choir boy the young Beck was interested in music from an early age, becoming a competent pianist and guitarist by the age of 11. His first main band was the Tridents, who made a name for themselves locally. After leaving them Beck took on the seemingly awesome task of stepping into the shoes of Eric Clapton, who had recently departed from the 60s R&B pioneers, the Yardbirds. Clapton had a fiercely loyal following, but Beck soon had them gasping with his amazing guitar pyrotechnics, utilizing feedback and distortion. Beck stayed with the Yardbirds adding colour and excitement to all their hits until October 1966. The tension between Beck and joint lead guitarist Jimmy Page was finally resolved during a US tour. Beck walked out and never returned. His solo career was launched in March 1967 with an unexpected pop single, 'Hi-Ho Silver Lining', wherein his unremarkable voice was heard on a singalong number that was saved by his trademark guitar solo. The record was a sizeable hit and has demonstrated its perennial appeal to party-goers by re-entering the charts on several occasions since. The follow-up, 'Tallyman', was also a minor hit, but by now Jeff's ambitions lay in other directions. From being a singing, guitar-playing, pop star he relaunched a career that led him to become one of the world's leading rock guitarists. The Jeff Beck Group, formed in 1968, consisted of Beck, Rod Stewart (vocals), Ron Wood (bass), Nicky Hopkins (piano) and Mickey Waller (drums). This powerhouse quartet released *Truth*, which became a major success in the USA, resulting in the band undertaking a number of arduous tours. The second album, *Cosa Nostra Beck-Ola*, had similar success,

although Stewart and Wood had now departed for the Faces. Beck also contributed some sparkling guitar and received equal billing with Donovan on the hit 'Goo Goo Barabajagal (Love Is Hot)'. In 1968 Beck's serious accident with one of his hot-rod cars put him out of action for almost 18 months. A recovered Beck formed another group with Cozy Powell, Max Middleton and Bob Tench, and recorded two further albums, *Rough And Ready* and *Jeff Beck Group*. Beck was now venerated as a serious musician and master of his instrument, and figured highly in various guitarist polls. In 1973 the erratic Beck musical style changed once again and he formed the trio Beck, Bogert And Appice with the two former members of Vanilla Fudge. Soon after Beck introduced yet another musical dimension, this time forming an instrumental band. The result was the excellent *Blow By Blow*, thought by many to be his best work. His guitar playing revealed extraordinary technique, combining rock, jazz and blues styles. *Blow By Blow* was a million seller and its follow-up, *Wired*, enjoyed similar success. Having allied himself with some of the jazz/rock fraternity Beck teamed up with Jan Hammer for a frantic live album, after which he effectively retired for three years. He returned in 1980 with *There And Back* and, now rejuvenated, he found himself riding the album charts once more. During the 80s Beck's appearances were sporadic, though he did guest on Tina Turner's *Private Dancer* and work with Robert Plant and Jimmy Page on the Honeydrippers' album. The occasional charity function aside, he has spent much of his leisure time with automobiles (in one interview Beck stated that he could just as easily have been a car restorer). In the mid-80s he toured with Rod Stewart and was present on his version of 'People Get Ready', though when *Flash* arrived in 1985, it proved his least successful album to date. The release of a box-set in 1992, chronicling his career, was a fitting tribute to this accomplished guitarist and his numerous guises (the latest of which had been guitarist on Spinal Tap's second album). Following an award in 1993 for his theme music (with Jed Stoller) for the Anglia TV production *Frankie's House* he released *Crazy Legs*, a tribute to the music of Gene Vincent. For this, Beck abandoned virtuosity, blistering solos and jazz stylings for a clean, low-volume rock 'n' roll sound demonstrating once more his absolute mastery of technique. He also made his acting debut, playing Brad the serial killer in *The Comic Strip Presents ... Gregory: Diary Of A Nutcase*.

●ALBUMS: *Truth* (EMI 1968)★★★, *Cosa Nostra Beck-Ola* (EMI 1969)★★, *Rough And Ready* (Epic 1971)★★, *Jeff Beck Group* (Epic 1972)★★, *Blow By Blow* (Epic 1975)★★★★, *Wired* (Epic 1976)★★, *Jeff Beck With The Jan Hammer Group Live* (Epic 1977)★, *There And Back* (Epic 1980)★★, *Flash* (Epic 1985)★★, with Terry Bozzio, Tony Hymas *Jeff Beck's Guitar Shop* (Epic 1989)★★, *Crazy Legs* (Epic 1993)★★★.

●COMPILATIONS: *Beckology* CD box set (Epic 1992)★★★★.

BEDFORD, DAVID

A graduate from London's Royal Academy of Music in London, this accomplished musician achieved considerable acclaim for his striking arrangements on Kevin Ayers' debut, *Joy Of A Toy* in 1969. Their working relationship was maintained on several subsequent releases and Bedford was also a member of the singer's backing group, the Whole World, prior to embarking on an independent recording career. The artist's first solo offering, *Nurses Song With Elephants*, was released in 1972. This eclectic, experimental collection featured former Whole World guitarist, Mike Oldfield, one of several fruitful collaborations that Bedford enjoyed. Roy Harper was another artist to benefit from the arranger's intuitive talent, exemplified in such stellar achievements as 'Me And My Woman' (*Stormcock*) and 'When An Old Cricketer Leaves The Crease (*HQ*). Bedford's 1974 release, *Star's End*, featured a composition commissioned by the Royal Philharmonic Orchestra, while the following year he completed *The Orchestral Tubular Bells*, a classical interpretation of Oldfield's multi-million-selling album, and *The Rime Of The Ancient Mariner*, a musical portrayal of the famous Samuel Taylor Coleridge poem. Literature also provided the inspiration for *The Odyssey*, but such ambitious projects lacked the humility the artist bestowed on his external work. Bedford's grandiose performances fell from favour in the late 70s, but he remains a respected and imaginative figure, arranging studio orchestration for various musicians and groups.

●ALBUMS: *Nurses Song With Elephants* (1972)★★★, *Star's End* (Virgin 1974)★★★, *The Orchestral Tubular Bells* (Virgin 1975)★★, *The Rime Of The Ancient Mariner* (Virgin 1975)★★, *The Odyssey* (Virgin 1976)★★, *Instructions For Angels* (1977)★★, *Rigel 9* (Charisma 1988)★★, *Star Clusters Nebulae And Places In Devon* (1993)★★.

BEE GEES

This hugely successful Anglo/Australian trio comprised the twins Maurice and Robin Gibb (b. 22 December 1949, Isle Of Man, British Isles) and their elder brother Barry Gibb (b. 1 September 1946, Isle Of Man, British Isles). Originating from a showbusiness family based in Manchester, England, they played as a child act in several of the city's cinemas. In 1958, the Gibb family emigrated to Australia and the boys performed regularly as a harmony trio in Brisbane, Queensland. Christened the Bee Gees, an abbreviation of Brothers Gibb, they signed to the Australian label Festival Records and released a series of singles written by the elder brother. While their single 'Spicks And Specks' was topping the Australian charts, the brothers were already on their way to London for a fateful audition before Robert Stigwood, a director of NEMS Enterprises, the company owned by Beatles svengali Brian Epstein. This, in turn, led to a record contract with Polydor and the swift release of 'New York Mining Disaster, 1941'. The quality of the single with its evocative, intriguing lyrics and striking harmony provoked premature comparison with the Beatles and gained the group a UK hit. During this period the trio was supplemented by Australian friends Colin Peterson (drums) and Vince Melouney (guitar). The second UK single, 'To Love Somebody', departed from the narrative power of their previous offering towards a more straightforward ballad style. Although the disc failed to reach the Top 40, the enduring quality of the song was evinced by a number of striking cover versions, most notably by Nina Simone, Eric Burdon And The Animals and Janis Joplin. The Beatlesque songs on their outstanding acclaimed UK debut, *The Bee Gees First* garnered further comparisons. Every track was a winner, from the delightfully naïve 'Cucumber Castle' to the sublime 'Please Read Me', while 'Holiday' had the beautiful stark quality of McCartney's 'Yesterday'. The 14 tracks were all composed by the twins and Barry, still aged only 17 and 19, respectively. By October 1967, the group had registered their first UK number 1 with the moving 'Massachusetts', which showcased their ability as arrangers to particular effect. Aware of the changes occurring in the pop firmament, the group bravely experimented with different musical styles and briefly followed the Beatles and the Rolling Stones along the psychedelic road. Their progressive forays confused their audience, however, and the double album *Odessa* failed to match the work of their major rivals. Their singles remained adventurous and strangely eclectic, with the unusual tempo of 'World' followed by the neurotic romanticism of 'Words'. Both singles hit the Top 10 in the UK but signs of commercial fallibility followed with the relatively unsuccessful double a-side 'Jumbo'/'The Singer Not The Song'. Masters of the chart comeback, the group next turned to a heart-rending ballad about the final hour of a condemned prisoner. 'I've Gotta Get A Message To You' gave them their second UK number 1 and sixth consecutive US Top 20 hit. The stark but startling 'First Of May' followed, again revealing the Bee Gees' willingness to tackle a mood piece in favour of an easily accessible melodic ballad. To complete their well-rounded image, the group showed their talent as composers, penning the Marbles' Top 10 UK hit 'Only One Woman'.

Without question, the Bee Gees were one of the most accomplished groups of the late 60s, but as the decade ended they fell victim to internal bickering and various pressures wrought by international stardom. Maurice Gibb married pop star Lulu and the group joined the celebrity showbusiness elite with all its attendant trappings of drink and drugs. Dissent among the brotherhood saw Robin Gibb embark on a solo career with brief success while the twins retained the group name. Remarkably, they ended the 60s with another change of style emerging with an authentic country standard in 'Don't Forget To Remember'. With Colin Peterson still in tow, Maurice and Barry worked on a much-publicized but ultimately insubstantial film, *Cucumber Castle*. This fractious period ended with a ludicrous series of law suits in which the drummer had the audacity to claim rights to the Bee Gees name. A year of chaos and missed opportunities ensued during which the group lost much of their impetus and following. Maurice and Barry both released one single each as soloists, but their efforts were virtually ignored. Their career in the UK was in tatters but after reuniting with Robin in late 1970 they went on to have two major US hits with 'Lonely Days' and the chart-topping 'How Can You Mend A Broken Heart'.

After a brief flurry of transatlantic hits in 1972 with 'My World' and 'Run To Me', the group's appeal diminished to an all-time low. Three hitless years saw them reduced to playing in cabaret at such inauspicious venues as the Batley Variety Club in Yorkshire. A switch from Polydor Records to Robert Stigwood's new label RSO encouraged the group to adopt a more American sound with the album *Life In A Tin Can*. Determined to explore a more distinctive style, the group were teamed with famed producer Arif Mardin. *Mr. Natural*, recorded in London, indicated a noticeable R&B/soul influence which was extended on 1975's *Main Course*. Now ensconced in Miami, the group gathered together a formidable backing unit featuring Alan Kendall (guitar), Dennis Bryon (drums) and Blue Weaver (keyboards). 'Jive Talkin'', a pilot single from the album, zoomed to number 1 in the US and brought the trio back to the Top 10 in Britain. Meanwhile, fellow RSO artist Olivia Newton-John enjoyed a US hit with the group's country ballad 'Come On Over'. The Bee Gees were well and truly back.

The changes in their sound during the mid-70s was nothing short of remarkable. They had virtually reinvented themselves, with Mardin encouraging them to explore their R&B roots and experiment with falsetto vocals. The effect was particularly noticeable on their next US Top 10 hit 'Nights On Broadway' (later a hit for Candi Staton). The group were perfectly placed to promote and take advantage of the underground dance scene in the USA, and their next album, *Children Of The World*, went platinum. The attendant single 'You Should Be Dancing' reached number 1 in the USA, while the follow-up, 'Love So Right', hit number 3. Not content to revitalize their own career the trio's soundtrack contributions also provided massive hits for Yvonne Elliman ('If I Can't Have You') and Tavares ('More Than A Woman'). The Bee Gees' reputation as the new gods of the discotheque was consummated on the soundtrack of the movie *Saturday Night Fever*, which sold in excess of 30 million copies. In their most successful phase to date, the group achieved a quite staggering run of six consecutive chart toppers: 'How Deep Is Your Love', 'Stayin' Alive', 'Night Fever', 'Too Much Heaven', 'Tragedy' and 'Love You Inside Out'. Their grand flurry continued with the movie *Grease*, for which they pro-

duced the chart-topping title track by Frankie Valli. Having already received Beatles comparisons during their early career, it was ill-advised of the group to take the starring role in the movie *Sgt. Pepper's Lonely Hearts Club Band*. The film proved an embarrassing detour for both the brothers and their co-star Peter Frampton.

As the 70s ended the Bee Gees increasingly switched their interests towards production. Although they released two further albums, *Spirits Having Flown* (1979) and *Living Eyes* (1981), far greater attention was being focused on their chart-topping younger brother Andy Gibb. A multi-million dollar dispute with their mentor Robert Stigwood was settled out of court, following which the group contributed to another movie soundtrack, *Stayin' Alive*. With the group's activities put on hold, it was Barry who emerged as the most prolific producer and songwriter. He duetted with Barbra Streisand on the chart-topping 'Guilty' and composed and sang on 'Heartbreaker' with Dionne Warwick. The brothers, meanwhile, also wrote the Kenny Rogers and Dolly Parton US chart topper 'Islands In The Stream' and Diana Ross's excellent Motown pastiche, 'Chain Reaction'. Seemingly content to stay in the background masterminding platinum discs for others, they eventually reunited in 1987 for the hugely successful *ESP*. The indisputable masters of melody, their 'comeback' single 'You Win Again' was warmly received by usually hostile critics who applauded its undoubted craftsmanship. The single gave the group their fifth UK number 1, a full eight years after their last chart topper, 'Tragedy'. Sadly, the death of younger brother Andy the following year added a tragic note to the proceedings. In deference to their brother's death they declined to attend an Ivor Novello Awards ceremony in which they were honoured for their Outstanding Contribution to British Music.

Looking back over the Bee Gees' career, one cannot fail to be impressed by the sheer diversity of their talents and their remarkable ability to continually reinvent themselves again and again. Like that other great family group the Beach Boys, they have survived family feuds, dissension, tragic death, harsh criticism, changes in musical fashion and much else to become one of pop's ineffable institutions. Throughout all the musical changes they have undergone, the one constant has been their vocal dexterity, strength and an innate ability to arrange some wondrous pop melodies. The Bee Gees have received more than their share of mocking criticisms but they have ignored it and continued with their art. One cannot ignore the legacy of their performing, songwriting and production activities. It represents one of the richest tapestries in the entire history of modern popular music. This appeared to be recognized at the 1997 Brit awards which was followed by a glut of press and television promotion for their *Still Waters* album, which became a sizeable hit. The brothers Gibb have shown controlled dignity in taking years of critism on the chin, but only in the late 90s does it appear that from all corners their work is applauded.

●ALBUMS: *Barry Gibb And The Bee Gees Sing And Play 14 Barry Gibb Songs* (Leedon 1965)★★, *Spicks And Specks* (Leedon 1966)★★, *The Bee Gees First* (Polydor 1967)★★★★, *Horizontal* (Polydor 1968)★★★★, *Idea* (Polydor 1968)★★★, *Odessa* (Polydor 1969)★★★, *Cucumber Castle* (Polydor 1970)★★, *Two Years On* (Polydor 1970)★★, *Trafalgar* (Polydor 1971)★★, *To Whom It May Concern* (Polydor 1972)★★, *Life In A Tin Can* (RSO 1973)★★, *Mr Natural* (RSO 1974)★★, *Main Course* (RSO 1975)★★★★, *Children Of The World* (RSO 1976)★★★, *Here At Last ... Bee Gees Live* (RSO 1977)★★, *Saturday Night Fever* soundtrack (RSO 1977)★★★★, *Sgt. Pepper's Lonely Hearts Club Band* (1978)★, *Spirits Having Flown* (RSO 1979)★★★, *Living Eyes* (RSO 1981)★★, *Stayin' Alive* (1983)★★, *ESP* (Warners 1987)★★★, *High Civilisation* (Warners 1991)★★, *Size Isn't Everything* (1993)★★, *Still Waters* (Polydor 1997)★★★.

●COMPILATIONS: *Rare Precious And Beautiful* (Polydor 1968)★★★, *Rare Precious And Beautiful Vol. 2* (Polydor 1968)★★, *Rare Precious And Beautiful Vol. 3* (Polydor 1969)★★, *Best Of The Bee Gees* (Polydor 1969)★★★★, *Best Of The Bee Gees Vol. 2* (Polydor 1973)★★★★, *Bee Gees Gold Volume One* (RSO 1976)★★★★, *Bee Gees Greatest* (RSO 1979)★★★★, *The Early Days Vol. 1* (Hallmark 1979)★★, *The Early Days Vol. 2* (Hallmark 1979)★★, *The Early Days Vol. 3* (Hallmark 1979)★, *Very Best Of The Bee Gees* (Polydor 1990)★★★★, *Tales From The Brothers Gibb (A History In Song)* (Polydor 1990)★★★★.

●VIDEOS: *Bee Gees: Video Biography* (Virgin Vision 1988), *Very Best Of The Bee Gees* (Video Collection 1990), *One For All Tour Volume 1* (Video Collection 1990), *One For All Tour Volume 2* (Video Collection 1990).

●FURTHER READING: *The Official Sgt. Pepper's Lonely Hearts Club Band Scrapbook*, Robert Stigwood and Dee Anthony. *The Bee Gees: A Photo Biography*, Kim Stevens. *The Bee Gees*, Suzanne Munshower. *Sgt. Pepper's Lonely Hearts Club Band*, Henry Edwards. *The Incredible Bee Gees*, Dick Tatham. *The Bee Gees*, Larry Pryce. *Bee Gees: The Authorized Biography*, Barry, Robin and Maurice Gibb as told to David Leaf.

BEES MAKE HONEY

Bees Make Honey were formed in London in 1972 by blues/jazz musician Barry Richardson (bass/vocals). Deke O'Brien (guitar/vocals), Mick Molloy (guitar/vocals), Ruan O'Lochlainn (piano/guitar/saxophone) and Bob Gee (drums) joined him in the band who then took over the residency at the Tally Ho from Eggs Over Easy. With the aid of Brinsley Schwarz, these acts established the genre known as 'pub rock'. Former Man/Help Yourself pianist Malcolm Morley took over from O'Lochlainn in 1973, but he in turn was replaced by Kevin McAlea. The arrival of Rod Demick (ex-Wheels/Demick And Armstrong) allowed Richardson to concentrate on vocals and saxophone, talents expressed on the band's sole album, *Music Every Night*. Sadly, the unit's live prowess could not be captured in the studio and the set was not a commercial success. By that point Fran Byrne was the drummer. In 1974 he joined Richardson and Demick in a reshaped line-up completed by Willie Findlayson (guitar/vocals, ex-Writing On The Wall) and former Skid Row pair Ed Dean (guitar) and Kevin McAlea (piano). Two albums were completed before Bees Make Honey split up in autumn that year. Findlayson and Demick formed Meal Ticket, Byrne joined Ace and McAlea later worked with Kate Bush. Meanwhile Richardson formed the Barry Richardson Band, continuing the musicianly 'roots' genre so typified in this group's work.

●ALBUMS: *Music Every Night* (EMI 1972)★★★.

BELL AND ARC

Formed in 1970 by songwriters John Turnbull (guitar/vocals) and Mickey Gallagher (keyboards/vocals), one-time colleagues in Skip Bifferty. Their new venture, originally known simply as Arc, was completed by Tommy Duffy (bass) and Dave Trudex (drums), although the latter was replaced by Rob Tait (ex-Battered Ornaments) prior to the recording of *Arc At This*. The quartet was then invited to back singer Graham Bell, another Skip Bifferty acolyte, on a projected album. This in turn inspired a new epithet, Bell And Arc, but their sole release sadly failed to capture the live sparkle displayed on tours supporting Genesis and the Who. Drummer Alan White, later of Yes, replaced Tait late in 1971, but the quintet broke up the following year. Bell then resumed his solo career while Gallagher and Turnbull pursued separate paths with among others, Glencoe and Peter Frampton, before reuniting in Ian Dury's Blockheads.

●ALBUMS: as Arc *Arc At This* (Decca 1971)★★, *Bell And Arc* (Charisma 1971)★★.

BELL, ARCHIE, AND THE DRELLS

This vocal soul group was formed by Archie Bell (b. 1 September 1944, Henderson, Texas, USA), with friends, James Wise (b. 1 May 1948, Houston, Texas, USA), Willie Parnell (b. 12 April 1945, Houston, Texas, USA), L.C. Watts and Cornelius Fuller at the Leo Smith Junior High School, in Houston, Texas. By the time their first record was made for the Ovid label in 1967, the group consisted of Bell, Wise, Huey 'Billy' Butler and Joe Cross. The single, produced by their manager Skippy Lee Frazier, was released by Atlantic Records. Although initially a poor seller, it found real success after the b-side was given airplay. The song 'Tighten Up' sold in excess of three million copies and reached number 1 in both the US R&B and pop charts. By this time Bell, who had been drafted into the army, was recuperating from a wound received in Vietnam. The Drells continued recording, now with the production team of Gamble And Huff. For live performances, fake 'Archie Bells' were enlisted and whenever possible, the real Bell would join them in the studio. These sessions produced three more hits 'I Can't Stop Dancing', 'Doin' The Choo-Choo' and '(There's Gonna Be A) Showdown'. Paradoxically the singles were less successful once Bell left the forces. 'Here I Go Again', an early Atlantic master, became a belated UK chart hit in 1972. Reunited with Gamble and Huff in 1975, they enjoyed several R&B successes on their TSOP/Philadelphia International label, including 'Let's Groove (Part 1)' (1976) and 'Soul City Walk' (1975) which entered the UK Top 20 in 1976. Archie Bell recorded a solo album for the Becket label in 1981 and charted with 'Any Time Is Right'. He still actively pursues a singing career within the US east coast 'beach music' scene.

●ALBUMS: *Tighten Up* (Atlantic 1968)★★★, *I Can't Stop Dancing* (Atlantic 1968)★★★, *There's Gonna Be A Showdown* (Atlantic 1969)★★★, *Dance All Your Troubles Away* (TSOP 1976)★★★, *Where Will You Go, When The Party's Over* (TSOP 1976)★★, *Hard Not To Like It* (TSOP 1977)★★★. Solo: Archie Bell *I Never Had It So Good* (Becket 1981)★★.

●COMPILATIONS: *Artists Showcase: Archie Bell* (DM Streetsounds 1986)★★★.

BELL, CHRIS

b. Memphis, Tennessee, USA, d. 27 December 1978. Singer/guitarist Bell spent his formative years in local bands, before working as an engineer at the city's Ardent Studios. Here he recorded several original compositions which attracted owners John Fry and Terry Manning, who operated a concurrent record label. Inspired by their interest, Bell formed Big Star with friends Andy Hummel, Jody Stephens and Alex Chilton (ex-Box Tops). *No.1 Record* (1971) exposed his love of Beatles-styled melodies, but Bell quit the group the following year, disillusioned with Ardent's distribution deal with the ailing Stax label. In 1973 he resumed recording with the aid of Stephens. Three tracks followed, including 'I Am The Cosmos'. The following year Bell travelled to Chateau D'Herouville in France where he completed an album's worth of material. The results were mixed at George Martin's AIR Studio, but despite their excellence, the performances failed to secure a recording contract. Having returned to Memphis the depressed singer ceased performing, opting to work for his family's fast-food restaurant chain. However, in 1977, Car Records in New York issued 'I Am The Cosmos', backed by 'You And Your Sister'. Both sides showed Bell's melodic muse and the single generated considerable interest. He formed a new group but on 27 December 1978 his car struck a telephone pole en route from a rehearsal. Bell was killed instantly. Awareness of his work has been maintained through continued interest in Big Star and This Mortal Coil's recording of 'You And Your Sister'. In 1992 Rykodisc released all the available Bell masters on *I Am The Cosmos*.

●COMPILATIONS: *I Am The Cosmos* (Rykodisc 1992)★★★.

BELL, MADELINE

b. 23 July 1942, Newark, New Jersey, USA. Bell arrived in the UK in 1962 with the cast of *Black Nativity*, a gospel show, but remained to embark on a solo career. Although early releases veered towards MOR, the singer's mid-60s recordings, including 'I Really Got Carried Away' and 'Doin' Things Together With You', were among Britain's strongest home-grown soul singles. A respected session vocalist, her powerful tones were also heard on numerous pop releases alongside Doris Troy, Lesley Duncan and Rosetta Hightower. Bell later secured consistent success as a member of Blue Mink, and has more recently forged a lucrative career singing jingles for television advertisements, during which time she has released two singles, in 1982 duetting with Dave Martin on 'East Side West Side' and 'I'm Not Really Me Without You'. In 1991, she appeared in a UK stage production of *The Cotton Club*.

●ALBUMS: *Bell's A'Poppin'* (Philips 1967)★★★, *Doin' Things* (Philips 1969)★★★, *Madeline Bell* (1971)★★, *16 Star Tracks By Madeline Bell* (1971)★★★, *Comin' Atcha* (Victor 1974)★★★, *This Is One Girl* (Pye 1976)★★, with John Telfer *Rubadub-Pop Goes The Nursery Rhymes* (Rubberband 1984)★.

BELL, MAGGIE

b. 12 January 1945, Glasgow, Scotland. Bell's career began in the mid-60s as the featured singer in several resident dancehall bands. She made her recording debut in 1966, completing two singles, with Bobby Kerr, under the name Frankie And Johnny. Bell then joined guitarist Leslie Harvey, another veteran of the same circuit, in Power, a hard-rock group which evolved into Stone The Crows. This earthy, soul-based band, memorable for Harvey's imaginative playing and Bell's gutsy, heart-felt vocals, became a highly popular live attraction and helped the singer win several accolades. Bell's press release at the time insisted that she would loosen her vocal chords by gargling with gravel! The group split up in 1973, still rocked by Harvey's tragic death the previous year. Bell embarked on a solo career with *Queen Of The Night*, which was produced in New York by Jerry Wexler and featured the cream of the city's session musicians. The anticipated success did not materialize and further releases failed to reverse this trend. The singer did have a minor UK hit with 'Hazell' (1978), the theme tune to a popular television series, but 'Hold Me', a tongue-in-cheek duet with B.A. Robertson, remains her only other chart entry. Bell subsequently fronted a new group, Midnight Flyer, but this tough, highly underrated singer, at times redolent of Janis Joplin, has been unable to secure a distinctive career but can still be seen on the blues club circuit.

●ALBUMS: *Queen Of The Night* (Super 1974)★★★, *Suicide Sal* (Polydor 1975)★★★.

●COMPILATIONS: *Great Rock Sensation* (Polydor 1977)★★★.

BELL, THOM

b. 1941, Philadelphia, Pennslyvania, USA. Born into a middle-class family, Bell studied classical piano as a child. In 1959 he teamed-up with school friend Kenny Gamble in a vocal duo and soon afterwards joined the latter's harmony group, the Romeos. By the time he was 19 years old, Bell was working with Chubby Checker and for three years conducted and arranged the singer's material. Bell accompanied him on live dates, contributed original songs and later joined Checker's production company. The office shared a building with Cameo Records and when the former venture folded, Bell worked for the label as a session pianist. It was here he met the Delfonics, and when their manager, Stan Watson, formed his Philly Groove outlet in 1968, Bell's shimmering production work for the group resulted in some of sweet soul's finest moments, including 'La La Means I Love You' (1968) and 'Didn't I Blow Your Mind This Time' (1970).

Bell then resumed his relationship with Kenny Gamble, who with Leon Huff, was forging the classic Philadelphia sound. Thom's brilliant arrangements for the O'Jays and Jerry Butler were particularly innovative, but his definitive work was saved for the Stylistics. Between 1971 and 1974 Bell fashioned the group's finest releases - 'You Are Everything' (1971), 'Betcha By Golly Wow' and 'I'm Stone In Love With You' (both 1972) - without descending into the bathos that lesser artists provided for the hapless quintet on his departure. Elsewhere, Bell enjoyed success with a revitalized (Detroit) Spinners, the Bee Gees and Johnny Mathis, and continued his remarkable career as a producer, arranger and songwriter. Despite the soft, almost luxurious, sound he fashioned for his acts, this craftsman skilfully avoided MOR trappings.

BELL, WILLIAM

b. William Yarborough, 16 July 1939, Memphis, Tennessee, USA. Having recorded in 1957 as part of the Del Rios, Bell emerged on the fledgling Stax label with 'You Don't Miss Your Water' (1961), a cornerstone in the development of country R&B. Military service sadly undermined his career, and on its resumption he found the label bursting with competition. His original songs, often composed with either Steve Cropper or Booker T. Jones, included 'Share What You've Got' (1966), 'Everyday Will Be Like A Holiday' (1967) and 'Eloise' (1967), while his effective homage to Otis Redding, 'A Tribute To A King', was genuinely moving. 'Private Number', a sumptuous duet with Judy Clay, provided one of his best-remembered releases, but a further US hit followed with 'I Forgot To Be Your Lover' (1968), which was remade into a US Top 10 pop hit by Billy Idol in 1986 as 'To Be A Lover'. Bell moved to Atlanta, Georgia, in 1969 where he set up his Peach Tree label. His biggest hit came on signing to Mercury when 'Tryin' To Love Two' (1976) was a US Top 10 single. During the 80s he enjoyed R&B successes on Kat Family and Wilbe, still endeavouring to develop southern soul styles.

●ALBUMS: *The Soul Of A Bell* (Stax 1967)★★★★, *Tribute To A King* (Stax 1968)★★★★, *Bound To Happen* (1969)★★★, *Wow … William Bell* (1971)★★★, *Phases Of Reality* (1973)★★★, *Relating* (1974)★★★, *Coming Back For More* (Mercury 1977)★★★, *It's Time You Took Another Listen* (Mercury 1977)★★★, *Survivor* (1983)★★, *Passion* (Tout Ensemble 1985)★★★, *On A Roll* (Wilbe 1989)★★★, *Bedtime Stories* (1992)★★★.

●COMPILATIONS: *Do Right Man* (Charly 1984)★★★, *The Best Of William Bell* (Warners 1988)★★★★, *A Little Something Extra* (Stax 1991)★★★, with Judy Clay, Mavis Staple, Carla Thomas *Duets* (1994)★★★.

BELLAMY BROTHERS

Howard (b. 2 February 1946, Darby, Florida, USA) and David (b. 16 September 1950, Darby, Florida, USA). Bellamy became one of the top country acts of the 80s after beginning their career in pop and soul. The brothers' father played bluegrass music but David Bellamy's first professional job was as keyboardist with the soul band the Accidents in the mid-60s, backing artists including Percy Sledge. The brothers formed the band Jericho in 1968, but disbanded three years later. They then began writing songs for other artists, and David's 'Spiders And Snakes' was a Top 3 pop hit for Jim Stafford in 1973-74. The Bellamy Brothers signed to Warner Brothers Records the following year and in 1976 reached the top of the US charts and the UK Top 10 with 'Let Your Love Flow'. Although they continued to release albums and singles for the next few years, their days as a pop act were over. In 1979 the double-entendre-titled 'If I Said You Had A Beautiful Body (Would You Hold It Against Me)?' became the first of 10 country number singles for the group. This became their biggest hit in the UK where it made the Top 3. By the late 80s, having transferred to Curb Records, the brothers still recorded Top 10 country singles on a regular basis, and enjoyed a strong following. To date in their long and successful career (including 12 country number 1s) they remain an enigma; often their material is lightweight and their stage act is strangely static. 'Kids Of The Baby Boom Time' trivializes Kennedy's assassination, while 'Jesus Is Coming' has the line, 'Jesus is coming and boy is he pissed.' In 1995 they updated 'Old Hippie' with 'Old Hippie (The Sequel)': it is to be hoped that they are not planning to update all their novelty hits.

●ALBUMS: *Bellamy Brothers* (Warners 1976)★★, *Let Your Love Flow* (Warners 1976)★★★, *Plain And Fancy* (Warners 1977)★★, *Beautiful Friends* (Warners 1978)★★, *The Two And Only* (Warners 1979)★★, *You Can Get Crazy* (Warners 1980)★★, *Sons Of The Sun* (Warners 1980)★★, *When We Were Boys* (1982)★★, *Strong Weakness* (1983)★★, *Restless* (MCA 1984)★★, *Howard And David* (MCA 1986)★★, *Country Rap* (MCA 1987)★★, *Crazy From The Heart* (1987)★★, *Rebels Without A Clue*

(1988)★★, *Rolling Thunder* (1990)★★, *Rip Off The Knob* (Intersound 1993)★★, *Heartbreak Overload* (Intersound 1994)★★, *Sons Of Beaches* (Intersound 1995)★★, *The Bellamy Brothers Dancin'* (Bellamy Brothers 1996)★★, *A Tropical Christmas* (Bellamy Brothers 1996)★★.

●COMPILATIONS: *The Bellamy Brothers' Greatest Hits* (MCA 1982)★★★, *Bellamy Brothers' Greatest Hits Vol. 2* (MCA 1986)★★, *Bellamy Brothers' Greatest Hits Vol. 3* (MCA 1989)★★, *Best Of The Best* (Intersound 1992)★★★.

●VIDEOS: *Best Of The Best* (Start Video 1994).

BETTS, RICHARD 'DICKIE'

b. 12 December 1943, Jacksonville, Florida, USA. Formerly with Tommy Roe's Romans, this exceptional guitarist was also a member of the Second Coming, a Jacksonville group which featured bassist Berry Oakley. Both musicians joined the Allman Brothers Band at its inception in 1969 and Richard's melodic lines provided the foil and support for leader Duane Allman's inventive slide soloing. Allman's tragic death in 1971 allowed Betts to come forward, a responsibility he shouldered admirably on the group's excellent *Brothers And Sisters* album. The country flavour prevalent on several of the tracks, most notably 'Ramblin' Man', set the tone for Dickie's solo career. *Highway Call* was released in 1974 but its promise was overshadowed by the parent group's own recordings. Betts formed a new group, Great Southern, in 1976, but their progress faltered when the guitarist was drawn into the resurrected Allman fold. In 1981, Betts formed BHLT with Jimmy Hall (from Wet Willie), Chuck Leavell, Butch Trucks and David Goldflies, but they too were doomed to a premature collapse and the guitarist withdrew from active work. However, in the late 80s Betts was signed to Epic, the outlet for whom Gregg Allman was recording, prompting rumours of a reunion. Betts was part of the 1989 reformation of the Allman Brothers.

●ALBUMS: *Highway Call* (Capricorn 1974)★★★, *Dickie Betts And The Great Southern* (Arista 1977)★★, *Atlanta Burning Down* (Arista 1978)★★, *Pattern Disruptive* (Epic 1988)★★.

BIG STAR

Formed in Memphis, Tennessee, USA, in 1971, Big Star's reputation and influence far outweigh any commercial rewards they enjoyed during their brief career. They evolved when ex-Box Tops singer Alex Chilton joined a local group, Ice Water - Chris Bell (d. 27 December 1978; guitar/vocals), Andy Hummel (bass) and Jody Stephens (drums). The realigned quartet made an impressive debut with *#1 Record*, which skilfully synthesized British pop and 60s-styled Los Angeles harmonies into a taut, resonant sound. Its commercial potential was marred by poor distribution while internal friction led to Bell's departure late in 1972. This talented artist was killed in December 1978 as a result of a car crash. Although the remaining trio dissolved

Big Star in 1973, they reconvened later in the year for a rock writer's convention where the resultant reaction inspired a more permanent reunion. *Radio City* lacked the polish of its predecessor, but a sense of urgency and spontaneity generated a second excellent set, of which the anthemic 'September Gurls' proved an undoubted highlight. Corporate disinterest once again doomed the project and an embittered Big Star retreated to Memphis following a brief, ill-starred tour on which John Lightman had replaced a disaffected Hummel. Chilton and Stephens then began work on a projected third album with the assistance of Steve Cropper (guitar), Jim Dickinson (piano) and Tommy McLure (bass), but sessions proved more fractured than ever and the group broke up without officially completing the set. *3rd* has subsequently appeared in various guises and mixes, yet each betrays Chilton's vulnerability as a series of bare-nerved compositions show his grasp of structure slipping away and providing a template for the singer's equally erratic solo career. In 1993 Chilton and Stephens re-formed the band with two members of the Posies for a one-off gig at Missouri University that was so successful that the band stayed together for a brief tour of the UK in the same year.

●ALBUMS: *#1 Record* (Ardent 1972)★★★★, *Radio City* (Ardent 1974)★★★★, *3rd* (PVC 1978)★★★★, *3rd/Sister Lovers* (Ryko 1992), *Live* rec. 1974 (Ryko 1992)★★★★, *Columbia Live At Missouri University 4/25/93* (1993)★★★.

BIG YOUTH

b. Manley Augustus Buchanan, February 1955, Jamaica, West Indies. A stylistic and artistic innovator of the highest order, Big Youth started adult life, following a youth of extreme poverty, as a cab driver. He subsequently found employment as a mechanic working in the Skyline and Sheraton hotels in Kingston. He practised while at work, listening to his voice echo around the empty rooms, and would sometimes be allowed to take the microphone at dances and thereby gain some experience. His popularity grew steadily until Big Youth became the resident DJ for the Lord Tippertone sound system (one of the top Kingston sounds in the early 70s), where he clashed regularly with other top DJs and gradually built a reputation. It was not too long before he was approached by record producers. Unfortunately his early attempts, notably the debut cut 'Movie Man', released on Gregory Isaacs and Errol Dunkley's African Museum label, failed to capture this live magic. Further sides such as 'The Best Big Youth', 'Tell It Black' and 'Phil Pratt Thing' helped to marginally enhance his reputation. But his first recording for Keith Hudson in 1972 changed everything. Hudson was a producer who understood DJs, knew how to present them properly and was one of the first to record U-Roy and Dennis Alcapone. The memorable 'S.90 Skank' stayed at number 1 in Jamaica for many weeks. Celebrating the West Kingston cult of the motorbike (the S.90 was a Japanese model), it opened with the sounds of an actual bike being revved up in the studio, and continued with Youth proclaiming 'Don't you ride like lightning or you'll crash like thunder'. For the next few years he really did ride like lightning and Bob Marley was the only artist to approach his popularity. Even the latter could not lay claim to Youth's unique distinguishing feature, front teeth inlaid with red green and gold jewels. Representing the authentic sound of the ghetto, Big Youth set new standards for DJs to say something constructive on record as well as exhort dancers to greater heights. The stories he told gave penetrating insights into the downtown Kingston ghettoes and into the mind of Rastafarian youth. His debut set featured rhythms from previous Dennis Brown and Gregory Isaacs recordings, though by *Hit The Road Jack*, Youth had moved on to covering soul standards in his distinctive style. Hit followed hit and while he always gave his best for other producers, his self-produced records were even better. He formed his Negusa Nagast (Amharic for King of Kings) and Augustus Buchanan labels in 1973 for greater artistic and financial control of his career, and many of these records' stark, proud lyrics set against jagged, heavy rhythms still sound as stunning 20 years after their initial release. He held little appeal outside of the Jamaican market, perhaps because he was too raw and uncompromising, but his innovations are still reverberating through reggae and rap. Though his records and live appearances are now few and far between, Youth has remained at the top for longer than any other DJ apart from U-Roy, and he is still respected and revered by the reggae cogniscenti.

●ALBUMS: *Screaming Target* (Trojan 1973)★★★★★, *Reggae Phenomenon* (Negusa Nagast 1974)★★★, *Dreadlocks Dread* (Klik 1975)★★★★, *Natty Cultural Dread* (Trojan 1976)★★★, *Hit The Road Jack* (Trojan 1976)★★★, *Isaiah First Prophet Of Old* (Front Line 1978)★★★, *The Chanting Dread Inna Fine Style* (Heartbeat 1983)★★★, *Live At Reggae Sunsplash* (Sunsplash 1984)★★★, *A Luta Continua* (Heartbeat 1985)★★★, *Manifestation* (Heartbeat 1988)★★★.

●COMPILATIONS: *Everyday Skank - The Best Of Big Youth* (Trojan 1980)★★★, *Some Great Big Youth* (Heartbeat 1981)★★★, *Jamming In The House Of Dread* (ROIR 1991).

BIRKIN, JANE

b. 14 December 1946. The unlikely recording success of actress Jane Birkin came about in 1969 as a result of her association with French composer Serge Gainsbourg. He had originally recorded a track with Brigette Bardot titled 'Je T'Aim . . . Moi Non Plus' but, as he explained at the time, 'She thought it was too erotic and she was married'. Birkin had no such reservations and expertly simulated the sensual heavy breathing and loving moans that gave the disc its notoriety. Originally released in the UK by Philips/Fontana, the company dissociated itself from the disc's controversial matter by ceasing production while the record was number 2 in

the charts. The ever-opportunistic entrepreneur Phil Solomon gratefully accepted the banned composition which was reissued on his Major Minor label and reached number 1 in late 1969. An album, which included such sensual numbers as '69 Année Erotique' and '18-39', was subsequently issued before Gainsbourg reverted to less newsworthy recording ventures. 'Je T'Aime . . .' re-entered the UK charts in 1974. In 1996 she released an album of songs written by her ex-partner.

●ALBUMS: *Jane Birkin And Serge Gainsbourg* (Fontana 1969)★★★, *Jane B* (Phonogram 1974)★★★, *Di Doo Dah* (Phonogram 1975)★★, *Versions Jane* (Discovery 1996)★★★.

BISHOP, ELVIN

b. 21 October 1942, Tulsa, Oklahoma, USA. Bishop moved to Chicago in his teens to study at university. An aspiring guitarist, he became one of several young white musicians to frequent the city's blues clubs and in 1965 he joined the house band at one such establishment, Big John's. This group subsequently became known as the Paul Butterfield Blues Band, and although initially overshadowed by guitarist Michael Bloomfield, it was here that Bishop evolved a distinctive, if composite style. Bishop was featured on four Butterfield albums, but he left the group in 1968 following the release of *In My Own Dream*. By the following year he was domiciled in San Francisco, where his own group became a popular live fixture. Bishop was initially signed to Bill Graham's Fillmore label, but these and other early recordings achieved only local success. In 1974, Richard 'Dickie' Betts of the Allman Brothers Band introduced the guitarist to Capricorn Records which favoured the hippie/hillbilly image Bishop had nurtured and investigated his mélange of R&B, soul and country influences. Six albums followed, including *Let It Flow*, *Juke Joint Jump* and a live album set, *Live! Raisin' Hell*, but it was a 1975 release, *Struttin' My Stuff*, which proved most popular. It included the memorable 'Fooled Around And Fell In Love' which, when issued as a single, reached number 3 in the US chart. The featured voice was that of Mickey Thomas, who later left the group for a solo career and subsequently became frontman of Jefferson Starship. The loss of this powerful singer undermined Bishop's momentum and his new-found ascendancy proved short-lived. Bishop's career suffered a further setback in 1979 when Capricorn filed for bankruptcy. Although he remains a much-loved figure in the Bay Area live circuit, the guitarist's recorded output has been thin on the ground during the last ten years, most recently on the Alligator label with Dr. John on *Big Fun* and *Ace In The Hole*.

●ALBUMS: *The Elvin Bishop Group* (Fillmore 1969)★★, *Feel It* (Fillmore 1970)★★, *Rock My Soul* (Fillmore 1972)★★, *Let It Flow* (Capricorn 1974)★★★, *Juke Joint Jump* (Capricorn 1975)★★★, *Struttin' My Stuff* (Capricorn 1975)★★★★, *Hometown Boy Makes Good!*

(Capricorn 1976)★★, *Live! Raisin' Hell* (Capricorn 1977)★★★, *Hog Heaven* (Capricorn 1978)★★★, *Is You Is Or Is You Ain't My Baby* (1982)★★, *Big Fun* (Alligator 1988)★★★, *Ace In The Hole* (Alligator 1995)★★★.
●COMPILATIONS: *The Best Of Elvin Bishop: Crabshaw Rising* (Epic 1972)★★, *Tulsa Shuffle: The Best Of ...* (Columbia 1994)★★★★.

BISHOP, STEPHEN

b. 14 November 1951, San Diego, California, USA. While he had mastered both piano and trombone, it was an older brother's gift of an electric guitar that launched a vocational flight whereby an unprepossessing, bespectacled 14-year-old became a highly popular songwriter of US pop. In 1967, he formed his first group, the Weeds, who taped some Beatles-inspired demos in Los Angeles before disbanding. During a consequent seven-year search for a solo recording contract, Bishop worked as a tunesmith for a publishing house before landing a contract in 1976 via the patronage of Art Garfunkel. Indeed, his debut album for ABC Records, *Careless*, was much in the style of his champion. It also employed the cream of Los Angeles session players. Fortunately for ABC, it was nominated for a Grammy and, like the succeeding *Bish,* hovered in the lower reaches of the national Top 40 for several months. The spin-off singles (particularly 'On And On' from *Careless)* also fared well. The Four Tops, Chaka Khan and Barbra Streisand covered his compositions and Bishop gained studio assistance from Khan, Garfunkel, Gary Brooker, Steve Cropper, Phil Collins and other stars. He returned these favours by contributing to Collins' *Face Value* (1981), and composing 'Separate Lives', the Englishman's duet with Marilyn Martin from the movie *White Nights.*
Bishop's own performances on film included the theme songs to *National Lampoon's Animal House* ('Dream Girl'), *Roadie* ('Your Precious Love' with Yvonne Elliman), 1982's *Tootsie* 'It Might Be You', a non-original) and *China Syndrome*. In common with the ubiquitous Garfunkel, he also tried his hand as a supporting actor - notably in 1980's *The Blues Brothers* and *Kentucky Fried Movie* - but his musicianship remains Bishop's calling card. Although his 80s albums have been commercially erratic, he has extended his stylistic range - as exemplified by *Red Cab To Manhattan*, which embraced both a stab at big band jazz ('This Is The Night') and 'Don't You Worry', a tribute to the Beatles. *Bowling In Paris* featured contributions from Eric Clapton, Phil Collins, Sting and Randy Crawford.
●ALBUMS: *Careless* (ABC 1976)★★★, *Bish* (ABC 1978)★★★, *Red Cab To Manhattan* (Warners 1980)★★★, *Bowling In Paris* (Atlantic 1989)★★★.
●COMPILATIONS: *The Best Of Bish* (1988)★★★.

BLACK OAK ARKANSAS

A sextet formed in the late 60s, Black Oak Arkansas took its name from the USA town and state where singer Jim 'Dandy' Mangrum (b. 30 March 1948) was born. The other members of the group hailed from nearby towns: Ricky Reynolds (b. 28 October 1948, Manilan, Arkansas, USA; guitar), Stanley Knight (b. 12 February 1949, Little Rock, Arkansas, USA; guitar), Harvey Jett (b. Marion, Arkansas, USA; guitar), Pat Daugherty (b. 11 November 1947, Jonesboro, Arkansas, USA; bass) and drummer Wayne Evans, replaced on the third album by Thomas Aldrich (b. 15 August, 1950, Jackson, Mississippi, USA). Before forming the band, the future members were part of a gang that shared a house. At first calling themselves the Knowbody Else, the group recorded an unsuccessful album for Stax Records in 1969. Two years later they changed their name and signed with Atco Records, for whom they recorded a self-titled album that introduced them to the US charts. Touring steadily, this hard rock/southern boogie band built a core following, yet its records never matched its concert appeal. Of their 10 US-charting albums between 1971 and 1976, *High On The Hog* proved the most commercially successful, peaking at number 52. It featured the best-selling 1974 Top 30 single, 'Jim Dandy' (sung by female vocalist Ruby Starr, who reappeared on the 1976 *Live! Mutha* album). In 1975, guitarist Jett was replaced by James Henderson (b. 20 May 1954, Jackson, Mississippi, USA) and the following year, after switching to MCA Records, Black Oak Arkansas had only one further minor chart single, 'Strong Enough To Be Gentle'. By 1977 only Mangrum remained from the original band and although they signed to Capricorn Records, there was no further record success. Mangrum did, however, keep variations of the group on the road during the 80s as well as recording a solo album in 1984. The catalogue was reissued in 1995 by Sequel Records.
●ALBUMS: as the Knowbody Else *The Knowbody Else* (Stax 1969)★★, *Black Oak Arkansas* (Atco 1971)★★, *Keep The Faith* (Atco 1972)★★, *If An Angel Came To See You, Would You Make Her Feel At Home?* (Atco 1972)★★, *Raunch 'N' Roll/Live* (Atlantic 1973)★★★, *High On The Hog* (Atco 1973)★★, *Street Party* (Atco 1974)★★, *Ain't Life Grand* (Atco 1975)★★, *X-Rated* (MCA 1975)★, *Live! Mutha* (Atco 1976)★, *Balls of Fire* (MCA 1976)★, *10 Year Overnight Success* (MCA 1976)★, *Race With The Devil* (Capricorn 1977)★, *I'd Rather Be Sailing* (Capricorn 1978)★, *Black Attack Is Back* (Capricorn 1986)★. Solo: Jim Dandy *Ready As Hell* (Capricorn 1984).
●COMPILATIONS: *The Best Of Black Oak Arkansas* (Atco 1977)★★, *Early Times* (1993)★, *Hot & Nasty: The Best Of* (1993)★★.

BLACK SABBATH

Group members Terry 'Geezer' Butler (b. 17 July 1949, Birmingham, England; bass), Tony Iommi (b. 19 February 1948, Birmingham, England; guitar), Bill Ward (b. 5 May 1948, Birmingham, England; drums) and 'Ozzy' Osbourne (b. 3 December 1948, Birmingham, England; vocals) were originally known as Earth, a name they changed to Black Sabbath in 1969. The members of this band grew up together in the Midlands of England, and their name hints at the heavy, doom-laden and yet ingenious music they produced. The name had first been invoked as a song title used by Polka Tulk, a pre-Earth blues outfit featuring Iommi, Ward, Butler and Osbourne. It does not come from a book by the occult writer Denis Wheatley, as is often stated, but from the cult horror film of that title. However, many of Sabbath's songs deal with alternative beliefs and ways of life in keeping with Wheatley's teachings. The title track of *Paranoid* confronts mental instability, and other songs are concerned with the effects of cocaine and marijuana. The line-up was unchanged until 1973 when Rick Wakeman, keyboard player for Yes, was drafted in to play on *Sabbath Bloody Sabbath*. By 1977 personnel difficulties within the band were beginning to take their toll, and the music was losing some of its earlier orchestral, bombastic sheen, prompting Ozzy Osbourne to pursue a solo career the following year. He was replaced by ex-Savoy Brown member Dave Walker until Ronnie James Dio accepted the job. Dio had been a central figure in the early 70s band Elf, and spent three years with Ritchie Blackmore's Rainbow. However, Dio's tenure with the band was short, and he left in 1982. The replacement vocalist was Ian Gillan. It is this Sabbath incarnation that is commonly regarded as the most disastrous for band and fans alike, with *Born Again* failing to capture any of the original vitality of the group. By 1986, Iommi was the only original member of the band, which now consisted of Geoff Nichols (b. Birmingham, England; keyboards), who had been the group's keyboard player since 1980 while he was still a member of Quartz, Glenn Hughes (b. England; vocals), Dave Spitz (b. New York, USA; bass), and Eric Singer (b. Cleveland, Ohio, USA; drums). This was an accomplished combination, Singer having been a member of the Lita Ford band, and Glenn Hughes having worked with Trapeze and Deep Purple. In 1986 the surprisingly blues-sounding *Seventh Star* was released, the lyrics and music for which had been written by Iommi. In the first of a succession of personnel changes, Hughes left the band to be replaced by Ray Gillen, an American singer who failed to record anything with them. Tony Martin (ex-Alliance) was the vocalist on 1987's powerful *The Eternal Idol* and 1988's *Headless Cross,* the album that the skilled and renowned drummer Cozy Powell produced and on which he appeared. Martin has intermittently remained with them since that time and has been replaced at various times by Rob Halford (Judas Priest), Osbourne and Dio, as a sort of permanent understudy. By late 1991 the band was suffering from flagging record sales and declining credibility, so Iommi recruited their original bassist, Butler, and attempted to persuade drummer Bill Ward to rejoin. Ward, however, was not interested; Cozy Powell was still recuperating after being crushed by his horse, and so Vinnie Appice became Sabbath's new drummer. (Bev Bevan of ELO

had been part of the band for *Born Again*, and returned at various times. Other temporary drummers have included Terry Chimes of the Clash.) After much speculation, a return to the band by Ronnie Dio completed the 1982/3 line-up. Ozzy's attempts, meanwhile, to re-form the original group for a 1992 tour faltered when the others demanded an absolutely equal share in the spoils. In 1994 a tribute album, *Nativity In Black*, was released, which featured appearances from all four original members in various guises, plus Megadeth, White Zombie, Sepultura, Biohazard, Ugly Kid Joe, Bruce Dickinson, Therapy?, Corrosion Of Conformity and Type O Negative. Spurred by the new interest in the group, the Powell, Iommi and Nichols line-up, with Tony Martin returning as singer and Neil Murray on bass, completed *Forbidden* in 1995. It was recorded in Wales and Los Angeles with Body Count guitarist Ernie C. producing and Ice-T providing vocals on 'Illusion Of Power'. The line-up in 1996 of this ever-changing unit was Iommi, Martin, Murray and Bobby Rondinelli (drums). Butler formed GZR.
●ALBUMS: *Black Sabbath* (Vertigo 1970)★★★, *Paranoid* (Vertigo 1970)★★★★, *Master Of Reality* (Vertigo 1971)★★★, *Black Sabbath Vol. 4* (Vertigo 1972)★★★, *Sabbath Bloody Sabbath* (World Wide Artists 1974)★★★, *Sabotage* (NEMS 1975)★★★, *Technical Ecstasy* (Vertigo 1976)★★★, *Never Say Die* (Vertigo 1978)★★★, *Heaven And Hell* (Vertigo 1980)★★★, *Live At Last* (NEMS 1980)★★, *Mob Rules* (Vertigo 1981)★★, *Live Evil* (Vertigo 1982)★★, *Born Again* (Vertigo 1983)★★, *Seventh Star* (Vertigo 1986)★★★, *The Eternal Idol* (Vertigo 1987)★★, *Headless Cross* (IRS 1989)★★, *Tyr* (IRS 1990)★★, *Dehumanizer* (IRS 1992)★★, *Cross Purposes* (EMI 1994)★★, *Forbidden* (IRS 1995)★★.
●COMPILATIONS: *We Sold Our Soul For Rock 'n' Roll* (NEMS 1976)★★, *Greatest Hits* (NEMS 1980)★★★, *Collection: Black Sabbath* (Castle 1985)★★★★, *Blackest Sabbath* (Vertigo 1989)★★, *Backtrackin'* (Backtrackin' 1990)★★, *The Ozzy Osbourne Years* 3-CD box set (Essential 1991)★★★★, *Between Heaven And Hell* (Raw Power 1995)★★★, *Sabbath Stones* (IRS 1996)★★, *Under The Wheels Of Confusion 1970-1987* (Essential 1997)★★★★.
●VIDEOS: *Never Say Die* (VCL 1986), *The Black Sabbath Story Vol. 1 (1970-1978)* (Castle Music Pictures 1992), *Under Wheels Of Confusion 1970-1987* 4-CD box set (Castle Music Pictures 1996).
●FURTHER READING: *Black Sabbath*, Chris Welch.

BLACK WIDOW

A progressive rock band from Leicester, England, the group was formed as soul band Pesky Gee in 1966 by Jim Gannon (vocals/guitar/vibraphone) with Kay Garrett (vocals), Kip Trevor (vocals/guitar/harmonica), Zoot Taylor (keyboards), Clive Jones (woodwind), Bob Bond (bass) and Clive Box (drums). Pesky Gee made one album for Pye, before re-forming without Garrett as Black Widow. The band's first album and its elaborate

stage act (choreographed by members of Leicester's Phoenix Theatre company) were based by Gannon on research into black magic rituals. Black Widow's 'Come To The Sabbat' appeared on the CBS sampler, *The Rock Machine Turns You On*, which was a Top 20 hit in 1969. The group toured throughout Europe and appeared at the Isle of Wight Festivals of 1969 and 1970. A debut album reached the Top 40 in the UK and after its release Romeo Challenger and Geoff Griffiths replaced Box and Bond. Later albums abandoned the witchcraft theme and were unmemorable. On *Three*, John Culley from Cressida replaced Gannon who later worked with Trevor on an abortive project to turn the *Black Widow* stage show into a Broadway musical. Gannon went on to play with songwriter Kenny Young in Fox and Yellow Dog before joining Sherbet and moving to Australia where he leads a club band called Bop Till You Drop. Trevor worked as a session singer and is now a music publisher while Challenger plays drums for Showaddywaddy.
●ALBUMS: *Sacrifice* (Columbia 1970)★★★, *Black Widow* (Columbia 1971)★★, *Three* (Columbia 1971)★★. Solo: *Pesky GeeExclamation Mark!* (Pye/Dawn 1969)★★.

BLACKBYRDS

The original Blackbyrds were formed in 1973 by jazz trumpeter Donald Byrd. A doctor of ethnomusicology, Byrd lectured at Washington, DC's Howard University and the group, named after *Black Byrd*, the artist's million-seller, was drawn from his students. The Blackbyrds' debut album charted in the soul, jazz and pop listings, while the follow-up, *Flying Start*, featured their 1975 US Top 10 single, 'Walking In Rhythm'. This infectious performance became the group's first major success, by which point founder members Kevin Toney (keyboards) and Keith Killgo (vocals/drums) had been joined by Joe Hall (bass), Orville Saunders (guitar) and Jay Jones (flute/saxophone). The following year the group hit the US charts again with 'Happy Music' reaching the Top 20. Sadly, the unit's adventurousness gave way to a less spirited direction. The compulsive rhythmic pulse became increasingly predictable as the group, once so imaginative, pursued a style reliant on a safe and tested formula, the repetitiveness of which brought about their demise.
●ALBUMS: *The Blackbyrds* (Fantasy 1974)★★★, *Flying Start* (Fantasy 1974)★★★★, *Cornbread, Earl And Me* (Fantasy 1975), *City Life* (Fantasy 1975)★★, *Unfinished Business* (Fantasy 1976)★★, *Action* (Fantasy 1977)★★, *Better Days* (Fantasy 1980)★★.
●COMPILATIONS: *Nightgroves - The Blackbyrds Greatest Hits* (Fantasy 1978)★★★, *The Best Of The Blackbyrds Volume 1* (Fantasy 1988)★★★★, *The Best Of The Blackbyrds Volume 2* (Fantasy 1988)★★★.

BLACKFOOT SUE

Previously known as Gift and led by twin brothers Tom (bass/keyboards/vocals) and Dave Farmer (both b. 2 March 1952, Birmingham, England; drums), this group was completed by Eddie Galga (b. 4 September 1951, Birmingham, England; lead guitar/keyboards) and Alan Jones (b. 5 January 1950, Birmingham, England; guitar/vocals). The quartet scored a UK Top 5 hit in 1972 with 'Standing In The Road', but although its rhythmic performance appealed successfully to pop and rock audiences, Blackfoot Sue proved unable to retain such a deft balance. They scored a minor hit the same year with 'Sing Don't Speak', but heavier elements displayed on subsequent albums were derided by commentators viewing the group as a purely 'teeny-bop' attraction. Blackfoot Sue broke up following the release of *Strangers* which appeared in the midst of the punk boom, with several members going on to soft-rock group Liner.
●ALBUMS: *Nothing To Hide* (Jam 1973)★★, *Gun Running* (Passport 1975)★, *Strangers* (Passport 1977)★.

BLACKWELL, CHRIS

b. 22 June 1937, London, England, the son of Middleton Joseph Blackwell, a distant relative of the power behind the Crosse & Blackwell food empire. Chris moved to Jamaica at the age of six months with his family, who settled in the affluent area of Terra Nova. Three years later he returned to England to attend prep. school and subsequently enrolled at Harrow public school. A mediocre scholar, he failed to get to university and spent the late 50s commuting between London and Kingston, uncertain of what to do with his life. During the summer of 1958 he was stranded on a coral reef near the Hellshire Beaches. Dehydrated and sunburnt, he was rescued by members of a small Rastafarian community. He never forgot that formative incident and, in later life, displayed every willingness to deal directly with Rasta musicians and introduce their philosophy and culture to European and American audiences. Blackwell was one of the first to record Jamaican rhythm and blues for his R&B and Island labels, and he achieved the very first number 1 hit in Jamaica with Laurel Aitken's 'Little Sheila'/'Boogie In My Bones'. Through his mother's friendship with writer Ian Fleming, Blackwell entered the film business during the early 60s, and worked with producer Harry Saltzman on the set of *Dr No*. Although he was offered the opportunity to work on further Bond films, Blackwell declined this invitation and instead returned to music. He has subsequently purchased Ian Fleming's former mansion in Jamaica. In May 1962 he founded Island Records in London, borrowing the name from Alec Waugh's 50s novel, *Island In the Sun*. One of his early successes was with the Spencer Davis Group and he looked after Steve Winwood's interests for many years with Traffic and his solo work. After leasing master recordings from Jamaican producers such as Leslie Kong, Coxsone Dodd and King Edwards, he issued them in the UK through Island. The company boasted a number of subsidiaries, including Jump Up,

Black Swan and, most notably, Sue, co-managed by producer Guy Stevens. Blackwell bought and promoted his own records, delivering them in his Mini Cooper. Early signings included a host of Jamaican talent: Owen Gray, Jimmy Cliff, Derrick Morgan, Lord Creator and Bob Morley (aka Bob Marley). However, it was 14-year-old Millie Small who provided Blackwell with his first UK breakthrough away from the West Indian and mod audiences. The infectious 'My Boy Lollipop' sold six million copies, and precipitated Blackwell's move into the mainstream UK pop/R&B market.

Blackwell continued to build up Island Records during the 60s and 70s simply by having a remarkably 'good ear'. He knew what he liked and chose well from a slew of 'progressive' groups and, it seemed, largely lost interest in Jamaican music - Island's catalogue was now handled by Trojan Records. Important artists and groups signed and nurtured by Blackwell included Spooky Tooth, Free, John Martyn, Cat Stevens and Fairport Convention. However, he signed up and promoted Bob Marley And The Wailers in 1972 as if they were one of his rock bands and because of Island's huge influence (and the eye catching Zippo sleeve for *Catch A Fire*) the rock audience was forced to accept reggae on its own terms - and they liked what they heard. The story of Bob Marley And The Wailers has been well documented, and Island continued to promote reggae music throughout the 70s, 80s and 90s, always giving the music and its performers the type of promotion and profile that they so rarely received elsewhere. Such attention was almost invariably deserved and nearly all of the first division Jamaican (and UK) reggae artists have worked with Island Records at one time or another. Blackwell sold Island records to Polygram in 1989 for £300 million and pocketed a sizeable fortune (approximately £100 million). Since then he has invested in tourist hotels and was listed in the *Sunday Times* annual survey as the 108th richest man in the UK. Blackwell's reputation for nurturing talent and persevering with his artists has long been legendary and his contribution to exposing reggae music to a wider audience is inestimable.

●ALBUMS: Various *Pressure Drop* 7-LP box set (Mango/Island 1987)★★★, *Tougher Than Tough - The Story Of Jamaican Music* 4-CD box set (Mango/Island 1993)★★★★.

BLODWYN PIG

During its short life, Blodwyn Pig made a valuable contribution to the British blues boom in the late 60s. The band was formed when Mick Abrahams (b. 7 April 1943, Luton, Bedfordshire, England; guitar) left the fast-rising Jethro Tull in 1969. His energetic and fluid playing blended well with the rest of the band, Jack Lancaster (saxophone), Andy Pyle (bass) and Ron Berg (drums). The fine debut *Ahead Rings Out* with its famous pig cover was a critical success, containing a healthy mixture of various styles of progressive blues. The Tull-

influenced 'Ain't Ya Comin Home' and the superb slide guitar of 'Dear Jill' were but two highlights. Lancaster's lengthy 'The Modern Alchemist' showcased his jazz influence and saxophone skills. The band were a prolific live attraction, and Abrahams delighted the crowds with his exceptional showpiece, 'Cats Squirrel', probably the only time that a Cream number had been 'borrowed' and improved upon. Abrahams' solo was superior to Eric Clapton's, although this was a millstone he constantly attempted to shed. The second album showed great moments, notably Abrahams' punchy 'See My Way'. Lancaster's advanced long pieces such as 'San Francisco Sketches', ultimately gave the band a split direction. Abrahams departed and was replaced by Pete Banks, formerly of Yes, and Larry Wallis. Their direction was now led by Lancaster and they changed their name to Lancaster's Bomber, and finally, Lancaster, before they crash-landed shortly afterwards. Four years later, Abrahams and Lancaster re-formed Blodwyn Pig again, with Pyle and ex-Tull drummer Clive Bunker, but they had hardly started when the signs that their day was long-past became evident. While Lancaster eventually carved out a career as a producer, Abrahams set up his own financial consultancy business. However, Abrahams was not able to forsake the music business for too long and subsequently resurrected the group in the early 90s to play club dates, performing new material, utilizing the services of Dick Heckstall-Smith, plus former Piggies, Clive Bunker and Andy Pyle. In 1993 *Lies* appeared on Abrahams' own label and the informative CD notes contain an invaluable Pete Frame family tree. The line-up of the band in addition to Abrahams comprised: David Lennox, keyboards; Mike Summerland, bass; Jackie Challoner, vocals; and Graham Walker, drums.

●ALBUMS: *Ahead Rings Out* (Chrysalis 1969)★★★★, *Getting To This* (Chrysalis 1970)★★★, *Lies* (A New Day 1994)★★, *All Tore Down* (Indigo 1996)★★.

BLONDIE

Blondie was formed in New York City in 1974 when Deborah Harry (b. 1 July 1945, Miami, Florida, USA; vocals), Chris Stein (b. 5 January 1950, Brooklyn, New York, USA; guitar), Fred Smith (bass) and Bill O'Connor (drums) abandoned the revivalist Stilettos for an independent musical direction. Backing vocalists Julie and Jackie, then Tish and Snookie, augmented the new group's early line-up, but progress was undermined by the departure of Smith for Television and the loss of O'Connor. Newcomers James Destri (b. 13 April 1954; keyboards), Gary Valentine (bass) and Clement Burke (b. 24 November 1955, New York, USA; drums) joined Harry and Stein in a reshaped unit that secured a recording contract through the aegis of producer Richard Gottehrer. Originally released on the Private Stock label, *Blondie* was indebted to both contemporary punk and 60s girl groups, adeptly combining melody with purpose. Although not a runaway commercial success, the album did engender interest, particularly in the UK, where the group became highly popular. Internal disputes resulted in the departure of Gary Valentine, but the arrival of Frank Infante (guitar) and Nigel Harrison (b. Princes Risborough, Buckinghamshire, England; bass) triggered the group's most consistent period. Having freed themselves from the restrictions of Private Stock and signed to Chrysalis Records, *Plastic Letters* contained two UK Top 10 hits in 'Denis' and '(I'm Always Touched By Your) Presence Dear' while *Parallel Lines*, produced by pop svengali Mike Chapman, included the UK chart-topping 'Heart Of Glass' and 'Sunday Girl' (both 1979, yet the latter did not even chart in the USA). Although creatively uneven, *Eat To The Beat* confirmed Blondie's dalliance with disco following 'Heart Of Glass' and the set spawned two highly successful singles in 'Union City Blue' and 'Atomic'. 'Call Me', produced by Giorgio Moroder, was taken from the soundtrack of the film *American Gigolo* and reached number 1 in both the UK and USA. *Autoamerican* provided two further US chart toppers in 'The Tide Is High' and 'Rapture' while the former song, originally recorded by reggae group the Paragons, reached the same position in Britain. However, despite this commercial ascendancy, Blondie was beset by internal difficulties, as the media increasingly focused on their photogenic lead singer. The distinction between the group's name and Harry's persona became increasingly blurred, although a sense of distance between the two was created with the release of her solo album, *Koo Koo*. *The Hunter*, a generally disappointing set which Harry completed under duress, became Blondie's final recording, their tenure ending when Stein's ill health brought an attendant tour to a premature end. The guitarist was suffering from the genetic disease pemphigus and between 1983 and 1985, both he and Debbie Harry absented themselves from full-time performing. The latter then resumed her solo career, while former colleague Burke briefly joined the Eurythmics for their *Revenge* album, before teaming up with Harrison, Steve Jones (ex-Sex Pistols), Tony Fox Sales and Michael Des Barres in Chequered Past. In June 1997, Harry re-formed the group to record new material and tour.

●ALBUMS: *Blondie* (Private Stock 1976)★★★, *Plastic Letters* (Chrysalis 1978)★★★, *Parallel Lines* (Chrysalis 1978)★★★★, *Eat To The Beat* (Chrysalis 1979)★★, *Autoamerican* (Chrysalis 1980)★★, *The Hunter* (Chrysalis 1982)★★.
●COMPILATIONS: *The Best Of Blondie* (Chrysalis 1981)★★★, *Once More Into The Bleach* (Chrysalis 1988)★★★, *The Complete Picture - The Very Best Of Deborah Harry And Blondie* (Chrysalis 1991)★★★★, *Blonde And Beyond* (Chrysalis 1993)★★★, *The Essential Collection* (EMI Gold 1997)★★★★.
●VIDEOS: *Blondie - Live* (CIC Video 1986), *Eat To The Beat* (Chrysalis Music Video 1988), *Best Of Blondie* (Chrysalis Music Video 1988).

●FURTHER READING: *Rip Her To Shreds: A Look At Blondie*, Paul Sinclair. *Blondie*, Fred Schruers. *Blondie*, Lester Bangs. *Making Tracks: The Rise Of Blondie*, Debbie Harry, Chris Stein and Victor Bockris.

BLOODROCK

One of the more prolific but ultimately least appealing of those west coast US bands playing in the acid rock period, Bloodrock imbued their music with the same lack of imagination that inspired their album titles (the first three of which ran sequentially, *Bloodrock I*, *Bloodrock II* and *Bloodrock III*). Comprising Jim Rutledge (vocals), Lee Pickens (guitar), Nick Taylor (guitar), Steve Hill (keyboards), Eddie Grundy (bass) and Rick Cobb (drums), the group was masterminded by Grand Funk Railroad manager Terry Knight. However, he saw vastly reduced dividends from his labours with Bloodrock, who always seemed a little out of step with their contemporaries. While others were throwing themselves into wanton experimentalism, Bloodrock seemed to gaze eternally at their own navels and produce ponderous whimsy as a result. By the advent of the 1973 album *USA*, Texan guitarist John Nitzinger had begun to write songs for the group, without ever joining them on a full-time basis. They might well have benefitted from his more sustained imput, but by the mid-70s even the long-suffering Capitol Records had called time on the band. Ironically, their final album, *Whirlwind Tongues*, was considered by many to be their finest release. Both Pickens and Rutledge subsequently started solo careers, but these proved just as unsuccessful.

●ALBUMS: *Bloodrock* (Capitol 1969)★★, *Bloodrock 2* (Capitol 1970)★★, *Bloodrock 3* (Capitol 1971)★★, *Passages* (Capitol 1972)★★, *Live* (Capitol 1972)★, *USA* (Capitol 1973)★★, *Whirlwind Tongues* (Capitol 1974)★★.
●COMPILATIONS: *D.O.A.* (Capitol 1989)★★.

BLOODSTONE

An R&B self-contained band from Kansas City, Missouri, USA. Sweet soul stand-up vocal groups were all the rage in the early 70s and Bloodstone, although a self-contained band, with its falsetto-led and vocally harmonized hits were a part of the phenomenon along with the Moments, Chi-lites, and Stylistics, among others. Original members were Charles McCormick (lead vocal/bass guitar), Charles Love (lead vocal/guitar), Willis Draffen (vocal/guitar), Henry Williams (vocal/percussion), Roger Durham, Eddie Summers (drummer). Bloodstone became hitmakers in the USA by the unusual route of being discovered by an English producer, Mike Vernon, who recorded them in the UK. Their biggest hits, on the London label in the USA, came early in their career from 1973-74, namely 'Natural High' (number 4 R&B, number 10 pop), 'Never Let You Go' (number 7 R&B, number 43 pop), 'Outside Woman' (number 2 R&B, number 34 pop), and 'My Little Lady' (number 4 R&B, number 57 pop). In the UK charts, 'Natural High' was the only entry, peaking at number 40. The group moved to the Isley Brothers' T-Neck label in 1982, and immediately had a Top 5 R&B hit with 'We Go A Long Way Back'. Their pop success remained behind them, however, but Bloodstone continued to appear on the R&B charts until 1984, when they disbanded.

●ALBUMS: *Bloodstone* (London 1972)★★, *Natural High* (London 1973)★★★, *Never Let You Go* (London 1973)★★★, *Unreal* (London 1973)★★★, *I Need Time* (London 1974)★★★, *Riddle Of The Sphinx* (London 1974)★★★, *Train Ride To Hollywood* (London 1975)★★★, *Do You Wanna Do A Thing* (London 1976)★★★, *Don't Stop* (Motown 1978)★★★, *We Go A Long Way Back* (T-Neck 1982)★★★, *Party* (T-Neck 1984)★★.
●COMPILATIONS: *Greatest Hits* (Columbia 1985)★★★.

BLUE (70s)

This Glasgow-based group made its debut in 1973 when Timmy Donald (b. 29 September 1946, Bristol, Avon, England; drums, ex-White Trash) joined two former members of the Poets, Hugh Nicholson (b. 30 July 1949, Rutherglen, Strathclyde, Scotland; guitar/vocals) and Ian MacMillan (b. 16 October 1947, Paisley, Strathclyde, Scotland; bass/vocals). Their debut album showcased an engaging, melodic rock and continued the style forged by Nicholson during his brief spell in the Marmalade. *Life In The Navy* introduced a new addition to the line-up, Robert 'Smiggy' Smith (b. 30 March 1946, Kiel, Germany; guitar), but this second set lacked the charm of its predecessor. The unit was briefly disbanded, but re-emerged in 1977 with a Top 20 single, 'Gonna Capture Your Heart'. Charlie Smith (drums) and David Nicholson (guitar) had replaced Donald and 'Smiggy', but despite completing two further albums, Blue was unable to repeat this success and latterly broke up.

●ALBUMS: *Blue* (Polydor 1973)★★★, *Life In The Navy* (Rocket 1974)★★, *Another Night Time Flight* (Rocket 1977)★★, *Fool's Party* (Rocket 1979)★★.

BLUE MINK

When four UK session men, a leading songwriter and an in-demand girl singer pooled their resources in 1969, the result was a new hit group, Blue Mink. The original line-up comprised: Madeline Bell (vocals), Roger Cook (vocals), Alan Parker (guitar), Roger Coulam (organ), Herbie Flowers (bass) and Barry Morgan (drums). With Cook And (Roger) Greenaway (alias David And Jonathan) providing the material, the group enjoyed a run of hits from 1969-73 beginning with the catchy anti-racist plea 'Melting Pot' and continuing with 'Good Morning Freedom', 'Our World', 'Banner Man', 'Stay With Me', 'By The Devil' and 'Randy'. With so much talent and experience in the group it seemed inevitable that they would drift off into extra-curricular projects and when the hits stopped they enjoyed continued success as session musicians, writers and soloists.

●ALBUMS: *Blue Mink* (Regal 1969)★★★, *A Time Of Change* (Regal 1972)★★★, *Live At The Talk Of The Town* (Regal 1972)★★, *Only When I Laugh* (EMI 1973)★★★, *Fruity* (EMI 1974)★★, *Attention* (Phonogram 1975)★★.
●COMPILATIONS: *Hit Making Sounds* (Gull 1977)★★, *Collection: Blue Mink* (Action Replay 1987)★★★.

BLUE OYSTER CULT

The genesis of Blue Öyster Cult lay in the musical ambitions of rock writers Sandy Pearlman and Richard Meltzer. Based in Long Island, New York, the pair put together a group - known variously as the Soft White Underbelly and Oaxaca - to perform their original songs. By 1969 the unit, now dubbed the Stalk-Forrest Group, had established around Eric Bloom (b. 11 December 1944; guitar/vocals), Donald 'Buck Dharma' Roeser (b. 12 November 1947; guitar/vocals), Allen Lanier (b. 25 June 1986; keyboards/guitar), Joe Bouchard (b. 9 November 1948; bass/vocals) and Albert Bouchard (drums). The quintet completed a single, 'What Is Quicksand', before assuming their Blue Öyster Cult appellation. Early releases combined Black Sabbath-styled riffs with obscure lyricism, which engendered an 'intelligent heavy metal' tag. Cryptic titles, including 'A Kiss Before The Redap' and 'OD'd On Life Itself' compounded an image - part biker, part occult - assiduously sculpted by Pearlman, whose clean production technique also removed any emotional inflections. 'Career Of Evil' from *Secret Treaties* - co-written by Patti Smith - showed an increasing grasp of commercial hooklines, which flourished on the international Byrds-sounding hit, '(Don't Fear) The Reaper'. Smith continued her association with the band on *Agents Of Fortune*, contributing to 'Debbie Denise' and 'The Revenge Of Vera Gemini'. A romantic companion to Allen Lanier, she later added 'Shooting Shark' to the band's repertoire for *Revolution By Night* and single release. Fantasy writer Michael Moorcock, meanwhile, contributed to *Mirrors* and *Cultosaurus Erectus*. However, the release of the live *Some Enchanted Evening* had already brought the group's most innovative era to an end, despite an unlikely hit single, 'Joan Crawford Has Risen From The Grave', drawn from *Fire Of Unknown Origin* (which included another composition co-written with Moorcock). Sustained by continued in-concert popularity, notably on the *Black And Blue* tour with Black Sabbath, elsewhere predictability had crept into their studio work. Former road crew boss Rick Downey replaced Al Bouchard in 1981, while the following year Roeser completed a solo album, *Flat Out*, as the Cult's own recordings grew noticeably less prolific. *Imaginos* in 1988 was the band's re-interpretation of a Bouchard solo album which had never been released. Though of dubious origins, critics welcomed it as the band's best work for several years. Afterwards Joe Bouchard would leave the group to form Deadringer with Neal Smith (ex-Alice Cooper), Dennis Dunaway, Charlie Huhn and Jay Johnson. 1992 saw the group write and perform the majority of the soundtrack album to the *Bad Channels* horror film.

●ALBUMS: *Blue Öyster Cult* (Columbia 1971)★★★, *Tyranny And Mutation* (Columbia 1973)★★★, *Secret Treaties* (Columbia 1974)★★, *On Your Feet Or On Your Knees* (Columbia 1975)★★, *Agents Of Fortune* (Columbia 1976)★★★★, *Spectres* (Columbia 1977)★★, *Some Enchanted Evening* (Columbia 1978)★★, *Mirrors* (Columbia 1979)★★, *Cultosaurus Erectus* (Columbia 1980)★★, *Fire Of Unknown Origin* (Columbia 1981)★★, *Extraterrestial Live* (Columbia 1982)★, *The Revolution By Night* (Columbia 1983)★, *Club Ninja* (Columbia 1985)★, *Imaginos* (Columbia 1988)★★★, soundtrack *Bad Channels* (Moonstone 1992)★★. Solo: Donald Roeser *Flat Out* (Portrait 1982)★★, *Workshop Of The Telescopes* (Columbia 1995)★★.

●COMPILATIONS: *Career Of Evil - The Metal Years* (Columbia 1990)★★★, *Cult Classic* (Herald 1994)★★★.

●VIDEOS: *Live 1976* (Castle Music Pictures 1991).

BLUE STARS

This 70s vocal group quintet featured Louis De Carlo (lead and first tenor), Tony Millone (lead and second tenor), Jack Scandura (lead and second tenor), Bobby Thomas (lead and baritone) and Ken Mewes (lead and bass). Formed in Queens, New York, USA, in 1974, they drew membership from several previous local groups, including Ricky And The Hallmarks (Scandura), the Devotions, Mr. Bassman and Symbols (De Carlo), Jordan And The Fascinations and Boulevards (Thomas) and Fulton Fish Market (Millone). Soon after they started rehearsing their a cappella and doo-wop harmonies, Millone departed to be replaced by Larry Galvin (himself formerly of the Velvet Five). Their first year together produced three singles for the local Arcade Records outlet, cover versions of the Channels' 'My Love Will Never Die', the Flamingos' 'I Only Have Eyes For You' and the Heartbeats' 'Your Way'. They retired soon afterwards, however, with three of the band going on to the Blendairs. Backing Johnny 'Ace' Acuino in this more R&B-orientated vehicle, Galvin, Scandura and Mewes added Eddie Conway to the line-up. By 1976 Mewes had been replaced by Sam Wood (the former Sparrows Quartette bass singer), and the Blendairs readied themselves for recording sessions. Just as they did so, Acuino received the call to rejoin his old working partner Elvin Bishop, but it was too late to stop the release of their 'Sweet Sue' single (this time a Crows cover version). Conway left the group in 1977, but by the following year the members elected to press ahead with a sound that retreated back to their original love of doo-wop and vocal records. Beverly Warren, another former member of Ricky And The Hallmarks, joined at the same time as Al Vieco, who had previously worked with Galvin in side-project Oasis. The first recording with the reshuffled line-up was 'He's Gone' for Story Untold Records in 1978. Two further singles followed, 'Gee Whizz' and 'Don't Leave Me', before Wood retired

and the Blendairs ground to a halt. However, by 1983 they had been reactivated, but this time they returned to their original title, the Blue Stars. The new members were Jay Ortsman (bass) and Bix Boyle (second tenor), joining Anthony Millone (returning on first tenor), Bobby Thomas (now just baritone) and Jack Scandura (lead). They continued to play concerts in the New York area but with the passing of the years the line-up soon evolved to feature Rick Wakeman (not the UK keyboard player) and Don Raphael with Scandura, Galvin and Millone. They did little recording work, but managed to pay the bills by supporting artists such as Little Caesar and the Medallions on the oldies circuit. However, they broke up once more in 1990, just before the release of their acclaimed *Blue Velvet A Cappella* collection. Most of the former members continue to be involved in low-key live bands of some nature, and so further reunions can hardly be ruled out.

●ALBUMS: *Reunion* (Clifton 1989)★★★, *Blue Velvet A Cappella* (Clifton 1991)★★★★.

BLUE, BARRY

b. Ronald Roker. During the early 70s singing in public was secondary to his composing skills - which peaked commercially with an international smash in 1972's 'Storm In A Teacup' (co-written with Lynsey de Paul) for the Fortunes. His confidence boosted by this syndication, Blue sought more prestigious customers. As it turned out, the act that derived most benefit from his songwriting talents was himself; 1973 was his richest year, with '(Dancing) On A Saturday Night' and 'Do You Wanna Dance' reaching the UK Top 10. The following year brought more minor chart entries with 'School Love' and 'Miss Hit And Run' - and after 'Hot Shot' completed a five-week chart run, Blue disappeared from the public eye.

●COMPILATIONS: *Dancing On A Saturday Night - The Very Best Of* (1993)★★.

BLUES BROTHERS

Formed in 1978, this US group was centred on comedians John Belushi (b. 24 January 1949, Chicago, Illinois, USA, d. 5 March 1982, Los Angeles, California, USA) and Dan Aykroyd (1 July 1952, Ottawa, Ontario, Canada). Renowned for contributions to the satirical *National Lampoon* team and television's *Saturday Night Live*, the duo formed this 60s-soul-styled revue as a riposte to disco. Taking the epithets Joliet 'Jake' Blues (Belushi) and Elwood Blues (Aykroyd), they embarked on live appearances with the assistance of a crack backing group, which included Steve Cropper (guitar), Donald 'Duck' Dunn (bass) and Tom Scott (saxophone). *Briefcase Full Of Blues* topped the US charts, a success that in turn inspired the film *The Blues Brothers* (1980). Although reviled by several music critics, there was no denying the refreshing enthusiasm the participants brought to R&B and the venture has since acquired a cult status. An affectionate, if anarchic, tribute to soul and R&B, it featured cameo appearances by Aretha Franklin, Ray Charles, John Lee Hooker and James Brown. Belushi's death from a drug overdose in 1982 brought the original concept to a premature end, since when Aykroyd has continued a successful acting career, notably in *Ghostbusters*. However, several of the musicians, including Cropper and Dunn, later toured and recorded as the Blues Brothers Band. The original Blues Brothers have also inspired numerous copy-cat/tribute groups who still attract sizeable audiences, over 15 years after the film's release. In August 1991, interest in the concept was again boosted with a revival theatre production in London's West End.

●ALBUMS: *Briefcase Full Of Blues* (Atlantic 1978)★★, *The Blues Brothers* film soundtrack (Atlantic 1980)★★★, *Made In America* (Atlantic 1980)★★, as the Blues Brothers Band *The Blues Brothers Band Live* (1990)★, *Red, White & Blues* (1992)★.

●COMPILATIONS: *The Best Of The Blues Brothers* (Atlantic 1981)★★.

●VIDEOS: *Live At Montreux* (WEA Music Video 1990), *Things We Did Last Summer* (Brave World 1991).

●FILMS: *The Blues Brothers* (1980).

BLUES IMAGE

Known mainly for their 1970 US number 4 hit 'Ride Captain Ride', Blues Image was a quintet from Tampa, Florida, USA. Formed in the mid-60s, the group began as a trio featuring Mike Pinera (b. 29 September 1948, Tampa, Florida, USA; guitar/vocals), Joe Lala (b. Tampa, Florida, USA; drums) and Manuel Bertematti (b. 1946, Tampa, Florida, USA; percussion). In 1966 bassist Malcolm Jones (b. Cardiff, Wales) joined and the group took the name Blues Image. Frank 'Skip' Konte, originally from Canyon City, California, was enlisted in 1968, at which time the group relocated to New York City. The band opened their own club, The Image, where besides booking some of the top acts of the day they were able to provide themselves with a ready-made venue for the Blues Image's performances. Signed to Atco Records in 1969, they recorded their self-titled debut album, which landed at number 112 in the US album charts. The following year, the band released *Open*, which did not do well despite the inclusion of the band's hit single. A third album was issued in 1970, minus Pinera (who briefly joined Iron Butterfly), but proved unsuccessful. The group disbanded upon that record's release, and although Atco issued two more singles, neither charted. Some members of the group started a new band called Manna. Konte joined Three Dog Night in 1974. Lala became renowned as a session drummer and percussionist, working with, among others, Crosby, Stills, Nash And Young, Manassas, Joe Walsh and Harry Chapin. Pinera joined Ramatam in 1972, then he and Bertematti formed the New Cactus Band in 1973, which recorded one album for Atlantic Records. Pinera started a short-lived band called Thee Image in 1975 and recorded two solo albums for

Capricorn Records and Spector Records in 1978-79. He took to the 60s revival circuit in the 80s and in 1990 was linked somewhat ironically with a new recording by Tiny Tim.

●ALBUMS: *Blues Image* (Atco 1969)★★, *Open* (Atco 1970)★★, *Red White And Blues Image* (Atco 1970)★★.

BLUNSTONE, COLIN

b. 24 June 1945, St Albans, Hertfordshire, England. The former lead vocalist of 60s pop group the Zombies possessed a unique creamy-breathy voice that contributed greatly to their success. Two of his performances, 'She's Not There' and 'Time Of The Season', have since become pop classics. He started a promising solo career initially as Neil MacArthur and then reverted to his own name with *One Year* in 1971. This Rod Argent-produced record included sensitive arrangements and exquisite vocals to Tim Hardin's 'Misty Roses' and Denny Laine's 'Say You Don't Mind'; the latter became a UK Top 20 hit. *Ennismore* in 1972 was his finest work, a faultless, almost continuous suite of songs which included two further UK chart hits, 'How Could We Dare To Be Wrong' and 'I Don't Believe In Miracles'. After two further albums Blunstone kept a low profile. He was guest vocalist on four Alan Parsons Project albums: *Pyramid* (1978), *Eye In The Sky* (1983), *Ammonia Avenue* (1983) and *Vulture Culture* (1984). As a soloist he resurfaced in 1981 as vocalist with Dave Stewart's hit remake of Jimmy Ruffin's 'What Becomes Of The Broken Hearted', and the following year had a minor hit with Smokey Robinson's 'Tracks Of My Tears'. During the 80s he attempted further commercial success with Keats, but the conglomeration folded shortly after the debut album. His 1991 album, *Sings His Greatest Hits*, was a collection of his most popular songs, re-recorded with his former colleagues, including Rod Argent and Russ Ballard. Further activity was demonstrated when he sang the title track on the charity EP *Every Living Moment*. 1995 proved to be something of a landmark year for Blunstone with three albums issued. In the space of a few months his various live BBC recordings were issued, a superb compilation was lovingly put together by Legacy/Epic records and finally a new studio album was recorded: *Echo Bridge*. The shy and nervous Blunstone has not become part of the rock cognoscenti, and, therefore, has so far never reached his full potential.

●ALBUMS: *One Year* (Epic 1971)★★★, *Ennismore* (Epic 1972)★★★★, *Journey* (Epic 1974)★★★, *Planes* (Rocket 1976)★★★, *Never Even Thought* (Rocket 1978)★★, *Late Nights In Soho* (Rocket 1979)★★, with Keats *Keats* (EMI 1984)★★, *Echo Bridge* (Permanent 1995)★★, *Live At The BBC* (Windsong 1995)★★★.

●COMPILATIONS: *Miracles* (Pickwick 1979)★★★, *Sings His Greatest Hits* (JSE 1991)★★★, *Some Years: It's The Time Of Colin Blunstone* (Epic/Legacy 1995)★★★★.

BOB AND MARCIA

Bob Andy and Marcia Griffiths had two UK chart entries at the turn of the 70s - the first, a version of Nina Simone's 'Young, Gifted And Black', was a UK Top 5 hit in 1970 on reggae producer Harry J's self-titled label, and the follow-up, 'Pied Piper', reached number 11 on the Trojan label. Both Andy and Griffiths were hugely popular artists in Jamaica in their own right before and after their pop crossover success, but neither felt that this particular interlude was successful for them, especially in financial terms. It is sad that these two hits have become the only records for which they are known outside of reggae music circles. Sadder still, that their best duet of the period, the timeless 'Always Together', which they recorded for Coxsone Dodd, failed to make any impression outside Jamaica.

●ALBUMS: *Young, Gifted And Black* (Harry J 1970)★★★, *Pied Piper* (Harry J 1971)★★★, *Really Together* (I-Anka 1987)★★★.

BOLAN, MARC

b. Mark Feld, 30 September 1947, Hackney, London, England, d. 16 September 1977. A former model in the halcyon 'Mod' era, Bolan began his singing career during the mid-60s folk boom. Initially dubbed 'Toby Tyler', he completed several unsuccessful demo discs before reportedly adopting his new surname from (Bo)b Dy(lan). The artist's debut single, 'The Wizard' (1965), revealed an early penchant for pop mysticism whereas its follow-up, 'The Third Degree', was indebted to R&B. Its b-side, 'San Francisco Poet', gave first airing to the distinctive, tremulous vocal warble for which Bolan became renowned and which flourished freely on his third single, 'Hippy Gumbo'. This slow, highly stylized performance, produced by new manager Simon Napier-Bell, made no commercial impression, but was latterly picked up by the pirate station Radio London, whose disc jockey John Peel became a pivotal figure in Bolan's history. A series of demos was also undertaken at this point, several of which surfaced on *The Beginning Of Doves* (1974) and, with overdubs, on *You Scare Me To Death* (1981), but plans for a fourth single were postponed following the failure of its predecessor. Frustrated at his commercial impasse, the artist then opted to join Napier-Bell protégés John's Children in 1967. He composed their best-known single, 'Desdemona', but left the line-up after a matter of months to form Tyrannosaurus Rex. Here Bolan gave full range to the 'underground' poetic folk mysticism, redolent of author J.R.R. Tolkien, that 'Hippy Gumbo' had suggested. Such pretensions gave way to unabashed pop when the unit evolved into T. Rex three years later. Between 1970 and 1973 this highly popular attraction enjoyed a run of 10 consecutive Top 5 singles, but Bolan's refusal to alter the formula of his compositions resulted in an equally spectacular decline. Bolan was, nonetheless, one of the few established musicians to embrace punk, and a contemporary television series, *Marc*, revived a flagging public profile. This ascendancy ended abruptly in September 1977 when the artist, as a passenger in a car driven by singer Gloria Jones, was killed when they crashed into a tree on Barnes Common, London.

●ALBUMS: *The Beginning Of Doves* (Track 1974)★★, *You Scare Me To Death* (Cherry Red 1981)★★, *Beyond The Rising Sun* (Cambra 1984)★★, *Love And Death* (Cherry Red 1985)★★, *The Marc Shows* television recordings (Marc On Wax 1989)★★★.

●COMPILATIONS: *Best Of The 20th Century Boy* (K-Tel 1985)★★★★.

●VIDEOS: *On Video* (Videoform 1984), *Marc* (Channel 5 1989), *The Ultimate Collection* (Telstar Video 1991), *T. Rex Double Box Set* (Virgin Vision 1991), *Born To Boogie* (PMI 1991), *20th Century Boy* (Polygram Music Video 1991), *The Groover Live In Concert* (MIA 1995).

●FURTHER READING: *The Warlock Of Love*, Marc Bolan. *The Marc Bolan Story*, George Tremlett. *Marc Bolan: Born To Boogie*, Chris Welch and Simon Napier-Bell. *Electric Warrior: The Marc Bolan Story*, Paul Sinclair. *Marc Bolan: The Illustrated Discography*, John Bramley and Shan. *Marc Bolan: Wilderness Of The Mind*, John Willans and Caron Thomas. *Twentieth Century Boy*, Mark Paytress. *Marc Bolan: The Legendary Years*, John Bramley and Shan.

BONEY M

In 1976, German-based producer/composer Frank Farian invented a group to front a single he had already recorded, 'Baby Do You Wanna Bump?', which sold well in Belgium and Holland. The line-up was Marcia Barrett (b. 14 October 1948, Jamaica; vocals), Bobby Farrell (b. 6 October 1949, Aruba, West Indies; vocals), Liz Mitchell (b. 12 July 1952, Clarendon, Jamaica; vocals) and Maizie Williams (b. 25 March 1951, Monserrat, West Indies; vocals). Between 1976 and 1977, the group enjoyed four UK Top 10 hits with 'Daddy Cool', 'Sunny', 'Ma Baker' and 'Belfast'. Their peak period, however, was 1978 when the chart-topping 'Rivers Of Babylon'/'Brown Girl In The Ring' spent 40 weeks on the UK chart, becoming the second best-selling UK single in history at that time. Its follow-up, 'Rasputin', climbed to number 2 and Boney M ended 1978 with the festive chart-topper 'Mary Boy's Child - Oh My Lord'. They experienced similarly phenomenal success in Europe (over 50 million total sales). Their unusual choice of material was emphasized the following year with a revival of Creation's 'Painter Man', which reached the Top 10. The singalong 'Hooray Hooray It's A Holi-Holiday' and 'Gotta Go Home'/'El Lute' were their last Top 20 hits, after which their appeal declined. However, the commercial power of their catalogue is emphasized by their third number 1 album, *The Magic Of Boney M*, which neatly punctuated their extraordinary hit career in 1980.

●ALBUMS: *Take The Heat Off Me* (Atlantic 1976)★, *Love*

For Sale (Atlantic 1977)★, *Night Flight To Venus* (Atlantic 1978)★★, *Oceans Of Fantasy* (Atlantic 1979)★, *Boonoonoonoos* (Atlantic 1981)★, *Eye Dance* (Carrere 1986)★.
●COMPILATIONS: *The Magic of Boney M* (Atlantic 1980)★★, *The Best Of 10 Years* (Stylus 1986)★★.
●VIDEOS: *Gold* (1993).
●FURTHER READING: *Boney M*, John Shearlaw.

BOOMTOWN RATS

One of the first new wave groups to emerge during the musical shake-ups of 1977, Boomtown Rats were also significant for spearheading an interest in young Irish rock. Originally formed in 1975, the group comprised Bob Geldof (b. Robert Frederick Zenon Geldof, 5 October 1954, Dun Laoghaire, Eire; vocals), Gerry Roberts (vocals/guitar), Johnnie Fingers (keyboards), Pete Briquette (bass) and Simon Crowe (drums). Before moving to London, they signed to the recently established Ensign Records, which saw commercial possibilities in their high energy yet melodic work. Their self-titled debut album was a UK chart success and included two memorable singles, 'Looking After No. 1' and 'Mary Of The Fourth Form', which both reached the UK Top 20. The following summer, their *A Tonic For The Troops* was released to critical acclaim. Among its attendant hit singles were the biting 'She's So Modern' and quirky 'Like Clockwork'. By November 1978, a third hit from the album, the acerbic, urban protest 'Rat Trap', secured them their first UK number 1. In spite of their R&B leanings, the group were initially considered in some quarters as part of the punk upsurge and were banned in their home country. The band received considerable press thanks to the irrepressible loquaciousness of their lead singer, who made the press regard him as an individual, and certainly not a punk. A third album, *The Fine Art Of Surfacing*, coincided with their finest moment, 'I Don't Like Mondays', the harrowing true-life story of an American teenage girl who wounded eight children and killed her school janitor and headmaster. The weirdest aspect of the tale was her explanation on being confronted with the deed: 'I don't like Mondays, this livens up the day.' Geldof adapted those words to produce one of pop's most dramatic moments in years, with some startlingly effective piano-work from the appropriately named Johnnie Fingers. A massive UK number 1, the single proved almost impossible to match, as the energetic but average follow-up, 'Someone's Looking At You', proved. Nevertheless, the Rats were still hitting the Top 5 in the UK and even released an understated but effective comment on Northern Ireland in 'Banana Republic'. By 1982, however, the group had fallen from critical and commercial grace and their subsequent recordings seemed passé. For Geldof, more important work lay ahead with the founding of Band Aid and much-needed world publicity on the devastating famine in Ethiopia. The Rats performed at the Live Aid concert on 13 July 1985 before bowing out the following year at Dublin's Self Aid benefit.
●ALBUMS: *The Boomtown Rats* (Ensign 1977)★★★, *A Tonic For The Troops* (Ensign 1978)★★★, *The Fine Art Of Surfacing* (Ensign 1979)★★★, *Mondo Bongo* (Ensign 1981)★★, *V Deep* (Ensign 1982)★★, *In The Long Grass* (Ensign 1984)★★.
●COMPILATIONS: *Greatest Hits* (Ensign 1987)★★, *Loudmouth - The Best Of The Boomtown Rats And Bob Geldof* (Vertigo 1994)★★★.
●VIDEOS: *A Tonic For The Troops* (VCL 1986), *On A Night Like This* (Spectrum 1989).
●FURTHER READING: *The Boomtown Rats: Having Their Picture Taken*, Peter Stone. *Is That It*, Bob Geldof.

BOOTHE, KEN

b. 1948, Kingston, Jamaica, West Indies. Boothe began his recording career with Winston 'Stranger' Cole in the duo Stranger And Ken, releasing titles including 'World's Fair', 'Hush', 'Artibella' and 'All Your Friends' during 1963-65. When the rocksteady rhythm began to evolve during 1966 Boothe recorded 'Feel Good'. He released a series of titles for Clement Dodd's Studio One label which revealed him to be an impassioned, fiery vocalist in an occasionally mannered style ultimately derived from US soul. During this period he was often referred to as the Wilson Pickett of Jamaican music. He continued recording with Dodd until 1970, releasing some of his best and biggest local hits. He made records for other producers at the same time, including Sonia Pottinger's Gayfeet label, for which he recorded the local hit 'Say You' in 1968. By the following year he had switched again, this time to Leslie Kong's Beverley's label where he stayed until 1971, notching up two more local hits with 'Freedom Street' and 'Why Baby Why', as well as several other singles and an album. He then freelanced during the early 70s for various producers, including Keith Hudson, Herman Chin-Loy, Randy's and George 'Phil' Pratt. During the same period he began an association with former Gaylad, B.B. Seaton, which resulted in an album in 1971. At this point in time he was hugely popular with Jamaican audiences, particularly teenage girls, who loved his emotive voice and good looks. When he started working with the pianist/vocalist/producer Lloyd Charmers in 1971 it was not long before the hits started to flow again, first in Jamaica and then in the UK charts. 'Everything I Own', a David Gates composition, topped the UK chart in November 1974. The follow-up, 'Crying Over You' also charted, reaching the number 11 position in February 1975. Pop singer Boy George covered Charmers' and Boothe's version of 'Everything I Own' when he reached the UK chart with the song in 1987. Boothe sadly failed to capitalize on this success, having continued to record for a variety of Jamaican producers throughout the late 70s and 80s. He has also produced his own material with occasional commercial success. He regularly appears on Jamaican oldies shows, usually singing his classic 60s and 70s material, and remains one of the great Jamaican soul voices.

●ALBUMS: *Mr. Rock Steady* (Studio One 1968)★★★, *More Of Ken Boothe* (Studio One 1968)★★★, *A Man And His Hits* (Studio One 1970)★★★, *Freedom Street* (Beverley's 1971)★★★, *The Great Ken Boothe Meets B.B. Seaton And The Gaylads* (1971)★★★, *Black Gold And Green* (Trojan 1973)★★★, *Everything I Own* (Trojan 1974)★★★, *Let's Get It On* (Trojan 1974)★★★, *Blood Brothers* (Trojan 1975)★★★, *Live Good* (Liberty 1978)★★★, *Who Gets Your Love* (Trojan 1978)★★★, *I'm Just A Man* (Bunny Lee 1979)★★★, *Showcase* (Justice 1979)★★★, *Reggae For Lovers* (Mountain 1980)★★★, *Imagine* (Park Heights 1986)★★, *Don't You Know* (Tappa 1988)★★, *Power Of Love* (1993)★★.

●COMPILATIONS: *Ken Boothe Collection* (Trojan 1987).

BOSTON

As a result of home-made demos recorded by the enterprising Tom Scholz (b. 10 March 1947, Toledo, Ohio, USA), one of the finest AOR albums of all time was created. The tapes impressed Epic Records and Scholz joined with friends, Fran Sheehan (b. 26 March 1949, Boston, Massachusetts, USA; bass), Brad Delp (b. 12 June 1951, Boston, Massachusetts, USA; guitar/vocals), Barry Goudreau (b. 29 November 1951, Boston, Massachusetts, USA; guitar) and Sib Hashian (b. 17 August 1949, Boston, Massachusetts, USA; drums). The name Boston was adopted and their first release was a US Top 3 album which eventually sold 16 million copies in the USA alone and spent two years in the US charts. The memorable single, 'More Than A Feeling', was an instant classic, containing all the ingredients of adult-orientated rock; upfront guitar, powerful lead vocal with immaculate harmonies and heavy bass and drums. Two years later they repeated the formula virtually note for note with *Don't Look Back* (featuring the same futuristic space-craft masquerading as guitars on the cover) which also topped the US charts. During this time Scholz, formerly a product designer for the Polaroid Company, invented a mini-amplifier marketed as the Rockman. Goudreau later grew tired of the band's lengthy sabbaticals and released a solo album before quitting to form Orion. Never a prolific band, Boston, in the guise of Scholz and Delp, returned seven years later with *Third Stage* which spawned two further US hit singles, 'Amanda' (which reached number 1) and 'We're Ready'. Those fans wanting to replace worn copies of the previous albums merely had to purchase this one. It too went straight to the top spot giving Boston a unique record in rock history, combining the biggest-selling debut album with three number 1 albums and total sales of over 50 million. *Walk On* was a disappointing fourth album..

●ALBUMS: *Boston* (Epic 1976)★★★★, *Don't Look Back* (Epic 1978)★★★, *Third Stage* (MCA 1986)★★★, *Walk On* (MCA 1994)★★. Solo: Barry Goudreau *Barry Goudreau* (Portrait 1980)★★.

BOWIE, DAVID

b. David Robert Jones, 8 January 1947, Brixton, London, England. One of the great enigmas of popular music and certainly the most mercurial, Bowie underwent a veritable odyssey of career moves and minor crises before establishing himself as a major performer. He began playing saxophone during his teens, initially with various school groups. School also contributed to his future pop star career in a more bizarre way as a result of a playground fight, which left the singer with a paralysed pupil (being stabbed in the eye with a school compass). Consequently, he had eyes of a different colour, an accident that later enhanced his otherworldly image. In the early 60s, however, his style was decidedly orthodox, all mod clothes and R&B riffs. Over the next few years, he went through a succession of backing groups including the King Bees, the Manish Boys, the Lower Third and the Buzz. In late 1966, he changed his surname owing to the imminent emergence of Davy Jones of the Monkees. During that same period, he came under the wing of manager Kenneth Pitt, who nurtured his career for the remainder of the decade. A contract with the fashionable Decca subsidiary Deram saw Bowie achieve some high-profile publicity but subsequent singles and a well-promoted debut album failed to sell. Bowie even attempted a cash-in novelty number, 'The Laughing Gnome', but the charts remained resilient to his every move. Bowie persisted with mime classes while Pitt financed a television film, *Love You Till Tuesday*, but it was never shown on a major network. For a time, the star-elect performed in cabaret and retained vocal inflexions that betrayed a strong debt to his idol Anthony Newley.

As the 60s wound to a close Bowie seemed one of the least likely pop idols of the new decade. He was known only because of numerous advertisements in the British music press, as an artist who had released many records for many labels without success. The possibility of reinventing himself as a 70s pop star seemed remote at best, but in the autumn of 1969 he finally broke through with 'Space Oddity', released to coincide with the American moon launch. The novel tale of Major Tom, whose sojourn in space disorientates him to such a degree that he chooses to remain adrift rather than return to Earth, was a worthy UK Top 10 hit. Unfortunately, Bowie seemed unable to follow up the single with anything similarly clever and when 'The Prettiest Star' flopped, most critics understandably dismissed him as a one-hit-wonder. Only weeks earlier, the American duo Zager And Evans had enjoyed a bigger hit with the transatlantic chart-topper 'In The Year 2525', the theme of which bore superficial similarities to Bowie's tale, each dealing with possible future events and containing a pat moral. The fate of Zager And Evans (instant obscurity) weighed heavily over Bowie's fragile pop career, while an interesting album named after his hit provided few clues to his future.

A remarkable series of changes in Bowie's life, both personal and professional, occurred in 1970. His brother Terry had been committed to a mental institution; his father died and, soon after, David married art student Angela Barnett, and finally he dispensed with the services of his loyal manager Kenneth Pitt, who was replaced by the more strident Tony De Fries. Amid this period of flux, Bowie completed his first major work, an extraordinary album entitled *The Man Who Sold The World*. With musical assistance from guitarist Mick Ronson, drummer Mick Woodmansey and producer Tony Visconti on bass, Bowie employed an arrestingly heavy sound, aided by the eerie synthesizer work of Ralph Mace to embellish his chillingly dramatic vocals. Lyrically, the album brilliantly complemented the instrumentation and Bowie worked through a variety of themes including sexual perversion ('The Width Of A Circle'), mental illness ('All The Madmen'), dystopianism ('Saviour Machine') and Nietzschean nihilism ('The Supermen'). All these leitmotifs were reiterated on later albums. The package was completed with a striking cover revealing Bowie lounging seductively in a flowing dress. The transvesticism again provided a clue to the later years when Bowie habitually disguised his gender and even publicized his bisexuality.

With the svengali-like De Fries aggressively promoting his career, Bowie was signed to RCA Records for a reportedly large advance and completed *Hunky Dory* in 1971. The album was lighter in tone than its predecessor with Bowie reverting to acoustic guitar on some tracks and exploring a more commercial, yet still intriguing, direction. There was the catchy 'Changes', the futuristic 'Life On Mars', tributes to Bob Dylan and the Velvet Underground, and the contrastingly celebratory 'Kooks' and sombre 'The Bewlay Brothers'. *Hunky Dory* was an excellent album yet modest seller. Bowie took full advantage of his increasingly hip media profile by embarking on a UK tour in which his outrageous costume, striking vocals and treasure trove of new material revealed the artist in full flow. Up until this point, Bowie had experimented with diverse ideas, themes and images that coalesced effectively, though not necessarily coherently. The complete fusion was revealed in June 1972 on the album *The Rise And Fall Of Ziggy Stardust And The Spiders From Mars*. Here, Bowie embraced the persona of an apocalyptic rock star whose rise and fall coincides with the end of the world. In addition to the doom-laden breeziness of 'Five Years', there were the now familiar space-age themes ('Starman', 'Lady Stardust', 'Moonage Daydream') and the instant encore ('Rock 'N' Roll Suicide').

By this point, Bowie was deemed to have the Midas touch and his production talents brought rewards for his old hero Lou Reed (*Transformer* and the single 'Walk On The Wild Side') and a resurrected Mott The Hoople who had their first hit with 'All The Young Dudes'. The track 'Oh You Pretty Things' (from *Hunky Dory*) had already provided a hit for Peter Noone and an equally unlikely artist, Lulu, enjoyed a Top 10 smash courtesy of 'The Man Who Sold The World'. Meanwhile, Bowie had undertaken a world tour and achieved a UK number 1 album with *Aladdin Sane*, another concept work which centred on global destruction as its main plot. While still at his peak, Bowie shocked the rock world on 4 July 1974 by announcing his retirement from the stage of London's Hammersmith Odeon. It later transpired that it was not Bowie who was retiring, but his now overused persona, Ziggy Stardust. Taking stock, Bowie took an unlikely detour by recording an album of his favourite mid-60s songs. *Pin Ups* proved a patchy collection though there were some memorable moments including a hit reworking of the Merseys' 'Sorrow', a frantic reading of the Rolling Stones' 'Let's Spend The Night Together' and an interesting cover of the Kinks' neglected song 'Where Have All The Good Times Gone'.

After recording a US broadcast television special at London's Marquee club titled 'The 1980 Floor Show', Bowie produced his next work *Diamond Dogs*. Having failed to receive permission to use the title *1984*, he nevertheless adapted George Orwell's famous novel as the basis for his favourite forays into dystopianism, sexuality and doomed love. There were even some delightful flashes from the novel neatly translated into rock by Bowie. Julia, described as 'a rebel from the waist downwards' by the book's anti-hero Winston Smith, becomes the hot tramp of 'Rebel Rebel' (itself a hit single). What the album lacked was the familiar sound of the Spiders From Mars and especially the cutting guitar work of Mick Ronson. A massive tour of USA and Canada saw the 'Diamond Dogs' spectacle at its most excessive and expansive, but the whole project was hampered by the production budget. Beneath the spectacle, the music tended to be somewhat forgotten, a view reinforced by the release of the critically panned *David Live* in 1974.

Bowie's popularity was as great as ever in the mid-70s when he effectively righted the wrongs of history by taking 'Space Oddity' to number 1, six years after its initial UK chart entry. That same year, he also enjoyed his first US number 1, 'Fame', which featured the voice and co-composing skills of John Lennon. The song appeared on his next album, *Young Americans*, which saw the emergence of a new Bowie, successfully tackling Philadelphia soul. Meanwhile, there were significant changes in his business life with Tony De Fries finally falling from favour amid an acrimonious lawsuit. During the same period, Bowie's often stormy marriage to Angie was dissolved. As ever in Bowie's life, personal upheavals coincided with creative endeavour and he was busy working on Nicholas Roeg's film *The Man Who Fell To Earth*, in which he was given the leading role of the displaced alien marooned on Earth. The movie received mixed reviews. Returning to London, Bowie was reprimanded in the liberal music press for allegedly displaying a Nazi salute and suggesting that his home country needed a 'new Hitler'. His fascist flirtation was partly provocative and perhaps related to the self-grandeur stemming from his heavy use of cocaine during the period. The image was crystallized in the persona of the Thin White Duke, the icy character who came to life on his next album, *Station To Station*. An austere yet opaque production, the album anticipated the next phase of his career when he worked with Brian Eno.

The duo relocated to Berlin for a cycle of albums which displayed Bowie at his least commercial and most ambitious. *Low* and *Heroes*, both released in 1977, were predominantly instrumental works whose mood was strongly influenced by Eno's minimalist electronics. Surprisingly, segments from each album found their way onto a live album *Stage*, a considerable improvement upon its predecessor, *David Live*. Following a best-forgotten appearance in the movie *Just A Gigolo*, Bowie concluded his collaborative work with Eno on 1979's *Lodger*. Generally regarded as the least impressive of the Eno triology, it nevertheless contained some strong songs, including 'Boys Keep Swinging' and 'Repetition'. Bowie's thespian pursuits continued with a critically acclaimed starring role in the Broadway production of *The Elephant Man*. During the show's run in Chicago, Bowie released an album of new material which leaned closer to the rock mainstream. *Scary Monsters (And Super Creeps)* was adventurous, with its modern electro-pop and distorted electric guitar, provided by former King Crimson helmsman Robert Fripp. The album contained the reflective 'Ashes To Ashes', a fascinating track, which included references to one of Bowie's earlier creations, Major Tom. Coincidentally, the Major brought Bowie his first UK number 1 since 'Space Oddity'.

The early 80s saw Bowie taking on a series of diverse projects including an appearance in Bertolt Brecht's *Baal*, surprise chart collaborations with Queen ('Under Pressure') and Bing Crosby ('Peace On Earth/Little Drummer Boy') and two more starring roles in the films *The Hunger* and the critically acclaimed *Merry Christmas Mr Lawrence*. A switch of record label from RCA to EMI saw Bowie release his most commercial work since the early 70s with *Let's Dance,* produced by Nile Rodgers of Chic. In striking contrast to his recent excursions with Eno and previous doom-laden imagery, the work showed Bowie embracing a new positivism with upbeat, uplifting songs that were both slick and exciting. Even his interviews revealed a more open, contented figure intent upon stressing the positive aspects of life, seemingly without ambiguity. The title track of the album gave Bowie his third solo UK number 1 and effectively revitalized his recording career in the process. The 'Serious Moonlight' tour which accompanied the album, played to over two million people and garnered excellent reviews. That same year (1983) he had two further hits both narrowly missing the top spot in the UK charts with 'China Girl' and 'Modern Love'. In

the meantime, Bowie's influence could be detected in the work of a number of younger artists who had fallen under the spell of his various aliases. Gary Numan, the Human League, Japan and Bauhaus each displayed aspects of his music and imagery with varying results. Similarly the New Romantics from Visage, Ultravox and Spandau Ballet to the New Pop of Culture Club were all descendants of the one time glam rocker and Thin White Duke.

Bowie quickly followed up *Let's Dance* with the anti-climactic *Tonight*, which attracted universally bad reviews but managed to spawn a hit single with 'Blue Jean'. During 1985, Bowie was chiefly in demand as a collaborator, first with the Pat Metheny Group on 'This Is Not America' (from the film *The Falcon And The Snowman*) and next with Mick Jagger on a reworking of Martha And The Vandellas' 'Dancing In The Street' for Live Aid. The following year was dominated by Bowie's various acting pursuits. The much-publicized movie *Absolute Beginners* divided the critics, but the strong title track provided Bowie with a major hit. He also starred in the fantasy film *Labyrinth* and sang the theme of the anti-nuclear war cartoon film *When The Wind Blows*. In 1987 Bowie returned to his roots by teaming up with former classmate Peter Frampton for the 'Glass Spider' tour. The attendant album, *Never Let Me Down*, was again poorly received, as speculation grew that Bowie was at last running dry of musical ideas and convincing new personae. Never predictable, Bowie decided to put a group together in 1989 and called upon the services of Reeves Gabrels (guitar), Tony Sales (bass) and Hunt Sales (drums) - the two brothers having previously worked with Iggy Pop and Todd Rundgren. The unit took their name from the title song of their new album, *Tin Machine*, a set that displayed some good, old-fashioned guitar work, occasionally bordering on heavy metal. Bowie also took his band on the road with a tour of deliberately 'low-key' venues, Bowie expressing a desire to play in 'sweaty' clubs and get back to his roots. It was an interesting experiment but neither the album nor the tour did much to increase Bowie's critical standing in the late 80s. Ironically, it was the re-release of his back catalogue on CD that brought a more positive response from his followers and in order to promote the campaign Bowie set out on an acoustic 'greatest hits' tour. *Black Tie White Noise* was his strongest album in years and entered the UK album charts at number 1. Enlisting Nile Rodgers again as producer the crisp production worked on stand-out tracks such as the romantic 'Don't Let Me Down And Down', Cream's 'I Feel Free' and Morrissey's 'I Know It's Going To Happen Someday'. At the beginning of the 90s this album served as a milestone and worthwhile tribute to a career that had encapsulated a staggering number of musical and image changes, spanning nearly 25 years. In May 1995 Bowie signed a major recording contract with Virgin Records Ame. His first release was *Outside*, a collaboration with Brian Eno that received mixed reviews and disappointing sales. In his 50th year the dance/techno-inspired *Earthling* was issued. For once, the cracks were beginning to show - Bowie ceases to be an innovator, instead he merely becomes an imitator. If the dance/tecno beat was stripped away to reveal the real Bowie it would have been a more satisfying album.

●ALBUMS: *David Bowie* (Deram 1967)★★, later reissued as *The World Of David Bowie*, *David Bowie* aka *Man Of Words, Man Of Music* (RCA Victor 1969)★★★, later reissued as *Space Oddity*, *The Man Who Sold The World* (RCA Victor 1971)★★★, *Hunky Dory* (RCA Victor 1972)★★★★★, *The Rise And Fall Of Ziggy Stardust And The Spiders From Mars* (RCA Victor 1972)★★★★★, *Aladdin Sane* (RCA Victor 1973)★★★★, *Pin Ups* (RCA Victor 1973)★★★, *Diamond Dogs* (RCA Victor 1974)★★★★, *David Live* (RCA Victor 1974)★, *Young Americans* (RCA Victor 1975)★★★, *Station To Station* (RCA Victor 1976)★★★, *Low* (RCA Victor 1977)★★★★, *Heroes* (RCA Victor 1977)★★★★, *Stage* (RCA Victor 1978)★★, *Lodger* (RCA Victor 1979)★★, *Scary Monsters (And Super Creeps)* (RCA Victor 1980)★★★★, *Christiane F.* film soundtrack (1982)★★, *Rare* (RCA 1983)★★, *Let's Dance* (EMI America 1983)★★★, *Ziggy Stardust - The Motion Picture* film soundtrack (RCA 1983)★★, *Tonight* (EMI America 1984)★, *Never Let Me Down* (EMI America 1987)★, with Tin Machine *Tin Machine* (EMI USA 1989)★★, with Tin Machine *Tin Machine II* (London 1991)★★, with Tin Machine *Oy Vey Baby* (EMI 1992)★, *Black Tie White Noise* (Arista 1993)★★★, *The Buddha Of Suburbia* television soundtrack (1993)★★, *Santa Monica* (Trident 1994),★★, *Outside* (Virgin 1995)★★★, *Earthling* (RCA 1996)★★.

●COMPILATIONS: *Images 1966-67* (Decca 1973)★★, *Changesonebowie* (RCA 1976)★★★★★,*Best Of David Bowie* (K-Tel 1981)★★★, *Changestwobowie* (RCA 1981)★★, *Golden Years* (RCA 1983)★★★, *Fame And Fashion (All Time Greatest Hits)* (RCA 1984)★★★, *Love You Til Tuesday* (Deram 1984)★★, *Changesbowie* (EMI 1990)★★★, *The Gospel According To ...* (1993)★★, *The Singles Collection* (EMI 1993)★★★★★.

●VIDEOS: *Richochet, Video Hits, David Bowie - Video EP* (Virgin Vision 1983), *Serious Moonlight* (Videoform 1984), *Ziggy Stardust And The Spiders From Mars* (Thorn-EMI 1984), *Live* ●VIDEOS: *David Bowie* (Videoform 1984), *Video EP: David Bowie* (PMI 1986), *Serious Moonlight 2* (Channel 5 1986), *Jazzin' For Blue Jean* (Video Collection 1987), *Day In Day Out* (PMI 1987), *Glass Spider Vol. 1* (Video Collection 1988), *Glass Spider Vol. 2* (Video Collection 1988), *Love You Till Tuesday* (Channel 5 1989), *David Bowie: The Video Collection* (1993), *David Bowie: Black Tie White Noise* (1993).

●FURTHER READING: *The David Bowie Story*, George Tremlett. *David Bowie: A Portrait In Words And Music*, Vivian Claire. *The David Bowie Biography*, Paul Sinclair. *David Bowie Black Book: The Illustrated Biography*, Miles and Chris Charlesworth. *Bowie In His Own Words*, Miles. *David Bowie: An Illustrated Discography*, Stuart Hoggard. *David Bowie: Profile*, Chris Charlesworth. *David Bowie:*

An Illustrated Record, Roy Carr and Charles Shaar Murray. *Free Spirit*, Angie Bowie. *David Bowie: The Pitt Report*, Kenneth Pitt. *David Bowie: A Chronology*, Kevin Cann. *David Bowie: A Rock 'N' Roll Odyssey*, Kate Lynch. *Bowie*, Jerry Hopkins. *David Bowie: The Concert Tapes*, Pimm Jal de la Parra. *David Bowie: The Starzone Interviews*, David Currie. *Stardust*, Tony Zanetta. *In Other Words ... David Bowie*, Kerry Juby. *David Bowie: The Archive*, Chris Charlesworth. *Alias David Bowie*, Peter Gillman and Leni. *Backstage Passes: Life On The Wild Side With David Bowie*, Angie Bowie. *The Bowie Companion*, Elizabeth Thomson and David Gutman (eds.).

●FILMS: *The Man Who Fell To Earth* (1976), *Just A Gigolo* (1978), *The Hunger* (1983), *Merry Christmas Mr Lawrence* (1983), *Ziggy Stardust And The Spiders From Mars 1973 performance* (1983), *Into The Night* (1984), *Absolute Beginners* (1985), *Labyrinth* (1986), *Twin Peaks: Fire Walk With Me* (1992).

BOXER

Formed in 1975, Boxer featured two former members of Patto, Mike Patrick McCarthy/Mike Patto (b. 22 September 1942, Glasgow, Scotland, d. 4 March 1979; vocals) and Ollie Halsall (b. 14 March 1949, Southport, Merseyside, England, d. 29 May 1992; guitars). The line-up was completed by two experienced musicians, Keith Ellis (bass, ex-Koobas; Juicy Lucy; and Van Der Graaf Generator) and Tony Newman (drums, ex-Sounds Incorporated; Jeff Beck; and May Blitz). *Below The Belt* is better recalled for the controversy surrounding its tasteless 'nude' cover rather than the hard rock unveiled within. The original Boxer broke up when a second album, *Bloodletting*, was withdrawn and not released until 1979. The singer re-established the group in 1977 with Chris Stainton (keyboards, ex-Grease Band), Adrian Fisher (guitar, ex-Sparks), Tim Bogert (bass, ex-Vanilla Fudge) and Eddie Tuduri (drums). Boxer was dissolved following the release of the disappointing *Absolutely*. Mike Patto resumed work with the ad hoc unit, Hinkley's Heroes, but died in 1979 following a long battle with throat cancer.

●ALBUMS: *Below The Belt* (Virgin 1975)★★★, *Absolutely* (Epic 1977)★★, *Bloodletting* (Virgin 1979)★★.

BOYS OF THE LOUGH

This Irish-Scottish group formed in 1967 and were well-known for their arrangements of Celtic music. The original line-up of Robin Morton (b. 24 December 1939, Portadown, Northern Ireland; vocals, concertina, bodhran), Cathal McConnell (b. 8 June 1944, Enniskillen, County Fermanagh, Northern Ireland; flute, vocals, whistle), and Tommy Gunn (b. Derrylin, County Fermanagh, Northern Ireland; fiddle, bones, vocals) adopted the name Boys Of The Lough during a recording session for a television programme. After a tour of Scotland and England, Gunn left the trio, leaving McConnell and Morton to continue as a duo. In 1988, at the Aberdeen Folk Festival, they performed with another duo, Aly Bain and Mike Whelans. This became the new line-up of the group. Dick Gaughan then replaced Whelans in 1972, and in this guise appeared at the Cambridge Folk Festival in the same year, to considerable acclaim. In 1973, Gaughan left to pursue a solo career. He was in turn replaced by Dave Richardson (b. 20 August 1948, Corbridge, Northumberland, England; guitar, mandolin, cittern, concertina, tenorbanjo, hammerdulcimer), for the group's forthcoming American tour. The group then toured regularly for the next few years, on both sides of the Atlantic. In 1979, Morton left, to be replaced by Tich Richardson, brother of Dave, on guitar. This line-up toured worldwide into the 80s, but in September 1984, Riachardson was killed in a car accident. In February 1985 Christy O'Leary (b. 7 June 1955, Rathcoole, Co. Dublin, Eire; uillean pipes/vocals) joined, followed by John Coakley (b. 30 July 1951, Cork, Eire; guitar/piano). From this point, the Irish music in their act took a greater precedence. In February 1988, they celebrated their 21st Anniversary with a concert at New York's Carnegie Hall which was released as an album the following year on the Sage Arts label. Despite the personnel changes, they have retained their popularity, and the standard of musicianship has remained consistently high. The group continue to tour the USA regularly, with the various individual members undertaking their own projects concurrently. In Bain's case this has involved much television work, including *Down Home* in 1985, *Aly Bain And Friends* in 1989, and *Push The Boat Out* in 1991. Morton, meanwhile, went on to head Temple Records in Edinburgh.

●ALBUMS: *The Boys Of The Lough* (1973)★★★, *Second Album* (Trailer 1973)★★★, *Recorded Live* (Transatlantic 1975)★★★, *Lochaber No More* (Transatlantic 1975)★★★, *The Piper's Broken Finger* (Transatlantic 1976)★★★, *Good Friends-Good Music* (Transatlantic 1977)★★★, *Wish You Were Here* (Transatlantic 1978)★★★, *Regrouped* (Topic 1980)★★, *In The Tradition* (Ross 1981)★★★, *Open Road* (Ross 1983)★★, *Far, Far From Home* (Auk 1986)★★, *Welcoming Paddy Home* (Lough 1986)★★★, *Farewell And Remember Me* (Lough 1987)★★★, *Sweet Rural Shade* (Lough 1988)★★★, *Live At Carnegie Hall* (Sagem 1990)★★★, *The Fair Hills Of Ireland* (1993)★★★. Solo: Robin Morton And Cathal McConnell *An Irish Jubilee* (1969)★★★. Cathal McConnell *On Lough Erne's Shore* (1978)★★★. Aly Bain *Aly Bain-Mike Whelans* (1971)★★★, Aly Bain (Whirlie 1985)★★★, *Down Home Vol.1* (1985)★★★, *Down Home Vol.2* (1985)★★★, *Aly Bain Meets The Cajuns* (Lismor 1988) *The Fair Hills Of Ireland* (1992)★★★, *The Day Dawn* (1994)★★★.

●COMPILATIONS: *Gaelic Folk, Vol.1* (1978)★★★, *Gaelic Folk, Vol.2* (1978)★★★.

BRAND X

Brand X was one of the most commercially successful of the British jazz/rock groups of the late 70s and early 80s. *Moroccan Roll* reached number 37 in the UK album chart in May 1977 while *Is There Anything About* crept in at number 93 in September 1982. The original line-up of the band was John Goodsall (guitar), Robin Lumley (keyboards), Percy Jones (bass, ex-Liverpool Scene), Phil Collins (drums) and Maurice Pert (percussion). This was the band that Collins considered second only to Weather Report. There were similarities, especially in that each group of musicians had great technical ability and a desire to play popular music; but Brand X's individuality came through in their compositions. They produced sharp arrangements of appealing melodies, often with a gangling counterpoint provided by Jones' slurred fretless bass lines. Collins and Pert could contribute anything from the lightest colouring to a furiously propulsive rhythm and both Goodsall and Lumley were exciting soloists. All the musicians were also busy with studio work and Collins had been expanding his role with Genesis after Peter Gabriel's departure. He had also released a solo album and, as his second career as a solo artist took off, he left Brand X, to be replaced by Chuck Burgi, and then by Mike Clarke. A little later Percy Jones left and was replaced by John Gilbin.

●ALBUMS: *Unorthodox Behaviour* (Charisma 1976)★★★, *Livestock* (Charisma 1977)★★★, *Moroccan Roll* (Charisma 1977)★★★, *Masques* (Charisma 1978)★★★, *Product* (Charisma 1979)★★★, *Do They Hurt* (Charisma 1980)★★★, *Is There Anything About* (Columbia 1982)★★★, *Live At The Roxy LA 1979* (Zok 1996)★★.

●COMPILATIONS: *The Plot Thins - A History Of* (1992)★★★.

BRASS CONSTRUCTION

Led by keyboards player and singer Randy Muller (b. Guyana), Brass Construction was a leading group in the disco movement of the 70s. Muller originally formed the band in Brooklyn, New York, as Dynamic Soul, mixing funk, salsa and reggae rhythms with a more orthodox jazz line-up to create a highly danceable sound. Renamed Brass Construction, the nine-piece group was signed by United Artists in 1975. The members included Michael Grudge (b. Jamaica) and Jesse Ward Jnr. (saxophones), Wayne Parris (b. Jamaica) and Morris Price (trumpets), Joseph Arthur Wong (b. Trinidad; guitar), Wade Williamson (bass), Larry Payton (drums) and percussionist Sandy Billups. With infectious polyrhythms and minimal, chanted vocals, the group's first release, 'Movin'', topped the R&B charts and was a pop Top 20 hit. It was followed by 'Changin'', 'Ha Cha Cha' and 'L-O-V-E-U', all best-sellers. Later singles were less successful although successive Brass Construction albums rode the disco boom. Muller also wrote for and produced New York disco group Skyy and B.T. Express. The group's popularity dwindled in the 80s, although the remix craze brought numerous versions of its early hits into the clubs in 1988 including 'Ha Cha Cha (Acieed Mix)'.

●ALBUMS: *Brass Construction* (United Artists 1976)★★★, *II* (United Artists 1976)★★, *III* (United

Artists 1977)★★, *IV* (United Artists 1979)★★, *V* (Liberty 1980)★★, *VI* (United Artists 1980)★★, *Attitudes* (Liberty 1982)★★, *Conversations* (Capitol 1983)★★, *Renegades* (Capitol 1984)★★, *Conquest* (Capitol 1985)★★.
●COMPILATIONS: *Movin' - The Best Of Brass Construction* (Syncopate 1988)★★★.

BREAD

Bread was formed in 1969 when David Gates (b. 11 December 1940, Tulsa, Oklahoma, USA), a leading Los Angeles session musician, produced an album for the Pleasure Faire, a group which included vocalist/guitarist Rob Royer. Songwriter James Griffin (b. Memphis, Tennessee, USA) contributed several compositions to the set and the three aspirants then decided to pool resources. All were assured multi-instrumentalists, and although not a commercial success, their debut album established a penchant for melodious soft-rock. Mike Botts (b. Sacramento, California, USA; drums) augmented the group for *On The Water*, which included the million-selling 'Make It With You', while *Manna* spawned a further gold disc with 'If', later successfully revived by actor/singer Telly Savalas. Royer was then replaced by keyboard veteran Larry Knechtel (b. Bell, California, USA), but Bread's smooth approach was left unruffled as they achieved further international success with immaculate pop songs, 'Baby I'm-A Want You' (1971), 'Everything I Own' and 'Guitar Man' (both 1972). However, increasing friction between Gates and Griffin led to the group's collapse later that year. The combatants embarked on solo careers while Botts joined the Linda Ronstadt Band, but the late period quartet reconvened in 1976 for *Lost Without Your Love*, the title track of which reached the US Top 10. Guitarist Dean Parks augmented the line-up when Griffin resumed his independent direction, but *The Goodbye Girl* failed to emulate its predecessors and Bread was again disbanded.
●ALBUMS: *Bread* (Elektra 1969)★★, *On The Waters* (Elektra 1970)★★, *Manna* (Elektra 1971)★★★, *Baby I'm-A Want You* (Elektra 1972)★★★, *Guitar Man* (Elektra 1972)★★★, *Lost Without Your Love* (Elektra 1977)★★★, *The Goodbye Girl* (Elektra 1978)★★.
●COMPILATIONS: *The Best Of Bread* (Elektra 1972)★★★, *The Best Of Bread Volume 2* (Elektra 1974)★★, *The Sound Of Bread* (Elektra 1977)★★, *The Very Best Of Bread* (Telstar 1987)★★★.

BRETT MARVIN AND THE THUNDERBOLTS

This UK skiffle-cum-blues jugband act was comprised of Graham Hine (guitar, vocals), Jim Pitts (guitar, vocals, harmonica), John Lewis aka Jona Lewie (keyboards/vocals), Pete Gibson (trombone, vocals, percussion), Dave Arnott (drums) and percussionists Keith Trussell and Big John Randall. A group of teachers and pupils from Crawley, Sussex, England, banded together, little knowing that nearly thirty years later they would still be treating audiences to a unique brand of music. Their debut album aroused novelty-based interest, but the unit only enjoyed commercial success after adopting the pseudonym Terry Dactyl And The Dinosaurs. An ensuing single, 'Seaside Shuffle', reached number 2 in 1972, but the Thunderbolts reverted to their original name when subsequent releases failed to emulate its success. Lewie embarked on a solo career following the group's first break-up. Various permutations of this band continue to gig on the club scene where their brand of loose blues and R&B is hugely popular. In not compromising their music they have built a loyal following and regularly feature onstage, in addition to regular instruments, their own bizarre inventions such as the Zobstick, the Lager Prone and the Electric Ironing Board. In 1993 the line-up on *Boogie Street* in addition to Hine, Pitts, Gibson, Trussell and Randell (now their road manager) added Taffy Davies (vocals, piano, clarinet, mandolin) and Pete Swan (bass).
●ALBUMS: *Brett Marvin And The Thunderbolts* (Sonet 1970)★★★, *Twelve Inches Of Brett Marvin* (Sonet 1971)★★, *Best Of Friends* (Sonet 1971)★★, *Alias Terry Dactyl* (Sonet 1972)★★, *Ten Legged Friend* (Sonet 1973)★★, *Boogie Street* (Exson 1993)★★.

BREWER AND SHIPLEY

Songwriters Mike Brewer (b. 1944, Oklahoma City, Oklahoma, USA) and Tom Shipley (b. 1942, Mineral Ridge, Ohio, USA) began their careers together in Los Angeles during the mid-60s, after several years' performing as solo artists on the folk club circuit. One of their compositions, 'The Keeper Of The Keys', was recorded by H.P. Lovecraft, and the song also appeared on the duo's own first album, *Down On LA*, which was comprised of demo tapes made for Good Sam Music and picked up by A&M Records. A competent pop/rock selection, the album led to the duo signing with Kama Sutra and greater critical success with *Weeds*, which featured cameo appearances by Mike Bloomfield, Jerry Garcia and Nicky Hopkins. *Tarkio* and *Shake Off The Demon* also benefited from an all-star cast, although such support did not deflect from Brewer and Shipley's close harmony, soft-rock style. In 1971 they enjoyed a surprise US hit when 'One Toke Over The Line' reached number 10, but the song was banned on radio due to its drug connotations. The duo then left their Bay Area for rural Missouri, but subsequent releases lacked the charm of previous work. The partnership was dissolved during the late 70s, but Shipley later worked as a studio engineer, most notably for Joni Mitchell on *Dog Eat Dog* (1985), *Chalk Mark On A Rainstorm* (1988) and *Night Ride Home* (1991).
●ALBUMS: *Down In LA* (A&M 1968)★★★, *Weeds* (Kama Sutra 1969)★★★, *Tarkio* (Kama Sutra 1971)★★★, *Shake Off The Demon* (Kama Sutra 1971)★★★, *Rural Space* (Kama Sutra 1973)★★★, *Brewer And Shipley* aka *ST-11261* (Kama Sutra 1974)★★★, *Welcome To Riddle Bridge*

(Capitol 1975)★★★, *Not Far From Free* (1978)★★. Solo: Michael Brewer *Beauty Lies* (Full Moon 1983)★★.
●COMPILATIONS: *The Best Of Brewer And Shipley* (Kama Sutra 1976)★★★.

BRINSLEY SCHWARZ

The roots of this enduringly popular attraction lay in Kippington Lodge, a Tunbridge Wells-based pop group. Formed in 1965, they completed five varied, if light-weight, singles under the direction of producer Mark Wirtz. The initial line-up - Brinsley Schwarz (guitar/vocals), Barry Landerman (organ/vocals), Nick Lowe (b. 25 March 1949, Woodbridge, Suffolk, England; bass/vocals) and Pete Whale (drums) - remained intact until 1968 when Bob Andrews replaced Landerman, who had joined Vanity Fare. Dissatisfied with their con-servative image, the group began emphasizing original material. In October 1969 they emerged with a new drummer, Bill Rankin, and had renamed themselves in deference to their lead guitarist. The quartet secured a management deal with the ambitious Famepushers agency, but were engulfed by controversy when British journalists were flown to witness the Brinsleys' debut appearance, bottom-of-the-bill at New York's Fillmore East. The plan failed in the wake of a shaky perfor-mance and the group was perceived as a hype. Their debut album, *Brinsley Schwarz*, was pleasant but unde-manding, and did little to dispel suspicions. However, a second collection, ironically entitled *Despite It All*, showed more promise as the group began shedding its derivative side and emerged with a distinctive style.

A second guitarist, Ian Gomm (b. 17 March 1947, Ealing, London, England), was added prior to *Silver Pistol*, arguably the group's most unified and satisfying release. It preceded a period when the Brinsleys popu-larized 'pub rock', a back-to-basics genre that reviled the pomposity perceived in more commercial contempo-raries. Having enjoyed a resident slot at the Tally Ho pub in Kentish Town, north London, the group then performed extensively throughout the country. Their extended sets featured a number of different influ-ences, be it the Band, reggae, rock 'n' roll or soul and this melting pot, in turn, inspired some of Nick Lowe's finest songs. *Nervous On The Road* featured the exquisite 'Don't Lose Your Grip On Love', while '(What's So Funny 'Bout) Peace, Love and Understanding', later revived by Elvis Costello, made its debut on *The New Favourites Of Brinsley Schwarz*. This exceptional selec-tion was produced by Dave Edmunds, but despite crit-ical plaudits, it failed to sell. The group was tiring and broke up in March 1975, unable to escape the 'good-time' niche they had ploughed. Schwarz and Andrews later joined Graham Parker And The Rumour while Ian Gomm and Nick Lowe embarked on solo careers.
●ALBUMS: *Brinsley Schwarz* (United Artists 1970)★★★, *Despite It All* (United Artists 1970)★★★, *Silver Pistol* (United Artists 1972)★★★★, *Nervous On The Road* (United Artists 1972)★★★, *Please Don't Ever Change*

(United Artists 1973)★★★, *The New Favourites Of Brinsley Schwarz* (United Artists 1974)★★★★.
●COMPILATIONS: *Original Golden Greats* (United Artists 1974)★★★★, *The Fifteen Thoughts Of Brinsley Schwarz* (United Artists 1978)★★★★.

BRISTOL, JOHNNY

b. Morgantown, North Carolina, USA. Bristol's career began within the nascent Tamla/Motown circle. He first recorded in 1960 as part of the duo of Johnny And Jackie (Jackie Beavers, whom Bristol met while in the US Air Force). On Gwen Gordy and Harvey Fuqua's Tri-Phi label, they recorded the original version of 'Someday We'll Be Together' (1961), which was a run-away success for the Supremes in 1969. Bristol remained with the company, and over the next 10 years, in a partnership with Harvey Fuqua, forged a successful career as a producer and songwriter with Edwin Starr, David Ruffin, Detroit Spinners, Stevie Wonder and Junior Walker. Bristol left Motown in 1973, and joined CBS as house producer, but, despite that, was still unable to get them to release his solo album. He eventually achieved this by negotiating an outside con-tract with MGM, and relaunched his performing career with an international smash, 'Hang On In There Baby' (1974). Despite a prolific work-rate, he was unable to repeat that early hit, except for a UK Top 40 hit in 1980, duetting with Ami Stewart on 'My Guy - My Girl'. After making singles for Ariola and Handshake Records in the 80s he briefly recorded for Ian Levine's Motor City label in 1989, issuing two UK singles.
●ALBUMS: *Hang On In There Baby* (MGM 1974)★★★, *Bristol's Creme* (Atlantic 1976)★★, *Free To Be Me* (Ariola Hansa 1981)★.
●COMPILATIONS: *The Best Of Johnny Bristol* (Polydor 1988)★★.

BRONCO

Vocalist Jess Roden, formerly of the Alan Bown Set, instigated this excellent group in 1970. Kevin Hammond (guitar/vocals), John Pasternak (bass) - both ex-Band Of Joy, Robbie Blunt (guitar) and Pete Robinson (drums) completed the line-up which made its debut that year with *Country Home*. The quintet offered a relaxed, sympathetic setting for the singer's soulful delivery, best exemplified on *Ace Of Sunlight*, which featured support from Ian Hunter and Mick Ralphs from Mott The Hoople, and Fotheringay's Trevor Lucas. Despite their promise, Bronco was unable to secure a sound commercial footing and the departure of Roden for a solo career effectively killed the group. Blunt subsequently joined Silverhead and appeared in several short-lived aggregations before securing wide-spread recognition with his work for Robert Plant.
●ALBUMS: *Country Home* (Island 1970)★★, *Ace Of Sunlight* (Island 1971)★★★, *Smokin' Mixture* (Polydor 1973)★★.

BROOKER, GARY

b. 29 May 1945, Essex, England. The ex-Paramount and the former lead vocalist/pianist of Procol Harum embarked on a solo career immediately after their demise. His solo albums were mainly unsuccessful and sold only moderately. Brooker's distinctive voice and excellent keyboard ability has kept him busy both as a session player and as a member of touring bands. He was a regular member of Eric Clapton's band during the late 80s, but spent more time becoming a fishing champion. Brooker has achieved rock immortality by being the vocalist and co-writer of the legendary hit 'A Whiter Shade of Pale'. A full circle was completed in 1991 when Brooker re-formed Procol Harum.
●ALBUMS: *No Fear Of Flying* (Chrysalis 1979)★★, *Lead Me To The Water* (Mercury 1982)★★, *Echoes In The Night* (Mercury 1985)★★.

BROOKLYN DREAMS

This disco-influenced soul trio, with roots spreading back to the doo-wop era via their impressive vocal formation, formed in Los Angeles, California, USA, in the mid-70s. All three members had known each other previously, Joe 'Bean' Esposito and Ed Hokenson having both attended Erasmus High School in Brooklyn, New York. Bruce Sudano was also raised in the Brooklyn area, and had sung with Alive And Kickin' earlier in the decade. Originally named the Movements, then Little Mike And The Mysteries and Alfalfa, they decided on Brooklyn Dreams as a nod to their east coast origins. They signed to Millennium Records after A&R executive Jimmy Ienner heard their first demo. They were sent to work on their debut album, from which sessions the single, 'Sad Eyes', was released. This made number 63 in the *Billboard* charts in November 1978, before the group embarked on a world tour supporting disco diva Donna Summer. Their biggest chart single arrived in March of the following year, when 'Music, Harmony And Rhythm', a title that summed up the basis of the band's appeal, reached number 57. However, even greater success awaited their first joint studio venture with Summer, January 1979's 'Heaven Knows', which made US number 4. Such lofty heights were never achieved by the group in its own right, however, with 'Make It Last', which stalled at number 69 the following March, the nearest they came. They continued to perform and write until 1983 when, with four albums behind them, they disbanded. All three remained in the music business however, with Sudano (who married Summer) and Hokenson producing and writing together, while Esposito produced advertising and radio jingles.
●ALBUMS: *Brooklyn Dreams* (Millennium 1978)★★★.

BROOKS, ELKIE

b. Elaine Bookbinder, 25 February 1946, Salford, Manchester, England. Brooks began her career as 'Manchester's answer to Brenda Lee' before touring the UK during the early 60s with the Eric Delaney Band. Her early records included sympathetic versions of 'Hello Stranger' and 'The Way You Do The Things You Do', first recorded, respectively, by Barbara Lewis and the Temptations, but the singer was unable to secure a deserved commercial breakthrough. In 1970, she joined Dada, a 12-piece jazz-rock act that also featured Robert Palmer (vocals) and Pete Gage (guitar). These three artists subsequently formed the core of Vinegar Joe, a highly popular soul/rock act that completed three powerful albums during the early 70s. The group was dissolved in 1974, following which Elkie embarked on a solo career. She enjoyed two UK Top 10 hits with 'Pearl's A Singer' and 'Sunshine After The Rain' (both 1977), but her once raucous approach, redolent of Tina Turner, became increasingly tempered by MOR trappings. 'Fool If You Think It's Over' and 'Nights In White Satin' (both 1982) enhanced the singer's reputation for dramatic cover versions, but 'No More The Fool', composed by Russ Ballard, revived her contemporary standing by reaching the UK Top 5 in 1986. An attendant album achieved double-gold status, while a follow-up set, *Bookbinder's Kid*, emphasized this revitalization by including further songs by Ballard and material by Bryan Adams. By the 90s Brooks was firmly established as one of Britain's leading singers, and in 1993 embarked on a 49-date UK tour. As well as the old favourites such as 'Lilac Wine' and 'Don't Cry Out Loud', her programme included several numbers made famous by artists such as Billie Holiday, Dinah Washington, and Peggy Lee.
●ALBUMS: *Rich Man's Woman* (A&M 1975)★★★, *Two Days Away* (A&M 1977)★★★, *Shooting Star* (A&M 1978)★★★, *Live And Learn* (A&M 1979)★★★, *Pearls* (A&M 1981)★★★, *Pearls II* (A&M 1982)★★, *Minutes* (A&M 1984)★★, *Screen Gems* (EMI 1984)★★, *No More The Fool* (Legend 1986)★★, *Bookbinder's Kid* (Legend 1988)★★★, *Inspiration* (Telstar 1989)★★, *'Round Midnight* (1993)★★, *Pearls III* (1993)★★, *Circles* (Permanent 1995)★★.
●COMPILATIONS: *The Very Best Of Elkie Brooks* (A&M 1986)★★★, *Collection: Elkie Brooks* (Castle 1987)★★★, *The Early Years 1964-1966* (C5 1987)★★, *Priceless-Very Best Of Elkie Brooks* (Pickwick 1991)★★★, *We've Got Tonight* (Spectrum 1995)★★★.
●VIDEOS: *We've Got Tonight* (Video Collection 1987), *No More The Fool* (Gold Rushes 1987), *Pearls - The Video Show* (A&M Sound Pictures 1988).

BROTHERHOOD OF MAN

This pop vocal group was formed in London in 1969 by songwriter Tony Hiller. The lead singer was Tony Burrows, veteran of such groups as the Ivy League, the Flower Pot Men and Edison Lighthouse. The group's first success was Hiller's 'United We Stand', a UK Top 10 hit in 1970. With a changing personnel, the group continued to record for Deram and Dawn in the early 70s but its career only revived when it was chosen to represent the UK in the 1976 Eurovision Song Contest. Appearing as an Abba-inspired male/female quartet led by Martin Lee and Lee Sheridan, Brotherhood Of Man's breezy rendition of 'Save Your Kisses For Me' won the competition and became an international hit, even reaching the Top 30 in America. The group followed with a series of UK successes including the number 1 hits, 'Angelo' and 'Figaro', co-written by Hiller with Lee and Sheridan. Thereafter, their popularity dwindled and by the 80s Brotherhood Of Man was relegated to the lucrative though uninspiring scampi-and-chips nightclub circuit, although 'Lightning Flash' in 1982 was a minor hit.

●ALBUMS: *Love & Kisses From The Brotherhood Of Man* (Pye 1976)★★, *B For Brotherhood* (Pye 1978)★★, *Singing A Song* (PRT 1979)★★, *Sing 20 Number One Hits* (Warwick 1980)★★, *Lightning Flash* (Epic 1983)★★.
●COMPILATIONS: *The Best Of The Brotherhood Of Man* (Spot 1983)★★, *20 Great Hits* (Prestige 1992)★★.

BROUGHTON, EDGAR, BAND

The London 'underground' scene welcomed the anarchic, revolutionary and irreverent Broughtons into an active fraternity during the early days of 1969. The band comprised Edgar Broughton (b. 24 October 1947, Warwick, Warwickshire, England; guitar/vocals), Steve Broughton (b. 20 May 1950, Warwick, Warwickshire, England; drums/vocals) and Arthur Grant (bass/guitar/vocals). Edgar's growling voice was similar to that of Captain Beefheart and they regularly featured his 'Dropout Boogie' in their act. Following their arrival in London they played at a number of small club gigs arranged by Blackhill Enterprises. They were given a wider audience by playing at the famous Blind Faith free concert in Hyde Park, where the Broughtons incited the crowd to a frenzy with an exhaustive rendition of the favourite, 'Out Demons, Out'. Despite the exposure that BBC disc jockey John Peel gave the band on his pioneering UK radio show *Top Gear*, the political and sexual themes of their songs had dated by the early 70s, although the band soldiered on for a number of years, maintaining a defiant political stance that gained acceptance with a loyal core of British and German rock fans. Into the early 90s Broughton could still be found performing part-time as part of a late 60s revival show and on the London pub circuit.

●ALBUMS: *Wasa Wasa* (Harvest 1969)★★★★, *Sing Brother Sing* (Harvest 1970)★★★, *The Edgar Broughton Band* (Harvest 1971)★★★, *In Side Out* (Harvest 1972)★★, *Oora* (Harvest 1973)★★, *Bandages* (NEMS 1975)★★, *Parlez-Vous English* (Infinity 1979)★★, *Live Hits Harder* (1979)★★, *Superchip* (See For Miles 1996)★★.
●COMPILATIONS: *A Bunch Of 45s* (Harvest 1975)★★, *As Was* (EMI 1988)★★, *Document Series Presents ... Classic Album & Single Tracks 1969-1973* (1992)★★★.

BROWNE, DUNCAN

b. 1946, England, d. 28 May 1993. Browne emerged during the mid-60s as half of Lorel, a 'flower-power' duo signed to the Immediate label, but embarked on a solo career when their projected single was shelved. His resultant album, *Give Me Take You*, showed a performer now in a singer-songwriter mould and, although burdened by Andrew Loog Oldham's elaborate string arrangement, the record was widely acclaimed. Browne later joined Mickie Most's Rak label and secured a UK Top 30 single in 1972 when the haunting 'Journey' reached number 23. A second low-key interlude ensued before the artist resurfaced in Metro, a synthesized pop act that enjoyed airplay success with 'Criminal World'. Browne left the group following their debut album and resumed his own career with *Wild Places*. He scored a minor hit in 1986 when 'Theme From The Travelling Man', the signature tune from a popular television series, reached the UK charts. Browne continued writing music for film, theatre and television until his death in May 1993 from cancer.

●ALBUMS: *Give Me Take You* (1968)★★★, *Duncan Browne* (RAK 1973)★★★, *Wild Places* (Logo 1978)★★★, *Streets Of Fire* (1979)★★★, *Planet Earth* (1986)★★★, *Music From The Travelling Man* (1986)★★, *Songs Of Love And War* (Zomart 1994)★★★.

BROWNE, JACKSON

b. 9 October 1948, Heidelberg, Germany, but resident of Los Angeles, California, from the age of three. Introduced to folk music while in his teens, Browne began writing songs at the instigation of two high school friends, Greg Copeland and Steve Noonan. The youngsters frequented the Paradox club, a favoured haunt of traditional musicians, where Jackson was introduced to the Nitty Gritty Dirt Band. He joined the group in February 1966, only to leave within six months, but some of his early compositions appeared on their subsequent albums. An ensuing deal with Nina Music, the publishing arm of Elektra Records, resulted in several of Browne's songs being recorded by the label's acts, including Tom Rush and the aforementioned Noonan. Jackson had meanwhile ventured to New York, where he accompanied singer Nico during her engagement at the Dom, a club owned by Andy Warhol. The singer's *Chelsea Girl* set featured three Browne originals, but their relationship quickly soured and the young musician retreated to California. In 1968 Jackson began work on a solo album, but both it and a projected 'supergroup', revolving around the artist, Ned Doheny and Jack Wilce, were later abandoned. Undeterred, Browne continued to frequent the Los Angeles clubs and music fraternity until a demo tape resulted in a recording deal with the newly established Asylum Records. *Jackson Browne/Saturate Before Using* confirmed that the artist's potential had not withered during earlier prevarications. David Crosby added sterling support to a set including the composer's own readings of 'Jamaica Say You Will' and 'Rock Me On The Water', previously covered by the Byrds and Brewer And Shipley, respectively, and 'Doctor My Eyes', an up-tempo performance that reached the US Top 10, but became an even bigger hit in the hands of the Jackson Five. Browne also drew plaudits for 'Take It Easy', which he wrote with Glenn Frey during a spell when they shared an apartment and penury. The song was a major success for the latter's group, the Eagles, and in turn inspired several subsequent collaborations including 'Nightingale', 'Doolin' Dalton' and 'James Dean'. Jackson's own version of 'Take It Easy' appeared on *For Everyman*, which also featured 'These Days', one of the singer's most popular early songs. The album introduced a long-standing relationship with multi-instrumentalist David Lindley, but although the punchy 'Redneck Friend' became a regional hit, the set was not a commercial success. *Late For The Sky* was an altogether stronger collection, on which Browne ceased relying on older material and in its place offered a more contemporary perspective. Extensive touring helped bring the artist a much wider audience and in 1975 he produced Warren Zevon's debut album for Asylum, infusing a measure of consistency to the performer's jaundiced wit and delivery. These facets contrasted with Browne's own, rather languid approach, which he attempted to reverse by employing producer Jon Landau for *The Pretender*. The resultant sense of contrast enhanced much of the material, including 'Here Come Those Tears Again' and the anthemic title track. One of the benchmarks of 70s American rock, this homage to blue-collar values became a staple part of AOR radio, while its poignancy was enhanced by the suicide of Jackson's wife, Phyllis, in March 1976. *The Pretender* earned a gold disc and the singer's newfound commercial appeal was emphasized with *Running On Empty*.

However, Browne did not meekly repeat the formula of its predecessor and in place of its homogeneous sheen was a set recorded at different locations during a tour. The album included material written by Danny O'Keefe and Danny Kortchmar, as well as an affectionate reading of 'Stay', originally recorded by Maurice Williams And The Zodiacs. This performance reached number 20 in the US, but fared better in the UK, climbing to number 12 and providing the singer with his only British hit to date. Despite its rough edges, *Running On Empty* became the singer's most popular release, closing a particular chapter in his career. During the late 70s Jackson pursued a heightened political profile through his efforts on behalf of the anti-nuclear lobby. In partnership with Graham Nash and Bonnie Raitt he organized several cross-country benefits culminating in a series of all-star concerts at New York's Madison Square Garden. The best of these were later compiled on *No Nukes*.

It was 1980 before Browne completed a new studio album, but although *Hold On* was undeniably well-crafted, it lacked the depth of earlier work. Nonetheless two of its tracks, 'Boulevard' and 'That Girl Could Sing', became Top 20 hits in America while in 1982 the singer reached number 7 with 'Somebody's Baby', a song taken from the soundtrack of *Fast Times At Ridgemont High*. Commitments to social causes and his personal life only increased Browne's artistic impasse and *Lawyers In Love* was a major disappointment. It did, however, contain 'Tender Is The Night', which combined the strength of early work to a memorable hookline. *Lives In The Balance*, which addressed the Reagan presidential era, showed a greater sense of accomplishment, a feature continued on *World In Motion*. Following his publicized break-up with actress Daryl Hannah he recorded an album of deeply powerful and introspective lyrics, much in keeping with *The Pretender* in 1976. *I'm Alive* clearly demonstrated that after more than twenty years of writing songs, it is possible to remain as sharp and fresh as ever. In songs such as the title track, 'Yeah now I'm rolling down California five, with your laughter in my head / I'm gonna have to block it out somehow to survive 'cause those dreams are dead / And I'm alive', simple yet moving lyrics show Browne resigned to a failed relationship. In 'Sky Blue And Black' he revisits old territory, with what can be seen as a 1993 version of 'Sleep's Dark And Silent Gate'; in the song he accepts failure: 'When the touch of a lover ends, and the soul of the friend begins / there's a need to be separate and a need to be one'. *Looking East* was limp and lifeless and a bitter disappointment for those expecting another *I'm Alive*. Jackson Browne rightly remains a highly regarded singer-songwriter, as testified by the numerous acts who have turned to his work over the years. The craftsmanship of his lyrics and melody assures him a devoted audience, and like Neil Young there is a feeling that the best may still be yet to come. *Looking East* by Browne's standards was a poor album, more noticeable after following in the wake of *I'm Alive*.

●ALBUMS: *Jackson Browne* aka *Saturate Before Using* (Asylum 1972)★★★★, *For Everyman* (Asylum 1973)★★★★, *Late For The Sky* (Asylum 1974)★★★★, *The Pretender* (Asylum 1976)★★★★, *Running On Empty* (Asylum 1977)★★★, *Hold Out* (Asylum 1980)★★, *Lawyers In Love* (Asylum 1983)★★★, *Lives In The Balance* (Asylum 1986)★★, *Worlds In Motion* (Elektra 1989)★★, *I'm Alive* (Elektra 1994)★★★★, *Looking East* (Elektra 1996)★★.

BROWNSVILLE STATION

This Detroit-based quartet - Cub Koda (guitar/harmonica), Michael Lutz (guitar/vocals), Bruce Nazarian (guitar/synthesiser) and Henry Week (drums/vocals) - forged its early reputation as a superior 'oldies' group. Their attention to 'roots' music was later fused to an understanding of pop's dynamics, exemplified in 'Smokin' In The Boys' Room' (1973), which reached number 3 in the US charts and the UK Top 30 the following year. Subsequent releases lacked the quartet's early sense of purpose and the band was latterly dissolved. Koda later fronted several 'revival'-styled units while proclaiming his love of R&B and blues through columns in USA collectors' magazines.

●ALBUMS: *Brownsville Station* (Palladium 1970)★★★, *No B.S.* (1970)★★★, *A Night On The Town* (Big Tree 1972)★★, *Yeah!* (Big Tree 1973)★★, *School Punks* aka *Smokin' In The Boys' Room* (Big Tree 1974)★★★, *Motor City Connection* (Big Tree 1975)★★, *Brownsville Station* (Private Stock 1977)★★, *Air Special* (1980)★★.

BRUCE, JACK

b. John Symon Asher, 14 May 1943, Glasgow, Lanarkshire, Scotland. Formerly a piano student at the Royal Scottish Academy of Music he was awarded a RSAM scholarship for cello and composition. Bruce has utilized his brilliant bass playing to cross and bridge free jazz and heavy rock, during spells with countless musical conglomerations. As a multi-instrumentalist he also has a great fondness for the piano, cello and acoustic bass, and is highly accomplished on all these instruments. At 19 years of age he moved to London and joined the R&B scene, first with Alexis Korner's band and then as a key member of the pioneering Graham Bond Organisation. Following brief stints with John Mayall's Bluesbreakers and Manfred Mann, Bruce joined with his former colleague in the Bond band, Ginger Baker, who together with Eric Clapton, formed Cream. The comparatively short career of this pivotal band reached musical heights that have rarely been bettered. During this time Bruce displayed and developed a strident vocal style and considerable prowess as a harmonica player. However, it was his imaginative and sometimes breathtaking bass playing that appealed. He popularized an instrument that had previously not featured prominently in rock music. Dozens of young players in the 70s and 80s cited Bruce as being the reason for them taking up the bass guitar. Upon the break-up of Cream, Bruce released an exemplary solo album, *Songs For A Tailor*. A host of top jazz/rock musicians were present on what was his most successful album. On this record he continued the songwriting partnership with Pete Brown that had already produced a number of Cream classics, 'White Room', 'Politician', 'I Feel Free', 'Sunshine Of Your Love' and 'SWLABR' (She Was Like A Bearded Rainbow). Brown's imaginative and surreal lyrics were the perfect foil to Jack's furious and complex bass patterns. Evocative songs such as 'Theme For An Imaginary Western' and 'The Weird Of Hermiston' enabled Bruce's ability as a vocalist to shine, with piercing clarity.

Throughout the early 70s, a series of excellent albums and constantly changing line-ups gave him a high profile. His involvement with Tony Williams' Lifetime and his own 'supergroup', West Bruce And Laing, further enhanced his position in the jazz and rock world. A further aggregation, Jack Bruce And Friends, included jazz guitarist Larry Coryell and former Jimi Hendrix drummer Mitch Mitchell. During this busy and fruitful period Bruce found time to add vocals to Carla Bley's classic album *Escalator Over The Hill*, and Bley was also a member of the 1975 version of the Jack Bruce Band. In 1979 he toured as a member of John McLaughlin's Mahavishnu Orchestra. The 80s started with a new Jack Bruce Band which featured former Bakerloo, Colosseum and Humble Pie guitarist Dave 'Clem' Clempson and David Sancious. They found particular favour in Germany and played there regularly. The ill-fated heavy rock trio BLT formed in 1981 with guitarist Robin Trower and drummer Bill Lordan but folded after two albums. Their debut, *BLT*, reached the US Top 40. During the 80s Bruce kept a low profile after having experienced severe drug problems in the 70s. In 1987 the perplexing album *Automatic* appeared. This obviously low-budget work had Bruce accompanied by a Fairlight machine, an odd coupling for a musician whose previous collections had consistently teamed him with highly talented drummers. Much more impressive was 1990's *A Question Of Time* which attempted to restore Bruce's now lapsed career to its former glory. Other than his long-term admirers Bruce has found it difficult to reach a wide new audience. Those that have followed his career understand his major shifts from jazz to heavy rock, but his position in today's musical climate is hard to place. His vocal work accompanied by his emotional piano playing has been his particularly strong point of late. In 1994 he formed BBM, with Gary Moore and Baker. Two parts Cream, the unit might have been more aptly called Semi-Skimmed. This was his most rock-orientated project for many years and showed clearly that Bruce was in sparkling form, fit and well. Bruce remains forever (probably because of Cream) the most renowned and respected of rock bassists.

●ALBUMS: *Songs For A Tailor* (Polydor 1969)★★★★, *Things We Like* (Polydor 1970)★★★, *Harmony Row* (Polydor 1971)★★★, *Out Of The Storm* (Polydor 1974)★★★, *How's Tricks* (RSO 1977)★★★, *I've Always Wanted To Do This* (Epic 1980)★★★, with Robin Trower *Truce* (Chrysalis 1982)★★★, *Automatic* (President 1987)★★, *A Question Of Time* (Epic 1990)★★★, *And Friends Live At The Bottom Line* (Traditional Line 1992)★★★, *Something Else* (1993)★★★, *Cities Of the Heart* (CMP 1994)★★★★, with Paul Jones *Alexis Korner Memorial Concert Vol 1* (Indigo 1995)★★★.

●COMPILATIONS: *Jack Bruce At His Best* (Polydor 1972)★★★, *Greatest Hits* (Polydor 1980)★★★, *Willpower* (Polydor 1989)★★★, *The Collection* (Castle 1992)★★★, with BBM *Around the Next Dream* (Virgin 1994)★★★.

BUBBLE PUPPY

One of the last groups signed to the legendary International Artists label, Bubble Puppy also gave the company its most substantial hit, 'Hot Smoke And Sasafrass'. More mainstream than many of their contemporaries, this Texan quartet's debut album, *A Gathering Of Promises*, showed traces of Jimi Hendrix, Cream and Moby Grape. An unstable unit, Bubble Puppy moved labels to ABC in 1970 and changed their name to Demian. Their eponymous album relied on progressive styles at the expense of melody and this aggregation was allowed to wither away. Rod Prince, the Puppy's lead guitarist, re-established the group in 1977 under the title Sirius, and the resultant release, *Electric Flow*, recalled something of the old group's erstwhile fire. Ten years later he re-emerged with a reconstituted Bubble Puppy and an album, *Wheels Go Round*, which bore a kinship with ZZ Top.

●ALBUMS: *A Gathering Of Promises* (International Artists 1969)★★, as Demian *Demian* (ABC 1971)★★, as Sirius *Electric Flow* (1977)★★, *Wheels Go Round* (One Big Guitar 1987)★★.

BUCHANAN, ROY

b. 23 September 1939, Ozark, Alabama, USA, d. 14 August 1988. The son of a preacher, Buchanan discovered gospel music through the influence of travelling revivalists. This interest engendered his love of R&B and having served an apprenticeship playing guitar in scores of minor groups, he secured fame on joining Dale Hawkins in 1958. Although Buchanan is often erroneously credited with the break on the singer's much-lauded 'Suzie Q', contributions on 'My Babe' and 'Grandma's House', confirmed his remarkable talent. Buchanan also recorded with Freddie Cannon, Bob Luman and the Hawks, and completed several low-key singles in his own right before retiring in 1962. However, he re-emerged in the following decade with *Roy Buchanan*, an accomplished, versatile set that included a slow, hypnotic rendition of the C&W standard 'Sweet Dreams'. *Loading Zone* was an accomplished album and contained two of his finest (and longest) outings; the pulsating 'Green Onions' featured shared solos with the song's co-composer Steve Cropper and the extraordinary 'Ramon's Blues' (again with Cropper). His trademark battered Fender Telecaster guitar gave a distinctive treble-sounding tone to his work. A series of similiarly crafted albums were released, before the guitarist again drifted out of the limelight. His career was rekindled in 1986 with *When A Guitar Plays The Blues*, but despite enjoying the accolades of many contemporaries, including Robbie Robertson, Buchanan was never comfortable with the role of virtuoso. A shy, reticent individual, he made several unsuccessful suicide attempts before hanging himself in a police cell in 1988, following his arrest on a drink-driving charge.

●ALBUMS: *Roy Buchanan* (Polydor 1972)★★★, *Second Album* (Polydor 1973)★★★, *That's What I'm Here For* (Polydor 1974)★★★, *In The Beginning* (Polydor 1974)★★★, *Rescue Me* (Polydor 1975)★★, *Live Stock* (Polydor 1975)★★, *A Street Called Straight* (Polydor 1976)★★★, *Loading Zone* (Polydor 1977)★★★, *You're Not Alone* (Polydor 1978)★★, *My Babe* (Waterhouse 1981)★★, *When A Guitar Plays The Blues* (Alligator 1986)★★★, *Dancing On The Edge* (Alligator 1987)★★, *Hot Wires* (Alligator 1987)★★.

●COMPILATIONS: *Early Roy Buchanan* (Krazy Kat 1989)★★★, *Sweet Dreams: The Anthology* (Mercury Chronicles 1992)★★★★, *The Early Years* (Krazy Kat/Interstate 1993)★★★.

●VIDEOS: *Custom Made* (Kay Jazz 1988).

BUCKLEY, TIM

b. 14 February 1947, Washington, DC, USA, d. 29 June 1975. This radiant talent began his solo career in the folk clubs of Los Angeles. He was discovered by manager Herb Cohen who secured the singer's recording deal with the prestigious Elektra label. *Tim Buckley* introduced the artist's skills, but his vision flourished more fully on a second selection, *Goodbye And Hello*. Although underscored by arrangements now deemed over-elaborate, the set features 'Morning Glory', one of Buckley's most evocative compositions, as well as the urgent 'I Never Asked To Be Your Mountain', a pulsating performance that indicated his future inclinations. With *Happy Sad* the singer abandoned the use of poetic metaphor, characteristic of its predecessor, to create a subtle, more intimate music. He forsook the services of long-time lyricist Larry Beckett, while Lee Underwood (guitar) and David Friedman (vibes) sculpted a sympathetic backdrop to Buckley's highly personal, melancholic compositions. This expansive style was maintained on *Blue Afternoon* and *Lorca*, but while the former largely consisted of haunting, melodious folk-jazz performances, the latter offered a more radical, experimental direction. Its emphasis on improvisation inspired the free-form *Starsailor*, an uncompromising, almost atonal work, on which the singer's voice functioned as an extra instrument in a series of *avant garde* compositions. The set included the delicate 'Song To The Siren', which was successfully revived by This Mortal Coil in 1983. Buckley's work was now deemed uncommercial and, disillusioned, he sought alternative employment, including a spell as a chauffeur for Sly Stone. Paradoxically, the soul singer's brand of rhythmic funk proved significant, and when Buckley re-emerged with *Greetings From LA*, it marked a newfound fascination with contemporary black music. Sexually frank, this pulsating set was a commercial success, although its power was then diluted over two subsequent releases of only intermittent interest. Tim Buckley died in June 1975, having ingested a fatal heroin/morphine cocktail. His influence has increased with time and a recent archive selection, *Dream Letter*, culled from the singer's 1968 London performances, is a fitting testament to his impassioned creativity. Renewed interest in Buckley came in the early 90s when many of his albums were well reviewed when reissued on CD.

●ALBUMS: *Tim Buckley* (Elektra 1966)★★★, *Goodbye And Hello* (Elektra 1967)★★★, *Happy Sad* (Elektra

1968)★★★★, *Blue Afternoon* (Straight 1969)★★★★, *Lorca* (Elektra 1969)★★★, *Starsailor* (Straight 1970)★★★, *Greetings From LA* (Warners 1972)★★★, *Sefronia* (DiscReet 1974)★★, *Look At The Fool* (DiscReet 1975)★★, *Dream Letter-Live In London 1968* (Demon 1990)★★★★, *The Peel Sessions* (Strange Fruit 1991)★★★, *Live At The LA Troubadour 1969* (Edsel 1994)★★★, *Honeyman* 1973 live recording (Edsel 1995)★★★.
●COMPILATIONS: *The Best Of Tim Buckley* (Rhino 1983)★★★.

BUDGIE

This hard rock group was formed in Cardiff, Wales, by John Burke Shelley (b. 10 April 1947, Cardiff, South Glamorgan, Wales; bass/acoustic guitar/lead vocals) and Ray Phillips (b. 1 March 1949; drums) in 1968. Joined by Tony Bourge (b. 23 November 1948, Cardiff, South Glamorgan, Wales; lead guitar/vocals) the trio established a substantial following in the south Wales college and club circuit and were subsequently signed to MCA Records. Plying their trade in a basic, heavy riffing style, the standard was set with the first single, charmingly entitled 'Crash Course To Brain Surgery'. The vagaries of early 70s British album artwork were typified by the treatment given to Budgie's releases and promotional material depicted ludicrous images of a budgerigar variously posed, dressed as a fighter pilot (staring nobly out into the far horizon), a Nazi Gestapo officer, or as a squadron of fighter budgies flying in formation, tearing into combat. Founder member Phillips quit in 1974 before the recording of their fourth album and was replaced by Pete Boot (b. 30 September 1950, West Bromwich, Staffordshire, England), who in turn departed that year before Steve Williams took over. The exiled drummer formed Ray Phillips' Woman back in Wales, then Tredegar in 1982. With the success of *In For The Kill*, Budgie won over a wider audience, although they were held in higher esteem in Europe during this period. Their sixth album, *If I Was Brittania I'd Waive The Rules*, was their first on A&M Records. *Impeckable* was the last to feature Bourge, who left in 1978, joining Phillips in Tredegar. He was replaced by former George Hatcher Band guitarist John Thomas. The group's popularity grew in the USA, resulting in Budgie's touring there for two years, with Rob Kendrick (ex-Trapeze) standing in for Thomas. Returning to Britain, and now signed to RCA, Budgie found themselves fitting in well with the new heavy rock scene, and despite being label-less for much of the mid-80s, their reputation and influence on a younger generation of musicians brought them consistent work until Shelley wound up the group in 1988. He subsequently worked with a new trio, Superclarkes. Phillips used the name Six Ton Budgie (from a journalist who commented that the original band sounded more like a 'Six Ton Budgie') for a new line-up featuring his son, Justin, on guitar, who still play out regularly with versions of his former group's standards.

●ALBUMS: *Budgie* (MCA 1971)★★, *Squawk* (MCA 1972)★★, *Never Turn Your Back On A Friend* (MCA 1973)★★, *In For The Kill* (MCA 1974)★★, *Bandolier* (MCA 1975)★★, *If I Was Brittania I'd Waive The Rules* (A&M 1976)★★, *Impeckable* (A&M 1978)★★, *Power Supply* (Active 1980)★★, *Nightflight* (RCA 1981)★★, *Deliver Us From Evil* (RCA 1982)★★.
●COMPILATIONS: *Best Of* (MCA 1976)★★, *An Ecstacy Of Fumbling: The Definitive Anthology* (Repertoire 1996)★★★.

BUFFETT, JIMMY

b. 25 December 1946, Pascagoula, Mississippi, USA, but raised in Mobile, Alabama. Country rock singer Buffett describes his songs as '90 per cent autobiographical', a statement attested to by his narratives of wine, women and song. He is 'the son of the son of a sailor', and he describes his grandfather's life in 'The Captain And The Kid'. His father was a naval architect, who often took Buffett on sailing trips. Buffett studied journalism at the University of Southern California, and described those years and his urge to perform in 'Migration'. Working as the Nashville correspondent for *Billboard* magazine, he built up the contacts that led to his first albums on Barnaby Records. The albums were not well produced and the best song was one he re-recorded, 'In The Shelter'. On a train journey, he and Jerry Jeff Walker wrote the poignant 'Railroad Lady', which has been recorded by Lefty Frizzell and Merle Haggard. Buffett settled in Key West and although initially involved in smuggling, he changed his ways when offered $25,000 to make an album for ABC Records. He went to Nashville, recorded *A White Sport Coat And A Pink Crustacean* for $10,000 and bought a boat with the remainder. The album included several story-songs about misdemeanours ('The Great Filling Station Holdup', 'Peanut Butter Conspiracy'), together with the lazy feel of 'He Went To Paris', which was recorded by Waylon Jennings. His humorous 'Why Don't We Get Drunk And Screw?' was written under the pseudonym of Marvin Gardens, who made imaginary appearances on Buffett's one-man concerts. *Living And Dying In 3/4 Time* included his US Top 30 hit, 'Come Monday'. Its ban in the UK by the BBC because of a reference to Hush Puppies shoes led to a shrewd Jonathan King cover, referring to tennis shoes instead. Buffett's 1974 album, *AIA*, was named after the access road to the beach in Florida and he commented, 'I never planned to make a whole series of albums about Key West. It was a natural process.' Buffett wrote the music for a film about cattle rustlers, *Rancho Deluxe*, scripted by Buffett's brother-in-law Tom McGuane. McGuane described Buffett's music as lying 'at the curious hinterland where Hank Williams and Xavier Cugat meet', and Buffett was the first person to consistently bring Caribbean rhythms to Nashville. (David Allan Coe, who recorded an attack on him called 'Jimmy Buffett', nevertheless copied his style.)
In 1975, Buffett formed the Coral Reefer Band and their

first album together, *Havana Daydreaming*, included a song about the boredom of touring: 'This Hotel Room'. His next album, arguably his best, *Changes In Latitudes, Changes In Attitudes*, included the million-selling single 'Margaritaville'. A bitter verse about 'old men in tank tops' was initially omitted, but was included on Buffett's irrepressible concert album, *You Had To Be There*. Buffett made the US Top 10 with *Son Of A Son Of A Sailor*, which included 'Cheeseburger In Paradise', a US pop hit, and 'Livingston Saturday Night', which was featured in the film *FM*. Buffett continued to record prolifically, moving over to contemporary rock sounds, but his songs began to lack sparkle. The best tracks on two of his albums were remakes of standards, 'Stars Fell On Alabama' and 'On A Slow Boat To China'. His *Hot Water* album included guest appearances by Rita Coolidge, the Neville Brothers, James Taylor and Steve Winwood, but it failed to restore him to the charts. Buffett is a major concert attraction, especially in Florida where he addresses his fans as 'Parrotheads'. Indeed, the magnificent 72-track, 4-CD box set *Boats Beaches, Bars And Ballads*, includes the Parrothead Handbook. *Fruitcakes* included two hilarious tracks, 'Everybody's Got A Cousin In Miama' and 'Fruitcakes' itself. The excessive length of both tracks (over seven minutes each) indicated that Buffett was ignoring potential radio and video play and merely playing for his fans. His songs continue to reflect his Key West lifestyle and to quote 'He Went To Paris': 'Some of it's tragic and some of it's magic, but I had a good life all the way.'

●ALBUMS: *Down To Earth* (Barnaby 1970)★★, *A White Sport Coat And A Pink Crustacean* (ABC 1973)★★★, *Living And Dying In 3/4 Time* (ABC 1974)★★, *A1A* (ABC 1974)★★★, *Rancho DeLuxe* soundtrack (United Artists 1975)★★★, *Havana Daydreaming* (ABC 1976)★★★, *High Cumberland Jubilee* (Barnaby 1976)★★★, *Changes In Latitudes, Changes In Attitudes* (ABC 1977)★★★, *Son Of A Son Of A Sailor* (ABC 1978)★★★, *You Had To Be There* (ABC 1978)★★★, *Volcano* (MCA 1979)★★★, *Coconut Telegraph* (MCA 1980)★★, *Somewhere Over China* (MCA 1981)★★, *One Particular Harbour* (MCA 1982)★★, *Fast Times At Ridgemont High* (Full Moon/Asylum 1982)★★, *Riddles In The Sand* (MCA 1984)★★, *Last Mango In Paris* (MCA 1985)★★, *Floridays* (MCA 1986)★★, *Hot Water* (MCA 1988)★★, *Off To See The Lizard* (MCA 1989)★★, *Always* soundtrack (MCA 1990)★★, *Live Feeding Frenzy* (MCA 1990)★★, *Before The Beach* (Margaritaville/MCA 1993)★★, *Fruitcakes* (MCA 1994)★★★★, *Barometer Soup* (Margaritaville/MCA 1995)★★★★, *Banana Wind* (Margaritaville 1996)★★★★, *Christmas Island* (Margaritaville 1996)★★★.

●COMPILATIONS: box set *Songs You Know By Heart - Greatest Hits* (MCA 1985)★★★★, *Boats Beaches, Bars And Ballads* 4-CD box set (MCA 1992)★★★★, *All The Great Hits* (Prism Leisure 1994)★★★.

●FURTHER READING: *The Jimmy Buffett Scrapbook*, Mark Humphrey with Harris Lewine.

BURNETTE, ROCKY

b. Jonathan 'Rocky' Burnette, 12 June 1953, Memphis, Tennessee, USA. Burnette was the son of pioneering rock 'n' roll trio member Johnny Burnette and nephew of fellow member Dorsey Burnette. Dorsey's son Billy Burnette (later a solo performer and member of Fleetwood Mac) was born within a few weeks of Rocky and some sources like to claim that Johnny and Dorsey coined the term 'Rockabilly' in their honour. This does seem to be unlikely, however. Like his father, Rocky was a keen fisherman who claimed that when his father died in 1964 (drowned in a boating accident) he went fishing himself rather than attend the funeral. He had also been a close friend of Elvis Presley until his father had fallen out with him over a publishing agreement, and the family had moved to California. He started out in the music business around 1967 as a teenage songwriter, working for Acuff-Rose publishers. His songs were later recorded by the Osmonds and David Cassidy, for whom he wrote on a production line basis. After graduating in 1971 he studied theatre, cinematography and the Bible at college, before returning to music to release his first solo album for Curb in the early 70s, which was only available in the US. His one solo hit was 'Tired Of Toein' The Line', written in less than 20 minutes and recorded at Rockfield studios in Wales. A surprise hit on both sides of the Atlantic, he nevertheless declined to provide a follow-up. He re-emerged in 1982 with *Heart Stopper* before putting together his New Rock 'N' Roll Trio, which consisted of Paul Burlinson (bass, the only surviving member of the original trio) and Johnny Black (brother of original Presley bass player Bill Black), and Tony Austin, to record *Get Hot Or Go Home* at Sun Studios, Memphis.

●ALBUMS: *Son Of Rock And Roll* (EMI 1980)★★★, *Heart Stopper* (EMI 1982)★★★, *Get Hot Or Go Home* (EMI 1983)★★★.

BURNING SPEAR

b. Winston Rodney, 1948, St. Ann's Bay, Jamaica, West Indies. Burning Spear, who appropriated the name from former Mau Mau leader Jomo Kenyatta, then president of Kenya, entered the music business in 1969 after fellow St. Ann's artist Bob Marley organised an audition for him with his erstwhile producer Coxsone Dodd. The three songs Spear sang for Dodd that Sunday afternoon included his eventual debut, 'Door Peep', a sombre, spiritual chant quite unlike anything that had so far emerged in the music, although a reference point may perhaps be found in the Ethiopians and Joe Higgs. 'Door Peep' and other early Spear recordings like 'We Are Free' and 'Zion Higher' emerged in the UK on the Bamboo and Banana labels. Spear continued to make records for Dodd until 1974, including 'Ethiopians Live It Out', 'This Population' and 'New Civilisation', nearly all in a serious, cultural style, mostly without any commercial success, although 'Joe Frazier' (aka 'He

Prayed') did make the Jamaican Top 5 in 1972. Most of these songs can be found on the two albums Spear completed for Dodd. In 1975 Ocho Rios sound system owner Jack Ruby (real name Laurence Lindo) approached the singer, and the two, along with pick-up backing vocalists Rupert Wellington and Delroy Hines, began working on the material that eventually emerged as *Marcus Garvey* (1975), in honour of the great St. Ann's-born pan-Africanist. 'Marcus Garvey' and 'Slavery Days' were released as singles, perfectly capturing the mood of the times and becoming huge local hits. The public were at last ready for Burning Spear and when the album finally emerged it was hailed as an instant classic. Spear became recognized as the most likely candidate for the kind of international success Bob Marley And The Wailers were beginning to enjoy, and soon *Marcus Garvey* had been snapped up by Island Records which released it in the UK with an added track and in remixed form. This tampering with the mix, including the speeding up of several tracks, presumably in order to make the album more palatable to white ears, raised the hackles of many critics and fans. Its popularity caused Island to release a dubwise companion set entitled *Garvey's Ghost* (1976). Rodney began to release music on his own Spear label at the end of 1975, the first issue being another classic, 'Travelling' (actually a revision of the earlier Studio One album track 'Journey'), followed by 'Spear Burning' (1976), 'The Youth' (1976), 'Throw Down Your Arms' (1977), the 12-inch 'Institution' (1977), 'Dry And Heavy' (1977), 'Free' (1977) and 'Nyah Keith' (1979). He also produced 'On That Day' by youth singer Burning Junior, and 'Love Everyone' by Phillip Fullwood, both in 1976. That same year Jack Ruby released 'Man In The Hills', followed by the album of the same name, again on Island, which marked the end of their collaboration. Spear also dropped Willington and Hines. 1977 saw the release of *Dry & Heavy*, recorded at Harry J's Studio, which satisfyingly reworked many of his Studio One classics, including 'Swell Headed', 'Creation Rebel', 'This Race' and 'Free Again'. In October that year he made an electrifying appearance at London's Rainbow Theatre, backed by veteran trumpeter Bobby Ellis and the UK reggae band Aswad. Island released an album of the performance that inexplicably failed to capture the excitement generated.

In 1978 Spear parted with Island and issued *Marcus Children*, arguably his best album since *Marcus Garvey*, released in the UK on Island Records' subsidiary One Stop as *Social Living*, again using members of Aswad alongside the usual Kingston session men. In 1980 he signed to EMI who issued his next album, the stunning *Hail H.I.M.*, produced by Spear and Family Man Barrett at Bob Marley's Tuff Gong studio, on his own Burning Spear subsidiary. Two excellent dubs of *Social Living* and *Hail H.I.M.* also appeared as *Living Dub Vols. 1* and *2*, mixed by engineer Sylvan Morris. Throughout the following years to the present, Spear has continued to

release albums regularly, as well as touring the USA and elsewhere. *Resistance*, nominated for a Grammy in 1984, was a particularly strong set highlighting Spear's impressive, soulful patois against a muscular rhythmic backdrop. *People Of The World* similarly saw his backing group, the Burning Band, which now encompassed an all-female horn section, shine. His 1988 set, *Mistress Music*, added rock musicians, including former members of Jefferson Airplane, though artistically it was his least successful album. *Mek We Dweet*, recorded at Tuff Gong studios, was a return to his unique, intense style. His lyrical concerns - black culture and history, Garveyism and Rasta beliefs, and universal love - have been consistently and powerfully expressed during his recording career.

●ALBUMS: *Studio One Presents Burning Spear* (Studio One 1973)★★★, *Rocking Time* (Studio One 1974)★★★, *Marcus Garvey* (Mango/Island 1975)★★★★★, *Man In The Hills* (Fox-Wolf/Island 1976)★★★★, *Garvey's Ghost* (Mango/Island 1976)★★★★, *Dry & Heavy* (Mango/Island 1977)★★★★, *Burning Spear Live* (Island 1977)★★★, *Marcus Children* aka *Social Living* (Burning Spear/One Stop 1978)★★★★, *Living Dub* (Burning Spear/Heartbeat 1979)★★★, *Hail H.I.M.* (Burning Spear/EMI 1980)★★★, *Living Dub Vol. 2* (Burning Spear 1981)★★★, *Farover* (Burning Spear/ Heartbeat 1982)★★★, *Fittest Of The Fittest* (Burning Spear/ Heartbeat 1983)★★★, *Resistance* (Heartbeat 1985)★★★★, *People Of The World* (Slash/Greensleeves 1986)★★★, *Mistress Music* (Slash/Greensleeves 1988)★★, *Live In Paris: Zenith '88* double album (Slash/Greensleeves 1989)★★★, *Mek We Dweet* (Mango/ Island 1990)★★★, *Jah Kingdom* (Mango/Island 1992)★★★, *The World Should Know* (Mango/Island 1993)★★★, *Rasta Business* (Heartbeat 1996)★★★.

●COMPILATIONS: *Reggae Greats* (Island 1985)★★★★, *Selection* (EMI 1987)★★★★, *100th Anniversary Marcus Garvey* and *Garvey's Ghost* (Mango/Island 1990)★★★★, *Chant Down Babylon: The Island Anthology* (Island 1996)★★★★.

BUTLER, JERRY

b. 8 December 1939, Sunflower, Mississippi, USA. Jerry, older brother of Billy Butler, moved to Chicago as a child and was later part of the city's burgeoning gospel circuit. He subsequently joined several secular groups, including the Roosters, an aspiring trio of Sam Gooden and Richard and Arthur Brooks. Butler then suggested they add his friend, Curtis Mayfield, on guitar. Now called the Impressions, the quintet secured a Top 3 US R&B hit with the haunting 'For Your Precious Love' (1958). However, the label credit, 'Jerry Butler And The Impressions', caused friction within the group. A second single, 'Come Back My Love', was less successful and Butler left for a solo career. His early releases were minor hits until 'He Will Break Your Heart' reached number 1 in the US R&B and number 7 in the pop charts in 1960. The song was written by

Mayfield who added guitar and sang backing vocals. Their differences clearly resolved, two subsequent hits, 'Find Another Girl' and 'I'm A Telling You' (both 1961), featured the same partnership. Mayfield's involvement lessened as the Impressions' own career developed, but Jerry's chart run continued. 'Make It Easy On Yourself' (1962) and 'I Stand Accused' (1964) were among his finest singles. Butler switched to Mercury in 1966 where he honed the style that won him his 'Ice Man' epithet. 'Hey Western Union Man' and 'Only The Strong Survive' topped the soul chart in 1968 and 1969, while duets with Gene Chandler and Brenda Lee Eager punctuated his early 70s recordings. With his brother, Billy Butler, he formed the Butler Writers Workshop, which encouraged aspiring songwriters and musicians, amongst whom were Marvin Yancey and Chuck Jackson of the Independents and Natalie Cole. Jerry's Motown releases preceded a more successful spell with Philadelphia Int., while the 80s saw his work appear on Fountain and CTI. *Up On Love* (1980) mixes the best of his Vee Jay singles with that first Impressions' hit. Butler is now an elected official in Chicago.

●ALBUMS: *Jerry Butler Esquire* (Abner 1959)★★★, *He Will Break Your Heart* (Vee Jay 1960)★★★, *Love Me* (Vee Jay 1961)★★, *Aware Of Love* (Vee Jay 1961)★★★, *Moon River* (Vee Jay 1962)★★, *Folk Songs* (Vee Jay 1963)★★, *Need To Belong* (Vee Jay 1964)★★★, with Betty Everett *Delicious Together* (Vee Jay 1964)★★★, *Soul Artistry* (Mercury 1967)★★★, *Mr. Dream Merchant* (Mercury 1967)★★★, *Jerry Butler's Golden Hits Live* (Mercury 1968)★★, *Just Beautiful* (Mercury 1968)★★★, *The Soul Goes On* (Mercury 1968)★★★, *The Ice Man Cometh* (Mercury 1968)★★★★, *Ice On Ice* (Mercury 1970)★★★★, *You & Me* (Mercury 1970)★★★, *Special Memory* (Mercury 1970)★★★, *Jerry Butler Sings Assorted Sounds By Assorted Friends And Relatives* (Mercury 1971)★★★, with Gene Chandler *Gene & Jerry - One & One* (Mercury 1971)★★★, *The Sagittarious Movement* (Mercury 1971)★★★, *The Spice Of Life* (Mercury 1972)★★★, *Melinda* (Mercury 1972)★★★, *Introducing The Ice Man Band* (Mercury 1972)★★★, with Brenda Lee Eagar *The Love We Have, The Love We Had* (Mercury 1973)★★★, *The Power Of Love* (Mercury 1973)★★★, *Sweet Sixteen* (Mercury 1974)★★★, *Love's On The Menu* (Motown 1976)★★, *Make It Easy On Yourself* (Motown 1976), *Suite For The Single Girl* (Motown 1977)★★, with Thelma Houston *Thelma And Jerry* (Motown 1977)★★, with Houston *Two To One* (Motown 1978)★★, *It All Comes Out In My Song* (Motown 1978)★★, *Nothing Says I Love You Like I Love You* (PIR 1978)★★★, *Best Love I Ever Had* (PIR 1981)★★★, *Ice 'N Hot* (Fountain 1982)★★, *Time & Faith* (1993)★★★, *Simply Beautiful* (Valley Vue 1994)★★★.

●COMPILATIONS: *The Best Of Jerry Butler* (1962)★★★, *More Of The Best Of Jerry Butler* (1965)★★★, *Best Of Jerry Butler* (Mercury 1970)★★★★, *The Vintage Years* double album shared with the Impressions (Sire 1977)★★★, *Up On Love* (1980)★★★, *Only The Strong Survive* (Club 1985)★★★★, *Whatever You Want* (Charly 1986)★★★★, *Soul Workshop* (Charly 1986)★★★★, *The Legendary Philadelphia Hits* (Mercury 1987)★★★★, *Iceman: The Mercury Years* (Mercury 1992)★★★★.

BUTTS BAND

Formed in 1972, the Butts Band included two former members of the Doors, Robbie Krieger (b. 8 January 1946, Los Angeles, California, USA; guitar) and John Densmore (b. 1 December 1945, Los Angeles, California, USA; drums). After the 1973 dissolution of the Doors, the two musicians teamed up with vocalist Jess Roden, formerly of Bronco. Roy Davies (keyboards) and Philip Chen (bass) were added to the line-up. One of the first white American groups to specialize in reggae music, the group signed to Blue Thumb Records. The self-titled debut album did not chart. For the second and final album, *Hear And Now*, Krieger and Densmore fired the rest of the band and formed a completely new line-up, featuring Michael Stull (guitar, keyboards), Alex Richman (keyboards, vocals), Karl Ruckner (bass) and Mike Berkowitz (drums). It, too, failed to chart and the group disbanded in 1975. Krieger, Densmore returned to their solo careers and Roden, recorded a number of solo albums for Island Records.

●ALBUMS: *The Butts Band* (Blue Thumb 1974)★★, *Hear And Now* (ABC 1975)★★.

BUZZCOCKS

Originally formed in Manchester in February 1976, the group consisted of Pete Shelley (b. Peter McNeish, 17 April 1955; vocals/guitar), Howard Devoto (b. Howard Trafford; vocals), Steve Diggle (bass) and John Maher (drums). Taking their name from a Time Out review of *Rock Follies*, a support spot on the Sex Pistols' infamous 'Anarchy' tour prefaced the Buzzcocks debut recording, the EP *Spiral Scratch*, which included one of punk's most enduring anthems, 'Boredom'. The quartet's undeveloped promise was momentarily short-circuited when Devoto sensationally left in February 1977, only to resurface later that year with Magazine. A reshuffled Buzzcocks, with Shelley taking lead vocal and Garth Davies (later replaced by Steve Garvey) on bass, won a major recording contract with United Artists. During the next three years, they recorded some of the finest pop-punk singles of their era, including the Devoto/Shelley song 'Orgasm Addict' and, after the split, Shelley's 'What Do I Get?', 'Love You More', the classic 'Ever Fallen In Love (With Someone You Shouldn't've)', 'Promises' (with Diggle), 'Everybody's Happy Nowadays' and Diggle's 'Harmony In My Head'. After three albums and nearly five years on the road, the group fell victim to disillusionment and Shelley quit for a solo career. Steve Diggle re-emerged with Flag Of Convenience, but neither party could reproduce the best of the Buzzcocks. With hindsight, the Buzzcocks' influence upon British 'indie-pop' of the late 80s ranks alongside that of the Ramones or the Velvet

Underground. The group re-formed in October 1989, then again in 1990 with former Smiths' drummer Mike Joyce added to their ranks. For their first major tour since the break-up, 1993's 35-date itinerary, Shelley and Diggle were joined by Tony Arber (bass) and Phil Barker (drums). Garvey was said to be a family man in New York, while Maher was unable to commit because of his devotion to motor racing. The Buzzcocks continue to be feted by the cognoscenti, and support tours with Nirvana and a genuinely riveting comeback album (*Trade Test Transmissions*) added to their legacy, although a disappointing live album failed to convince.
●ALBUMS: *Another Music In A Different Kitchen* (United Artists 1978)★★★★, *Love Bites* (United Artists 1978)★★★, *A Different Kind Of Tension* (United Artists 1979)★★★, *Trade Test Transmissions* (Castle 1993)★★★, *French* (IRS 1995)★★, *All Set* (IRS 1996)★★.
●COMPILATIONS: *Singles - Going Steady* (EMI 1981)★★★★, *Lest We Forget* (ROIR 1988)★★★, *Live At The Roxy, April '77* (Absolutely Free 1989)★★★, *The Peel Sessions Album* (Strange Fruit 1990)★★★, *Time's Up* rec. 1976 (Document 1991)★★, *Product* 3-CD box set (EMI 1989)★★★, *Operator's Manual - Buzzcocks Best* (EMI 1991)★★★★, *Entertaining Friends* (EMI 1992)★★★, *Chronology* (EMI 1997)★★★.
●VIDEOS: *Auf Wiedersehen* (Ikon Video 1989), *Live Legends* (Castle Music Pictures 1990).
●FURTHER READING: *Buzzcocks: The Complete History*, Tony McGartland.

BYRON, DAVID
b. David Garrick, 29 January 1947, Essex, England, d. 28 February 1985. Byron began his music career as vocalist with the Stalkers, an Essex-based act which, by 1969, had evolved into Uriah Heep. Although subjected to critical denigration, the group became one of the 70s' leading hard rock/heavy metal attractions, thanks in part to the singer's powerful delivery. In 1975, Byron completed a solo album, *Take No Prisoners*, as excessive alcohol consumption put his position within the line-up under increasing pressure. He was fired the following year, but hopes of an artistic rebirth with Rough Diamond proved ill-founded, and this highly touted attraction featuring Dave Clempson broke apart within a year. Bereft of a regular group, he completed *Baby Faced Killer*, but the set appeared during the height of the punk boom, and was not a commercial success. A similar fate befell the ensuing Byron Band whose ill-focused *On The Rocks* did little to further their leader's progress. They dissolved soon after its release, after which the disconsolate vocalist attempted to sustain his career, with increasingly faltering results. He died in 1985 as a result of a heart attack.
●ALBUMS: *Take No Prisoners* (Bronze 1975)★★, *Baby Faced Killer* (Arista 1977)★, *This Day And Age* (Arista 1980)★, as the Byron Band: *On The Rocks* (Creole 1981)★, *Bad Widow* (Rockport 1984)★.

CACTUS
Formed in 1969, the original Cactus consisted of Rusty Day (vocals), Jim McCarty (guitar, ex-Mitch Ryder and Buddy Miles' Express), and two former members of Vanilla Fudge, Tim Bogert (bass) and Carmine Appice (drums). Their exciting, uncompromising brand of hard rock was best displayed on *One Way ... Or Another*, but internal disputes hampered their progress. Day and McCarty left to join Detroit in 1971, but although a reshaped line-up completed *Restrictions*, the initial rhythm section abandoned their creation to form Beck, Bogert And Appice. Recent arrival Duane Hitchins (keyboards) then instigated the New Cactus Band with Mike Pinera (guitar, ex-Iron Butterfly), Roland Robinson (bass) and Jerry Norris (drums), but the group disintegrated in 1973.
●ALBUMS: *Cactus* (Atco 1970)★★, *One Way ... Or Another* (Atco 1971)★★★, *Restrictions* (Atco 1971)★★, *'Ot 'N' Sweaty* one side recorded live (Atco 1972)★★, *Son Of Cactus* (Atco 1973)★★.
●COMPILATIONS: *Cactology: The Cactus Collection* (Rhino 1996)★★★.

CADOGAN, SUSAN
b. Alison Susan Cadogan, c.1959, Kingston, Jamaica, West Indies. Cadogan studied to be and qualified as a librarian. Her singing inspired the Jamaican Broadcasting DJ Jerry Lewis to introduce her to Lee Perry. Cadogan recorded at the Black Ark Studios a version of Millie Jackson's soul hit, 'Hurts So Good'. In 1974 the single appeared through Dennis Harris' DIP International label and topped the reggae chart in the UK. The success of the single led to the Magnet label licensing the tune and taking the song into the Top 5 of the pop chart in April 1975. Whilst Cadogan enjoyed the benefit of her success the Black Wax label released, 'Love My Life', which failed to emulate the providence of her debut. The Magnet label released the official follow-up, 'Love Me Baby', which although a Top 20 hit marked the end of Cadogan's foray into the UK pop charts. Trojan Records signed her and released a compilation of cover versions including 'Fever', 'Don't You Burn Your Bridges', 'Congratulations' and 'In The Ghetto'. The production was in a similar vein to John Holt's *1000 Volts* series and proved a commercial success. The single 'How Do You Feel The Morning After' intensified her notoriety but was followed by intermittent output. By 1982 she successfully recorded cover

versions of the soul classics, 'Piece Of My Heart' and 'Tracks Of My Tears'. In 1983, with Hawkeye producing, she recorded 'Love Me' and in combination with Ruddy Thomas the chart-topping, '(You Know How To Make Me) Feel So Good'. She returned in fine style with the Mad Professor who in 1992 recorded an album hailing her comeback. The Professor also utilized her re-recording of 'Hurts So Good' for U-Roy's 'The Hurt Is Good', from his Ariwa Records' *Smile A While*. It was Cadogan's rendition of the song that inspired a successful cover version in 1995 by Jimmy Somerville and in turn regenerated an interest in the original.

●ALBUMS: *Doing It Her Way* (Magnet 1975)★★★, *Hurt So Good* (Trojan 1976)★★★, *Soulful Reggae* (Ariwa 1992)★★★, *Chemistry Of Love* (Imp 1995)★★★.

CAFÉ SOCIETY

The predecessor to Tom Robinson's solo career, Café Society might well have developed on their own account, had the fates not conspired against them. The band were formed in 1973 with Hereward Kaye and Ray Doyle, and picked up residencies at the Troubadour Club and Bunjies in London's Earl's Court and Charing Cross districts. There they were seen by the Kinks' Ray Davies, who signed them to his new label, Konk. However, such good auspices turned sour when Davies insisted on producing an album to his own satisfaction, rather than the ambitions of the folk rock-fixated group. Absent for much of the period due to the Kinks' touring commitments, Davies imposed electric instruments on Café Society and the results were not impressive. The set was eventually released in 1975, by which time Robinson had become disillusioned with the whole process and left to form the Tom Robinson Band (TRB) with Danny Kurstow. However, the bad blood between Davies and Robinson continued, and it took Robinson several months to disentangle himself from Konk, with Davies maintaining an interest in his publishing rights throughout the TRB period. He was as bitter about the whole affair as Robinson too, penning the words 'Tried to be gay / But it didn't pay / So he bought a motorbike instead' on 'Prince Of Punks', the b-side to the Kinks' 1977 single, 'Father Christmas'. Hereward Kaye, meanwhile, resurfaced in the 90s as the lyricist for stage musical *Moby Dick*.

●ALBUMS: *Café Society* (Konk 1975)★★.

CALE, J.J.

b. Jean Jacques Cale, 5 December 1938, Tulsa, Oklahoma, USA. This mercurial artist began performing professionally in the 50s as guitarist in a western swing group. With the advent of rock 'n' roll he led his own group, Johnnie Cale And The Valentines, before moving to Nashville late in the decade for an unsuccessful career in country music. He subsequently settled in Los Angeles, thereby joining fellow Tulsa ex-patriots Leon Russell, Carl Radle and Chuck Blackwell. Cale played in bar bands, worked as a studio engineer

and recorded several low-key singles before collaborating with songwriter Roger Tillison on a psychedelic album, *A Trip Down Sunset Strip*. Credited to the Leathercoated Minds, this tongue-in-cheek selection has since become a cult favourite.

An impoverished Cale returned to Tulsa in 1967. He remained an obscure local talent for three years but his fortunes changed dramatically when Eric Clapton recorded 'After Midnight', a song Cale had written and released as a single in 1965. 'It was like discovering oil in your own backyard,' he later commented. Producer Audie Ashworth then invited him to Nashville where he completed the excellent *Naturally*. The completed tape was then forwarded to Leon Russell, who released it on his fledgling Shelter label. The concise, self-confident album, arguably Cale's best, featured a re-recording of 'After Midnight', as well as several equally enchanting compositions including 'Call Me The Breeze', 'Magnolia' and 'Crazy Mama', which became a US Top 30 hit. His laconic, almost lachrymose delivery quickly became a trademark, while the sympathetically light instrumental support from veterans David Briggs (keyboards), Norbert Putnam (bass) and Tim Drummond (drums), previously members of Area Code 615, enhanced its intimate atmosphere. *Naturally* created a style from which Cale has rarely strayed and while some critics detected a paucity of ideas, others enthuse over its hypnotic charm.

Really confirmed the high quality of the artist's compositions. Marginally tougher than its predecessor, it included the R&B-flavoured 'Lies' and featured contributions from the Muscle Shoals team of Barry Beckett (keyboards), David Hood (bass) and Roger Hawkins (drums). While *Okie* and *Troubadour* lacked its immediacy, the latter contained the singer's own version of 'Cocaine', another song popularized by Clapton, who also recorded 'I'll Make Love To You Anytime' from *Five*. Although Cale has remained a somewhat shy and reticent figure, his influence on other musicians has been considerable. Mark Knopfler of Dire Straits appropriated much of his delivery from Cale's self-effacing style, yet while such devotees enjoyed massive commercial success, the originator entered a period of semi-retirement following an ill-fated dalliance with a major label. Despite the inclusion of the popular 'Money Talks' and the acquisition of Cale's back-catalogue, Cale's two albums for Phonogram, *Grasshopper* and *8*, failed to sell in the quantities anticipated and he asked to be released from his contract. The artist re-emerged in 1989 with *Travel Log*, which was issued on Silvertone, a British independent label. Devotees were relieved to hear little had changed, the songs were still largely based on 12-bar structures, his guitar style retained its rhythmic, yet relaxed pulse, while Cale's warm, growling voice was as distinctive as ever. Cale is an artist who would lose fans if he dared to change and even though the waiting time between each album can be agonizing he never fails. *Closer To You* and *Guitar Man* were both (fortunately) more of the same and, as usual, faultless musicians gave him support. On the former release ex-Little Feat keyboardist Bill Payne, bassists Tim Drummond and Larry Taylor were featured among the array of names.

●ALBUMS: *Naturally* (Shelter 1971)★★★, *Really* (Shelter 1972)★★★, *Okie* (Shelter 1974)★★★, *Troubadour* (Shelter 1976)★★★, *Five* (Shelter 1979)★★★, *Shades* (Shelter 1981)★★★, *Grasshopper* (Mercury 1982)★★, *8* (Mercury 1983)★★, *Travel Log* (Silvertone 1989)★★★, *Ten* (1992)★★★, *Closer To You* (Virgin 1994)★★★, *Guitar Man* (Virgin 1996)★★★.

●COMPILATIONS: *Special Edition* (Mercury 1984)★★★, *La Femme De Mon Pote* (Mercury 1984)★★★, *Nightriding* (Nightriding 1988)★★★, *Anyway The Wind Blows: The Anthology* (Mercury Chronicles 1997)★★★★.

CALE, JOHN

b. 9 March 1940, Crynant, West Glamorgan, Wales. Cale was a student of viola and keyboards at London's Goldsmith's college when introduced to electronic music. In 1963 he won a Leonard Bernstein scholarship to study modern composition at the Eastman Conservatory in Massachusetts, but later moved to New York where he joined the Dream Syndicate. It was during this period that Cale began playing rock and the following year he met Lou Reed through a mutual association with Pickwick Records. Sceptical of the company's desire for exploitative releases, the duo left to form a group that later evolved into the Velvet Underground. Cale remained with this highly influential act until 1968, during which time his experimental predisposition combined with Reed's grasp of pop's traditions to create a truly exciting lexicon, embodied to perfection in 'Sister Ray' from *White Light/White Heat*. Cale's contribution to the group should not be underemphasized, a fact enhanced by the shift in style that followed his summary dismissal from the line-up. He produced *The Marble Index* for Nico, the first of several collaborations, and the Stooges, before embarking on a solo career with *Vintage Violence*. Those anticipating a radical set were pleasantly surprised by the melodic flair that marked its content. However, *Church Of Anthrax*, a rather unsatisfactory pairing with Terry Riley, and the imaginative *The Academy In Peril*, reaffirmed his experimental reputation. While working for the Warners label in studio production and A&R, he assembled a backing band with Lowell George and Richard Hayward (both ex-Little Feat). Together they recorded the haunting *Paris 1919*, which continued the popular style of Cale's debut and remains, for many, the artist's finest work. Cameos on albums by Nick Drake and Mike Heron preceded a spell with UK-based Island Records. Cale's first album for the label, *Fear*, included a selection of compositions both overpoweringly dense and also light-hearted. It featured Brian Eno, who also contributed to the follow-up *Slow Dazzle* and appeared with Cale, Nico and Kevin Ayers (as

ACNE) on *June 1 1974*. Such a punishing schedule undermined Cale's creativity, a fact exemplified in the disappointing *Helen Of Troy*, but his production on Patti Smith's *Horses* (1975) nonetheless enhanced the urgency of this exemplary work. Now fêted by the punk audience, Cale's own recordings increasingly borrowed ideas rather than introducing them and he hit an artistic trough with the onstage beheading of a chicken, which led to his band walking out on him. However, *Music For A New Society* marked a renewed sense of adventure. The personal tribulations of the 70s now behind him, Cale continued to offer innovative music, and *Words For The Dying* matched his initial work for purpose and imagination. *Songs For 'Drella*, a 1990 collaboration with Lou Reed as a tribute to their recently deceased former mentor, Andy Warhol, was lauded by critics and audiences alike. Cale was part of the Velvet Underground reunion in 1993 but old wounds between himself and Reed resurfaced, and Cale was soon back to recording his idiosyncratic solo albums.

●ALBUMS: *Vintage Violence* (Columbia 1970)★★★, with Terry Riley *Church Of Anthrax* (Columbia 1971)★★★, *The Academy In Peril* (Reprise 1972)★★★, *Paris 1919* (Reprise 1973)★★★★, *Fear* (Island 1974)★★★, as ACNE *June 1 1974* (Island 1974)★★, *Slow Dazzle* (Island 1975)★★★, *Helen Of Troy* (Island 1975)★★, *Sabotage/Live* (Spy 1979)★★, *Honi Soit* (A&M 1981)★★, *Music For A New Society* (Ze 1982)★★★, *Caribbean Sunset* (Ze 1984)★★, *John Cale Comes Alive* (Ze 1984)★★★, *Artificial Intelligence* (Beggars Banquet 1985)★★★, *Words For The Dying* (Land 1989)★★★, with Lou Reed *Songs For 'Drella* (Warners 1990)★★★★, with Brian Eno *Wrong Way Up* (Land 1990)★★★, *Even Cowgirls Get The Blues* (1991)★★, *Fragments Of A Rainy Season* (Hannibal 1992)★★★, with Bob Neuwirth *Last Day On Earth* (MCA 1994)★★★, *Paris S'Eveille* (Crepuscule 1995)★★★, *23 Solo Pieces For La Naissance De L'Amour* (Crepuscule 1995)★★★, *Walking On Locusts* (Hannibal/Ryko 1996)★★★.

●COMPILATIONS: *Guts* (Island 1977)★★★★, *Seducing Down The Door: A Collection 1970-1990* (Rhino 1994)★★★★, *The Island Years* (Island 1996)★★★.

●VIDEOS: *Songs For Drella* (Warner Music Video 1991).

CALIFORNIA, RANDY

b. Randy Wolfe, 20 February 1951, Los Angeles, California, USA, d. 2 January 1997. California was best known for his often lustrous rock guitar work and fine songwriting ability with the west coast band Spirit. He kept the band name alive for nearly 30 years with numerous line-ups. His solo career started in 1972 during one of Spirit's many break-ups, with the perplexing *Captain Kopter And The Fabulous Twirlybirds*. This Jimi Hendrix-inspired outing featured versions of the Beatles' 'Day Tripper' and 'Rain', and Paul Simon's 'Mother And Child Reunion'. The accompanying band featured Ed Cassidy from Spirit and Clit McTorious (alias Noel Redding) playing bass. California has since made a few albums bearing his name, but none have appealed to a market outside the loyal cult of kindred spirits. He always needed a band or a 'family' around him, even though he was very direct and opinionated in his work. California, for better or worse, will always be joined at the hip to Spirit, way beyond his tragic death by drowning in 1997, even if most of their time was spent in limbo. Such is spiritualism. He was a gentle soul and a true cosmic hippy.

●ALBUMS: *Captain Kopter And The Fabulous Twirlybirds* (Epic 1972)★★★, *Euro American* (Beggars Banquet 1982)★★★, *Restless* (Vertigo 1985)★★, *Shattered Dreams* (Line Records 1986)★★.

CALIFORNIANS

Despite their name, this rock band was formed in the Midlands, England, during the mid-70s. Comprising Mike Brookes, P.J. Habberly, John O'Hara (ex-O'Hara's Playboys) and Robert Trewis, the band made its debut for CBS Records in 1967 with 'Little Ship With A Red Sail'. Dressed in matching white pullovers, the succession of singles for Decca Records and Fontana Records that followed nevertheless featured some credible, energized rock 'n' roll. Their first release for Decca, a version of Warren Zevon's 'Follow Me', was well received before they attempted a cover of another strong American single, Spanky And Our Gang's 'Sunday Will Never Be The Same'. Subsequent releases were heavily influenced by the growing psychedelia boom, a fact reflected in titles such as 'The Cooks Of Cakes And Kindness'. By the end of the 60s the band had disappeared from view, leaving behind a final single, 'Golden Apples', which saw them return to CBS. No album was ever released.

CALVERT, ROBERT

b. *c.*1945, Pretoria, South Africa, d. 14 August 1988. Domiciled in London's bohemian Ladbroke Grove/Portobello Road area, Calvert became acquainted with Hawkwind, one of the area's atypical 'underground' attractions. His poetry readings became part of the group's act during the early 70s and in 1972 he joined the line-up as an official member. Calvert wrote and originally sang 'Silver Machine', their Top 3 hit, although by that point his vocal had been over-dubbed. He left Hawkwind the following year, but three of the group - Dave Brock (guitar), Lemmy (bass) and Simon King (drums) - joined ex-Pink Fairies Twink (drums) and Paul Rudolph (guitar) on *Captain Lockheed And The Starfighters*, the artist's highly praised solo debut. His second set, *Lucky Leif And The Longships*, which featured science-fiction writer Michael Moorcock, was produced by Brian Eno, but it proved less popular than its predecessor. Calvert returned to the Hawkwind fold in 1977, but left again at the end of the decade. Two more solo albums, blending science fiction with rock ensued, before this respected performer succumbed to a heart attack on 14 August 1988.

●ALBUMS: *Captain Lockheed And The Starfighters* (United Artists 1974)★★★, *Lucky Leif And The Longships* (United Artists 1975)★★★, *Hype* (A-Side 1980)★★, *Freq* (Flicknife 1984)★★, *Test Tube Conceived* (Demi-Monde 1986)★★, *Blueprints From The Cellar* (Beat Goes On 1992)★★★, *Live At The Queen Elizabeth Hall* (Clear 1993)★★.

CAMEL

Formed in the spring of 1972 by former members of Philip Goodhand-Tait's backing band, Camel comprised Doug Ferguson (b. 4 April 1947, Carlisle, Cumbria, England; bass), Andy Ward (b. 28 September 1952, Epsom, Surrey, England; drums) and Andy Latimer (b. 17 May 1947, Guildford, Surrey, England; guitar, flute, vocals) and Peter Bardens (b. 19 June 1945, Westminster, London, England; keyboards). Bardens, whose pedigree included stints with Them and Shotgun Express, dominated the group's sound to the extent that they came to be known as Peter Bardens' Camel, in deference to Peter Frampton's Camel. As regular performers on the UK college circuit, it took an adaptation of the Paul Gallico children's story, *The Snow Goose*, to put this foremost progressive band into the UK Top 30 album chart. After the release of *Moonmadness*, Ferguson departed, to be replaced by ex-Caravan member Richard Sinclair. They consolidated their position with the Top 30 albums *Rain Dances* and *Breathless*. Although their success preceded the rise of the punk/new wave movement, the band's image as outdated progressive rockers threatened their future. However, they survived, but not without some changes to the line-up and consequently, the style of music. Peter Bardens' replacement by Jan Schelhaas (another ex-Caravan member) made the biggest impact, leaving room for lighter song structures typified on *The Single Factor*. The group continued to record and perform well into the 80s when the final line-up, now led by the only remaining original member Latimer and comprising Ton Scherpenzeel (keyboards), Christopher Rainbow (vocals), Paul Burgess (drums) and Colin Bass (bass), closed proceedings with the live set, *Pressure Points*. *Never Let Go* was recorded during their 20th anniversary tour and released in 1993.

●ALBUMS: *Camel* (MCA 1973)★★, *Mirage* (Deram 1974)★★, *The Snow Goose* (Decca 1975)★★★, *Moonmadness* (Decca 1976)★★★, *Rain Dances* (Decca 1977)★★★, *A Live Record* (Decca 1978)★★, *Breathless* (Decca 1978)★★, *I Can See Your House From Here* (Decca 1979)★★★, *Nude* (Decca 1981)★★★, *The Single Factor* (Decca 1982)★★, *Stationary Traveller* (Decca 1984)★★, *Pressure Points* (Decca 1984)★★, *Never Let Go* (Camel Productions 1993)★★, *Harbour Of Tears* (Camel Productions 1996)★★.

●COMPILATIONS: *The Camel Collection* (Castle 1985)★★★.

●VIDEOS: *Pressure Points (Camel Live)* (Polygram Music Video 1984).

CAMPBELL, GLEN

b. Glen Travis Campbell, 22 April 1936, Delight, Arkansas, USA. Campbell came from a musical family and began his career with his uncle's Dick Bills Band in 1954 before forming Glen Campbell And The Western Wranglers, four years later. By the end of the 50s he had moved to Los Angeles, where he became a renowned session player and one of the finest guitarists in Hollywood. After briefly joining the Champs, he released a solo single, 'Too Late To Worry - Too Blue To Cry', which crept into the US Hot 100. Ever in demand, he took on the arduous task of replacing Brian Wilson on touring commitments with the Beach Boys. Campbell's period as a Beach Boy was short-lived and he soon returned to session work and recording, even enjoying a minor hit with Buffy Sainte-Marie's 'The Universal Soldier'. By 1967, Capitol Records were pushing Campbell seriously as an artist in his own right. The breakthrough came with an accomplished version of John Hartford's 'Gentle On My Mind', which won a Grammy Award for Best Country 'n' Western Recording of 1967. Campbell's finest work was recorded during the late 60s, most notably a superb trilogy of hits written by Jim Webb. 'By The Time I Get To Phoenix', 'Wichita Lineman' and 'Galveston' were richly evocative compositions, full of yearning for towns in America that have seldom been celebrated in the annals of popular music. By this stage of his career, Campbell was actively pursuing television work and even starred with John Wayne in the film *True Grit* (1969). He recorded some duets with country singer Bobbie Gentry, including a revival of the Everly Brothers' 'All I Have To Do Is Dream', which proved a worldwide smash hit. Further hits followed, including 'Honey Come Back', 'It's Only Make Believe' and 'Dream Baby'. There was a second film appearance in *Norwood* (1970) and another duet album, this time with Anne Murray. Campbell's hit record output slowed somewhat in the early 70s, but by the mid-decade he found second wind and belatedly registered his first US number 1 single with 'Rhinestone Cowboy'. Two years later he repeated that feat with a version of Allan Touissant's 'Southern Nights'. Numerous hit compilations followed and Campbell found himself still in demand as a duettist with such artists as Rita Coolidge and Tanya Tucker. By the late 70s, he had become a C&W institution, regularly releasing albums, touring and appearing on television. In 1988, he returned to his young provider Jim Webb for the title track to *Still Within The Sound Of My Voice*. Campbell's career is most remarkable for its scope. A brilliant guitarist, star session player, temporary Beach Boy, first-class interpreter, television personality, strong vocalist, in-demand duettist and C&W idol, he has run the gamut of American music and rarely faltered.

●ALBUMS: *Too Late To Worry, Too Late To Cry* (Capitol 1963)★★★, *The Astounding 12-String Guitar Of Glen Campbell* (Capitol 1964)★★★, *The Big Bad Rock Guitar Of Glen Campbell* (Capitol 1965)★★★, *Gentle On My Mind* (Capitol 1967)★★★, *By The Time I Get To Phoenix* (Capitol 1967)★★★, *Hey, Little One* (Capitol 1968)★★★, *A New Place In The Sun* (Capitol 1968)★★★, *Bobbie Gentry And Glen Campbell* (Capitol 1968)★★★, *Wichita Lineman* (Capitol 1968)★★★, *That Christmas Feeling* (Capitol 1968)★★, *Galveston* (Capitol 1969)★★★, *Glen Campbell - Live* (Capitol 1969)★★, *Try A Little Kindness* (Capitol 1970)★★★, *Oh Happy Day* (Capitol 1970)★★★, *Norwood* film soundtrack (Capitol 1970)★★, *The Glen Campbell Goodtime Album* (Capitol 1970)★★★, *The Last Time I Saw Her* (Capitol 1971)★★★, *Anne Murray/Glen Campbell* (Capitol 1971)★★★, *Glen Travis Campbell* (Capitol 1972)★★★, *I Knew Jesus (Before He Was A Star)* (Capitol 1973)★★★, *Reunion (The Songs Of Jimmy Webb)* (Capitol 1974)★★★, *Rhinestone Cowboy* (Capitol 1975)★★, *Bloodline* (Capitol 1976)★★★, *Southern Nights* (Capitol 1977)★★★, with the Royal Philharmonic Orchestra *Live At The Royal Festival Hall* (Capitol 1978)★★★, *Basic* (Capitol 1978)★★★, *Somethin' 'Bout You Baby I Like* (Capitol 1980)★★★, *It's The World Gone Crazy* (Capitol 1981)★★★★, *Old Home Town* (Atlantic 1983)★★★, *Letter To Home* (Atlantic 1984)★★★, *Just A Matter Of Time* (Atlantic 1986)★★★, *No More Night* (Word 1988)★★★, *Still Within The Sound Of My Voice* (MCA 1988)★★★, *Walkin' In The Sun* (Capitol 1990)★★★★, *Unconditional Love* (Capitol Nashville 1991)★★★, *Somebody Like That* (Liberty 1993)★★★, *The Rhinestone Cowboy Live In Concert* (Summit 1995)★★★.

●COMPILATIONS: *Glen Campbell's Greatest Hits* (Capitol 1971)★★★, *The Best Of Glen Campbell* (Capitol 1976)★★★, *Twenty Golden Greats* (1987)★★, *Country Boy* (MFP 1988)★★, *The Complete Glen Campbell* (Stylus 1989)★★★.

●VIDEOS: *Live At The Dome* (80s), *Glen Campbell Live* (Channel 5 1988), *An Evening With* (Music Club Video 1989), *Glen Campbell* (Castle Music Pictures 1991).

●FURTHER READING: *The Glen Campbell Story*, Freda Kramer. *Rhinestone Cowboy: An Autobiography*, Glen Campbell with Tom Carter.

●FILMS: *The Cool Ones* (1967), *True Grit* (1969), *Norwood* (1970).

CAMPBELL, JUNIOR

b. William Campbell, 31 May 1947, Glasgow, Scotland. The former lead singer of Marmalade began a promising solo career in 1972 with the stirring 'Hallelujah Freedom'. Combining much of the melody of Marmalade, this soul-influenced single made the UK Top 10. The following year similar success came with 'Sweet Illusion'. The chart singles stopped and Campbell's direction moved towards back-room production. In the early 80s he wrote the theme music to award-winning UK television children's programmes, notably *Thomas The Tank Engine* (narrated by Ringo Starr) and *Tugs*.

●ALBUMS: *Second Time Around* (Deram 1977)★★.

CAN

Formed in Cologne, Germany and originally known as Inner Space, this experimental unit was founded by two students of modern classical music, Irmin Schmidt (b. 29 May 1937, Berlin, Germany; keyboards) and Holger Czukay (b. 24 March 1938, Danzig, Germany; bass). The group embraced a rock-based perspective with the addition of Michael Karoli (b. 29 April 1948, Straubing, Lower Bavaria, Germany; guitar), Jaki Liebezeit (b. 26 May 1938, Dresden, Germany; drums) and the inclusion in this early line-up of David Johnson (flute).

The arrival of black American vocalist Malcolm Mooney coincided with the adoption of a new name, Can. Johnson left the group in December 1968 as the unit began work on their official debut album. *Monster Movie* introduced many of Can's subsequent trademarks: Schmidt's choppy, percussive keyboard style, Karoli's incisive guitar and the relentless, hypnotic pulse of its rhythm section. At times reminiscent of a Teutonic Velvet Underground, the set's highlight was the propulsive 'You Doo Right', a 20-minute excerpt from a 12-hour improvisatory session. The group completed several other masters, later to appear on *Can Soundtracks* and *Delay 1968*, prior to the departure of Mooney. He was replaced by Kenji 'Damo' Suzuki (b. 16 January 1950, Japan), whom Liebezeit and Czukay had discovered busking outside a Munich cafe. *Tago Mago*, a sprawling, experimental double set, then followed, the highlight of which was the compulsive 'Hallelujah'. However, despite retaining a penchant for extended compositions, Can also began exploring a more precise, even ambient direction on *Ege Bamyasi* and *Future Days*. Suzuki left the group in 1973, and although they flirted with other featured vocalists, Can remained a quartet for some time. In 1976 the group had an unlikely UK Top 30 hit with 'I Want More', a song written by their live sound mixer Peter Gilmore, who also guested on several tracks from the attendant album, *Flow Motion*. Can was later augmented by two former members of Traffic, Rosko Gee (bass) and Reebop Kwaku Baah (percussion), but the departure of Czukay signalled their demise. The group completed *Out Of Reach* without him, but the bassist returned to edit their next release, *Can*. These largely disappointing releases made little impact and the unit split up at the end of 1978.

Holger Czukay then pursued a successful solo career with a series of excellent solo albums and fruitful partnerships with David Sylvian and the Eurythmics. Irmin Schmidt completed several film soundtracks, Jaki Liebezeit formed his own group, the Phantom Band, and worked with systems musician Michael Rother, while Karoli recorded an excellent solo set. The four musicians remained in close contact and a re-formed Can, complete with Malcolm Mooney, returned to the studio in 1987. The fruits of their renewed relationship appeared two years later in the shape of the excellent *Rite Time*.

●ALBUMS: *Monster Movie* (United Artists 1969)★★★★, *Can Soundtracks* film soundtrack (United Artists 1970)★★★, *Tago Mago* (United Artists 1971)★★★★, *Ege Bamyasi* (United Artists 1972)★★★★, *Future Days* (United Artists 1973)★★★★, *Soon Over Babaluma* (United Artists 1974)★★★★, *Landed* (Virgin 1975)★★★, *Flow Motion* (Virgin 1976)★★★, *Saw Delight* (Virgin 1977)★★★, *Out Of Reach* (Lightning 1978)★★, *Can -* later released as *Inner Space* (Laser 1979)★★, *Rite Time* (Mercury 1989)★★★, *The Peel Sessions* (Strange Fruit 1995)★★★. Solo: Michael Karoli with Polly Eltes *Deluge* (Spoon 1984)★★★★. Jaki Liebezeit *Phantom Band* (Sky 1980)★★★, with Phew and Holger Czukay *Phew* (Pass 1981)★★★, with Phantom Band *Freedom Of Speech* (Sky 1981)★★★, with Phantom Band *Nowhere* (Spoon 1984)★★★. Irwin Schmidt *Film Musik* (Spoon 1980)★★★, with Bruno Spoerri *Toy Planet* (Spoon 1981)★★★, *Film Musik Volume 2* (Spoon 1981)★★★, *Rote Erde* (Teldec 1983)★★★, *Film Musik Volumes 3&4* (Spoon 1984)★★★, *Music At Dusk* (Warners 1987)★★★. Damo Suzuki with Dunkelziffer *In The Night* (Forty Five 1984)★★.

●COMPILATIONS: *Limited Edition* (United Artists 1974)★★★, *Unlimited Edition* (Caroline 1976)★★★, *Opener* (Sunset 1976)★★, *Cannibalism* (United Artists 1978)★★★★, *Incandescence* (Virgin 1981)★★, *Delay 1968* (Spoon 1981)★★★, *Onlyou* (Pure Freude 1982)★★★, *Prehistoric Future* (Tago Mago 1985)★★★, *Cannibalism 2* (1993)★★★, *Anthology 1968-1993* (1997)★★★★.

CANDLEWICK GREEN

This pop group from Liverpool, England, had one hit in 1974 with 'Who Do You Think You Are'. Consisting of Jimmy Nunnen, Tony Webb, Alan Leyland, Lennie Coswell and Andy Bell, they started their career in 1973 with the Decca single 'Doggie'. This was followed by 'Sunday Kinda Monday', before the aforementioned hit. Subsequent releases 'Leave A Little Love', and 'Everyday Of My Life' rapidly disappeared with their authors following their fate soon after. Their live radio appearances on BBC radio programmes such as those hosted by David Hamilton did little to enhance their credibility and put them firmly in the middle of the road, with no audience.

CAPALDI, JIM

b. 24 August 1944, Evesham, Worcestershire, England. The son of a music teacher, Capaldi studied piano and sang from an early age but it was drums that ultimately attracted his attention. Following his membership of the Hellions (with Dave Mason) and Deep Feeling (with Chris Wood), he befriended Steve Winwood, who was still with the Spencer Davis Group. Traffic was formally launched in 1967, and during its turbulent stop-go eight year history, became one of the leading progressive bands. Capaldi made his name during this time as the perfect lyricist for Winwood's innovative musical ideas. During Winwood's enforced absence through peritonitis in 1972, Capaldi released a solo album, *Oh How We Danced*. Its respectable showing in the US charts enabled him to continue to record albums at regular intervals. *Short Cut Draw Blood* in 1974 proved to be his finest work, containing two hit singles: 'Its All Up To You' and a lively version of Boudleaux Bryant's 'Love Hurts'. He toured with his band the Space Cadets in 1976 to average response. He eventually moved to Brazil, effectively ending his lucrative songwriting partnership with Steve Winwood. Often known as 'Gentleman' Jim Capaldi, he has an affectionate rather than important place in musical history. He returned in 1989 with the album *Some Came Running* and contributed to Winwood's multi-million selling *Roll With It* the same year. In 1990 he again collaborated with Winwood on the album *Refugees Of The Heart* and co-wrote the US hit 'One And Only Man'. The full circle was completed in 1994 when Traffic re-formed for a major world tour and an underrated album *Far From Home*. In 1996 Capaldi won a BMI Award for 'Love Will Keep Us Alive', co-written with Peter Vale and recorded by the Eagles. He contributed to Winwood's disappointing 1997 album *Junction 7*.

●ALBUMS: *Oh How We Danced* (Island 1972)★★★★, *Whale Meat Again* (Island 1974)★, *Short Cut Draw Blood* (Island 1975)★★★★, *Play It By Ear* (Island 1977)★★, *The Contender* (Polydor 1978)★★★, *Electric Nights* (Polydor 1979)★★, *The Sweet Smell Of Success* (Carrere 1980)★★, *Let The Thunder Cry* (Carrere 1981)★★, *Fierce Heart* (Atlantic 1983)★★★, *One Man Mission* (Warners 1984)★★, *Some Come Running* (Island 1989)★★.

●FURTHER READING: *Keep On Running: The Steve Winwood Story*, Chris Welch. *Back In The High Life: A Biography Of Steve Winwood*, Alan Clayson.

CAPTAIN AND TENNILLE

Toni Tennille (b. 8 May 1943, Montgomery, Alabama, USA) co-wrote the 1972 rock musical *Mother Earth*. When it was staged in Los Angeles, the house band included keyboards player Daryl Dragon, (b. 27 August 1942, Los Angeles, California, USA), the son of conductor Carmen Dragon. The duo teamed up and toured as part of the Beach Boys' backing group before writing and producing 'The Way I Want To Touch You', their first recording as Captain And Tennille. The first hit was the jaunty 'Love Will Keep Us Together' (1975) a Neil Sedaka composition which established the group as a close harmony favourite of Top 40 radio programmers. That song sold a million copies as did 'Lonely Night (Angel Face)'and 'Muskrat Love'. 'You Never Done It Like That' (1978) was their last Top 10 record before they moved from A&M to the Casablanca label. The sensual slow ballad 'Do That To Me One More Time' reached number 1 in the USA in 1979 (number 7 in the UK, where they were not as successful with any of their singles), but afterwards the hits tailed off. By now, however, Captain And Tennille were established in television, with their own primetime series which was fol-

lowed in the 80s by a daytime show hosted by Tennille with Dragon as musical director. Toni Tennille later made solo albums of standard ballads. A reunited pair issued *Twenty Years Of Romance* in 1995.

●ALBUMS: *Love Will Keep Us Together* (A&M 1975)★★★, *Por Amor Viviremos* (A&M 1975)★★, *Song Of Joy* (A&M 1976)★★, *Come In From The Rain* (A&M 1977)★★, *Dream* (A&M 1978)★★, *Make Your Move* (Casablanca 1979)★★, *Keeping Our Love Warm* (Casablanca 1980)★★, *Twenty Years Of Romance* (K-Tel 1995)★★. Solo: Toni Tennille *More Than You Know* (Mirage 1984)★★★, *Moonglow* (1986)★★, *All Of Me* (Gaia 1987)★★, *Do It Again* (Prestige 1990)★★, *Things Are Swingin'* (1994)★★.

●COMPILATIONS: *Greatest Hits* (A&M 1977)★★, *20 Greatest Hits* (MFP 1980)★★.

●FURTHER READING: *Captain And Tennille*, James Spada.

CAPTAIN BEYOND

Based in Los Angeles, this Anglo-American 'supergroup' was formed in 1972 around Rod Evans (b. 19 January 1947, Edinburgh, Scotland; vocals, ex-Deep Purple), Bobby Caldwell (drums, ex-Johnny Winter) and two former members of Iron Butterfly, Larry 'Rhino' Rheinhart (b. 7 July 1948, Florida, USA; guitar) and Lee Dorman (b. 15 September 1945, St. Louis, Missouri, USA; bass). Although *Captain Beyond* established the unit's hard-rock style, this initial line-up proved incompatible and Caldwell was replaced by Marty Rodriguez for *Sufficiently Breathless*. The departure of Evans precipitated a lengthy period of inactivity but in 1976 the remaining trio was joined by Willy Daffern (vocals), Reese Wynans (keyboards, ex-Stevie Ray Vaughan) and Guille Garcia (percussion). This final version broke up following the release of *Dawn Explosion*.

●ALBUMS: *Captain Beyond* (Capricorn 1972)★★, *Sufficiently Breathless* (Capricorn 1973)★★★, *Dawn Explosion* (Capricorn 1977)★★.

CARAVAN

Formed in Canterbury, England, in 1968, Caravan evolved from the Wilde Flowers, a seminal local attraction which had included Robert Wyatt, Kevin Ayers and Hugh Hopper, each later of the Soft Machine. Pye Hastings (b. 21 January 1947, Tominavoulin, Bamffshire, Scotland; guitar/vocals), David Sinclair (b. 24 November 1947, Herne Bay, Kent, England; keyboards), Richard Sinclair (b. 6 June 1948, Canterbury, Kent, England; bass/vocals) and Richard Coughlan (b. 2 September 1947, Herne Bay, Kent, England; drums) forged the original Caravan line-up whose gift for melody and imaginative improvisation was made apparent on an excellent debut album. The haunting 'Place Of My Own' and 'Love Song With Flute' were particularly impressive and set the tone for much of the quartet's early work. *If I Could Do It All Over Again, I'd Do It All Over You* continued their blend of wistfulness and the *avant garde*, but it was not until *In The Land Of Grey*

And Pink that the quartet achieved due commercial plaudits. Its extended title track contrasted the quirky economy of 'Golf Girl' and the set remains, for many, Caravan's finest album. Dave Sinclair then joined Matching Mole, but the unit was reshaped around Steve Miller, formerly of Delivery, for *Waterloo Lily*. However, a period of frantic activity saw Richard Sinclair leave for Hatfield And The North, before the prodigal David returned to augment a line-up of Hastings, Coughlan, John Perry (b. 19 January 1947, Auburn, New York, USA; guitar) and Geoff Richardson (b. 15 July 1950, Hinckley, Leicestershire, England; viola/violin). An ensuing rigorous touring schedule was punctuated by *For Girls Who Go Plump In The Night* and *Symphonia*, but further personnel changes undermined the group's early charm. Although *Cunning Stunts* provided a surprise US chart entry, Caravan were blighted by their concern for technical perfection. Although increasingly confined to a post-progressive rock backwater inhabited by fellow distinctly English acts National Health and Anthony Phillips, the irrepressible Hastings continued to lead the group into the 80s. The original quartet was reunited for *Back To Front*, Caravan's last new recording to date, although live appearances have since been made. A flurry of activity in 1991 saw Caravan performing once more, with the addition of Richard Sinclair's amalgamation of former Caravan and Camel members undertaking a series of low-key London club dates under the name of Caravan Of Dreams. A new album from Sinclair, Coughlan, Geoffrey Richardson, Jimmy and Pye Hastings and Jim Levington was issued in 1995 and found particular favour in Japan.

●ALBUMS: *Caravan* (Verve 1968)★★★, *If I Could Do It All Over Again, I'd Do It All Over You* (Decca 1970)★★★, *In The Land Of Grey And Pink* (Deram 1971)★★★, *Waterloo Lily* (Deram 1972)★★★★, *For Girls Who Grow Plump In The Night* (Deram 1973)★★★, *Caravan And The New Symphonia* (Deram 1974)★★, *Cunning Stunts* (Decca 1975)★★★, *Blind Dog At St. Dunstan's* (BTM 1976)★★★, *Better By Far* (Arista 1977)★★, *The Album* (Kingdom 1980)★★, *The Show Of Our Lives* (Decca 1981)★★, *Back To The Front* (Kingdom 1982)★★, *Live At The Paris Theatre, 1975* (1991)★★, *Live 1990* (1993)★★, *Cool Water* (HTD 1994)★★, *Battle Of Hastings* (HTD 1995)★★★. Solo: Richard Sinclair *Caravan Of Dreams* (1992)★★.

●COMPILATIONS: *The Canterbury Tales* (Decca 1976)★★★★, *Collection: Caravan* (Kingdom 1984)★★★, *And I Wish I Weren't Stoned, Don't Worry* (See For Miles 1985)★★★, *The Best Of Caravan* (C5 1987)★★★, *Canterbury Collection* (Kingdom 1987)★★★, *The Best Of* (1993)★★★.

CARMEN, ERIC

b. 11 August 1949, Cleveland, Ohio, USA. A veteran of several aspiring Midwest groups, Carmen first achieved success with the Raspberries. This melodious quartet drew inspiration from British 60s pop and scored notable US hits with 'Go All The Way', 'I Wanna Be With You' and 'Let's Pretend'. Carmen wrote and sang lead on each of these releases and was the sole member to prosper commercially when the group was dissolved in 1975. The following year Carmen scored an international hit with a dramatic ballad, 'All By Myself'. Although he enjoyed two further US Top 20 entries with 'Never Gonna Fall In Love Again' (1976) and 'Change Of Heart' (1978), the artist was unable to sustain a consistent momentum. He returned to the US Top 10 in 1987 with the single 'Hungry Eyes' (from the film *Dirty Dancing*), and the following year reached number 3 with 'Make Me Lose Control'. Carmen remains a cultured and versatile performer, although his recent work lacks the panache of his early releases.

●ALBUMS: *Eric Carmen* (Arista 1975)★★★, *Boats Against The Current* (Arista 1977)★★, *Change Of Heart* (Arista 1978)★★, *Tonight You're Mine* (Arista 1980)★★, *Eric Carmen* (Geffen 1985)★★.

●COMPILATIONS: *The Best Of Eric Carmen* (Arista 1988)★★★.

CARPENTERS

This brother-and-sister duo featured Richard Carpenter (b. 15 October 1946, New Haven, Connecticut, USA; piano) and Karen Carpenter (b. 2 March 1950, New Haven, Connecticut, USA, d. 4 February 1983; vocals/drums). During 1963, Richard appeared at various New Haven clubs and bars in an instrumental trio. After his family relocated to Los Angeles, he studied piano and backed his sister, who was signed to the small local label Magic Lamp in 1965. With assistance from Wes Jacobs (bass/tuba) and session bassist Joe Osborn, Karen recorded one single 'I'll Be Yours'. Retaining Jacobs, the brother and sister team next formed a predominantly jazz/instrumental unit known as the Richard Carpenter Trio. After winning a battle of the bands contest at the Hollywood Bowl they were duly signed to RCA Records, but no material was issued. In 1967, Jacobs left the group to study music and Richard and Karen teamed up with a friend, John Bettis, in the short-lived Spectrum. The following year, A&M Records president Herb Alpert heard some demos that they had recorded and signed the brother-and-sister duo, now called the Carpenters. In late 1969, their debut album *Offering* was issued, but failed to chart. A harmonic version of the Beatles 'Ticket To Ride' subsequently climbed to number 54 in the US singles charts early the following year, and this set their hit career in motion. A wonderful reading of Burt Bacharach and Hal David's 'Close To You', complete with a superbly understated piano arrangement, took them to number 1 in the USA. The song was a massive hit all over the world and ushered in an era of chart domination by the wholesome duo. Towards the end of 1970, they were back at number 2 in the US singles chart with the Paul Williams/Roger Nichols composition, 'We've Only Just Begun'. Once more, the track highlighted Karen's crystal-clear diction, overladen with intricated harmonies and a faultless production. Throughout 1971, the duo consolidated their success with such Top 3 US hits as 'For All We Know', 'Rainy Days And Mondays' and 'Superstar'/'Bless The Beasts And Children'. They also received Grammy Awards for Best New Artist and Best Vocal Performance, as well as launching their own television series, *Make Your Own Kind Of Music*.

Between 1972-73, the group's run of hits was unrelenting, with 'Goodbye To Love' (the remarkable guitar solo is played by Tony Palusao), 'Sing' and 'Yesterday Once More' all reaching the US Top 10, while the irresistibly melodic 'Top Of The World' climbed to number 1. All of these songs (with the exception of 'Sing') were composed by Richard Carpenter and his former bassist John Bettis. A cover of the Marvelettes/Beatles 'Please Mr Postman' brought the Carpenters back to number 1 in the summer of 1974, and that same year they played before President Richard Nixon at the White House. Although they continued to chart regularly with such smashes as 'Only Yesterday', there was a noticeable decline in their Top 40 performance during the second half of the 70s. Personal and health problems were also taking their toll. Richard became addicted to prescription drugs and eventually entered a clinic in 1978 to overcome his addiction. Karen, meanwhile, was suffering from the slimmers' disease anorexia nervosa, a condition from which she never recovered.

The latter part of the 70s saw the duo tackle some unlikely material, including covers of Herman's Hermits' 'There's A Kind Of Hush' and Klaatu's 'Calling Occupants Of Interplanetary Craft'. The latter fared particularly well in the UK, reaching number 10 and convincing many that the duo could adapt any song to their distinctive style. Anxious to improve her own standing as a singer, Karen subsequently completed a solo album during 1979 but it was destined to remain unreleased. Thereafter, she reunited with Richard for another Carpenters album, *Made In America*, and that same year the duo registered their final US Top 20 hit with 'Touch Me When We're Dancing'. The group's low profile during the early 80s coincided with Karen's increasingly poor health and weak state. On 4 February 1983 she was discovered unconscious at her parents' home in New Haven and died in hospital that morning of a cardiac arrest. The coroner's report revealed the cause of death as 'heartbeat irregularities brought on by chemical imbalances associated with anorexia nervosa'. Following his sister's death, Richard moved into production. In the meantime, various Carpenters compilations were issued as well as a posthumous studio album, *Voice Of The Heart*. Richard returned to recording with 1987's Time, on which he sang lead, with guest appearances by such notable female vocalists as Dusty Springfield and Dionne Warwick. In late 1989, he supervised the remixing and release of an ambitious 12-CD anthology of the Carpenters' recordings. During their heyday they were passed over by many critics as being too bland and 'nice'. Following a reappraisal in the early 90s their standing in popular music today is high.

●ALBUMS: *Offering* later reissued as *Ticket To Ride* (A&M 1969)★★, *Close To You* (A&M 1970)★★★★, *The Carpenters* (A&M 1971)★★★★, *A Song For You* (A&M 1972)★★★, *Now And Then* (A&M 1973)★★, *Horizon* (A&M 1975)★★★, *Live In Japan* (A&M 1975)★★, *A Kind Of Hush* (A&M 1976)★★, *Live At The Palladium* (A&M 1976)★★, *Passage* (A&M 1977)★★, *Christmas Portrait* (A&M 1978)★, *Made In America* (A&M 1981)★★, *Voice Of The Heart* (A&M 1983)★★★, *An Old Fashioned Christmas* (A&M 1984)★. Solo: Richard Carpenter *Time* (A&M 1987)★. Karen Carpenter *Karen Carpenter* (A&M 1996)★★.

●COMPILATIONS: *The Singles 1969-73* (A&M 1973)★★★★, *Collection* (A&M 1976)★★★★, *The Singles 1974-78* (A&M 1978)★★★★, *Silver Double Disc Of The Carpenters* (A&M 1979)★★, *The Best Of The Carpenters* (World 1981)★★, *The Carpenters Collection - The Very Best Of The Carpenters* (EMI 1984)★★★★, *Lovelines* (A&M 1989)★★, *The Compact Disc Collection* 12-CD box set (A&M 1989)★★★, *From The Top (1965-82)* 4-CD set (A&M 1992)★★★.

●VIDEOS: *Yesterday Once More* (A&M Sound Pictures 1986), *Only Yesterday (Richard & Karen Carpenter's Greatest Hits)* (Channel 5 1990).

●FURTHER READING: *The Carpenters: The Untold Story*, Ray Coleman

CARR, IAN

b. 21 April 1933, Dumfries, Scotland. Carr taught himself trumpet from the age of 17. Between 1952 and 1956 he studied English literature at Newcastle University, and has had a career as writer, broadcaster, teacher and musician, all furthering the cause of jazz. Between 1960 and 1962 he played with the EmCee Five, the Newcastle bop quintet, before moving to London to work with tenor saxophonist Don Rendell. The Rendell-Carr group lasted until 1969, recording five albums and making international tours. Carr left to form Nucleus, which followed Miles Davis into the world of amplified jazz rock. *Elastic Rock*, their debut, was released in 1970. Tours followed, including Europe and the USA. Leonard Feather wrote, 'Many listeners and critics have agreed that Nucleus has been a seminal influence on jazz-rock groups in Europe and elsewhere'. In 1973 his book on contemporary UK jazz, *Music Outside*, was published. Carr's sometimes academic approach to music has resulted in long compositions, including *Solar Plexus* (1971) and *Labyrinth* (1974). In 1982 he became an associate professor at the Guildhall School of Music in London and was given the Calabria award for 'outstanding contribution in the field of jazz'. The same year saw the publication of his acclaimed biography of Miles Davis. This book has now become one of the standard works on Miles Davis. In 1986 he composed *Spirit Of Place* for Tony Coe and Eberhard Weber. His *Jazz: The Essential Companion* (co-written with Digby Fairweather and Brian Priestley) was for some time the most in-depth jazz encyclopedia available in the UK, although some registered disquiet at Carr's apparent lack of sympathy for free improvisation, harmolodics and the black *avant garde*. In 1987 Carr also worked with the Mike Gibbs Orchestra and was the featured soloist with the Hamburg Radio Orchestra under Gibbs' direction.

Carr's recent projects include a trilogy of jazz compositions inspired by his years in Newcastle-upon-Tyne. The first piece, *Old Heartland*, inspired by the highly underrated novelist Sid Chaplin, was recorded in 1988; the second part is called *Going Home* which was performed alongside Alan Plater's play of the same name; and the third, a suite entitled *North Eastern Song Lives*, was commissioned by Jazz North East to mark their 25th anniversary and first performed in Newcastle in October 1991. Since then, Carr has had a further jazz biography published, *Keith Jarrett: The Man And His Music*, and has performed with the United Jazz And Rock Ensemble. Carr is one the most literate and emotional artists to come out of the fertile 60s UK jazz scene.

●ALBUMS: with Don Rendell *Shades Of Blue* (1965)★★★★, with Rendell *Phase III* (1968)★★★, with Rendell, Neil Ardley *Greek Variations* (1970)★★★, *Belladonna* (Core 1972)★★★, *Old Heartland* (MMC 1988)★★★. see also Nucleus discography.

●FURTHER READING: *Music Outside-Contemporary Jazz In Britain*, Ian Carr. *Miles Davis*, Ian Carr. *Keith Jarrett: The Man And His Music*, Ian Carr.

CARTER, CLARENCE

b. 14 January 1936, Montgomery, Alabama, USA. Carter's earliest releases were as half of the duo, Clarence And Calvin. Also known as the C And C Boys, the blind duo made seven singles, the last of which was recorded at Fame's Muscle Shoals studio. When his partner, Calvin Thomas (aka Scott), suffered serious injury in a car accident in 1966, Carter became a solo act. (Calvin Scott himself later reappeared as a solo act to record two Dave Crawford-produced Atco singles in 1969/70 and a Clarence Paul-produced 1971 album for Stax, *I'm Not Blind ... I Just Can't See*, from which two singles were also culled.) 'Tell Daddy', released in January 1967, began a fruitful spell of Fame-produced hits by Carter, released on the Atlantic label. Noteworthy were 'Thread The Needle', 'Looking For A Fox' and 'Slip Away' where the singer combined his outstanding voice with his skill as an arranger and musician. 'Patches', first recorded by Chairmen Of The Board, was a UK number 2 and a US number 4 in 1970, but despite further strong offerings, Clarence was unable to sustain the momentum. He remained with Fame until 1973, where he also helped guide Candi Staton, who was now his wife, before moving to ABC Records the subsequent year. Further recordings on Venture and Big C took Carter's career into the 80s and of late the artist has found a sympathetic outlet with the Ichiban label.

Despite being blinded as a child, he developed a distinctive guitar style which complemented his earthy delivery, and was just as comfortable on keyboards, writing songs or arranging sessions. The first two albums, *This Is Clarence Carter* and *The Dynamic Clarence Carter* show off his versatile talent to good effect.

●ALBUMS: *This Is Clarence Carter* (Atlantic 1968)★★★, *The Dynamic Clarence Carter* (Atlantic 1969)★★★, *Testifyin'* (Atlantic 1969)★★★, *Patches* (Atlantic 1970)★★★, *Sixty Minutes With Clarence Carter* (1973)★★, *Real* (1974)★★, *Loneliness And Temptation* (1975)★★★, *Heart Full Of Song* (ABC 1976)★★★, *I Got Caught* (ABC 1977)★★★, *Let's Burn* (Venture 1981)★★★, *Messin' With My Mind* (Ichiban 1985)★★★, *Dr. CC* (Ichiban 1986)★★★, *Hooked On Love* (Ichiban 1987)★★★, *Touch Of Blues* (Ichiban 1989)★★★, *Between A Rock And A Hard Place* (Ichiban 1990)★★★, *Have You Met Clarence Carter ... Yet?* (1992)★★★, *I Couldn't Refuse* (Ron 1995)★★★.

●COMPILATIONS: *The Best Of Clarence Carter* (Atlantic 1971)★★★, *Soul Deep* (Edsel 1984)★★★, *The Dr.'s Greatest Prescriptions* (Ichiban 1991)★★, *Snatching It Back: The Best Of ...* (Sequel 1995)★★★.

CARTHY, MARTIN

b. 21 May 1940, Hatfield, Hertfordshire, England. Carthy began his career as an actor but in 1959 became a skiffle guitarist and singer with the Thameside Four. He made his first solo recording on the collection *Hootenanny In London* (1963), singing 'Your Baby 'As Gone Down The Plug Hole', later revived by Cream. By now, Carthy was recognized as a virtuoso folk guitarist and was resident at London's top folk club the Troubadour. There, he taught songs to visiting Americans including Bob Dylan and Paul Simon, who adapted 'Lord Franklin' and 'Scarborough Fair' for their own records. With Leon Rosselson, Carthy recorded as the Three City Four before making his first solo album for Fontana. On *Byker Hill* there was equal billing for violinist Dave Swarbrick, with whom Carthy was touring the folk clubs. From 1969-72, he was a member of the folk rock band Steeleye Span with whom he first played electric guitar. Carthy later joined the more traditional vocal group the Watersons which also included his wife Norma Waterson. In the 80s he toured and recorded with Brass Monkey, a band formed by John Kirkpatrick. Carthy also took part in concept albums by the Albion Country Band (1972) and in the Transports, the 'folk opera' created by Peter Bellamy. Essentially, though, Carthy is at his best as a soloist or in partnership with Swarbrick with whom he toured again in 1989. In the 90s some of his work with his daughters Eliza and Norma Waterson was particularly inspiring.

●ALBUMS: *Martin Carthy* (Fontana 1965)★★★, *Second Album* (Fontana 1966)★★★, with Dave Swarbrick *Byker Hill* (Fontana 1967)★★★★, with Swarbrick *But Two Came By* (Fontana 1968)★★★, with Swarbrick *Prince Heathen* (Fontana 1970)★★★, with Swarbrick *Selections* (Pegasus 1971)★★★, *Landfall* (Philips 1971)★★★★,

Sweet Wivelsfield (Deram 1974)★★★, *Shearwater* (Topic 1975)★★★, *Crown Of Horn* (Topic 1976)★★★, *Because It's There* (1979)★★★, *Out Of The Cut* (Topic 1982)★★★, *Right Of Passage* (Topic 1989)★★★★, with Swarbrick *Life And Limb* (Special Delivery/Topic 1990)★★★, with Swarbrick *Skin & Bone* (1992)★★★★.
●COMPILATIONS: *This Is Martin Carthy* (Philips 1972)★★★★, *Rigs Of The Time - The Best Of...* (1993)★★★, *The Collection* (Green Linnet 1994)★★★★.
●VIDEOS: *British Fingerstyle Guitar* (1994).

CASSIDY, DAVID

b. 12 April 1950, New York, USA. The son of actor Jack Cassidy, David pursued a showbusiness career and received his big break after being cast in *The Partridge Family*. The television series was inspired by the life of another hit group, the Cowsills, and it was not long before the Partridge Family began registering hits in their own right. Cassidy appeared as lead vocalist on their earnest 1970 US chart-topper, 'I Think I Love You'. Further hits followed and, in October 1971, Cassidy was launched as a solo artist. One month later he was number 1 in the USA with a revival of the Association's 'Cherish'. Cassidy was classic teen-idol material but was ambivalent about the superficiality of his image and attempted to create a more adult sexual persona by appearing semi-naked in the pages of *Rolling Stone*. The publicity did not help his career at home, but by mid-1972 he was finding even greater success as a soloist in the UK, where teen-idols were suddenly in the ascendant. That year, he climbed to number 2 in Britain with 'Could It Be Forever' and enjoyed a solo chart-topper with a revival of the Young Rascals' 'How Can I Be Sure?' The more R&B-style 'Rock Me Baby' just failed to reach the Top 10 in the UK and peaked at number 38 in the USA. It was his last hit in his home country. By 1973, Cassidy was concentrating on the UK market and his efforts were rewarded with the Top 3 'I Am A Clown' and the double-sided 'Daydreamer'/'The Puppy Song' gave him his second UK number 1. His ability to raid old catalogues and recycle well-known songs to teenage audiences was reflected through further successful covers, including the Beatles' 'Please Please Me' and the Beach Boys' 'Darlin''. By the mid-70s, it was clear that his teen-idol days were reaching their close, so he switched to serious acting, appearing in Tim Rice and Andrew Lloyd Webber's *Joseph And The Amazing Technicolor Dreamcoat*. In 1985, he made a surprise return to the UK Top 10 with the self-penned 'The Last Kiss', which featured backing vocals from George Michael. Two years later, he took over from Cliff Richard in the lead role of Dave Clark's musical *Time*. His teen-idol mantle was meanwhile passed on to his younger brother Shaun Cassidy. In 1993, the two brothers, along with veteran singer Petula Clark, boosted audiences considerably when they joined the Broadway production of Willy Russell's musical *Blood Brothers*.

●ALBUMS: *Cherish* (Bell 1972)★★, *Could It Be Forever* (Bell 1972)★★, *Rock Me Baby* (Bell 1973)★★, *Dreams Are Nothin' More* (Bell 1973)★★, *Cassidy Live* (Bell 1974)★, *The Higher They Climb* (RCA 1975)★★, *Romance* (Arista 1985)★★, *His Greatest Hits, Live* (Starblend 1986)★, *David Cassidy* (Enigma 1990)★★.
●COMPILATIONS: *Greatest Hits* (MFP 1977)★★★.
●FURTHER READING: *Meet David Cassidy*, James A. Hudson. *David Cassidy Annual 1974*, no editor listed. *The David Cassidy Story*, James Gregory. *David In Europe: Exclusive! David's Own Story In David's Own Words*, David Cassidy. *C'mon Get Happy... Fear And Loathing On The Partridge Family Bus*, David Cassidy..

CAT MOTHER AND THE ALL NIGHT NEWSBOYS

The original line-up of this eclectic quintet included Larry Israel Packer (vocals, guitar, harmonica, mandolin), Charlie Chin (guitar, banjo, vocals), Bob Smith (keyboards, vocals, drums), Roy 'Bones' Michaels (bass, guitar, banjo, vocals) and Michael Equine (drums). Packer was a former member of the New York Rock 'N' Roll Ensemble, while Michaels had served in the Au Go Go Singers, a clean-cut folk ensemble that also included Stephen Stills and Richie Furay, both of whom later appeared in Buffalo Springfield. Chin, another coffee-house acolyte, coincidentally supplied the distinctive banjo coda on the latter group's exemplary 'Bluebird'. Cat Mother's debut album, which was produced by Jimi Hendrix, reflected contrasting backgrounds. Chin then left the group, which sought a more receptive audience on America's west coast. Their music reflected a good-time, almost communal, spirit, but a notorious insta-bility undermined their undoubted potential. A 1973 release, *Last Chance Dance*, marked the end of the group's recording career, although they remained a popular live attraction for several years. Late arrival Charlie Harcourt was the only former member to prosper on Cat Mother's demise when he latterly joined Lindisfarne.

●ALBUMS: *The Street Giveth ... And The Street Taketh Away* (Polydor 1969)★★★, *Albion Doo Wah* (1970)★★, *Cat Mother* (1972)★★, *Last Chance Dance* (United Artists 1973)★★.

CATE BROTHERS

A duo composed of twin brothers Ernie and Earl Cate (b. 26 December 1942, Fayetteville, Arkansas, USA), the Cate Brothers specialized in southern soul music and enjoyed brief popularity in the late 70s. Ernie (piano/vocals) and Earl (guitar/vocals) signed to Asylum Records in 1975 and released their first album, a self-titled effort, using numerous studio musicians, among them Memphis legends Steve Cropper and Donald 'Duck' Dunn, Timothy B Schmit (ex-Poco and the Eagles), Nigel Olsson of Elton John's band, Klaus Voormann and Levon Helm of the Band. The album charted in 1976 and the single 'Union Man' reached number 24. The brothers' second album, *In One Eye And Out The Other*, also charted in 1976, as did one other single, 'Can't Change My Heart'. Although there were no other commercial successes, two further albums were recorded, 1977's *The Cate Brothers Band* and *Fire On The Tracks*, the last for Atlantic in 1979. In the early 80s the two brothers and members of the current edition of their group joined Levon Helm and three other original members of the Band in a reformation of the latter group, the entire quartet replacing guitarist Robbie Robertson. No further recordings have emerged since the 70s.

●ALBUMS: *The Cate Brothers* (Asylum 1975)★★★, *In One Eye And Out The Other* (Asylum 1976)★★★, *The Cate Brothers Band* (Asylum 1977)★★, *Fire On The Tracks* (Atlantic 1979)★★.

CAVALIERE, FELIX

b. 29 November 1944, Pelham, New York, USA. Formerly keyboard player/vocalist with the (Young) Rascals, Cavaliere was one of rock's definitive blue-eyed soul performers. By the 70s his group was embracing a cool jazz-rock and this crafted, smooth approach also marks the singer's solo releases. His debut album, *Felix Cavaliere*, was a promising affair, but the follow-up, *Destiny*, was even more accomplished, and featured contributions from former Rascals Dino Danelli and Buzz Feiten, and singer Laura Nyro. A third collection followed in 1979, from which 'Only A Lonely Heart Sees' was a US hit single at the start of the new decade. However, Cavaliere has since been unable to fulfil his undoubted potential and in 1988 he, Danelli and Gene Cornish were reunited for a national Rascals tour. That year he moved to Nashville and pursued a writing career that included music for advertising and record production (including B.B. King, Isaac Hayes and Rufus Thomas). In 1995 he went on tour with Ringo Starr.

●ALBUMS: *Felix Cavaliere* (Bearsville 1974)★★, *Destiny* (Bearsville 1975)★★★, *Castles In The Air* (Epic 1979)★★.

●COMPILATIONS: *A Rascal Alone* (See For Miles 1988)★★★.

CBGB's

CBGB's is almost as intrinsic to the development of American alternative rock music as the guitar. A downtown, 300-capacity New York nightclub/venue, its legendary status grew quickly among aficionados of the city's 'No Wave' scene, and the subsequent punk movement. Established in December 1963, the venue was founded by owner Hilly Kristal (b. *c.*1931), giving it the name Country, Bluegrass, Blues and Other Music for Uplifting Gourmandizers, though the last sections of these initials were soon dropped. Previously it had been a low-rent drinking establishment. The club came into its own in the mid-70s, when Television manager Terry Ork brought in new groups. A who's who of New York music quickly followed, including Patti Smith, Blondie,

Richard Hell, Ramones, Dead Boys, Talking Heads and the Cramps. A second generation also saw the light of day through CBGB's, including Sonic Youth and the Swans. In 1993 20th Anniversary Celebrations were held, with some of the venue's favourite artists taking part in the celebrations, including Joan Jett, the Damned, David Byrne and more recent graduates, Jesus Lizard and J. Mascis (Dinosaur Jr). The Dictators, Tuff Darts and the Shirts all reunited for the occasion. Other notable attractions over the years have included Guns N'Roses, AC/DC, Pearl Jam, and the Spin Doctors. Though many like Joey Ramone retain fond memories of its illustrious past as a 'birthplace', the venue remains popular to this day because of the booking policy, whereby bands receive 80% of the door minus expenses.

●ALBUMS: *Live At CBGBs* (1976)★★★.

●FURTHER READING: *This Ain't No Disco*, Roman Kozak.

CCS

CCS - Collective Consciousness Society - was an unlikely collaboration between blues traditionalist Alexis Korner (b. 19 April 1928, Paris, France. d. January 1984; vocals/guitar), producer Mickie Most and arranger John Cameron. Formed in 1970, the group revolved around Korner and longtime associate Peter Thorup (vocals), plus several of Britain's leading jazz musicians, including Harry Beckett, Henry Lowther, Kenny Wheeler, Les Condon (trumpets), Johnnie Watson, Don Lusher (trombones), Ronnie Ross, Danny Moss (saxophones), Ray Warleigh (flute), Herbie Flowers, Spike Heatley (basses), Barry Morgan and Tony Carr (drums) and Bill Le Sage (tuned percussion). Although the exact line-up was determined by availability, the unit's commercial, brass-laden sound remained intact over three albums. CCS enjoyed several hit singles, each of which was marked by Korner's distinctive growl. Their version of Led Zeppelin's 'Whole Lotta Love', which served as the theme to BBC television's *Top Of The Pops*, reached number 13 in 1970, and the following year the group enjoyed two UK Top 10 entries with 'Walkin'' and 'Tap Turns On The Water'. CCS was dissolved in 1973 when Korner and Thorup formed Snape with Boz Burrell (bass) and Ian Wallace (drums), two former members of King Crimson.

●ALBUMS: *CCS* aka *Whole Lotta Love* (RAK 1970)★★★, *CCS (2)* (RAK 1972)★★★, *The Best Band In The Land* (RAK 1973)★★★.

●COMPILATIONS: *The Best Of CCS* (RAK 1977)★★★.

CHAIRMEN OF THE BOARD

Briefly known as the Gentlemen, this Detroit-based quartet was instigated by General Norman Johnson (b. 23 May 1944, Norfolk, Virginia, USA). A former member of the Showmen, he left that group in 1968 intent on a solo path, but instead joined Danny Woods (b. 10 April 1944, Atlanta, Georgia, USA), Harrison Kennedy (b.

Canada) and Eddie Curtis (b. Philadelphia, Pennsylvania, USA) in this budding venture. Signed to the newly formed Invictus label, the group secured an international hit with their debut single, 'Give Me Just A Little More Time'. His elated performance established the General's emphatic delivery, which combined the emotional fire of the Four Tops' Levi Stubbs with the idiomatic 'trilling' of Billy Stewart. Its follow-up, the vibrant '(You've Got Me) Dangling On A String', was a more substantial hit in the UK than America, the first of several releases following this pattern. Such commercial contradictions did not detract from the excellence of 'Everything's Tuesday', 'Pay To The Piper' (both 1971) and 'I'm On My Way To A Better Place' (1972) as the group furthered its impressive repertoire. Although Johnson provided the most recognizable voice, Woods and Kennedy also shared the lead spotlight, while the overall sound varied from assertive R&B to the melancholia of 'Patches', later a hit for Clarence Carter. The group ceased recording in 1971, but singles continued to appear until 1976 while a final album, Skin I'm In (1974), was also compiled from old masters. Curtis left Invictus altogether but the remaining trio each issued solo albums. Johnson also worked with stablemates the Honey Cone and 100 Proof, while he and Woods, kept the Chairmen name afloat with live performances.

The General subsequently signed with Arista, where he enjoyed a series of late 70s R&B hits before reuniting with Woods. Releases including 'Down At The Beach Club' (1981) and 'On The Beach' (1982), reflect their enduring popularity on the American 'beach'/vintage soul music scene.

●ALBUMS: as the Chairmen Of The Board Chairmen Of The Board (Invictus 1969)★★★, In Session (Invictus 1970)★★, Men Are Getting Scarce (Bittersweet) (Invictus 1972)★★, Skin I'm In (Invictus 1974)★★★, as General Johnson And The Chairmen Success (1981)★★, A Gift Of Beach Music (1982)★★. Solo: General Johnson Generally Speaking (Invictus 1972)★★, General Johnson (Invictus 1976)★★★. Harrison Kennedy Hypnotic Music (Invictus 1972)★★. Danny Woods Aries (Invictus 1972)★★.

●COMPILATIONS: Salute The General (HDH/Demon 1983)★★★, A.G.M. (HDH/Demon 1985)★★★, Soul Agenda (1989)★★, Greatest Hits (HDH/Fantasy 1991)★★★★.

CHAPIN, HARRY

b. 7 December 1942, New York, USA, d. 16 July 1980. The son of a big band drummer, Chapin played in the Brooklyn Heights Boys' Choir and during his teens formed a group with his brothers, Tom and Stephen. Immensely talented as a writer and film-maker, he directed the Oscar-nominated Legendary Champions in 1968, after which he returned to music. In 1971, he formed a group with John Wallace (bass), Ron Palmer (guitar) and Tim Scott (cello) and played in various clubs in New York. The following year, he was signed to Elektra Records and his debut Heads And Tales and the

six-minute single 'Taxi' enjoyed minor success in the US charts. Chapin's strength as a writer was already emerging in the form of fascinating narrative songs, which often had a twist in the tale. 'W-O-L-D', an acute observation of the life of a local disc jockey, went on to become something of an FM radio classic. In 1974, Chapin secured the US Christmas number 1 single with the evocative 'Cat's In The Cradle', a moral warning on the dangers of placing careerism above family life. In the song, the neglectful father realizes too late that he has no relationship with his son, who abandons him in his old age. Despite the quality of the recording, it made surprisingly little headway in the UK, failing even to reach the Top 40. With a series of albums, strongly narrative in tone, it was clear that Chapin was capable of extending himself and in 1975 he wrote the Broadway musical revue, The Night That Made America Famous. That same year, he also won an Emmy award for his musical work on the children's television series, Make A Wish. By 1976, Chapin was still enjoying immense success in his homeland and his double live album Greatest Stories - Live received a gold record award. During the late 70s, he became increasingly involved in politics and was a delegate at the 1976 Democratic Convention. He also played many benefit concerts, raising millions of dollars in the process. In 1980, he switched labels to the small Boardwalk. The title track to his album Sequel, which was a story sequel to his first hit 'Taxi', gave him his final US Top 30 entry. On 16 July, while travelling to a benefit concert, his car was hit by a truck in Jericho, New York, and the singer was killed. A Harry Chapin Memorial Fund was subsequently launched in honour of his memory.

●ALBUMS: Heads And Tales (Elektra 1972)★★★, Sniper And Other Love Songs (Elektra 1972)★★, Short Stories (Elektra 1974)★★★, Verities And Balderdash (Elektra 1974)★★★★, Portrait Gallery (Elektra 1975)★★★, Greatest Stories - Live (Elektra 1976)★★, On The Road To Kingdom Come (Elektra 1976)★★, Dance Band On The Titanic (Elektra 1977)★★★, Living Room Suite (Elektra 1978)★★, Legends Of The Lost And Found - New Greatest Stories Live (Elektra 1979)★★, Sequel (Boardwalk 1980)★★★, The Last Protest Singer (Sequel 1989)★★.

●COMPILATIONS: Anthology (Elektra 1985)★★★.

●FURTHER READING: Taxi: The Harry Chaplin Story, Peter M. Coan.

CHAPMAN, MICHAEL

b. 24 January 1941, Leeds, Yorkshire, England. A former teacher of art and photography, Chapman emerged from the relative obscurity of Britain's folk club circuit with his 1968 debut, Rainmaker. This exceptional release, which contrasted excellent acoustic performances with a handful of rock-based pieces, revealed a gifted songwriter/guitarist and established his lachrymose delivery. Fully Qualified Survivor, the artist's next collection, reached the Top 50 in the UK charts in March 1970, and included the emotional 'Postcards Of

Scarborough' which remains his best-known work. Among the featured musicians was guitarist Mick Ronson, whose impressive contributions led to his subsequent collaborations with David Bowie. Chapman meanwhile continued to forge his mildly eccentric path, and following the release of his fourth album, *Wrecked Again*, toured the USA with long-time associate Rick Kemp. However, their partnership was dissolved upon their return when the bassist joined Steeleye Span. In 1973 Chapman switched record labels from Harvest to Deram, but releases there failed to maintain his early promise. The collapse of Criminal Records, the company responsible for several of his late 70s recordings, was a further blow, but Chapman maintained his popularity through live appearances. Chapman's work as a solo artist from the late 70s and early 80s was admirably captured on *Almost Alone*, which included new performances of 'Kodak Ghosts', 'Northern Lights' and 'Dogs Got More Sense'. A brief reunion with Kemp in the latter part of this period resulted in the single, 'All Day, All Night'/'Geordie's Down The Road' (1983). Later work has seen him sign to the Coda label, performing New Age music (a tag that Chapman reportedly despises), enabling him to demonstrate these exemplary guitar skills. After recovering from a heart attack in August 1991, and playing alongside Kemp in his band Savage Amusement, Chapman resumed his customary treks across the UK, recording a new album in 1993, *Still Making Rain* and hit a late peak with *Navigation* in 1996. *Dreaming Out Loud* was another good album, but was slightly marred by the loss of 'acousticity' of his guitar. Chapman's songs have greater impact in a 'wooden' environment. His voice, however, has ripened beautifully. Rob Beattie in Q magazine perceptively summed up Chapman's voice as 'a delivery that makes John Martyn sound like a Shakespearian voice coach'. Both artists remain painfully ignored yet hugely talented.

●ALBUMS: *Rainmaker* (Harvest 1968)★★★, *Fully Qualified Survivor* (Harvest 1970)★★★★, *Window* (Harvest 1971)★★★, *Wrecked Again* (Harvest 1972)★★★, *Millstone Grit* (Gama 1973)★★★, *Deal Gone Down* (Gama 1974)★★★, *Pleasures Of The Street* (Gama 1975)★★★, *Savage Amusement* (Gama 1976)★★, *The Man Who Hated Mornings* (Gama 1977)★★★, *Playing Guitar The Easy Way* guitar tutor (Criminal 1978)★★★, *Life On The Ceiling* (Criminal 1978)★★, *Looking For Eleven* (Criminal 1980)★★★, *Almost Alone* (Black Crow 1981)★★★★, with Rick Kemp *Original Owners* (Konnexion 1984)★★, *Heartbeat* (Coda 1987)★★★, *Still Making Rain* (Making Waves 1993)★★★, *Navigation* (Planet Plan 1996)★★★★, *Dreaming Out Loud* (Demon 1997)★★★.

●COMPILATIONS: *Lady On The Rocks* (1974)★★, *Michael Chapman Lived Here From 1968-72* (Cube 1977)★★★★, re-released as*The Best Of (1968 - 1972)* (See For Miles 1988)★★★★.

CHAPMAN, ROGER

b. Roger Maxwell Chapman, 8 April 1942, Leicester, England. 'Chappo' sprang howling in the world's face as frontman for Family in 1966, having already worked in the business for eight years. He had progressed from local groups covering the likes of Ray Charles and the Coasters to a Beatle-esque sojourn in Germany with the (UK) Exciters. When Ric Grech left the Exciters to join the Leicester-based Farinas, Chapman followed. Changing their name to Family they moved to London in 1966, where their tight arrangements, augmented by the singular combination of violin and saxophone, laid a solid base for Chapman's searing delivery, and they had an immediate impact on the 'underground' scene. When Family broke up in 1973 the Chapman/Whitney songwriting partnership was continued in Streetwalkers, producing some memorable live performances (including supporting the Who at Charlton in 1976) and a couple of excellent hard rock albums. However, after three years of mixed success and fluctuating line-ups the partnership was dissolved. Chapman's first solo output, *Chappo*, in 1979 (produced by David Courtney) and accompanying tour were well received. The mid-80s saw an occasional UK gig and some less successful albums, but 1989's acclaimed *Walking The Cat* demonstrated Chapman's resilience and energy. Supported by Bob Tench (who had been a stable element in Streetwalkers), Alvin Lee and Mick Moody, it marked a return to form, continued in 1991 with *Hybrid and Lowdown*. *Kiss My Soul* in 1996 was a triumphant album - his best for many years, with a full production sound that enabled Chapman's voice to cut through like cheese-wire. 'Habit Of A Lifetime' and 'Into The Bright' were highly commercial (it even prompted a single release for the latter) but others like 'A Cat Called Kokomo' and 'One More Whiskey' were funkier, bluesier, less cluttered and more like the Chapman we know.

●ALBUMS: *Chappo* (Arista 1979)★★★, *Live In Hamburg* (Acrobat 1979)★★★, *Mail Order Magic* (Kamera 1980)★★, *Hyenas Only Laugh For Fun* (Teldec 1981)★★, as the Shortlist *The Riffburgler Album* (1981)★★, *He Was She Was* (Polydor 1982)★★, as the Riffburglers *Swag* (1983)★★, *Mango Crazy* (1983)★★, *The Shadow Knows* (1984)★★★, *Zipper* (1986)★★, *Techno Prisoners* (1987)★★, *Walking The Cat* (1989)★★★, *Hybrid And Lowdown* (1991)★★★, *Under No Obligation* (1992)★★, *King Of The Shouters* (1994)★★, *Kiss My Soul* (Essential 1996)★★★.

●COMPILATIONS: *Kick It Back* (1993)★★★.

CHAS AND DAVE

These veterans of the English rock scene joined forces in 1975 to create novelty material in the cockney idiom. Chas Hodges (b. 28 December 1943, London, England) had played piano with the Outlaws, Cliff Bennett And The Rebel Rousers and Heads, Hands And Feet. Dave

Peacock (b. 24 May 1945, London, England) was a guitarist with rock 'n' roll revival and country bands before joining up with Hodges to record *One Fing And Annuver* for Retreat, a label owned by session guitarist Big Jim Sullivan. Adding drummer Mick Burt (b. 23 August 1943), the group signed to EMI in 1977. 'Strummin'' was a minor hit but the group reached the Top 20 in 1979 with 'Gertcha!', a rollicking composition that had featured in a UK television beer commercial. An even more successful effort in the same vein was 'Rabbit', which appeared on Chas And Dave's own Rockney label. In 1981 and 1982 the duo provided football songs for Cup finalists Tottenham Hotspur, in 'Ossie's Dream' and 'Tottenham Tottenham'. The duo extended their sporting interests to snooker on 1987's 'Romford Rap', credited to the Matchroom Mob. A more sentimental side was displayed on their biggest hit, 'Ain't No Pleasing You' (1982) and during the 80s Chas And Dave appeared frequently on television light entertainment shows and regularly released raucous party records. Their rock roots were not entirely lost, however, and *Oily Rags* (released by Signature) included 'Holy Cow' and 'Mailman Bring Me No More Blues' in amongst the cockney ditties.

●ALBUMS: *One Fing 'N' Annuver* (Retreat 1976)★★★, *Rockney* (EMI 1978)★★, *Don't Give A Monkey's* (EMI 1979)★★, *Live At Abbey Road* (EMI 1981)★★, *Chas And Dave's Christmas Jamboree Bag* (Rockney 1981)★★, *Mustn't Grumble* (Rockney 1982)★★, *Job Lot* (Rockney 1982)★★★, *Chas And Dave's Knees Up - Jamboree Bag Number 2* (Rockney 1983)★★, *Well Pleased* (Rockney 1984)★★, *Oily Rags* (Signature 1985)★★, *Jamboree Bag Number 3* (Rockney 1985)★★, *Buddy* (Autograph 1985)★★, *Christmas Carol Album* (Telstar 1986)★★, *On The Road* (Rockney 1986)★★, *Flying* (Bunce 1987)★★.

●COMPILATIONS: *All The Best From Chas And Dave* (K-Tel 1988)★★★.

●FURTHER READING: *The Rock & Roll Years Of Chas Before Dave*, Chas Hodges.

CHASE, BILL

b. 1935, Boston, Massachusetts, USA, d. 9 August 1974, Jackson, Minnesota, USA. In the mid-50s Chase studied trumpet at Berklee College Of Music under Herb Pomeroy. Towards the end of the decade he played with Maynard Ferguson, Stan Kenton and Woody Herman. Throughout the 60s he frequently returned to the Herman band but turned increasingly to jazz-rock, later forming his own band Chase in 1971; three years later he toured with a re-formed version of the band. It was while on tour that, on 9 August 1974, he and other members of the band - John Emma (guitar), Walter Clark (drums) and Wally York (keyboards) - were killed in an airplane crash.

●ALBUMS: with Maynard Ferguson *A Message From Newport* (1958)★★★★, with Woody Herman *Woody's Winners* (1965)★★★, as Chase *Chase* (Epic 1971)★★★, *Ennea* (Epic 1972)★★★, *Pure Music* (Epic 1974)★★★.

CHEAP TRICK

One of rock's most entertaining attractions, Cheap Trick formed in Chicago, Illinois, USA, in 1973. Rick Nielsen (b. 22 December 1946, Rockford, Illinois, USA; guitar/vocals) and Tom Petersson (b. Peterson, 9 May 1950, Rockford, Illinois, USA; bass/vocals) began their careers in various high school bands, before securing a recording deal as members of Fuse. This short-lived outfit folded on completing a debut album, and the duo subsequently formed a new group with Thom Mooney and Robert 'Stewkey' Antoni from the recently disbanded Nazz. Mooney was subsequently replaced by drummer Brad Carlson (aka Bun E. Carlos, b. 12 June 1951, Rockford, Illinois, USA), and with the departure of 'Stewkey', the initial Cheap Trick line-up was completed by vocalist Randy 'Xeno' Hogan. He in turn was replaced by Robin Zander (b. 23 January 1952, Loves Park, Illinois, USA; guitar/vocals), a former colleague of Carlson in the short-lived Toons. Relocated to America's Midwest, the quartet followed the gruelling bar band circuit before a series of demonstration tapes secured a recording contract. Although *Cheap Trick* is generally regarded as a disappointment, it introduced the group's inventive flair and striking visual image. The heart-throb good looks of Zander and Petersson clashed with Carlos' seedy garb, while Nielsen's odd-ball costume - baseball cap, bow-tie and monogrammed sweater - compounded this unlikely contrast. Having spent a frenetic period supporting Queen, Journey and Kiss, Cheap Trick completed a second collection within months of their debut. *In Color* offered a smoother sound in which a grasp of melody was allowed to flourish and established the group's ability to satisfy visceral and cerebral demands. It contained several engaging performances, including 'I Want You To Want Me', 'Hello There' and 'Clock Strikes Ten', each of which became in-concert favourites. *Heaven Tonight* consolidated the group's unique approach while 'Surrender' contained the consummate Cheap Trick performance, blending the British pop of the Move with the urgent riffing of the best of America's hard rock. *At Budokan* followed a highly successful tour of Japan, and this explosive live set became the quartet's first platinum disc, confirming them as a headline act in their own right. However, *Dream Police* added little to the sound extolled on the previous two studio releases, and indeed the title song was originally recorded for the group's debut album. Producer George Martin did little to deflect this sterility on *All Shook Up*, while *Found All The Parts*, a mini-album culled from out-takes, suggested internal problems. A disaffected Petersson left the group in 1982, but although Pete Comita initially took his place, the latter quickly made way for Jon Brant (ex-Ruffians). Neither *One On One*, nor the Todd Rundgren-produced *Next Position Please* halted Cheap Trick's commercial slide, but *Standing On The Edge* offered hopes of a renaissance. A 1986 recording, 'Mighty Wings', was used on the soundtrack of the successful *Top Gun* film, while the return of Petersson the same year re-established the group's most successful line-up. *Lap Of Luxury* achieved multi-platinum status when an attendant single, 'The Flame', topped the US chart in 1988 while *Busted* scaled similar heights, confirming Cheap Trick's dramatic resurrection as a major US act.

●ALBUMS: *Cheap Trick* (Epic 1977)★★★, *In Color* (Epic 1977)★★★, *Heaven Tonight* (Epic 1978)★★★★, *Cheap Trick At Budokan* (Epic 1979)★★★★, *Dream Police* (Epic 1979)★★★, *Found All The Parts* (Epic 1980)★★, *All Shook Up* (Epic 1980)★★, *One On One* (Epic 1982)★★, *Next Position Please* (Epic 1983)★★, *Standing On The Edge* (Epic 1985)★★★, *The Doctor* (Epic 1986)★★, *Lap Of Luxury* (Epic 1988)★★★, *Busted* (Epic 1990)★★★, *Woke Up With A Monster* (Warners 1994)★★, *Budokan 2* rec. 1978 (Epic/Sony 1994)★★, *Cheap Trick* (Red Ant 1997)★★.

●COMPILATIONS: *The Collection* (Castle 1991)★★★★, *Greatest Hits* (Epic 1992)★★★, *Sex, America, Cheap Trick* 4-CD box set (Epic 1996)★★★★.

●VIDEOS: *Every Trick In The Book* (CMV Enterprises 1990).

CHEECH AND CHONG

Richard 'Cheech' Marin (b. 1946, Watts, Los Angeles, California, USA) became acquainted with Tommy Chong (b. 24 May 1940, Edmonton, Alberta, Canada) while fleeing to escape induction into the US Army. The latter was a noted musician, having performed in Bobby Taylor And The Vancouvers, but the duo's plans for a rock group were sidelined on discovering an aptitude for comedy. A residency at the famed Los Angeles Troubador venue resulted in a recording contract, through which a succession of albums established their unique humour. Drawing upon their rock backgrounds, Cheech And Chong pursued subjects apposite to hippie culture - long hair, drugs, sex and police harassment - in a manner indebted to comedian Lenny Bruce and the San Francisco-based *avant garde* troupe, the Committee. Initially fêted by those whose lifestyles provided their subject matter, the duo won a Best Comedy Album Grammy for *Los Cochinos*, and later enjoyed three US hit singles with 'Basketball Jones Featuring Tyrone Shoelaces', 'Sister Mary Elephant (Shudd-Up!)' and 'Earache My Eye Featuring Alice Bowie'. In 1979 they began a film career with *Up In Smoke*, the first of several such ventures, and while under the influence of MTV and a concurrent video boom, began placing a greater emphasis on music. *Get Out Of My Room* included 'Born In East LA', a satirical reworking of Bruce Springsteen's 'Born In The USA'. The duo's song referred to a true-life incident wherein a Latin-American, legally domiciled in the USA, was deported to Mexico when he was unable to prove his citizenship during an immigration raid. 'Born In East LA' became a hit single and inspired a film of the same name. Following their break-up in the late 80s Richard Marin has gone on to enjoy great suc-

cess as a comedy actor and had a major role as a hyena voice in *The Lion King*.

●ALBUMS: *Cheech And Chong* (Ode 1971)★★, *Big Bambu* (Ode 1972)★★, *Los Cochinos* (Ode 1973)★★, *Cheech & Chong's Wedding Album* (Ode 1974)★★, *Sleeping Beauty* (Ode 1976)★★, *Six* (1977)★★, *Up In Smoke* film soundtrack (Warners 1978)★, *Let's Make A New Dope Deal* (Warners 1980)★★, *Get Out Of My Room* (MCA 1986)★★.

●COMPILATIONS: *Greatest Hit* (1993)★★.

CHELSEA

Formed in London, England, in 1977, this punk band consisted of vocalist Gene October, the only constant in a myriad of line-ups, Brian James (guitar), Geoff Myles (bass) and Chris Bashford (drums). Like many of their immediate peers Chelsea were a band with a strong social conscience. Specializing in sub-three minute vitriolic outbursts on unemployment, inner city decay and the destruction of British society under Margaret Thatcher, their lyrics were always more interesting than their music. The songs generally formed a similar pattern of up-tempo numbers, marred by basic studio techniques (October's delivery, occasionally gruesome, was nevertheless the glue in the formula). Taken as a body of work the songs become jarring, but individually their music is exciting and energetic. Their most noteworthy song is 'Right To Work', although it later transpired that the basis of the song was anti-union. They continued to record throughout the 80s with an ever-changing line-up and an image as anachronistic as their music.

●ALBUMS: *Chelsea* (Step Forward 1979)★★★, *Alternative Hits* (Step Forward 1980)★★, *Evacuate* (IRS 1982)★★, *Rocks Off* (Jungle 1986)★★, *Under Wraps* (IRS 1989)★★.

●COMPILATIONS: *Just For The Record* (Step Forward 1985)★★, *Backtrax* (Illegal 1988)★★, *Unreleased Stuff* (Clay 1989)★.

●VIDEOS: *Live At The Bier Keller* (Jettisoundz 1984).

●FILMS: *Jubilee* (1978).

CHI-LITES

Formed in Chicago in 1960 and originally called the Hi-Lites, the group featured Eugene Record (b. 23 December 1940, Chicago, Illinois, USA), Robert Lester (b. 1942, McComb, Mississippi, USA), Creadel Jones (b. 1939, St. Louis, Missouri, USA) and Marshall Thompson (b. April 1941, Chicago, Illinois, USA). Imbued with the tradition of doo-wop and street corner harmony, Record and Lester came together with Clarence Johnson in the Chanteurs, who issued a single on Renee Records in 1959. The trio then teamed with Marshall Thompson and Creadel 'Red' Jones, refugees from another local group, the Desideros. The resultant combination was dubbed the Hi-Lites and a series of releases followed. 'I'm So Jealous' from late 1964 introduced the group's new name, Marshall And The Chi-Lites, the amended suffix celebrating their 'Windy City' origins. Johnson left the group later that year and with the release of 'You Did That To Me', the quartet became simply the Chi-Lites. Further singles confirmed a growing reputation while their arrival at Brunswick Records in 1968 pitched them alongside the cream of Chicago's soul hierarchy. Record formed a songwriting partnership with Barbara Acklin, a combination responsible for many of his group's finest moments. 'Give It Away' (1969) became the Chi-Lites' first US national hit, and introduced a string of often contrasting releases. Although equally self-assured on up-tempo songs, the group became noted for its slower, often sentimental performances. The wistful 'Have You Seen Her' (1971), which reached number 3 on both sides of the Atlantic, highlighted Record's emotive falsetto and later singles, including the US number 1, 'Oh Girl' (1972) and 'Homely Girl' (1974) continued this style. Although American pop success eluded the Chi-Lites' later work, in the UK they hit the Top 5 with 'It's Time For Love' (1975) and 'You Don't Have To Go' (1976). Their continuity was maintained despite several line-up changes. Creadel Jones left the group in 1973, but his successor, Stanley Anderson, was latterly replaced by Willie Kensey. Doc Roberson subsequently took the place of Kensey. The crucial change came in 1986 when Eugene Record left for a short-lived solo career. David Scott and Danny Johnson replaced him but the original quartet of Record, Jones, Lester and Thompson, re-formed in 1980. The title track of *Bottoms Up* became a Top 10 soul single but further releases failed to sustain that success. The group continued as a trio on Jones' retirement, but by the end of the decade Record once again left the group, leaving Thompson with the Chi-Lites' name.

●ALBUMS: *Give It Away* (Brunswick 1960)★★★, *(For God's Sake) Give More Power To The People* (Brunswick 1971)★★★★, *A Lonely Man* (Brunswick 1972)★★★, *A Letter To Myself* (Brunswick 1973)★★★, *The Chi-Lites* (Brunswick 1973)★★★, *Toby* (Brunswick 1974)★★★, *Half A Love* (Brunswick 1975)★★, *Happy Being Lonely* (Mercury 1976)★★★, *The Fantastic Chi-Lites* (Mercury 1977)★★★, *Heavenly Body* (Chi-Sound 1980)★★, *Me And You* (Chi-Sound 1982)★★, *Bottoms Up* (Larc 1983)★★★, *Changing For You* (R&B/Redbus 1983)★★.

●COMPILATIONS: *The Chi-Lites Greatest Hits* (Brunswick 1972)★★★★, *The Chi-Lites Greatest Hits Volume Two* (Brunswick 1975)★★★, *The Best Of The Chi-Lites* (Kent 1987)★★★, *Greatest Hits* (Street Life 1988)★★★, *Very Best Of The Chi-Lites* (BR Music 1988)★★★, *The Chi-Lites Greatest Hits* (Rhino 1992)★★★★, *Have You Seen Her? The Very Best Of ...* (Pickwick 1995)★★★.

CHIC

Arguably *the* band of the disco generation, Chic was built around Nile Rodgers (b. 19 September 1952, New York, USA; guitar) and Bernard Edwards (b. 31 October 1952, Greenville, Carolina, USA, d. 18 April 1996, Tokyo, Japan; bass). During the 60s Rodgers had played

in a rock group, New World Rising, before joining the Apollo Theatre house band. Edwards had played with several struggling musicians prior to meeting his future partner through a mutual friend. They both joined the Big Apple Band in 1971, which subsequently toured, backing hit group New York City. Chic evolved out of a collection of demos that Edwards and Rodgers had recorded. Two female singers, Norma Jean Wright and Luci Martin, were added to the line-up, along with Tony Thompson, a former drummer with LaBelle. Wright later left for a solo career and was replaced by Alfa Anderson. The quintet scored an immediate hit with 'Dance Dance Dance (Yowsah, Yowsah, Yowsah)' (1977), which introduced wit and sparkling instrumentation to the maligned disco genre. In 1978 'Le Freak' became the biggest-selling single in Atlantic/WEA's history, with a total of over four million copies moved. Chic's grasp of melody was clearly apparent on 'I Want Your Love' (1979), while US number 1 'Good Times', with its ferocious bass riff, was not only a gold disc in itself, but became the sampled backbone to several 80s scratch and rap releases. Edwards' and Rodgers' skills were also in demand for outside projects and their handiwork was evident on 'Upside Down' (Diana Ross), 'We Are Family' (Sister Sledge) and 'Spacer' (Sheila B. Devotion). However, their distinctive sound grew too defined to adapt to changing fashions and Chic's later work was treated with indifference. Edwards' solo album, *Glad To Be Here*, was a disappointment, and Rodgers' effort, *Adventures In The Land Of Groove*, fared little better. However, Rodgers' unique work on David Bowie's 'Let's Dance' provided much of the track's propulsive bite. Rodgers later produced Madonna's first major hit, 'Like A Virgin', while Edwards took control of recording the Power Station, the Duran Duran offshoot that also featured Tony Thompson. Edwards also provided the backbone to Robert Palmer's 1986 hit, 'Addicted To Love'. In 1992 the duo re-formed Chic as a rebuff to the rap and techno-dance styles, releasing a single, 'Chic Mystique', and an album. Sadly Chic's revival looks to have ended with the death of Bernard Edwards in 1996, but their influence on dance music (especially its rhythms) ensures a place in pop history.

●ALBUMS: *Chic* (Atlantic 1977)★★★, *C'Est Chic* (Atlantic 1978)★★★, *Risqué* (Atlantic 1979)★★★★, *Real People* (Atlantic 1980)★★★★, *Take It Off* (Atlantic 1981)★★★★, *Tongue In Chic* (Atlantic 1982)★★★, *Believer* (Atlantic 1983)★★★, *Chic-Ism* (Warners 1992)★★★.

●COMPILATIONS: *Les Plus Grands Succès De Chic - Chic's Greatest Hits* (Atlantic 1979)★★★★, *Freak Out - The Greatest Hits of Chic And Sister Sledge* (Telstar 1987)★★★, *Megachic - The Best Of Chic* (Warners 1990)★★★★, *Dance Dance Dance: The Best Of Chic* (Atlantic 1991)★★★★.

CHICAGO

Formed in 1966 in Chicago, Illinois, USA, Chicago was a consistent hit-making group throughout the 70s and

80s. The band was initially called the Missing Links, next becoming the Big Thing and then, the same year, Chicago Transit Authority, at the suggestion of manager Jim Guercio. The original line-up was Terry Kath (b. 31 January 1946, Chicago, USA, d. 23 January 1978; guitar/vocals), Peter Cetera (b. 13 September 1944, Chicago, USA; bass/vocals), Robert Lamm (b. 13 October 1944, Brooklyn, New York, USA; keyboards/vocals), Walter Parazaider (Walt Perry) (b. 14 March 1945, Chicago, USA; saxophone), Danny Seraphine (b. 28 August 1948, Chicago, USA; drums), James Pankow (b. 20 August 1947, Chicago, USA; trombone) and Lee Loughnane (b. 21 October 1941, Chicago, USA; trumpet). The horn section set the group apart from other mid-60s rock bands, although *Chicago Transit Authority* was preceded on record by similar sounding groups such as Blood, Sweat And Tears and the Electric Flag. During 1967 and 1968 Guercio built the band's reputation, particularly in the Los Angeles area, where they played clubs such as the Whisky A-Go-Go. In January 1969 Guercio landed the group a contract with Columbia Records, largely through his reputation as producer of Blood, Sweat And Tears and the Buckinghams. With jazz influences the group released its self-titled album in 1969. Although it never made the Top 10 the album stayed on the US charts for 171 weeks. The group also enjoyed singles hits with 'Does Anybody Really Know What Time It Is' and 'Beginnings'. In 1970 the group shortened its name to Chicago. Still working in the jazz-rock idiom they released *Chicago II*. Henceforth each of the group's albums would receive a number as its title, up to *Chicago 21* by 1991, with the sole exceptions of their fourth album, the four-record boxed set *Chicago At Carnegie Hall*, their twelfth, titled *Hot Streets*, and their fifteenth and twentieth, greatest hits volumes. Each album cover has featured a different interesting treatment of the group's logo, and many have won graphic design awards. By the early 70s Chicago began breaking away from its jazz sound toward more mainstream pop, resulting in such light-rock staples as 'Colour My World', the 1976 transatlantic number 1 'If You Leave Me Now' and the 1982 number 1 'Hard To Say I'm Sorry'. Five consecutive Chicago albums topped the charts between 1972 and 1975; however, the group experienced a sales slump in the late 70s only to rebound in the early 80s.

In 1974 Lamm recorded a poor-selling solo album. That same year the group added Brazilian percussionist Laudir de Oliveira to the line-up. The following year the group toured with the Guercio-managed Beach Boys. In 1977, after *Chicago X* was awarded a Best Album Grammy, Guercio and the group parted ways. On 23 January 1978 founding member Kath was killed by a self-inflicted accidental gunshot wound. The group continued, with Donnie Dacus (ex-Stephen Stills sideman) joining on guitar (he left the following year and was replaced by Chris Pinnick; Pinnick left in 1981, when Bill Champlin, ex-Sons Of Champlin, joined on keyboards). In 1981, Chicago was dropped by Columbia and signed to Full Moon Records, distributed by Warner Brothers Records. Also that year, Cetera released a solo album, which was a mild success. After leaving the group in 1985 (his replacement was Jason Scheff, son of Elvis Presley bassist Jerry Scheff), he released two further solo albums, the first of which yielded two number 1 singles, 'Glory Of Love' and 'The Next Time I Fall', the latter a duet with Amy Grant. Switching to Reprise Records in 1988, Chicago was still considered a major commercial force despite having long abandoned their original jazz-rock roots. In 1995 the perplexing *Night And Day* was released; on this collection the big band era was given the Chicago treatment with mixed results.

●ALBUMS: *Chicago Transit Authority* (Columbia 1969)★★★★, *Chicago II* (Columbia 1970)★★★, *Chicago III* (Columbia 1971)★★★, *Chicago At Carnegie Hall* (Columbia 1971)★★, *Chicago V* (Columbia 1972)★★★, *Chicago VI* (Columbia 1973)★★★, *Chicago VII* (Columbia 1974)★★★, *Chicago VIII* (Columbia 1975)★★★★, *Chicago X* (Columbia 1976)★★, *Chicago XI* (Columbia 1977)★★, *Hot Streets* (Columbia 1978)★★★, *Chicago 13* (Columbia 1979)★★, *Chicago XIV* (Columbia 1980)★★, *Chicago 16* (Full Moon 1982)★★, *Chicago 17* (Full Moon 1984)★★, *Chicago 18* (Warners 1987)★★, *Chicago 19* (Reprise 1988)★★, *Chicago 21* (Reprise 1991)★★, *Night And Day* (Giant 1995)★★★.

●COMPILATIONS: *Chicago IX - Chicago's Greatest Hits* (Columbia 1975)★★★★, *Chicago - Greatest Hits, Volume II* (Columbia 1981)★★★, *Greatest Hits 1982-1989* (Reprise 1989)★★★, *The Heart Of Chicago* (Warners 1989)★★★, *Group Portrait* (Columbia/Legacy 1991)★★★★, *The Very Best Of Chicago* (Arcade 1996)★★★.

●VIDEOS: *And The Band Played On* (Warner Reprise 1994), *In Concert At The Greek Theatre* (Warner Music Vision 1994).

CHICORY TIP

Hailing from Maidstone, Kent, in England, this pop quartet was formed in 1968 by singer Peter Hewson (b. 1 September 1950, Gillingham, Kent, England). The rest of the group comprised Barry Mayger (b. 1 June 1950, Maidstone, Kent, England; bass), Brian Shearer (b. 4 May 1951, Lewisham, London, England; drums) and Dick Foster (guitar). Foster was replaced in October 1972 by Rod Cloutt (b. 26 January 1949, Gillingham, Kent, England; lead guitar/synthesizer/organ). Chicory Tip's main claim to fame was a gnawingly infectious piece of pop ephemera titled 'Son Of My Father' which topped the UK charts for three weeks in early 1972. In the USA the band were marketed as Chicory, the same song made a respectable number 91. The record was something of a combined star effort having been written by the soon-to-be-famous disco producer Giorgio Moroder. The distinctive synthesizer backing on the disc was played by another producer-elect, Chris Thomas. Finally, the man who actually produced the

record was Roger Easterby, manager of another seasoned pop outfit, Vanity Fare. Although Chicory Tip had a low-key image, they rode the glam rock wagon long enough to enjoy two further UK Top 20 hits with 'What's Your Name?' (1972) and 'Good Grief Christina' (1973).
●ALBUMS: *Son Of My Father* (Columbia 1972)★★.

CHILD

This British teen band from the late 70s comprised Timothy Atack (b. 5 April 1959, Wakefield, Yorkshire, England; drums), Graham Robert Bilbrough (b. 23 March 1958, Fairburn, Yorkshire, England; lead vocals/rhythm guitar), Keith Atack (b. 5 April 1959, Wakefield, Yorkshire, England; lead guitar), Mike McKenzie (b. 20 August 1955, Edinburgh, Scotland; bass guitar). They charted in the UK with three uninspired cover versions of 'When You Walk In The Room', 'It's Only Make Believe' (both 1978) and 'Only You (And You Alone)' (1979). Two albums were also released of non-original material. Sold entirely as a visual band and aimed at the young female teenage market, the group worked for 18 months.
●ALBUMS: *Child: The First Album* (Ariola Hansa 1978)★★, *Total Recall* (Ariola Hansa 1979)★★.

CHILLI WILLI AND THE RED HOT PEPPERS

Although fondly recalled as a leading 'pub rock' attraction, Chilli Willi began life as a folksy-cum-country duo comprising Martin Stone (b. 11 December 1946, Woking, Surrey, England; guitar, mandolin, vocals) and Phil 'Snakefinger' Lithman (b. 17 June 1949, Tooting, London, England; guitar, lapsteel, fiddle, piano, vocals). Both were former members of Junior's Blues Band, an aspiring early 60s group, but while Lithman moved to San Francisco, Stone joined the Savoy Brown Blues Band and Mighty Baby. The friends were reunited on *Kings Of The Robot Rhythm*, an informal, enchanting collection which featured assistance from blues singer Jo-Ann Kelly and several members of Brinsley Schwarz. In December 1972 the duo added Paul 'Dice Man' Bailey (b. 6 July 1947, Weston-super-Mare, Somerset, England; guitar, saxophone, banjo), Paul Riley (b. 3 October 1951, Islington, London, England; bass) and Pete Thomas (b. 9 August 1954, Sheffield, Yorkshire, England; drums) and over the ensuing two years, the quintet became one of Britain's most compulsive live attractions. Despite its charm, incorporating many diverse American styles such as blues, country, western swing, rock and R&B, *Bongos Over Balham* failed to capture the group's in-concert passion and a disillusioned Chilli Willi disbanded in February 1975. Pete Thomas later joined the Attractions, Paul Riley played with Graham Parker's band, while Bailey helped form Bontemps Roulez. Martin Stone joined the Pink Fairies prior to leaving music altogether, while Lithman returned to San Francisco where, as Snakefinger, he resumed his earlier association with the Residents.

●ALBUMS: *Kings Of The Robot Rhythm* (Revelation 1972)★★★, *Bongos Over Balham* (Mooncrest 1974)★★★.
●COMPILATIONS: *I'll Be Home* (Proper 1997)★★★.

CHILLIWACK

This was the third version of a Canadian, Vancouver-based group previously known as the Classics and the Collectors. Claire Lawrence (woodwind, harmonica, vocals), Bill Henderson (guitar, recorder, vocals), Glenn Miller (bass, vocals) and Ross Turney (drums) abandoned the latter name in 1971 and embarked on a new direction. Chilliwack's eponymous debut album acknowledged this transition by including a restructured version of 'Seventeeth Summer', a track previously associated with the Collectors. Their third release, *All Over You*, provided a major Canadian hit single in 'Ground Hog', and Chilliwack subsequently became one of the country's most popular home-grown talents. Their often melodious hard-rock was best heard on *Dreams Dreams Dreams*, but inconsistent material and an unstable personnel (Henderson became the lone original member), hampered a wider success.
●ALBUMS: *Chilliwack* i (Mushroom 1971)★★★, *All Over You* (A&M 1972)★★, *Chilliwack* ii (1972)★★, *Chilliwack* iii (1974)★★, *Rockerbox* (1975)★★, *Dreams Dreams Dreams* (Mushroom 1977)★★★, *Lights From The Valley* (Mushroom 1978)★★, *Breakdown In Paradise* (1980)★★, *Wanna Be A Star* (Millenium 1981)★★, *Opus X* (Millenium 1982)★★.

CHILTON, ALEX

b. 28 December 1950, Memphis, Tennessee, USA. Chilton began singing and playing guitar while still at school and absorbed the raw-edged cry of local soul singers. His first work experience was with Ronnie And The DeVilles, singing Stax-styled R&B. Teamed with multi-instrumentalist Bill Cunningham (whose older brother was in the Hombres and wrote 'Let It All Hang Out'), he fronted the Box Tops on guitar and vocals, mixing pop and soul in equal measure. Producer Dan Penn discovered them and recorded 'The Letter', released in late summer 1967 on Bell Records and reaching number 1 in both the UK and US charts. 'Cry Like A Baby' (1968) and 'Soul Deep' (1969) were quintessential blue-eyed Motown. In 1969 the Box Tops broke up. Chilton joined forces with Chris Bell, an old high school buddy obsessed with British beat music. They named themselves after a store across the street from the Ardent studio: Big Star Foodmarkets. *No 1 Record* (1971) (on the Ardent label, distributed by Stax) was a brilliant debut, with scintillating guitars and fresh melodies. Bell departed, but the tougher sound of *Radio City* (1972) was an improvement, if anything. Unfortunately, a foul-up over distribution meant the albums became cult items rather than the pop successes they deserved to be. Chilton disappeared into New York, doing production work (Chris Stamey, Tav Falco's Panther Burns) and releasing erratic solo albums

(*Like Flies On Sherbert*). Requested by the Cramps for production work - a telling recognition from new wavers with a greater sense of tradition than anyone guessed - he did a startling job on *Songs The Lord Taught Us* (1980), actually setting up in Sam Philips' legendary studio, using more reverb than even Philips would have countenanced. *High Priest* and a 1988 tour showed that Alex Chilton was still using his R&B roots to good effect, voice and guitar exhibiting their characteristic nervy edge. Chilton's standing and cult status continues to rise, even by doing nothing. *1970* built upon that reputation even though it contained a dreadful version of the Archies' 'Sugar Sugar', a perfect pop song the point of which even Chilton seems to have missed.

●ALBUMS: with Big Star *#1 Record* (Ardent 1972)★★★★, with Big Star *Radio City* (Ardent 1974)★★★★, with Big Star *3rd* (PVC 1978)★★★★, *Like Flies On Sherbert* (Aura 1980)★★, *Document* (Aura 1986)★★, *Stuff* (1986)★★, *Lost Decade* (Fan Club 1986)★★, *Bach's Bottom* (Line 1987)★★, *High Priest* (New Rose 1987)★★★, *Black List* (New Rose 1990)★★, with Big Star *Live* live radio broadcast from 1974 (Ryko 1992)★★★, with Big Star *Sister Lovers* rec. 1975 (Ryko 1992)★★★★, *Clichés* (New Rose 1994)★★, *A Man Called Destruction* (Ardent 1995)★★, *1970* (Revola 1996)★★★.

●COMPILATIONS: *19 Years: A Collection Of Alex Chilton* (Rhino 1991)★★★★.

CHINN AND CHAPMAN

Mike Chapman (b. 15 April 1947, Queensland, Australia) and Nicky Chinn (b. 16 May 1945, London, England) teamed up to form a songwriting partnership while the former was a member of the group Tangerine Peel and the latter a garage owner. With the encouragement of the Rak Records boss, Mickie Most, they later composed a string of hits in the early 70s for such acts as New World, Sweet, Gary Glitter, Mud, Suzi Quatro and Smokie. The duo became one of the most successful songwriting teams of the era and obtained a reputation in the UK that was only matched in the 80s by the team of Stock, Aitken And Waterman. Mike Chapman emerged as an influential force in moulding Blondie for the pop market, providing production credit on such hits as 'Heart Of Glass', 'The Tide Is High', 'Sunday Girl', 'Atomic' and 'Rapture'. Chinn and Chapman inaugurated the Dreamland label in 1979 which folded two years later. Chapman later worked with Pat Benatar, Exile ('Kiss You All Over', a US number 1 and a Chinn/Chapman composition), Nick Gilder ('Hot Child In The City', a US number 1), the Knack ('My Sharona' a US number 1), Patti Smith and Lita Ford. During this time the duo's songwriting skills earned them a US number 1 in 1982 with 'Mickey' for Toni Basil.

CHISWICK RECORDS

This pioneering independent label was founded in London, England, in 1975 by Ted Carroll and Roger Armstrong. Partners in Rock On, a record stall in Soho market, in London, they were inspired by innovative US 50s outlets such as Sun and Chess Records. Chiswick's first signing, the Count Bishops, were a gutsy R&B band and their EP *Speedball*, captured the prevailing 'pub rock' mood. Trevor Churchill joined the Chiswick board soon afterwards and his record industry experience facilitated licensing deals. The fledgling label issued vintage material by Vince Taylor and Link Wray as well as punk singles by the Hammersmith Gorillas, the 101ers (with Joe Strummer), and Johnny And The Self Abusers, which featured three future members of Simple Minds. Motörhead, Radio Stars and the Radiators (From Space) were among Chiswick's first acts to release an album. In 1978 the label signed a distribution deal with EMI Records. Hit singles by Rocky Sharpe And The Replays, Sniff 'N' The Tears and a revived Damned followed. In the meantime Carroll, Armstrong and Churchill had established Ace Records as an outlet for reissues. The new label eventually superseded Chiswick, which was gradually wound down after its deal with EMI expired in 1981. Chiswick's final release, barring commemorative sets, appeared in 1984, but its combination of newly recorded acts and prime repackages is maintained on another Ace Records subsidiary, Big Beat.

●COMPILATIONS: *The Chiswick Story* (Chiswick 1993)★★★, *Good Clean Fun* (Chiswick 1995)★★★.

CHRISTIE

This UK pop trio was formed around vocalist/bassist/songwriter Jeff Christie, previously with several groups, including the Outer Limits and the Epics. Vic Elmes (guitar) and Mike Blakely (drums), members of the latter attraction, completed the line-up which enjoyed a UK number 1 hit in May 1970 with the ebullient 'Yellow River'. The song was initially intended for the Tremeloes, who featured Mike's brother Alan Blakely, but when they prevaricated Christie decided to record it himself. However, although a follow-up, 'San Bernadino' reached the UK Top 10, the trio, by now featuring Paul Fenton on drums, was unable to sustain a lasting career and a 1972 release, 'Iron Horse', was their final chart entry.

●ALBUMS: *Yellow River* (Columbia 1970)★★.

CHRISTIE, TONY

b. Anthony Fitzgerald, 25 April 1944, Conisborough, Yorkshire, England. Christie was a self-taught guitarist who became a professional singer in 1964. By the time he made his BBC Radio debut three year later, he had acquired vocal mannerisms similar to those of Tom Jones, and this attracted the interest of songwriters Mitch Murray and Peter Callender, who provided Christie with his first UK Top 30 entry in 1970 with 'Las Vegas'. Next came the title track to *I Did What I Did For Maria*, a number 2 UK hit which cleared the way for the million-selling 'Is This The Way To Amarillo' (written by Howard Greenfield and Neil Sedaka), which topped charts throughout Europe while managing only to break into the UK Top 20. Touring Australasia and South Africa for much of 1972, Christie's chart placings tailed off until a minor hit with 'Avenues And Alleyways' sparked off robust sales for 1973's *With Loving Feeling*. To a lesser degree, he did it again in 1975 with 'Drive Safely Darlin'' and an in-concert offering. A 'best of' selection the following year rounded off his career as a serious chart contender - though he was heard on the *Evita* studio cast album in 1978. However, his refusal of a part in the London stage production led to a schism with his manager, Harvey Lisberg, resulting in Christie continuing to earn his living on the cabaret/supper club circuit.

●ALBUMS: *I Did What I Did For Maria* (MCA 1971)★★★, *With Loving Feeling* (MCA 1973)★★, *Live* (MCA 1975)★★, *Ladies Man* (RCA 1983)★★.

●COMPILATIONS: *The Best Of Tony Christie* (MCA 1976)★★★, *Golden Greats* (MCA 1985)★★★, *Baby I'm A Want You* (Cambra 1986)★★, *The Very Best Of ...* (Music Club 1995)★★★.

CITY BOY

Based in Birmingham, England, pop-rock group City Boy started out as a four-piece acoustic folk band playing in the pubs and clubs of the Midlands in the early 70s. The original line-up was 'Lol' Lawrence Mason (vocals), Steve Broughton (guitar), Mike Slamer (guitar) and Max Thomas (guitar). They turned professional in 1975 and started writing their own songs (mainly the work of Broughton). Thomas took up keyboards in addition to guitar, and after being signed to Phonogram Records, they recruited Chris Dunn (bass) and Roger Kent (drums) who was soon replaced by Roy Ward. They had released several albums without success before they made a breakthrough in 1978 when '5-7-0-5' made the UK Top 10. They had two more hits, including 'The Day The Earth Caught Fire'. Dunn and Broughton were ejected from the band at this point after attempting to convince City Boy to concentrate on pop songs rather than progressive rock. Dunn managed Tight Fit before setting up rental companies in Nashville and New York, while Broughton went on to write for Cyndi Lauper, Junior and Stacie Lattislaw. A further City Boy single emerged on the band's own City Boy label in 1982, after which they broke up. Mason went on to form the Maisonettes, who had their own hit single with 'Heartache Avenue', but faded quickly after. From there he wrote songs for artists including Samantha Fox, and won the Radio Times' radio comedy award for *Total Accident* in 1991. Slamer formed Streets with Steve Walsh in Atlanta before going on to session and production work with Angry Anderson (ex-Rose Tattoo) and World War III, and then writing scores for television and film. Thomas returned to mathematics teaching in England. Drummer Ward, whose vocal had graced '5-7-0-5', continued to work with producer Robert

Mutt Lange, singing the 'behind-the-scenes' lead on Tight Fit's UK number 1, 'The Lion Sleeps Tonight'. Afterwards he was blacklisted in the industry after being (wrongly) blamed for leaking the story. He also drummed for Tokyo Charm.

●ALBUMS: *City Boy* (Vertigo 1976)★★, *Dinner At The Ritz* (Vertigo 1977)★★, *Young Men Gone West* (Vertigo 1977)★★★, *Book Early* (Vertigo 1978)★★, *The Day The Earth Caught Fire* (Vertigo 1979)★★, *Heads Are Rolling* (Vertigo 1980)★★.

CLANCY

Formed in London, England in 1975, Clancy was comprised of Dave Skinner (keyboards/vocals), Ernie Graham (guitar/vocals), Dave Vasco (guitar/vocals), Jim Cuomo (saxophone), Sam Mitchell (dobro), Colin Bass (bass/vocals), Barry Ford (drums/vocals) and Gaspar Lawal (percussion). Skinner was already renowned as a session musician, working with, among others, Bryan Ferry, and had previously been a member of Uncle Dog. Ernie Graham had been a member of Eire Apparent and Help Yourself and had completed a solo album in 1971. Gaspar Lawal's credits included work with Graham Bond, Joan Armatrading, Stephen Stillis and Viv Stanshall. Clancy quickly became a popular live attraction, blending skilled musicianship with the relaxed, good time, atmosphere of contemporaries Kokomo and 'pub rock' favourites Bees Make Honey. They secured a major record deal with Warner Brothers Records, but sadly their two albums for the company failed to recreate the atmosphere of live performances. They split up in 1976, after which Skinner and Lawal resumed their careers as session musicians while Graham worked with Nick Lowe.

●ALBUMS: *Seriously Speaking* (Warners 1975)★★, *Everyday* (Warners 1975)★★.

CLARK, GENE

b. 17 November 1941, Tipton, Missouri, USA, d. 24 May 1991. After playing in various teenage groups, Clark was offered a place in the sprawling New Christy Minstrels in late 1963. He stayed long enough to contribute to two albums, *Merry Christmas* and *Land Of Giants*, before returning to Los Angeles, where he teamed up with Jim (Roger) McGuinn and David Crosby in the Jet Set. This fledgling trio evolved into the Byrds. At that point Clark was the leading songwriter in the group and contributed significantly to their first two albums. Classic Clark songs from this period include 'I Feel A Whole Lot Better', 'Here Without You' and 'Set You Free This Time'. Following the release of 'Eight Miles High' in March 1966, he dramatically left the group, citing fear of flying as the major cause.

Under the auspices of producer Jim Dickson, Clark recorded a solo album, *Echoes (With The Gosdin Brothers)*, which remains one of the best 'singer-songwriter' albums of its era. However, it failed to sell, effectively putting Clark's solo career in jeopardy. At this time Clark also recorded two albums with Doug Dillard as Dillard and Clark. At the end of 1968, following Crosby's dismissal from the Byrds, Clark was re-enlisted but left within weeks due to his long-standing aerophobia. Revitalizing his career in 1971 with *White Light*, Clark seemed a prime candidate for singer-songwriter success, but middling sales and a lack of touring forestalled his progress. A recorded reunion with the original Byrds in late 1973 temporarily refocused attention on Clark. Soon, he was back in the studio recording a solo album for Asylum Records with producer Thomas Jefferson Kaye. *No Other* (1974) was a highly acclaimed work, brilliantly fusing Clark's lyrical power with an ethereal mix of choral beauty and rich musicianship provided by some of the finest session players in Hollywood. Sales again proved disappointing, prompting Clark to record a less complex album for RSO, which was reasonably publicized but fared no better.

The irresistible lure of the original Byrds brought Gene back together with two of his former colleagues in the late 70s. McGuinn, Clark And Hillman enjoyed brief success, but during the recording of their second album *City* (1980), history repeated itself and Clark left amid some acrimony. After this he mainly recorded for small labels, occasionally touring with other ex-Byrds as well as solo. He collaborated with Carla Olson, formerly of the Textones. After years of ill health Clark died in 1991.

●ALBUMS: *Echoes (With The Gosdin Brothers)* (Columbia 1967)★★★★, reissued as *Gene Clark With The Goseden Brothers* (Edsel 1997), *White Light* (A&M 1972)★★★, *Roadmaster* (A&M 1972)★★★, *No Other* (Asylum 1974)★★★★, *Two Sides To Every Story* (RSO 1977)★★, *Firebyrd* (Takoma 1984)★★ reissued as *This Byrd Has Flown* (Edsel 1995), with Carla Olson *So Rebellious A Lover* (Demon 1987)★★★, with Carla Olson *Silhouetted In Light* (Demon 1992)★★★.

●COMPILATIONS: *Amercian Dreamer 1964 - '74* (1993)★★★★.

CLARK, GUY

b. 6 November 1941, Rockport, Texas, USA. Clark has achieved considerably more fame as a songwriter than as a performer, although he is revered by his nucleus of fans internationally. Brought up in the hamlet of Monahans, Texas, Clark worked in television during the 60s, and later as a photographer - his work appeared on albums released by the Texan-based International Artists Records. He briefly performed in a folk trio with Kay K.T. Oslin, and began writing songs for a living, moving to Los Angeles, which he eventually loathed, but which inspired one of his biggest songs, 'LA Freeway', a US Top 100 hit for Jerry Jeff Walker. Clark then wrote songs such as his classic 'Desperados Waiting For A Train', which was covered by acts as diverse as Tom Rush and Mallard (the group formed by ex-members of Captain Beefheart's Magic Band) and the brilliant train song, 'Texas 1947', by Johnny Cash.

His first album, *Old No. 1*, was released in 1975, and included 'Freeway', 'Desperados' and '1947', as well as several more songs of similarly high quality, like 'Let It Roll'. Despite receiving virtually unanimous and well-deserved critical acclaim, it failed to chart on either side of the Atlantic. Clark's 1976 follow-up album, *Texas Cooking*, was no more successful, although it again contained classic songs such as 'The Last Gunfighter Ballad' and 'Virginia's Real'. Among those who contributed to these albums simply because they enjoyed Clark's music were Emmylou Harris, Rodney Crowell, Steve Earle, Jerry Jeff Walker, Hoyt Axton and Waylon Jennings.

By 1978, Clark had moved labels to Warner Brothers Records, and released *Guy Clark*, which included four songs from other writers, among them Rodney Crowell's 'Viola', 'American Dream' and Townes Van Zandt's 'Don't You Take It Too Bad', while the harmonizing friends this time included Don Everly, Gordon Payne (of the Crickets) and K.T. Oslin. A three year gap then ensued before 1981's *The South Coast Of Texas*, which was produced by Rodney Crowell. Clark wrote two of the songs with Crowell, 'The Partner Nobody Chose' (a US country Top 40 single) and 'She's Crazy For Leavin'', while the album also included 'Heartbroke', later covered by Ricky Skaggs. 1983 brought *Better Days*, again produced by Crowell, which included vintage classics like 'The Randall Knife' and 'The Carpenter', as well as another US country chart single, 'Homegrown Tomatoes' and Van Zandt's amusing 'No Deal', but Clark was still unable to penetrate the commercial barriers that had long been predicted by critics and his fellow musicians. He began to work as a solo troubadour, after various unsuccessful attempts to perform live with backing musicians. At this point he developed the intimate show that he brought to Europe several times during the latter half of the 80s. This resulted in his return to recording with *Old Friends*, appearing on U2's label, Mother Records. The usual array of 'heavy friends' were on hand, including Harris, Crowell, Rosanne Cash and Vince Gill, but only two of the 10 tracks were solely written by Clark. Among the contributions were Joe Ely's 'The Indian Cowboy', and Van Zandt's 'To Live Is To Fly'. Even with the implied patronage of U2, at the time one of the biggest acts in the world, Clark enjoyed little more success than he had previously experienced.

On stage, Clark is introverted, performing his material in an unplugged, unadorned and underrated way, with the aid of constant cigarettes and mumbled introductions. Time and time again, Clark's album *Old No 1* is cited by critics and performers as a landmark work. Many musicians, including Lyle Lovett, Nanci Griffith and Emmylou Harris, have acknowledged his contribution to American music and, to quote the title of one of his more recent songs, it is 'Stuff That Works'.

●ALBUMS: *Old No. 1* (RCA 1975)★★★★, *Texas Cookin'* (RCA 1976)★★★, *Guy Clark* (Warners 1978)★★★, *The*

South Coast Of Texas (1981)★★★, *Better Days* (1983)★★★, *Old Friends* (Mother 1989)★★, *Boats To Build* (Asylum 1992)★★★, *Dublin Blues* (Asylum 1995)★★★.
●COMPILATIONS: *Best Of Guy Clark* (RCA 1982)★★★.

CLARKE, JOHN COOPER

b. 25 January 1949, Salford, Manchester, England. With a 1965-style Bob Dylan suit and sunglasses and quick-fire delivery, Clarke enjoyed a brief vogue as a 'punk poet'. His usually comedic compositions showed the influence of the punning wordplay of Roger McGough, combined with the tougher 'hip' approach of the American beats. Clarke recited his poetry in local folk clubs and working with Rick Goldstraw's group, the Ferretts, he began to mix his poems with musical backing. Goldstraw's involvement with the independent label, Rabid Records led, in 1977, to Clarke recording the co-produced Martin Hannett single, 'Psycle Sluts' - ' ... those nubile nihilists of the north circular the lean leonine leatherette lovelies of the Leeds intersection luftwaffe angels locked in a pagan paradise - no cash a passion for trash...' With the onset of punk, Clarke found himself encountering livelier audiences when he shared a bill with the Buzzcocks. The popularity of his performances with such audiences led to an increase in the phenomenon of the 'punk poet', giving rise to the careers of such 'second generation' artists as Attila The Stockbroker, Seething Wells and Joolz. After touring with Be-Bop DeLuxe, he was signed to Epic Records where Bill Nelson produced his debut album. The single 'Gimmix' became a UK Top 40 hit in 1979. Again produced by Martin Hannett and with backing music by the Invisible Girls, it also appeared on *Snap Crackle And Bop*, along with 'Beasley Street', described by one reviewer as 'an English 'Desolation Row''. Clarke went into semi-retirement later in the 80s, forming a domestic partnership with ex-Velvet Underground singer Nico. In the 90s Clarke became active again on the pub and club circuit and is engaged in various film and book projects (his 1992 documentary, *Ten Years In An Open Necked Shirt*, was shown on UK television's Channel Four).
●ALBUMS: *Disguise In Love* (Epic 1978)★★★, *Snap Crackle And Bop* (Epic 1979)★★★, *Zip Style Method* (Epic 1982)★★★.
●COMPILATIONS: *Qu'est Le Maison De Fromage* (Rabid 1980)★★★, *Me And My Big Mouth* (Epic 1981)★★★.
●FURTHER READING: *Ten Years In An Open Necked Shirt*, John Cooper Clarke.

CLARKE, STANLEY

b. 21 July 1951, Philadelphia, Pennsylvania, USA. Clarke started on violin, then transferred to cello, double bass and finally the bass guitar. After formal training at school and at the Philadelphia Musical Academy, his first experience was in funk outfits; he then got a taste for playing jazz working with Horace

Silver for six months in 1970. He played with tenor saxophonist Joe Henderson and with Pharoah Sanders on the latter's *Black Unity*. A spell with Chick Corea and his Return For Forever band reminded Clarke of his aptitude for the electric bass, and he became a pioneer of fusion as 'cosmic' as it was commercial: *Journey To Love* (1975) had glossy production a million miles from Sanders' abrasive poly-rhythms. A partnership with George Duke, also a fugitive from acoustic jazz, provided audiences with spectacular virtuoso work-outs. Gifted with jaw-dropping technique, Clarke's rise to fame coincided with a period when demonstrating 'chops' was considered to be at the cutting edge of the music. His slapping style has produced a host of imitators, though none can quite match his speed and confidence. In 1995 he formed Rite Of Strings with guitarist Al DiMeola and violinist Jean-Luc Ponty.
●ALBUMS: with Pharoah Sanders *Black Unity* (Impulse 1972)★★★, with Return To Forever *Return To Forever* (Polydor 1972)★★★★, *Stanley Clarke* (Nemperor 1974)★★★★, *Journey To Love* (Nemperor 1975)★★★, *School Days* (Nemperor 1976)★★, *Modern Man* (Nemperor 1978)★★, *I Wanna Play For You* (Nemperor 1979)★★, *Rocks, Pebbles And Sand* (Epic 1980)★★, *You/Me Together* (Epic 1980)★★, with George Duke *The Clarke/Duke Project* (Epic 1981)★★★, *Let Me Know You* (Epic 1982)★★, with Duke *The Clarke/Duke Project II* (Epic 1983)★★★, *Time Exposure* (Epic 1984)★★, *Find Out* (Epic 1985)★★, *Hideaway* (Epic 1986)★★, *Shieldstone* (Optimism 1987)★★, *If This Bass Could Only Talk* (Epic 1988)★★★, with Duke *3* (Epic 1990)★★★, *East River Drive* (1993)★★★, with Al DiMeola, Jean-Luc Ponty *The Rite Of Strings* (IRS 1995)★★★.
●COMPILATIONS: *The Collection* (Castle 1990)★★★.

CLASH

The Clash at first tucked in snugly behind punk's loudest noise, the Sex Pistols (whom they supported on 'the Anarchy tour'), and later became a much more consistent and intriguing force. Guitarist Mick Jones (b. 26 June 1955, London, England) had formed London SS in 1975, whose members at one time included bassist Paul Simonon (b. 15 December 1956, London, England) and drummer Nicky 'Topper' Headon (b. 30 May 1955, Bromley, Kent, England). Joe Strummer (b. John Graham Mellor, 21 August 1952, Ankara, Turkey) had spent the mid-70s fronting a pub-rock group called the 101ers, playing early rock 'n' roll style numbers such as 'Keys To Your Heart'. The early line-up of the Clash was completed by guitarist Keith Levene but he left early in 1976 with another original member, drummer Terry Chimes, whose services were called upon intermittently during the following years. They signed to CBS Records and during three weekends they recorded *The Clash* in London with sound engineer Mickey Foote taking on the producer's role. In 1977 *Rolling Stone* magazine called it the 'definitive punk album' and elsewhere it was recognized that they had brilliantly distilled the anger, depression and energy of mid-70s England. More importantly, they had infused the message and sloganeering with strong tunes and pop hooks, as on 'I'm So Bored With The USA' and 'Career Opportunities'. The album reached number 12 in the UK charts and garnered almost universal praise. CBS were keen to infiltrate the American market and Blue Öyster Cult's founder/lyricist Sandy Pearlman was brought in to produce *Give 'Em Enough Rope*. The label's manipulative approach failed and it suffered very poor sales in the USA but in the UK it reached number 2, despite claims that its more rounded edges amounted to a sell out of the band's earlier much-flaunted punk ethics. They increasingly embraced reggae elements, seemingly a natural progression of their anti-racist stance, and had a minor UK hit with '(White Man) In Hammersmith Palais' in July 1978, following it up with the frothy punk-pop of 'Tommy Gun' - their first Top 20 hit. Their debut album was finally released in the USA as a double set including tracks from their singles and it sold healthily before *London Calling*, produced by the volatile Guy Stevens, marked a return to almost top form. They played to packed houses across the USA early in 1980 and were cover stars in many prestigious rock magazines. Typically, their next move was over-ambitious and the triple set, *Sandinista!*, was leaden and too sprawling after the acute concentration of earlier records. It scraped into the UK Top 20 and sales were disappointing despite CBS making it available at a special cut-price. The experienced rock producer Glyn Johns was brought in to instigate a tightening-up and *Combat Rock* was as snappy as anticipated. It was recorded with Terry Chimes on drums after Headon had abruptly left the group. Chimes was later replaced by Pete Howard. 'Rock The Casbah', a jaunty, humorous song written by Headon, became a Top 10 hit in the USA and reached number 30 in the UK, aided by a sardonic video. During 1982 they toured the USA supporting the Who at their stadium concerts. Many observers were critical of a band that had once ridiculed superstar status, for becoming part of the same machinery. A simmering tension between Jones and Strummer eventually led to bitterness and Jones left in 1983 after Strummer accused him of becoming lazy. He told the press: 'He wasn't with us any more.' Strummer later apologized for lambasting Jones and admitted he was mainly to blame for the break-up of a successful songwriting partnership: 'I stabbed him in the back,' was his own honest account of proceedings. The Clash struggled without Jones' input, despite the toothless *Cut The Crap* reaching number 16 in the UK charts in 1985. Mick Jones formed Big Audio Dynamite with another product of the 70s London scene, Don Letts, and for several years became a force merging dance with powerful, spiky pop choruses. Strummer finally disbanded the Clash in 1986 and after a brief tour with Latino Rockabilly War and a period playing rhythm guitar with the Pogues, he turned almost full-time to acting and

production. He supervised the soundtrack to the film *Sid And Nancy*, about the former Sex Pistols bassist Sid Vicious and his girlfriend Nancy Spungen. In 1988 the Clash's most furious but tuneful songs were gathered together on the excellent compilation, *The Story Of The Clash*. They made a dramatic and unexpected return to the charts in 1991 when 'Should I Stay Or Should I Go?', originally a UK number 17 hit in October 1982, was re-released by CBS after the song appeared in a Levi's jeans television advertisement. Incredibly, the song reached number 1, thereby prompting more reissues of Clash material and fuelling widespread rumours of a band reunion, which came to nought.

●ALBUMS: *The Clash* (Columbia 1977)★★★★, *Give 'Em Enough Rope* (Columbia 1978)★★★, *London's Calling* double album (Columbia 1979)★★★★, *Sandinista!* (Columbia 1980)★★, *Combat Rock* (Columbia 1982)★★, *Cut The Crap* (Columbia 1985)★.

●COMPILATIONS: *The Story Of The Clash* (Columbia 1988)★★★★, *The Singles Collection* (Columbia 1991)★★★.

●VIDEOS: *This Is Video Clash* (CBS-Fox 1985) *Rude Boy* (Hendring Video 1987).

●FURTHER READING: *The Clash: Before & After*, Pennie Smith. *The Clash*, Miles and John Tobler. *Joe Strummer With The 101'ers & The Clash*, Julian Leonard Yewdall. *Last Gang In Town: Story Of The Clash*, Marcus Gray.

CLAYTON, LEE

b. 29 October 1942, Russelville, Alabama, USA. Clayton moved to Oak Ridge, Tennessee when aged four. His father encouraged his musical abilities and, when aged only 10, he played steel guitar on radio. Clayton's background is told in his song 'Industry'. Between 1966 and 1969 and after a short-lived marriage, he flew jet fighters in the US Air Force, which is described in his song 'Old Number Nine'. Clayton moved to Nashville, determined to make his name as a songwriter. The 'outlaw' scene was in its infancy and Clayton's song, 'Ladies Love Outlaws', was a US country hit for Waylon Jennings and later recorded by the Everly Brothers. His 1973 *Lee Clayton* is regarded as a classic of 'outlaw country'. Jennings and Willie Nelson have both recorded his erotic love song, 'If You Can Touch Her At All'. Clayton, however, became penniless trying to establish his own band and then followed a nomadic existence. Eventually, he developed a more strident, electric sound, employing the Irish guitarist Philip Donnolly, to record dark albums full of disillusionment. The melancholy 'A Little Cocaine' is about the downfall of a friend, and his own drug habits made him unreliable. In the 80s Clayton wrote two books and one stage play, *Little Boy Blue*, all autobiographical. He returned to recording with a fine album recorded live in Oslo, *Another Night*, but the songs were familiar. Bono of U2 was reported to have said, 'There's only one country singer who has influenced me and he's an unknown feller called Lee Clayton.' Maverick UK record company

Edsel had similar faith when they reissued three Clayton albums in 1996.

●ALBUMS: *Lee Clayton* (MCA/Edsel 1973)★★★★, *Border Affair* (Capitol/Edsel 1978)★★★, *Naked Child* (Capitol/Edsel 1979)★★★, *The Dream Goes On* (Capitol 1981)★★, *Another Night* (Provogue 1989)★★★, *Spirit Of The Twilight* (Provogue 1994)★★★.

CLAYTON, MERRY

b. Mary Clayton. This powerful American vocalist made her debut in 1963 with 'The Doorbell Rings', before recording a version of 'The Shoop Shoop Song (It's In His Kiss)', a song later popularized by Betty Everett and Cher. Clayton went on to record further singles before beginning a successful career as a session singer. She appeared on several Joe Cocker releases, but is best known for her impassioned appearance on the Rolling Stones' 'Gimmie Shelter'. A member of Ray Charles' Raelettes during the late 60s, Clayton then resumed her solo work and scored several R&B hits including 'After All This Time' (1971) and 'Oh No Not My Baby' (1973). She subsequently enjoyed sporadic success. 'Yes', from the film *Dirty Dancing* reached the US Top 50 in 1988, but latterly Clayton has also pursued an acting vocation with roles in *Maid To Order* and television's *Cagney And Lacey*. She performed cabaret-style with Marianne Faithfull and Darlene Love as '20th Century Pop' in 1996.

●ALBUMS: *Gimme Shelter* (Ode 1970)★★, *Merry Clayton* (Ode 1971)★★, *Celebration* (Ode 1973)★★, *Keep Your Eye On The Sparrow* (Ode 1975)★★.

CLEAR BLUE SKY

A trio of Mark Sheater (bass), John Simmons (guitar) and Ken White (drums), Clear Blue Sky were a progressive rock/hard rock group formed in the UK at the beginning of the 70s. After playing extensively on their native Essex pub circuit they were spotted at an Acton youth club by Patrick Campbell-Lyons of Nirvana (UK). Through him they signed to Vertigo Records in 1970, though no member of the band was older than 18, and they began working on sessions for their debut album. A self-titled collection of fairly energetic but otherwise unremarkable selections, which was re-titled *Play It Loud* for European distribution, it failed to engender a breakthrough into the rock mainstream. Although work was begun on a follow-up collection, and recordings completed, Vertigo decided not to release it and the group broke up in 1972.

●ALBUMS: *Clear Blue Sky* (Vertigo 1971)★★.

CLEMPSON, DAVE

b. 5 September 1949, Tamworth, Staffordshire, England. Guitarist Dave 'Clem' Clempson achieved early recognition as a member of Bakerloo, an inventive blues-based trio which completed an excellent album for the Harvest label. In October 1969 he replaced James Litherland in Colosseum with whom he remained for two years. Clempson then joined Humble Pie, whose brand of brash rock contrasted with that of his previous jazz-rock employers. *Smokin'* (1972) and *Eat It* (1973) offered his most emphatic work, but by 1975 the quartet was losing its direction. Clempson then formed Strange Brew with bassist Greg Ridely and drummer Cozy Powell, but this short-lived unit dissolved when the latter broke his wrist. Having briefly joined Steve Marriott's All Stars, the guitarist formed Rough Diamond with ex-Uriah Heep singer David Byron. This ill-fated venture collapsed in 1977 with Byron embarking on a solo career. The remaining musicians became known as Champion but Clempson's nomadic path was resumed in 1979 when he departed to join Roger Chapman. During the 80s Clempson played some of his finest work with Jack Bruce and was particularly popular in Germany. In 1994 he was part of *Cities Of The Heart*, the album to celebrate Bruce's 50th birthday. He is one of the most accomplished rock guitarists to come out of the late 60s blues boom. His speedy precision playing is faultless, and rarely boring.

CLIFF, JIMMY

b. James Chambers, 1948, St. Catherine, Jamaica, West Indies. One of the great popularizers of reggae music, Jimmy Cliff blazed a trail into rock that Bob Marley later followed, but without ever capitalizing on his great advantages as a singer-songwriter, nascent film star and interpreter of other people's material. Raised by his father, Cliff first moved to Kingston in 1962 after the dream of a musical career seduced him from his studies. An early brace of singles, 'Daisy Got Me Crazy', with Count Boysie, and 'I'm Sorry', for sound system operator Sir Cavalier, did little to bring him to the public's attention. His career began in earnest when a song he had written himself, 'Hurricane Hattie', describing the recent arrival in South America of the self-same meteorological disaster, became a local hit. He was still only 14 years old.

Cliff subsequently emerged as a ska singer for producer Leslie Kong in 1963, singing 'King Of Kings' and 'Dearest Beverly' in a hoarse, raucous voice. He can be seen in this fledgling role on the video *This Is Ska*, shot in 1964. The same year Cliff joined a tour, promoted by politician Eward Seaga and headlined by Byron Lee And The Dragonaires, with the intention of exporting reggae music to the wider world. Though it later collapsed in acrimony, the jaunt at least brought Cliff to the attention of Island Records' boss Chris Blackwell, and in the mid-60s the young singer moved to London. By 1968 Cliff was being groomed as a solo star to the underground rock market. Musicians teamed with him included Mott The Hoople's Ian Hunter and vocalists including Madeline Bell and P.P. Arnold. The shift away from the conventional reggae audience was confirmed by a cover of Procul Harum's 'Whiter Shade of Pale' and appearances alongside the Incredible String Band and Jethro Tull on Island samplers.

In 1968 Cliff chanced his arm in Brazil, representing Jamaica in the International Song Festival. His entry, 'Waterfall' (a flop in England), earned him a considerable following in South America. More importantly the sojourn gave him the chance to take stock and write new material. He finally broke through in 1969 with 'Wonderful World, Beautiful People', a somewhat over-produced single typical of the era, which he had written in Brazil. 'Vietnam' was a small hit the following year, and was described by Bob Dylan as not only the best record about the war, but the best protest song he had heard. Paul Simon went one step further in his praises; after hearing the song he travelled to Kingston and booked the same rhythm section, studio and engineer to record 'Mother And Child Reunion' - arguably the first US reggae song. In local terms, however, its success was outstripped by 'Wild World', a cover of the Cat Stevens song, the link between the two singers perhaps strengthened by a shared Muslim faith.

While the albums *Jimmy Cliff*, *Hard Road To Travel* and particularly *Another Cycle* were short on roots credibility, his next move, as the gun-toting, reggae-singing star of *The Harder They Come* (1972), was short on nothing. Cliff, with his ever-present five-point star T-shirt, was suddenly Jamaica's most marketable property. *The Harder They Come* was the island's best home-grown film, and its soundtrack one of the biggest selling reggae records of all time. Cliff seemed set for super-stardom. Somehow it never happened: his relationship with Island soured and deals with EMI, Reprise and CBS failed to deliver him to his rightful place. In fact, his star began to wane directly as Bob Marley signed to Island. The company executed the same marketing process for both artists - rebellion, great songwriting, hipness - but it was Marley who embodied the new spirit of reggae and reaped the rewards. Cliff's artistic fortunes were revived, ironically enough, by the recruitment of Wailers producer Joe Higgs as his bandleader. Despite their merits, Cliff's excellent records for his own Sunpower label did not really connect. To many outside the reggae world he remains best known for writing the beautiful tear-jerker 'Many Rivers To Cross', a massive hit for UB40. However, his popularity on the African continent is enormous, arguably greater than that of any other reggae artist, Marley included. He is similarly venerated in South America, whose samba rhythms have helped to inform and enrich his latter-day material. His 90s albums *Images* and *Breakout*, which highlight, as ever, his plaintive, gospel-tinged delivery, offer ample evidence to dislodge the widely held belief (particularly in the West) that he is a perennial under-achiever.

●ALBUMS: *Jimmy Cliff* (Trojan 1969)★★★, *Wonderful World, Beautiful People* (A&M 1970)★★★★, *Hard Road To Travel* (Trojan/A&M 1970)★★★, *Another Cycle* (Island 1971)★★★, *The Harder They Come* film soundtrack (Mango/Island 1972)★★★★, *Unlimited* (EMI 1973, Trojan 1990)★★★, *Struggling Man* (Island 1974)★★★, *Brave Warrior* (EMI 1975)★★★, *Follow My Mind* (Reprise 1976)★★, *Give Thanx* (Warners. 1978)★★, *Oh Jamaica* (EMI 1979)★★, *I Am The Living* (Warners 1980)★★, *Give The People What They Want* (Oneness/Warners 1981)★★, *House Of Exile* (1981)★★, *Special* (Columbia 1982)★★, *The Power And The Glory* (Columbia 1983)★★★, *Can't Get Enough Of It* (Veep 1984)★★★, *Cliff Hanger* (Dynamic/Columbia 1985)★★, *Sense Of Direction* (Sire 1985)★★★, *Hang Fire* (Dynamic/Columbia 1987)★★★, *Images* (Cliff Sounds 1989)★★★, *Save Our Planet Earth* (Musidisc 1990)★★, *Breakout* (Cliff Sounds 1993)★★★, *The Cool Runner Live In London* (More Music 1995)★★.
●COMPILATIONS: *The Best Of Jimmy Cliff* (Island 1974)★★★★, *The Best Of Jimmy Cliff In Concert* (Reprise 1977)★★★, *The Collection* (EMI 1983)★★★, *Jimmy Cliff* (Trojan 1983)★★★, *Reggae Greats* (Island 1985)★★★, *Fundamental Reggae* (See For Miles 1987)★★★, *The Best Of Jimmy Cliff* (Mango/Island 1988)★★★★.
●VIDEOS: *Bongo Man* (Hendring Video 1989).
●FILMS: *The Harder They Come* (1972).

CLIMAX BLUES BAND

Originally known as the Climax Chicago Blues Band, this long-enduring group comprised Colin Cooper (b. 7 October 1939, Stafford, England; vocals/saxophone), Peter Haycock (b. 4 April 1952, Stafford, England; vocals/guitar), Richard Jones (keyboards), Arthur Wood (keyboards), Derek Holt (b. 26 January 1949, Stafford, England; bass) and George Newsome (b. 14 August 1947, Stafford, England; drums). They made their recording debut in 1969 with *The Climax Chicago Blues Band* which evoked the early work of John Mayall and Savoy Brown. Its somewhat anachronistic approach gave little indication of a potentially long career. Jones departed for university prior to the release of *Plays On*, which displayed a new-found, and indeed sudden, sense of maturity. A restrictive adherence to 12-bar tempos was replaced by a freer, flowing pulse, while the use of wind instruments, in particular on 'Flight', inmplied an affiliation with jazz-rock groups like Colosseum and Blodwyn Pig.

In 1970 CCBB switched labels to Harvest. Conscious of stereotyping in the wake of the blues' receding popularity, the group began emphasizing rock-based elements in their work. *A Lot Of Bottle* and *Tightly Knit* reflected a transitional period where the group began wooing the affections of an American audience responsive to the unfettered styles of Foghat or ZZ Top. Climax then embarked on a fruitful relationship with producer Richard Gottehrer who honed the group's live sound into an economic, but purposeful, studio counterpart. *Rich Man*, their final album for Harvest, and *Sense Of Direction* were the best examples of their collaboration. Richard Jones rejoined the band in 1975 having been a member of the Principal Edwards Magic Theatre since leaving university. The band enjoyed a surprise UK hit single when 'Couldn't Get It Right' reached number 10 in 1976, but the success proved temporary. Although they have pursued a career into the 90s, the Climax Blues Band have engendered a sense of predictability and consequently lost their eminent position as a fixture of America's lucrative FM rock circuit. In 1994 the line-up retained only Cooper from the original band, who had recruited George Glover (keyboards/vocals), Lester Hunt (guitar/vocals), Roy Adams (drums) and Neil Simpson (bass). Their live album *Blues From The Attic*, however, sounded remarkably fresh for a band who have been gigging for so long.

●ALBUMS: *Climax Chicago Blues Band* (Parlophone 1969)★★, *Plays On* (Parlophone 1969)★★★, *A Lot Of Bottle* (Harvest 1970)★★, *Tightly Knit* (Harvest 1971)★★★, *Rich Man* (Harvest 1972)★★★, *FM/Live* (Polydor 1973), *Sense Of Direction* (Polydor 1974)★★★, *Stamp Album* (BTM 1975)★★★, *Gold Plated* (BTM 1976)★★, *Shine On* (Warners 1978)★★★, *Real To Reel* (Warners 1979)★★★, *Flying The Flag* (Warners 1980)★★★, *Lucky For Some* (Warners 1981)★★, *Sample And Hold* (Virgin 1983)★★, *Total Climax* (1985)★★, *Drastic Steps* (Clay 1988)★★, *Blues From The Attic* (HTD 1994)★★★.

●COMPILATIONS: *1969-1972* (Harvest 1975)★★★, *Best Of The Climax Blues Band* (RCA 1983)★★★, *Loosen Up (1974-1976)* (See For Miles 1984)★★★, *Couldn't Get It Right* (C5 1987)★★, *25 Years 1968-1993* (Repertoire 1996)★★★.

CLOVER

Formed in Mill Valley, California, USA, when bassist Johnny Ciambotti joined John McFee (b. 18 November 1953, Santa Cruz, California, USA; guitar/pedal steel guitar/vocals), Alex Call (guitar/vocals) and Mitch Howie (drums) in the Tiny Hearing Aid Company. Having decided on a less cumbersome name, the quartet made its debut as Clover in July 1967 and soon became a popular attraction in the region's thriving dancehalls. *Clover* consolidated their reputation as a feisty bar band, although a primitive production undermined its charm. *Forty-Niner* was a marked improvement, but although its informality was both varied and infectious, the group was unable to break out of its now stifling good-time niche. The band were featured in an early Levis television advertisement singing 'Route 66'. A dispirited Howie left the line-up which was then bolstered by the addition of Huey (Louis) Lewis (vocals/harmonica), Sean Hopper (keyboards/vocals) and Mickey Shine (drums) but fortunes remained unchanged until 1976 when the group came to the UK at the urging of Nick Lowe. Clover quickly became a popular attraction in their adopted homeland, during which time they accompanied Elvis Costello on *My Aim Is True*. However, despite completing two promising albums, Clover were unable to make a significant breakthrough and returned to the USA in 1978 where they folded. McFee subsequently joined the Doobie Brothers while Lewis and Hooper eventually achieved considerable commercial success as Huey Lewis And The News.

●ALBUMS: *Clover* (Liberty 1970)★★, *Forty-Niner* (Liberty 1971)★★★, *Unavailable* (Vertigo 1977)★★★, *Love On The Wire* (Vertigo 1977)★★★.

●COMPILATIONS: *Clover Chronicle - The Best Of The Fantasy Years* (DJM 1979)★★★, *The Best Of Clover* (Mercury 1986)★★★.

COBHAM, BILLY

b. 16 May 1944, Panama. Cobham began playing drums while growing up in New York City, to where his family had moved while he was still a small child. He studied at the city's High School of Music before entering military service. In the army he played in a band and by the time of his discharge had achieved a high level of proficiency. In the late 60s he played in the New York Jazz Sextet and with Horace Silver. In 1969 he formed a jazz-rock band, Dreams, with Michael and Randy Brecker. The growing popularity of jazz rock kept Cobham busy with recording dates, including some with Miles Davis, and he then joined the Mahavishnu Orchestra, one of the most influential and highly regarded jazz-rock bands. *Birds Of Fire*'s success owes as much to Cobham's extraordinary drumming as it does to McLaughlin's stellar guitar. In 1973 Cobham capitalized upon his international fame by forming his own band and continued to lead fusion bands for the next several years. He played all around the world, at festivals and in concert, teaching and presenting drum clinics. In 1984 he and McLaughlin were reunited in a new version of the Mahavishnu Orchestra. A technically accomplished jazz rock drummer, Cobham's rhythmic dexterity and all-round ability has resulted in many copyists. For all his spectacular pyrotechnics, however, Cobham's talent runs deep and his abilities as a teacher and clinician ensure that his methods are being handed on to future generations of drummers.

●ALBUMS: with Horace Silver *Serenade To A Soul Sister* (1968), with Miles Davis *A Tribute To Jack Johnson* (Columbia 1970)★★★★, *Dreams* (1970), with the Mahavishnu Orchestra *The Inner Mounting Flame* (Columbia 1972)★★★★, with the Mahavishnu Orchestra *Birds Of Fire* (Columbia 1973)★★★★, with the Mahavishnu Orchestra *Between Nothingness And Eternity* (Columbia 1973)★★★, *Spectrum* (Atlantic 1973)★★★★, *Total Eclipse* (Atlantic 1974)★★, *Crosswinds* (Atlantic 1974)★★★, *Life And Times* (Atlantic 1976)★★, *Live - On Tour In Europe* (Atlantic 1976)★★, *Inner Conflicts* (Atlantic 1978)★★★, *Simplicity Of Expression-Depth Of Thought* (Columbia 1979)★★★, *B.C.* (Columbia 1979)★★★, *Flight Time* (Inak 1981)★★★, *Stratus* (Inak 1981)★★★, *Smokin'* (Elektra 1983)★★★, *Warning* (GRP 1985)★★★, *Power Play* (GRP 1986)★★★, *Picture This* (GRP 1987)★★★, *Same Ol Love* (GRP 1987)★★★, *Live On Tour In Europe* (Atlantic 1988)★★★, *By Design* (1992)★★★, *The Traveller* (WMD 1994)★★★.

●COMPILATIONS: *Best Of Billy Cobham* (Columbia 1980)★★★, *Billy's Best Hits* (GRP 1987)★★★, *Best Of Billy Cobham* (Atlantic 1988)★★★.

COCHISE

This melodic British country rock group - Stewart Brown (vocals), Mick Grabham (guitar, ex-Plastic Penny), B.J. Cole (b. 17 June 1946, London, England; pedal steel), Rick Wills (bass) and Willie Wilson (drums) - made its recording debut in 1970. The confidence displayed on *Cochise* continued on its successor, *Swallow Tales*, where a grasp of contemporary Americana was enhanced by several supporting musicians, including Tim Renwick and Cal Batchelor. Their rapport with drummer Wilson resurfaced in a subsequent group, Quiver. Cochise broke up in 1972 following the release of *So Far*. Cole and Wills became respected session musicians; the latter was also a member of several bands including (Peter) Frampton's Camel, Roxy Music and later versions of the Small Faces, while Grabham joined Procol Harum where he remained until their break-up in 1977.
●ALBUMS: *Swallow Tales* (Liberty 1970)★★★, *Cochise* (United Artists 1971)★★★, *So Far* (United Artists 1972)★★.
●COMPILATIONS: *The Best Of* (1992)★★★.

COCKBURN, BRUCE

b. 27 May 1945, Ottawa, Canada. This singer-songwriter has long been heralded as Canada's best-kept secret. His numerous early albums (10 from 1970 to 1979) were tainted by a strong devotional feel, tied to their author's Christian beliefs. However, after his breakthrough single 'Wondering Where The Lions Are' (from *Dancing In The Dragon's Jaws*), his lyrical gaze had turned to the body politic. Cockburn had travelled prolifically throughout several continents, and this had opened his mind to a different strata of subjects: 'I always go around with my notebook open in my mind'. His experiences abroad became the core of his work, particularly *World Of Wonders*. One song, 'They Call It Democracy', was turned down by MTV until the accompanying video removed the names of several high profile corporate concerns. More recent work has embraced environmental concerns, from the destruction of the rain forests ('If A Tree Falls'), to the Chernobyl nuclear disaster ('Radium Rain'). A prolific writer, Cockburn now lives in Toronto, a divorcee who enjoys horse riding and the company of his teenage daughter. He is enormously popular in his homeland yet his brand of folk rock remains only a cult item elsewhere. Even the weight of producer T-Bone Burnett, mixer Glyn Johns and Columbia Records could not make *Dart To The Heart* a commercial success in other territories.
●ALBUMS: *Bruce Cockburn* (True North 1970)★★, *High Winds White Sky* (True North 1971)★★, *Sunwheel Dance* (True North 1972)★★, *Night Vision* (True North 1973)★★★, *Salt Sun And Time* (True North 1974)★★, *Joy Will Find A Way* (True North 1975)★★★, *Circles In The Stream* (True North 1977)★★, *In The Falling Dark* (True North 1977)★★, *Further Adventures Of* (True North 1978)★★★, *Dancing In The Dragon's Jaws* (True North 1980)★★★★, *Rumours Of Glory* (True North 1980)★★★, *Humans* (True North 1980)★★★, *Inner City Front* (True North 1981)★★★, *Trouble With Normal* (True North 1983)★★★, *Stealing Fire* (True North 1984)★★★★, *World Of Wonders* (True North 1986)★★★, *Big Circumstance* (True North 1989)★★★, *Live* (True North 1990)★★★, *Nothing But A Burning Light* (Columbia 1992)★★★★, *Dart To The Heart* (Columbia 1994)★★★, *The Charity Of Night* (Rykodisc 1996)★★★.
●COMPILATIONS: *Mummy Dust/Resumé* (True North 1981)★★★★, *Waiting For A Miracle* (singles collection)(Revolver 1987)★★★★.

COCKER, JOE

b. John Robert Cocker, 20 May 1944, Sheffield, Yorkshire, England. The capricious but brilliant Cocker is felt by many to be the finest white soul singer Britain has yet produced. His rollercoaster career started in 1961 with a little-known local band the Cavaliers, who changed their name to the clumsier Vance Arnold And The Avengers and became known as a warm-up for big names such as the Hollies during the beat boom of 1963. Joe was spotted and offered a one single deal by Decca. This excellent record, a cover of the Beatles 'I'll Cry Instead' failed to sell and he was dropped. The sturdy Cocker refused to give in and formed the first Grease Band in 1966, comprising Vernon Nash (piano), Dave Memmott (drums), Frank Myles (guitar) and his future musical partner Chris Stainton (bass). After two years of solid club gigs building a reputation, they were rewarded with a recording session; however, only Cocker and Stainton were needed and the rest of the band were told to stay at home. The single 'Marjorine' was a minor hit and Cocker and Stainton assembled a new Grease Band with Mickey Gee (guitar), Tommy Reilly (drums) and Tommy Eyre (keyboards). Once again a session was arranged; this time Gee and Reilly were banished. The resulting single took an age to record with session musicians including Jimmy Page and B.J. Wilson. The single, John Lennon and Paul McCartney's 'With A Little Help From My Friends', went straight to the top of the UK charts in 1968. This *tour de force* features the finest bloodcurdling scream on record, and 25 years later, was still a turntable hit.
The Grease Band had now enlisted the talented guitarist Henry McCullough (ex-Eire Apparent) who was able to copy Page's solo admirably. The band recorded their debut album with assistance from Steve Winwood and Jimmy Page and although it failed to chart in the UK it was a hit in the USA. Cocker and his band started touring America in 1969, and became huge stars through exposure on the *Ed Sullivan Show* and constant performing. The highlight of that year was Cocker's performance at the Woodstock Festival. Few would deny that Cocker was one of the stars of the event; his astonishing delivery of 'With A Little Help From My Friends'

is captured on the film of the festival. Joe stayed in the USA for many months. By the end of 1969 he had a further two hits with Dave Mason's 'Feelin' Alright' and Leon Russell's 'Delta Lady', together with another solid and successful album *Joe Cocker*.

The 70s began with the famous Mad Dogs And Englishmen tour. Over 60 dates were played in as many days. A subsequent film and double album were released, although it was reported that Cocker was bankrupted by the whole charade. He then slid into a drink-and-drug stupor that lasted through most of the decade. Such was his stamina that he still regularly performed and continued to have hit records in America. In the UK he was largely forgotten apart form a loyal core of fans. He was deported from Australia during a 1972 tour, and was often so drunk onstage he was barely able to perform, even after throwing up in front of the audience. In the recording studio he was still able to find some magic and among the highlights of his catalogue of hits were Gregg Allman's 'Midnight Rider', 'You Are So Beautiful' and 'Put Out The Light'. His albums were patchy with only *I Can Stand A Little Rain* (1974) being totally satisfying. Amazingly, he survived the decade, and apart from a minor hit guesting with the Crusaders on 'I'm So Glad I'm Standing Here Today', little was heard from him until 1982. It was stated that it took two years for the alcohol to drain out of his body, but true or not, a thinner, older Cocker was seen promoting his best album for years, the critically well-received *Sheffield Steel*. Despite the plaudits, commercially the album was a comparative failure. Cocker had little time to worry about its dismal showing for within weeks he was back at the top of the US charts duetting with Jennifer Warnes with the soundtrack to the film *An Officer And A Gentlemen*. The song 'Up Where We Belong' also restored him to the UK singles chart in 1983 after an absence of 13 years. He celebrated it with a belated return to his home town for a memorable concert. *Civilized Man* was another disappointment but while his albums are less successful, his live performances are electrifying. His most satisfying recent album was *Unchain My Heart*; Cocker's interpretation of his mentor Ray Charles' classic was released as a single but was only a moderate hit. *Night Calls* contained the Bryan Adams song 'Feels Like Forever' and interesting Cocker reworkings of the Beatles' 'You've Got To Hide Your Love Away' and Blind Faith's 'Can't Find My Way Home'. A strong publicity campaign was behind his anniversary tour in 1994; it was fortunate that the tour was accompanied by his best album in years, *Have A Little Faith*. It was preceded by 'The Simple Things' and further hit singles poured forth as the album scaled the charts in most countries. A sympathetic television documentary in 1994 portrayed a shy but very together human being. A wiser and sober Cocker continues into the 90s with his amazing voice intact and a constitution as strong as Sheffield steel. He paid tribute to himself in 1996 with *Organic*, an album containing many remakes

from his catalogue. This further emphasized his great ear for a good songwriter, regardless of a song's chart placing. Prime examples are Winwood's 'Cant Find My Way Back Home, Billy Preston's 'You Are So Beautiful' and John Sebastian's 'Darlin' Be Home Soon'. Cocker could sing the alphabet and make it sound exciting.

●ALBUMS: *With A Little Help From My Friends* (Regal Zonophone 1969)★★★★, *Joe Cocker!* (Regal Zonophone 1970)★★★★, *Mad Dogs And Englishmen* (A&M 1970)★★★★, *Cocker Happy* (Fly 1971)★★★, *Something To Say* (Cube 1973)★★, *I Can Stand A Little Rain* (Cube 1974)★★, *Jamaica Say You Will* (Cube 1975)★★, *Stingray* (A&M 1976)★★★, *Live In LA* (Cube 1976)★★, *Luxury You Can Afford* (Asylum 1978)★★★, by the Crusaders *Standing Tall* (MCA 1981)★★, *Sheffield Steel* (Island 1982)★★★, *Space Captain* (Cube 1982)★★, *Countdown Joe Cocker* (Cube 1982)★★, *An Officer And A Gentleman* film soundtrack (Island 1983)★★, *A Civilized Man* (Capitol 1984)★★, *Cocker* (Capitol 1986)★★, *Unchain My Heart* (Capitol 1987)★★★, *One Night Of Sin* (Capitol 1989)★★, *Joe Cocker Live* (Capitol 1990)★★, *Night Calls* (Capitol 1992)★★, *Have A Little Faith* (Capitol 1994)★★★, *Organic* (Parlophone 1996)★★★.

●COMPILATIONS: *Greatest Hits Volume 1* (Hallmark 1978)★★★, *Joe Cocker Platinum Collection* (Cube 1981)★★★, *The Very Best Of Joe Cocker* (Telstar 1986)★★★, *Joe Cocker Collection* (Castle 1986)★★★, *Best Of Joe Cocker* (K-Tel 1988)★★★, *Connoisseur's Cocker* (1991)★★★, *Joe Cocker: The Legend* (1992)★★★★, 4-CD box set *The Long Voyage Home* (A&M 1995)★★★★.

●VIDEOS: *Mad Dogs And Englishmen* (A&M Sound Pictures 1988), *Have A Little Faith* (1995).

●FURTHER READING: *Joe Cocker: With A Little Help From My Friends*, J.P. Bean.

●FILMS: *Mad Dogs And Englishmen*.

COCKNEY REBEL

Formed in 1973 by the strongly opinionated ex-journalist Steve Harley (b. Steven Nice, 27 February 1951, South London, England). Following his advertisement in a music paper he recruited Jean-Paul Crocker, Paul Avron Jeffreys (b. 13 February 1952, d. 21 December 1988 in the Lockerbie air disaster), Milton Reame-James and Stuart Elliott. Visually they looked like early Roxy Music with a strong David Bowie influence. Their debut hit 'Judy Teen' was a confident start, but one that was spoilt by the self-destructive Harley. He antagonized the music press and shortly afterwards disbanded his group. The most stable line-up was with Jim Cregan (guitar, ex-Family), George Ford (keyboards), Lindsay Elliott (percussion), Duncan McKay (keyboards) and Stuart Elliott, the drummer from the original band. Their first two albums remain their best and most satisfying works with Harley venturing into dangerous fields with his Dylanesque lyrics, winning him few critical friends. They reached the UK number 1 position with the sparkling 'Make Me Smile (Come Up And See Me)', now billed as Steve Harley And Cockney Rebel.

Harley's limited but interesting vocal range was put to the test on George Harrison's 'Here Comes the Sun', which made the UK Top 10 in 1976. Harley spent most of the next few years living in America and returned to the lower echelons of the charts in 1983 with 'Ballerina (Prima Donna)'. Ironically this was the second time he had visited the charts with a song containing the words 'Prima Donna' (in 1976 'Love's A Prima Donna' had similar success). Harley returned to the best-sellers in 1986 duetting with Sarah Brightman in the title song from *The Phantom Of The Opera*, a part that Harley was originally scheduled to play. That year he attempted a comeback after being signed by Mickie Most. Little was heard until 1988 when a UK television commercial used one of his early hits 'Mr Soft'. This prompted a compilation album of the same name. In 1992 Harley returned to the UK Top 50 with the re-released 'Make Me Smile (Come Up And See Me)' and embarked on a major tour. Five years elapsed until another album arrived, this time with an unremarkable cover of Dylan's 'Love Minus Zero'.

●ALBUMS: *The Human Menagerie* (EMI 1973)★★★, *Psychomodo* (EMI 1974)★★★, *The Best Years Of Our Lives* (EMI 1975)★★, *Love's A Prima Donna* (EMI 1976)★★, *Face To Face - A Live Recording* (EMI 1977)★★, *Hobo With A Grin* (EMI 1978)★★. Solo: Steve Harley *Poetic Justice* (Castle 1996)★★.

●COMPILATIONS: *Timeless Flight* (EMI 1976)★★, *The Best Of Steve Harley And Cockney Rebel* (EMI 1980)★★★, *Mr Soft - Greatest Hits* (Connoisseur 1988)★★★, *Make Me Smile, The Best Of Steve Harley And Cockney Rebel* (1992)★★★.

COHEN, LEONARD

b. 21 September 1934, Montreal, Canada. A graduate in English Literature from McGill and Columbia Universities, Cohen first made an impression as a novelist. *The Favourite Game* (1963) and *Beautiful Losers* (1966) offered the mixture of sexual and spiritual longing, despair and black humour, prevalent in his lyrics. Two early songs, 'Suzanne' and 'Priests', were recorded by folk singer Judy Collins, and the former was also included on *The Songs Of Leonard Cohen*, the artist's impressive debut. The weary loneliness portrayed by his intonation was enhanced by the barest of accompaniment, while the literate, if bleak, subject matter endeared the artist to a generation of 'bedsit' singer-songwriter aficionados. The album also featured 'Sisters Of Mercy' and 'Hey, That's No Way To Say Goodbye', two haunting compositions destined to become classics of the genre. *Songs From A Room* maintained a similar pattern, but despite the inclusion of 'Story Of Isaac' and 'Bird On A Wire', lacked the commercial impact of its predecessor. The appeal of Cohen's lugubrious delivery had noticeably waned by the release of *Songs Of Love And Hate*, yet it contained two of his finest compositions in 'Joan Of Arc' and 'Famous Blue Raincoat'. The inclusion of 'Dress Rehearsal Rag', one of the artist's earliest songs, suggested an aridity and it was four years before Cohen completed another studio set. *New Skin For The Old Ceremony* showed his talent for wry, often chilling, observations undiminished and included the disconsolate 'Chelsea Hotel', an account of Cohen's sexual encounter with singer Janis Joplin. A second impasse in the artist's career ended in 1977 with *Death Of A Ladies' Man*, an unlikely collaboration with producer Phil Spector. Although Cohen's songs retained their accustomed high standard, a grandiose backing proved ill-fitting and he later disowned the project. *Recent Songs* and *Various Positions* were excellent, if underrated collections, but the singer's career seemed confined to a small, committed audience until Jennifer Warnes, a former backing vocalist, released *Famous Blue Raincoat* in 1987. This commercially successful celebratory set was comprised solely of Cohen's songs and served as a timely reminder of his gifts. His own next set, *I'm Your Man*, was thus afforded widespread attention and attendant live performances formed the core of a BBC television documentary. It revealed Cohen's artistry intact and suggested that his major compositions have grown in stature with the passing of time. This was confirmed by the excellent *The Future* on which Cohen sounded confident and fresh with lyrics as biting and interesting as ever.

●ALBUMS: *The Songs Of Leonard Cohen* (Columbia 1968)★★★★, *Songs From A Room* (Columbia 1969)★★★, *Songs Of Love And Hate* (Columbia 1971)★★★, *Live Songs* (Columbia 1973)★★★, *New Skin For The Old Ceremony* (Columbia 1974)★★★, *Death Of A Ladies' Man* (Columbia 1977)★★★, *Recent Songs* (Columbia 1979)★★★, *Various Positions* (Columbia 1985)★★★, *I'm Your Man* (Columbia 1988)★★★★, *The Future* (Columbia 1992)★★★★, *Cohen Live* (Columbia 1994)★★★.

●COMPILATIONS: *Greatest Hits* (Columbia 1975)★★★★, *The Best Of Leonard Cohen* (Columbia 1976)★★★★, tribute album *Tower Of Song: The Songs Of Leonard Cohen* (A&M 1995)★★.

●VIDEOS: *Songs From The Life Of Leonard Cohen* (CMV Enterprises 1989).

●FURTHER READING: *Beautiful Losers*, Leonard Cohen. *Selected Poems 1956-1968*, Leonard Cohen. *The Favourite Game*, Leonard Cohen. *Flowers For Hitler*, Leonard Cohen. *The Spice-box Of Earth*, Leonard Cohen. *Death Of A Ladies Man*, Leonard Cohen. *Leonard Cohen: Prophet Of The Heart*, L.S. Dorman and C.L Rawlins. *Stranger Music, Selected Poems And Songs*, Leonard Cohen. *Leonard Cohen: A Life In Art*, Ira Nadel.

●FILMS: *Bird On A Wire* (1972).

COLD BLOOD

A popular live attraction in their native San Francisco, Cold Blood featured the powerful, bluesy voice of Lydia Pense and echoed the hard, brassy sound of Tower Of Power. Formed in 1968, the group - Larry Field (guitar), Paul Matute (keyboards), Danny Hull (saxophone),

Jerry Jonutz (saxophone), David Padron (trumpet), Larry Jonutz (trumpet), Paul Ellicot (bass), Frank J. David (drums), plus Pense - was signed to impresario Bill Graham's San Francisco label Fillmore the following year. Two albums resulted from this relationship before the group moved to Reprise Records. Later releases failed to recapture the gritty quality of those early records, although their final album was produced by guitarist Steve Cropper. Most of the group then dropped out from active performing, but a late-period drummer, Gaylord Birch, later worked with Santana, the Pointer Sisters and Graham Central Station.

●ALBUMS: *Cold Blood* (San Francisco 1969)★★★, *Sysiphus* (San Francisco 1971)★★★, *First Taste Of Sin* (Reprise 1972)★★, *Thriller!* (Reprise 1973)★★, *Lydia* (Warners 1974)★★, *Lydia Pense And Cold Blood* (ABC 1976)★★.

COLEMAN, ORNETTE

b. 19 March 1930, Fort Worth, Texas, USA. The evolution of any art form is a complex process and it is always an over-simplification to attribute a development to a single person. If there is anyone apart from Louis Armstrong for whom that claim could be made, however, Ornette Coleman would be a tenable candidate. Charlie Parker and John Coltrane were great forces for progress, but they focused and made viable certain concepts that were already in the air and which only awaited some exceptionally talented artist to give them concrete shape. They accelerated evolution, but did not change the direction of jazz in the way that Armstrong and Coleman seem to have done. Of course, certain elements of Coleman's music, including free improvisation, had been tried previously and he certainly did not reject what had gone before: his playing is well-rooted in the soil of Parker's bop tradition, and in R&B - Coleman's playing is a logical development from both, but he set the melody free and jolted jazz out of its 30-year obsession with chords. His role is somewhat analogous to that of Arnold Schoenberg in European classical music, although, unlike Schoenberg, Coleman did not forge a second set of shackles to replace the ones he burst. Those who do not recognize Coleman's contribution to music select two sticks from his early career with which to beat him. The first is that, when he acquired his first saxophone at the age of 14, he thought the low C on the alto was the A in his instruction book. Of course, he discovered his mistake after a while, but the realization of his error caused him to look at pitch and harmony in a fresh way, and this started the process which led to a style based on freely moving melody unhindered by a repetitive harmonic sub-structure, and, eventually, to the theory of harmolodics. The second was that, when in Pee Wee Crayton's band, he was playing so badly that he was paid to keep silent. Crayton remembered it slightly differently: he said that Coleman was quite capable of playing the blues convincingly, but chose not to, so Crayton told him forcefully that that's what he was paid to do. In 1946 Coleman had taken up the tenor saxophone and joined the 'Red' Connors band. He played in blues and R&B bands for some time, sat in with Stan Kenton on one occasion, and in 1949 took the tenor chair in a touring minstrel show. He recorded several of his own tunes in Natchez, Mississippi, in the same year, but these have never resurfaced. He was stranded in New Orleans, where he found it hard to get anyone to play with him, and eventually hooked up with Crayton's band, which took him to Los Angeles in 1950. He took a number of jobs unconnected with music, but continued his study of theory when he could. In the early and mid-50s he began to establish contact with musicians who were in sympathy with his ideas, such as Bobby Bradford, Ed Blackwell and Don Cherry, and in 1958 he recorded for Contemporary in Los Angeles. He met John Lewis, who arranged for the Coleman quartet - then comprising Cherry, Charlie Haden and Billy Higgins - to play a two-week engagement at New York's Five Spot Cafe; this turned into a legendary 54-month stay during which Coleman was physically assaulted by an irate bebop drummer, described as 'psychotic' by Miles Davis, and hailed as the saviour of jazz by others. Lewis also secured Coleman a recording contract with Atlantic Records, where he made a series of influential but controversial albums, most notably *Free Jazz*, a collective improvisation for double quartet. After signing him, Atlantic sponsored Coleman and Don Cherry at the Lennox School of Jazz. At this time he earned the admiration of classical composer/academics like Gunther Schuller, who involved him in a number of Third Stream works (e.g. on the John Lewis album *Jazz Abstractions*). During 1963/4 he went into retirement, learning trumpet and violin, before appearing again in 1965 with the highly influential trio with David Izenzon and Charles Moffett that he had introduced on the 1962 *Town Hall* album. It was during the currency of this trio that Coleman began to promote his 'classical' writing (*Saints And Soldiers*). Also in the mid-60s, Coleman turned his attention to writing film scores, the best-known of which is *Chappaque Suite*, which features Pharoah Sanders. He also made a guest appearance - on trumpet! - on Jackie MacLean's *Old And New Gospel*. In 1968 a second saxophonist, Dewey Redman, was added to the group, and Izenzon and Moffett were replaced by Jimmy Garrison and Elvin Jones, John Coltrane's former bassist and drummer.

By the end of the 60s, Coleman was again playing with his early associates, such as Haden, Cherry, Bradford, Higgins and Blackwell, various combinations of which can be heard on *Crisis*, *Paris Concert*, *Science Fiction* and *Broken Shadows*. In the mid-70s Coleman began using electric guitars and basses and some rock rhythms with a band that eventually evolved into Prime Time, which continues to this day. The theory of harmolodics has underpinned his music for the last 20 years in particular. Even musicians who have worked with Coleman extensively confess that they do not understand what the theory is about, but there are some threads which can be discerned: two of the most readily understood are that all instruments have their own peculiar, natural voice and should play in the appropriate range, regardless of conventional notions of key, and, secondly, that there is a sort of democracy of instruments, whereby the distinction between soloist and accompanist, leader and sidemen, front-line instruments and rhythm section, is broken down. Coleman is such a powerful improviser that in performance the soloist-accompanist division often remains, but the concept of harmolodics has been quite influential, and is evident in the music of James 'Blood' Ulmer, Ronald Shannon Jackson and the Decoding Society (Ulmer and Jackson were both members of the proto-Prime Time and Coleman guests on the former's 1978 *Tales Of Captain Black*) and Pinski Zoo. While Coleman is seen by many as the father of free jazz his music has never been as abstract, as centred on pure sound as that of the Chicago AACM circle or of many European exponents of improvised music. His playing is always intensely personal, with a 'human vocalized' sound especially notable on alto, and there is usually a strong, if fluid, rhythmic feel which has become increasingly obvious with Prime Time. There is often a sense of a tonal centre, albeit not one related to the European tempered system, and melodically, both as a writer and improviser, he evinces an acute talent for pleasing design. This he manages without the safety-net of a chord-cycle: instead of the more traditional method of creating symmetrical shapes within a pre-existing structure, his improvisations are based on linear, thematic development, spinning out open-ended, spontaneous compositions which have their own rigorous and indisputable internal logic. Since the mid-70s, with Prime Time and its immediate predecessors, this method began to give way to a more fragmented style, the edgy but elegant depth of emotion being replaced by an intensely agitated feel which sometimes seems to cloak an element of desperation. His 1987 double album, *In All Languages*, featured one disc by a re-formed version of the classic late 50s/early 60s quartet, and one by Prime Time, with most themes common to both records, and is an ideal crash-course in Coleman's evolution. As a composer he has written a number of durable themes, such as 'Beauty Is A Rare Thing', 'Focus On Sanity', 'Ramblin'', 'Sadness', 'When Will The Blues Leave', 'Tears Inside' and the ravishing 'Lonely Woman' as well as the massive and rather baffling suite *Skies Of America* written for his group and a symphony orchestra. In the 80s and early 90s he turned increasingly to his notated musics, writing a series of chamber and solo pieces that, excepting *Prime Time/Time Design* (for string quartet and percussion), remain unrecorded.

●ALBUMS: *Something Else!* (Contemporary 1958)★★★, *Tomorrow Is The Question* (Contemporary 1959)★★★, *The Shape Of Jazz To Come* (Atlantic 1959)★★★★, *Change Of The Century* (Atlantic 1960)★★★★, *This Is Our Music* (Atlantic 1961)★★★★, *Free Jazz* (Atlantic 1961)★★★★, *Ornette!* (Atlantic 1962)★★★★, *Ornette On Tenor* (Atlantic 1962)★★★, *The Town Hall Concert 1962* (1963)★★★★, *The Music Of Ornette Coleman* (RCA 1965)★★★, *Chappaque Suite* (1965)★★★, *The Great London Concert* aka *An Evening With Ornette Coleman* (1966)★★★, *At The Golden Circle, Volumes 1 & 2* (Blue Note 1966)★★★, *The Empty Foxhole* (Blue Note 1966)★★★, *Music Of Ornette Coleman* aka *Saints And Soldiers* (1967)★★★, *The Unprecedented Music Of Ornette Coleman* (1967)★★★, *New York Is Now!* (Blue Note 1968)★★★, *Love Call* (Blue Note 1968)★★★, *Ornette At 12* (Impulse 1969)★★★, *Crisis* (Impulse 1969)★★★, *Friends And Neighbours* (1970)★★★, *The Art Of Improvisers* rec. 1959-61 (Atlantic 1970)★★★, *Twins* rec. 1959-61 (Atlantic 1972)★★★, *Science Fiction* (1972)★★★, *Skies Of America* (1972)★★★, *To Whom Who Keeps A Record* (Atlantic 1975)★★★, *Dancing In Your Head* (1976)★★★, *Body Meta* (1976)★★★, *Paris Concert* rec. 1971 (1977)★★★, *Coleman Classics Volume One* rec. 1958 (1977)★★★, with Charlie Haden *Soapsuds, Soapsuds* (1977)★★★, *Broken Shadows* rec. 1971-72 (Moon 1982)★★★, *Of Human Feelings* rec. 1979 (1982)★★★, *Who's Crazy* (Affinity 1983)★★★, *Opening The Caravan Of Dreams* (1985)★★★, *Prime Time/Time Design* (1985)★★★, with Pat Metheny *Song X* (Geffen 1986)★★★, *In All Languages* (1987)★★★, *Virgin Beauty* (1988)★★★, *Live In Milano 1968* (1989)★★★, *Jazzbuhne Berlin 88* rec. 1988 (1990)★★★, *Naked Lunch* (1992)★★★, *Languages* (1993)★★★, *The Empty Foxhole* (Connoisseur 1994)★★★, with Prime Time *Tone Dialing* (Verve 1995)★★★.

●COMPILATIONS: *Beauty Is A Rare Thing: The Complete Atlantic Recordings* 6-CD box set (Rhino/Atlantic 1993)★★★★.

●FURTHER READING: *Ornette Coleman*, Barry McCrae. *Four Lives In The Bebop Business*, A.B. Spellman.

COLEMAN, RAY

b. 15 June 1937, Leicester, Leicestershire, England, d. 10 September 1996. Editor and journalist Ray Coleman managed to instil a sense of formality and professionalism to that most nebulous of critical forms, rock journalism, throughout his long career. He brought the tabloid banner headlines of Fleet Street and the intrepid determinism of the front-line reporter to his editorship of *Melody Maker* throughout the 60s and 70s. The son of a Polish immigrant, he started his apprenticeship as a copy boy for the *Leicester Evening Mail*. His other major interest at this time was chess, and he duly managed to sneak in match reports concerning his successes into the same paper. Always intending to become a Fleet Street reporter, he worked on court and business diaries for Brighton and Manchester regional papers, but also began to string for the *Melody Maker*. That journal was already a familiar fixture in the family household, as Coleman's brother was a semi-professional jazz guitarist. He was eventually offered a full-time post with the *Melody Maker*, but still yearned to become a reporter for the *Daily Telegraph*. However, when his ambitions were frustrated, he transferred his energies back into the entertainment industry. Where previously music journalism had been conducted on a fanzine-like basis, Coleman was responsible for the more questioning, if never hectoring, tone adopted by the *Melody Maker*. After supporting the rise of traditional jazz musicians such as Chris Barber, Acker Bilk and Kenny Ball, he also spotted and nurtured the ascendancy of the Beatles. He became a confidante of both that group and its manager Brian Epstein, and was part of the Beatles entourage when it toured the USA. He soon became assistant editor of the title under Jack Hutton, who was impressed by his forceful style and his unwillingness to be put off the scent of his targets. His prose, though never particularly elegant, was both succinct and rigorously accurate - many musicians happily submitted to interviews knowing that the misquotes that were a feature of many articles would not be a danger with Coleman. It also became easy to spot Coleman headlines - 'Beatle Mania!' and 'Would You Let Your Sister Go With A Rolling Stone' successfully importing populist tabloid values (although he was clearly cast in the Fleet Street mould, he was a life-long socialist). In 1965 he took the editorship of another IPC title, *Disc*, before returning to *Melody Maker* five years later when Hutton left to start the rival weekly, *Sounds*. The paper immediately prospered under his hands, its circulation rising to 200,000 in the 70s. However, having successfully charted the rise of rock bands such as Led Zeppelin and Genesis, Coleman found himself less able to provide adequate coverage of the punk boom. Despite commissioning writers such as Caroline Coon, Coleman's finger, to use his own ironic phrase, was no longer on the pulse. His editorship of *Melody Maker* had spanned a decade, 1971-81, the last two years indirectly as a senior editor. After a period as publisher, Coleman became a freelance author, writing his first book about Gary Numan (1982), and then a much more prestigious, and acclaimed, two-volume set about John Lennon. These were officially sanctioned by Cynthia Lennon and Yoko Ono. Further biographies followed of Eric Clapton, Brian Epstein, Bill Wyman, Gerry Marsden (Gerry And The Pacemakers), the Carpenters and Frank Sinatra. He was working on a biography of Phil Collins at the time of his death from kidney cancer in 1996.

COLLINS, BOOTSY

b. William Collins, 26 October 1951, Cincinnati, Ohio, USA. This exceptional showman was an integral part of the JBs, the backing group fashioned by James Brown to replace the Famous Flames. Between 1969 and 1971, the distinctive Bootsy basswork propelled some of the era's definitive funk anthems. Collins was later part of the large-scale defection in which several of Brown's most valued musicians switched to George Clinton's Parliament/Funkadelic organization. The bassist's popularity inspired the formation of Bootsy's Rubber Band, a spin-off group featuring such Brown/Clinton associates as Fred Wesley, Maceo Parker and Bernie Worrell. Collins' outrageous image - part space cadet, part psychedelic warlord - emphasized a mix of funk and fun encapsulated in 'Psychoticbumpschool' (1976), 'The Pinocchio Theory' (1977) and 'Bootzilla' (1978), a US R&B chart-topper. The internal problems plaguing the Clinton camp during the early 80s temporarily hampered Collins' career although subsequent releases reveal some of his erstwhile charm. Collins and the Bootzilla Orchestra were employed for the production of Malcolm McLaren's 1989 album *Waltz Darling* and by the early 90s the Rubber Band had started touring again.

●ALBUMS: *Stretchin' Out In Bootsy's Rubber Band* (Warners 1976)★★★, *Ahh...The Name Is Bootsy, Baby!* (Warners 1977)★★★, *Bootsy? Player Of The Year* (Warners 1978)★★★, *This Boot Is Made For Fonk-n* (Warners 1979)★★, *Ultra Wave* (Warners 1980)★★★, *The One Giveth, The Count Taketh Away* (Warners 1982)★★★, *What's Bootsy Doin'?* (Columbia 1988)★★★, *Blasters Of The Universe* (Rykodisc 1994)★★★.

●COMPILATIONS: *Back In The Day: The Best Of ...* (Warners 1995)★★★★.

COLLINS, SHIRLEY AND DOLLY

Shirley Elizabeth Collins (b. 5 July 1935, Hastings, East Sussex, England) and Dolly Collins (b. 6 March 1933, Hastings, East Sussex, England). Shirley Collins was established as a leading English folk singer following her discovery by a BBC researcher. She accompanied archivist Alan Lomax on a tour of southern American states before making her recording debut in 1959 with *False True Lovers*, issued on Folkways Records. In 1964 she completed *Folk Roots, New Routes* with guitarist Davey Graham, an ambitious album that challenged the then-rigid boundaries of British folk music. Shirley's first solo album, *The Power Of The True Love Knot*, was a sumptuous evocation of medieval England. This enthralling collection featured sister Dolly's sympathetic arrangements and atmospheric flute organ. The Collins sisters were then signed to the nascent Harvest label for whom they recorded two excellent albums that maintained the atmosphere of their earlier collection. The songs ranged from those by Robert Burns to Robin Williamson, while the presence of David Munrow's Early Music Consort gave *Anthems In Eden* an authoritative air. The sisters continued to work together but Shirley was increasingly drawn into the Albion Country Band circle following her marriage to bassist Ashley Hutchings. The group, an offshoot of the Steeleye Span/Young Tradition axis, provided the backing on Shirley's *No Roses* and she continued to sing with related projects the Etchingham Steam Band and the Albion Dance Band. Her divorce from Hutchings precluded further involvement and the singer retired from music for several years following a third collaboration with her sister. Shirley Collins returned to performing during the late 80s.

●ALBUMS: *Sweet Primroses* (Topic 1967), *The Power Of The True Love Knot* (Polydor 1968)★★★★, *Anthems In Eden* (Harvest 1969)★★★★, *Love, Death And The Lady* (Harvest 1970), *For As Many As Will* (Topic 1974)★★★. Solo: Shirley Collins *False True Lovers* (Folkways 1959)★★★,*Sweet England* (Folkways 1959)★★★, with Davey Graham *Folk Roots, New Routes* (Righteous 1964)★★★, *No Roses* (Pegasus 1971)★★★, *Adieu To Old England* (Topic 1974)★★★, *Amaranth* (Harvest 1976)★★★★, combines one side of newly recorded material with the 'Anthems In Eden' suite from the above 1969 release, *The Sweet Primroses* (plus *Heroes in Love* EP) (Topic 1995)★★★.

●COMPILATIONS: *A Favourite Garland* (1974)★★★, *Fountain Of Snow* (1992)★★★.

COMMANDER CODY AND HIS LOST PLANET AIRMEN

Although renowned for its high-energy rock, the Detroit/Ann Arbor region also formed the focal point for this entertaining country rock band. The first of several tempestuous line-ups was formed in 1967, comprising Commander Cody (b. George Frayne IV, 19 July 1944, Boise City, Idaho, USA; piano), John Tichy (b. St. Louis, Missouri, USA; lead guitar), Steve Schwartz (guitar), Don Bolton aka the West Virginia Creeper (pedal steel), Stephen Davis (bass) and Ralph Mallory (drums). Only Frayne, Tichy and Bolton remained with the group on their move to San Francisco the following year. The line-up was completed on the Airmen's debut album, *Lost In The Ozone* by Billy C. Farlowe (b. Decatur, Alabama, USA; vocals/harp), Andy Stein (b. 31 August 1948, New York, USA; fiddle/saxophone), Billy Kirchen (b. 29 January 1948, Ann Arbor, Michigan, USA; lead guitar), 'Buffalo' Bruce Barlow (b. 3 December 1948, Oxnard, California, USA; bass) and Lance Dickerson (b. 15 October 1948, Livonia, Michigan, USA; drums). This earthy collection covered a wealth of material, including rockabilly, western swing, country and jump R&B, a pattern sustained on several subsequent releases. Despite attaining a US Top 10 single with 'Hot Rod Lincoln' (1972), the group's allure began to fade as their albums failed to capture an undoubted in-concert prowess. Although *Live From Deep In The Heart Of Texas* and *We've Got A Live One Here* redressed the balance, what once seemed so natural became increasingly laboured as individual members grew disillusioned. John Tichy's departure proved crucial and preceded an almost total desertion in 1976. The following year Cody released his first solo album, *Midnight Man*, before convening the New Commander Cody Band. Cody And Farlowe re-formed the Lost Planet Airmen in the 90s.

●ALBUMS: *Lost In The Ozone* (Paramount 1971)★★★, *Hot Licks, Cold Steel And Trucker's Favourites* (Paramount 1972)★★★, *Country Casanova* (Paramount 1973)★★★, *Live From Deep In The Heart Of Texas* (Paramount 1974)★★★★, *Commander Cody And His Lost Planet Airmen* (Warners 1975)★★, *Tales From The Ozone* (Warners 1975)★★, *We've Got A Live One Here!* (Warners 1976)★★★, *Let's Rock* (Special Delivery 1987)★★, *Sleazy Roadside Stories* rec. live 1973 (1988)★★★, *Aces High* (1992)★★; as the Commander Cody Band *Rock 'N' Roll Again* (Arista 1977)★★, *Flying Dreams* (1978)★★, *Lose It Tonight* (1980)★★.

●COMPILATIONS: *The Very Best Of Commander Cody And His Lost Planet Airmen* (See For Miles 1986)★★★, *Cody Returns From Outer Space* (Edsel 1987)★★★, *Too Much Fun - The Best Of Commander Cody* (MCA 1990)★★★.

COMMODORES

The Commodores were formed at Tuskagee Institute, Alabama, USA, in 1967, when two groups of students merged to form a six-piece band. Lionel Richie (b. 20 June 1949, Tuskegee, Alabama, USA; keyboards/saxophone/vocals), Thomas McClary (b. 6 October 1950; guitar) and William King (b. 30 January 1949, Alabama, USA; trumpet) had been members of the Mystics; Andre Callahan (drums), Michael Gilbert (bass) and Milan Williams (b. 28 March 1949, Mississippi, USA; keyboards) previously played with the Jays. Callahan and Gilbert were replaced, respectively, by Walter 'Clyde' Orange (b. 10 December 1947, Florida, USA and Ronald LaPread (b. 1950, Florida, USA), before the Commodores moved to New York in 1969, where they became established as a club band specializing in funk instrumentals. A year later, they recorded an album for Atlantic Records, left unissued at the time but subsequently released as *Rise Up*, which included instrumental covers of recent R&B hits, plus some original material.

In 1972, the group's manager, Bernie Ashburn, secured them a support slot on an American tour with the Jackson Five, and the Commodores were duly signed to Motown Records. They continued to tour with the Jackson Five for three years, after which they supported the Rolling Stones on their 1975 US tour. By this time, their mix of hard-edged funk songs and romantic ballads, the latter mostly penned and sung by Richie, had won them a national following. The instrumental 'Machine Gun' gave them their first US hit, followed by 'Slippery When Wet'.

The Commodores soon found consistent success with Richie's smooth ballads; 'Sweet Love', 'Just To Be Close To You' and 'Easy' all enjoyed huge sales between 1975 and 1977. Although Clyde Orange's aggressive 'Too Hot To Trot' broke the sequence of ballads in 1977, the Commodores were increasingly regarded as a soft-soul outfit. This perception was underlined when Richie's sensitive love song to his wife, 'Three Times A Lady', became a number 1 record in the US and UK, where it was Motown's biggest-selling record to date. The follow-up, 'Sail On', introduced a country flavour to Richie's work, and he began to receive commissions to write material for artists like Kenny Rogers. After 'Still' gave them another US pop and soul number 1 in 1979, confirming the Commodores as Motown's best-selling act of the 70s, the group attempted to move into a more experimental blend of funk and rock on *Heroes* in 1980. The commercial failure of this venture, and the success of Lionel Richie's duet with Diana Ross on 'Endless Love', persuaded him to leave the group for a solo career. The remaining Commodores were initially overshadowed by the move, with the replacement Kevin Smith unable to emulate Richie's role in live performances.

In 1984, Thomas McClary also launched a solo career with an album for Motown. He was replaced by Englishman J.D. Nicholas (b. 12 April 1952, Watford, Hertfordshire, England), formerly vocalist with Heatwave, and this combination was featured on the group's enormous 1985 hit 'Nightshift', an affecting tribute to Marvin Gaye and Jackie Wilson which successfully captured Gaye's shifting, rhythmic brand of soul. Later that year, the Commodores left Motown for Polydor, prompting Ronald LaPread to leave the band. Their new contract began promisingly with a major US soul chart hit, 'Goin' To The Bank' (1986), but subsequent releases proved less successful. The group made an unexpected return to the UK chart in 1988 when 'Easy' was used on a television commercial for the Halifax Building Society, reaching number 15. The Commodores have lost much of their status as one of America's most popular soul bands.

●ALBUMS: *Machine Gun* (Motown 1974)★★★★, *Caught In The Act* (Motown 1975)★★★, *Movin' On* (Motown 1975)★★★, *Hot On The Tracks* (Motown 1976)★★★, *Commodores* aka *Zoom* (Motown 1977)★★★, *Live!* (Motown 1977)★★★, *Natural High* (Motown 1978)★★★, *Midnight Magic* (Motown 1979)★★★, *Heroes* (Motown 1980)★★★, *In The Pocket* (Motown 1981)★★★, *13* (Motown 1983)★★★, *Nightshift* (Motown 1985)★★★, *United* (Polydor 1986)★★, *Rise Up* (Blue Moon 1987)★★, *Rock Solid* (Polydor 1988)★★.
●COMPILATIONS: *Greatest Hits* (Motown 1981)★★★★, *Love Songs* (K-Tel 1982)★★, *Anthology* (Motown 1983)★★★, *The Best Of The Commodores* (Telstar 1985)★★★, *14 Greatest Hits* (1993)★★★, *The Very Best Of the Commodores* (Motown 1995)★★★★.
●VIDEOS: *Cover Story* (Stylus Video 1990).

COMUS

This experimental act was comprised of Bobbie Watson (vocals/percussion), Glen Goring (guitar/vocals), Roger Wooton (guitar/vocals), Colin Pearson (violin), Andy Hellaby (bass), Gordon Caxon (drums) and Rob Young (percussion/oboe/flute). Nominally a folk group, Comus brought a unique perspective to the genre on *First Utterance*, released on the progressively minded Dawn Records. The songs' subject matter - witchcraft, murder, rape - echoed the themes of some traditional

material, but the group attempted to weld this perspective to a genuinely disturbing, and contemporary, sound. Treated vocals emphasized the often horrific lyrics while musically Comus fused melodic gifts to insightful playing. By contrast *To Keep From Crying* was more orthodox. The departures of Goring, Pearson and Young robbed the group of its intensity, and although the use of studio musicians on woodwind instruments helped maintain the spirit of its predecessor, the set was burdened by a rock-orientated rhythm section. Comus broke up soon after its release.
●ALBUMS: *First Utterance* (Dawn 1971)★★★, *To Keep From Crying* (Virgin 1974)★★.

CONCERT FOR BANGLA DESH, THE

Moved by the famine-blighted Bangla Desh, Indian master musician Ravi Shankar turned to his best-known pupil for possible aid. Galvanized, George Harrison hurriedly recorded his 'Bangla Desh' single and organized a gala benefit concert at Madison Square Gardens, New York, on 1 August 1971. The former Beatles star was firmly in the ascendancy following *All Things Must Pass* and its attendant single, 'My Sweet Lord', and the cast assembled included Leon Russell, Billy Preston and Badfinger, as well as Shankar. However Harrison's greatest coup was persuading a then reclusive Bob Dylan to make a rare, scheduled live appearance, his first since the Isle Of Wight Festival two years previously. The singer was in sparkling form, as evinced by powerful renditions of 'Mr. Tambourine Man', 'Blowin' In The Wind' and 'A Hard Rain's Gonna Fall'. Indeed all of the performers played strong sets - Preston's 'That's The Way God Planned It' was especially memorable - generating considerable goodwill about the project at the outset. The resultant film, complete with rehearsal material, proved highly popular and a corresponding three-album set, complete with commemorative book, continued to sell well over the ensuing years. However, controversy reared several months later over the proceeds from the event. Rancour was such that it discoloured the entire proceedings and *The Concert For Bangla Desh* became synonymous with good intentions going bad. Its well-publicized tribulations nonetheless helped the Live Aid organizers avoid similar pitfalls.
●ALBUMS: *Concert For Bangla Desh* (Apple 1972)★★★.

CONGREGATION

This British mixed choir and accompanying orchestra was a one-shot studio creation of composers Roger Cook and Roger Greenaway. It was fronted by session vocalist Brian Keith (ex-Plastic Penny) for 'Softly Whispering I Love You' which, hinged on an eminently hummable melody, went to number 4 in the UK chart, and was a 1972 Christmas hit. Too cumbersome for concert tours, Congregation was laid to rest after the single's television promotions but the song was successfully revived by Paul Young in 1989.

COODER, RY

b. Ryland Peter Cooder, 15 March 1947, Los Angeles, California, USA. One of rock's premier talents, Cooder mastered the rudiments of guitar while still a child. He learned the techniques of traditional music from Rev. Gary Davis and by the age of 17 was part of a blues act with singer Jackie DeShannon. In 1965 he formed the Rising Sons with Taj Mahal and veteran Spirit drummer Ed Cassidy, but this promising group broke up when the release of a completed album was cancelled. However the sessions brought Ry into contact with producer Terry Melcher, who in turn employed the guitarist on several sessions, notably with Paul Revere And The Raiders. Cooder enjoyed a brief, but fruitful, association with Captain Beefheart And His Magic Band. His distinctive slide work is apparent on the group's debut album, *Safe As Milk*, but the artist declined an offer to join on a permanent basis. Instead he continued his studio work, guesting on sessions for Randy Newman, Little Feat and Van Dyke Parks, as well as to the soundtracks of *Candy* and *Performance*. Cooder also contributed to the Rolling Stones' album *Let It Bleed*, and was tipped as a likely replacement for Brian Jones until clashes with Keith Richard, primarily over the authorship of the riff to 'Honky Tonk Woman', precluded further involvement.

Cooder's impressive debut album included material by Lead Belly, Sleepy John Estes and Blind Willie Johnson, and offered a patchwork of Americana which became his trademark. A second collection, *Into The Purple Valley*, established his vision more fully and introduced a tight but sympathetic band, which included longstanding collaborators Jim Keltner and Jim Dickinson. By contrast, several selections employed the barest instrumentation, resulting in one of the artist's finest releases. The rather desolate *Boomer's Story* completed Cooder's early trilogy and in 1974 he released the buoyant *Paradise And Lunch*. His confidence was immediately apparent on the reggae interpretation of 'It's All Over Now' and the silky 'Ditty Wa Ditty', and it was this acclaimed collection that established him as a major talent. A fascination with 30s topical songs was now muted in favour of a greater eclecticism, which in turn anticipated Cooder's subsequent direction. *Chicken Skin Music* was marked by two distinct preoccupations. Contributions from Flaco Jiminez and Gabby Pahuini enhanced its mixture of Tex-Mex and Hawaiian styles, while Cooder's seamless playing and inspired arrangements created a sympathetic setting. The guitarist's relationship with Jiminez was maintained on a fine in-concert set, *Showtime*, but Cooder then abandoned this direction with the reverential *Jazz*. This curiously unsatisfying album paid homage to the dixieland era, but a crafted meticulousness denied the project life and its creator has since disowned it.

Cooder then embraced a more mainstream approach with *Bop Till You Drop*, an ebullient, rhythmic, yet rock-based collection, reminiscent of Little Feat. The album, which included cameo-performances from soul singer Chaka Khan, comprised several urban R&B standards, including 'Little Sister', 'Go Home Girl' and 'Don't Mess Up A Good Thing'. Its successor, *Borderline*, offered similar fare, but when the style was continued on a third release, *The Slide Area*, a sense of weariness became apparent. Such overtly commercial selections contrasted with Cooder's soundtrack work. *The Long Riders*, plus *Paris, Texas* and *Crossroads* owed much to the spirit of adventure prevalent in his early work, while the expansive tapestry of these films allowed a greater scope for his undoubted imagination. It was five years before Cooder released an official follow-up to *The Slide Area* and although *Get Rhythm* offered little not already displayed, it re-established purpose to his rock-based work. This inventive, thoughtful individual has embraced both commercial and ethnic styles with equal dexterity, but has yet to achieve the widespread success that his undoubted talent deserves. In 1992, Cooder had joined up with Nick Lowe, Jim Keltner and John Hiatt to record and perform under the name of Little Village. In the mid-90s he was acclaimed for his successful collaborations with V.M. Bhatt on *A Meeting By the River* in 1993 and with Ali Farka Toure on *Talking Timbuktu* in 1994.

●ALBUMS: *Ry Cooder* (Reprise 1970)★★★, *Into The Purple Valley* (Reprise 1971)★★★★, *Boomer's Story* (Reprise 1972)★★★★, *Paradise And Lunch* (Reprise 1974)★★★★, *Chicken Skin Music* (Reprise 1976)★★★★, *Showtime* (Warners 1976)★★★, *Jazz* (Warners 1978)★★, *Bop Till You Drop* (Warners 1979)★★★, *Borderline* (Warners 1980)★★★, *The Long Riders* film soundtrack (Warners 1980)★★★, *The Border* film soundtrack (MCA 1980)★★★, *Ry Cooder Live* (Warners 1982)★★★, *The Slide Area* (Warners 1982)★★, *Paris, Texas* film soundtrack (Warners 1985)★★★, *Alamo Bay* film soundtrack (Slash 1985)★★★, *Blue City* film soundtrack (Warners 1986)★★, *Crossroads* film soundtrack (Warners 1987)★★, *Get Rhythm* (Warners 1987)★★, *Johnny Handsome* film soundtrack (Warners 1989)★★★, with Little Village *Little Village* (Reprise 1992)★★, *Trespass* film soundtrack (1993)★★, with V.M. Bhatt *A Meeting By The River* (1993)★★★, with Ali Farka Toure *Talking Timbuktu* (World Circuit 1994)★★★★, *Geronimo* film soundtrack (Columbia 1994)★★★.

●COMPILATIONS: *Why Don't You Try Me Tonight?* (Warners 1985)★★★, *Music By ...* (Reprise 1995)★★★.

COOK AND GREENAWAY

Sons of Bristol, England, Roger Cook (b. 19 August 1940, Bristol, Avon, England) and Roger Greenaway (b. 23 August 1938, Bristol, Avon, England) sang with the Kestrels, a close harmony pop group whose easy professionalism guaranteed, if not hit parade placings, then regular employment on mid-60s package tours and variety seasons. Setting themselves up in London as session musicians and songwriters, the pair's tenacity paid off when 'You've Got Your Troubles' charted for the Fortunes in 1965. This established them as a middle-of-the-road hit factory (sometimes in collaboration with other writers), with a knack for infectious and hummable melodies with lyrics more impressive in sound than meaning. Their compositions included 'Softly Whispering I Love You' (Congregation), 'Home Lovin' Man' (Andy Williams), 'My Baby Loves Lovin'' (White Plains) and 1972's extraordinary success, 'I'd Like To Teach The World To Sing' (the New Seekers). As David And Jonathan, the two Rogers themselves succeeded twice in 1966's UK Top 20 with a cover of the Beatles' 'Michelle' and their own 'Lovers Of The World Unite' but, with the failure of subsequent discs (including 'Softly Whispering I Love You'), they ceased public appearances as a duo. They then functioned separately as occasional recording artists - as instanced by Cook's *Study* album and Greenaway's 1970 smash with 'Gimme Dat Ding' (as one of the Pipkins) - but this was incidental to the team's composition and production work for other acts, for the purposes of which Cookaway Music was formed. With no existence beyond recording and television studios, some Cookaway acts (Congregation, Harley Quinne) were created simply to front specific projects. The most enduring of these was Blue Mink, assembled in 1969 with Cook and Madeline Bell as lead vocalists for a four-year chart run, mostly with Cook-Greenaway numbers. During this period, the team illuminated commercial breaks on British television with jingles extolling the virtues of Typhoo Tea, Woodpecker Cider and other products. Nevertheless, Greenaway and Cook, without rancour, were no longer composing together by 1975. The following year, Cook alone supervised sessions for the Chanter Sisters (for whom he and Herbie Flowers wrote 'Side Show') and Nana Mouskouri, and '7-6-5-4-3-2-1 (Blow Your Whistle)' by the Rimshots was attributed only to him. Disgruntled with the British tax system and the narrow-minded attitude of some UK radio and television producers, he migrated to Nashville to infiltrate the country market, penning US country number 1's for artists such as Crystal Gayle ('Talking In Your Sleep') and Don Williams ('I Believe In You' and 'Love Is On A Roll'), all published by his own Cook House company. Greenaway also came up with a country number 1 for Gayle with 'It's Like We Never Said Goodbye' in 1980, but it was business as usual in continuing to compose advertising jingles for such companies as Allied Carpets, Asda and British Gas, and having a creative hand in post-Cook hits such as those of the Drifters, David Dundas, Our Kid, Dana and Claude Francois. In 1983, Greenaway was appointed chairman of Britain's Performing Right Society and in 1995 he took charge of the European office for ASCAP. In 1992 Cook teamed up with Hugh Cornwall (Stranglers) and guitarist Andy West to release *CCW* on the UFO label, under the moniker Cornwall, Cook & West.

COOK, ROGER

b. *c.*1937, Bristol, England. Roger Cook has enjoyed two parallel but equally successful careers; one as a writer and performer of pop songs, the other as a widely celebrated writer of country songs for the Nashville community. Despite these achievements, he doubtless remains best-known for co-writing 'I'd Like To Teach The World To Sing', a song adopted for a worldwide Coca Cola advertising campaign, which he co-wrote with Roger Greenaway. Cook first met Greenaway when his group, the Sapphires, shared a manager with Greenaway's Kestrels. When the Sapphires folded, Cook formed a duo known as John And Julie. They played pantomime and summer seasons together, and had a recording contract with Norrie Paramor, before 'Julie' became pregnant and left to get married. Afterwards, Cook joined Greenaway in the Kestrels when one of their members dropped out. Eventually, the two decided to start writing songs together, the first result being 'You've Got Your Troubles'. They planned to record it together with Beatles producer George Martin, but a rival version by the Fortunes took the chart honours. Now recording as David And Jonathan, they had their own chart hits in 1966 with 'Lovers Of The World Unite' and 'Michelle'. Cook then wrote 'Melting Pot' for Blue Mink, a largely studio-based group with which he was associated for several years. He subsequently became a songwriter at Mills Music and Dick James Music. There he met Elton John - then still Reg Dwight - who later recorded a version of 'Skyline Pigeon' which Cook and Greenaway published. In 1970 Cook and Greenaway wrote a song, 'True Love And Apple Pie', as a single for the artist Susan Shirley. Although it flopped, they rejigged the same tune and presented it to Coca Cola for worldwide success as 'I'd Like To Teach The World To Sing'. Two versions of the song, one by a rapidly assembled group known as the Hilltop Singers, the other by the New Seekers, became US Top 10 hits. As Cook remembers: 'I wanted to disown the song. I must admit I got to like it when it sold several million records and the money started rolling in.' Eventually, after breaking up the partnership with Greenaway, Cook settled in Nashville. There he began to write for country artists, his biggest success being Crystal Gayle's 'Talking In Your Sleep', co-written with Bobby Wood. He settled in Nashville permanently in 1976, setting up a series of publishing companies. He continued to enjoy further hits as a writer, including Don Williams' number 1, 'Love Is On A Roll', co-written with John Prine. Cook returned to the UK in 1990, and has continued to write and develop plans for a stage musical written with Joe Brown about the skiffle boom.

COOLIDGE, RITA

b. 1 May 1944, Nashville, Tennessee, USA, from mixed white and Cherokee Indian parentage. Coolidge's father was a baptist minister and she first sang radio jingles in

Memphis with her sister Priscilla. Coolidge recorded briefly for local label Pepper before moving to Los Angeles in the mid-60s. There she became a highly regarded session singer, working with Eric Clapton, Stephen Stills and many others. She had a relationship with Stills and he wrote a number of songs about her including 'Cherokee', 'The Raven' and 'Sugar Babe' In 1969-70, Coolidge toured with the Delaney And Bonnie and Leon Russell (*Mad Dogs & Englishmen*) troupes. Russell's 'Delta Lady' was supposedly inspired by Coolidge. Returning to Los Angeles, she was signed to a solo recording contract by A&M. Her debut album included the cream of LA session musicians (among them Booker T. Jones, by now her brother-in-law) and it was followed by almost annual releases during the 70s. Coolidge also made several albums with Kris Kristofferson to whom she was married between 1973 and 1979. The quality of her work was uneven since the purity of her natural voice was not always matched by subtlety of interpretation. Her first hit singles were a revival of the Jackie Wilson hit 'Higher And Higher' and 'We're All Alone', produced by Booker T. in 1977. The following year a version of the Temptations' 'The Way You Do The Things You Do' reached the Top 20. Coolidge was less active in the 80s although in 1983 she recorded a James Bond movie theme, 'All Time High' from *Octopussy*.

●ALBUMS: *Rita Coolidge* (A&M 1971)★★★, *Nice Feelin'* (A&M 1971)★★, *The Lady's Not For Sale* (A&M 1972)★★★, with Kris Kristofferson *Full Moon* (A&M 1973)★★★, *Fall Into Spring* (A&M 1974)★★★, with Kris Kristofferson *Breakaway* (Monument 1974)★, *It's Only Love* (A&M 1975)★★, *Anytime Anywhere* (A&M 1977)★★★★, *Love Me Again* (A&M 1978)★★★, with Kris Kristofferson *Natural Act* (A&M 1979)★★, *Satisfied* (A&M 1979)★★, *Heartbreak Radio* (A&M 1981)★★, *Never Let You Go* (A&M 1983)★★, *Inside The Fire* (A&M 1988)★★, *All Time High* (1993)★★, *Cherokee* (Permanent 1995)★★.

●COMPILATIONS: *Greatest Hits* (A&M 1981)★★★.

COREA, CHICK

b. Armando Anthony Corea, 12 June 1941, Chelsea, Massachusetts, USA. After a very musical home environment, pianist Corea's first notable professional engagements were in the Latin bands of Mongo Santamaría and Willie Bobo (1962-63), playing a style of music that continues to influence him today. Joining Blue Mitchell's band in 1964, he spent two years with the trumpeter, and had a chance to record some of his own compositions on Blue Note Records. Corea's first recordings appeared in 1966 with *Tones For Joan's Bones*, and show a pianist influenced mainly by hard-bop. In 1968, he joined Miles Davis for the trumpeter's first real experiments with fusion. Playing on some of Davis's most important albums, Corea's electric piano became integral to the new sound. Leaving Davis in 1970 to explore free music within an acoustic setting, he

formed Circle with Dave Holland, Barry Altschul, and later Anthony Braxton. Although Circle lasted only a year, it managed to make some important recordings before Corea, now involved in Scientology, became interested in a style with more widespread appeal. Forming the first of three bands called Return To Forever in 1971, he played a Latin-influenced fusion featuring the vocalist Flora Purim and percussionist Airto Moreiro, before he changed the band's line-up to produce a more rock-orientated sound in the mid-70s. The final Return To Forever hinted at classical music with string and brass groups, but disbanded in 1980 after only moderate success. After playing with numerous top musicians in the early 80s (including Herbie Hancock and Michael Brecker), since 1985 he has concentrated on his Akoustic and Elektric Bands and now records for GRP Records. Joined by John Patitucci (bass) and Dave Weckl (drums), he is presently involved in a music that challenges the extremes of virtuosity, mixing passages of complex arrangement with solos in the fusion style.

●ALBUMS: *Tones For Joan's Bones* (1966)★★★, *Bliss* (1967)★★★, with Roy Haynes, Miroslav Vitous *Now He Sings, Now He Sobs* (Blue Note 1968)★★★★, with Haynes, Vitous *Circling In* (1968),★★★ *Is 69* (1969)★★★, *Sun Dance* (1969)★★★, *The Song Of Singing* (Blue Note 1970)★★★★, with Circle *Circulus* (1970)★★★, with Circle *Paris Concert* (1971)★★★, *A.R.C.* (ECM 1971)★★★, *Early Circle* (Blue Note 1971)★★★, *Piano Improvisations Vols. 1 & 2* (ECM 1971)★★★★, with Return To Forever *Inner Space* (Polydor 1972)★★★★, with Return To Forever *Return To Forever* (ECM 1972)★★★★, with Gary Burton *Crystal Silence* (ECM 1973)★★★★, with Return To Forever *Light As A Feather* (Polydor 1973)★★★★, with Return To Forever *Hymn Of The Seventh Galaxy* (Polydor 1973)★★★★, with Return To Forever *Where Have I Known You Before* (Polydor 1974)★★★, *Chick Corea* (Blue Note 1975)★★★★, with Return To Forever *No Mystery* (Polydor 1975)★★, *Chick Corea Quartet: Live In New York City, 1974* (1976)★★★, with Return To Forever *The Leprechaun* (Polydor 1976)★★★★, *My Spanish Heart* (Polydor 1976)★★★★, *Before Forever* (1977)★★★, *The Mad Hatter* (Polydor 1978)★★★, *Friends* (Polydor 1978)★★★, *Secret Agent* (1978)★★★, with Burton *Duet* (1979)★★★★, *An Evening With Herbie Hancock And Chick Corea* live 1978 recordings (Columbia 1979)★★★, *Corea/Hancock* (Polydor 1979)★★★, *Delphi 1: Solo Piano Improvisations* (Polydor 1979)★★★, *Crystal Silence* (ECM 1979)★★★, *In Concert, Zurich, October 28, 1978* (ECM 1980)★★★, *Delphi 2 & 3* (1980), *Tap Step* (Warners 1980)★★★, *Three Quartets* (Warners 1981)★★★, *Trio Music* (ECM 1981)★★★★, *Touchstone* (Streych 1982),★★★ with Nicolas Economou *On Two Pianos* (1982)★★★, with Friedrich Gulda *The Meeting* (1982)★★★, *Again And Again (The Joburg Sessions)* (Elektra 1983)★★★, *Children's Songs* (ECM 1983)★★★★, with Burton *Lyric Suite For Sextet* (ECM 1983)★★★, *Trio*

Music, Live In Europe (ECM 1984)★★★★, *Septet* (ECM 1985)★★★, with Steve Kujala *Voyage* (ECM 1985)★★★★, *Early Days* 1969 recordings (LRC 1986)★★★, *Elektric Band* (GRP 1986)★★★, *Light Years* (GRP 1987)★★, *Eye Of The Beholder* (GRP 1988)★★★, *Chick Corea Akoustic Band* (GRP 1989)★★★, *Inside Out* (GRP 1990)★★★, *Beneath The Mask* (GRP 1991)★★, *Alive* (GRP 1991)★★★, with Bobby McFerrin *Play* (1992)★★★, *Inner Space* (Atlantic 1993)★★★, *Paint The World* (GRP 1993)★★★, *Expressions* (GRP 1994)★★★, with Chick Corea Quartet *Time Warp* (Stretch 1995)★★★, *Remembering Bud Powell* (Stretch 1997)★★★.
●COMPILATIONS: *Verve Jazz Masters* (Verve 1979)★★★, *The Best Of Return To Forever* (Columbia 1980)★★★★, *Chick Corea Works* (ECM 1985)★★★★.
●VIDEOS: *Live In Madrid* (Channel 5 1987), *Inside Out* (GRP Video 1992).

CORTINAS

Originally an R&B band, the Cortinas were formed during July 1976 in Bristol, England, by Jeremy Valentine (vocals), Nick Sheppard (guitar), Mike Fewins (guitar), Dexter Dalwood (bass) and Daniel Swan (drums). The advent of the late 70s 'new wave' brought a change to their usual live set of 60s cover versions, which were replaced with self-penned tracks like 'Television Families' and 'I Wanna Have It With You'. The remainder were given the 'punk treatment', which created an exciting live spectacle. In the beginning of June 1977, 'Fascist Dictator' was released on the Step Forward label, perfectly capturing the raw energy of the time, although it lacked any real originality. This new-found popularity brought with it problems, as many of their hometown gigs ended in trouble, prompting the band to cut their ties with punk. Consequently, the live set saw a return to cover versions, where even 'Fascist Dictator' was excluded. *True Romances* was released on CBS Records in 1978 and contained a remake of Smokey Robinson's 'First I Look At The Purse', together with 12 originals. The album had lost the power and bite of previous offerings, the result being mediocre. One last single 'Heartache' was extracted before they split at the end of the year. Mike Fewins joined Essential Bop, whereas Nick Sheppard formed the Spics, two of the most prominent new wave bands to emerge from Bristol in 1979.
●ALBUMS: *True Romances* (Columbia 1978)★★.

CORYELL, LARRY

b. 2 April 1943, Galveston, Texas, USA. Coryell grew up in the state of Washington. He first worked as a guitarist in 1958 when he formed a rock 'n' roll band with keyboard player Michael Mandel. In 1965 he relocated to New York and joined Chico Hamilton's band, overlapping with the legendary guitarist Gabor Szabo, whom he eventually replaced. In 1966 he formed Free Spirits with American Indian tenor player Jim Pepper. He toured with Gary Burton (1967-68) and played on

Herbie Mann's *Memphis Underground* (1968). Coryell was impressed with the exploits of Jimi Hendrix and Eric Clapton with Cream, and his performance on Michael Mantler's *Jazz Composers Orchestra* project in 1968 was scarifying electric guitar at its best. Coryell's early solo albums featured strong support from Elvin Jones and Jim Garrison (*Lady Coryell*), and John McLaughlin and Billy Cobham (*Spaces*). *Fairyland*, recorded live at Montreux in 1971 with soul veterans Chuck Rainey (bass) and Bernard 'Pretty' Purdie (drums), a power trio format, was packed with sublime solos. *Barefoot Boy*, recorded the same year at Electric Lady Studios (built by Hendrix), was notable for its simultaneous use of non-pareil jazz drummer Roy Haynes and electric feedback and distortion. Coryell formed Eleventh House with Mandel, honing his experimental music into a dependable showcase for his virtuosity. Coryell, seeming to have sensed that a spark had gone, broke up the band and gave up electricity for a while. He began playing with other guitarists - Philip Catherine, McLaughlin, Paco De Lucia and John Scofield. He played on Charles Mingus's *Three Or Four Shades Of Blue* in 1977 and recorded arrangements of Stravinsky for Nippon Phonogram. In the mid-80s Coryell started playing electric again, with Bunny Brunel (bass) and Alphonse Mouzon (drums). In 1990 he recorded with Don Lanphere, using his considerable name to spotlight an old friend's rekindled career, and produced easy, unassuming acoustic jazz. Despite his extraordinary technique and his early promise, Coryell has never really created his own music, instead playing with undeniable finesse in a variety of contexts.
●ALBUMS: with Michael Mantler *Jazz Composers Orchestra* (1968)★★★, *Lady Coryell* (Vanguard 1969)★★★★, *Coryell* (Vanguard 1969)★★★, *Spaces* (Vanguard 1970)★★★, *Fairyland* (1971)★★★, *Larry Coryell At The Village Gate* (Vanguard 1971)★★★★, *Barefoot Boy* (Philips 1971)★★★, *Offering* (Vanguard 1972)★★★, *The Real Great Escape* (Vanguard 1973)★★★, *Introducing The Eleventh House* (Vanguard 1974)★★★, *The Restful Mind* (Vanguard 1975)★★★, *Planet End* (Vanguard 1976)★★★, *Level One* (Arista 1976)★★★, *Basics* 1968 recordings (1976)★★, *Aspects* (Arista 1976)★★★, *Lion And The Ram* (1976)★★★, with Steve Kahn *Two For The Road* (1976)★★★, with Philip Catherine *Twin House* (Elektra 1976)★★★★, *Back Together* (Warners 1977)★★★, *Splendid* (1978)★★★, *European Impressions* (1978)★★★, *Standing Ovation* (1978)★★★★, *Return* (Vanguard 1979)★★★, with John Scofield, Joe Beck *Tributaries* (Novus 1979)★★★, *Bolero* (String 1981)★★★, *'Round Midnight* (1983)★★★, *Scheherazade* (1984)★★★, with Brian Keane *Just Like Being Born* (Flying Fish 1984)★★★, *The Firebird And Petrouchka* (Philips 1984)★★★, with Emily Remler *Together* (Concord 1986)★★★, *Coming Home* (Muse 1986)★★★, *Equipoise* (Muse 1987)★★★, *Toku Du* (Muse 1988)★★★, *A Quiet Day In Spring* (Steeplechase 1988)★★★, *Just Like Being Born* (Flying Fish 1989)★★★,

Don Lanphere/Larry Coryell (1990)★★★, *Plays Ravel And Gershwin* (Soundscreen 1990)★★★, *Shining Hour* (Muse 1991)★★★, *Twelve Frets To One Octave* (Shanachie 1991)★★★, *Live From Bahia* (CTI 1992)★★★, *Fallen Angel* (CTI 1994)★★★.

COVINGTON, JULIE

b. *c.*1950, England. An actress and singer, Covington had the original hit version of 'Don't Cry For Me Argentina' from Andrew Lloyd Webber and Tim Rice's *Evita*. A student at Cambridge University, her performance in the 1967 Footlights Revue led to an appearance on David Frost's UK television show, singing a song by Pete Atkin and Clive James. Covington was subsequently signed to EMI's Columbia label, recording *Beautiful Changes*. During the 70s, she pursued a career in the theatre and in 1976 was cast with Rula Lenska and Charlotte Cornwell as a vocal group in the television series *Rock Follies*. With music by Sue Lloyd-Jones and Roxy Music's Andy Mackay, the group had a hit album on Island and a Top 10 single, 'O.K.?' in 1977. Covington's performance in *Rock Follies* won her the role of Evita Peron in the studio version of the musical and she had a number 1 hit with 'Don't Cry For Me Argentina' (1977), the big ballad from the show. Covington now signed to Virgin to make a solo album with all-star sidemen like Richard Thompson, John Cale and Steve Winwood. It included a version of Alice Cooper's 'Only Women Bleed' which reached the Top 20 in 1977. The next year she was guest vocalist on the Albion Band's *Rise Up Like The Sun*, and also sang on Richard And Linda Thompson's *First Light* album. Her only later recording was 'When Housewives Had The Choice' (1989), the theme for a selection of ballads featured on a 50s BBC Radio show. She continues to work in the theatre and as an occasional broadcaster.
●ALBUMS: *Beautiful Changes* (Columbia 1970)★★, *Julie Covington* (Virgin 1978)★★★.

COYNE, KEVIN

b. 27 January 1944, Derby, England. A former art student, psychiatric therapist and social worker, Coyne also pursued a singing career in local pubs and clubs. His fortunes flourished on moving to London where he joined Siren, a group later signed to disc jockey John Peel's Dandelion label. Coyne left the band in 1972, and having completed the promising *Case History*, switched outlets to Virgin the following year. *Marjory Razor Blade* emphasized his idiosyncratic talent in which the artist's guttural delivery highlighted his lyrically raw compositions. Taking inspiration from country blues, Coyne successfully constructed a set of invective power and his obstinate quest for self-effacement was confirmed on *Blame It On The Night*. Although showing a greater sophistication, this enthralling set was equally purposeful and introduced a period marked by punishing concert schedules. Coyne formed a group around Zoot Money (keyboards), Andy Summers (guitar), Steve

Thompson (bass) and Peter Wolf (drums) to promote *Matching Head And Feet* and this line-up later recorded *Heartburn*. This period was captured to perfection on the live *In Living Black And White*, but escalating costs forced the singer to abandon the band in 1976. His work was not out of place in the angst-ridden punk era, while a 1979 collaboration with former Slapp Happy vocalist Dagmar Krause, *Babble*, was an artistic triumph. Coyne parted company with Virgin during the early 80s, but recordings for Cherry Red Records, including *Pointing The Finger* and *Politicz* showed an undiminished fire. *Peel Sessions*, a compendium of radio broadcasts from between 1974 and 1990, is a testament to the artist's divergent styles and moods.
●ALBUMS: *Case History* (Dandelion 1972)★★★, *Marjory Razor Blade* (Virgin 1973)★★★★, *Blame It On The Night* (Virgin 1974)★★★★, *Matching Head And Feet* (Virgin 1975)★★★, *Heartburn* (Virgin 1976)★★★, *In Living Black And White* (Virgin 1977)★★★★, *Dynamite Daze* (Virgin 1978)★★★, *Millionaires And Teddy Bears* (Virgin 1978)★★★, *Beautiful Extremes* (Virgin 1978)★★★, with Dagmar Krause *Babble* (Virgin 1979)★★★★, *Bursting Bubbles* (Virgin 1980)★★★, *Sanity Stomp* (Virgin 1980)★★, *Pointing The Finger* (Cherry Red 1981)★★★, *Politicz* (Cherry Red 1982)★★★, *Beautiful Extremes Etcetera* (Cherry Red 1983)★★★, *Wild Tiger Love* (Golden Hind 80s)★★, *Stumbling Onto Paradise* (Golden Hind 80s)★★★, *Elvira: Songs From The Archives* (Golden Hind 80s)★★★, *Romance-Romance* (Zabo 80s)★★★, *Legless In Manila* (Collapse 1984)★★★, *Everybody's Naked* (AVM 1990)★★, *Peel Sessions* (1991)★★★, *Let's Do It* unissued 1970 tracks (JVC 1995)★★.
●COMPILATIONS: *Dandelion Years* (Butt 1982)★★★.
●FURTHER READING: *Show Business*, Kevin Coyne.

CRAZY HORSE

Crazy Horse evolved in 1969 when singer Neil Young invited Danny Whitten (guitar), Billy Talbot (b. New York, USA; bass) and Ralph Molina (b. Puerto Rico; drums) - all formerly of struggling local attraction the Rockets - to accompany him on his second album, *Everybody Knows This Is Nowhere*. The impressive results inspired an attendant tour, but although the group also contributed to Young's *After The Goldrush*, their relationship was sundered in the light of Whitten's growing drug dependency. *Crazy Horse*, completed with the assistance of Jack Nitzsche and Nils Lofgren, featured several notable performances, including the emotional 'I Don't Want To Talk About It', later revived by Rod Stewart and Everything But The Girl. Whitten succumbed to a heroin overdose in November 1972, but although Talbot and Molina kept the group afloat with various different members, neither *Loose* or *At Crooked Lake* scaled the heights of their excellent debut. Reunited with Young for *Tonight's The Night* and *Zuma*, and buoyed by the arrival of guitarist Frank Stampedro (b. West Virginia, USA), the group reclaimed its independence with the excellent *Crazy Moon*. Although

Crazy Horse has since abandoned its own career, their role as the ideal foil to Young's ambitions was amply proved on the blistering *Ragged Glory* (1991) and *Sleeps With Angels* (1994) and further joint billing with Ian McNabb on some tracks on his excellent 1994 album *Head Like A Rock*.

●ALBUMS: *Crazy Horse* (Reprise 1970)★★★★, *Loose* (Reprise 1971)★★★, *Crazy Horse At Crooked Lake* (1973)★★★, *Crazy Moon* (1978)★★★.

CREACH, 'PAPA' JOHN

b. 28 May 1917, Beaver Falls, Pennsylvania, USA, d. 22 February 1994, Los Angeles, California, USA. John Creach began his career as a fiddle player upon his family's move to Chicago in 1935. He later toured the Midwest of the USA as a member of cabaret attraction the Chocolate Music Bars, but settled in California in 1945. Creach played in the resident band at Palm Springs' Chi Chi Restaurant, undertook session work and entertained tourists on a luxury liner before securing a spot at the Parisian Room in Los Angeles. He was 'discovered' at this venue by Joey Covington, drummer in Hot Tuna and Jefferson Airplane, and by October 1970 Creach was a member of both groups. His tenure was not without controversy; many aficionados resented this intrusion, but although he left the former group two years later, 'Papa' John remained with the latter act until 1975, surviving their transformation into Jefferson Starship. *Papa John Creach* featured support from many bay area acolytes, including Jerry Garcia, Carlos Santana and John Cipollina, while *Filthy* was notable for 'Walking The Tou Tou', effectively a Hot Tuna master. *Zulu (Playing My Fiddle For You)* marked Creach's growing estrangement from the 'Airplane' family and was his final release on their in-house Grunt label. Successive releases failed to achieve the profile of those early recordings, but Creach remained an enduring live attraction in Los Angeles throughout the 70s. He was awarded the Blues Foundation's W.C. Handy Award in 1993, shortly before his death.

●ALBUMS: *Papa John Creach* (Grunt 1971)★★, *Filthy* (Grunt 1972)★★★, *Zulu (Playing My Fiddle For You)* (Grunt 1974)★★, *I'm The Fiddle Man* (Buddah 1975)★★, *Rock Father* (Buddah 1976)★★, *The Cat And The Fiddle* (DJM 1977)★★, *Inphasion* (DJM 1978)★★.

CROCE, JIM

b. 10 January 1943, Philadelphia, Pennsylvania, USA, d. 20 September 1973. Originally a university disc jockey, Croce played in various rock bands before moving to New York in 1967 where he performed in folk clubs. By 1969, he and his wife Ingrid (b. 27 April 1947, Philadelphia, Pennsylvania, USA) were signed to Capitol Records for *Approaching Day*. The album's failure led to Croce's returning to Pennsylvania and taking on work as a truck driver and telephone engineer. Meanwhile, he continued with songwriting and, after sending demo tapes to former college friend and

New York record producer Tommy West, Croce secured a new contract with the ABC label. Croce's second album, *You Don't Mess Around With Jim*, provided him with a US Top 10 hit in the title track and, along with 'Operator (That's Not The Way It Feels)', helped establish Croce as a songwriter of distinction. In July 1973, he topped the US charts with the narrative 'Bad Boy Leroy Brown'. Exactly two months later, he died in a plane crash at Natchitoches, Louisiana. In the wake of his death he registered a Top 10 hit with 'I Got A Name', which was featured in the film *The Last American Hero*. The contemplative 'Time In A Bottle' was released in late 1973 and became the final US number 1 of the year. It was a fitting valediction. During 1974, further releases kept Croce's name in the US charts, including 'I'll Have To Say I Love You In A Song' and 'Workin' At The Car Wash Blues'.

●ALBUMS: *Approaching Day* (Capitol 1969)★★, *You Don't Mess Around With Jim* (ABC 1972)★★★, *Life And Times* (ABC 1973)★★★, *I Got A Name* (ABC 1973)★★★.

●COMPILATIONS: *Photographs And Memories - His Greatest Hits* (ABC 1974)★★★, *The Faces I've Been* early rec. 1961-71 (Lifesong 1975,)★★, *Time In A Bottle - Jim Croce's Greatest Love Songs* (Lifesong 1977)★★, *Collection* (Castle 1986)★★★★.

●FURTHER READING: *The Faces I've Been*, Jim Croce. *Jim Croce: The Feeling Lives On*, Linda Jacobs.

CROSBY AND NASH

Formed in 1972 by David Crosby (b. 14 August 1941, Los Angeles, California, USA) and Graham Nash (b. 2 February 1942, Blackpool, Lancashire, England), this highly successful duo was an offshoot of the supergroup Crosby, Stills, Nash And Young. Initially, they specialized in intimate all-acoustic shows characterized by stoned anecdotes and inspired vocals. Fresh from the concert floor, they recorded *Graham Nash/David Crosby* which included some of their best work, most notably Nash's 'Immigration Man' and Crosby's superb question and answer songs, 'Where Will I Be' and 'Page 43'. It was three years before the CSN&Y wheel of fortune again brought together Crosby And Nash as a recording duo. After appearing on albums by Neil Young, James Taylor and Carole King, they reactivated their partnership, switched from Atlantic to ABC Records and set about recording *Wind On The Water*. Released in 1975, the album was a solid set with Crosby particularly strong on the autobiographical 'Carry Me' and the a capella choral 'A Critical Mass'. An extensive tour saw them using videos sanctioned by Greenpeace to highlight the plight of the whale. The following year the less successful *Whistling Down The Wire* was released and the group recorded a live album featuring an extended jazz version of Crosby's 'Déja Vu'. A Crosby, Stills And Nash reunion was followed by solo projects and drug problems for Crosby. Following his release from jail, Crosby announced in 1989 that he and Nash were recording and planning to tour. Instead, Stills returned again, and in 1992 they were singing together, immaculately. Surprisingly their debut has never received a proper CD reissue.

●ALBUMS: *Graham Nash/David Crosby* (Atlantic 1972)★★★★, *Wind On The Water* (Polydor 1975)★★★, *Whistling Down The Wire* (Polydor 1976)★★★, *Crosby/Nash Live* (Polydor 1977)★★.

●COMPILATIONS: *The Best Of Crosby And Nash* (Polydor 1978)★★★.

CROSBY, DAVID

b. David Van Cortlandt Crosby, 14 August 1941, Los Angeles, California, USA. Hailing from a high society family in Hollywood, Crosby dropped out of acting school in the early 60s to sing in coffeehouses in New York and California. Along the way he played informally with a number of influential musicians including Travis Edmunson, Fred Neil, Dino Valenti, Paul Kantner and David Freiberg. After a short-lived stint in the commercialized folk unit the Les Baxter Balladeers he returned to Los Angeles and became the protégé of producer/manager Jim Dickson. Towards the end of 1963, Crosby demoed several songs for a projected solo album including covers of Ray Charles' 'Come Back Baby' and Hoyt Axton's 'Willie Gene', which later surfaced on the archive compilation *Early LA*. After failing to secure a record deal with Warner Brothers Records, Crosby stumbled upon two like-minded rock 'n' roll enthusiasts at Hollywood's Troubadour club. Jim McGuinn and Gene Clark were folk musicians with a strong interest in the Beatles and after joining forces with Crosby in the Jet Set, they systematically refined their unusual style for mass consumption. With the arrival of bassist Chris Hillman and drummer Michael Clarke, the Jet Set became the Byrds, one of the most important and influential American groups of the 60s. Crosby remained with them for three years, and his rhythm guitar work, arranging skills and superb harmonic ability greatly contributed to their international success. By 1966, he was emerging as their spokesman onstage and during the succeeding two years contributed a significant number of songs to their repertoire including 'What's Happening?!?!', 'Renaissance Fair', 'Why' and 'Everybody's Been Burned'. However, his outspokenness and domineering tendencies eventually resulted in his dismissal in 1967.

After a sabbatical in which he produced Joni Mitchell's debut album, Crosby resurfaced as part of rock's celebrated 'supergroup' Crosby, Stills And Nash. With the addition of singer/guitarist Neil Young, they became one of the most critically acclaimed and commercially successful albums artists of their era. Crosby wrote some of their most enduring songs including 'Guinevere', 'Long Time Gone' and 'Déja Vu'. During their peak period he finally recorded his solo album, *If I Could Only Remember My Name*. An extraordinary work by any standard, the album featured guest appearances from his various confederates including several members of the Grateful Dead and Jefferson Airplane. Arguably one of the all-time great albums, the work was essentially a mood piece with Crosby using guitar and vocal lines to superb effect. On 'Music Is Love' and 'What Are Their Names?' the songs were built from single riffs and developed towards a startling crescendo of instrumentation and vocal interplay. Crosby's lyrical skill was in evidence on the electric 'Cowboy Movie' (a western allegory of the CSN&Y saga with Rita Coolidge cast as a manipulative Indian girl), plus the moving 'Traction In The Rain' (with Joni Mitchell on dulcimer) and the poignant 'Laughing' (inspired by the beatific and controversial Maharishi Mahesh Yogi). Finally, there were a number of choral experiments, culminating in the eerie Gregorian chanting of 'I'd Swear There Was Somebody Here'.

Crosby continued to work with Graham Nash, Stephen Stills and Neil Young in various permutations but by the end of the decade he was alone, playing before small audiences and severely dependent upon heroin. In 1980, a completed album was rejected by Capitol Records and during the next few years Crosby became one of the most notorious drug abusers in popular music history. A series of arrests for firearm offences and cocaine possession forced him into a drug rehabilitation centre but he absconded, only to be arrested again. Finally, he was imprisoned in 1985, long after many of his friends had declared that his death was imminent. Jail provided his salvation, however, and when he emerged a year later, corpulent and clean, he engaged in a flurry of recording activity with his former colleagues. The decade ended with the release of his long-awaited second solo album, *Oh Yes I Can*, and a strong selling autobiography, *Long Time Gone*, which documented the highs and excesses of his singular career. Following further activity in the 90s with Stills and Nash, Crosby worked with Phil Collins, following their meeting on the set of the movie *Hook*, in which they both appeared. The result was *Thousand Roads*, an accessible if overtly slick album, which produced a Crosby/Collins minor UK hit with 'Hero', which fared much better in the USA. Crosby has additionally been playing more acting roles and was seen in the television series *Rosanne*. In the mid-90s with his drug-taking days well behind him, Crosby suffered complications with his diabetes and was seriously ill awaiting a kidney donor. The man who had courted death so many times was given his ninth life with a new kidney. A worthy live album was issued during his convalescence in 1995 and he further celebrated being alive with the birth of a child in May that year.

●ALBUMS: *If I Could Only Remember My Name* (Atlantic 1971)★★★★★, *Oh Yes I Can* (Atlantic 1989)★★★, *Thousand Roads* (Atlantic 1993)★★★, *It's All Coming Back To Me Now* (Atlantic 1995)★★★, *King Biscuit Flower Hour Presents: David Crosby* (BMG 1996)★★★.

●FURTHER READING: *Long Time Gone*, David Crosby and Carl Gottlieb. *Timeless Flight*, Johnny Rogan.

CROSBY, STILLS, NASH AND YOUNG

David Crosby (b. 14 August 1941, Los Angeles, California, USA), Stephen Stills (b. 3 January 1945, Dallas, Texas, USA) and Graham Nash (b. 2 February 1942, Blackpool, Lancashire, England) first came together in the 1969 supergroup Crosby, Stills And Nash before recruiting Neil Young (b. 12 November 1945, Toronto, Canada). That same year, the quartet appeared at the Woodstock festival and established a format of playing two sets, one acoustic and one electric, which showed off their musicianship to remarkable effect. Instant superstars, their 1970 album, *Deja Vu*, was one of the biggest sellers of the year and one of the most celebrated works of the early 70s. Its power came from the combined brilliance of the contributors and included some of their finest material, at a time when they were at their most inventive. Stills, the maestro, offered the startling 'Carry On' with its driving rhythm and staggering high harmony, plus the stark melancholia of '4 + 20'. Young contributed the suitably maudlin 'Helpless' and an ambitious song suite, 'Country Girl', which remains one of his most underrated songs. Nash's 'Teach Your Children', with Jerry Garcia on steel guitar, was the group's personal favourite and remained a permanent number in their live set over the years. Finally, Crosby provided the jazz-influenced title track and the raw, searing 'Almost Cut My Hair', one of the great anti-establishment songs of the period. There was even a US Top 10 single, courtesy of their reading of Joni Mitchell's 'Woodstock'.

During the summer of 1970, National Guardsmen opened fire on demonstrators at Kent State University and killed four students. Crosby handed Young a magazine reporting the incident and watched in fascination as the song 'Ohio' emerged. Recorded within 24 hours of its composition, the song captured the foursome at their most musically aggressive and politically relevant. Sadly, it was to remain a frustrating statement of all they might have achieved had they remained together. A series of concerts produced the double set *Four Way Street*, which revealed the group's diversity in contrasting acoustic and electric sets. By the time of its release in 1971, the group had scattered in various directions to pursue solo projects.

Their unexpected and untimely departure left a huge gap in the rock marketplace. During 1971, they were at their peak and could command gold records as soloists or in a variety of other permutations of the original foursome. Many saw them as the closest that America reached in creating an older, second generation Beatles. Part of their charm came from the fact that their ranks contained former members of the Buffalo Springfield, the Hollies and the Byrds. Wherever they played part of the audience's psychological response contained elements of that old fanaticism which is peculiar to teenage heroes. While other contemporaneous groups such as the Band might claim similar musical excellence or stylistic diversity, they could never match the charisma or messianic popularity of CSN&Y. The supergroup were perfectly placed in the late 60s/early 70s defining their time with a ready-made set of philosophies and new values which were liberally bestowed on their audience. They brilliantly reflected the peace, music and love ideal, as popularized by the Woodstock promoters. While other groups exploited the hippie ideal, CSN&Y had the courage to take those ideas seriously. At every concert and on every record they eulogized those precepts without a trace of insincerity. It was a philosophy exemplified in their lifestyles and captured in neo-romantic compositions of idealism and melancholia. A brittle edge was added with their political commentaries, both in interviews and on record, where civil unrest in Chicago, Ohio and Alabama were pertinent subjects.

With such cultural and commercial clout, it was inconceivable that the quartet would not reconvene and, during 1974, they undertook a stupendous stadium tour. A second studio album, *Human Highway*, originally begun in Hawaii and resumed after their tour, produced some exceptionally strong material but was shelved prior to completion. Two years later, Crosby And Nash attempted to join forces with the short-lived Stills/Young Band only to have their harmony work erased amid acrimony and misunderstanding. By the late 70s, the CSN&Y concept had lost its appeal to punk-influenced music critics who regarded the quartet's romanticism as narcissism, their political idealism as naïve and their technical perfection as elitist and clinical. It was a clear case of historical inevitability - one set of values replacing another. Remarkably, it was not until 1988 that the quartet at last reunited for *American Dream*, their first studio release for 18 years. It was a superlative work, almost one hour long and containing some exceptionally strong material including the sardonic title track, the brooding 'Night Song', Crosby's redemptive 'Compass' and Nash's epochal 'Soldiers Of Peace'. This time around, however, there was no accompanying CSN&Y tour and the prospects of a third studio album seem decidedly remote.

●ALBUMS: *Deja Vu* (Atlantic 1970)★★★★, *Four Way Street* (Atlantic 1971)★★★, *American Dream* (Atlantic 1989)★★★.

●COMPILATIONS: *So Far* (Atlantic 1974)★★★, *Crosby Stills And Nash* 4-CD box set (Atlantic 1991)★★★★★.

●FURTHER READING: *Prisoner Of Woodstock*, Dallas Taylor. *Crosby Stills Nash & Young: The Visual Documentary*, Johnny Rogan.

CRUSADERS

This remarkably versatile group was formed in Houston, Texas, as the Swingsters. During the 50s, Wilton Felder (b. 31 August 1940, Houston, Texas, USA; reeds), Wayne Henderson (b. 24 September 1938, Houston, Texas, USA; trombone), Joe Sample (b. 1

February 1939, Houston, Texas, USA; keyboards) and Nesbert 'Stix' Hooper (b. 15 August 1938, Houston, Texas, USA; drums), forged a reputation as an R&B group before moving to California. Known as the Jazz Crusaders, they were signed by the Pacific label for whom they recorded a series of melodious albums. In 1970 the quartet truncated their name to the Crusaders in deference to an emergent soul/funk perspective. In truth the group exaggerated facets already prevalent in their work, rather than embark on something new. A 1972 hit, 'Put It Where You Want It', established a tight, precise interplay and an undeniably rhythmic pulse. The song was later recorded by the Average White Band, the kind of approval confirming the Crusaders' newfound status. Henderson left the group in 1975, and several session musicians, including master guitarist Larry Carlton, augmented the remaining nucleus on their subsequent recordings. In 1979 the Crusaders began using featured vocalists following the success of 'Street Life'. This international hit helped launch Randy Crawford's solo career, while a further release, 'I'm So Glad I'm Standing Here Today', re-established Joe Cocker. Although Hooper left the line-up in 1983, and was replaced by Leon Ndugu Chancler, Felder and Sample continued the group's now accustomed pattern. The Good And Bad Times, released in 1986, celebrated the Crusaders 30th anniversary and featured several 'special guests' including jazz singer Nancy Wilson.

●ALBUMS: as the Jazz Crusaders Freedom Sound (Pacific 1961)★★★, Looking Ahead (Pacific 1962)★★★, At The Lighthouse (Pacific 1963)★★★, Tough Talk (Pacific 1963)★★★, Heat Wave (Pacific 1965)★★★, Chile Con Soul (Pacific 1966)★★★, Lighthouse 66 (Pacific 1966)★★★, Talk That Talk (Pacific 1966)★★★, Lighthouse 68 (Pacific 1968)★★★, Uh Hah (Pacific 1968)★★★, Powerhouse (Pacific 1969)★★★, Lighthouse 69 (Pacific 1969)★★★, Old Socks New Shoes, New Socks Old Shoes (Chisa 1970)★★★; as the Crusaders Pass The Plate (Chisa 1971)★★★, Crusaders 1 (Blue Thumb 1972)★★★★, Hollywood (1972)★★★, Second Crusade (Blue Thumb 1973)★★★★, Unsung Heroes (Blue Thumb 1973)★★★, Scratch (Blue Thumb 1974)★★★, Southern Comfort (Blue Thumb 1974)★★★, Chain Reaction (Blue Thumb 1975)★★★★, Those Southern Nights (Blue Thumb 1976)★★, Young Rabbits (1976)★★★, Free As The Wind (Blue Thumb 1977)★★★, Images (Blue Thumb 1978)★★★, Street Life (MCA 1979)★★★, Rhapsody And Blues (MCA 1980)★★★, with Joe Cocker Standing Tall (MCA 1981)★★, Live Sides (1981)★★, with B.B. King and the Royal Philharmonic Orchestra Royal Jam (MCA 1982)★★, Ongaku-Kai: Live In Japan (Crusaders 1982)★★★, Free As The Wind (ABC 1983)★★, Ghetto Blaster (MCA 1984)★★★, The Good And Bad Times (MCA 1986)★★★, Life In The Modern World (MCA 1988)★★★, Healing The Wounds (GRP 1991)★★★.

●COMPILATIONS: Best Of The Crusaders (Blue Thumb 1976)★★★★, The Vocal Album (MCA 1987)★★★, The Story So Far (1988)★★★, Sample A Decade (Connoisseur Collection 1989)★★★, The Golden Years (1992)★★★, The Greatest Crusade 2-CD (Calibre 1995)★★★★, Soul Shadows (Connoisseur Collection 1995)★★★.

CURVED AIR

Originally emerging from the classically influenced progressive band Sisyphus, Curved Air formed in early 1970 with a line-up comprising Sonja Kristina (b. 14 April 1949, Brentwood, Essex, England; vocals), Darryl Way (b. 17 December 1948, Taunton, Somerset, England; violin), Florian Pilkington Miksa (b. 3 June 1950, Roehampton, London, England), Francis Monkman (b. 9 June 1949, Hampstead, London, England; keyboards) and Ian Eyre (b. 11 September, Knaresborough, Yorkshire, England; bass). After establishing themselves on the UK club circuit, the group were signed by Warner Brothers Records for a much-publicized advance of £100,000. Their debut album, Air Conditioning, was heavily promoted and enjoyed a particular curiosity value as one of rock's first picture disc albums. In the summer of 1971, the group enjoyed their sole UK Top 5 hit with 'Back Street Luv', while their Second Album cleverly fused electronic rock and classical elements to win favour with the progressive music audience. By the time of Phantasmagoria, Eyre had left the group because of musical differences: he wanted to capitalize on the success of the hit single with a follow-up; the group wanted a more folky, esoteric direction. Mike Wedgewood (b. 19 May 1956, Derby, England) joined, during which time Monkman and Way were in disagreement over musical direction and presentation. By October 1972, both had left the group and Kristina was the sole original member and the line-up consistently changed thereafter. One new member, teenager Eddie Jobson (b. 28 April 1955) later left to join Roxy Music, replacing Brian Eno. Following a two-year hiatus during which Kristina rejoined the cast of the musical Hair, the group was reactivated, with Way returning, for touring purposes. Two further albums followed before the unit dissolved in 1977. Kristina pursued a largely unsuccessful solo career in music and acting - although her 1991 album Songs From The Acid Folk augurs well for the future. Monkman went on to form Sky, while latter-day drummer Stewart Copeland (b. 16 July 1952, Alexandria, Egypt) joined the successful Police.

●ALBUMS: Air Conditioning (Warners 1970)★★★, Second Album (Warners 1971)★★★, Phantasmagoria (Warners 1972)★★, Air Cut (Warners 1973)★★, Curved Air Live (Deram 1975)★★, Midnight Wire (BTM 1975)★★, Airborne (SBT 1976)★★, Live At The BBC (Band Of Joy 1995)★★. Solo: Sonja Kristina Sonja Kristina (Chopper 1980)★★, Songs From The Acid Folk (Total 1991)★★★.

●COMPILATIONS: The Best Of Curved Air (Warners 1976)★★★.

DADA

Formed in 1970, this superior British jazz rock act comprised Robert Palmer (vocals), Elkie Brooks (vocals), Jimmy Chambers (vocals), Paul Korda (vocals), Pete Gage (guitar/bass), Don Shinn (keyboards), Ernie Lauchlan (horns), Malcolm Cambell (woodwind), Barry Duggan (woodwind) and Martin Harryman (drums). Palmer was previously a member of the Alan Bown Set, Brooks had enjoyed a solo recording career since 1964 and Gage was formerly of Geno Washington's Ram Jam Band. Dada became a popular act on the UK university circuit but the unit proved to constricting for the members' individual musical ambitions. They split up in 1971 when Palmer, Brooks and Gage left to form Vinegar Joe.
●ALBUMS: *Dada* (Atco 1970)★★★.

DADDY LONGLEGS

This US act initially comprised Steve Hayton (guitar/vocals), Cliff Carrison (drums) and Kurt Palomaki (bass/clarinet/vocals). The trio spent its early months on a farm in New York state, before moving location to New Mexico. The promise of work in films brought the group to Europe in 1969, and although such plans were later aborted, they decided to settle in England. Daddy Longlegs showcased their appealing brand of good-time, country-influenced rock before the line-up was expanded to accommodate vocalist Mo Armstrong. Both he and Hayton then left the group, following which the drummer and bassist were joined by Peter Arneson (piano) and Gary 'Norton' Holderman (guitar), the latter of whom had worked with Carrison in Slim's Blues Band. *Oakdown Farm* was released on the renowned Vertigo label, but progress was hampered by further changes in personnel. Daddy Longlegs disbanded in 1972, following which Arneson teamed with former members of Gracious and the Greatest Show On Earth in the pop group, Taggett.
●ALBUMS: *Daddy Longlegs* (Warner Bros 1970)★★, *Oakdown Farm* (Vertigo 1971)★★★, *Three Musicians* (Polydor 1972)★★, *Shifting Sands* (Polydor 1972)★★.

DALTON, KATHY

Dalton was originally a member of the Gas Company, a folk rock act based in Los Angeles, USA, who released 'Blow Your Mind' in 1965. As Kathleen Yesse she joined ex-Gas Company singer Greg Dempsey in the Daughters Of Albion before embarking on a solo career in 1973. *Amazin'*, issued on Frank Zappa/Herb Cohen's Discreet label, featured stellar support from Little Feat, but the material rarely rose above average. The set was reissued the following year with the addition of its new title track. Dalton's recording career ended when Discreet broke up.
●ALBUMS: *Amazin'* (Discreet 1973)★★, as *Boogie Bands And One Night Stands* (Discreet 1974)★★.

DAMNED

Formed in 1976, this UK punk group comprised Captain Sensible, Rat Scabies (b. Chris Miller, 30 July 1957, Surrey, England; drums), Brian James (b. Brian Robertson, England; guitar) and Dave Vanian (b. David Letts, England; vocals). Scabies and James had previously played in the unwieldy punk ensemble London SS and, joined by Sensible, a veteran of early formations of Johnny Moped, they backed Nick Kent's Subterrancans. The Damned emerged in May 1976 and two months later they were supporting the Sex Pistols at the 100 Club. After appearing at the celebrated Mont de Marsan punk festival in August, they were signed to Stiff Records one month later. In October they released what is generally regarded as the first UK punk single, 'New Rose', which was backed by a frantic version of the Beatles' 'Help'. Apart from being dismissed as a support act during the Sex Pistols' ill-fated Anarchy tour, they then released UK punk's first album, *Damned Damned Damned*, produced by Nick Lowe. The work was typical of the period, full of short, sharp songs played at tremendous velocity, which served to mask a high level of musical ability (some critics, unable to believe the speed of the band, wrongly accused them of having speeded up the studio tapes). During April 1977 they became the first UK punk group to tour the USA. By the summer of that year, they recruited a second guitarist, Lu Edmunds; and soon afterwards, drummer Rat Scabies quit. A temporary replacement, Dave Berk (ex-Johnny Moped), deputized until the recruitment of London percussionist Jon Moss. In November their second album, *Music For Pleasure*, produced by Pink Floyd's Nick Mason, was mauled by the critics and worse followed when they were dropped from Stiff's roster. Increasingly dismissed for their lack of earnestness and love of pantomime, they lost heart and split in early 1978. The members went in various directions: Sensible joined the Softies, Moss and Edmunds formed the Edge, Vanian teamed up with Doctors Of Madness and James founded Tanz Der Youth. The second part of the Damned story reopened one year later when Sensible, Vanian and Scabies formed the Doomed. In November 1978 they became legally entitled to use the name Damned and, joined by ex-Saints bass player Algy Ward, they opened this new phase of their career with their first Top 20 single, the storming 'Love Song'. Minor hits followed, including the equally visceral 'Smash It Up' and the more sober but still affecting 'I Just Can't Be Happy Today'. Both were included on *Machine Gun*

Etiquette, one of the finest documents of any band of this generation, as the group again became a formidable concert attraction. When Ward left to join Tank he was replaced by Paul Gray, from Eddie And The Hot Rods. The group continued to reach the lower regions of the chart during the next year while Captain Sensible simultaneously signed a solo deal with A&M Records. To everyone's surprise, not least his own, he zoomed to number 1 with a novel revival of 'Happy Talk', which outsold every previous Damned release. Although he stuck with the group for two more years, he finally left in August 1984 due to the friction his parallel career was causing. However, during that time the Damned remained firmly on form. *The Black Album* was an ambitious progression, while singles such as 'White Rabbit' (a cover of Jefferson Airplane's psychedelic classic) and 'History Of The World' revealed a band whose abilities were still well above the vast majority of their peers. *Strawberries* announced a more pop-orientated direction, but one accommodated with aplomb. With Sensible gone, a third phase in the group's career ushered in Roman Jugg (guitar/keyboards), who had already been playing on tour for two years, and new member Bryn Merrick (bass), joining the core duo of Scabies and Vanian. Subsequent releases now pandered to a more determined assault on the charts. In 1986 they enjoyed their biggest ever hit with a cover of Barry Ryan's 'Eloise' (UK number 3). Another 60s pastiche, this time a rather pedestrian reading of Love's 'Alone Again Or', gave them a further minor UK hit. However, the authenticity of the Damned's discography from here on in is open to question, while their back-catalogue proved ripe for exploitation by all manner of compilations and poorly produced live albums, to further muddy the picture of a genuinely great band. *Phantasmagoria* and more particularly the lacklustre *Anything* failed to add anything of note to that legacy. The band continue to tour into the 90s, sometimes with Sensible and lately without Scabies, and there are numerous side projects to entertain aficionados, but it is unlikely that the Damned will ever match their early 80s phase.
●ALBUMS: *Damned Damned Damned* (Stiff 1977)★★★★, *Music For Pleasure* (Stiff 1977)★★, *Machine Gun Etiquette* (Chiswick 1979)★★★, *The Black Album* (Chiswick 1980)★★★, *Strawberries* (Bronze 1982)★★★, *Phantasmagoria* (MCA 1985)★★, *Anything* (MCA 1986)★★, *Not Of This Earth* (Cleopatra 1996) released in UK as *I'm Alright Jack & The Beans Talk* (Marble Orchid 1996)★★.
●COMPILATIONS: *The Best Of The Damned* (Chiswick 1981)★★★, *Live At Shepperton* (Big Beat 1982)★★, *Not The Captain's Birthday Party* (Stiff 1986)★★, *Damned But Not Forgotten* (Dojo 1986)★★, *Light At The End Of The Tunnel* (MCA 1987)★★, *Mindless, Directionless Energy* (ID 1987)★★, *The Long Lost Weekend: Best Of Vol. 1 & 2* (Big Beat 1988)★★★, *Final Damnation* (Essential 1989)★★, *Totally Damned (Live And Rare)* (Dojo 1991)★★, *Skip Off*

School To See The Damned - The Stiff Singles (Stiff 1992)★★★, *School Bullies* (Receiver 1993)★★, *Sessions Of The Damned* (Strange Fruit 1993)★★, *Eternally Damned - The Very Best Of ...* (MCI 1994)★★★, *The Radio 1 Sessions* (Strange Fruit 1996)★★★.
●VIDEOS: *Light At The End Of The Tunnel* (1987).
●FURTHER READING: *The Damned: The Light At The End Of The Tunnel*, Carol Clerk.

DANA

b. Rosemary Brown, 30 August 1951, Belfast, Northern Ireland. Pop vocalist Dana was 19 years old when she won the Eurovision Song Contest in 1970 with the ballad 'All Kinds Of Everything'. It reached number 1 in many countries, including Ireland, South Africa, Australia and the UK, selling over a million copies worldwide. She had sporadic UK chart successes with, 'Who Put The Lights Out', 'Please Tell Him That I Said Hello', 'It's Gonna Be A Cold Cold Christmas' and 'Fairy Tale', all Top 20 hits, before switching to a career consisting of mainly pantomime, acting and numerous guest appearances on various television shows.
●ALBUMS: *All Kinds Of Everything* (Decca 1970)★★★, *Love Songs And Fairy Tales* (GTO 1977)★★, *The Girl Is Back* (GTO 1979)★★, *Everything Is Beautiful* (Warwick 1981)★★, *Magic* (Creole 1982)★★, *Please Tell Him That I Said Hello* (Spot 1984)★★, *Totally Yours* (Word 1985)★★, *If I Give My Heart To You* (Ritz 1985)★★, *Let Their Be Love* (1985)★★, *No Greater Love* (Priority 1988)★★.
●COMPILATIONS: *World Of Dana* (Decca 1974)★★★.
●FURTHER READING: *Dana: An Autobiography*, Dana.

DANDO SHAFT

Formed in Coventry, England, in 1968, at a time when hippie culture was in full swing, the original members of the group were Kevin Dempsey (b. 29 May 1950, Coventry, West Midlands, England; guitar), Martin Jenkins (b. 17 July 1946, London, England; violin), Dave Cooper (vocals/guitar), Roger Bullen (bass), and Ted Kay (percussion). After moving to London, the unit received a boost with the inclusion of Polly Bolton. In the early 70s the albums *Dando Shaft* and *Lantaloon* included such titles as 'The Harp Lady I Bombed' and 'The Magnetic Beggar', testifying to Dando Shaft's own particular brand of humour. During 1972 the band tried to become a rock group, but this caused dissension, and Dempsey and Bolton left to form a duo, eventually moving to the USA. Subsequently, Jenkins went on to Hedgehog Pie who recorded for Rubber records of Newcastle-upon-Tyne. When Rubber decided to record Jenkins and Dave Cooper, the addition of Dempsey, Bolton and Kay made it into a Dando Shaft reunion. During the late 80s Jenkins and Dempsey reunited in Whippersnapper, and performed the occasional Dando song. In 1989 an Italian promoter caused the group to re-form for a week's worth of what they described as 'funky' concerts. At around the same time, archive label See For Miles issued a revival compilation. A live disc of

their continental performances. is projected for release.
●ALBUMS: *An Evening With Dando Shaft* (Youngblood 1970)★★★, *Dando Shaft* (RCA Neon 1971)★★★, *Lantaloon* (RCA 1972)★★, *Kingdom* (Rubber 1977)★★.
●COMPILATIONS: *Reaping The Harvest* (See For Miles 1990)★★★.

DARROW, CHRIS

b. 1944, South Falls, Dakota, USA. A founder member of the fabled Kaleidoscope, this versatile multi-instrumentalist left the group in 1968 to join the Nitty Gritty Dirt Band. The following year Darrow helped form the Corvettes, an underrated country rock group who later backed Linda Ronstadt on a tour to promote her *Hand Sewn* album. Darrow then began a solo career with *Artist Proof*, and also found employment as a studio musician. He contributed to releases by John Stewart, John Fahey and others, as well as appearing on several Tamla/Motown sessions. A second album, *Chris Darrow*, reaffirmed his eclectic nature and featured cameos by Dolly Collins and Alan Stivell, while the equally crafted *Under My Own Disguise* followed in 1974. Darrow's subsequent profile has been more low key. He was involved in the brief Kaleidoscope reunion (1976), which in turn led to the formation of another short-term group, Rank Strangers, whose album appeared the following year. Having helped launch the career of guitarist Toulouse Engelheart, Darrow then completed another solo release, *Fretless*. By preferring to work on a small-scale circuit, Darrow has retained an integrity at the expense of the wider recognition his talent deserves.
●ALBUMS: *Artist Proof* (1971)★★, *Chris Darrow* (United Artists 1973)★★★, *Under My Own Disguise* (United Artists 1974)★★★, *Fretless* (1979)★★★, *A South California Drive* (1980)★★★.

DARTS

After the demise of UK's John Dummer Blues Band, Iain Thompson (bass) and drummer John Dummer joined forces with Hammy Howell (keyboards), Horatio Hornblower (b. Nigel Trubridge; saxophone) and singers Rita Ray, Griff Fender (Ian Collier), bassist Den Hegarty and Bob Fish (ex-Mickey Jupp Band) as revivalists mining the vocal harmony seam of rock 'n' roll. Dave Kelly, an ex-Dummer guitarist, was a more transient participant. Bursting upon metropolitan clubland in the late 70s, Darts were championed by pop historian and Radio London disc jockey Charlie Gillett who helped them procure a Magnet Records contract. Their debut single - a medley of 'Daddy Cool' and Little Richard's 'The Girl Can't Help It' - ascended the UK Top 10 in 1977, kicking off three years of entries in both the singles and albums lists that mixed stylized self-compositions (e.g. 'It's Raining', 'Don't Let It Fade Away') with predominant revamps of such US hits as the Cardinals' 'Come Back My Love', the Ad-Libs' 'Boy From New York City', 'Get It' (Gene Vincent) and 'Duke Of Earl' (Gene

Chandler). After the eventual replacement of Hegarty with Kenny Edwards in 1979, their records were less successful. Without the television commercial coverage that sent the Jackie Wilson original to number 1 a few years later, Darts' version of 'Reet Petite' struggled to number 51 while 'Let's Hang On' - also 1980 - was their last *bona fide* smash - and 'White Christmas'/'Sh-Boom' the first serious miss. With the exit of Howell (to higher education) and Dummer (to form the ribald True Life Confessions), Darts were still able to continue in a recognizable form but were no longer hit parade contenders. As leader of Rocky Sharpe And The Replays, Hegarty had hovered between 60 and 17 in the UK singles list until 1983 when his post as a children's television presenter took vocational priority. Keeping the faith longer, Ray and Collier produced a 1985 album for the Mint Juleps, an a cappella girl group who had been inspired initially by Darts.
●ALBUMS: *Darts* (Magnet 1977)★★, *Everyone Plays Darts* (Magnet 1978)★★, *Dart Attack* (Magnet 1979)★★.
●COMPILATIONS: *Amazing Darts* (Magnet 1978)★★, *Greatest Hits* (Magnet 1983)★★★.

DAVE AND ANSELL COLLINS

A Jamaican duo who topped the UK charts in 1971 with 'Double Barrel', which was written and produced by Winston Riley. The duo comprised Dave Barker, a session vocalist and sometime pioneering DJ, and keyboard player Ansell Collins. Both had worked for Lee Perry in the late 60s before joining forces. 'Double Barrel' was one of the first reggae hits in the US. The follow-up, 'Monkey Spanner', was also a UK Top 10 hit. However, they split shortly after the release of their sole album. Ansell, who had previously worked solo in the late 60s, continued to record for small reggae labels throughout the 80s, principally as a session musician. Barker became a UK resident and fronted several short-lived soul bands. The duo briefly reunited as Dave And Ansell Collins in 1981 but to little effect.
●ALBUMS: *Double Barrel* (Techniques/Trojan 1972)★★★, *In The Ghetto* (Trojan 1975)★★★.
●COMPILATIONS: *Classic Tracks* (Classic Tracks 1988)★★★.

DAVIES, DAVE

b. 3 February 1947, London, England. The younger brother of Ray Davies has for almost 30 years stood in the shadow of his talented brother. By Ray's own admission, Dave is a highly underrated lead guitarist. Interestingly, while the elder Davies has yet to release a solo record, Dave had a UK number 3 hit with 'Death Of A Clown' in 1967 and followed it with a Top 20 placing, 'Susannah's Still Alive'. Both songs were lyrically strong; the former ranks with the best of the Kinks' work, the latter was a clever tale of a frustrated spinster. In 1967 Dave set about recording a solo album which did not see the light of day until almost 20 years later when parts were released as *The Album That Never*

Was. He released three disappointing guitar-laden albums in the 80s during one of the Kinks' many hiatuses. The hate/love relationship with his elder brother has been heavily documented in the press over the past years. In Ray's recent biography *X-Ray* Dave is considerably overlooked; his chance came with the publication of his autobiography in 1996. In *Kink* Dave subtly sniped back at his brother. Among other revelations the younger Davies annouced he was bisexual. Much more interesting, however, was his lengthy interview with Peter Doggett in the UK's *Record Collector* magazine. The younger Davies now resides in the USA and at present spends more time tracking down UFOs than making music. His musical activity has been mostly confined to working with John Carpenter on two film soundtracks, *Village Of The Damned* and *The Mouth Of Madness*.
●ALBUMS: *Dave Davies (AFL-1)* (RCA 1980)★★, *Glamour* (RCA 1981)★★, *Chosen People* (Warners 1983)★★, *The Album That Never Was* (PRT 1988)★★★.
●FURTHER READING: *Kink: An Autobiography*, Dave Davies.

DAVIS, SPENCER

b. 17 July 1941, Swansea, Wales. The nominal leader of the Spencer Davis Group resumed a solo career in 1968 after managerial disagreements thwarted a liaison with Plastic Penny guitarist Mick Grabham and session pianist Kirk Duncan (co-writer of the last group single, 'Short Change'). During a subsequent sojourn in Germany, Davis recorded 'Aquarius' from *Hair* before migrating to California, where he gained employment as a singing guitarist in venues such as Los Angeles' Troubadour. Later, he was accompanied by bottleneck guitarist Pete Jamieson with whom he made the all-acoustic *It's Been So Long* (1970). With guitarists Jon Mark and Alun Davies, Davis contributed to Chicago sessions for an album by Mississippi Fred McDowell. An amalgamation of Mark and Spencer came to nought but the Davis and Davies duo's assault on the folk scene was more fruitful. A more ambitious collaboration with an Australasian rhythm section and 'Sneaky' Pete Kleinow (who had produced 1972's US-only *Mousetrap*) quietly died when a re-formed Spencer Davis Group recorded two albums before likewise disintegrating. After putting his languages degree to use as a technical translator in the mid-70s, Davis accepted a post on Island's west coast staff. He speculated later in other areas of entertainment, landing a 1983 video contact with Fleetwood Mac, and, the following year, releasing another album - which included a duet with Dusty Springfield on 'Private Number'. In 1988 Davis returned to Britain for a Blues Reunion tour with Pete York and Zoot Money and has played in Germany with various line-ups in the 90s. The most recent line-up features York, together with Miller Anderson (vocals/guitar, ex-Keef Hartley Band) and Colin Hodgkinson (bass).
●ALBUMS: *It's Been So Long* (United Artists 1970)★★★, *Mousetrap* (1972)★★, *Crossfire* (Allegiance 1984)★.

DAVIS, TYRONE

b. 4 May 1938, Greenville, Mississippi, USA. One of the great unknowns of soul music, Davis has been a consistent chartmaker for over 20 years. This former Freddie King valet was discovered working in Chicago nightclubs by pianist Harold Burrage. 'Can I Change My Mind' (1968), Davis's first chart entry, was originally recorded as a b-side, but its success determined his musical direction. A singer in the mould of Bobby Bland and Z.Z. Hill, Davis was at his most comfortable with mid-paced material, ideal for the classic 'Windy City' orchestrations enhancing the mature delivery exemplified on 'Is It Something You've Got' and 'Turn Back The Hands Of Time', a US number 3. During the early 70s his producers began to tinker with this formula. 'I Had It All The Time' (1972) offered a tongue-in-cheek spoken introduction while the beautifully crafted 'Without You In My Life' (1973), 'There It Is' (1973) and 'The Turning Point' (1975) emphasized rhythmic punch without detracting from Tyrone's feather-light vocals. The artist's work continued to enjoy success; 'In The Mood' (1979) and 'Are You Serious' (1982) were both substantial R&B hits and he has since remained an active performer. As the singer's extensive catalogue suggests, he is also greatly underrated.
●ALBUMS: *Can I Change My Mind* (Dakar 1969)★★★, *Turn Back The Hands Of Time* (Dakar 1970)★★★, *I Had It All The Time* (Dakar 1972)★★★, *Without You In My Life* (Dakar 1973)★★★, *It's All In The Game* (Dakar 1974)★★★, *Home Wrecker* (Dakar 1975)★★★, *Turning Point* (1976)★★★, *Love And Touch* (Columbia 1976)★★, *Let's Be Closer Together* (Columbia 1977)★★, *I Can't Go On This Way* (Columbia 1978)★★, *In The Mood With Tyrone Davis* (Columbia 1979)★★, *Can't You Tell It's Me* (1979)★★, *I Just Can't Keep On Going* (1980)★★, *Tyrone Davis* (Highrise 1983)★★★, *Something Good* (1983)★★★, *Sexy Thing* (1985)★★★, *Man Of Stone* (1987)★★★, *Pacifier* (1987)★★, *Flashin' Back* (1988)★★, *Come On Over* (1990)★★, *I'll Always Love You* (Ichiban 1991)★★★, *Something's Mighty Wrong* (1992)★★★, *You Stay On My Mind* (Ichiban 1994)★★★, *Simply Tyrone Davis* (Malaco 1996)★★★.
●COMPILATIONS: *Greatest Hits* (Dakar 1972)★★★, *The Tyrone Davis Story* (Kent 1985)★★★, *In The Mood Again* (Charly 1989)★★★, *The Best Of Tyrone Davis* (Rhino 1992)★★★★.

DAWN

Formed in 1970 by singer Tony Orlando (b. 1945, New York, USA) when a demo of 'Candida', co-written by Toni Wine, arrived on his desk. Orlando elected to record it himself with support from Tamla/Motown session vocalists Telma Hopkins and Joyce Vincent, and hired instrumentalists. On Bell Records, this single was attributed to Dawn, despite the existence of 14 other professional acts of that name - which is why, after 'Candida' and 'Knock Three Times' topped international charts, the troupe came to be billed as 'Tony Orlando and Dawn', three more million-sellers later. Though the impetus slackened with 'What Are You Doing Sunday' and a 'Happy Together'/'Runaway' medley (with Del Shannon), the irresistible 'Tie A Yellow Ribbon Round The Old Oak Tree' proved *the* hit song of 1973. With typical bouncy accompaniment and downhome libretto - about a Civil War soldier's homecoming - it has amassed hundreds of cover versions. The 'Say Has Anybody Seen My Sweet Gypsy Rose' follow-up exuded a ragtime mood that prevailed throughout the associated album, and Dawn's *New Ragtime Follies* variety season in Las Vegas was syndicated on television spectaculars throughout the globe - although such exposure could not prevent the comparative failure of 1974's 'Who's In The Strawberry Patch With Sally'. After moving to Elektra/Asylum, the group had their last US number 1 - with 'He Don't Love You', a rewrite of a Jerry Butler single from 1960. Another revival - of Marvin Gaye and Tammi Terrell's 'You're All I Need To Get By' - was among other releases during their less successful years.

●ALBUMS: *Candida* (Bell 1970)★★★, *Dawn Featuring Tony Orlando* (Bell 1971)★★, *Tuneweaving* (Bell 1973)★★★, *Dawn's New Ragtime Follies* (Bell 1973)★★, *Prime Time* (Bell 1974)★★★, *Golden Ribbons* (Bell 1974)★★, *He Don't Love You (Like I Love You)* (Elektra 1975)★★★,*Skybird* (Arista 1975)★★, *To Be With You* (Elektra 1976)★★.

●COMPILATIONS: *Greatest Hits* (Arista 1975)★★★, *The Best Of Tony Orlando And Dawn* (Rhino 1995)★★★.

DE PAUL, LYNSEY

b. 11 June 1950, London, England. On leaving Hornsey Art College, De Paul worked initially as a cartoonist, but it was as a designer of record sleeves that she first took an interest in songwriting, having studied piano while at school. Though MAM Records signed her as a vocalist, singing in public was always secondary to her composing skills - even when she began a patchy five year UK Top 40 run with the sparkling 'Sugar Me' in 1972. In the same year the Fortunes climbed the US Hot 100 with her 'Storm In A Teacup'. Her confidence boosted by this syndication, she flew to Los Angeles to explore vocational opportunities. Incidental to this expedition was De Paul's romance with the actor James Coburn. On returning to London, she commenced a more light-hearted affair with Ringo Starr who bashed tambourine on 'Don't You Remember When', a ballad she wrote and produced for Vera Lynn. When her affair with Starr finished, Lynsey penned 'If I Don't Get You (The Next One Will)' as its requiem. Less personal outpourings surfaced on hit singles such as 'Getting A Drag', a topical dig at glam-rock. In 1974 she became the first woman to win an Ivor Novello award - with 'Won't Somebody Dance With Me' - gaining another with the theme to the UK television series *No Honestly*. Shortly after 'Rock Bottom', her duet with Mike Moran,

was runner-up in 1977's Eurovision Song Contest, she was voted Woman Of The Year for Music by the Variety Club of Great Britain. However, a subsequent season at the London Palladium was marred by harrowing legal wrangles with Don Arden, her former manager. A depressive illness, not unrelated to the case, preceded a comeback-of-sorts as an actress in an ITV mock-up of a 40s dance band show with Alvin Stardust and Zoot Money. Later roles included the starring role in a thriller in a Bromley theatre, and as The Princess in a 1983 staging of *Aladdin* in London's West End.

●ALBUMS: *Lynsey Sings* (1974)★★, *No Honestly* (Hallmark 1977)★★, *Tigers And Fireflies* (Polydor 1979)★★.

●COMPILATIONS: *Greatest Hits* (Repertoire 1994)★★, *Just A Little Time* (Music De Luxe 1995)★★.

DEAD BOYS

One of the first wave punk/no wave bands in the USA, the Dead Boys formed in Cleveland, Ohio, in 1976 but relocated to New York the following year. They won their spurs playing the infamous Bowery club, CBGB's. The band consisted of Stiv Bators (vocals), Jimmy Zero (rhythm guitar), Cheetah Chrome (b. Gene Connor; lead guitar), Jeff Magnum (bass) and Johnny Blitz (drums). The group took its cue from Iggy Pop And The Stooges by being as menacing, snarling and aggressive as possible. Signed to Sire Records in 1977, they released their debut album, the appropriately titled *Young, Loud And Snotty*, one of the very earliest US punk records, which included the band's anthem, 'Sonic Reducer'. It was followed a year later by the less convincing *We Have Come For Your Children*, produced by Felix Pappalardi. The band sundered in 1980 (*Night Of The Living Dead Boys* is a posthumous live issue), with Bators recording a pair of solo albums before invoking Lords Of The New Church with former Damned and Sham 69 member, Brian James. He was killed in an automobile accident in France in June 1990.

●ALBUMS: *Young, Loud And Snotty* (Sire 1977)★★★, *We Have Come For Your Children* (Sire 1978)★★, *Night Of The Living Dead Boys* (Bomp 1981)★★.

●COMPILATIONS: *Younger, Louder And Snottier* (Necrophilia 1989)★★★.

DEAD END KIDS

This Scottish teenybop group was discovered by hit-maker and producer Barry Blue who tried to market them as a more aggressive version of the Bay City Rollers. From Ayrshire, Davey, Allan, Ricky, Colin and Robbie toured as support act to the Rollers and released their debut Blue-produced single on CBS Records in 1977. A version of the old Honeycombs' chart-topper 'Have I The Right', it went to number 6 in the UK. Their debut album, *Breakout*, was released later that year and contained their theme song, 'Tough Kids'.

●ALBUMS: *Breakout* (1977)★★.

DEAF SCHOOL

An art-rock band that practically started the Liverpool new wave scene single-handed, Deaf School were formed in January 1974 by a large group of students at Liverpool Art College. The original line-up extended to 15 but the basic 12 were singers Bette Bright (b. Ann Martin, Whitstable, Kent, England), Ann Bright, Hazel Bartram, and Eric Shark (b. Thomas Davis), Enrico Cadillac Jnr, (b. Steve Allen), guitarists Cliff Hanger (b. Clive Langer) and Roy Holder, bassist Mr Average (b. Steve Lindsay), keyboards player the Rev. Max Ripple (b. John Wood), drummer Tim Whittaker and saxophonists Ian Ritchie and Mike Evans. Ann Bright soon left to get married and she was quickly followed by Bartram, Evans and Holder, the last of whom was fired. The remaining eight-piece line-up developed an entertaining blend of rock music and almost vaudevillian stage theatrics. This combination helped them win a *Melody Maker* Rock Contest in which the prize was a recording contract with WEA Records. The debut - *Second Honeymoon* - came out in August 1976 (by which time former Stealers Wheel guitarist Paul Pilnick had been added to the line-up). Hugely popular, particularly in Liverpool, their audience contained a host of names who later became famous in their own right. Two more albums and three singles emerged before the band finally dissolved after Bette Bright appeared in the *Great Rock 'N' Roll Swindle*, recorded two singles for Radar and a third for Korova with her backing band The Illuminations (variously Glen Matlock, Rusty Egan, Henry Priestman, Clive Langer, and Paul Pilnick). In 1981 she married Suggs from Madness. Eric Shark gave up music to run a shop in Liverpool; Enrico Cadillac reverted to his real name and formed the Original Mirrors; Clive Langer formed the Boxes but had more success as a producer; Steve Lindsay replaced Holly Johnson in Big In Japan, went on to the Secrets and then found limited success with the Planets; the Rev. Max Ripple became the head of the Fine Art department at Goldsmiths College in London; Tim Whittaker concentrated on session work with such Liverpool luminaries as Pink Military; Ian Ritchie finished up with Jane Aire; Steve Lindsay released a solo single ('Mr Average') while still in Deaf School, and another as Steve Temple in 1981, before forming the Planets. Steve Allen later joined with Steve Nieve in Perils Of Plastic. Various ex-Deaf School kids have also turned up in the deliberately dreadful Portsmouth Sinfonia. In 1988 Cadillac, Bright, Shark, Langer, Lindsay and Ripple reformed for five sell-out shows to celebrate the 10th anniversary of their demise, a concert commemorated with the 1988 release of *2nd Coming*.

● ALBUMS: *Second Honeymoon* (Warners 1976)★★★, *Don't Stop The World* (Warners 1977)★★, *English Boys Working Girls* (Warners 1978)★★, *2nd Coming: Liverpool '88* (Demon 1988)★★.

DEE, KIKI

b. Pauline Matthews, 6 March 1947, Bradford, England. Having begun her career in local dancebands, this popular vocalist made her recording debut in 1963 with the Mitch Murray-penned 'Early Night'. Its somewhat perfunctory pop style was quickly replaced by a series of releases modelled on US producer Phil Spector before Kiki achieved notoriety for excellent interpretations of contemporary soul hits, including Tami Lynn's 'I'm Gonna Run Away From You' and Aretha Franklin's 'Runnin' Out Of Fools'. Her skilled interpretations secured a recording deal with Tamla/Motown Records, the first white British act to be so honoured. However, although lauded artistically, Kiki was unable to attain due commercial success, and the despondent singer sought cabaret work in Europe and South Africa. Her career was revitalized in 1973 on signing up with Elton John's Rocket label. He produced her 'comeback' set, *Loving And Free*, which spawned a UK Top 20 entry in 'Amoureuse', while Kiki subsequently scored further chart success with 'I Got The Music In Me' (1974) and 'How Glad I Am' (1975), fronting the Kiki Dee Band - Jo Partridge (guitar), Bias Boshell (piano), Phil Curtis (bass) and Roger Pope (drums). Her duet with John, 'Don't Go Breaking My Heart', topped the UK and US charts in 1976, and despite further minor UK hits, the most notable of which was 'Star', which reached number 13 in 1981, this remains her best-known performance. She took a tentative step into acting by appearing in the London stage musical, *Pump Boys And Dinettes* in 1984. Kiki Dee's career underwent yet another regeneration in 1987 with *Angel Eyes*, which was co-produced by David A. Stewart of the Eurythmics. She has since appeared in Willy Russell's award-winning musical, *Blood Brothers* in London's West End, and was nominated for a Laurence Olivier Award for her performance in 1989. In 1993 she had a number 2 single with Elton John, 'True Love'. In 1995 *Almost Naked* was her 'unplugged' album and although commercial success continued to elude her it was one of her best albums. Her voice has matured to the point of having an edge of rasping. Notable tracks were Joni Mitchell's 'Carey' and a slowed down reworking of 'Don't Go Breaking My Heart' which gave the song greater depth than the earlier version.

● ALBUMS: *I'm Kiki Dee* (Fontana 1968)★★, *Great Expectations* (Tamla Motown 1970)★★, *Loving And Free* (Rocket 1973)★★★, *I've Got The Music In Me* (Rocket 1974)★★★, *Kiki Dee* (Rocket 1977)★★★, *Stay With Me* (Rocket 1979)★★★, *Perfect Timing* (Ariola 1980)★★, *Angel Eyes* (Columbia 1987)★★★, *Almost Naked* (Tickety-Boo 1995)★★★.

● COMPILATIONS: *Patterns* (Philips International 1974)★★★, *Kiki Dee's Greatest Hits* (Warwick 1980)★★★, *The Very Best Of Kiki Dee* (Rocket 1994)★★★.

● FILMS: *Dateline Diamonds* (1965).

DEEP PURPLE

Deep Purple evolved in 1968 following sessions to form a group around former Searchers drummer Chris Curtis (b. 26 August 1942, Liverpool, England). Jon Lord (b. 9 June 1941, Leicester, England; keyboards) and Nick Simper (b. 14 April 1945, Southall, England; bass), veterans, respectively, of the Artwoods and Johnny Kidd And The Pirates, joined guitarist Ritchie Blackmore (b. 14 April 1945, Weston-Super-Mare, England) in rehearsals for this new act, initially dubbed Roundabout. Curtis dropped out within days, and when Dave Curtis (bass) and Bobby Woodman (drums) also proved incompatible, two members of Maze, Rod Evans (b 19 January 1947, Edinburgh, Scotland; vocals) and Ian Paice (b. 29 June 1948, Nottingham, England; drums), replaced them. Having adopted the Deep Purple name following a brief Scandinavian tour, the quintet began recording their debut album, which they patterned on US group Vanilla Fudge. *Shades Of Deep Purple* thus included dramatic rearrangements of well-known songs, including 'Hey Joe' and 'Hush', the latter becoming a Top 5 US hit when issued as a single. Lengthy tours ensued as the group, all but ignored at home, steadfastly courted the burgeoning American concert circuit. *The Book Of Taliesyn* and *Deep Purple* also featured several excellent reworkings, notably 'Kentucky Woman' (Neil Diamond) and 'River Deep Mountain High' (Ike And Tina Turner), but the unit also drew acclaim for its original material and the dramatic interplay between Lord and Blackmore. In July 1969 both Evans and Simper were axed from the line-up, which was then buoyed by the arrival of Ian Gillan (b. 19 August 1945, Hounslow, Middlesex, England; vocals) and Roger Glover (b. 30 November 1945, Brecon, Wales; bass) from the pop group Episode Six. Acknowledged by aficionados as the 'classic' Deep Purple line-up, the reshaped quintet made its album debut on the grandiose *Concerto For Group And Orchestra*, scored by Lord and recorded with the London Philharmonic Orchestra. Its orthodox successor, *Deep Purple In Rock*, established the group as a leading heavy metal attraction and introduced such enduring favourites as 'Speed King' and 'Child In Time'. Gillan's powerful intonation brought a third dimension to their sound and this new-found popularity in the UK was enhanced when an attendant single, 'Black Night', reached number 2. 'Strange Kind Of Woman' followed it into the Top 10, while *Fireball* and *Machine Head* topped the album chart. The latter included the riff-laden 'Smoke On The Water', now lauded as a seminal example of the hard rock oeuvre, and was the first release on the group's own Purple label. Although the platinum-selling *Made In Japan* captured their live prowess in full flight, relations within the band grew increasingly strained, and *Who Do We Think We Are?* marked the end of this highly successful line-up. The departures of Gillan and Glover robbed Deep Purple of an expressive frontman and

imaginative arranger, although David Coverdale (b. 22 September 1951, Saltburn, Lancashire, England; vocals) and Glenn Hughes (b. 21 August 1952, Cannock, Scotland; bass, ex-Trapeze) brought a new impetus to the act. *Burn* and *Stormbringer* both reached the Top 10, but Blackmore grew increasingly dissatisfied with the group's direction and in May 1975 left to form Rainbow. US guitarist Tommy Bolin (b. 18 April 1951, Sioux City, USA, d. 4 December 1976, Miami, Florida, USA), formerly of the James Gang, joined Deep Purple for *Come Taste The Band*, but his jazz/soul style was incompatible with the group's heavy metal sound, and a now-tiring act folded in 1976 following a farewell UK tour. Coverdale then formed Whitesnake, Paice and Lord joined Tony Ashton in Paice, Ashton And Lord, while Bolin died of a heroin overdose within months of Purple's demise. Judicious archive and 'best of' releases kept the group in the public eye, as did the high profile enjoyed by its several ex-members. Pressure for a reunion bore fruit in 1984 when Gillan, Lord, Blackmore, Glover and Paice completed *Perfect Strangers*. A second set, *House Of Blue Lights*, ensued, but recurring animosity between Gillan and Blackmore resulted in the singer's departure following the in-concert *Nobody's Perfect*. Former Rainbow vocalist, Joe Lynn Turner, was brought into the line-up for *Slaves And Masters* as Purple steadfastly maintained their revitalized career. Gillan rejoined in 1993 only to quit, yet again, shortly afterwards, while his old sparring partner, Blackmore, also bailed out the following year, to be briefly replaced by Joe Satriani. The line-up that recorded the credible *Purpendicular* in 1996 was Steve Morse on guitar, with Lord, Gillan, Glover and Paice.

●ALBUMS: *Shades Of Deep Purple* (Parlophone 1968)★★, *The Book Of Taliesyn* (Harvest 1969)★★★, *Deep Purple* (Harvest 1969)★★★, *Concerto For Group And Orchestra* (Harvest 1970)★★, *Deep Purple In Rock* (Harvest 1970)★★★★, *Fireball* (Harvest 1971)★★★★, *Machine Head* (Purple 1972)★★★★, *Made In Japan* (Purple 1973)★★★, *Who Do We Think We Are?* (Purple 1973)★★★, *Burn* (Purple 1974)★★★, *Stormbringer* (Purple 1975)★★★, *Come Taste The Band* (Purple 1975)★★★, *Made In Europe* (Warners 1976)★★★, *Perfect Strangers* (Polydor 1984)★★★, *House Of Blue Light* (Polydor 1987)★★★, *Nobody's Perfect* (Polydor 1988)★★, *Slaves And Masters* (RCA 1990)★★, *The Battle Rages On* (RCA 1993)★★★, *The Final Battle* (RCA 1994)★★★, *Come Hell Or High Water* (RCA 1994)★★, *Purpendicular* (RCA 1996)★★★, *Mark III, The Final Concerts* (Connoisseur 1996)★★.

●COMPILATIONS: *24 Carat Purple* (Purple 1975)★★★★, *Last Concert In Japan* (EMI 1977)★★★, *Powerhouse* (Purple 1977)★★★, *When We Rock, We Rock And When We Roll, We Roll* (Warners 1978)★★★★, *Singles: As & Bs* (Harvest 1978)★★★, *Deepest Purple* (Harvest 1980)★★★, *Live In London: Deep Purple* (Harvest 1982)★★, *Anthology: Deep Purple* (Harvest 1985)★★★★, *Scandinavian Nights* (Connoisseur

1988)★★, *Knebworth '85* (Connoisseur 1991)★★, *Anthology 2* (EMI 1991)★★, *On The Wings Of A Russian Foxbat: Live In California 1976* (Connoisseur 1995)★★, *The Collection* (EMI Gold 1997)★★★★.
●VIDEOS: *California Jam* (1984), *Video Singles* (1987), *Bad Attitude* (1988), *Concert For Group And Orchestra* (1988), *Deep Purple* (1988), *Doing Their Thing* (1990), *Scandinavian Nights* (1990).
●FURTHER READING: *Deep Purple: The Illustrated Biography*, Chris Charlesworth.

DELANEY AND BONNIE

Delaney Bramlett (b. 1 July 1939, Pontotoc, Mississippi, USA) first came to prominence as a member of the Shindigs, the house band on US television's *Shindig*. As well as recording with the group, Delaney made several unsuccessful solo singles prior to meeting Bonnie Lynn (b. 8 November 1944, Acton, Illinois, USA) in California. His future wife had already sung with several impressive figures including Little Milton, Albert King and Ike And Tina Turner. The couple's first album, *Home*, produced by Leon Russell and Donald 'Duck' Dunn, was only released in the wake of *Accept No Substitute* (1969). This exemplary white-soul collection featured several excellent Delaney compositions, including 'Get Ourselves Together' and 'Love Me A Little Bit Longer'. An expanded ensemble, which featured Bobby Keys (saxophone), Jim Price (trumpet), Bobby Whitlock (guitar), Carl Radle (bass) and Jim Keltner (drums) alongside the Bramletts, then toured America with Blind Faith. The Bramletts' refreshing enthusiasm inspired guitarist Eric Clapton, who guested with the revue in Britain. This period was documented on their *On Tour* (1970) collection and a powerful single, 'Comin' Home'. Lavish praise by the media and from George Harrison and Dave Mason was undermined when the backing group walked out to join Joe Cocker's *Mad Dogs And Englishmen* escapade. *To Bonnie From Delaney* (1970), recorded with the Dixie Flyers and Memphis Horns, lacked the purpose of previous albums. *Motel Shot*, an informal, documentary release, recaptured something of the duo's erstwhile charm, but it was clear that they had not survived the earlier defections. *Together* (1972) introduced their new deal with Columbia Records, but the couple's marriage was now collapsing and they broke up later that year. Delaney subsequently released several disappointing albums for MGM Records and Prodigal but Bonnie's three collections for Capricorn showed a greater urgency and she took to singing gospel when she become a born-again Christian. Overwhelmed by their brief spell in the spotlight, the duo is better recalled for the influence they had on their peers.
●ALBUMS: *Accept No Substitute - The Original Delaney & Bonnie* (Elektra 1969)★★★, *Home* (1969)★★, *Delaney & Bonnie & Friends On Tour With Eric Clapton* (Atco 1970)★★★★, *To Bonnie From Delaney* (Atco 1970)★★★, *Motel Shot* (Atco 1971)★★★, *D&B Together* (Columbia 1972)★★, *Country Life* (1972)★★.
●COMPILATIONS: *Best Of Delaney And Bonnie* (Atco 1973)★★★, *Best Of Delaney And Bonnie* (Rhino 1990)★★★.
●FILMS: *Catch My Soul* (1974).

DELFONICS

Formed in Philadelphia, USA, in 1965 and originally known as the Four Gents the Delfonics featured William Hart (b. 17 January 1945, Washington, DC, USA), Wilbert Hart (b. 19 October 1947, Philadelphia, Pennsylvania, USA), Randy Cain (b. 2 May 1945, Philadelphia, Pennsylvania, USA) and Ritchie Daniels. An instigator of the Philly Sound, the above line-up evolved out of an earlier group, the Veltones. The Delfonics' early releases appeared on local independent labels until their manager, Stan Watson, founded Philly Groove. Cut to a trio on Daniels' conscription, their distinctive hallmarks, in particular William Hart's aching tenor, were heard clearly on their debut hit, 'La La Means I Love You'. It prepared the way for several symphonic creations, including 'I'm Sorry', 'Ready Or Not Here I Come' (both 1968) and 'Didn't I (Blow Your Mind This Time)' (1970). Much of the credit for their sumptuous atmosphere was due to producer Thom Bell's remarkable use of brass and orchestration. It provided the perfect backdrop for Hart's emotive ballads. 'Trying To Make A Fool Out Of Me' (1970), the group's 10th consecutive R&B chart entry, marked the end of this relationship, although Bell later continued this style with the (Detroit) Spinners and Stylistics. The Delfonics meanwhile maintained a momentum with further excellent singles. In 1971 Cain was replaced by Major Harris, whose subsequent departure three years later coincided with the Delfonics' downhill slide. Unable to secure a permanent third member, the Harts were also bedevilled by Philly Groove's collapse. Singles for Arista (1978) and Lorimar (1979) were issued, but to negligible attention.
●ALBUMS: *La La Means I Love You* (Philly Groove 1968)★★★, *The Sound Of Sexy Soul* (Philly Groove 1969)★★★, *The Delfonics* (Philly Groove 1970)★★★, *Tell Me This Is A Dream* (Philly Groove 1972)★★★, *Alive And Kicking* (1974)★★.
●COMPILATIONS: *The Delfonics Super Hits* (Philly Groove 1969)★★★, *Symphonic Soul - Greatest Hits* (Charly 1988)★★★★.

DELLS

A soul vocal and close harmony group formed in 1953 as the El-Rays when the members - Johnny Funches (lead), Marvin Junior (b. 31 January 1936, Harrell, Arkansas, USA; tenor), Verne Allison (b. 22 June 1936, Chicago, Illinois, USA; tenor), Lucius McGill (b. 1935, Chicago, Illinois, USA; tenor), Mickey McGill (b. 17 February 1937, Chicago, Illinois, USA; baritone) and Chuck Barksdale (b. 11 January 1935, Chicago, Illinois,

USA; bass) - were all high school students. As the El-Rays the group released one record on the Chess label, 'Darling Dear I Know' in 1953. After a name change they recorded 'Tell The World' in 1955, which was only a minor hit, but a year later they released 'Oh What A Night' (number 4 in the R&B chart), one of the era's best-loved black harmony performances and the Dells' last hit for 10 years. In 1965 they returned to the R&B chart with 'Stay In My Corner'. Three years later under the guidance of producer Bobby Miller, a re-recorded version of this song effectively relaunched their career when it became a US Top 10 hit. An enchanting medley of 'Love Is Blue' and 'I Can Sing A Rainbow' (1969) was their sole UK hit in 1969 but a further re-recording, this time of 'Oh What A Night', introduced a string of successful releases in the US including 'Open Up My Heart' (1970), 'Give Your Baby A Standing Ovation' (1973) and 'I Miss You' (1974). The Dells continued to prosper through the 70s and early 80s, surviving every prevalent trend in music. Just as noteworthy was the members' own relationship which survived almost intact from their inception. Lucius McGill left when they were still known as the El-Rays and the only further change occurred in 1958 when Funches was replaced by ex-Flamingo Johnny Carter (b. 2 June 1934, Chicago, Illinois, USA). Marvin Junior took over as lead and Carter took first tenor. Funches gave his reason for leaving as being 'tired of the constant touring'. The Dells' enduring music is a tribute to their longevity.

●ALBUMS: *Oh What A Nite* (1959)★★★, *It's Not Unusual* (1965)★★★, *There Is* (Cadet 1968)★★★★, *Stay In My Corner* (Cadet 1968)★★★, *Musical Menu/Always Together* (Cadet 1969)★★★, *Love Is Blue* (Cadet 1969)★★★, *Like It Is, Like It Was* (Cadet 1970)★★★, *Oh, What A Night* (Cadet 1970)★★★, *Freedom Means* (Cadet 1971)★★★, *Dells Sing Dionne Warwick's Greatest Hits* (Cadet 1972)★★, *Sweet As Funk Can Be* (Cadet 1972)★★★, *Give Your Baby A Standing Ovation* (Cadet 1973)★★★, with the Dramatics *The Dells Vs The Dramatics* (Cadet 1974)★★★★, *The Mighty Mighty Dells* (Cadet 1974)★★★, *No Way Back* (1975)★★★, *They Said It Couldn't Be Done, But We Did It* (Mercury 1977)★★, *Love Connection* (Mercury 1977)★★★, *New Beginnings* (ABC 1978)★★, *Face To Face* (ABC 1979)★★★, *I Touched A Dream* (20th Century 1980)★★★, *Whatever Turns You On* (20th Century 1981)★★, *One Step Closer* (1984)★★, *The Second Time* (1988)★★, *Music From The Motion Picture: The Five Heartbeats* (Virgin 1991)★★★.

●COMPILATIONS: *The Best Of The Dells* (1973)★★★★, *Cornered* (1977)★★★, *Rockin' On Bandstand* (1983)★★★, *From Streetcorner To Soul* (1984)★★★, *Breezy Ballads And Tender Tunes* (1985)★★★, *On Their Corner/The Best Of ...* (Chess/MCA 1992)★★★★.

DENNY, SANDY

b. Alexandra Elene Maclean Denny, 6 January 1947, Wimbledon, London, England, d. 21 April 1978, London, England. A former student at Kingston Art College where her contemporaries included John Renbourn and Jimmy Page, Sandy Denny forged her early reputation in such famous London folk clubs as Les Cousins, Bunjies and the Scots Hoose. Renowned for an eclectic repertoire, she featured material by Tom Paxton and her then boyfriend Jackson C. Frank, as well as traditional English songs. Work from this early period was captured on two 1967 albums, *Sandy And Johnny* (with Johnny Silvo) and *Alex Campbell & His Friends*. The following year the singer spent six months as a member of the Strawbs. Their lone album together was not released until 1973, but this melodic work contained several haunting Denny vocals and includes the original version of her famed composition, 'Who Knows Where The Time Goes'. In May 1968 Sandy joined Fairport Convention with whom she completed three excellent albums. Many of her finest performances date from this period, but when the group vowed to pursue a purist path at the expense of original material, the singer left to form Fotheringay. This accomplished quintet recorded a solitary album before internal pressures pulled it apart, but Sandy's contributions, notably 'The Sea', 'Nothing More' and 'The Pond And The Stream', rank among her finest work.

Denny's debut album, *North Star Grassman And The Ravens*, contained several excellent songs, including 'Late November' and the expansive 'John The Gun', as well as sterling contributions from the renowned guitarist Richard Thompson, who appeared on all of the singer's releases. *Sandy* was another memorable collection, notable for the haunting 'It'll Take A Long Time' and a sympathetic version of Richard Farina's 'Quiet Joys Of Brotherhood', a staple of the early Fairport's set. Together, these albums confirmed Sandy as a major talent and a composer of accomplished, poignant songs. *Like An Old Fashioned Waltz*, which included the gorgeous 'Solo', closed this particular period. Sandy married Trevor Lucas, her partner in Fotheringay, who was now a member of Fairport Convention. Despite her dislike of touring, she rejoined the group in 1974. A live set and the crafted *Rising For The Moon* followed, but Denny and Lucas then left in December 1975. A period of domesticity ensued before the singer completed *Rendezvous*, a charming selection which rekindled an interest in performing. Plans were made to record a new set in America, but following a fall down the staircase at a friend's house she died from a cerebral haemorrhage on 21 April 1978. Denny is recalled as one of Britain's finest singer-songwriters and remembered for work that has grown in stature over the years. Her effortless and smooth vocal delivery still sets the standard for many of today's female folk-based singers.

●ALBUMS: *The North Star Grassman And The Ravens* (Island 1971)★★★, *Sandy* (Island 1972)★★★★, *Like An Old Fashioned Waltz* (Island 1973)★★★, *Rendezvous* (Island 1977)★★★, *The BBC Sessions 1971-1973* (Strange Fruit 1997)★★★★.

●COMPILATIONS: *The Original Sandy Denny*

(Mooncrest 1984)★★★, *Who Knows Where The Time Goes* (Island 1986)★★★★, *The Best Of Sandy Denny* (Island 1987)★★★, with Trevor Lucas *The Attic Tracks 1972 - 1984 Outtakes and Rarities* (Special Delivery 1995)★★★★, *The Best Of ...* (Island 1996)★★★★.

●FURTHER READING: *Meet On The Ledge*, Patrick Humphries.

DENVER, JOHN

b. Henry John Deutschendorf Jnr., 31 December 1943, Roswell, New Mexico, USA. One of America's most popular performers during the 70s, Denver's rise to fame began when he was 'discovered' in a Los Angeles nightclub. He initially joined the Back Porch Majority, a nursery group for the renowned New Christy Minstrels but, tiring of his role there, left for the Chad Mitchell Trio where he forged a reputation as a talented songwriter.

With the departure of the last original member, the Mitchell Trio became known as Denver, Boise and Johnson, but their brief lifespan ended when John embarked on a solo career in 1969. One of his compositions, 'Leaving On A Jet Plane', provided an international hit for Peter, Paul And Mary, and this evocative song was the highlight of Denver's debut album, *Rhymes And Reasons*. Subsequent releases, *Take Me To Tomorrow* and *Whose Garden Was This*, garnered some attention, but it was not until the release of *Poems, Prayers And Promises* that the singer enjoyed popular acclaim when one of its tracks, 'Take Me Home, Country Roads', broached the US Top 3 and became a UK Top 20 hit for Olivia Newton-John in 1973. The song's undemanding homeliness established a light, almost naïve style, consolidated on the albums *Aerie* and *Rocky Mountain High*. 'I'd Rather Be A Cowboy' (1973) and 'Sunshine On My Shoulders' (1974) were both gold singles, while a third million-seller, 'Annie's Song', secured Denver's international status when it topped the UK charts that same year and subsequently became an MOR standard, as well as earning the classical flautist James Galway a UK number 3 hit in 1978. Further US chart success came in 1975 with two number 1 hits, 'Thank God I'm A Country Boy' and 'I'm Sorry'. Denver's status as an all-round entertainer was enhanced by many television spectaculars, including *Rocky Mountain Christmas*, and further gold-record awards for *An Evening With John Denver* and *Windsong*, ensuring that 1975 was the artist's most successful year to date.

He continued to enjoy a high profile throughout the rest of the decade and forged a concurrent acting career with his role in the film comedy *Oh, God* with George Burns. In 1981 his songwriting talent attracted the attention of yet another classically trained artist, when opera singer Placido Domingo duetted with Denver on 'Perhaps Love'. However, although Denver became an unofficial musical ambassador with tours to Russia and China, his recording became less prolific as increasingly he devoted time to charitable work and ecological interests. Despite the attacks by music critics, who have deemed his work to be bland and saccharine, Denver's cute, simplistic approach has nonetheless achieved a mass popularity that is the envy of many artists.

●ALBUMS: *Rhymes & Reasons* (RCA 1969)★★★, *Take Me To Tomorrow* (RCA 1970)★★★, *Whose Garden Was This* (RCA 1970)★★★, *Poems, Prayers And Promises* (RCA 1971)★★★, *Aerie* (RCA 1971)★★★, *Rocky Mountain High* (RCA 1972)★★★★, *Farewell Andromeda* (RCA 1973)★★, *Back Home Again* (RCA 1974)★★★★, *An Evening With John Denver* (RCA 1975)★★★★, *Windsong* (RCA 1975)★★★★, *Rocky Mountain Christmas* (RCA 1975)★★, *Live In London* (RCA 1976)★★, *Spirit* (RCA 1976)★★★★, *I Want To Live* (RCA 1977)★★, *Live At The Sydney Opera House* (RCA 1978)★★, *John Denver* (RCA 1979)★★★★, with the Muppets *A Christmas Together* (RCA 1979)★★, *Autograph* (RCA 1980)★★★, *Some Days Are Diamonds* (RCA 1981)★★★, with Placido Domingo *Perhaps Love* (Columbia 1981)★★, *Seasons Of The Heart* (RCA 1982)★★★, *It's About Time* (RCA 1983)★★★, *Dreamland Express* (RCA 1985)★★, *One World* (RCA 1986)★★, *Higher Ground* (RCA 1988)★★, *Stonehaven Sunrise* (1989)★★, *The Flower That Shattered The Stone* (Windstar 1990)★★, *Earth Songs* (Music Club 1990)★★, *Different Directions* (Concord 1992)★★.

●COMPILATIONS: *The Best Of John Denver* (RCA 1974)★★★, *The Best Of John Denver Volume 2* (RCA 1977)★★★, *The John Denver Collection* (Telstar 1984)★★★, *Greatest Hits Volume 3* (RCA 1985)★★★, *The Rocky Mountain Collection* (BMG 1997)★★★★.

●VIDEOS: *A Portrait* (Telstar 1994), *The Wildlife Concert* (Sony 1995).

●FURTHER READING: *John Denver*, Leonore Fleischer. *John Denver*, David Dachs. *John Denver: Rocky Mountain Wonderboy*, James Martin. *Take Me Home: An Autobiography*, John Denver with Arthur Tobier.

DEODATO

b. Eumir Deodato Almeida, 21 June 1942, Rio de Janeiro, Brazil. As a child, Deodato taught himself to play keyboards and graduated to playing in local pop bands in his teens. He also worked as a session musician (keyboards, bass, guitar) before recording under his own name. His first success came in Brazil, accompanying Astrud Gilberto. He won a prize at the Rio Song Festival for his composition, 'Spirit Of Summer', before emigrating to California in 1967. There he quickly established himself as a musical arranger, handling these chores for Roberta Flack's Chapter Two in 1970. He also appeared on recordings by Frank Sinatra, Bette Midler, Aretha Franklin, Roberta Flack and others. He then signed as a solo artist to the New York-based CTI Records and found success with his first release, an adaptation of Richard Strauss's 'Also Sprach Zarathustra', which had recently been used as the title music to Stanley Kubrick's film, *2001*. Deodato's jazz version (originally intended for label-mate Bob James as *his* CTI debut) was an international smash, hitting number 2 on the US Top 100 and number 7 in the UK, also collecting the 1973 Grammy Award for 'Best Pop Instrumental Performance'. After two albums for CTI (*Prelude* and *Deodato 2*) and with the label in difficulties (ironically caused by the success of 'Also Sprach Zarathustra') Deodato moved to MCA for three albums, recording *First Cuckoo*, *Whirlwinds* and *Very Together*, the latter causing dancefloor activity thanks to 'Peter Gunn'. A further move to Warner Brothers Records. revived his career, with 'Whistle Bump' and 'Night Cruiser' afforded almost anthem status in the UK. In 1979 he embarked on a highly successful production career, revitalizing the fortunes of Kool And The Gang with *Ladies Night* and *Celebration* in particular. After one further album for Warners in 1984 he switched to Atlantic, recording *Somewhere Out There* in 1989. The previous year he had produced the debut solo album from Dexys Midnight Runners' star, Kevin Rowland.

●ALBUMS: *Prelude* (CTI 1973)★★★, *Deodato 2* (CTI 1974)★★★, *The First Cuckoo* (MCA 1976)★★★★, *Very Together* (MCA 1976)★★, *Whirlwinds* (MCA 1977)★★, *Love Island* (Warners 1978)★★, *Night Cruiser* (Warners 1980)★★, *Happy Hour* (Warners 1982)★★, *Motion* (Warners 1984)★★, *Somewhere Out There* (Atlantic 1989)★★.

DEREK AND THE DOMINOS

Eric Clapton (b. 30 March 1945, Ripley, Surrey, England), formed this short-lived band in May 1970 following his departure from the supergroup Blind Faith and his brief involvement with the down-home loose aggregation of Delaney And Bonnie And Friends. He purloined three members of the latter; Carl Radle (d. May 30 1980; bass), Bobby Whitlock (keyboards/vocals) and Jim Gordon (drums). Together with Duane Allman on guitar they recorded *Layla And Other Assorted Love Songs*, a superb double album. The band were only together for a year, during which time they toured the UK, playing small clubs, toured the USA, and imbibed copious amounts of hard and soft drugs. It was during his time with the Dominos that Eric became addicted to heroin. This however, did not detract from the quality of the music. In addition to the classic 'Layla' the album contained Clapton's co-written compositions mixed with blues classics like 'Key To The Highway' and a sympathetic reading of Jimi Hendrix's 'Little Wing'. The subsequent live album, recorded on their USA tour, was a further demonstration of their considerable potential had they been able to hold themselves together.

●ALBUMS: *Layla And Other Assorted Love Songs* (Polydor 1970)★★★★, *In Concert* (Polydor 1973)★★★.

DERRINGER, RICK

b. Richard Zehringer, 5 August 1947, Fort Recovery, Ohio, USA. Originally a member of the chart-topping McCoys ('Hang On Sloopy' etc.), Derringer went on to produce two of their later albums, paving the way for his new career. Along with his brother Randy, Rick formed the nucleus of Johnny Winter's backing group. After producing four of Winter's albums, he joined the Edgar Winter Group and produced their best-selling, *They Only Come Out At Night*. Meanwhile, Derringer finally recorded his first solo album, the heavy metal-tinged *All American Boy*. Vinny Appice (later of Black Sabbath), joined in 1976. Appice, plus band colleagues Danny Johnson (guitar) and Kenny Aaronson (bass) eventually departed to form Axis after the release of *Live* in 1977. For his part, after several albums with the group Derringer, he reverted to solo billing and appeared as guest guitarist on albums by Steely Dan (he was the Ricky mentioned in 'Ricky Don't Lose That Number'), Bette Midler, Todd Rundgren, Donald Fagen, Kiss, Cyndi Lauper, Meat Loaf, Barbra Streisand and 'Weird Al' Yankovic. Afterwards, he turned his attention to production and soundtrack work. However, in the 90s he returned to solo recording, having turned down several previous attempts to lure him. It was Mike Varney at Shrapnel Records who finally won the day, teaming him with bassist and co-producer Kevin Russell for *Back To The Blues* and *Electra Blues*.

●ALBUMS: *All American Boy* (Blue Sky 1974)★★★, *Spring Fever* (Blue Sky 1975)★★, *Derringer* (Blue Sky 1976)★★, *Sweet Evil* (Blue Sky 1977)★★, *Live* (Blue Sky 1977)★★★, *If You Weren't So Romantic, I'd Shoot You* (Columbia 1978)★★, *Guitars And Women* (Columbia 1979)★★, *Face To Face* (Columbia 1980)★★, *Good Dirty Fun* (Passport 1983)★★, *Back To The Blues* (Shrapnel 1993)★★★, *Electra Blues* (Shrapnel 1994)★★★, *Tend The Fire* (Code Blue 1996)★★★.

DETROIT EMERALDS

Formed in Little Rock, Arkansas, USA, by bothers; Abrim, Ivory, Cleophus and Raymond Tilmon. The Emeralds' first hit, 'Show Time' (1968) reached the US R&B Top 30. By the time 'Do My Right' (1971) reached the Soul Top 10, the line-up had been reduced to a trio of Abrim, Ivory and mutual friend James Mitchell, (b. Perry, Florida, USA). The group secured their biggest US successes in 1972 with 'You Want It, You Got It' and 'Baby Let Me Take You (In My Arms)' but the following year 'Feel The Need In Me', which failed to crack *Billboard*'s Hot 100, peaked at number 4 in the UK chart. Three further UK hits followed, including, in 1977, a re-recorded version of that 1973 best-seller; but at home the Emeralds' career was waning. By 1977 Abrim Tilmon was the last remaining original member; but died from a heart attack five years later.

●ALBUMS: *Do Me Right* (Westbound 1971)★★, *You Want, It You Got It, Feel The Need* (Westbound 1972)★★★, *I'm In Love With You* (Westbound 1973)★★★, *Feel The Need* (Atlantic 1973)★★, *Abe James And Ivory* (1973)★★, *Let's Get Together* (Atlantic 1978)★★.

●COMPILATIONS: *Do Me Right/You Want It You Got It* (1993)★★★, *I'm In Love With You/Feel The Need* (1993)★★★.

DETROIT SPINNERS

Formed in Ferndale High School, near Detroit, Michigan, USA, and originally known as the Domingoes, Henry Fambrough (b. 10 May 1935, Detroit, Michigan, USA), Robert 'Bobby' Smith (b. 10 April 1937, Detroit, Michigan, USA), Billy Henderson (b. 9 August 1939, Detroit, Michigan, USA), Pervis Jackson and George Dixon became the Spinners upon signing with the Tri-Phi label in 1961. (The prefix 'Motown' and/or 'Detroit' was added in the UK to avoid confusion with the Spinners folk group.) Although not a member, producer and songwriter Harvey Fuqua sang lead on the group's debut single, 'That's What Girls Are Made For', which reached number 5 in the US R&B chart and broached the pop Top 30. Edgar 'Chico' Edwards then replaced Dixon, but although Fuqua took the quintet to Motown in 1963, they were overshadowed by other signings and struggled to gain a commercial ascendancy. 'I'll Always Love You' was a minor US hit in 1965, but it was not until 1970 that the Spinners scored a major success when the Stevie Wonder composition, 'It's A Shame', reached the Top 20 in both the USA and the UK. The following year the group moved to Atlantic on the suggestion of Aretha Franklin. However, lead singer G.C. Cameron, who had replaced Edwards, opted to remain at Motown and thus new singer Philippe Wynne (b. Philip Walker, 3 April 1941, Detroit, Michigan, USA, d. 14 July 1984) was added to the line-up. His expressive falsetto lent an air of distinctiveness to an already crafted harmony sound and, united with producer Thom Bell, the Spinners completed a series of exemplary singles which set a benchmark for 70s sophisticated soul. 'I'll Be Around', 'Could It Be I'm Falling In Love' (both 1972), 'One Of A Kind (Love Affair)' and 'Mighty Love Part 1' (both 1973) were each R&B chart toppers, while 'Then Came You', a collaboration with Dionne Warwick, topped the US pop chart. 'Ghetto Child' (1973) and 'The Rubberband Man' (1976) provided international success as the quintet deftly pursued a sweet, orchestrated sound which nonetheless avoided the sterile trappings of several contemporaries. The early Atlantic singles featured smooth-voiced Smith as lead, but later singles featured the baroque stylings of Wynne. New lead John Edwards replaced Wynne when the latter left for a solo career in 1977, but the Spinners continued to enjoy hits, notably with 'Working My Way Back To You/Forgive Me Girl' which reached number 1 in the UK and number 2 in the USA. A medley of 'Cupid' and 'I've Loved You For A Long Time' reached both countries' respective Top 10s in 1980, but an ensuing unstable line-up undermined the group's career during the 80s.

●ALBUMS: *Party - My Pad* (Motown 1963)★★, *The Original Spinners* (Motown 1967)★★★, *The Detroit Spinners* (Motown 1968)★★★, *Second Time Around* (V.I.P. 1970)★★★, *The (Detroit) Spinners* (Atlantic 1973)★★★★, *Mighty Love* (Atlantic 1974)★★★★, *New And Improved* (Atlantic 1974)★★★, *Pick Of The Litter* (Atlantic 1975)★★★★, *(Detroit) Spinners Live* (Atlantic 1975)★★★, *Happiness Is Being With The (Detroit) Spinners* (Atlantic 1976)★★★, *Yesterday, Today And Tomorrow* (Atlantic 1977)★★, *8* (Atlantic 1977)★★, *From Here To Eternally* (Atlantic 1979)★★, *Dancin' And Lovin'* (Atlantic 1980)★★, *Love Trippin'* (Atlantic 1980)★★, *Labour Of Love* (Atlantic 1981)★★, *Can't Shake This Feelin'* (Atlantic 1982)★★, *Grand Slam* (Atlantic 1983)★★, *Cross Fire* (Atlantic 1984)★★, *Lovin' Feelings* (Atco 1985)★★.
●COMPILATIONS: *The Best Of The Detroit Spinners* (Motown 1973)★★★★, *Smash Hits* (Atlantic 1977)★★★★, *The Best Of The Spinners* (Atlantic 1978)★★★★, *20 Golden Classics - The Detroit Spinners* (Motown 1980)★★★, *Golden Greats - Detroit Spinners* (Atlantic 1985)★★★, *A One Of A Kind Love Affair: The Anthology* (Atlantic 1991)★★★★.

DEVO

Formed during 1972 in Akron, Ohio, this US new wave band, who fitted the term better than most, comprised Gerald Casale (bass, vocals), Alan Myers (drums), Mark Mothersbaugh (vocals, keyboards, guitar), Bob Mothersbaugh (guitar, vocals), and Bob Casale (guitar, vocals). The philosophical principle on which Devo operated, and from which they took a shortened name, was devolution: the theory that mankind, rather than progressing, has actually embarked on a negative curve. The medium they pioneered to present this was basic, electronic music, with strong robotic and mechanical overtones. The visual representation and marketing exaggerated modern life, with industrial uniforms and neo-military formations alongside potato masks and flower-pot headgear. Their debut album was among their finest achievements; a synthesis of pop and sarcastic social commentary. Produced by Brian Eno, it caught the prevailing wind of America's new wave movement perfectly. It also offered them their biggest UK hit in a savage take on the Rolling Stones' '(I Can't Get No) Satisfaction'. It wasn't until their third studio album, however, that Devo confirmed they were no novelty act. *Freedom Of Choice* contained Devo standards 'Girl You Want' and 'Whip It', the latter giving them a million-selling single. At the peak of their powers, Devo inspired and informed many, not least one of Neil Young's great albums, *Rust Never Sleeps*. However, as the 80s unfolded the band seemed to lose its bite, and *New Traditionalists* signalled a creative descent. Successive albums were released to diminishing critical and commercial returns, and after *Shout* songwriters Gerald Casale and Mark Mothersbaugh moved into soundtrack work. Devo had previously performed the theme to Dan Ayckroyd's movie *Doctor Detroit*, and they added to this with TV work on *Pee-Wee's Playhouse* and *Davis Rules*. Mothersbaugh had also recorded a pair of solo studio LPs, largely consisting of keyboard doodlings and 'atmosphere' pieces. These arrived at the same time as Devo's first original work together in four years, *Total*

Devo, which saw Myers replaced by David Kendrick (ex-Gleaming Spires; Sparks). Devo's absence had not, however, made critics' hearts grow fonder. As was unerringly pointed out, the band had long since lost its status as innovators, and been surpassed by a generation of electronic outfits it had helped to inspire. Despite falling out of fashion as the 80s wore on, Devo nevertheless saw themselves venerated in the new decade by bands who hailed their early work as a significant influence. Nirvana covered an obscure Devo recording, 'Turnaround', and both Soundgarden and Superchunk offered remakes of 'Girl You Want'. A new wave tribute album, *Freedom Of Choice*, adopting the band's own 1980 title, included the latter. Gerald Casale was bemused by the sudden attention: 'I think we were the most misunderstood band that ever came down the pike because behind the satire, our message was a humanistic one, not an inhumane one. If there's any interest in Devo now, it's only because it turned out that what was called an art-school smartass joke - this de-evolution rap, about man devolving - now seems very true as you look around.'

●ALBUMS: *Q: Are We Not Men? A: We Are Devo!* (Warners 1978)★★★★, *Duty Now For The Future* (Warners 1979)★★★, *Freedom Of Choice* (Warners 1980)★★★, *Devo Live* mini-album (Warners 1981)★, *New Traditionalists* (Warners 1981)★★★, *Oh No, It's Devo* (Warners 1982)★★★, *Shout* (Warners 1984)★★, *Total Devo* (Enigma 1988)★★, *Smooth Noodle Maps* (Enigma 1990)★★. Solo: Mark Mothersbaugh *Muzik For Insomniaks Vols. 1 & 2* (Enigma 1988).

●COMPILATIONS: *E-Z Listening Disc* (Rykodisc 1987)★★, *Now It Can Be Told* (Enigma 1989)★★★, *Greatest Hits* (Warners 1990)★★★★, *Greatest Misses* (Warners 1990)★★★, *Hard Core Devo* (Rykodisc 1990)★★, *Hardcore Devo 1974-77, Volumes 1 & 2* (Fan Club 1991)★★, *Live: The Mongoloid Years* (Rykodisc 1992)★★.

DIAMOND, NEIL

b. Noah Kaminsky, 24 January 1941, Brooklyn, New York, USA. With a career as a hitmaker stretching across three decades, Diamond has veered between straightforward pop, a progressive singer-songwriter style and middle-of-the-road balladry. He attended the same high school as Neil Sedaka and Bobby Feldman of the Strangeloves and began songwriting as a young teenager. He made his first records in 1960 for local label Duel with Jack Packer as Neil And Jack. After college, Diamond became a full-time songwriter in 1962, recording unsuccessfully for CBS before 'Sunday And Me', produced by Leiber And Stoller for Jay And The Americans, brought his first success as a composer in 1965. The following year, Diamond made a third attempt at a recording career, joining Bert Berns' Bang label. With Jeff Barry and Ellie Greenwich as producers, he released 'Solitary Man' before the catchy 'Cherry Cherry' entered the US Top 10. In 1967 the Monkees

had multi million-sellers with Diamond's memorable 'I'm A Believer' and 'A Little Bit Me, A Little Bit You'. Like his own 1967 hit, 'Thank The Lord For The Night', these songs combined a gospel feel with a pop melody. In the same year, Diamond also showed his mastery of the country-tinged ballad with 'Kentucky Woman'.

After a legal dispute with Bang, Diamond signed to MCA Records' Uni label, moving from New York to Los Angeles. After a failed attempt at a progressive rock album (*Velvet Gloves And Spit*) he began to record in Memphis and came up with a series of catchy, and simple hits, including 'Sweet Caroline' (1969), 'Holly Holy' and two number 1s, 'Cracklin Rosie' (1970) and 'Song Sung Blue' (1972). At the same time, Diamond was extending his range with the semi-concept album *Tap Root Manuscript* (on which Hollywood arranger Marty Paich orchestrated African themes) and the confessional ballad, 'I Am ... I Said', a Top 10 single on both sides of the Atlantic. He was also much in demand for live shows and his dynamic act was captured on *Hot August Night*. Soon after its release, Diamond announced a temporary retirement from live appearances, and spent the next three years concentrating on writing and recording. He moved into film work, winning a Grammy award for the soundtrack of *Jonathan Livingston Seagull* to which his long-time arranger Lee Holdridge also contributed. *Beautiful Noise* (on his new label, CBS) was a tribute to the Brill Building songwriting world of the 50s and 60s. It cost nearly half a million dollars to make and was produced by Robbie Robertson. Diamond also appeared in *The Last Waltz*, the star-studded tribute movie to the Band.

In 1978, he recorded his first duet since 1960 and his biggest hit single. The wistful 'You Don't Bring Me Flowers' had previously been recorded solo by both Diamond and Barbra Streisand but after a disc jockey had spliced the tracks together, producer Bob Gaudio brought the pair together for the definitive version which headed the US chart. Now at the peak of his success, Diamond accepted his first film acting role in a remake of *The Jazz Singer*. The film was undistinguished although Diamond's performance was credible. The soundtrack album sold a million, in part because of 'America', a rousing, patriotic Diamond composition which he later performed at the Statue Of Liberty centenary celebrations. During the 80s, he increasingly co-wrote songs with Gilbert Becaud, David Foster and above all Carole Bayer Sager and Burt Bacharach. They collaborated on the ballad 'Heartlight' (1982), inspired by the film *E.T.* The next year, UB40 revived one of his earliest songs, 'Red Red Wine' and had a UK number 1. There were also disputes with CBS, which insisted on changes to two of Diamond's proposed albums, bringing in Maurice White to produce *Headed For The Future*. However, 'The Best Years Of Our Lives', written by Diamond alone, showed a return to the form of the 70s while he worked on his 1991 album with leading contemporary producers Don Was and Peter Asher.

Diamond has neither courted nor has been fully accepted by the *cognoscenti*; his track record however speaks volumes: almost 60 hits in the USA, over 30 charting albums and one of the Top 20 most successful artists ever in the USA. His success in the UK is comparable, with 26 charting albums and a fiercely loyal fan base. In 1993 Diamond released one of his finest records in a long time, *Up On The Roof*. His interpretation of songs by the great songwriters of the Brill Building was an outstanding tribute. His 1996 release *Tennessee Moon* was a complete departure from the safe limits of AOR pop; easily his most interesting album in years, it scaled the country music charts and introduced a totally new audience to Diamond. What was all the more remarkable was that his voice has the timbre of a natural country singer; maybe he should have entered this territory years ago.

●ALBUMS: *The Feel Of Neil Diamond* (Bang 1966)★★, *Just For You* (Bang 1967)★★★, *Velvet Gloves And Spit* (Uni 1968)★★, *Brother Love's Travelling Salvation Show* (Uni 1969)★★★, *Touching You, Touching Me* (Uni 1969)★★★, *Gold* (Uni 1970)★★★, *Shilo* (Bang 1970)★★, *Tap Root Manuscript* (Uni 1970)★★★★, *Do It* (Bang 1971)★★, *Stones* (Uni 1971)★★★, *Moods* (Uni 1972)★★★, *Hot August Night* (MCA 1972)★★★★, *Rainbow* (MCA 1973)★★★, *Jonathan Livingston Seagull* (Columbia 1974)★★, *Serenade* (Columbia 1974)★★★, *Beautiful Noise* (Columbia 1976)★★★★, *Love At The Greek* (Columbia 1977)★★★, *I'm Glad You're Here With Me Tonight* (Columbia 1977)★★★, *You Don't Bring Me Flowers* (Columbia 1978)★★★★, *September Morn* (Columbia 1980)★★★, *The Jazz Singer* (Capitol 1980)★★★★, *On The Way To The Sky* (Columbia 1981)★★★, *Heartlight* (Columbia 1982)★★★, *Primitive* (Columbia 1984)★★★, *Headed For The Future* (Columbia 1986)★★★, *Hot August Night II* (Columbia 1987)★★, *The Best Years Of Our Lives* (Columbia 1989)★★★, *Lovescape* (Columbia 1991)★★★, *The Christmas Album* (Columbia 1992)★★★, *Up On The Roof (Songs From The Brill Building)* (Columbia 1993)★★★, *Live In America* (Columbia 1994)★★★, *Tennessee Moon* (Columbia 1996)★★★★.

●COMPILATIONS: *Neil Diamond's Greatest Hits* (Bang 1968)★★★, *Double Gold* (Bang1973)★★★, *His 12 Greatest Hits* (MCA 1974)★★★★, *And The Singer Sings His Song* (MCA 1976)★★★, *20 Golden Greats* (EMI 1978)★★★, *Diamonds* (MCA 1981)★★, *Classics: The Early Years* (Columbia 1983)★★★, *Red Red Wine* (Pickwick 1988)★★, *Touching You Touching Me* (MCA 1988)★★, *The Greatest Hits 1966 - 1992* (Columbia 1993)★★★★, *The Very Best Of ...* (Pickwick 1996)★★★, *In My Lifetime* 3-CD box set (Columbia 1996)★★★★.

●VIDEOS: *Neil Diamond: The Christmas Special* (1993), *The Roof Party* (Columbia 1994).

●FURTHER READING: *Neil Diamond*, Suzanne K. O'Regan. *Solitary Star: Biography Of Neil Diamond*, Rich Wiseman.

●FILMS: *The Jazz Singer* (1980).

DICKIES

Formed in 1977 in Los Angeles, California, USA, the Dickies were a punk rock band which specialized in speedy renditions of humorous songs, many of which were cover versions of earlier rock hits. The group consisted of Chuck Wagon (keyboards), guitarist Stan Lee (guitar), Billy Club (bass), Leonard Graves Phillips (vocals) and Karlos Kaballero (drums). Wearing fashionably ludicrous, often grotesque clothing, the Dickies quickly became one of the most popular of the original LA punk bands, and were signed to A&M Records in 1978. In addition to their self-penned songs, the Dickies' early recordings included such previously bombastic numbers as the Moody Blues' 'Nights In White Satin' and Black Sabbath's 'Paranoid', played at a furious pace and often clocking in at under two minutes. During their career they also covered the Monkees, Led Zeppelin and others. Their original material often took its cue from cult b-movies, similar in style and attitude to New York's Ramones. After a prolific recording schedule in the early 80s, the Dickies kept a low profile for the rest of the decade and were still recording new material in 1988, although they were no longer in the spotlight. Jonathan Melvoin (b. 6 December 1961, Los Angeles, California, USA, d. 12 July 1996) was in the band towards the end of their career, later joining the Smashing Pumpkins.

●ALBUMS: *The Incredible Shrinking Dickies* (A&M 1979)★★★, *Dawn Of The Dickies* (A&M 1979)★★★, *Stukas Over Disneyland* (1983)★★★, *We Aren't The World!* (1986)★★, *Second Coming* (Enigma 1988)★★, *Live In London-Locked 'N' Loaded* (Receiver 1991)★★.

DICKSON, BARBARA

b. 27 September 1947, Dunfermline, Fife, Scotland. Dickson earned her initial reputation during the 60s as part of Scotland's flourishing folk scene. An accomplished singer, she tackled traditional and contemporary material and enjoyed a fruitful partnership with Archie Fisher. In the 70s she encompassed a wider repertoire and became a popular MOR artist in the wake of her contributions to Willy Russell's *John, Paul, George, Ringo And Bert*, a successful London West End musical She enjoyed a UK Top 10 single in 1976 with 'Answer Me', while two later releases, 'Another Suitcase In Another Hall' (1977) and 'January February' (1980), also broached the UK Top 20. In 1983, the Dickson/Russell combination scored again when she won a Laurence Olivier Award for her portrayal of Mrs Johnstone in his widely applauded musical *Blood Brothers*. Dickson maintained her popularity through assiduous television and concert appearances and in 1985 had a number 1 hit with 'I Know Him So Well', a duet with Elaine Paige from the London musical *Chess*. Its success confirmed Barbara Dickson as one of Britain's leading MOR attractions. In 1993 Dickson received renewed critical acclaim when she recreated her original role in the current West End revival of *Blood Brothers*. Two years later she played in cabaret at London's Café Royal, and appeared in the television dramas *Band Of Gold* and *Taggart*. Her recording career is shared with her acting duties and she is able to choose her projects. *Dark End Of The Street* was a personal selection of songs she wanted to record, most notably her credible interpretations of Dan Penn's title track and the Bryants' 'Love Hurts'.

●ALBUMS: with Archie Fisher *The Fate Of O'Charlie* (Trailer 1969)★★★, with Fisher *Thro' The Recent Years* (1969)★★★, *From The Beggar's Mantle* (Decca 1972)★★, *Answer Me* (RSO 1976)★★★, *Morning Comes Quickly* (RSO 1977)★★★, *Sweet Oasis* (Columbia 1978)★★★, *The Barbara Dickson Album* (Epic 1980)★★★, *I Will Sing* (Decca 1981)★★, *You Know It's Me* (Epic 1981)★★, *Here We Go (Live On Tour)* (Epic 1982)★★, *All For A Song* (Epic 1982)★★, *Tell Me It's Not True* adapted from the stage musical *Blood Brothers* (Legacy 1983)★★★, *Heartbeats* (Epic 1984)★★, *The Right Moment* (K-Tel 1986)★★, *After Dark* (Theobald Dickson 1987)★★★, *Coming Alive Again (Album)* (Telstar 1989)★★, with Elaine Paige *Together* (1992)★★, *Don't Think Twice It's Alright* (1993)★★★, *Parcel Of Rogues* (Castle 1994)★★★, *Dark End Of The Street* (Transatlantic 1995)★★★.

●COMPILATIONS: *The Barbara Dickson Songbook* (K-Tel 1985)★★, *Gold* (K-Tel 1985)★★★, *The Very Best Of Barbara Dickson* (Telstar 1986)★★★, *The Barbara Dickson Collection* (Castle 1987)★★★.

DILLARDS

Brothers Rodney (b. 18 May 1942, East St. Louis, Illinois, USA; guitar/vocals) and Doug Dillard (b. 6 March 1937, East St. Louis, Illinois, USA; banjo/vocals) formed this seminal bluegrass group in Salem, Missouri, USA. Roy Dean Webb (b. 28 March 1937, Independence, Missouri, USA; mandolin/vocals) and former radio announcer Mitch Jayne (b. 7 May 1930, Hammond, Indiana, USA; bass) completed the original line-up which, having enjoyed popularity throughout their home state, travelled to Los Angeles in 1962 where they secured a recording deal with the renowned Elektra label. *Back Porch Bluegrass* and *The Dillards Live! Almost!* established the unit as one of America's leading traditional acts, although purists denigrated a sometimes irreverent attitude. *Pickin' & Fiddlin'*, a collaboration with violinist Byron Berline, was recorded to placate such criticism. The Dillards shared management with the Byrds and, whereas their distinctive harmonies proved influential to the latter group's development, the former act then began embracing a pop-based perspective. Dewey Martin (b. 30 September 1942, Chesterville, Ontario, Canada), later of Buffalo Springfield, added drums on a folk rock demo which in turn led to a brace of singles recorded for the Capitol label. Doug Dillard was unhappy with this new direction and left to form a duo with ex-Byrd Gene Clark. Herb Peterson joined the Dillards in 1968 and, having

resigned from Elektra, the reshaped quartet completed two exceptional country rock sets, *Wheatstraw Suite* and *Copperfields*. The newcomer was in turn replaced by Billy Rae Latham for *Roots And Branches*, on which the unit's transformation to full-scale electric instruments was complete. A full-time drummer, Paul York, was now featured in the line-up, but further changes were wrought when founder member Jayne dropped out following *Tribute To The American Duck*. Rodney Dillard has since remained at the helm of a capricious act, which by the end of the 70s, returned to the traditional music circuit through the auspices of the respected Flying Fish label. He was also reunited with his prodigal brother in Dillard-Hartford-Dillard, an occasional sideline, which also featured John Hartford.

●ALBUMS: *Back Porch Bluegrass* (Elektra 1963)★★★, *The Dillards Live! Almost!* (Elektra 1964)★★★, with Byron Berline *Pickin' & Fiddlin'* (Elektra 1965)★★★, *Wheatstraw Suite* (Elektra 1969)★★★★, *Copperfields* (Elektra 1970)★★★, *Roots And Branches* (Anthem 1972)★★, *Tribute To The American Duck* (1973)★★★, *The Dillards Versus The Incredible LA Time Machine* (Sonet 1977)★★, *Mountain Rock* (1978)★★, *Decade Waltz* (Flying Fish 1979)★★, *Homecoming & Family Reunion* (Flying Fish 1979)★★★, *Let It Fly* (Vanguard 1990)★★★.

●COMPILATIONS: *Country Tracks* (Elektra 1974)★★★, *I'll Fly Away* (Edesl 1988)★★★.

●VIDEOS: *A Night In The Ozarks* (Hendring 1991).

●FURTHER READING: *Everybody On The Truck*, Lee Grant.

DIMEOLA, AL

b. 22 July 1954, Jersey City, New Jersey, USA. After learning the drums at a very early age, DiMeola was inspired by the Beatles to take up the guitar, at the age of nine. Private lessons continued until, at the age of 15, he was performing in a C&W context. A growing interest in jazz led DiMeola to enter Berklee College Of Music in 1971, but he soon left to join Barry Miles' fusion group, returning in 1974 to study arranging. He was invited by Chick Corea to join his popular and influential Return To Forever. During this time DiMeola made a name for himself with his furious and sometimes spellbinding playing. It was 1976 before DiMeola began working as a leader and recording for Columbia, mostly in a jazz-rock style. In 1982 and 1983 he recorded two flamenco-influenced albums with John McLaughlin and Paco de Lucia, as part of an acoustic trio. The Al DiMeola Project was born in 1985 and remains his most celebrated venture. Recording on Manhattan and touring internationally, this group mixed his delicate, classically influenced acoustic guitar with the futuristic synthesizer work of Phil Markowitz and ethnic percussion of Airto Moreiro to form a new and influential sound. In 1995 he formed Rite Of Strings, a trio with bassist Stanley Clarke and violinist Jean-Luc Ponty.

●ALBUMS: *Land Of The Midnight Sun* (Columbia

1976)★★, *Elegant Gypsy* (Columbia 1977)★★★, *Casino* (Columbia 1978)★★★, *Splendido Hotel* (Columbia 1979)★★★★, *Roller Jubilee* (Columbia 1980)★★★, *Electric Rendevous* (Columbia 1982)★★★, *Tour De Force Live* (Columbia 1982)★★★★, *Scenario* (Columbia 1983)★★★★, *Cielo e Terra* (EMI 1983)★★★★, *Soaring Through A Dream* (EMI 1985)★★★, *Tiramu Su* (EMI 1988)★★★, *Heart Of The Immigrants* (Tomato 1993)★★★, *Kiss My Axe* (Tomato 1993)★★★, *World Sinfonia* (Tomato 1993)★★★, *Orange And Blue* (Verve 1994)★★★, with Stanley Clarke, Jean-Luc Ponty *The Rite Of Strings* (IRS 1995)★★★, *Paco De Lucia, Al DiMeola, John McLaughlin* (Verve 1996)★★★.
●COMPILATIONS: *The Best Of Al DiMeola* (Manhattan 1993)★★★.

DISCO TEX AND THE SEX-O-LETTES

Led by Sir Monti Rock III (b. Joseph Montanez Jnr.) whose camp posturings in an extravagant white pimp suit made him a favourite in the gay and straight disco clubs in the USA and UK during the 70s, the group was put together by producer Bob Crewe. They had two highly influential hits on the Chelsea label in the US and UK charts with the irresistible 'Get Dancin'' (1974) hitting the US and UK Top 10, and 'I Wanna Dance Wit' Choo (Doo Dat Dance), Part One' (1975) making the UK Top 10 and US Top 30.
●ALBUMS: *Disco Tex And The Sex-O-Lettes* (Chelsea 1975)★★.
●COMPILATIONS: *Get Dancin'* (Start 1989)★★.

DISTEL, SACHA

b. 28 January 1933, Paris, France. This scion of a well-heeled showbusiness family was a professional jazz guitarist at the age of 16, often sitting in with distinguished Americans visiting Parisian clubland. With the Modern Jazz Quartet sincerely loud in his praise, Distel was recognized as one of his country's foremost jazz instrumentalists by the mid-50s. He also gained publicity for his liaisons with Brigitte Bardot and beatnik icon Juliet Greco. He also became a businessman with interests in music publishing.
In 1956, his debut single 'Shoubi-dou-bidou' made the French hit parade. His marriage to skiing champion Francie Breaud in 1963, and the birth of their son, Laurent, did not affect the growth of a following that had extended beyond France to North America, where he starred in his own television spectacular. Nevertheless, he continued recording a French-language version (with cover girl Johanna Shimus) of Frank Sinatra and Nancy Sinatra's 'Somethin' Stupid' in 1967. His biggest moment on disc, however, was with 'Raindrops Keep Falling On My Head', an Oscar-winning number from the film *Butch Cassidy And The Sundance Kid*, which outsold the B.J. Thomas original in the UK chart, where it peaked at number 10 in January 1970, making no less than three re-entries throughout

that year. An attendant album sold well in Britain and the USA, and Distel remained a top cabaret draw throughout the world. In 1993, he co-starred with the television hostess and compère, Rosemarie Ford, on the UK tour of *Golden Songs Of The Silver Screen*.
●ALBUMS: *Sacha Distel* (Warners 1970)★★★, *Love Is All* (Pye 1976)★★★, *Forever And Ever* (1978)★★★, *20 Favourite Love Songs* (1979)★★★, *From Sacha With Love* (Mercury 1979)★★, *Move Closer* (Towerbell 1985)★★, *More And More* (Warners 1987)★★★, *Dedications* (1992)★★★.
●COMPILATIONS: *Golden Hour Of Sacha Distel* (Golden Hour 1978)★★★★, *The Sacha Distel Collection* (Pickwick 1980)★★★★.

DOG SOLDIER

A UK rock quintet of the mid-70s, Dog Soldier comprised Miller Anderson (guitar/vocals), Paul Bliss (bass), Derek Griffiths (guitar), Keef Hartley (drums) and Mel Simpson (keyboards). The group were very much Hartley's project after having established his reputation as a first class blues/rock drummer with John Mayall's Bluesbreakers and the Artwoods. He had already had one attempt at forming his own group, the Keef Hartley Band, but with Dog Soldier he linked up with former Artwoods colleague Griffiths (who in the interim had worked with Mike Cotton Sound and Satisfaction). Anderson was one survivor from the Keef Hartley Band, having also worked with the Voice, At Last The 1958 Rock 'N' Roll Show and Hemlock. Anderson proved to be by far the most talented member of the band, both as a musician and songwriter. However, Dog Soldier's sole album for United Artists Records in 1975 (there was also a single, 'Pillar To Post'), failed to ignite commercially and prompted Hartley to forgo his ambitions for a solo career. Largely inactive Hartley has returned to carpentry as a career. Anderson now performs regularly as a solo acoustic artist.
●ALBUMS: *Dog Soldier* (United Artists 1975)★★.

DOLAN, JOE

b. 16 October 1943, Mullingar, West Meath, Eire. After appearing on local radio, Dolan began singing professionally in early 1962. His acccomplished backing group, the Drifters, comprised his brother Ben Dolan (saxophone), Tommy Swarbrigg (trumpet), Jimmy Horan (bass guitar), Joey Gilheaney (trumpet) Des Doherty (keyboards) and Donal Aughey (drums). After signing a record deal with Pye, the band recorded a promising cover of Burt Bacharach's 'The Answer To Everything', which reached the Irish Top 10 in 1964. During the mid-60s Dolan and the Drifters established themselves as one of the most successful Irish showbands of their era. At their peak they enjoyed a string of hits in Eire including 'My Own Peculiar Way', 'Aching Breaking Heart', 'Two Of A Kind', 'Pretty Brown Eyes', 'House With The Whitewashed Gable' and 'Tar And

Cement'. The latter was unfortunate not to cross over into the UK charts, and was followed by the fragmentation of the original Drifters, several of whom reappeared in the Times. It was not until Dolan recorded solo, with the specific intent of becoming successful in Britain, that he won through. Mike Hazelwood and Albert Hammond of the Family Dogg provided the crucial hit with 'Make Me An Island', which reached number 3 in the summer of 1969. Subsequent hits from the songwriting partnership included the plaintive 'Teresa' and the up-tempo 'You're Such A Good Looking Woman'. As late as 1976 Dolan was back at number 1 in the Irish charts with 'Sister Mercy'. The following year, 'I Need You' repeated the feat and also infiltrated the UK Top 50. Dolan remains a regular performer on the Irish dancehall circuit.

●ALBUMS: *The Answer To Everything* (1969)★★★, *Lady In Blue* (Pye 1975)★★★, *Crazy Woman* (Pye 1977)★★★, *I Need You* (Pye 1977)★★★, *Turn Out The Light* (Pye 1980), *It's You, It's You, It's You* (Ritz 1986)★★★, *Always On My Mind* (Harmac 1989)★★★.

●COMPILATIONS: *At His Best* (K-Tel 1988)★★★, *Golden Hour Of Joe Dolan, Vols. 1 & 2* (Golden Hour 1988)★★★, *More And More* (1993)★★★.

DOLLAR

Under the aegis of producer Trevor Horn, this UK singing duo were designed to appeal to much the same market as Guys And Dolls before, and Bucks Fizz after them. Attired in stylish but not too way-out costumes for *Top Of The Pops*, Thereze Bazaar and David Van Day (b. 28 November 1957) made a promising start with 1978's 'Shooting Star' (number 14 in the UK). For the next four years, it was unusual for the latest Dollar single to miss the Top 20. With vocals floating effortlessly above layers of treated sounds, the team's biggest work included: 'Love's Gotta Hold On Me', a revival of the Beatles' 'I Wanna Hold Your Hand', 'Mirror Mirror (Mon Amour)', 'Give Me Back My Heart' and the futuristic 'Videotheque'. By 1982, however, sales had become erratic, and, coupled with failure to crack the US charts, as well as Bazaar and Van Day's growing antagonism towards each other, Dollar signed off with a 'best of' compilation harrying the album lists. While Van Day managed a small hit with 'Young Americans Talking' in 1983, overall lack of record success as individuals prompted a reunion in 1986, but only 'O L'Amour' has since made more than minor impact.

●ALBUMS: *Shooting Stars* (Carrere 1979)★★, *The Dollar Album* (Warners 1982)★★.

●COMPILATIONS: *The Very Best Of Dollar* (Carrere 1982)★★.

DOOBIE BROTHERS

This enduring act evolved from Pud, a San Jose-based trio formed in March 1970 by Tom Johnson (b. Visalia, California, USA; guitar) and John Hartman (b. 18 March 1950, Falls Church, Virginia, USA; drums). Original bassist Greg Murphy was quickly replaced by Dave Shogren (b. San Francisco, California, USA). Patrick Simmons (b. 23 January 1950, Aberdeen, Washington, USA; guitar) then expanded the line-up, and within six months the group had adopted a new name, the Doobie Brothers, in deference to a slang term for a marijuana cigarette. Their muted debut album, although promising, was commercially unsuccessful and contrasted with the unit's tougher live sound. A new bassist, Tiran Porter and second drummer, Michael Hossack (b. 18 September 1950, Paterson, New York, USA), joined the group for *Toulouse Street*, which spawned the anthem-like (and successful) single, 'Listen To The Music'. This confident selection was a marked improvement on its predecessor, while the twin-guitar and twin-percussionist format inspired comparisons with the Allman Brothers Band. A third set, *The Captain And Me*, contained two US hits, 'Long Train Running' and 'China Grove', which have both become standard radio classics, while *What Were Vices...*, a largely disappointing album, did feature the Doobies' first US chart-topper, 'Black Water'. By this point the group's blend of harmonies and tight rock was proving highly popular, although critics pointed to a lack of invention and a reliance on proven formula. Michael Hossack was replaced by Keith Knudsen (b. 18 October 1952, Ames, Iowa, USA) for *Stampede*, which also introduced ex-Steely Dan guitarist, Jeff 'Skunk' Baxter (b. 13 December 1948, Washington, DC, USA). In April 1975, his former colleague, Michael McDonald, (b. 2 December 1952, St. Louis, Missouri, USA; keyboards, vocals) also joined the Doobies when founder member Johnson succumbed to a recurrent ulcer problem. Although the guitarist rejoined the group in 1976, he left again the following year. The arrival of McDonald heralded a new direction. He gradually assumed control of the group's sound, instilling the soul-based perspective revealed on the excellent *Minute By Minute* and its attendant US number 1 single, the ebullient 'What A Fool Believes'. Both Hartman and Baxter then left the line-up, but McDonald's impressive, distinctive voice proved a unifying factor. *Takin' It To The Streets* and its titled hit single maintained a high standard. *One Step Closer* featured newcomers John McFee (b. 18 November 1953, Santa Cruz, California, USA; guitar), Cornelius Bumpus (b. 13 January 1952; saxophone, keyboards) and Chet McCracken (b. 17 July 1952, Seattle, Washington, USA; drums), yet it was arguably the group's most accomplished album. Willie Weeks subsequently replaced Porter, but by 1981 the Doobies' impetus was waning. They split in October the following year, with McDonald and Simmons embarking on contrasting solo careers. Johnson released a solo album in 1979 *Everything You've Heard Is True* and a second in 1981, *Still Feels Good To Me*. However, a re-formed unit, comprising the *Toulouse Street* line-up, plus long-time conga player Bobby Lakind, completed a 1989 release, *Cycles*, on which traces of their one-time verve are still apparent. They found a similar audience and 'The Doctor' made the US Top 10. In 1993 a remixed version of 'Long Train Running' put them back in the charts, although to many 70s fans the Ben Liebrand production added little to the original classic. The Doobie Brothers remain critically underrated, their track record alone making them one of the major US rock bands of the 70s. *Rockin' Down The Highway*, a live album retrospective, demonstrates a sizeable catalogue of hits that are perfect for a live environment.

●ALBUMS: *The Doobie Brothers* (Warners 1971)★★, *Toulouse Street* (Warners 1972)★★★, *The Captain And Me* (Warners 1973)★★★★, *What Were Once Vices Are Now Habits* (Warners 1974)★★★, *Stampede* (Warners 1975)★★★, *Takin' It To The Streets* (Warners 1976)★★★★, *Livin' On The Fault Line* (Warners 1977)★★★, *Minute By Minute* (Warners 1980)★★★★, *One Step Closer* (Warners 1981)★★, *Cycles* (Capitol 1989)★★, *Brotherhood* (Capitol 1991)★, *Rockin' Down The Highway* (Legacy 1996)★★★.

●COMPILATIONS: *The Best Of The Doobie Brothers* (Warners 1976)★★★, *The Best Of The Doobies Volume 2* (Warners 1981)★★★, *Very Best Of The Doobie Brothers* (1993)★★★★.

DOUGLAS, CARL

Jamaican-born Carl Douglas was working with producer Biddu during 1974 when the necessity to record a b-side to 'I Want To Give You My Everything', resulted in 'Kung Fu Fighting', a song which apparently took only 10 minutes to record. When the Douglas composition was presented to the A&R department at Pye Records, they wisely elevated the song to an a-side. Capturing the contemporary interest in Kung Fu in films and magazines, and bestowed with a catchy chorus, the song topped the charts in both the UK and USA. Douglas, gamely dressed in martial arts garb, executed his 'hoo!' and 'haaa!' grunts while performing the song and kept up the novelty long enough to chart again with 'Dance The Kung Fu'. Three years later, Douglas made a return to the UK charts with the Top 30 hit, 'Run Back', since when little has been heard of him.

●ALBUMS: *Carl Douglas* (Pye 1975)★★, *Kung Fu Fighter* (Pye 1976)★★, *Run Back* (Pye 1977)★, *Keep Pleasing Me* (Pye 1978)★.

●COMPILATIONS: *Kung Fu Fighting* (Spectrum 1995)★★.

DR. FEELGOOD

The most enduring act to emerge from the much touted 'pub rock' scene, Dr. Feelgood was formed in 1971. The original line-up included Lee Brilleaux (b. 1953, d. 7 April 1994; vocals/harmonica), Wilko Johnson (b. John Wilkinson, 1947; guitar), John B. Sparks (b. 1953; bass), John Potter (piano) and 'Bandsman' Howarth (drums). When the latter pair dropped out, the remaining trio recruited a permanent drummer in John 'The Big Figure' Martin. Initially based in Canvey Island, Essex, on the Thames estuary, Dr. Feelgood broke into the London circuit in 1974. Brilleaux's menacing personality complemented Johnson's propulsive, jerky stage manner, while the guitarist's staccato style, modelled on Mick Green of the Pirates, emphasized the group's idiosyncratic brand of rhythm and blues. Their debut album, *Down By The Jetty*, was released in 1974, but despite critical approbation, it was not until the following year that the quartet secured due commercial success with *Stupidity*. Recorded live in concert, this raw, compulsive set topped the UK charts and the group's status seemed assured. However, internal friction led to Johnson's departure during sessions for a projected fourth album and although his replacement, John 'Gypie' Mayo, was an accomplished guitarist, he lacked the striking visual image of his predecessor. Dr. Feelgood then embarked on a more mainstream direction which was only intermittently successful. 'Milk And Alcohol' (1978) gave them their sole UK Top 10 hit, but they now seemed curiously anachronistic in the face of the punk upheaval. In 1981 Johnny Guitar replaced Mayo, while the following year both Sparks and the Big Figure decided to leave the line-up. Brilleaux meanwhile continued undeterred, and while Dr. Feelgood could claim a loyal audience, it was an increasingly small one. However, they remained a popular live attraction in the USA where their records also achieved commercial success. In 1993 Brilleaux was diagnosed as having lymphoma and, owing to the extensive treatment he was receiving, had to break the band's often-inexorable touring schedule for the first time in over 20 years. He died the following year.

●ALBUMS: *Down By The Jetty* (United Artists 1975)★★★★, *Malpractice* (United Artists 1975)★★★, *Stupidity* (United Artists 1976)★★★, *Sneakin' Suspicion* (United Artists 1977)★★, *Be Seeing You* (United Artists 1977)★★★, *Private Practice* (United Artists 1978)★★★, *As It Happens* (United Artists 1979)★★★, *Let It Roll* (United Artists 1979)★★, *A Case Of The Shakes* (United Artists 1980)★★, *On The Job* (Liberty 1981)★★, *Fast Women And Slow Horses* (Chiswick 1982)★★, *Mad Man Blues* (I.D. 1985)★★★, *Doctor's Orders* (Demon 1986)★★, *Brilleaux* (Demon 1986)★★, *Classic Dr. Feelgood* (Stiff 1987)★★, *Live In London* (Grand 1990)★★★, *The Feelgood Factor* (1993)★★, *Down At The Doctors* (Grand 1994)★★.

●COMPILATIONS: *Casebook* (Liberty 1981)★★, *Case History - The Best Of Dr. Feelgood* (EMI 1987)★★★, *Singles (The UA Years)* (Liberty 1989)★★★, *Looking Back* 4-CD (EMI 1995)★★★.

DR. HOOK

Sporting denims and buckskin, Dr. Hook And The Medicine Show epitomized much of the countrified and 'laid-back' style that was in vogue during the early 70s, but though their material was sung in a dixie drawl and three members were genuine southerners, they began as a New Jersey bar band with one-eyed Dr. Hook (b.

Ray Sawyer, 1 February 1937, Chicksaw, Alabama, USA; vocals), Denis Locorriere (b. 13 June 1949, New Jersey, USA; guitar/vocals), George Cummings (b. 1938; lead/slide guitar), William Francis (b. 1942; keyboards) and Jay David (b. 1942; drums). One evening they impressed a talent scout looking for an outfit to record *Playboy* cartoonist Shel Silverstein's film score to *Who's Harry Kellerman And Why Is He Saying These Terrible Things About Me?* (1970), and later backed Silverstein's singing on record. As a result, the band were signed to CBS. Almost immediate international success followed with 'Sylvia's Mother' from their debut album. The follow-up, *Sloppy Seconds*, was also penned entirely by Silverstein, and was attended by a hit single that cited portrayal on 'The Cover Of The *Rolling Stone*' (which was dogged by a BBC ban in the UK) as the zenith of the group's ambition - which they later achieved.

Augmented by Rik Elswit (b. 1945; guitar) and Jance Garfat (b. 1944; bass), they embarked on a punishing touring schedule with a diverting act riven with indelicate humour that came to embrace an increasing number of their own compositions. Some were included on *Belly Up* - and the US-only *Fried Face*, their last album before transferring to Capitol - and the first with new drummer John Wolters. By then, the popularity of the group - as plain Dr. Hook - on the boards gave false impressions of their standing in market terms. This was better expressed in the title *Bankrupt*, the fifth album. However, a revival of Sam Cooke's 'Only 16', redressed the balance financially, by rocketing up the US Hot 100. A year later this feat was repeated on a global scale with the title track of *A Little Bit More*. Next came a UK number 1 with 'When You're In Love With A Beautiful Woman' from the million-selling *Pleasure And Pain*. With Locorriere taking the lion's share of lead vocals by then, 1979's *Sometimes You Win* was the wellspring of two more smashes - though a third, 'The Ballad Of Lucy Jordan', was eclipsed for slight Top 50 honours in Britain by Marianne Faithfull's cover.

Throughout the 80s, Dr. Hook's chart strikes were confined mainly to North America (even if a 1981 concert album was taped in London), becoming more sporadic as the decade wore on. Indeed, Sawyer's concentration on solo records, and Locorriere's efforts as a Nashville-based songwriter had all but put the tin lid on Dr. Hook by 1990.

●ALBUMS: *Dr. Hook And the Medicine Show* (Columbia 1972)★★★, *Sloppy Seconds* (Columbia 1972)★★★, *Belly Up* (Columbia 1973)★★, *Fried Face* (Columbia 1974)★★, *Bankrupt* (Capitol 1975)★★, *A Little Bit More* (Capitol 1976)★★★, *Making Love And Music* (Capitol 1977)★★, *Pleasure And Pain* (Capitol 1978)★★★, *Sometimes You Win* (Capitol 1979)★★★, *Rising* (Casablanca 1980)★★, *Live In The UK* (Capitol 1981)★★, *Players In The Dark* (Casablanca 1982)★★.

●COMPILATIONS: *Greatest Hits* (Capitol 1980)★★★, *Completely Hooked-The Best Of Dr. Hook* (Columbia

1992)★★★, *Pleasure And Pain: The History Of Dr. Hook* 3-CD box set (EMI 1996)★★★.
●VIDEOS: *Completely Hooked* (PMI 1992).

DR. JOHN
b. Malcolm John Rebennack, 21 November 1940, New Orleans, Louisiana, USA. Dr. John has built a career since the 60s as a consummate New Orleans musician, incorporating funk, rock 'n' roll, jazz and R&B into his sound. Rebennack's distinctive vocal growl and virtuoso piano playing brought him acclaim among critics and fellow artists, although his commercial successes have not equalled that recognition. Rebennack's musical education began in the 40s when he accompanied his father to blues clubs. At the age of 14 he began frequenting recording studios, and wrote his first songs at that time. By 1957 he was working as a session musician, playing guitar, keyboards and other instruments on recordings issued on such labels as Ace, Ric, Rex and Ebb. He made his first recording under his own name, 'Storm Warning', for Rex during that same year. His first album was recorded for Rex in 1958, and others followed on Ace and AFO Records with little success. In 1958 he also co-wrote 'Lights Out', recorded by Jerry Byrne, and toured with Byrne and Frankie Ford.

By 1962 Rebennack had already played on countless sessions for such renowned producers as Phil Spector, Harold Battiste, H.B. Barnum and Sonny Bono (later of Sonny And Cher). Rebennack formed his own bands during the early 60s but they did not take off. By the mid-60s Rebennack had moved to Los Angeles, where he fused his New Orleans roots with the emerging west coast psychedelic sound, and he developed the persona Dr. John Creux, The Night Tripper. The character was based on one established by singer Prince La La, but Rebennack made it his own through the intoxicating brew of voodoo incantations and New Orleans heritage. An album, *Zu Zu Man*, for A&M Records, did not catch on when released in 1965.

In 1968 Dr. John was signed to Atco Records and released *Gris Gris*, which received critical acclaim but did not chart. This exceptional collection included the classic 'Walk On Gilded Splinters' and inspired several similarly styled successors, winning respect from fellow musicians, resulting in Eric Clapton and Mick Jagger guesting on a later album. The same musical formula and exotic image were pursued on follow-up albums *Babylon* and *Remedies*. Meanwhile, he toured on the rock festival and ballroom circuit and continued to do session work. In 1971, Dr. John charted for the first time with *Dr. John, The Night Tripper (The Sun, Moon And Herbs)*. The 1972 *Gumbo* album, produced by Jerry Wexler, charted, as did the single, 'Iko Iko'. His biggest US hit came in 1973 with the single 'Right Place, Wrong Time', which reached number 9; the accompanying album, *In The Right Place*, was also his best-selling, hitting number 24. These crafted, colourful albums featured the instrumental muscle of the Meters, but despite a newfound popularity, the artist parted from his record label, Atlantic, and subsequent work failed to achieve a similar status.

During that year he toured with the New Orleans band the Meters, and recorded *Triumvirate* with Michael Bloomfield and John Hammond. The single 'Such A Night' also charted in 1973. Dr. John continued to record throughout the 70s and 80s, for numerous labels, among them United Artists, Horizon and Clean Cuts, the latter releasing *Dr. John Plays Mac Rebennack*, a solo piano album, in 1981. In the meantime, he continued to draw sizeable audiences as a concert act across the USA, and added radio jingle work to his live and recording work (he continued to play on many sessions). He recorded *Bluesiana Triangle* with jazz musicians Art Blakey and David 'Fathead' Newman and released *In A Sentimental Mood*, a collection of interpretations of standards including a moody duet with Rickie Lee Jones, on Warner Brothers Records. Despite employing a low-key approach to recording, Dr. John has remained a respected figure. His live appearances are now less frequent, but this irrepressible artist continues his role as a tireless champion of Crescent City music.

●ALBUMS: *Gris Gris* (Atco 1968)★★★★, *Babylon* (Atco 1969)★★★, *Remedies* (Atco 1970)★★★, *Dr. John, The Night Tripper (The Sun, Moon And Herbs)* (Atco 1971)★★★, *Dr. John's Gumbo* (Atco 1972)★★★★, *In The Right Place* (Atco 1973)★★★, with John Hammond, Mike Bloomfield *Triumvirate* (Columbia 1973)★★★, *Desitively Bonnaroo* (Atco 1974)★★★, *Hollywood Be Thy Name* (United Artists 1975)★★, *Cut Me While I'm Hot* (1975)★★, *City Lights* (Horizon 1978)★★★, *Tango Palace* (Horizon 1979)★★, *Love Potion* (1981)★★, *Dr. John Plays Mac Rebennack* (Clean Cuts 1982)★★★, *The Brightest Smile In Town* (Clean Cuts 1983)★★★, with Chris Barber *Take Me Back To New Orleans* (1983)★★★, *Such A Night - Live In London* (Spindrift 1984)★★★, *In A Sentimental Mood* (Warners 1989)★★, *Going Back To New Orleans* (1992)★★★, *Television* (GRP 1994)★★, *Afterglow* (Blue Thumb 1995)★★.

●COMPILATIONS: *I Been Hoodood* (Edsel 1984)★★★, *In The Night* (Topline 1985)★★★, *Zu Zu Man* (Topline 1987)★★★, *Bluesiana Triangle* (1990)★★★, *Mos' Scocious* 2-CD (Rhino 1994)★★★★, *The Best Of ...* (Rhino 1995)★★★★.

●FURTHER READING: *Dr. John: Under A Hoodoo Moon*, Mac Rebennack with Jack Rummel.

DRAKE, NICK

b. 19 June 1948, Burma, d. 25 November 1974. Born into an upper middle-class background, Drake was raised in Tanworth-in-Arden, near Birmingham. Recordings made at his parents' home in 1967 revealed a blossoming talent, indebted to Bert Jansch and John Renbourn, yet clearly a songwriter in his own right. He enrolled at Fitzwilliam College in Cambridge, and during this spell met future associate Robert Kirby.

Drake also made several live appearances and was discovered at one such performance by Fairport Convention bassist, Ashley Hutchings, who introduced the folk singer to their producer Joe Boyd. A series of demos were then completed, part of which surfaced on the posthumous release *Time Of No Reply*, before Drake began work on his debut album.

Five Leaves Left was a mature, melodic collection which invoked the mood of Van Morrison's *Astral Weeks* or Tim Buckley's *Happy Sad*. Drake's languid, almost unemotional intonation contrasted with the warmth of his musical accompaniment, in particular Robert Kirby's temperate string sections. Contributions from Richard Thompson (guitar) and Danny Thompson (bass) were equally crucial, adding texture to a set of quite remarkable compositions. By contrast *Bryter Layter* was altogether more worldly, and featured support from emphatic, rather than intuitive, musicians. Lyn Dobson (flute) and Ray Warleigh (saxophone) provided a jazz-based perspective to parts of a selection which successfully married the artist's private and public aspirations. Indisputably Drake's most commercial album, the singer was reportedly stunned when it failed to reap due reward and the departure of Boyd for America accentuated his growing misgivings. A bout of severe depression followed, but late in 1971 Nick resumed recording with the harrowing *Pink Moon*. Completed in two days, its stark, almost desolate atmosphere made for uncomfortable listening, yet beneath its loneliness lay a poignant beauty. Two songs, 'Parasite' and 'Place To Be' dated from 1969, while 'Things Behind The Sun' had once been considered for *Bryter Layter*. These inclusions suggested that Drake now found composing difficult, and it was 1974 before he re-entered a studio. Four tracks were completed, of which 'Black Eyed Dog', itself a metaphor for death, seemed a portent of things to come. On 25 November 1974, Nick Drake was found dead in his bedroom. Although the coroner's verdict was suicide, relatives and acquaintances feel that his overdose of a prescribed drug was accidental. Interest in this ill-fated performer has increased over the years and his catalogue contains some of the era's most accomplished music. Drake is now seen as a hugely influential artist.

●ALBUMS: *Five Leaves Left* (Island 1969)★★★★, *Bryter Layter* (Island 1970)★★★★, *Pink Moon* (Island 1972)★★★.

●COMPILATIONS: *Heaven In A Wild Flower* (Island 1985)★★★★, *Fruit Tree* 4-LP (Island 1979)★★★★, *Time Of No Reply* (Hannibal 1986)★★★, *Way To Blue* (Island 1994)★★★★.

●FURTHER READING: *Nick Drake*, David Housden.

DRANSFIELD, ROBIN AND BARRY

Brothers Robin (guitar, banjo, vocals) and Barry Dransfield (fiddle, guitar, mandolin, gimbri, cello, vocals), both born in Harrogate, Yorkshire, England, were popular folk traditionalists who enjoyed a high profile during the 70s. They began singing and playing together in 1962, as part of a Leeds-based bluegrass band, the Crimple Mountain Boys. The group only lasted for three years, at the end of which Robin and Barry decided to concentrate on indigenous British music. Barry turned professional in 1966, having been a civil servant. Robin waited until 1969 before joining him, having performed in clubs while holding down a teaching post. *Rout Of The Blues*, its title track the first song they had worked on together, was released by Bill Leader Records in 1970. Their rising profile saw them invited to join Steeleye Span at this time, an offer they declined, though they did become close allies of Ashley Hutchings. They appeared at London's Royal Albert Hall Festival in 1971 and, in addition to Barry's fiddle tunes, contributed four tracks to the ensuing album, including 'Who's The Fool Now' and 'The Waters Of Tyne'. After touring America and participating in the *Morris On* project, the brothers then formed their own folk rock band. *Fiddler's Dream* (1976), with contributions from Brian Harrison, was the result, followed by the more traditional *Popular To Contrary Belief* (1977). Although they remained popular in mainland Europe, the brothers gradually became disillusioned with the non-stop touring. 'Neither of us was stuck with music. Robin was a teacher and I was perfectly capable of making a living as a carpenter,' he recalled. Both have subsequently released solo albums.

●ALBUMS: *Rout Of The Blues* (Bill Leader 1970)★★★, *Lord Of All I Behold* (Bill Leader 1971)★★★, *The Fiddler's Dream* (Free Reed 1976)★★★, *Popular To Contrary Belief* (Free Reed 1977)★★★.

DUKE, GEORGE

b. 12 January 1946, San Rafael, California, USA. Duke studied the piano at school (where he ran a Les McCann-inspired Latin band) and emerged from the San Francisco Conservatory as a Bachelor of Music in 1967. From 1965-67 he was resident pianist at the Half Note, accompanying musicians such as Dizzy Gillespie and Kenny Dorham. This grounding served as a musical education for the rest of his life. He arranged for a vocal group, the Third Wave, and toured Mexico in 1968. In 1969 he began playing with French violinist Jean-Luc Ponty, using electric piano to accompany Ponty's plugged-in violin. He played on *King Kong*, an album of music Frank Zappa composed for Ponty. He then joined Zappa's group in 1970, an experience that transformed his music. As he put it, previously he had been too 'musically advanced' to play rock 'n' roll piano triplets. Zappa encouraged him to sing and joke and use electronics. Together they wrote 'Uncle Remus' for *Apostrophe* (1972), a song about black attitudes to oppression. His keyboards contributed to a great edition of the Mothers Of Invention - captured in the outstanding *Roxy & Elsewhere* (1975) - which combined fluid jazz playing with rock and *avant garde* sonorities. In 1972 he toured with Cannonball Adderley (replacing

Joe Zawinul). Duke had always had a leaning towards soul jazz and after he left Zappa, he went for full-frontal funk. *I Love The Blues She Heard My Cry* (1975) combined a retrospective look at black musical forms with warm good humour and freaky musical ideas: a duet with Johnny Guitar Watson was particularly successful. Duke started duos with fusion power-drummer Billy Cobham, and virtuoso bassist Stanley Clarke, playing quintessential 70s jazz rock: amplification and much attention to 'chops' being the order of the day. Duke always had a sense of humour: 1978's 'Dukey Stick' sounded like a Funkadelic record. The middle of the road beckoned, however, and by *Brazilian Love Affair* (1979) he was merely providing high class background music. In 1982 *Dream On* showed him happily embracing west coast hip easy listening. However, there has always been an unpredictable edge to Duke. The band he put together for the Wembley Nelson Mandela concert in London backed a stream of soul singers, and his arrangement of 'Backyard Ritual' on Miles Davis's *Tutu* (1986) was excellent. He collaborated with Clarke again for the funk-styled 3 and in 1992 he bounced back with the jazz fusion *Snapshot* followed by the orchestral suite *Enchanted Forest* in 1996 and *Is Love Enough?* in 1997.

●ALBUMS: *Jazz Workshop of San Francisco* (1966)★★★, with Jean-Luc Ponty *Live In Los Angeles* (1969)★★★, *The Inner Source* (1971)★★★, *Feel* (MPS 1975)★★★, *The Aura WIll Prevail* (MPS 1975)★★★, *I Love The Blues, She Heard My Cry* (MPS 1975)★★★, with Billy Cobham *Live - On Tour In Europe* (Atlantic 1976)★★★, *Liberated Fantasies* (MPS 1976)★★★, *From Me To You* (Epic 1977)★★★, *Reach For It* (Epic 1977)★★★, *Don't Let Go* (Epic 1978)★★, *Follow The Rainbow* (Epic 1979)★★, *Master Of The Game* (Epic 1979)★★, *A Brazilian Love Affair* (Epic 1979)★★★, *Primal* (MPS 1979)★★★, *Secret Rendevous* (Epic 1979)★★★, with Clarke *Clarke Duke Project* (1981)★★★★, *Dream On* (Epic 1982)★★, *Guardian Of The Light* (Epic 1983)★★★, with Clarke *The Clarke/Duke Project II* (Epic 1983)★★★★, *1976 Solo Keyboard Album* (Epic 1983)★★★, *Thief In The Night* (Elektra 1985)★★★, *Night After Night* (Elektra 1989)★★★, with Duke *3* (Epic 1990)★★★, *Reach For It* (Sony 1991)★★★, *Snapshot* (Warners 1992)★★★, *Enchanted Forest: Muir Woods Suite* (Warners 1996)★★★, *Is Love Enough* (Warners 1997)★★★.

●COMPILATIONS: *The Collection* (Castle 1991)★★★.

DUNBAR, AYNSLEY

b. 10 January 1946, Lancaster, Lancashire, England. This respected drummer served his musical apprenticeship in numerous Merseybeat bands, including Derry Wilkie And The Pressmen, Freddie Starr And The Flamingos and the Excheckers. Dunbar joined the Mojos in March 1965, but the following year he replaced Hughie Flint in John Mayall's Bluesbreakers. His skills were apparent on the group's *A Hard Road* (1967) and a later recording, 'Rubber Duck', which

formed the b-side of a Bluesbreakers' single. This propulsive instrumental is memorable for its fiery drum solo. Aynsley briefly joined the Jeff Beck Group in April 1967, before leaving six months later to pursue a career with his own quartet, the Aynsley Dunbar Retaliation. This compulsive, blues-based attraction was responsible for four excellent albums, but their leader left the line-up in 1969 to form a larger, brass-based unit, Aynsley Dunbar's Blue Whale. The unit's lone album included a version of Frank Zappa's 'Willie The Pimp', a coincidental inclusion given that Dunbar then joined the former's group, the Mothers Of Invention. A member between 1970 and 1972, Dunbar then defected with four other members to form Flo And Eddie. By this point Aynsley had become an established session musician, contributing to albums by David Bowie (*Pin-Ups*), Lou Reed (*Berlin*) and Ian Hunter (*All American Alien Boy*). He joined Journey in 1974, but left four years later in order to replace John Barbata in Jefferson Starship. Dunbar remained with this successful act until 1982, since when he has maintained a lower professional profile.
●ALBUMS: *Aynsley Dunbar's Blue Whale* (Warners 1970)★★.

DUNCAN, LESLEY

This UK-born singer and songwriter became popular in the commercial side of the folk music field. Although starting out as a songwriter, and married to record producer Jimmy Horowitz, she became better known for her work as a session singer, especially during the 70s. It was Elton John's version of her composition 'Love Song', on his album *Tumbleweed Connection*, that inspired her to record *Sing Children Sing*. Her own albums suffered from a lack of commercial success, which was at odds with her popularity as a backing singer on a host of albums by acts as diverse as Long John Baldry, Tim Hardin, Donovan, the Alan Parson's Project, Pink Floyd, on *Dark Side Of The Moon*, and even Bunk Dogger. After her two releases on CBS, she left the label, and subsequent releases were on GM Records. Her reluctance to perform live did not help to raise her public profile. Apart from providing backing vocals for an album by Exiled, in 1980, her name has sadly been missing from sleevenote credits.
●ALBUMS: *Sing Children Sing* (Columbia 1971)★★★, *Earth Mother* (Columbia 1972)★★★, *Everything Changes* (GM 1974)★★★, *Moonbathing* (GM 1975)★★★, *Maybe It's Lost* (GM 1977)★★★.

DUNDAS, DAVID

b. *c*.1945, Oxford, England. The son of the Marquess of Zetland, Dundas' original vocation in life was as an actor, mainly playing minor roles on stage, television and film, at one point working alongside Judy Geeson and David Niven in *Prudence And The Pill* (1968). Eschewing the actor's life, Dundas' claim to fame in the music world came when, as an advertising jingle writer,

his work for the Brutus jeans advert on UK television spawned the hit single 'Jeans On'. The Dundas composition was fleshed out with help from Roger Greenaway, and released on the Air/Chrysalis label, eventually reaching number 3 in the UK charts in the summer of 1976. The tune also reached the US Top 20 in January the following year. His only other UK chart entry came in 1977 with 'Another Funny Honeymoon' which reached number 29. He released two, for the most part, unremarkable albums for Chrysalis before taking up a career as a composer. His recent credits include the scores for *Dark City*, *Withnail And I* (with Rick Wentworth) and *How To Get Ahead In Advertising*.
●ALBUMS: *David Dundas* (Air 1977)★★, *Vertical Hold* (Air 1978)★★.

DUROCS

Formed in 1979, this San Francisco-based act was comprised of Ron Nagle (vocals/keyboards) and Scott Mathews (guitar/drums). Both musicians brought considerable experience to the project; Nagle, who founded the pioneering Mystery Trend, composed incidental music to several horror films, notably *The Exorcist* and co-wrote 'Don't Touch Me There', a best-seller for the Tubes. Mathews, meanwhile, was an ex-member of several groups, including the Elvin Bishop Band and the Hoodoo Rhythm Devils. The duo's songs were recorded by Michelle Phillips and Barbra Streisand, and having built a recording studio, the Pen, completed *The Durocs*, which took its name from a breed of pig noted for its large ears and genitals. The album was a strong effort but sold poorly, and the project was abandoned when Capitol Records refused to release a second set. Undeterred, the duo continued to compose and record together, and later released a single under a new name, the Profits. Their version of 'I'm A Hog For You Baby' continued the porcine metaphor, as did its Proud Pork Productions credit. Music notwithstanding, Nagle has since become one of the USA's leading exponents of ceramic art.
●ALBUMS: *The Durocs* (Capitol 1979)★★★.

DURY, IAN

b. 12 May 1942, Upminster, Essex, England. The zenith of Dury's musical career, *New Boots And Panties*, came in 1977, when youth was being celebrated amid power chords and bondage trousers - he was 35 at the time. Stricken by polio at the age of seven, he initially decided on a career in art, and until his 28th birthday taught the subject at Canterbury School of Art. He began playing pubs and clubs in London with Kilburn And The High Roads, reinterpreting R&B numbers and later adding his own wry lyrics in a semi-spoken cockney slang. The group dissolved and the remainder became a new line-up called the Blockheads. In 1975 Stiff Records signed the group and considered Dury's aggressive but honest stance the perfect summary of the contemporary mood. The Blockheads' debut and finest moment, *New Boots And Panties*, received superlative reviews and spent more than a year in the UK albums chart. His dry wit, sensitivity and brilliant lyrical caricatures were evident in songs like 'Clever Trevor', 'Wake Up And Make Love To Me' and his tribute to Gene Vincent, 'Sweet Gene Vincent'. He lampooned the excesses of the music business on 'Sex And Drugs And Rock And Roll' and briefly crossed over from critical acclaim to commercial acceptance with the UK number 1 'Hit Me With Your Rhythm Stick' in December 1979. *Do It Yourself* and *Laughter* were similarly inspired although lacking the impact of his debut, and by his third album he had teamed up with Wilko Johnson (ex-Dr. Feelgood) and lost the co-writing services of pianist Chaz Jankel. He continued to work towards a stronger dance context and employed the masterful rhythm section of Sly Dunbar and Robbie Shakespeare on *Lord Upminster* which also featured the celebrated jazz trumpeter Don Cherry. He continued to make thoughtful, polemic records in the 80s and audaciously suggested that his excellent song, 'Spasticus Autisticus', should be adopted as the musical emblem of the Year Of The Disabled. Like many before him, he turned to acting and appeared in several television plays and films in the late 80s. In 1989 he wrote the musical *Apples* with another former member of the Blockheads, Mickey Gallagher. In the 90s Dury was seen hosting a late night UK television show *Metro* and continued to tour, being able to dictate his own pace.

●ALBUMS: *New Boots And Panties* (Stiff 1977)★★★★, *Do It Yourself* (Stiff 1979)★★★, *Laughter* (Stiff 1980)★★★, *Lord Upminster* (Polydor 1981)★★★, *Juke Box Dury* (Stiff 1981)★★, *4,000 Weeks Holiday* (Polydor 1984)★★★, *The Bus Driver's Prayer And Other Stories* (1992)★★★.

●COMPILATIONS: *Greatest Hits* (Fame 1981)★★★, *The Best Of ...* (Repertoire 1995)★★★, *Reasons To Be Cheerful* (Repertoire 1996)★★★.

EAGLES

Formed in Los Angeles, California, in 1971, this highly successful unit consisted of musicians drawn from singer Linda Ronstadt's backing group. Of the original quartet, Bernie Leadon (b. 19 July 1947, Minneapolis, Minnesota, USA; guitar/vocals) boasted the most prodigious pedigree, having embraced traditional country music with the Scottsville Squirrel Barkers, before bringing such experience to rock as a member of Hearts And Flowers, Dillard And Clark and the Flying Buritto Brothers. Randy Meisner (b. 8 March 1947, Scottsbluff, Nabraska, USA; bass/vocals) was formerly of Poco and Rick Nelson's Stone Canyon Band; Glenn Frey (b. 6 November 1948, Detroit, Michigan, USA; guitar/vocals) had recorded as half of Longbranch Pennywhistle; while Don Henley (b. 22 July 1947, Gilmer, Texas, USA; drums/vocals) had led Texas-based aspirants Shiloh. Such pedigrees ensured interest in the new venture, which was immediately signed to David Geffen's nascent Asylum label. *The Eagles*, recorded in London under the aegis of producer Glyn Johns, contained 'Take It Easy', co-written by Frey and Jackson Browne and 'Witchy Woman', both of which reached the US Top 20 and established the quartet's meticulous harmonies and relaxed, but purposeful country rock sound. Critical reaction to *Desperado*, an ambitious concept album based on a western theme, firmly established the group as leaders in their field and contained several of their most enduring compositions including the pleadingly emotional title track. The follow-up, *On The Border*, reasserted the unit's commerciality. 'Best Of My Love' became their first US number 1 while new member Don Felder (b. 21 September 1947, Topanga, California, USA; guitar/vocals), drafted from David Blue's backing group in March 1974, considerably bolstered the Eagles' sound. The reshaped quintet reached superstar status with *One Of These Nights*, the title track from which also topped the US charts. This platinum-selling album included 'Lyin' Eyes', now considered a standard on Gold format radio, and the anthemic 'Take It To The Limit'. The album also established the Eagles as an international act; each of these tracks had reached the UK Top 30, but the new-found pressure proved too great for Leadon who left the line-up in December 1975. He subsequently pursued a low-key career with the Leadon-Georgiades band. His replacement was Joe Walsh (b. 20 November 1947, Wichita, Kansas, USA), former lead guitarist with the James Gang and a successful solo artist in his own right. His somewhat surprising induction was tempered by the knowledge that he shared the same manager as his new colleagues. The choice was ratified by the powerful *Hotel California*, which topped the US album charts for eight weeks and spawned two number 1 singles in the title track and 'New Kid In Town'. The set has become the Eagles' most popular collection, selling nine million copies worldwide in its year of release alone (by 1996, 14 million in the USA), as well as appearing in many 'all time classic' albums listings. A seasonal recording, 'Please Come Home For Christmas', was the quintet's sole recorded offering for 1978 and internal ructions the following year resulted in Meisner's departure. His replacement, Timothy B. Schmit (b. 30 October 1947, Sacramento, California, USA), was another former member of Poco, but by this point the Eagles' impetus was waning. *The Long Run* was generally regarded as disappointing, despite containing a fifth US number 1 in 'Heartache Tonight', and a temporary hiatus taken at the end of the decade became a fully-fledged break in 1982 when longstanding disagreements could not be resolved. Henley, Frey and Felder began solo careers with contrasting results, while Walsh resumed the path he had followed prior to joining the group.

Although latterly denigrated as representing 70s musical conservatism and torpidity, the Eagles' quest for perfection and committed musical skills rightly led to their becoming one of the era's leading acts. It was no surprise that they eventually re-formed, after months of speculation. The resulting album proved that they were still one of the world's most popular acts. Their 1994/5 tour of the USA was (apart from the Rolling Stones parallel tour) the largest grossing on record. With the over-indulgences of the 70s behind them, it is an exciting prospect to look forward to an Eagles album of new songs, written with the patina of age. In the meantime the public are happy to continue to purchase their two greatest hits packages: *Volume 1* has now overtaken Michael Jackson's *Thriller* as the biggest-selling album of all time, with 24 million units in the USA alone.

●ALBUMS: *The Eagles* (Asylum 1972)★★★, *Desperado* (Asylum 1973)★★★★, *On The Border* (Asylum 1974)★★★★, *One Of These Nights* (Asylum 1975)★★★, *Hotel California* (Asylum 1976)★★★★★, *The Long Run* (Asylum 1979)★★, *Eagles-Live* (Asylum 1980)★★, *Hell Freezes Over* (Geffen 1994)★★★.

●COMPILATIONS: *Their Greatest Hits 1971-1975* (Asylum 1976)★★★★, *Greatest Hits Volume 2* (Asylum 1982)★★★, *Best Of The Eagles* (Asylum 1985)★★★.

●VIDEOS: *Hell Freezes Over* (Geffen Home Video 1994).

●FURTHER READING: *The Eagles*, John Swenson. *The Long Run: The Story Of The Eagles*, Marc Shapiro.

EARTH, WIND AND FIRE

The origins of this colourful, imaginative group date back to the 60s and Chicago's black music session circle. Drummer Maurice White (b. 19 December 1941,

Memphis, Tennessee, USA) appeared on sessions for Etta James, Fontella Bass, Billy Stewart and more, before joining the Ramsey Lewis Trio in 1965. He left four years later to form the Salty Peppers, which prepared the way for an early version of Earth Wind and Fire.

The new group - Verdine White (b. 25 July 1951, Illinois, USA; bass), Michael Beale (guitar), Wade Flemmons (vocals), Sherry Scott (vocals), Alex Thomas (trombone), Chet Washington (tenor saxophone), Don Whitehead (keyboards) and Yackov Ben Israel (percussion) - embarked on a diffuse direction, embracing jazz, R&B and funk, as well as elements of Latin and ballad styles. The extended jam, 'Energy', from their second album, was artistically brave, but showed a lack of cohesion within the group. White then abandoned the line-up, save his brother, and pieced together a second group around Ronnie Laws (b. 3 October 1950, Houston, Texas, USA; saxophone/guitar), Philip Bailey (b. 8 May 1951, Denver, Colorado, USA; vocals), Larry Dunn (b. Lawrence Dunhill, 19 June 1953, Colorado, USA; keyboards), Roland Battista (guitar) and Jessica Cleaves (b. 1948; vocals). He retained the mystic air of the original group but tightened the sound immeasurably, blending the disparate elements into an intoxicating 'fire'. Two 1974 releases, *Head To The Sky* and *Open Our Eyes* established the group as an album act, while the following year 'Shining Star' was a number 1 hit in both the US R&B and pop charts. Their eclectic mixture of soul and jazz was now fused to an irresistible rhythmic pulse, while the songs themselves grew ever more memorable. By the end of the decade they had regular successes with such infectious melodious singles as 'Fantasy', 'September', 'After The Love Has Gone' and 'Boogie Wonderland', the latter an energetic collaboration with the Emotions. A further recording, 'Got To Get You Into My Life', transformed the song into the soul classic composer Paul McCartney had originally envisaged.

The line-up of Earth, Wind And Fire remained unstable. Philip Bailey and Ronnie Laws both embarked on solo careers as new saxophonists, guitarists and percussionists were added. White's interest in Egyptology and mysticism provided a visual platform for the expanded group, particularly in their striking live performances. However, following 11 gold albums, 1983's *Electric Universe* was an unexpected commercial flop, and prompted a four-year break. A slimline core quintet, comprising the White brothers, Andrew Woolfolk, Sheldon Reynolds and Philip Bailey, recorded *Touch The World* in 1987 but they failed to reclaim their erstwhile standing. *Heritage* (1990) featured cameos from rapper MC Hammer and Sly Stone, in an attempt to shift White's vision into the new decade.

●ALBUMS: *Earth, Wind And Fire* (Warners 1971)★★, *The Need Of Love* (Warners 1972)★★, *Last Days And Time* (Columbia 1972)★★, *Head To The Sky* (Columbia 1973)★★★, *Open Our Eyes* (Columbia 1974)★★★★,

That's The Way Of The World (Columbia 1975)★★★★, *Gratitude* (Columbia 1975)★★★, *Spirit* (Columbia 1976)★★★, *All And All* (Columbia 1977)★★★, *I Am* (ARC 1979)★★★, *Faces* (ARC 1980)★★★, *Raise!* (ARC 1981)★★★, *Powerlight* (Columbia 1983)★★★, *Electric Universe* (Columbia 1983)★★, *Touch The World* (Columbia 1987)★★★, *Heritage* (Columbia 1990)★★, *Millennium* (1993)★★★, *Greatest Hits Live, Tokyo Japan* (Rhino 1996)★★.

●COMPILATIONS: *The Best Of Earth, Wind And Fire, Volume 1* (ARC 1978)★★★★, *The Collection* (K-Tel 1986)★★★, *The Best Of Earth, Wind And Fire, Volume 2* (Columbia 1988)★★★★, *The Eternal Dance* (1993)★★★, *The Very Best Of* (1993)★★★.

EDDIE AND THE HOT RODS

Formed in 1975, this quintet from Southend, Essex, England, originally comprised Barrie Masters (vocals), Lew Lewis (harmonica), Paul Gray (bass), Dave Higgs (guitar), Steve Nicol (drums) plus 'Eddie', a short-lived dummy that Masters pummelled onstage. After one classic single, 'Writing On The Wall', Lewis left, though he appeared on the high energy 'Horseplay', the flip-side of their cover of Sam The Sham And The Pharoahs' 'Wooly Bully'. Generally regarded as a younger, more energetic version of Dr. Feelgood, the Rods pursued a tricky route between the conservatism of pub rock and the radicalism of punk. During the summer of 1976, the group broke house records at the Marquee Club with a scorching series of raucous, sweat-drenched performances. Their power was well captured on a live EP which included a cover of ? And The Mysterians' '96 Tears' and a clever amalgamation of the Rolling Stones' 'Satisfaction' and Them's 'Gloria'. The arrival of guitarist Graeme Douglas from the Kursaal Flyers gave the group a more commercial edge and a distinctive jingle-jangle sound. A guest appearance on former MC5 singer Robin Tyner's 'Till The Night Is Gone' was followed by the strident 'Do Anything You Want To Do', which provided a Top 10 hit in the UK. A fine second album, *Life On The Line*, was striking enough to suggest a long term future, but the group fell victim to diminishing returns. Douglas left, followed by Gray, who joined the Damned. Masters disbanded the group for a spell but re-formed the unit for pub gigs and small label appearances.

●ALBUMS: *Teenage Depression* (Island 1976)★★★★, *Life On The Line* (Island 1977)★★★, *Thriller* (Island 1979)★★, *Fish 'N' Chips* (EMI America 1980)★★, *Gasoline Days* (Creative Man 1996)★★.

●COMPILATIONS: *The Curse Of The Rods* (Hound Dog 1990)★★★, *Live And Rare* (Receiver 1993)★★, *The Best Of … The End Of The Beginning* (Island 1995)★★★.

EDMUNDS, DAVE

b. 15 April 1944, Cardiff, Wales. The multi-talented Edmunds has sustained a career for many years by being totally in touch with modern trends while main-taining a passionate love for music of the 50s and 60s, notably rockabilly, rock 'n' roll and country music. He first came to the public eye as lead guitarist of Love Sculpture with an astonishing solo played at breakneck speed on their only hit, Khatchaturian's 'Sabre Dance'. At the end of the 60s Edmunds built his own recording studio, Rockfield. The technical capabilities of Rockfield soon became apparent, as Edmunds became a masterful producer working with Shakin' Stevens, the Flamin' Groovies and Brinsley Schwarz. The latter's bass player was Nick Lowe, and they formed a musical partnership that lasted many years. Edmunds' own recordings were few, but successful. He brilliantly reproduced the sound of his rock 'n' roll heroes and had hits with Smiley Lewis's 'I Hear You Knocking', the Ronettes' 'Baby, I Love You' and the Chordettes, 'Born To Be With You'. The first was a worldwide hit selling several million copies and topping the UK charts. In 1975 his debut *Subtle As A Flying Mallet* was eclipsed by his credible performance in the film *Stardust*, and he wrote and sang on most of the Jim McLaine (David Essex) tracks. *Get It* in 1977 featured the fast-paced Nick Lowe composition, 'I Knew the Bride' which gave Edmunds another hit. Lowe wrote many of the songs on *Tracks On Wax* in 1978, during a hectic stage in Edmunds' career when he played with Emmylou Harris, Carl Perkins, with his own band Rockpile, and appeared at the Knebworth Festival and the Rock For Kampuchea concert. *Repeat When Necessary* arrived in 1979 to favourable reviews; it stands as his best album. He interpreted Elvis Costello's 'Girls Talk', giving it a full production with layers of guitars, and the record was a major hit. Other outstanding tracks were 'Crawling From The Wreckage' written by Graham Parker, 'Queen Of Hearts' and the 50s sounding 'Sweet Little Lisa'.

The latter contained arguably one of the finest rocka-billy/country guitar solos ever recorded, although the perpetrator is Albert Lee and not Edmunds. The fickle public ignored the song and the album barely scraped into the Top 40. The following year Edmunds succeeded with Guy Mitchell's 50s hit 'Singin' The Blues' and the road-weary Rockpile released their only album, having been previously prevented from doing so for contractual reasons. The regular band of Edmunds, Lowe, Billy Bremner and Terry Williams was already a favourite on the UK pub-rock circuit. Their *Seconds Of Pleasure* was unable to do justice to the atmosphere they created at live shows, although it was a successful album. In 1981 Edmunds charted again, teaming up with the Stray Cats and recording George Jones' 'The Race Is On', although a compilation of Edmunds' work that year failed to sell. His style changed for the Jeff Lynne-produced *Information* in 1983; not surprisingly he sounded more like Lynne's ELO. As a producer he won many friends by crafting the Everly Brothers' comeback albums *EB84* and *Born Yesterday* and he wrote much of the soundtrack for *Porky's Revenge*. He was pro-

ducer of the television tribute to Carl Perkins; both Edmunds and George Harrison are long-time admirers, and Edmunds cajoled the retiring Harrison to make a rare live appearance. During the mid-80s Edmunds worked with the Fabulous Thunderbirds, Jeff Beck, Dr. Feelgood, k.d. lang and Status Quo. His own music was heard during his first tour for some years together with the live *I Hear You Rockin'*, although more attention was given to Edmunds for bringing Dion back into the centre stage with live gigs and an album. Edmunds has made a major contribution to popular music by working creatively, mostly in the background, surfacing occasionally with his own product. This demonstrates a man without ego and one who has always put a love of music first and as the most important end product.
●ALBUMS: *Subtle As A Flying Mallet* (RCA 1975)★★★, *Get It* (Swansong 1977)★★★, *Tracks On Wax* (Swansong 1978)★★★, *Repeat When Necessary* (Swansong 1979)★★★★, as Rockpile *Seconds Of Pleasure* (F-Beat 1980)★★★, *Twangin'* (Arista 1981)★★★, *D.E.7th* (Arista 1982)★★★, *Information* (Arista 1983)★★, *Riff Raff* (Arista 1984)★★, *I Hear You Rockin'* (Arista 1987)★★★, *Closer To The Flame* (Capitol 1990)★★, *Plugged In* (Columbia 1994)★★★.
●COMPILATIONS: *The Best Of Dave Edmunds* (Swansong 1981)★★★★, *The Original Rockpile Vol. 2* (Harvest 1987)★★★, *The Complete Early Edmunds* (EMI 1991)★★★, *Chronicles* (Connoisseur 1995)★★★★.
●FILMS: *Give My Regards To Broad Street* (1985).

EGAN, JOE

b. c.1944 Scotland. The former partner of Gerry Rafferty in Stealers Wheel, Egan recorded two low-key albums after their final disintegration. *Out Of Nowhere* contained the charming 'Back On The Road Again', a turntable hit on UK radio. Both albums were similar in structure to the three Stealers Wheel collections and demonstrated the considerable songwriting ability of Egan, who sadly was unable to find his own 'Baker Street'. After a number of years of musical inactivity Egan worked with Rafferty by adding some backing vocals on his 1993 album *On A Wing & A Prayer*. He also benefitted from the use of the Rafferty/Egan composition 'Stuck In The Middle With You' in the film *Reservoir Dogs* that same year.
●ALBUMS: *Out Of Nowhere* (Ariola 1979)★★★, *Map* (Ariola 1981)★★.

EGAN, WALTER

b. 12 July 1948, Jamaica, New York, USA. An accomplished singer, guitarist and songwriter, Egan first attracted attention on a UK tour, accompanying former Kaleidoscope member Chris Darrow. Their association helped introduce the younger musician to the Los Angeles-based fraternity and he achieved due recognition when one of his songs, 'Hearts On Fire', was recorded by Gram Parsons. He then formed the short-lived Southpaw, which also included Jules Shear and

Stephen Hague. In 1976 Egan embarked on a solo career. *Fundamental Roll* was produced by Fleetwood Mac mainstays Lindsay Buckingham and Stevie Nicks, while the former was also responsible for overseeing a second set, *Not Shy*. This entertaining album included 'Magnet And Steel', Egan's solo hit single which reached number 8 in the US chart. His brand of pop-cum-country grew progressively less popular and after the release of the *Wild Exhibitions* in 1983, the artist released no further albums throughout the 80s.
●ALBUMS: *Fundamental Roll* (Columbia 1977)★★★, *Not Shy* (Columbia 1978)★★★, *Hi Fi* (Polydor 1979)★★★, *The Last Stroll* (Edge 1980)★★, *Wild Exhibitions* (Backstreet 1983)★★.

EGG

Egg was formed in July 1968 by Dave Stewart (keyboards), Hugh Montgomery 'Mont' Campbell (bass/vocals) and Clive Brooks (drums). The three musicians were all previous members of Uriel, a flower-power influenced group which had featured guitarist Steve Hillage. Egg recorded two albums, *Egg* and *The Polite Force*, between 1970 and 1972. Stylistically similar to the Soft Machine, these releases featured Stewart's surging keyboard work and a complex, compositional flair, bordering on the mathematical. The group's aficionados were thus stunned when Brooks abandoned this experimental path for the more orthodox, blues-based Groundhogs, and his departure resulted in Egg's demise. Stewart rejoined former colleague Hillage in the short-lived Khan, before replacing David Sinclair in Hatfield And The North. However, the three original members of Egg were later reunited for the final album, *The Civil Surface*, on the Virgin Records subsidiary label, Caroline, before dissolving again. Stewart and Campbell remained together in another experimental group, National Health, but then embarked on separate paths. The former has latterly enjoyed several hit singles by rearranging well-known 60s songs. 'It's My Party', a collaboration with singer Barbara Gaskin, topped the UK charts in 1981 but, for all their charm, such releases contrast with the left-field explorations of his earlier trio.
●ALBUMS: *Egg* (Nova 1970)★★★, *The Polite Force* (Deram 1970)★★★, *The Civil Surface* (Virgin 1974)★★★.
●COMPILATIONS: *Seven Is A Jolly Good Time* (See For Miles 1988)★★★.

EGGS OVER EASY

Formed in San Francisco, California, USA, in 1971, Eggs Over Easy was a popular attraction in the city's lively small club scene prior to arriving in London the following year. The quartet - Austin De Lone (guitar/vocals, ex-Southwind), Brien Hopkins (guitar/keyboards), Jack O'Hara (bass, ex-David Blue's American Patrol) and Bill Franz (drums) took up a residency at a former jazz haunt, the Tally Ho in Kentish Town, and in doing so established the genre known as 'pub rock'. Bees Make Honey, Brinsley Schwarz and Ducks DeLuxe followed in their wake. Eggs Over Easy returned to San Francisco in 1973 where they continued to forge an engaging blend of country, blues and rock styles. Sadly, their appeal as a live act did not transfer to their recordings. One-time Grootna vocalist Anna Rizzo often supplemented the band onstage and Hopkins subsequently forged a new group, the Reptile Brothers, with three ex-members of Rizzo's former act; Greg Dewey (ex-Mad River), Notcho Dewey and Vic Smith. Another member of the Reptiles, Tim Eshelman, worked in the Moonlighters, an offshoot of Commander Cody And His Lost Planet Airmen, which also featured De Lone. When Eggs Over Easy disbanded at the end of the 70s, De Lone and Eshelman made the Moonlighters a full-time project.

●ALBUMS: *Good And Cheap* (A&M 1972)★★, *I'm Gonna Put A Bar In The Back Of My Car And Drive Myself To Drink* (Buffalo 1976)★★.

ELECTRIC LIGHT ORCHESTRA

The original ELO line-up comprised Roy Wood (b. 8 November 1946, Birmingham, England; vocals, cello, woodwind, guitars), Jeff Lynne (b. 30 December 1947, Birmingham, England; vocals, piano, guitar) and Bev Bevan (b. Beverley Bevan, 25 November 1945, Birmingham, England; drums). They had all been members of pop group the Move, but viewed this new venture as a means of greater self-expression. Vowing to 'carry on where the Beatles' "I Am The Walrus" left off', they completed an experimental debut set with the aid of Bill Hunt (french horn) and Steve Woolam (violin). Despite their lofty ambitions, the group still showed traces of its earlier counterpart with Lynne's grasp of melody much in evidence, particularly on the startling '10538 Overture', a UK Top 10 single in 1972. Although Woolam departed, the remaining quartet added Hugh McDowell (b. 13 July 1953), Andy Craig (cellos), ex-Balls keyboardist Richard Tandy (b. 26 March 1948, Birmingham, England; bass, piano, guitar) and Wilf Gibson (b. 28 February 1945, Dilston, Northumberland, England; violin) for a series of indifferent live appearances, following which Wood took Hunt and McDowell to form Wizzard. With Craig absenting himself from either party, the remaining quartet maintained the ELO name with the addition of Mike D'Albuquerque (b. 24 June 1947, Wimbledon, London, England; bass/vocals) and cellists Mike Edwards (b. 31 May, Ealing, London, England) and Colin Walker (b. 8 July 1949, Minchinhampton, Gloucestershire, England). The reshaped line-up completed the transitional *ELO II* and scored a Top 10 single with an indulgent version of Chuck Berry's 'Roll Over Beethoven' which included quotes from Beethoven's 5th Symphony. ELO enjoyed a third hit with 'Showdown', but two ensuing singles, 'Ma Ma Ma Ma Belle' and 'Can't Get It Out Of My Head', surprisingly failed to chart. However, the latter song reached the US Top 10 which in turn helped its atten-

dant album, *Eldorado*, achieve gold status. By this point the group's line-up had stabilized around Lynne, Bevan, Tandy and the prodigal McDowell, Kelly Grouchett (bass), Mik Kaminski (violin) and Melvyn Gale (cello). They became a star attraction on America's lucrative stadium circuit and achieved considerable commercial success with *A New World Record*, *Out Of The Blue* and *Discovery*. Lynne's compositions successfully steered the line between pop and rock, inspiring commentators to compare his group with the Beatles. Between 1976 and 1981 ELO scored an unbroken run of 15 UK Top 20 singles, including 'Livin' Thing' (1976), 'Telephone Line' (1977), 'Mr. Blue Sky' (1978) 'Don't Bring Me Down' (1979) and 'Xanadu', a chart-topping collaboration with Olivia Newton-John, taken from the film of the same name. The line-up had now been slimmed to that of Lynne, Bevan, Tandy and Grouchett, but recurrent legal and distribution problems conspired to undermine ELO's momentum. *Time* and *Secret Messages* lacked the verve of earlier work and the group's future was put in doubt by a paucity of releases and Lynne's growing disenchantment. The guitarist's subsequent pursuit of a solo career signalled a final split, but in 1991 Bevan emerged with ELO 2. It remains doubtful that he can regain the heights scaled in the 70s when Lynne's songwriting talent seemed untenable.

●ALBUMS: *Electric Light Orchestra* aka *No Answer* (Harvest 1971)★★, *ELO II* (Harvest 1973)★★, *On The Third Day* (Warners 1973)★★★, *The Night The Lights Went On In Long Beach* (Warners 1974)★★, *Eldorado* (Warners 1975)★★★★, *Face The Music* (Jet 1975)★★★, *A New World Record* (Jet 1976)★★★, *Out Of The Blue* (Jet 1977)★★★★, *Discovery* (Jet 1979)★★★, with Olivia Newton-John *Xanadu* film soundtrack (Jet 1980)★★, *Time* (Jet 1981)★★, *Secret Messages* (Jet 1983)★★, *Balance Of Power* (Epic 1986)★★, *Electric Light Orchestra Part Two* (Telstar 1991)★, as ELO 2 *Moment Of Truth* (Edel 1994)★.

●COMPILATIONS: *Showdown* (Harvest 1974)★★★, *Ole ELO* (Jet 1976)★★★, *The Light Shines On* (Harvest 1976)★★★, *Greatest Hits* (Jet 1979)★★★★, *A Box Of Their Best* (1980)★★★, *First Movement* (Harvest 1986)★★, *A Perfect World Of Music* (Jet 1988)★★★, *Their Greatest Hits* (Epic 1989)★★★, *The Definitive Collection* (1993)★★★, *The Very Best Of ...* (Dino 1994)★★★, *The Gold Collection* (EMI 1996)★★★.

●FURTHER READING: *The Electric Light Orchestra Story*, Bev Bevan.

ELLIMAN, YVONNE

b. 29 December 1951, Hawaii, USA. American singer Yvonne Elliman played in the high school band in Hawaii before coming to London in 1969. She was singing at the Pheasantry folk club in the Kings Road, Chelsea, when the rising songwriters Tim Rice and Andrew Lloyd Webber chanced upon her. They offered her the part of Mary Magdalene in their new rock opera *Jesus Christ Superstar* and this brought her to the public's attention. She subsequently recreated the role in the film and earned a nomination for a Golden Globe award by the Foreign Press Association. The role also gave her her first hit single with 'I Don't Know How To Love Him', which was also the title of her 1972 debut for Polydor. Her co-star, Ian Gillan of Deep Purple, subsequently signed her to Purple's UK Label. Elliman then recorded an album for Decca in New York before returning to London to record a follow-up with the help of Pete Townshend. While appearing on Broadway in the American showing of *Jesus Christ Superstar* she met and married RSO president Bill Oakes. Through Oakes she was introduced to Eric Clapton and invited to sing backing vocals on the single he was then recording - 'I Shot The Sheriff'. She remained part of Clapton's band for his next five albums. She was also signed to RSO in her own right and recorded the solo *Rising Sun,* which was produced by Steve Cropper. Her next album, *Love Me,* featured a title track written by Barry Gibb and Robin Gibb and became a UK Top 10 hit. The Bee Gees then wrote some of their *Saturday Night Fever* tracks with Elliman in mind and she had a US chart topper with 'If I Can't Have You'. She has since concentrated on session work although she recorded a duet with Stephen Bishop in 1980 that narrowly missed the US charts.

●ALBUMS: *I Don't Know How To Love Him* (Polydor 1972)★★, *Food Of Love* (Decca 1973)★★, *Rising Sun* (RSO 1975)★★, *Love Me* (RSO 1976)★★, *Night Flight* (RSO 1978)★★, *Yvonne* (RSO 1979)★★.

●FILMS: *Jesus Christ Superstar* (1973).

ELLIS, DON

b. 25 July 1934, Los Angeles, California, USA, d. 17 December 1978. Appreciation of Ellis's work has increased since his death and he is now regarded by many as an important figure in jazz. From childhood he was fascinated with brass instruments and received a trumpet at the age of two. At junior high school he had his own quartet and at Boston university he was a member of the band. His first professional work was as a member of Ray McKinley's Glenn Miller Orchestra. After his national service, Don formed a small group playing coffeehouses in New York's Greenwich Village. By the late 50s he was playing with many name bands including those of Woody Herman, Lionel Hampton, Charles Mingus and Maynard Ferguson. Ellis also worked in small groups, enjoying the greater freedom of expression this allowed. In 1961/2 he was a member of George Russell's sextet. In Atlantic City, Ellis took up a teaching fellowship and it was there he developed and explored his interest in the complexities of Indian rhythm patterns. Ellis made a triumphant appearance at the 1966 Monterey Jazz festival with his 23-piece band. His completely original themes were scored using unbelievably complex notation. Customarily, most big band music was played at four beats to the bar but Ellis confidently and successfully experimented

with 5-beat bars, then 9-, 11-, 14-, 17-, 19- and even 27-beat bars. Mixing metres created difficulties for his rhythm sections so he taught himself to play drums in order that he might properly instruct his drummers. He also experimented with brass instruments, introducing the four-valve flügelhorn and superbone. During the late 60s the Don Ellis Orchestra was promoted as part of the great CBS progressive music campaign and he found himself performing at rock festivals and concerts. His music found favour with the Woodstock generation, who could also recognize him as an exciting pioneer. His CBS albums were all successful, his work being produced by both John Hammond and Al Kooper. Dubbed the 'Father of the Time Revolution' in jazz, Ellis's music was much more than complex. It was also undeniably joyous. Tunes like the 7/4 romp 'Pussy Wiggle Stomp', 'Barnum's Revenge' (a reworking of 'Bill Bailey') and 'Scratt And Fluggs' (a passing nod to country music's Lester Flatt and Earl Scruggs), are played with zesty enthusiasm, extraordinary skill and enormous good humour. Ellis's trumpet playing was remarkable, combining dazzling technique with a hot jazz feeling that reflected his admiration for Henry 'Red' Allen. He also experimented with electronic devices, such as a Ring Modulator, which transformed his trumpet into a generator of atavistic moans and shouts. Conversely, as he showed on *Haiku,* he could play with delicate charm and often deeply moving emotion. Ellis scored the music for 10 films, including *The French Connection* (1971), for which he won a Grammy. It is, however, his brilliantly ambitious and innovative 'eastern' music, notably 'Indian Lady' and 'Turkish Bath' that makes his work as important as John Coltrane's flirtation with the music of the mystic east. He is indubitably an outstanding figure destined for future reappraisal. Ellis stated 'I am not concerned whether my music is jazz, third stream, classical or anything else, or whether it is even called music. Let it be judged as Don Ellis noise'.

●ALBUMS: *How Time Passes* (Candid 1960)★★, *New Ideas* (New Jazz 1961)★★★★, *Essence* (Pacific Jazz 1962)★★★, *Jazz Jamboree No 1* (1962)★★★, *Live At Monterey* (Pacific Jazz 1966)★★★★, *Live In 3/2/3/4 Time* (Pacific Jazz 1967)★★★, *Electric Bath* (Columbia 1968)★★★★, *Shock Treatment* (Columbia 1968)★★★★, *Autumn* (Columbia 1969)★★★★, *The New Don Ellis Band Goes Underground* (Columbia 1969)★★, *Don Ellis At Fillmore* (Columbia 1970)★★★, *Tears Of Joy* (1971)★★★, *Connection* (1972)★★★, *Soaring* (1973)★★★, *Haiku* (1974)★★★★, *Star Wars* (1977)★★★, *Live At Montreux* (Atlantic 1978)★★★, *Out Of Nowhere* rec. 1961 (Candid 1989)★★★.

EMERSON, KEITH

b. 1 November 1944, Todmorden, Lancashire, England. Organist Emerson was briefly associated with several British club R&B attractions prior to joining soul singer P.P. Arnold's backing group in 1967. Known as the Nice, this unit later embarked on an independent career and quickly established itself as a leading progressive rock act. Emerson's keyboard dexterity and showmanship - he used knives to sustain notes during lengthy improvisations - was undoubtedly their focal point, a feature continued on his subsequent venture, the 'supergroup' Emerson, Lake And Palmer. Although deemed pretentious by critics, the trio became highly successful and maintained a rigorous recording schedule throughout the early 70s. Emerson's solo single, 'Honky Tonk Train Blues', recorded during a hiatus in the parent group's career, reached the UK Top 30 in 1976, but the artist did not pursue such ambitions full-time until ELP was dissolved in 1980. The artist scored the films *The Inferno* and *Nighthawks*, and completed a series of musicianly collections, but this facet of his work conflicted with other projects, notably Emerson, Lake And Powell and 3, with Carl Palmer and Robert Berry. In 1992, Emerson, Lake And Palmer re-formed, recording an album and preparing to hit the road once again.

●ALBUMS: *The Inferno* film soundtrack (Atlantic 1980)★★, *Nighthawks* film soundtrack (MCA 1981)★★, *Honky* film soundtrack (Chord 1985)★★, *Murderrock*, film soundtrack (Chord 1986)★★, *Best Revenge* film soundtrack (Chord 1986)★★, *Harmageddon/ China Free Fall* (Chord 1987)★★, *The Christmas Album* (Priority 1988)★★.

●COMPILATIONS: *The Emerson Collection* (Chord 1986)★★.

EMERSON, LAKE AND PALMER

One the most prominent supergroups of the early 70s, ELP comprised Keith Emerson (b. 1 November 1944, Todmorden, Lancashire, England; keyboards), Greg Lake (b. 10 November 1948, Bournemouth, Dorset, England; vocals/bass) and Carl Palmer (b. 20 March 1951, Birmingham, England; drums, percussion). Formerly, the super trio were, respectively, members of the Nice, King Crimson and Atomic Rooster. After making their debut at the Guildhall, Plymouth, they appeared at the much-publicized 1970 Isle of Wight Festival. That same year, they were signed to Island Records and completed their self-titled debut album. The work displayed their desire to fuse classical music influences with rock in determinedly flourishing style. Early the following year, at Newcastle's City Hall they introduced their arrangement of Mussorgsky's *Pictures At An Exhibition*. The concept album *Tarkus* followed some months later and revealed their overreaching love of musical drama to the full. The theme of the work was obscure but the mechanical armadillo, visualized on the sleeve, proved a powerful and endearing image. Extensive tours and albums followed over the next three years including *Trilogy*, *Brain Salad Surgery* and an extravagant triple live album. Having set up their own label and established themselves as a top-grossing live act, the members branched out into various solo ventures, reuniting for part of *Works*. This double album included their memorably dramatic reading of Aaron Copland's 'Fanfare For The Common Man' which took them close to the top of the British singles charts. With solo outings becoming increasingly distracting, the group released one final studio album, *Love Beach*, before embarking on a farewell world tour. With changes in the music industry wrought by punk and new wave groups, it was probably an opportune moment to draw a veil over their career. It was not until 1986 that a serious reformation was attempted but Carl Palmer (then in the highly successful Asia) would not be drawn. Instead, Emerson and Lake teamed up with hit drummer Cozy Powell. The collaboration produced one chart album *Emerson, Lake And Powell*, which included the pomp of Holst among the many classical influences. When Powell quit, Palmer regrouped with his colleagues for a projected album in 1987, but the sessions proved unfruitful. Instead, Emerson recruited Hush drummer Robert Berry for *To The Power Of Three*, which sold poorly. In the early 90s the original trio reformed and produced *Black Moon* followed by another live album. Whilst their concert tour was well attended no new ground was being broken and recent new material (notably *In The Hot Seat*) is but a pale shadow of their former material. Reaction to the new recording was tepid, indicating that the era of pomp rock is long gone.

●ALBUMS: *Emerson Lake & Palmer* (Island 1970)★★★, *Tarkus* (Island 1971)★★★★, *Pictures At An Exhibition* (Island 1971)★★★★, *Trilogy* (Island 1972)★★★, *Brain Salad Surgery* (Manticore 1973)★★★, *Welcome Back My Friends To The Show That Never Ends: Ladies And Gentlemen ... Emerson Lake & Palmer* (Manticore 1974)★★, *Works* (Atlantic 1977)★★, *Works, Volume Two* (Atlantic 1977)★★, *Love Beach* (Atlantic 1978)★★, *Emerson, Lake & Palmer In Concert* (Atlantic 1979)★★, *Black Moon* (Victory 1992)★★, *Live At The Royal Albert Hall* (1993)★★, *In The Hot Seat* (Victory 1994)★★. As Emerson, Lake And Powell: *Emerson, Lake & Powell* (Polydor 1986)★★. As 3: *To The Power Of Three* (1988)★★.

●COMPILATIONS: *The Best Of Emerson, Lake & Palmer* (Atlantic 1980)★★★, *The Atlantic Years* (Atlantic 1992)★★★, *Return Of The Manticore* 4-CD box set (Victory 1993)★★★★.

●VIDEOS: *Pictures At An Exhibition* (Castle Hendring 1990).

EMOTIONS

The Hutchinson sisters, Wanda (b. 17 December 1951; lead vocal), Sheila and Jeanette, first worked together in Chicago, Illinois, USA, as the Heavenly Sunbeams, then as the Hutchinson Sunbeams up to 1968. They recorded for several local companies prior to arriving at Stax on the recommendation of Pervis Staples of the Staple Singers. Their debut release for the label, 'So I Can Love You' (1969), reached the US Top 40, and introduced a series of excellent singles, including 'Show Me How' (1971) and 'I Could Never Be Happy' (1972).

Although Jeanette was briefly replaced by a cousin, Theresa Davis, she latterly returned to the line-up, while a fourth sister, Pamela, came into the group when Davis left. The Emotions moved to Columbia Records in 1976 and began working under the aegis of Maurice White of Earth, Wind And Fire. 'Best Of My Love' was a US number 1 the following year while the singers secured further success with 'Boogie Wonderland' (1979), an energetic collaboration with White's group. The Emotions continued to record into the 80s and if their material was sometimes disappointing, their harmonies remained as vibrant as ever.
●ALBUMS: *So I Can Love You* (Stax 1970)★★★, *Songs Of Love* (Stax 1971)★★★, *Untouched* (Stax 1972)★★★, *Flowers* (Columbia 1976)★★★, *Rejoice* (Columbia 1977)★★★, *Sunshine* (Stax 1977)★★★, *Sunbeam* (Columbia 1978)★★★, *Come Into Our World* (ARC 1979)★★★, *New Affair* (ARC 1981)★★, *If I Only Knew* (Motown 1985)★★.
●COMPILATIONS: *Heart Association - The Best Of The Emotions* (Columbia 1979)★★★★.

ENGLAND DAN AND JOHN FORD COLEY

Dan Seals (b. 8 February 1950, McCamey, Texas, USA) comes from a family of performing Seals. His father played bass for many country stars (Ernest Tubb, Bob Wills) and his brother, Jimmy, was part of the Champs and then Seals And Croft. His cousins include 70s country star Johnny Duncan and songwriters Chuck Seals ('Crazy Arms') and Troy Seals. Seals formed a partnership with John Ford Coley (b. 13 October 1951) and they first worked as Southwest F.O.B., the initials representing Freight On Board. The ridiculous name did not last, but Jimmy, not wanting them to be called Seals And Coley, suggested England Dan And John Ford Coley. Their first albums for A&M Records sold moderately well, but they struck gold in 1976 with a move to Big Tree Records. The single, 'I'd Really Love To See You Tonight', went to number 2 in the US charts and also made the UK Top 30, although its hook owed something to James Taylor's 'Fire And Rain'. The resulting album, *Nights Are Forever*, was a big seller and the pair opted for a fuller sound which drew comparisons with the Eagles. The title track, 'Nights Are Forever Without You', was another Top 10 single. With their harmonies, acoustic-based songs and tuneful melodies, they appealed to the same market as the Eagles and, naturally, Seals And Croft. They had further US hits with 'It's Sad To Belong', 'Gone Too Far', 'We'll Never Have To Say Goodbye Again' and 'Love Is The Answer'. When the duo split, Seals, after a few setbacks, became a country star. Coley found a new partner, but their 1981 album, *Kelly Leslie And John Ford Coley*, was not a success.
●ALBUMS: as Southwest F.O.B. *Smell Of Incense* (A&M 1968)★★, *England Dan And John Ford Coley* (A&M 1971)★★★, *Fables* (A&M 1971)★★, *I Hear The Music* (A&M 1976)★★, *Nights Are Forever* (Big Tree 1976)★★, *Dowdy Ferry Road* (Big Tree 1977)★★★, *Some Things Don't Come Easy* (Big Tree 1978)★★, *Dr. Heckle And Mr. Jive* (Big Tree 1979)★★, *Just Tell Me If You Love Me* (1980)★★.
●COMPILATIONS: *Best Of* (Big Tree 1980)★★★, *The Very Best* (Rhino 1997)★★★.

ENID

Influential art-rockers, formed in 1974 at experimental school Finchden Manor by keyboardist Robert John Godfrey (b. 30 July 1947, Leeds Castle, Kent, England) with guitarists Stephen Stewart and Francis Lickerish. The Enid's leader, Godfrey was educated at Finchden Manor (other alumni included Alexis Korner and Tom Robinson) and the Royal Academy Of Music. After starting a promising career as a concert pianist, Godfrey joined Barclay James Harvest as musical director in 1969 and moved them towards large orchestral works. He left BJH in 1972, then recorded a solo album, *The Fall Of Hyperion*, for Charisma in 1973. He returned to Finchden Manor to form the Enid in 1974, taking the name from a school in-joke. Supported by dynamic live shows, a debut album, *In The Region of the Summer Stars*, appeared in 1976. The simultaneous growth of punk 'put us in a cul-de-sac', according to Godfrey but, despite an ever-changing line-up, subsequent concept albums, rock operas and tours saw them increasing their cult audience and playing large venues. A move to Pye Records just as the label went bankrupt in 1980 broke up the band. Godfrey formed his own label, distribution and studio with Stewart. They functioned uncredited as the backing band on all Kim Wilde albums up to *Cambodia*, and re-formed as the Enid in 1983. Operating as independents, their following still grew, and the fifth album, *Something Wicked This Way Comes*, was their biggest success yet. Simultaneously, Godfrey began a collaboration with healer Matthew Manning on meditational music albums. In 1986, the group presented its eighth album, *Salome*, as a ballet at London's Hammersmith Odeon. By 1988, the band's popularity appeared to have peaked so, after two sold-out farewell gigs at London's Dominion Theatre, Godfrey split the band again. In 1990, based in an old house near Northampton, Godfrey re-emerged as manager of a new band, Come September, for whom he writes the material, but does not perform.
●ALBUMS: *The Fall Of Hyperion* (Charisma 1973)★★, *In The Region Of The Summer Stars* (EMI 1976)★★★, *Aerie Faerie Nonsense* (EMI 1978)★★★, *Touch Me* (Pye 1979)★★★, *Six Pieces* (Pye 1979)★★★, *Rhapsody In Rock* (Pye 1980)★★★, *Something Wicked This Way Comes* (Enid 1983)★★★, *Live At Hammersmith Volumes 1 & 2* (Enid 1984)★★, *The Spell* (Hyperion 1984)★★★, *Fand Symphonic Tone Poem* (Enid 1985)★★★, *Salome* (Enid 1986)★★★, *Lovers And Fools* (Dojo 1987)★★★, *Reverberations* (1987)★★★, *The Seed And The Sower* (Enid 1988)★★★, *Final Noise* (Wonderful Music 1990)★★★,

Tripping The Light Fantastic (Mantella 1995)★★★.
●VIDEOS: *Stonehenge Free Festival 1984* (Visionary 1995).

ENO, BRIAN

b. Brian Peter George St. Baptiste de la Salle Eno, 15 May 1948, Woodbridge, Suffolk, England. While studying at art schools in Ipswich and Winchester, Eno fell under the influence of *avant garde* composers Cornelius Cardew and John Cage. Although he could not play an instrument, Eno liked tinkering with multi-track tape recorders and in 1968 wrote the limited edition theoretical handbook, *Music For Non Musicians*. During the same period he established Merchant Taylor's Simultaneous Cabinet which performed works by himself and various contemporary composers, including Christian Wolff, La Monte Young, Cornelius Carden and George Brecht. This experiment was followed by the formation of a short-lived *avant garde* performance group, the Maxwell Demon.

After moving to London, Eno lived in an art commune and played with Carden's Scratch Orchestra, the Portsmouth Sinfonia and his own group. As a result of his meeting with saxophonist Andy Mackay, Eno was invited to join Roxy Music in January 1971 as a 'technical adviser', but before long his powerful visual image began to rival that of group leader Bryan Ferry. It was this fact that precipitated his departure from Roxy Music on 21 June 1973. That same day, Eno began his solo career in earnest, writing the strong 'Baby's On Fire'. Shortly afterwards, he formed a temporary partnership with Robert Fripp, with whom he had previously worked on the second album by Robert Wyatt's Matching Mole, *Little Red Record*. By November 1973, their esoteric *No Pussyfooting* was released, and a tour followed. With the entire Roxy line-up, bar Ferry, Eno next completed *Here Come The Warm Jets*, which was issued less than three months later in January 1974. It highlighted Eno's bizarre lyrics and quirky vocals. A one-off punk single 'Seven Deadly Finns' prompted a tour with the Phil Rambow-led Winkies. On the fifth date, Eno's right lung collapsed and he was confined to hospital. During his convalescence, Eno visited America, recorded some demos with Television and worked with John Cale on *Slow Dazzle* and later *Helen Of Troy*. His fraternization with former members of the Velvet Underground reached its apogee at London's Rainbow Theatre on 1 June 1974 when he was invited to play alongside Cale, Kevin Ayers and Nico, abetted by Robert Wyatt and Mike Oldfield. An souvenir album of the event was subsequently issued.

A second album *Taking Tiger Mountain (By Strategy)* was followed by several production credits on albums by Robert Wyatt, Robert Calvert and Phil Manzanera. This, in turn, led to Eno's experiments with environment-conscious music. He duly formed the mid-price label Obscure Records whose third release was his own *Discreet Music*, an elongated synthesizer piece conceived during a period of convalescence from a road accident. During the same period, he completed *Another Green World*, a meticulously crafted work that displayed the continued influence of John Cage. A further album with Robert Fripp followed, called *Evening Star*. After performing in Phil Manzanera's group 801, Eno collaborated with painter Peter Schmidt on a concept titled 'Oblique Strategies', which was actually a series of cards designed to promote lateral thinking.

During a hectic 18-month period, Eno recorded 120 tracks, the sheer bulk of which temporarily precluded the completion of his next album. In the meantime, he began a fruitful alliance with David Bowie on a trilogy of albums: *Low*, *Heroes* and *Lodger*. Even with that workload, however, he managed to complete his next solo work, *Before And After Science*. An unusually commercial single followed with 'King's Lead Hat'. The title was an anagram of Talking Heads and Eno later worked with that group as producer on three of their albums. Eno then turned his attention to soundtrack recordings before returning to ambient music. *Music For Films* was a pot-pourri of specific soundtrack material allied to pieces suitable for playing while watching movies. The experiment was continued with *Music For Airports*. Throughout this period, Eno remained in demand as a producer: and/or collaborator on albums by Ultravox, Cluster, Harold Budd, Devo and Talking Heads. In 1979 Eno moved to New York where he began making a series of vertical format video installation pieces. Numerous exhibitions of his work were shown throughout the world accompanied by his ambient soundtracks.

During the same period he produced the *No New York* album by New York No Wave *avant garde* artists the Contortions, DNA, Teenage Jesus And The Jerks, and Mars. Two further Talking Heads album productions followed culminating in 1981 with the Top 30 album, *My Life In The Bush Of Ghosts*, a fascinating collaboration with the Talking Heads' David Byrne, that fused 'found voices' with African rhythms. In 1980 Eno forged an association with Canadian producer/engineer Daniel Lanois. Between them they produced *Voices*, by Eno's brother Roger, and a collaboration with Harold Budd, *The Plateaux Of Mirror*. This assocaition with Lanois culminated in the highly successful U2 albums, *The Unforgettable Fire*, *The Joshua Tree*, *Achtung Baby* and *Zooropa*. In critic Tim de Lisle's words Eno's involvement converted them (U2) from earnestness to gleeful irony. In 1990 Eno completed a collaborative album with John Cale, *Wrong Way Up*. The following year there was some confusion when Eno released *My Squelchy Life*, which reached some record reviewers, but was withdrawn, revised, and re-released in 1992 as *Nerve Net*. As Eno's first album of songs for 15 years, it fused 'electronically-treated dance music, eccentric English pop, cranky funk, space jazz, and a myriad of other, often dazzling sounds'. For *The Shutov Assembly* (1992), Eno returned to the ambient style he first introduced in

1975 with *Discreet Music*, and which was echoed 10 years later on his *Thursday Afternoon*. The album was conceived for Moscow painter Sergei Shutov, who had been in the habit of working to the accompaniment of Eno's previous music. *Neroli* (1993), was another hour's worth of similar atmospheric seclusion. In 1995 he was again working with David Bowie on *Outside* in addition to projects with Jah Wobble on *Spanner* and sharing the composing credits with Bono, Adam Clayton and Larry Mullen Jr. on *Passengers: Original Soundtracks 1*. Eno's back-catalogue remains a testament to his love of esoteria, ever-shifting musical styles and experimentation.

●ALBUMS: with Robert Fripp *No Pussyfooting* (Island 1973)★★★, *Here Come The Warm Jets* (Island 1974)★★★★, with John Cale, Kevin Ayers, Nico *June 1st 1974* (Island 1974)★★, *Taking Tiger Mountain (By Strategy)* (Island 1974)★★★★, *Another Green World* (Island 1975)★★★★, *Discreet Music* (Island 1975)★★★, with Fripp *Evening Star* (Island 1975)★★★, with Phil Manzanera *801 Live* (Island 1976)★★, *Before And After Science* (Polydor 1977)★★★★, with Cluster *Cluster And Eno* (Sky 1978)★★★, *Music For Films* (Polydor 1978)★★★, with Moebius And Roedelius *After The Heat* (Sky 1979)★★★, *Ambient 1: Music For Airports* (Polydor/EG 1979)★★★★, with Harold Budd *Ambient 2: The Plateaux Of Mirror* (Polydor/EG 1980)★★★, with Jon Hassell *Fourth World Vol i: Possible Musics* (Polydor/EG 1980)★★★, with David Byrne *My Life In The Bush Of Ghosts* (EG 1981)★★★★, *Ambient 4: On Land* (Editions 1982)★★★, with Daniel Lanois, Roger Eno *Apollo: Atmospheres And Soundtracks* (EG 1983)★★★, with Budd, Lanois *The Pearl* (Editions 1984)★★★, with Michael Brook, Lanois *Hybrid* (Editions 1985)★★★, with Roger Eno *Voices* (Editions 1985)★★★, *Thursday Afternoon* (EG 1985)★★★, with Cale *Wrong Way Up* (Land 1990)★★★★, *Nerve Net* (1992)★★★, *The Shutov Assembly* (1992)★★★, *Neroli* (1993)★★★, with Jah Wobble *Spanner* (All Saints 1995)★★★, *Passengers: Original Soundtracks 1* (Island 1995)★★★.

●COMPILATIONS: with Moebius, Roedelius And Plank *Begegnungen* (Sky 1984)★★★, *Begegnungen ii* (Sky 1985)★★★, with Cluster *Old Land* (Sky 1986)★★★, *More Blank Than Frank* (EG 1986)★★★★, *Desert Island Selection* (EG 1986)★★★★.

●VIDEOS: *Thursday Afternoon* (Hendring). *Excerpt From The Khumba Mele* (Hendring). *Mistaken Memories Of Medieval Manhattan* (Hendring).

●FURTHER READING: *Music For Non-Musicians*, Brian Eno. *Roxy Music: Style With Substance - Roxy's First Ten Years*, Johnny Rogan. *More Dark Than Shark* Brian Eno and Russell Mills. *Brian Eno: His Music And The Vertical Colour Of Sound*, Eric Tamm. *A Year With Swollen Appendices*, Brian Eno.

ENTWISTLE, JOHN

b. John Alec Entwistle, 9 October 1944, Chiswick, London, England. As bassist (and occasional French horn player) in the Who, Entwistle provided the neces-

sary bedrock to the group's individual sound. His immobile features and rigid stage manner provided the foil to his colleagues' impulsive pyrotechnics, yet paradoxically it was he who most enjoyed performing live. The sole member to undergo formal musical tuition, having played the French horn with the Middlesex Youth Orchestra, Entwistle quickly asserted his compositional talent, although such efforts were invariably confined to b-sides and occasional album tracks. His songs included 'Doctor Doctor', 'Someone's Coming' and 'My Wife', but he is generally recalled for such macabre offerings as 'Boris The Spider', 'Whiskey Man' and his two contributions to *Tommy*: 'Fiddle About' and 'Cousin Kevin'. These performances enhanced a cult popularity and several were gathered on *The Ox*, titled in deference to the bassist's nickname. Entwistle released his first solo album, *Smash Your Head Against The Wall*, in 1971. It contained a new version of 'Heaven And Hell', a perennial in-concert favourite and the set attracted considerable attention in the USA. *Whistle Rymes*, a pun on his often misspelled surname, confirmed the bassist's new-found independence with what is perhaps his strongest set to date, containing within such entertaining dark tales of peeping Toms, isolation, suicide and nightmares. The following album, *Rigor Mortis Sets In*, paid homage to 50s rock 'n' roll and although an ambitious tour to support its release was set up it had to be abandoned when the whole venture proved too costly. Entwistle then compiled the Who's archive set, *Odds And Sods*, before forming a new group, Ox, but the attendant album, *Mad Dog*, was poorly received. He subsequently worked as musical director on two soundtrack sets, *Quadrophenia* and *The Kids Are Alright*, before completing his 1981 release, *Too Late The Hero*, which featured former James Gang/Eagles' guitarist, Joe Walsh. While Entwistle's solo career has since been deferred, his stature as an important rock bass player was enhanced by his outstanding performance on the Who's 1973 double album, *Quadrophenia*.

●ALBUMS: *Smash Your Head Against The Wall* (Track 1971)★★★, *Whistle Rymes* (Track 1972)★★★, *Rigor Mortis Sets In* (Track 1973)★★, as John Entwistle's Ox *Mad Dog* (Decca 1975)★★, *Too Late The Hero* (Warners 1981)★★.

●COMPILATIONS: *The Ox* (Track 1971)★★★, *Anthology* (Repertoire 1996)★★★, *Thunderfingers: The Best Of ...* (Rhino 1997)★★★.

ERICKSON, ROKY

b. Roger Erkynard Erickson, 15 July 1947, Dallas, Texas, USA. Erickson came to the fore in the infamous Thirteenth Floor Elevators. He composed 'You're Gonna Miss Me', the group's most popular single, while his feverish voice and exciting guitar-work provided a distinctive edge. This influential unit broke up in disarray during 1968 as Erickson began missing gigs. Arrested on a drugs charge, he faked visions to avoid imprisonment, but was instead committed to Rusk State

Hospital for the Criminally Insane. He was released in 1971 and began a low-key solo career, recording several singles with a new backing group, Bleib Alien. In 1980 the guitarist secured a deal with CBS Records but the resultant album, *Roky Erickson And The Aliens*, was a disappointment and compromised the artist's vision for a clean, clear-cut production. Erickson's subsequent releases have appeared on several labels. Their quality has varied, befitting a mercurial character who remains a genuine eccentric - he has persistently claimed that he is from the planet Mars. His music borrows freely from horror and science fiction films and, when inspired, he is capable of truly powerful performances. Erickson was imprisoned in 1990 for stealing mail, but his plight inspired Sire Records' *Where The Pyramid Meets The Eye*, wherein 19 acts, including R.E.M., Jesus And Mary Chain, ZZ Top and the Butthole Surfers interpreted many of his best-known songs, the proceeds of which should ameliorate his incarceration. Following his release from a mental institution Erickson recorded *All That May Do My Rhyme*, and against all expectations and fully expecting a drug-wrecked casualty record it was one of his better efforts. Like Syd Barrett and Peter Green, Erickson may never return to our cosy and supposedly sane world, but unlike Green and Barrett he is at least still attempting to make new music.

● ALBUMS: *Roky Erickson And The Aliens* (Columbia 1980)★★★, *The Evil One* (415 Records 1981)★★★, *Clear Night For Love* (New Rose 1985)★★, *Don't Slander Me* (Enigma/Pink Dust 1986 (US), Demon 1987 (UK))★★★, *Gremlins Have Pictures* (Enigma/Pink Dust 1986 (US), Demon 1987 (UK))★★, *I Think Of Demons* adds two tracks to *Roky Erickson And The Aliens* (Edsel 1987)★★★, *Casting The Runes* (Five Hours Back 1987)★★, *The Holiday Inn Tapes* (Fan Club 1987)★★, *Openers* (5 Hours Back 1988)★★, *Live At The Ritz, 1987* (New Rose/Fan Club 1988)★★, *Mad Dog* (Swordfish 1992)★★, *All That May Do My Rhyme* (Trance Syndicate 1995)★★★.

● COMPILATIONS: *You're Gonna Miss Me: The Best Of Roky Erickson* (Restless 1991)★★★★.

ESSEX, DAVID

b. David Albert Cook, 23 July 1947, London, England. Originally a drummer in the semi-professional Everons, Essex subsequently turned to singing during the mid-60s, and recorded a series of unsuccessful singles for a variety of labels. On the advice of his influential manager, Derek Bowman, he switched to acting and after a series of minor roles received his big break upon winning the lead part in the stage musical *Godspell*. This was followed by a more familiar role in the authentic 50s-inspired film *That'll Be The Day* and its sequel *Stardust*. The former reactivated Essex's recording career and the song he composed for the film, 'Rock On', was a transatlantic Top 10 hit. It was in Britain, however, that Essex enjoyed several years as a pin-up teen idol. During the mid-70s, he registered two UK number 1s, 'Gonna Make You A Star' and 'Hold Me

Close', plus the Top 10 hits 'Lamplight', 'Stardust' and 'Rollin' Stone'. After parting with producer Jeff Wayne, Essex continued to chart, though with noticeably diminishing returns. As his teen appeal waned, his serious acting commitments increased, most notably with the role of Che Guevara in the production of *Evita*. The musical also provided another Top 5 hit with the acerbic 'Oh, What A Circus'. His lead part in the film *Silver Dream Machine* resulted in a hit of the same title. Thereafter, Essex took on a straight non-singing part in *Childe Byron*. The Christmas hit, 'A Winter's Tale', kept his chart career alive, as did the equally successful 'Tahiti'. The latter anticipated one of his biggest projects to date, an elaborate musical *Mutiny* (based on *Mutiny On The Bounty*). In 1993, after neglecting his showbusiness career while he spent two a half years in the African region as an ambassador for Voluntary Service Overseas, Essex embarked on a UK concert tour, and issued *Cover Shot*, a collection of mostly 60s songs. In the same year he played the part of Tony Lumpkin in Oliver Goldsmith's comedy, *She Stoops To Conquer*, in London's West End. In 1994 he continued to tour, and released an album produced by Jeff Wayne. It included a duet with Catherine Zeta Jones on 'True Love Ways', and the VSO-influenced 'Africa', an old Toto number. Despite pursuing two careers, Essex has managed to achieve consistent success on record, in films and stage.

● ALBUMS: *Rock On* (Columbia 1973)★★★, *David Essex* (Columbia 1974)★★★, *All The Fun Of The Fair* (Columbia 1975)★★, *Out On The Street* (Columbia 1976)★★, *On Tour* (Columbia 1976)★★, *Gold And Ivory* (Columbia 1977)★★, *Hold Me Close* (Columbia 1979)★★, *Imperial Wizard* (Mercury 1979)★★, *The David Essex Album* (Columbia 1979)★★, *Silver Dream Racer* (Mercury 1980)★, *Hot Love* (Mercury 1980)★★, *Be-Bop - The Future* (Mercury 1981)★★, *Stage Struck* (Mercury 1982)★★, *Mutiny!* (Mercury 1983)★★, *The Whisper* (Mercury 1983)★★, *This One's For You* (Mercury 1984)★★, *Live At The Royal Albert Hall* (1984)★★, *Centre Stage* (K-Tel 1986)★★, *Touching The Ghost* (Lamplight 1989)★★, *Cover Shot* (1993)★★, *Back To Back* (1994)★★.

● COMPILATIONS: *The David Essex Collection* (Pickwick 1980)★★★, *The Very Best Of David Essex* (TV Records 1982)★★★, *Spotlight On David Essex* (1993)★★★, *The Best Of ...* (Columbia 1996)★★★.

● VIDEOS: *Live At The Royal Albert Hall* (Polygram 1984).

● FURTHER READING: *The David Essex Story*, George Tremlett.

● FILMS: *That'll Be The Day* (1975), *Stardust* (1976), *Silver Dream Machine* (1980).

EVERETT, KENNY

b. Maurice James Christopher Cole, 25 December 1944, Liverpool, England, d. 4 April 1995, London, England. Everett was a maverick disc jockey and comedian whose headlong broadcasting style broke established rules and outraged establishment figures. His sense of humour was a reaction to the stress of being an introverted and delicate child in Liverpool's dockside area. His first tapes earned him brief exposure on BBC Radio's Home Service, but his personal audition with Derek Chinnery (later controller of Radio 1) was a disaster. He sent the tapes to pirate station Radio London, and was immediately taken on as a disc jockey. Since pirate radio was 'of unproven legality' in the UK, all the disc jockeys adopted pseudonyms, thus did Maurice Cole become Kenny Everett. It was at Radio London that the Kenny And Cash broadcasting partnership with Dave Cash was born, later reprised on London's Capital Radio. He was sacked from Radio London for insulting behaviour on air. He then worked for a short time on BBC Light Programme's *Where It's At*. When the Marine Offences Act finished off the pirates, the BBC filled the void with the creation of Radio 1 in September 1967. A number of ex-pirate disc jockeys were taken on, including Everett. He hosted various shows and gained a loyal following for his anarchic style before being dismissed in 1970 for a remark about the wife of the Minister of Transport. Two years later he was taken back into the BBC fold, with the proviso that the show be pre-recorded (at his home studio in Wales) so that it could be vetted before broadcast.

He found a new outlet in 1973 at London's Capital Radio, the first independent commercial music station. Initially pre-recording his shows in Wales, he moved to London to revive 'Kenny And Cash' on Capital's breakfast show. His progress faltered when, 18 months after joining Capital, he took an overdose of sleeping pills. Although it was probably an accident, Everett had a history of fast living in the music business, and was under severe psychological pressure. Mixing the high life with daily breakfast broadcasting took its toll, and his marriage (at the age of 21) to Lee Middleton was under severe strain as Everett faced up to and made public his homosexuality. He switched to weekend shows, and started developing some of the characters later made famous by television. His shows were a breathless whirlwind of music, gags, jingles and vignettes, and they earned him a break on television in 1978 with Thames Television's *The Kenny Everett Video Show*. Everett's imagination and character expanded to fill every inch of the medium, frequently working on adrenalin rather than using a script. Surprisingly, the show transferred to the BBC in 1982 as *The Kenny Everett Television Show*, and also earned him a following in the USA and Australia. The show lasted until 1988. Meanwhile he had also been sacked again from BBC Radio (Radio 2 this time) for telling a rude joke about Margaret Thatcher. He went back to Capital as part of their new Capital Gold oldies station, which became his broadcasting home for the rest of his life. His work inspired many of today's disc jockeys and broadcasters.

●ALBUMS: *Captain Kremmen (Greatest Adventure Yet)* (Columbia 1980)★★, *Kenny Everett Naughty Joke Box* (Relax 1984)★★.
●FILMS: *Dateline Diamonds* (1965).

FACES

Formed from the ashes of the defunct UK mod group the Small Faces, this quintet comprised Ronnie Lane (b. 1 April 1946, Plaistow, London, England; bass), Kenny Jones (b. 16 September 1948, Stepney, London, England; drums), Ian McLagan (b. 12 May 1945, London, England; organ), Rod Stewart (b. 10 January 1945, Highgate, London, England; vocals) and Ron Wood (b. 1 June 1947; guitar). The latter two members were originally part of Jeff Beck's group. the Faces' 1970 debut *First Step* reflected their boozy, live appeal in which solid riffing and strong gutsy vocals were prominent. Their excellent follow-up, *Long Player*, enhanced their appeal with its strong mix of staunch rock songs. Throughout this period, Rod Stewart had been pursuing a solo career which took off in earnest in the summer of 1971 with the worldwide success of the chart-topping single 'Maggie May'. At that point, the Faces effectively became Stewart's backing group. Although they enjoyed increasingly commercial appeal with *A Nod's As Good As A Wink...To A Blind Horse* and a string of memorable good-time singles, including 'Stay With Me' and 'Cindy Incidentally', there was no doubt that the focus on Stewart unbalanced the unit. Lane left in 1973 and was replaced by Tetsu Yamauchi. Despite further hits with 'Pool Hall Richard', 'You Can Make Me Dance Sing Or Anything' and a live album to commemorate their Stateside success, the band clearly lacked unity. In 1975, Stewart became a tax exile and by the end of the year announced that he had separated from the group. Wood went on to join the Rolling Stones, while the remaining members briefly teamed up with Steve Marriott in an ill-fated reunion of the Small Faces. The band unexpectedly reunited for a one-off appearance at the Brit Awards in February 1993. They performed with Rod Stewart with Bill Wyman taking over Ronnie Lane's role on bass.

●ALBUMS: *First Step* (Warners 1970)★★★, *Long Player* (Warners 1971)★★★★, *A Nod's As Good As A Wink ... To A Blind Horse* (Warners 1971)★★★, *Ooh La La* (Warners 1973)★★★, *Coast To Coast: Overture And Beginners* (Mercury 1974)★★★.
●COMPILATIONS: *The Best Of The Faces* (Riva 1977)★★★.

FACTORY (UK)

The Oak Records label has long been famed for its popularity among collectors, and the Factory's sole 1971 single, 'Time Machine'/'Castle On The Hill', is no exception, regularly fetching over £100 when offered for sale to collectors . Different from the band of the same name who recorded for MGM Records and CBS Records at the end of the 60s, this UK band featured Laurie Cooksey (drums), Geoff 'Jaffa' Peckham (bass), Andy Quinta (vocals) and Tony Quinta (12-string acoustic guitar). Peckham was later replaced on bass by Steve Kinch. Before forming Factory the Quinta brothers had been part of the school band Perfect Turkey, who also recorded an acetate single ('Stones'/'Perfect Turkey Blues') for Oak. The Factory's single was issued in a limited pressing of 99, helping to make it one of the label's most elusive releases. However, the Factory's main claim to fame came much later in their career. They persevered without issuing further records until 1976, and were supported at one of their final performances by the Sex Pistols. The Quinta brothers and Kinch subsequently formed Head On, after which Andy Quinta and Kinch continued the punk connection by joining Hazel O'Connor's band.

FAIRPORT CONVENTION

The unchallenged inventors of British folk rock have struggled through tragedy and changes, retaining the name that now represents not so much who is in the band, but what it stands for. The original group of 1967 comprised Iain Matthews (b. Ian Matthews MacDonald, 16 June 1946, Scunthorpe, Lincolnshire, England; vocals), Judy Dyble (b. 13 February 1949, London, England; vocals), Ashley Hutchings (b. 26 January 1945, Muswell Hill, London, England; bass), Richard Thompson (b. 3 April 1949, London, England; guitar/vocals), Simon Nicol (b. 13 October 1950, Muswell Hill, London, England; guitar/vocals) and Martin Lamble (b. 28 August 1949, St. Johns Wood, London, England, d. 12 May 1969; drums). The band originally came to the attention of the London 'underground' club scene by sounding like a cross between the Jefferson Airplane and the Byrds. As an accessible alternative, people immediately took them to their hearts. American producer Joe Boyd signed them and they released the charming 'If I Had A Ribbon Bow'. On their self-titled debut they introduced the then little-known Canadian songwriter Joni Mitchell to a wider audience. The album was a cult favourite, but like the single, it sold poorly. Judy Dyble departed and was replaced by former Strawbs vocalist, Sandy Denny (b. Alexandra Denny, 6 January 1948, Wimbledon, London, England, d. 21 April 1978). Denny brought a traditional folk-feel to their work which began to appear on the superlative *What We Did On Our Holidays*. This varied collection contained some of their finest songs: Denny's version of 'She Moved Through The Fair', her own 'Fotheringay', Matthews' lilting 'Book Song', the superb 'I'll Keep It With Mine' and Thompson's masterpiece 'Meet On The Ledge'. This joyous album was bound together by exemplary musicianship, of partic-

ular note was the guitar of the shy and wiry Thompson. Matthews left soon after its release, unhappy with the traditional direction the band were pursuing. Following the album's critical acclaim and a modest showing in the charts, they experienced tragedy a few months later when their Transit van crashed, killing Martin Lamble and their friend and noted dressmaker Jeannie Franklyn. *Unhalfbricking* was released and, although not as strong as the former, it contained two excellent readings of Bob Dylan songs, 'Percy's Song' and 'Si Tu Dois Partir' (If You Gotta Go, Go Now). Denny contributed two songs, 'Autopsy' and the definitive, and beautiful, 'Who Knows Where The Time Goes'. More significantly, *Unhalfbricking* featured guest musician, Dave Swarbrick, on fiddle and mandolin. The album charted, as did the second Dylan number; by now the band had opened the door for future bands like Steeleye Span, by creating a climate that allowed traditional music to be played in a rock context. The songs that went on their next album were premiered on John Peel's BBC radio show *Top Gear*. An excited Peel stated that their performance would 'sail them into uncharted waters'; his judgement proved correct. The live set was astonishing - they played jigs and reels, and completed all 27 verses of the traditional 'Tam Lin', featuring Swarbrick, now a full-time member, plus the debut of new drummer, Dave Mattacks (b. March 1948, Edgware, Middlesex, England). The subsequent album *Liege And Lief* was a milestone; they had created British folk rock in spectacular style. This, however, created problems within the band and Hutchings left to form Steeleye Span and Denny departed to form Fotheringay with ex-Eclection and future husband Trevor Lucas. Undeterred, the band recruited Dave Pegg on bass and Swarbrick became more prominent both as lead vocalist and as an outstanding fiddle player. From their communal home in Hertfordshire they wrote much of the next two albums' material although Thompson left before the release of *Angel Delight*. They made the *Guinness Book Of Records* in 1970 with the longest-ever title: 'Sir B. McKenzies's Daughter's Lament For The 77th Mounted Lancer's Retreat From The Straits Of Loch Knombe, In The Year Of Our Lord 1727, On The Occasion Of The Announcement Of Her Marriage To The Laird Of Kinleakie'. *Full House* was the first all-male Fairport album and was instrumentally strong with extended tracks like 'Sloth' becoming standards. The concept album *Babbacombe Lee*, although critically welcomed, failed to sell and Simon Nicol left to form the Albion Band with Ashley Hutchings. Swarbrick struggled on, battling against hearing problems. With such comings and goings of personnel it was difficult to document the exact changes. The lack of any animosity from ex-members contributed to the family atmosphere, although by this time record sales were dwindling. Sandy Denny rejoined, as did Dave Mattacks (twice), but by the end of the 70s the name was put to rest. The family tree specialist Pete Frame has documented their incredible array of line-ups. Their swan-song was at Cropredy in Oxfordshire in 1979. Since then an annual reunion has taken place and is now a major event on the folk calendar. The band have no idea which ex-members will turn up! They have continued to release albums, making the swan-song a sham. With Swarbrick's departure, his position was taken by Ric Sanders in 1985 who rapidly quietened his dissenters by stamping his own personality on the fiddler's role. Some of the recent collections have been quite superb, including *Gladys Leap*, with Simon Nicol back on lead vocals, and the instrumental *Expletive Delighted*. With the release in 1990 of *The Five Seasons*, the group had established the longest-lasting line-up in their history. The nucleus of Pegg, Nicol, Saunders, Mattacks and Allcoock were responsible for *Jewel In The Crown* (named after their favourite Tandoori takeaway). Nicol's voice sounded like it had been matured in a wooden cask and fuelled the suggestion that he should perhaps have been the lead vocalist right from the beginning. This was their best selling and undoubtedly finest album in years and dispels any thought of old folkies growing outdated and staid. The Fairports are as much a part of the folk music tradition as the music itself.

●ALBUMS: *Fairport Convention* (Polydor 1968)★★★, *What We Did On Our Holidays* (Island 1969)★★★★, *Unhalfbricking* (Island 1969)★★★★, *Liege And Lief* (Island 1969)★★★★, *Full House* (Island 1970)★★★★, *Angel Delight* (Island 1971)★★★, *Babbacombe Lee* (Island 1971)★★★, *Rosie* (Island 1973)★★★, *Nine* (Island 1973)★★, *Live Convention (A Moveable Feast)* (Island 1974)★★, *Rising For The Moon* (Island 1975)★★, *Gottle O'Geer* (Island 1976)★, *Live At The LA Troubadour* (Island 1977)★★, *A Bonny Bunch Of Roses* (Vertigo 1977)★★, *Tipplers Tales* (Vertigo 1978)★★, *Farewell, Farewell* (Simons 1979)★★★, *Moat On The Ledge: Live At Broughton Castle* (Woodworm 1981)★★★, *Gladys' Leap* (Woodworm 1985)★★★, *Expletive Delighted* (Woodworm 1986)★★★, *House Full* (Hannibal 1986)★★, *Heyday: The BBC Radio Sessions 1968-9* (Hannibal 1987)★★★, *'In Real Time' - Live '87* (Island 1987)★★, *Red And Gold* (New Routes 1989)★★, *Five Seasons* (New Routes 1991)★★, *25th Anniversary Concert* (Wormwood 1994)★★★, *Jewel In The Crown* (Woodworm 1995)★★★★, *Old New Borrowed Blue* (Woodworm 1996)★★★.

●COMPILATIONS: *History Of Fairport Convention* (Island 1972)★★★★, *The Best Of Fairport Convention* (1988)★★★★, *The Woodworm Years* (Woodworm 1992)★★★.

●VIDEOS: *Reunion Festival Broughton Castle 1981* (Videotech 1982), *Cropredy 39 August 1980* (Videotech 1982), *A Weekend In The Country* (Videotech 1983), *Cropredy Capers* (Intech Video 1986), *In Real Time* (Island Visual Arts 1987), *It All Comes Round Again* (Island Visual Arts 1987), *Live At Maidstone 1970* (Musikfolk 1991).

●FURTHER READING: *Meet On The Ledge*, Patrick Humphries. *The Woodworm Era: The Story Of Today's*

Fairport Convention, Fred Redwood And Martin Woodward. *Richard Thompson: Strange Affair*, Patrick Humphries.

FAIRWEATHER

This Welsh quintet - Andy Fairweather-Low (b. 2 August 1950, Ystrad Mynach, Cardiff, Wales; vocals/guitar), Neil Jones (guitar), Blue Weaver (keyboards), Clive Taylor (bass) and Dennis Bryon (drums) - evolved from the ashes of the pop group Amen Corner. Although the new unit was determined to plough a more progressive furrow, they reached number 6 in the UK charts with 'Natural Sinner' in July 1970. Fairweather was unable to rid itself of a 'teenybopper' tag, and split up on completing their lone album. Blue Weaver later became a respected session musician, appearing with such disparate acts as the Strawbs, the Bee Gees and the Pet Shop Boys, while Andy Fairweather-Low pursued a solo career.

●ALBUMS: *Beginning From An End* (RCO 1971)★★.

FAIRWEATHER-LOW, ANDY

b. 2 August 1950, Ystrad Mynach, Cardiff, Wales. This Welsh guitarist and singer took over Dave Edmunds' sales assistant job at the music shop Barrett's Of Cardiff in the mid-60s, which enabled him to mix with the musicians on the local scene. He recruited a number of these to form the pop/soul band Amen Corner. It was Low's intention to play guitar in the group but as they had too many guitarists and no vocalists, he had to take on the singing duties and became a teen-idol in Britain as the band enjoyed a run of hit singles. When the band split, Low and the brass section formed Fairweather who signed to RCA Records' new progressive label Neon. They immediately blew their underground 'cool' by having a big hit single with 'Natural Sinner', but after a couple of less successful singles they too broke up. Low retired to Wales to concentrate on writing and playing for his own amusement. He returned in 1975 with an album and hit single 'Reggae Tune'. Another memorable big hit with 'Wide Eyed And Legless' highlighted his characteristic voice. Low's subsequent releases, including a 1986 single on the Stiff label, failed to chart and he spent more time playing on sessions and live gigs including some with Roger Waters. He also sang with the all-star ARMS band during 1987 to raise money for research in to multiple sclerosis. In 1990, Low toured with Chris Rea and in December 1991 with George Harrison and Eric Clapton (Japanese tour). He is currently playing in Clapton's band as well as being his musical arranger (appearing on *Unplugged*) and is regularly called upon for other prestigious gigs throughout the rock world.

●ALBUMS: as Fairweather *Beginning From An End* (RCO 1971)★★, *Spider Jivin'* (A&M 1974)★★★, *La Booga Rooga* (A&M 1975)★★, *Be Bop 'N' Holla* (A&M 1976)★★, *Mega-Shebang* (Warners 1980)★★.

FAMILY

Highly respected and nostalgically revered, Family were one of Britain's leading progressive rock bands of the late 60s and early 70s. They were led by the wiry yet vocally demonic Roger Chapman (b. 8 April 1942, Leicester, England), a man whose stage presence could both transfix and terrify his audience, who would duck from the countless supply of tambourines he destroyed and hurled into the crowd. Chapman was ably supported by Rick Grech (b. 1 November 1946, Bordeaux, France, d. 16 March 1990; violin, bass), Charlie Whitney (b. 24 June 1944, Leicester, England; guitar), Rob Townsend (b. 7 July 1947, Leicester, England; drums) and Jim King (b. Kettering, Northamptonshire, England; flute, saxophone). The band was formed in 1962 and known variously as the Roaring Sixties and the Farinas, finally coming together as Family in 1967 with the arrival of Chapman and Townsend. Their first album released in 1968 was given extensive exposure on John Peel's influential BBC radio programme, resulting in this Dave Mason-produced collection becoming a major cult record. Chapman's remarkable strangulated vibrato caused heads to turn. Following the release of their most successful album *Family Entertainment* they experienced an ever-changing personnel of high pedigree musicians when Rick Grech departed to join Blind Faith in 1969, being replaced by John Weider, who in turn was supplanted by John Wetton in 1971, then Jim Cregan in 1972. Poli Palmer (b. John Palmer, 25 May 1943) superseded Jim King in 1969 who was ultimately replaced by Tony Ashton in 1972. Throughout this turmoil they maintained a high standard of recorded work and had singles success with 'No Mules Fool', 'Strange Band', 'In My Own Time' and the infectious 'Burlesque'. Family disintegrated after their disappointing swan-song *Its Only A Movie*, Chapman and Whitney departing to form Streetwalkers. While their stage performances were erratic and unpredictable, the sight of Roger Chapman performing their anthem 'The Weaver's Answer' on a good night was unforgettable.

●ALBUMS: *Music In A Doll's House* (Reprise 1968)★★★★, *Family Entertainment* (Reprise 1969)★★★★, *A Song For Me* (Reprise 1970)★★★, *Anyway* (Reprise 1970)★★★, *Fearless* (Reprise 1971)★★★★, *Bandstand* (Reprise 1972)★★★★, *It's Only A Movie* (Reprise 1973)★★, *Peel Sessions* (Strange Fruit 1988)★★, *In Concert* (Windsong 1991)★★★★.

●COMPILATIONS: *Old Songs New Songs* (Reprise 1971)★★★★, *Best Of Family* (Reprise 1974)★★★, *Singles A's and B's* (See For Miles 1991)★★★★.

FANNY

Warner Brothers Records claimed in 1970 that their recent signing Fanny were the 'first all-female rock group'. They sustained a career for four years on that basis, throwing off all rivals to the throne, including Birtha, whose tasteless publicity handout stated 'Birtha has balls'. Formerly Wild Honey, the name Fanny was suggested by George Harrison to their producer Richard Perry. It was only later in their career that the group realized how risqué their name was internationally. Comprising Jean Millington (b. 1950, Manila, California, USA; bass/vocals), June Millington (b. 1949, Manila, California, USA; guitar/vocals), Alice de Buhr (b. 1950, Mason City, Iowa, USA; drums) and Nickey Barclay (b. 1951, Washington, DC, USA; keyboards), their blend of driving hard rock and rock 'n' roll was exciting, although they were always a second division act. They were more popular in the UK where they toured regularly, recording albums at Apple and Olympic studios. June Millington was replaced in 1974 by Patti Quatro from the Pleasure Seekers, the sister of Suzi Quatro. None of their albums charted in the UK and their sales in the USA were minimal. Their second album, *Charity Ball* was their best work, giving them a US Top 40 hit with the title song. Ironically, their biggest hit 'Butter Boy' came as they fragmented in 1975.

●ALBUMS: *Fanny* (Reprise 1970)★★★, *Charity Ball* (Reprise 1971)★★★, *Fanny Hill* (Reprise 1972)★★★, *Mother's Pride* (Reprise 1973)★★, *Rock 'N' Roll Survivors* (Casablanca 1974)★★. Solo: June And Jean Millington *Millington* (United Artists 1977)★★.

FARNHAM, JOHN

b 1 July 1949, Dagenham, Essex, England. Farnham has sustained a successful career in Australia for over three decades. Having initial success in 1968 with 'Sadie', a throwaway pop song, his manager pushed Farnham into the pop limelight with 13 subsequent hit singles. He was voted Australia's 'King of Pop' five years in a row between 1969 and 1973, and was also active in a variety of stage shows and musicals. However, for the second half of the 70s his career seemed dead, and it was not until mid-1980 that he re-emerged with another hit record, a unique rendition of the Beatles' 'Help'. He formed his own band and went back on the road until 1982 when he was asked to sing with the Little River Band, replacing original singer Glenn Shorrock. Despite adding some bite to its music, Farnham was unable to assist the band in repeating its earlier successes and so he resumed his solo career. For his comeback, *Whispering Jack*, Farnham sifted through hundreds of songs from local and international writers, which proved fruitful as it became the largest-selling album in Australia's history. The record deserved its success as the songs were varied and strong, and it showcased Farnham's excellent singing voice. Because of his earlier successes, his fans continued to support him and, unlike other performers, he was not afraid to change and move in new directions. The single 'You're The Voice' was a Top 10 hit in the UK in 1987. While his next album, *Age Of Reason*, repeated the success formula of the first, Farnham remains highly successful in his native country. *Romeo's Heart* in 1996 became his fastest-selling album.

●ALBUMS: *Sadie* (1968)★★, *Looking Through A Tear* (1970)★★, *Christmas Is John Farnham* (1970)★★, *Everybody Oughta Sing A Song* (1971)★★, *JF Sings The Shows* (1972)★★, with Alison Durbin *Together* (1972)★★, *Hits Magic And Rock 'N' Roll* (1973)★★, *JF Sings The Hits Of 1973* (1973)★★, *Uncovered* (RCA 1981)★★, *Whispering Jack* (RCA 1987)★★★, *Age Of Reason* (Wheatley 1988)★★★, *Chain Reaction* (RCA 1990)★★, *Full House* (RCA 1992)★★, *Romeo's Heart* (BMG 1996)★★.

●COMPILATIONS: *Best Of John Farnham* (1981)★★★.

●VIDEOS: *Classic Jack Live* (BMG 1989), *Chain Reaction-Live In Concert* (BMG 1991).

FAUST

Producer/advisor Uwe Nettelbeck formed this group in Wumme, Germany in 1971. The initial line-up - Werner Diermaier, Jean Herve Peron, Rudolf Sosna, Hans Joachim Irmler, Gunther Wusthoff and Armulf Meifert - worked from a custom-built studio, sited in a converted schoolhouse. *Faust* was a conscious attempt to forge a new western 'rock' music wherein fragments of sound were spliced together to create a radical collage. Released in a clear sleeve and clear vinyl, the album was viewed as an experimental masterpiece, or grossly self-indulgent, dependent on taste. *So Far* proved less obtuse, and the group subsequently secured a high-profile recording deal with Virgin. *The Faust Tapes*, a collection of private recordings reassembled by a fan in the UK, retailed at the price of a single (49p) and this inspired marketing ploy not unnaturally generated considerable interest. The label also issued *Outside The Dream Syndicate* on which the group accompanied Tony Conrad, a former colleague of John Cale. Faust's music remained distanced from mainstream acceptance, as evinced on *Faust 4*, and subsequent recordings, as well as items drawn from their back catalogue, were later issued by Recommended Records, specialists in *avant garde* recordings. Faust remained active throughout the 70s and 80s, albeit with a different line-up. In 1988 they reduced the price of admission to those persons arriving at live concerts with a musical instrument who were prepared to play it during the performance. *Rien*, their first album in years, was a return to ambient noise; 'challenging' is a good word to describe it.

●ALBUMS: *Faust* (Polydor 1972)★★, *So Far* (Polydor 1972)★★★, *The Faust Tapes* (Virgin 1973)★★★, with Tony Conrad *Outside The Dream Syndicate* (Virgin 1973)★★★, *Faust 4* (Virgin 1973)★★, *One* (Recommended 1979)★★, *Rien* (Table Of The Elements 1996)★★, *You Know Us* (Table Of The Elements 1997)★★.

●COMPILATIONS: *Munich And Elsewhere* (Recommended 1986)★★★.

FELICIANO, JOSÉ

b. 10 September 1945, Lares, Puerto Rico. After early fame as a flamenco-style interpreter of pop and rock material, Feliciano turned more to mainstream Latin music, becoming one of the most popular artists in the Spanish-speaking world. He was born blind and as a child moved to New York's Spanish Harlem. He learned guitar and accordion and from 1962 performed a mixture of Spanish and American material in the folk clubs and coffeehouses of Greenwich Village. Signed to RCA, he released a gimmicky single 'Everybody Do The Click' before recording an impressive debut album in 1964. Its impassioned arrangements of recent hits were continued on *Feliciano!* With jazz bassist Ray Brown among the backing musicians, Feliciano's Latin treatment of the Doors' 'Light My Fire' became his first hit. It was followed by a version of Tommy Tucker's R&B standard 'Hi Heel Sneakers' and such was Feliciano's popularity that he was chosen to sing 'The Star-Spangled Banner' at the 1968 baseball World Series. However, the application of his characteristic Latin-jazz styling to the US national anthem caused controversy among traditionalists.

In the UK, where he recorded a 1969 live album, Feliciano's version of the Bee Gees' 'The Sun Will Shine' was a minor hit, but the 70s saw RCA promoting Feliciano's Spanish-language material throughout Latin America. He recorded albums in Argentina, Mexico and Venezuela and had a television show syndicated throughout the continent. He also sang the theme music to the television series *Chico And The Man*. In parallel with the Latin albums, Feliciano continued to record English-language songs, notably on *Compartments*, produced by Steve Cropper. In 1976, Feliciano switched labels to Private Stock where producer Jerry Wexler was brought in to recreate the feeling of Feliciano's early work on Sweet Soul Music. When Motown set up its own Latin music label in 1981 Feliciano headed the roster, recording the Rick Jarrard-produced *Romance In The Night* as well as Grammy-winning Latin albums. In 1987 he signed a three-pronged deal with EMI to record classical guitar music and English pop (*I'm Never Gonna Change*) as well as further Spanish-language recordings (*Tu Immenso Amor*). He also pursued his jazz interests, and one of his more recent albums, *Steppin' Out,* was recorded for Optimism. He joined Polygram Latino records in 1995 and released *El Americano* in 1996.

●ALBUMS: *The Voice And Guitar Of José Feliciano* (RCA 1964)★★, *A Bag Full Of Soul* (RCA 1965)★★★, *Feliciano!* (RCA 1968)★★★★, *Souled* (RCA 1969)★★★, *Feliciano 10 To 23* (RCA 1969)★★, *Alive Alive-O* (RCA 1969)★★, *Fireworks* (RCA 1970)★★, *That The Spirit Needs* (RCA 1971)★★, *José Feliciano Sings* (RCA 1972)★★, *Compartments* (RCA 1973)★★, *And The Feeling's Good* (RCA 1974)★★, *Just Wanna Rock 'N' Roll* (RCA 1975)★★, *Sweet Soul Music* (RCA 1976)★★★, *Jose Feliciano* (Motown

1981)★★, *Escenas De Amor* (Latino 1982)★★, *Romance In The Night* (Latino 1983)★★, *Los Exitos De José Feliciano* (Latino 1984)★★, *Sings And Plays The Beatles* (RCA 1985)★★, *Tu Immenso Amor* (EMI 1987)★★★, *I'm Never Gonna Change* (EMI 1989)★★, *Steppin' Out* (Optimism 1990)★★★, *El Americano* (Polygram 1996)★★★.
●COMPILATIONS: *Encore!* (RCA 1971)★★★, *The Best Of José Feliciano* (RCA 1985)★★★, *Portrait* (Telstar 1985)★★★, *And I Love Her* (Camden 1996)★★★.

FERGUSON, JAY

b. John Ferguson, 10 May 1947, Burbank, California, USA. The former lead singer of seminal progressive rock band Spirit and hard rock quartet Jo Jo Gunne, Ferguson's debut album was well received but sold poorly. However, two years later the sparkling 'Thunder Island' made the US Top 10. The accompanying album stands as his best work. His name often appeared as session singer on other albums amidst the occasional (and usually abortive) Spirit reunions.
●ALBUMS: *All Alone In The End Zone* (Asylum 1976)★★★, *Thunder Island* (Asylum 1978)★★★, *Real Life Ain't This Way* (Asylum 1979)★★, *White Noise* (Capitol 1982)★★.

FERRY, BRYAN

b. 26 September 1945, Washington, Tyne & Wear, England. Ferry began his musical career in local group the Banshees, following which he enrolled at Newcastle-upon-Tyne University where he formed R&B group the Gas Board, whose ranks included Graham Simpson and John Porter. After studying Fine Art under Richard Hamilton, Ferry briefly worked as a teacher before forming Roxy Music. During their rise to fame, he plotted a parallel solo career, beginning in 1973 with *These Foolish Things*, an album of favourite cover versions. At the time, the notion of recording an album of rock standards was both innovative and nostalgic. Ferry recorded half an album of faithful imitations, leaving the other half to more adventurous arrangements. Some of the highlights included a revival of Ketty Lester's obscure 'Rivers Of Salt', a jaunty reading of Elvis Presley's 'Baby I Don't Care' and a remarkable hit version of Bob Dylan's 'A Hard Rain's A-Gonna Fall'. The album received mixed reviews but effectively paved the way for similar works including David Bowie's *Pin Ups* and John Lennon's *Rock 'N' Roll*. Ferry continued the cover game with *Another Time Another Place*, which was generally less impressive than its predecessor. Two stylish pre-rock numbers that worked well were 'Smoke Gets In Your Eyes' and 'Funny How Time Slips Away'. A gutsy revival of Dobie Gray's 'The In Crowd' brought another UK Top 20 hit. By 1976, Ferry had switched to R&B covers on *Let's Stick Together* which, in addition to the hit Wilbert Harrison title track, featured a rousing re-run of the Everly Brothers' 'The Price Of Love'. It was not until 1977 that Ferry finally wrote an album's worth of songs for a solo work. *In Your Mind* spawned a couple

of minor hits with 'This Is Tomorrow' and 'Tokyo Joe'. That same spring, Ferry appeared on the soundtrack of *All This And World War II* singing the Beatles' She's Leaving Home'. The following year, he retired to Montreux to complete the highly accomplished *The Bride Stripped Bare*. Introspective and revelatory, the album documented his sense of rejection following separation from his jet-setting girlfriend, model Jerry Hall. The splendid 'Sign Of The Times' presented a Dadaist vision of life as total bleakness: 'We live, we die . . . we know not why'. The track 'Can't Let Go', written at a time when he considered giving up music, maintained the dark mood. It was another seven years before Ferry recorded solo again. In the meantime, he married society heiress Lucy Helmore, abandoning his lounge lizard image in the process. The 1985 comeback *Boys And Girls* was stylistically similar to his work with Roxy Music and included the hits 'Slave To Love' and 'Don't Stop The Dance'. After a further two-year break, Ferry collaborated with guitarist Johnny Marr on 'The Right Stuff' (adapted from the Smiths' instrumental, 'Money Changes Everything'). The album *Bete Noire* was a notable hit indicating that Ferry's muse was still very much alive, even though his solo work continues to be eclipsed by the best of Roxy Music. *Mamouna* suffered from a lack of sparkle; Ferry seems to have become so good at what he does that he ceases to put any energy or emotion into the songs. The production is excellent, his singing is excellent but someone needs to remind him that emotion is necessary, too.
●ALBUMS: *These Foolish Things* (Island 1973)★★★, *Another Time Another Place* (Island 1974)★★, *Let's Stick Together* (Island 1976)★★★, *In Your Mind* (Polydor 1977)★★★, *The Bride Stripped Bare* (Polydor 1978)★★★★, *Boys And Girls* (EG 1985)★★★, *Bete Noire* (Virgin 1987)★★, *Taxi* (Virgin 1993)★★, *Mamouna* (Virgin 1994)★★.
●COMPILATIONS: *The Compact Collection* 3-CD box set (1992)★★★★.
●VIDEOS: *Bryan Ferry And Roxy Music* (Virgin 1995).
●FURTHER READING: *Roxy Music: Style With Substance - Roxy's First Ten Years*, Johnny Rogan.

FIREFALL

Firefall were a second generation US country rock band in the tradition of Poco and the Eagles. Formed during the genre's heyday the initial line-up was comprised of ex-Flying Burrito Brothers members Rick Roberts (b. 1950, Florida, USA; guitar/vocals) and Michael Clarke (b. Michael Dick, 3 June 1943, New York, USA; drums, also ex-Byrds), ex-Spirit Mark Andes (b. 19 February 1948, Philadelphia, Pennsylvania, USA; bass), Jock Bartley (guitar/vocals), David Muse (keyboards/saxophone/flute) and Larry Burnett (guitar/vocals). Their debut was a refreshing though laid-back affair, and in addition to three US hit singles the album contained a version of the Stephen Stills/Chris Hillman song 'It Doesn't Matter', with alternative lyrics by Roberts.

Their first three albums were all strong sellers and for a brief time Firefall were one of the biggest-selling artists in their genre. *Luna Sea* contained a further major US hit with the memorable 'Just Remember I Love You'. While their instrumental prowess was faultless their inability to progress significantly was their ultimate failing, although *Elan* demonstrated a will to change, with the sparkling hit 'Strange Way' which featured a breathy jazz-influenced flute solo. They continued to produce sharply engineered albums with Muse playing an increasingly important role adding other instruments, giving a new flavour to a guitar-dominated genre. They experienced hits even beyond the era of mainstream country rock.

●ALBUMS: *Firefall* (Atlantic 1976)★★★, *Luna Sea* (Atlantic 1977)★★, *Elan* (Atlantic 1978)★★★, *Undertow* (Atlantic 1980)★★, *Clouds Across The Sun* (Atlantic 1981)★★, *Break Of Dawn* (Atlantic 1983)★★.

●COMPILATIONS: *Best Of* (Atlantic 1981)★★★, *The Greatest Hits* (1993)★★★.

FIRESIGN THEATRE

Formed in Los Angeles, USA in 1967, this satirical/comedy group consisted of Philip Proctor, Peter Bergman, David Ossman and Phil Austin. The quartet's work drew on a multitude of disparate sources, encompassing 30s radio serials, W.C. Fields, Lord Buckley, the Marx Brothers and contemporary politics. Their surreal humour found favour with the late 60s' 'underground' audience, but despite punning wordplay and sharp wit, many cultural references were too obtuse for widespread appeal. Produced by Gary Usher, they were used to provide the spectacular gunshot effects on 'Draft Morning' on the Byrds' *Notorious Byrd Brothers*. They subsequently completed the film script for *Zacharia* (1970), 'the first electric Western', but the final draft bore little relation to their original intention. A series of adventurous albums, including *How Can You Be In Two Places At Once When You're Not Anywhere At All*, *Don't Crush That Dwarf, Hand Me The Pliers* and *I Think We're All Bozos On This Bus* are among the quartet's most popular collections, while *Dear Friends* included several highlights from their radio shows. During the 70s the group also pursued independent projects, with Ossman recording *How Time Flies* (1973), Austin *The Roller Maidens From Outer Space* (1974), and Proctor and Bergman completing *TV Or Not TV* (1973), *What This Country Needs* (1975) and *Give Us A Break* (1978). Their prolific output slackened towards the end of the decade, but the Firesign Theatre subsequently found a sympathetic haven at Rhino Records. Another series of excellent albums ensued, before the group began transferring their routines to video.

●ALBUMS: *Waiting For The Electrician* (Columbia 1968)★★, *How Can You Be In Two Places At Once When You're Not Anywhere At All* (Columbia 1969)★★★★, *Don't Crush That Dwarf, Hand Me The Pliers* (Columbia 1970)★★★★, *I Think We're All Bozos On This Bus* (Columbia 1971)★★★, *Dear Friends* (Columbia 1972)★★, *Not Insane Or Anything You Want To* (Columbia 1972)★★, *The Tale Of The Giant Rat Of Sumatra* (Columbia 1974)★★, *Everything You Know Is Wrong* (Columbia 1974)★★★★, *In The Next World You're On Your Own* (Columbia 1975)★★★, *Just Folks, A Firesign Chat* (Butterfly 1977)★★, *Pink Puffins In A Pelican's World* (1978)★★, *Live At The Roxy* (1980)★★, *Fighting Clowns* (1980)★★★, *Anything You Want To* (1981)★★★, *Carter/Reagan* (1982)★★★, *Lawyer's Hospital* (1982)★★★, *Shakespeare's Lost Comedie* (1982)★★★, *Nick Danger In The Three Faces Of Owl* (1984)★★★, *Eat Or Be Eaten* (1985)★★★.

●COMPILATIONS: *Forward Into The Past* (Columbia 1976)★★★★.

FIRST CLASS

This studio group was conceived by John Carter and Ken Lewis in 1974. Carter And Lewis were formerly the leaders of Carter-Lewis And The Southerners and the Ivy League, and were prolific songwriters, session singers and hitmakers. They assembled some of the UK's finest studio musicians to record the summery 'Beach Baby' which made the UK Top 20 in the summer of 1974. The cast included singer Tony Burrows, previously in the Ivy League with Carter/Lewis, and the man chosen to lead the touring version of their 1967 studio group, the Flowerpot Men. Burrows also sang on records by White Plains, Edison Lighthouse, Pipkins, the Brotherhood Of Man and others. In 1970 he made *Top Of The Pops* history by appearing on one show with three different groups. Others on the record included John Carter himself, Del John, and Chas Mills completing the vocal harmonies plus Spencer James on guitar, Clive Barrett on keyboards, Robin Shaw on bass, and Eddie Richards on drums. The follow-ups to 'Beach Baby' - 'Dreams Are Ten A Penny' and the old Ivy League hit 'Funny How Love Can Be' - were flops and the band was dismantled in 1976. Carter went on to form another studio group - Ice. In the early 80s the First Class name was resurrected for a cover of Brenton Wood's 'Gimme Little Sign' on Sunny Records. The label suggests that the British Surf mafia of Carter and company were involved but personnel details are not known.

●COMPILATIONS: *The First Class/SST* (See For Miles 1996)★★.

FISCHER Z

A vehicle for the talents of musician/songwriter John Watts, Fischer Z was a bridge between new wave pop and the synthesizer wave of the early 80s. Watts and three other musicians performed on their first two albums, but by the time of the third Watts had taken over the keyboards and was co-producing as well. The first two singles, 'Wax Dolls' and 'Remember Russia', were both well received. The latter even boasted a Ralph Steadman cartoon illustration on the sleeve.

However, it was 'The Worker' in 1979 that gave them their sole single success. In 1982 Watt started recording under his own name. However, singles like 'I Smelt Roses In The Underground' and 'Mayday Mayday' attracted little interest.

●ALBUMS: *Word Salad* (United Artists 1979)★★★, *Going Deaf For A Living* (United Artists 1980)★★, *Red Skies Over Paradise* (Liberty 1981)★★, *Reveal* (Arista 1988)★★★, *Destination Paradise* (1992)★★★, *Kamikaze Shirt* (Welfare 1994)★★★, Solo: John Watts *One More Twist* (EMI 1982)★★★, *The Iceberg Model* (EMI 1983)★★★.

●COMPILATIONS: *Going Red For A Salad (UA Years 1979-1982)* (Capitol 1990)★★★.

●VIDEOS: *John Watts And The Cry* (Dubious 1988).

FISCHER, LARRY 'WILD MAN'

b. 1945. Fischer was a prominent fixture on Los Angeles' Sunset Strip during the late 60s. This imposing figure, part-eccentric, part-LSD casualty, was renowned for composing songs to order in return for small change. He became associated with Frank Zappa who produced Larry's uncompromising debut, *An Evening With Wild Man Fischer*. Contemporary opinion was divided on its merits. Some critics deemed it voyeuristic, while others proclaimed it a work of art and a valid documentary. Caught in the middle was an ecstatic performer, elated that his 50s-style compositions were finally recorded. Fischer made several live appearances with Zappa's group, the Mothers Of Invention, but it was seven years before he recorded again. Having completed a single, advertising the Rhino Records store, he was signed to their fledgling label. Three further albums continued the disquieting atmosphere of that first release.

●ALBUMS: *An Evening With Wild Man Fischer* (Bizarre 1968)★★, *Wild Mania* (Rhino 1978)★★, *Pronounced Normal* (Rhino 1981)★★, *Nothing Crazy* (Rhino 1984)★★.

FITZGERALD, PATRICK

Best known for 'Safety Pin In My Heart', a slightly crass but enduring snapshot of the late 70s new wave UK scene, punk poet Fitzgerald was lauded in some circles on his arrival as 'the new Bob Dylan', praise that was rather excessive, although Fitzgerald's performances deserve to be elevated above the stature of also-ran beneath the greater impact made by John Cooper Clarke. 'Safety Pin' was included on his debut five-track EP for Small Wonder Records in January 1978. Following two further singles, 'Backstreet Boys' and 'Paranoid Ward', he signed to Polydor Records in 1979. His first single for the label, 'All Sewn Up', featured John Maher of the Buzzcocks on drums, who was also in place for the accompanying debut album. However, his popularity dissolved quickly and by the 80s his studio work was received by a dwindling audience. 1986's *Tunisia Twist* was a brave attempt at commercial renewal, before he faded from view. Taking a job as a

waiter at the House Of Commons, he then relocated to Normandy in France in 1988. However, he found himself disenchanted and unable to find gainful employment, and so returned to England three years later. He started playing gigs again, and also launched an acting career, the most high profile engagement of which was a version of Moliere's *The Miser* at Stratford. In 1994 he was said still to be plotting a musical comeback, making ends meet with temporary market research work.

●ALBUMS: *Grubby Stories* (Polydor 1979)★★★, *Gifts And Telegrams* (Red Flame 1982)★★, *Drifting Toward Violence* (Red Flame 1984)★★, *Tunisia Twist* (1986)★★★.

●COMPILATIONS: *Treasures From The Wax Museum* (1993)★★★, *Safety-Pin Stuck In My Heart* (Anagram 1994)★★★.

FLACK, ROBERTA

b. 10 February 1937, Asheville, North Carolina, USA. Born into a musical family, Flack graduated from Howard University with a BA in music. She was discovered singing and playing jazz in a Washington nightclub by pianist Les McCann who recommended her talents to Atlantic Records. Two classy albums, *First Take* and *Chapter Two*, garnered considerable acclaim for their skilful, often introspective, content before Flack achieved huge success with a poignant version of folksinger Ewan MacColl's ballad, 'First Time Ever I Saw Your Face'. Recorded in 1969, it was a major international hit three years later, following its inclusion in the film *Play Misty For Me*. Further hits came with 'Where Is The Love?' (1972), a duet with Donny Hathaway, and 'Killing Me Softly With His Song' (1973), where Flack's penchant for sweeter, more MOR-styled compositions gained an ascendancy. Her cool, almost unemotional style benefited from a measured use of slow material, although she seemed less comfortable on up-tempo songs. Flack's self-assurance wavered during the mid-70s, but further duets with Hathaway, 'The Closer I Get To You' (1978) and 'You Are My Heaven' (1980), suggested a rebirth. She was shattered when her partner committed suicide in 1979, but in the 80s Flack enjoyed a fruitful partnership with Peabo Bryson which reached a commercial, if sentimental, peak with 'Tonight I Celebrate My Love' in 1983. Roberta Flack remains a crafted, if precisionist, performer.

●ALBUMS: *First Take* (Atlantic 1970)★★★★, *Chapter Two* (Atlantic 1970)★★★, *Quiet Fire* (Atlantic 1971)★★, *Roberta Flack And Donny Hathaway* (Atlantic 1972)★★, *Killing Me Softly* (Atlantic 1973)★★, *Feel Like Making Love* (Atlantic 1975)★★, *Blue Lights In The Basement* (Atlantic 1978)★★, *Roberta Flack* (Atlantic 1978)★★, *Roberta Flack Featuring Donny Hathaway* (Atlantic 1980)★★★, with Peabo Bryson *Live And More* (Atlantic 1980)★★, *Bustin' Loose* (MCA 1981)★★, *I'm The One* (Atlantic 1982)★★, with Bryson *Born To Love* (Capitol 1983)★★★, *Oasis* (Atlantic 1988)★★, *Set The Night To Music* (Atlantic 1991)★★, *Roberta* (Atlantic/East West 1995)★★★.

●COMPILATIONS: *Best Of Roberta Flack* (Atlantic

1980)★★★, *Softly With These Songs: The Best Of ...* (Atlantic 1993)★★★.
●FURTHER READING: *Roberta Flack: Sound Of Velvet Melting*, Linda Jacobs.
●FILMS: *Body Rock* (1984).

FLAMIN' GROOVIES

This unflinchingly self-assured act evolved from an aspiring San Francisco-based garage band, the Chosen Few. Roy Loney (b. 13 April 1946, San Francisco, California, USA; vocals), Tim Lynch (b. 18 July 1946, San Francisco, California, USA; guitar), Cyril Jordan (b. 1948, San Francisco, California, USA; guitar), George Alexander (b. 18 May 1946, San Mateo, California, USA; bass) and Ron Greco (drums) subsequently flirted with a new appellation, Lost And Found, before breaking up in the summer of 1966. All of the group, bar Greco, reassembled several months later as the Flamin' Groovies. New drummer Danny Mihm (b. San Francisco, California, USA) joined from another local act, Group 'B', and the new line-up embarked on a direction markedly different from the city's prevalent love of extended improvisation. The Groovies remained rooted in America's immediate beat aftermath and bore traces of the Lovin' Spoonful and the Charlatans. Having completed a promising private pressing, the group recorded their official debut, *Supersnazz*, which also revealed a strong debt to traditional rock 'n' roll. The group's subsequent albums, *Flamingo* and *Teenage Head*, were influenced by Detroit's MC5 and offered a more contemporary perspective. The latter set drew complementary reviews and was compared favourably with the Rolling Stones' *Sticky Fingers*, but it marked the end of the original line-up. Loney and Lynch were replaced, respectively, by Chris Wilson and James Farrell. Denigrated at home, the Groovies enjoyed a cult popularity in Europe and a series of superb recordings, including the seminal anti-drug song, 'Slow Death', were recorded during a brief spell in Britain. Several of these performances formed the basis of *Shake Some Action*, the Groovies' majestic homage to 60s pop, which remains their finest and most accomplished work. New drummer David Wright had replaced a disaffected Mihm, while the group's harmonies and reverberating instrumental work added an infectious sparkle. The group then adopted former Charlatan Mike Wilhelm in place of Farrell. However, subsequent releases relied on a tried formula where a series of cover versions disguised a lack of original songs. The Groovies were then perceived as a mere revival band and the resultant frustration led to the departure of Wilson, Wilhelm and Wright. Jordan and Alexander continued relatively undeterred, adding Jack Johnson (guitar) and Paul Zahl (drums) from Roky Erickson's backing band. The reconstituted Groovies toured Europe, Australia and New Zealand and completed a handful of new recordings, including *One Night Stand*. However, despite promises of a greater prolificacy, the group has been unable to secure a permanent recording contract. Paradoxically, Roy Loney has enjoyed a flourishing performing career, honing a style not dissimilar to that of *Supersnazz* and *Flamingo*.
●ALBUMS: *Sneakers* (Snazz 1968)★★, *Supersnazz* (Epic 1969)★★★, *Flamingo* (Kama Sutra 1970)★★★, *Teenage Head* (Kama Sutra 1971)★★★, *Shake Some Action* (Sire 1976)★★★★, *Flamin' Groovies Now* (Sire 1978)★★★, *Jumpin' In The Night* (Sire 1979)★★★, *One Night Stand* (Sire 1986)★★.
●COMPILATIONS: *Still Shakin'* (Buddah 1976)★★, *Slow Death - Live* aka *Bucketful Of Brains* (1983)★★★, *Studio '68* (1984)★★, *Studio '70* (1984)★★, *The Rockfield Sessions* (1989)★★, *Live At The Festival Of The Sun* (Aim 1995)★★.
●FURTHER READING: *A Flamin' Saga: The Flamin' Groovies Histoire & Discographie* Jea-Pierre Poncelet. *Bucketfull Of Groovies* Jon Storey.

FLASH CADILLAC AND THE CONTINENTAL KIDS

Formed in Colorado, USA in 1969, Flash Cadillac And The Continental Kids were one of several groups to parody 50s rock in the wake of Sha Na Na. The original line-up - Flash Cadillac (Kenny Moe) (vocals), Sam McFadin (guitar/vocals), Linn Phillips (guitar/vocals), George Robinson (saxophone), Kris Angelo (keyboards/vocals), Warren 'Butch' Knight (bass/vocals) and Ricco Masino (drums) - later moved to Los Angeles where they met pop svengali Kim Fowley. The group made a successful appearance in the film *American Graffiti* before releasing a promising debut album which contained respectable readings of rock 'n' roll favourites. A second set, *No Face Like Chrome*, contained material indebted to 50s, 60s and 70s styles and was arguably reminiscent of Britain's 'pub rock' groups. Although they enjoyed two minor US hits with 'Dancin' On A Saturday Night' and 'Good Times Rock 'n' Roll', Flash Cadillac were unable to escape a revivalist tag and broke up without realizing their full potential.
●ALBUMS: *Flash Cadillac And The Continental Kids* (Epic 1973)★★★, *There's No Face Like Chrome* (Epic 1974)★★★, *Sons Of Beaches* (Private Stock 1975)★.

FLEETWOOD MAC

The original Fleetwood Mac was formed in July 1967 by Peter Green (b. Peter Greenbaum, 29 October 1946, Bethnel Green, London, England; guitar) and Mick Fleetwood (b. 24 June 1947, Redruth, Cornwall, England; drums), both of whom had recently left John Mayall's Bluesbreakers. They secured a recording contract with Blue Horizon Records on the strength of Green's reputation as a blues guitarist before the label's overtures uncovered a second guitarist, Jeremy Spencer (b. 4 July 1948, Hartlepool, Cleveland, England), in a semi-professional group, the Levi Set. A temporary bassist, Bob Brunning, was recruited into the line-up, until a further Mayall acolyte, John McVie (b.

26 November 1945, London, England; bass), was finally persuaded to join the new unit. Peter Green's Fleetwood Mac, as the group was initially billed, made its debut on 12 August 12 1967 at Windsor's National Jazz And Blues Festival. Their first album, *Fleetwood Mac*, released on Blue Horizon in February the following year, reached the UK Top 5 and established a distinctive balance between Green's introspective compositions and Spencer's debt to Elmore James. A handful of excellent cover versions completed an album that was seminal in the development of the British blues boom of the late 60s.

The group also enjoyed two minor hit singles with 'Black Magic Woman', a hypnotic Green composition later popularized by Santana, and a delicate reading of 'Need Your Love So Bad', first recorded by Little Willie John. Fleetwood Mac's second album, *Mr. Wonderful*, was another triumph, but while Spencer was content to repeat his established style, Green, the group's leader, extended his compositional boundaries with several haunting contributions, including the heartfelt 'Love That Burns'. His guitar playing, clean and sparse but always telling, was rarely better, while McVie and Fleetwood were already an instinctive rhythm section. *Mr. Wonderful* also featured contributions from Christine Perfect (b. 12 July 1943, Birmingham, England), pianist from Chicken Shack, and a four-piece horn section, as the group began to leave traditional blues behind. A third guitarist, Danny Kirwan (b. 13 May 1950, London, England), was added to the line-up in September 1968. The quintet had an immediate hit when 'Albatross', a moody instrumental reminiscent of 'Sleep Walk' by Santo And Johnny, topped the UK charts. The single, which reached number 2 when it was reissued in 1973, was the group's first million-seller.

Fleetwood Mac then left Blue Horizon, although the company subsequently issued *Blues Jam At Chess*, on which the band jammed with several mentors, including Buddy Guy, Otis Spann and Shakey Horton. Following a brief interlude on Immediate Records, which furnished the hypnotic 'Man Of The World', the quintet made their debut on Reprise with 'Oh Well', their most ambitious single to date, and the superb *Then Play On*. This crafted album unveiled Kirwan's songwriting talents and his romantic leanings offset the more worldly Green. Although pictured, Jeremy Spencer was notably absent from most of the sessions, although his eccentric vision was showcased on a self-titled solo album.

Fleetwood Mac now enjoyed an international reputation, but it was a mantle too great for its leader to bear. Peter Green left the band in May 1970 as his parting single, the awesome 'The Green Manalishi', became another Top 10 hit. He was replaced by Christine Perfect, now married to John McVie, and while his loss was an obvious blow, Kirwan's songwriting talent and Spencer's sheer exuberance maintained a measure of continuity on a fourth album, *Kiln House*. However, in 1971 the group was rocked for a second time when Spencer disappeared midway through an American tour. It transpired he had joined a religious sect, the Children Of God and while Green deputized for the remainder of the tour, a permanent replacement was found in a Californian musician, Bob Welch.

The new line-up was consolidated on two melodic albums, *Future Games* and *Bare Trees*. Neither release made much impression with UK audiences who continued to mourn the passing of the Green-led era, but in America the group began to assemble a strong following for their new-found transatlantic sound. However, further changes occurred when Kirwan's chronic stage-fright led to his dismissal. Bob Weston, a guitarist from Long John Baldry's backing band, was his immediate replacement, while the line-up was also bolstered by former Savoy Brown vocalist, Dave Walker. The group, however, was unhappy with a defined frontman and the singer left after only eight months, having barely completed work on their *Penguin* album. Although not one of the band's strongest collections, it does contain an excellent Welch composition, 'Night Watch'.

The remaining quintet completed another album, *Mystery To Me*, which was released at the time of a personal nadir within the group. Weston, who had been having an affair with Fleetwood's wife, was fired midway through a prolonged US tour and the remaining dates were cancelled. Their manager, Clifford Davis, assembled a bogus Mac to fulfil contractual obligations, thus denying the 'real' group work during the inevitable lawsuits. Yet despite the inordinate pressure, Perfect, Welch, McVie and Fleetwood returned with *Heroes Are Hard To Find*, a positive release which belied the wrangles surrounding its appearance. Nonetheless the controversy proved too strong for Welch, who left the group in December 1974, robbing Fleetwood Mac of an inventive songwriter.

It was while seeking prospective recording studios that Fleetwood was introduced to Stevie Nicks and Lindsey Buckingham via the duo's self-named album. Now bereft of a guitarist, he recalled Buckingham's expertise and invited him to replace Welch. Lindsey accepted on condition that Nicks also join, thus cementing Fleetwood Mac's most successful line-up. *Fleetwood Mac*, released in 1975, was a promise fulfilled. The newcomers provided easy, yet memorable compositions with smooth harmonies while the British contingent gave the group its edge and power. A succession of stellar compositions, including 'Over My Head', 'Say You Love Me' and the dramatic 'Rhiannon', confirmed a perfect balance had been struck giving the group their first in a long line of US Top 20 singles. The quintet's next release, *Rumours*, proved more remarkable still. Despite the collapse of two relationships - the McVies were divorced, Buckingham and Nicks split up - the group completed a remarkable collection which laid bare the traumas within, but in a manner neither maudlin nor pitiful. Instead the ongoing drama was charted by several exquisite songs; 'Go Your Own Way', 'Don't Stop', 'Second Hand News' and 'Dreams', which retained both melody and purpose. An enduring release, *Rumours* has sold upwards of 25 million copies and is second to Michael Jackson's *Thriller* as the best-selling album of all time.

Having survived their emotional anguish, Fleetwood Mac was faced with the problem of following up a phenomenon. Their response was *Tusk*, an ambitious double set that showed a group unafraid to experiment, although many critics damned the collection as self-indulgent. The title track, a fascinating instrumental, was an international hit, although its follow-up, 'Sara', a composition recalling the style of *Rumours*, was better received in the USA than the UK. An in-concert selection, *Fleetwood Mac: Live*, was released as a stop-gap in 1980 as rumours of a complete break-up flourished. It was a further two years before a new collection, *Mirage*, appeared by which point several members were pursuing independent ventures. Buckingham and Nicks, in particular, viewed their own careers with equal importance and *Mirage*, a somewhat self-conscious attempt at creating another *Rumours*, lacked the sparkle of its illustrious predecessor. It nonetheless yielded three successful singles in 'Hold Me', 'Gypsy' and Buckingham's irrepressible 'Oh Diane'.

Five years then passed before a new Fleetwood Mac album was issued. *Tango In The Night* was a dramatic return to form, recapturing all the group's flair and invention with a succession of heartwarming performances in 'Little Lies', 'Family Man' and 'You And I (Part 2)'. Christine McVie contributed a further highpoint with the rhythmic singalong 'Anyway'. The collection was, however, Lindsey Buckingham's swansong, although his departure from the band was not officially confirmed until June 1988. By that point two replacement singer/guitarists, ex-Thunderbyrd Rick Vito (b. 1950) and Billy Burnette (b. 7 May 1953), had joined the remaining quartet. The new line-up's debut, *Behind The Mask*, ushered in a new decade and era for this tempestuous group, that gained strength from adversity and simply refused to die. Its success confirmed their status as one of the major groups in the history of popular music. In recent years the the release of *The Chain*, compiled by Fleetwood, gave the band greater critical acclaim than it had received of late. In September 1995 Fleetwood self-promoted the excellent *Peter Green's Fleetwood Mac: Live At The BBC*. This was a project that was dear to his heart as during the promotion it became clear that Fleetwood still has great emotional nostalgia for the original band and clearly regrets the departure of Green and the subsequent turn of events. A month later a new Fleetwood Mac album was released to muted reviews and minimal sales. The addition of ex-Traffic guitarist Dave Mason and Bekka Bramlett b. 1970, USA (daughter of Delaney And Bonnie) for the album *Time* failed to ignite any spark. The dismal reaction to *Time* must have prompted Fleetwood to rethink where the band wanted to go. He had made no secret of the fact that he longed for the days of Green and the latter-day line-up of Nicks and Buckingham. Some diplomacy must have occurred behind closed doors because in the Spring of 1997 it was announced that the famous *Rumours* line-up had reunited and were recording together.

●ALBUMS: *Fleetwood Mac* (Columbia/Blue Horizon 1968)★★★★, *Mr. Wonderful* (Columbia/Blue Horizon 1968)★★★, *English Rose* (Epic 1969)★★★, *Then Play On* (Reprise 1969)★★★★, *Blues Jam At Chess* aka *Fleetwood Mac In Chicago* (Blue Horizon 1969)★★★, *Kiln House* (Reprise 1970)★★★, *Future Games* (Reprise 1971)★★★, *Bare Trees* (Reprise 1972)★★, *Penguin* (Reprise 1973)★★, *Mystery To Me* (Reprise 1973)★★, *Heroes Are Hard To Find* (Reprise 1974)★★★, *Fleetwood Mac* (Reprise 1975)★★★★, *Rumours* (Warners 1977)★★★★, *Tusk* (Warners 1979)★★★, *Fleetwood Mac Live* (Warners 1980)★★, *Mirage* (Warners 1982)★★★, *Live In Boston* (Shanghai 1985)★★, *London Live '68* (Thunderbolt 1986)★, *Tango In The Night* (Warners 1988)★★★, *Behind The Mask* (Warners 1989)★★★, *Live At The Marquee* rec. 1967 (Sunflower 1992)★, *Live* rec. 1968 (Abracadabra 1995)★, *Peter Green's Fleetwood Mac: Live At The BBC* (Fleetwood/Castle 1995)★★★★, *Time* (Warners 1995)★. Solo: Danny Kirwan *Second Chapter* (DJM 1976)★★, *Midnight In San Juan* (DJM 1976)★, *Hello There Big Boy* (DJM 1979)★. Jeremy Spencer *Jeremy Spencer* (Reprise 1970)★★, *Jeremy Spencer And The Children Of God* (Columbia 1973)★, *Flee* (Atlantic 1979)★. Mick Fleetwood *The Visitor* (RCA 1981)★, *I'm Not Me* (RCA 1983)★. John McVie *John McVie's Gotta Band With Lola Thomas* (Warners 1992)★. Christine McVie *Christine Perfect* (Blue Horizon 1970)★★★, *Christine McVie* (Warners 1984)★★.

●COMPILATIONS: *The Pious Bird Of Good Omen* (Columbia/Blue Horizon 1969)★★, *The Original Fleetwood Mac* (Columbia/Blue Horizon 1971)★★, *Fleetwood Mac's Greatest Hits* (Columbia 1971)★★★★, *The Vintage Years* (Sire 1975)★★★, *Albatross* (Columbia 1977)★★★, *Man Of The World* (Columbia 1978)★★, *Best Of* (Reprise 1978)★★★, *Cerurlean* (Shanghai 1985)★★, *Greatest Hits: Fleetwood Mac* (Columbia 1988)★★★, *The Blues Years* (Essential 1991)★★★, *The Chain* CD box set (Warners 1992)★★★, *The Early Years* (Dojo 1992)★★, *Fleetwood Mac Family Album* (Connoisseur 1996)★★, *The Best Of ...* (Columbia 1996)★★★.

●VIDEOS: *Fleetwood Mac* (Warners 1981), *In Concert - Mirage Tour* (Spectrum 1983), *Peter Green's Fleetwood Mac: The Early Years 1967-1970* (PNE 1995).

●FURTHER READING: *Fleetwood Mac: The Authorized History*, Samuel Graham. *Fleetwood Mac: Rumours 'N' Fax*, Roy Carr and Steve Clarke. *Fleetwood Mac*, Steve Clarke. *The Crazed Story Of Fleetwood Mac*, Stephen Davis. *Fleetwood Mac: Behind The Masks*, Bob Brunning. *Fleetwood: My Life And Adventures With Fleetwood Mac*, Mick Fleetwood with Stephen Davis. *Peter Green: The Biography*, Martin Celmins.

FLINTLOCK

This UK teenybop band of the mid-70s was led by heart-throb drummer Mike Holoway, introduced to television audiences via the children's science fiction programme *The Tomorrow People*. The series told the story of several teenagers who had evolved beyond the rest of humanity and acted as guardians to its fate. Holoway appeared as Mike Bell in the fourth series of the programme, a would-be pop star both on screen and off, with an affected cockney accent. In one serial, 'The Heart Of Sogguth', Holoway performed with Flintlock on a musical piece with a supposedly mind-controlling beat heralding the arrival of extra-terrestrials. However, Flintlock's music was as cardboard as the sets and they achieved only one hit with 'Dawn' in 1976 despite much exposure from children's magazines such as *Look In*.
●ALBUMS: *On The Way* (Pinnacle 1975)★★, *Hot From The Lock* (Pinnacle 1976)★★, *Tears 'N' Cheers* (Pinnacle 1977)★, *Stand Alone* (Pinnacle 1979)★.

FLO AND EDDIE

Lead singers (and songwriters) of the Turtles, Marc Volman and Howard Kaylan took their name - the Phlorescent Leech and Eddie - from two of their roadies when the group split up in 1970. The Turtles' brand of innocent folk pop could not survive in the new sex-and-drug-oriented climate of rock. As if to advertise the change, they joined counter-cultural supremo Frank Zappa for tours and recordings. In his role as circus-master, Zappa had the pair perform hilarious routines about backstage groupie shenanigans (*Fillmore East June 1971*) and act desperate, on-the-road pop stars in the film *200 Motels* (1972). Zappa wrote suitably operatic lines for their strong voices and the results - though they dismayed fans of the 'serious' Mothers Of Invention - are undeniably effective. The sleeve of *Just Another Band From LA* (1972) - with Zappa reduced to a puppet in Kaylan's hand - seems to imply they had taken control of the group. They certainly split amidst much animosity, leaving Zappa just as his accident at the Rainbow Theatre, London, had made him wheel-chair-bound. The comedy albums they released subsequently - *Flo & Eddie, Immoral Illegal & Fattening, Moving Targets* - haven't the punch of their work with Zappa, nor did the pair seem capable of recreating the catchy pop they wrote for the Turtles. However, they did enliven the rock scene with an animated satirical film, *Cheap,* and a weekly three-hour radio show, *Flo & Eddie By The Fireside,* which originated on LA's KROQ but was syndicated all over the States by 1976. They also supplied their powerful falsettos to give Marc Bolan's voice a lift on many T. Rex hits. Their careers dived in the 80s, but the Marc Bolan revival, in the 90s, brought their voices back to the airwaves (albeit only as backing), and Jason Donovan brought the Turtles' evergreen 'Happy Together' back to the charts in 1991.
●ALBUMS: *Flo & Eddie* (Warners 1973)★★, *Immoral Illegal & Fattening* (Columbia 1974)★★★, *Moving Targets* (Columbia 1976)★★.

FLOATERS

Originally from Detroit, USA, Charles Clark (Libra), Larry Cunningham (Cancer), Paul Mitchell (Leo), Ralph Mitchell (Aquarius) and latterly, Jonathan 'Mighty Midget' Murray, who joined the group in 1978, were responsible for one of soul's more aberrant moments. 'Float On', with its astrological connotations and Barry White-influenced machismo, was saved from utter ignominy by a light, almost ethereal melody line which was effective enough to provide the group with a US number 2 and a UK number 1 hit single in 1977. The Floaters could not survive the gimmick and although two further singles reached the R&B Top 50, this often-ridiculed performance remains their lasting testament.
●ALBUMS: *Floaters* (ABC 1977)★★★, *Magic* (ABC 1978)★★, *Into The Future* (ABC 1979)★★.

FLOCK

Although they were formed in 1966 (Chicago, Illinois, USA) it was not until 1969 that Flock burst upon a most receptive market. CBS Records had successfully taken the lion's share of the progressive boom and for a short time Flock became one of their leading products. The original band comprised Jerry Goodman (violin), Fred Glickstein (guitar/vocals), Tom Webb and Rick Canoff (saxophones), Ron Karpman (drums), Jerry Smith (bass) and Frank Posa (trumpet). Their blend of jazz and rock improvisations soon exhausted audiences as the solos became longer and longer. Jerry Goodman was the outstanding musician, stunning fans with his furious and brilliant electric violin playing. Their version of the Kinks' 'Tired Of Waiting For You' was memorable if only for the fact that they managed to turn a three minute pop song into a magnum opus lasting, on occasions, over 10 minutes. Goodman left in 1971 to team up with John McLaughlin in the Mahavishnu Orchestra.
●ALBUMS: *The Flock* (Columbia 1969)★★★, *Dinosaur Swamps* (Columbia 1970)★, *Inside Out* (1975)★.
●COMPILATIONS: *Rock Giants* (1982)★★.

FLOWERS, HERBIE

As a session musician, Flowers' many performances have ensured his reputation as one of the world's most in-demand bass players (with the occasional request for trumpet playing). He found fame in the late 60s with the session players' 'supergroup' Blue Mink, enjoying success with the international hit 'Melting Pot'. His songwriting talents brought him fame with the novelty number 1 hit for Clive Dunn, 'Grandad' in January 1971. Flowers' performance on Lou Reed's UK Top 10/US Top 20 hit 'Walk On The Wild Side' (*Transformer* 1972) produced one of rock's most distinctive bass lines. His later work with the virtuoso group Sky, with John Williams, Kevin Peek, Tristan Fry and Francis

Monkman, brought him worldwide fame. Flowers also performed as part of one of the later line-ups of T. Rex in the late 70s. His many studio credits throughout his career have included work for David Bowie (*Space Oddity* 1969, *Diamond Dogs* 1974 and *David Live* 1974), CCS (*CCS* 1970), Melanie (*Candles In The Rain* 1970), Elton John (*Madman Across The Water* 1971 and *A Single Man* 1978), Cat Stevens (*Foreigner* 1973), Ginger Baker (*Eleven Sides Of Baker* 1977), Roy Harper (*Bullinamingvase* 1977), Ian Gomm (*Summer Holiday* 1978), Jeff Wayne (*War Of The Worlds* 1978), Steve Harley (*Hobo With A Grin* 1978), Roger Daltry (*McVicar* 1980), George Harrison (*Gone Troppo* 1982) and Paul McCartney (*Give My Regards To Broad Street* 1984). Along the way he has also managed to release two solo albums on Philips and EMI Note.
●ALBUMS: *Plant Life* (Philips 1975)★★, *A Little Potty* (Note 1980)★★.

FLYING BURRITO BROTHERS

The Flying Burrito Brothers initially referred to an informal group of Los Angeles musicians, notably Jesse Davis and Barry Tashain. The name was appropriated in 1968 by former Byrds Gram Parsons (b. 5 November 1946, Waycross, Georgia USA, d. 19 September 1973; guitar/vocals) and Chris Hillman (b. 4 December 1942, Los Angeles, California, USA; guitar/vocals) for a new venture that would integrate rock and country styles. 'Sneaky' Pete Kleinow (pedal steel), Chris Ethridge (bass) plus various drummers completed the line-up featured on *The Gilded Palace Of Sin*, where the founding duo's vision of a pan-American music flourished freely. The material ranged from the jauntily acerbic 'Christine's Tune' to the maudlin 'Hippy Boy', but its highlights included Parsons' emotional reading of two southern soul standards, 'Dark End Of The Street' and 'Do Right Woman', and his own poignant 'Hot Burrito #1' and the impassioned 'Hot Burrito #2'. The album's sense of cultural estrangement captured a late 60s restlessness and reflected the rural traditions of antecedents the Everly Brothers. This artistic triumph was never repeated. *Burrito Deluxe*, on which Bernie Leadon replaced Ethridge and Michael Clarke (b. Michael Dick, 3 June 1944, Texas, USA), formerly of the Byrds, became the permanent drummer, showed a group unsure of direction as Parsons' role became increasingly questionable. He left for a solo career in April 1970 and with the arrival of songwriter Rick Roberts, the Burritos again asserted their high quality. The underrated *The Flying Burrito Brothers* was a cohesive, purposeful set, marked by the inclusion of Roberts' 'Colorado', Gene Clark's 'Tried So Hard' and Merle Haggard's 'White Line Fever', plus several other excellent Roberts originals. Unfortunately, the group was again bedevilled by defections. In 1971 Leadon joined the Eagles while Kleinow opted for a career in session work, but Hillman, Clarke and Roberts were then buoyed by the arrival of Al Perkins (pedal steel), Kenny

Wertz (guitar), Roger Bush (bass) and Byron Berline (fiddle). *The Last Of The Red Hot Burritos* captured the excitement and power of the group live. The septet was sundered in 1971 with Wertz, Bush and Berline forming Country Gazette, Hillman and Perkins joining Manassas while Roberts embarked on a solo career before founding Firefall with Clarke. However, much to the consternation of Hillman, Pete Kleinow later commandeered the Burritos' name and in 1975 completed *Flying Again* with Chris Ethridge, Gene Parsons (guitar/vocals) and Gib Guilbeau (fiddle). The last-named joined Kleinow in a full-scale reactivation during the 80s. The arrival of country veteran John Bleland has provided the group with a proven songwriter worthy of the early, pioneering line-up.
●ALBUMS: *The Gilded Palace Of Sin* (A&M 1969)★★★★★, *Burrito DeLuxe* (A&M 1970)★★★, *The Flying Burrito Brothers* (A&M 1971)★★★, *The Last Of The Red Hot Burritos* (A&M 1972)★★★, *Flying Again* (Columbia 1975)★★, *Airborne* (Columbia 1976)★★, *Close Encounters On The West Coast* (1978)★★, *Live In Tokyo, Japan* (1978)★★, *Flying High* (1980)★★, *Back To The Sweethearts Of The Rodeo* (1988)★★★, *Southern Tracks* (Dixie Frog 1990)★★★, *Eye Of A Hurricane* (1993)★★★.
●COMPILATIONS: *Live In Amsterdam* (Bumble 1973)★★★, *Bluegrass Special* (Ariola 1975)★★, *Close Up The Honky Tonks* (A&M 1974)★★★★, *Honky Tonk Heaven* (A&M 1972)★★, *Hot Burrito - 2* (A&M 1975)★★, with Gram Parsons *Sleepless Nights* (A&M 1976)★★★, *Dim Lights, Thick Smoke And Loud, Loud Music* (Edsel 1987)★★★, *Hollywood Nights 1979-1981* (Sundown 1990)★★★, *Out Of The Blue* (Polygram Chronicles 1996)★★★.

FOCUS

A former Amsterdam Conservatory student, Thijs van Leer (keyboards/flute/vocals) with Martin Dresden (bass) and philosophy graduate Hans Cleuver (drums) backed Robin Lent, Cyril Havermans and other Dutch singers before 1969's catalytic enlistment of guitarist Jan Akkerman, veteran of the progressive unit Brainbox. The new quartet's first collective essay as recording artists was humble - accompaniment on a Dutch version of *Hair* - but, heartened by audience response to a set that included amplified arrangements of pieces by Bartok and Rodrigo, Focus released a *bona fide* album debut with a spin-off single, 'House Of The King', that sold well in continental Europe. However, aiming always at the English-speaking forum, the group engaged Mike Vernon to produce *Moving Waves* which embraced vocal items (in English) and melodic if lengthy instrumentals. The album included the startling 'Hocus Pocus', a UK Top 20 hit. After reshuffles in which only van Leer and Akkerman surfaced from the original personnel, the group stole the show at British outdoor festivals, and a slot on BBC television's *Old Grey Whistle Test* assisted the passage of the glorious 'Sylvia', into the UK Top 5; *Focus III* and earlier album also reached the upper echelons of the charts. After stoking up modest interest in North America, 1973 began well with each member figuring in respective categories in the more earnest music journals' popularity polls. An in-concert album from London and *Hamburger Concerto* both marked time artistically and, following 1975's *Mother Focus*, Akkerman left to concentrate on the solo career that he had pursued parallel to that of Focus since his *Profile* in 1973. With several solo efforts, Van Leer was also well-placed to do likewise but elected instead to stick with a latter-day Focus in constant flux which engaged in a strange studio amalgamation with P.J. Proby before its final engagement in Terneuzen in 1978. Akkerman and Van Leer guided Focus through a 1985 album before the 1972 line-up re-formed solely for a Dutch television special five years later.

●ALBUMS: *In And Out Of Focus* (Polydor 1971)★★★, *Moving Waves* (Blue Horizon 1971)★★★★, *Focus III* (Polydor 1972)★★★, *At The Rainbow* (Polydor 1973)★★, *Hamburger Concerto* (Polydor 1974)★★, *Mother Focus* (Polydor 1975)★★, *Ship Of Memories* (Harvest 1977)★★, *Focus Con Proby* (Harvest 1977)★★★.

●COMPILATIONS: *Greatest Hits* (Fame 1984)★★, *Hocus Pocus: The Best Of ...* (EMI 1994)★★★.

FOGELBERG, DAN

b. 13 August 1951, Peoria, Illinois, USA. Having learned piano from the age of 14, Fogelberg moved to guitar and songwriting. Leaving the University of Illinois in 1971 he relocated to California and started playing on the folk circuit, at one point touring with Van Morrison. A move to Nashville brought him to the attention of producer Norbert Putnam. Fogelberg released *Home Free* for Columbia shortly afterwards. This was a very relaxed album, notable for the backing musicians involved, including Roger McGuinn, Jackson Browne, Joe Walsh and Buffy Sainte-Marie. Despite the calibre of the other players, the album was not a success, and Fogelberg, having been dropped by Columbia, returned to session work. Producer Irv Azoff, who was managing Joe Walsh, signed Fogelberg and secured a deal with Epic. Putnam was involved in subsequent recordings by Fogelberg. In 1974, Fogelberg moved to Colorado, and a year later released *Souvenirs*. This was a more positive album, and Walsh's production was evident. From here on, Fogelberg played the majority of the instruments on record, enabling him to keep tight control of the recordings, but inevitably it took longer to finish the projects. Playing support to the Eagles in 1975 helped to establish Fogelberg. However, in 1977, due to appear with the Eagles at Wembley, he failed to show on-stage, and it was later claimed that he had remained at home to complete recording work on *Netherlands*. Whatever the reason, the album achieved some recognition, but Fogelberg has enjoyed better chart success in the USA than in the UK. In 1980, 'Longer' reached number 2 in the US singles charts, while in the UK it did not even

reach the Top 50. Two other singles, 'Same Auld Lang Syne' and 'Leader Of The Band', both from *The Innocent Age*, achieved Top 10 places in the USA. The excellent *High Country Snows* saw a return to his bluegrass influences and was in marked contrast to the harder-edged *Exiles* which followed. From plaintive ballads to rock material, Fogelberg is a versatile writer and musician who continues to produce credible records and command a loyal cult following.

●ALBUMS: *Home Free* (Columbia 1973)★★, *Souvenirs* (Full Moon 1974)★★★, *Captured Angel* (Full Moon 1975)★★, *Netherlands* (Full Moon 1977)★★, with Tim Weisberg *Twin Sons Of Different Mothers* (Full Moon 1978)★★★★, *Phoenix* (Full Moon 1979)★★★★, *The Innocent Age* (Full Moon 1981)★★★★, *Windows And Walls* (Full Moon 1984)★★, *High Country Snows* (Full Moon 1985)★★★, *Exiles* (Full Moon 1987)★★, *The Wild Places* (Full Moon 1990)★★, *Dan Fogelberg Live - Greetings From The West* (Full Moon 1991)★★, *River Of Souls* (Sony 1993)★★.

●COMPILATIONS: *Greatest Hits* (Full Moon 1983)★★★, *Starbox* (1993)★★★.

FOGERTY, JOHN

b. 28 May 1945, Berkeley, California, USA. As the vocalist and composer with Creedence Clearwater Revival, one of the most successful acts of its era, Fogerty seemed assured of a similar status when he began a solo career in 1972. However his first release, *Blue Ridge Rangers*, was a curiously understated affair, designed to suggest the work of a group. The material consisted of country and gospel songs, two tracks from which, 'Jambalaya (On The Bayou)' and 'Hearts Of Stone', became US hit singles in 1973. Despite the exclusion of original songs and its outer anonymity, the work was clearly that of Fogerty, whose voice and instrumentation were unmistakable.

The first of many problems arose when the singer charged that his label, Fantasy Records, had not promoted the record sufficiently. He demanded a release from his contract, but the company claimed the rights to a further eight albums. This situation remained at an impasse until Asylum Records secured Fogerty's North American contract, while Fantasy retained copyright for the rest of the world. *John Fogerty* was duly released in 1975 and this superb collection contained several classic tracks, notably 'Almost Saturday Night' and 'Rockin' All Over The World' which were successfully covered, respectively, by Dave Edmunds and Status Quo. However, Fogerty's legal entanglements still persisted and although a single, 'Comin' Down The Road', was released from a prospective third album, *Hoodoo*, it was never issued. It was 1985 before the artist re-emerged with the accomplished *Centerfield*, which topped the US album charts and provided an international hit single in 'The Old Man Down The Road'. The set also included two powerful rock songs, 'Mr. Greed' and 'Zanz Kan't Danz', which Fantasy owner Saul

Zaentz assumed was a personal attack. He sued Fogerty for $142 million, claiming he had been slandered by the album's lyrics, and filed for the profits from 'The Old Man Down The Road', asserting the song plagiarised CCR's 'Run Through The Jungle'. Fogerty's riposte was a fourth album, *Eye Of A Zombie* which, although failing to scale the heights of its predecessor, was the impetus for a series of excellent live performances. Since then the artist has maintained a lower profile, and success-fully secured a decision against Zaentz's punitive action. *Blue Moon Swamp* was a welcome return to form, and the reviews were generally excellent, although the material was not radically different from his chosen past of rock/country. Possibly his popularity is greater than his product.

●ALBUMS: *The Blue Ridge Rangers* (Fantasy 1973)★★★, *John Fogerty* (Fantasy 1975)★★★, *Centerfield* (Warners 1985)★★★, *Eye Of A Zombie* (Warners 1986)★★, *Blue Moon Swamp* (Warners 1997)★★★.

FOGHAT

Although British in origin, Foghat relocated to the USA, where this boogie-blues band built a large following during the 70s. The band originally consisted of 'Lonesome' Dave Peverett (b. 1950, London, England; guitar/vocals), Tony Stevens (b. 12 September 1949, London, England; bass), Roger Earl (b. 1949; drums) and guitarist Rod Price. Peverett and Earl had been members of Savoy Brown, the British blues band. They left and immediately settled in the USA with the new unit, where Foghat signed with Bearsville Records, owned by entrepreneurial manager Albert Grossman. Their self-titled debut album reached the US charts, as did the single, a cover of Willie Dixon's blues standard 'I Just Want To Make Love To You'. (A live version of that song also charted, in 1977.) The group held on to its formula for another dozen albums, each on Bearsville and each a chart item in the USA. Of those, the 1977 live album was the most popular. The band underwent several personnel changes, primarily bassists, with Price being replaced by Erik Cartwright in 1981. In the mid-90s the band were still active, regularly gigging in the USA.

●ALBUMS: *Foghat* i (Bearsville 1972)★★, *Foghat* ii (Bearsville 1973)★★, *Energized* (Bearsville 1974)★★★, *Rock And Roll Outlaws* (Bearsville 1974)★★★, *Fool For The City* (Bearsville 1975)★★, *Night Shift* (Bearsville 1976)★★★, *Foghat Live* (Bearsville 1977)★★★, *Stone Blue* (Bearsville 1978)★★★, *Boogie Motel* (Bearsville 1979)★★★, *Tight Shoes* (Bearsville 1980)★, *Girls To Chat And Boys To Bounce* (Bearsville 1981)★, *In The Mood For Something Rude* (Bearsville 1982)★, *Zig-Zag Walk* (Bearsville 1983)★, *Return Of The Boogie Man* (Modern 1994)★.

●COMPILATIONS: *The Best Of Foghat* (Rhino 1988)★★★, *The Best Of Foghat, Volume 2* (Rhino 1992)★★★.

FORD, MARTYN

b. 28 April 1944, Rugby, England. One of the most diverse conductors in the field, Ford studied at the Royal Academy of Music. He formed the New Sinfonia in 1970, which was renamed the Martyn Ford Orchestra. Before entering the UK Top 40 in spring 1977 as an orchestra conductor, Ford led an increasingly fuller life throughout the 70s as an arranger and session musician. Among his responsibilities were conducting and arranging the music for *Tommy*, working on the *Live And Let Die* soundtrack, supervising horn sections on albums by Shawn Phillips, Suntreader and Nasty Pop, and plucking mandolin for Sharon Forrester and the Spencer Davis Group (on 1974's *Living In A Back Street*). His orchestra provided the strings on Lou Reed's 'Walk On The Wild Side', with production by Herbie Flowers. His reputation spread like a forest fire in the 70s and he worked with some of the decade's top acts including Wings, (as the Black Dyke Mills Band), the Grateful Dead, Barclay James Harvest, Blue Mink, Elton John ('Blue Eyes' and 'Princess'), Bryan Ferry, Cliff Richard, Man, Paul McCartney, the Rolling Stones, Kate Bush, Phil Collins, Art Garfunkel, Caravan, Jerry Lee Lewis, Yes, Toto and Led Zeppelin. He arranged and conducted Johnny Nash's 'I Can See Clearly Now' and conducted Harry Nilsson's hit 'Without You'. He was also signed to Mountain Records and the Martyn Ford Orchestra's 'Let Your Body Go Downtown' reached number 38 in the UK at the height of disco fever. Album spin-offs were notable for suggestive buzz-word song titles (e.g. 'Horny') and duplication of previously-issued tracks. However, none spawned a follow-up hit, and the versa-tile Ford returned to a lucrative career as a leading arranger, including his most recent success with the theme music to the UK television series *Naturewatch*. He is a music advisor to the Arts Council.

●ALBUMS: Martyn Ford Orchestra *Smoovin'* (Mountain 1976)★★, *Going To A Disco* (Mountain 1977)★★, *Take Me To The Dance* (Mountain 1978)★★, *Hot Shoe* (Mountain 1978)★★. Selected albums arranged and conducted by: The London Symphony Orchestra and The Royal Choral Society *Classic Rock* (K-Tel)★★★, *The Second Movement* (K-Tel)★★★, *Rock Classics* (K-Tel)★★★★, *Suite London* (K-Tel)★★★, see entries for ratings; Phil Collins: *Face Value* (Virgin), *Hello I Must Be Going* (Virgin), *No Jacket Required* (Virgin), Toto: *Toto IV* (Columbia), Elton John: *Blue Moves*, Mike Oldfield: *Five Miles Out*, Cliff Richard: *Silver*, Grateful Dead: *Terrapin Station* (Arista), Rolling Stones: *Goats Head Soup*, Procol Harum: *Grand Hotel*, Amy Grant: *A Christmas Album*, Harry Nilsson *Son Of Schmilsson*, Barclay James Harvest: *And Other Short Stories* (Harvest), *Baby James Harvest* (Harvest).

FORMERLY FAT HARRY

Formed in England in 1971, Formerly Fat Harry revolved around the talents of US expatriates Gary Peterson (vocals, guitar, keyboards), Phil Greenberg (vocals, guitar) and Bruce Barthol (bass, ex-Country Joe And The Fish). Saxophonist George Khan (formerly of Battered Ornaments) and Laurie Allen (drums) completed the featured line-up on *Formerly Fat Harry*, a pleasant country rock, good time music set which anticipated the 'pub rock' boom. Unfortunately, the group failed to make commercial headway and they split up when the core members returned to the USA. Allen subsequently worked with Gong, Lol Coxhill and Robert Wyatt. George Khan, also known as Nisar Ahmet Khan, played on several jazz rock features by Annette Peacock and Mike Westbrook before leading Mirage (1977).

●ALBUMS: *Formerly Fat Harry* (Harvest 1971)★★★.

FOTHERINGAY

The folk rock group Fotheringay was formed in 1970 by singer Sandy Denny upon her departure from Fairport Convention, and drew its name from one of her compositions for that group. Trevor Lucas (guitar/vocals), Gerry Conway (drums - both ex-Eclection), Jerry Donahue (guitar) and Pat Donaldson (bass; both ex-Poet And The One Man Band) completed the line-up responsible for the quintet's lone album. This impressive, folk-based set included several superior Denny originals, notably 'Nothing More', 'The Sea' and 'The Pond And The Stream', as well as meticulous readings of Gordon Lightfoot's 'The Way I Feel' and Bob Dylan's 'Too Much Of Nothing'. Although criticized contemporaneously as constrained, *Fotheringay* is now rightly viewed as a confident, accomplished work. However, the album failed to match commercial expectations and pressures on Denny to undertake a solo career - she was voted Britain's number 1 singer in *Melody Maker*'s 1970 poll - increased. Fotheringay was disbanded in 1971 during sessions for a projected second set. Some of its songs surfaced on the vocalist's debut album, *The Northstar Grassman* and whereas Donaldson and Conway began session work, Lucas and Donahue resurfaced in Fairport Convention.

●ALBUMS: *Fotheringay* (Island 1970)★★★.

●FURTHER READING: *Meet On The Ledge*, Patrick Humphries.

FRAMPTON, PETER

b. 22 April 1950, Beckenham, Kent, England. The former 'Face of 1968', with his pin-up good looks as part of the 60s pop group the Herd, Frampton grew his hair longer and joined Humble Pie. His solo career debuted with *Wind Of Change* in 1971, although he immediately set about forming another band, Frampton's Camel, to carry out US concert dates. This formidable unit consisted of Mike Kellie (drums), Mickey Gallagher (keyboards) and Rick Wills (bass), all seasoned players from Spooky Tooth, Cochise and Bell And Arc, respectively. *Frampton* in 1975 was a great success in the USA, while in the UK he was commercially ignored. The following year a double set, *Frampton Comes Alive* scaled the US chart and stayed on top for a total 10 weeks, in four

visits during a record-breaking two-year stay. The record became the biggest-selling live album in history and to date has sold over 12 million copies. Quite why the record was so successful has perplexed many rock critics. Like Jeff Beck, Frampton perfected the voice tube effect and used this gimmick on 'Show Me The Way'. The follow-up *I'm In You*, sold in vast quantities, although compared to the former it was a flop, selling a modest 'several million'. Again Frampton found little critical acclaim, but his records were selling in vast quantities. He continued to reach younger audiences with aplomb. In 1978 he suffered a near fatal car crash, although his fans were able to see him in the previously filmed *Sgt Pepper's Lonely Hearts Club Band*. Frampton played Billy Shears alongside the Bee Gees in the Robert Stigwood extravaganza that was a commercial and critical disaster. When he returned in 1979 with *Where I Should Be*, his star was dwindling. The album garnered favourable reviews, but it was his last successful record. Even the short-haired image for *Breaking All The Rules* failed, with only America, his loyal base, nudging it into the Top 50. Following *The Art Of Control* Frampton 'disappeared' until 1986, when he was signed to Virgin Records and released the synthesizer-laced *Premonition*. He returned to session work thereafter. Later on in the decade Frampton was found playing guitar with his former schoolfriend David Bowie on his *Never Let Me Down*. In 1991 he was allegedly making plans to re-form Humble Pie with Steve Marriott, but a week after their meeting in New York, Marriott was tragically burnt to death in his home. He diverted his interest to the other great success of his career in 1995 by releasing *Frampton Comes Alive II*.

●ALBUMS: *Wind Of Change* (A&M 1972)★★★, *Frampton's Camel* (A&M 1973)★★★, *Somethin's Happening* (A&M 1974)★★, *Frampton* (A&M 1975)★★, *Frampton Comes Alive!* (A&M 1976)★★★★, *I'm In You* (A&M 1977)★★, *Where I Should Be* (A&M 1979)★★, *Breaking All The Rules* (A&M 1981)★★, *The Art Of Control* (A&M 1982)★★, *Premonition* (Atlantic 1986)★, *When All The Pieces Fit* (Atlantic 1989)★★, *Show Me The Way* (1993)★★, *Peter Frampton* (Relativity 1994)★★★, *Frampton Comes Alive II* (El Dorado/IRS 1995).

●COMPILATIONS: *Shine On: A Collection* (1992)★★★.

●FURTHER READING: *Frampton!: An Unauthorized Biography*, Susan Katz. *Peter Frampton*, Marsha Daly. *Peter Frampton: A Photo Biography*, Irene Adler.

FREE

Formed in the midst of 1968's British blues boom, Free originally comprised Paul Rodgers (b. 17 December 1949, Middlesbrough, Cleveland, England; vocals), Paul Kossoff (b. 14 September 1950, London, England, d. 19 March 1976; guitar), Andy Fraser (b. 7 August 1952, London, England; bass) and Simon Kirke (b. 28 July 1949, Shrewsbury, Shropshire, England; drums). Despite their comparative youth, the individual musicians were seasoned performers, particularly Fraser, a former member of John Mayall's Bluesbreakers. Free gained early encouragement from Alexis Korner, but having completed an excellent, earthy debut album, *Tons Of Sobs*, the group began honing a more individual style with their second set. The injection of powerful original songs, including 'I'll Be Creeping', showed a maturing talent, while Rodgers' expressive voice and Kossoff's stinging guitar enhanced a growing reputation. The quartet's stylish blues rock reached its commercial peak on *Fire And Water*. This confident collection featured moving ballads; 'Heavy Load', 'Oh I Wept' and compulsive, up-tempo material, the standard-bearer of which is 'All Right Now'. An edited version of this soulful composition reached number 2 in the UK and number 4 in the US in 1970, since when the song has become one of pop's most enduring performances, making periodic reappearances in the singles chart. A fourth set, *Highway*, revealed a more mellow perspective highlighted by an increased use of piano at the expense of Kossoff's guitar. This was due, in part, to friction within the group, a factor exacerbated when the attendant single, 'The Stealer', failed to emulate its predecessor's success. Free broke up in May 1971, paradoxically in the wake of another hit single, 'My Brother Jake', but regrouped in January the following year when spin-off projects faltered, although Kossoff and Kirke's amalgamation (Kossoff, Kirke, Tetsu And Rabbit) proved fruitful. A sixth album, *Free At Last*, offered some of the unit's erstwhile fire and included another UK Top 20 entrant, 'Little Bit Of Love'. However, Kossoff's increasing ill health and Fraser's departure for the Sharks undermined any new-found confidence. A hastily convened line-up consisting of Rodgers, Kirke, John 'Rabbit' Bundrick (keyboards) and Tetsu Yamauchi (b. 1946, Fukuoka, Japan; bass) undertook a Japanese tour, but although the guitarist rejoined the quartet for several British dates, his contribution to Free's final album, *Heartbreaker*, was muted. Kossoff embarked on a solo career in October 1972; Wendel Richardson from Osibisa replaced him on a temporary basis, but by July the following year Free had ceased to function. Rodgers and Kirke subsequently formed Bad Company.

●ALBUMS: *Tons Of Sobs* (Island 1968)★★★, *Free* (Island 1969)★★★, *Fire And Water* (Island 1970)★★★★, *Highway* (Island 1970)★★★, *Free Live* (Island 1971)★★, *Free At Last* (Island 1972)★★, *Heartbreaker* (Island 1973)★★.

●COMPILATIONS: *The Free Story* double album (Island 1974)★★★★, *Completely Free* (Island 1982)★★★, *All Right Now* (Island 1991)★★★, *Molton Gold: The Anthology* (Island 1993)★★★★.

●VIDEOS: *Free* (1989).

FRIEDMAN, DEAN

This New Jersey, USA-born vocalist found instant success on both sides of the Atlantic with a mixture of sentimental ballads and joyful pleasant tunes about

romance. He had a US hit with 'Ariel' which made ripples in Europe, but his 1978 record 'Lucky Stars', reached the Top 3 position in the UK and made him a household name. A lack of promotion and sporadic record releases led to declining sales (due mainly to problems at the Lifesong, GTO label), although 'Lydia' gave him his last notable chart hit, reaching the UK Top 40. Although he briefly recorded for the Epic label, releasing *Rumpled Romeo* in 1982, throughout the 80s he released occasional singles on minor labels. One track 'The Lakelands' was included on a compilation album which sold a quarter of a million units. He reappeared in 1990 writing and performing the soundtrack to a low-budget British horror film, *I Bought A Vampire Motorcycle*.

●ALBUMS: *Dean Friedman* (Lifesong 1977)★★, *Well, Well, Said The Rocking Chair* (Lifesong 1978)★★, *Rumpled Romeo* (Epic 1982)★★.

●COMPILATIONS: *Very Best Of Dean Friedman* (Music Club 1991)★★★.

FRIEDMAN, KINKY

b. Richard Friedman, 31 October 1944, Palestine, Texas, USA. Friedman, a Jew in Texas, remarks, 'Cowboys and Jews have a common bond. They are the only two groups to wear their hats indoors and attach a certain importance to it.' Friedman, whose father was a university lecturer, first recorded as part of the surfing band, King Arthur And The Carrots, in 1966. One of the Carrots, Jeff Shelby, became Little Jewford Shelby in Friedman's band, the Texas Jewboys, the name satirising Bob Wills' Texas Playboys. Chuck Glaser of the Glaser Brothers took him to Nashville for his first album, *Sold American*. The title song combined the qualities of Ralph McTell's 'Streets Of London' with Phil Ochs' 'Chords Of Fame' and has been recorded by Glen Campbell and Tompall Glaser, the latter version being co-produced by Friedman. His Jewishness was emphasized in songs like 'We Refuse The Right To Refuse Service To You' and 'Ride 'Em Jewboy'. Friedman's single, 'Carryin' The Torch', an offbeat look at the Statue of Liberty, was produced by Waylon Jennings. *Kinky Friedman* was a patchy mixture of blasphemy and ballads, and included a good-natured romp produced by Willie Nelson, 'They Ain't Makin' Jews Like Jesus Anymore'. A hoarse recording of 'Sold American', recorded as part of Bob Dylan's Rolling Thunder Revue, was included on *Lasso From El Paso*. Buck Owens, who published 'Okie From Muskogee', refused to allow the album to be called Asshole From El Paso. 'Ol' Ben Lucas', about nose-picking, features Eric Clapton's guitar-picking, while 'Men's Room, L.A.' is about a shortage of toilet paper and features Ringo Starr as Christ wanting to use the toilet. Friedman's own career never shone as bright as the 3D portrait of Christ he had at his home and, in 1977, he dropped his touring band and went solo. He also improved his diction so that his insults could be understood. He sang the title song of the film *Skating On Thin Ice,* and he was murdered in his acting role in *Easter Sunday*, a film starring Dorothy Malone and Ruth Buzzi. Friedman has become a perceptive writer writing on country music for *Rolling Stone* and his novel, *Greenwich Killing Time*, is about a country singer turned detective. Friedman briefly returned to performing to promote this anthology, although his live sets merely reprised his old material. In recent years he has become a successful writer of crime novels, and he tries to write a new novel each year. Friedman says his autobiography will be printed backwards, like old Jewish texts. He also intends to write a mystery in which one of Willie Nelson's ex-wives is out to kill him - and has the full co-operation of the participants for this! On his promotional tours for his books he goes 'singing the song that made me infamous and reading from the books that made me respectable'.

●ALBUMS: *Sold American* (Vanguard 1973)★★★, *Kinky Friedman* (ABC 1975)★★, *Lasso From El Paso* (Epic 1976)★★★, *Kinky Friedman Live At The Lone Star* (80s), *Old Testaments And New Revelations* (Fruit Of The Tune 1993)★★★, *From One Great American To Another* (Fruit Of The Tune 1995)★★★.

●FURTHER READING: *Greenwich Killing Time*, Kinky Friedman. *A Case Of Lone Star*, Kinky Friedman. *When The Cat's Away*, Kinky Friedman. *Frequent Flyer*, Kinky Friedman. *Musical Chairs*, Kinky Friedman. *The Kinky Freidman Crime Club*. Kinky Friedman. *Elvis, Jesus And Coca Cola*, Kinky Friedman. *More Kinky Friedman*, Kinky Friedman. *Armadillos And Old Lace*, Kinky Friedman. *God Bless John Wayne*, Kinky Friedman.

FRIJID PINK

Kelly Green (vocals/harmonica), Gary Ray Thompson (guitar), Thomas Beaudry (bass), Larry Zelanka (keyboards) and Rick Stevens (drums) emerged from the hard rock circuit in Detroit, USA. In 1970 they scored a surprise transatlantic hit with their powerhouse interpretation of 'The House Of The Rising Sun', based on the Animals' highly original arrangement, but to which they added a searing, guitar-strewn approach, reminiscent of contemporaries the MC5 and Stooges. The single reached number 7 in the US and number 4 in the UK, but the group's subsequent chart entries, 'Sing A Song For Freedom' and 'Heartbreak Hotel' (both 1971), were confined to the lower regions of the US chart. It confirmed a suspicion that the song, rather than the group, was responsible for that first flush of success. By the time of their final album in 1975 for Fantasy Records only Stevens remained from the original line-up.

●ALBUMS: *Frijid Pink* (Parrot 1970)★★, *Defrosted* (Parrot 1970)★★, *Earth Omen* (1972)★★, *All Pink Inside* (Fantasy 1975)★★.

FRIPP, ROBERT

b. 16 May 1946, Wimbourne, Dorset, England. Guitarist, composer and producer, Fripp began his diverse career in the small, but flourishing, circuit centred on Bournemouth, Dorset. He subsequently joined the League Of Gentlemen, a London-based group renowned for backing visiting American singers, and later founded Giles Giles And Fripp with brothers Pete and Mike Giles. This eccentric trio completed one album, *The Cheerful Insanity of Giles Giles And Fripp* in 1968 before evolving into King Crimson, the progressive act though which the artist forged his reputation. Between 1969 and 1974, Fripp led several contrasting versions of this constantly challenging group, during which time he also enjoyed an artistically fruitful collaboration with Brian Eno. *No Pussyfooting* (1972) and *Evening Star* (1974) were among the era's leading *avant garde* recordings, the former of which introduced the tape loop and layered guitar technique known as 'Frippertronics', which later became an artistic trademark. During this period Fripp also produced several experimental jazz releases, notably by Centipede, and having disbanded King Crimson at a time 'all English bands in that genre should have ceased to exist', Fripp retired from music altogether. He re-emerged in 1977, contributing several excellent passages to David Bowie's *Heroes*, before playing on, and producing, Peter Gabriel's second album. Fripp provided a similar role on Daryl Hall's *Sacred Songs*, before completing *Exposure*, on which the artist acknowledged the concurrent punk movement. Simpler and more incisive than previous work, its energetic purpose contrasted the measured, sculpted approach of King Crimson, whom Fripp nonetheless surprisingly reconstituted in 1981. Three well-received albums followed, during which time the guitarist pursued a parallel, more personal, path leading a group bearing another resurrected name, the League Of Gentlemen. Both units were disbanded later in the decade, and Fripp subsequently performed and gave tutorials under a 'League Of Crafty Guitarists' banner and recorded with former Police member Andy Summers. Now married to singer and actress Toyah Wilcox, this highly talented individual has doggedly followed an uncompromising path, resulting in some highly individual, provocative music. He constantly seeks new and interesting musical ventures, his most recent being an album with David Sylvian. In 1994 he reunited with King Crimson for a mini-album and tour.

●ALBUMS: as Giles Giles And Fripp *The Cheerful Insanity Of Giles Giles And Fripp* (Deram 1968)★★★, with Brian Eno *No Pussyfooting* (1975)★★★, with Eno *Evening Star* (1976)★★★; *Exposure* (Polydor 1979)★★★★, *God Save The Queen, Under Heavy Manners* (Polydor 1980)★★, with League Of Gentlemen *Let The Power Fall* aka *The League Of Gentlemen* (Polydor 1981)★★★, with Andy Summers *I Advance Masked* (A&M 1982)★★★★, *Bewitched* (A&M 1984)★★★, with League Of Gentlemen *God Save The King* (Editions 1985)★★★, with Toyah *The Lady And The Tiger* (Editions 1986)★★★, with League Of Crafty Guitarists *Robert Fripp And The League Of Crafty Guitarists Live* (Editions 1986)★★★, *Network*

(Editions 1987)★★★, *Live II* (Editions 1990)★★★, *Show Of Hands* (Editions 1991)★★★, with David Sylvian *The First Time* (1993)★★★, *Soundscapes - Live In Argentina* (Discipline 1995)★★★, *A Blessing Of Tears* (Discipline 1995)★★★, with League Of Crafty Guitarists *Intergalactic Boogie Express* (Discipline 1995)★★★, *Radiophonics* (Discipline 1996)★★★.
●FURTHER READING: *Robert Fripp: From King Crimson To Guitar Craft*, Eric Tamm.

FUNKADELIC

George Clinton (b. 22 July 1941, Kannapolis, North Carolina, USA), established this inventive, experimental group out of the 1969 line-up of the Parliaments - Raymond Davis (b. 29 March 1940, Sumter, South Carolina, USA), Grady Thomas (b. 5 January 1941, Newark, New Jersey, USA), Calvin Simon (b. 22 May 1942, Beckley, West Virginia, USA), Clarence 'Fuzzy' Haskins (b. 8 June 1941, Elkhorn, West Virginia, USA), plus the backing group; Bernard Worrell (b. 19 April 1944, Long Beach, New Jersey, USA; keyboards), William Nelson Jnr. (b. 28 January 1951, Plainfield, New Jersey, USA; bass), Eddie Hazel (b. 10 April 1950, Brooklyn, New York, USA, d. 23 December 1992; lead guitar), Lucius Ross (b. 5 October 1948, Wagram, North Carolina, USA; rhythm guitar) and Ramon 'Tiki' Fulwood (b. 23 May 1944, Philadelphia, Pennsylvania, USA; drums) - when contractual problems prevented the use of their original name. Bandleader Clinton seized the opportunity to reconstruct his music and the result laced hard funk with a heady dose of psychedelia; hence the name Funkadelic. Primarily viewed as an album-orientated vehicle, the group's instinctive grasp of such contrasting styles nonetheless crossed over into their singles. Although few managed to enter the R&B Top 30, Funkadelic consistently reached the chart's lower placings. In 1977 Clinton moved from the Westbound label to Warner Brothers Records and the following year the compulsive 'One Nation Under A Groove' was a million-seller. By this point the distinctions between Funkadelic and Parliament were becoming increasingly blurred and the former secured another major hit in 1979 with '(Not Just) Knee Deep'. Several offshoot projects, Bootsy's Rubber Band, Parlet and the Brides Of Funkenstein, also emanated from within the burgeoning corporation, but a protracted contractual wrangle with Warners ended with legal action. Three long-time associates, Clarence Haskins, Calvin Simon and Grady Thomas, then broke away, taking the Funkadelic name with them. Despite an early R&B hit, 'Connections And Disconnections', they were unable to maintain their own direction and the group later dissolved. In 1993 the band were favourably reappraised and courted by the soul and dance cognoscenti.
●ALBUMS: *Funkadelic* (Westbound 1970)★★★, *Free Your Mind ... And Your Ass Will Follow* (Westbound 1970)★★★, *Maggot Brain* (Westbound 1971)★★★★, *America Eats Its Young* (Westbound 1972)★★★, *Cosmic Slop* (Westbound 1973)★★★, *Standing On The Verge Of Getting It On* (Westbound 1974)★★★, *Let's Take It To The Stage* (Westbound 1975)★★★★, *Tales Of Kidd Funkadelic* (Westbound 1976)★★★, *Hardcore Jollies* (Warners 1976)★★★, *One Nation Under A Groove* (Warners 1978)★★★★, *Uncle Jam Wants You* (Warners 1979)★★★, *The Electric Spanking Of War Babies* (Warners 1981)★★★★.
●COMPILATIONS: *The Best Of The Early Years - Volume One* (Westbound 1977)★★★★, *The Best Of ... 1976-1981* (Charly 1994)★★★★.

G

GADD, STEVE

b. 4 September 1945, Rochester, New York, USA. Gadd was taught the drums by an uncle from the age of three: he enjoyed Sousa marches and worked with a drum corps. He spent two years at Manhattan's School of Music before going on to study at the Eastman College in Rochester after which he was drafted into the army. While there he spent three years in an army band. After leaving the services his first professional work was with the trumpeter Chuck Mangione before he joined Chick Corea's Return To Forever in 1975. Corea described him as bringing 'orchestral and compositional thinking to the drum kit while at the same time having a great imagination and a great ability to swing'. Gadd worked extensively in the New York studios from the early 70s onwards and was able to provide the perfect accompaniment for a diverse series of sessions. He developed his own style of linear drumming in which no two drums are sounded at the same time. He played for many artists from Charles Mingus via George Benson to Paul Simon with whom he toured in 1991, directing the large group of percussionists on the *Rhythm Of The Saints* tour. So ubiquitous did he become that it was his sound that was sampled for the earlier drum machines. In 1976 he played in the influential funk band Stuff along with other session musicians like Eric Gale and Richard Tee. Throughout the 80s Gadd continued with a busy studio schedule but also played in the straight jazz Manhattan Jazz Quintet.
●ALBUMS: with George Benson *In Concert* (1975)★★★, *My Spanish Heart* (1976)★★★, with Carla Bley *Dinner Music* (1976)★★★, with Stuff *Stuff* (Warners 1976)★★★, *Friends* (Warners 1978)★★★, *The Mad Hatter* (1978)★★★, with Chick Corea *Three Quartets* (Warners 1981)★★★, with Al DiMeola *Electric Rendezvous* (Columbia 1982)★★, with Manhattan Jazz Quintet *Manhattan Jazz Quintet* (1986)★★★, *Gaddabout* (King 1986)★★★, *Autumn Leaves* (1986)★★★, with Paul Simon *Rhythm Of The Saints* (Warners 1989)★★.

GALLAGHER AND LYLE

Benny Gallagher (vocals/guitar) and Graham Lyle (vocals/guitar) were both born in Largs, Ayrshire, Scotland. Having sung with several nascent beat groups, they began a songwriting career with 'Mr. Heartbreak's Here Instead', a 1964 single for Dean Ford And The Gaylords. The duo later moved to London where they joined the Apple label as in-house com-

posers. One of their songs, 'International', was recorded by Mary Hopkin.

In 1969 the pair joined McGuinness Flint for whom they wrote two successful singles, 'When I'm Dead And Gone' (1970) and 'Malt And Barley Blues' (1971), before leaving the group for an independent career. Several well-crafted, if low-key, albums followed, which showcased the duo's flair for folk-styled melody, but it was not until 1976 that they enjoyed a commercial breakthrough. *Breakaway* spawned two major hits in 'I Wanna Stay With You' and 'Heart On My Sleeve', both of which reached number 6 in the UK. Further recognition of their compositional talents was endorsed by Art Garfunkel taking a cover version of the album's title track into the US Top 40, but the act was curiously unable to sustain its newfound profile. Gallagher and Lyle parted following the release of *Lonesome No More* in order to pursue different projects. Graham Lyle later found a new partner, Terry Britten, with whom he composed 'What's Love Got To Do With It' and 'Just Good Friends' which were recorded, respectively, by Tina Turner and Michael Jackson. Both have continued a successful career as songwriters.
●ALBUMS: *Gallagher And Lyle* (A&M 1972)★★, *Willie And The Lap Dog* (A&M 1973)★★, *Seeds* (A&M 1973)★★, *The Last Cowboy* (A&M 1974)★★★, *Breakaway* (A&M 1976)★★★, *Love On The Airwaves* (A&M 1977)★★, *Showdown* (A&M 1978)★★, *Gone Crazy* (1979)★★, *Lonesome No More* (Mercury 1979)★★.
●COMPILATIONS: *The Best Of Gallagher And Lyle* (A&M 1980)★★★, *Heart On My Sleeve* (A&M 1991)★★★.

GALLAGHER, RORY

b. 2 March 1949, Ballyshannon, Co. Donegal, Eire, d. 15 June 1995. Having served his musical apprenticeship in the Fontana and Impact Showbands, Gallagher put together the original Taste in 1965. This exciting blues-based rock trio rose from regional obscurity to the verge of international fame, but broke up, acrimoniously, five years later. Gallagher was by then a guitar hero and embarked on a solo voyage supported by Gerry McAvoy (bass) and Wilgar Campbell (drums). He introduced an unpretentious approach, which marked a career that deftly retained all the purpose of the blues without erring on the side of reverence. Gallagher's early influences were Lonnie Donegan, Woody Guthrie, Chuck Berry and Muddy Waters and he strayed very little from that path of influence.
The artist's refreshing blues guitar work which featured his confident bottleneck playing was always of interest and by 1972 Gallagher was a major live attraction. Campbell was replaced by Rod De'ath following the release of *Live In Europe*, while Lou Marrin was added on keyboards. This line-up remained constant for the next six years and was responsible for Gallagher's major commercial triumphs *Blueprint* and *Irish Tour '74*. De'ath and Martin left the group in 1978. Former Sensational Alex Harvey Band drummer Ted McKenna joined the

ever-present McAvoy but was in turn replaced by Brendan O'Neill. Former Nine Below Zero member and blues harmonica virtuoso Mark Feltham became a full time 'guest', as Gallagher quietly got on with his career. Shunning the glitzy aspect of the music business, he toured America over 30 times in addition to touring the globe. twice. His record sales reached several millions and he retained a fiercely loyal following. He had the opportunity to record with his heroes such as Donegan, Waters, Jerry Lee Lewis and Albert King and his love of his homeland resulted in contributions to the work of the Fureys, Davy Spillane and Joe O'Donnell. Gallagher retained his perennial love for the blues, his original Stratocaster guitar (now badly battered) and the respect of many for his uncompromising approach. He died following complications after a liver transplant in 1995.

●ALBUMS: *Rory Gallagher* (Polydor 1971)★★★, *Deuce* (Polydor 1971)★★★, *Live! In Europe* (Polydor 1972)★★★, *Blueprint* (Polydor 1973)★★★★, *Tattoo* (Polydor 1973)★★★★, *Irish Tour '74* (Polydor 1974), *Saint ... And Sinner* (Polydor 1975)★★★, *Against The Grain* (Chrysalis 1975)★★★, *Calling Card* (Chrysalis 1976)★★★, *Photo Finish* (Chrysalis 1978)★★★, *Top Priority* (Chrysalis 1979)★★★, *Stage Struck* (Chrysalis 1980)★★★, *Jinx* (Chrysalis 1982)★★★, *Defender* (Demon 1987)★★, *Fresh Evidence* (Castle 1990)★★.

●COMPILATIONS: *In The Beginning* (Emerald 1974)★★★, *The Story So Far* (Polydor 1976)★★★, *The Best Years* (1976)★★★, *Best Of Rory Gallagher And Taste* (Razor 1988)★★★★, *Edged In Blue* (1992)★★★, *Rory Gallagher Boxed* 4-CD set (1992)★★★.

GARCIA, JERRY

b. 1 August 1942, San Francisco, California, USA, d. 9 August 1995, Forest Knolls, California, USA. The mercurial guitarist of the Grateful Dead was able to play with two or three other conglomerations without it affecting his career as leader of one of rock music's legendary bands. For four decades Garcia was a leading light on the west coast musical scene - he was credited on Jefferson Airplane's *Surrealistic Pillow* as 'musical and spiritual adviser' and known locally as 'Captain Trips'. In addition to his session work with the Airplane, he worked with David Crosby, Paul Kantner, Jefferson Starship, New Riders Of The Purple Sage and Crosby, Stills, Nash And Young as well as various spin-offs involving David Nelson, John Kahn (b. 1948, d. 30 May 1996), Merl Saunders and Howard Wales. Garcia was equally at home on banjo and pedal-steel guitar, and had the ability to play two entirely different styles of music without a hint of musical overlap (rock 'n' roll/blues and country/bluegrass). His flowing manner was all the more remarkable given that the third finger of his left hand was missing, owing to an accident as a child. Garcia was known and loved as a true hippie who never 'sold out'. Following his heroin addiction and much publicized near-death in 1986, Garcia philosophically stated, 'I'm 45 years old, I'm ready for anything, I

didn't even plan on living this long so all this shit is add-on stuff.' But he continued touring and recording, with the Dead and on his own, until shortly before his death from a heart attack during a stay at a treatment centre near his home in Marin County, California (see Grateful Dead entry).

●ALBUMS: *Hooteroll* (Douglas 1971)★★, *Garcia* (Warners 1972)★★★, with Merl Saunders *Live At Keystone* (Fantasy 1973)★★, *Garcia* (Round 1974)★★★, *Old And In The Way* (Round 1975)★★★, *Reflections* (Reflections 1976)★★, *Cats Under The Stars* (Arista 1978)★★★, *Run For The Roses* (Arista 1982)★★★, *Keystone Encores, Vols. 1 & 2* (Fantasy 1988)★★, as the Jerry Garcia Acoustic Band *Almost Acoustic* (Grateful Dead 1989)★★★, *Jerry Garcia Band* (Arista 1991)★★★, with David Grisman *Not For Kids Only* (Acoustic Disc 1993)★★★, with Grisman *Shady Grove* (Acoustic 1996)★★★.

●FURTHER READING: *Garcia - A Signpost To A New Space*, Charles Reich and Jann Wenner. *Grateful Dead - The Music Never Stopped*, Blair Jackson. *Captain Trips: The Life And Fast Times Of Jerry Garcia*, Sandy Troy.

GARFUNKEL, ART

b. 5 November 1941, Queens, New York City, USA. The possessor of one of the most pitch-perfect voices in popular music has had a sparse recording career since the demise of Simon And Garfunkel. The break-up of one of the most successful post-war singing duos was due in part to Garfunkel's desire to go into acting, and Paul Simon's understandable resentment that Art took the glory on his compositions like 'Bridge Over Troubled Water'. While Simon had the songs, Garfunkel possessed *the* voice. The split would be revisited in 'The Breakup', included on Garfunkel's 1993 set, *Up 'Til Now*, though by this time the two parties had made their peace. In terms of personal history, Garfunkel can lay claim to a masters degree in mathematics, and the fact that he has embarked upon a mission to walk all the way across the USA, in 100-mile increments. His solo recording career actually started while he was singing with Simon as the Duo Tom And Jerry. Two singles were released under the name of Artie Garr, 'Dream Alone' in 1959 and 'Private World' the following year.

Garfunkel's acting career landed him substantial parts in *Catch 22*, *Carnal Knowledge*, *Bad Timing* and *Good To Go*. During this time his recorded output, although sporadic, was of a consistently high quality. His debut *Angel Clare* contained the beautiful 'All I Know', which was a Top 10 US hit. In the UK two of his records made the top spot, a luscious 'I Only Have Eyes For You' and the Mike Batt theme for *Watership Down*, 'Bright Eyes'. In 1978 '(What A) Wonderful World' featured the additional voices of James Taylor and Paul Simon, fuelling rumours of a reunion. They appeared together occasionally both on television and on record, but it was not until October 1981 that the historic Central Park concert occurred. The duo struggled through a world tour, opening up old wounds; until once again they parted company. Since then Garfunkel has released occasional albums, the best moments of which are largely attributable to the songwriting of Jim Webb.

●ALBUMS: *Angel Clare* (Columbia 1973)★★★, *Breakaway* (Columbia 1975)★★★, *Watermark* (Columbia 1978)★★★, *Fate For Breakfast* (Columbia 1979)★★★, *Scissors Cut* (Watermark 1981)★★★, *Lefty* (Columbia 1988)★★★, *Up 'Til Now* (Columbia 1993)★★, *The Very Best Of - Across America* (Virgin 1996)★★★.

GARRETT, LEIF

b. 8 November 1961, Hollywood, California, USA. Blond teen vocalist Garrett had already been seen in the film *Walking Tall* in 1973. He also appeared in both sequels before signing to Atlantic Records. He hit the US Top 20 with a remake of the Beach Boys' 'Surfin' USA', in 1977. His US chart career continued with updates of Dion's 'Runaround Sue' and 'The Wanderer' and Paul Anka's 'Put Your Head On My Shoulder', before he moved to the Scotti Brothers label in 1978 and achieved his biggest hit, 'I Was Made For Dancing', a Top 10 smash in both the UK and US in 1979. He was instrumental in promoting the skateboard craze in the mid to late 70s in the UK.

●ALBUMS: *Leif Garrett* (Atlantic 1977)★★, *Feel The Need* (Scotti Brothers 1978)★, *Same Goes For You* (Scotti Brothers 1979)★, *My Movie Of You* (Scotti Brothers 1981)★.

●FILMS: *Walking Tall* (1973).

GATES, DAVID

b. 11 December 1940, Tulsa, Oklahoma, USA. Having played in a hometown high school band alongside Leon Russell, Gates followed his former colleague to Los Angeles. He initially pursued a career as a rockabilly singer, recording a series of locally issued singles including 'Swinging Baby Doll' (1958), which featured Russell on piano, and 'My Baby's Gone Away' (1961). He later switched to studio work, and appearances on sessions for Duane Eddy and Pat Boone preceded a fruitful period in the budding 'girl-group' genre. Gates produced and/or composed a string of excellent releases, notably Merry Clayton's 'Usher Boy', the Murmaids' 'Popsicles And Icicles', Dorothy Berry's 'You're So Fine' (all 1963), Shelly Fabares' 'He Don't Love Me' and Connie Stevens' 'A Girl Never Knows' (both 1964). Having founded, then closed, the short-lived Planetary label in 1966, Gates switched his attentions to the emergent west coast group scene. He produced material for Captain Beefheart and the Gants, while work with a harmony act, the Pleasure Fair in 1968, led to the formation of Bread. For three years Gates led this highly popular attraction, composing many of their best-known songs including 'Make It With You', 'If', 'Baby I'm A Want You' and 'Everything I Own'. He began a solo career in 1973, but despite two albums of a similar high quality, the artist failed to sus-

tain this level of success. A short-lived Bread reunion was equally ill-starred, suggesting that Gates' brand of soft, melodic pop was now out of fashion. He did enjoy a US Top 20 hit in 1978 with 'Goodbye Girl' but ensuing releases were less well received and Gates has now reportedly retired from music altogether.

●ALBUMS: *First Album* (Elektra 1973)★★, *Never Let Her Go* (Elektra 1975)★★★, *Goodbye Girl* (Elektra 1978)★★★, *Songbook* (Elektra 1979)★★, *Falling In Love Again* (Elektra 1980)★★, *Take Me Now* (Arista 1981)★★, *Love Is Always Seventeen* (Discovery 1994)★★.

GAYNOR, GLORIA

b. 7 September 1947, Newark, New Jersey, USA. The 'Queen Of The Discotheques' spent several years struggling on the east coast circuit prior to finding success. A 1965 single, produced by Johnny Nash, preceded her spell as a member of the Soul Satisfiers. Gaynor was discovered singing in a Manhattan nightclub by her future manager, Jay Ellis. He teamed with producers Tony Bongiovia and Meco Monardo to create an unswerving disco backbeat that propelled such exemplary Gaynor performances as 'Never Can Say Goodbye' (1974) and 'Reach Out I'll Be There' (1975). Her crowning achievement followed in 1979 when 'I Will Survive' topped both the UK and US charts. This emotional performance, later adapted as a gay movement anthem, rose above the increasingly mechanical settings her producers were fashioning for the disco market. 'I Am What I Am', another song with militant implications, was a UK hit in 1983, but the singer was too closely tied to a now dying form and her later career suffered as a result.

●ALBUMS: *Never Can Say Goodbye* (MGM 1975)★★★, *Experience Gloria Gaynor* (MGM 1975)★★★, *I've Got You* (Polydor 1976)★★, *Glorious* (Polydor 1977)★★, *Love Tracks* (Polydor 1979)★★★, *I Have A Right* (Polydor 1979)★★★, *Stories* (Polydor 1980)★★, *I Kinda Like Me* (Polydor 1981)★★, *Gloria Gaynor* (Polydor 1982)★★, *I Am Gloria Gaynor* (Chrysalis 1984)★★, *The Power Of Gloria Gaynor* (Stylus 1986)★★.

●COMPILATIONS: *Greatest Hits* (Polydor 1982)★★★, *I Will Survive: Greatest Hits* (1993)★★★.

GEILS, J., BAND

Formed in Boston, Massachusetts, USA in 1969, the group - J. Geils (b. Jerome Geils, 20 February, 1946, New York, USA; guitar), Peter Wolf (b. 7 March 1947, Bronx, New York, USA; vocals), Magic Dick (b. Richard Salwitz, 13 May 1945, New London, Connecticut, USA; harmonica), Seth Justman (b. 27 January 1951, Washington, DC, USA; keyboards), Danny Klein (b. 13 May 1946, New York, USA; bass) and Stephan Jo Bladd (b.31 July 1942, Boston, Massachusetts; drums) - was originally known as the J. Geils Blues Band. Their first two albums established a tough, raw R&B which encouraged comparisons with Butterfield Blues Band. Versions of songs by Albert Collins, Otis Rush and John Lee Hooker showed an undoubted flair, and with Wolf as an extrovert frontman, they quickly became a popular live attraction. *Bloodshot*, a gold US album, introduced the group to a wider audience, but at the same time suggested a tardiness which marred subsequent releases. The major exception was *Monkey Island* where Wolf, Geils and Magic Dick reclaimed the fire and excitement enlivening those first two albums. The group moved from the Atlantic label to EMI at the end of the 70s and secured a massive international hit in 1982 with the leering 'Centrefold'. Now divorced from its blues roots, the J. Geils Band was unsure of its direction, a factor emphasized in 1984 when Wolf departed for a solo career, midway through a recording session. The group completed a final album, *You're Gettin' Even, While I'm Gettin' Old*, without him.

●ALBUMS: *J. Geils Band* (Atlantic 1971)★★★, *The Morning After* (Atlantic 1971)★★★, *Live - Full House* (Atlantic 1972)★★★, *Bloodshot* (Atlantic 1973)★★, *Ladies Invited* (Atlantic 1973)★★★, *Nightmares ... And Other Tales From The Vinyl Jungle* (Atlantic 1974)★★, *Hotline* (Atlantic 1975)★★, *Live - Blow Your Face Out* (Atlantic 1976)★★, *Monkey Island* (Atlantic 1977)★★★, *Sanctuary* (Atlantic 1978)★★★, *Love Stinks* (EMI 1980)★★★, *Freeze Frame* (EMI 1981)★★★, *Showtime!* (EMI 1982)★★★, *You're Gettin' Even While I'm Gettin' Old* (EMI 1984)★★, with Magic Dick *Little Car Blues* (Rounder 1996)★★★.

●COMPILATIONS: *The Best Of The J. Geils Band* (Atlantic 1979)★★★.

GENERATION X

UK punk group Generation X emerged during the punk explosion of 1976. Billy Idol (b. William Broad, 30 November 1955, Stanmore, Middlesex, England; vocals) had previously worked with Tony James (bass/vocals) in the short-lived Chelsea. With Bob Andrews (guitar/vocals) and John Towe (drums), Generation X made their performing debut in London during December 1976. By the following May, Towe was replaced on drums by Mark Laff, while record companies sought their hand. Eventually they signed with Chrysalis Records. The group soon arrived in the lower regions of the UK chart with 'Your Generation' and 'Ready Steady Go'. The latter, strange for a punk group, was an affectionate tribute to the 60s, full of references to Bob Dylan, the Beatles, the Rolling Stones and Cathy McGowan (the legendary presenter of the UK music programme, *Ready Steady Go!*). Following 'Friday's Angels' in June 1979, former Clash drummer Terry Chimes stepped in for Laff. The group lasted until 1981, but were soon regarded as a rock band in punk garb. Their biggest commercial success was with the 1979 single 'King Rocker', which reached number 11 in the UK. Idol later went on to solo stardom, departed drummer John Towe reappeared in the Adverts, Terry Chimes rejoined the Clash, while Tony James reinvented himself in Sigue Sigue Sputnik.

●ALBUMS: *Generation X* (Chrysalis 1978)★★★, *Valley Of The Dolls* (Chrysalis 1979)★★, as Gen X *Kiss Me Deadly* (Chrysalis 1981)★★.

●COMPILATIONS: *Best Of Generation X* (Chrysalis 1985)★★★, *The Original Generation X* (MBC 1987)★★, *Generation X Live* (MBC 1987)★★, *Perfect Hits (1975-81)* (Chrysalis 1991)★★★.

GENTLE GIANT

Formed in 1969 by the Shulman brothers; Derek (b. 11 February 1947, Glasgow, Scotland; vocals/guitar/bass), Ray (b. 3 December 1949, Portsmouth, Hampshire, England; vocals/bass/violin) and Phil (b. 27 August 1937, Glasgow, Scotland; saxophone), on the collapse of their previous group, Simon Dupree And The Big Sound. Kerry Minnear (b. 2 January 1948, Shaftsbury, Dorset, England; keyboards/vocals), Gary Green (b. 20 November 1950, Muswell Hill, London, England; guitar/vocals) and Martin Smith (drums) completed the first Gentle Giant line-up which eschewed the pop/soul leanings of its predecessor for an experimental, progressive style reminiscent of Yes and King Crimson. The sextet was signed to the renowned Vertigo label in 1970 and, teamed with producer Tony Visconti, completed a debut album that offered all the hallmarks of their subsequent recordings. This ambitious set blended hard rock and classics with an adventurous use of complex chord changes which, if not commercially successful, indicated a quest for both excellence and originality. Although deemed pretentious by many commentators, there was no denying the ambition and individuality this release introduced. Smith left the line-up following *Acquiring The Taste*, but although his replacement, Malcolm Mortimore, appeared on *Three Friends*, a motorcycle accident forced the newcomer's departure. John 'Pugwash' Weathers (b. 2 February 1947, Carmarthen, Glamorganshire, Wales), veteran of Eyes Of Blue, Graham Bond and Pete Brown's Piblokto!, joined Gentle Giant for *Octopus*, arguably their best-known release. However, an attendant tour ended with the departure of Phil who retired from music altogether. The group then switched outlets to WWA, but encountered problems in America when *In A Glass House* was deemed too uncommercial for release there. *The Power And The Glory* proved less daunting and in turn engendered a new recording deal with Chrysalis. The ensuing *Free Hand* became Gentle Giant's best-selling UK album, but this ascendancy faltered when *Interview* invoked the experimental style of earlier releases. A double set, *Playing The Fool*, confirmed the quintet's in-concert dexterity, but subsequent albums unsuccessfully courted an AOR audience. *Civilian* was a conscious attempt at regaining former glories, but the departure of Minnear, by this point the band's musical director, signalled their demise. Gentle Giant split up in 1980 and several former members have pursued low-key careers. Ray Shulman has become a highly successful producer, working with such diverse acts as the Sugarcubes, the Sundays and Ian McCulloch. Brother Derek moved to

New York to become director of A&R at Polygram.

●ALBUMS: *Gentle Giant* (Vertigo 1970)★★★, *Acquiring The Taste* (Vertigo 1971)★★★, *Three Friends* (Vertigo 1972)★★★, *Octopus* (Vertigo 1973)★★, *In A Glass House* (WWA 1973)★★, *The Power And The Glory* (WWA 1974)★★, *Free Hand* (Chrysalis 1975)★★★, *Interview* (Chrysalis 1976)★★★, *The Official 'Live' Gentle Giant - Playing The Fool* (Chrysalis 1977)★★★, *The Missing Piece* (Chrysalis 1977)★★, *Giant For A Day* (Chrysalis 1978)★★, *Civilian* (Chrysalis 1980)★★, *Live-Playing The Fool* (Essential 1989)★★.

●COMPILATIONS: *Giant Steps (The First Five Years)* (Vertigo 1975)★★★, *Pretentious (For The Sake Of It)* (Vertigo 1977)★★, *Greatest Hits* (Vertigo 1981)★★★, *In Concert* (Windsong 1995)★★, *Out Of The Woods: The BBC Sessions* (Band Of Joy 1996)★★.

GEORDIE

From the north east of England, Brian Johnson (b. 5 October 1947, Newcastle, England; vocals), Victor Malcolm (guitar), Tom Hill (bass) and Brian Gibson (drums) started life as a poor man's Slade. Their unconsciously professional style was based on the pop end of the hard rock spectrum, with a stage act that included an audience participation opus, the dialectal 'Geordie's Lost His Liggy', which involved Johnson hoisting Malcolm onto his shoulders. After one single for Regal Zonophone, 'Don't Do That', tickled the hit parade, they were signed by EMI Records, whose faith was justified when 'All Because Of You' from 1973's *Hope You Like It* made the UK Top 20. Two lesser entries - 'Can You Do It' and 'Electric Lady' - followed, and the group's albums sold steadily if unremarkably. Geordie's power as a concert attraction outlasted this chart run, and when the going got rough in the watershed year of 1976-77, the quartet signed off with *Save The World* - a consolidation rather than development of their derivative music. They were remembered not for their hits but as the *alma mater* of Johnson who, after a lean period in which he was heard in a vacuum cleaner commercial, replaced the late Bon Scott in AC/DC.

●ALBUMS: *Hope You Like It* (EMI 1973)★★★, *Masters Of Rock* (EMI 1974)★★, *Don't Be Fooled By The Name* (EMI 1974)★★, *Save The World* (EMI 1976)★★.

●COMPILATIONS: *Featuring Brian Johnson* (Red Bus 1981)★★.

GERMS

Los Angeles, California, USA, punk band the Germs were formed in April 1977. The original members were Darby Crash (b. Paul Beahm; vocals), Pat Smear (guitar), Lorna Doom (bass) and Belinda Carlisle (drums), later of the Go-Gos. She soon left and was replaced by a succession of percussionists, including future X drummer D.J. Bonebrake and Don Bolles of 45 Grave. The group's first single, 'Forming', was issued on What? Records in 1977 and is considered by some to be the first example of the post-punk 'hardcore' genre,

later popularized by bands such as Black Flag and the Dead Kennedys. Their next single was issued on Slash Records, which in 1979 released the group's only album, *GI*. The group disbanded in early 1980 but reformed later that year. A week after their first reunion concert, however, singer Crash died of a heroin overdose. The catalyst to a thousand US punk bands, though few modelled themselves on Crash's legendary self-destructive nature, the Germs were only ever going to provide a musical flashpoint rather than a career blueprint. A tribute album was issued in 1996 featuring White Zombie, Courtney Love, the Melvins, Mudhoney and others.

●ALBUMS: *GI* (Slash 1979)★★★.

●COMPILATIONS: *What We Do Is Secret* (Slash 1981)★★, *Germicide* (ROIR 1982)★★, *MIA* (Slash 1994)★★.

GIBB, ANDY

b. 5 March 1958, Manchester, England, d. 10 March 1988, Oxford, England. Following the international success of his three elder brothers in the Bee Gees, Andy appeared as a star in his own right in 1977. Emerging at the beginning of the disco boom, he scored three consecutive US number 1 hits with his first three chart entries. 'I Just Want To Be Your Everything', '(Love Is) Thicker Than Water' and 'Shadow Dancing' made him one of the most commercially successful recording artists of his era and for a time he even eclipsed his illustrious brothers in popularity. Six further hits followed, including a collaboration with Olivia Newton-John ('I Can't Help It') before Gibb moved into television work. The pressure of living with the reputation of his superstar brothers, coupled with immense wealth and a hedonistic bent, brought personal problems and he became alarmingly reliant upon cocaine. Within months of his brothers' autumnal and highly successful reunion in the late 80s, tragedy struck when the 30-year-old singer died of an inflammatory heart virus at his home. It was the end of a career that had brought spectacular success in a remarkably short period.

●ALBUMS: *Flowing Rivers* (RSO 1977)★★, *Shadow Dancing* (RSO 1978)★★, *After Dark* (RSO 1980)★★.

●COMPILATIONS: *Andy Gibb's Greatest Hits* (RSO 1981)★★.

GIBBONS, STEVE

b. c.1942, Birmingham, England. Gibbons was the quintessential product of the English beat group era, with a powerful vocal style and a quiverful of imaginative and intelligent compositions. He started in 1958 as the vocalist with the Dominettes. After several changes of line-up this became the Uglys in 1962. With Dave Pegg (later of Fairport Convention) on bass the group recorded unsuccessfully for Pye and later for MGM. In 1969, the Uglys split and Gibbons joined ex-Moody Blues member Denny Laine and Trevor Burton, formerly of the Move, in Balls, an abortive attempt by ex-Move manager Tony Secunda to create a Brum 'supergroup'. With the aid of session guitarists Albert Lee and Chris Spedding, Balls made *Short Stories* for Secunda's Wizzard label before disbanding in 1971. Gibbons next briefly joined the Idle Race which evolved into the Steve Gibbons Band, which has continued with line-up changes to this day. The early line-up included Burton (bass), Dave Carroll and Bob Wilson on guitars and Bob Lamb (drums). Their debut album appeared on Roger Daltrey's Goldhawk label in 1976 and the following year Gibbons had a Top 20 hit with Chuck Berry's 'Tulane', from *Caught In The Act* produced by Kenny Laguna. Soon afterwards Lamb quit the band to concentrate on running his own studio, where he produced the early work of another local band, UB40. In the early 80s the Steve Gibbons Band recorded two albums for RCA Records with Gibbons maintaining his imaginative and witty approach to co-songwriting, as the titles 'Biggles Flys Undone', 'B.S.A.' and 'Somebody Stole My Synthesiser' suggest. Burton left the band around this time but Gibbons continued to be a popular live performer, especially in the Birmingham area. His later albums appeared infrequently on small UK labels.

●ALBUMS: *Any Road Up* (Goldhawk 1976)★★★, *Rolling On* (Polydor 1977)★★★, *Caught In The Act* (Polydor 1977)★★★, *Down In The Bunker* (Polydor 1978)★★★★, *Street Parade* (RCA 1980)★★★, *Saints And Sinners* (RCA 1981)★★★, *On The Loose* (Magnum Force 1986)★★★, *Not On The Radio* (1991)★★★.

●COMPILATIONS: *Best Of* (Polydor 1980)★★★.

GILDER, NICK

b. 7 November 1951, London, England. Gilder is best known for the 1978 hit 'Hot Child In The City', which reached number 1 in the US. Gilder moved to Vancouver, Canada, at the age of 10 and in high school formed a band called Throm Hortis. Gilder joined the band Sweeney Todd in 1971, and they charted with 'Roxy Roller' in 1976 (a second version of that song, also by Sweeney Todd featuring Bryan Adams on vocals, charted a month after the Gilder-sung version).With band member Jim McCulloch, Gilder relocated to Los Angeles and signed as a solo artist to Chrysalis Records. 'Hot Child In The City' was his first and greatest success, followed by two lesser chart singles, 'Here Comes The Night' and 'Rock Me'. Gilder also placed two albums on the chart, *City Nights* and *Frequency* but he was unable to repeat his success after the end of the 70s, despite further albums for Casablanca Records and RCA Records.

●ALBUMS: *You Know Who You Are* (Chrysalis 1977)★★, *City Nights* (Chrysalis 1978)★★★, *Frequency* (Chrysalis 1979)★★, *Rock America* (Casablanca 1980)★★, *Nick Gilder* (RCA 1985)★★.

GILLAN, IAN

b. 19 August 1945, Hounslow, Middlesex, England. Heavily influenced by Elvis Presley, vocalist Gillan formed his first band at the age of 16. In 1962 he was invited to join local semi-professional R&B band the Javelins, who eventually split up in March 1964. Gillan next formed the Hickies, but abandoned the project to join established soul band, Wainwright's Gentlemen. Soon he was unhappy with this group and he readily accepted an invitation to join the fully professional outfit, Episode Six, in May 1965. A succession of tours and singles failed to produce any domestic chart placings, however, and by early 1969 the band was beginning to disintegrate. In May of the same year Gillan, and Roger Glover (b. 30 November 1945, Brecon, South Wales; bass) were recruited to join Deep Purple, forming the legendary 'Mk II' line-up with Ritchie Blackmore, Jon Lord and Ian Paice. Deep Purple gradually established themselves as a major rock band, helped by their dynamic live show and an aggressive sound characterized by a mix of long instrumentals and Gillan's powerful vocals. The latter part of 1972 saw Deep Purple, acknowledged as the biggest-selling rock band in the world, enter the *Guinness Book Of Records* as the loudest pop group of the day. Their status was consolidated with the release of the live album, *Made In Japan*. In August 1972 Gillan decided to leave the band, but was persuaded to remain with them until June 1973. By the time of his last show with Deep Purple on 28 June, he had already purchased the De Lane Lea studio in London, and it was on this venture that he concentrated on leaving the band, forming Kingsway Studios. He recorded a solo album in 1974 for the Purple label, to whom he was still signed, but it was rejected as too radical a musical departure, and has never been released. After a brief attempt to launch Ian Gillan's Shand Grenade, which included Glover, in late 1975, it was the Ian Gillan Band which began recording *Child In Time* in the first days of 1976. The line-up was Gillan, Ray Fenwick (guitar), Mike Moran (keyboards), Mark Nauseef (drums) and John Gustafson (bass). This first album was much lighter in tone than Deep Purple, but included some excellent songs. The next two albums, now with Colin Towns on keyboards, demonstrated a notable jazz-rock influence, particularly on *Clear Air Turbulence*, which was also distinguished by its striking Chris Foss-designed cover. None of these albums was particularly successful commercially, and after a disappointing tour in spring 1978, Gillan disbanded the group.

Within just a few months of dissolving the Ian Gillan Band, he was back in the studio with a new outfit, inspired by a Towns' song, 'Fighting Man'. New members Leon Genocky (drums), Steve Byrd (guitar) and John McCoy (bass) joined Ian Gillan and Towns to record *Gillan* in summer 1978. The lack of a record deal meant that this excellent album was never released in the UK, although several of the tracks did appear on the next album, *Mr. Universe*, recorded early in 1979 with Pete Barnacle on drums. The title track was based on a song of the same name that Ian Gillan had recorded with Episode Six. The album as a whole marked the return of the imposing frontman to solid rock music. In so doing, this collection was instrumental in developing the New Wave Of British Heavy Metal, a label even more applicable to Gillan's next album, *Glory Road*. Now with Bernie Torme on guitar and former Episode Six drummer Mick Underwood, Gillan produced one of his finest albums, the first copies of which contained a second, free album, *For Gillan Fans Only*. After the slightly disappointing *Future Shock*, Torme left to be replaced by guitarist Janick Gers of White Spirit, who featured on *Double Trouble*, a double album comprising one studio and one live album, recorded mainly at the 1981 Reading rock festival, at which the band were appearing for the third consecutive year, a testimony to their popularity. Summer 1982 saw the release of *Magic*, another album of quality though sadly also the group's last. After many years of speculation and rumour, a Deep Purple reformation seemed imminent and Gillan wound up his band amid a certain amount of acrimony and uncertainty, early in 1983. Finding that he had ended Gillan somewhat prematurely, he joined Black Sabbath, a move he claims was motivated by financial necessity. Artistically, the time he spent with this band is deplored by both Gillan and Sabbath fans. After one album and a tour with Sabbath, the much talked about Deep Purple reunion took off and Gillan had his opportunity to escape. After eleven years apart, and all with successful, if turbulent careers during that time, the essential question remained whether or not the various members of the band would be able to get on with each other. A successful tour and a sell-out British concert at the 1985 Knebworth Festival seemed to suggest the reunion had worked, but by the time of the next album, *House Of The Blue Light*, it was clear that the latent tensions within the band were beginning to reappear. Between Deep Purple tours, and adding to the speculation about a break-up, Gillan and Glover recorded an album together; a curious but thoroughly enjoyable collection of material; it seemed to fulfil a need in both musicians to escape from the confines of the parent band. The 1988/1989 Deep Purple tour revealed the true extent of the rift between the members, and Gillan's departure was formally announced in May 1989. It was effectively over from January, when he was informed that he need not attend rehearsals for the next album. Gillan's response was to perform a short tour as his alter ego, Garth Rockett, in spring 1989, before recording vocals for the Rock Aid Armenia version of 'Smoke On The Water', in July. By the end of 1989 Gillan had assembled a band to record a solo album, which he financed himself to escape record company pressures, and recorded under his own name to avoid the politics of group decisions. The line-up featrued Steve Morris (guitar), from the Garth Rockett tour; Chris Glen (bass) and Ted McKenna (drums), both formerly of the Michael Schenker Group; Tommy Eyre (keyboards); Mick O'Donoghue (ex-Grand Prix; rhythm guitar) and Dave Lloyd (ex-Nutz, Rage and 2am;

backing vocals/percussion). The album, *Naked Thunder*, released in July 1990, was labelled middle-of-the-road by some critics, while Gillan himself described it as 'hard rock with a funky blues feel.' After touring in support of it, Gillan returned to the studio to prepare a second solo album. Now formulating a highly productive partnership with Steve Morris, he recruited Brett Bloomfield (bass) and Leonard Haze (ex-Y&T; drums) and produced an excellent album as a four-piece rock band, blending straightforward music with Gillan's often bizarre sense of humour and offbeat lyrics. *Toolbox* was released in October 1991 to critical acclaim. Gillan rejoined Deep Purple in 1992, undertook new recording sessions with the band and toured, before yet again quitting. However, the career decision taken in 1994 was indeed a strange one, seeing him reunited with his very first band, the Javelins, for a moribund collection of 60s covers. However, Gillan's durability alone makes him a central player in the British rock tradition, despite such occasional lapses.

●ALBUMS: as Ian Gillan Band *Child In Time* (Oyster 1976)★★★, *Clear Air Turbulence* (Island 1977)★★, *Scarabus* (Scarabus 1977)★★, *I.G.B. Live At The Budokan* (Island 1978)★★. With Gillan *Gillan* (Eastworld 1978)★★, *Mr. Universe* (Acrobat 1979)★★, *Glory Road* (Virgin 1980)★★★★, *Future Shock* (Virgin 1981)★★★, *Double Trouble* (Virgin 1982)★★★, *Magic* (Virgin 1982)★★★, *Live At The Budokan* (Virgin 1983)★★, *What I Did On My Vacation* (Virgin 1986)★★, *Live At Reading 1980* (Raw Fruit 1990)★★.

●COMPILATIONS: With Episode Six *Put Yourself In My Place* (PRT 1987)★★. With Black Sabbath *Born Again* (Vertigo 1983)★. With Gillan/Glover *Accidentally On Purpose* (Virgin 1988)★★. As Garth Rockett *Story Of* (Rock Hard 1990)★★★. As Ian Gillan *Naked Thunder* (East West 1990)★★★, *Very Best Of* (Music Club 1991)★★★, *Trouble: The Best Of* (Virgin 1991)★★★, *Toolbox* (East West 1991)★★★, *The Japanese Album* (East West 1993)★★★. With the Javelins *Raving ... With The Javelins* (RPM 1994)★★.

●VIDEOS: *Gillan Live At The Rainbow 1978* (Spectrum 1988), *Ian Gillan Band* (Spectrum 1990), *Ian Gillan Live* (Castle 1992). As Garth Rockett And The Moonshiners *Live* (Fotodisk 1990).

●FURTHER READING: *Child In Time: The Life Story Of The Singer From Deep Purple*, Ian Gillan with David Cohen..

GILMOUR, DAVID

b. 6 March 1944, Cambridge, England. The solo career of the Pink Floyd lead guitarist and now lead vocalist started in 1978 with a self-titled debut. The material was recorded during a perilously long Pink Floyd hiatus and amid rumours of a break-up. The album was well-received and made a respectable showing in the UK and US charts. *About Face* came in 1984 after the official and acrimonious split of the band. During that year Gilmour was very active; he performed at the Live Aid concert

with Bryan Ferry and played a major role in Ferry's *Bête Noire* and Grace Jones' *Slave To The Rhythm*. In 1987 Gilmour reunited with Nick Mason and decided to use the Pink Floyd title. As Rick Wright had also been hired it seemed legitimate, until Roger Waters objected. Gilmour has been involved in a subtle war of words with Waters ever since. Waters at present has lost title to the name (he does not want to use it anyway) and Gilmour now leads the band. His confidence both as a writer and as a leader has notably grown in stature. Pink Floyd march on.
●ALBUMS: *David Gilmour* (Harvest 1978)★★★, *About Face* (Harvest 1984)★★.

GILTRAP, GORDON
b. 6 April 1948, East Peckham, Tonbridge, Kent, England. A renowned and innovative guitarist, Giltrap came through the early days of the UK folk revival, and established himself in rock music circles. His first guitar was a present, at the age of 12, from his mother. Leaving school aged 15, he wanted to pursue a career in art, but had insufficient qualifications, so spent time working on building sites. As his interest and ability developed, he started playing regularly at Les Cousin's, in London's Greek Street. There he met a number of singers and musicians who later became household names in the folk and blues world. Names such as Bert Jansch, John Renbourn, John Martyn and Al Stewart were just a few such notables. Although still only semi-professional, Giltrap signed a deal with Transatlantic Records and released *Early Days* and *Portrait*. Playing the college, folk club and university circuit, and establishing a growing following, Giltrap had begun to write mainly instrumental pieces by the 70s. This change of direction led to *Visionary*, an album based on the work of William Blake, the 18th century English artist and poet. By now Giltrap was receiving favourable reviews for his style blending classical and rock music, and this led to him being commissioned to write for a number of special events. 'Heartsong', from *Perilous Journey*, just failed to broach the Top 20 in the British singles charts in 1978. The tune, a Giltrap composition, was later used by BBC Television, as the theme tune to the *Holiday* programme during the 80s. The album from which it came reached the Top 30 in the British charts, while the following year, 1979, 'Fear Of The Dark' narrowly failed to make the Top 50 singles chart. In 1979, he composed, for London's Capital Radio, an orchestral piece to commemorate 'Operation Drake', a two-year round-the-world scientific expedition following in the footsteps of Sir Francis Drake. This resulted in the premiere, in 1980, of the 'Eyes Of The Wind Rhapsody' with the London Philharmonic Orchestra, conducted by Vernon Handley. Many of Giltrap's other compositions have been used for UK television work, on programmes such as ITV's *Wish You Were Here*, *The Open University*, and, in 1985, the television drama *Hold The Back Page*, and other subsequent television films. Giltrap now tours

regularly with Ric Sanders in addition to solo work, and has also duetted with John Renbourn, and Juan Martin. *The Best Of Gordon Giltrap - All The Hits Plus More*, includes a previously unreleased track, 'Catwalk Blues', which was recorded live at Oxford Polytechnic. As well as performing, recording and owning a guitar shop Giltrap is a regular contributor to *Guitarist* magazine and has written a book on the history of Hofner guitars.
●ALBUMS: *Early Days* (Transatlantic 1968)★★★, *Gordon Giltrap* (Transatlantic 1968)★★★, *Portrait* (Transatlantic 1969)★★★, *Testament Of Time* (1971)★★★, *Giltrap* (1973)★★★, *Visionary* (1976)★★★, *Perilous Journey* (1977)★★★, *Fear Of The Dark* (1978)★★★, *Performance* (1980)★★★, *The Peacock Party* (PVK 1981)★★★, *Live* (Electric 1981)★★, *Airwaves* (1982)★★★, *Elegy* (Filmtrax 1987)★★, *A Midnight Clear* (Filmtrax 1987)★★★, *Gordon Giltrap-Guitarist* (1988)★★★, *Mastercraftsmen* (1989)★★, with Ric Sanders *One To One* (Nico Polo 1989)★★★, with Martin Taylor *A Matter Of Time* (Prestige 1991)★★★, *On A Summer's Night - Live* (1993)★★★.
●COMPILATIONS: *The Very Best Of Gordon Giltrap* (1988)★★★, *The Best Of Gordon Giltrap - All The Hits Plus More* (Prestige 1991)★★★.

GLENCOE
Based in London, England, Glencoe was formed in 1971 by two ex-members of Forevermore; Mick Travis (guitar/vocals) and Stewart Francis (drums). Graham Maitland (keyboards/vocals), who had previously played with Francis in 60s act Hopscotch, and Norman Watt-Roy (bass; ex-Greatest Show On Earth) completed the early line-up. In 1972 Francis was replaced by John Turnbull (ex-Skip Bifferty and Bell And Arc). Glencoe then became a highly popular live attraction, renowned for thoughtful, melodic, unpretentious rock music. *Glencoe* fully captured their talents, but sadly *The Spirit Of Glencoe* was a marked disappointment. The group split up in 1974. Francis joined Sharks, while Maitland moved to the USA where he pursued a songwriting career. Watt-Roy and Turnbull formed Loving Awareness with Mickey Gallagher and Charley Charles, a group that in 1977 became the Blockheads, backing group to Ian Dury.
●ALBUMS: *Glencoe* (Columbia 1972)★★★, *The Spirit Of Glencoe* (Columbia 1973)★★.

GLITTER BAND
Formed as a backing group for UK pop singer Gary Glitter, the Glitter Band also enjoyed a period of fame in their own right. The group's line-up comprised John Springate, Tony Leonard, Gerry Shephard, Pete Phipps and Harvey Ellison. Their gimmick and distinctive musical punch lay in the employment of two drummers. At the height of the glitter fad they secured a series of Top 10 UK hits, including 'Angel Face', 'Just For You', 'Let's Get Together Again', 'Goodbye My Love' and 'People Like You And People Like Me'. They split-up in

February 1977, but briefly reunited in 1981 in order to tour with their former mentor.

●ALBUMS: *Hey!* (Bell 1974)★★, *Rock 'N' Roll Dudes* (Bell 1975)★★, *Listen To The Band* (Bell 1975)★★, *Paris Match* (Bell 1977)★★.

●COMPILATIONS: *Greatest Hits* (Bell 1976)★★, *People Like You, People Like Me* (Bell 1977)★★, *Hits Collection* (Grab It 1990)★★★.

GLITTER, GARY

b. Paul Gadd, 8 May 1940, Banbury, Oxfordshire, England. The elder statesman of the 70s UK glam rock scene, Glitter began his career in a skiffle group, Paul Russell And The Rebels. He then became Paul Raven, under which name he recorded an unsuccessful debut for Decca Records, 'Alone In The Night'. His cover of 'Tower Of Strength' lost out to Frankie Vaughan's UK chart-topper, after which he spent increasingly long periods abroad, particularly in Germany. During the late 60s, having been signed to MCA Records by his former orchestral backing leader and now MCA head Mike Leander, he attempted to revitalize his career under the names Paul Raven and Monday, the latter of which was used for a version of the Beatles' 'Here Comes The Sun', which flopped. Seemingly in the autumn of his career, he relaunched himself as Gary Glitter, complete with thigh-high boots and a silver costume. His debut for Bell Records, 'Rock 'N' Roll Part 2' unexpectedly reached number 2 in the UK and climbed into the US Top 10. Although he failed to establish himself in America, his career in the UK traversed the early 70s, stretching up until the punk explosion of 1977. Among his many UK Top 10 hits were three number 1 singles: 'I'm The Leader Of The Gang (I Am)', 'I Love You Love Me Love' and 'Always Yours'. An accidental drug overdose and bankruptcy each threatened to end his career, but he survived and continues to play regular concerts in the UK. In recent years the now sober figure of Glitter is courted favourably by the media and is a minor legend.

●ALBUMS: *Glitter* (Bell 1972)★★, *Touch Me* (Bell 1973)★★, *Remember Me This Way* (Bell 1974)★★, *Always Yours* (MFP 1975)★★, *GG* (Bell 1975)★★, *I Love You Love* (Hallmark 1977)★★, *Silver Star* (Arista 1978)★★, *The Leader* (GTO 1980)★★, *Boys Will Be Boys* (Arista 1984)★.

●COMPILATIONS: *Greatest Hits* (Bell 1976)★★★, *Gary Glitter's Golden Greats* (GTO 1977)★★★, *The Leader* (GTO 1980)★★, *Gary Glitter's Gangshow* (Castle 1989)★★, *Many Happy Returns - The Hits* (1992)★★, *The Glam Years: Part 1* (Repertoire 1995)★★★, *The Glam Years* (Repertoire 1996)★★★.

●VIDEOS: *Gary Glitter's Gangshow* (Hendring 1989), *Gary Glitter Story* (Channel 5 1990), *Rock'n'Roll's Greatest Show: Gary Glitter Live* (PMI 1993).

●FURTHER READING: *The Gary Glitter Story*, George Tremlett. *Leader: The Autobiography Of Gary Glitter*, Gary Glitter with Lloyd Bradley.

GLOBAL VILLAGE TRUCKING COMPANY

One of several groups to emerge from London's alternative scene of the early 70s, the Global Village Trucking Company came to national prominence in 1973. The quintet - Jon Owen (guitar, vocals), Jimmy Lascelles (keyboards), Mike Medora (harmonica, guitar, vocals), John McKenzie (bass) and Simon Stewart (drums) - were featured on the 'benefit' release, *Greasy Truckers Live At Dingwalls*. Three years later the band was augmented by Peter Kitley (guitar), Jim Cuomo (saxophone), Jeremy Lacalles (percussion) and vocalists Caromay Dixon and Monica Garelts for *Global Village Trucking Company*. This album reflected the free spirit the collective brought to their music, but it was not a commercial success. The group slipped from the limelight upon the advent of punk.

●ALBUMS: *Greasy Truckers Live At Dingwalls* (Greasy Truckers 1973)★★, *Global Village Trucking Company* (Caroline 1976)★★.

GODLEY AND CREME

This highly talented duo were formed in 1976, having already enjoyed an illustrious career in British pop. Kevin Godley (b. 7 October 1945, Manchester, England; vocals/drums) and Lol Creme (b. 19 September 1947, Manchester, England; vocals/guitar) had previously been involved with such groups as the Mockingbirds, Hotlegs and, most crucially, 10cc. After leaving the latter, they intended to abandon mainstream pop in favour of a more elaborate project. The result was a staggeringly overblown triple album *Consequences*, whose concept was nothing less than 'The Story Of Man's Last Defence Against An Irate Nature'. The work was lampooned in the music press, as was the duo's invention of a new musical instrument the 'Gizmo' gadget, which had been used on the album. As their frustrated manager Harvey Lisberg sagely noted: 'They turned their back on huge success. They were brilliant, innovative - and what did they do? A triple album that goes on forever and became a disaster'. An edited version of the work was later issued but also failed to sell. By 1981, the duo reverted to a more accessible approach for the excellent UK Top 10 hit 'Under My Thumb', a ghost story in song. Although they enjoyed two more singles hits with 'Wedding Bells' and 'Cry', it was as video makers that they found their greatest success. Their monochrome video of 'Cry' won many awards and is a classic of the genre. This film superimposes a series of faces which gradually change. Visage, Duran Duran, Toyah, the Police and Herbie Hancock were some of the artists that used their services. Then, in 1984, they took the rock video form to new heights with their work with Frankie Goes To Hollywood. Godley And Creme are presently regarded as arguably the best in their field.

●ALBUMS: *Consequences* (Mercury 1977)★★, *L*

(Mercury 1978)★★, *Freeze Frame* (Polydor 1979)★★, *Ismism* (Polydor 1981)★★, *Birds Of Prey* (Polydor 1983)★★, *The History Mix Volume 1* (Polydor 1985)★★★, *Goodbye Blue Sky* (Polydor 1988)★★.
●COMPILATIONS: *The Changing Face Of 10cc And Godley And Creme* (Polydor 1987)★★★.
●VIDEOS: *Changing Faces-The Very Best Of 10cc And Godley And Creme* (Polygram 1988), *Cry* (Polygram 1988), *Mondo Video* (Virgin 1989).

GOLD, ANDREW

b. 2 August 1951, Burbank, California, USA. This accomplished guitarist/vocalist/keyboard player was the son of two notable musicians. His father, Ernest Gold, composed several film scores, including *Exodus*, while his mother, Marni Nixon, provided the off-screen singing voice for actors Audrey Hepburn and Natalie Wood in *My Fair Lady* and *West Side Story*, respectively. Andrew Gold first drew attention as a member of Los Angeles-based acts, Bryndle and the Rangers. Both groups also featured guitarist Kenny Edwards, formerly of the Stone Poneys, and the pair subsequently pursued their careers as part of Linda Ronstadt's backing group. Gold's skills as a musician and arranger contributed greatly to several of her releases, including *Prisoner In Disguise* (1975) and *Hasten Down The Wind* (1976), while sessions for Carly Simon, Art Garfunkel and Loudon Wainwright were also undertaken. Gold completed his solo debut in 1975 and the following year he enjoyed a transatlantic hit with 'Lonely Boy'. A follow-up single, 'Never Let Her Slip Away', reached number 5 in the UK, while other chart entries included 'How Can This Be Love' and 'Thank You For Being A Friend'. However the artist was unable to circumvent an increasingly sterile sound and was dropped by his label in the wake of the disappointing *Whirlwind*. Gold continued to tour with Ronstadt as part of her back-up band before forming Wax with Graham Gouldman in 1986. In 1992 Undercover had a major UK hit with a dance version of 'Never Let Her Slip Away'.
●ALBUMS: *Andrew Gold* (Asylum 1976)★★★, *What's Wrong With This Picture?* (Asylum 1977)★★, *All This And Heaven Too* (Asylum 1978)★★, *Whirlwind* (Asylum 1980)★★.
●COMPILATIONS: *Never Let Her Slip Away* (1993)★★★.

GOLDEN EARRING

Formed in The Hague, Netherlands, in 1961 by George Kooymans (b. 11 March 1948, The Hague, Netherlands; guitar/vocals) and Rinus Gerritsen (b. 9 August 1946, The Hague, Netherlands; bass/vocals) along with Hans Van Herwerden (guitar) and Fred Van Der Hilst (drums). The group, initially known as the Golden Earrings, subsequently underwent several changes before they secured a Dutch Top 10 hit with their debut release, 'Please Go' (1965). By this point Kooymans and Gerritsen had been joined by Frans Krassenburg (vocals), Peter De Ronde (guitar) and Jaap Eggermont

(drums) and the revitalized line-up became one of the most popular 'nederbeat' attractions. Barry Hay (b. 16 August 1948, Fyzabad, India; lead vocals/flute/saxophone/guitar) replaced Krassenburg in 1966, while De Ronde also left the group as they embraced a more radical direction. The group's first Dutch number 1 hit, 'Dong-Dong-Di-Ki-Di-Gi-Dong', came in 1968 and saw them branching out from their homeland to other European countries as well as a successful tour of the USA. Eggermont left the group to become a producer and was eventually supplanted by Cesar Zuiderwijk (b. 18 July 1948, The Hague, Netherlands) in 1969 as Golden Earring began courting an international audience with their compulsive *Eight Miles High*, which featured an extended version of the famous Byrds' song.

After years of experimenting with various music styles, they settled for a straight, hard rock sound and in 1972 Golden Earring were invited to support the Who on a European tour. They were subsequently signed to Track Records and the following year had a Dutch number 1/UK Top 10 hit with 'Radar Love' which subsequently found its way into the US Top 20 in 1974. Despite this, they were curiously unable to secure overseas success, which was not helped by a consistently unstable line-up. Robert Jan Stips augmented the quartet between 1974 and 1976 and on his departure Eelco Gelling joined as supplementary guitarist. By the end of the decade, however, the group had reverted to its basic line-up of Kooymans, Gerritsen, Hay and Zuiderwijk which continued to forge an imaginative brand of rock and their reputation as a top European live act was reinforced by *Second Live*. With the release of *Cut* in 1982, Golden Earring earned themselves a US Top 10 hit with 'Twilight Zone'. This was followed by a triumphant tour of the United States and Canada, where further chart success was secured with 'Lady Smiles'. With various members able to indulge themselves in solo projects, Golden Earring have deservedly earned themselves respect throughout Europe and America as the Netherland's longest surviving and successful rock group.
●ALBUMS: *Just Ear-rings* (Polydor 1965)★★★, *Winter Harvest* (Polydor 1966)★★★, *Miracle Mirror* (Polydor 1968)★★★, *On The Double* (Polydor 1969)★★★, *Reflections* (Polydor 1969)★★★, *Highlights From On The Double* (Polydor 1969)★★★, *Eight Miles High* (Polydor 1969)★★★, *Golden Earring (Wall Of Dolls)* (Polydor 1970)★★★, *Golden Earring* Box 5-LP box set (Polydor 1970)★★★★, *Seven Tears* (Polydor 1971)★★★, *Pophistory Vol 16* (Polydor 1971)★★★, *Together* (Polydor 1972)★★★, *Moontan* (Polydor 1973)★★★, *Switch* (Polydor 1975)★★★, *To The Hilt* (Polydor 1975)★★★, *Rock Of The Century* (Polydor 1976)★★★, *Contraband* (Polydor 1976)★★★, *Mad Love* (1977)★★★, *Live* (Polydor 1977)★★★, *Grab It For A Second* (Polydor 1978)★★★, *No Promises ... No Debts* (Polydor 1979)★★★, *Prisoner Of The Night* (Polydor 1980)★★★, *Second Live* (Polydor 1981)★★★, *Cut* (Mercury 1982)★★★, *Live*

Tracks (Polydor 1983)★★★, *N.E.W.S. (North East West South)* (21 Records 1984)★★★, *Live And Pictured* (Polydor 1984)★★★, *Something Heavy Going Down - Live From The Twilight Zone* (21 Records 1984)★★★, *The Hole* (21 Records 1986)★★★, *Keeper Of The Flame* (Jaws 1989)★★★, *Bloody Buccaneers* (Columbia 1991)★★★, *The Naked Truth* (Columbia 1992)★★★, *Face It* (Columbia 1994). Solo: George Kooymans *Jojo* (Polydor 1971)★★, *Solo* (Ring 1987)★★. Barry Hay *Only Parrots, Frogs And Angels* (Polydor 1972)★★★, *Victory Of Bad Taste* (Ring 1987)★★. Rinus Gerritsen and Michel Van Dijk *De G.V.D. Band* (Atlantic 1978)★★, *Labyrinth* (1985)★★.

●COMPILATIONS: *Hits Van De Golden Earrings* (Polydor 1967)★★★, *Greatest Hits* (Polydor 1968)★★★★, *Best Of Golden Earring* (1970)★★★, *Greatest Hits Volume 2* (Polydor 1970)★★★, *Superstarshine Vol. 1* (Polydor 1972)★★★, *Hearring Earring* (1973)★★★, *The Best Of Golden Earring* (Polydor 1974)★★★, *The Best Ten Years: Twenty Hits* (Arcade 1975)★★★, *Fabulous Golden Earring* (Polydor 1976)★★★, *The Golden Earring Story* (1978)★★★, *Greatest Hits Volume 3* (Polydor 1981)★★★, *Just Golden Earrings* (Polydor 1990)★★★, *The Complete Singles Collection 1 1965-1974* (Arcade 1992)★★★★, *The Complete Singles Collection 1975-1991* (Arcade 1992)★★★★,

GOLDIE (70s)

b. Goldie Zelkowitz, 1943, Brooklyn, New York, USA. The one-time leader of Goldie And The Gingerbreads, an all-girl US group briefly based in Britain, Zelkowitz embarked on a solo career, as Goldie, in October 1965. She was initially signed to Andrew Loog Oldham's Immediate label but although an original Mick Jagger/Keith Richard song was touted as her debut, the singer's first single was a version of Goffin/King's 'Goin' Back'. However the record was quickly withdrawn when the composers objected to its amended lyric, and Goldie switched outlets for her second release, 'I Do'. This expressive vocalist found it hard to attain any commercial momentum and by the late 60s she had returned to the USA. Now known as Genya Ravan, the artist joined an ambitious 10-piece jazz-rock band, Ten Wheel Drive, before continuing her solo career in 1972. *Urban Desire* and *And I Mean It* captured a performer inspired by the freedom punk had afforded, yet one whose past was equally influential on newer female artists, including Debbie Harry and Patti Smith. Ravan later produced the Dead Boys' album *Young Loud And Snotty*.

●ALBUMS: *Genya Ravan With Baby* (1972)★★, *They Love Me/They Love Me Not* (1973)★★, *Goldie Zelkowitz* (1974)★★, *Urban Desire* (1978)★★★, *And I Mean It* (1979)★★★.

GOLDSBORO, BOBBY

b. 18 January 1941, Marianna, Florida, USA. Goldsboro first came to prominence as a guitarist in Roy Orbison's touring band in 1960. His major chart breakthrough as a solo singer occurred in 1964 with the self-penned US Top 10 hit 'See The Funny Little Clown'. During the mid-60s, he also enjoyed minor US hits with such compositions as 'Whenever He Holds You', 'Little Things' (a UK hit for Dave Berry), 'Voodoo Woman', 'It's Too Late' and 'Blue Autumn'. His international status was assured in 1968 with the elegiacal 'Honey', a Bobby Russell composition, perfectly suited to Goldsboro's urbane, but anguished vocal style. The song dominated the US number 1 position for five weeks and was arguably the unluckiest single never to reach number 1 in the UK, twice reaching the number 2 slot, in 1968 and 1975. Goldsboro enjoyed further hits in the early 70s, most notably 'Watching Scotty Grow' and the risqué 'Summer (The First Time)'. In an attempt to extend his appeal, Goldsboro subsequently turned to country music, and met with considerable success in the 80s.

●ALBUMS: *Honey* (United Artists 1968)★★★, *Word Pictures* (United Artists 1968)★★★, *Today* (United Artists 1969)★★★, *Muddy Mississippi Line* (United Artists 1970)★★★, *We Gotta Start Lovin'* (United Artists 1971)★★★, *Come Back Home* (United Artists 1971)★★, *10th Anniversary Album* (United Artists 1974)★★, *Goldsboro* (1977)★★, *Roundup Saloon* (1982)★★.

●COMPILATIONS: *Solid Goldsboro* (United Artists 1967)★★★, *Summer The First Time* (United Artists 1973)★★★, *Best Of Bobby Goldsboro* (MFP 1983)★★★★, *The Very Best Of Bobby Goldsboro* (C5 1988)★★★★.

GONG

Although not officially applied to a group until 1971, the name Gong had already appeared on several projects undertaken by guitarist Daevid Allen, a founder-member of the Soft Machine. After relocating to Paris, Allen recorded two idiosyncratic albums before establishing this anarchic, experimental ensemble. Gilli Smyth aka Shanti Yoni (vocals), Didier Malherbe aka Bloomdido Bad De Grasse (saxophone/flute), Christian Tritsch aka The Submarine Captain (bass) and Pip Pyle (drums) had assisted Allen on his solo collection *Banana Moon* (1971), but Gong assumed a more permanent air when the musicians moved into a communal farmhouse in Sens, near Fontainbleu, France. Lauri Allen replaced Pyle as the group completed two exceptional albums, *Continental Circus* and *Camembert Electrique*. Musically, these sets expanded on the quirky, *avant garde* nature of the original Soft Machine, while the flights of fancy undertaken by their leader, involving science fiction, mysticism and 'pot-head pixies', emphasized their hippie-based surrealism. Subsequent releases included an ambitious 'Radio Gnome Invisible' trilogy; *Flying Teapot, Angel's Egg* and *You*. This period of the Gong story saw the band reach the peak of their commercial success with stunning, colourful live performances, plus the roles of newcomers Steve Hillage (guitar), Mike Howlett (bass) and Tim Blake (synthesizer) emphasized the group's long-

ignored, adept musicianship. During this period however, Allen had became estranged from his creation with Hillage becoming increasingly perceived as the group leader, resulting in the guitarist leaving the group in July 1975. Gong subsequently abandoned his original, experimental vision in favour of a tamer style. Within months Hillage, who had enjoyed great success with his solo album, *Fish Rising*, had begun a solo career, leaving Pierre Moerlen, prodigal drummer since 1973, in control of an increasingly tepid, jazz-rock direction. Mike Howlett left soon after to pursue a successful career in studio production and was replaced by Hanny Rowe. The guitarist role was filled by former Nucleus and Tempest member Allan Holdsworth. After a period of inaction in the early 80s the Gong name was used in performances alongside anarcho space/jazz rock group Here And Now, before being swallowed whole by the latter. In doing so, it returned to its roots appearing at free festivals, new age and neo-hippie gatherings. Often billed with various appendages to the name, by the late 80s and 90s Gong was once more under the control of its original leader.
●ALBUMS: *Magick Brother, Mystic Sister* (BYG 1969)★★, *Continental Circus* (Philips 1971)★★★, *Camembert Electrique* (BYG 1971)★★★★, *Radio Gnome Invisible Part 1-The Flying Teapot* (Virgin 1973)★★★★, *Radio Gnome Invisible Part 2-Angel's Egg* (Virgin 1973)★★★, *You* (Virgin 1974)★★★, *Shamal* (Virgin 1976)★★, *Gazeuse* (Virgin 1977)★★, *Gong Est Mort -Vive Gong* (Tapioca 1977)★★, *Expresso 2* (Virgin 1978)★★, *Downwind* (Arista 1979)★★, *Time Is The Key* (Arista 1979)★★, *Pierre Moerlen's Gong, Live* (Arista 1980)★★, *Leave It Open* (Arista 1981)★★, *Breakthrough* (Arc/Eulenspiegel 1986)★★, *Second Wind* (LIDLP 1988)★★, *Floating Anarchy* (Decal 1990)★★, *Live Au Bataclan 1973* (Mantra 1990)★★★, *Live At Sheffield 1974* (Mantra 1990)★★★, *25th Birthday Party* (Voiceprint 1995)★★, *The Peel Sessions* (Strange Fruit 1995)★★★, *Shapeshifter +* (Viceroy 1997)★★.
●COMPILATIONS: *Live Etc.* (Virgin 1977)★★, *A Wingful Of Eyes* (Virgin 1987)★★★, *The Mystery And The History Of The Planet G**g* (Demi-Monde 1989)★★★, *The Best Of ...* (Nectar Masters 1995)★★★.
●VIDEOS: *Gong Maison* (1993).

GOODIES

One of the few British television comedy acts to put together a consistent run of hit records, the Goodies were Bill Oddie (b. 7 July 1941, Rochdale, Lancashire, England), Graeme Garden (b. 18 February 1943, Aberdeen, Scotland) and Tim Brooke-Taylor (b. 17 July 1940, Buxton, Derbyshire, England). All three were educated at Cambridge University and were involved in the Footlights Revue in the early 60s, although not all at the same time. Oddie and Brooke-Taylor then joined the Cambridge Circus Show (with John Cleese) and toured worldwide. They then moved on to the BBC radio show *I'm Sorry I'll Read That Again* where they were eventu-

ally joined by Graeme Garden (who replaced Graham Chapman). Brooke-Taylor also spent time in the theatre and made films before starting to work in television on programmes such as *At Last The 1948 Show*. Oddie wrote and performed for programmes like *That Was The Week That Was* and *Twice A Fortnight* before meeting up with Brooke-Taylor again, and Garden (now a qualified doctor after medical training at Kings College Hospital, London) in the comedy programme *Broaden Your Mind*. Oddie, a prolific songwriter, also entered the recording world on Parlophone including a passable stab at pop with 'Nothing Better To Do' (a lament about Mods And Rockers fighting). The three teamed up for their own comedy show which was originally to have been called *Narrow Your Mind* but was eventually broadcast as *The Goodies* starting on the BBC on 8 November 1970. Several series were broadcast throughout the 70s and a number of spin-offs including several hit singles were created including 'The In Betweenies', 'Funky Gibbon', and 'Black Pudding Bertha', the first two of which both made the UK Top 10. In 1980 they left the BBC for Independent Television but the Goodies soon went their separate ways. Oddie, a keen ornithologist, has written several books on the subject and appears regularly on television in this guise or in general factual programmes. He also hosts a jazz programme (another of his passions) on radio. Oddie's performance, impersonating Joe Cocker's 'With A Little Help From My Friends' was a classic moment. Garden works in radio quizzes and game shows but has also used his medical background to present some light-hearted health and fitness programmes. Brooke-Taylor has worked successfully in television situation comedies.
●ALBUMS: *Goodies Sing Songs* (Decca 1973)★★, *The New Goodies LP* (Bradley's 1975)★★, *Nothing To Do With Us* (Island 1976)★★, *The Goodies' Beastly Record* (EMI 1978)★★.
●COMPILATIONS: *The World Of The Goodies* (1975)★★★, *The Goodies' Greatest* (Bradley's 1976)★★★.
●VIDEOS: *Kitten Kong* (1970).

GOODMAN, STEVE

b. 25 July 1948, Chicago, Illinois, USA, d. 20 September 1984. An engaging singer-songwriter from Chicago, Goodman was a favourite among critics, although his albums rarely achieved the commercial success which reviews suggested they deserved. His first appearance on record came in 1970 on *Gathering At The Earl Of Old Town* an album featuring artists who regularly performed at a Chicago folk club, the Earl Of Old Town, which was run by an enthusiast named Earl Plonk. Released initially on Dunwich Records and later by Mountain Railroad, the album included three tracks by Goodman, 'Right Ball', 'Chicago Bust Rag' (written by Diane Hildebrand) and his classic train song, 'City Of New Orleans'. By 1972, Goodman's talent had been spotted by Kris Kristofferson, who recommended him to Paul Anka. Anka, who was an admirer of Kris Kristofferson, convinced Buddah (the label to which Anka was signed at the time) to also sign Goodman, while Goodman in turn recommended his friend and fellow singer-songwriter, John Prine, to both Anka and Kristofferson, resulting in Atlantic signing Prine. Unfortunately for Goodman, Prine's career took off and Goodman remained a cult figure. He made two excellent albums for Buddah. *Steve Goodman* (which was produced by Kristofferson) included his two best known songs in commercial terms, 'You Never Even Call Me By My Name', which was David Allan Coe's breakthrough country hit in 1975, and 'City Of New Orleans', a 1972 US Top 20 hit for Arlo Guthrie which was also covered by dozens of artists. Recorded in Nashville, the album featured many Area Code 615 musicians including Charlie McCoy and Kenny Buttrey. It was followed by *Somebody Else's Troubles* (produced by Arif Mardin) which featured musicians including David Bromberg, Bob Dylan (under the alias Robert Milkwood Thomas) and members of the Rascals.

Although his album had failed thus far to chart, Goodman quickly secured a new deal with Asylum, a label which specialized in notable singer-songwriters. While his next two self-produced albums, *Jessie's Jig And Other Favourites* (1975) and *Words We Can Dance To* (1976), were minor US hits, 1977's *Say It In Private* (produced by Joel Dorn and including a cover of the Mary Wells classic written by Smokey Robinson, 'Two Lovers'), 1979's *High And Outside* and 1980's *Hot Spot* failed to chart, and his days on major labels ended at this point. By this time, Goodman, who had been suffering from leukemia since the early 70s, was often unwell, but by 1983, he had formed his own record label, Red Pajamas, with the help of his (and Prine's) manager, Al Bunetta. The first album to be released on the label was a live collection covering 10 years of performances by Goodman. *Artistic Hair*'s sleeve pictured him as almost bald, due to the chemotherapy he was receiving. Soon afterwards came *Affordable Art*, which also included some live tracks and at least one out-take from an Asylum album, and with John Prine guesting. Goodman's final album, *Santa Ana Winds*, on which Emmylou Harris and Kris Kristofferson guested, included two songs he co-wrote with Jim Ibbotson and Jeff Hanna of the Nitty Gritty Dirt Band, 'Face On The Cutting Room Floor' and 'Queen Of The Road', but in September 1984, he died from kidney and liver failure following a bone marrow transplant operation. In 1985, Red Pajamas Records released a double album *Tribute To Steve Goodman*, on which many paid their musical respects to their late friend, including Prine, Bonnie Raitt, Arlo Guthrie, John Hartford, Bromberg, Richie Havens and the Nitty Gritty Dirt Band. It is highly likely that the largely excellent catalogue of this notable performer will be re-evaluated in the future - while he cannot be aware of the posthumous praise he has received, few would regard it as less than well deserved.

●ALBUMS: *Gathering At The Earl Of Old Town* (Dunwich 1970)★★★, *Steve Goodman* (Buddah 1972)★★★★, *Somebody Else's Trouble* (Buddah 1973)★★★, *Jessie's Jig And Other Favourites* (Asylum 1975)★★★★, *Words We Can Dance To* (Asylum 1976)★★★★, *Say It In Private* (Asylum 1977)★★★, *High And Outside* (1979)★★★, *Hot Spot* (1980)★★★, *Artistic Hair* (1983)★★★, *Affordable Art* (Red Pajamas 80s)★★, *Santa Ana Winds* (Red Pajamas 80s)★★.
●COMPILATIONS: *No Big Surprise - The Steve Goodman Anthology* (Red Pajamas 1995)★★★.

GORDON, ROBERT

b. 1947, Washington, DC, USA. Gordon was briefly a leading light during the 70s rediscovery of pop's roots. His own preferences for rockabilly and soul became apparent onstage when, after moving to New York in 1970, he began singing with various groups including Tuff Darts with whom he was heard among other acts on a concert album from the celebrated CBGB's club. As a solo artist, he was produced by Richard Gottehrer and signed to Private Stock. On a 1977 album with Link Wray, the ghost of the 50s faced the spirit of the 70s in state-of-the-art workouts of old chestnuts like 'Summertime Blues', Frankie Ford's 'Sea Cruise' and the tie-in single, 'Red Hot'. Hopes of a hit via Bruce Springsteen's 'Fire', the single from *Fresh Fish Special*, were dashed by a cover from the better-known Pointer Sisters but, transferring to RCA, Gordon tried again with help from Gottehrer, Chris Spedding and the cream of Nashville session players on *Rockabilly Boogie*, which contained 'The Catman', a self-penned tribute to Gene Vincent. A promotional tour of North America and Europe stoked up much revivalist fervour, and guaranteed a fair hearing for *Bad Boy*, highlighted by arrangements of Conway Twitty's 'It's Only Make Believe' and Joe Brown's 'A Picture Of You'. However, most consumers favoured the original sounds to Gordon's remakes and stylized homages - though few quarrelled over his integrity and taste.

●ALBUMS: *Robert Gordon With Link Wray* (Private Stock 1977)★★, *Fresh Fish Special* (Private Stock 1978)★★, *Rock Billy Boogie* (RCA 1979)★★, *Bad Boy* (RCA 1980)★★, *Are You Gonna Be The One* (RCA 1981)★★, *Live At Lone Star* (New Rose 1989)★★.
●COMPILATIONS: *Too Fast To Live, Too Young To Die* (1982)★★, *Robert Gordon Is Red Hot* (Bear Family 1989)★★★, *Red Hot 1977-1981* (Razor & Tie 1995)★★★.

GOULDMAN, GRAHAM

b. 10 May 1945, Manchester, England. Gouldman began his recording career with the Whirlwinds, before forming the Mockingbirds with drummer Kevin Godley. One of Graham's compositions, 'For Your Love', was scheduled as the new group's first single, but when their label rejected it the song was passed on to the Yardbirds. Their version topped the charts and this fruitful songwriter/client relationship continued with

'Heart Full Of Soul' and 'Evil Hearted You'. Gouldman also penned a series of exemplary British pop hits for the Hollies ('Look Through Any Window', 'Bus Stop'), Herman's Hermits ('No Milk Today'), Wayne Fontana ('Pamela Pamela') and Jeff Beck ('Tallyman'), but paradoxically the Mockingbirds failed to find a similar commercial success. The artist began a solo career with 'Stop Or Honey I'll Be Gone' (1966), but was again unable to make an impact as a performer. An album blending versions of old and new songs, *The Graham Gouldman Thing*, was only issued in the USA but it served as the spur to a brief period domiciled in New York working under the auspices of producers Jerry Kasenetz and Jeff Katz. He joined the late period Mindbenders where he collaborated with guitarist Eric Stewart. An unreleased album for Giorgio Gomelsky's Marmalade label brought Gouldman into contact with ex-Mockingbird Kevin Godley and talented instrumentalist Lol Creme. Their studio experiments created the hit group Hotlegs, which soon evolved into 10cc, one of the most consistent hit groups of the 70s. Gouldman remained a member throughout the group's history, but re-embraced outside interests at the end of the decade. He scored the cartoon film *Animalympics* and later enjoyed a minor hit with 'Sunburn'. He produced albums by the Ramones and Gilbert O'Sullivan and in 1986 formed Wax with Andrew Gold. 10cc re-formed in 1991.

●ALBUMS: *The Graham Gouldman Thing* (1968)★★, *Animalympics* (1980)★.

GRACIOUS

British progressive act Gracious - Alan Cowderoy (guitar/vocals), Paul Davis (guitar/vocals), Martin Kitcat (keyboards/vocals), Tim Wheatley (bass) and Robert Lipson (bass) - made its recording debut in 1968 with 'Once In A Windy Day', issued by Polydor Records. A second single, 'Beautiful', followed in 1969 when Gracious supported the Who on a national UK tour. In 1970 the group was signed by the feted Vertigo Records, for which they completed *Gracious!*, a bold synthesis of classic and symphonic influences, progressive hard rock and judicious use of the mellotron. 'Fugue In 'D' Minor' is representative of their mock-baroque ambitions. Davis then sang on the film soundtrack of *Jesus Christ Superstar*, before rejoining his colleagues for *This Is ... Gracious!!*. This equally ambitious set was issued on a budget-price label, which undermined the group's music and confidence and Gracious disbanded soon after its release. Alan Cowderoy subsequently worked behind the scenes at Stiff Records.

●ALBUMS: *Gracious!* (Vertigo 1970)★★★, *This Is ... Gracious!!* (Phillips International 1972)★★★.

GRAHAM CENTRAL STATION

Formed in San Francisco in late 1972 by Larry Graham (b. 14 August 1946, Beaumont, Texas, USA), erstwhile bassist in Sly And The Family Stone. The core of the group: David Vega (lead guitar), Hershall Kennedy (keyboards), Willie Sparks and Patrice Banks (both drums), were former members of Hot Chocolate (USA), a local band Graham was producing, while a second keyboard player, Robert Sam, was drafted in from Billy Preston's touring ensemble. Musically, Graham Central Station emulated the rhythmic funk of Sly And The Family Stone, but lacked their perception. Renowned as one of the era's flashiest live attractions, the group's shows included light panels programmed to oscillate in time to their pulsating sound. Although their initial albums enjoyed critical and commercial success, later releases failed to capitalize on this in-concert popularity and in 1980 Graham embarked on a solo career.

●ALBUMS: *Graham Central Station* (Warners 1974)★★★, *Release Yourself* (Warners 1974)★★★, *Ain't No 'Bout-A-Doubt It* (Warners 1975)★★★, *Mirror* (Warners 1976)★★★, *Now Do U Wanta Dance* (Warners 1977)★★★, *My Radio Sure Sounds Good To Me* (Warners 1978)★★★, *Star Walk* (Warners 1979)★★. Solo: Larry Graham *One In A Million You* (Warners 1980)★★, *Just Be My Lady* (Warners 1981)★★, *Sooner Or Later* (Warners 1982)★★, *Victory* (Warners 1983)★★.

GRAND FUNK RAILROAD

Formed in 1968, Grand Funk Railroad were the first American heavy rock 'power trio' to reach massive fame, while alienating another large segment of the rock audience and critics at the same time. The group consisted of guitarist Mark Farner (b. 29 September 1948, Flint, Michigan, USA), bassist Mel Schacher (b. 3 April 1951, Owosso, Michigan, USA) and drummer Don Brewer (3 September 1948, Flint, Michigan, USA). The group was a spin-off of Terry Knight And The Pack, a popular soul-rock group in the Michigan area in the mid-60s. Farner and Brewer had both been members of that band (Brewer had also belonged to the Jazz Masters prior to the Pack). Following a single release on the small Lucky Eleven label, 'I (Who Have Nothin)', which reached number 46 in the US, the Pack were joined by Schacher, formerly of ? And The Mysterians. At this point Knight stopped performing to become the band's manager, renaming it Grand Funk Railroad (the name was taken from the Michigan landmark the Grand Trunk Railroad). The new trio signed with Capitol Records in 1969 and immediately began making its name by performing at several large pop festivals. Their first singles made the charts but Grand Funk soon proved its real strength in the album market. *On Time* reached number 27 in 1969, followed by the number 11 *Grand Funk* in 1970. By the summer of that year they had become a major concert attraction, and their albums routinely reached the Top 10 for the next four years. Of those, 1973's *We're An American Band* was the biggest seller, reaching number 2. The group's huge success is often attributed to the public relations expertise of manager Knight. In 1970, for example, Knight reportedly paid $100,000 for a huge billboard in New York

City's Times Square to promote the group's *Closer To Home*, which subsequently became their first Top 10 album, reaching number 6 and spawning the FM radio staple title track. That promotional campaign backfired with the press, however, which dismissed the band's efforts despite spiralling success with the public. In June 1971, for example, Grand Funk became only the second group (after the Beatles) to sell out New York's Shea Stadium. Their recordings sold in greater quantity even as many radio stations ignored their releases. 1970's *Live Album* reached number 5 and included another concert and radio favourite in Farner's 'Mean Mistreater'. The next year saw the release of *Survival* and *E Pluribus Funk*, the latter most notable for its round album cover. In 1972 the group fired Knight, resulting in a series of lawsuits involving millions of dollars. (they hired John Eastman, father of Linda McCartney, as their new manager). In 1973 the group shortened its name officially to Grand Funk, and added a fourth member, keyboardist Craig Frost (b. 20 April 1948, Flint, Michigan, USA). Now produced by Todd Rundgren, they finally cracked the singles market, reaching number 1 with album title track 'We're An American Band', a celebration of its times on the road. In 1974 a major revision of Little Eva's 'Loco-motion' also reached the top (the first time in US chart history that a cover of a song that had previously reached number 1 also ascended to that position). In 1975, with their popularity considerably diminished, the group reverted to its original name of Grand Funk Railroad. The following year they signed with MCA Records and recorded *Good Singin', Good Playin'*, produced by Frank Zappa. When it failed to reach the Top 50, Farner left for a solo career. The others stayed together, adding guitarist Billy Elworthy and changing their name to Flint, a group who failed to derive commercial success with their solitary album. Grand Funk, this time consisting of Farner, Brewer and bassist Dennis Bellinger, re-formed for two years in 1981-83 and recorded *Grand Funk Lives* and *What's Funk?* for the Full Moon label. Failing to recapture former glories, they split again. Farner returned to his solo career and Brewer and Frost joining Bob Seger's Silver Bullet Band.

●ALBUMS: *On Time* (Capitol 1969)★★★, *Grand Funk* (Capitol 1970)★★★, *Closer To Home* (Capitol 1970)★★★, *Live* (Capitol 1970)★★, *Survival* (Capitol 1971)★★, *E Pluribus Funk* (Capitol 1971)★★★, *Phoenix* (Capitol 1972)★★★, *We're An American Band* (Capitol 1973)★★★, *Shinin' On* (Capitol 1974)★★, *All The Girls In The World Beware!!!* (Capitol 1974)★★, *Caught In The Act* (MCA 1975)★★, *Good Singin', Good Playin'* (MCA 1976)★★★, *Grand Funk Lives* (Full Moon 1981)★★, *What's Funk?* (Full Moon 1983)★★.

●COMPILATIONS: *Mark, Don & Mel 1969-71* (Capitol 1972)★★, *Grand Funk Hits* (Capitol 1976)★★★, *The Best Of Grand Funk Railroad* (Capitol 1990)★★★, *More Of The Best Of Grand Funk Railroad* (Capitol 1991)★★, *The Collection* (Castle 1992)★★★.

GRANT, EDDY

b. Edmond Montague Grant, 5 March 1948, Plaisance, Guyana, West Indies. Grant was 24 years old, with several hits to his credit, when he left the Equals to form his own production company. After producing other acts, he made his own debut in 1977 with *Message Man*. It was certainly a solo effort. Not only did he sing and play every note, but it was recorded in his own studio, the Coach House, and released on his own label, Ice Records. Grant had developed his own sound - part reggae, part funk, strong musical motifs, strong melodies - pop with credibility. More than 10 years after the Equals' first hit, 'Living On The Front Line' (1979) was a UK number 11 hit, and the now dreadlocked Grant had found himself a whole new audience. 'Do You Feel My Love' and 'Can't Get Enough Of You' kept him in the UK Top 20. In 1982 he moved his home and studio to Barbados, signed Ice Records to RCA, and achieved a memorable UK number 1 hit with 'I Don't Wanna Dance'. The following year 'Electric Avenue' reached number 2 on both sides of the Atlantic, and the parent album *Killer On The Rampage* proved his biggest seller. The huge hits eluded him for four years until he stormed back in January 1988 with 'Gimme Hope Jo'anna', as if he had never been away. The dressing of the anti-Apartheid message in the apparent simplicity of a pop song was typically inspired.

●ALBUMS: *Message Man* (Ice 1977)★★★, *Walking On Sunshine* (Ice 1979)★★★, *Love In Exile* (Ice 1980)★★★, *Can't Get Enough* (Ice 1981)★★★, *Live At Notting Hill* (Ice 1981)★★, *Paintings Of The Soul* (Ice 1982)★★★, *Killer On The Rampage* (Ice/RCA 1982)★★★, *Can't Get Enough* (Ice/RCA 1983)★★★, *Going For Broke* (Ice/RCA 1984)★★, *Born Tuff* (Ice 1987)★★, *File Under Rock* (Parlophone 1988)★★.

●COMPILATIONS: *All the Hits: The Killer At His Best* (K-Tel 1984)★★, *Hits* (Starr 1988)★★, *Walking On Sunshine (The Best Of Eddy Grant)* (Parlophone 1989)★★★.

●VIDEOS: *Live In London* (PMI 1986), *Walking On Sunshine* (PMI 1989).

GRANT, PETER

b. 5 April 1935, London, England, d. 21 November 1995. Best known as the heavyweight manager of UK rock group Led Zeppelin, Grant began his career as a wrestler under the name Count Massimo. He also enjoyed spells as an actor, deputizing for Robert Morley and appearing in the UK television series *Dixon Of Dock Green* and the *Benny Hill Show*. Grant learned his trade in the pop business from the notorious Don Arden, then went on to manage his own acts. His first discoveries, the Flintstones and the She Trinity, were unsuccessful, but the New Vaudeville Band did a little better. He was then approached by manager Simon Napier-Bell with a view to overseeing the career of the fragmenting Yardbirds. This eventually resulted in the management of Led Zeppelin. Under Grant's tutelage they became one of the biggest-selling albums bands in the world. Grant's speciality was the American tour, from which he gained his charges enormous amounts of money. During his heyday, Grant was one of the fiercest and most feared entrepreneurs in the rock business, a reputation that often worked to led Zeppelin's advantage. During the 70s, he co-managed other acts, including Bad Company and Maggie Bell, who appeared on Led Zeppelin's Swansong label, which was also co-owned by Grant. However, the label failed to establish an identity beyond Led Zeppelin. Grant, like many others, fell victim to the excesses that were associated with Led Zeppelin at their most decadent, and spent most of the 80s in relative retirement at his 15th-century manor house in Sussex. During this time he suffered heart problems, although in the mid-90s he was to be seen at music business functions. He died following a heart attack at his home in 1995.

GRAVY TRAIN

Typifying the excesses that have frequently been denounced in their genre, UK progressive rock band Gravy Train recorded a series of albums for Vertigo Records and Dawn Records in the early 70s bedecked in grandiose, conceptual artwork. The group's core members were Norman Barrett (vocals/guitar), Barry Davenport (drums), J.D. Hughes (woodwind/keyboards/vocals) and Les Williams (bass/vocals). Their first, self-titled 1970 album was dominated by Hughes' flute melodies, which earned the group initial comparisons to Jethro Tull, as well as extended rock riffs. One of the songs, 'Tribute To Syd', was an obvious salute to the genius of Syd Barrett. The follow-up collection, which sold poorly, was *Ballad Of A Peaceful Man*. Despite its relative lack of success, many critics considered it to be far superior to the group's debut, with its complex arrangements, strong musical values and disciplined vocals attracting particular praise. Though they continued to draw crowds on their extensive UK touring schedule, Vertigo became frustrated with their lack of record sales, leading to a move to Dawn. *Second Birth* is considered by most to be a disappointing effort, lacking the focus and drive of its predecessor. For their final album, 1974's *Staircase To The Day*, the group experimented with Greek folk and classical signatures (notably on the Bach-inspired title-track), while Roger Dean supplied the cover artwork. The group utilized a wide variety of collaborators for this album, including Russell Cordwell (drums), Jim Frank (drums), George Lynon (guitar), Pete Solley (synthesizer) and Mary Zinovieff (synthesizer/violin). Original drummer Davenport had now left, and the rest of the band elected to close their career after further moderate sales.
●ALBUMS: *Gravy Train* (Vertigo 1970)★★★, *Ballad Of A Peaceful Man* (Vertigo 1971)★★★, *Second Birth* (Dawn 1973)★★, *Staircase To The Day* (Dawn 1974)★★★.

GRAY, DOBIE

b. Leonard Victor Ainsworth, 26 July 1942, Brookshire, Texas, USA. Although Gray had already been recording for a number of years, the anthem-like 'The In Crowd' (1965) was his first major hit. This compulsive, if boastful, single was followed by 'See You At The Go-Go' (1965), but it was eight years before the singer secured another chart entry. In the interval Gray worked as an actor, appearing in productions of *Hair* and the controversial play *The Beard*. In the early 70s Gray sang lead for a hard rock group, Pollution; they recorded three albums that were well received, but were commercial failures. He also recorded several demos for songwriter Paul Williams, whose brother Mentor, a producer, was responsible for relaunching Dobie's singing career. 'Drift Away' (US Top 5 in 1973), provided an artistic and commercial success which the singer followed with further examples of progressive southern rock/soul. However, despite minor successes for labels, Capricorn and Infinity, Gray was unable to find a distinctive direction and his newfound promise was left unfulfilled.
●ALBUMS: *Drift Away* (MCA 1973)★★★, *Loving Arms* (MCA 1973)★★, *Hey Dixie* (MCA 1974)★★, *New Ray Of Sunshine* (Capricorn 1975)★★, *Dobie Gray* (Capricorn 1976)★★, *Midnight Diamond* (Infinity 1979)★★.
●COMPILATIONS: *Sings For In Crowders That Go-Go* (Kent 1987)★★★.

GREASE

Released in 1978 and adapted from a stage play, this endearingly simple musical became one of the decade's most spectacular successes. Set in a high school during the early 60s, the plot recalled those of the Annette/Frankie Avalon 'beach' movies. Stars John Travolta and Olivia Newton-John meet during the summer break, but their affair seems doomed when the former plays up to his 'tough-guy' image, fearful of the admonishment of fellow gang members. Naturally, the pair are together at the end and only the occasional sexual innuendo - and co-star Stockard Channing's pregnancy - indicate the film is a product of a later decade. What elevated *Grease* from mere formula was Travolta, then riding on the crest of success from *Saturday Night Fever*, and a succession of memorable songs. He paired with Newton-John on 'You're The One That I Want' and 'Summer Nights', which together topped the UK singles chart in 1978 for a total of 16 weeks. Travolta's solo release, 'Sandy', reached number 2, a position equalled by Newton-John with 'Hopelessly Devoted To You'. The soundtrack album, meanwhile, spent 13 consecutive weeks at the top of the album charts.

GRECH, RIC

b. 1 November 1945, Bordeaux, France, d. 16 March 1990. Bassist Ric (sometimes Rick) Grech embraced professional music in 1965 when he joined Leicester-based group, the Farinas (also using the names X-Citers and Roaring Sixties), which later evolved into Family. Prior to that he had played with the Leicester City Youth Orchestra. By doubling on violin, Grech added considerable texture to an already inventive, exciting attraction but abandoned them in rancorous circumstances during an American tour. Grech then joined Blind Faith where an understanding forged with Steve Winwood continued with spells in Airforce (1970) and Traffic (1970-71) and on many other albums as a session player with Winwood. He found time during this hectic period to produce Rosetta Hightower and carry out sessions with the Faces and Fairport Convention. After leaving Traffic in December 1971 the bassist was later a member of the Crickets, alongside guitarist Albert Lee, and he also appeared on a session basis for Jim Capaldi, Vivian Stanshall, Chuck Berry, Muddy Waters, Gordon Jackson, Graham Bond and Streetwalkers, the latter featuring former Family colleagues Roger Chapman and John Whitney. Grech then moved to America where an association with Gram Parsons resulted in his composing 'Kiss The Children' and 'Las Vegas' and co-producing G.P. with the singer. The bassist then performed at Eric Clapton's famous Rainbow Concert and briefly joined KGB with Mike Bloomfield and Ray Kennedy. On his return to the UK he formed a country rock band Square Dance Machine but drug problems increasingly undermined his career. Years of sustained abuse took their toll on his liver and he died in 1990. Grech was a musician who was able to embrace many styles and play them all with conviction. The combination of violin and bass was in itself interesting, but to be musically at home with country, jazz, blues, folk, soul and rock, was remarkable.

● ALBUMS: on which Grech appeared include, Family *Music In A Dolls House* (Reprise 1968), *Family Entertainment* (Reprise 1969). Blind Faith *Blind Faith* (Polydor 1969). Gordon Jackson *Thinking Back* (Marmalade 1969), *Airforce* (Polydor 1970), *Airforce 2* (Polydor 1970). Harold McNair *The Fence* (B&B 1970). Traffic *Welcome To The Canteen* (Island 1971), *The Low Spark Of High Heeled Boys* (Island 1971). Rosetta Hightower *Rosetta Hightower* (Columbia 1971). Graham Bond *Holy Magick* (Vertigo 1971). Crickets *Bubblegum, Bop, Ballads & Boogies* (Philips 1972). Chuck Berry *The London Sessions* (Chess 1972). Muddy Waters *The London Sessions* (Chess 1972). Jim Capaldi *Oh How We Danced* (Island 1972). Gram Parsons *G.P.* (Reprise 1972). *Eric Clapton's Rainbow Concert* (RSO 1973). Bee Gees *Life In A Tin Can* (RSO 1973). Crickets *Remnants* (Vertigo 1973). Rod Stewart *Smiler* (Mercury 1974). Eddie Harris *In The UK* (Atlantic 1974). Vivian Stanshall *Men Opening Umbrellas Ahead* (Warners 1974). Crickets *Long Way From Lubbock* (Mercury 1974). Ron Wood and Ronnie Lane *Mahoney's Last Stand* (Atlantic 1976). For ratings on these albums please refer to the individual entries.

● COMPILATIONS: *Ric Grech: The Last Five Years* a collection drawn from several groups with which Grech appeared (RSO 1973)★★★.

GREEN, AL

b. Al Greene, 13 April 1946, Forrest City, Arkansas, USA. Having served his musical apprenticeship in the Greene Brothers, a fraternal gospel quartet, this urbane singer made his first recordings in 1960. Four years later he helped form the Creations with Curtis Rogers and Palmer Jones. These two companions subsequently wrote and produced 'Back Up Train', a simple, effective ballad and a 1967 R&B hit for his new group, Al Greene And The Soul Mates. Similar releases fared less well, prompting Green's decision to work solo. In 1969 he shared a bill with bandleader Willie Mitchell, who took the singer to Hi Records. The combination of a crack house band, Mitchell's tight production and Green's silky, sensuous voice, resulted in some of soul's definitive moments. The combination took a little time to gel, but with the release of 'I Can't Get Next To You' (1970), they were clearly on course. Previously a hit for the Temptations, this slower, blues-like interpretation established an early pattern. However, the success of 'Tired Of Being Alone' (1971), a Green original, introduced a smoother perspective. A US number 11 and a UK number 4, it was followed by 'Let's Stay Together' (1971), 'I'm Still In Love With You' (1972), 'Call Me (Come Back Home)', 'Here I Am (Come And Take Me)' (both 1973), each of which increased Green's stature as a major artist. His personal life, however, was rocked in October 1974. Following an argument, his girlfriend, Mary Woodson, burst in while the singer was taking a bath and poured boiling grits over his back. She then shot herself dead. Although he occasionally recorded gospel material, a scarred and shaken Green vowed to devote more time to God. His singles, meanwhile, remained popular, 'L-O-V-E (Love)' and 'Full Of Fire' were both R&B chart toppers in 1975, but his work grew increasingly predictable and lacked the passion of his earlier records. The solution was drastic. The partnership with Mitchell was dissolved and Green opened his own recording studio, American Music. The first single was the majestic 'Belle' (a US R&B Top 10 hit), although the accompanying album was a departure from his commercial formula and something of a 'critics favourite' as were the later Hi collections. The failure of further singles suggested that the problem was more than simply a tired working relationship. In 1979 Green fell from a Cincinnati stage, which he took as a further religious sign. *The Lord Will Make A Way* was the first of several gospel-only recordings, which included a 1985 reunion with Mitchell for *He Is The Light*. Green has since continued to record sacred material. A practising minister, he nonetheless reached the UK singles chart in 1989 with the distinctly secular, 'Put A Little Love In Your Heart'. His Hi albums, *Al Green Gets Next To You*, *Let's Stay Together*, *I'm Still In Love With You* and *Call Me*, are particularly recommended. *Greatest Hits* and *Take Me To The River – Greatest Hits Volume Two* offer the simplest overview with the first mentioned being reissued on CD in an expanded form with 15 tracks. *Truth 'N' Time* (1978) best represents the post-Mitchell, pre-gospel recordings. *Don't Look Back* was a sparkling return after many years away from recording new R&B/soul material, and some critics rated it as high as albums such as *Let's Stay Together*. The USA release was delayed for over three years, until *In Good Hands* was issued containing eight tracks from *Don't Look Back*.

●ALBUMS: *Back Up Train* (1967)★★, *Green Is Blues* (Hi 1970)★★★, *Al Green Gets Next To You* (Hi 1970)★★★★, *Let's Stay Together* (Hi 1972)★★★★, *I'm Still In Love With You* (Hi 1972)★★★★, *Call Me* (Hi 1973)★★★★, *Livin' For You* (Hi 1973)★★★★, *Al Green Explores Your Mind* (Hi 1974)★★★★, *Al Green Is Love* (Hi 1975)★★★, *Full Of Fire* (Hi 1976)★★★, *Have A Good Time* (Hi 1976)★★★, *The Belle Album* (Hi 1977)★★★★, *Truth 'N' Time* (Hi 1978)★★★★, *The Lord Will Make A Way* (Myrrh 1980)★★★, *Higher Plane* (Myrrh 1981)★★★, *Tokyo Live* (Hi 1981)★★★★, *Precious Lord* (Myrhh 1982)★★, *I'll Rise Again* (Myrrh 1983)★★★, *Trust In God* (Myrrh 1984)★★★, *Going Away* (A&M 1985)★★★, *White Christmas* (Hi 1986)★★, *Soul Survivor* (A&M 1987)★★★, *I Get Joy* (A&M 1989)★★★, *Don't Look Back* (RCA 1993)★★★, *In Good Hands* (MCA 1995)★★★.

●COMPILATIONS: *Greatest Hits* (Hi 1975)★★★★★, *The Cream Of Al Green* (Hi 1980)★★★★, *Spotlight On Al Green* (PRT 1981)★★★★, *Take Me To The River (Greatest Hits Volume 2)* (Hi 1987)★★★★, *Hi-Life - The Best Of Al Green* (K-Tel 1988)★★★, *Love Ritual: Rare & Previously Unreleased 1968-1976* (Hi 1989)★★★★, *You Say It!* (Hi 1990)★★★, *Christmas Cheers* nine tracks plus 12 by Ace Cannon (Hi 1991)★★, *One In A Million* (Word/Epic 1991)★★★★, *The Flipside Of Al Green* (1993)★★★.

●VIDEOS: *Gospel According To Al Green* (Rhapsody 1995).

GREEN, PETER

b. Peter Greenbaum, 29 October 1946, Bethnal Green, London, England. Having served an apprenticeship in various semi-professional groups, including the Muskrats and the Tridents, Peter Green became one of several guitarists who joined John Mayall's Bluesbreakers as a temporary substitute for Eric Clapton during the latter's late 1965 sabbatical. When Mayall's preferred choice returned to the fold, Green joined Peter Bardens (organ), Dave Ambrose (bass) and Mick Fleetwood (drums) in a short-lived club band, the Peter B's. The quartet completed one single for Columbia Records: 'If You Wanna Be Happy'/'Jodrell Blues' in February 1966. The b-side, an instrumental, showcased Green's already distinctive style. The entire unit subsequently formed the instrumental core to the Shotgun Express, backing singers Rod Stewart and Beryl Marsden, but the guitarist found this role too restrictive and left after a matter of weeks. Green rejoined Mayall in July 1966 when Clapton left to form Cream. Over the next 12 months Green made several telling contributions to the Bluesbreakers' recordings, most notably on

the group's third album, *A Hard Road*. This powerful release featured two of the guitarist's compositions, of which 'The Supernatural', a riveting instrumental, anticipated the style he would forge later in the decade. The seeds of Green's own group were sown during several sessions without Mayall and a Bluesbreakers 'solo' single, 'Curly', was released in March 1967. Two months later Green left to form his own group with drummer Mick Fleetwood. The two musicians added a second guitarist, Jeremy Spencer, to form Fleetwood Mac, whose line-up was eventually completed by another former Mayall sideman, John McVie. Fleetwood Mac became one of the most popular groups of the era, developing blues-based origins into an exciting, experimental unit. Green's personality, however, grew increasingly unstable and he became estranged from his colleagues. 'Pete should never have taken acid,' Fleetwood later recalled. 'He was charming, amusing, just a wonderful person (but) off he went and never came back.'

Green has followed an erratic course since leaving the group in May 1970. His solo debut, *The End Of The Game*, was a perplexing collection, consisting of six instrumentals, each of which were little more than jams. An atmospheric single, 'Heavy Heart', followed in June 1971, while a collaboration with one Nigel Watson, 'Beasts Of Burden', was issued the following year. Green also made sporadic session appearances but following a cameo role on Fleetwood Mac's *Penguin* album, the guitarist dropped out of music altogether. The mid-70s proved particularly harrowing; this tormented individual was committed to two mental institutions in the wake of his unsettled behaviour. Green returned to active recording in 1979 with *In The Skies*, a light but optimistic collection which showed traces of his erstwhile fire and included a version of 'A Fool No More', first recorded by Fleetwood Mac. A second album, *Little Dreamer*, offered a more blues-based perspective while two further releases attempted to consolidate the artist's position.

In 1982 Green, now calling himself Greenbaum, began touring with a group named Kolors, but the results were unsatisfactory. A hastily concocted album consisting of out-takes and unfinished demos was issued, the last to bear the guitarist's name as leader. A collaboration with former Mungo Jerry singer Ray Dorset aside, this once-skilful musician again abandoned music. Nicknamed the 'Wizard' by local children, Green lived a hermit-like existence, shunning any links with his past. Rumours frequently circulated about his return to the music business, but most were instigated by tabloid journalists pining for his reappearance. In 1995 Gary Moore recorded an album of Peter Green tracks, *Blues For Greeny*. In 1996 rumours were confirmed that Greeney was becoming active again. He had purchased a guitar, was keen to play some old blues material, showed up onstage at a Gary Moore gig and best of all played live in May 1996. In August he played with the Splinter

Group, Cozy Powell (drums), Nigel Watson (guitar) and Neil Murray (bass) at the Guildford Blues Festival. Although shakey on some numbers he excelled on two familiar Freddie King songs, 'The Stumble' and 'Going Down'. His new manager Stuart Taylor stated about Peter's future, back in music; 'I am cautiously optimistic'. An album from the Splinter group was released in June 1997, and although flawed it demonstrates Green's commitment to regaining the crown he never sought in the first place: the UK's finest ever white blues guitarist.

●ALBUMS: *The End Of The Game* (Reprise 1970)★★, *In The Skies* (PVK 1979)★★★, *Little Dreamer* (PVK 1980)★★★, *Whatcha Gonna Do* (PVK 1981)★★, *Blue Guitar* (Creole 1981)★★, *White Sky* (Headline 1982)★★, *Kolors* (Headline 1983)★★, *Legend* (Creole 1988)★★, tribute album *Rattlesnake Guitar: The Music Of Peter Green* (Coast To Coast 1995)★★★, *The Peter Green Splinter Group* (Snapper 1997)★★.

●FURTHER READING: *Peter Green: The Biography*, Martin Celmins.

GREENBAUM, NORMAN

b. 20 November 1942, Malden, Massachusetts, USA. Greenbaum first tasted minor US chart fame as the founder of Los Angeles jug band Dr. West's Medicine Show And Junk Band, who achieved a minor hit with the novelty 'The Eggplant That Ate Chicago'. After the break-up of the group in 1967, Greenbaum effectively retired from the music business to run a dairy farm (he later recorded 'Milk Cow Blues'). In 1970, however, one of his recordings, 'Spirit In The Sky', unexpectedly scaled the US charts, finally reaching number 3 and later hitting the top in the UK. It was a startling single of its era, highlighted by a memorable fuzz guitar riff and some spirited backing vocals and handclaps. Although Greenbaum was teased out of retirement to record a couple of albums, he remained the quintessential one-hit-wonder chart-topper. In 1986, 16 years after his finest moment, the British group Doctor And The Medics revived 'Spirit In The Sky', which hit number 1 in the UK for the second occasion.

●ALBUMS: *Spirit In The Sky* (Reprise 1970)★★, *Back Home* (1971)★.

GREENSLADE

Formed in 1972 by ex-Colosseum members Dave Greenslade (b. 18 January 1943, Woking, Surrey, England; keyboards) and Tony Reeves (b. 18 April 1943, London, England). The line-up was completed by ex-Episode Six and Alan Bown Set member Dave Lawson (keyboards/vocals) and Andrew McCulloch (drums). Their four well-received albums all proved to be moderately successful - the strong emphasis on keyboard sounds with a hint of classical roots was perfect for the progressive rock market of the early 70s. Their distinctive album covers were illustrated and calligraphed by Roger Dean. Dave Clempson, another ex-Colosseum

member, joined them for *Spyglass Guest* and alongside new recruit, violinist Graham Smith, the organ-dominated sound became less prominent. Reeves departed and returned for the second time to his main interest as record producer, where he became a highly respected figure. Six months after their last album Greenslade dismantled the band as managerial and legal problems continued. He embroiled himself in television music scores, where he has found great success. His solo *Cactus Choir* in 1976 sold only moderately. Greenslade re-formed briefly in 1977 with yet another ex-Colosseum member, Jon Hiseman, who together with Tony Reeves and Mick Rodgers, lasted only one tour. Their intricate and occasionally brilliant music was out of step with the burgeoning punk scene.

●ALBUMS: *Greenslade* (Warners 1973)★★★, *Bedside Manners Are Extra* (Warners 1973)★★★, *Spyglass Guest* (Warners 1974)★★★, *Time And Tide* (Warners 1975)★★★.

GREENSLADE, DAVE

b. 18 January 1943, Woking, Surrey, England. Former member of Colosseum and founder of the progressive jazz/rock group, Greenslade. In 1979 he collaborated with fantasy artist/writer Patrick Woodroffe in an lavish and expensive concept double album, *The Pentateuch Of The Cosmogony*. Released at the 'wrong' end of the 70s, it was doomed to failure, yet in recent times it has achieved a notoriety as an valued artefact amongst collectors. Throughout the 80s and into the 90s, he has carved out a successful career composing theme music for British film and television.

●ALBUMS: *Cactus Choir* (Warners 1976)★★, *The Pentateuch Of The Cosmogony* (EMI 1979)★★, *Terry Pratchett's From The Discworld* (Virgin 1994)★★★.

GREYHOUND

Greyhound evolved from the Rudies, subsequently known as Freddie Notes And The Rudies. The band was formed by Danny Smith and Freddie Notes in the second half of the 60s. Working with Dandy Livingstone, then known as Dandy they had a hit in 1969 with, 'Night Train'. They enjoyed hits in the reggae charts including 'Down On The Farm' and a version of Clarence Carter's, 'Patches'. Their version of the Bobby Bloom hit, 'Montego Bay' was almost a crossover hit. While collectively known as the Rudies they released *Unity* and *Montego Bay*, both of which were titled after their hit singles. In the early 70s Freddie left the band and was replaced by Glenroy Oakley. It was at this time that the transformation took place. Trojan Records had several unsuccessful attempts at recording a live album but the release of *Trojan Reggae Party Volume One* resolved this with musical backing provided by Greyhound. The group accompanied a host of top reggae artists at the show as well as performing, 'You Made Me So Very Happy' and 'Move On Up'. By June 1971 the new line-up had a Top 10 hit with 'Black And

White' a song that has since been covered by Gregory Isaacs, the Maytones and King Sounds (who also covered 'Patches'). A tour to promote the album named after their first hit proved to be a success. In January 1972 the group covered Danny Williams' number 1 hit, 'Moon River' and entered the UK Top 20. Their sound had by now been diluted and the addition of strings did nothing to enhance the recordings. The final hit, 'I Am What I Am',, a plea for recognition in a white-dominated society peaked at number 20 in March of that same year. A combination of the Pioneers and Greyhound, known as the Uniques, released a cover version of Paul Simon's, 'Mother And Child Reunion' followed by 'Lonely For Your Love'. The singles did not reap the rewards they deserved and resulted in confusion with the group which featured Slim Smith, Lloyd Charmers and Jimmy Riley. The release of 'Floating' did not match the success of the earlier recordings in either the reggae or national chart although the later output had more of a reggae feel. Disillusioned with the lack of promotion, a change of labels ensued and despite national airplay the follow-up releases, 'Wily', 'Only Love Can Win' and 'Dream Lover', failed to attain chart status. Shortly after the release of *Mango Rock* the group disbanded and Sonny Binns joined the Cimarons while the others emerged as Dansak who toured the UK in 1974 with Jimmy Cliff and Dave Barker.

●ALBUMS: as Freddie Notes And The Rudies *Unity* (Trojan 1969)★★, as Freddie Notes And The Rudies *Montego Bay* (Trojan 1970)★★★, *Black And White* (Trojan 1971)★★★, *Mango Rock* (Trans Atlantic 1975)★★.

●COMPILATIONS: *Black And White* (Tring 1990)★★.

GROUNDHOGS

The original Groundhogs emerged in 1963 when struggling UK beat group the Dollarbills opted for a more stylish name; Tony 'T.S.' McPhee (b. 22 March 1944, Humberstone, Lincolnshire, England; guitar), John Cruickshank (vocals/harp), Bob Hall (piano), Pete Cruickshank (b. 2 July 1945, Calcutta, India; bass) and Dave Boorman (drums) also adopted a 'John Lee' prefix in honour of mentor John Lee Hooker, whom the quintet subsequently backed in concert and on record. John Lee's Groundhogs recorded two singles before breaking up in 1966. McPhee completed several solo tracks with producer Mike Vernon before rejoining Pete Cruickshank in Herbal Mixture, a short-lived pseudo-psychedelic group. In 1968 the two musicians formed the core of a re-formed Groundhogs alongside Steve Rye (vocals/harmonica) and Ken Pustelnik (drums). The new unit made its debut with the rudimentary *Scratching The Surface*, but were then reduced to a trio by Rye's departure. A second set, *Blues Obituary*, contained two tracks, 'Mistreated' and 'Express Man', which became in-concert favourites as the group embarked on a more progressive direction. This was confirmed with *Thank Christ For The Bomb*, the Groundhogs' powerful 1970 release which cemented a growing popularity.

McPhee composed the entire set and his enthusiasm for concept albums was maintained with its successor, *Split*, which examined schizophrenia. Arguably the group's definitive work, this uncompromising selection included the stage classic, 'Cherry Red'. Pustelnik left the group following the release of *Who Will Save The World?* in 1972. Former Egg drummer Clive Brooks (b. 28 December 1949, London, England) was an able replacement, but although the Groundhogs continued to enjoy fervent popularity, their subsequent recordings lacked the fire of those early releases. The trio was also beset by managerial problems and broke up in 1975, although McPhee maintained the name for two disappointing releases, *Crosscut Saw* and *Black Diamond*. The guitarist resurrected the Groundhogs' sobriquet in 1984 in the wake of interest in an archive release, *Hoggin' The Stage*. Although Pustelnik was one of several musicians McPhee used for touring purposes, the most effective line-up was completed by Dave Anderson on bass, formerly of Hawkwind, and drummer Mike Jones. McPhee has in recent years appeared as a solo performer as part of a 70s nostalgia tour together with various incarnations of his respected band. A fitting testament as the Groundhogs' story endures mainly through a live reputation second to none.

●ALBUMS: *Scratching The Surface* (Liberty 1968)★★, *Blues Obituary* (Liberty 1969)★★★, *Thank Christ For The Bomb* (Liberty 1970)★★★, *Split* (Liberty 1971)★★★★, *Who Will Save The World?* (United Artists 1972)★★★, *Hogwash* (United Artists 1972)★★★, *Solid* (WWA 1974)★★, *Crosscut Saw* (United Artists 1976)★★, *Black Diamond* (United Artists 1976)★★, *Razor's Edge* (Conquest 1985)★★, *Back Against The Wall* (Demi-Monde 1987)★★, *Hogs On The Road* (Demi-Monde 1988)★★, as Tony McPhee's Groundhogs *Who Said Cherry Red?* (Indigo 1996)★★.

●COMPILATIONS: *Groundhogs Best 1969-1972* (United Artists 1974)★★★, *Hoggin' The Stage* double album (Psycho 1984)★★★, *Moving Fast, Standing Still*, comprises McPhee solo album *2 Sides Of* plus *Razor's Edge* (Raw Power 1986)★★, *No Surrender* (Total 1990)★★, *Classic Album Cuts 1968 - 1976* (1992)★★★, *The Best Of ...* (EMI Gold 1997)★★★.

GROSVENOR, LUTHER

b. 23 December 1949, Evesham, Worcestershire, England. Grosvenor's flowing and biting lead guitar lines were widely heard when he was a member of heavy progressive rockers Spooky Tooth in the late 60s. Tracks such as 'Better By You, Better Than Me' benefitted greatly from his memorable riffs. When Spooky Tooth disintegrated, Grosvenor released the obligatory solo album. He became much in demand as a session player and briefly joined Stealer's Wheel; consequently, his credible debut *Under Open Skies* was overlooked. In mid-1973 he joined Mott the Hoople, by which time he had aquired the bizarre moniker 'Ariel Bender'. After less than two years with Mott he left to form the heavier-sounding Widowmaker with Steve Ellis (ex-Love Affair). He drifted out of the music business over the past decade but following a session on the Peter Green tribute album *Rattlesnake Guitar* in 1996, Grosvenor obviously became enthused about playing again and recorded a new album in 1996.

●ALBUMS: *Under Open Skies* (Island 1971)★★★, *Floodgates* (Brilliant Recording Co 1996)★★.

GRYPHON

Originally called Spellthorn, Gryphon were formed in 1971 by Royal College of Music students Richard Harvey (b. 25 September 1953, Enfield, Middlesex, England; keyboards, woodwinds, mandolin) and Brian Gulland (b. 30 April 1951, Maidstone, Kent, England; renaissance wind instruments, bassoon, keyboards, vocals). Harvey had eschewed an offer to join the London Philharmonia Orchestra in order to pursue his vision of a blend of medieval music and progressive rock. The group had also comprised Graeme Taylor (b. 2 February 1954, Stockwell, London, England; guitar, keyboards, recorder) and David Oberlé (b. 9 January 1953, Farnborough, Kent, England; drums, percussion, flageolet, vocals). Gryphon started their career playing folk clubs, moving on to the usual rock venues and colleges, in addition to performing at special events such as the Victoria & Albert Museum. Their style made the group unique on the UK rock scene in the early 70s, with Gulland's Crumhorn solos making a refreshing change from the usual guitar sound of the day. By 1973 they were performing a mixture of minstrel airs and Beatles songs, and even a version of 'Chattanooga Choo Choo'. With the addition of a bassist, Philip Nestor (b. 1952, Epsom, Surrey, England), Gryphon were, by the time of *Midnight Mushrumps*, performing a lengthy composition, commissioned by Peter Hall of the London National Theatre, and moving into a more traditional rock style. By 1975 the group had joined Yes on a tour of the USA and Gryphon's line-up began to suffer various personnel changes. Taylor had left the group that year (later to join Home Service) and was replaced by Bob Foster; Alex Baird (ex-Contraband) was added as a drummer; and Malcolm Bennett, who had replaced Nestor was, in turn, supplanted by Jonathan Davie. Very soon the group had begun to lose its sense of originality and subsequently broke up in the face of the emerging punk rock explosion. Harvey moved into the field of commercial jingles and television and film soundtracks, including the collaboration with Elvis Costello for Alan Bleasdale's *G.B.H.* television play.

●ALBUMS: *Gryphon* (1973)★★★, *Midnight Mushrumps* (1974)★★★, *Red Queen To Gryphon Three* (Arista 1974)★★★, *Raindance* (1975)★★, *Treason* (Harvest 1977)★★. Solo: Richard Harvey *Divisions On A Ground* (1975)★★, with Stanley Myers *L'Amant De Lady Chatterley* (1981)★★, with Elvis Costello *G.B.H.* (1991)★★.

●COMPILATIONS: *The Collection* (Curio 1991)★★★.

GUESS WHO

The Guess Who was Canada's most popular rock band of the 60s and early 70s. The group had its roots in a band called Chad Allan And The Reflections, formed in Winnipeg, Canada, in 1962. That group itself came out of two others, Allan And The Silvertones and the Velvetones. The original line-up of Chad Allan And The Reflections consisted of Allan (b. Allan Kobel; guitar/vocals), Jim Kale (bass), Randy Bachman (guitar), Bob Ashley (piano) and Garry Peterson (drums). Their first single, 'Tribute To Buddy Holly', was released on the Canadian American label in Canada in 1962. Singles for the Quality and Reo labels followed. By 1965 the group had changed its name to Chad Allan and the Expressions and recorded a cover of Johnny Kidd And The Pirates' 'Shakin' All Over', released on Quality Records in Canada and picked up by Scepter Records in the USA. It became a number 1 single in Canada and number 22 in the USA. Ashley left the group and was replaced by Burton Cummings, formerly of the Canadian group the Deverons, who shared lead vocal duties with Allan for a year. In 1966 the group released its first album, *Shakin' All Over*. In order to give the impression to potential buyers that the group was English, Quality printed 'Guess Who?' on the cover, prompting the group to take those words as its new name. In 1966 Allan departed from the group. He was briefly replaced by Bruce Decker, another ex-Deveron, who quickly left, leaving the group as a quartet with Cummings as chief vocalist.

Although they faded from the US charts for three years, the Guess Who remained popular in Canada. In 1967 they had their first UK chart single with 'His Girl', on the King label. A brief, disorganized UK tour left the group in debt, and it returned to Canada, recording Coca-Cola commercials and appearing on the television programme *Let's Go*, which boosted their Canadian popularity even further. They continued to release singles in Canada on Quality, and on Amy and Fontana Records in the USA. In 1968, with financial backing from producer Jack Richardson, the Guess Who recorded *Wheatfield Soul* in New York, released in Canada on Richardson's own Nimbus 9 label. The third single from the album, 'These Eyes', written by Cummings and Bachman, reached number 1 in Canada and earned the group a US contract with RCA Records. The single reached number 6 in the USA in spring of 1969. That year, the group's second album, *Canned Wheat Packed By The Guess Who*, also charted, as did 'Laughing', the b-side of 'These Eyes', itself a Top 10 hit, and 'Undun', which reached number 22 in the US. The group's busy year was wrapped up with a number 5 single, 'No Time'.

In March 1970, the hard-rocking 'American Woman' became the Guess Who's only US number 1 The b-side 'No Sugar Tonight' also received considerable radio airplay. *American Woman* became the group's only Top 10 album in the US during this time. In July 1970 Bachman left the group, finding the group's rock lifestyle incompatible with his Mormon religion. He resurfaced first with Chad Allan in a new group called Brave Belt and finally with Bachman Turner Overdrive (minus Allan), which itself - ironically - became a popular hard rock group in the 70s. A Guess Who album recorded while Bachman was still in the group was cancelled. Bachman was replaced in the Guess Who by guitarists Kurt Winter and Greg Leskiw. Another US Top 10 single, 'Share The Land', finished up 1970 for the group. They continued to release charting singles and albums in the early 70s, including 'Albert Flasher' and 'Rain Dance' in 1971, and their *Greatest Hits* reached number 12. In 1972 Leskiw and Kale left the group, replaced by Don McDougall and Bill Wallace, respectively. In 1974 Winter and McDougall left, replaced by Domenic Troiano, former guitarist of the James Gang. That year, the single 'Clap For The Wolfman', written for US disc jockey Wolfman Jack, reached number 6 in the USA. It proved to be the group's final hit. In 1975 Cummings disbanded the Guess Who and began a solo career.

In 1979 a new Guess Who group, featuring Allan, Kale, McDougall and three new members, recorded and toured but were not successful. Similar regroupings (minus Cummings) also failed. A 1983 Guess Who reunion aroused some interest and resulted in an album and concert video, and Bachman and Cummings toured together in 1987, failing to win large audiences.

●ALBUMS: *Shakin' All Over* (1965)★★, *It's Time* (1966)★★, *A Wild Pair* (King 1967)★★, *Wheatfield Soul* (RCA 1969)★★★, *Canned Wheat Packed By The Guess Who* (RCA 1969)★★★, *American Woman* (RCA 1970)★★, *Share The Land* (RCA 1970)★★★, *So Long, Bannatyne* (RCA 1971)★★★, *Rockin'* (RCA 1972)★★, *Live At The Paramount (Seattle)* (RCA 1972)★, *Artificial Paradise* (RCA 1973)★★, *#10* (RCA 1973)★★, *Road Food* (RCA 1974)★★, *Flavours* (RCA 1975)★, *Power In The Music* (RCA 1975)★★, *Lonely One* (Intersound 1995)★★.

●COMPILATIONS: *The Best Of The Guess Who* (RCA 1971)★★★, *The Best Of The Guess Who, Volume II* (RCA 1974)★★, *The Greatest Of The Guess Who* (RCA 1977)★★★.

GUTHRIE, ARLO

b. 10 July 1947, Coney Island, New York, USA. The eldest son of folksinger Woody Guthrie, Arlo was raised in the genre's thriving environment. His lengthy ballad, 'Alice's Restaurant Massacre', was the outcome of being arrested for being a litter lout in 1965. It was a part humorous song, part narrative, and achieved popularity following the artist's appearance at the 1967 Newport Folk Festival. The composition became the cornerstone of Arlo's debut album, and inspired a feature film, but the attendant publicity obscured the performer's gifts for melody. An early song, 'Highway In The Wind', was successfully covered by Hearts And Flowers as Arlo emerged from under the shadow of his father. *Running*

Down The Road, produced by Van Dyke Parks, indicated a newfound maturity, but his talent truly flourished on a series of excellent 70s recordings, notably *Hobo's Lullaby*, *Last Of The Brooklyn Cowboys*, and *Amigo*. Although offering a distillation of traditional music - wedding folk and country to ragtime, blues and Latin - such recordings nonetheless addressed contemporary concerns. 'Presidential Rag' was a vitriolic commentary on Watergate and 'Children Of Abraham' addressed the Arab/Israeli conflict. The singer enjoyed a US Top 20 hit with a reading of Steve Goodman's 'City Of New Orleans' (1972) and, if now less prolific, Arlo Guthrie remains a popular figure on the folk circuit as well as an imposing sight with his full mane of grey hair. He returned to the site of his most famous song in 1995 with a reworked (even longer!) reprise, 'The Massacre Revisited'.

●ALBUMS: *Alice's Restaurant* (Reprise 1967)★★★★, *Arlo* (Reprise 1968)★★, *Running Down The Road* (Reprise 1969)★★★, *Alice's Restaurant* film soundtrack (Reprise 1969)★★, *Washington County* (Reprise 1970)★★★, *Hobo's Lullaby* (Reprise 1972)★★★, *Last Of The Brooklyn Cowboys* (Reprise 1973)★★★, *Arlo Guthrie* (Reprise 1974)★★★, with Pete Seeger *Together In Concert* (Reprise 1975)★★, *Amigo* (Reprise 1976)★★★★, *One Night* (Warners 1978)★★, *Outlasting The Blues* (Warners 1979)★★★★, *Power Of Love* (Warners 1981)★★★, with Pete Seeger *Precious Friend* (Warners 1982)★★★, *Someday* (Rising Son 1986)★★★, *All Over The World* (Rising Son 1991)★★★, *Son Of The Wind* (Rising Son 1992)★★★, *Mystic Journey* (Rising Son 1996)★★★.

●COMPILATIONS: *The Best Of Arlo Guthrie* (Warners 1977)★★★.

●FILMS: *Alice's Restaurant* (1969).

HACKETT, STEVE

b. 12 February 1950, London, England. Formerly a member of various minor groups, Canterbury Glass, Heel Pier, Sarabande and Quiet World, Hackett joined Genesis as guitarist in 1971. He replaced Anthony Phillips, and stayed with the group during their successful mid-70s progressive rock period, recording with the group from *Nursery Cryme* (1971) to the live double album, *Seconds Out* (1977). By the time the latter was released, Hackett had recently left the group. Having previously released his first solo effort, *Voyage Of The Acolyte* two years earlier, Hackett had decided to pursue a full time solo career. He achieved modest success with a string of albums, including the UK Top 10 *Defector*, but his following remained largely static and of interest only to die-hard Genesis fans. He joined former Yes guitarist Steve Howe and Max Bacon (vocals) in GTR in 1986, issuing a self-titled album which reached the US Top 20, and an accompanying single, 'When The Heart Rules The Mind' reached number 14. In the UK the album barely made the Top 40, indicating that Hackett's reputation as 'former Genesis guitarist' overshadowed all his work.
●ALBUMS: *Voyage Of The Acolyte* (Charisma 1975)★★★, *Please Don't Touch* (Charisma 1978)★★★, *Spectral Mornings* (Charisma 1979)★★★, *Defector* (Charisma 1980)★★★, *Cured* (Charisma 1981)★★★, *Highly Strung* (Charisma 1983)★★★, *Bay Of Kings* (Lamborghinin 1983)★★★, *Till We Have Faces* (Lamborghini 1984)★★, *Momentum* (Start 1988)★★, *Guitar Noir* (1993)★★, *Blues With A Feeling* (Permanent 1994)★★.
●COMPILATIONS: *The Unauthorised Biography* (1992)★★★.

HALL AND OATES

Like their 60s predecessors the Righteous Brothers (and their 90s successor Michael Bolton), Hall And Oates' string of hits was proof of the perennial appeal of white soul singing. The duo achieved their success through the combination of Hall's falsetto and Oates' warm baritone. A student at Temple University, Daryl Hall (b. Daryl Franklin Hohl, 11 October 1949, Pottstown, Pennsylvania, USA) sang lead with the Temptones and recorded a single produced by Kenny Gamble in 1966. Hall subsequently made solo records and formed soft-rock band Gulliver with Tim Moore, recording one album for Elektra. In 1969 he met Oates (b. 7 April 1949, New York, USA), a former member of

Philadelphia soul band the Masters. The two began to write songs together and were discovered by Tommy Mottola, then a local representative of Chappell Music. He became their manager and negotiated a recording deal with Atlantic. Their three albums for the label had star producers (Arif Mardin on *Whole Oates* and Todd Rundgren for *War Babies*) but sold few copies. However, *Abandoned Luncheonette* included the first version of one of Hall And Oates' classic soul ballads, 'She's Gone'. The duo came to national prominence with the million-selling 'Sara Smile', their first single for RCA. It was followed by the tough 'Rich Girl' which reached number 1 in the USA in 1977. However, they failed to capitalize on this success, dabbling unimpressively in the currently fashionable disco style on *X-Static*. The turning point came with the Hall and Oates-produced *Voices*. The album spawned four hit singles, notably a remake of the Righteous Brothers' 'You've Lost That Lovin' Feelin'. It also included the haunting 'Every Time You Go Away', a big hit for Paul Young in 1985. For the next five years the pair could do no wrong, as hit followed hit. Among their best efforts were 'Maneater', the pounding 'I Can't Go For That (No Can Do)', 'Out Of Touch' (co-produced by Arthur Baker) and 'Family Man' (a Mike Oldfield composition). On *Live At The Apollo* they were joined by Temptations members Eddie Kendricks and David Ruffin. This was the prelude to a three-year hiatus in the partnership, during which time Hall recorded his second solo album with production by Dave Stewart. Reunited in 1988, Hall And Oates had a big US hit with 'Everything Your Heart Desires' on Arista. On the 1990 hit 'So Close', producers Jon Bon Jovi and Danny Kortchmar added a strong rock flavour to their sound.
●ALBUMS: *Whole Oates* (Atlantic 1972)★★, *Abandoned Luncheonette* (Atlantic 1973)★★★, *War Babies* (Atlantic 1974)★★, *Hall & Oates* (RCA 1975)★★, *Bigger Than Both Of Us* (RCA 1976)★★, *Beauty On A Back Street* (RCA 1977)★★★, *Along The Red Ledge* (RCA 1978)★★★, *Livetime* (RCA 1978)★★, *X-Static* (RCA 1979)★★, *Voices* (RCA 1980)★★★, *Private Eyes* (RCA 1981)★★★★, *H₂O* (RCA 1982)★★★★, *Bim Bam Boom* (RCA 1984)★★★, *Live At The Apollo* (RCA 1985)★★★, *Ooh Yeah!* (Arista 1988)★★, *Change Of Season* (Arista 1990)★★, *Whole Oats* (1993)★★, *Really Smokin'* (1993)★★. Solo: Daryl Hall *Sacred Songs* (RCA 1980)★★, *Three Hearts In The Happy Ending Machine* (RCA 1986)★★, *Soul Alone* (Epic 1993)★★★.
●COMPILATIONS: *The Atlantic Collection* (Rhino 1996)★★★★.

HAMMER, JAN

b. 17 April 1948, Prague, Czechoslovakia, he trained as a jazz pianist before winning a scholarship to Berklee College in Boston, Massachusetts, USA, in 1968. In 1970, he played with Elvin Jones and Sarah Vaughan. Hammer next joined the Mahavishnu Orchestra, as well as playing synthesizers on albums by Santana, Billy Cobham and others. After leader John McLaughlin temporarily disbanded the orchestra, Hammer and violinist Jerry Goodman made a 1974 album for Nemperor. This was followed by Hammer's own composition, *The First Seven Days*, a concept album based on the creation of the earth. During the late 70s, he was one of a loose aggregation of New York-based musicians creating various types of jazz-rock fusion.

Among his more important collaborations were those with Jeff Beck on *Wired* and *There And Back*. Hammer also toured with Beck. He later made a record with Journey guitarist Neil Schon and another with jazz guitarist John Abercrombie before finding a wider audience through his work in television music. Hammer was responsible for the theme to *Miami Vice*, one of the most successful police series of the 80s. Released as a single, it went to number 1 in the USA (UK number 5) in 1985. He followed it in 1987 with 'Crocketts Theme', which made number 2 in the UK yet failed completely in the USA. This new role dominated his later work - Hammer wrote the music for *Eurocops* - and in 1991 he even composed special background music for a best-selling computer game. Hammer's biggest hit was sadly tarnished during 1991 and 1992 when it was oddly used as the theme music for a major television advertising campaign for a UK bank.

●ALBUMS: *Like Children* (Nemperor 1974)★★★, *First Seven Days* (1975)★★★, *Oh Yeah* (1976)★★★, *Live With Jeff Beck* (Epic 1977), *Timeless* (1978)★★★, *Melodies* (1979)★★, *Black Sheep* (1979)★★, *Neil Schon And Jan Hammer* (1981)★★, *Untold Passion* (Columbia 1982)★★, *Night* (1984)★★, *Escape From TV* (MCA 1987)★★★, *Snapshots* (MCA 1989)★★★, *Country & Eastern Music* (1993)★★, *Behind The Mind's Eye* (1993)★★.
●COMPILATIONS: *The Early Years* (Coulmbia 1988)★★★.
●VIDEOS: *Beyond The Mind's Eye* (1982).

HAMMILL, PETER

In 1967 Peter Hammill (b. 5 November 1948, Ealing, London, England; vocals/piano/guitar) formed Van Der Graaf Generator in Manchester, England, with university friends Hugh Banton (keyboards/bass) and Guy Evans (drums). The band collapsed without making any recordings, but in 1968 it was re-formed with David Jackson on saxophone. Hammill had intended to release a solo album, but the new Van Der Graaf Generator seized on his material, the result being the celebrated *Aerosol Grey Machine*. The band always enjoyed greater success in Europe than in the UK, and broke up for the second and final time in 1972. Its dissolution gave Hammill the opportunity to continue with the limited success he had already found in his solo career, which he now pursued again. He has maintained a prolific output ever since, counting contemporary artists such as Peter Gabriel, Nick Cave, Marc Almond, David Bowie, Mark E. Smith (Fall) and John Lydon (Sex Pistols/Public Image Limited) among his many admirers. It is the quality rather than the quantity of his work that ensures that more mainstream artists return to him for inspiration again and again. The various stages of his work have been analogized as progressive rock (Van Der Graaf Generator), lo-fi pre-punk (his 70s albums, particularly *Nadir's Big Chance*) and the search for the perfect exposition of the love song (much of his subsequent output). Despite writing pieces for ballets and undertaking an opera version of Edgar Allan Poe's 'The Fall Of The House Of Usher', he has never fully escaped the legacy of Van Der Graaf Generator. He had described this hindrance as a 'monkey on my back', which militates against his subsequent artistic divergence. He has achieved a commendable level of autonomy in his work - he owns his own studio and record label, and is quietly proud of what he calls his 'bloody-mindedness . . . my reputation for quitting, doing something entirely different the moment success began to beckon.' Perhaps the best introductions to this vividly expressive and wildly eclectic artist are *Soft* and *Hard*, released in the mid-90s, which feature his own self-deprecating commentaries on the origins of each song.

●ALBUMS: *Fool's Mate* (Charisma 1971)★★★, *Chameleon In The Shadow Of Night* (Charisma 1973)★★★, *The Silent Corner And The Empty Stage* (Charisma 1974)★★★, *In Camera* (Charisma 1974)★★, *Nadir's Big Chance* (Charisma 1975)★★★, *Over* (Charisma 1977)★★★, *The Future Now* (Charisma 1978)★★★, *ph7* (Charisma 1979)★★★, *A Black Box* (S Type 1980)★★★, *Sitting Targets* (Virgin 1981)★★★, *Enter K* (Naive 1982)★★★, *Patience* (Naive 1983)★★★, *Loops And Reels* (Sofa 1983)★★★, *The Love Songs* (Charisma 1984)★★★, *The Margin - Live* (Foundry 1985)★★★, *Skin* (Foundry 1986)★★★, *And Close As This* (Virgin 1986)★★★★, *In A Foreign Town* (Enigma 1988)★★★, *Out Of Water* (Enigma 1990)★★★, *Room Temperature Live* (1990)★★★, *No Way Out* (1990)★★★, *The Fall Of The House Of Usher* (World Chief 1991)★, *Fireships* (Fie! 1992)★★, *The Noise* (1993)★★, with Guy Evans *Spur Of The Moment* (Red Hot 1993)★★★, *There Goes The Daylight* (1994)★★★, *Peter Hammill And The K Group The Margin, Roaring Forties* (1994)★★★, *The Peel Sessions* (Windsong 1995)★★★, *X My Heart* (Fie! 1996)★★★.
●COMPILATIONS: *The Calm After The Storm* (Virgin 1993)★★★, *After The Show* (1996)★★★.
●VIDEOS: *In The Passionskirche, Berlin MVMXCII* (Studio 1993).
●FURTHER READING: *The Lemming Chronicles*, David Shaw-Parker. *Killers, Angels, Refugees*, Peter Hammill. *Mirrors, Dreams And Miracles*, Peter Hammill.

HAMMOND, ALBERT

b. c.1943, England. Hammond spent most of his boyhood in Gibraltar where he began entertaining professionally at 13. With a brother, he formed the Diamond Boys but, on returning to England, he secured a job with Los Cuico Ricardos, a mariachi combo. In 1966, a meeting with Mike Hazelwood, a Radio Luxembourg presenter, led to a productive songwriting collaboration. After 1968's international success with 'Little Arrows' for Leapy Lee, they scored domestically with the Pipkins' 'Gimme Dat Ding' - commissioned (like 'Little Arrows') for *Oliver And The Overlord*, an award-winning children's television series. The pair also sang with Magic Lantern and Family Dogg - whose 'Way Of Life' reached the UK Top 10 in 1969 - prior to crossing to Los Angeles to better hawk their collective and separate wares before more prestigious customers. With compositions of less infantile stamp than 'Gimme Dat Ding', Hammond became, in 1971, the first artist contracted to the Mums label. Its supremo, Bobby Roberts' outlay was mitigated when the second Hammond single, 'It Never Rains In Southern California', sold a million in the USA alone and, after a two-year wait, 'Free Electric Band' also did well, even gaining a toehold on the UK Top 20. His last major hit was in the USA with 'I'm A Train'. Hammond lacked 'image', and so the success or failure of his records depended solely on their commercial suitability; his initial triumphs were not matched by anything issued since. Yet, with 'The Air That I Breathe' (with Hazelwood) for the Hollies, '99 Miles From LA' for Art Garfunkel, the Carpenters' 1976 hit, 'I Need To Be In Love' and 1977's 'When I Need You' (with Carole Bayer Sager) for Leo Sayer, he continued to register hits as a major songwriter.

●ALBUMS: *It Never Rains In Southern California* (Mum 1973)★★, *Free Electric Band* (Mum 1973)★★★, *Albert Hammond* (Mum 1974)★★.

HANCOCK, HERBIE

b. 12 April 1940, Chicago, Illinois, USA. Growing up in a musical household, Hancock studied piano from the age of seven and gave his first public performance just two years later. Although he played classical music at his debut Hancock's interest lay mostly in jazz. During high school and college he played in semi-professional bands and on occasion accompanied visiting jazzmen, including Donald Byrd. It was with Byrd that Hancock first played in New York, in 1961, recording with him and as leader of his own small group. Among the tunes on this later album was 'Watermelon Man', a Hancock original that appealed to more than the usual jazz audience. A version of the song, by Mongo Santamaría, reached the US Top 10. During the early and mid-60s Hancock led bands for club engagements and record dates but the move which really boosted his career and international recognition was joining the quintet led by Miles Davis, with whom he stayed for more than five years. Towards the end of the stint with Davis, the band began its move into jazz-rock. Hancock felt comfortable in this style and in 1968 formed a sextet to pursue his own concepts. With musicians such as Julian Priester, Buster Williams and Eddie Henderson, and playing much original material composed by Hancock, the band became one of the most popular and influential of the jazz-rock movement in the early 70s. From 1969

Hancock made extensive use of electronic piano and other electronic keyboard instruments, including synthesizers. In 1973 economic pressures compelled Hancock to cut the band to a quartet, which featured Bennie Maupin, who had also been in the bigger group. The new group's music was again fusion, but this time leaned more towards jazz-funk. Whether by good fortune or through astute observation of the music scene, Hancock's first album with the quartet, *Headhunters*, was widely accepted in the burgeoning disco scene and achieved substantial sales. Throughout the rest of the 70s Hancock's music was concentrated in this area with occasional returns to jazz for record dates. By the end of the decade, however, his popularity in the disco market was such that he cut down still further on straight jazz performances. Certain albums he made, with Chick Corea and with his own band, V.S.O.P (a re-creation of the Davis quintet except with Freddie Hubbard in place of Miles), suggested that he retained an interest, however peripheral, in jazz. His numerous disco successes included 'You Bet Your Love', a UK Top 20 hit in 1979, and in collaboration with the group Material he recorded *Future Shock*, one track from which 'Rockit', reached the UK Top 10 in 1983 and made the top spot in the USA. In 1986 Hancock played and acted in the film *'Round Midnight*; he also wrote the score, for which he won an Academy Award. Subsequently, he became more active in jazz, touring with Williams, Ron Carter, Michael Brecker and others. Although the career moves made by Hancock over the years have tended to alienate the hardcore jazz fans who applauded his earlier work with Davis, his popularity with the disco and related audiences has not been achieved at the expense of quality. All of his successes in this area have been executed to the highest musical and other professional standards; the pop video accompanying 'Rockit' was an award winner. In his use of synthesizers, voice-box and other state-of-the-art electronic devices, Hancock has displayed far-reaching inventiveness, setting standards for the pop industry. Where his jazz work is concerned, he has displayed an intelligent approach to his material. If the music is often cerebral, it is rarely without heart; indeed, the V.S.O.P. band's recreations have been notable for their integrity and a measure of passionate intensity that at times matches that of the original. *The New Standard* was an interesting concept album. On this Hancock gave interpretations of songs by rock singer-songwriters such as Peter Gabriel, the Eagles' Don Henley, John Lennon, Paul McCartney, Stevie Wonder, Prince and lo and behold, Nirvana's Kurt Cobain.

●ALBUMS: *Takin' Off* (Blue Note 1962)★★★★, *My Point Of View* (Blue Note 1963)★★★★, *Inventions And Dimensions* (Blue Note 1963)★★★, *Empyrean Isles* (Blue Note 1964)★★★★, *Maiden Voyage* (Blue Note 1965)★★★★, *Blow Up* (MGM 1967)★★★, *Speak Like A Child* (Blue Note 1968)★★★, *The Prisoner* (Blue Note 1969)★★★, *Mwandishi* (Warners 1971)★★★★, *Crossings* (Warners 1972)★★★★, *Sextant* (Columbia 1973)★★★★,

Headhunters (Columbia 1974)★★★★★, *Thrust* (Columbia 1974)★★★, *Man-Child* (Columbia 1975)★★★★, *V.S.O.P.* (Columbia 1976)★★★★, *V.S.O.P.: The Quintet* (Columbia 1977)★★★★, *An Evening With Herbie Hancock And Chick Corea* (Columbia 1978)★★★, *Feets Don't Fail Me Now* (Columbia 1979)★★, *Mr Hands* (Columbia 1980)★★★, *Hancock Alley* (Manhattan 1980)★★★, *Quartet* (Columbia 1982)★★★, *Future Shock* (Columbia 1983)★★★★, *Hot And Heavy* (Premier 1984),★★ *Herbie Hancock And The Rockit Band* (Columbia 1984)★★★, with Dexter Gordon *'Round Midnight* film soundtrack (Columbia 1986)★★★, with Wayne Shorter, Ron Carter, Wallace Roney, Tony Williams *A Tribute To Miles* (QWest/Reprise 1994)★★★, *Dis Is Da Drum* (Mercury 1995)★★★, *The New Standard* (Verve 1996)★★★.
●COMPILATIONS: *Greatest Hits* (Columbia 1980)★★★, *A Jazz Collection* (Sony 1991)★★★, *Best Of Vol. 2* (1992)★★★, *Mwandishi: The Complete Warner Bros. Recordings* (Warners 1994)★★★.
●VIDEOS: *Herbie Hancock And The Rockit Band* (Columbia 1984).

HARDIN AND YORK
Drummer Pete York (b. 15 August 1942, Middlesborough, Cleveland, England) and singing keyboard *wunderkind* Eddie Hardin (b. 1949, England) left the Spencer Davis Group in October 1968 to team up as 'the smallest big band in the world' - as a duo they certainly achieved an impressive depth of sound coupled with strong melodic emphasis on their three albums, which also reflected jazz leanings and proficient creative parameters. At their 1969 apogee, the pair could fill moderate-sized auditoriums in Europe especially Germany, but most regarded them as a reliable support to bigger acts. After participating with Hardin in a fleeting reformation of the Davis group in 1973, York played at various continental jazz and blues festivals. In the late 80s, one of his most inspired ventures was leading bands of well-known British musicians in annual 'Blues Reunion' tours. Those old pals assisting him included Zoot Money, Chris Farlowe and Spencer Davis. Highlights of Hardin's journey through the 80s were his and drummer Zak Starkey's *Musical Version Of Wind In The Willows* - with Donovan and the Who's John Entwistle among guest players - and solo albums (and attendant concerts) of new age persuasion.
●ALBUMS: *Tomorrow Today* (Bell 1969)★★, *The Smallest Big Band In The World* (Bell 1970)★★★, *For The World* (Bell 1971)★★.

HARLEY, STEVE
(see Cockney Rebel)

HARPER, ROY
b. 12 June 1941, Rusholme, Manchester, England. Although introduced to music through his brother's skiffle group, Harper's adolescence was marked by a harrowing spell in the Royal Air Force. Having secured a discharge by feigning insanity, he drifted between mental institutions and jail, experiences which left an indelible mark on later compositions. Harper later began busking around Europe, and secured a residency at London's famed Les Cousins club on returning to Britain. His debut album, *The Sophisticated Beggar* (1966), was recorded in primitive conditions, but contained the rudiments of the artist's later, highly personal, style. *Come Out Fighting Genghis Smith* was released as the singer began attracting the emergent underground audience, but he was unhappy with producer Shel Talmy's rather fey arrangements. He was also subsequently unhappy with the cover shot, preferring the reinstated image used on the reissued album of a baby being born, complete with umbilical chord (sic). *Folkjokeopus* contained the first of Harper's extended compositions, 'McGoohan's Blues', but the set as a whole was considered patchy. *Flat, Baroque And Berserk* (1970) introduced the singer's long association with the Harvest label. Although he later castigated the outlet, they allowed him considerable artistic licence on this excellent album, considered by Harper as his first 'real work', offered contrasting material, including the uncompromising 'I Hate The White Man' and 'Tom Tiddler's Ground', as well as the jocular 'Hell's Angels', which featured support from the Nice. The latter was one of the first songs to feature a wah wah linked to an acoustic guitar. *Stormcock*, arguably the performer's finest work, consists of four lengthy, memorable songs which feature sterling contributions from arranger David Bedford and guitarist Jimmy Page. The latter remained a close associate, acknowledged on 'Hats Off To Harper' from *Led Zeppelin III*, and he appeared on several succeeding releases, including *Lifemask* and *Valentine*. Although marred by self-indulgence, the former was another remarkable set, while the latter reaffirmed Harper's talent for shorter compositions. An in-concert album, *Flashes From The Archives Of Oblivion* completed what was arguably the artist's most rewarding period. *HQ* (1975) introduced Trigger, Harper's short-lived backing group consisting of Chris Spedding (guitar), Dave Cochran (bass) and Bill Bruford (drums). The album included 'When An Old Cricketer Leaves The Crease', in which a colliery brass band emphasized the melancholia apparent in the song's cricketing metaphor. A second set, *Commercial Break*, was left unreleased on the group's demise. The singer's next release, *Bullinamingvase*, centred on the ambitious 'One Of Those Days In England', but it is also recalled for the controversy surrounding the flippant 'Watford Gap' and its less-than-complimentary remarks about food offered at the subject's local service station. The song was later removed. It was also during this period that Harper made a memorable cameo appearance on Pink Floyd's *Wish You Were Here*, taking lead vocals on 'Have A Cigar'. Harper's subsequent work, while notable, has lacked the passion of this period and *The*

Unknown Soldier, a bleak and rather depressing set, was the prelude to a series of less compulsive recordings, although his 1990 album, *Once*, was critically acclaimed as a return to form. Roy Harper remains a challenging, eccentric talent who has steadfastly refused to compromise his art. Commercial success has thus eluded him, but he retains the respect of many peers and a committed following. *Death Or Glory* was an emotional record that bemoaned the ending of his long relationship with his lover. In the mid-90s he was often to be found performing with his son Nick (Nick Harper), a similarly talented individual with an uncanny musical resemblance to his father. The elder Harper should, however, be both flattered and proud.

Most of Harper's back catalogue has been sensitively reissued on the small Science Friction label. Clearly, this record company cares passionately about Harper. The ambitious release of a series of albums chronicling his performances live at the BBC reaffirms what a talent he is. Songs such as 'Forever', 'I Hate The White Man', 'Another Day', 'Too Many Movies', 'Home' and the glorious 'Highway Blues' have all stood the test of time. He is cantankerous and opinionated but through all this he is a highly intelligent poet and a hopeless romantic. Mostly, his work is hugely underrated.

●ALBUMS: *The Sophisticated Beggar* (Strike 1966)★★, *Come Out Fighting Genghis Smith* (Columbia 1967)★★★, *Folkjokeopus* (Liberty 1969)★★, *Flat, Baroque And Berserk* (Harvest 1970)★★★, *Stormcock* (Harvest 1971)★★★★, *Lifemask* (Harvest 1973)★★★★, *Valentine* (Harvest 1974)★★★, *Flashes From The Archives Of Oblivion* (Harvest 1974)★★★, *HQ* retitled *When An Old Cricketer Leaves The Crease* (Harvest 1975)★★★, *Bullinamingvase* (Harvest 1977)★★★★, *The Unknown Soldier* (Harvest 1980)★★, *Work Of Heart* (Public 1981)★★★, with Jimmy Page *Whatever Happened To Jugula* (Beggars Banquet 1985)★★, *Born In Captivity* (Hardup 1985)★★★, *In Between Every Line* (Harvest 1986)★★, *Descendants Of Smith* (EMI 1988)★★★, *Loony On The Bus* (Awareness 1988)★★, *Once* (Awareness 1990)★★★, *Death Or Glory?* (Awareness 1992)★★★, *The BBC Tapes Vol. 1* (Science Friction 1997)★★★★, *The BBC Tapes Vol. 2* (Science Friction 1997)★★★★, *The BBC Tapes Vol. 3* (Science Friction 1997)★★★★, *The BBC Tapes Vol. 4* (Science Friction 1997)★★★, *The BBC Tapes Vol. 5* (Science Friction 1997), *The BBC Tapes Vol. 6* (Science Friction 1997).

●COMPILATIONS: *Harper 1970-1975* (Harvest 1978)★★★★.

HARRISON, GEORGE

b. 25 February 1943, Liverpool, England. As the youngest member of the Beatles, Harrison was constantly overshadowed by John Lennon and Paul McCartney. Although 'Don't Bother Me' (*With The Beatles*), 'I Need You' (*Help!*) and 'If I Needed Someone' (*Rubber Soul*) revealed a considerable compositional talent, such contributions were swamped by his col-

leagues' prodigious output. Instead, Harrison honed a distinctive guitar style, modelled on rockabilly mentor Carl Perkins, and was responsible for adding the sitar into the pop lexicon through its complementary use on 'Norwegian Wood'. Harrison's infatuation with India was the first outward sign of his growing independence, while his three contributions to *Revolver*, noticeably 'Taxman' and 'I Want To Tell You', showed a newfound musical maturity. The Indian influence continued on the reflective 'Within You, Without You'. He flexed solo ambitions with the would-be film soundtrack, *Wonderwall* and the trite *Electronic Sounds*, but enhanced his stature as a skilled songwriter with the majestic 'While My Guitar Gently Weeps' (*The Beatles*) and 'Something' (*Abbey Road*). Sales of the latter composition exceeded one million when issued as a single in 1969. Harrison also produced releases for Billy Preston, Jackie Lomax and the Radha Krishna Temple and performed on the concurrent Delaney And Bonnie tour before commencing work on *All Things Must Pass*. This treble album consisted of material stockpiled over the years and featured several high quality compositions including 'Awaiting On You All', 'I'd Have You Anytime' (co-written with Bob Dylan) and 'Beware Of Darkness'. These selections were, however, eclipsed by 'My Sweet Lord', which deftly combined melody with mantra and deservedly soared to the top of the US and UK charts. Its lustre was sadly removed in later years when the publishers of the Chiffons' 1964 hit, 'She's So Fine', successfully sued for plagiarism. Harrison's next project was 'Bangla Desh', a single inspired by a plea from master musician Ravi Shankar to aid famine relief in the Indian subcontinent. Charity concerts, featuring Harrison, Dylan, Preston, Eric Clapton and Leon Russell, were held at New York's Madison Square Gardens in August 1971, which in turn generated a film and boxed-set. Legal wrangles blighted Harrison's altruism and it was 1973 before he resumed recording. Whereas *All Things Must Pass* boasted support from Derek And The Dominos, Badfinger and producer Phil Spector, *Living In The Material World* was more modest and consequently lacked verve. The album nonetheless reached number 1 in the US, as did an attendant single, 'Give Me Love (Give Me Peace On Earth)', but critical reaction was noticeably muted. A disastrous US tour was the unfortunate prelude to *Dark Horse*, the title of which was inspired by Harrison's new record label. His marriage to Patti Boyd now over, the set reflected its creator's depression and remains his artistic nadir. Although poorly received, *Extra Texture* partially redressed the balance, but the fact that its strongest track, 'You', dated from 1971, did not escape attention. *Thirty-Three And A Third* and *George Harrison* continued this regeneration; the latter was a particularly buoyant collection, but the quality still fell short of his initial recordings.

During this period George became involved with his personal heroes, the Monty Python comedy team, in

the production of *Life Of Brian*. His financing of the film ensured its success and cemented a long-lasting relationship with the troupe. In 1980 the artist's parent label, Warner Brothers Records, rejected the first version of *Somewhere In England*, deeming its content below standard. The reshaped collection included 'All Those Years Ago', George's homage to the murdered John Lennon, which featured contributions from Paul McCartney and Ringo Starr. The song reached the UK Top 3 when issued as a single, a position reflecting the subject matter rather than faith in the artist. *Gone Troppo* was issued to minimal fanfare from both outlet and creator, and rumours flourished that it marked the end of Harrison's recording career. He pursued other interests, notably with his company Handmade Films which included such productions as *Time Bandits* (1981), *The Long Good Friday* (1982), *Water* (1985), *Mona Lisa* (1986) and *Shanghai Surprise* (1986), occasionally contributing to the soundtracks. During this time George cultivated two hobbies which took up a great deal of his life: motor racing and gardening. He was tempted back into the studio to answer several low-key requests, including Mike Batt's adaptation of *The Hunting Of The Snark* and the *Greenpeace* benefit album. He joined the all-star cast saluting Carl Perkins on the television tribute *Blue Suede Shoes*, and in 1986 commenced work on a projected new album. Production chores were shared with Jeff Lynne, and the care lavished on the sessions was rewarded the following year when Harrison's version of Rudy Clark's 'Got My Mind Set On You' reached number 2 in the UK and number 1 in the US. The intentionally Beatles-influenced 'When We Was Fab' was another major success, while *Cloud Nine* itself proved equally popular, with Lynne's grasp of commerciality enhancing George's newfound optimism. Its release completed outstanding contracts and left this unpredictable artist free of obligations, although several impromptu live appearances suggest his interest in music is now rekindled. This revitalization has also seen Harrison play a pivotal role within the Traveling Wilburys, an *ad hoc* 'supergroup' initially comprising himself, Lynne, Dylan, Tom Petty and Roy Orbison. Harrison made his first tour for many years in Japan during January 1992 with his long-time friend Eric Clapton giving him support. He reappeared onstage in England at a one-off benefit concert in April 1992. In 1995 the UK press seemed to delight in the fact that had hit hard times caused by various business ventures and ill advice from people he used as advisors. The Beatles reunion in 1995 for the *Anthology* series banished any thoughts of bankrupcy. A further bonus came in January 1996 when he was awarded $11.6 million following litigation against Denis O'Brien and his mishandling of Harrison's finances. Harrision's tact and the way he has dealt with his inner self should not be underestimated; the 'quiet' Beatle does seem to have this part of his life totally sorted out.
●ALBUMS: *Wonderwall* (Apple 1968)★★, *Electronic Sound* (Zapple 1969)★★, *All Things Must Pass* (Apple 1970)★★★★, with other artists *The Concert For Bangla Desh* (Apple 1972)★★★, *Living In The Material World* (Apple 1973)★★★, *Dark Horse* (Apple 1974)★, *Extra Texture* (Apple 1975)★★, *Thirty Three And A Third* (Dark Horse 1976)★★★, *George Harrison* (Dark Horse 1979)★★★, *Somewhere In England* (Dark Horse 1981)★★, *Gone Troppo* (Dark Horse 1982)★, *Cloud Nine* (Dark Horse 1987)★★★, *Live In Japan* (1992)★★.
●COMPILATIONS: *The Best Of George Harrison* (Parlophone 1977)★★★, *Best Of Dark Horse 1976-1989* (Dark Horse 1989)★★★.
●FURTHER READING: *George Harrison Yesterday And Today*, Ross Michaels. *I Me Mine*, George Harrison. *I Me Mine: Limited Edition*, George Harrison. *Fifty Years Adrift*, George Harrison and Derek Taylor. *Dark Horse: The Secret Life Of George Harrison*, Geoffrey Giuliano. *The Quiet One: A Life Of George Harrison*, Alan Clayson. *The Illustrated George Harrison*, Geoffrey Giuliano.
●FILMS: *A Hard Day's Night* (1964), *Help!* (1965), *Magical Mystery Tour* (1968), *Let It Be* (1971)

HARRISON, MIKE

b. 3 September 1945, Carlisle, Cumberland, England. Vocalist/pianist Harrison began his career in the early 60s as a member of local act the Ramrods. In 1965 he joined the VIPs, who later evolved into Art (1967), then Spooky Tooth (1968). In each of these acts Harrison's distinctive voice was well to the fore, notably on Spooky Tooth's 'Sunshine Help Me' and 'Better By You, Better Than Me'. *Mike Harrison* was recorded following this group's disintegration. Here the singer was supported by Junkyard Angels, a Carlisle-based group led by ex-VIPs' guitarist Frank Kenyon and completed by Ian Herbert (guitar/vocals), Peter Batley (bass) and Ken Iverson (drums). Harrison's powerful intonation - part Joe Cocker, part Stevie Winwood - raises this rather disappointing set which failed to recreate a personal chemistry between the leader and sidemen. *Smokestack Lightning* was an excellent collaboration with various Muscle Shoals session musicians, including Barry Beckett (keyboards) and David Hood (bass), both of whom later joined Traffic. In 1972 Harrison joined a re-formed Spooky Tooth - which also featured Ian Herbert - but left again in 1974. The low-key *Rainbow Rider* ensued before Harrison teamed with former Joe Cocker pianist Chris Stainton. After spending some time in Canada he now works in a warehouse. Harrison has now left music altogether, a sad waste of one of the finest heavy rock voices the UK has produced.
●ALBUMS: *Mike Harrison* (Island 1971)★★, *Smokestack Lightning* (Island 1972)★★★, *Rainbow Rider* (Good Ear 1975)★★★.

HARTMAN, DAN

b. 4 November 1951, Harrisburg, Pennsylvania, USA, d. 22 March 1994, Westport, Connecticut, USA. Hartman's multi-instrumental talents and light tenor were first

heard by North America at large when he served bands led, together and separately, by Johnny Winter and Edgar Winter. Employment by the latter from 1973-77 brought the greatest commercial rewards - principally via Hartman's co-writing all selections on the Edgar Winter Group's *They Only Come Out At Night*, which contained the million-selling single, 'Frankenstein'. He was also in demand as a session player by artists including Todd Rundgren, Ian Hunter, Rick Derringer, Stevie Wonder and Ronnie Montrose. Riding the disco bandwagon, Hartman next enjoyed international success with the title track to *Instant Replay* and another of its singles, 'This Is It' (both of which were among the first records to be released on 12-inch vinyl). However, after the relative failure of *Relight My Fire* in 1979, he retired from stage centre to concentrate on production commissions - some carried out in his own studio, the Schoolhouse, in Westport, Connecticut. Among his production and songwriting clients were the Average White Band, Neil Sedaka, .38 Special, James Brown (notably with the 1986 hit 'Living In America'), Muddy Waters, Diana Ross, Chaka Khan and Hilly Michaels. In 1985 he returned to the US Top 10 with the soul concoction, 'I Can Dream About You' (for the *Streets Of Fire* film soundtrack) which he followed with two lesser hits prior to another withdrawal to the sidelines of pop. Having been diagnosed HIV Positive, his last major production projects included tracks for Holly Johnson and Tina Turner's hugely successful *Foreign Affair* set. He died from AIDS-related complications in 1994, just as his career was being reappraised (his material was much sampled by dance bands, notably Black Box on their huge hit 'Ride On Time', while Take That took his 'Relight My Fire' to the UK number 1 spot).
●ALBUMS: *Images* (Blue Sky 1976)★★, *Instant Replay* (Blue Sky 1978)★★★, *Relight My Fire* (Blue Sky 1980)★★, *I Can Dream About You* (MCA 1985)★★, *White Boy* (1986)★★, *New Green Clear Blue* (RCA 1989)★★.

HATFIELD AND THE NORTH

Formed in 1972, Hatfield And The North was comprised of musicians active in England's musically incestuous, experimental fringe. The original line-up - David Sinclair (b. 24 November 1947, Herne Bay, Kent, England; keyboards), Phil Miller (b. 22 January 1949, Barnet, Hertfordshire, England; guitar), Richard Sinclair (b. 6 June 1948, Canterbury, Kent, England; bass/vocals) and Pip Pyle (b. 4 April 1950, Sawbridgeworth, Hertfordshire, England; drums) - was drawn from ex-members of Caravan, Matching Mole and Delivery, but within months David Sinclair left to join Caravan and was replaced by Dave Stewart (b. 30 December 1950, Waterloo, London, England), previously in Egg and Khan. Taking their name from the first signpost out of London on the A1 trunk road, the group completed two albums, influenced by Soft Machine, that adeptly combined skilled musicianship with quirky melodies. Their extended instrumental passages, par-

ticularly Stewart's deft keyboard work, were highly impressive, while their obtuse song titles, including 'Gigantic Land Crabs In Earth Takeover Bid' and '(Big) John Wayne Socks Psychology On The Jaw', emphasized an air of detached intellectualism. However, their chosen genre was losing its tenuous appeal and, unable to secure a sure commercial footing, the quartet split up in June 1975. Stewart and Miller then formed National Health, Pyle became a session drummer while Sinclair abandoned professional music altogether until re-emerging in the early 90s with Caravan Of Dreams.
●ALBUMS: *Hatfield And The North* (Virgin 1974)★★★, *The Rotters' Club* (Virgin 1975)★★★.
●COMPILATIONS: *Afters* (Virgin 1980)★★★, *Live* (1993)★★.

HAWKWIND

Befitting a group associated with community and benefit concerts, Hawkwind was founded in the hippie enclave centred on London's Ladbroke Grove during the late 60s. Dave Brock (b. Isleworth, Middlesex, England; guitar/vocals), Nik Turner (b. Oxford, Oxfordshire, England; saxophone/vocals), Mick Slattery (guitar), Dik Mik (b. Richmond, Surrey; electronics), John Harrison (bass) and Terry Ollis (drums) were originally known as Group X, then Hawkwind Zoo, prior to securing a recording contract. Their debut, *Hawkwind*, was produced by Dick Taylor, former guitarist with the Pretty Things, who briefly augmented his new protégés on Slattery's departure. Indeed Hawkwind underwent many personnel changes, but by 1972 had achieved a core consisting of Brock, Turner, Del Dettmar (b. Thornton Heath, Surrey, England; synthesizer), Lemmy (b. Ian Kilmister, 24 December 1945, Stoke-on-Trent, Staffordshire, England; bass), Simon King (b. Oxford, Oxfordshire, England; drums), Stacia (b. Exeter, Devon, England; dancer) and poet/writer Robert Calvert (b. c.1945, Pretoria, South Africa, d. 14 August 1988; vocals). One part-time member was science fiction writer Michael Moorcock who helped organize some of Hawkwind's concert appearances and often deputized for Calvert when the latter was indisposed. This role was extended to recording credits on several albums. The group's chemically blurred science-fiction image was made apparent in such titles as *In Search Of Space* and *Space Ritual*. They enjoyed a freak UK pop hit when the compulsive 'Silver Machine' soared to number 3, but this flirtation with a wider audience ended prematurely when a follow-up single, 'Urban Guerilla', was hastily withdrawn in the wake of a terrorist bombing campaign in London. Hawkwind continued to shed personalities; Calvert left, and rejoined, Dettmar was replaced by Simon House (ex-High Tide), but the group lost much of its impetus in 1975 when Lemmy was fired on his arrest on drugs charges during a North American tour. The bassist subsequently formed Motörhead. Although the group enjoyed a period of relative stability following the release of

Astounding Sounds, Amazing Music, it ended in 1977 with the firing of founder-member Turner and two latter additions, Paul Rudolph (ex-Deviants and Pink Fairies) and Alan Powell. The following year Simon House left to join David Bowie's band before Brock, Calvert and King assumed a new name, the Hawklords, to avoid legal and contractual complications. The group reverted to using its former appellation in 1979, by which time Calvert had resumed his solo career. An undaunted Hawkwind pursued an eccentric path throughout the 80s. Dave Brock remained at the helm of a flurry of associates, including Huw Lloyd Langton, who played guitar on the group's debut album, Tim Blake (synthesizer) and drummer Ginger Baker. Nik Turner also reappeared in the ranks of a group which has continued to enjoy a committed following, despite the bewildering array of archive releases obscuring the group's contemporary standing. In 1990 they underwent a resurgence in popularity thanks primarily to the growth of the rave culture and their album, *Space Bandits*, reflected this new, young interest. It also saw the return of Simon House and the inclusion for the first time of a female vocalist, Bridgett Wishart (ex-Hippy Slags). However, when their next album started to copy rave ideas, it became obvious that they were running out of inspiration, with *Palace Springs* containing no less than five new versions of early tracks. In 1992 they set off to America for a successful tour, but on their return fell apart. Eventually reduced to a three-piece they became totally dance/rave-orientated and subsequent releases had little in common with the classic days gone by. It is sad that a band celebrating 25 years in business had become so easily embroiled in current musical trends as opposed to setting them.

●ALBUMS: *Hawkwind* (Liberty 1970)★★★, *In Search Of Space* (United Artists 1971)★★★, *Doremi Fasol Latido* (United Artists 1972)★★, *Space Ritual Alive* (United Artists 1973)★★, *Hall Of The Mountain Grill* (United Artists 1974)★★★, *Warrior On The Edge Of Time* (United Artists 1975)★★★, *Astounding Sounds Amazing Music* (Charisma 1976)★★★, *Quark, Strangeness And Charm* (Charisma 1977)★★, *25 Years On* (Charisma 1978)★★, *PXR 5* (Charisma 1979)★★★, *Live 1979* (Bronze 1980)★★, *Levitation* (Bronze 1980)★★★, *Sonic Attack* (RCA 1981)★★★, *Church Of Hawkwind* (RCA 1982)★★★, *Choose Your Masques* (RCA 1982)★★★, *Zones* (Flicknife 1983)★★★, *The Chronicle Of The Black Sword* (Flicknife 1985)★★★, *The Xenon Codex* (GWR 1988)★★★, *Night Of The Hawk* (Powerhouse 1989)★★★, *Space Bandits* (GWR 1990)★★★, *Palace Springs* (GWR 1991)★★, *Electric Tepee* (Essential 1992)★★★, *It Is The Business Of The Future To Be Dangerous* (Essential 1993)★★★, *The Business Trip* (Emergency Broadcast Systems 1994)★★, *Future Reconstructions: Ritual Of The Solstice* (Emergency Broadcast Systems 1996)★★★. Solo: Alan Davey *Captured Rotation* (Emergency Broadcasting Systems 1996)★★★.

●COMPILATIONS: *Road Hawks* (United Artists 1976)★★★, *Masters Of The Universe* (United Artists 1977)★★★, *Repeat Performances* (Charisma 1980)★★★, *Friends And Relations* (Flicknife 1982)★, *Twice Upon A Time - Friends And Relations Vol. 2* (Flicknife 1983)★★, *Text Of The Festival Live 70/72* (Illuminated 1983)★★, *Independent Days* mini-album (Flicknife 1984)★, *Bring Me The Head Of Yuri Gagarin* (Demi-Monde 1985)★★, *In The Beginning* (Demi-Monde 1985)★★, *Space Ritual Volume 2* (American Phonograph 1985)★★★, *Anthology - Hawkwind Volumes 1, 2 and 3* (Samurai 1985-1986)★★★, *Live 70/73* (Dojo 1986)★★, *The Collection* (Castle 1986)★★★★, *Angels Of Death* (RCA 1986)★★★, *Early Daze/Best Of* (Thunderbolt 1987)★★, *Out And Intake* (Flicknife 1987)★★, *Stasis: The UA Years* (EMI 1990)★★, *Mighty Hawkwind Classics* (Anagram 1992)★★★, *Lord Of Light* (Cleopatra 1993)★★★.

●VIDEOS: *Night Of The Hawks* (1984), *Chronicle Of The Black Sword* (1986), *Live Legends* (1990), *Treworgy Tree Fayre* (1990), *The Academy* (1991), *Promo Collection* (1992), *Hawkwind: The Solstice At Stonehenge 1984* (1993).

●FURTHER READING: *This Is Hawkwind, Do Not Panic*, Kris Tate.

HAYES, ISAAC

b. 20 August 1942, Covington, Tennessee, USA. Hayes' formative years were spent playing piano and organ in various Memphis clubs. He fronted several groups, including Sir Isaac And The Doo-dads, the Teen Tones and Sir Calvin And His Swinging Cats, and recorded a handful of rudimentary singles. However, it was not until 1964 that he was able to attract the attention of the city's premier soul outlet, Stax Records. Having completed a session with Mar-Keys saxophonist Floyd Newman, Hayes was invited to remain as a stand-in for Booker T. Jones. He then established a songwriting partnership with David Porter and enjoyed success with Sam And Dave's 'Hold On I'm Comin'', 'Soul Man' and 'When Something Is Wrong With My Baby'. The team also wrote for Carla Thomas ('B-A-B-Y') and Johnnie Taylor ('I Had A Dream', 'I Got To Love Somebody's Baby'). They were responsible for the formation of the Soul Children as a vehicle for their songwriting. Hayes nonetheless remained a frustrated performer, and an afterhours, jazz-based spree resulted in his debut, *Presenting Isaac Hayes* (1967). *Hot Buttered Soul*, released in 1969, established the artist's reputation, its sensual soliloquies and shimmering orchestration combined in a remarkable, sophisticated statement. The artist also attained notoriety for his striking physical appearance - his shaven head and gold medallions enhanced a carefully cultivated mystique. However, *The Isaac Hayes Movement, To Be Continued* (both 1970) and *Black Moses* (1971) were less satisfying artistically as the style gradually degenerated into self-parody. *Shaft* (1971), a highly successful film soundtrack, is considered by many to be Hayes' best work. Its theme also became an international hit single and its enduring qualities were emphasized when the song reached number 13 in the

UK in the hands of Eddy And The Soul Boys (1985). However, subsequent film scores, *Tough Guys* (1973) and *Truck Turner* (1974) were less interesting. Hayes left Stax in 1975 following a much publicized row over royalties, and set up his own Hot Buttered Soul label. Declared bankrupt the following year, he moved to the Polydor and Spring labels, where his prolific output continued. In 1981, however, he retired for five years before re-emerging with 'Ike's Rap', a Top 10 US R&B single that partially revitalized his reputation. Many of Hayes' original Enterprise albums have been reissued in CD format by UK Ace under their reactivated Stax logo.

●ALBUMS: *Presenting Isaac Hayes* later reissued as *In The Beginning* (1967)★★, *Hot Buttered Soul* (Stax 1969)★★★★, *The Isaac Hayes Movement* (Enterprise 1970)★★, *To Be Continued* (Stax 1970)★★, *Shaft* (Stax 1971)★★★★, *Black Moses* (Stax 1971)★★, *Live At The Sahara Tahoe* (Stax 1973)★★, *Joy* (Stax 1973)★★, *Tough Guys* (Stax 1974)★★, *Truck Turner* (Stax 1974)★★, *Chocolate Chip* (Stax 1975)★★★, *Use Me* (Stax 1975)★★, *Disco Connection* (HBS 1976)★★, *Groove-A-Thon* (HBS 1976)★, *Juicy Fruit (Disco Freak)* (HBS 1976)★, with Dionne Warwick *Man And A Woman* (HBS 1977)★, *New Horizon* (Polydor 1977)★, *Memphis Movement* (1977)★, *For The Sake Of Love* (Polydor 1978)★, *Don't Let Go* (Polydor 1979)★★, with Millie Jackson *Royal Rappin'* (Polydor 1980)★★, *And Once Again* (Polydor 1980)★★, *Light My Fire* (1980)★★, *A Lifetime Thing* (1981)★★, *U Turn* (Columbia 1986)★★, *Love Attack* (Columbia 1988)★★, *Branded* (Pointblank 1995)★★, *Raw And Refined* (Pointblank 1995)★★.

●COMPILATIONS: *The Best Of* (Enterprise 1975)★★★, *The Isaac Hayes Chronicle* (1978)★★★, *Hotbed* (1978)★★, *Enterprise - His Greatest Hits* (1980)★★★★, *Isaac's Moods* (Stax 1988)★★★, *The Collection* (Connoisseur Collection 1995)★★★.

HAYWARD, JUSTIN

b. 14 October 1946, Swindon, Wiltshire, England. As singer and guitarist with the Moody Blues, Hayward was responsible for the international hit 'Nights In White Satin' which has since been elevated to classic status. He pursued a solo career while the parent group was in occasional temporary retirement. After the first 'break-up' of the group, Hayward teamed up with fellow Moody's songwriter John Lodge as the Blue Jays between December 1974 and January 1977. During this period they achieved a UK Top 10 hit with 'Blue Guitar' (1975). Hayward's most successful solo offering, 'Forever Autumn', reached the UK Top 5 and was taken from Jeff Wayne's 1978 best-selling concept album, *The War Of The Worlds*.

●ALBUMS: with John Lodge *Blue Jays* (Threshold 1975)★★★, *Songwriter* (Deram 1977)★★, *Nightflight* (Decca 1980)★★, *Moving Mountains* (Towerbell 1985)★★, with Mike Batt and the London Philharmonic Orchestra *Classic Blue* (Filmtrax 1989)★★.

HEAD EAST

An example of stubborn belligerence ensuring longevity despite limited musical identity, Head East persevered on the Midwest, USA, circuit for several years, releasing a sequence of competent hard rock albums without ever making the transition to international fame which peers such as REO Speedwagon enjoyed. Comprising John Schlitt (vocals), Mike Somerville (guitar), Roger Boyd (keyboards), Dan Birney (bass) and Steve Huston (drums), after forming in St. Louis, Missouri, they cultivated a highly commercial hard rock sound which made them perfect for AOR radio. Critics were less appreciative of their earnest, hard driving sound (reflected in lyrics which dwelled on domestic and romantic themes), but their live following by the end of the 70s was considerable. Accordingly, their best album of this period was the 1979 *Live* set, attaining the group's highest chart placing at US number 65. In the early 80s the group attempted to restrain their sound and convert their local popularity into national chart placings, but despite cover versions of material by Russ Ballard, they never made the transition. For *US No 1* Schlitt, Somerville and Birney all left, with their replacements being Dab Odum (vocals), Tony Gross (guitar) and Mark Boatman (bass). Eventually A&M Records, their home since 1975, became frustrated by their lack of national success and dropped the group. One further album emerged for an independent in 1982, but the group broke up following its release. A late 80s reunion saw the release of *Choice Of Weapons*, but this lacked the original spirit of the band and fared poorly.

●ALBUMS: *Flat As A Pancake* (A&M 1975)★★★, *Get Yourself Up* (A&M 1976)★★★, *Gettin' Lucky* (A&M 1977)★★★, *Head East* (A&M 1978)★★★, *Live* (A&M 1979)★★★, *A Different Kind Of Crazy* (A&M 1979)★★, *US No 1* (A&M 1980)★★, *Onwards And Upwards* (Allegiance 1982)★★, *Choice Of Weapons* (Dark Heart 1989)★★.

HEADS, HANDS AND FEET

Formed in 1970, from Poet And The One Man Band, a promising unit which folded on the demise of their record label. Tony Colton (b. 11 February 1942, Tunbridge Wells, Kent, England; vocals), Ray Smith (b. 9 July 1943, London, England; guitar), Albert Lee (b. 21 December 1943, Leominster, Herefordshire, England; guitar) and Pete Gavin (b. 9 September 1946, London, England; drums) were joined by Mike O'Neil (keyboards) and Chas Hodges (b. 11 November 1943, London, England; bass; ex-Outlaws and Cliff Bennett) for a debut designed to indicate the disparate influences of such talented individuals. A double album in America, the British version was whittled to a single album to emphasize their musicianship. O'Neil left the group prior to *Tracks* which offered a greater emphasis on rock than its country-tinged predecessor. However, relationships within the group grew strained and Heads, Hands And Feet disbanded in December 1972, prior to the release of *Old Soldiers Never Die*. Colton and Smith pursued successful careers as songwriters and producers, while Gavin, Hodges and Lee were reunited in the Albert Lee Band. The guitarist later found fame accompanying Emmylou Harris and Eric Clapton, while Hodges formed half of the popular Chas And Dave duo. Rediscovered tapes surfaced in the 90s and were packaged and released much to the delight of a small and devoted fanbase.

●ALBUMS: *Heads, Hands And Feet* (1971)★★★, *Tracks* (1972)★★★, *Old Soldiers Never Die* (Atlantic 1973)★★, *Home From Home (The Missing Album)* (See For Miles 1995)★★.

HEART

This durable US rock band features the talents of sisters Ann (b. 19 June 1951, San Diego, California, USA) and Nancy Wilson (b. 16 March 1954, San Francisco, California, USA). The elder sister had released two singles as Ann Wilson And The Daybreaks on a local label in 1967. After a series of unreleased demos she took her sister to Vancouver, Canada, in search of a backing band. There they found bassist Steve Fossen (b. 15 November 1949) and guitarist Roger Fisher (b. 14 February 1950), and Heart was born (two initial monikers, the Army and White Heart, were rejected). After *Dreamboat Annie* emerged on Mushroom Records in 1976, their second single, 'Crazy On You', brought them to public attention. Michael Derosier (b. 24 August 1951, Canada) had previously become the band's first permanent drummer. They maintained their high profile when *Little Queen* and the single, 'Barracuda', became mainstays in the US charts. By the time *Dog And Butterfly* arrived in 1978, the professional relationships within the band had escalated to ones of a more personal nature, with Nancy Wilson dating guitarist Fisher, while sister Ann was involved with his brother, Mike. Mike Fisher, who had once been part of the group's embryonic line-up, had now become their unofficial manager. However, before sessions for *Bebe Le Strange* on Epic were complete, the relationships had soured and Roger Fisher left the band, leaving the group bereft of the lead guitar which had previously been so prominent in the group's formula. The guitar parts were covered on tour by Nancy and multi-instrumentalist Howard Leese (b. 13 June 1953, Canada), who became a permanent member. By the time they resurfaced with *Private Audition* in 1983, Fossen and Derosier were also on the verge of departure. Their replacements were Mark Andes (b. 19 February 1948, Philadelphia, USA; ex-Spirit) and Denny Carmassi (ex-Montrose and Sammy Hagar), though their efforts on *Passionworks* were not enough to inspire any kind of revival in Heart's fortunes. Their confidence was bolstered, however, when Ann's duet with Mike Dean (Loverboy) produced 'Almost Paradise...Love Theme

From Footloose', which rose to number 7 in the US charts. When Epic allowed their contract to lapse, Heart joined Capitol in 1985, seemingly with their career in its death throes. The new label brought about a transformation in the band's image, projecting them as a more rock-orientated concern, but could hardly have expected the turnaround in Heart's fortunes that resulted. *Heart* gave them a number 1 in the US, and highly lucrative singles 'What About Love' and 'Never', before 'These Dreams' finally achieved the equivalent number 1 slot in the singles chart. The follow-up, *Bad Animals*, was almost as successful, stalling at number 2. While both Wilson sisters continued to work on soundtrack cuts, the most profitable of which was Ann's duet with Robin Zander (Cheap Trick) 'Surrender To Me', Nancy married *Rolling Stone* writer Cameron Crowe. Heart's success continued with the long-conceived *Brigade* in 1990, from which 'All I Wanna Do Is Make Love To You' (written by Robert John 'Mutt' Lange) became a Top 10 hit in the UK and a number 1 in the US. Both Wilson sisters then became involved in solo projects, while former companions Fossen, Roger Fisher and Derosier embarked on a new dual career with Alias, who had two big US single hits in 1990. The sisters returned as Heart in 1993, backed by Schuyler Deale (bass), John Purdell (keyboards), Denny Carmassi (drums) and Lease (guitar) and found themselves with another hit on their hands in 'Will You Be There (In The Morning)', which preceded *Desire Walks On*. *The Road Home* was an acoustic live album with production by John Paul Jones, released to mark the band's 20th anniversary.

●ALBUMS: *Dreamboat Annie* (Mushroom 1976)★★★★, *Little Queen* (Portrait 1977)★★★, *Dog And Butterfly* (Portrait 1978)★★★★, *Magazine* (Mushroom 1978)★★, *Bebe Le Strange* (Portrait 1980)★★★, *Greatest Hits/Live* (Portrait 1981)★★★, *Private Audition* (Epic 1982)★★, *Passionworks* (Epic 1983)★★, *Heart* (Capitol 1985)★★, *Bad Animals* (Capitol 1987)★★, *Brigade* (Capitol 1990)★★, *Rock The House Live!* (Capitol 1991)★★, *Desire Walks On* (Capitol 1993)★★, *The Road Home* (Capitol 1995)★★★.

●COMPILATIONS: *Heart Box Set* (Capitol 1990)★★, *Greatest Hits* (Capitol 1997)★★★.

●VIDEOS: *If Looks Could Kill* (1988), *The Road Home* (Capitol 1995).

HEARTBREAKERS

The Heartbreakers were formed in New York in 1975 when Richard Hell, former bassist with Television, joined forces with Johnny Thunders (guitar/vocals) and Jerry Nolan (drums), disaffected members of the New York Dolls. The new act made one live appearance as a trio before adding Walter Lure (guitar/vocals) to the line-up. The original Heartbreakers enjoyed cult popularity, but by the following year the mercurial Hell left to found the Voidoids. Drafting Billy Rath as his replacement, the quartet later moved to London, eager to embrace its nascent punk movement. They supported the Sex Pistols on the aborted Anarchy tour (December 1976) and were then signed to the ailing Track Records. 'Chinese Rocks', a paean to heroin co-written by Dee Dee Ramone of the Ramones, and the subsequent *L.A.M.F.*, gave an indication of the group's 'wrong side of the tracks' rock 'n' roll strengths, but was marred by Speedy Keen's unfocused production. Nolan left the band in disgust, but returned to fulfil outstanding commitments. The Heartbreakers then severed connections with Track, but having broken up in November 1977, re-formed the following year with new drummer Ty Styx. The name was subsequently dropped and resurrected on several occasions, notably in 1984, but such interludes vied with Thunders' other, equally temporary, outlets, until he was found dead in mysterious circumstances in April 1991.

● ALBUMS: *L.A.M.F.* (Track 1977)★★, *Live At Max's Kansas City* (Max's Kansas City 1979)★★, *D.T.K. Live At The Speakeasy* (Jungle 1982)★★, *Live At The Lyceum Ballroom 1984* (ABC 1984)★★, *L.A.M.F. Revisited* remixed version of their debut (Jungle 1984)★★★.

● COMPILATIONS: *D.T.K. - L.A.M.F.* (Jungle 1984)★★★.

HEAVY METAL KIDS

Formed in London, England, in 1973, Heavy Metal Kids consisted of Gary Holton (vocals), Mickey Waller (guitar), Ron Thomas (bass) and Keith Boyce (drums). Signing to Atlantic Records the band released their self-titled debut album in 1974. Quickly gaining popularity on the live club circuit in and around the London area, playing brash street metal, the band followed up with *Anvil Chorus* in 1975. This featured keyboard player Danny Peyronel and the semi-legendary 'Cosmo' on guitar joining the quartet. The album also contained the utterly outrageous 'Call The Cops'. However, Holton's volatile nature got the band into trouble at various gigs, breaking his leg on an ill-fated American tour. Subsequently dropped by Atlantic Records, the band nevertheless released a third and final album. *Kitsch* appeared on RAK Records in 1977, and was again dominated by tough, street metal tunes. It still did not give the band the break it needed and they folded shortly after its release. Holton went on to a short-lived solo career which saw him (very) briefly join the Damned, release a solo album in Europe and have a minor hit single with 'Catch A Falling Star' in 1984, before setting out to pursue an acting career. He will be best remembered for his role as Wayne, in the television series, *Auf Wiedersehen Pet*. He died of a drugs overdose during the filming of the series.

● ALBUMS: *Heavy Metal Kids* (Atlantic 1974)★★, *Anvil Chorus* (Atlantic 1975)★★, *Kitsch* (RAK 1977)★★.

HELL, RICHARD

b. Richard Myers, 2 October 1949, Lexington, Kentucky, USA. A seminal figure on New York's emergent punk scene, Hell embodied the fierce nihilism of the genre.

In 1971 he was a founder member of the Neon Boys with guitarist Tom Verlaine. Hell first performed several of his best-known songs, including 'Love Comes In Spurts', while in this group. He also published a handful of poems, under his own name, during this period. The Neon Boys subsequently mutated into Television where Hell's torn clothing, the result of impoverishment, inspired Malcolm McLaren's ideas for the Sex Pistols. Personality clashes resulted in Hell's departure in 1975. He then formed the Heartbreakers with former New York Dolls guitarist Johnny Thunders and drummer Jerry Nolan, but once again left prematurely. Hell reappeared in 1976 fronting his own unit, Richard Hell and the Voidoids, with twin-lead guitarists, Bob Quine and Ivan Julian, alongside drummer Marc Bell. The quartet's debut EP appeared later that year - Stiff Records secured the rights in Britain - and the set quickly achieved underground popularity. One particular track, 'Blank Generation', achieved anthem-like proportions as an apposite description of punk, but Hell intended the 'blank' to be filled by the listener's personal interpretation. A re-recorded version of the same song became the title track of the Voidoids dazzling debut album, which also featured the terse, but extended epic, 'Another World', and a fiery interpretation of John Fogerty's 'Walk Upon The Water'. Raw, tense and edgy, with Richard intoning 'cut-up'-styled lyrics delivered in a style ranging from moan to scream, *Blank Generation* is one of punk's definitive statements. Bell's departure for the Ramones in 1978 undermined the group's potential and Quine subsequently left to pursue a successful career as a session musician and sometime Lou Reed sideman. A three-year gap ensued, during which Hell only issued one single, the Nick Lowe-produced 'The Kid With The Replaceable Head'. An EP combining two new songs with a brace of Neon Boys masters served as a prelude to *Destiny Street*, another compulsive selection on which the artist's lyricism flourished. Quine returned to add highly expressive guitar work while Material drummer Fred Maher supplied a suitably crisp frame. Despite the power of this release, Hell once again withdrew from recording. Indeed on his liner notes to *R.I.P.*, a compilation drawn from all stages in his career, Hell declared it a swan-song. Instead he opted for film work, the most notable example of which was his starring role in Susan Seidelman's *Smithereens*. Sporadic live appearances did continue, some of which were reflected on *Funhunt*, a composite of three Voidoid line-ups (1977, 1979 and 1985) which, despite its poor quality, is enthralling. In 1991 Hell resumed recording as part of the Dim Stars, a group completed by Thurston Moore and Steve Shelley (from Sonic Youth) and Don Fleming (Gumball etc.). A live three-single set, issued on Sonic Youth's Ecstatic Peace label, was succeeded by *3 New Songs*, an EP credited to Hell, but comprising Dim Stars recordings. A 1993 album, *Dim Stars*, showed Hell's powers undiminished. In 1995 he was said to be working on a novel with guitarist Quine, excerpts from which were released in spoken word format as *Go Now*.

●ALBUMS: *Blank Generation* (Sire 1977)★★★★, *Destiny Street* (Red Star 1982)★★★, *Go Now* spoken word (Codex 1995)★★.

●COMPILATIONS: *R.I.P.* cassette only (ROIR 1984)★★★, *Funhunt* cassette only (ROIR 1990)★★★.

HELLO

From north London, England, Bob Bradbury (guitar/vocals), Keith Marshall (guitar/vocals), Vic Faulkner (bass) and Jeff Allen (drums) were signed to Bell Records in 1974 by glam-rock *eminence grise*, Mike Leander. A version of Chuck Berry's 'Carol' paved the way for a second single - a revival of the Exciters'/Billie Davis's 'Tell Him' - to infiltrate the UK Top 10, and they were named as 'Brightest Hope For 1975' in a *Disc* readers poll. This breakthrough was dampened by a subsequent flop in 'Games Up' (composed by the Glitter Band) but Russ Ballard's 'New York Groove' at number 12 in autumn 1975 stayed the further decline that was heralded by poor sales for 'Star-Studded Sham' from *Keep Us Off The Streets*. This collection was a poor effort of covers and previously issued singles.

●ALBUMS: *Keep Us Off The Streets* (Bell 1975)★★.

●COMPILATIONS: *The Glam Years 1971-1979* (Biff 1987)★★, *New York Groove - The Best Of* (1993)★★.

HELM, LEVON

b. Mark Levon Helm, 26 May 1942, Marvell, Arkansas, USA. Drummer Helm was part of the Ron Hawkins Quartet and when he graduated, he and Hawkins moved to Canada and they developed into Ronnie Hawkins And The Hawks. When the group left Hawkins, they began playing the bars and clubs in their own right and recorded for Atlantic Records as Levon And The Hawks. In 1965 Bob Dylan invited them to accompany him on concert dates - and they enhanced his work, both on record and onstage. They also made their own records as the Band. Their first albums, *Music From Big Pink* and *The Band*, feature American music at its best and encompass many styles, little of which could have been predicted before they met Dylan. When the Band disbanded, Helm, who had developed into an fine, intense vocalist, made solo albums and took acting roles. He was brilliantly cast as Loretta Lynn's father in the film *Coal Miner's Daughter* and, after recording 'Blue Moon Of Kentucky' for the soundtrack album, he used the same musicians for a country album, *American Son*. Helm played good ol' boys in several other films and was also featured as Jesse James on the concept album, *The Legend Of Jesse James*, and he was a drummer alongside Ringo Starr when the latter formed his All-Starr Band in 1990. The Band re-formed in 1991 and relationships may have been strained when Helm published his no-holds-barred autobiography, *This Wheel's On Fire*, in 1993.

●ALBUMS: *Levon Helm And The RCO All-Stars* (ABC 1977)★★★, *Levon Helm* (ABC 1978)★★, *American Son* (MCA 1980)★★★, *Levon Helm* (Capitol 1982)★★.

●FURTHER READING: *This Wheel's On Fire*, Levon Helm with Stephen Davis. *Across The Great Divide: The Band And America*, Barney Hoskyns.

HELMS, JIMMY

b. 1944, Florida, USA. A versatile individual, Helms was a member of the Fort Jackson Army Band during his spell in the forces. He forged a singing career after his national service, and was a frequent performer on the popular *Merv Griffin* US televison show. He also appeared in the hippie musical *Hair*. Helms' only notable chart success came in 1973 with the smooth and soulful 'Gonna Make You An Offer You Can't Refuse', the title of which was taken from a line in the Francis Ford Coppola movie, *The Godfather*. The record faltered in the US charts but reached the UK Top 10. He was, however, unable to repeat this one-off hit.

●ALBUMS: *Gonna Make You An Offer* (Cube 1974)★★★, *Songs I Sing* (1975)★★.

HELP YOURSELF

Formed in 1969, founder members Malcolm Morley (guitar/vocals) and Dave Charles (drums/vocals) met in an embryonic version of Sam Apple Pie. Richard Treece (guitar/vocals) and Ken Whaley (bass) completed the original Help Yourself line-up which made its recording debut in 1971. This promising debut was succeeded by *Strange Affair* on which the group's penchant for extended improvisation, reminiscent of America's classic west coast tradition, flourished more freely, notably with 'American Woman'. Paul Burton had replaced Whaley for this release, the latter having joined Ducks DeLuxe, and this line-up was augmented by guitarists Ernie Graham and Jo Jo Glemser. A third Help Yourself album, *Beware The Shadow*, consolidated their impressive style, highlighted by the epic 'Reaffirmation', before the group's prodigal bassist rejoined his colleagues for the aptly titled *The Return Of Ken Whaley*. This 1973 album was, however, Help Yourself's last release. All of the group, bar Morley, later joined Deke Leonard's Iceberg, while the guitarist, who was also an accomplished keyboards player, began a spell with Man. The itinerant Whaley subsequently joined him there. Treece later joined the Flying Aces.

●ALBUMS: *Help Yourself* (Liberty 1971)★★★, *Strange Affair* (United Artists 1972)★★★, *Beware The Shadow* (United Artists 1972)★★★, *The Return Of Ken Whaley/Happy Days* (United Artists 1973)★★★.

HENLEY, DON

b.22 July 1947, Gilmer, Texas, USA. Drummer and vocalist Henley entered music as a member of the Four Speeds and Felicity, the latter of which became known as Shiloh on moving to Los Angeles, California, in 1969. This country rock unit completed an album under the aegis of producer Kenny Rogers, but split up when

Henley joined Linda Ronstadt's touring band. This group, in turn, formed the basis for the Eagles, which became one of America's most popular acts during the 70s. Henley's distinctive voice took lead on the bulk of their best-known songs, many of which he also co-composed. He enjoyed his first taste of single chart success without the Eagles when a duet recorded with Stevie Nicks, 'Leather And Lace', reached the US Top 10. Although surprised when the Eagles' problems led to a permanent break, Henley shook off its legacy with the excellent *I Can't Stand Still*. A songwriting partnership with guitarist Danny Kortchmar resulted in several strong compositions, notably the acerbic 'Dirty Laundry' (1982) which reached number 3 in the USA. A second set, *Building The Perfect Beast*, proved highly popular, attaining platinum status in 1985 and spawning two US Top 10 singles in 'The Boys Of Summer' and 'All She Wants To Do Is Dance'. His skill as a perceptive songwriter was enhanced by the release of *The End Of The Innocence*, which underlined the artist's ever maturing skills. Henley was back with the Eagles in 1994 showing that the passage of time had not diminished their extraordinary popularity.

●ALBUMS: *I Can't Stand Still* (Asylum 1982)★★★★, *Building The Perfect Beast* (Geffen 1984)★★★★, *The End Of The Innocence* (Geffen 1989)★★★.
●COMPILATIONS: *Actual Miles* (Geffen 1996)★★★.

HENRY, STUART

b. 1942, Edinburgh, Scotland, d. 24 November 1976, Luxembourg. One of the most popular disc jockeys on British airwaves during the 70s, Stuart Henry spent six years as an actor following training at the Glasgow College Of Dramatic Art. However, he was lured away from that occupation with the offer of a job as a pirate disc jockey with Radio Scotland. A subsequent offer to join BBC Radio 1 came in 1967 which Henry, who suffered from seasickness, was happy to accept. His early shows included slots such as 'She's Leaving Home', which attempted to trace missing adolescents, emphasizing a heartfelt concern for his fellow man and woman that never deserted him. He also campaigned against nuclear testing and introduced an environmental talk-in. Among the more extrovert disc jockeys of his generation, he was usually pictured in a caftan and beads, and his shows regularly attracted audiences of 11 million and upwards in the early 70s. However, his show was axed during a BBC shake-up in 1974, at which time he defected to Radio Luxembourg. Although unstated, part of the reason for the BBC sacking him was owing to his slight slurring of speech - they believed it to be the result of cannabis usage, when in fact it signalled the onset of multiple sclerosis. In 1982 fellow Radio Luxembourg disc jockey Tony Prince encouraged him to make his condition public as misplaced accusations of on-air insobriety threatened to wreck his career. His former model wife, Ollie, whom he married in 1976, began to help him during his broad-

casts as his condition worsened. To their credit, Radio Luxembourg insisted that as long as he could talk, he would still have a job with their station, and *The Stuart And Ollie Show* continued for many years. When the station closed in 1992 they started a pop news service for local radio and contributed to rock nostalgia magazine *Gold*. Eventually the disease left him utterly incapacitated and he died in November 1995 with Ollie still his constant nurse and companion.

HIGH TIDE

Heavy/psychedelic progressive British band formed in 1969 by Tony Hill (ex-Misunderstood; guitar/vocals/keyboards), Simon House (violin/piano), Roger Hadden (drums/organ) and Peter Pavli (ex-White Rabbit; bass). Signed to the Clearwater production agency they obtained a recording contract with Liberty Records who were eager to join the progressive rock bandwagon that had been milked dry by other record companies. High Tide was a more than credible debut, complete with Mervyn Peake-styled sleeve illustrations. 'Walking Down Their Outlook' features Hill's Jim Morrison-like vocals although longer tracks such as 'Pushed But Not Forgotten' allowed House and Hill to stretch out and improvise - always a feature of their live performances - with lead guitar and violin competing with each other. They played their first live concert with fellow Clearwater band, Hawkwind. After two albums with Liberty they were dropped, and a poor second album sold badly. After numerous tours they became involved with Arthur Brown, Magic Muscle, and the post-Arthur Brown band, Rustic Hinge. By 1972 Hadden was suffering from mental problems and was placed in hospital where he remains to this day. Hill then went on to work with Drachen Theaker while Pavli and House joined the Third Ear Band. Pavli soon involved himself in a number of musical projects with Robert Calvert and Michael Moorcock, House meanwhile joined Hawkwind and later David Bowie's band. In 1987 House and Pavli re-formed High Tide and have overseen various other related projects and releases. Hill released a solo album, *Playing For Time*, in 1991, while House again joined up with Hawkwind and Magic Muscle.

●ALBUMS: *Sea Shanties* (Liberty 1969)★★★★, *High Tide* (Liberty 1970)★★★, *Ancient Gates* (80s)★★, *Interesting Times* (High Tide 1987)★★, *Precious Cargo* (Cobra 1989)★★, *The Flood* (High Tide 1990)★★, *A Fierce Native* (High Tide 1990)★★. Solo: Tony Hill *Playing For Time* (1991)★★★.

HILL, DAN

b. Daniel Hill Jnr., 3 June 1954, Toronto, Ontario, Canada. Hill achieved success when a soft ballad co-written by Hill and Barry Mann, reached number 3 in 1977, and 'Can't We Try', a duet with Vonda Sheppard, climbed to number 6 in 1987. Hill and his parents moved to Canada during the 50s and he discovered music in his teens, gravitating toward vocalists such as Frank Sinatra. Hill became a professional musician at the age of 18, playing at clubs and trying to sell his demo tapes to uninterested record labels. He gradually became popular in Canada, and signed to 20th Century Fox Records in the USA. His self-titled debut album just missed the US Top 100 in 1975 and his first chart single in the US was 'Growin' Up', in 1976. But the follow-up introduced Hill to a larger audience. It was the president of the publishing company for which he worked who teamed him with Mann, resulting in the success of 'Sometimes When We Touch'. Hill's album, *Longer Fuse*, which included that single, was also his biggest seller, reaching number 21 in 1977. The Hill-Mann collaboration was followed by a few lesser chart singles for Hill and it seemed he had disappeared from the music scene in the early 80s after recording two albums for Epic Records. In 1987, however, he collaborated with female singer Vonda Sheppard and returned to the Top 10. Hill placed one further single in the chart in early 1988 and had Top 10 hits in *Billboard*'s 'Adult' chart that year with 'Carmelia' and in 1990 with 'Unborn Heart'.

●ALBUMS: *Dan Hill* i (20th Century 1975)★★, *Longer Fuse* (20th Century 1977)★★★, *Hold On* (20th Century 1978)★★, *Frozen In The Night* (20th Century 1978)★★, *If Dreams Had Wings* (Epic 1980)★★, *Partial Surrender* (Epic 1981)★★, *Dan Hill* ii (Columbia 1987)★★.

●COMPILATIONS: *The Best Of Dan Hill* (20th Century 1980)★★★.

HILLAGE, STEVE

b. 2 August 1951, England. Guitarist Hillage played with Uriel in December 1967 alongside Mont Campbell (bass), Clive Brooks (drums) and Dave Stewart (organ). This trio carried on as Egg when Hillage went to college. He returned to music in April 1971, forming Khan with Nick Greenwood (bass), Eric Peachey (drums) and Dick Henningham. Dave Stewart also joined but they had little success and split in October 1972. Hillage then joined Kevin Ayers' touring band Decadence, before linking up with French-based hippies Gong, led by Ayers' ex-Soft Machine colleague Daevid Allen. Hillage injected much-needed musicianship into the band's blend of mysticism, humour and downright weirdness. In 1975 he released his first solo album *Fish Rising*, recorded with members from Gong, which marked the start of his writing partnership with long-time girlfriend Miquette Giraudy.

On leaving Gong in 1976, Hillage developed his new age idealism on the successful *L*, produced by Todd Rundgren, and featuring Rundgren's Utopia. *Motivation Radio* utilized the synthesizer skills of Malcom Cecil, of synthesizer pioneer group Tonto's Expanding Headband, and included an inspired update of Buddy Holly's 'Not Fade Away'. *Live Herald* featured one side of new studio material which developed a funkier feel on *Open* in 1979. *Rainbow Dome Musick* was an instrumental experiment

in ambient atmospherics. In the 80s, Hillage moved into production work, including albums by Robin Hitchcock and Simple Minds. In 1991 Hillage returned to recording and live performance as the leader of System 7, a loose aggregation of luminaries including disc jockey Paul Oakenfield, Alex Paterson of the Orb and Mick MacNeil of Simple Minds. As the line-up would suggest, System 7 produce ambient dance music, combining house beats with progressive guitar riffs and healthy bursts of soul and disco.

●ALBUMS: *Fish Rising* (Virgin 1975)★★★, *L* (Virgin 1976)★★★, *Motivation Radio* (Virgin 1977)★★★, *Green* (Virgin 1978)★★★, *Live Herald* (Virgin 1979)★★★, *Open* (Virgin 1979)★★★, *Rainbow Dome Musick* (Virgin 1979)★★★, *For To Next/And Not Or* (Virgin 1983)★★★, *System 7* (Ten 1991)★★★★.

HILLMAN, CHRIS

b. 4 December 1942, Los Angeles, California, USA. Originally a mandolin player of some distinction, Hillman appeared in the Scottsville Squirrel Barkers, the Blue Diamond Boys and the Hillmen before Jim Dickson offered him the vacant bassist's role in the fledgling Byrds in late 1964. The last to join that illustrious group, he did not emerge as a real force until 1967's *Younger Than Yesterday*, which contained several of his compositions. His jazz-influenced wandering bass lines won him great respect among rock *cognoscenti* but it soon became clear that he harked back to his country roots. After introducing Gram Parsons to the Byrds, he participated in the much-acclaimed *Sweetheart Of The Rodeo* and went on to form the highly respected Flying Burrito Brothers. A line-up with Stephen Stills in Manassas and an unproductive period in the ersatz supergroup Souther Hillman Furay Band was followed by two mid-70s solo albums of average quality. A reunion with Roger McGuinn and Gene Clark in the late 70s proved interesting but short-lived. During the 80s, Hillman recorded two low budget traditional bluegrass albums, *Morning Sky* and *Desert Rose*, before forming the excellent and highly successful Desert Rose Band. They enjoyed considerable but diminishing success and the unit folded in 1993. Hillman and Herb Pederson worked as a duo in the mid-90s and released a traditional flavoured album *Bakersfield Bound* in 1996.

●ALBUMS: *Slippin' Away* (Asylum 1976)★★★, *Clear Sailin'* (Asylum 1977)★★, *Morning Sky* (Sugar Hill 1981)★★★, *Desert Rose* (Sugar Hill 1984)★★★, with Herb Pederson *Bakersfield Bound* (Sugar Hill 1996)★★★, with Pedersen, Tony Rice, Larry Rice *Out Of The Woodwork* (Rounder 1996)★★★.

HODGKINSON, COLIN

b. 14 October 1945, Peterborough, England. Hodgkinson is a self-taught bass player who turned professional with a jazz trio in 1966. In 1969 he began a long association with Alexis Korner, during which time they played in everything from a duo to a big band. In 1972

Hodgkinson and Ron Aspery (reeds) took time off in Yorkshire to write music. The two were joined by drummer Ron Hicks in the trio Back Door in which Hodgkinson had an opportunity to display his amazing technical facility. The band toured Europe and the USA and played at the Montreux Jazz Festival. In 1978 he began another long association, this time with Jan Hammer. Though he had written a lot for Back Door, with Hammer he writes lyrics more than tunes. In the late 80s he also played with Brian Auger's Blues Reunion and in the mid-90s was constantly working, touring at times with various versions of the Spencer Davis Group. Hodgkinson is one of the few people who can make the solo bass sound quite unlike any other instrument. His solo version of 'San Francisco Bay Blues' is breathtakingly original.

●ALBUMS: with Alexis Korner *New Church* (1970)★★★, *Back Door* (1972)★★★, with Jan Hammer *Black Sheep* (1979)★★★, *Hammer* (1980)★★★, *Here To Stay* (1982)★★★, *City Slicker* (1986)★★★.

HOPKINS, NICKY

b. 24 February 1944, London, England, d. 6 September 1994, California, USA. A classically trained pianist at the Royal Academy Of Music, Hopkins embraced rock 'n' roll in 1960 when, inspired by Chuck Berry, he joined the Savages, a seminal pre-Beatles group led by Screaming Lord Sutch. In 1962 Hopkins accompanied singer Cliff Bennett and his Rebel Rousers during a residency at Hamburg's *Star Club*, before becoming a founder-member of Cyril Davies' R&B All Stars. The unit's debut release, 'Country Line Special', now regarded as a classic of British blues, owes much of its urgency to the pianist's compulsive technique. A lengthy spell in hospital undermined Hopkins' career, but he re-emerged in 1965 as one of the country's leading session musicians (although he was frequently referred to as the greatest unknown in popular music). His distinctive fills were prevalent on releases by the Who, Dusty Springfield, Tom Jones and the Kinks, the latter of whom paid tribute with 'Session Man' from *Face To Face*. Hopkins later released a version of that group's 'Mr. Pleasant', before completing the novelty-bound *Revolutionary Piano Of Nicky Hopkins*. Sterling contributions to *Their Satanic Majesties Request* established a rapport with the Rolling Stones which continued over successive releases including *Let It Bleed* (1969), *Exile On Main Street* (1972) and *Black And Blue* (1976). His distinctive piano opens the Stones' 'We Love You'.

Tired of unremitting studio work, the pianist joined the Jeff Beck Group in October 1968, but left the following year to augment the Steve Miller Band. After moving to California, Hopkins switched to the Quicksilver Messenger Service with whom he completed two albums, including *Shady Grove*, which featured his lengthy solo *tour de force*, 'Edward, The Mad Shirt Grinder'. This epithet reappeared on *Jammin' With*

Edward, an informal session dating from the Stones' *Let It Bleed* sessions, belatedly issued in 1971. Hopkins was also a member of Sweet Thursday, a studio-based group that included guitarist Jon Mark, before completing a second solo album, *The Tin Man Was A Dreamer* with assistance from George Harrison, Mick Taylor and Klaus Voorman. He also sessioned on John Lennon's *Imagine* and worked on countless albums by other rock stars of the 60s and 70s. His contribution to Jefferson Airplane's *Volunteers* was among his finest sessions. In 1979 Hopkins joined Night, a group that also featured vocalist Chris Thompson (ex-Manfred Mann's Earth Band) and future Pretenders and Paul McCartney guitarist Robbie McIntosh. However, the pianist left the line-up following the release of their debut album, returning to session playing by contributing to Ron Wood's 1981 release, *1,2,3,4*. As a resident of California his subsequent activities included informal work with local Bay Area musicians including fellow expatriate Pete Sears (former member of Jefferson Starship) and Merrell Fankhauser. Hopkins continued to be dogged by ill health in the 90s, his death coming on 6 September 1994 after complications following further stomach surgery.

●ALBUMS: *The Revolutionary Piano Of Nicky Hopkins* (CBS 1966)★★, *The Tin Man Was A Dreamer* (Columbia 1973)★★, *No More Changes* (1976)★★.

HOT CHOCOLATE

This highly commercial UK pop group was formed in Brixton, London, by percussionist Patrick Olive (b. 22 March 1947, Grenada), guitarist Franklyn De Allie and drummer Ian King. Songwriter/vocalist Errol Brown (b. 12 November 1948, Kingston, Jamaica) and bassist Tony Wilson (b. 8 October 1947, Trinidad, Jamaica) and pianist Larry Ferguson (b. 14 April 1948, Nassau, Bahamas) joined later in 1969. Following the departure of De Allie the group was signed to the Beatles' label Apple for an enterprising reggae version of the Plastic Ono Band's 'Give Peace A Chance'. They also provided label-mate Mary Hopkin with the hit 'Think About Your Children'. The following year, Hot Chocolate signed to Mickie Most's RAK label and again proved their songwriting worth by composing Herman's Hermits hit 'Bet Yer Life I Do'. In September 1970, Hot Chocolate enjoyed the first hit in their own right with the melodic 'Love Is Life'. Over the next year, they brought in former Cliff Bennett guitarist Harvey Hinsley (b. 19 January 1948, Northampton, England) and replacment drummer Tony Connor (b. 6 April 1948, Romford, Essex, England) to bolster the line-up. The Brown-Wilson songwriting team enabled Hot Chocolate to enjoy a formidable run of UK Top 10 hits including 'I Believe (In Love)', 'Brother Louie' (a US number 1 for Stories), 'Emma', 'A Child's Prayer', 'You Sexy Thing', 'Put Your Love In Me', 'No Doubt About It', 'Girl Crazy', 'It Started With A Kiss' and 'What Kinda Boy You Looking For (Girl)'. In the summer of 1987, they scored a number 1 UK hit with the Russ Ballard song 'So You Win Again'. Although Wilson had left in 1976, the group managed to sustain their incredible hit run. However, the departure of their shaven-headed vocalist and songwriter Errol Brown in 1987 was a much more difficult hurdle to overcome and it came as little surprise when Hot Chocolate's break-up was announced. Brown went on to register a hit with 'Personal Touch', and completed two albums.

●ALBUMS: *Cicero Park* (RAK 1974)★★, *Hot Chocolate* (RAK 1975)★★, *Man To Man* (RAK 1976)★★, *Every 1's A Winner* (RAK 1978)★★★, *Going Through The Motions* (RAK 1979)★★, *Class* (RAK1980)★★, *Mystery* (RAK 1982)★★, *Love Shot* (RAK 1983)★★.

●COMPILATIONS: *Hot Chocolate's Greatest Hits* (RAK 1976)★★, *20 Hottest Hits* (EMI 1979)★★★, *The Very Best Of Hot Chocolate* (EMI 1987)★★★, *Their Greatest Hits* (EMI 1993)★★★. Solo: Errol Brown *That's How Love Is* (Warners 1989)★★, *Secret Rendevous* (1992)★★.

●VIDEOS: *Greatest Hits* (Video Collection 1985), *Very Best Of* (Video Collection 1987).

HOT GOSSIP

Ostensibly a risqué dance troupe, Hot Gossip also made it to number 6 in the UK charts in November 1978 with the preposterous space fantasy, 'I Lost My Heart To A Starship Trooper'. The follow-up single was credited to Sarah Brightman And The Starship Troopers. Hot Gossip were formed by dance teacher Arlene Phillips, and appeared regularly at Maunkbury's nightclub in London before being spotted by the director of the *Kenny Everett Television Show* who was looking for a 'racier version of Pan's People'. Hot Gossip were best known thereafter for the inclusion of future Andrew Lloyd-Webber wife Sarah Brightman. Other members of the group included Chrissie Wickham, Floyd, Roy Gayle, Richard Lloyd King, Jane Newman, Julia Redburn, Kim Leeson, Perry Lister, Debbie Ash, Virginia Hartley and Alison Hierlehy. That list includes members from several different line-ups, including the splinter group Spinooch. Most subsequently returned to careers as dancers in West End shows, though Gayle, a British aerobic champion, retained his involvement in music by singing with London soul band Frank The Cat. Lister was briefly married to Billy Idol.

HOT TUNA

This US group represented the combination of two members of the Jefferson Airplane, Jack Casady (b. 13 April 1944, Washington, DC, USA; bass) and Jorma Kaukonen (b. 23 December 1940, Washington, DC, USA; guitar/vocals). The group evolved as a part-time extension of the Airplane with Kaukonen and Casady utilizing the services of colleagues Paul Kantner (guitar) and Spencer Dryden (drums) and other guests, displaying their talents as blues musicians. Stage appearances were initially integrated within the Airplane's performances on the same bill. During one of the

Airplane's rest periods, the duo began to appear in their own right, often as a rock trio with then Airplane drummer, Joey Covington. Having the name Hot Shit rejected, they settled on Hot Tuna and released a self-titled debut as a duo, with a guest appearance from harmonica player, Will Scarlet. Kaukonen has since rejected this stating that 'age-old rumors that we planned to call it Hot Shit are completely unfounded'. The set was drawn largely from traditional blues/ragtime material by Jelly Roll Morton and the Rev. Gary Davis, with Casady's booming and meandering bass lines interplaying superbly with Kaukonen's fluid acoustic guitar. By the time of their second album, another live set, they were a full-blown rock quartet with the addition of violinist Papa John Creach and Sammy Piazza on drums. This line-up displayed the perfect combination of electric and acoustic rock/blues for which Casady and Kaukonen had been looking. Creach had departed by the time *The Phosphorescent Rat* was recorded, and Piazza, who had left to join Stoneground was replaced by Bob Steeler in 1974. The music became progressively louder, so that by the time of their sixth album they sounded like a rumbling heavy rock traditional ragtime blues band. Kaukonen's limited vocal range added to this odd concoction, but throughout all this time the group maintained a hardcore following. In the late 70s the duo split, resulting in Casady embarking on an ill-advised excursion into what was perceived as 'punk' with SVT. Kaukonen continued with a solo career combining both electric and acoustic performances. At best Hot Tuna were excitingly different, at worst they were ponderous and loud. Selected stand-out tracks from their erratic repertoire were 'Mann's Fate' from *Hot Tuna*, 'Keep On Truckin'' and 'Sea Child' from *Burgers*, 'Song From The Stainless Cymbal' from *Hoppkorv*, and 'Hit Single #1' from *America's Choice*. Casady and Kaukonen reunited in 1991 with a workmanlike album that found little favour with the record-buying public.

●ALBUMS: *Hot Tuna* (RCA 1970)★★★, *First Pull Up Then Pull Down* (RCA 1971)★★★, *Burgers* (Grunt 1972)★★★★, *The Phosphorescent Rat* (Grunt 1973)★★, *America's Choice* (Grunt 1974)★★★, *Yellow Fever* (Grunt 1975)★★, *Hoppkorv* (Grunt 1976)★★★, *Double Dose* (Grunt 1978)★★★, *Final Vinyl* (Grunt 1980)★★★, *Splashdown* (Relix 1985)★★, *Pair A Dice Found* (Epic 1991)★★, *Live At Sweetwater* (1993), *Historic* (Relix 1993)★★, *Classic Electric* (Relix 1996), *Acoustic Hot Tuna* (Relix 1996).

●COMPILATIONS: *Trimmed And Burning* (Edsel 1994)★★★★, *Hot Tuna In A Can* 5-CD tin (Rhino 1996)★★★★.

HOTLEGS

This UK studio group was formed in 1970 and featured Kevin Godley (b. 7 October 1945, Manchester, England; vocals/drums), Lol Creme (b. 19 September 1947, Manchester, England; vocals/guitar) and Eric Stewart

(b. 20 January 1945, Manchester, England; vocals/guitar). Godley had previously played in the Mockingbirds, while Stewart was a former member of both Wayne Fontana And The Mindbenders and the Mindbenders. While working at Stewart's Strawberry Studios, the group completed a track, which caught the attention of Philips Records managing director, Dick Leahy. The result was a highly original UK Top 10 single 'Neanderthal Man' and an album, *Thinks School Stinks*. The group then returned to the studio, where they formed the nucleus of 10cc. Godley And Creme later enjoyed further success as a duo.

●ALBUMS: *Thinks School Stinks* (Fontana 1970)★★.

HOYLE, LINDA

Formerly lead vocalist with progressive act Affinity, Hoyle embarked on a brief solo career in 1971. *Pieces Of Me* is a superb showcase for the singer's dynamic style. Aided by guitarist Chris Spedding and Karl Jenkins (oboe), Jeff Clyne (bass) and John Marshall (drums) from Nucleus, Hoyle exhibits her grasp of a wide range of material, notably through interpretations of Laura Nyro's 'Lonely Women' and Nina Simone's 'Backlash Blues'. However, Hoyle opted to leave music following her marriage to Pete King, former musical director to saxophonist Ronnie Scott.

●ALBUMS: *Pieces Of Me* (Vertigo 1971)★★★.

HUDSON, KEITH

b. 1946, Kingston, Jamaica, West Indies, d. 14 November 1984, New York, USA. As a youth, Hudson attended Boys Town School where his fellow pupils included Bob Marley, Delroy Wilson, Ken Boothe and the Heptones, with whom he organized school concerts. From an early age, he was a sound system fanatic, and became an ardent follower of Coxsone Dodd's Downbeat. He also came to know members of the Skatalites, and gained entry to Studio One recording sessions by carrying Don Drummond's trombone. He was only 14 years old when he produced his first recording, an instrumental featuring members of the Skatalites which eventually saw release with a blank label in 1968, and two years later was re-used for Dennis Alcapone's 'Shades Of Hudson'. After leaving school, he served an apprenticeship in dentistry, and subsidized his early recordings with money earned from these skills. In late 1967, he opened his Inbidimts label with Ken Boothe's 'Old Fashioned Way', which subsequently became a number 1 in Jamaica. Over the next two years he released hits by Delroy Wilson ('Run Run') and John Holt ('Never Will I Hurt My Baby'). In 1970 he began to feature himself as a vocalist with 'Working Like A Slave' and 'Don't Get Confused', which caused a sensation at the time. Over the next two years, he had hits with U-Roy's 'Dynamic Fashion Way', Alton Ellis' 'Big Bad Boy', Dennis Alcapone's 'The Sky's The Limits', Big Youth's 'S.90 Skank' and Soul Syndicate's 'Riot', and released a host of other singles on his Imbidimts, Mafia, Rebind and other labels. His willingness to experiment was evident on U Roy's 'Dynamic Fashion Way', on which he re-employed the 'Old Fashioned Way' rhythm, added a string bass to lay a new bass-line, and over-dubbed saxophone to totally transform the track. For 'S.90 Skank' he arranged for a motorcycle to be surreptitiously brought into Byron Lee's recording studio so that he could record it being revved-up. It created such an impact on motorcycle-mad Jamaica that Coxsone Dodd, Lee Perry and other producers were soon wheeling motorcycles into their recording sessions.

In 1972 Hudson released his first LP, *Furnace*, on his Imbidimts label, which featured four songs by himself, together with DJ, instrumental and dub tracks. He followed this with *Class And Subject*, and though he continued to record other artists, from this point in time he concentrated on his own career. In 1973 he emigrated to London, issuing *Entering The Dragon*, which showed him continuing to experiment and develop, even if the results at this stage were inconsistent. In particular, his practice of utilizing one rhythm track for two or more different songs on one album was an innovation that only fully entered the reggae mainstream some ten years later. In 1974 he released *Flesh Of My Skin, Blood Of My Blood*, which still stands as a masterpiece. Sandwiched between two atmospheric instrumentals was a series of uplifting laments set to bare, understated rhythms, that sounded like nothing that had preceded them and nothing that has followed them, forcefully conveying not only a feeling of pain and oppression, but also an iron resolve to endure and defeat those obstacles. There were two further stunning releases in 1975: *Torch of Freedom* and *Pick A Dub*. The latter is simply one of the greatest dub albums ever issued, featuring versions of his classic singles plus covers of the Abyssinians' 'Satta Massa Gana' and 'Declaration Of Rights'. It also included both the vocal and dub cuts of his cover of the Dramatics' Stax hit, 'In The Rain', on which he makes the song wholly his own. *Torch Of Freedom* was another one-off stroke of genius, featuring an understated, introverted sound with a distinct soul influence for a series of songs on the theme of love, before eventually changing its focus for the final song, the visionary title track.

In 1976 he moved to New York and signed a four-year contract with Virgin Records, who had followed Islands' lead in signing reggae acts in response to increased interest in the music, primarily from a new, predominantly white audience. If Hudson had released a strong mainstream reggae album at this juncture, then he would probably have become at least as big a star as Burning Spear or Dennis Brown. However, Hudson's insatiable desire to keep moving artistically and try new things compelled him to follow his own direction, and what he duly delivered to Virgin was a fully blown soul album, *Too Expensive*. Virgin marketed it along with their reggae releases, but it sounded so out of step with prevailing tastes and expectations that it received a savaging at the hands of the press, and generated poor sales. In fact, it is a strong album let down only by two poor tracks and an irritating, thin saxophone sound. The reaction to the album severely strained Hudson's relationship with Virgin, and he released his next single, '(Jonah) Come Out Now', under the pseudonym of Lloyd Linberg on his wryly titled Tell A Tale label. Hudson had moved on again, returning to reggae and re-using the rhythm he had previously employed for 'The Betrayer' to build a classic track. Virgin were evidently underwhelmed by their artist's intention to make each album entirely different, and they terminated Hudson's contract. In October, he released another excellent single in Jamaica, 'Rasta Country', before starting Joint, his new label in New York.

In 1977 a dub album, Brand (aka The Joint) was issued, followed the next year by its companion vocal set, Rasta Communication, which included 'Rasta Country' and a remade 'Jonah'. The brilliant, militant songs, outstanding rhythms and inspired playing made both of these albums masterpieces. An unusual feature enhancing several tracks was the excellent slide guitar work of Willy Barratt, who added a ghostly shimmer to the sound. In 1979, he again preceded his new vocal album with its dub counterpart, but Nuh Skin Up Dub and From One Extreme To Another were less inspired than their predecessors and were marred by overuse of in-vogue synth-drums. Nevertheless, they still contained some fine music. That year, Hudson also issued a strong DJ album to back Brand, Militant Barry's Green Valley. 1981's Playing It Cool proved an excellent set, featuring new songs built over six of his earlier rhythms. In 1982 the disappointing Steaming Jungle was released. In early 1984 rumours circulated that Keith was recording with the Wailers in New York, but nothing was ever released. In August he was diagnosed as having lung cancer. He received radiation therapy, and appeared to be responding well to the treatment, but on the morning of 14 November he complained of stomach pains, collapsed and died. Very little of his music remains on catalogue, and at the time of writing not one of his albums has been released on compact disc. Hopefully this situation will change, and allow his music to be appreciated by a wider audience.

●ALBUMS: Class And Subject (1972)★★★, Entering The Dragon (1973)★★★, Flesh Of My Skin, Blood Of My Blood (Mamba 1974)★★★, Furnace (Imbidimts 1974)★★★, Torch Of Freedom (Altra 1975)★★★, Too Expensive (Virgin 1976)★★★, Rasta Communication (Joint 1978)★★★★, From One Extreme To Another (1979)★★, Playing It Cool (1981)★★★★, Steaming Jungle (1982)★★. Dub ●ALBUMS: Pick A Dub (1975)★★★, Brand/The Joint (Joint 1977)★★★★, Nuh Skin Up Dub (1979)★★. Productions: Militant Barry Green Valley (1979)★★★★. Various Furnace (1972)★★★, The Big J Of Reggae covers 1970-75 (1978)★★★, Studio Kinda Cloudy covers 1967-72 (Trojan 1988)★★★.

HUDSON-FORD

With the follow-up to their Ivor Novello award-winning composition, 'Part Of The Union', only a minor hit, UK-born bass guitarist John Ford and drummer Richard Hudson left the Strawbs in 1973 to try their luck as a duo. Though each of their albums spawned a UK Top 40 placing - 'Pick Up The Pieces', 'Burn Baby Burn' and 'Floating In The Wind' - each sold less than its predecessor, and lack of fan commitment to Hudson-Ford per se forced disbandment after a tour to promote Worlds Collide - on which Hudson played lead guitar. The pair were joined onstage by drummer Ken Laws and, on keyboards, Chris Parren who, with members of If, had assisted during the Worlds Collide sessions at Ringo Starr's Ascot studio. 1979 brought Ford and Hudson's belated and cynical crack at punk as the Monks - and a royalty-earning chart run with 'Nice Legs Shame About Her Face'. In 1989, Hudson was heard on a re-formed Strawbs album, Don't Say Goodbye.

●ALBUMS: Nickelodeon (A&M 1973)★★★, Free Spirit (A&M 1974)★★★, Worlds Collide (A&M 1975)★★★.

HUES CORPORATION

Formed in 1969 in Los Angeles, California, USA. Their name was taken as a pun on the Howard Hughes billion dollar corporation. They had been performing for five years when their biggest hit, 'Rock The Boat', arrived. The vocal trio consisted of Hubert Ann Kelly (b. 24 April 1947, Fairchild, Alabama, USA; soprano), St. Clair Lee (b. Bernard St. Clair Lee Calhoun Henderson, 24 April 1944, San Francisco, California, USA; baritone) and Fleming Williams (b. Flint, Michigan, USA; tenor). Their first record, 'Goodfootin'', was recorded for Liberty Records in 1970 but failed to hit. They signed with RCA Records in 1973 and made the charts with a song called 'Freedom For The Stallion'. 'Rock The Boat', originally a forgotten album track, was released in 1974 as the next single and reached number 1 in the US pop charts and number 6 in the UK, becoming one of the first significant disco hits. Tommy Brown (b. Birmingham, Alabama, USA), replaced Williams after the single hit and their only other chart success came later that same year with 'Rockin' Soul', which peaked at number 18 in the US chart and reached the Top 30 in the UK. The group continued to record in to the late 70s, but they were unable to sustain their early success. However, in 1983 'Rock The Boat' made another chart appearance when Forrest took the single to the UK Top 5 position.

●ALBUMS: Freedom For The Stallion (RCA 1974)★★, Love Corporation (RCA 1975)★★, I Caught Your Act (Warners 1977)★★, Your Place Or Mine (Warners 1978)★★.

HULL, ALAN

b. 20 February 1945, Newcastle-upon-Tyne, England, d. 17 November 1995. Alan Hull's career began as a founder-member of the Chosen Few, a Tyneside beat group which also included future Ian Dury pianist, Mickey Gallagher. Hull composed the four tracks constituting their output, before leaving to become a nurse and sometime folk singer. In 1967 Alan founded Downtown Faction, which evolved into Lindisfarne. This popular folk rock act had hit singles with 'Meet Me On The Corner' and the evocative latter-day classic 'Lady Eleanor', both of which Hull wrote (the latter for his wife). Their first two albums were critical and commercial successes. *Pipedream*, Hull's fine debut album, was recorded with assistance from many members of Lindisfarne, in 1973. Its content was more introspective than that of his group and partly reflected on the singer's previous employment in a mental hospital. Although Hull continued to lead his colleagues throughout the 70s and 80s, he pursued a solo career with later releases *Squire* and *Phantoms*, plus a one-off release on the Rocket label as Radiator, a group formed with the assistance of Lindisfarne drummer Ray Laidlaw. None of these albums were able to achieve the same degree of success as *Pipedream*, the second decade proved more low-key, including some time spent in local politics (he was a committed socialist), resulting in only one collection, *On The Other Side*. The live recording *Back To Basics* was a mixture of his great compositions such as the cruelly poignant 'Winter Song' and the previously mentioned 'Lady Eleanor' together with more recent material including the powerful yet beautiful ode to Mother Russia 'This Heart Of Mine'. Hull carved a small but solid niche as one of the UK's leading troubadours. He was still very active in the 90s performing his familiar catalogue to a small but loyal following throughout the UK. Known to be fond of a drink or three, he died when he had a heart attack on the way the back from his local pub. His final album was ironically one that could have seen his work re-appraised. The posthumous *Statues And Liberties* contained some excellent songs such as 'Statues & Liberties' and 'Treat Me Kindly'. His passionate voice was still intact. Hull never wasted a lyric, every line was meant to count, and even if we sometimes failed to understand, his intention was always honest and true, dark and humourous. His work deserves to endure.

●ALBUMS: *Pipedream* (Charisma 1973)★★★★, *Squire* (Warners 1975)★★★, with Radiator *Isn't It Strange* (Rocket 1977)★★★, *Phantoms* (Rocket 1979)★★★, *On The Other Side* (Black Crow 1983)★★★, *Another Little Adventure* (Black Crow 1988)★★★, *Back To Basics* (Mooncrest 1994)★★★, *Statues And Liberties* (Transatlantic 1996)★★★★.

●FURTHER READING: *The Mocking Horse*, Alan Hull.

HUMBLE PIE

An early example of the 'supergroup', Humble Pie was formed in April 1969 by Peter Frampton (guitar/vocals, ex-Herd), Steve Marriott (guitar/vocals, ex-Small Faces) and Greg Ridley (b. 23 October 1943, Carlisle, Cumbria, England; bass, ex-Spooky Tooth). Drummer Jerry

Shirley (b. 4 February 1952) completed the original line-up which had a UK Top 5 hit with its debut release, 'Natural Born Bugie'. The quartet's first two albums blended the single's hard-rock style with several acoustic tracks. Having failed to consolidate their early success, Humble Pie abandoned the latter, pastoral direction, precipitating Frampton's departure. He embarked on a prosperous solo career in October 1971, while his former colleagues, now bolstered by former Colosseum guitarist Dave Clempson, concentrated on wooing US audiences. This period was best captured on *Smokin'*, the group's highest ranking UK chart album. Humble Pie latterly ran out of inspiration and, unable to escape a musical rut, broke up in March 1975. Marriott then formed Steve Marriott's All Stars, which latterly included both Clempson and Ridley, while Shirley joined a new venture, Natural Gas. Tragically, Marriott died on 20 April 1991, following a fire at his Essex home.

●ALBUMS: *As Safe As Yesterday Is* (Immediate 1969)★★★, *Town And Country* (Immediate 1969)★★★, *Humble Pie* (A&M 1970)★★★, *Rock On* (A&M 1971)★★★, *Performance - Rockin' The Fillmore* (A&M 1972)★★, *Smokin'* (A&M 1972)★★, *Eat It* (A&M 1973)★★, *Thunderbox* (A&M 1974)★, *Street Rats* (A&M 1975)★, *On To Victory* (Jet 1980)★, *Go For The Throat* (Jet 1981)★.

●COMPILATIONS: *Crust Of Humble Pie* (EMI 1975)★★, *The Humble Pie Collection* (Castle 1994)★★★.

100 PROOF AGED IN SOUL

This short-lived quartet was formed in Detroit around Steve Mancha (b. Clyde Wilson, 25 December 1945, Walhalla, South Carolina, USA), Joe Stubbs, Don Hatcher and Eddie Anderson. The group was the culmination of several individual careers. Joe Stubbs, the brother of Four Tops' singer Levi, was the featured voice on the Falcons' hit, 'You're So Fine', prior to his spells in the Originals and the Contours. Mancha had recorded several solo singles and was a member of the Holidays, with Eddie Anderson. 100 Proof made its soul chart debut with 'Too Many Cooks (Spoil The Soup)' in 1969. The nursery-rhyme simplicity of 'Somebody's Been Sleeping' gave them a US Top 10 hit the following year. '90 Day Freeze' (1971) introduced a revamped group of Mancha, Hatcher, Ron Bykowski, Dave Case and Darnell Hughes, which remained intact until their outlet, Hot Wax, was wound down. Mancha revived his solo career under his real name as a gospel singer and also became involved in production work. A new 100 Proof appeared in 1976, but none of the original cast was involved.

●ALBUMS: *Somebody's Been Sleeping In My Bed* (Hot Wax 1970)★★★.

●COMPILATIONS: *Greatest Hits* (HDH/Fantasy 1990)★★★★.

HUNTER, IAN

b. 3 June 1946, Shrewsbury, Shropshire, England. Having served a musical apprenticeship in several contrasting groups, Hunter was employed as a contract songwriter when approached to audition for a new act recently signed by Island Records. Initially known as Silence, the band took the name Mott The Hoople on his installation and Hunter's gravelly vocals and image-conscious looks - omnipresent dark glasses framed by long Dylanesque curly hair - established the vocalist/pianist as the group's focal point. He remained their driving force until 1974 when, having collapsed from physical exhaustion, he left the now-fractious line-up to begin a career as a solo artist. Late-period Mott guitarist Mick Ronson quit at the same time and the pair agreed to pool resources for particular projects. Ronson produced and played on *Ian Hunter*, which contained the singer's sole UK hit, 'Once Bitten Twice Shy'. Having toured together as Hunter/Ronson with Peter Arnesen (keyboards), Jeff Appleby (bass) and Dennis Elliott (drums), the colleagues embarked on separate paths. *All American Alien Boy* contained contributions from Aynsley Dunbar, David Sanborn and several members of Queen, but despite several promising tracks, the set lacked the artist's erstwhile passion. *Overnight Angels* continued this trend towards musical conservatism, although Hunter aligned himself with the punk movement following a period of seclusion by producing *Beyond The Valley Of The Dolls* for Generation X. *You're Never Alone ...* marked his reunion with Ronson and subsequent live dates were commemorated on *Ian Hunter Live/Welcome To The Club* which drew material from their respective careers. Hunter's output during the 80s was minimal and in 1990 he resumed his partnership with Mick Ronson on *YUI Otra*. He made an appearance at the 1992 Freddy Mercury Aids benefit and in 1995 was once again tempted out of retirement to front Ian Hunter's Dirty Laundry, which featured ex-Crybabys Darrell Barth and Honest John Plain, plus Vom (ex-Doctor And The Medics), Casino Steele (ex-Hollywood Brats) and Glen Matlock (ex-Sex Pistols).

●ALBUMS: *Ian Hunter* (Columbia 1975)★★★, *All American Alien Boy* (Columbia 1976)★★, *Overnight Angels* (Columbia 1977)★★, *You're Never Alone With A Schizophrenic* (Chrysalis 1979)★★★, *Ian Hunter Live/Welcome To The Club* double album (Chrysalis 1980)★★★, *Short Back And Sides* (Chrysalis 1981)★★★, *All Of The Good Ones Are Taken* (Chrysalis 1983)★★★, with Mick Ronson *YUI Orta* (Mercury 1990)★★★, as Ian Hunter's Dirty Laundry *Ian Hunter's Dirty Laundry* (Norsk 1995)★★★, *The Artful Dodger* (Citadel 1997)★★★.

●COMPILATIONS: *Shades Of Ian Hunter* (Columbia 1979)★★★★, *The Collection* (Castle 1991)★★★, *The Very Best Of* (Columbia 1991)★★★.

●FURTHER READING: *Diary Of A Rock 'N' Roll Star*, Ian Hunter.

HUTCHINGS, ASHLEY

b. 26 January 1945, Southgate, Middlesex, England. Although largely remembered as the founder-member of Fairport Convention, where he was often afforded the nickname 'Tyger', Hutchings also went on to form Steeleye Span in 1970. He played on the first four Fairport Convention albums, ending with the classic *Liege And Lief*. Hutchings had grown unhappy with the increase in original material that the group was playing, at the expense of more traditional works. While with Fairport Convention he contributed to their one hit record, 'Si Tu Dois Partir', in 1969. After three albums with Steeleye Span, Hutchings formed the Albion Country Band, in 1971, and has led a succession of Albion Band line-ups ever since. The first of these line-ups was on *No Roses*, which included a total of 26 musicians, including himself and his then wife Shirley Collins. Many of the personnel involved have worked with Hutchings on other occasions, such as John Kirkpatrick, Barry Dransfield, Nic Jones, and the late Royston Wood, formerly of Young Tradition. With Hutchings the Albion Band became the first electric group to appear in plays at London's National Theatre. The group also 'electrified' Morris dancing, exemplified in *Morris On*, and *Son Of Morris On*. Hutchings has also done much work with former Fairport Convention members, Richard Thompson, and the late Sandy Denny. Hutchings has written and presented programmes on folk music for the BBC, and both he and the Albion Band were the subject of their own BBC television documentary in 1979. More recently, Hutchings wrote and acted in his own one-man show about song collector Cecil Sharp. The show has been performed nationwide since 1984. The presentation resulted in *An Evening With Cecil Sharp And Ashley Hutchings*. Hutchings continues to tour and record. It is not undeserved that he has been called the Father of Folk Rock in the UK.

●ALBUMS: with others *Morris On* (1972)★★★★, with John Kirkpatrick *The Compleat Dancing Master* (1974)★★★, *Kicking Up The Sawdust* (1977)★★★, *An Hour With Cecil Sharp And Ashley Hutchings* (1986)★★★, *By Gloucester Docks I Sat Down And Wept* (1987)★★★, the Ashley Hutchings All Stars *As You Like It* (Making Waves 1989)★★★, *A Word In Your Ear* (1991)★★★.

●COMPILATIONS: various artists *49 Greek Street* (1970)★★★, various artists *Clogs* (1971)★★★, with Shirley Collins *A Favourite Garland* (1974)★★★, with Richard Thompson *Guitar Vocal* (1976)★★★★, various artists *Buttons And Bows* (1984)★★★★, various artists *Buttons And Bows 2* (1985)★★★, with Sandy Denny *Who Knows Where The Time Goes?* (1985)★★★★, *The Guv'nor Vol. 1* (HTD 1994)★★★, *The Guv'nor Vol. 3* (HTD 1996).

HYMAN, PHYLLIS

b. Pittsburgh, Pennsylvania, USA, d. 30 June 1995. A singer, actress and fashion model, Hyman was one of several acts nurtured by vocalist Norman Connors. Although she had already secured a minor R&B hit with 'Baby I'm Gonna Love You' in 1976, a duet with Connors the following year, covering the Stylistics hit, 'Betcha By Golly Wow', brought the artist a wider audience. Although Hyman failed to reach the US pop Top 100, over the next 10 years she enjoyed 13 soul hits, including 'You Know How To Love Me' (1979) and 'Can't We Fall In Love Again' (1981). The latter release coincided with the singer's appearance in the Broadway musical, *Sophisticated Ladies*.

●ALBUMS: *Phyllis Hyman* (Buddah 1977)★★, *Somewhere In My Lifetime* (Arista 1979)★★★, *Sing A Song* (Buddah 1979)★★★, *You Know How To Love Me* (Arista 1979)★★★★, *Can't We Fall In Love Again* (Arista 1981)★★★★, *Goddess Of Love* (Arista 1983)★★★, *Living All Alone* (Philadelphia International 1986)★★★, *Prime Of My Life* (Philadelphia International 1991)★★★, *The Legacy Of Phyllis Hyman* (Arista 1996)★★★★.

●COMPILATIONS: *The Best Of Phyllis Hyman* (Arista 1986)★★★.

I ROY

b. Roy Reid, *c.*1949, Spanish Town, Jamaica, West Indies. With a voice like your favourite uncle telling you a slightly risqué story, I Roy, aka Roy Reid, aka Roy Senior, is one of the great originals of Jamaican music. Always the most intellectual of his peers, he arrived at the start of the 70s as an accomplished DJ with a neat line in storytelling and the ability to ride a rhythm as if it was first recorded for him and not simply 'borrowed' by him from a singer or group. He drew his name from U-Roy, the first truly popular reggae star and his first records were slightly derivative of the elder man's style, and also owed a little to another DJ pioneer, Dennis Alcapone. However, I Roy soon hit his stride and recorded a mighty series of singles for producer Gussie Clarke, including 'Black Man Time', 'Tripe Girl' and 'Magnificent Seven'. 'Brother Toby Is A Movie From London' emerged for Glen Brown; 'Dr Who' for Lee Perry and innumerable sides for Bunny Lee. His debut album *Presenting* was magnificent, collating most of his hits for Gussie Clarke. It remains a classic of its genre today. Further albums *Hell And Sorrow* and *Many Moods Of* were nearly as strong. In 1975 he became involved in an on-record slanging match with fellow DJ Prince Jazzbo, a bizarre name-calling affair that nonetheless presented the public with a new twist to such rivalries and helped maintain sales. In 1976 a liaison with producer Prince Tony Robinson brought I Roy a deal with Virgin Records and five albums were released: *General*, *Musical Shark Attack*, *World On Fire*, *Crisis Time* and *Heart Of A Lion*. By the early 80s I Roy had burnt out his lyrical store and was overtaken by younger, madder DJs. However, he is still to be found on on Ujama, the label owned by his old rival, Prince Jazzbo.

●ALBUMS: *Presenting* (Gussie/Trojan 1973)★★★★, *Hell & Sorrow* (Trojan 1974)★★★★, *Many Moods Of* (Trojan 1974)★★★★, *Truths & Rights* (Grounation 1975)★★★, with Prince Jazzbo *Step Forward Youth* (Live & Love 1975)★★★, *Can't Conquer Rasta* (Justice 1976)★★★, *Crisis Time* (Caroline/Virgin 1976)★★★, *Dread Baldhead* (Klik 1976)★★★, *Ten Commandments* (Micron 1977)★★★, *Heart Of A Lion* (Front Line 1977)★★★★, *Musical Shark Attack* (Front Line 1977)★★★, *The Best Of* (GG's 1977)★★★, *The Godfather* (Third World 1977)★★★, *The General* (Front Line 1977)★★★, *World On Fire* (Front Line 1978)★★★, *African Herbsman* (Joe Gibbs 1979)★★★, *Hotter Yatta* (Harry J 1980)★★★, *I Roy's Doctor Fish* (Imperial 1981)★★★, *Outer Limits*

(Intense/Hawkeye 1983)★★★, with Jah Woosh *We Chat You Rock* (Trojan 1987)★★★, *The Lyrics Man* (Witty 1990)★★★, with Prince Jazzbo *Head To Head Clash* (1990)★★★, *Straight To The Heart* reissue of *Truths & Rights* with four non I Roy dub tracks (Esoldun 1991)★★★.

●COMPILATIONS: *Crucial Cuts* (Virgin 1983)★★★, *Classic I Roy* (Mr. Tipsy 1986)★★★, *Crisis Time - Extra Version* (Front Line 1991)★★★, *Don't Check Me With No Lightweight Stuff (1972-75)* (Blood And Fire 1997)★★★.

IAN, JANIS

b. Janis Eddy Fink, 7 April 1951, New York, USA. A teenage prodigy, Ian first attracted attention when her early composition, 'Hair Of Spun Gold', was published in a 1964 issue of *Broadside* magazine. Performances at New York's Village Gate and Gaslight venues inspired a recording contract that began with the controversial 'Society's Child (Baby I've Been Thinking)'. Brought to national prominence following the singer's appearance on Leonard Bernstein's television show, this chronicle of a doomed, interracial romance was astonishingly mature and inspired a series of equally virulent recordings attacking the perceived hypocrisy of an older generation. Ian's dissonant, almost detached delivery, enhanced the lyricism offered on a series of superior folk-rock styles albums, notably *For All The Seasons Of Your Mind*. Later relocated in California, Janis began writing songs for other artists, but re-embraced recording in 1971 with *Present Company*. *Stars* re-established her standing, reflecting a still personal, yet less embittered, perception. The title song was the subject of numerous cover versions, while 'Jesse' provided a US Top 10 hit for Roberta Flack. *Between The Lines* contained the evocatively simple 'At Seventeen', Ian's sole US chart topper, and subsequent releases continued to reflect a growing sophistication. *Night Rains* featured two film theme songs, 'The Foxes' and 'The Bell Jar', although critics began pointing at an increasingly maudlin, self pity. The artist's impetus noticeably waned during the 80s and Janis Ian seemed to have retired from music altogether. However, she re-emerged in 1991 giving live performances and appearing on a British concert stage for the first time in 10 years. Her 1995 album *Revenge* moves firmly into smooth pop, but do not be misled for Ian's lyrics are as personal, biting and original as ever.

●ALBUMS: *Janis Ian* (Verve 1967)★★, *For All The Seasons Of Your Mind* (Verve 1967)★★★, *The Secret Life Of J. Eddy Fink* (1968)★★, *Present Company* (Capitol 1971)★★, *Stars* (Columbia 1974)★★★, *Between The Lines* (Columbia 1975)★★★★, *Aftertones* (Columbia 1976)★★★, *Miracle Row* (Columbia 1977)★★, *Night Rains* (Columbia 1979)★★, *Restless Eyes* (Columbia 1981)★★, *Breaking Silence* (1993)★★★, *Revenge* (Grapevine 1995)★★★.

●COMPILATIONS: *The Best Of Janis Ian* (Columbia 1980)★★, *Society's Child: The Anthology* (Polydor 1995)★★★, *Live On The Test 1976* (Nighttracks / Windsong 1995)★★.

●FURTHER READING: *Who Really Cares?*, Janis Ian.

IF

This ambitious, multi-instrumentalist jazz-rock ensemble made its recording debut in 1970. Leader Dick Morrissey (saxophones/flute) was already a well-established figure in UK jazz circles, having led a quartet which included Phil Seaman and Harry South. Having flirted with pop and rock through an association with the Animals and Georgie Fame, Morrissey formed this new venture with guitarist Terry Smith, J.W. Hodgkinson (vocals), Dave Quincy (alto saxophone), John Mealing (keyboards), Jim Richardson (bass) and Dennis Elliott (drums) completing the initial line-up. They recorded four powerful, if commercially moribund, albums before internal pressures undermined progress. Mealing, Richardson and Elliott - the latter of whom later joined Foreigner - abandoned the group in 1972, while by the release of If's final album in 1975 only Morrissey remained from the founding septet. Although they enjoyed great popularity in Europe, the group was never able to achieve consistent commercial success, although the saxophonist subsequently enjoyed a fruitful partnership with guitarist Jim Mullen as Morrissey/Mullen.

●ALBUMS: *If* (Capitol 1970)★★★, *If2* (Capitol 1970)★★★, *If3* (Capitol 1971)★★★, *If4* aka *Waterfall* (Capitol 1972)★★, *Double Diamond* (Capitol 1973)★★★, *Not Just Another Bunch Of Pretty Faces* (Capitol 1974)★★★, *Tea Break Is Over, Back On Your Heads* (Gull 1975)★★★.

●COMPILATIONS: *This Is If* (Capitol 1973)★★, *God Rock* (1974)★★, *Forgotten Roads: The Best Of If* (Sequel 1995)★★★.

IGGY POP

b. James Jewel Osterburg, 21 April 1947, Ypsilanti, Michigan, USA. The emaciated 'Godfather Of Punk', Iggy Pop was born just west of Detroit to an English father and raised in nearby Ann Arbor. He first joined bands while at high school, initially as a drummer, most notably with the Iguanas in 1964 where he picked up the nickname Iggy. The following year he joined the Denver blues-styled Prime Movers, but a year after that dropped out of the University Of Michigan to travel to Chicago and learn about the blues from former Howlin' Wolf and Paul Butterfield Blues Band drummer, Sam Lay. On returning to Detroit as Iggy Stooge, and further inspired after seeing the Doors, he formed the Psychedelic Stooges with Ron Asheton of the Chosen Few. Iggy was vocalist and guitarist, Asheton initially played bass, and they later added Asheton's brother Scott on drums. Before the Chosen Few, Ron Asheton had also been in the Prime Movers with Iggy. The Psychedelic Stooges made their debut on Halloween night, 1967, in Ann Arbor. The same year Iggy also made his acting debut in a long forgotten Françoise De Monierre film that also featured Nico. Meanwhile Dave Alexander joined on bass and the word 'Psychedelic' was dropped from their name. Ron switched to guitar leaving Iggy free to concentrate on singing and showmanship. The Stooges were signed to Elektra Records in 1968 by A&R man Danny Fields (later manager of the Ramones). They recorded two albums (the first produced by John Cale) for the label which sold moderately at the time but later became regarded as classics, featuring such quintessential Iggy numbers as 'No Fun' and 'I Wanna Be Your Dog'. Steven MacKay joined on saxophone in 1970 in-between the first and second albums as did Bill Cheatham on second guitar. Cheatham and Alexander left in August 1970 with Zeke Zettner replacing Alexander and James Williamson replacing Cheatham - but the Stooges broke up not long afterwards as Iggy fought a heroin problem. Stooge fan David Bowie tried to resurrect Iggy's career and helped him record *Raw Power* in London in the summer of 1972 (as Iggy and the Stooges, with Williamson on guitar, Scott Thurston on bass, and the Ashetons, who were flown in when suitable British musicians could not be found). The resultant album included the nihilistic anthem 'Search And Destroy'. Bowie's involvement continued (although his management company Mainman withdrew support because of constant drug allegations) as Iggy sailed through stormy seas (including self-admission to a mental hospital). The popular, but poor quality, live *Metallic KO* was released in France only at the time. Iggy Pop live events had long been a legend in the music industry, and it is doubtful whether any other artist has sustained such a high level of abject self destruction onstage. It was his performance on British television slot *So It Goes*, for example, that ensured the programme would never air again. After *Raw Power* there were sessions for *Kill City*, although it was not released until 1978, credited then to Iggy Pop and James Williamson. It also featured Thurston, Hunt and Tony Sales, Brian Glascock (ex-Toe Fat and later in the Motels), and others. The Stooges had folded again in 1974 with Ron Asheton forming New Order (not the same as the UK band) and then Destroy All Monsters. Steve MacKay later died from a drugs overdose and Dave Alexander from alcohol abuse. Thurston also joined the Motels. Interest was stirred in Iggy with the arrival of punk, on which his influence was evident. (Television recorded the tribute 'Little Johnny Jewel'.) In 1977 Bowie produced two studio albums - *The Idiot* and *Lust For Life* - using Hunt and Tony Sales, with Bowie himself, unheralded, playing keyboards. Key tracks from these two seminal albums include 'Night Clubbin'', 'The Passenger', and 'China Girl' (co-written with and later recorded by Bowie). Iggy also returned one of the several favours he owed Bowie by guesting on backing vocals for *Low*. In the late 70s Iggy signed to Arista Records and released some rather average albums with occasional assistance from Glen Matlock

(ex-Sex Pistols) and Ivan Kral. He went into (vinyl) exile after 1982's autobiography and the Chris-Stein produced *Zombie Birdhouse*. During his time out of the studio he cleaned up his drug problems and married. He started recording again in 1985 with Steve Jones (ex-Sex Pistols) featuring on the next series of albums. He also developed his acting career (even taking lessons) appearing in *Sid And Nancy*, *The Color Of Money*, *Hardware*, and on television in *Miami Vice*. His big return came in 1986 with the Bowie-produced *Blah Blah Blah* and his first ever UK hit single, 'Real Wild Child', a cover of Australian Johnny O'Keefe's 50s rocker. His rejuvenated *Brick By Brick* album featured Guns N'Roses guitarist Slash, who co-wrote four of the tracks, while his contribution to the *Red Hot And Blue* AIDS benefit was an endearing duet with Debbie Harry on 'Well Did You Evah?'. This was followed in 1991 by a duet with the B-52's Kate Pierson, who had also featured on *Brick By Brick*. 1993's *American Caesar*, from its jokily self-aggrandising title onwards, revealed continued creative growth, with longer spaces between albums now producing more worthwhile end results than was the case with his 80s career. Throughout he has remained the consummate live performer, setting a benchmark for at least one generation of rock musicians.

●ALBUMS: with the Stooges *The Stooges* (Elektra 1969)★★★★, with the Stooges *Fun House* (Elektra 1970)★★★★, as Iggy And The Stooges *Raw Power* (Columbia 1973)★★★★, as Iggy And The Stooges *Metallic KO* (Import 1974)★★, *The Idiot* (RCA 1977)★★★★, *Lust For Life* (RCA 1977)★★★★, with James Williamson *Kill City* (Bomp 1978)★★★, *TV Eye Live* (RCA 1978)★★, *New Values* (Arista 1979)★★, *Soldier* (Arista 1980)★★, *Party* (Arista 1981)★★, *Zombie Birdhouse* (Animal 1982)★★, *Blah Blah Blah* (A&M 1986)★★★, *Instinct* (A&M 1988)★★, *Brick By Brick* (Virgin 1990)★★★, *American Caesar* (Virgin 1993)★★★, *Naughty Little Doggie* (Virgin 1996)★★★.

●COMPILATIONS: *Choice Cuts* (RCA 1984)★★★, *Compact Hits* (A&M 1988)★★★, *Suck On This!* (Revenge 1993)★★, *Live NYC Ritz '86* (Revenge 1993)★★, *Best Of ... Live* (MCA 1996)★★, *Nude & Rude: The Best Of ...* (Virgin 1996)★★★★, *Pop Music* (BMG/Camden 1996)★★★.

●FURTHER READING: *The Lives And Crimes Of Iggy Pop*, Mike West. *I Need More: The Stooges And Other Stories*, Iggy Pop with Anne Wehrer. *Iggy Pop: The Wild One*, Per Nilsen and Dorothy Sherman.

INGRAM, LUTHER

b. Luther Thomas Ingram, 30 November 1944, Jackson, Tennessee, USA. This singer-songwriter's professional career began in New York with work for producers Jerry Leiber and Mike Stoller. Several unsuccessful singles followed, including 'I Spy For The FBI', which failed in the wake of Jamo Thomas's 1966 hit version. Ingram then moved to Koko Records, a tiny independent label later marketed by Stax. Ingram's career flourished in the wake of this arrangement. With Mack Rice he helped compose 'Respect Yourself' for the Staple Singers, while several of his own releases were R&B hits. The singer's finest moment came when his 1972 recording of the classic Homer Banks, Raymond Jackson and Carl Hampton song, '(If Loving You Is Wrong) I Don't Want To Be Right'. This tale of infidelity was later recorded by Rod Stewart, Millie Jackson and Barbara Mandrell, but neither matched the heart-breaking intimacy Ingram brought to his superb original version. It went on to sell over a million copies and reached number 3 in the US pop charts. The haunting 'I'll Be Your Shelter (In Time Of Storm)' then followed as the artist proceeded to fashion a substantial body of work. His undoubted potential was undermined by Koko's financial problems, but after eight years in the commercial wilderness, Ingram returned to the R&B chart in 1986 with 'Baby Don't Go Too Far'.

●ALBUMS: *I've Been Here All The Time* (Koko 1972)★★, *(If Loving You Is Wrong) I Don't Want To Be Right* (Koko 1972)★★★, *Let's Steal Away To The Hideaway* (Koko 1976)★★★, *Do You Love Somebody* (Koko 1977)★★, *It's Your Night* (QWest 1983)★★, *Luther Ingram* (Profile 1986)★★, *It's Real* (Warners 1989)★★.

INNER CIRCLE

Inner Circle first emerged in the early 70s, comprising brothers Ian and Roger Lewis (guitars) and three future members of Third World, Stephen 'Cat' Coore, Ritchie Daley and Michael 'Ibo' Cooper. As Third World reassembled, the Lewis brothers recruited drummer Calvin McKenzie, keyboard players Charles Farquharson and Bernard 'Touter' Harvey. Together they won the prestigious 'Best Band Contest' on the *Johnny Golding Show*. Although they later enjoyed moderately successful album sales and a hit single, 'I See You', it wasn't until the brothers brought in singer Jacob 'Killer' Miller that they became a viable commercial proposition. Miller, a child prodigy, who had created a series of classic roots records ('Tenement Yard', 'Forward Jah Jah Children') before joining Inner Circle, was somewhat rotund, and the Lewis brothers were hardly skinny either: the trio made a formidable, imposing combination. Early albums showed the band fusing dancefloor rhythms and reggae to reasonable success. However, in 1976 they signed to Capitol Records releasing two albums for the label, *Reggae Thing* and *Ready For The World*, rising rapidly up the reggae hierarchy in the process. At one point Miller was more popular in Jamaica than Bob Marley, the band playing the now-legendary Peace Concert in 1978 above him on the bill.

Everything Is Great, their first album for Island gave the band an overdue international hit with its title song, and its disco rhythms made it a huge seller in Europe. 'Stop Breaking My Heart' was also a hit single, and *New Age Music* consolidated their position. However, disaster struck in 1980 when Jacob Miller was killed in a car crash. The remainder of Inner Circle quit, with the

Lewis brothers and Harvey eventually opening a studio in Miami. In 1987 the band got itchy feet, and recorded an album for RAS, *One Way*, with new singer Carlton Coffey. US dates were critically acclaimed, and the band, with the addition of Lance Hall (drums) and Lester Adderley (guitar), signed to WEA/Metronome. *Identified*, their first LP for the label, brought the band to wider recognition with 'Bad Boys', which was employed as the theme to the US television series *Cops*. In 1993 pop success eventually returned with 'Sweat (A La La La La Long)', a catchy, upbeat single from the *Bad To the Bone* album. Bright, unsentimental, and thoroughly professional, Inner Circle deserve their long overdue success.

●ALBUMS: *Dread Reggae Hits* (Top Ranking 1973)★★★, *Heavy Reggae* (Top Ranking 1974)★★★, *Blame It On The Sun* (Trojan 1975)★★★, *Rock The Boat* (Trojan 1975)★★★, *Reggae Thing* (Capitol 1976)★★★, *Ready For The World* (Capitol 1977)★★★, *Everything Is Great* (Island 1978)★★★★, *New Age Music* (Island 1979)★★★, *One Way* (RAS 1987)★★★, *Identified* (Warners 1989)★★★★, *Bad To The Bone* (RAS 1993)★★★.

●COMPILATIONS: *Reggae Greats* (Island 1985)★★★.

ISLAND RECORDS

Chris Blackwell, the son of a wealthy plantation owner and Crosse and Blackwell food family, founded this label in Jamaica in 1961. Its early, low-key singles were imported into Britain where several were subsequently issued by Starlite. Blackwell opened a UK office the following year, instigating the famed 'WI' (West Indian) prefix with Lord Creator's 'Independent Jamaica'. Island's ensuing releases included material by the Maytals, Jackie Edwards and the Skatalites and over the next four years they encompassed the shift in styles from jump R&B, through ska, to rock steady. In 1963 Island secured the UK rights to the New York-based Sue label and although the agreement was later rescinded, the appellation was kept as an outlet for material licensed from a variety of sources, including Vee Jay, Ace and Kent. Although most of its recordings were distributed independently, Island enjoyed a marketing agreement with Fontana. Thus, their first chart success - Millie's 'My Boy Lollipop' (1964) - bore the latter's label, a feature also prevalent on their first pop signing, the Spencer Davis Group. Such diversification was later shown by releases on Island by Wynder K. Frog, the V.I.Ps (later Spooky Tooth) and Kim Fowley, but the company did not undertake a fully fledged switch to rock until 1967 and the formation of Traffic, which Blackwell also managed. The group achieved three UK Top 10 hits but, more importantly, also established Island as a force within the nascent album market. Having assigned its West Indian catalogue to Trojan, the label now welcomed many of the era's best-loved 'underground' acts, including Jethro Tull, Fairport Convention and Free, and by 1970 was firmly established as one of Britain's leading labels. Judicious production deals with companies including Chrysalis, Bronze and EG, brought further success with, among others, Roxy Music, King Crimson and Uriah Heep, but Island's eminent position was undermined later in the decade when several such enterprises themselves opted for independence. Blackwell developed a reputation for nurturing talent and persevering with his artists. John Martyn was with Island for many years, although major success eluded him. Cat Stevens by contrast became one of the most successful singer-songwriters of the 70s. By this point the company had exhumed its interest in Jamaican music with the Wailers' *Catch A Fire*. Island's relationship with group leader Bob Marley, which was maintained until his death, was largely responsible for introducing reggae into the rock mainstream. By the late 70s the company's diverse catalogue included the Chieftains, Inner Circle and Eddie And The Hot Rods, but a flirtation with punk act the Slits incurred the wrath of Blackwell, who returned from a recently founded US office to take charge of UK operations. U2 became the label's most impressive signing of this period, but long-time artists Robert Palmer and Stevie Winwood also enjoyed considerable success, while Island was also responsible for transforming Grace Jones from cult act into international star. The departure of all three individuals was another major blow, but Island nonetheless boasted a roster including Tom Waits, the Christians, Julian Cope and Anthrax at the time of its 25th Anniversary celebrations in 1987. However, two years later, Blackwell sold his company to A&M, ending Island's tenure as an independent outlet. In the 90s Island continued to maintain its reggae and hip hop reputation although it was the Cranberries that became the label's strongest act. In 1996 Wille Nelson became the first ever country artist to sign to the label.

●COMPILATIONS: *Island Story* (Island 1987)★★★, *Island Life* (Island 1988)★★★.

ISLEY BROTHERS

Three brothers, O'Kelly (b. 25 December 1937, d. 31 March 1986), Rudolph (b. 1 April 1939) and Ronald Isley (b. 21 May 1941) began singing gospel in their hometown of Cincinnati, USA, in the early 50s, accompanied by their brother Vernon, who died in a car crash around 1957. Moving to New York the following year, the trio issued one-shot singles before being signed by the RCA Records production team, Hugo And Luigi. The Isleys had already developed a tight vocal unit, with Rudolph and O'Kelly supporting Ronald's strident tenor leads in a call-and-response style taken directly from the church. The self-composed 'Shout' - with a chorus based on an ad-libbed refrain which had won an enthusiastic response in concert - epitomized this approach, building to a frantic crescendo as the brothers screamed out to each other across the simple chord changes. 'Shout' sold heavily in the black market, and has since become an R&B standard, but RCA's attempts to concoct

a suitable follow-up were unsuccessful. The group switched labels to Wand in 1962, where they scored a major hit with an equally dynamic cover of the Top Notes' 'Twist And Shout', an arrangement that was subsequently copied by the Beatles. In the fashion of the times, the Isleys were forced to spend the next two years recording increasingly contrived rewrites of this hit, both on Wand and at United Artists. A brief spell with Atlantic Records in 1964 produced a classic R&B record, 'Who's That Lady?', but with little success. Tired of the lack of control over their recordings, the Isleys formed their own company, T-Neck Records, in 1964 - an unprecedented step for black performers. The first release on the label, 'Testify', showcased their young lead guitarist, Jimi Hendrix, and allowed him free rein to display his virtuosity and range of sonic effects. But the record's experimental sound went unnoticed at the time, and the Isleys were forced to abandon both T-Neck and Hendrix, and sign a contract with Motown Records. They were allowed little involvement in the production of their records and the group were teamed with the Holland/Dozier/ Holland partnership, who effectively treated them as an extension of the Four Tops, and fashioned songs for them accordingly. This combination reached its zenith with 'This Old Heart Of Mine' in 1966, a major hit in the USA, and a belated chart success in Britain in 1968. UK listeners also reacted favourably to 'Behind A Painted Smile' and 'I Guess I'll Always Love You' when they were reissued at the end of the 60s. Such singles were definitive Motown; a driving beat, an immaculate house band and several impassioned voices. But although the Isleys' records always boasted a tougher edge than those by their stablemates, little of their work for Motown exploited their gospel and R&B heritage to the full.

Tired of the formula and company power games, the Isley's reactivated T-Neck in 1969 along with a change of image from the regulation mohair suits to a freer, funkier 'west coast' image, reflected in their choice of repertoire. At this point too, they became a sextet, adding two younger brothers, Ernie (b. 7 March 1952; guitar) and Marvin (bass) as well as a cousin, Chris Jasper (keyboards). While their mid-60s recordings were enjoying overdue success in Britain, the Isleys were scoring enormous US hits with their new releases, notably 'It's Your Thing' and 'I Turned You On'. These records sported a stripped-down funk sound, inspired by James Brown And The JBs, and topped with the brothers' soaring vocal harmonies. They issued a succession of ambitious albums in this vein between 1969 and 1972, among them a live double set which featured extended versions of their recent hits, and *In The Beginning*, a collection of their 1964 recordings with Jimi Hendrix.

In the early 70s, the Isleys incorporated a variety of rock material by composers like Bob Dylan, Stephen Stills and Carole King into their repertoire. Their dual role as composers and interpreters reached a peak in

1973 on *3+3*, the first album issued via a distribution agreement with CBS Records. The record's title reflected the current make-up of the group, with the three original vocalists supported by a new generation of the family, Ernie (guitar/drums), Marvin and Chris Jasper. Ernie Isley's powerful, sustained guitarwork, strongly influenced by Jimi Hendrix, became a vital ingredient in the Isleys' sound, and was featured heavily on the album's lead single, 'That Lady', a revamped version of their unheralded 1964 single on Atlantic. *3+3* also contained soft soul interpretations of material by Seals And Croft, James Taylor and the Doobie Brothers. An important key track was the Isleys' own 'Highway Of My Life', which demonstrated Ronald's increasing mastery of the romantic ballad form.

Having established a winning formula, the Isleys retained it through the rest of the 70s, issuing a succession of slick, impressive soul albums which were divided between startlingly tough funk numbers and subdued Ronald Isley ballads. *The Heat Is On* in 1975 represented the pinnacle of both genres: the angry lyrics of 'Fight The Power', a US Top 10 single, contrasted sharply with the suite of love songs on the album's second side, aptly summarized by the title of one of the tracks, 'Sensuality'. 'Harvest For The World' (1976) proved to be one of the Isleys' most popular recordings in Britain, with its stunning blend of dance rhythm, melody and social awareness. This song hit the charts in 1988 with the Christians. In the late 70s, the increasing polarization of the rock and disco markets ensured that while the Isleys continued to impress black record buyers, their work went largely unheard in the white mainstream. 'The Pride', 'Take Me To The Next Phase', 'I Wanna Be With You' and 'Don't Say Goodnight' all topped the specialist black music charts without registering in the US Top 30, and the group responded in kind, concentrating on dance-flavoured material to the exclusion of their ballads. 'It's A Disco Night', a UK hit in 1980, demonstrated their command of the idiom, but a growing sense of self-parody infected the Isleys' music in the early 80s. Conscious of this decline, Ernie and Marvin Isley and Chris Jasper left the group in 1984 to form the successful Isley, Jasper, Isley combination. The original trio soldiered on, but the sudden death of O'Kelly Isley from a heart attack on 31 March 1986 brought their 30-year partnership to an end. Ronald and Rudolph dedicated their next release, *Smooth Sailin'*, to him, and the album produced another black hit in Angela Wimbush's ballad, 'Smooth Sailin' Tonight'. Wimbush now assumed virtual artistic control over the group, and she wrote and produced their 1989 release *Spend The Night,* which was effectively a Ronald Isley solo album. The artistic innovations of the Isley Brothers, continued by the second generation of the family in Isley/Jasper/Isley, belie the conservatism of their releases since the late 70s. Their 1996 release *Mission To Please* attempted to move them into the same smooth urban soul field as Keith Sweat and Babyface. The group represented the apogee of gospel-inspired soul on their early hits; pioneered the ownership of record labels by black artists; and invented a new funk genre with their blend of dance rhythms and rock instrumentation in the early 70s. Their series of US hits from the 50s to the 90s is one of the major legacies of black American music.

●ALBUMS: *Shout* (RCA Victor 1959)★★★, *Twist And Shout* (Wand 1962)★★★★, *The Fabulous Isley Brothers-Twisting And Shouting* (1964)★★, *Take Some Time Out-The Famous Isley Brothers* (United Artists 1964)★★, *This Old Heart Of Mine* (Tamla 1966)★★, *Soul On The Rocks* (Tamla 1967)★★, *It's Our Thing* (T-Neck 1969)★★★, *Doin' Their Thing* (Tamla 1969)★★★, *The Brothers: Isley* (T-Neck 1969)★★★, *Live At Yankee Stadium* (T-Neck 1969)★★, *Get Into Something* (T-Neck 1970)★★★, *Givin' It Back* (T-Neck 1971)★★★, *Brother Brother Brother* (T-Neck 1972)★★★, *Live* (T-Neck 1972)★★★, *3+3* (T-Neck 1973)★★★★, *Live It Up* (T-Neck 1974)★★★, *The Heat Is On* (T-Neck 1975)★★★★, *Harvest For The World* (T-Neck 1976)★★★, *Go For Your Guns* (T-Neck 1977)★★★, *Showdown* (T-Neck 1978)★★★, *Winner Takes All* (T-Neck 1979)★★★, *Go All The Way* (T-Neck 1980)★★★, *Grand Slam* (T-Neck 1981)★★★, *Inside You* (T-Neck 1981)★★★, *The Real Deal* (T-Neck 1982)★★★, *Between The Sheets* (T-Neck 1983)★★★, *Masterpiece* (Warners 1985)★★★, *Smooth Sailin'* (Warners 1987)★★★, *Spend The Night* (Warners 1989)★★, *Tracks Of Life* (Warners 1992)★★★, *Live* (1993)★★, *Mission To Please* (Island 1996)★★.

●COMPILATIONS: *In The Beginning* (1970)★★, *Rock Around The Clock* (1975)★★, *Super Hits* (Motown 1976)★★★, *Forever Gold* (Epic 1977)★★★★, *The Best Of The Isley Brothers* (United Artists 1978)★★★, *Timeless* (Epic 1979)★★★, *Let's Go* (Stateside 1986)★★, *Greatest Motown Hits* (Motown 1987)★★★, *Beautiful Ballads* (Epic Legacy 1995)★★, *Funky Family* (Epic Legacy 1995)★★, *Early Classics* (Spectrum 1996)★★★, *The Complete UA Sessions* (EMI 1996)★★★.

IT'S A BEAUTIFUL DAY

This San Francisco-based unit centred on the virtuoso skills of violinist David LaFlamme, formerly of Dan Hicks And His Hot Licks. Patti Santos (b. 16 November 1949, d. 1989; vocals), Hal Wagenet (guitar), Linda LaFlamme (b. 5 April 1941: keyboards), Mitchell Holman (bass) and Val Fluentes (drums) completed the line-up which won a major recording contract in the wake of its appearance on Cream's farewell concert bill. *It's A Beautiful Day* was marked by the inclusion of 'White Bird', the haunting opening track with which the act is inexorably linked. The instrumental 'Bombay Calling' and 'Wasted Union Blues' were other stand-out tracks. Elsewhere, a pot-pourri of musical styles revealed their undoubted versatility, a facet continued on *Marrying Maiden*. However, the appeal of the leader's extravagant soloing quickly paled as numerous departures undermined an early sense of purpose, rendering later releases, *Choice Quality Stuff* and *Live At Carnegie Hall* superfluous. LaFlamme later abandoned his creation as a protracted lawsuit with former manager Matthew Katz destroyed any lingering enthusiasm. Late period members Bud Cockrell (bass) and David Jenkins (guitar) resurfaced in Pablo Cruise, while both LaFlamme and Santos enjoyed low-key solo careers. The violinist briefly resuscitated the band in 1978 under the sarcastic title It Was A Beautiful Day. Santos was killed in a car accident in 1989.

●ALBUMS: *It's A Beautiful Day* (Columbia 1969)★★★, *Marrying Maiden* (Columbia 1970)★★, *Choice Quality Stuff/Anytime* (Columbia 1971)★★, *It's A Beautiful Day At Carnegie Hall* (Columbia 1972)★★, *It's A Beautiful Day ... Today* (Columbia 1973)★, *1001 Nights* (Columbia 1974)★★.

●COMPILATIONS: *It's A Beautiful Day* (Columbia 1979)★★.

JACK THE LAD

This offshoot of Lindisfarne, comprising Billy Mitchell (guitar/vocals), Simon Cowe (guitar/vocals), Ray Laidlaw (drums) and Rod Clements (bass), was formed in 1973. The quartet recorded some rock 'n' jig material with Maddy Prior's vocals, before Clements left for session and production work. Ian Walter Fairburn (fiddle) and Phil Murray (bass) were recruited for *The Old Straight Track*, a song cycle of 'Geordie' electric folk songs. After the failure of this somewhat experimental project, the group returned to philosophical good time material, and, in 1976, signed for United Artists. Cowe assisted in the preparation of *Jackpot*, but had left before the band recorded the dense, commercial album which was produced by Tom Allom. Despite having a loyal cult following on the college and club circuit, Jack The Lad disbanded shortly after Laidlaw's departure to Radiator, playing a few farewell gigs with Eric Green on drums. In 1993, after several CD releases, and Lindisfarne's impending 25th anniversary, Jack The Lad re-formed in two forms: the original band, and as a festival act which included Mitchell, Fairburn and Murray.

●ALBUMS: *It's Jack The Lad* (Charisma 1974)★★, *The Old Straight Track* (Charisma 1974)★★★, *Rough Diamonds* (Charisma 1975)★★★, *Jackpot* (United Artists 1976)★★★, *Back On The Road Again* (Mah Mah 1994)★★.

JACKS, TERRY

b. *c.*1953, Winnipeg, Canada. Jacks was a former member of the hit group Poppy Family, and a well-known session player. While working in the studio with the Beach Boys, he attempted to persuade them to record 'Le Moribund', a song about a dying man by French composer Jacques Brel. When the group declined, Jacks himself recorded the English translation by Rod McKuen, retitled 'Seasons In The Sun'. A smash hit in Canada, it subsequently reached number 1 in both the US and UK charts. Although Jacks enjoyed one further hit with a cover of Brel's 'If You Go Away', no other successes followed.

●ALBUMS: *Seasons In The Sun* (Bell 1974)★★.

JACKSON FIVE

The Jackson Five comprised five brothers, Jackie (b. Sigmund Esco Jackson, 4 May 1951), Tito (b. Toriano Adaryll Jackson, 15 October 1953), Jermaine (b. 11

December 1954), Marlon (b. 12 March 1957) and Michael Jackson (b. 29 August 1958). Raised in Gary, Indiana, USA, by their father Joe, a blues guitarist, they began playing local clubs in 1962, with youthful prodigy Michael as lead vocalist. Combining dance routines influenced by the Temptations with music inspired by James Brown, they first recorded for the Indiana-based Steeltown label before auditioning for Motown Records in 1968. Bobby Taylor recommended the group to Motown, although the company gave Diana Ross public credit for their discovery. A team of Motown writers known as the Corporation composed a series of songs for the group's early releases, all accentuating their youthful enthusiasm and vocal interplay. Their debut single for Motown, 'I Want You Back', became the fastest-selling record in the company's history in 1969, and three of their next five singles also topped the American chart. Michael Jackson was groomed for a simultaneous solo recording career, which began in 1971, followed by similar excursions for Jermaine and elder brother Jackie. As the group's appeal broadened, they became the subjects of a cartoon series on American television, *The Jackson 5*, and hosted a television special, *Goin' Back To Indiana*.

After the dissolution of the Corporation in 1971, the group recorded revivals of pop and R&B hits from the 50s, and cover versions of other Motown standards, before being allowed to branch out into more diverse material, such as Jackson Browne's 'Doctor My Eyes'. They also began to record their own compositions in the early 70s, a trend which continued until 1975, by which time they were writing and producing most of the songs on their albums.

The Jackson Five reached the peak of their popularity in Britain when they toured there in 1972, but after returning to America they suffered decreasing record sales as their music grew more sophisticated. By 1973, they had dropped the teenage stylings of their early hits, concentrating on a cabaret approach to their live performances while on record they perfected a harder brand of funk. The group's recording contract with Motown expired in 1975. Feeling that the label had not been promoting their recent records, they signed to Epic Records. Jermaine Jackson, however, who was married to the daughter of Motown boss Berry Gordy, chose to leave the group and remain with the company as a solo artist. Gordy sued the Jackson Five for alleged breach of contract in 1976, and the group were forced to change their name to the Jacksons. The case was settled in 1980, with the brothers paying Gordy $600,000, and allowing Motown all rights to the 'Jackson Five' name.

●ALBUMS: *Diana Ross Presents The Jackson 5* (Motown 1970)★★★, *ABC* (Motown 1970)★★★★, *Third Album* (Motown 1970)★★★, *Christmas Album* (Motown 1970)★★, *Maybe Tomorrow* (Motown 1971)★★, *Goin' Back To Indiana* (Motown 1971)★★, *Lookin' Through The Windows* (Motown 1972)★★★, *Skywriter* (Motown 1973)★★★, *Get It Together* (Motown 1973)★★★, *Dancing Machine* (Motown 1974)★★★, *Moving Vibrations* (Motown 1975)★★★, *Joyful Jukebox Music* (Motown 1976)★★★.

●COMPILATIONS: *Greatest Hits* (Motown 1971)★★★★, *Anthology* (Motown 1976)★★★★, *Soulstation! - 25th Anniversary Collection* 4-CD box set (Motown 1995)★★★★, *Early Classics* (Spectrum 1996)★★★.

●FURTHER READING: *Jackson Five*, Charles Morse. *The Jacksons*, Steve Manning. *Pap Joe's Boys: The Jacksons' Story*, Leonard Pitts. *The Magic And The Madness*, J. Randy Taraborrelli. *The Record History: International Jackson Record Guide* , Ingmar Kuliha.

JACKSONS

Jackie (b. Sigmund Esco Jackson, 4 May 1951, Gary, Indiana, USA), Tito (b. Toriano Adaryll Jackson, 15 October 1953, Gary), Marlon (b. Marlon David Jackson, 12 March 1957, Gary), Michael (b. Michael Joseph Jackson, 29 August 1958, Gary) and Randy Jackson (b. Steven Randall Jackson, 20 October 1962, Gary) changed their collective name from the Jackson Five to the Jacksons in March 1976, following their departure from Motown Records. At the same time, Randy Jackson replaced his brother Jermaine, handling percussion and backing vocals. The group's new recording contract with Epic offered them a more lucrative deal than they had received from Motown, though at first they seemed to have exchanged one artistic strait-jacket for another. Their initial releases were written, arranged and produced by Gamble And Huff, whose expertise ensured that the Jacksons sounded professional, but slightly anonymous. 'Enjoy Yourself' and 'Show You The Way To Go' were both major hits in the US charts, and the latter also topped the UK sales listing. The group's second album with Gamble And Huff, *Goin' Places*, heralded a definite decline in popularity. *Destiny* saw the Jacksons reassert control over writing and production, and produced a string of worldwide hit singles. 'Blame It on The Boogie' caught the mood of the burgeoning disco market, while the group's self-composed 'Shake Your Body (Down To The Ground)' signalled Michael Jackson's growing artistic maturity.

The success of Michael's first adult solo venture, *Off The Wall* in 1979, switched his attention away from the group. On *Triumph* (1980), they merely repeated the glories of their previous album, although the commercial appeal of anything bearing Michael's voice helped singles like 'Can You Feel It?', 'Heartbreak Hotel' and 'Lovely One' achieve success on both sides of the Atlantic. The Jacksons' 1981 US tour emphasized Michael's dominance over the group, and the resulting *Live* included many of his solo hits alongside the brothers' joint repertoire. Between 1981 and the release of *Victory* in 1984, Michael issued *Thriller*, the best-selling album of all time (total sales by 1992, 40 million units). When the Jacksons' own effort was released, it became apparent that he had made only token contributions to the record, and its commercial fortune suffered accordingly. 'State Of Shock', which paired Michael with Mick Jagger, was a US hit, but sold in smaller quantities than expected. Hysteria surrounded the group's 'Victory Tour' in the summer of 1984; adverse press comment greeted the distribution of tickets, and the Jacksons were accused of pricing themselves out of the reach of their black fans. Although they were joined onstage by their brother Jermaine for the first time since 1975, media and public attention was focused firmly on Michael. Realising that they were becoming increasingly irrelevant, the other members of the group began to voice their grievances in the press; as a result, Michael Jackson expressed that he would not be working with his brothers in future. The Jacksons struggled to come to terms with his departure, and it was five years before their next project was complete. *2300 Jackson Street* highlighted their dilemma: once the media realized that Michael was not involved, they effectively boycotted its release.

●ALBUMS: *The Jacksons* (Epic 1976)★★★, *Goin' Places* (Epic 1977)★★★, *Destiny* (Epic 1979)★★★★, *Triumph* (Epic 1980)★★★, *Live* (Epic 1981)★★★, *Victory* (Epic 1984)★★★, *2300 Jackson Street* (Epic 1989)★★.

JAM

This highly successful late 70s and early 80s group comprised Paul Weller (b. 25 May 1958, Woking, Surrey, England; vocals/guitar), Bruce Foxton (b. 1 September 1955, Woking, Surrey, England; bass/vocals) and Rick Buckler (b. Paul Richard Buckler, 6 December 1955, Woking, Surrey, England; drums). After gigging consistently throughout 1976, the group were signed to Polydor Records early the following year. Although emerging at the peak of punk, the Jam seemed oddly divorced from the movement. Their leader, Paul Weller, professed to voting Conservative (although he would later switch dramatically to support the Labour Party), and the group's musical influences were firmly entrenched in the early Who-influenced mod style. Their debut, 'In The City', was a high energy outing, with Weller displaying his Rickenbacker guitar to the fore. With their next record, 'All Around The World' they infiltrated the UK Top 20 for the first time. For the next year, they registered only minor hits, including 'News Of The World' (their only single written by Foxton) and a cover of the Kinks' 'David Watts'. A turning point in the group's critical fortunes occurred towards the end of 1978 with the release of 'Down In The Tube Station At Midnight'. This taut, dramatic anti-racist song saw them emerge as social commentators par excellence. *All Mod Cons* was widely acclaimed and thereafter the group rose to extraordinary heights. With *Setting Sons*, a quasi-concept album, Weller fused visions of British colonialism with urban decay and a satirical thrust at suburban life. The tone and execution of the work recalled the style of the Kinks' Ray Davies, whose class-conscious vignettes of the 60s had clearly influenced Weller. The superbly constructed 'Eton Rifles', lifted from the album, gave the Jam their first UK Top 10 single in late 1979. Early the following year, they secured their first UK number 1 with 'Going Underground', indicating the enormous strength of the group's fan base. By now they were on their way to topping music paper polls with increasing regularity. Throughout 1982, the Jam were streets ahead of their nearest rivals but their parochial charm could not be translated into international success. While they continued to log number 1 hits with 'Start' and 'Town Called Malice', the US market remained untapped. In late 1982, the group's recent run of UK chart-toppers was interrupted by 'The Bitterest Pill (I Ever Had To Swallow)' which peaked at number 2. Weller then announced that the group were to break up, and that he intended to form a new band, the Style Council. It was a shock decision, as the group were still releasing some of the best music to come out of Britain and were most certainly at their. peak. Their final single, the exuberant, anthemic 'Beat Surrender' entered the UK chart at number 1, an extraordinary conclusion to a remarkable but brief career. After the mixed fortunes of the Style Council Weller embarked on a solo career, a move Foxton made immediately after the Jam's dissolution. Buckler and Foxton worked together briefly in Time U.K., with Foxton then joining Stiff Little Fingers and Buckler retiring from the music industry as a furniture restorer. The latter two sued Weller for alleged unpaid royalties. This was resolved in 1996 when Weller purchased all remaining interests from the Foxton and Buckler.

●ALBUMS: *In The City* (Polydor 1977)★★★★, *This Is The Modern World* (Polydor 1977)★★★, *All Mod Cons* (Polydor 1978)★★★★, *Setting Sons* (Polydor 1979)★★★★, *Sound Affects* (Polydor 1980)★★★★, *The Gift* (Polydor 1982)★★★, *Dig The New Breed* (Polydor 1982)★★★, *Live Jam* (Polydor 1993)★★★.

●COMPILATIONS: *Snap!* (Polydor 1983)★★★★, *Greatest Hits* (Polydor 1991)★★★★, *Extras* (Polydor 1992)★★★, *The Jam Collection* (Polydor 1996)★★★★.

●VIDEOS: *Video Snap* (Polygram 1984)★★★, *Transglobal Unity Express* (Channel 5 1988)★★★, *Greatest Hits* (Polygram 1991)★★★, *Little Angels: Jam On Film* (1994)★★★, *The Jam Collection* (Polydor 1996)★★★★, *Direction, Reaction, Creation* 4-CD box set (Polydor 1997)★★★★.

●FURTHER READING: *The Jam: The Modern World By Numbers*, Paul Honeyford. *Jam*, Miles. *The Jam: A Beat Concerto, The Authorized Biography*, Paolo Hewitt. *About The Young Idea: The Story Of The Jam 1972-1982*, Mike Nicholls. *Our Story*, Bruce Foxton and Rick Buckler with Alex Ogg. *Keeping The Flame*, Steve Brookes.

JAMES GANG

Formed in 1967 in Cleveland, Ohio, USA, the embryonic James Gang was comprised of Glenn Schwartz (guitar/vocals), Tom Kriss (bass/vocals) and Jim Fox (drums/vocals). Schwartz left in April 1969 to join Pacific Gas And Electric, but Joe Walsh proved a more than competent replacement. *Yer Album* blended group originals with excellent interpretations of material drawn from Buffalo Springfield ('Bluebird') and the Yardbirds ('Lost Women'). The group enjoyed the approbation of Pete Townshend, who admired their mature cross-section of British and 'west coast' rock. Kriss was replaced by Dale Peters for *The James Gang Rides Again*, an excellent, imaginative amalgamation of rock, melody and instrumental dexterity. Here Walsh emerged as the group's director, particularly on the second side which also marked his maturation as a songwriter. Keyboards were added to create a dense, yet more fluid sound as the group embraced themes drawn from country and classical music. *Thirds* was another highlight, including the excellent 'Walk Away', but when a retreat to hard rock proved unconvincing, Walsh quit to pursue solo ambitions. He later found fame as a member of the Eagles. Two Canadians - Roy Kenner (vocals) and Dom Troiano (guitar) - joined Fox and Peters for *Straight Shooter* and *Passin' Thru*, but both sets were viewed as disappointing. Troiano was then replaced by Tommy Bolin, formerly of Zephyr, whose exemplary technique provided new bite and purpose. *Bang*, which featured eight of the newcomer's songs, was a marked improvement, but still lacked the verve and conviction of the Walsh era. *Miami*, released in July 1974, coincided with Bolin's departure to Deep Purple, following which the James Gang was dissolved. The ever optimistic Fox and Peters resurrected the name the following year, adding Bubba Keith (vocals) and Richard Shack (guitar), but finally dropped the name following the undistinguished *Jesse Come Home*.

●ALBUMS: *Yer Album* (BluesWay 1969)★★★, *The James Gang Rides Again* (ABC 1970)★★★★, *Thirds* (ABC 1971)★★★, *James Gang Live In Concert* (ABC 1971)★★★, *Straight Shooter* (ABC 1972)★★, *Passin' Thru'* (ABC 1972)★★, *Bang* (Atco 1974)★★, *Miami* (Atco 1974)★★, *Newborn* (Atco 1975)★★, *Jesse Come Home* (1976)★★.

●COMPILATIONS: *The Best Of The James Gang Featuring Joe Walsh* (ABC 1973)★★★, *16 Greatest Hits* (ABC 1973)★★★, *The True Story Of The James Gang* (See For Miles 1987)★★★.

JAMES, BOB

b. 23 December 1939, Marshall, Michigan, USA. James played the piano from the age of four and eventually gained an MA in Composition from the University of Michigan in 1962. He worked as musical director and accompanist with vocalist Sarah Vaughan until 1968. In 1973 Quincy Jones introduced him to Creed Taylor who was forming his CTI label. James became his arranger and producer working on albums with Dionne Warwick, Roberta Flack, Eric Gale, Grover Washington and Quincy Jones, as well as producing four solo works. In 1976 he moved to CBS as Director of Progressive

A&R and worked with musicians as diverse as Joanne Brackeen and Santamaria. In 1986 James worked with saxophonist David Sanborn on *Double Vision*. James has also written musical scores for Broadway and for films including *The Selling Of The President* and *Serpico*. The television series *Taxi* used 'Angela' from the 1978 *Touchdown* as its theme.

●ALBUMS: *One* (CTI 1974)★★, *Two* (CTI 1975)★★, *Three* (CTI 1976)★★, *BJ4* (CTI 1977)★★, *Heads* (Tappan Zee 1977)★★, *Touchdown* (Tappan Zee 1978)★★★, *Lucky Seven* (Tappan Zee 1979)★★★, *One On One* (Tappan Zee 1979)★★★, *H* (Tappan Zee 1980)★★★, *All Around The Town* (Tappan Zee 1981)★★★, *Sign Of The Times* (Tappan Zee 1981)★★★, *Hands Down* (Tappan Zee 1982)★★★, *Two Of A Kind* (Capitol 1982)★★★, *The Genie* (Columbia 1983)★★★, *Foxie* (Tappan Zee 1983)★★★, *12* (Tappan Zee 1984)★★★, *Double Vision* (Warners 1986)★★★, *Obsession* (Warners 1986)★★★, *Ivory Coast* (Warners 1988)★★★, *Cool* (Warners 1992)★★★, with Kirk Whalum *Joined At The Hip* (Warners 1996)★★★, *Straight Up* (Warners 1996)★★★.

JAMES, JIMMY, AND THE VAGABONDS

Jimmy James (b. September 1940, Jamaica), enjoyed local success with two self-composed singles, 'Bewildered And Blue' and 'Come Softly To Me', before arriving in England in 1964. He joined the multi-racial Vagabonds - Wallace Wilson (lead guitar), Carl Noel (organ), Matt Fredericks (tenor saxophone), Milton James (baritone saxophone), Phillip Chen (bass), Rupert Balgobin (drums) and Count Prince Miller (vocals/MC) - and the new unit became a leading attraction at UK soul venues during the 60s. The group was managed and produced by the early Who mentor, Peter Meaden. Although they failed to secure a substantial chart hit, the Vagabonds' early albums were impressive, infectious re-interpretations of contemporary releases, featuring material by the Impressions, the Miracles and Bobby Bland. Such a function, however enthusiastic, lost its impetus when the original artists gained popular acclaim. 'Red Red Wine' gave the group a belated, if minor, success in 1968, but the unit was latterly dubbed *passé*. Chen later enjoyed a fruitful association with Rod Stewart, while James scored two hits in 1976 alongside another set of Vagabonds with 'I'll Go Where The Music Takes Me' and 'Now Is The Time', the latter of which reached the UK Top 5. The singer has since pursued a career as a cabaret attraction.

●ALBUMS: *The New Religion* (1966)★★★, *Open Up Your Soul* (1968)★★★, one side only *London Swings* (1968), *You Don't Stand A Chance* (Pye 1975)★★, *Now* (Pye 1976)★★, *Life* (Pye 1977)★★, *Dancin' Till Dawn* (PRT 1979)★★.

●COMPILATIONS: *This Is Jimmy James* (1968)★★★, *Golden Hour Of Jimmy James* (Golden Hour 1979)★★.

JAMES, TOMMY

b. 29 April 1947, Dayton, Ohio, USA. After the disbandment of Tommy James And The Shondells, James, the lead singer, produced New York group Alive And Kicking, whose 'Tighter And Tighter' reached the US Top 10. James himself then launched his solo career and after three minor hits, returned to the upper echelons of the chart with 'Draggin' The Line'. Although the follow-up, 'I'm Comin' Home' scraped into the *Billboard* Top 40, it was another nine years before he charted again with 'Three Times In Love'. In the meantime, he pursued a variety of club dates, trading on a healthy repertoire of past Shondells hits.

●ALBUMS: *Tommy James* (Roulette 1970)★★, *Christian Of The World* (Roulette 1971)★★, *My Head, My Bed And My Red Guitar* (Roulette 1971)★★, *In Touch* (Fantasy 1976)★, *Midnight Rider* (Fantasy 1977)★, *Three Times In Love* (Milennium 1980)★★, *A Night In Big City* (Aura 1995)★★, *Tommy James Greatest Hits Live* (Aura 1996)★★.

●COMPILATIONS: *Tommy James : The Solo Years (1970-1981)* (Rhino 1991)★★★.

JARRETT, KEITH

b. 8 May 1945, Allentown, Pennsylvania, USA. Growing up in a highly musical family, Jarrett displayed startling precocity and was playing piano from the age of three. From a very early age he also composed music and long before he entered his teens was touring as a professional musician, playing classical music and his own compositions. He continued with his studies at Berklee College Of Music in the early 60s but was soon leading his own small group. From the mid-60s he was based in New York where he was heard by Art Blakey who invited him to join his band. Jarrett stayed with Blakey for only a few months but it was enough to raise his previously low profile. In 1966 he joined Charles Lloyd's quartet which made his name known internationally, thanks to extensive tours of Europe and visits to the Soviet Union and the Far East. It was with this quartet that he befriended Jack DeJohnette. During his childhood Jarrett had also played vibraphone, saxophone, flute and percussion instruments, and he resumed performing on some of these instruments in the late 60s. In 1969 he joined Miles Davis, playing organ for a while, before turning to electric piano. This was during the jazz/fusion period and although the best music from this group was never recorded they released *Live At The Fillmore* and *Live-Evil*. By now, word was out that Jarrett was one of the most exciting new talents in the history of jazz piano. During his two years with Davis he also found time to record under his own name, enhancing his reputation with a succession of fine albums with Charlie Haden, Dewey Redman, Paul Motian and others. After leaving Davis he resumed playing acoustic piano and established a substantial following for his music, which he has described as 'uni-

versal folk music'. *Facing You* created a considerable response and was a brilliant demonstration of speed, dynamics and emotion. The now familiar Jarrett characteristic of brilliantly adding styles was first aired on this album. Country, folk, classical, blues and rock were given brief cameos, this was a remarkable solo debut. Subsequently, Jarrett has become a major figure not only in furthering his own music but in 'showing the way' for contemporary jazz and in particular the growth of ECM Records and the work of Manfred Eicher. Eicher and Jarrett complement each other like no other business partnership. Jarrett's success with huge sales of his albums enabled ECM to expand. Eicher in turn will record and release anything Jarrett wishes, such is their trust in each other. He has often worked and recorded with artists including Jan Garbarek, Gary Burton, Palle Danielsson and Jon Christensen. It is with DeJohnette and bassist Gary Peacock, he regularly returns to playing with. Known as the 'standards trio', there can be few units currently working that have such intuition and emotional feeling of each others musical talent. Albums such as *Changes*, *Standards Vol. 1* and *Vol. 2*, *Live Standards* and *The Cure* represent the finest possibilities of an acoustic jazz trio. Jarrett's greatest achievement, however, is as the master of improvised solo piano. It is in this role that Jarrett has arguably created a musical genre. His outstanding improvisational skills have led to his ability to present solo concerts during which he might play works of such a length that as few as two pieces will comprise an entire evening's music. His pivotal and often breathtaking *Solo Concerts: Bremen and Lausanne* released in 1973, received numerous accolades in the USA and Europe. Similarly in 1975 *The Koln Concert* was a huge success becoming a million plus seller. It remains his biggest selling work and is a must for any discerning music collection, even though it was recorded on a badly tuned piano. In Ian Carr's excellent biography, Jarrett explains that in addition to feeling unwell on the day of the concert the right piano did not arrive in time. Instead he had to make do by restricting his improvisation to the middle keys as the top end was shot and the bass end had no resonance. Additionally the ambitious multi-album set *The Sun Bear Concerts* are rich journeys into the improvisational unknown. Jarrett's solo improvised work has not resulted in his turning his back on composing and he has written and recorded music for piano and string orchestra resulting in albums such as *In The Light* and *The Celestial Hawk*. His interest in this form of music has added to his concert repertoire and during the 80s, in addition to solo and continuing small group jazz concerts he also played and recorded classical works. Jarrett's continuing association with ECM Records has helped advance his constantly maturing musical persona. Technically flawless, Jarrett's playing style draws upon many sources reaching into all areas of jazz while simultaneously displaying a thorough understanding of and deep feeling for the western classical form. Unquestionably one of the most dazzling improvising talents the world of music has ever known, Jarrett is also remarkable for having achieved recognition from the whole musical establishment as well as the jazz audience while also enjoying considerable commercial success.

●ALBUMS: *Life Between The Exit Signs* (Vortex 1967)★★, *Restoration Ruin* (Vortex 1968)★★, *Somewhere Before* (Atlantic 1968)★★, with Gary Burton *Gary Burton And Keith Jarrett* (Atlantic 1970)★★★, with Jack DeJohnette *Ruta And Daitya* (ECM 1971)★★★, *The Mourning Of A Star* (Atlantic 1971)★★, *Facing You* (ECM 1971)★★★★★, *Expectations* (Columbia 1972)★★★, *Fort Yawuh* (Impulse 1973)★★★, *In The Light* (ECM 1973)★★★, *Solo Concerts: Bremen And Lausanne* (ECM 1973)★★★★★, *Treasure Island* (Impulse 1974)★★★, with Jan Garbarek *Belonging* (ECM 1974)★★★★, with Garbarek *Luminessence* (ECM 1974)★★★, *Death And The Flower* (Impulse 1975)★★★, *Arbour Zena* (ECM 1975)★★★, *The Köln Concert* (ECM 1975)★★★★★, *Sun Bear Concerts* (ECM 1976)★★★★, *Mysteries* (Impulse 1976)★★★, *The Survivor's Suite* (ECM 1976)★★★★, *Silence* (Impulse 1976)★★★, *Shades* (Impulse 1976)★★★, *Byablue* (Impulse 1977)★★★, *My Song* (ECM 1977)★★★★, *Nude Ants* (ECM 1979)★★★★, *Personal Mountains* (ECM 1979)★★★, *Expectations* (Columbia 1979)★★★, *The Moth And The Flame* (ECM 1980)★★★, *The Celestial Hawk* (ECM 1980)★★★, *Invocations* (ECM 1980)★★★, *Concerts Bregenz And München* (ECM 1981)★★★★, *Concerts (Bregenz)* (ECM 1982)★★★★, *Bop-Be* (Impulse 1982)★★, *Standards Vol. 1* (ECM 1983)★★★★, *Changes* (ECM 1983)★★★, *Backhand* (Impulse 1983)★★★, *Eyes Of The Heart* (ECM 1985)★★★, *Spirits* (ECM 1985)★★★, *Standards Live* (ECM 1985)★★★★, *Sacred Hymns* (ECM 1985)★★★, *Staircase* (1985)★★★★, *Still Live* (ECM 1986)★★★, *Book Of Ways* (ECM 1986)★★★, *Hymns Spheres* (ECM 1986)★★, *Dark Intervals* (ECM 1988)★★★, *Standards Vol. 2* (ECM 1988)★★★★, *The Well Tempered Clavier Book* (ECM 1988)★★, *J.S. Bach Das Wohltemperierte Klavier Buch 1* (ECM 1988)★★★, *Changeless* (ECM 1989)★★★, *Treasure Island* (Impulse 1989)★★, *Paris Concert* (ECM 1990)★★★★, *J.S. Bach Das Wohltemperierte Klavier Buch 2* (ECM 1991)★★★★, *Tribute* (ECM 1991)★★★★, *The Cure* (ECM 1992)★★★★, *Vienna Concert* (ECM 1992)★★★★, *Bye Bye Blackbird* (ECM 1993)★★★★, with Gary Peacock, Paul Motian *At The Deer Head Inn* (ECM 1994)★★★, *Standards In Norway* (ECM 1995)★★★, *At The Blue Note* (ECM 1995)★★★★, with the Stuttgart Chamber Orchestra *W.A. Mozart Piano Concertos Nos. 21, 23, 17. Masonic Funeral Music* (ECM 1996)★★★.

●COMPILATIONS: *Best Of Keith Jarrett* (Impulse 1979)★★, *Works* (ECM 1989)★★★.

●FURTHER READING: *Keith Jarrett: The Man And His Music* Ian Carr.

JEFFERSON STARSHIP

Formerly the Jefferson Airplane, the band evolved into the Jefferson Starship after Paul Kantner (b. 17 March 1941, San Francisco, California, USA; guitar/vocals) had previously released *Blows Against The Empire* in 1970, billed as Paul Kantner And The Jefferson Starship. His fascination with science fiction no doubt led the Airplane to metamorphose into a Starship. The official debut was *Dragonfly* in 1974, which became an immediate success. The band played with a freshness and urgency that had been missing on recent Airplane releases. Joining Kantner on this album were Grace Slick (b. Grace Barnett Wing, 30 October 1939, Chicago, Illinois, USA; vocals), Papa John Creach (b. 28 May 1917, Beaver Falls, Pennsylvania, USA; violin), former Quicksilver Messenger Service bassist David Freiberg (b. 24 August 1938, Boston, Massachusetts, USA; vocals/keyboards), Craig Chaquico (b. 26 September 1954; lead guitar), ex-Turtles member John Barbata (drums) and Pete Sears (bass/keyboards). Among the tracks were 'Ride The Tiger', which was accompanied by an imaginatively graphic, early video and 'Hyperdrive', a Slick magnum opus featuring Chaquico's frantic screaming guitar. Old Airplane fans were delighted to hear Marty Balin guesting on one track with his own composition 'Caroline', and further cheered when he joined the band at the beginning of 1975. *Red Octopus* later that year became their most successful album and ended up selling several million copies and spending a month at the top of the US charts. The flagship track was Balin's beautiful and seemingly innocent 'Miracles'. This was the first known pop lyric to feature reference to cunnilingus with Balin singing 'I had a taste of the real world, when I went down on you' and Slick innocently responding in the background with 'Mmm, don't waste a drop of it, don't ever stop it'.

Soon afterwards, Kantner and Slick separated; she moved in with Skip Johnson, the band's lighting engineer, and eventually married him. Later that year Slick was regularly in the news when her drinking problems got out of control. *Spitfire* and *Earth* continued their success, although the band had now become a hard rock outfit. Balin's lighter 'Count On Me' was a US Top 10 hit in 1978. That year, Slick was asked to leave the band, to be allowed to return when she dried out. She was eventually dismissed in 1978, closely followed by Balin, who left towards the end of a turbulent year. He was replaced by Mickey Thomas and further changes were afoot when stalwart drummer Aynsley Dunbar (b. 1946, Liverpool, England) joined in place of Barbata. *Freedom From Point Zero* and the US Top 20 hit 'Jane', at the end of 1979, bore no resemblance to the musical style towards which remaining original member Kantner had attempted to steer them. He suffered a stroke during 1980, but returned the following spring together with a sober Grace Slick. Both *Modern Times* (1981) and *Winds Of Change* (1982), continued the success, although by now the formula was wearing thin. Kantner found his role had diminished and released a solo album later that year. He continued with them throughout the following year, although he was openly very unsettled.

Towards the end of 1984 Kantner performed a nostalgic set of old Airplane songs with Balin's band, amid rumours of a Jefferson Airplane reunion.

The tension broke in 1985 when, following much acrimony over ownership of the band's name, Kantner was paid off and took with him half of the group's moniker. Kantner claimed the rights to the name, although he no longer wanted to use the title, as his reunion with Balin and Casady in the KBC Band demonstrated. In defiance his former band performed as Starship Jefferson, but shortly afterwards became Starship. Both Thomas and Freiberg left during these antagonistic times, leaving Slick the remaining original member after the incredible changes of the previous few years. The new line-up added Denny Baldwin on drums and recorded *Knee Deep In The Hoopla* in 1985, which became their most successful album since *Red Octopus*. Two singles from the album, 'We Built This City' (written by Bernie Taupin) and 'Jane', both reached number 1 in the USA. The following year they reached the top spot on both sides of the Atlantic with the theme from the film *Mannequin*, 'Nothing's Gonna Stop Us Now'. Their image is now of slick perpetrators of AOR, performing immaculate music for the MTV generation (on which China Kantner was a presenter). Now, having gone full circle, Grace Slick departed in 1989 to join Kaukonen, Casady, Balin and Kantner in . . . the Jefferson Airplane. Kantner still carries the Starship banner, and in the mid-90s still had Balin and Casady in tow. A new live album was issued in 1995.

●ALBUMS: *Dragonfly* (Grunt 1974)★★★, *Red Octopus* (Grunt 1975)★★★★, *Spitfire* (Grunt 1976)★★★, *Earth* (Grunt 1978)★★, *Freedom At Point Zero* (Grunt 1979)★★, *Modern Times* (RCA 1981)★★, *Winds Of Change* (Grunt 1982)★★, *Nuclear Furniture* (Grunt 1984)★★; as Starship *Knee Deep In The Hoopla* (RCA 1985)★★, *No Protection* (RCA 1987)★★, *Love Among The Cannibals* (RCA 1989)★, *Deep Space/Virgin Sky* (Intersound 1995)★.

●COMPILATIONS: featuring Jefferson Airplane and Starship *Flight Log (1966-1976)* (Grunt 1977)★★★★, *Gold* (Grunt 1979)★★★★, *Jefferson Starship: The Collection* (1992)★★★.

JENNINGS, WAYLON

b. Wayland Arnold Jennings, 15 June 1937, Littlefield, Texas, USA. Jennings' mother wanted to christen him Tommy but his father, William Alvin, insisted that the family tradition of W.A. must be maintained. His father played guitar in Texas dance halls and Jennings' childhood hero was Ernest Tubb, with whom he later recorded. When only 12 years old, he started as a radio disc jockey and then, in Lubbock, befriended an aspiring Buddy Holly. In 1958, Holly produced his debut single 'Jole Blon' and they co-wrote 'You're The One', a Holly demo that surfaced after his death. Jennings played bass on Holly's last tour, relinquishing his seat for that fatal plane journey to the Big Bopper. Jennings named his son, Buddy, after Holly and he

recalled their friendship in his 1976 song, 'Old Friend'. Much later (1996) he contributed a poignant version of 'Learning The Game' with Mark Knopfler to the Buddy Holly tribute album *notfadeaway*. After Holly's death, Jennings returned to radio work in Lubbock, before moving to Phoenix and forming his own group, the Waylors. They began a two-year residency at a new Phoenix club, J.D's, in 1964. The album of their stage repertoire has worn well, but less satisfying was Jennings' album for A&M, *Don't Think Twice*. 'Herb Alpert heard me as Al Martino,' says Waylon, 'and I was wanting to sound like Hank Williams'. Bobby Bare heard the A&M album and recommended Jennings to record producer Chet Atkins. Jennings started recording for RCA in 1965 and made the US country charts with his first release, 'That's The Chance I'll Have To Take'. He co-wrote his 1966 country hit, 'Anita, You're Dreaming' and developed a folk-country style with 'For Loving Me'. He and Johnny Cash shared two wild years in Nashville, so it was apt that he should star in *Nashville Rebel*, a dire, quickly made film. Jennings continued to have country hits - 'Love Of The Common People', 'Only Daddy That'll Walk The Line' and, with the Kimberlys, 'MacArthur Park'. However, he was uncomfortable with session men, no matter how good they were, he felt the arrangements were overblown. He did his best, even with the string-saturated 'The Days Of Sand And Shovels', which was along the lines of Bobby Goldsboro's 'Honey'. When Jennings was ill with hepatitis, he considered leaving the business, but his drummer Richie Albright, who has been with him since 1964, talked him into staying on. Jennings recorded some excellent Shel Silverstein songs for the soundtrack of *Ned Kelly*, which starred Mick Jagger, and the new Jennings fell into place with his 1971 album, *Singer Of Sad Songs*, which was sympathetically produced by Lee Hazlewood. Like the album sleeve, the music was darker and tougher, and the beat was more pronounced. Such singles as 'The Taker', 'Ladies Love Outlaws' and 'Lonesome, On'ry And Mean' showed a defiant, tough image. The cover of *Honky Tonk Heroes* showed the new Jennings and the company he was keeping. His handsome looks were overshadowed by dark clothes, a beard and long hair, which became more straggly and unkempt with each successive album.

The new pared-down, bass-driven, no frills allowed sound continued on *The Ramblin' Man* and his best album, *Dreaming My Dreams*. The title track is marvellously romantic, while the album also included 'Let's All Help The Cowboys (Sing The Blues)', an incisive look at outlaw country with great phased guitar, 'Are You Sure Hank Done It This Way?', and a tribute to his roots, 'Bob Willis Is Still The King'. *Wanted: The Outlaws* and its hit single, 'Good Hearted Woman', transformed both Willie Nelson and Waylon Jennings' careers, making them huge media personalities in the USA. The first of the four 'Waylon And Willie' albums is the best, including the witty 'Mammas, Don't Let Your Babies

Grow Up To Be Cowboys' and 'I Can Get Off On You'. In reality, Nelson reveals a constant habit in his autobiography, while Jennings admits to 21 years' addiction in an ode bidding farewell to drugs, in his audiobiography, *A Man Called Hoss*. Jennings was tired of his mean and macho image even before it caught on with the public. He topped the US country charts for six weeks and also made the US Top 30 with a world-weary song for a small township, 'Luckenbach, Texas', which is filled with disillusionment. Further sadness followed on 'I've Always Been Crazy' and 'Don't You Think This Outlaw Bit's Done Got Out Of Hand?'. He aged quickly, acquiring a lined and lived-in face which, ironically, enhanced his image. His voice became gruffer but it was ideally suited to the stinging 'I Ain't Living Long Like This' and 'It's Only Rock & Roll'. His theme for *The Dukes Of Hazzard* made the US Top 30 but the outlaw deserved to be convicted for issuing such banal material as 'The Teddy Bear Song' and an embarrassing piece with Hank Williams Jnr., 'The Conversation'. The latter was included on *Waylon And Company*, which also featured duets with Emmylou Harris and actor James Garner. Jennings has often recorded with his wife, Jessi Colter; he and Johnny Cash had a hit with 'There Ain't No Good Chain Gang' and made an underrated album, *Heroes*. His two albums with Nelson, Cash and Kris Kristofferson as the Highwaymen were highly successful, but in early 1993 it was anounced that the quartet would no longer work together. Jennings and Cash had major heart surgery at the same time and recuperated in adjoining beds. A change to MCA and to producer Jimmy Bowen in 1985 had improved the consistency of his work, including two brilliant reworkings of Los Lobos' 'Will The Wolf Survive?' and Gerry Rafferty's 'Baker Street'. His musical autobiography, *A Man Called Hoss* (Waylon refers to everyone as 'hoss'), included the wry humour of 'If Ole Hank Could Only See Us Now'. Despite his poor health, Jennings still looks for challenges and *Waymore's Blues (Part II)* was produced by Don Was. His thought-provoking 'I Do Believe' on the *Red Hot And Country* video, showed him at his best, questioning what religion was all about. Willie and Waylon will be remembered as outlaws and certainly they did shake the Nashville establishment by assuming artistic control and heralding a new era of grittier and more honest songs. Whether they justify being called outlaws is a moot point - Jerry Lee Lewis is more rebellious than all the so-called Nashville outlaws put together. Bear Family have repackaged Jennings' recordings in a 15-album series, *The Waylon Jennings Files*, which include many previously unissued titles.
●ALBUMS: *Waylon Jennings At J.D's* (Bat 1964)★★, *Don't Think Twice* (A&M 1965)★★, *Waylon Jennings - Folk/Country* (RCA 1966)★★, *Leaving Town* (RCA 1966)★★, *Nashville Rebel* (RCA 1966)★★★, *Waylon Sings Ol' Harlan* (RCA 1967)★★, *The One And Only Waylon Jennings* (RCA 1967)★★★, *Love Of The Common People* (RCA 1967)★★, *Hangin' On* (RCA 1968)★★, *Only The Greatest* (RCA 1968)★★★, *Jewels* (RCA 1968)★★★, *Waylon Jennings* (RCA 1969)★★★, with the Kimberlys *Country Folk* (RCA 1969)★★★, *Just To Satisfy You* (RCA 1969)★★★, *Ned Kelly* soundtrack (1970)★★, *Waylon* (RCA 1970)★★★, *Singer Of Sad Songs* (RCA 1970)★★★, *The Taker/Tulsa* (RCA 1971)★★★, *Cedartown, Georgia* (1971)★★, *Good Hearted Woman* (RCA 1972)★★★, *Ladies Love Outlaws* (RCA 1972)★★★, *Lonesome, On'ry And Mean* (RCA 1973)★★★, *Honky Tonk Heroes* (RCA 1973)★★★★, *This Time* (RCA 1974)★★★, *The Ramblin' Man* (RCA 1974)★★, *Dreaming My Dreams* (RCA 1975)★★★★, *Mackntosh And T.J.* (RCA 1976)★★★, with Willie Nelson, Jessi Colter, Tompall Glaser *Wanted:The Outlaws* (RCA 1976)★★★, *Are You Ready For The Country?* (RCA 1976)★★★, *Waylon 'Live'* (RCA 1976)★★, *Ol' Waylon* (RCA 1977)★★★, with Nelson *Waylon And Willie* (RCA 1978)★★★, with Colter, John Dillon, Steve Cash *White Mansions* (1978)★★★, *I've Always Been Crazy* (RCA 1978)★★★, *The Early Years* (MCA 1979)★★, *What Goes Around Comes Around* (RCA 1979)★★★, *Waylon Music* (RCA 1980)★★★, *Music Man* (RCA 1980)★★, with Colter *Leather And Lace* (RCA 1981)★★, with Nelson *WWII* (RCA 1982)★★★, with Colter *The Pursuit Of D.B. Cooper* soundtrack (1982)★★, *Black On Black* (RCA 1982)★★, *It's Only Rock & Roll* (RCA 1983)★★★, *Waylon And Company* (RCA 1983)★★, with Nelson *Take It To The Limit* (RCA 1983)★★, *Never Could Toe The Mark* (RCA 1984)★★, *Turn The Page* (RCA 1985)★★, *Will The Wolf Survive?* (MCA 1985)★★★★, with Nelson, Johnny Cash, Kris Kristofferson, *Highwayman* (Columbia 1985)★★★, with Cash *Heroes* (Columbia 1986)★★★, *Hangin' Tough* (MCA 1987)★★★, *A Man Called Hoss* (MCA 1987)★★, *Full Circle* (MCA 1988)★★★, with Cash, Kristofferson, Nelson *Highwayman 2* (Columbia 1990)★★★, *The Eagle* (RCA 1990)★★★, with Nelson *Clean Shirt* (RCA 1991)★★, *Too Dumb For New York City - Too Ugly For L.A.* (RCA 1992)★★★, *Cowboys, Sisters, Rascals & Dirt* (RCA 1993)★★★, *Waymore's Blues (Part II)* (RCA 1994)★★, with Nelson, Cash and Kristofferson *The Road Goes On Forever* (Liberty 1995)★★, *Ol' Waylon Sings Ol' Hank* (WJ 1995)★★★, *Right For The Time* (Justice 1996)★★★.
●COMPILATIONS: *Silver Collection* (RCA 1992)★★★, *Only Daddy That'll Walk The Line* (Camden 1993)★★★, *The Essential Waylon Jennings* (RCA 1997)★★★★.
●VIDEOS: *Renegade Outlaw Legend* (1991), *The Lost Outlaw Performance* (1991), *America* (1992).
●FURTHER READING: *Waylon Jennings*, Albert Cunniff. *Waylon - A Biography*, R. Serge Denisoff. *Waylon And Willie*, Bob Allen. *The Waylon Jennings Discography*, John L. Smith (ed.).

JET

This UK group was formed in 1974 by two former members of the psychedelic pop-orientated John's Children, Andy Ellison (vocals) and Chris Townson (drums), alongside Martin Gordon (bass/vocals), David O'List (guitar - erstwhile Nice and Roxy Music member) and Peter Oxendale (keyboards). They recorded one album

that failed to set the music scene alight, despite a rigorous touring schedule. O'List once more demonstrated his inability to remain in a stable group and was later replaced by Ian McLeod. Oxendale soon followed him (to Gary Glitter's Glitter Band) supplanted by ex-Sparks guitarist Trevor White. After CBS Records' unwillingness to finance another album, Jet disintegrated in the summer of 1976. After briefly going their separate ways, the trio of Ellison, Gordon and McLeod (followed later on by White), found a new lease of life in 1977 when they regrouped as the Radio Stars.
●ALBUMS: *Jet* (Columbia 1975)★★.

JETHRO TULL

Jethro Tull was formed in Luton, England, in 1967 when Ian Anderson (b. 10 August 1947, Edinburgh, Scotland; vocals/flute) and Glenn Cornick (b. 24 April 1947, Barrow-in-Furness, Cumbria, England; bass), members of a visiting Blackpool blues group, John Evan's Smash, became acquainted with Mick Abrahams (b. 7 April 1943, Luton, Bedfordshire, England; guitar/vocals) and Clive Bunker (b. 12 December 1946, Blackpool, Lancashire, England; drums), Abrahams' colleague in local attraction, McGregor's Engine, completed the original line-up which made its debut in March the following year with 'Sunshine Day'. This commercially minded single, erroneously credited to Jethro Toe, merely hinted at developments about to unfold. A residency at London's famed Marquee club and a sensational appearance at that summer's Sunbury Blues Festival confirmed a growing reputation, while 'Song For Jeffrey', the quartet's first release for the Island label, introduced a more representative sound. Abrahams' rolling blues licks and Anderson's distinctive, stylized voice combined expertly on *This Was* - for many Tull's finest collection. Although the material itself was derivative, the group's approach was highly exciting, with Anderson's propulsive flute playing, modelled on jazzman Raahsan Roland Kirk, particularly effective. The album reached the UK Top 10, largely on the strength of Tull's live reputation in which the singer played an ever-increasing role. His exaggerated gestures, long, wiry hair, ragged coat and distinctive, one-legged stance cultivated a compulsive stage personality to the extent that, for many spectators, Jethro Tull was the name of this extrovert frontman and the other musicians merely his underlings. This impression gained credence through the group's internal ructions. Mick Abrahams left in November 1968 and formed Blodwyn Pig. When future Black Sabbath guitarist Tony Iommi proved incompatible, Martin Barre (b. 17 November 1946) joined Tull for *Stand Up*, their excellent chart-topping second album. The group was then augmented by John Evan (b. 28 March 1948; keyboards), the first of Anderson's Blackpool associates to be invited into the line-up. *Benefit* duly followed and this period was also marked by the group's three UK Top 10 singles, 'Living In The Past', 'Sweet Dream' (both 1969) and

'The Witch's Promise' (1970). Cornick then left to form Wild Turkey and Jeffrey Hammond-Hammond (b. 30 July 1946), already a legend in Tull's lexicon through their debut single, 'Jeffrey Goes To Leicester Square' and 'For Michael Collins, Jeffrey And Me', was brought in for *Aqualung*. Possibly the group's best-known work, this ambitious concept album featured Anderson's musings on organized religion and contained several tracks that remained long-standing favourites, including 'My God' and 'Locomotive Breath'.

Clive Bunker, the last original member, bar Anderson, left in May 1971. A further John Evan-era acolyte, Barriemore Barlow (b. 10 September 1949), replaced him as Jethro Tull entered its most controversial period. Although *Thick As A Brick* topped the US chart and reached number 5 in the UK, critics began questioning Anderson's reliance on obtuse concepts. However, if muted for this release, the press reviled *A Passion Play*, damning it as pretentious, impenetrable and the product of an egotist and his neophytes. Such rancour obviously hurt. Anderson retorted by announcing an indefinite retirement, but continued success in America, where the album became Tull's second chart-topper, doubtless appeased his anger. *War Child*, a US number 2, failed to chart in the UK, although *Minstrel In The Gallery* proved more popular. *Too Old To Rock 'N' Roll, Too Young To Die* marked the departure of Hammond-Hammond in favour of John Glascock (b. 1953, London, England, d. 17 November 1979), formerly of the Gods, Toe Fat and Chicken Shack. Subsequent releases, *Songs From The Wood* and *Heavy Horses*, reflected a more pastoral sound as Anderson abandoned the gauche approach marking many of their predecessors. David Palmer, who orchestrated each Tull album, bar their debut, was added as a second keyboards player as the group embarked on another highly successful phase culminating in November 1978 when a concert at New York's Madison Square Garden was simultaneously broadcast around the world by satellite. However, Glascock's premature death in 1979 during heart surgery ushered in a period of uncertainty, culminating in an internal realignment. In 1980 Anderson began a projected solo album, retaining Barre and new bassist Dave Pegg (ex-Fairport Convention), but adding Eddie Jobson (ex-Curved Air and Roxy Music; keyboards) and Marc Craney (drums). Longtime cohorts Barlow, Evan and Palmer were left to pursue their individual paths. The finished product, *A*, was ultimately issued under the Jethro Tull banner and introduced a productive period that saw two more group selections, plus Anderson's solo effort, *Walk Into Light*, issued within a two-year period. Since then Jethro Tull has continued to record and perform live, albeit on a lesser scale, using a nucleus of Anderson, Barre and Pegg. *Catfish Rising* in 1991, although a disappointing album, was a return to their blues roots. *Roots To Branches* was a return to the standard Tull progressive rock album, full of complicated time changes, and fiddly new age and Arabian intros and codas. Squire Anderson has also become a renowned entrepreneur, owning tracts of land on the west coast of Scotland and the highly successful Strathaird Salmon processing plant.

●ALBUMS: *This Was* (Chrysalis 1968)★★★★, *Stand Up* (Chrysalis 1969)★★★★, *Benefit* (Chrysalis 1970)★★★, *Aqualung* (Chrysalis 1971)★★★, *Thick As A Brick* (Chrysalis 1972)★★★, *A Passion Play* (Chrysalis 1973)★★, *War Child* (Chrysalis 1974)★★, *Minstrel In The Gallery* (Chrysalis 1975)★★★, *Too Old To Rock 'N' Roll Too Young To Die* (Chrysalis 1976)★★, *Songs From The Wood* (Chrysalis 1977)★★★, *Heavy Horses* (Chrysalis 1978)★★★, *Live - Bursting Out* (Chrysalis 1978)★★, *Storm Watch* (Chrysalis 1979)★★, *A* (Chrysalis 1980)★★, *The Broadsword And The Beast* (Chrysalis 1982)★★, *Under Wraps* (Chrysalis 1984)★★, *Crest Of A Knave* (Chrysalis 1987)★★★, *Rock Island* (Chrysalis 1989)★★, as the John Evan Band *Live '66* (A New Day 1990)★★, *Live At Hammersmith* (Raw Fruit 1990)★★, *Catfish Rising* (Chrysalis 1991)★★, *A Little Light Music* (Chrysalis 1992)★★, *Nightcap* (Chrysalis 1993)★★, *In Concert* (Windsong 1995)★★★, *Roots To Branches* (Chrysalis 1995)★★.

Ian Anderson Solo: *Walk Into Light* (Chrysalis 1983)★★, *Divinities: Twelve Dances With God* (EMI 1995)★★.

●COMPILATIONS: *Living In The Past* (Chrysalis 1972)★★★★, *M.U.: Best Of Jethro Tull* (Chrysalis 1976)★★★, *Repeat, The Best Of Jethro Tull - Volume II* (Chrysalis 1977)★★★, *Original Masters* (Chrysalis 1985)★★★, *20 Years Of Jethro Tull* 3-CD box set (Chrysalis 1988)★★★★, *25th Anniversary Box Set* 4-CD box set (Chrysalis 1992)★★★★, *The Anniversary Collection* (Chrysalis 1993)★★★.

●VIDEOS: *Slipstream* (Chrysalis 1981), *20 Years Of Jethro Tull* (Virgin 1988), *25th Anniversary Video* (PMI 1993).

JIGSAW

Barrie Bernard (b. 27 November 1944, Coventry, Midlands, England; bass), Tony Campbell (b. 24 June 1944, Rugby, Midlands, England; guitar), Des Dyer (b. 22 May 1948, Rugby, Midlands, England; vocals/drums) and Clive Scott (b. 24 February 1945, Coventry, Midlands, England; keyboards/vocals) became Jigsaw in 1966. Bernard came from Pinkerton's Assorted Colours, while Campbell had previously played in the Mighty Avengers. Scott and Dyer were a successful songwriting team - Engelbert Humperdinck covered their material - but it took the band nine years and 13 singles before their big hit, 'Sky High'. It was the theme to *The Man From Hong Kong*, and was the first release on the band's own label Splash. 'Sky High' was a worldwide hit. It was number 1 twice in Japan, thanks to a popular wrestler adopting it as his theme tune. Jigsaw enjoyed continuing success there, but elsewhere their star shone less brightly and in 1977 'If I Have To Go Away' only reached number 36 in the UK.

●ALBUMS: *Leathersdale Farm* (1970), *Sky High* (Splash 1975)★★★, *Jigsaw* (Spalsh 1977)★★★.

JO JO GUNNE

Formed by Jay Ferguson (b. John Ferguson, 10 May 1947, Burbank, California, USA; vocals/piano) and Mark Andes (b. 19 February 1948, Philadelphia, Pennsylvania, USA; bass/vocals), following their departure from Spirit in 1971. This hard rock quartet were completed by Matthew Andes (guitar/vocals) and Curly Smith (drums). Their contagious debut single 'Run Run Run' was an instant success, reaching number 6 in the UK. Shortly after, Andes was replaced by Jimmy Randall. Unfortunately, they were unable to progress musically, and their four albums are all a very similar pattern of average hard rock. *Bite Down Hard* is the most powerful album, particularly in 'Rock Around the Symbol' and 'Ready Freddy'. *Jumpin' The Gunne* featured a tacky album cover - with a photo montage depicting the band in bed together watching obese naked females flying through their window. The band broke up in 1974.

●ALBUMS: *Jo Jo Gunne* (Asylum 1972)★★★, *Bite Down Hard* (Asylum 1973)★★★★, *Jumpin' The Gunne* (Asylum 1973)★★, *So ... Where's The Show?* (Asylum 1974)★★.

JOBRAITH

b. Bruce Campbell, 1949, California, USA, d. 1985, New York, USA. In 1973 Jobraith became the first overtly gay star to be signed, and marketed as such, by a major label. Jobraith was cagey about his past, claiming to have come from Outer Space; he was in fact from California and had initially pursued a career in the theatre - he played the bisexual Woof in the LA and Broadway productions of *Hair*. Manager Jerry Brandt, who ran New York's Electric Circus, discovered Jobraith via an unsolicited demo tape. At the time of glam rock and 'bisexual chic' Brandt felt 'it's gay time and I think the world is ready for a true fairy.' David Geffen at Elektra Records reportedly paid the singer a £500,000 advance, and spent thousands on promotional stunts which included hiring the Paris Opera House for a three day showcase in December 1973. Journalists mocked this highly theatrical stage debut, and his two albums fared just as badly with press and public alike. Featuring guest appearances from Peter Frampton and Led Zeppelin's John Paul Jones, the music was a poor pastiche of David Bowie circa *The Man Who Sold The World*, and the lyrics, dependent on camp innuendo, rather than explicitly gay, were delivered in a grating fake cockney whine. Brandt dropped the group unceremoniously when they were halfway through an American tour, and Jobraith tried unsuccessfully to return to acting. By the late 70s he had moved into the Chelsea Hotel and performed a regular solo spot at a New York restaurant. He died of an AIDS-related illness in 1985.

●ALBUMS: *Jobraith* (Elektra 1973)★★, *Creatures Of The Street* (1974)★★.

JOHN, ELTON

b. Reginald Kenneth Dwight, 25 March 1947, Pinner, Middlesex, England. At the age of four, the young Reg started taking piano lessons. This launched a talent, which via the Royal Academy Of Music led him to become the most successful rock pianist in the world, one of the richest men in Britain and one of the world's greatest rock stars. John formed his first band Bluesology in the early 60s and turned professional in 1965 when they secured enough work backing touring American soul artists. Long John Baldry joined the band in 1966, which included Elton Dean on saxophone and Caleb Quaye on lead guitar. As the forceful Baldry became the leader, John became disillusioned with being a pub pianist and began to explore the possibilities of a music publishing contract. Following a meeting set up by Ray Williams of Liberty Records at Dick James Music, the shy John first met Bernie Taupin, then an unknown writer from Lincolnshire. Realizing they had uncannily similar musical tastes they began to communicate by post only, and their first composition 'Scarecrow' was completed. This undistinguished song was the first to bear the John/Taupin moniker; John had only recently adopted this name, having dispensed with Reg Dwight in favour of the more saleable title borrowed from the first names of his former colleagues Dean and Baldry.

In 1968 John and Taupin were signed by Dick James, formerly of Northern Songs, to be staff writers for his new company DJM at a salary of £10 per week. The songs were slow to take off, although Roger Cook released their 'Skyline Pigeon' and Lulu sang 'I've Been Loving You Too Long' as a potential entry for the Eurovision Song Contest. One hopes that John was not too depressed when he found that 'Boom-Bang-A-Bang' was the song chosen in its place. While the critics liked his own single releases, none were selling. Only 'Lady Samantha' came near to breaking the chart, which is all the more perplexing as it was an excellent, commercial-sounding record. In June 1969 Empty Sky was released, and John was still ignored, although the reviews were reasonably favourable. During the next few months he played on sessions with the Hollies (notably the piano on 'He Ain't Heavy He's My Brother') and made budget recordings for cover versions released in supermarkets. Finally, his agonizingly long wait for recognition came the following year when Gus Dudgeon produced the outstanding Elton John. Among the tracks were 'Border Song' and the classic 'Your Song'. The latter provided Elton's first UK hit, reaching number 2, and announced the emergence of a major talent. The momentum was maintained with Tumbleweed Connection but the following soundtrack, Friends and the live 17-11-70 were major disappointments to his fans. These were minor setbacks, as over the next few years Elton John became a superstar. His concerts in America were legendary as he donned ridiculous outfits and outrageous spectacles.

At one stage between 1972 and 1975 he had seven consecutive number 1 albums, variously spawning memorable hits including 'Rocket Man', 'Daniel', 'Saturday Night's Alright For Fighting', 'Goodbye Yellow Brick Road', 'Candle In The Wind' and the powerful would-be suicide note, 'Someone Saved My Life Tonight'.

He was partly responsible for bringing John Lennon and Yoko Ono back together again following his Madison Square Garden concert in 1975 and became Sean Lennon's godfather. In 1976 he topped the UK charts with a joyous duet with Kiki Dee, 'Don't Go Breaking My Heart', and released a further two million selling albums Here And There and Blue Moves. The phenomenal pattern continued as Elton courted most of the rock cognoscenti. Magazine articles peeking into his luxury home revealed an astonishing wardrobe, and a record collection so huge that he would never be able to listen to all of it. By 1979 the John/Taupin partnership went into abeyance as Taupin moved to Los Angeles. John started writing with pianist and bandleader Tony Osborne's son, Gary. The partnership produced few outstanding songs, however. The most memorable during that time was the solo 'Song For Guy', a beautiful instrumental written in tribute to the Rocket Records motorcycle messenger who was killed.

Elton entered an uncomfortable phase in his life; he remained one of pop's most newsworthy figures, openly admitting his bisexuality and personal insecurities about his weight and baldness. It was this vulnerability that made him such a popular personality. His consumerism even extended to rescuing his favourite football club, Watford. He purchased the club and invested money in it, and under his patronage their fortunes changed positively. His albums during the early 80s were patchy, and only when he started working exclusively with Taupin again did his record sales pick up. The first renaissance album was Too Low For Zero in 1983 which scaled the charts as did the triumphant 'I'm Still Standing'. John ended the year in much better shape and married Renate Blauel the following February. During 1985 he appeared at Wham's farewell concert, and the following month he performed at the historic Live Aid giving a particularly strong performance, now as one of rock's elder statesmen. He completed the year with another massive album, Ice On Fire. In January 1986 he and Taupin contested a lengthy court case for back royalties against DJM. However, the costs of the litigation were prohibitive and the victory at best pyrrhic. Towards the end of that year John collapsed onstage in Australia and entered an Australian hospital for throat surgery in January. During this time the UK gutter press were having a field day, speculating on John's possible throat cancer and his rocky marriage. The press had their pound of flesh when it was announced that Renate and John had separated. In 1988 he released the excellent Reg Strikes Back and the fast-tempo boogie, 'I Don't Want To Go On With You Like That'. Meanwhile, the Sun newspaper made serious allegations against the singer, which prompted a libel suit. Considering the upheavals in his personal life and regular sniping by the press John sounded in amazingly good form and was performing with the energy of his early 70s extravaganzas. In September, almost as if he were closing a chapter of his life, Elton auctioned at Sotheby's 2000 items of his personal memorabilia including his boa feathers, 'Pinball Wizard' boots and hundreds of pairs of spectacles. In December 1989, John accepted a settlement (reputedly £1 million, although never confirmed) from the *Sun*, thus forestalling one of the most bitter legal disputes in pop history. He appeared a sober figure, now divorced, he concentrated on music and recorded two more outstanding albums *Sleeping With The Past* and *The One*.

In April 1991 the *Sunday Times* announced that John had entered the list of the top 200 wealthiest people in Britain. He added a further £300,000 to his account when he yet again took on the UK press and won, this time the *Sunday Mirror*, for an alleged incident with regard to bulimia. In 1993 an array of guest musicians appeared on John's *Duets*, including Bonnie Raitt, Paul Young, k.d. lang, Little Richard and George Michael. Five new songs by the artist (written with Tim Rice) graced the soundtrack to 1994's Disney blockbuster, *The Lion King*, the accompanying album reaching number 1 in the US charts. In 1995 John confronted the media and gave a series of brave and extremely frank confessional interviews with regard to his past. He confessed to sex, drugs, food and rock 'n' roll. Throughout the revelations he maintained a sense of humour and it paid him well. By confessing, his public seemed to warm further to him. He rewarded his fans with one of his best albums, *Made In England*. With ease it scaled the charts throughout the world. With or without his now substantial wealth Elton John has kept the friendship and admiration of his friends and peers. He remains an outstanding songwriter and an underrated pianist and together with the Beatles and Rolling Stones is Britain's most successful artist of all time. He has ridden out all intrusions into his private life from the media with considerable dignity and maintained enormous popularity. Above all he is able to mock himself in down-to-earth fashion.

●ALBUMS: *Empty Sky* (DJM 1969)★★, *Elton John* (DJM 1970)★★★★, *Tumbleweed Connection* (DJM 1970)★★★★, *Friends* film soundtrack (Paramount 1971)★, *17-11-70* (DJM 1971)★★, *Madman Across The Water* (DJM 1971)★★★, *Honky Chateau* (DJM 1972)★★★★, *Don't Shoot Me I'm Only The Piano Player* (DJM 1973)★★★, *Goodbye Yellow Brick Road* (DJM 1973)★★★★, *Caribou* (DJM 1974)★★, *Captain Fantastic And The Brown Dirt Cowboy* (DJM 1975)★★★, *Rock Of The Westies* (DJM 1975)★★★★, *Here And There* (DJM 1976)★★, *Blue Moves* (Rocket 1976)★★, *A Single Man* (Rocket 1978)★★★, *London And New York* (repressing of *Here And There*, Hallmark 1978)★★, *Victim Of Love* (Rocket 1979)★★, *21 At 33* (Rocket 1980)★★, *Lady Samantha* (Rocket 1980)★★★, *The Fox* (Rocket 1981)★★, *Jump Up* (Rocket 1982)★★, *Too Low For Zero* (Rocket 1983)★★★, *Breaking Hearts* (Rocket 1984)★★, *Ice On Fire* (Rocket 1985)★★★, *Leather Jackets* (Rocket 1986)★★, *Live In Australia* (Rocket 1987)★★, *Reg Strikes Back* (Rocket 1988)★★★, *Sleeping With The Past* (Rocket 1989)★★★, *The One* (Rocket 1992)★★★, *Duets* (MCA 1993)★★, *Made In England* (Mercury/Rocket 1995)★★★★, *Live In Australia* (MCA 1996)★★.

●COMPILATIONS: *Greatest Hits* (DJM 1974)★★★★, *Greatest Hits Volume 2* (DJM 1977)★★★, *The Elton John Live Collection* (Pickwick 1979)★★, *The Elton John Box Set* (DJM 1979)★★★, *The Very Best Of Elton John* (K-Tel 1980)★★★, *The Album* (Hallmark 1981)★★, *Love Songs* (TV 1982)★★★★, *The New Collection* (Everest 1983)★★, *The New Collection Vol 2* (Premier 1984)★★, *The Very Best Of Elton John* (Rocket 1990)★★★★, *Rare Masters* (1992)★★, *Love Songs* (Mercury/Rocket 1995)★★★★.

●VIDEOS: *Live In Central Park - New York* (1986), *The Video Singles* (1987), *Night Time Concert* (1988), *Live In Australia 1 & 2* (1988), *The Afternoon Concert* (1988), *Very Best Of Elton John* (1990), *Single Man In Concert* (1991), *Live - World Tour 1992* (1993), *Live In Australia* (J2 Communications 1995).

●FURTHER READING: *Bernie Taupin: The One Who Writes The Words For Elton John: Complete Lyrics*, Bernie Taupin. *Elton John*, Cathi Stein. *A Conversation With Elton John And Bernie Taupin*, Paul Gambaccini. *Elton John*, Dick Tatham and Tony Jasper. *Elton John Discography*, Paul Sobieski. *Elton John: A Biography In Words & Pictures*, Greg Shaw. *Elton John: Reginald Dwight & Co*, Linda Jacobs. *Elton: It's A Little Bit Funny*, David Nutter. *The Elton John Tapes: Elton John In Conversation With Andy Peebles*, Elton John. *Elton John: The Illustrated Discography*, Alan Finch. *Elton John 'Only The Piano Player', The Illustrated Elton John Story*, Chris Charlesworth. *Elton John: A Biography*, Barry Toberman. *Two Rooms: A Celebration Of Elton John & Bernie Taupin*, Elton John and Bernie Taupin. *A Visual Documentary*, Nigel Goodall. *Candle In The Wind*, no author listed. *Elton John: The Biography*, Philip Norman. *The Many Lives Of Elton John*, Susan Crimp and Patricia Burstein. *The Complete Lyrics Of Elton John And Bernie Taupin*, no author listed. *Elton John: 25 Years In The Charts*, John Tobler. *Rocket Man: The Encyclopedia Of Elton John*, Claude Bernardin and Tom Stanton.

JOHNSON, LINTON KWESI

b. 1952, Chapelton, Jamaica, West Indies. Johnson's family emigrated to London in 1963, and he quickly developed a keen awareness of both literature and politics, culminating in a degree in sociology at Goldsmith's College, London, in 1973. An interest in poetry manifested itself in two books, *Voices Of The Living And The Dead* (1974) and *Dread Beat And Blood* (1975), both written in a style that put on paper the patois spoken in black Britain, often with a rhythm reminiscent of Jamaican DJs. Johnson also wrote about reggae for *New Musical Express*, *Melody Maker* and *Black Music*, as well as being writer-in-residence for the London Borough of Lambeth and heavily involved in the *Race Today* co-operative newspaper. Experiments with reggae bands at his poetry readings culminated in 1977's *Dread Beat An' Blood* recorded as Poet And The Roots, an album that virtually defined the 'dub poetry' genre. An intoxicating mixture of Johnson's lucid, plain-spoken commonsense and rhetoric, and Dennis Bovell's intriguing dub rhythms, it sold well. In 1978 Johnson changed labels from Virgin to Island and issued the strong *Forces Of Victory*, this time under his own name. Johnson became a media face, introducing radio histories of reggae and cropping up on television arts shows, but to his credit he did not exploit his position, preferring instead to remain politically active at grass roots level in Brixton, London. *Bass Culture* was a more ambitious project that met a mixed reception, with tracks including the love-chat 'Lorraine' and the title song offering a far broader sweep of subjects than his previous work. *LKJ In Dub* contained Dennis Bovell dub mixes of tracks from his two Island albums. In the same year *Inglan Is A Bitch*, his third book, was published and he also opened a record label, LKJ, which introduced Jamaican poet Michael Smith to a UK audience. In the early 80s Johnson seemed to tire of the 'dub poet' tag and became far less active in the music business. In 1986 he issued *In Concert With The Dub Band*, a double live set which consisted chiefly of older material. He finally returned to the studio in 1990 to record *Tings An' Times* for his own label, a more reflective, slightly less brash set. While Johnson has undoubtedly added a notch to reggae's canon in providing a solid focus for the dub poetry movement, offering an alternative stance to that of straightforward reggae DJs, he appears to view his musical involvement as secondary to his political and social activities, and is not therefore the 'name' in the media he might have been. However, no other artist would have tackled subjects like 'Black Petty Booshwah' (petit-bourgeois) or 'Inglan' (England) Is A Bitch', and for that, his place in reggae history is assured.

●ALBUMS: as Poet And The Roots *Dread Beat An' Blood* (Front Line 1978)★★★, *Forces Of Victory* (Island 1979)★★★★, *Bass Culture* (Island 1980)★★★★, *LKJ In Dub* (Island 1980)★★★, *Making History* (Island 1984)★★★★, *Linton Kwesi Johnson Live* (Rough Trade 1985)★★★, *In Concert With The Dub Band* (LKJ 1986)★★★, *Tings An' Times* (LKJ 1990)★★★★, *LKJ In Dub Vol. 2* (1992)★★★, *A Cappalla Live* (LKJ 1997)★★★.
●COMPILATIONS: *Reggae Greats* (Island 1985)★★★★.

JOHNSON, WILKO

b. John Wilkinson, *c*.1950. A native of Canvey Island, Essex, England, Johnson played in several local groups, including the Roamers and the Heap, prior to a gaining a degree in English Literature at Newcastle-upon-Tyne University. He returned to music with Dr. Feelgood, a gritty R&B band, which became one of the leading attractions of the mid-70s' 'pub rock' phenomenon. The group's early sound was indebted to Johnson's punchy guitar style, itself inspired by Mick Green of the Pirates, while his striking appearance - black suit and pudding-bowl haircut - combined with jerky, mannequin movements, created a magnetic stage persona. Internal friction led to the guitarist's departure in 1976, but the following year he formed the Solid Senders with keyboards player John Potter, a founder member of Dr. Feelgood, Steve Lewins (bass) and Alan Platt (drums). However, despite securing a prestigious deal with Virgin, Johnson was unable to regain the success he enjoyed with his erstwhile unit and the band was dissolved following their lone, but excellent, album. Wilko then replaced Chas Jankel in Ian Dury's Blockheads, but resumed his solo career having contributed to *Laughter* (1980). A promising act with Canvey Island associate Lew Lewis ensued - Johnson's idol Mick Green was also briefly a member - but commercial indifference doomed its potential. Subsequent line-ups appeared on a variety of outlets as the artist became increasingly hidebound to a diminishing pub and club circuit. His 1991 *Don't Let Your Daddy Know*, was recorded live at Putney's Half Moon pub.
●ALBUMS: *Solid Senders* (Virgin 1978)★★★, *Ice On The Motorway* (Nighthawk 1981)★★★, *Watch Out* (Waterfront 1986)★★★, *Barbed Wire Blues* (Jungle 1988)★★★, *Don't Let Your Daddy Know* (1991)★★.

JOHNSTON, BRUCE

b. *c*.1943, Los Angeles, California, USA. An early associate of Sandy Nelson and Phil Spector, whom he often supported on keyboards, Johnston enjoyed a spell backing Richie Valens before recording 'Take This Pearl' as half of Bruce And Jerry. He then wrote and played piano on several records by singer Ron Holden, before embracing the surfing craze in 1962 with 'Do The Surfer Stomp'. The following year he began a fruitful partnership with songwriter/producer Terry Melcher which not only engendered the excellent *Surfin' 'Round The World*, but a series of well-crafted studio projects. The duo took control of releases by the Ripchords, notably 'Three Window Coupe', and the Rogues, as well as completing several singles as Bruce And Terry. In April 1965 Johnston joined the Beach Boys as an on-tour replacement for Brian Wilson. He made his recording debut with the group on 'California Girls', but the artist's songwriting skills did not flourish until 1969 when 'The Nearest Faraway Place' surfaced on *20/20*. Johnston's melodramatic approach prevailed on 'Deidre' and 'Tears In The Morning' (*Sunflower*), but 'Disney Girls 1957' (*Surf's Up*) captured the balance between evocation and sentimentality. Johnston also guested on albums by numerous acts, including Sagittarius, (American) Spring and Roger McGuinn. He officially left the Beach Boys in 1972, although his services were still called upon during recording sessions.

Johnston then joined former partner Melcher in Equinox Productions, and worked with such disparate acts as Jack Jones, the Hudson Brothers and Sailor. However, this period is best recalled for 'I Write The Songs', his multi-million selling composition, first recorded by the Captain And Tennille, which was a hit for both David Cassidy and, especially, Barry Manilow. Having completed the largely disappointing *Goin' Public*, Bruce returned to the Beach Boys camp in 1978 by producing their *L.A. Light Album*. He has since remained an integral part of the line-up and is often credited as mediator during recurrent internal strife.

●ALBUMS: as Bruce Johnston Surfing Band *Surfer's Pajama Party* (1963)★★★, *Surfin' 'Round The World* (1963)★★★, *Goin' Public* (Columbia 1977)★.

JONES, QUINCY

b. 14 March 1933, Chicago, Illinois, USA. Jones began playing trumpet as a child and also developed an early interest in arranging, studying at the Berklee College Of Music. When he joined Lionel Hampton in 1951 it was as both performer and writer. With Hampton he visited Europe in a remarkable group which included rising stars Clifford Brown, Art Farmer, Gigi Gryce and Alan Dawson. Leaving Hampton in 1953, Jones wrote arrangements for many musicians, including some of his former colleagues and Ray Anthony, Count Basie and Tommy Dorsey. Mostly, he worked as a freelance but had a stint in the mid-50s as musical director for Dizzy Gillespie, one result of which was the 1956 album *World Statesman*. Later in the 50s and into the 60s Jones wrote charts and directed the orchestras for concerts and record sessions by several singers, including Frank Sinatra, Billy Eckstine, Brook Benton, Dinah Washington (an association that included the 1956 album *The Swingin' Miss 'D'*), Johnny Mathis and Ray Charles, whom he had known since childhood. He continued to write big band charts, composing and arranging albums for Basie, *One More Time* (1958-59) and *Li'l Ol' Groovemaker...Basie* (1963). By this time, Jones was fast becoming a major force in American popular music. In addition to playing he was busy writing, arranging and was increasingly active as a record producer. In the late 60s and 70s he composed scores for about 40 feature films and hundreds of television shows. Among the former were *The Pawnbroker* (1965), *In Cold Blood* (1967) and *In The Heat Of The Night* (1967) while the latter included the long-running *Ironside* series and *Roots*. Other credits for television programmes include *The Bill Cosby Show*, *NBC Mystery Series*, *The Jesse Jackson Series*, *In The House* and *Mad TV*. He continued to produce records featuring his own music played by specially assembled orchestras. As a record producer Jones had originally worked for Mercury's Paris-based subsidiary Barclay but later became the first black vice-president of the company's New York division. Later, he spent a dozen years with A&M Records before starting up his own label, Qwest.

Despite suffering two brain aneurysms in 1974 he showed no signs of letting up his high level of activity. In the 70s and 80s in addition to many film soundtracks he produced successful albums for Aretha Franklin, George Benson, Michael Jackson, the Brothers Johnston and other popular artists. With Benson he produced *Give Me The Night*, while for Jackson he helped to create *Off The Wall* and *Thriller*, the latter proving to be the best-selling album of all time. He was also producer of the 1985 number 1 charity single 'We Are The World'. Latterly, Jones has been involved in film and television production, not necessarily in a musical context. As a player, Jones was an unexceptional soloist; as an arranger, his attributes are sometimes overlooked by the jazz audience, perhaps because of the manner in which he has consistently sought to create a smooth and wholly sophisticated entity, even at the expense of eliminating the essential characteristics of the artists concerned (as some of his work for Basie exemplifies). Nevertheless, with considerable subtlety he has fused elements of the blues and its many offshoots into mainstream jazz, and has found ways to bring soul to latter-day pop in a manner that adds to the latter without diminishing the former. His example has been followed by many although few have achieved such a level of success. A major film documentary, *Listen Up: The Lives Of Quincy Jones*, was released in 1990, and five years later Jones received the Jean Hersholt Humanitarian Award at the Academy Awards ceremony in Los Angeles. This coincided with *Q's Jook Joint*, a celebration of his 50 years in the music business with re-recordings of selections from his extraordinarily varied catalogue. The album lodged itself at the top of the *Billboard* jazz album chart for over four months.

●ALBUMS: *Quincy Jones With The Swedish/U.S. All Stars* (Prestige 1953)★★★, *This Is How I Feel About Jazz* (ABC 1957)★★★, *Go West Man* (ABC 1957)★★★, *The Birth Of A Band* (Mercury 1959)★★★, *The Great Wide World Of Quincy Jones* (Mercury 1960)★★★, *Quincy Jones Live At Newport* (Mercury 1961)★★★, *I Dig Dancers* (Mercury 1961)★★★, *Quintessence* (Impulse 1961)★★★, *Big Band Bossa Nova* (Mercury 1962)★★★, *Brand New Bag* (Mercury 1963)★★★, *Hip Hits* (Mercury 1963)★★★, *The Boy In The Tree* (1963)★★★, *Quincy Jones Explores The Music Of Henry Mancini* (Mercury 1964)★★★, *Golden Boy* (Mercury 1964)★★★, *Quincy Plays For Pussycats* (Mercury 1965)★★★, *The Pawnbroker* (Mercury 1965)★★★, *Walk Don't Run* (Mainstream 1966)★★★, *The Slender Thread* (Mercury 1966)★★★, *The Deadly Affair* (Verve 1967)★★★, *Enter Laughing* (Liberty 1967)★★★, *In The Heat Of The Night* (United Artists 1967)★★★, *In Cold Blood* (Colgems 1967)★★★, *Banning* (1968)★★★, *For The Love Of Ivy* (ABC 1968)★★★, *The Split* (1968)★★★, *Jigsaw* (1968)★★★, *A Dandy In Aspic* (1968)★★★, *The Hell With Heroes* (1968)★★★, *MacKennas Gold* (RCA 1969)★★★, *The Italian Job* (Paramount 1969)★★★, *The Lost Man* (1969)★★★, *Bob & Carol & Ted & Alice* (Bell 1969)★★★, *John And Mary*

(A&M 1969)★★★, *Walking In Space* (A&M 1969)★★★, *Gula Matari* (A&M 1970)★★★, *The Out Of Towners* (United Artists 1970)★★★, *Cactus Flower* (Bell 1970)★★★, *The Last Of The Hot Shots* (1970)★★★, *Sheila* (1970)★★★, *They Call Me Mr Tibbs* (United Artists 1970)★★★, *Smackwater Jack* (A&M 1971)★★★, *The Anderson Tapes* (1971)★★★, *Dollars* (1971)★★★, *Man And Boy* (1971)★★★, *The Hot Rock* (Prophesy 1972)★★★, *Ndeda* (Mercury 1972)★★★, *The New Centurians* (1972)★★★, *Come Back Charleston Blue* (Atco 1972)★★★, *You've Got It Bad Girl* (A&M 1973)★★★, *Body Heat* (A&M 1974)★★★, *This Is How I Feel About Jazz* (Impulse 1974)★★★, *Mellow Madness* (A&M 1975)★★★, *I Heard That!* (A&M 1976)★★★, *Roots* (A&M 1977)★★★, *Sounds ... And Stuff Like That* (A&M 1978)★★★, *The Wiz* (MCA 1978)★★★, *Go West, Man* (Impulse 1978)★★★, *The Dude* (A&M 1981)★★★, *The Color Purple* (Qwest 1985)★★★, *Back On The Block* (Qwest 1989)★★★, *Listen Up, The Lives Of Quincy Jones* (Qwest 1990)★★★, with Miles Davis *Live At Montreux* rec. 1991 (Reprise 1993)★★★★, *Q's Jook Joint* (Qwest 1995)★★★★.
●VIDEOS: *Miles Davis And Quincy Jones: Live At Montreux* (1993).
●FURTHER READING: *Quincy Jones*, Raymond Horricks.

JONES, RICKIE LEE

b. 8 November 1954, Chicago, Illinois, USA. Jones emerged from a thriving Los Angeles bohemian subculture in 1979 with a buoyant debut album, peppered with images of streetwise characters and indebted, lyrically, to beat and jazz styles. The set included 'Chuck E.'s In Love', a US Top 5 single, and 'Easy Money', a song covered by Little Feat guitarist Lowell George. Other selections bore a debt to Tom Waits to whom Jones was briefly romantically linked. Although *Rickie Lee Jones* garnered popular success and critical plaudits, the singer refused to be rushed into a follow-up. Two years later, *Pirates*, a less instantaneous, yet more rewarding collection, offered a greater perception and while still depicting low-rent scenarios, Jones revealed a hitherto hidden emotional depth. *Girl At Her Volcano*, a collection of live material and studio out-takes, marked time until the release of *The Magazine* in 1984. The ambitious work confirmed the artist's imagination and blended her accustomed snappy, bop-style ('Juke Box Fury', 'It Must Be Love') with moments of adventurousness, in particular the multi-part 'Rorschachs'. The album also confirmed Jones as an expressive vocalist, at times reminiscent of Laura Nyro. However, it was six years before a further album, *Flying Cowboys*, was issued and, while lacking the overall strength of its predecessors, the record maintained its creator's reputation for excellence. The set also marked a fruitful collaboration with Glasgow group, the Blue Nile. *Naked Songs* was her contribution to the unplugged phenomenon.
●ALBUMS: *Rickie Lee Jones* (Warners 1979)★★★★, *Pop Pop* (Geffen 1981)★★, *Pirates* (Warners 1981)★★★★, *Girl At Her Volcano* (Warners 1982)★★, *The Magazine* (Warners 1984)★★★, *Flying Cowboys* (Geffen 1990)★★★, *Traffic From Paradise* (1993)★★★, *Naked Songs: Live And Acoustic* (Reprise 1995)★★.
●VIDEOS: *Naked Songs* (Warner Music Vision 1996).

JOURNEY

This US rock group was formed in 1973 by ex-Santana members Neil Schon (b. 27 February 1954, San Mateo, California, USA; guitar) and Gregg Rolie (b. 1948; keyboards), with the assistance of Ross Valory (b. 2 February 1949, San Francisco, USA; ex-Steve Miller band; bass) and Prairie Prince (b. 7 May 1950, Charlotte, North Carolina, USA; drums, ex-Tubes). George Tickner was added later as rhythm guitarist and lead vocalist. On New Year's Eve the same year, they made their live debut in front of 10,000 people at San Fransisco's Winterland. The following day they played to 10 times as many at an open-air festival in Hawaii. In February 1974 Prince returned to the Tubes and was replaced by Aynsley Dunbar (b. 10 January 1946, Liverpool, Lancashire, England; ex-Jeff Beck, John Mayall, Frank Zappa, etc.). Initially they specialized in jazz-rock, complete with extended and improvised solo spots. This style can clearly be heard on their first three albums. In 1975 Tickner left (for medical school) and was eventually replaced by ex-Alien Project vocalist Steve Perry (b. 22 January 1953, Hanford, California, USA) following a brief tenure by Robert Fleischmann. The switch to highly sophisticated pomp rock occurred with the recording of *Infinity*, when Roy Thomas Baker was brought in as producer to give the band's sound a punchy and dynamic edge. The album was a huge success, reaching number 21 on the *Billboard* charts and gaining a platinum award. Dunbar was unhappy with this new style and quit for Jefferson Starship, to be replaced by Steve Smith (b. 21 August 1954, Los Angeles, California, USA). *Evolution* followed and brought the band their first Top 20 hit, 'Lovin', Touchin', Squeezin''. *Captured* was a live double album that surprised many of the critics, being far removed from their technically excellent and clinically produced studio releases; instead, it featured cranked-up guitars and raucous hard rock, eventually peaking at number 9 in the US album chart. Founder member Rolie departed after its release, to be replaced by Jonathan Cain (b. 26 February 1950, Chicago, Illinois, USA), who had previously played with the Babys. Cain's arrival was an important landmark in Journey's career, as his input on the writing side added a new dimension to the band's sound. *Escape* was the pinnacle of the band's success, reaching number 1 and staying in the chart for over a year. It also spawned three US Top 10 hit singles in the form of 'Who's Crying Now', 'Don't Stop Believin'', and 'Open Arms'. The follow-up, *Frontiers*, was also successful, staying at number 2 on the *Billboard* album chart for nine weeks; 'Separate Ways', culled as a single from it, climbed to number 8 in the singles chart. After a series of internal disputes the band reduced to a three-man nucleus of Schon, Cain and Perry to record *Raised On Radio* (though they were joined on live dates by Randy Jackson and Mike Baird on drums and bass). This was Journey's last album, before Schon and Cain joined forces with John Waite's Bad English in 1988. Smith fronted a fusion band, Vital Information, before teaming up with ex-Journey members Rolie and Valory to form Storm in 1991. Perry concentrated on his long-awaited second solo album. A *Greatest Hits* compilation was posthumously released to mark the band's passing, since when only a November 1991 reunion to commemorate the death of promoter Bill Graham has seen the core members regroup. This continued with new albums in 1996 and 1997 which saw the band religiously refusing to adapt or change from a style of music that has now dated.

●ALBUMS: *Journey* (Columbia 1975)★★★, *Look Into The Future* (Columbia 1976)★★★, *Next* (Columbia 1977)★★★, *Infinity* (Columbia 1978)★★★, *Evolution* (Columbia 1979)★★★, *Departure* (Columbia 1980)★★★, *Dream After Dream* (Columbia 1980)★★, *Captured* (Columbia 1981)★★★, *Escape* (Columbia 1981)★★★★, *Frontiers* (Columbia 1983)★★★, *Raised On Radio* (Columbia 1986)★★★, *Trial By Fire* (Columbia 1996)★★, *Into The Fire* (Columbia 1997)★★.

●COMPILATIONS: *In The Beginning* (Columbia 1979)★★, *Greatest Hits/Best Of Journey* (Columbia 1988)★★★★, *Time* 3-CD box set (Columbia 1992)★★★★.

JUDAS JUMP

Formed in 1970, Judas Jump was the confluence of two leading UK 'teenybop' groups. Andy Bown (vocals/piano) and Henry Spinetti (drums) had been members of the Herd, while Alan Jones and Mike Smith (both saxophone), were the brass section of Amen Corner. Trevor Williams (lead guitar), Adrian Williams (vocals) and Charlie Harrison (bass) completed the line-up. Plans to name the band Septimus were abandoned on Smith's premature departure. Although *Scorch* showed promise, Judas Jump's mixture of pop and progressive styles ultimately proved too unwieldy and they broke up within a year of their inception. Bown, who overdubbed much of the album in deference to what he perceived as incompetence, later embarked on a solo career. Harrison led a chequered career working for Leo Sayer, Frankie Miller, Roger McGuinn, Al Stewart and finally ending up in the ranks of Poco in 1977.

●ALBUMS: *Scorch* (Parlophone 1970)★★.

JUDGE DREAD

Real name Alex Hughes, Kent-born Judge Dread was a bouncer in London clubs at the end of the 60s and became familiar with reggae through his work, where he had run into (not literally!) the likes of Derrick Morgan and Prince Buster. In 1969 Buster had a huge

underground hit with the obscene 'Big 5', a version of Brook Benton's 'Rainy Night In Georgia'. It was clear there was a yawning gap waiting to be filled when Buster failed effectively to follow his hit, so Hughes, aka Judge Dread (a name borrowed from a Prince Buster character) plunged in. His first single, 'Big Six' went to number 11 in 1972, and spent more than half the year in the charts. No-one heard it on air: it was a filthy nursery rhyme. 'Big Seven' did better than 'Big Six', and from this point on Dread scored hits with 'Big Eight', a ridiculous version of 'Je T'Aime', and a string of other novelty reggae records, often co-penned by his friend, Fred Lemon. Incidentally, 'Big Six' was also a hit in Jamaica. Five years and 11 hits later (including such musical delicacies as 'Y Viva Suspenders' and 'Up With The Cock'), the good-natured Hughes, one of just two acts to successfully combine music-hall with reggae (the other was Count Prince Miller, whose 'Mule Train' rivalled Dread for sheer chutzpah), had finally ground to a halt in chart terms. He can still be found occasionally working the clubs, and has also sought employment as a local newspaper columnist in Snodland, Kent.

●ALBUMS: *Dreadmania: It's All In The Mind* (Trojan 1972)★★★, *Working Class 'Ero* (Trojan 1974)★★★, *Bedtime Stories* (Creole 1975)★★★, *Last Of The Skinheads* (Cactus 1976)★★★, *40 Big Ones* (Creole 1977)★★★, *Reggae And Ska* (TTR 1980)★★★, *Rub-A-Dub* (Creole 1981)★★★, *Not Guilty* (Creole 1984)★★, *Live And Lewd* (Skank 1988)★★, *Never Mind Up With The Cock, Here's Judge Dread* (Tring 1994)★★, *Ska'd For Life* (Magnum 1996)★★, *Dread White And Blue* (Skank 1996)★★★.

●COMPILATIONS: *The Best Of Judge Dread* (Klik 1976)★★★, *The Best Worst Of Judge Dread* (Creole 1978)★★★, *The Legendary Judge Dread Vol. 1* (Link 1989)★★★, *The Legendary Judge Dread Vol. 2* (Link 1989)★★★, *The Very Worst Of Judge Dread* (Creole 1991)★★★, *The Big 24* (Trojan 1994)★★★, *Big 14* (Hallmark 1995)★★★, *Greatest Hits* (K-Tel 1997)★★★, *Big Hits* (Summit 1997)★★★.

JUICY LUCY

Juicy Lucy was formed in 1969 when three ex-members of the Misunderstood - Ray Owen (vocals), Glen 'Ross' Campbell (steel guitar) and Chris Mercer (tenor saxophone) - were augmented by Neil Hubbard (guitar), Keith Ellis (bass) and Pete Dobson (bass). The sextet enjoyed a surprise hit single with their fiery reading of Bo Diddley's 'Who Do You Love', a track featured on the group's first, and best-known, album. The cover became a sexist classmate of Jimi Hendrix's *Electric Ladyland*, and featured a naked busty woman languishing on a banquet table, amid a glut of various sliced and squashed fruits. Owen was later replaced by former Zoot Money singer Paul Williams, one of several changes afflicting the group. Their brand of blues-rock became more predictable as one by one the original cast dropped out. A fourth album, *Pieces*, was completed by a reshaped unit of Williams, Mick Moody (guitar), Jean Roussal (keyboards) and ex-Blodwyn Pig members Andy Pyle (bass) and Ron Berg (drums), but this was the final line-up of Juicy Lucy, which broke up soon afterwards.

●ALBUMS: *Juicy Lucy* (Vertigo 1969)★★★, *Lie Back And Enjoy It* (Vertigo 1970)★★, *Get A Whiff A This* (Bronze 1971)★★, *Pieces* (Polydor 1972)★★.
●COMPILATIONS: *Who Do You Love: The Best Of* (Sequel 1990)★★.

JUPP, MICKEY

b. *c.*1940, Essex, England. Guitarist Jupp began his recording career as a member of the Orioles, a beat group based in Southend, Essex, England. By the end of the 60s he was fronting Legend, an act bedeviled by instability, but which anticipated the pub-rock style of Dr. Feelgood and Ducks Deluxe. The former act recorded one of Jupp's compositions, 'Cheque Book', and the artist in turn became one of the early signings to the nascent Stiff label. *Juppanese* enjoyed support from the entire Rockpile line-up, but despite assiduous touring, the guitarist was unable to escape cult status. *Mickey Jupp's Legend* featured Southend contemporaries Gary Brooker, Chris Copping and B.J. Wilson, but this newly recorded selection of material drawn from his previous group failed to capture their original informality. Jupp then left Stiff, but subsequent releases failed to expand upon an already well-honed niche.

●ALBUMS: *Juppanese* (Stiff 1978)★★★, *Mickey Jupp's Legend* (Stiff 1978)★★, *Long Distance Romancer* (1979)★★, *Some People Can't Dance* (A&M 1982)★★, *Shampoo, Haircut And Shave* (A&M 1983)★★, *X* (Waterfront 1988)★★, *As The Years Go By* (On The Beach 1991)★★.

KANDIDATE

This expansive UK disco and soul group came together in 1976 comprising members from two previous soul bands: Hot Wax (who went on to become Hi Tension) and 70% Proof. They were signed to Mickie Most's RAK label and he also produced their recordings. Their debut 'Don't Wanna Say Goodnight' was a minor hit in 1978 and this was followed by three more charting singles, including the number 11 hit, 'I Don't Wanna Lose You' (1979). The line-up of the band was Teeroy (vocals/keyboards), Ferdi (bass), Alex Bruce (percussion), St Lloyd Phillips (drums/vocals), Tamby (guitar/vocals), Phil Fearon (guitar) and Bob Collins (percussion/vocals). Of these, only Fearon (b. 30 July 1956, Jamaica) had any further chart success after Kandidate split. He built his own recording studio and had a string of hits in the mid-80s under his own name and the group name Galaxy.

KANSAS

This US group was formed in 1972 after David Hope (b. *c.*1951, Kansas, USA; bass) and Phil Ehart (b. 1951, Kansas, USA; drums/percussion) changed the name of their band, White Clover, to Kansas, recruiting Kerry Livgren (b. 18 September 1949, Kansas, USA; guitar/vocals), Robert Steinhardt (b. *c.*1951, Michigan, USA; violin/strings/vocals), Steve Walsh (b. *c.*1951, St. Joseph, Missouri, USA; keyboards/vocals) and Richard Williams (b. *c.*1951, Kansas, USA; guitars). Although an American band, Kansas were heavily influenced from the outset by British rock of the time, such as Yes and Genesis, and this was evident in the lyrics of their primary songwriter, Walsh. Kansas released their debut in 1974, and the following two albums attained gold record status, guaranteeing the band a high profile in the USA (although no Kansas albums made the charts in the UK). By 1977 the band had tired of the progressive rock pigeonhole into which the music press was forcing them, and decided to try a more commercial approach. Their popularity was confirmed on 27 June 1978 when they attended a ceremony at the Madison Square Gardens in New York at which the organization UNICEF named the band Deputy Ambassadors of Goodwill. In the early 80s Walsh decided to leave the band after he became unhappy with the increasingly commercial sound they were producing. He released the solo set, *Schemer Dreamer*, which featured other members of Kansas. He was replaced by John Elefante

(b. *c*.1958, Levittown, New York, USA; keyboards/vocals) who wrote four of the songs on *Vinyl Confessions*. The band split in 1983 following two unsuccessful albums. Livgren and Hope had become born-again Christians, the former releasing *Seeds Of Change*, a commercially disastrous solo effort based on his religious experiences. In October 1986 Walsh, Ehart and Williams re-formed Kansas with Steve Morse, lately of Dixie Dregs (guitar), and Billy Greer (bass). This reunion was celebrated with the release of *Power*, an album that rejected the jazz-rock feel of earlier releases in favour of a heavier sound. Their first studio album in seven years was released in May 1995.

●ALBUMS: *Kansas* (Kirshner 1974)★★★, *Song For America* (Kirshner 1975)★★★, *Masque* (Kirshner 1976)★★★, *Leftoverture* (Kirshner 1977)★★★, *Point Of Know Return* (Kirshner 1977)★★★★, *Two For The Show* (Kirshner 1978)★★★, *Monolith* (Kirshner 1979)★★★, *Audio-Visions* (Kirshner 1980)★★★, *Vinyl Confessions* (Kirshner 1982)★★, *Drastic Measures* (Columbia 1983)★★, *Power* (MCA 1986)★★, *In The Spirit Of Things* (MCA 1988)★★, *Live At The Whisky* (1993)★, *Freaks Of Nature* (Intersound 1995)★★.

●COMPILATIONS: *The Best Of Kansas* (Columbia 1984)★★★.

KANTNER, PAUL

b. 17 March 1941, San Francisco, California, USA. Kantner abandoned ambitions of a career in folk music on becoming a founder-member of Jefferson Airplane in 1965. Although this revered unit was initially a vehicle for lead singer Marty Balin, his influence was gradually eclipsed by those of Kantner and new vocalist Grace Slick, particularly when the pair became linked romantically. An early predilection for love songs was replaced by an espousal of hip politics and science fiction; the latter was a particular Kantner favourite. *Volunteers* included 'Wooden Ships', written with David Crosby and Stephen Stills, and a collaboration reflecting a growing desire among many musicians to break the constraints of a single group. *Blows Against The Empire*, credited to Paul Kantner with Jefferson Starship, enshrined this desire by featuring contributions from Slick, Crosby, Jerry Garcia and Graham Nash. Although the storyline was slight - a group of friends hijack Earth's first starship - it contained several excellent songs, notably 'Have You Seen The Stars Tonite' and 'A Child Is Coming'. The album was nominated for a Hugo science fiction award. Kantner and Slick used several of the same artists on *Sunfighter* and although the duo remained members of Jefferson Airplane, many queried their long-standing commitment in the light of the superior material appearing on 'outside' projects. *Baron Von Tollbooth And The Chrome Nun* emphasized their growing independence and when the parent group disintegrated, Kantner and Slick assembled a permanent Jefferson Starship line-up. Kantner remained at the helm of this highly popular attraction until October

1980 when he suffered a brain haemorrhage, but resumed his role upon making a full recovery. In 1983, he recorded *Planet Earth Rock And Roll Orchestra*, an ambitious sequel to his solo debut which was produced by the Durocs team and featured many Bay Area acolytes. The soundtrack to an as yet unrealized science fiction novel, the set appeared as relations within the parent band soured to the extent that Kantner left the following year. In 1985, he rejoined two former Airplane colleagues, Marty Balin and Jack Casady, in KBC, but this much heralded unit was a great disappointment. Kantner was a member of the re-formed Airplane in the late 80s.

●ALBUMS: *Blows Against The Empire* (RCA 1970)★★★★, with Grace Slick *Sunfighter* (Grunt 1971)★★★, with Grace Slick, David Freiberg *Baron Von Tollbooth And The Chrome Nun* (Grunt 1973)★★, *Planet Earth Rock And Roll Orchestra* (RCA 1983)★★★.

KAUKONEN, JORMA

b. 23 December 1940, Washington, DC, USA. The solo career of the former Jefferson Airplane lead guitarist started after the demise of the Airplane splinter group Hot Tuna in 1978. Kaukonen went back to his roots as a solo acoustic performer in small clubs. Four years earlier, he had released an outstanding recording, *Quah*, joined by Tom Hobson and produced by Jack Casady. The album was well received and although not released in the UK, enough copies were imported to satisfy the small but enthusiastic market. On this album Kaukonen displayed an intensity that had been hidden during his years with the Airplane. The autobiographical 'Song For The North Star' and the emotive 'Genesis' were two outstanding examples. On *Barbeque King* he was joined by Denny DeGorio (bass) and John Stench (drums), otherwise known as Vital Parts, in a not too successful attempt to work again within a rock group. During his solo years Kaukonen's reputation as an acoustic guitarist has grown considerably; his love for ragtime blues continued to find a small and loyal audience fascinated to watch a six-foot, body-tattooed Scandinavian playing such delicate music. In 1989, Kaukonen was cajoled into re-forming the Jefferson Airplane, where once again he sacrificed his love of 'wooden' music for the power of his biting and frantic lead guitar playing. In 1990, he and Casady reconvened as Hot Tuna.

●ALBUMS: *Quah* (Grunt 1975)★★★★, *Jorma* (RCA 1980)★★★, *Barbeque King* (RCA 1980)★★, *Magic* (Relix 1985)★★★, *Too Hot To Handle* (Relix 1987)★★★, with Tom Constanten *Embryonic Journey* (Relix 1995)★★★, *The Land Of Heroes* (American Heritage/Relix 1996)★★★.

KC AND THE SUNSHINE BAND

This racially integrated band was formed in Florida, USA, in 1973 by Harry Wayne (KC) Casey (b. 31 January 1951, Hialeah, Florida, USA; vocals, keyboards) and Richard Finch (b. 25 January 1954, Indianapolis,

Indiana, USA; bass). Arguably the cornerstone of the Miami-based TK label, the duo wrote, arranged and produced their own group's successes, as well as those of singer George McCrae. The Sunshine Band enjoyed several hits, including 'Queen Of Clubs' (1974, UK Top 10), three consecutive US number 1s with 'Get Down Tonight', 'That's The Way (I Like It)' (both 1975) and '(Shake, Shake, Shake), Shake Your Body' (1976), each of which displayed an enthusiastic grasp of dance-based funk. The style was exaggerated to almost parodic proportions on 'I'm Your Boogie Man' (1977, a US number 1) and 'Boogie Shoes' (1978), but a crafted ballad, 'Please Don't Go', in 1979, not only reversed this bubblegum trend, but was a transatlantic smash in the process (a UK number 1 in 1992 for K.W.S.). That same year KC duetted with Teri DeSario on the US number 2 hit, 'Yes, I'm Ready' on the Casablanca label. Although the group numbered as many as 12 on its live appearances, its core revolved around Jerome Smith (b. 18 June 1953, Hialeah, Florida, USA; guitar), Robert Johnson (b. 21 March 1953, Miami, Florida, USA; drums) and its two songwriters. The team moved to Epic/CBS Records after the collapse of the TK organization in 1980. Any benefit this accrued was hampered by a head-on car crash in January 1982 which left Casey paralyzed for several months. Their fortune changed the following year when the group found themselves at the top of the UK charts with 'Give It Up'. It did not reach the US charts until the following year, and was by then credited to 'KC'. Casey and Finch subsequently seem to have lost the art of penning radio-friendly soul/pop.

●ALBUMS: *Do It Good* (TK 1974)★★★, *KC And The Sunshine Band* (TK 1975)★★★, as the Sunshine Band *The Sound Of Sunshine* (TK 1975)★★, *Part Three* (TK 1976)★★★★, *I Like To Do It* (Jay Boy 1977)★★★, *Who Do Ya (Love)* (TK 1978)★★, *Do You Wanna Go Party* (TK 1979)★★, *Painter* (Epic 1981)★★, *All In A Night's Work* (Epic 1983)★★, *Get Down Live!* (Intersound 1995)★★. Solo: Wayne Casey/KC *Space Cadet* (1981)★★, *KC Ten* (Meca 1984)★★.

●COMPILATIONS: *Greatest Hits* (TK 1980)★★★, *The Best Of* (Roulette 1990)★★★★.

KELLY, JO ANN

b. 5 January 1944, Streatham, London, England, d. 21 October 1990. This expressive blues singer, sister of Blues Band guitarist Dave Kelly, was renowned as one of the finest of the genre. She made her recording debut in 1964 on a privately pressed EP and appeared on several specialist labels before contributing a series of excellent performances to guitarist Tony McPhee's Groundhogs recordings, issued under the aegis of United Artists. Her self-titled solo album displayed a hard, gritty vocal delivery evocative of Memphis Minnie and confirmed the arrival of a major talent. In 1969, the singer appeared live with Mississippi Fred McDowell and later made several tours of the USA.

Kelly became a constituent part of the British blues circuit, recording with the John Dummer Blues Band, Chilli Willi And The Red Hot Peppers and Stefan Grossman. In 1972, she completed an album with Woody Mann, John Miller and acoustic guitarist John Fahey, before forming a group, Spare Rib, which performed extensively throughout the UK. Kelly recorded a second solo album, *Do It*, in 1976 and maintained her popularity throughout the 70s and 80s with appearances at European blues festivals and judicious live work in Britain. Her last performance was at a festival in Lancashire in August 1990, when she was given the award for Female Singer of the Year by the British Blues Federation. Having apparently recovered from an operation in 1989 to remove a malignant brain tumour, she died in October 1990.

●ALBUMS: *Jo Ann Kelly* (CBs 1969)★★★, *Jo Ann Kelly, With Fahey, Mann And Miller* (1972)★★★, with Pete Emery *Do It* (Red Rag 1976)★★★, *It's Whoopie* (1978)★★, with Mississippi Fred McDowell *Standing At The Burying Ground* (1984)★★, *Just Restless* (1984)★★★, *Women In (E)Motion* rec. 1988 (Indigo/Traditon & Moderne 1995)★★★.

●COMPILATIONS: with Tony McPhee *Same Thing On Our Minds* (Sunset 1969)★★, *Retrospect 1964-1972* (Connoisseur 1990)★★★.

KENDRICKS, EDDIE

b. 17 December 1939, Union Springs, Alabama, USA, d. 5 October 1992, Alabama, USA. Kendricks was a founder member of the Primes in the late 50s, an R&B vocal group that moved to Detroit in 1960 and formed the basis of the Temptations. His wavering falsetto vocals were an essential part of the group's sound throughout their first decade on Motown Records. He was singled out as lead vocalist on their first major hit, 'The Way You Do The Things You Do', and was also given a starring role on the 1966 US number 29 'Get Ready'. David Ruffin gradually assumed the leadership of the group, but in 1971 Kendricks was showcased on 'Just My Imagination', one of their most affecting love ballads. Kendricks chose this moment to announce that he was leaving the Temptations, weary of the production extravaganzas which Norman Whitfield was creating for the group. His initial solo albums failed to establish a distinctive style, and it was 1973 before he enjoyed his first hit, with an edited version of the disco classic, 'Keep On Truckin''. The accompanying album, *Eddie Kendricks*, was in more traditional style, while *Boogie Down!* had Kendricks displaying emotion over a succession of dance-oriented backing tracks. Rather than repeat a winning formula, Kendricks bravely chose to revise his sound on *For You* in 1974. The first side of the album was a masterful arrangement of vocal harmonies, with Eddie submerged by the backing. 'Shoeshine Boy' was extracted as a single, and followed 'Keep On Truckin'' and 'Boogie Down' to the summit of the soul charts. *The Hit Man* and *He's A Friend* repeated the experiment with less conviction, and by the time he left Motown for Arista in 1978, Kendricks had been forced to submit to the prevailing disco current. After a run of uninspiring efforts, *Love Keys* on Atlantic in 1981 was a welcome return to form, teaming the singer with the Muscle Shoals horns and the Holland/Dozier/Holland production team. Poor sales brought this liaison to an end, and Kendricks returned to the Temptations fold for a reunion tour and album in 1982. When this venture was completed, he formed a duo with fellow ex-Temptation David Ruffin, and the pair were showcased at Live Aid as well as on a live album by Hall And Oates. This exposure allowed them to secure a contract as a duo, and *Ruffin And Kendricks* in 1988 represented the most successful blending of their distinctive vocal styles since the mid-60s. Kendricks died of lung cancer in 1992, after having already had his right lung removed the previous year.

●ALBUMS: *All By Myself* (Tamla 1971)★★★, *People...Hold On* (Tamla 1972)★★★, *Eddie Kendricks* (Tamla 1973)★★★, *Boogie Down!* (Tamla 1974)★★★, *For You* (Tamla 1974)★★★, *The Hit Man* (Tamla 1975)★★★, *He's A Friend* (Tamla 1976)★★★, *Goin' Up In Smoke* (Tamla 1976)★★★, *Slick* (Tamla 1977)★★★, *Vintage '78* (Arista 1978)★★, *Something More* (Arista 1979)★★, *Love Keys* (Atlantic 1981)★★★, with David Ruffin *Ruffin And Kendricks* (RCA 1988)★★★.

●COMPILATIONS: *At His Best* (Motown 1990)★★★.

KENNY

Former employees at a banana warehouse in Enfield, Middlesex, England, Richard Driscoll (vocals), Yan Style (guitar), Christopher Lacklison (keyboards), Chris Redburn (bass) and Andy Walton (drums) were collectively known as Chufff (sic), a group of glam-rock latecomers who, after a 1974 showcase at London's exclusive Speakeasy, signed with manager Peter Walsh. In doing so, they acquired a new name - and a producer in Mickie Most who, with the highest calibre of session musicians, arrangers and songwriters at his disposal, guided them with mathematical precision to transient success. This was despite the confusion of an Irish singer called Kenny who was also signed to Most's Rak Records at this time. Chris Spedding and Clem Cattini were among those heard anonymously on the group Kenny's four UK smashes. All inconsequentially catchy and topped with a trademark falsetto in unison with Driscoll, these were 'The Bump' (a dance craze ditty that fought off competition from a b-side version by the Bay City Rollers) 'Fancy Pants', 'Baby I Love You OK' and autumn 1975's Top 20 swansong, Bill Martin and Phil Coulter's 'Julie Ann'. This chart run was rounded off neatly when the hits and some makeweight tracks were lumped together on a collection which bubbled under the album Top 50 in January 1976. They later provided the backing to the theme tune for UK Television's popular *Minder* series, sung by Dennis Waterman. Redburn is now a successful road haulage

businessman and still gigs with Andy Walton as the Legendary Old Brown Growlers. Style runs his own PA hire company.

●ALBUMS: *The Sound Of Super K* (RAK 1975)★★.
●COMPILATIONS: *The Best Of ...* (Repertoire 1995)★★.

KILBURN AND THE HIGH ROADS

An important link between 'pub rock' and punk, Kilburn And The High Roads were formed in November 1970 by art lecturer Ian Dury (b. 12 May 1942, Upminster, Essex, England; vocals) and Russell Hardy (b. 9 September 1941, Huntingdon, Cambridgeshire, England; piano). As a frontman, Dury cut an almost Dickensian figure, with his growling, half-spoken vocals, squat figure, polio stricken leg and a withered hand, encased in a black leather glove. In fact, throughout the band's entire history their visual image was the antithesis of the prevalent glitter and glam-pop fashion. The initial line-up included Ted Speight (guitar), Terry Day (drums) and two former members of the Battered Ornaments, George Khan (saxophone) and Charlie Hart (bass). By 1973, despite a series of fluctuating line-ups, Dury and Russell had eventually settled down with a collection of musicians comprising: Keith Lucas (b. 6 May 1950, Gosport, Hampshire, England; guitar - a former art-school pupil of Dury's), Davey Payne (b. 11 August 1944, Willesden, London, England; saxophone), David Newton-Rohoman (b. 21 April, 1948, Guyana, South America; drums) and Humphrey Ocean (bass). The last subsequently left the Kilburns to concentrate on a successful career as an artist and was replaced by Charlie Sinclair in January 1974. The group's early repertoire consisted of rock 'n' roll favourites mixed with early 50s Tin Pan Alley pop, but this was later supplemented and supplanted by original material utilizing Dury's poetry, mostly depicting the loves and lives of every day east London folk. The Kilburns were, by this point, enshrined on London's 'pub rock' circuit. Managed by Charlie Gillett, they completed an album for the Raft label. This good fortune suffered a setback when the album's release was cancelled after the label went bankrupt. Warner Brothers Records, the parent company, chose to drop the group from its roster (but later released the sessions as *Wotabunch* in the wake of Dury's solo success). By late spring 1974, Gillett had left the scene, as had Hardy, who was replaced by Rod Melvin. Later that year they signed to the Dawn label, and released two superb singles, 'Rough Kids'/'Billy Bentley (Promenades Himself In London)' and 'Crippled With Nerves'/ 'Huffety Puff'. The subsequent album, *Handsome*, released the following year, was a huge disappointment, largely due to the bland production which captured little of the excitement and irreverence of a Kilburns gig. The album marked the end of this particular era as the group then disintegrated. Keith Lucas embraced punk with the formation of 999, performing under the name of Nick Cash, while Dury, Melvin and Payne became founder members of a revitalized unit, Ian Dury And The Kilburns. Ted Speight was also involved in this transitional band, during which time the singer introduced 'What A Waste' and 'England's Glory', two songs better associated with Ian Dury And The Blockheads, the group with which he found greater, long-deserved success.

●ALBUMS: *Handsome* (Dawn 1975)★★, *Wotabunch* (Warners 1978)★★.

●COMPILATIONS: *The Best Of Kilburn And The High Roads* (Warners 1977)★★★.

KING CRIMSON

Arguably progressive rock's definitive exponents, King Crimson was formed in January 1969 out of the ashes of the eccentric Giles, Giles And Fripp. Robert Fripp (b. 1946, Wimbourne, Dorset, England; guitar) and Mike Giles (b. 1 March 1942; Bournemouth, Dorset, England; drums) were joined by Ian McDonald (b. 25 June 1946, London, England; keyboards), before former Gods member Greg Lake (b. 10 November 1948, Bournemouth, Dorset, England; vocals/bass), completed the first official line-up. A fifth addition to the circle, Pete Sinfield, supplied lyrics to the guitarist's compositions. The group's debut album, *In The Court Of The Crimson King*, drew ecstatic praise from critics and a glowing, well-publicized testimonial from the Who's Pete Townshend. An expansive use of mellotron suggested a kinship with the Moody Blues, but Fripp's complex chord progressions, and the collection's fierce introduction '21st Century Schizoid Man', revealed a rare imagination.

This brief courtship with critical popularity ended with *In The Wake Of Poseidon*. Damned as a repeat of its predecessor, the album masked internal strife which saw McDonald And Giles depart to work as a duo and Greg Lake leave to found Emerson, Lake And Palmer. Having resisted invitations to join Yes, Fripp completed the album with various available musicians including Gordon Haskell (b. 27 April 1946, Bournemouth, Dorset, England; bass/vocals) and Mel Collins (saxophone), both of whom remained in the group for *Lizard*. Drummer Andy McCullough completed this particular line-up, but both he and Haskell left the group when the sessions terminated. Boz Burrell (bass/vocals - Fripp taught Burrell how to play the instrument) and Ian Wallace (drums) replaced them before the reshaped quartet embarked on a punishing touring schedule. One studio album, *Islands*, and a live selection, *Earthbound*, emanated from this particular version of King Crimson which collapsed in April 1972. Collins, Wallace and Burrell then pursued studio-based careers although the bassist later found fame with Bad Company. With Sinfield also ousted from the ranks, Fripp began fashioning a new, more radical line-up. John Wetton (b. 12 June 1950, Derby, England), formerly of Family, assumed the role of bassist/vocalist while Bill Bruford left the more lucrative ranks of Yes to become King Crimson's fourth drummer. Percussionist Jamie Muir and violinist David Cross (b. 23 April 1949, Plymouth, Devon, England) completed the innovative unit unveiled on *Larks Tongues In Aspic*, but were discarded over the next two years until only Fripp, Wetton and Bruford remained for the exemplary *Red*.

'King Crimson is completely over for ever and ever', Fripp declared in October 1974 as he embarked on an idiosyncratic solo career. However, in 1981 the guitarist took a surprisingly retrograde step, resurrecting the name for a unit comprising himself, Bruford, Tony Levin (bass) and Adrian Belew (guitar). The albums which followed, *Discipline*, *Beat* and *Three Of A Perfect Pair*, showed both adventure and purpose, belying the suspicion that the group would rest on previous laurels. It was, however, a temporary interlude and Fripp subsequently resumed his individual pursuits and established a new unit, the League Of Gentlemen. King Crimson, a group that married invention and ambition while avoiding the trappings prevailing in rock's experimental arena, may nonetheless prove Fripp's crowning achievement. Fripp reconvened King Crimson in 1994 with the line-up of Belew, Trey Gunn (stick and backing vocals), Levin, Bruford and Pat Mastelotto (acoustic/electric percussion) and a new album *Thrak* appeared the following year.

●ALBUMS: *In The Court Of The Crimson King* (Island 1969)★★★★, *In The Wake Of Poseidon* (Island 1970)★★★, *Lizard* (Island 1970)★★★, *Islands* (Island 1971)★★, *Earthbound* (Island 1972)★★, *Larks Tongues In Aspic* (Island 1973)★★★★, *Starless And Bible Black* (Island 1974)★★★, *Red* (Island 1974)★★★★, *USA* (Island 1975)★★★, *Discipline* (EG 1981)★★★, *Beat* (EG 1982)★★★, *Three Of A Perfect Pair* (EG 1984)★★★, *Thrak* (Virgin 1995)★★★, *Vroom* (Discipline 1995), *B'Boom* (Discipline 1995), *THRaKaTTak* (Discipline 1996).

●COMPILATIONS: *A Young Person's Guide To King Crimson* (Island 1976)★★★, *The Compact King Crimson* (EG 1986)★★★, *The Essential King Crimson - Frame By Frame* (EG 1991)★★★★, *The Great Deceiver* (1992)★★★.

KING, CAROLE

b. Carole Klein, 9 February 1942, Brooklyn, New York, USA. A proficient pianist from the age of four, King was a prolific songwriter by her early teens. When friend and neighbour Neil Sedaka embarked on his recording career, she followed him into the New York milieu, recording demos, singing back-up and even helping arrange occasional sessions. As a student at Queen's College, New York, she met future partner and husband Gerry Goffin whose lyrical gifts matched King's grasp of melody. She completed a handful of singles, including 'The Right Girl' (1958), 'Baby Sittin'', 'Queen Of The Beach' (1959), prior to recording 'Oh Neil' (1960), a riposte to Sedaka's 'Oh Carol'. Although not a hit, her record impressed publishing magnate Don Kirshner, who signed the Goffin/King team to his Aldon Music empire. They scored notable early success with the

Shirelles ('Will You Still Love Me Tomorrow'), Bobby Vee ('Take Good Care Of My Baby') and the Drifters ('Up On The Roof') and were later responsible for much of the early output on Dimension, the company's in-house label. The duo wrote, arranged and produced hits for Little Eva ('The Locomotion') and the Cookies ('Chains' and 'Don't Say Nothin' Bad About My Baby') while a song written with Bobby Vee in mind, 'It Might As Well Rain Until September', provided King with a solo hit in 1962. Although this memorable and highly evocative song barely reached the US Top 30, it climbed to number 3 in the UK. However, two follow-up singles fared less well. The Goffin/King oeuvre matured as the 60s progressed, resulting in several sophisticated, personalized compositions, including 'A Natural Woman' (Aretha Franklin), 'Goin' Back' (Dusty Springfield and the Byrds) and 'Pleasant Valley Sunday' (the Monkees). The couple also established the short-lived Tomorrow label, but their disintegrating marriage was chronicled on King's 1967 single, 'The Road To Nowhere', the year they dissolved their partnership.

King then moved to Los Angeles and having signed to Lou Adler's Ode label, formed the City with ex-Fugs duo Danny Kortchmar (guitar) and Charles Larkey (bass). (The latter became King's second husband.) The trio's lone album included the artist's versions of 'I Wasn't Born To Follow' and 'That Old Sweet Roll (Hi De Ho)', covered, respectively, by the Byrds and Blood, Sweat And Tears. King began a solo career in 1970 with *Writer*, before fully asserting her independence with *Tapestry*. This radiant selection contained several of the singer's most incisive compositions, notably 'You've Got A Friend', a US number 1 for James Taylor, 'It's Too Late', a US chart-topper for King, and 'So Far Away'. Unlike many of her former production-line contemporaries, King was able to shrug off teen preoccupations and use her skills to address adult doubts and emotions. *Tapestry* has now sold in excess of 15 million copies worldwide and established its creator as a major figure in the singer-songwriter movement. However, the delicate balance it struck between perception and self-delusion became blurred on *Music* and *Rhymes And Reasons*, which were regarded as relative disappointments. Each set nonetheless achieved gold disc status, as did *Fantasy*, *Wrap Around Joy* (which contained her second US number 1, 'Jazzman') and *Thoroughbred*. The last marked the end of King's tenure at Ode and she has since failed to reap the same commercial success. Her first release of the 80s, *Pearls*, comprised 'classic' Goffin/King songs, a release which many interpreted as an artistic impasse. Certainly King subsequently pursued a less frenetic professional life, largely restricting her live appearances to fund-raising concerns. In the early 90s she had relocated to Ireland. Her recordings also became more measured and if *Speeding Time* or *City Streets* lacked the cultural synchronization *Tapestry* enjoyed with the post-Woodstock audience, her songwriting skills were still in evidence. In the USA *Tapestry*

exceeded 10 million copies sold in July 1995.

●ALBUMS: *Writer* (Ode 1970)★★★, *Tapestry* (Ode 1971)★★★★, *Music* (Ode 1971)★★★, *Rhymes And Reasons* (Ode 1972)★★★, *Fantasy* (Ode 1973)★★★★, *Wrap Around Joy* (Ode 1974)★★★, *Really Rosie* (Ode 1975)★★★, *Thoroughbred* (Ode 1976)★★★, *Simple Things* (Capitol 1977)★★, *Welcome Home* (Avatar 1978)★★, *Touch The Sky* (Capitol 1979)★★, *Pearls (Songs Of Goffin And King)* (Capitol 1980)★★, *One To One* (Atlantic 1982)★★, *Speeding Time* (Atlantic 1984)★★★, *City Streets* (Capitol 1989)★★, *In Concert* (Quality 1994)★★.

●COMPILATIONS: *Her Greatest Hits* (Ode 1973)★★★, *Carole King, A Natural Woman - The Ode Collection 1968-1976* (Legacy 1995)★★★★.

●VIDEOS: *In Concert* (Wienerworld 1994).

●FURTHER READING: *Carole King*, Paula Taylor. *Carole King: A Biography In Words & Pictures*, Mitchell S. Cohen.

KING, JONATHAN

b. 6 December 1944, London, England. While studying for his finals at Cambridge University, King hit the charts in 1965 with his plaintive protest song 'Everyone's Gone To The Moon'. That song has been a radio hit ever since. Although the catchy follow-up 'Green Is The Grass' failed, the English student was already revealing his entrepreneurial talents by discovering and writing for others. Hedgehopper's Anonymous gave him his second protest hit with 'It's Good News Week', while King next took on Manfred Mann with an unsuccessful cover of Bob Dylan's 'Just Like A Woman'. A perennial pop columnist and socialite, he impressed Decca Records' managing director Sir Edward Lewis who took on his talent-spotting services. King discovered, named and produced Genesis' first album, but the group soon moved to Tony Stratton-Smith's Charisma label. King, meanwhile, was releasing occasionally quirky singles like 'Let It All Hang Out' and another Dylan cover 'Million Dollar Bash'. He was also an inveterate pseudonymous hit maker, heavily involved in such studio novelty numbers as the Piglets' 'Johnny Reggae', Sakkarin's 'Sugar Sugar', the Weathermen's 'The Same Old Song' and St. Cecilia's 'Leap Up And Down (Wave Your Knickers In The Air)'.

In 1972, King launched UK Records, best remembered for its hits courtesy of 10cc rather than the label boss's latest wealth of pseudonyms, which included Shag ('Loop Di Love'), Bubblerock ('Satisfaction'), 53rd And 3rd ('Chick-A-Boom'), 100 Ton And A Feather ('It Only Takes A Minute') and Sound 9418 ('In The Mood'). He also scored a major hit in his own name during 1975 with the summer smash 'Una Paloma Blanca'. Despite his array of unlikely hits, King had many failures and as a label manager could do little with the careers of either Ricky Wilde or the Kursaal Flyers. Apart from the odd witty parody such as his reading of Cat Stevens' 'Wild World', juxtaposed to the provocative tune of the Pet

Shop Boys' 'It's A Sin', King has worked hard maintaining a high-media profile via newspaper columns, radio appearances and his BBC television programme, *Entertainment USA*. He established his own music business newpaper in 1993, the *Tip Sheet*. Always controversial, King thrives on conflict and remains a lively member of the music business.

●ALBUMS: *Or Then Again* (Decca 1965)★★, *Try Something Different* (Decca 1972)★★, *A Rose In A Fisted Glove* (UK 1975)★★, *JK All The Way* (UK 1976)★★, *Anticloning* (1992)★★.

●COMPILATIONS: *King Size King* (PRT 1982)★★, *The Butterfly That Stamped* (Castle 1989)★★, *The Many Faces Of Jonathan King* (1993)★★.

KINGFISH

Formed in 1974 in San Francisco, California, USA, Kingfish were one of the city's most popular live attractions during the late 70s. Founder-members Matt Kelly (guitar/vocals) and Chris Herold (drums) first worked together in the 60s in the New Delhi River Band. In 1968 they formed Horses who recorded an album for White Whale Records. This group's lead guitarist Bobby Hoddinot joined Kelly and Herold in 1973 in Lonesome Janet, along with Nick Ward (keyboards). When Dave Torbert (bass, ex-New Riders Of The Purple Sage and New Delhi Blues Band) was added to the line-up in 1974, Lonesome Janet became known as Kingfish. Ward died in 1974, after which Grateful Dead guitarist/vocalist Bob Weir joined the remaining musicians, boosting their popularity overnight. *Kingfish* captures their relaxed, bar band style, but it disguised internal disharmony. Weir left soon after its completion and *Live'N'Kicking* featured a four-piece group. Dave Perber replaced Herold for *Trident*, which also introduced newcomers Mike O'Neil (guitar) and Barry Flast (keyboards). Perber then left, and Mark Neilson became the group's third drummer for *Two For The Sun*. Kingfish disbanded officially in 1979, although Kelly and Flast subsequently revived the name during the 80s. *Kingfish* (1985) featured assistance from John Lee Hooker and Mike Bloomfield, as well as Bob Weir, who resumed his association with the group, albeit on a part-time basis. *Live From The Sweetwater* proved their in-concert sparkle had not disappeared.

●ALBUMS: *Kingfish* (Round 1976)★★★, *Live'N'Kicking* (Jet 1977)★★★, *Trident* (Jet 1978)★★, *Two For The Sun* (Krishner 1979)★★, *Kingfish* (Relix 1985)★★, *Live From The Sweetwater* (Relix 1986)★★★.

KINKS

It is ironic that one of Britain's most enduring and respected groups spawned from the beat boom of the early 60s has for the best part of two decades received success, adulation and financial reward in the USA. Today this most 'English' institution can still fill a vast stadium in any part of the USA, while in Britain, a few thousand devotees watch their heroes perform in a comparatively small club or hall. The Kinks is the continuing obsession of one of Britain's premier songwriting talents, Raymond Douglas Davies (b. 21 June 1944, Muswell Hill, London, England; vocals/guitar/piano). Originally known as the Ravens, the Kinks formed at the end of 1963 with a line-up comprising: Dave Davies (b. 3 February 1947, Muswell Hill, London; guitar/vocals) and Peter Quaife (b. 31 December 1943, Tavistock, Devon, England; bass), and were finally joined by Mick Avory (b. 15 February 1944, London; drums). Their first single 'Long Tall Sally' failed to sell, although they did receive a lot of publicity through the efforts of their shrewd managers Robert Wace, Grenville Collins and Larry Page. Their third single, 'You Really Got Me', rocketed to the UK number 1 spot, boosted by an astonishing performance on the UK television show *Ready Steady Go*. This and its successor, 'All Day And All Of The Night', provided a blueprint for hard rock guitar playing, with the simple but powerful riffs supplied by the younger Davies. Over the next two years Ray Davies emerged as a songwriter of startling originality and his band were rarely out of the best-sellers list. Early in 1965, the group returned to number 1 with the languid 'Tired Of Waiting For You'. They enjoyed a further string of hits that year, including 'Everybody's Gonna Be Happy', 'Set Me Free', 'See My Friend' and 'Till The End Of The Day'. Despite the humanity of his lyrics, Davies was occasionally a problematical character, renowned for his eccentric behaviour. The Kinks were equally tempestuous and frequently violent. Earlier in 1965, events had reached a head when the normally placid drummer, Mick Avory, attacked Dave Davies onstage with the hi-hat of his drum kit, having been goaded beyond endurance. Remarkably, the group survived such contretemps and soldiered on. A disastrous US tour saw them banned from that country, amid further disputes.

Throughout all the drama, Davies the songwriter remained supreme. He combined his own introspection with humour and pathos. The ordinary and the obvious were spelled out in his lyrics, but, contrastingly, never in a manner that was either. 'Dedicated Follower Of Fashion' brilliantly satirized Carnaby Street narcissism while 'Sunny Afternoon' (another UK number 1) dealt with capitalism and class. 'Dead End Street' at the end of 1966 highlighted the plight of the working class poor: 'Out of work and got no money, a Sunday joint of bread and honey', while later in that same song Davies comments 'What are we living for, two-roomed apartment on the second floor, no money coming in, the rent collector knocks and tries to get in'. All these were embraced with Davies' resigned laconic music-hall style. Their albums prior to *Face To Face* had contained a staple diet of R&B standards and comparatively harmless Davies originals. With *Face To Face* and *Something Else*, however, he set about redefining the English character, with sparkling wit and steely nerve. One of Davies' greatest songs was the final track on the latter;

'Waterloo Sunset' was a simple but emotional *tour de force* with the melancholic singer observing two lovers (many have suggested actor Terence Stamp and actress Julie Christie, but Davies denies this) meeting and crossing over Hungerford Bridge in London. It narrowly missed the top of the charts, as did the follow-up, 'Autumn Almanac', with its gentle chorus, summing up the English working class of the 50s and 60s: 'I like my football on a Saturday, roast beef on Sunday is all right, I go to Blackpool for my holiday, sit in the autumn sunlight'.

Throughout this fertile period, Ray Davies, along with John Lennon/Paul McCartney and Pete Townshend, was among Britain's finest writers. But by 1968 the Kinks had fallen from public grace in the UK, despite remaining well respected by the critics. Two superb concept albums, *The Kinks Are The Village Green Preservation Society* and *Arthur Or The Decline And Fall Of The British Empire*, failed to sell. This inexplicable quirk was all the harder to take as they contained some of Davies' finest songs. Writing honestly about everyday events seemingly no longer appealed to Davies' public. The former was likened to Dylan Thomas's *Under Milk Wood*, while *Arthur* had to compete with Pete Townshend's *Tommy*. Both were writing rock operas without each other's knowledge, but as Johnny Rogan states in his biography of the Kinks: 'Davies' celebration of the mundane was far removed from the studious iconoclasm of *Tommy* and its successors'. The last hit single during this 'first' age of the Kinks was the glorious 'Days'. This lilting and timeless ballad is another of Davies' many classics and was a major hit for Kirsty MacColl in 1989.

Pete Quaife permanently departed in 1969 and was replaced by John Dalton. The Kinks returned to the UK best-sellers lists in July 1970 with 'Lola', an irresistible fable of transvestism, which marked the beginning of their breakthrough in the USA by reaching the US Top 10. The resulting *Lola Vs Powerman And The Moneygoround Part One* was also a success there. On this record Davies attacked the music industry and in one track, 'The Moneygoround', openly slated his former managers and publishers, while alluding to the lengthy high court action in which he had been embroiled. The group now embarked on a series of huge US tours and rarely performed in Britain, although their business operation centre and recording studio, Konk, was based close to the Davies' childhood home in north London. Having signed a new contract with RCA in 1971 the band had now enlarged to incorporate a brass section, amalgamating with the Mike Cotton Sound. Following the interesting country-influenced *Muswell Hillbillies*, however, they suffered a barren period. Ray experienced drug and marital problems and their ragged half-hearted live performances revealed a man bereft of his driving, creative enthusiasm. Throughout the early 70s a series of average, over-ambitious concept albums appeared as Davies' main outlet. *Preservation Act I*, *Preservation Act II*, *Soap Opera* and *Schoolboys In Disgrace* were all thematic, and *Soap Opera* was adapted for British television as *Starmaker*. At the end of 1976 John Dalton departed, as their unhappy and comparatively unsuccessful years with RCA ended. A new contract with Arista Records engendered a remarkable change in fortunes. Both *Sleepwalker* (1977) and *Misfits* (1978) were excellent and successful albums; Ray had rediscovered the knack of writing short, punchy rock songs with quality lyrics. The musicianship of the band improved, in particular, Dave Davies, who after years in his elder brother's shadow, came into his own with a more fluid style.

Although still spending most of their time playing to vast audiences in the USA, the Kinks were adopted by the British new wave, and were cited by many punk bands as a major influence. Both the Jam ('David Watts') and the Pretenders ('Stop Your Sobbing') provided reminders of Davies' 60s songwriting skill. The British music press, then normally harsh on 60s dinosaurs, constantly praised the Kinks and helped to regenerate a market for them in Europe. Their following albums continued the pattern started with *Sleepwalker*, hard-rock numbers with sharp lyrics. Although continuing to be a huge attraction in the USA they have so far never reappeared in the UK album charts, although they are regular victims of ruthless 'Greatest Hits' packages. As Ray Davies' stormy three-year relationship with Chrissie Hynde of the Pretenders drew to its close, so the Kinks appeared unexpectedly back in the UK singles chart with the charming 'Come Dancing'. The accompanying video and high publicity profile prompted the reissue of their entire and considerable back catalogue. Towards the end of the 80s the band toured sporadically amid rumours of a final breakup. In 1990 the Kinks were inducted into the Rock 'n' Roll Hall of Fame, at the time only the fourth UK group to take the honour behind the Beatles, Rolling Stones and the Who. During the ceremony both Pete Quaife and Mick Avory were present. Later that year they received the Ivor Novello award for 'outstanding services to British music'. After the comparative failure of *UK Jive* the band left London Records, and after being without a recording contract for some time signed with Sony in 1991. Their debut for that label was *Phobia*, a good album that suffered from lack of promotion (the public still perceiving the Kinks as a 60s band). A prime example was in 'Scattered', as good a song as Davies has ever written, which when released was totally ignored apart from a few pro-Kinks radio broadcasters. Following the commercial failure of *Phobia* the band were released from their contract and put out *To The Bone*, an interesting album on their own Konk label, which satisfied long-standing fans. This unplugged session was recorded in front of a small audience at their own headquarters in Crouch End, north London, and contained semi-acoustic versions of some of Davies' classic songs. Both brothers had autobiographies published in the 90s, Ray came first with the cleverly constructed *X-Ray* and Dave responded with *Kink*, a pedestrian, though revealing, book in 1996. Whether or not they can maintain their reputation as a going concern beyond the mid-90s, Ray Davies has made his mark under the Kinks' banner as one of the most perceptive and prolific popular songwriters of our time. His catalogue of songs observing ordinary life is one of the finest available. Much of the Britpop movement from the mid-90s acknowledged a considerable debt to Davies as one of the key influences. Bands such as Supergrass, Oasis, Cast and especially Damon Alban of Blur are some of the Kinks' most admiring students.

●ALBUMS: *Kinks* (Pye 1964)★★★, *Kinda Kinks* (Pye 1965)★★★, *The Kink Kontroversy* (Pye 1966)★★★, *Face To Face* (Pye 1966)★★★★, *Live At The Kelvin Hall* (Pye 1967)★, *Something Else* (Pye 1967)★★★★★, *The Kinks Are The Village Green Preservation Society* (Pye 1968)★★★★★, *Arthur Or The Decline And Fall Of The British Empire* (Pye 1969)★★★★, *Lola Versus Powerman And The Moneygoround, Part One* (Pye 1970)★★★, *Percy* film soundtrack (Pye 1971)★★, *Muswell Hillbillies* (RCA 1971)★★★★, *Everbody's In Showbiz, Everybody's A Star* (RCA 1972)★★★ *Preservation Act 1* (RCA 1973)★★, *Preservation Act 2* (RCA 1974)★★, *Soap Opera* (RCA 1975)★★, *Schoolboys In Disgrace* (RCA 1975)★★★, *Sleepwalker* (Arista 1977)★★★, *Misfits* (Arista 1978)★★★★, *Low Budget* (Arista 1979)★★★, *One For The Road* (Arista 1980)★★★, *Give The People What They Want* (Arista 1982)★★★, *State Of Confusion* (Arista 1983)★★★, *Word Of Mouth* (Arista 1984)★★, *Think Visual* (London 1986)★★, *The Road* (London 1988)★★, *UK Jive* (London 1989)★★, *Phobia* (Columbia 1993)★★★, *To The Bone* (Konk 1994)★★★, *To The Bone (USA)* (Guardian 1996)★★★★.

●COMPILATIONS: *Well Respected Kinks* (Marble Arch 1966)★★★★, *The Kinks* double CD (Pye 1970)★★★★, *A Golden Hour Of The Kinks* (Golden Hour 1973)★★★★, *All The Good Times* 4-LP box set (Pye 1973)★★★★, *The Kinks File* (Pye 1977)★★★★, *Greatest Hits* (PRT 1983)★★★, *The Ultimate Collection* (Castle 1989)★★★★, *The EP Collection* (See For Miles 1990)★★★★, *Fab Forty: The Singles Collection, 1964-70* (Descal 1991)★★★★, *Tired Of Waiting For You* (Rhino 1995)★★★.

●FURTHER READING: *The Kinks: The Sound And The Fury*, Johnny Rogan. *The Kinks: The Official Biography*, Jon Savage. *You Really Got Me: The Kinks Part One*, Doug Hinman. *X-Ray*, Ray Davies. *Kink: An Autobiography*, Dave Davies. *The Kinks: Well Respected Men*, Neville Marten and Jeffrey Hudson.

Kiss

Following the demise of Wicked Lester, Kiss was formed in 1972 by Paul Stanley (b. Paul Eisen, 20 January 1950, Queens, New York, USA; rhythm guitar/vocals) and Gene Simmons (b. Chaim Witz, 25 August 1949, Haifa, Israel; bass/vocals), who went on to recruit Peter Criss (b. Peter Crisscoula, 27 December 1947, Brooklyn, New York, USA; drums/vocals) and Ace Frehley (b. Paul Frehley, 22 April 1951, Bronx, New York, USA; lead guitar/vocals). At their second show at the Hotel Diplomat, Manhattan, 1973, Flipside producer Bill Aucoin offered the band a management contract, and within two weeks they were signed to Neil Bogart's recently established Casablanca Records. In just over a year, Kiss had released their first three albums with a modicum of success. In the summer of 1975 their fortunes changed with the release of *Alive*, which spawned their first US hit single, 'Rock 'N' Roll All Nite'. The appeal of Kiss has always been based on their live shows: the garish greasepaint make-up, outrageous costumes, and pyrotechnic stage effects, along with their hard rocking anthems, combined to create what was billed as 'The Greatest Rock 'n' Roll Show On Earth'. Their live reputation engendered a dramatic upsurge in record sales, and *Alive* became their first certified platinum album in the USA. *Destroyer* proved just as successful, and also gave them their first US Top 10 single, earning Peter Criss a major songwriting award for the uncharacteristic ballad, 'Beth'. Subsequent releases, *Rock And Roll Over*, *Love Gun* and *Alive II*, each certified platinum, confirmed the arrival of Kiss as major recording artists. By 1977 Kiss had topped the prestigious Gallup poll as the most popular act in the USA. They had become a marketer's dream. Kiss merchandise included: make-up kits, masks, board games, and pinball machines. *Marvel Comics* produced two superhero cartoon books, and even a full length science-fiction film, *Kiss Meet The Phantom Of The Park*, was produced. The ranks of their fan club, the Kiss Army, had swollen to a six figure number. In 1978 all four group members each produced a solo album released on the same day, a feat never before envisaged, let alone matched. At the time this represented the biggest shipment of albums from one 'unit' to record stores in the history of recorded music. The albums enjoyed varying degrees of success; Ace Frehley's record came out on top and included the US hit single, 'New York Groove'. Gene Simmons, whose album featured an impressive line-up of guests including Cher, Donna Summer, Bob Seger and Janis Ian, had a hit single in the UK with 'Radioactive', which reached number 41 in 1978. After the release of *Dynasty* in 1979, which featured the worldwide hit single, 'I Was Made For Lovin' You', cracks appeared in the ranks. Peter Criss left to be replaced by session player Anton Fig, who had previously appeared on Frehley's solo album. Fig played drums on the 1980 release *Unmasked* until a permanent replacement was found in the form of New Yorker Eric Carr (b. 12 July 1950, d. 24 November 1991), who made his first appearance during the world tour of 1980. A fuller introduction came on *Music From The Elder*, an album that represented a radical departure from traditional Kiss music and included several ballads, an orchestra and a choir. It was a brave attempt to break new ground but failed to capture the imagination of the

record-buying public. Frehley, increasingly disenchanted with the musical direction of the band finally left in 1983. The two albums prior to his departure had featured outside musicians. Bob Kulick, who had contributed to the studio side of *Alive II* and played on Stanley's solo album, supplied the lead work to the four previously unreleased tracks on the *Killers* compilation of 1982 and Vincent Cusano (later to become Vinnie Vincent) was responsible for lead guitar on the 1982 release, *Creatures Of The Night*. By 1983 the popularity of the band was waning and drastic measures were called for. The legendary make-up which had concealed their true identities for almost 10 years was removed on MTV in the USA. Vinnie Vincent made his first official appearance on *Lick It Up*, an album which provided Kiss with their first Top 10 hit in the UK. The resurgence of the band continued with *Animalize*. Vincent had been replaced by Mark St. John (b. Mark Norton), a seasoned session player and guitar tutor. His association with the band was short-lived, however, as he was struck down by Reiters Syndrome. Bruce Kulick, the brother of longtime Kiss cohort Bob, was drafted in as a temporary replacement on the 1984 European Tour and subsequently became a permanent member when it became apparent that St. John would not be able to continue as a band member. Further commercial success was achieved with *Asylum* and *Crazy Nights*, the latter featuring their biggest UK hit single, 'Crazy, Crazy Nights', which peaked at number 4 in 1987 and was followed by a further two Top 40 hit singles, 'Reason To Live' and 'Turn On The Night'. *Hot In The Shade* succeeded their third compilation album, *Smashes, Thrashes And Hits,* and included their highest charting hit single in the USA, 'Forever', which reached number 4 in 1990. Work on a new Kiss album with producer Bob Ezrin was delayed following Eric Carr's illness due to complications from cancer. He died on 24 November 1991, in New York, at the age of 41. Despite this setback, Kiss contributed a cover of Argent's classic, 'God Gave Rock 'N' Roll To You', to the soundtrack of the film, *Bill And Ted's Bogus Journey*, and brought in replacement drummer Eric Singer (ex-Black Sabbath; Badlands). 1994, meanwhile, brought the *Kiss My Ass* tribute album, with contributions from Lenny Kravitz, Stevie Wonder, Garth Brooks, Lemonheads, Faith No More, Dinosaur Jr, Rage Against The Machine and others. The interest in *Kiss My Ass* led to an historic reunion for *MTV Unplugged*. A stable unit with Bruce Kulick (guitar) and Eric Singer (drums) together with Simmons and Stanley appeared to be on the cards but Frehley and Criss stepped back in for a reunion tour. So successful was the tour that Kulick and Singer were naturally a little put out and both quit. This was even more irritating for them as a new (unreleased) studio album *Carnival Of Souls* featured Kulick and Singer. With a history spanning three decades, Kiss's impact on the consciousness of a generation of music fans remains huge.
●ALBUMS: *Kiss* (Casablanca 1974)★★★, *Hotter Than Hell* (Casablanca 1974)★★, *Dressed to Kill* (Casablanca 1975)★★★, *Alive* (Casablanca 1975)★★★, *Destroyer* (Casablanca 1976)★★★★, *Rock And Roll Over* (Casablanca 1976)★★, *Love Gun* (Casablanca 1977)★★★, *Alive II* (Casablanca 1977)★★★, *Dynasty* (Casablanca 1979)★★, *Unmasked* (Casablanca 1980)★★, *Music From The Elder* (Casablanca 1981)★★, *Creatures Of The Night* (Casablanca 1982)★★, *Lick It Up* (Vertigo 1983)★★, *Animalize* (Vertigo 1984)★★, *Asylum* (Vertigo 1985)★★, *Crazy Nights* (Vertigo 1987)★★, *Hot In The Shade* (Vertigo 1989)★★, *Revenge* (Mercury 1992)★★★, *Alive III* (Mercury 1993)★★, *MTV Unplugged* (Mercury 1996)★★★.
●COMPILATIONS: *The Originals* (Casablanca 1976)★★★, *Double Platinum* (Casablanca 1978)★★★, *Killers* (Casablanca 1982)★★★, *Smashes, Thrashes And Hits* (Vertigo 1988)★★★, *Revenge* (Mercury 1992)★★, *You Wanted The Best, You Got The Best* (Mercury 1996)★★★★, *Greatest Kiss* (Mercury 1996)★★★.
●VIDEOS: *Animalize* (Embassy Home Video 1986), *The Phantom Of The Park* (IVS 1987), *Exposed* (Polygram 1987), *Crazy Crazy Nights* (Channel 5 1988), *Age Of Chance* (Virgin Vision 1988), *X-Treme Close Up* (1992), *Konfidential* (1993), *Kiss My A*** (Polygram 1994), *Unplugged* (Polygram 1996).
●FURTHER READING: *Still On Fire*, Dave Thomas. *Kiss: The Greatest Rock Show On Earth*, John Swenson. *Kiss: The Real Story Authorized*, Peggy Tomarkin. *Kiss*, Robert Duncan.

KLAATU

Klaatu was a Canadian rock trio led by vocalist, songwriter and drummer Terry Draper, who formed the group *c*.1975 along with John Woloschuk and Dee Long. The group's main claim to fame was that for a brief period a rumour circulated that Klaatu might actually be the Beatles in disguise. The first single by Klaatu - whose name was that of the robot alien in the 1951 film *The Day The Earth Stood Still* - was 'Doctor Marvello/California Jam', a minor hit in Canada on Daffodil Records and picked up in the USA by Island Records. Switching to Capitol Records in 1976, the group released a single titled 'Calling Occupants Of Interplanetary Craft'. Along with its b-side 'Sub Rosa Subway' and the accompanying album, *Klaatu* (titled *3:47 E.S.T.* in Canada), the band's sound closely resembled that of the latter-day Beatles, and when the group included no biographical material with its recordings, and supplied its record company with no information about themselves, a US journalist surmised that it might very well *be* the Beatles. The group did nothing to stem the rumours and *Rolling Stone* named Klaatu 'hype of the year' for 1977. While the story aided sales of the group's debut album, when it was revealed that Klaatu was indeed just Klaatu, sales of their future recordings diminished. The song 'Calling Occupants...' did eventually attain chart status in the hands of the Carpenters when, in 1977, it reached the US Top 40 and UK Top 10.

Klaatu meanwhile, carried on working until 1981 when, after releasing four further albums, the group eventually disbanded. Dee Long is very successful in software animation technology, Draper has his own roofing business and Woloschuk is an accountant.

●ALBUMS: *Klaatu* (Capitol 1976)★★★, *Hope* (Capitol 1977)★★, *Sir Army Suit* (Capitol 1978)★★, *Endangered Species* (Capitol 1980)★★, *Magentalane* (1981)★★.

KLARK KENT

Whether this Klark Kent is the same man who works as a reporter for the *Daily Planet* is unclear. His close friend Stewart Copeland (b. 16 July 1952, Alexandria, Egypt), drummer with the Police tells us that Kent 'dabbles in politics, religion and anthropology'. He owns a huge multi-national company called the Kent Foundation, whose sinister influence is behind many world events. Kent is unable to tour because an unpleasant odour emitted from his body makes him intolerable to other musicians. . . The truth is, of course, that Kent and Copeland are one and the same. In 1978 when the Police were still waiting for their major breakthrough, Copeland was looking for some extra-curricular activities, having previously been cited as a member of the unrealized group the Moors Murderers. Creating the *alter ego* of Kent, his first single 'Don't Care' was released on Kryptone in 1978 and later reissued on A&M when it was a minor hit. The follow-up 'Too Kool To Kalypso' (back on the Krypton label) was pressed in lurid Kryptonite green; two more singles and a solitary mini-album followed, before Kent disappeared allowing Copeland to write film music and continue drumming with the Police.

●ALBUMS: *Klark Kent* (A&M 1980)★★.

KNACK

Formed in Los Angeles in 1978, the Knack comprised Doug Fieger (vocals/guitar), Prescott Niles (bass), Berton Averre (guitar) and Bruce Gary (drums). Taking their name from a cult British movie of the 60s, they attempted to revive the spirit of the beat-boom with matching suits, and short songs boasting solid, easily memorable riffs. After garnering considerable media attention for their club appearances on the Californian coastline in early 1979, they became the fortuitous recipients of a record company bidding war, which ended in their signing to Capitol Records. The fact that this was the Beatles' US label was no coincidence, for the Knack consistently employed imagery borrowed from the 'Fab Four', both in their visual appearance and record sleeves. Their prospects were improved by the recruitment of renowned pop producer Mike Chapman, who had previously worked with Blondie. During the summer of 1979, the Knack's well-publicized debut single 'My Sharona' promptly topped the US charts for six weeks, as well as reaching the UK Top 10 and selling a million copies. The first album, *The Knack*, was a scintillating pop portfolio, full of clever hooks and driving

rhythms and proved an instant hit, selling five million copies in its year of release. Implicit in the Knack's abrupt rise were the seeds of their imminent destruction. In adapting 60s pop to snappy 70s production, they had also spiced up the standard boy/girl love songs with slightly more risqué lyrics for their modern audience. Critics, already suspicious of the powerful record company push and presumptuous Beatles comparisons, pilloried the group for their overt sexism in such songs as 'Good Girls Don't' as well as reacting harshly to Fieger's arrogance during interviews. At the height of the critical backlash, the Knack issued the apologetically titled *But The Little Girls Understand*, a sentiment that proved over-optimistic. Both the sales and the songs were less impressive and by the time of their third album, *Round Trip*, their powerpop style seemed decidedly outmoded. By the end of 1981, they voluntarily disbanded with Fieger attempting unsuccessfully to rekindle recent fame with Taking Chances, while the others fared little better with the ill-fated Gama. A reunion in 1991 resulted in the forgettable *Serious Fun*.

●ALBUMS: *The Knack* (Capitol 1979)★★★, *But The Little Girls Understand* (Capitol 1980)★★, *Round Trip* (Capitol 1981)★★, *Serious Fun* (Charisma 1991)★★.

●COMPILATIONS: *The Best Of ...* (1993)★★.

KNIGHT, GLADYS, AND THE PIPS

Gladys Knight (b. 28 May 1944, Atlanta, Georgia, USA), her brother Merald 'Bubba' (b. 4 September 1942, Atlanta, Georgia, USA), sister Brenda and cousins Elenor Guest and William Guest (b. 2 June 1941, Atlanta, Georgia, USA) formed their first vocal group in their native Atlanta in 1952. Calling themselves the Pips, the youngsters sang supper-club material in the week, and gospel music on Sundays. They first recorded for Brunswick in 1958, with another cousin to the Knights, Edward Patten (b. 2 August 1939) and Langston George making changes to the group line-up the following year when Brenda and Elenor left to get married. Three years elapsed before their next sessions, which produced a version of Johnny Otis' 'Every Beat Of My Heart' for the small Huntom label. This song, which highlighted Knight's bluesy, compelling vocal style, was leased to Vee Jay Records when it began attracting national attention, and went on to top the US R&B charts. By this time, the group, now credited as Gladys Knight And The Pips, had signed a long-term contract with Fury Records, where they issued a re-recording of 'Every Beat Of My Heart' which competed for sales with the original release. Subsequent singles such as 'Letter Full Of Tears' and 'Operator' sealed the group's R&B credentials, but a switch to the Maxx label in 1964 - where they worked with producer Van McCoy - brought their run of successes to a halt. Langston George retired from the group in the early 60s, leaving the quartet line-up which survived into the 80s.

In 1966, Gladys Knight and the Pips were signed to Motown's Soul subsidiary, where they were teamed up with producer/songwriter Norman Whitfield. Knight's tough vocals left them slightly out of the Motown mainstream, and throughout their stay with the label the group were regarded as a second-string act. In 1967, they had a major hit single with the original release of 'I Heard It Through The Grapevine', an uncompromisingly tough performance of a song that became a Motown standard in the hands of its author Marvin Gaye in 1969. 'The Nitty Gritty' (1968) and 'Friendship Train' (1969) proved equally successful, while the poignant 'If I Were Your Woman' was one of the label's biggest-selling releases of 1970. In the early 70s, the group slowly moved away from their original blues-influenced sound towards a more middle-of-the-road harmony blend. Their new approach brought them success in 1972 with 'Neither One Of Us (Wants To Say Goodbye)'. Later that year, Knight and The Pips elected to leave Motown for Buddah, unhappy at the label's shift of operations from Detroit to Hollywood. At Buddah, the group found immediate success with the US chart-topper 'Midnight Train To Georgia', an arresting soul ballad, while major hits like 'I've Got To Use My Imagination' and 'The Best Thing That Ever Happened To Me' mined a similar vein. In 1974, they performed Curtis Mayfield's soundtrack songs for the film *Claudine*; the following year, the title track of *I Feel A Song* gave them another soul number 1. Their smoother approach was epitomized by the medley of 'The Way We Were/Try To Remember' which was the centrepiece of *Second Anniversary* in 1975 - the same year that saw Gladys and the group host their own US television series.

Gladys made her acting debut in *Pipedream* in 1976, for which the group recorded a soundtrack album. Legal problems then dogged their career until the end of the decade, forcing Knight and the Pips to record separately until they could sign a new deal with CBS. *About Love* in 1980 teamed them with the Ashford And Simpson writing/production partnership, and produced a strident piece of R&B social comment in 'Bourgie Bourgie'. Subsequent releases alternated between the group's R&B and MOR modes, and hits like 'Save The Overtime (For Me)' and 'You're Number One In My Book' (1983) and, after a move to MCA Records, 'Love Overboard' (1988), demonstrated that they could work equally well in either genre. The latter song earned them a Grammy award for the Best R&B performance in early 1989. Following this, Knight and the Pips split. Merald remained with Knight as she achieved a UK Top 10 that year with the James Bond movie song, 'Licence To Kill'.
●ALBUMS: *Letter Full Of Tears* (Fury 1961)★★, *Gladys Knight And The Pips* (Maxx 1964)★★, *Everybody Needs Love* (Soul 1967)★★★, *Feelin' Bluesy* (Soul 1968)★★★, *Silk 'N' Soul* (Soul 1969)★★★, *Nitty Gritty* (Soul 1969)★★★, *All In A Knight's Work* (Soul 1970)★★★, *If I Were Your Woman* (Soul 1971)★★★, *Standing Ovation* (Soul 1972)★★★, *Neither One Of Us* (Soul 1973)★★★★, *All I Need Is Time* (Soul 1973)★★★, *Imagination* (Buddah 1973)★★★★, *Knight Time* (Soul 1974)★★, *Claudine* (Buddah 1974)★★★, *I Feel A Song* (Buddah 1974)★★★, *A Little Knight Music* (Soul 1975)★★★, *Second Anniversary* (Buddah 1975)★★★, *Bless This House* (Buddah 1976)★★, *Pipe Dreams* soundtrack (Buddah 1976)★★, *Still Together* (Buddah 1977)★★★, *About Love* (Columbia 1980)★★, *Touch* (Columbia 1981)★★★, *That Special Time Of Year* (Columbia 1982)★★, *Visions* (Columbia 1983)★★★, *Life* (Columbia 1985)★★★, *All Our Love* (MCA 1987)★★★. Solo: Gladys Knight *Miss Gladys Knight* (Columbia 1979)★★, *Good Woman* (MCA 1991)★★★. The Pips *At Last - The Pips* (1979)★★, *Callin'* (1979)★★.
●COMPILATIONS: *Greatest Hits* (Soul 1970)★★★★, *Anthology* (Motown 1974)★★★★, *Best Of* (Buddah 1976)★★★★, *30 Greatest* (K-Tel 1977)★★★, *The Collection - 20 Greatest Hits* (1984)★★★, *The Singles Album* (Polygram 1989)★★★, *17 Greatest Hits* (1992)★★★.

KOKOMO (UK)

Formed in 1973, this blue-eyed soul band was made up from the remnants of several British groups. Vocalists Dyan Birch, Paddie McHugh and Frank Collins were ex-members of Arrival, a superior pop harmony band, while Neil Hubbard (guitar) and Alan Spenner (bass) had previously worked with Joe Cocker's Grease Band. The line-up was completed by further formidable musicians, Tony O'Malley (piano), Jim Mullen (guitar), Terry Stannard (drums), Joan Linscott (congas) and journeyman saxophonist Mel Collins. A popular live attraction, Kokomo's acclaimed debut album suggested a future akin to that of the Average White Band. However, the group failed to sustain its promise and quickly ran out of inspiration, possibly because of the conflict of so many strong musical ideas and styles. This line-up split in January 1977, but a reconstituted version of the band appeared on the London gig circuit in the early 80s and recorded one album. The fluctuating activity of the group saw yet another reunion in the latter part of the 80s. This incarnation faltered when Alan Spenner died in August 1991.
●ALBUMS: *Kokomo* (Columbia 1975)★★★, *Rise And Shine* (Columbia 1976)★★, *Kokomo* (Columbia 1982)★★. Solo:Tony O'Malley *Naked Flame* (Jazz House 1995)★★★.
●COMPILATIONS: *The Collection* (1992)★★★.

KONGOS, JOHN

This singing multi-instrumentalist left his native South Africa for London in 1966. After leading a group called Scrub through several unsuccessful singles, he was signed as a solo artist by Dawn Records who released 1969's *Confusions About Goldfish*. A transfer to Fly two years later and the services of producer Gus Dudgeon and engineer Roy Thomas Baker gave Kongos a fleeting taste of pop fame when 'He's Gonna Step On You Again' and 'Tokoloshe Man' each bounded to number four in the UK charts. These highly inventive singles and their

associated album were blessed with studio assistance from a cast that included Lol Coxhill, Mike Moran, Ray Cooper, Caleb Quaye and Ralph McTell. Kongos' uncompromising lyrics were born of the socio-political state back home paralleling a flavour of the Transvaal in backing tracks that anticipated the fusions of Johnny Clegg in the 80s. In 1990, the Happy Mondays covered 'Tokoloshe Man' (as 'Step On'), reaching the UK Top 5.
●ALBUMS: *Kongos* (Fly 1971)★★★.
●COMPILATIONS: *Tokoloshe Man Plus ...* (See For Miles 1990)★★★.

KOOPER, AL

b. 5 February 1944, Brooklyn, New York, USA. Kooper embarked upon a professional music career in 1959 as guitarist in the Royal Teens, who had enjoyed a novelty hit the previous year with 'Short Shorts'. He became a noted New York session musician and later forged a successful songwriting partnership with Bobby Brass and Irwin Levine. Their collaborations included 'This Diamond Ring', a chart-topper for Gary Lewis And The Playboys, 'I Must Be Seeing Things' (Gene Pitney) and 'The Water Is Over My Head' (the Rockin' Berries). In 1965, producer Tom Wilson asked Kooper to attend a Bob Dylan session. With Mike Bloomfield already installed on guitar, the eager musician opted for organ, an instrument with which he was barely conversant. Dylan nonetheless loved his instinctive touch which breathed fire into 'Like A Rolling Stone' and its attendant *Highway 61 Revisited* album. Kooper maintained his links with Dylan over the years, guesting on *Blonde On Blonde* (1966), *New Morning* (1970) and *Under The Red Sky* (1990).

Kooper became involved in several electric folk sessions, notably for Tom Rush *(Take A Little Walk With Me)* and Peter, Paul And Mary *(Album)*. His solo version of 'I Can't Keep From Crying Sometimes' appeared on an Elektra label sampler, *What's Shakin'*, and his reading of 'Parchman Farm' was issued as a single in 1966. The organist was then invited to join the Blues Project, which became one of America's leading urban R&B acts. Kooper left the group in 1967 to found Blood, Sweat And Tears, one of the originals of US jazz-rock, with whom he remained for one album before internal unrest resulted in his dismissal. He accepted a production post at Columbia Records, before recording the influential *Super Session* with Mike Bloomfield and Stephen Stills. This successful informal jam inspired several inferior imitations, not the least of which was the indulgent *Live Adventures Of Al Kooper And Mike Bloomfield*, which featured cameos by Elvin Bishop and the then relatively unknown Carlos Santana when Bloomfield was unable to finish the schedule. Kooper's solo career was effectively relaunched with *I Stand Alone*, but in keeping with many of his albums, this promising set was marred by inconsistency. A limited vocalist, his best work relied on his imaginative arrangements, which drew on the big band jazz of

Maynard Ferguson and Don Ellis (whom he produced), and the strength of the supporting cast. *You Never Know Who Your Friends Are* and *New York City (You're A Woman)* were among his most popular releases. His double set *Easy Does It* contained a superb slowed-down version of Ray Charles' 'I Got A Woman', resplendent with an exquisite jazz-piano solo introduction. Kooper, however, remained best-known for his role as a catalyst. He appeared on *Electric Ladyland* (Jimi Hendrix) and *Let It Bleed* (Rolling Stones) and produced the debut albums by Nils Lofgren and the Tubes. He established his own label, Sounds Of The South, in Atlanta, Georgia, and secured international success with early protégés Lynyrd Skynyrd.

During the 70s, Kooper became involved in several Blues Project reunions and the following decade he formed Sweet Magnolia, an *ad hoc* group comprising several studio musicians. In 1982, he completed *Championship Wrestling*, his first solo album for five years, which featured contributions from guitarist Jeff 'Skunk' Baxter (Steely Dan and Doobie Brothers). Al Kooper has since pursued an active career recording computerized soundtrack music, but in 1991 produced *Scapegoats* for Green On Red. Now happily living in Nashville, Kooper has been a major background personality in American rock for more than 30 years and has made a considerable contribution.
●ALBUMS: with Mike Bloomfield, Stephen Stills *Super Session* (Columbia 1968)★★★★, *The Live Adventures Of Al Kooper And Mike Bloomfield* (Columbia 1969)★★, *I Stand Alone* (Columbia 1969)★★, *You Never Know Who Your Friends Are* (Columbia 1969)★★, with Shuggie Otis *Kooper Session* (Columbia 1970)★★, *Easy Does It* (Columbia 1970)★★★, *Landlord* (1971)★★, *New York City (You're A Woman)* (Columbia 1971)★★★, *A Possible Projection Of The Future/Childhood's End* (Columbia 1972)★, *Naked Songs* (1973)★★, *Unclaimed Freight* (Columbia 1975)★★, *Act Like Nothing's Wrong* (United Artists 1977)★★, *Championship Wrestling* (1982)★★, *Live: Soul Of A Man* (Music Masters 1995)★★★.
●COMPILATIONS: *Al's Big Deal* (Columbia 1989)★★★.
●FURTHER READING: *Backstage Pass*, Al Kooper with Ben Edmonds.

KOSSOFF, PAUL

b. 14 September 1950, Hampstead, London, England, d. 19 March 1976. The son of English actor David Kossoff, Paul was an inventive, impassioned guitar player who was initially a member of Black Cat Bones, a nascent late 60s blues band which included drummer Simon Kirke. In 1968, both musicians became founder members of Free and later worked together in Kossoff, Kirke, Tetsu And Rabbit, a spin-off project which completed a lone album in 1971 during a hiatus in the parent group's career. Free was reconstituted in 1972, but Kossoff's tenure during this second phase was blighted by recurring drug and related health problems. Absent on portions of several tours, Kossoff finally left the group to pursue a solo career. *Back Street Crawler* contained several excellent performances, notably 'Molten Gold', but it was two years before the guitarist was well enough to resume live work. He accompanied John Martyn on a 1975 tour before assembling a new group, also entitled Back Street Crawler. The quintet completed one album but projected concerts were cancelled when Kossoff suffered a near-fatal heart attack. Specialists forbade an immediate return, but plans were hatched for a series of concerts the following year. However, in March 1976, Paul Kossoff died in his sleep during a flight from Los Angeles to New York. On Jim Capaldi's 1975 solo album, *Short Cut Draw Blood*, two songs were reputedly written in tribute to Kossof: 'Seagull' and 'Boy With A Problem'. Kossoff played lead guitar on the latter, presumably oblivious to the poignant lyrics.

●ALBUMS: *Back Street Crawler* (Island 1973)★★★, *Live In Croydon, June 15th 1975* (Repertoire 1995)★★.

●COMPILATIONS: *Koss* (DJM 1977)★★★, *The Hunter* (Street Tunes 1983)★★, *Leaves In The Wind* (Street Tunes 1983)★★, *Blue Soul* (Island 1986)★★★, *The Collection* (Hit Label 1995)★★★.

KOTTKE, LEO

b. 11 September 1945, Athens, Georgia, USA. This inventive guitarist drew inspiration from the country-blues style of Mississippi John Hurt and having taken up the instrument as an adolescent, joined several aspiring mid-60s groups. Induction into the US Navy interrupted his progress, but the artist was discharged following an accident that permanently damaged his hearing. Kottke subsequently ventured to Minneapolis where a spell performing in the city's folk clubs led to a recording deal. *Circle Round The Sun* received limited exposure via two independent outlets, but his career did not fully flourish until 1971 when John Fahey invited Kottke to record for his company, Takoma. *Six And Twelve String Guitar* established the artist as an exciting new talent, with a style blending dazzling dexterity with moments of introspection. Kottke's desire to expand his repertoire led to a break with Fahey and a major deal with Capitol Records. *Mudlark* included instrumental and vocal tracks, notably a version of the Byrds' 'Eight Miles High', and while purists bore misgivings about Kottke's languid, sonorous voice, his talent as a guitarist remained unchallenged. Several excellent albums in a similar vein ensued, including *Greenhouse*, which boasted an interpretation of Fahey's 'Last Steam Engine Train', and the in-concert *My Feet Are Smiling*. Prodigious touring enhanced Kottke's reputation as one of America's finest acoustic 12-string guitarists, although he was unable to convert this standing into commercial success. He later switched labels to Chrysalis, but by the 80s had returned to independent outlets on which his crafted approach has continued to flourish.

●ALBUMS: *12-String Blues: Live At The Scholar Coffee House* (Oblivion 1968)★★★, *Six And Twelve String Guitar* (Takoma/Sonet 1971)★★★, *Circle Round The Sun* (Symposium 1970)★★★, *Mudlark* (Capitol 1971)★★★, *Greenhouse* (Capitol 1972)★★★★, *My Feet Are Smiling* (Capitol 1973)★★★★, *Ice Water* (Capitol 1974)★★★★, *Dreams And All That Stuff* (Capitol 1975)★★, *Chewing Pine* (Capitol 1975)★★★, *Leo Kottke* (Chrysalis 1976)★★★★, *Burnt Lips* (Chrysalis 1979)★★★, *Balance* (Chrysalis 1979)★★, *Leo Kottke Live In Europe* (Chrysalis 1980), *Guitar Music* (Chrysalis 1981)★★★, *Time Step* (Chrysalis 1983)★★★★, *A Shout Towards Noon* (Private Music 1986)★★★, *Regards From Chuck Pink* (Private Music 1988)★★★★, *My Father's Face* (Private Music 1989)★★★, *That's What* (Private Music 1990)★★★, *Great Big Boy* (Private Music 1991)★★★, *Peculiaroso* (Private Music 1994)★★★, *Live* (Private Music 1995)★★★, *Standing In My Shoes* (Private Music 1997)★★★★.

●COMPILATIONS: *Leo Kottke 1971-1976 - Did You Hear Me?* (Capitol 1976)★★★, *The Best Of Leo Kottke* (Capitol 1977)★★★, *The Best Of Leo Kottke* (EMI 1979)★★★, *Essential Leo Kottke* (Chrysalis 1991)★★★★.

KURSAAL FLYERS

Formed in Southend, Essex, England, the Kursaal Flyers - Paul Shuttleworth (vocals), Graeme Douglas (guitar), Vic Collins (guitar/steel guitar/vocals), Richie Bull (bass/vocals), and Will Birch (drums) - secured the approbation of producer Jonathan King who signed the quintet to his label, UK. *Chocs Away* and *The Great Artiste* enjoyed considerable praise for their grasp of melodic pop, and the group also became a popular live attraction, with Shuttleworth's 'spiv' persona an undoubted focal point. The Kursaals attained commercial success after joining CBS. 'Little Does She Know' reached the Top 20 in 1975 although the group struggled to find a suitable follow-up. Barry Martin replaced Douglas when the latter joined Eddie And The Hot Rods, but the unit disintegrated following *Five Live Kursaals*. Will Birch subsequently formed the Records, but having compiled the commemorative *In For A Spin*, reunited the Flyers for *Former Tour De Force Is Forced To Tour*.

●ALBUMS: *Chocs Away* (UK 1975)★★★, *The Great Artiste* (UK 1975)★★★, *Golden Mile* (Columbia 1976)★★★, *Five Live Kursaals* (Columbia 1977)★★, *Former Tour De Force Is Forced To Tour* (Waterfront 1988)★★.

●COMPILATIONS: *The Best Of The Kursaal Flyers* (Teldec 1983)★★★, *In For A Spin* (Edsel 1985)★★★.

L

Sweethearts Of The Apollo (Atlantic 1963)★★★, Sleigh Bells, Jingle Belles (Atlantic 1963)★★, On Stage (Atlantic 1964)★★, Over The Rainbow (Atlantic 1966)★★; as LaBelle LaBelle (1971)★★★, Moonshadow (1972)★★★, Pressure Cookin' (1973)★★★★, Nightbirds (Epic 1974)★★★★, Phoenix (Epic 1975)★★, Chameleon (Epic 1976)★★, Burnin' (1991)★★.
●COMPILATIONS: The Early Years (1993)★★★, Over The Rainbow - The Atlantic Years (1994)★★★.

LABELLE

This popular soul act evolved from two friends, Patti LaBelle (b. Patricia Holte, 24 May 1944, Philadelphia, Pennsylvania, USA) and Cindy Birdsong (b. 15 December 1939, Camden, New Jersey, USA) who sang together in a high school group, the Ordettes. In 1962, they teamed up with two girls from another local attraction, the Del Capris - Nona Hendryx (b. 18 August 1945, Trenton, New Jersey, USA) and Sarah Dash (b. 24 May 1942, Trenton, New Jersey, USA). Philadelphia producer Bobby Martin named the quartet after a local label, Bluebell Records, becoming Patti LaBelle And The Blue-Belles. Infamous for their emotional recordings of 'You'll Never Walk Alone', 'Over The Rainbow' and 'Danny Boy', the quartet also wrung a fitting melodrama from 'I Sold My Heart To The Junkman' and 'Down The Aisle (Wedding Song)'. This almost kitchen-sink facet has obscured more lasting work, of which 'Groovy Kind Of Love' (later a hit for the Mindbenders) is a fine example. Cindy Birdsong left the group in 1967 to replace Florence Ballard in the Supremes but the remaining trio stayed together despite failing commercial fortunes. Ex-patriot Briton, Vicki Wickham, a former producer on UK television's pop show Ready Steady Go!, became their manager and suggested the trio drop their now-anachronistic name and image and embrace a rock-orientated direction. Having supported the Who on a late 60s concert tour, LaBelle then accompanied Laura Nyro on Gonna Take A Miracle, a session which inspired their album debut. One of the few female groups to emerge from the passive 60s to embrace the radical styles of the next decade, their album releases won critical praise, but the trio did not gain commercial success until the release of Nightbirds. The 1975 single 'Lady Marmalade (Voulez-Vous Coucher Avec Moi Ce Soir?)' was an international hit single produced by Allen Toussaint and composed by Bob Crewe and Kenny Nolan. Subsequent singles, however, failed to emulate this achievement. Phoenix and Chameleon were less consistent, although the group continued to court attention for their outlandish, highly visual, stage costumes. LaBelle owed much of its individuality to Nona Hendryx, who emerged as an inventive and distinctive composer. Her sudden departure in 1976 was a fatal blow and the group broke apart. Patti embarked on a solo career and has since enjoyed considerable success.
●ALBUMS: as Patti LaBelle And The Blue-Belles

LAKE

This multi-national rock band was formed in Hamburg, Germany, in 1973. Initial members included Ian Cussick (b. Scotland; vocals), Geoff Pacey (b. England; keyboards), Bernie Whelan (b. Ireland; trumpet), plus four European partners (three German, one Italian). Despite innumerable line-up shuffles Lake's harmonic, neo-orchestral approach to rock music remained intact, which led to a glowing and growing international reputation. Their self-titled 1976 debut album enhanced this impression further, and sold over 400,000 copies in Germany. A fierce retinue of gigs included several open air concerts throughout mainland Europe, dates at the London Marquee in England and a 40-concert tour of the US (where the album charted). After a live album they returned to the studio in 1978 for Lake II, which was promoted by an appearance on the UK's Old Grey Whistle Test television programme and support slots with Genesis and Bob Dylan. They were also voted the best rock band in several German music polls. The constantly revolving line-ups continued to make their history confusing, and by the late 70s the group's personnel included James Hopkins-Harrison (d. May 1991; vocals), Alex Conti (guitar) and Detlef Petersen (keyboards). By 1981 the band decided that, having failed to capitalize on their initial success, it was time to go their separate ways. Conti went on to a solo career, while other members became embroiled in session work. There was subsequently a brief and successful reunion of various former members in 1983.
●ALBUMS: Lake (Columbia 1976)★★★, Live (Columbia 1977)★★, Lake II (Columbia 1978)★★, Paradise Island (Columbia 1979)★★, Ouch (1980)★★, Hot Day (1981)★, Live/On The Run (1982)★★.

LANE, RONNIE

b. 1 April 1946, London, England, d. 4 June 1997, Trinidad, Colorado, USA. A founder-member of the Small Faces and Faces, Lane left for a highly stylized solo career in 1973. He formed a backing group, Slim Chance, which included (Benny) Gallagher And (Graham) Lyle, and had a UK Top 20 hit with the effervescent 'How Come?', in 1974. In the same year 'The Poacher' was a UK Top 40 hit, but the group were unable to maintain their chart success. Ronnie's debut, Anymore For Anymore, was a finely honed mixture of good-time original songs and folksy cover versions, the most impressive of which was Lane's reading of Derroll

Adams' 'Roll On Babe'. Lane's progress, however, faltered on an ambitious tour, the Passing Show, with its attendant fire-eaters and jugglers. Financial burdens caused its abandonment and the original Slim Chance broke up in disarray. A new line-up was later convened around Brian Belshaw (bass - formerly of Blossom Toes), Steve Simpson (guitar/mandolin), Ruan O'Lochlainn (keyboards/saxophone), Charlie Hart (keyboards/accordion) and Colin Davey (drums). Two excellent albums, *Ronnie Lane's Slim Chance* and *One For The Road*, confirmed the promise of that first collection. The singer disbanded his group in 1977, although several ex-members, including Gallagher, Lyle and Hart, appeared on *Rough Mix*, Ronnie's excellent collaboration with Who guitarist Pete Townshend. This critically acclaimed release was preceded by *Mahoney's Last Stand*, a less satisfying venture with former Faces member Ron Wood. Although Lane completed another stylish collection, *See Me* in 1979, his progress was blighted by the debilitating disease, multiple sclerosis. Over the years Lane's condition deteriorated considerably and he lived in comparative poverty, although efforts were made to raise money for him through various rock benefits. Despite his illness, he still managed to play live in the USA and embarked on a tour in Japan during 1990. He finally lost his battle against the disease in 1997, dying at his adopted home in Trinidad, Colorado, where he lived with his wife and stepchildren.

●ALBUMS: *Anymore For Anymore* (GM 1973)★★★, *Ronnie Lane's Slim Chance* (GM 1974)★★★★, *One For The Road* (GM 1975)★★★★, with Ron Wood *Mahoney's Last Stand* (Atlantic 1976)★★★, with Pete Townshend *Rough Mix* (Polydor 1977)★★★★, *See Me* (Gem 1979)★★★.

LAST POETS

Coming out of the poverty-stricken ghetto of Harlem, New York, in the mid-60s, there are many who claim the Last Poets to be the first hip hop group proper. Comprising Suliaman El Hadi, Alafia Pudim, Nilijah, Umar Bin Hassan (aka Omar Ben Hassan - as with other personnel name alterations occurred frequently) and Abio Dun Oyewole, the Last Poets formed on 19 May 1968 (Malcolm X's birthday). Hassan was not actually an original member, joining the band after seeing them perform on campus and insisting on membership. Together, the Last Poets recorded powerful protest gems like 'Niggas Are Scared Of Revolution' and 'White Man's Got A God Complex'. Their legacy, that of the innovative use of rap/talk over musical backing, has born obvious fruit in subsequent generations of hip hop acts. Oyewole left after their debut album. They re-formed in 1984, with two 12-inch singles, 'Super Horror Show' and 'Long Enough', although the group was still split into two separate camps. More recently Hassan released a solo LP featuring Bootsy Collins, Buddy Miles and others, after a period of seclusion, and drug and family problems. He has been keeping company with rap stars

like Arrested Development and Flavor Flav, and also starred in John Singleton's *Poetic Justice* film. While not bitter about failing to reap the financial rewards that subsequent rappers have done, Hassan remains philosophical: 'As far as I'm concerned we made a market, for those young boys to have their careers . . . I understand that some brothers are still trying to find their manhood. But it ain't about drive-by shootings. That's madness. Self-destruction. Real gangsters don't go around shooting everybody'. Another former Last Poet, Jalal Nuridin, who released an album alongside Kool And The Gang and Eric Gale under the title Lightnin' Rod (*Hustlers Convention*), went on to become mentor to the UK's acid jazz fusion team, Galliano. Incidentally, this is a different Last Poets to the one comprising David Nelson, Felipe, Luciano and Gylan Kain who titled themselves the Original Last Poets and recorded an album for Juggernaut in 1971.

●ALBUMS: *The Last Poets* (Douglas 1970)★★★, *This Is Madness* (Douglas 1971)★★★, *Oh My People* (Celluloid 1985)★★★, *Freedom Express* (Acid Jazz 1989)★★★, *Scattarap/Home* (Bond Age 1994)★★★, *Holy Terror* (Ryko 1995)★★★. Solo: Oyewole *25 Years* (Rykodisk 1995)★★★. Umar Bin Hassan *Be Bop Or Be Dead* (Axiom 1993)★★★. Jalal Nuridin As Lightnin' Rod *Hustlers Convention* (Douglas 1973)★★★.

●COMPILATIONS: *Right On!* (Collectables 1986)★★★.

LAST WALTZ, THE

By 1976, years of road life coupled with personal excess had taken its toll of the Band. Famed as Bob Dylan's backing group and creators of milestone albums, *Music From Big Pink* and *The Band*, the group was beset by internal problems. They decided to host a farewell Thanksgiving Day concert at San Francisco's Winterland Ballroom which would be filmed for posterity by Martin Scorsese. The extravaganza not only featured some of the Band's best-known material, including 'The Night They Drove Old Dixie Down' and 'The Weight', the group was clearly inspired to invest the songs with renewed vigour. *The Last Waltz* was also a showcase for acts with whom they associated themselves. One of their early inspirations, Muddy Waters, provided a searing rendition of 'Mannish Boy' and Ronnie Hawkins, whom the Band backed in an earlier incarnation, the Hawks, offered an explosive 'Who Do You Love'. San Francisco-based poet Lawrence Ferlingetti brought a literary air to the proceedings - much to Band drummer Levon Helm's chagrin - whereas contributions from Joni Mitchell, Neil Young, Eric Clapton and Van Morrison were more in keeping with the notion of a rock concert. The arrival of Bob Dylan wrought images of his tours with the Band in 1966 and 1972, and the event closed with an all-cast version of the hymnal 'I Shall Be Released'. A commemorative three-album set formed a précis of the evening's proceedings. *The Last Waltz* film also featured newly recorded material, shot in a studio some months following the concert. Interview footage with Band members was also included, much of which reflected a jaded perception of their history and the project itself. Only guitarist/composer Robbie Robertson, the prime mover of the film, showed real enthusiasm. Nonetheless, *The Last Waltz* is an endearing tribute to one of rock's most fascinating groups and, given the advent of punk the following year, acts as a eulogy to an entire generation of musicians.

●ALBUMS: *The Last Waltz* (Warners 1977)★★★.

LAWRENCE, SYD

b. 26 June 1923, Shotton, Flintshire, Wales. As a child Lawrence studied violin but began playing cornet with a brass band. In 1941, he became a professional musician, playing dance music but then entered the Royal Air Force. During his military service he became a member of the RAF Middle East Command Dance Orchestra. After the war, he played with, among others, Ken Mackintosh and Geraldo. In 1953, he joined the BBC Northern Dance Orchestra, where he remained for 15 years. Towards the end of his stint with the orchestra Lawrence formed a rehearsal band, playing the kind of dance music and swing popularized in the late 30s and 40s by American bands, especially that led by Glenn Miller. Over the next few months Lawrence found that his rehearsal band was attracting a growing audience which was especially appreciative of the Miller music he had transcribed from records. In 1969, he made the decision to form a full-time professional band and has remained in the business ever since. Although in its original concept Lawrence's band played highly derivative music, it was done with such spirit and enthusiasm that he has successfully retained an audience for concerts and records.

●ALBUMS: *Syd Lawrence And The Glenn Miller Sound* (1971)★★★, *Something Old, Something New* (Philips 1972)★★★, *My Favourite Things* (1973)★★★, *Singin' 'N' Swingin'* (1975)★★★, *Great Hits Of The 30s, Volume 1* (1975)★★★, *Ritual Fire Dance* (1975)★★★, *Band Beat* (BBC 1976)★★★, *Disco Swing* (1976)★★★, *Swing Classics* (Philips 1982)★★★, *Remember Glenn Miller* (Ditto 1983)★★★, *Holland Special* (Philips 1986)★★★, *Big Band Swing* (Philips 1988).

●COMPILATIONS: *The Syd Lawrence Collection* (1976)★★★, *Spotlight On The Syd Lawrence Orchestra* (1977)★★★.

LEANDER, MIKE

b. 30 June 1941, England, d. 18 April 1996, Spain. Leander, a respected composer and songwriter, will best be remembered by rock and pop fans for his contribution to the ascendancy of Gary Glitter in the 70s. Leander played drums, piano and guitar as a child before giving up legal studies to pursue a music career in composition at the Trinity College Of Music in London. He joined Decca Records as musical director at the age of 20, after studio work with artists including

the Rolling Stones and Phil Spector. While at Decca his achievements included arranging the string section for the Beatles' 'She's Leaving Home' (from *Sgt. Pepper's Lonely Hearts Club Band*). Other production, composition and arranging credits included Joe Cocker, Marianne Faithfull, Alan Price, Shirley Bassey, Gene Pitney and Roy Orbison. In the USA the Drifters took Leander's version of 'Under The Boardwalk' to number 1. It was his work with Gary Glitter, however, which gave him his most high-profile success in the UK. As well as writing most of Glitter's successful songs, Leander also discovered the then Paul Raven in 1965 when he was working as a warm-up act. They chose the stage name Gary Glitter together and developed the high camp persona with which the artist would take the stage. Leander also came up with the visual image of shoulder pads, high stack-heeled boots, outlandish hair and garish costumes with which Glitter would be associated long into the 90s. Leander and Glitter wrote their first song together, the enduring 'Rock And Roll', then a sequence of successful singles including 'I Didn't Know I Loved You (Till I Saw You Rock And Roll)', 'Oh Yes, You're Beautiful' and 'I Love You Love Me Love'. They also worked together on Glitter's signature tune, the hugely successful 'I'm The Leader Of The Gang (I Am)' - remaining unconcerned about clumsy parentheses getting in the way of otherwise snappy song titles. Leander married model Penny Carter in 1974, and continued to win awards for his compositions outside of his work with Glitter, including one for the role of executive producer on Andrew Lloyd Webber and Tim Rice's *Jesus Christ Superstar*. Leander was also a member of the MCC and a keen cricket supporter, but he retired to Majorca at the end of the 70s. A musical for the West End, *Matador*, was considered a relative failure in 1991. He returned again three years later with a series of cassettes featuring actors reading the work of Henry Miller and extracts from the *Kama Sutra*.

LED ZEPPELIN

This pivotal quartet was formed in October 1968 by British guitarist Jimmy Page (b. James Patrick Page, 9 January 1944, Heston, Middlesex, England) following the demise of his former band, the Yardbirds. John Paul Jones (b. John Baldwin, 3 June 1946, Sidcup, Kent, England; bass/keyboards), a respected arranger and session musician, replaced original member Chris Dreja, but hopes to incorporate vocalist Terry Reid floundered on a contractual impasse. The singer unselfishly recommended Robert Plant (b. 20 August 1948, West Bromwich, West Midlands, England), then frontman of struggling Midlands act Hobbstweedle, who in turn introduced drummer, John Bonham (b. 31 May 1948, Birmingham, England, d. 25 September 1980) when first choice B.J. Wilson opted to remain with Procol Harum. The quartet gelled immediately and having completed outstanding commitments under the name 'New Yardbirds', became Led Zeppelin following an off-the-cuff quip by the Who's Keith Moon, who remarked that they would probably go down like a lead Zeppelin when rating their prospects. Armed with a prestigious contract with Atlantic Records, the group toured the USA supporting Vanilla Fudge prior to the release of their explosive debut *Led Zeppelin*, which included several exceptional original songs, including; 'Good Times, Bad Times', 'Communication Breakdown', 'Dazed And Confused' - a hold-over from the Yardbirds' era, and skilled interpretations of R&B standards 'How Many More Times?' and 'You Shook Me'. The set vied with Jeff Beck's *Truth* as the definitive statement of English heavy blues/rock, but Page's meticulous production showed a greater grasp of basic pop dynamics, resulting in a clarity redolent of 50s rock 'n' roll. His staggering dexterity was matched by Plant's expressive, beseeching voice, a combination that flourished on *Led Zeppelin II*. The group was already a headline act, drawing sell-out crowds across the USA, when this propulsive collection confirmed an almost peerless position. The introductory track, 'Whole Lotta Love', a thinly-veiled rewrite of Willie Dixon's 'You Need Love', has since become a classic, while 'Livin' Lovin' Maid' and 'Moby Dick', Bonham's exhibition piece, were a staple part of the quartet's early repertoire. Elsewhere, 'Thank You' and 'What Is And What Should Never Be' revealed a greater subtlety, a factor emphasized more fully on *Led Zeppelin III*. Preparation for this set had been undertaken at Bron-Y-Aur cottage in Snowdonia (immortalized in 'Bron-Y-Aur Stomp') and a resultant pastoral atmosphere permeated the acoustic-based selections, 'That's The Way' and 'Tangerine'. 'The Immigrant Song' and 'Gallow's Pole' reasserted the group's traditional fire and the album's release confirmed Led Zeppelin's position as one of the world's leading attractions. In concert, Plant's sexuality and Adonis-like persona provided the perfect foil to Page's more mercurial character, yet both individuals took full command of the stage, the guitarist's versatility matched by his singer's unfettered roar.

Confirmation of the group's ever-burgeoning strengths appeared on *Led Zeppelin IV*, also known as 'Four Symbols', the 'Runes Album' or 'Zoso', in deference to the fact that the set bore no official title. It included the anthemic 'Stairway To Heaven', a group *tour de force*. Arguably the definitive heavy-rock song, it continues to win polls and the memorable introduction remains every guitar novice's first hurdle. The approbation granted this ambitious piece initially obscured other contents, but the energetic 'When The Levee Breaks' is now also lauded as a masterpiece, particularly for Bonham's drumming. 'Black Dog' and 'Rock 'N' Roll' saw Zeppelin at their immediate best, while 'The Battle Of Evermore' was marked by a vocal contribution from Sandy Denny. *IV* was certified as having sold 16 million copies in the USA by March 1996. However, the effusive praise this album generated was notably more muted for *Houses Of The Holy*. Critics queried its musically

diverse selection - the set embraced folk ballads, reggae and soul - yet when the accustomed power was unleashed, notably on 'No Quarter', the effect was inspiring. A concurrent US tour broke all previous attendance records, the proceeds from which helped finance an in-concert film, issued in 1976 as *The Song Remains The Same*, and the formation of the group's own record label, Swan Song. Bad Company, the Pretty Things and Maggie Bell were also signed to the company, which served to provide Led Zeppelin with total creative freedom. *Physical Graffiti*, a double set, gave full rein to the quartet's diverse interests with material ranging from compulsive hard-rock ('Custard Pie' and 'Sick Again') to pseudo-mystical experimentation ('Kashmir'). The irrepressible 'Trampled Underfoot' joined an ever-growing lexicon of peerless performances while 'In My Time Of Dying' showed an undiminished grasp of progressive blues. Sell-out appearances in the UK followed the release, but rehearsals for a projected world tour were abandoned in August 1975 when Plant sustained multiple injuries in a car crash. A new album was prepared during his period of convalescence, although problems over artwork delayed its release. Advance orders alone assured *Presence* platinum status, yet the set was regarded as a disappointment and UK sales were notably weaker. The 10-minute maelstrom, 'Achilles Last Stand', was indeed a remarkable performance, but the remaining tracks were competent rather than fiery and lacked the accustomed sense of grandeur. In 1977 Led Zeppelin began its rescheduled US tour, but on 26 July news reached Robert Plant that his six-year-old son, Karac, had died of a viral infection. The remaining dates were cancelled amid speculation that the group would break up.

They remained largely inactive for over a year, but late in 1978 flew to Abba's Polar recording complex in Stockholm. Although lacking the definition of earlier work, *In Through The Out Door* was a strong collection on which John Paul Jones emerged as the unifying factor. Two concerts at Britain's Knebworth Festival were the prelude to a short European tour on which the group unveiled a stripped-down act, inspired, in part, by the punk explosion. Rehearsals were then undertaken for another US tour, but in September 1980, Bonham was found dead following a lengthy drinking bout. On 4 December, Swansong announced that the group had officially retired, although a collection of archive material, *Coda*, was subsequently issued. Jones later became a successful producer, notably with the Mission, while Plant embarked on a highly successful solo career, launched with *Pictures At Eleven*. Page scored the film *Death Wish 2* and, after a brief reunion with Plant and the Honeydrippers project in 1984, he inaugurated the short-lived Firm with Paul Rogers. He then formed the Jimmy Page Band with John Bonham's son, Jason, who in turn drummed with Led Zeppelin on their appearance at Atlantic's 25th Anniversary Concert in 1988. Despite renewed interest in the group's career, particularly in the wake of the retrospective *Remasters*, entreaties to make this a permanent reunion have been resisted. However, in 1994 Page and Plant went two thirds of the way to a reformation with their ironically titled *Unledded* project, though John Paul Jones was conspicuous by his absence (for want of an invitation). Although their commercial success is unquestionable, Led Zeppelin are now rightly recognized as one of the most influential bands of the rock era and their catalogue continues to provide inspiration to successive generations of musicians.

●ALBUMS: *Led Zeppelin* (Atlantic 1969)★★★★, *Led Zeppelin II* (Atlantic 1969)★★★★, *Led Zeppelin III* (Atlantic 1970)★★★★, *Led Zeppelin IV* (Atlantic 1971)★★★★, *Houses Of The Holy* (Atlantic 1973)★★★, *Physical Graffiti* (Swan Song 1975)★★★, *Presence* (Swan Song 1976)★★★, *The Song Remains The Same* film soundtrack (Swan Song 1976)★★, *In Through The Out Door* (Swan Song 1979)★★★, *Coda* (Swan Song 1982)★★.

●COMPILATIONS: *Led Zeppelin* 4-CD box set (Swan Song 1991)★★★★, *Remasters* (Swan Song 1991)★★★★, *Remasters II* (Swan Song 1993)★★★.

Page And Plant: *Unledded* (Fontana 1994)★★★.

●VIDEOS: *The Song Remains The Same* (1986).

●FURTHER READING: *Hammer Of The Gods*, Stephen Davis. *Led Zeppelin: A Celebration*, Dave Lewis. *Led Zeppelin*, Michael Gross and Robert Plant. *Led Zeppelin*, Howard Mylett. *Led Zeppelin: In The Light 1968-1980*, Howard Mylett and Richard Bunton. *Led Zeppelin In Their Own Words*, Paul Kendall. *Led Zeppelin: A Visual Documentary*, Paul Kendall. *Led Zeppelin: The Book*, Jeremy Burston. *Jimmy Page: Tangents Within A Framework*, Howard Mylett. *Led Zeppelin: The Final Acclaim*, Dave Lewis. *Illustrated Collector's Guide To Led Zeppelin*, Robert Godwin. *Led Zeppelin: Heaven & Hell*, Charles Cross and Erik Flannigan. *Stairway To Heaven*, Richard Cole with Richard Trubo. *Led Zeppelin: Breaking And Making Records*, Ross Clarke. *Led Zeppelin: The Definitive Biography*, Ritchie Yorke. *On Tour With Led Zeppelin*, Howard Mylett (ed.). *Led Zeppelin*, Chris Welch. *The Essential Guide To The Music Of ...*, Dave Lewis.

LEE, ALBERT

b. 21 December 1943, Leominster, Herefordshire, England. Lee is a country rock guitarist of breathtaking ability. If a poll of polls were taken from leading guitarists in the field, Lee would be the likely winner. During the early 60s he was the guitarist of the R&B-influenced Chris Farlowe And The Thunderbirds. He departed in 1967, as by then offers of session work were pouring in. During that time he joined Country Fever, playing straight honky-tonk country music before recording as Poet And The One Man Band with Chas Hodges (later of Chas And Dave). The unit evolved into Heads Hands And Feet, a highly respected band, playing country/rock. It was during this stage in his career that Lee became a 'guitar hero'; he was able to

play his Fender Telecaster at breakneck speed and emulate and outshine his American counterparts. Lee played with the Crickets in 1973-74 and spent an increasing amount of time in America, eventually moving out there. After appearing on a reunion album with Chris Farlowe in 1975, he joined Emmylou Harris's Hot Band, replacing one of his heroes, the legendary James Burton. During the late 70s and early 80s Lee performed in touring bands with Eric Clapton, Jackson Browne, Jerry Lee Lewis and Dave Edmunds. His solo on 'Sweet Little Lisa' on Edmund's *Repeat When Necessary* is a superb example of the man's skill. Lee played a major part in the historic reunion of the Everly Brothers at London's Royal Albert Hall in 1983, and he continues to be a member of their regular touring band. He has made only two solo albums, both of which are impressive outings from one of Britain's finest guitarists.

●ALBUMS: *Hiding* (A&M 1979)★★★, *Albert Lee* (Polydor 1983)★★★, *Speechless* (MCA 1987)★★★, and Hogan's Heroes *Live At Montreux* rec. 1992 (Round Tower 1994)★★★.

LEE, ALVIN

b. 19 December 1944, Nottingham, England. Guitarist Lee began his professional career in the Jaybirds, a beat-trio popular both locally and in Hamburg, Germany. In 1966, an expanded line-up took a new name, Ten Years After, and in turn became one of Britain's leading blues/rock attractions with Lee's virtuoso solos its main attraction. His outside aspirations surfaced in 1973 with *On The Road To Freedom*, a collaboration with American Mylon Lefevre, which included support from George Harrison, Steve Winwood and Mick Fleetwood. When Ten Years After disbanded the following year, the guitarist formed Alvin Lee & Co. with Neil Hubbard (guitar), Tim Hinkley (keyboards), Mel Collins (saxophone), Alan Spenner (bass) and Ian Wallace (drums). Having recorded the live *In Flight*, Lee made the first of several changes in personnel, but although he and Hinkley were joined by Andy Pyle (bass, ex-Blodwyn Pig) and Bryson Graham (drums) for *Pump Iron!*, the group struggled to find its niche with the advent of punk. Lee toured Europe fronting Ten Years Later (1978-80) and the Alvin Lee Band (1980-81), before founding a new quartet, known simply as Alvin Lee, with Mick Taylor (guitar, ex-John Mayall/Rolling Stones), Fuzzy Samuels (bass, ex-Crosby, Stills, Nash And Young) and Tom Compton (drums). This promising combination promoted *RX-5*, but later split. In 1989, Lee reconvened the original line-up of Ten Years After to record *About Time*. Lee released *Zoom* in 1992 with Sequel Records, after finding the majaor companies were not interested. Although offering nothing new, it was a fresh and well-produced record, and featured George Harrison on backing vocals.

●ALBUMS: with Mylon Lefevre *On The Road To Freedom* (Columbia 1973)★★★, *In Flight* (Columbia 1975)★★★,

Pump Iron! (Columbia 1975)★★, *Rocket Fuel* (Polydor 1978)★★, *Ride On* (Polydor 1979)★★★, *Free Fall* (Avatar 1980)★★, *RX-5* (Avatar 1981)★★★, *Detroit Diesel* (21 Records 1986)★★★, *Zoom* (Sequel 1992)★★, *Nineteen Ninety Four* (Magnum Music 1994)★★, *I Hear You Rockin'* (Viceroy 1994)★★★, *Pure Blues* (Chrysalis 1995)★★★.

LEE, ARTHUR

b. 1944, Memphis, Tennessee, USA. Lee's musical career began in Los Angeles with Arthur Lee And The LAGs. This instrumental group - Lee (organ), Johnny Echols (guitar), Alan Talbot (saxophone), Roland Davis (drums) - was inspired by Booker T. And The MGs as demonstrated by their lone single, 'The Ninth Wave' (1963). Lee also pursued a career as a songwriter, composing two surfing songs, 'White Caps' and 'Ski Surfin' Sanctuary', and 'My Diary', a local R&B hit for singer Rosa Lee Brooks which featured Jimi Hendrix on guitar. Lee then began an association with producer Bob Keene's group of labels, writing 'I've Been Trying' for protégé Little Ray and performing 'Luci Baines' - 'Twist And Shout' clone, with a new group, the American Four. Lee also composed 'Everybody Jerk' and 'Slow Jerk' for a thriving bar-band, Ronnie And The Pomona Casuals. Both songs appeared on the unit's lone album and featured Lee on lead vocals. The all-pervasive success of the Byrds inspired Lee to form a folk rock band, initially dubbed the Grass Roots, but later known as Love. He led this erratically brilliant group throughout its tempestuous history, but temporarily abandoned the name in 1972 for his solo album, *Vindicator*. This energized set featured support from Band-Aid, which included Frank Fayad (bass), Don Poncher (drums) and guitarists Craig Tarwarter (Ex-Daily Flash and Jeff Simmons) and Charles Karp. The collection polarized opinion; some bemoaned its unsubtle approach, while others praised its exciting aggression. Lee then joined Paul A. Rothschild's Buffalo label, but a completed album was shelved when the company folded. Lee subsequently resurrected Love. The singer resumed his solo career in 1977 with a four-track EP, which included the haunting 'I Do Wonder'. These tracks later formed the basis of a second album, *Arthur Lee*, but its newer material showed a sad lack of direction. The singer undertook another comeback in 1992 with *Arthur Lee And Love*, issued on the independent French outlet, New Rose. It included the captivating 'Five String Serenade', later covered by Mazzy Star, but the overall set was again marred by baffling inconsistancy. An attendent promotional tour provided flashes of Lee's former genius, particularly his appearance at the Creation label's 10th anniversary concert. In 1994 he formed yet another incarnation of Love, releasing 'Girl On Fire'/'Midnight Sun' on the independent Distortions label. He remains an enigmatic figure on America's West Coast and both he and his groups have retained their cult following. Any stable musical unions are unlikely as Lee now suffers from parkinson's disease. In 1996 he was impri-

sioned with an 8 year sentence for threatening his neighbours with a gun.
●ALBUMS: *Vindicator* (A&M 1972)★★, *Arthur Lee* (Beggars Banquet 1981)★★, as Arthur Lee And Love *Arthur Lee And Love* (New Rose 1992)★★.

LENNON, JOHN

b. 9 October 1940, Liverpool, England, d. 8 December 1980, New York, USA. John Winston Ono Lennon has been exhumed in print more than any other popular musical figure, including the late Elvis Presley, of whom Lennon said that he 'died when he went into the army'. Such was the cutting wit of a deeply loved and sadly missed giant of the 20th century. As a member of the world's most successful group ever, he changed lives for the better. Following the painful collapse of the Beatles, he came out a wiser but angrier person. Together with his wife Yoko Ono, he attempted to transform the world through non-musical means. To many they appeared as naïve crackpots, Ono in particular has been victim of some appalling insults in the press. One example shown in the film *Imagine* depicts the cartoonist Al Capp being both hostile and dangerously abusive. Their bed-in in Amsterdam and Montreal, their black bag appearances onstage, their innocent flirting with political activists and radicals, all received massive media attention. These events were in search of world peace, which regrettably was unachievable. What Lennon did achieve, however, was to educate us all to the idea of world peace. During the Gulf War of 1991, time and time again various representatives of those countries who were initially opposed to war (and then asked for a ceasefire), unconsciously used Lennon's words; 'Give Peace A Chance'. The importance of that lyric could never have been contemplated, when a bunch of mostly stoned members of the Plastic Ono Band sat on the floor of the Hotel La Reine and recorded 'Give Peace A Chance', a song that has grown in stature since its release in 1969.

Lennon's solo career began a year earlier with *Unfinished Music No 1 - Two Virgins*. The sleeve depicted him and Ono standing naked, and the cover became better known than the disjointed sound effects contained within. Three months later Lennon continued his marvellous joke on us, with *Unfinished Music No 2 - Life With The Lions*. One side consisted of John and Yoko calling out to each other during her stay in a London hospital while pregnant. Lennon camped by the side of her bed during her confinement and subsequent miscarriage. Four months after 'Give Peace a Chance', 'Cold Turkey' arrived via the Plastic Ono Band, consisting of Lennon, Ono, Eric Clapton, Klaus Voorman and drummer Alan White. This raw rock song about heroin withdrawal was also a hit, although it failed to make the Top 10. Again, Lennon's incorrigible wit worked when he sent back his MBE to the Queen, protesting about the Biafran war, Britain supporting the American involvement in Vietnam and 'Cold Turkey' slipping down the charts. In February 1970, a cropped-headed Lennon was seen performing 'Instant Karma' on the BBC Television programme *Top Of The Pops*; this drastic action was another anti-war protest. This Phil Spector-produced offering was his most melodic post-Beatles song to date and was his biggest hit thus far in the UK and the USA. The release of *John Lennon - Plastic Ono Band* in January 1971 was a shock to the system for most Beatles' fans. This stark 'primal scream' album was recorded following treatment with Dr. Arthur Janov. It is as brilliant as it is disturbing. Lennon poured out much of his bitterness from his childhood and adolescence, neat and undiluted. The screaming 'Mother' finds Lennon grieving for her loss and begging for his father. Lennon's Dylanesque 'Working Class Hero' is another stand-out track; in less vitriolic tone he croons: 'A working class hero is something to be, if you want to be a hero then just follow me'. The irony is that Lennon was textbook middle-class and his agony stemmed from the fact that he *wanted* to be working class. The work was a cathartic exorcism for Lennon, most revealing on 'God', in which he voiced the heretical, 'I don't believe in the Beatles . . . ', before adding, 'I just believe in me, Yoko and me, and that's reality.' More than any other work in the Lennon canon, this was a farewell to the past. The album was brilliant, and 20 or more years later, it is regarded as his finest complete work.

1971 was his most creative year; following the album was another strong single, 'Power To The People', and after his move to New York, *Imagine* was released in October. Whilst the album immediately went to number 1 internationally, it was a patchy collection. The attack on Paul McCartney in 'How Do You Sleep?' was laboured over in the press and it took two decades before another track, 'Jealous Guy', was accepted as a classic, and only then after Bryan Ferry's masterly cover became a number 1 hit. Lennon's resentment towards politicians was superbly documented in 'Gimme Some Truth' when he spat out, 'I'm sick and tired of hearing things from uptight, short-sighted, narrow-minded hypocrites'. The title track, however, remains as one of his greatest songs. Musically 'Imagine' is extraordinarily simple, but the combination of that simplicity and the timeless lyrics make it one of the finest songs of the century. A Christmas single came in December, 'Happy Christmas (War Is Over)', another song destined for immortality and annual reissue. Again, an embarrassingly simple message: 'War is over if you want it'. The following year *Sometime In New York City* was issued; this double set contained a number of political songs, and was written during the peak of Lennon's involvement with hippie-radical, Jerry Rubin. Lennon addresses numerous problems with angry lyrics over deceptively melodic songs. The lilting and seemingly innocent 'Luck Of The Irish' is one example of melody with scathing comment. The album's strongest track is yet another song with one of

Lennon's statement-like titles: 'Woman Is the Nigger Of The World'. Once again he was ahead of the game, making a bold plea for women's rights a decade before it became fashionable. The following year he embarked on his struggle against deportation and the fight for his famous 'green card'. At the end of a comparatively quiet 1973, Lennon released *Mind Games*, an album that highlighted problems between him and Yoko. Shortly afterwards, Lennon left for his 'lost weekend' and spent many months in Los Angeles in a haze of drugs and alcohol. During a brief sober moment he produced Nilsson's *Pussycats*. At the end of a dreadful year, John released *Walls And Bridges*, which contained more marital material and a surprise US number 1, 'Whatever Gets You Through The Night'; a powerful rocker with Lennon sounding in complete control. That month (November 1974), he made his last ever concert appearance when he appeared onstage at Madison Square Garden with Elton John. That night Lennon was reunited with Ono and, in his words, 'the separation failed'.

Rock 'N' Roll was released the next year; it was a tight and energetic celebration of many of his favourite songs, including 'Slippin' And Slidin'', 'Peggy Sue' and a superb 'Stand By Me'. The critics and public loved it and it reached number 6 on both sides of the Atlantic. Following the birth of their son Sean, Lennon became a house husband, while Ono looked after their not inconsiderable business interests. Five years later, a new album was released to a relieved public and went straight to number 1 virtually worldwide. The following month, with fans still jubilant at Lennon's return, he was suddenly brutally murdered by a gunman outside his apartment building in Manhattan. Almost from the moment that Lennon's heart stopped in the Roosevelt Hospital the whole world reacted in unprecedented mourning, with scenes usually reserved for royalty and world leaders. His records were re-released and experienced similar sales and chart positions to that of the Beatles' heyday. While all this happened, one could 'imagine' Lennon calmly looking down on us, watching the world's reaction, and having a celestial laugh.

●ALBUMS: *Unfinished Music No1 - Two Virgins* (Apple 1968)★, *Unfinished Music No2 - Life With The Lions* (Zapple 1969)★, *The Wedding Album* (Apple 1969)★, *The Plastic Ono Band; Live Peace In Toronto 1969* (Apple 1970)★★★, *John Lennon Plastic Ono Band* (Apple 1971)★★★★★, *Imagine* (Apple 1971)★★★★, *Sometime In New York City* (Apple 1972)★★★, *Mind Games* (Apple 1973)★★★, *Walls And Bridges* (Apple 1974)★★★, *Rock 'N' Roll* (Apple 1975)★★★, *Double Fantasy* (Geffen 1980)★★★, *Heartplay - Unfinished Dialogue* (Polydor 1983)★, *Milk And Honey* (Polydor 1984)★★, *Live In New York City* (Capitol 1986)★★, *Menlove Ave* (Capitol 1986)★★, *The Last Word* (Baktabak 1988)★, *Imagine - Music From The Motion Picture* (Parlophone 1988)★★, *John & Yoko: The Interview* (BBC 1990)★.

●COMPILATIONS: *Shaved Fish* (Apple 1975)★★★★,

The John Lennon Collection (Parlophone 1982)★★★★★, *The Ultimate John Lennon Collection* (Parlophone 1990)★★★★.

●VIDEOS: *The Bed-In* (PMI 1991), *The John Lennon Video Collection* (PMI 1992), *One To One* (BMG 1993).

●FURTHER READING: *In His Own Write*, John Lennon. *The Penguin John Lennon*, John Lennon. *Lennon Remembers: The Rolling Stone Interviews*, Jann Wenner. *The Lennon Factor*, Paul Young. *The John Lennon Story*, George Tremlett. *John Lennon: One Day At A Time: A Personal Biography Of The Seventies*, Anthony Fawcett. *A Twist Of Lennon*, Cynthia Lennon. *John Lennon: The Life & Legend*, Editors Of Sunday Times. *John Lennon In His Own Words*, Miles . *A Spaniard In The Works*, John Lennon *Lennon: What Happened!*, Timothy Green (ed.). *Strawberry Fields Forever: John Lennon Remembered*, Vic Garbarini and Brian Cullman with Barbara Graustark. *John Lennon: Death Of A Dream*, George Carpozi. *The Lennon Tapes: Andy Peebles In Conversation With John Lennon And Yoko Ono*, Andy Pebbles. *The Ballad Of John And Yoko*, Rolling Stone Editors. *The Playboy Interviews With John Lennon And Yoko Ono*, John Lennon. *John Lennon: In My Life*, Peter Shotton and Nicholas Schaffner. *Loving John*, May Pang. *Dakota Days: The Untold Story Of John Lennon's Final Years*, John Green. *The Book Of Lennon*, Bill Harry. *John Ono Lennon 1967-1980*, Ray Coleman. *John Winston Lennon 1940-1966*, Ray Coleman. *Come Together: John Lennon In His Own Time*, Jon Wiener. *John Lennon: For The Record*, Peter McCabe and Robert D. Schonfeld. *The Lennon Companion: 25 Years Of Comment*, Elizabeth M. Thomson and David Gutman. *Imagine John Lennon*, Andrew Solt and Sam Egan. *Skywriting By Word Of Mouth*, John Lennon. *The Lives Of John Lennon*, Albert Goldman. *John Lennon My Brother*, Julia Baird. *The Other Side Of Lennon*, Sandra Shevey. *Days In The Life: John Lennon Remembered*, Philip Norman. *The Murder Of John Lennon*, Fenton Bresler. *The Art & Music Of John Lennon*, John Robertson. *In My Life: John Lennon Remembered*, Kevin Howless and Mark Lewisohn. *John Lennon: Living On Borrowed Time*, Frederic Seaman. *Let Me Take You Down: Inside The Mind Of Mark Chapman*, Jack Jones. *The Immortal John Lennon 1940-1980*, Michael Heatley. *John Lennon*, William Ruhlmann. *AI: Japan Through John Lennon's Eyes (A Personal Sketchbook)*, John Lennon.

●FILMS: *A Hard Day's Night* (1964), *Help* (1965), *Magical Mystery Tour* (1968), *Let It Be* (1971).

LEWIE, JONA

b. *c.*1943, England. A former member of Brett Marvin And The Thunderbolts and Terry Dactyl And The Dinosaurs, Lewie was one of several unconventional artists signed to the Stiff label. *On The Other Hand There's A Fist* maintained the quirky approach of earlier acts, but despite an appearance on the highly publicized *Be Stiff* tour, the artist remained largely unknown until 1980 when 'You'll Always Find Me In The Kitchen At Parties' broached the UK Top 20. A follow-up release,

'Stop The Cavalry', reached number 3 later that year when its nostalgic brass arrangement proved popular in the Christmas market. However, a subsequent album, *Heart Skips Beat*, failed to consolidate this success. 'Stop The Cavalry' continues to be an annual favourite during the Christmas season, thanks to its inclusion on compilation albums.

●ALBUMS: *On The Other Hand There's A Fist* (Stiff 1980)★★★, *Heart Skips Beat* (Stiff 1982)★★★.

●COMPILATIONS: *Gatecrasher* (Sonet 1979)★★★.

LEYTON BUZZARDS

This new wave/pop group was formed by Geoffrey Deanne (b. 10 December 1954, London, England; vocals) and David Jaymes (b. 28 December 1954, Woodford, Essex, England; bass). They recruited Kevin Steptoe (drums) and Dave Monk (guitar). From playing R&B covers on the pub circuit, they changed direction in 1976 after witnessing the new punk movement at the Roxy Club in London. By the following year they had secured a record deal with Small Wonder Records, releasing the single '19 & Mad', and changing surnames to the likes of Nick Nayme (Deanne) to reinforce their new image. After the single, Monk was replaced by Vernon Austin. After entering The Band Of Hope And Glory contest, jointly sponsored by the *Sun* newspaper and BBC Radio 1, they won the final at the London Palladium. Their prize was a recording contract with Chrysalis. The result was the band's best-remembered moment, as 'Saturday Night (Beneath The Plastic Palm Trees)' saw them appearing on *Top Of The Pops*, celebrating band members' former weekend drinking and fighting antics. Shortening their name to the Buzzards, they were unable to capitalize on their early success, though their last Chrysalis single 'We Make A Noise' featured a cover designed by Monty Python's Terry Gilliam. The contract-fulfilling *Jellied Eels To Record Deals* compiled early singles, demos, and radio session tracks. Their final recording was a one-off single for WEA Records titled 'Can't Get Used To Losing You', before Deane and Jaymes set up the more successful, salsa-flavoured Modern Romance.

●ALBUMS: *Jellied Eels to Record Deals* (Chrysalis 1979)★★.

LIEUTENANT PIGEON

From Coventry, England, this 'novelty' group evolved from the minor local band, Stavely Makepiece. Lieutenant Pigeon's line-up comprised Robert Woodward (piano), Stephen Johnson (bass) and Nigel Fletcher (drums). Their single, 'Mouldy Old Dough', an instrumental occasionally punctuated by the deadpan refrain of the title, was issued in January 1972. It was revived the following autumn and topped the UK charts for four weeks. The single had actually been recorded in Woodward's front room and featured his 60-year-old mother, Hilda, on piano. Although strong candidates for one-hit-wonder status, the group managed one more

UK Top 20 hit, 'Desperate Dan'. An attempt to incorporate disco music on 'And The Fun Goes On' failed to reach the charts and afterwards Lieutenant Pigeon returned to obscurity as a genuine chart curio, at least in the UK. However, the group enjoyed further success abroad, with 1974's 'I'll Take You Home' becoming their third Australian number 1 single. The group finally broke up in 1978, with Fletcher joining two unsuccessful groups, Tasty and Oakie. He subsequently worked for British Rail before reuniting with former bandmate Steve Johnson (also of Tasty) on his Mediatrax documentary video production unit. Johnson also recorded as Class 50, while Woodward still works on freelance studio projects.
●ALBUMS: *Mouldy Old Music* (Decca 1973)★★, *Pigeon Pie* (Decca 1974)★, *Pigeon Party* (Decca 1974)★.

LIGHTFOOT, GORDON
b. 17 November 1938, Orillia, Ontario, Canada. Lightfoot moved to Los Angeles during the 50s where he studied at Hollywood's Westlake College of Music. Having pursued a short-lived career composing jingles for television, the singer began recording demos of his own compositions which, by 1960, owed a considerable debt to folk singers Pete Seeger and Bob Gibson. Lightfoot then returned to Canada and began performing in Toronto's Yorktown coffeehouses. His work was championed by several acts, notably Ian And Sylvia and Peter, Paul And Mary. Both recorded the enduring 'Early Morning Rain', which has since become a standard, while the latter group also enjoyed a hit with his 'For Lovin' Me'. Other successful compositions included 'Ribbon Of Darkness', which Marty Robbins took to the top of the US country chart, while such renowned artists as Bob Dylan, Johnny Cash, Elvis Presley and Jerry Lee Lewis have all covered Lightfoot's songs. Having joined the Albert Grossman management stable, the singer made his debut in 1966 with the promising *Lightfoot*. *The Way I Feel* and *Did She Mention My Name* consolidated the artist's undoubted promise, but it was not until 1970 that he made a significant commercial breakthrough with *Sit Down Young Stranger*. Producer Lenny Waronker added an edge to Lightfoot's approach which reaped an immediate benefit with a US Top 5 hit, 'If You Could Read My Mind'. The album also included the first recording of Kris Kristofferson's 'Me And Bobbie McGee'. A series of crafted albums enhanced his new-found position and in 1974 the singer secured a US number 1 with the excellent 'Sundown'. Two years later 'The Wreck Of The Edmund Fitzgerald' peaked at number 2, but although Lightfoot continued to record mature singer-songwriter-styled material, his increasing reliance on safer, easy-listening perspectives proved unattractive to a changing rock audience. Gordon Lightfoot nonetheless retains the respect of his contemporaries, although his profile lessened quite considerably during the 80s.
●ALBUMS: *Lightfoot* (United Artists 1966)★★★, *Early*

Lightfoot (United Artists 1966)★★★, *The Way I Feel* (United Artists 1967)★★★, *Did She Mention My Name* (United Artists 1968)★★★, *Back Here On Earth* (United Artists 1969)★★, *Sunday Concert* (United Artists 1969)★★★, *Sit Down Young Stranger* aka *If You Could Read My Mind* (Reprise 1970)★★★★, *Summer Side Of Life* (Reprise 1971)★★, *Don Quixote* (Reprise 1972)★★★, *Old Dan's Records* (Reprise 1972)★★, *Sundown* (Reprise 1974)★★★, *Cold On The Shoulder* (Reprise 1975)★★, *Summertime Dream* (Reprise 1976)★★★, *Endless Wire* (Warners 1978)★★, *Dream Street Rose* (Warners 1980)★★, *Shadows* (Warners 1982)★★, *Salute* (Warners 1983)★★★, *East Of Midnight* (Warners 1986)★★★, *Waiting For You* (1993)★★★.
●COMPILATIONS: *The Very Best Of Gordon Lightfoot* (United Artists 1974)★★★, *Gord's Gold* (Reprise 1975)★★★, *The Best Of Gordon Lightfoot* (Warners 1981)★★★, *Gord's Gold, Volume 2* (Warners 1988)★★.
●FURTHER READING: *Gordon Lightfoot*, Alfrieda Gabiou. *If You Could Read My Mind*, Maynard Collins.

LIMMIE AND THE FAMILY COOKING
Led by Limmie Snell (b. Dalton, Alabama, USA), this vocal trio was hugely popular on the UK disco scene in the mid-70s. Limmie's first musical influence was gospel but at the age of 11 he made a series of novelty records as Lemmie B. Good. He next formed a singing group with his sisters Jimmy and Martha. After an initial recording for Phil Spector's Scepter label, they were signed to Avco, where Steve Metz and Sandy Linzer produced the catchy 'You Can Do Magic', a UK Top 10 hit in 1973. This was followed by the less successful 'Dreamboat', but the next year the trio had another UK best seller with a revival of the Essex's 1963 hit 'A Walking Miracle'. More pop than soul, Limmie And the Family Cooking next recorded a version of the 50s hit 'Lollipop'. Despite its failure, the group remained a favourite with British disco audiences and appeared on soul revival bills in the UK over the next decade.

LINDISFARNE
This Newcastle, UK-based quintet - Alan Hull (b. 20 February 1945, Newcastle-upon-Tyne, Tyne And Wear, England, d. 18 November 1995; vocals/guitar/piano), Simon Cowe (b. 1 April 1948, Jesmond Dene, Tyne And Wear, England; guitar), Ray Jackson (b. 12 December 1948, Wallsend, Tyne And Wear, England; harmonica/mandolin), Rod Clements (b. 17 November 1947, North Shields, Tyne And Wear, England; bass/violin) and Ray Laidlaw (b. 28 May 1948, North Shields, Tyne And Wear, England; drums) - was originally known as the Downtown Faction, but took the name Lindisfarne in 1968. Their debut *Nicely Out Of Tune*, was issued the following year and this brash mixture of folk rock and optimistic harmonies is arguably the group's most satisfying set. The album contained the wistful and lyrically complex 'Lady Eleanor'. Their

popularity flourished with the release of *Fog On The Tyne* the humorous title track celebrating life in Newcastle and containing such verses as; 'Sitting in a sleazy snack-bar sucking sickly sausage rolls'. The number 1 album's attendant single, 'Meet Me On The Corner', reached the UK Top 5 in 1972 where it was followed by a re-released 'Lady Eleanor'. *Fog On The Tyne* was produced by Bob Johnston, and although they pursued this relationship on a third selection, *Dingly Dell*, the group was unhappy with his work and remixed the set prior to release. The final results were still disappointing, creatively and commercially, and tensions within the line-up were exposed during an ill-fated tour of the USA. In 1973, Laidlaw, Cowe and Clements left for a new venture, Jack The Lad. Kenny Craddock (keyboards), Charlie Harcourt (guitar), Tommy Duffy (bass) and Paul Nichols (drums) were brought in as replacements but this reconstituted line-up lacked the charm of its predecessor and was overshadowed by Alan Hull's concurrent solo career. A 1974 release, *Happy Daze*, offered some promise, but Lindisfarne was disbanded the following year. The break, however, was temporary and the original quintet later resumed working together. They secured a recording deal with Mercury Records and in 1978 enjoyed a UK Top 10 single with 'Run For Home'. Despite further releases, Lindisfarne was unable to repeat this success and subsequently reached an artistic nadir with *C'mon Everybody*, a medley of rock 'n' roll party favourites with six of the group's own best-known songs saved for the finale. In November 1990, Lindisfarne were back in the UK charts, joined together with the England international footballer, and fellow Geordie, Paul Gascoigne. Their reworked, and inferior, version of 'Fog On The Tyne' reached number 2. Although they are now restricted to only the occasional chart success, the group's following remains strong, particularly in the north-east of England, and is manifested in their annual Christmas concerts. Until his death Hull maintained an independent solo career although he still performed Lindisfarne classics, as heard on his *Back To Basics* in 1994.

●ALBUMS: *Nicely Out Of Tune* (Charisma 1970)★★★, *Fog On The Tyne* (Charisma 1971)★★★★, *Dingly Dell* (Charisma 1972)★★★, *Lindisfarne Live* (Charisma 1973)★★, *Roll On Ruby* (Charisma 1973)★★, *Happy Daze* (Warners 1974)★★★, *Back And Fourth* (Mercury 1978)★★★, *Magic In The Air* (Mercury 1978)★★, *The News* (Mercury 1979)★★, *Sleepless Night* (LMP 1982)★★, *LindisfarneTastic Live* (LMP 1984)★★, *LindisfarneTastic Volume 2* (LMP 1984)★★, *Dance Your Life Away* (River City 1986)★★, *C'mon Everybody* (Stylus 1987)★★, *Peel Sessions* (Strange Fruit 1988)★★★, *Amigos* (Black Crow 1989)★★, *Elvis Lives On The Moon* (Essential 1993)★★, *Another Fine Mess* (Grapevine 1995)★★. Solo: Ray Jackson *In The Night* (Mercury 1980)★★. Rod Clements with Bert Jansch *Leather Launderette* (Black Crow 1988)★★.

●COMPILATIONS: *Take Off Your Head* (Rubber 1974)★★, *Finest Hour* (Charisma 1975)★★★, *Singles Album* (1981)★★★, *The Best Of Lindisfarne* (Virgin 1989)★★★, *Buried Treasures Vol. 1* (Virgin 1993)★★, *Buried Treasures Vol. 2* (Virgin 1993)★★, *On Tap* (Essential 1994)★★.

LITTLE FEAT

The compact rock 'n' roll funk displayed by Little Feat put them out of step with other Californian rock bands of the early 70s. By combining elements of country, folk, blues, soul and boogie they unwittingly created a sound that became their own, and has to date never been replicated or bettered. The band comprised Lowell George (b. 13 April 1945, Hollywood, California, USA, d. 29 June 1979) who had already found experience with the earthy garage band the Standells and with the Mothers Of Invention, plus, Roy Estrada (b. Santa Ana, California, USA; bass), Bill Payne (b. 12 March 1949, Waco, Texas, USA; keyboards) and Richie Haywood (drums). Although they signed to the mighty Warner Brothers Records in 1970, no promotional push was given to the band until their second album in 1972. The public later latched on to the debut, *Little Feat*. It remains a mystery why the band were given such a low profile. George had already been noticed as potentially a major songwriter; two of his songs were taken by the Byrds, 'Truck Stop Girl' and 'Willin''.

The debut sold poorly and quite inexplicably, as did their second and third albums. The band were understandably depressed and began to fragment. Lowell began writing songs with John Sebastian amid rumours of a planned supergroup adding Phil Everly. Fortunately, their record company made a further advance to finance *Feats Don't Fail Me Now*; the revised band was now Paul Barrere (b. 3 July 1948, Burbank, California, USA; guitar), Kenny Gradney (b. New Orleans, Louisiana, USA; bass) and Sam Clayton (b. New Orleans, Louisiana, USA; percussion). Deservedly, they made the album charts in the USA, although the excellent material was no better than their three previous albums. *Feats Don't Fail Me Now* marked the growth of other members as credible songwriters and George's role began to diminish. The European critics were unanimous in praising the band in 1975 on the 'Warner Brothers Music Show'. This impressive package tour contained Graham Central Station, Bonaroo, Tower Of Power, Montrose, Little Feat and the headliners, the Doobie Brothers, who were then enjoying unprecedented acclaim and success. Without exaggeration, Little Feat blew everyone off the stage with a series of outstanding concerts, and from that moment on they could do no wrong. *The Last Record Album* in 1975 contained Lowell's finest (albeit short) winsome love song, 'Long Distance Love'; the sparseness of the guitar playing and the superb change of tempo with drum and bass, created a song that courted melancholy and tenderness. The opening question and answer line, 'Ah Hello, give me missing persons, tell me what is it that you need, I said oh, I need her so, you've got to stop your teasing', is full of emotional pleading.

George, meanwhile, was overindulging with drugs, and his contribution to *Time Loves A Hero* was minimal. Once again they delivered a great album, featuring the by now familiar and distinctive cover artwork by Neon Park. Following the double live *Waiting For Columbus*, the band disintegrated and George started work on his solo album, *Thanks, I'll Eat It Here* (which sounded like a Little Feat album); two notable tracks were 'Missing You', and '20 Million Things To Do'. During a solo concert tour George had a heart attack and died; years of abuse had taken their toll. The remaining band re-formed for a benefit concert for his widow and at the end of a turbulent year the barrel was scraped to release *Down On The Farm*. The record became a considerable success, as did the compilation *Hoy-Hoy*.

In 1988, almost a decade after they broke up, the band re-formed and *Let It Roll* became their biggest album by far. The band had ex-Pure Prairie League Craig Fuller taking Lowell's place, and the musical direction was guided by the faultless keyboard playing of Bill Payne. A second set from the re-formed band came in 1990, and although it disappointed many, it added fuel to the theory that this time they intended to stay together. *Shake Me Up* finally buried the ghost of George, as the critics accepted that the band was a credible force once again and could claim rightful ownership of both its name and history, without forgetting Lowell George's gigantic contribution. Fuller was not present on *Ain't Had Enough Fun*, instead the band recruited a female lead singer, Shaun Murphy

●ALBUMS: *Little Feat* (Warners 1971)★★★, *Sailin' Shoes* (Warners 1972)★★★★, *Dixie Chicken* (Warners 1973)★★★★, *Feats Don't Fail Me Now* (Warners 1974)★★★★, *The Last Record Album* (Warners 1975)★★★★, *Time Loves A Hero* (Warners 1977)★★★★, *Waiting For Columbus* (Warners 1978)★★★, *Down On The Farm* (Warners 1979)★★★, *Let It Roll* (Warners 1988)★★, *Representing The Mambo* (Warnera 1990)★★, *Shake Me Up* (Polydor 1991)★★, *Ain't Had Enough Fun* (Zoo 1995)★★. Solo: Lowell George *Thanks I'll Eat It Here* (Warners 1979)★★★. Paul Barrere *On My Own Two Feet* (Warners/Mirage 1983)★★.

●COMPILATIONS: *Hoy Hoy* (Warners 1981)★★★★, *As Time Goes By - The Best Of Little Feat* (Warners 1986)★★★★.

LITTLE RIVER BAND

Prior to the success of AC/DC, Air Supply, Men At Work and INXS, the Little River Band were probably Australia's most successful international rock band. Evolving out of the group Mississippi, who had previously spent much time working in London, former members Graham Goble (b. 15 May 1947, Adelaide, South Australia, Australia; guitar), Beeb Birtles (b. Gerard Birtlekamp, 28 November 1948, Amsterdam, Netherlands; guitar) and Derek Pellicci (drums) met up

with Glen Shorrock (b. 30 June 1944, Rochester, Kent, England; vocals) in Melbourne in 1975. With a name change to the Little River Band and the addition of Rick Formosa (guitar) and Roger McLachlan (bass) the band boasted years of experience and chose the US west coast harmony and guitar sound as their major influence. They had immediate success in Australia with their first single and album. Under the guidance of Glen Wheatley (ex-Masters Apprentices), the band was soon aiming for the overseas market, the USA in particular, and by the end of 1976 they had enjoyed their first appearance in the US charts. With Formosa and McLachlan being replaced, respectively, by David Briggs (b. 26 January 1951, Melbourne, Victoria, Australia) and George McArdle (b. 30 November 1954, Melbourne, Victoria, Australia), the second album *Diamantina Cocktail* went gold in the USA in 1977, the first time an Australian act had managed this. The band followed this with another hugely successful album in 1978, *Sleeper Catcher*, and they found themselves also selling well in Latin-America and Europe, especially France. The band's popularity waned a little in Australia but continued unabated in the USA. In 1983, lead vocalist Glen Shorrock left to pursue a solo career and was replaced by John Farnham, one of Australia's most popular singers. By 1986 Farnham had left to pursue his solo career and the band continued with a low profile, playing live occasionally at upmarket venues but still releasing records. In 1988, with the return of Shorrock, the group signed to MCA Records, releasing *Get Lucky* two years later.

●ALBUMS: *Little River Band* (Harvest 1976)★★★, *Diamantina Cocktail* (Harvest 1977)★★★, *Sleeper Catcher* (Harvest 1978)★★, *First Under The Wire* (Capitol 1979)★★, *Backstage Pass* (Capitol 1980)★★, *Time Exposure* (Capitol 1981)★★, *The Net* (Capitol 1983)★★, *Playing To Win* (Capitol 1985)★★, *No Reins* (Capitol 1986)★★, *Monsoon* (MCA 1988)★★, *Too Late To Load* (1989)★, *Get Lucky* (MCA 1990)★★, *Worldwide Love* (Curb 1991)★★.

●COMPILATIONS: *Greatest Hits* (Capitol 1984)★★★, *The Best Of ...* (EMI 1997)★★★.

●VIDEOS: *Live Exposure* (PMI 1981).

LOFGREN, NILS

b. 21 June 1951, Chicago, Illinois, USA. In the late 60s, Lofgren first recorded as Paul Dowell And The Dolphin before forming Grin. The latter made several excellent albums during the early 70s and although a critics' favourite they never quite managed to receive the recognition they deserved. Lofgren, meanwhile, was already branching out into other ventures after making a guest appearance on Neil Young's *After The Goldrush*. He briefly teamed up with Young's backing group Crazy Horse for their critically acclaimed debut album. Lofgren's association with Young continued in 1973 when he was invited to join the *Tonight's The Night* tour. By now, Lofgren was a highly respected guitarist and it

was widely speculated that he might be joining the Rolling Stones as Mick Taylor's replacement. Instead, he signed to A&M Records as a solo artist and recorded a self-titled album, which included the tribute 'Keith Don't Go (Ode To The Glimmer Twin)'. The album was applauded on its release, as were Lofgren's solo tours during which he astounded audiences with his acrobatic skills, often propelling himself in the air from a trampoline. An 'official bootleg' from the tour, *Back It Up*, captured some of the excitement. Lofgren's *Cry Tough* displayed his power as a writer, arranger and musician. It was a best seller on both sides of the Atlantic and momentarily placed Lofgren on a level with the other acclaimed new guitar-playing artists such as Bruce Springsteen. With *I Came To Dance* and *Nils*, the singer/guitarist consolidated his position without breaking any new ground. The latter included some lyrics from Lou Reed which added some bite to the proceedings. By the end of the 70s, Lofgren left A&M and found himself recording for the MCA subsidiary, Backstreet. By the early 80s, his reputation as a solo artist had declined and it was generally accepted that his real genius lay as a 'right-hand man' to other artists. In early 1983 he embarked on Neil Young's *Trans* tour and the following year joined Bruce Springsteen's E Street Band. By this point, his solo standing was such that he was recording for an independent label, Towerbell. During the late 80s, he continued to work with Springsteen, but also undertook occasional low-key solo tours. In 1991, he ended a six-year hiatus from recording with *Silver Lining*, which included guest appearances from Springsteen and various members of Ringo Starr's All Starr Band. *Damaged Goods* was a surprisingly good album on which Lofgren reinvented his voice. Taking his range down one or two octaves to give him a sexy growl, Lofgren has either been drinking whiskey by the gallon, smoking ten thousand cigarettes a day or simply his voice has at last broken.
●ALBUMS: *Nils Lofgren* (A&M 1975)★★★★, *Back It Up (Official Bootleg)* (A&M 1976)★★★, *Cry Tough* (A&M 1976)★★★, *I Came To Dance* (A&M 1977)★★★, *Night After Night* (A&M 1977)★★, *Nils* (A&M 1979)★★★, *Night Fades Away* (Backstreet 1981)★★, *Wonderland* (MCA 1983)★★★, *Flip* (Towerbell 1985)★★★, *Code Of The Road* (Towerbell 1986)★★★, *Silver Lining* (Essential 1991)★★★, *Crooked Line* (Essential 1992)★★, *Live On The Test* (Windsong 1994)★★★, *Everybreath* (Permanent 1994)★★, *Damaged Goods* (Essential 1995)★★★.
●COMPILATIONS: *A Rhythm Romance* (A&M 1982)★★★, *Don't Walk, Rock* (Connoisseur 1990)★★, *The Best Of Nils Lofgren* (A&M 1992)★★★, *Shine Silently* (Spectrum 1995)★★, *Soft Fun, Tough Tears 1971-1979* (Raven 1995)★★★, *Steal Your Heart* (A&M 1996)★★★.
●VIDEOS: *Nils Lofgren* (Castle 1991).

LOGGINS AND MESSINA

This duo featured Kenny Loggins and Jim Messina (b. 5 December 1947, Maywood, California, USA). Following his premature departure from Poco, Messina intended to resume his career as a record producer, a role he had previously carried out by producing the final Buffalo Springfield album, *Last Time Around*. Songwriter Loggins, who had recently experienced success when the Nitty Gritty Dirt Band took his whimsical song 'House At Pooh Corner' into the US charts, was signed by CBS and was introduced to Messina who was now a staff producer. This started a partnership that lasted six years and produced numerous gold albums. By combining country rock with hints of Latin, Mexican and R&B, the duo hit upon a strong formula. All nine albums reached high US chart positions and spawned a number of hit singles including 'Your Mama Don't Dance' and 'My Music'. As seasoned performers, their regular tours of North America made them a major attraction during the first half of the 70s. Following an amicable split, Loggins embarked on a solo career. Messina, following three moderately successful albums, instigated the reformation of the much-loved Poco in 1989 to considerable acclaim and a successful album *Legacy*. A surprisingly fresh album was issued in 1996 covering Messina's entire career. Reworkings and new recordings of his back catalogue demonstrated a relaxed and mature voice, that has clearly improved with age.
●ALBUMS: *Kenny Loggins With Jim Messina Sittin' In* (Columbia 1972)★★★, *Loggins And Messina* (Columbia 1972)★★★★, *Full Sail* (Columbia 1973)★★, *On Stage* (Columbia 1974)★★★, *Mother Lode* (Columbia 1974)★★, *So Fine* (Columbia 1975)★★, *Native Sons* (Columbia 1976)★★, *Finale* (Columbia 1977)★★.
●COMPILATIONS: *The Best Of Friends* (Columbia 1976)★★★.

LONDON

As punk sent an electric shock through a complacent late 70s UK music scene, major labels were to be found signing acts, regardless of ability. London, like many other second division new wavers, were scooped up only to disappear after all the fuss had died down. Two releases in 1977, 'Everyone's A Winner' and 'No Time', were both of their time; punchy and urgent but ultimately lacking in substance. *Animal Games*, London's one and only album (and accompanying single) in 1978 followed suit, its power-pop feel lacking the true bite of punk's pioneers. Lead singer Riff Regan later had a stab at a solo career, while drummer Jon Moss joined the Edge before making his name in the early 80s with Culture Club.
●ALBUMS: *Animal Games* (MCA 1978)★★.

LOVE UNLIMITED

Formed in 1969 in San Pedro, California, USA, under the aegis of singer/producer Barry White, the group consisted of Diane Taylor, Linda James and her sister Glodean James who married White on 4 July 1974. The trio had an early hit with 'Walkin' In The Rain With The One I Love' (1972), an imaginatively arranged performance which married contemporary soul to the aura of the now-passed girl-group genre, reminiscent of the Shangri-Las. Love Unlimited's later releases included 'It May Be Winter Outside, (But In My Heart It's Spring)' (1973) and 'Under The Influence Of Love' (1974), both of which White had previously recorded with Felice Taylor. The care the producer lavished on such releases equalled that of his own, but despite further R&B hits, 'I Belong To You' (1974) was the trio's final US pop chart entry.

●ALBUMS: *Love Unlimited* (Uni 1972)★★, *Under The Influence Of...* (20th Century 1973)★★, *In Heat* (20th Century 1974)★★, *He's All I Got* (Unlimited Gold 1977)★★, *Love Is Back* (Unlimited Gold 1980)★★.

LOVE UNLIMITED ORCHESTRA

This 40-piece orchestra was pieced together by singer Barry White to back his girl trio protégés, Love Unlimited. The unit also supplied the silky backing to several of White's singles and enjoyed an international hit in 1974 in their own right with 'Love Theme'. Later releases, including 'Rhapsody In White' and 'Satin Soul', were less successful, although they did provide the theme song to the Dino DeLaurentis remake of *King Kong* (1977). One member, saxophonist Kenny G, later embarked on a solo career.

●ALBUMS: *Rhapsody In White* (20th Century 1974)★★, *Together Brothers* (20th Century 1974)★★, *White Gold* (20th Century 1974)★, *Music Maestro Please* (20th Century 1976)★, *My Sweet Summer Suite* (20th Century 1976)★, *My Musical Bouquet* (20th Century 1978)★, *Super Movie Themes* (1979)★, *Let 'Em Dance* (1981)★, *Welcome Aboard* (1981)★, *Rise* (1983)★.

LOWE, NICK

b. 25 March 1949, Woodbridge, Suffolk, England. Lowe has for many years been held in high esteem by a loyal band of admirers aware of his dexterity as producer, musician, vocalist and songwriter. His early apprenticeship as bass player/vocalist with Kippington Lodge, which evolved into Brinsley Schwarz, made him a seasoned professional by the mid-70s. He then started a career as record producer, making his debut with the Kursaal Flyers' *Chocs Away*, followed by Dr. Feelgood's *Malpractice*. He also owns up to being responsible for an appalling novelty record, 'We Love You', a parody of the Bay City Rollers, recorded under the name the Tartan Horde. He formed Stiff Records with Jake Riviera and Dave Robinson in 1976 and was an early pioneer of punk music. His own singles were unsuccessful, but he was critically applauded for the catchy 'So It Goes', backed with the prototype punk song, 'Heart Of The City'. He was an important catalyst in the career of Elvis Costello, producing his first five albums and composing a modern classic with 'What's So Funny 'Bout (Peace Love And Understanding)'. Lowe became a significant figure in the UK, producing albums for the Damned, Clover and Dave Edmunds. In 1977, Lowe co-founded

Rockpile and also managed to join the legendary 'Live Stiffs' tour. His own debut, *Jesus Of Cool* (US title: *Pure Pop For Now People*) was a critics' favourite and remains a strong collection of unpretentious rock 'n' pop. The hit single, 'I Love The Sound Of Breaking Glass', is still a disc jockey favourite, although the equally impressive 'Little Hitler' failed miserably. In 1979 he produced another important single, 'Stop Your Sobbing', by the Pretenders, and released another excellent collection, *Labour Of Lust*, which contained the sparkling 'Cruel To Be Kind' and 'Cracking Up'. Lowe was indeed cracking up, from a surfeit of alcohol, as his brother-in-arms Dave Edmunds intimated in the UK television documentary, *Born Fighters*. Towards the end of a hectic year he married Carlene Carter. In the early 80s, as well as continuing his work with Costello, he additionally produced albums with John Hiatt, Paul Carrack, Carlene Carter and the Fabulous Thunderbirds. His own recordings suffered and were rushed efforts. In 1986 he reunited with Costello for *Blood And Chocolate*, although his own albums were virtually ignored by the public. He returned in 1988 with *Pinker And Prouder Than Previous*, with contributions from Edmunds, but once again it was dismissed, making his catalogue of flop albums embarrassingly large, a fact that Lowe observes with his customary good grace and humour. In 1992 Lowe formed a loose band, Little Village, with Hiatt, Ry Cooder and Jim Keltner, whose debut album received a lukewarm response. Much better was *The Impossible Bird* with some of his best lyrics in years, notably 'Lover Don't Go' and 'Love Travels On A Gravel Road'.

●ALBUMS: *Jesus Of Cool* aka *Pure Pop For Now People* (Radar 1978)★★★★, *Labour Of Lust* (Radar 1978)★★★★, *Nick The Knife* (F-Beat 1982)★★★, *The Abominable Showman* (F-Beat 1983)★★★, *Nick Lowe And His Cowboy Outfit* (RCA 1984)★★★, *Rose Of England* (RCA 1985)★★★, *Pinker And Prouder Than Previous* (Demon 1988)★★★, *Party Of One* (Reprise 1990)★★★, *The Impossible Bird* (Demon 1994)★★★★.

●COMPILATIONS: *16 All Time Lowes* (Demon 1984)★★★★, *Nick's Knacks* (Demon 1986)★★★, *Basher: The Best Of Nick Lowe* (Demon 1989)★★★★, *The Wilderness Years* (Demon 1991)★★★.

●FILMS: *Americion* (1979).

LUNCH, LYDIA

b. Lydia Koch, 1959, Rochester, New York, USA. The provocative Lydia Lunch was a pivotal figure in New York's 'no wave' scene of the late 70s and has worked with an array of talent since then. After spells with Teenage Jesus And The Jerks and Beirut Slump (the latter were restricted to one US single, 'Try Me'), Lunch opted for the freedom of solo work with 1980's acclaimed *Queen Of Siam* on the Ze label. Her next project, Eight-Eyed Spy, toyed with funk and R&B while retaining her uncompromising vocal style and violent, experimental musical approach. Then came *13:13* on the Ruby label, which benefited from a harder production and more co-ordinated sound. In 1982 she shared a 12-inch EP with the Birthday Party on 4AD Records, *The Agony Is The Ecstasy*, revealing her increasing fascination with the baser instincts of human nature. Members of the Birthday Party also backed her on 'Some Velvet Morning', while Einsturzende Neubauten joined her for 'Thirsty'. This marriage of the New York and Berlin undergrounds was further developed on 'Der Karibische Western', on Zensor with Die Haut. Lunch continued her collaborative ventures in 1983, working with Danish band Sort Sol. 1984's *In Limbo*, a mini-album for Cabaret Voltaire's Doublevision label, reintroduced her to solo work, and she soon founded Widowspeak Productions in 1985 as an outlet to document her work, starting appropriately with the *Uncensored Lydia Lunch* cassette. This included 'Daddy Dearest' - a document of the abuse she suffered at the hands of her father. After a project with Michael Gira (Swans) entitled *Hard Rock* (a cassette on Ecstatic Peace), Lunch teamed up with New York art rock pranksters Sonic Youth for 'Death Valley '69', a menacing record concerning the Manson killings which launched Blast First Records in the UK. An equally sinister solo offering, *The Drowning Of Lady Hamilton*, was followed by a 10-inch EP recorded with No Trend, *Heart Of Darkness* (1985). The next release for Widowspeak was a limited edition box set, *The Intimate Diaries Of The Sexually Insane*, containing a cassette of chronic case histories, a magazine and a book, *Adulterers Anonymous*, co-written by Lunch. 1987's remixed and remastered double album retrospective, *Hysterie*, summarized her work from 1976-86, before she paired with the man behind Foetus and Clint Ruin, Jim Thirlwell, for the awesome Stinkfist project in 1989. That year also witnessed Harry Crews, an all-female wall of guitar sound group in which Lunch was joined by Sonic Youth bassist, Kim Gordon. 1993 was spent working on a film script, *Psychomenstruum*. Lunch, in conjunction with Thirlwell, has become known as an avid opponent of censorship. Her own work is uncompromisingly confrontational, including videos featuring explicit sexual activity. The politics of outrage remain her gospel.

●ALBUMS: *Queen Of Siam* (Ze 1980)★★★, with 8 Eyed Spy *Live* cassette only (ROIR 1981)★★★, with 8 Eyed Spy *8 Eyed Spy* (Fetish 1981)★★★, *13:13* (Ruby 1982)★★★, *In Limbo* (Doublevision 1984)★★★, *Uncensored Lydia Lunch* cassette only(Widowspeak 1985)★★★, *The Drowning Of Lady Hamilton* mini-album (Widowspeak 1985)★★★, *Honeymoon In Red* (Widowspeak 1988)★★★, *Oral Fixation* (Widowspeak 1989)★★★, with Harry Crews *Naked In Garden Hills* (Widowspeak 1989)★★★, *Drowning In Limbo* (Widowspeak 1989)★★★, *Conspiracy Of Women* (Widowspeak 1991)★★★, with Rowland S. Howard *Shotgun Wedding* (UFO 1991)★★★, with Exene Cervenka *Rude Hieroglyphics* (Rykodisk 1995)★★★, *The Uncensored ... Oral Fixation* (Atavistic 1996)★★★.

●COMPILATIONS: *Hysterie (1976-1986)* (Widowspeak 1986)★★★, *Crimes Against Nature* 3-CD set (Triple X)★★★.

●VIDEOS: *Lydia Lunch: The Gun Is Loaded* (1993).

●FURTHER READING: *Incriminating Evidence*, Lydia Lunch.

LYNYRD SKYNYRD

Formed in Jacksonville, Florida, in 1964, this US boogie/hard rock band took their (slightly corrupted) name from their Physical Education teacher, Leonard Skinner. The group initially comprised Ronnie Van Zant (b. 15 January 1948, Jacksonville, Florida, USA, d. 20 October 1977; vocals), Gary Rossington (b. 4 December 1951, Jacksonville, Florida, USA; guitar), Allen Collins (b. 19 July 1952, Jacksonville, Florida, USA, d. 23 January 1990; guitar, ex-Mods), Larry Jungstrom (bass) and Bob Burns (drums, ex-Me, You & Him), the quintet meeting through minor league baseball connections. Together they played under various names, including Noble Five, Wildcats, Sons Of Satan and My Backyard, releasing one single, 'Need All My Friends', in 1968, before changing their name to Lynyrd Skynyrd. After playing the southern states during the late 60s they released a second single, 'I've Been Your Fool', in 1971, after recording demos in Sheffield, Alabama. The group were discovered in Atlanta by Al Kooper in 1972 while he was scouting for new talent for his Sounds Of The South label. Signed for $9000, the group's ranks were swollen by the addition of Leon Wilkeson (b. 2 April 1952; bass), who replaced Jungstrom (who went on to work with Van Zant's brother, Donnie, in .38 Special). Kooper produced the group's debut album, *Pronounced Leh-Nerd Skin-Nerd*, which also featured former Strawberry Alarm Clock guitarist Ed King (originally standing in on bass for Wilkeson, who dropped out of the band for six months) and Billy Powell (b. 3 June 1952; keyboards). Their three-guitar line-up attracted a great deal of attention, much of it generated through support slots with the Who, and the combination of blues, honky tonk and boogie proved invigorating. Their momentous anthem, 'Free Bird' (a tribute to Duane Allman), included a superb guitar finale, while its gravity and durability were indicated by frequent reappearances in the chart years later. In 1974 the group enjoyed their biggest US hit with 'Sweet Home Alabama', an amusing and heartfelt response to Neil Young who had criticized the south in his compositions 'Southern Man' and 'Alabama'. After the release of parent album *Second Helping*, drummer Bob Burns was replaced by Artimus Pyle (b. 15 July 1948, Spartanburg, South Carolina, USA). The group were by now renowned as much for their hard-living as their music, and Ed King became the first victim of excess when retiring from the band in May 1975 (Van Zant's name was also regularly to be found in the newspapers through reports of bar brawls and confrontations with the law). *Gimme Back My Bullets* arrived in March of the following year, with production expertise from Tom

Dowd. In September 1976 Rossington was injured in a car crash, while Steve Gaines (b. 14 September 1949, Seneca, Missouri, d. 20 October 1977; guitar) became King's replacement. With their tally of gold discs increasing each year and a series of sell-out tours, the band suffered an irrevocable setback in late 1977. On 20 October, Van Zant, Gaines, his sister Cassie (one of three backing singers) and personal manager Dean Kilpatrick were killed in a plane crash *en route* from Greenville, South Carolina, to Baton Rouge, Louisiana. Rossington, Collins, Powell and Wilkeson were all seriously injured, but each would recover. That same month the group's new album, *Street Survivors*, was withdrawn as the sleeve featured an unintentionally macabre design of the band surrounded by flames. With their line-up devastated, the group dispersed and the remaining members went on to join the Rossington-Collins Band (with the exception of Pyle). In 1987 the name Lynyrd Skynyrd was revived for a 'reunion' tour featuring Rossington, Powell, Pyle, Wilkeson and King, with Ronnie's brother Johnny Van Zant (vocals) and Randell Hall (guitar). One of their performances was later issued as the live double set, *For The Glory Of The South*. Collins had earlier been paralyzed, and his girl-friend killed, during an automobile accident in 1986. When he died in 1990 from pneumonia, this only helped to confirm Lynyrd Skynyrd's status as a 'tragic' band. However, members were still performing and recording in the early 90s, after disentangling themselves from legal complications over the use of the name caused by objections from Van Zant's widow. The most spectacular aspect of this was a 20th anniversary performance live on cable television in February 1993, with Rossington, Powell, Wilkeson, King and Johnny Van Zant joined by guests including Peter Frampton, Brett Michaels (Poison), Charlie Daniels and Tom Kiefer (Cinderella), the latter having also written new songs with Rossington. Pyle was conspicuous by his absence, having been charged with a sexual assault on a four-year-old girl the previous year.

●ALBUMS: *Pronounced Leh-Nerd Skin-Nerd* (Sounds Of The South/MCA 1973)★★★, *Second Helping* (Sounds Of The South/MCA 1974)★★★★, *Nuthin' Fancy* (MCA 1975)★★★, *Gimme Back My Bullets* (MCA 1976)★★, *One More From The Road* (MCA 1976)★★★★, *Street Survivors* (MCA 1977)★★★★, *First And Last* rec. 1970-1972 (MCA 1978)★★★, *For The Glory Of The South* (MCA 1987)★★★, *Lynyrd Skynyrd 1991* (MCA 1991)★★★, *The Last Rebel* (MCA 1993)★★★, *Endangered Species* (Capricorn 1995)★★★, *Southern Knights* (CBH 1996)★★★, *Twenty* (SPV 1997)★★.

●COMPILATIONS: *Gold And Platinum* (MCA 1980)★★★★, *Best Of The Rest* (MCA 1982)★★★, *Legend* (MCA 1987)★★★, *Anthology* (Raw Power 1987)★★★, *Skynyrd's Innyrds* (MCA 1989)★★, *Definitive* 3-CD box set (MCA 1991)★★★★.

MACAULEY, TONY

b. Anthony Instone, 21 April 1944, Fulham, London, England. Originally a song-plugger for Essex Music, Macauley became one of the UK's leading pop composers of the late 60s and early 70s. He burst onto the scene in 1967 with two number 1 hits, 'Baby Now That I've Found You' for the Foundations and 'Let The Heartaches Begin' for Long John Baldry. With uncomplicated lyrics by John MacLeod, the songs were bouncy and melodic, setting the pattern for much of Macauley's subsequent output. The run of hits continued in 1968-69 with songs for Herman's Hermits ('I Can Take Or Leave Your Loving'), the Hollies ('Sorry Suzanne' with lyrics by Geoff Stephens) and the Foundations again ('Back On My Feet Again' and 'Build Me Up Buttercup'). Another good-time pop band, Johnny Johnson And The Bandwagon, became a vehicle for Macauley's compositions in 1970 when they recorded 'Sweet Inspiration' and 'Blame It On The Pony Express'. But his biggest songs of the year were Pickettywitch's 'That Same Old Feeling' and 'Love Grows (Where My Rosemary Goes)' by Edison Lighthouse, while the most accomplished was the reflective 'Home Lovin' Man', recorded by Andy Williams. During the early 70s, Macauley's progress was interrupted by a lengthy legal dispute with his publishers, which the songwriter won on appeal in 1974. The case had staggering implications for the music industry, presaging similar actions from Gilbert O'Sullivan and Elton John. Macauley's later successes were almost all in association with American artists. For the Drifters he wrote 'Kissin In The Back Row Of The Movies' and 'You're More Than A Number In My Little Red Book' and he helped to revive Duane Eddy's career by providing him with 'Play Me Like You Play Your Guitar'. Geoff Stephens rejoined Macauley for the biggest hits of this phase of his career and the pair provided a series of soft ballads for actor David Soul (star of television's *Starsky & Hutch*), the most successful of which were 'Goin' In With My Eyes Open' and the 1976 transatlantic number 1, 'Don't Give Up On Us'. With the arrival of disco, Macauley turned away from the pop scene to write stage musicals and film music but none of these projects achieved the popularity of his earlier hits.

MAGAZINE

The Buzzcocks vocalist Howard Devoto left that group in January 1977, although he continued to be involved on the fringe of their activities for some time. In April he met guitarist John McGeoch and together they started writing songs. They formed Magazine with Devoto on vocals, McGeoch on guitar, Barry Adamson on bass, Bob Dickinson on keyboards and Martin Jackson on drums. The group played their debut live gig at the closing night of the Electric Circus, Manchester, in the autumn of 1977 as a last-minute addition to the bill. Their moody, cold keyboards and harsh rhythms were in sharp contrast to the mood of the day: 'Everybody was playing everything ultra fast, as fast as they could. I thought we could begin to play slow music again.' They were signed to Virgin Records but Dickinson left in November and, as a result, their debut, 'Shot By Both Sides', was recorded by the four remaining members. Dave Formula was recruited in time to play on *Real Life*. Next to leave was Jackson who departed after their first tour. Paul Spencer came in temporarily before John Doyle was recruited in October 1978. This line-up remained for the next couple of years, although McGeoch was also playing with Siouxsie And The Banshees, and, along with Adamson and Formula, in Steve Strange's Visage. Their albums received universal acclaim but only their first single and 1980's 'Sweetheart Contract' dented the charts. As the latter was released McGeoch left to join Siouxsie full-time and Robin Simon (ex-Neo and Ultravox) was brought in on guitar. A tour of the USA and Australia - where a live album was recorded - led to Simon's departure and Ben Mandelson (ex-Amazorblades) came in for the band's last few months. The departure of Devoto in May 1981 signalled the unit's death knell. The body of work they left behind, however, is surprisingly enduring given its angular and experimental slant. Devoto went on to a solo career before forming Luxuria.
●ALBUMS: *Real Life* (Virgin 1978)★★★, *Secondhand Daylight* (Virgin 1979)★★★, *The Correct Use Of Soap* (Virgin 1980)★★★, *Play* (Virgin 1980)★★★, *Magic, Murder And The Weather* (Virgin 1981)★★★.
●COMPILATIONS: *After The Fact* (Virgin 1982)★★★, *Rays & Hail 1978-81* (Virgin 1987)★★★, *Scree: Rarities 1978-1981* (Virgin 1990)★★, *BBC Radio 1 Live In Concert* (Windsong 1993)★★★.

MAHAVISHNU ORCHESTRA

Led by guitarist John McLaughlin, (b. 4 January 1942, Yorkshire, England), between 1972 and 1976 the Mahavishnu Orchestra played a leading part in the creation of jazz/rock fusion music. Mahavishnu was the name given to McLaughlin by his Hindu guru Snr i Chimnoy, and the group's early work showed the influence of Indian ragas. The first line-up included several musicians who had played on McLaughlin's previous solo album, *Inner Mounting Flame*. The high-energy electric music created by keyboardist Jan Hammer, ex-Flock violinist Jerry Goodman, bassist Rick Laird and drummer Billy Cobham made *Birds Of Fire* a Top 20 hit in the USA. After releasing the live *Between Nothingness And Eternity*, whose lengthy 'Dreams' sequence featured spectacular duetting between the guitarist and Cobham, McLaughlin split the group. A year later he reformed Mahavishnu with an entirely new personnel. Jean-Luc Ponty replaced Goodman, Narada Michael Walden took over on drums, with Gayle Moran on keyboards/vocals, and there was also a four-piece string section. This group made *Apocalypse* with producer George Martin. In 1975, Ponty left and keyboardist Stu Goldberg played on the final albums. McLaughlin next decided to pursue classical Indian music more rigorously in the acoustic quartet Shakti, but Cobham and Hammer in particular carried on the Mahavishnu approach to jazz/rock in their later work. Moran played with Chick Corea's Return To Forever while Walden became a noted soul music producer in the 80s.
●ALBUMS: *The Inner Mounting Flame* (Columbia 1972)★★★★, *Birds Of Fire* (Columbia 1973)★★★★, *Between Nothingness And Eternity* (Columbia 1973)★★★, *Apocalypse* (Columbia 1974)★★, *Visions Of The Emerald Beyond* (Columbia 1975)★★★, *Inner Worlds* (Columbia 1976)★★★, *Adventures In Radioland* (Relativity 1987)★★★.

MAHOGANY RUSH

Recovering in hospital from a bad drugs experience, Frank Marino (b. 22 August 1954, Canada) claimed he was visited by an apparition of Jimi Hendrix. After leaving hospital he picked up a guitar for the first time and was able to play Hendrix riffs, or so the legend runs. The group was formed in Montreal during 1970 when Marino recruited bassist Paul Harwood and drummer Jim Ayoub to fulfil his desire to work in a power trio format. Their first three albums were derivative in the extreme; every component of Hendrix's unique style had been dismantled, adapted, then rebuilt under new song titles. Nevertheless, they were not condemned as copyists, but revered instead for paying tribute to the great man in such an honest and sincere fashion. By 1976 Marino had started to develop his own style, based on an extension of the Hendrix tricks he had already acquired. This is clearly evident on *Mahogany Rush IV* and *World Anthem*, released in 1976 and 1977, respectively. Eventually he outgrew the comparisons as his own style began to dominate the band's material. The name was amended to Frank Marino and Mahogany Rush, then to Frank Marino, following the release of *What's Next* and the departure of Ayoub.
●ALBUMS: *Maxoom* (Kotai 1971)★★, *Child Of The Novelty* (20th Century 1974)★★, *Strange Universe* (20th Century 1975)★★, *Mahogany Rush IV* (Columbia 1976)★★★, *World Anthem* (Columbia 1977)★★★, *Live*

(Columbia 1978)★★★, *Tales Of The Unexpected* (Columbia 1979)★★★, *What's Next* (Columbia 1980)★★★.

MAN

Man evolved from the Bystanders, a Swansea, Wales-based group specializing in close harmony pop. They latterly grew tired of this direction and, by 1969, were performing a live set at odds with their clean-cut recordings. Producer John Schroeder was inclined to drop the unit from his roster, but on hearing this contrary material, renewed their contract on the understanding they pursue a more progressive line. Micky Jones (b. 7 June 1946, Merthyr Tydfil, Mid-Glamorgan, Wales; lead guitar/vocals), Deke Leonard (b. Roger Leonard, Wales; guitar), Clive John (guitar/keyboards), Ray Williams (bass) and Jeff Jones (drums) completed Man's debut, *Revelation*, a concept album based on evolution. One of the tracks, 'Erotica', became a substantial European hit, but the single, which featured a simulated orgasm, was denied a British release. Man abandoned much of *Revelation*'s gimmicky frills for *2ozs Of Plastic With A Hole In The Middle*, which captured something of the group's live fire. Having suppressed the British feel prevalent on that first outing, the quintet was establishing its improvisatory preferences, akin to those associated with America's 'west coast' bands, exemplified by the Quicksilver Messenger Service. The first in a flurry of line-up changes began when Martin Ace (bass) and Terry Williams (drums) joined the group. *Man* and *Do You Like It Here Now, Are You Settling In?* contained several established stage favourites, including 'Daughter Of The Fireplace' and 'Many Are Called But Few Get Up', but the band only prospered as a commercial force with the release of *Live At the Padgett Rooms, Penarth*. This limited-issue set created considerable interest but coincided with considerable internal unrest. With the departure of Deke Leonard in pursuit of a solo career, the 1972 line-up of Micky Jones, Clive John, Will Youatt (b. Michael Youatt, 16 February, 1950, Swansea, West Glamorgan, Wales; bass/vocals), Phil Ryan (b. 21 October 1946, Port Talbot, West Galmorgan, Wales; keyboards) and Terry Williams (b. 11 January 1948, Swansea, West Glamorgan, Wales) released what is generally considered to be Man's most popular album, the live set, *Be Good To Yourself...At Least Once A Day*, which contained lengthy guitar/keyboard workouts typified by the classic track 'Bananas'. The next album, *Back To The Future* gave Man their highest UK album chart position, which was almost emulated the following year with *Rhinos, Winos And Lunatics*. The latter saw the return of Leonard and found Man at the height of their success. During this period the nomadic habits of various members were unabated due to the comings and goings between variously related groups such as Help Yourself, the Neutrons, Alkatraz and the Flying Aces. Throughout the band's history, Mickey Jones was Man's unifying factor as they lurched from one change to the next. Following the group's success in the USA promoting their well-received album, *Slow Motion*, an ill-fated project with Quicksilver's John Cippolina resulted in the unsatisfactory *Maximum Darkness*. The group's demise came in 1976 when, after the release of the *Welsh Connection*, having lost their momentum, the group ground to a halt. During the late 80s, Jones, Leonard, Ace and drummer John 'Pugwash' Weathers (ex-Gentle Giant), resuscitated the Man name, regularly appearing on the UK pub/club circuit and on the Continent. Terry Williams had in the meantime found security in Rockpile and Dire Straits. In 1993 the unit released their first studio album in 16 years, *The Twang Dynasty Road Goes On Forever*. Much-loved, the band's activities are still chronicled in Michael Heatley's fanzine, *The Welsh Connection*.

●ALBUMS: *Revelation* (Pye 1969)★★★, *2ozs Of Plastic With A Hole In The Middle* (Dawn 1969)★★★, *Man* aka *Man 1970* (Liberty 1970)★★, *Do You Like It Here Now, Are You Settling In?* (United Artists 1971)★★, *Live At The Padgett Rooms, Penarth* (United Artists 1972)★★★, *Be Good To Yourself ... At Least Once A Day* (United Artists 1972)★★★, *Back Into The Future* (United Artists 1973)★★, *Rhinos, Winos And Lunatics* (United Artists 1974)★★★, *Slow Motion* (United Artists 1974)★★★, *Maximum Darkness* (United Artists 1975)★★, *Welsh Connection* (MCA 1976)★★, *All's Well That Ends Well* (MCA 1977)★★, *Live At Reading 1983* (1993)★★, *The Twang Dynasty Road Goes On Forever* (1993)★★, *Call Down The Moon* (Hypertension 1995)★★.

●COMPILATIONS: *Golden Hour* (Pye 1973)★★, *Green Fly* (Latymer 1986)★★, *Perfect Timing (The UA Years: 1970-75)* (EMI 1991)★★★.

●FURTHER READING: *Mannerisms*, Martin Mycock. *Mannerisms II*, Martin Mycock.

MANASSAS

The multi-talented Stephen Stills founded this highly regarded unit in October 1971, during sessions for a projected album. Chris Hillman (guitar/vocals), Al Perkins (pedal steel guitar), both formerly of the Flying Burrito Brothers, and percussionist Jo Lala joined the singer's regular touring band of Paul Harris (b. New York, USA; keyboards), Calvin 'Fuzzy' Samuels (bass) and Dallas Taylor (drums), although Samuels was latterly replaced by Kenny Passarelli. The group's disparate talents were best displayed in their remarkably accomplished live shows and on *Manassas*, a diverse double-album selection brilliantly encompassing country, rock, R&B and Latin styles. The septet displayed a remarkable unity of purpose despite the contrasting material, a cohesion which endowed the set with its lasting quality. *Down The Road* could not quite match the standards set by the debut and Manassas was brought to an end in September 1973, with the sudden departure of Hillman, Perkins and Harris for the ill-fated Souther Hillman Furay Band. Many mourn the fact that Stills seemed at his most creative when fronting this band and those who were lucky enough to have seen them during their brief career can testify that they were indeed a spectacular rock/country/blues band.

●ALBUMS: *Manassas* (Atlantic 1972)★★★★, *Down The Road* (Atlantic 1973)★★★.

MANCHESTER, MELISSA

b. 15 February 1951, the Bronx, New York, USA. A former staff writer at Chappel Music and back-up singer for Bette Midler, Manchester launched her own career in 1973 with *Home To Myself*. Her intimate style showed a debt to contemporary New York singer-songwriters, but later releases, including her self-titled third album, were more direct. This collection, produced by Richard Perry and Vini Poncia, yielded the artist's first major hit, 'Midnight Blue' (US Top 10), and set the pattern for her subsequent direction which, if carefully performed, lacked the warmth of those early recordings. Success as a performer and songwriter continued into the 70s and 80s. 'Whenever I Call You Friend', co-written with Kenny Loggins, was a best-selling single for him in 1978, while in 1979 Melissa's second US Top 10 was achieved with 'Don't Cry Out Loud' (composed by Carole Bayer Sager and Peter Allen). Three years later she had another hit with 'You Should Hear How She Talks About You'. Although she has since diversified into scriptwriting and acting, Manchester remains a popular recording artist.

●ALBUMS: *Home To Myself* (Bell 1973)★★★, *Bright Eyes* (Bell 1974)★★★, *Melissa* (Arista 1975)★★★, *Better Days And Happy Endings* (Arista 1976)★★, *Help Is On The Way* (Arista 1976)★★, *Singin'* (Arista 1977)★★, *Don't Cry Out Loud* (Arista 1978)★★, *Melissa Manchester* (Arista 1979)★★, *For The Working Girl* (Arista 1980)★★, *Hey Ricky* (Arista 1982)★★, *Emergency* (Arista 1983)★★, *Mathematics* (MCA 1985)★★.

●COMPILATIONS: *Greatest Hits* (Arista 1983)★★★.

MANDEL, HARVEY

b. 11 March 1945, Detroit, Michigan, USA. This fluent, mellifluous guitarist was one of several young aspirants learning their skills in Chicago blues clubs. A contemporary of Paul Butterfield and Michael Bloomfield, Mandel was a member of both the Charlie Musselwhite and Barry Goldberg blues bands, before moving to the west coast in 1967. His debut album, *Christo Redentor*, was released the following year. This wholly instrumental set, which included contributions from Musselwhite, Graham Bond, and the Nashville musicians later known as Area Code 615, is arguably the guitarist's definitive release, but *Righteous* and *Baby Batter* are equally inventive. Between 1969 and 1971, Mandel was a member of Canned Heat wherein he struck an empathy with bassist Larry Taylor. Both subsequently joined John Mayall for *USA Union* and *Back To The Roots* before the guitarist formed the short-lived Pure Food And Drug Act. He also remained a popular session musician, contributing to albums by Love, the Ventures

and Don 'Sugarcane' Harris during this highly prolific period. Mandel continued to record his stylish solo albums throughout the early 70s, and was one of several candidates mooted to replace Mick Taylor in the Rolling Stones. The results of his audition are compiled on the group's 1976 album, *Black And Blue*. This dalliance with corporate rock was Harvey's last high-profile appearance. In 1985 he signed a recording deal with the newly founded Nuance label, but no new release has been forthcoming. Two subsequent releases on other small labels appealed only to his loyal following. The release of the 2-CD box set *The Mercury Years* once again directed us back to *Christo Redendor*, a modern classic of psychedelic wanderings and widely regarded as his finest moment.

●ALBUMS: *Christo Redentor* (Philips 1968)★★★★, *Righteous* (Philips 1969)★★★★, *Games Guitars Play* (Philips 1970)★★★, *Baby Batter* aka *Electric Progress* (Janus 1971)★★★, *The Snake* (Janus 1972)★★★★, *Shangrenade* (Janus 1973)★★★, *Feel The Sound Of ...* (Janus 1974)★★★, *Live Boot: Harvey Mandel Live In California* (Fresh Squeezed 1990)★★★, *Twist City* (Western Front 1993)★★★.

●COMPILATIONS: *Best Of ...* (Janus 1975)★★★, *The Mercury Years* (Mercury 1995)★★★.

MANDEL, JOHNNY

b. 23 November 1935, New York, USA. After playing trumpet and trombone while still in his pre-teenage years (a period in which he began to write music), Mandel played with various bands in and around New York, including those led by Boyd Raeburn and Jimmy Dorsey. In the mid- to late 40s Mandel played in the bands of Buddy Rich, Alvino Rey and others, and in the early 50s, he worked with Elliott Lawrence and Count Basie. He began to establish himself both as an arranger, contributing charts to the Basie and Artie Shaw bands, and also as a songwriter. By the mid-50s he was writing music for films and was working less in the jazz field, although his film music often contained echoes of his background. Much respected by singers and jazz instrumentalists, Mandel has a particular facility for ballads. He also orchestrated scores for Broadway and for television specials. His film work, from the 50s through to the 80s, includes music for *I Want To Live*, *The Third Voice*, *The Americanization Of Emily*, *The Sandpiper*, *The Russians Are Coming*, *Point Blank*, *MASH*, *The Last Detail*, *Escape To Witch Mountain*, *Freaky Friday*, *Agatha*, *Being There*, *The Baltimore Bullet*, *Caddyshack*, *Deathtrap*, *The Verdict*, *Staying Alive*, and *Brenda Starr* (1987). He also scored for television movies such as *The Trackers*, *The Turning Point Of Jim Molloy*, *A Letter To Three Wives*, *Christmas Eve*, *LBJ - The Early Years*, *Assault And Matrimony*, *Foxfire*, *Agatha*, *The Great Escape II - The Untold Story*, and *Single Men - Married Women* (1989). Among his songs are 'Emily', 'A Time For Love' and, perhaps his best-known, 'The Shadow Of Your Smile' (lyrics by Paul Francis Webster), written for

The Sandpiper (1965). The latter won a Grammy for song of the year, and the Oscar for best song.

MANFRED MANN CHAPTER THREE

Following the demise of Manfred Mann, Hugg (b. 11 August 1942, Andover, Hampshire, England; drums/vibraphone) and Mann (b. Manfred Lubowitz, 21 October 1940, Johannesburg, South Africa; keyboards) pursued their jazz/rock path by forming Chapter Three as a sideline to their lucrative career writing successful television jingles. This brave project was originally called Enamel and included Bernie Living (alto saxophone/flute), Steve York (bass), Craig Collinge (drums) and featured sessions from some of the finest contemporary jazz musicians including Harold Beckett, Derek Wadsworth, Chris Pyne and Dave Quincey. They immediately established themselves on the progressive rock circuit, but could not break out of the small club environment. Their two albums were excellent and imaginative but came as a considerable shock to those old fans who expected anything akin to Manfred Mann. The band was blighted with problems due to Mann and Hugg having to support the venture financially, and because of trying to establish themselves as something other than a pop group. Those that supported the endeavour were not disappointed, although Manfred soon returned to a more commercial path with Manfred Mann's Earth Band.

●ALBUMS: *Manfred Mann Chapter Three* (Vertigo 1969)★★★, *Manfred Mann Chapter Three Volume Two* (Vertigo 1970)★★★.

MANFRED MANN'S EARTH BAND

The fourth incarnation of Manfred Mann (the second being only a change of singer) has been the longest, surviving for almost 20 years. The original Earth Band was formed after Mann's bold attempt at jazz/rock with Manfred Mann Chapter Three had proved financially disastrous. The new band was comprised of Manfred (b. Manfred Lubowitz, 21 October 1940, Johannesburg, South Africa; keyboards), Mick Rogers (vocals/guitar), Colin Pattenden (bass) and Chris Slade (drums). Their debut was with the Bob Dylan song 'Please Mrs Henry' and following its poor showing they quickly released a version of Randy Newman's 'Living Without You', again to apathy. While the band gradually won back some of the fans who had deserted the Chapter Three project, it was not until their third offering, *Messin'*, that both success and acclaim arrived. The title track was a long, rambling but exciting piece, reminiscent of Chapter Three, but the band hit the mark with a superb interpretation of Holst's Jupiter, entitled 'Joybringer'. It became a substantial UK hit in 1973. From then on the band forged ahead with gradual rather than spectacular progress and built a loyal following in Europe and America. Their blend of rock still contained strong jazz influences, but the sound was wholeheartedly acces-

sible and rock based. *Solar Fire* featured yet another Dylan song, 'Father Of Day', complete with heavenly choir. Rogers departed in 1976. Just as Bruce Springsteen fever started, the band had a transatlantic hit with a highly original reading of his 'Blinded By The Light' with vocals from Chris Thompson. The record, with its lengthy, spacey instrumental introduction, reached the top spot in the US chart and worldwide sales exceeded two million.

The Roaring Silence became the band's biggest album, and featured the most assured line-up to date. Other hits followed, including the Robbie Robertson/John Simon composition 'Davey's On The Road Again' in 1978 and Dylan's 'You Angel You' and 'Don't Kill It Carol' in 1979. Further personnel changes came with Pat King (bass), ex-Wings and East Of Eden drummer Geoff Britton and Steve Waller (ex- Gonzalez). After a lengthy absence, they made the US chart in 1984 with 'Runner', featuring the vocals of the returning Mick Rogers. Mann's homage to his former homeland *Somewhere In Afrika* was well received that year, although *Criminal Tango*, a collection of non-originals, *Budapest* and *Masque* were commercial failures. The band remain highly popular in Germany and retain the respect of the critics, having never produced a poor album during their long career. Nine years elapsed before the release of *Soft Vengeance* in 1996.

●ALBUMS: *Manfred Mann's Earth Band* (Philips 1972)★★, *Glorified Magnified* (Philips 1972)★★★, *Messin'* (Vertigo 1973)★★★★, *The Good Earth* (Bronze 1974)★★★, *Nightingales And Bombers* (Bronze 1975)★★★, *The Roaring Silence* (Bronze 1976)★★★★, *Watch* (Bronze 1978)★★★, *Angel Station* (Bronze 1979)★★★, *Chance* (Bronze 1980)★★★, *Somewhere In Afrika* (Bronze 1983)★★★, *Budapest* (Bronze 1984)★★★, *Criminal Tango* (Ten 1986)★★★, *Masque* (Ten 1987)★★★, *Soft Vengeance* (Grapevine 1996)★★.

●COMPILATIONS: *The New Bronze Age* (1977)★★★, *Manfred Mann's Earth Band* (1992, 13-CD box set)★★★.

MANHATTAN TRANSFER

The original band was formed in 1969, performing good-time, jugband music. By 1972, the only surviving member was Tim Hauser (b. 1940, Troy, New York, USA; vocals), accompanied by Laurel Masse (b. 1954, USA; vocals) Alan Paul (b. 1949, Newark, New Jersey, USA; vocals) and Janis Siegel (b. 1953, Brooklyn, New York, USA; vocals). Although they covered a variety of styles, their trademark was their use of exquisite vocal harmony. Like their Atlantic stablemate, Bette Midler, they were selling nostalgia, and they were popular on the New York cabaret circuit. An unlikely pop act, they nonetheless charted on both sides of the Atlantic. It was symptomatic of their lack of crossover appeal that the hits were different in the UK and the USA. Their versatility splintered their audience. Fans of the emotive ballad, 'Chanson D'Amour', were unlikely to go for the brash gospel song 'Operator', or a jazz tune like 'Tuxedo

Junction'. In 1979, Cheryl Bentyne replaced Masse without noticeably affecting the vocal sound. Their stunning version of Weather Report's 'Birdland' remains a modern classic. The power of Manhattan Transfer is in their sometimes breathtaking vocal abilities, strong musicianship and slick live shows.

●ALBUMS: *Jukin'* (Capitol 1971/75)★★, *Manhattan Transfer* (Atlantic 1975)★★★★, *Coming Out* (Atlantic 1976)★★★, *Pastiche* (Atlantic 1978)★★★, *Live* (Atlantic 1978)★★, *Extensions* (Atlantic 1979)★★★, *Mecca for Moderns* (Atlantic 1981)★★★, *Bodies And Souls* (Atlantic 1983)★★★, *Bop Doo-Wop* (Atlantic 1985)★★★, *Vocalese* (Atlantic 1985)★★★, *Live In Tokyo* (Atlantic 1987)★★★, *Brasil* (Atlantic 1987)★★, *The Offbeat Of Avenues* (Columbia 1991)★★★, *Tonin'* (Atlantic 1995)★★★. Solo: Janis Siegel *Experiment In White* (1982)★★.

●COMPILATIONS: *Best Of Manhattan Transfer* (Atlantic 1981)★★★, *The Christmas Album* (Columbia 1992)★★, *The Very Best Of ...* (Rhino 1993)★★★★.

MANILOW, BARRY

b. Barry Alan Pincus, 17 June 1946, Brooklyn, New York, USA. An immensely popular singer, pianist and composer from the mid-70s onwards, Manilow studied music at the Juilliard School and worked as an arranger for CBS-TV. During the 60s, he also became a skilled composer of advertising jingles. In 1972 he served as accompanist to Bette Midler, then a cult performer in New York's gay bath-houses. Manilow subsequently arranged Midler's first two albums and gained his own recording contract with Bell. After an unsuccessful debut album, he took the powerful ballad 'Mandy' to number 1 in America. The song had previously been a UK hit for its co-writer Scott English, as 'Brandy'. This was the prelude to 10 years of remarkable hit parade success. With his strong, pleasant tenor, well-constructed love songs and ingratiating manner in live shows, Manilow was sneered at by critics but adored by his fans, who were predominantly female. Among the biggest hits were 'Could It Be Magic' (1975), 'I Write The Songs' (composed by the Beach Boys' Bruce Johnston (1976), 'Tryin' to Get The Feeling Again' (1976), 'Looks Like We Made It' (1977), 'Can't Smile Without You' (1978), the upbeat 'Copacabana (At The Copa)' (1978), 'Somewhere In The Night' (1979), 'Ships' (1979), and 'I Made It Through The Rain' (1980). Two albums, *2am Paradise Cafe* and *Swing Street*, marked a change of direction as Manilow underlined his jazz credentials in collaborations with Gerry Mulligan and Sarah Vaughan. He also appeared on Broadway in two one-man shows, the second of which, *Showstoppers* (1991), was a schmaltzy tribute to great songwriters of the past. During the 80s, Manilow was invited by the widow of one of those writers, Johnny Mercer, to set to music lyrics unpublished during Mercer's lifetime. A selection of these were recorded by Nancy Wilson on her 1991 album *With My Lover Beside Me*. In June 1994, the stage musical *Copacabana*, for which Manilow composed the music

and co-wrote the book, opened in London starring Gary Wilmot and Nicola Dawn. In the same year he was the supervising composer, and collaborated on several of the songs, for the animated feature *Thumbelina*.

●ALBUMS: *Barry Manilow* (Bell 1972)★★★, *Barry Manilow II* (Bell 1973)★★★, *Tryin' To Get The Feeling* (Arista 1975)★★★, *This One's For You* (Arista 1976)★★★, *Live* (Arista 1977)★★, *Even Now* (Arista 1978)★★★, *One Voice* (Arista 1979)★★★, *Barry* (Arista 1980)★★★, *If I Should Love Again* (Arista 1981)★★, *Oh, Julie!* (Arista 1982)★★, *Here Comes The Night* (Arista 1982)★★, *Barry Live In Britain* (Arista 1982)★★, *Swing Street* (Arista 1984)★★★, *2am Paradise Cafe* (Arista 1985)★★★, *Songs To Make The Whole World Sing* (Arista 1989)★★, *Live On Broadway* (Arista 1990)★★★, *Because It's Christmas* (Arista 1990)★★, *Showstoppers* (Arista 1991)★★★, *Hidden Treasures* (Arista 1993)★★★, *Singin' With The Big Bands* (Arista 1994)★★★, *Summer Of '78* (Arista 1996)★★★.

●COMPILATIONS: *Greatest Hits* (Arista 1978)★★★, *Greatest Hits Volume II* (Arista 1983)★★★, *The Songs 1975-1990* (Arista 1990)★★★, *The Complete Collection And Then Some* 4-CD set (1992)★★★.

●VIDEOS: *In Concert At The Greek* (Guild Home Video 1984), *Live On Broadway* (Arista 1990), *The Greatest Hits...And Then Some* (1994).

●FURTHER READING: *Barry Manilow*, Ann Morse. *Barry Manilow: An Autobiography*, Barry Manilow with Mark Bego. *Barry Manilow*, Howard Elson. *The Magic Of Barry Manilow*, Alan Clarke. *Barry Manilow For The Record*, Simon Weir. *The Barry Manilow Scrapbook: His Magical World In Works And Pictures*, Richard Peters. *Barry Manilow*, Tony Jasper.

MARLEY, BOB, AND THE WAILERS

This legendary vocal group originally comprised six members: Robert Nesta Marley (b. 6 February 1945, St. Anns, Jamaica, West Indies, d. 11 May 1981, Miami, Florida, USA), Bunny Wailer (b. Neville O'Riley Livingston, 10 April 1947, Kingston, Jamaica), Peter Tosh (b. Winston Hubert McIntosh, 19 October 1944, Westmoreland, Jamaica, d. 11 September 1987, Kingston, Jamaica), Junior Braithwaite, Beverley Kelso, and Cherry Smith. Bob Marley And The Wailers are the sole Jamaican group to have achieved global superstar status together with genuine penetration of world markets. The original vocal group was formed during 1963. After extensive tuition with the great vocalist Joe Higgs, they began their recording career later that year for Coxsone Dodd, although Marley had made two singles for producer Leslie Kong in 1962 - 'Judge Not' and 'One Cup Of Coffee'. Their first record, 'Simmer Down', released just before Christmas 1963 under the group name Bob Marley And The Wailers, went to number 1 on the JBC Radio chart in January 1964, holding that position for the ensuing two months and reputedly selling over 80,000 copies. This big local hit was followed by 'It Hurts To Be Alone', featuring Junior Braithwaite on lead vocal, and 'Lonesome Feeling', with lead vocal by Bunny Wailer. During the period 1963-66, the Wailers made over 70 tracks for Dodd, over 20 of which were local hits, covering a wide stylistic base; from covers of US soul and doo-wop with ska backing to the newer, less frantic 'rude-boy' sounds which presaged the development of rocksteady, and including many songs that Marley re-recorded in the 70s. In late 1965, Braithwaite left to go to America, and Kelso and Smith also departed that year.

On 10 February 1966, Marley married Rita Anderson, at the time a member of the Soulettes, later to become one of the I-Threes and a solo vocalist in her own right. The next day he left to join his mother in Wilmington, Delaware, returning to Jamaica in October 1966; the Wailers were now a vocal trio. They recorded the local hit 'Bend Down Low' at Studio One late in 1967 (though it was actually self-produced and released on their own label, Wail 'N' Soul 'M'). This and other self-produced output of the time is amongst the rarest, least reissued Wailers music, and catches the group on the brink of a new maturity; for the first time there were overtly Rasta songs. By the end of that year, following Bunny Wailer's release from prison, they were making demos for Danny Sims, the manager of soft-soul singer Johnny Nash, who hit the UK charts in April 1972 with the 1968 Marley composition, 'Stir It Up'. This association proved incapable of supporting them, and they began recording for producer Leslie Kong, who had already enjoyed international success with Desmond Dekker, the Pioneers, and Jimmy Cliff. Kong released several singles and an album called The Best Of The Wailers in 1970. By the end of 1969, wider commercial success still eluded them. Marley, who had spent the summer of 1969 working at the Chrysler car factory in Wilmington, Delaware, returned to Jamaica, and the trio began a collaboration with Lee Perry that proved crucially important to their future development. Not only did Perry help to focus the trio's rebel stance more effectively, but they worked with the bass and drum team of the Barrett brothers, Aston 'Family Man' (b. 22 November 1946, Kingston, Jamaica) and Carlton (b. 17 December 1950, Kingston, Jamaica, d. 1987, Kingston, Jamaica), who became an integral part of the Wailers' sound.

The music Bob Marley And The Wailers made with Perry during 1969-71 represents possibly the height of their respective collective powers. Combining brilliant new songs like 'Duppy Conqueror', 'Small Axe' and 'Sun Is Shining' with definitive reworkings of old material, backed by the innovative rhythms of the Upsetters and the equally innovative influence of Perry, this body of work stands as a zenith in Jamaican music. It was also the blueprint for Bob Marley's international success. The group continued to record for their own Tuff Gong label after the Perry sessions and came to the attention of Chris Blackwell, then owner of Island Records. Island had released much of the Wailers' early music from the Studio One period, although the label had concentrated on the rock market since the late 60s. Their first album for the company, Catch A Fire (1973), was packaged like a rock album, and targeted at the album market in which Island had been very successful. The band arrived in the UK in April 1973 to tour and appear on television. In July 1973 they supported Bruce Springsteen at Max's Kansas City club in New York. Backed by an astute promotional campaign, Catch A Fire sold well enough to warrant issue of Burnin', adding Earl 'Wire' Lindo to the group, which signalled a return to a militant, rootsy approach unencumbered by any rock production values whatsoever.

The rock/blues guitarist Eric Clapton covered 'I Shot The Sheriff' from this album, taking the tune to the number 9 position in the UK chart during the autumn of 1974, and reinforcing the impact of the Wailers in the process. Just as the band was poised on the brink of wider success internal differences caused Tosh and Livingston to depart, both embarking on substantial solo careers, and Lindo left to join Taj Mahal. The new Wailers band, formed mid-1974, included Marley, the Barrett brothers and Bernard 'Touter' Harvey on keyboards, with vocal harmonies by the I-Threes, comprising Marcia Griffiths, Rita Marley and Judy Mowatt. This line-up, with later additions, would come to define the so-called 'international' reggae sound that Bob Marley And The Wailers played until Marley's death in 1981. In establishing that form, not only on the series of albums recorded for Island but also by extensive touring, the band moved from the mainstream of Jamaican music into the global market. As the influence of Bob Marley spread, not only as a musician but also as a symbol of success from the so-called 'Third World', the music made locally pursued its own distinct course. 1975 was the year in which the group consolidated their position, with the release of the massively successful Natty Dread and rapturously received concerts at London Lyceum. These concerts attracted both black and white patrons; the crossover had begun. At the end of the year Marley achieved his first UK chart hit, the autobiographical 'No Woman No Cry'. His first live album, comprising material from the Lyceum concerts, was also released this year. He continued to release an album a year until his death, at which time a spokesman for Island Records estimated worldwide sales of $190 million. Marley survived an assassination attempt on 3rd December 1976, leaving Jamaica for 18 months early in 1977. In July he had an operation in Miami to remove cancer cells from his right toe.

His albums Exodus and Kaya enjoyed massive international sales. In April 1978, he played the One Love Peace Concert in Kingston, bringing the two leaders of the violently warring Jamaican political parties together in a largely symbolic peacemaking gesture. The band then undertook a huge worldwide tour that took in the USA, Canada, Japan, Australia and New Zealand. His own label, Tuff Gong, was expanding its interests, developing new talent. The album *Survival* was released to the usual acclaim, being particularly successful in Africa. The song 'Zimbabwe' was subsequently covered many times by African artists. In 1980, Marley and the Wailers played a momentous concert in the newly liberated Zimbabwe to an audience of 40,000. In the summer of 1980, his cancer began to spread; he collapsed at Madison Square Garden during a concert. Late in 1980 he began treatment with the controversial cancer specialist, Dr Josef Issels. By 3 May, the doctor had given up. Marley flew to Miami, Florida, where he died on 11 May. Marley was rightly celebrated in 1992 with the release of an outstanding CD box set chronicling his entire career, although his discography remains cluttered due to the legal ramifications of his estate. His global success had been an inspiration to all Jamaican atists; his name became synonymous with Jamaican music, of which he had been the first authentic superstar. His contribution is thus immense: his career did much to focus attention on Jamaican music and establish credibility for it. In addition, he was a charismatic performer, a great singer and superb songwriter; a hard act to follow for other Jamaican artists.

●ALBUMS: *Wailing Wailers* (Studio One 1965)★★★, *The Best Of The Wailers* (Beverley's 1970)★★★, *Soul Rebels* (Trojan/Upsetter 1970)★★★, *Catch A Fire* (Island 1973)★★★★, *Burnin'* (Island 1973)★★★★, *African Herbsman* (Trojan 1974)★★★, *Rasta Revolution* (Trojan 1974)★★★, *Natty Dread* (Island 1975)★★★★★, *Live!* later re-titled *Live At The Lyceum* (Island 1975)★★★★, *Rastaman Vibration* (Island 1976)★★★★, *Exodus* (Island 1977)★★★★, *Kaya* (Island 1978)★★★★, *Babylon By Bus* (Island 1978)★★★, *Survival* (Tuff Gong/Island 1979)★★★★, *Uprising* (Tuff Gong/Island 1980)★★★★, *Marley, Tosh Livingston & Associates* (Studio One 1980)★★★.

●COMPILATIONS: *In The Beginning* (Psycho/Trojan 1979)★★★, *Chances Are* (Warners 1981)★★★, *Bob Marley - The Boxed Set* 9-LP box set (Island 1982)★★★, *Confrontation* (Tuff Gong/Island 1983)★★★, *Legend* (Island 1984)★★★★★, *Mellow Mood* (Topline 1984)★★, *Reggae Greats* (Island 1985)★★★, *Soul Revolution I & II* the first UK release of the 70s Jamaican double album (Trojan 1988)★★★, *Interviews* (Tuff Gong 1988)★★, *Talkin' Blues* (Tuff Gong 1991)★★★, *All The Hits* (Rohit 1991)★★★, *Upsetter Record Shop Parts 1&2* (Esoldun 1992)★★★, *Songs Of Freedom* 4-CD box set (Island 1992)★★★★, *Never Ending Wailers* (RAS 1993)★★★, *Natural Mystic: The Legend Continues* (Island 1995)★★★★, *Power* (More Music 1995)★★★, *Soul Almighty - The Formative Years Vol 1* (JAD 1996)★★★.

●VIDEOS: *One Love Peace Concert* (Hendring 1988), *Live At The Rainbow* (Channel 5 1988), *Caribbean Nights* (Island 1988), *Legend* (Island 1991), *Time Will Tell* (1992), *The Bob Marley Story* (Island 1994).

●FURTHER READING: *Bob Marley: The Roots Of Reggae*, Cathy McKnight and John Tobler. *Soul Rebel - Natural Mystic*, Adrian Boot and Vivien Goldman. *Bob Marley: The Biography*, Stephen Davis. *Catch A Fire, The Life Of Bob Marley*, Timothy White. *Bob Marley: Reggae King Of The World*, Malika Lee Whitney. *Bob Marley: In His Own Words*, Ian McCann. *The Music Of Bob Marley*, Ian McCann. *Bob Marley: Music, Myth & The Rastas*, Henderson Dalrymple. *Bob Marley: Conquering Lion Of Reggae*, Stephen Davis. *The Illustrated Legend 1945-1981*, Barry Lazell. *Sprit Dancer*, Bruce W. Talamon.

MARRIOTT, STEVE

b. 30 January 1947, London, England, d. 20 April 1991, Arkesden, Essex, England. As a child actor, Marriott appeared in *The Famous Five* television series in the late 50s and made a West End theatre debut as the Artful Dodger in Lionel Bart's *Oliver!* in 1961. That same year, Decca engaged him as an Adam Faith soundalike for two unsuccessful singles. Next, as singing guitarist in the Moments, he had another miss with a sly cover of the Kinks' 'You Really Got Me' for the USA market. Then followed Steve Marriott and the Frantic Ones (amended to just the Frantics). This venture was, however, less lucrative than his daytime job in an East Ham music equipment shop where, in 1964, he met fellow mod Ronnie Lane (bass) with whom he formed the Small Faces after recruiting Kenny Jones (drums) and Jimmy Winston (keyboards). Knock-kneed and diminutive, Steve emerged as the outfit's public face, attacking the early smashes with a strangled passion revealing an absorption of R&B, and an exciting (if sometimes slipshod) fretboard style that belied the saccharine quality of such songs as 'Sha-La-La-La-Lee' and 'My Mind's Eye'. With Lane, he composed the unit's later output as well as minor hits for Chris Farlowe and P.P. Arnold.

On leaving the Small Faces in 1969, Marriott, as mainstay of Humble Pie, acquired both a solitary UK Top 20 entry and a reputation for boorish behaviour on BBC's *Top Of The Pops* before building on his previous group's small beginnings. In North America, by 1975, he earned a hard-rock stardom accrued over 22 USA tours when Humble Pie disbanded. He put himself forward as a possible replacement when Mick Taylor left the Rolling Stones, played concerts with his All-Stars (which included Alexis Korner) and recorded a patchy solo album before regrouping the Small Faces, but poor sales of two 'comeback' albums blighted their progress. A link-up with Leslie West was mooted and a new Humble Pie released two albums but, from the early 80s, Marriott was heard mostly on the European club circuit, fronting various short-lived bands, including Packet Of Three, with a repertoire that hinged on past glories. Shortly before he perished in a fire in his Essex home in April 1991, Marriot had been attempting to reconstitute Humble Pie with Peter Frampton. Frampton was among the many famous friends attending the funeral where the Small Faces' 'All Or Nothing' was played as Steve Marriott's requiem. Since his death his standing has steadily increased, cruel irony for a man who found it hard to get a recording contract for much of the past decade.

●ALBUMS: *Marriott* (A&M 1975)★★, *30 Seconds To Midnite* (Trax 1989)★★, with Packet Of Three *Live 23rd October 1985* (Zeus 1996)★★.

●FILMS: *Heavens Above* (1962), *Night Cargoes* (1962), *Live It Up* (1963), *Be My Guest* (1963).

MARSHALL HAIN

This UK pop duo consisted of Julian Marshall and Kit Hain, b. 15 December 1956, Cobham, Surrey, England, who enjoyed a hit in 1979 with the memorable 'Dancing In The City'. The equally smooth and emotional follow-up 'Coming Home' was also a minor hit. Their only album enlisted the credible support of Frank Ricotti (percussion), Dave Olney (guitar), Harold Fisher (drums) and Glen Nightingale (guitar). However, as their grip on the pop charts slackened the duo's record company cancelled their second album. Marshall left to play piano for the Flying Lizards and following the break-up of their personal relationship his partner embarked on a solo career. Hain's first release was 'The Joke's On You', for Harvest, before she signed to Decca and subsequently Mercury for several singles and albums. Kit Hain moved to the USA in 1985 and has forged a successful career as a songwriter. Her portfolio includes 'Fires Of Eden' for Cher, 'Back To Avalon' for Heart, 'Rip In Heaven' and 'Crash And Burn' for Til Tuesday, 'Further From Fantasy' for Annie Haslam, 'Remind My Heart' and 'Every Time We Fall' for Lea Salonga (Miss Saigon). Her songs have also been recorded by Roger Daltrey, Kiki Dee, Barbara Dickson, Nicki Gregoroff, Cheryl Beattie and Kim Criswell.

●ALBUMS: *Free Ride* (Harvest 1978)★★★. Kit Hain: *Spirits Walking Out* (Deram 1981)★★★, *School For Spies* (Mercury 1983)★★★.

MARSHALL TUCKER BAND

Formed in 1971 in South Carolina, USA, the Marshall Tucker Band was a 'southern-rock' style group which maintained modest popularity from the early to late 70s. The band consisted of Toy Caldwell (b. 1948, Spartanburg, South Carolina, USA, d. 25 February 1993, Moore, South Carolina, USA; lead guitarist), his brother, Tommy Caldwell, (b. 1950, Spartanburg, South Carolina, USA; bass), vocalist/keyboardist Doug Gray, rhythm guitarist George McCorkle, saxophonist/flautist Jerry Eubanks and drummer Paul Riddle. There was no member named Marshall Tucker; the group was named after the owner of the room in which they practised their music. Like the Allman Brothers Band, Wet Willie and several others, the band signed with Capricorn Records and established the southern rock style, which emphasized lengthy improvisations built around soul-influenced rock and boogie songs. Prior to the formation of the Marshall Tucker Band, from 1962-65, Toy Caldwell had played with a local group called the Rants. He was in the Marines from 1965-69, and then the Toy

Factory, which also included Gray and Eubanks. McCorkle (another ex-Rant), Riddle and Tommy Caldwell were then added in 1972, and the new name was adopted. The group's first Capricorn album was self-titled and reached number 29 in the USA in 1973. The following year *A New Life* and *Where We All Belong* were released, a two-album set featuring one studio and one live disc. Their highest-charting album, *Searchin' For A Rainbow*, came in 1975. Their first single to chart was 'This Ol' Cowboy', also in 1975.

Most of the group's albums were gold or platinum sellers through 1978, and the 1977 single 'Heard It In A Love Song' was their best-selling, reaching number 14 (although they were primarily considered an 'album' band). Following their 1978 *Greatest Hits* album, the band switched to Warner Brothers Records and released three final chart albums through 1981. The group continued to perform after the death of Tommy Caldwell in an auto crash on 28 April 1980, but never recaptured their 70s success. (Caldwell was replaced by Franklin Wilkie, ex-Toy Factory) By the early 80s they had largely disappeared from the national music scene. They released new albums, first on Mercury Records in 1988, and then on Sisapa Records in 1990, with no notable success. All of the group's Capricorn albums were reissued on the AJK Music label in the USA in the late 80s.

●ALBUMS: *The Marshall Tucker Band* (Capricorn 1973)★★★★, *A New Life* (Capricorn 1974)★★★, *Where We All Belong* (Capricorn 1974)★★★, *Searchin' For A Rainbow* (Capricorn 1975)★★★★, *Long Hard Ride* (Capricron 1976)★★★, *Carolina Dreams* (Capricorn 1977)★★★, *Together Forever* (Capricorn 1978)★★★, *Running Like The Wind* (Warners 1979)★★★, *Tenth* (Warners 1980)★★★, *Dedicated* (Warners 1981)★★★, *Tuckerized* (Warners 1981)★★★, *Just Us* (1983)★★, *Greetings From South Carolina* (1983)★★, *Still Holdin' On* (Mercury 1988)★★, *Southern Spirit* (Sisapa 1990)★★, *Still Smokin'* (1993)★★.

●COMPILATIONS: *Greatest Hits* (Capricorn 1978)★★★.

●VIDEOS: *This Country's Rockin'* (1993), *Then And Now, Cabin Fever* (1993).

MARTHA AND THE MUFFINS

The roots of this Canadian new wave band lie in the mid-70s, when Martha Johnson was the organist with Oh Those Pants, a 10-piece 60s covers/send-up band which also included future members of the Cads. This was followed by a spell in another Toronto band, the Doncasters, who specialized in revamping 60s garage band material. In 1977, Johnson joined up with Mark Gane (guitar), Carl Finkle (bass), Andy Haas (saxophone) and Tin Gane (drums) to form Martha And The Muffins. They were later joined by Martha Ladly, who initially played guitar but later moved to keyboards and trombone. The group sent a tape to New York journalist Glenn O'Brien, who referred them to the fledgling DinDisc Records label. This led to the release of their debut single, 'Insect Love'. Success followed in March 1980 with 'Echo Beach', which was a number 10 hit in the UK charts. Its escapist verses ('From 9 to 5 I have to spend my time at work/My job is very boring I'm an office clerk/The only thing that helps me pass the time away/Is knowing I'll be back at Echo Beach someday') remain popular to this day. Follow-ups, including 'Saigon' (with its double groove b-side - playable both backwards and forwards) fared less well. This resulted in Martha And The Muffins becoming denigrated as 'one-hit-wonders', when in actuality all their albums, particularly *Trance And Dance*, are deeply resonant collections of songwriting which endure as well as any 'pop new wave' of the period. In 1981, Ladly left to work with the Associates and later formed the Scenery Club who released two singles on DinDisc. (Ladly now runs Real World Records' design department.) Finkle was then replaced by Jocelyn Lanois, Daniel Lanois's sister. The Muffins signed to RCA Records and session player Clara Hurst played keyboards temporarily but joined the Belle Stars in 1982, at which time Martha And The Muffins broke up. Wife and husband team Johnson and Mark Gane formed M + M, who enjoyed a major US hit with 'Black Stations White Stations', and released *Danseparc* on RCA in 1984. They later released two albums as a duo (*Mystery Walk*, with production from Daniel Lanois, and *The World Is A Ball*), before moving to the UK. Following soundtrack work in Toronto for the film *Modern Gravity*, a further album, *Modern Lullaby*, was released in 1992, but their label went bankrupt shortly after its release. They have also recorded a children's album together, *Songs From The Treehouse*. The rest of the band now work variously as a driver for the Canadian Automobile Association (Tim Gane), architect and swimming pool designer (Finkle), graphic designer (Ladly), and art museum guard (Haas).

●ALBUMS: *Metro Music* (DinDisc 1980)★★★, *Trance And Dance* (DinDisc 1980)★★★, *This Is The Ice Age* (DinDisc 1981)★★★.

MASEKELA, HUGH

b. Hugh Rampolo Masekela, 4 April 1939, Witbank, Johannesburg, South Africa. South Africa's leading *émigré* trumpeter and bandleader was born into a musical family which boasted one of the largest jazz record collections in the city. One of Masekela's earliest memories is of winding up the household gramophone for his parents; by the age of 10, he was familiar with most of the 78s issued by Duke Ellington, Count Basie, Cab Calloway and Glenn Miller. Other early influences were the traditional musics of the Swazis, Zulus, Sutus and Shangaan, all of which he heard at weekend musical gatherings in the township and neighbouring countryside. A difficult and rebellious schoolboy, Masekela was frequently given to playing truant. On one such occasion, he saw Kirk Douglas in the Bix Beiderbecke bio-pic *Young Man With A Horn* - and decided there and then that he wanted to become a

trumpeter and bandleader when he grew up. His teacher, the anti-apartheid activist and Anglican priest Trevor Huddlestone, welcomed this enthusiasm and gave Masekela his first trumpet, a battered old instrument owned by a local bandleader. A year later, in 1955, Huddlestone was expelled from South Africa. In New York, he met Louis Armstrong, and enthused to him about Masekela's talents and persuaded Armstrong to send a trumpet over to Johannesburg for the boy. With trombonist Jonas Gwangwa, Masekela dropped out of school in 1955 to form his first group, the Merry Makers. His main influences at this time were the African-American bop trumpeters Dizzy Gillespie and Clifford Brown and by 1956, the Merry Makers were playing nothing but bop.

By 1958, apartheid had tightened up to the extent that it was very difficult for black bands to make a living - they were banned from the government-controlled radio and were not allowed to travel freely from one town to another. Masekela was obliged to leave the Merry Makers and join the African Jazz and Variety package tour (which also included his future wife, Miriam Makeba). Operated by a white man, Alfred Herbert, the troupe was able to circumvent some of the travel restrictions imposed on blacks and continued to tour the country. In 1959, with Makeba, Masekela left Herbert to join the cast of the 'township musical', *King Kong*. The same year, he formed the pioneering band, the Jazz Epistles, with Gwangwa and pianist Dollar Brand (now Abdullah Ibrahim). They became the first black band in South Africa to record an album, all previous releases having been 78s.

In 1960, the year of the Sharpeville massacre, the government extended the Group Areas Act to ban black musicians from working in inner city (that is, white) clubs. The move effectively ended the Jazz Epistles' ability to make a living, and Masekela decided the time had come to emigrate to the USA. With the help of Trevor Huddlestone and Harry Belafonte in New York, he obtained a passport and, after a brief period in London at the Guildhall School of Music, won a scholarship to New York's Manhattan School of Music.

Initially aspiring to become a sideman with Art Blakey, Masekela was instead persuaded by the drummer to form his own band, and put together a quartet which debuted at the Village Gate club in 1961. A year later, he recorded his first album, *Trumpet Africa*, a considerable critical success. In 1964, Masekela married Miriam Makeba, another of Belafonte's protégées (who divorced him a few years later to marry Black Panther activist Stokeley Carmichael). Continuing to lead his own band, Masekela also wrote arrangements for Makeba and toured with her backing group. Husband and wife became prominent critics of the South African regime, and donated part of their touring income to fund scholarships that enabled black musicians to leave South Africa. In 1964, Masekela also released his second solo album, *The Americanization Of Ooga Booga*, and appeared at the first Watts, Los Angeles, California Jazz Festival. In 1966, he linked up with old Manhattan School of Music classmate Stewart Levine to form the production company Chisa. The original idea was for Levine to be the artist and Masekela the producer, but the success of Chisa's debut release, an album called *The Emancipation Of Hugh Masekela,* led to a role-reversal. (The Levine-Masekela partnership continued throughout the 60s, 70s and 80s.)

In 1967, Masekela appeared at the legendary Monterey Jazz Festival and released two more albums, *Promise Of A Future* and *Coincidence*. Unable to find top-quality South African musicians with whom to work in the USA, Masekela became drawn into the lucrative area of lightweight jazz/pop. His first chart success in the genre was an instrumental version of 'Up Up And Away' in 1967, which reached number 71 in the US charts. In 1968, he had a number 1 hit with 'Grazin' In The Grass', selling four million copies. The follow-up, 'Puffin' On Down The Track', disappointingly only reached number 71. Not surprisingly, given the mood of the times, the latter two singles were widely perceived to carry pro-marijuana statements in their titles and, in autumn 1968, Masekela was arrested at his home in Malibu and charged with possession of the drug.

Despite the urging of the record business, Masekela refused to capitalize on the success of 'Grazin' In The Grass' with a lightweight album in the same vein, and instead recorded the protest album *Masekela,* which included track titles such as 'Fuzz' and 'Riot'.

In 1970, Masekela signed with Motown Records, who released the album *Reconstruction*. Also that year, he formed the Union of South Africa band with fellow *émigrés* Gwangwa and Caiphus Semenya. The band was short-lived, however, following the lengthy hospitalization of Gwangwa from injuries sustained in a car crash. Frustrated in his attempt to launch an American-based, South African line-up, Masekela visited London to record the album *Home Is Where The Music Is* with exiled South African saxophonist Dudu Pukwana. Deciding to reimmerse himself in his African roots, Masekela set off in late 1972 on a 'pilgrimage' to Senegal, Liberia, Zaire and other countries. He worked for a year in Guinea (where his ex-wife Makeba was now living) as a music teacher, then spent some months in Lagos, Nigeria, playing in Fela Anikulapo Kuti's band. He finally ended up in Ghana, where he joined the young highlife-meets-funk band Hedzolleh Soundz. Between 1974 and 1976, Masekela released five albums with the group - *Your Mama Told You Not To Worry, I Am Not Afraid, The Boys Doin' It, The African Connection* and *Colonial Man*. By 1975, however, leader and band had fallen out, with Hedzolleh accusing Masekela of financial mistreatment. In fact, the cost of supporting Hedzolleh in the USA during loss-making tours had drained Masekela's resources, and in 1976, he and Levine were obliged to wind up Chisa. Short of money, Masekela signed to A&M Records, where he recorded two lightweight

albums with label boss Herb Alpert - *The Main Event* and *Herb Alpert/Hugh Masekela.*

In 1980, with Makeba, Masekela headlined a massive Goin' Home outdoor concert in Lesotho. In 1982, in a similar venture, they appeared in neighbouring Botswana. Both concerts were attended by large numbers of black and white South Africans, who gave the duo heroes' welcomes. Masekela decided to settle in Botswana, 20 miles from the South African border, and signed to the UK label Jive, who flew over to him in a state-of-the-art mobile studio. The sessions resulted in the albums *Technobush* and *Waiting For The Rain*. In 1983, he made his first live appearance in London for over 20 years, at the African Sounds for Mandela concert at Alexandra Palace. In 1986, Masekela severed his links with Jive and returned to the USA, where he signed with Warner Brothers Records, releasing the album *Tomorrow*, and joining label-mate Paul Simon's Graceland world tour. In 1989, he co-wrote the music for the Broadway show *Sarafina*, set in a Soweto school during a state of emergency, and released the album *Up Township*.

●ALBUMS: *Jazz Epistles* (1959)★★★, *Trumpet Africa* (1962)★★★★, *The Americanization Of Ooga Booga* (1964)★★★, *The Emancipation Of Hugh Masekela* (1966)★★★, *Promise Of A Future* (1967)★★★, *Coincidence* (1967)★★★, *Hugh Masekela* (Fontana 1968)★★★, *Alive And Well At The Whiskey* (Uni 1968)★★★, *Reconstruction* (Motown 1970)★★★, *And The Union Of South Africa* (Rare Earth 1971)★★★, with Dudu Pukwana *Home Is Where The Music Is* (1972)★★★★, *Your Mama Told You Not To Worry* (1974)★★★, *I Am Not Afraid* (1974)★★★, *The Boys Doin' It* (1975)★★★, *The African Connection* (1975)★★★, *Colonial Man* (1976)★★★, with Herb Alpert *The Main Event* (A&M 1978)★★, *Herb Alpert/Hugh Masekela* (A&M 1979)★★, *Home* (1982)★★★, *Dollar Bill* (1983)★★★, *Technobush* (Jive 1984)★★★, *Waiting For The Rain* (Jive 1985)★★★, *Tomorrow* (Warners 1987)★★★, *Up Township* (Novus 1989)★★★, *Hope* (Triloka 1994)★★★, *Notes Of Life* (Sony 1996)★★★.

●COMPILATIONS: *Liberation* (Jive 1988)★★★.

●VIDEOS: *Notice To Quit (A Portrait Of South Africa)* (Hendring 1986), *Vukani* (BMG 1990).

MASON, DAVE

b. 10 May 1944, Worcester, England. Mason, the former guitarist of local bands the Hellions and Deep Feeling with Jim Capaldi, met Steve Winwood when he was employed as a road manager for the Spencer Davis Group. This legendary 60s R&B band was weakened in 1967 when Winwood, together with Mason, formed Traffic. They found instant success as one of the leaders of progressive pop in the late 60s, and went on to develop into a highly regarded unit in the 70s. Mason joined and left the band on numerous occasions. He subsequently settled in America in 1969 and enjoyed considerable success as a solo artist. His excellent debut album on Blue Thumb records, *Alone Together*, proved to be his most critically acclaimed work, and featured strong musical support from Leon Russell, Rita Coolidge and former Traffic colleague Jim Capaldi on well-crafted songs such as 'You Shouldn't Have Took More Than You Gave', 'Only You Know And I Know' and 'World In Changes'. Mason's melodic flair and fine guitar playing came to the fore on all eight tracks. The original record package was a triple-fold, cut-out, hole-punched cover that attempted to encourage the listener to hang it on the wall. His second venture without Traffic was a collaboration with 'Mama' Cass Elliot. The record suffered from Blue Thumb's poor marketing and indifferent reviews and was shortly offloaded as a cut-out. His next album Headkeeper also suffered, but this time Mason disowned it and referred to it as a bootleg. The content was dubious and consisted of poor live recordings and half-finished studio takes. In the court proceedings that followed Mason filed for bankruptcy and was able to be released from his contract. By 1973, Mason had permanently settled in America, and he signed a long-term contract with Clive Davis at CBS. The first record, It's Like You Never Left, was a return to the format of the debut, although reviews were mixed and erred on the side of average. The recruitment of a number of name LA musicians gave the album a full and varied sound. Graham Nash, Greg Reeves, Jim Keltner, Carl Radle, Lonnie Turner and Stevie Wonder were just some of the artists who participated. Mason found limited success in his adopted country, and produced a series of reasonably successful records in the 70s. He built a considerable following in the USA by constant touring and had a stable touring unit. The regular line-up included Rick Jaeger (drums), Mike Finnigan (keyboards/vocals), Jim Krueger (b. 1950, USA, d. 29 March 1993; guitar/vocals) and Bob Galub (bass), later replaced by Gerald Johnson from the Steve Miller Band. The CBS albums formed a steady pattern that contained mostly Mason originals, regularly sprinkled with versions of oldies. 'All Along The Watchtower', 'Bring It On Home To Me', 'Crying, Waiting, Hoping' were just three of the songs he sympathetically interpreted. Following a surprise US hit single with 'We Just Disagree' Mason's albums predictably became dull and Old Crest On A New Wave was the nadir. Mason kept a relatively low profile during the 80s playing acoustic gigs with Krueger, making one poor album in 1987 and another forgettable release on MCA in 1988. He was also heard on American television singing on Miller beer commercials. In 1993 after having lived on Mick Fleetwood's estate in California for a while he joined the latest version of Fleetwood Mac. He contributed a number of songs to their badly received album Time. Mason looked back over his career in a lengthy 1995 interview in Goldmine and philosophically accepted all the mistakes he has made with regard to bad business arrangements, drugs and alcohol; he has at least survived with his sanity.

●ALBUMS: Alone Together (Blue Thumb 1970)★★★★, Dave Mason And Cass Elliot (Blue Thumb 1971)★★★, Headkeeper (Blue Thumb 1972)★★, Dave Mason Is Alive! (Blue Thumb 1973)★★, It's Like You Never Left (Columbia 1973)★★★, Dave Mason (Columbia 1974)★★★, Split Coconut (Columbia 1975)★★, Certified Live (Columbia 1976)★★, Let It Flow (Columbia 1977)★★, Mariposa De Oro (Columbia 1978)★★, Old Crest On A New Wave (Columbia 1980)★★, Some Assembly Required (Maze 1987)★, Two Hearts (MCA 1988)★.

●COMPILATIONS: The Best Of Dave Mason (Columbia 1974)★★★, Dave Mason At His Very Best (Blue Thumb 1975)★★★, The Very Best Of Dave Mason (ABC 1978)★★★, Long Lost Friend: The Best Of Dave Mason (Sony/Legacy 1995)★★★.

●FURTHER READING: Keep On Running: The Steve Winwood Story, Chris Welch. Back In The High Life: A Biography Of Steve Winwood, Alan Clayson.

MATCHBOX

Named after a Carl Perkins' classic, Matchbox were one of several 70s rock 'n' roll revivalist bands from the UK to make the jump from club favourites to chart stars. The band was formed in 1971 by two former members of Contraband - bassist Fred Poke and his brother-in-law Jimmy Redhead. They were joined by an old school-friend of Poke's called Steve Bloomfield. Capable of playing almost any stringed instrument, Bloomfield had made a living as a session player for Pye and was on several Mungo Jerry hits. Matchbox's debut single came out on Dawn in 1973, after which Redhead's departure left a line-up of Wiffle Smith (vocals), Rusty Lipton (piano), Bob Burgos (drums), Bloomfield (guitars), and Poke (bass). They subsequently recorded Riders In The Sky for Charly (they had previously recorded a Dutch-only album on Rockhouse). Smith and Lipton then departed, and former Cruisers vocalist Gordon Waters joined. The band were signed to a minor label and completed Setting The Woods On Fire in just over two days in October 1977, but as the record company were virtually bankrupt Chiswick took over its distribution. By this time, however, Matchbox had signed up with Raw Records - which issued a single - and this led to complications. Chiswick did not promote the band because Matchbox were not signed to the label, and Raw declined to promote them because they did not own the album. In desperation the group bought themselves out of their contract and signed a new agreement with Magnet. At this point they had been joined by vocalist Graham Fenton, previously with the Wild Bunch, the Houseshakers and the Hellraisers, and now Redhead returned, along with another guitarist, Gordon Scott. The first Magnet single, 'Black Slacks', missed out, but the second - a Steve Bloomfield original called 'Rockabilly Rebel' - made the charts. A string of hit singles followed. One further line-up change came about when Bloomfield decided he did not want to tour anymore, and Dick Callan was brought in as a replacement for live appearances. Apart from Matchbox recordings, the group also put out a version of Freddie Cannon's 'Palisades Park' under the pseudonym Cyclone. Steve Bloomfield released a solo album entitled *Rockabilly Originals*. The group is known as Major Matchbox outside the UK.

●ALBUMS: *Riders In The Sky* (Charly 1978)★★★, *Setting The Woods On Fire* (Chiswick 1979)★★★, *Matchbox* (Magnet 1980)★★★, *Midnite Dynamos* (Magnet 1980)★★★, *Flying Colours* (Magnet 1981)★★★, *Crossed Line* (Magnet 1983)★★★, *Going Down Town* (Magnum Force 1985)★★★, *Rockabilly Rebel* (1993)★★★.

MATCHING MOLE

Matching Mole were formed by Robert Wyatt after he left Soft Machine in 1971. The name was conceived by a brilliant twist, by using a french translation of the name Soft Machine (La Machine Molle). He recruited David Sinclair (keyboards, ex-Caravan), Phil Miller (guitar, ex-Delivery) and Bill McCormick (bass, ex-Quiet Sun) to complete the line-up. Having secured a contract with CBS Records, the group embarked on recording sessions for their debut album, but soon lost the services of Sinclair. Dave Macrae was recruited as his replacement in time to complete the sessions. The result was the group's self-titled 1972 debut. Those already converted to Wyatt's esoteric and innovative musical ambitions were not disappointed. Two of the best tracks, 'O Caroline' and 'Signed Curtain' were combined on a single, though for obvious reasons the album's outstanding track, 'Instant Pussy', was not. A second album followed in 1973. *Matching Mole's Little Red Record* arrived packaged in a striking cover showing armed revolutionaries painted in the manner of post-war Soviet propaganda - demonstrating both Wyatt's growing politicization and sense of irony. Many have assumed that the group's subsequent career was blighted by Wyatt's disabling accident, after he fell from an apartment window in 1972. In actuality, the group was falling apart anyway, and the accident coincided with his decision to relaunch the group with new members. In the event, when he returned from recuperation in hospital he elected to pursue a solo career. Sinclair and Miller subsequently joined Hatfield And The North, who also included David Sinclair's brother Richard. McCormick returned to session work while Macrae joined Pacific Eardrum.

●ALBUMS: *Matching Mole* (Columbia 1972)★★★, *Matching Mole's Little Red Record* (Columbia 1973)★★★.

MATTHEWS SOUTHERN COMFORT

Formed in 1969 by former Fairport Convention singer/guitarist Iain Matthews, the group comprised Mark Griffiths (guitar), Carl Barnwell (guitar), Gordon Huntley (pedal steel guitar), Andy Leigh (bass) and Ray Duffy (drums). After signing to EMI Records, they recorded their self-titled debut album in late 1969. Country-tinged rather than folk, it nevertheless dis-

played Matthews' songwriting talents. In the summer of 1970, their next album, *Second Spring* reached the UK Top 40 and was followed by a winter chart-topper, 'Woodstock'. The single had been written by Joni Mitchell as a tribute to the famous festival that she had been unable to attend. Already issued as a single in a hard-rocking vein by Crosby, Stills, Nash & Young, it was a surprise UK number 1 for Matthews Southern Comfort. Unfortunately, success was followed by friction within the group and, two months later, Matthews announced his intention to pursue a solo career. One more album by the group followed, after which they truncated their name to Southern Comfort. After two further albums, they disbanded in the summer of 1972.

●ALBUMS: *Matthews Southern Comfort* (EMI 1969)★★★, *Second Spring* (UNI 1970)★★★, *Later That Same Year* (1970)★★. As Southern Comfort *Southern Comfort* (1971)★★, *Frog City* (1971)★★, *Stir Don't Shake* (1972)★★.

MATTHEWS, IAIN

b. Ian Matthews McDonald, 16 June 1946, Scunthorpe, Lincolnshire, England. Matthews sang with small-time Lincolnshire bands, the Classics, the Rebels and the Imps, before moving to London in 1966, as one of the vocalists in a British surfing band Pyramid, who recorded a few tracks for Deram Records. To supplement his income, Iain worked in a shoe shop in London's famous Carnaby Street. He learned of a vacancy for a vocalist in Fairport Convention, which he joined in 1967 before they had recorded (and before Sandy Denny joined them). He appeared on the group's first single 'If I Had A Ribbon Bow', released on Track and produced by Joe Boyd, and on their debut album on Polydor. Fairport then moved to Island Records in 1968, and Matthews appeared on their early breakthrough album, *What We Did On Our Holidays*, but left the group during the recording of mid-1969's *Unhalfbricking*, because it had become obvious to him that the group's new-found traditional folk rock direction would involve him less than its previous contemporary 'underground' work.

Matthews (who had changed his surname to avoid confusion with saxophonist Ian McDonald of King Crimson) then signed with starmakers Howard And Blaikley, who had been involved in the success story of Dave Dee, Dozy, Beaky, Mick And Tich. After making a solo album *Matthews Southern Comfort*, for MCA in 1970, a group, also called Matthews Southern Comfort, was formed around him, and released two more country rock albums, *Second Spring* and *Later That Same Year*. The group also topped the UK singles chart with their version of Joni Mitchell's 'Woodstock'. By 1971, Matthews had left the band, which continued with little success as Southern Comfort. Matthews, meanwhile, signed a solo recording contract with Vertigo, releasing two excellent but underrated solo albums, *If You Saw Through My Eyes* and *Tigers Will Survive*, both featuring many of his ex-colleagues from Fairport, before forming Plainsong, an ambitious quartet that included Andy Roberts (ex-Liverpool Scene), Dave Richards and Bob Ronga. Matthews was still obligated to make another album for Vertigo, but was unwilling to commit Plainsong to the label. As a result, he was given a small budget to make a contractual commitment album, *Journeys From Gospel Oak*, which Vertigo did not release but instead sold to Mooncrest, a label with which the album's producer Sandy Robertson was connected. Originally released in 1974, it became one of the earliest compact disc releases to feature Matthews' post-Fairport work. Plainsong then signed with Elektra, and released the magnificent *In Search Of Amelia Earhart* in 1972, before Bob Ronga left the band. During the recording of a second album (still unreleased, but supposedly titled *Plainsong III*, referring to the membership of the band rather than a third album), Matthews and Richards apparently fell out. To continue would have been difficult, and Matthews accepted an invitation to work with ex-Monkee Michael Nesmith in Los Angeles. An excellent solo album (organized and encouraged by Nesmith), *Valley Hi*, was followed by *Some Days You Eat The Bear*, which included the Tom Waits song, 'Ol' 55', which Matthews recorded a month earlier than labelmates the Eagles. He then signed with CBS for *Go For Broke* and *Hit And Run*, which were neither commercially successful nor artistically satisfactory. By 1978, Matthews was again 'available for hire', at which point Rockburgh (which was owned by Sandy Robertson) offered to re-sign him. The first fruit of this reunion was *Stealing Home*, on which the backing musicians included Bryn Haworth and Phil Palmer on guitar, and Pete Wingfield on piano. Robertson licensed the album for North America to a small Canadian label, Mushroom, which had been financed by the discovery of the group Heart. 'Shake It' was excerpted as a US single and reached the Top 10, but the founder and owner of Mushroom died suddenly, and the company virtually collapsed. A follow-up by Matthews, *Siamese Friends*, was already contracted to Mushroom, but swiftly vanished with little trace in the UK.

In 1980 came a third album for Rockfield, *A Spot Of Interference*, which was an ill-judged attempt to climb aboard the new wave. This also disappeared, and later that same year came *Discreet Repeat*, a reasonably selected double album 'Best Of' featuring post-Southern Comfort material, but this marked the parting of the waves between Matthews and Robertson. The former formed an unlikely band called Hi-Fi in Seattle, where he lived with ex-Pavlov's Dog vocalist David Surkamp. Two more contrasting vocal styles than those of Surkamp and Matthews could hardly be imagined, but the group made a live mini-album, *Demonstration Records*, in 1982, and followed it with a full-length studio album, *Moods For The Mallards* - both were released in the UK on the small independent label, Butt Records. In 1983, Matthews signed with Polydor in Germany for

a new album, *Shook*, which surprisingly remains unreleased in Britain, and more importantly from the artistic point of view, the USA. Matthews threw in the towel and took a job as an A&R man for Island Music in Los Angeles, but was made redundant in 1985. An appearance at the 1986 Fairport Convention Cropredy Festival in Oxfordshire convinced Matthews that he should return to singing, even though he had just ended a period of unemployment by starting to work for the noted new age label, Windham Hill. After a frustrating year during which it became clear that Matthews and the label were creatively at odds, Matthews left, but only after recording a vocal album for the predominantly instrumental label, *Walking A Changing Line* released in 1988, on which he interpreted a number of songs written by Jules Shear (ex-Funky Kings and Jules And The Polar Bears). While this was his best album to date according to Matthews, it sold little better than anything since *Stealing Home*.

In 1989, Matthews relocated to Austin, Texas, where he linked up with Mark Hallman, a guitarist and producer who had worked on 'Changing Line'. A cassette-only album by the duo, *Iain Matthews Live*, was made for sale at gigs, and Matthews signed in 1990 with US independent label Gold Castle, to which several comparative veterans, including Joan Baez and Karla Bonoff, were also contracted. *Pure And Crooked* was released in 1990, and later that same year, Matthews reunited with his Plainsong-era colleague, Andy Roberts, for a very popular appearance at the Cambridge Folk Festival. By 1992, Gold Castle had gone out of business, leaving Matthews, an exceptional vocalist, once again without a recording contract. In 1993 Matthews and Roberts released *Dark Side Of The Room* under the Plainsong moniker, which was funded by a German record-maker and supporter.

●ALBUMS: *If You Saw Through My Eyes* (Vertigo 1970)★★★, *Tigers Will Survive* (Vertigo 1971)★★★, *Journeys From Gospel Oak* (Mooncrest 1972)★★, *Valley Hi* (Elektra 1973)★★★, *Somedays You Eat The Bear* (Elektra 1974)★★★, *Go For Broke* (Columbia 1975)★★★, *Hit And Run* (Columbia 1977)★★, *Stealing Home* (Rockburgh 1978)★★, *Siamese Friends* (Rockburgh 1979)★★, *A Spot Of Interference* (Rockburgh 1980)★★, *Shook* (Polydor 1983)★★★, *Walking A Changing Line* (Windham Hill 1988)★★★, *Pure And Crooked* (Gold Castle 1990)★★, *Nights In Manhattan - Live* (1991)★★, *Orphans And Outcasts Vol. 1* (1991)★★, *Orphans And Outcasts Vol. 2* (1993)★★, *Dark Side Of The Room* (Watermelon 1994)★★★.

●COMPILATIONS: *Discreet Repeat* (1980)★★★.

●VIDEOS: *Compass And Chart Vol. 1* (Perfect Pitch 1994).

MATUMBI

Nowadays largely remembered for being home to Dennis Bovell's first musical adventures, Matumbi should nevertheless be considered in their own right as a leading voice in the UK's 70s reggae scene. Formed in south London in 1972 by Tex Dixon (vocals), he pulled together a nucleus that comprised Euton Jones (drums), Errol Pottinger (guitar), Eaton 'Jah' Blake (bass), Bevin Fagan and Nicholas Bailey (vocals), alongside the aforementioned Bovell (guitar). They took their name from the African word for 'rebirth', and in the customary manner of early UK reggae bands, first found employment backing visiting Jamaican musicians. After signing to Trojan early singles included 'Brother Louie' and 'Wipe Them Out', but it was the subsequent singles, 'After Tonight' and 'Man In Me', which brought them major commercial recognition. The latter was the biggest-selling UK reggae single of 1976. However, success almost immediately brought internal friction, exacerbated by Trojan's attitude. They were disquietened by the way individual members were partaking of several outside projects, rather than concentrating on establishing the band as a top name. An injunction was finally served, with the result that Baily and Dixon quit, the former, who went on to solo 'pop' successes with Nick Straker, being replaced by Webster Johnson (keyboards). Pottinger had already been replaced by Glaister Fagan, whilst Jah 'Bunny' Donaldson joined in 1976 for Euton Jones. The remaining members moved on to a contract with EMI subsidiary Harvest, bolstering their profile by joining Ian Dury And The Blockheads on tour. *Seven Seals* was an effective long playing debut, but it was the follow-up, *Point Of View*, with garnered most plaudits. The title track, a mix of reggae, soul and Glen Miller, reached the Top 40, and for a time it seemed Matumbi might occupy the commercial high ground that many UK reggae bands had aspired to. It was not to be, two albums followed but popular taste had bypassed Matumbi, and the members resumed their solo projects. Bunny joined the Cimarons, and Glaister Fagan and Eaton 'Jah' Blake came to be known as the Squad, seeing some chart success as such. Bovell pursued his own idiosyncratic vision working both inside and outside of the reggae medium.

● ALBUMS: *Seven Seals* (Harvest 1978)★★★, *Point Of View* (EMI 1979)★★★★, *Dub Planet* (Extinguish 1980)★★.

● COMPILATIONS: *Best Of* (Trojan 1978)★★★.

MCCARTNEY, PAUL

b. 18 June 1942, Liverpool, England. Although commitments to the Beatles not unnaturally took precedence, bassist/vocalist McCartney nonetheless pursued several outside projects during this tenure. Many reflected friendships or personal preferences, ranging from production work for Cliff Bennett, Paddy, Klaus And Gibson and the Bonzo Dog Doo-Dah Band to appearances on sessions by Donovan, Paul Jones and Steve Miller (on *Brave New World*). He also wrote 'Woman' for Peter And Gordon under the pseudonym Bernard Webb, but such contributions flourished more freely with the founding of Apple Records, where Paul guided the early careers of Mary Hopkin and Badfinger and enjoyed cameos on releases by Jackie Lomax and James Taylor. However, despite this well-documented independence, the artist ensured a critical backlash by timing the release of *McCartney* to coincide with that of the Beatles' *Let It Be* and his announced departure from the group. His low-key debut was labelled self-indulgent, yet its intimacy was a welcome respite from prevailing heavy rock, and in 'Maybe I'm Amazed', offered one of Paul's finest songs. *Ram*, credited to McCartney and his wife Linda (b. Linda Eastman, 24 September 1942, Scarsdale, New York, USA), was also maligned as commentators opined that the singer lacked an acidic riposte to his often sentimental approach. The album nonetheless spawned a US number 1 in 'Uncle Albert/Admiral Halsey', while an attendant single, 'Another Day', reached number 2 in the UK. Drummer Denny Seiwell, who had assisted on these sessions, was invited to join a projected group, later enhanced by former Moody Blues' member Denny Laine. The quartet, dubbed Wings, then completed *Wildlife*, another informal set marked by an indifference to dexterity and the absorption of reggae and classic rock 'n' roll rhythms. Having expanded the line-up to include Henry McCullough (ex-Grease Band; guitar), McCartney took the group on an impromptu tour of UK colleges, before releasing three wildly contrasting singles, 'Give Ireland Back To The Irish' (banned by the BBC), 'Mary Had A Little Lamb' and 'Hi Hi Hi'/'C Moon' (all 1972). The following year, Wings completed 'My Love', a sculpted ballad in the accepted McCartney tradition, and *Red Rose Speedway*, to that date his most formal set. Plans for the unit's fourth album were undermined by the defection of McCullough and Seiwell, but the remaining trio emerged triumphant from a series of productive sessions undertaken in a Lagos studio.

Band On The Run was undeniably a major achievement, and did much to restore McCartney's faltering reputation. Buoyed by adversity, the artist offered a passion and commitment missing from earlier albums and, in turn, reaped due commercial plaudits when the title song and 'Jet' reached both US and UK Top 10 positions. The lightweight but catchy, 'Junior's Farm' provided another hit single before a reconstituted Wings, which now included guitarist Jimmy McCulloch (d. 28 September 1979; ex-Thunderclap Newman and Stone The Crows) and Joe English (drums), completed *Venus And Mars*, *Wings At The Speed Of Sound* and the expansive on-tour collection, *Wings Over America*. Although failing to scale the artistic heights of *Band On The Run*, such sets re-established McCartney as a major figure and included best-selling singles such as 'Listen To What The Man Said' (1975), 'Silly Love Songs' and 'Let 'Em In' (both 1976). Although progress was momentarily undermined by the departures of McCulloch and English, Wings enjoyed its most spectacular success with 'Mull Of Kintyre' (1977), a saccharine paean to

Paul and Linda's Scottish retreat which topped the UK charts for nine consecutive weeks and sold over 2.5 million copies in Britain alone. Although regarded as disappointing, *London Town* nevertheless included 'With A Little Luck', a US number 1, but although Wings' newcomers Laurence Juber (guitar) and Steve Holly (drums) added weight to *Back To The Egg*, it, too, was regarded as inferior. Whereas the group was not officially disbanded until April 1981, McCartney's solo recordings, 'Wonderful Christmastime' (1979), 'Coming Up' (1980) and *McCartney II*, already heralded a new phase in the artist's career. However, if international success was maintained through duets with Stevie Wonder ('Ebony And Ivory'), Michael Jackson ('The Girl Is Mine') as well as 'Say Say Say' and 'Pipes Of Peace', attendant albums were marred by inconsistency. McCartney's feature film, *Give My Regards To Broadstreet*, was maligned by critics, a fate befalling its soundtrack album, although the optimistic ballad, 'No More Lonely Nights', reached number 2 in the UK. The artist's once-prolific output then noticeably waned, but although his partnership with 10cc guitarist Eric Stewart gave *Press To Play* a sense of direction, it failed to halt a significant commercial decline. *Choba B CCCP*, a collection of favoured 'oldies' solely intended for release in the USSR, provided an artistic respite and publicity, before a much-heralded collaboration with Elvis Costello produced material for the latter's *Spike* and McCartney's own *Flowers In The Dirt*, arguably his strongest set since *Venus And Mars*. Paradoxically, singles culled from the album failed to chart significantly, but a world tour, on which Paul and Linda were joined by Robbie McIntosh (ex-Pretenders; guitar), Wix (keyboards), Hamish Stuart (ex-Average White Band; bass/vocals) and Chris Whitten (drums), showed that McCartney's power to entertain was still intact. By drawing on material from the Beatles, Wings and solo recordings, this enduring artist demonstrated a prowess which spans over a quarter of a century. The extent of his diversity was emphasized by his collaboration with Carl Davis on the classical 'Liverpool Oratorio', which featured opera singer Dame Kiri Te Kanawa. *Off The Ground* received lukewarm reviews and soon dropped out of the charts after a brief run. The accompanying tour, however, was a different story. The ambitious stage show and effects undertook a world tour in 1993, and was one of the highest grossing tours in the USA during tht year. Various rumours circulated in 1994 about a reunion with the surviving members of his most famous group. Both he and Yoko Ono appeared to have settled their longstanding differences, as had George Harrison and McCartney. The success in 1994-95 of the *Beatles At The BBC* indicated a ripe time for some kind of musical reunion. This was partly acheived with the overdubbing of 'Free As A Bird' and 'Real Love' for the magnificent *Anthology* series in 1996. The profile of the Beatles had rarely been higher and this was celebrated in the new year honours list by a knighthood for

services to music to McCartney. Presumably this is in recognition for his outstanding work with Lennon.

No doubt spurred on by the *Anthology*, *Flaming Pie* sounds like Paul means it again. The addition of Steve Miller on three tracks adds some gutsy rock guitar credibility. Mostly however, it is a magnificent return to form. Jeff Lynne's production has been tempered to sound cooked to perfection, unlike some of his previous overbaked concoctions. This is most definitely for lovers of the Beatles' *White Album*. The varied content includes 'Heaven On A Sunday', with its descending acoustic guitar duelling with the ascending lead guitar of son James, and 'Used To Be Bad', an excellent simple up-tempo blues featuring, Miller in which he revels, both singers trade lines as their voices blend beautifully. Further varied content includes some Memphis soul with 'Souvenir' and 'In It For The Money' which never loses pace for one moment. The folk simplicity of 'Calico Skys' is topped by the exquisite 'Somedays', a heart-tugging love song to Linda, and one of his finest songs in many decades. The album should ideally be listened to as one piece, since in that context, it sounds like a minor masterpiece.

●ALBUMS: *McCartney* (Apple 1970)★★★, *Ram* (Apple 1971)★★★, with Wings *Wildlife* (Apple 1971)★★, with Wings *Red Rose Speedway* (Apple 1973)★★★, with Wings *Band On The Run* (Apple 1973)★★★★, with Wings *Venus And Mars* (Apple 1975)★★★★, with Wings *Wings At The Speed Of Sound* (Apple 1976)★★, with Wings *Wings Over America* (Parlophone 1976)★★★, with Wings *London Town* (Parlophone 1978)★★★, with Wings *Back To The Egg* (Parlophone 1979)★★★, *MacCartney II* (Parlophone 1980)★★, *Tug Of War* (Parlophone 1982)★★, *Pipes Of Peace* (Parlophone 1983)★★, *Give My Regards To Broad Street* (Parlophone 1984)★, *Press To Play* (Parlophone 1986)★★, *Choba B CCCP The Russian Album* (Parlophone 1989)★★, *Flowers In The Dirt* (1989)★★★, *Tripping The Live Fantastic* (Parlophone 1990)★★, *Unplugged - The Official Bootleg* (Parlophone 1991)★★★, *Off The Ground* (1992)★★, *Paul Is Live* (Parlophone 1993)★★, *Flaming Pie* (Parlophone 1997)★★★★.

●COMPILATIONS: *Wings Greatest Hits* (Parlophone 1978)★★★, *All The Best* (Parlophone 1987)★★★★.

●VIDEOS: *Paul Is Live In Concert On The New World Tour* (PMI 1994).

●FURTHER READING: *Body Count*, Francie Schwartz. *The Paul McCartney Story*, George Tremlett. *The Facts About A Pop Group: Featuring Wings*, David Gelly. *Paul McCartney In His Own Words*, Paul Gambaccini. *Paul McCartney: A Biography In Words & Pictures*, John Mendelsohn. *Paul McCartney & Wings*, Tony Jasper. *Hands Across The Water: Wings Tour USA*, no author listed. *Paul McCartney: Beatle With Wings*, Martin A. Grove. *Paul McCartney: Composer/ Artist*, Paul McCartney. *The Ocean View: Paintings And Drawings Of Wings American Tour April To June 1976*, Humphrey Ocean. *Paul McCartney: The Definitive Biography*, Chris Welch. *McCartney*, Chris Salewicz. *McCartney: The*

Biography, Chet Flippo. *Blackbird: The Life And Times Of Paul McCartney*, Geoffrey Giuliano. *Blackbird: The Unauthorized Biography of Paul McCartney*, Geoffrey Giuliano. *Paul McCartney: Behind The Myth*, Ross Benson. *McCartney: Yesterday & Today*, Ray Coleman.
●FILMS: *A Hard Day's Night* (1964), *Help* (1965), *Give My Regards To Broad Street* (1985).

McCoy, Van

b. 6 January 1944, Washington, DC, USA, d. 6 July 1979. This successful artist had been a member of several groups prior to announcing his solo career with 'Hey Mr DJ'. Released in 1959, the single was distributed by Sceptre Records, with which McCoy subsequently served in an A&R capacity. He also branched out into writing and production work, making contributions to hits by the Drifters, Gladys Knight And The Pips and Barbara Lewis. Following that, McCoy embarked on a fruitful relationship with Peaches And Herb. In 1968, he established VMP (Van McCoy Productions) and enjoyed further success with Jackie Wilson ('I Get The Sweetest Feeling') and Brenda And The Tabulations ('Right On The Tip Of My Tongue'). He later became the musical arranger for the Stylistics, on the departure of Thom Bell, and emphasized the sweet, sentimental facets of their sound. McCoy was also encouraged to record under his own name and, fronting the Soul Symphony, secured an international smash in 1975 with the multi-million-selling, disco-dance track, 'The Hustle'. This perky performance set the pattern for further releases but the style grew quickly anonymous. McCoy continued his successful production career with, among others, Faith, Hope And Charity, until his premature death from a heart attack in 1979.
●ALBUMS: *Soul Improvisations* (1972)★★, *From Disco To Love* (Buddah 1972)★★★, *Disco Baby* (Avco 1975)★★★, *The Disco Kid* (Avco 1975)★★, *The Real McCoy* (H&L 1976)★★★, *The Hustle* (H&L 1976)★★★, *Rhythms Of The World* (1976)★★, *My Favourite Fantasy* (MCA 1978)★★, *Van McCoy And His Magnificent Movie Machine* (1978)★★, *Sweet Rhythm* (H&L 1979)★★, *Lonely Dancer* (MCA 1979)★★.
●COMPILATIONS: *The Hustle And Best Of Van McCoy* (H&L 1976)★★★.

McCrae, George

b. 19 October 1944, West Palm Beach, Florida, USA. A member of a vocal group, the Stepbrothers, while at elementary school, McCrae later joined the Jivin' Jets. This unit broke up on his induction into the US Navy, but was re-formed by the singer on completing his service in 1967. McCrae's wife, Gwen McCrae, joined the line-up, but after six months the couple began work as a duo. Together they recorded two singles, the second of which, 'Lead Me On', won Gwen a contract as a solo artist with Columbia Records. She received sole credit on the song's ensuing re-release which reached the R&B Top 40. McCrae then began managing his wife's career,

but following an R&B Top 20 hit with 'For Your Love' (1973), the pair resumed their singing partnership. McCrae was responsible for one of soul's memorable releases when Gwen failed to meet a particular studio session. He was obliged to sing lead on 'Rock Your Baby', a melodic composition written and produced by Harry Wayne (KC) Casey and Rick Finch, the two protagonists of KC And The Sunshine Band. This soaring, buoyant song topped both the US and UK charts, while two further releases, 'I Can't Leave You Alone' (1974) and 'It's Been So Long' (1975) also reached the UK Top 10. McCrae's work was less well-received at home but he continued to manage and record with his wife, appearing on her US number 1 R&B hit 'Rockin' Chair' (1975). In 1984, George McCrae enjoyed a final minor UK chart entry with 'One Step Closer (To Love)', but is still recording and touring in the mid-90s.
●ALBUMS: *Rock Your Baby* (TK 1974)★★★, *George McCrae* i (TK 1975)★★★, *Diamond Touch* (TK 1977)★★★, *George McCrae* ii (TK 1978)★★★, *We Did It* (TK 1979)★★★. With Gwen McCrae *Together* (Cat 1975)★★★, *One Step Closer To Love* (1984)★★.
●COMPILATIONS: *The Best Of George McCrae* (1984)★★★, *The Best Of George And Gwen McCrae* (1993)★★★.

McDonald, Country Joe

b. 1 January 1942, El Monte, California, USA. Named Joe in honour of Joseph Stalin by his politically active parents, McDonald became immersed in Berkeley's folk and protest movement during the early 60s. In 1964, he made a low-key album with fellow performer Blair Hardman, and later founded the radical pamphlet, *Rag Baby*. An early copy included a four-track record that featured the original version of the singer's celebrated anti-Vietnam War song, 'I Feel Like I'm Fixin' To Die Rag'. In 1965, he formed the Instant Action Jug band, which later evolved into Country Joe And The Fish. This influential acid-rock band was one of the era's finest, but by 1969, McDonald had resumed his solo career. Two tribute albums, *Thinking Of Woody Guthrie* and *Tonight I'm Singing Just For You* (a selection of C&W favourites) presaged his first original set, *Hold On, It's Coming*, which was recorded in London with several British musicians. This was followed by *Quiet Days In Clichy*, the soundtrack to a film of Henry Miller's novel, and *War, War, War*, an evocative adaptation of the work of poet Robert Service. The acclaimed *Paris Sessions* was a critical success, but subsequent releases lacked the artist's early purpose. He has remained a popular live attraction and his commitment to political and environmental causes is undiminished, as exemplified on a 1989 release, *Vietnam Experience*.
●ALBUMS: *Country Joe And Blair Hardman* (1964)★★, *Thinking Of Woody Guthrie* (Vanguard 1970)★★★, *Tonight I'm Singing Just For You* (Vanguard 1971)★★★, *Hold On It's Coming* (Vanguard 1971)★★, *Quiet Days In Clichy* soundtrack (Sonet 1971)★★, *War, War, War* (Vanguard

1972)★★, *Incredible! Live!* (Vanguard 1972)★★, *The Paris Sessions* (Vanguard 1973)★★★, *Country Joe* (Vanguard 1975)★★★, *Paradise With An Ocean View* (Fantasy 1975)★★, *Love Is A Fire* (Fantasy 1976)★★, *Goodbye Blues* (Fantasy 1977)★★, *Rock 'N' Roll Music From The Planet Earth* (Fantasy 1978)★★, *Leisure Suite* (Fantasy 1979)★★, *On My Own* (Rag Baby 1981)★★, *Into The Fray* (Rag Baby 1982)★★, *Child's Play* (Rag Baby 1983)★★, *Animal Tracks* (Animus 1983)★★, *Peace On Earth* (Line 1989)★★, *Vietnam Experience* (Line 1989)★★.
●COMPILATIONS: *The Best Of Country Joe McDonald* (Vanguard 1973)★★★, *The Essential Country Joe McDonald* (Vanguard 1976)★★★, *A Golden Hour Of Country Joe McDonald* (Pye 1977)★★, *Collectors' Items-The First Three EP's* (Rag Baby 1981)★★, *Classics* (1992)★★★.

McFADDEN AND WHITEHEAD

Gene McFadden and John Whitehead (both b. 1948, Philadelphia, Pennsylvania, USA), were former members of the Epsilons, a group managed by Otis Redding, prior to joining the Philadelphia International label. Here they forged a career as producers, playing a major role in the development of the label's 'sound' and as songwriters, penning hits for Harold Melvin And The Blue Notes ('Bad Luck', 'Wake Up Everybody') and the O'Jays ('Back Stabbers'), ultimately being responsible for over 20 gold discs. As performers, MacFadden and Whitehead enjoyed an international smash with 'Ain't No Stoppin Us Now' (1979), a defiant, post-disco anthem, highlighted by the latter's magnificent, exhorting delivery. The duo's later releases, however, were less successful, and, after serving time in prison for tax evasion, Whitehead embarked on a solo career in 1988.
●ALBUMS: *McFadden And Whitehead* (Philadelphia International 1979)★★★, *I Heard It In A Love Song* (TSOP 1980)★★.

McGARRIGLE, KATE AND ANNA

Kate (b. 1944, St Sauveur, Montreal, Canada; keyboards, guitar, vocals), and her sister Anna (b. 1946, St. Sauveur, Montreal, Canada; keyboards, banjo, vocals), were brought up in the French quarter of Quebec. As a result they learned to sing and perform in both French and English. It was their father who first encouraged them in their musical pursuits, rewarding them with nickels when they learned harmonies from him. While still in Montreal, after mastering the guitar in their teens, the sisters became members of the Mountain City Four, before they went their separate ways, Anna to art college and Kate to McGill University to study engineering. As a duo, Kate and Anna came to public notice after other artists, including Linda Ronstadt and Maria Muldaur, recorded and performed their songs. Kate McGarrigle met Muldaur after moving to New York, and Muldaur recorded 'Work Song' as the final track on her debut album. When Ronstadt scored a hit with Anna's 'Heart Like A Wheel', record companies began to express an interest in the duo's talents. As a result, Muldaur's label, Warner Brothers Records, asked the McGarrigle sisters to record an album. *Kate And Anna McGarrigle*, their first release, was produced by Joe Boyd, and contained their own take of 'Heart Like A Wheel'. The album's disparate musical styles spanned everything save rock, yet that did not prevent *Melody Maker* magazine naming it the 1976 Rock Record Of The Year. Apart from *Dancer With Bruised Knees*, which made the Top 40 in the UK, none of their subsequent releases has had any significant impact in the charts in either the USA or Britain. The long break after *Love Over And Over* was put down to the strong-minded duo fighting the promotional machine that was building around them: 'We just weren't prepared to be in that mould, of "Hey, now you're being professional". It took a lot of the fun out of it.' However, they have retained a strong following and their concerts, albeit on a smaller scale, consistently sell out. They first came to the UK to perform in 1976, with Kate then married to Loudon Wainwright III, and they toured consistently until they arrived to support the release of *Love Over And Over*. In the meantime they had raised four children between them, penned movie soundtracks and written songs. The McGarrigle sisters have an instantly recognizable sound, with a distinctive harmonic blend, and incisive lyrics which defy expectations. Their early promise has never been realized, but they still command respect, and a loyal following.
●ALBUMS: *Kate And Anna McGarrigle* (Warners 1975)★★★★, *Dancer With Bruised Knees* (Warners 1977)★★★★, *Pronto Monto* (Warners 1978)★★★, *French Record* (Hannibal 1980)★★★★, *Love Over And Over* (Polydor 1982)★★★★, *Heartbeats Accelerating* (Private Music 1990)★★★★, *Matapedia* (Hannibal 1996)★★★★.

McGOVERN, MAUREEN

b. Maureen Therese McGovern, 27 July 1949, Youngstown, Ohio, USA. The possessor of 'one of the most technically proficient singing voices in all of pop', with a four-octave, coloratura range, as a young girl Maureen McGovern was influenced by Barbra Streisand. After graduating from high school in 1967, she worked as a typist, and perfomed folk songs in the evenings. She then embarked on a six-year tour of hotels and holiday camps in the Midwest of America, performing contemporary material with a rock band. She came to the attention of 20th Century-Fox Records, who signed her to a contract. Her first recording, in 1972, was Al Kasha and Joel Hirschhorn's 'The Morning After', which was used as the love theme for the 'disaster' film *The Poseidon Adventure*. It won an Academy Award for best song, and McGovern's version topped the US chart. In 1974, the media began calling her the 'disaster queen' after she sang the Oscar-winning 'We May Never Love Like This Again' (Kasha -Hirschhorn) on the soundtrack of *The Towering Inferno* (McGovern also played a cameo role in the picture), and 'Wherever

Love Takes Me' (Leslie Bricusse-Don Black), the theme from *Gold*, a British film starring Roger Moore and Susannah York, in which a South African gold mine is destroyed. Given her recent career history, it was hardly surprising that McGovern was cast as the singing nun, Sister Angelina, in the 'disaster-spoof' movie *Airplane!* in 1980. By that time, she had begun to be known in Britain through her version of 'The Continental', and reached the US Top 10 with 'Different Worlds', the theme from the television series *Angie*. She had also recorded 'Can You Read My Mind' (Bricusse-John Williams), the love theme from *Superman*. In the early 80s, as well as appearing in regional productions of *The Sound Of Music* and *South Pacific*, McGovern attracted much acclaim for her performance as the ingénue, Mabel, in Joe Papp's revival of *The Pirates Of Penzance* on Broadway. She replaced Karen Akers in the Tony Award-winning musical, *Nine*, toured with *Guys And Dolls*, and appeared in a revival of the two-hander musical, *I Do! I Do!* Around this time McGovern was beginning to establish herself as a classy nightclub performer, singing mainly a blend of jazz and beloved Broadway standards. In particular, she has come to be regarded by many as 'the quintessential interpreter of Gershwin', although her programmes also include songs by writers such as Sergio Mendes, John Lennon and Paul McCartney, and Shelby Flint. In 1989 McGovern made her solo debut at Carnegie Hall, and as Polly Peachum, with Sting as Macheath, in *3 Penny Opera* (a new production of *The Threepenny Opera*) on Broadway. In the early 90s, she made her London concert debut at the Barbican theatre, and also played in cabaret at the Pizza On The Park and the Café Royal. Her honours include a Canadian Gold Leaf Award (1973), an Australian Gold Award (1975), and the Grand Prize in the 1975 Tokyo Music Festival for her performance of Paul Williams' 'Even Better Than I Know Myself'. She continues into the 90s firmly established as a top attraction on the US caberet circuit.

●ALBUMS: *The Morning After* (20th Century 1973)★★★, *Nice To Be Around* (20th Century 1974)★★★, *Academy Award Performance* (20th Century 1975)★★★, *Maureen McGovern* (Warners 1979)★★★, *Christmas With Maureen McGovern* (80s)★★★, with Sarah Vaughan, Placido Domingo, Mandy Patinkin *Love Songs* (80s)★★★, *Another Woman In Love* (1987)★★★, *State Of The Heart* (1988)★★★, *Naughty Baby-Sings Gershwin* (1988)★★★, *Greatest Hits* (Curb 1990)★★★, *Baby I'm Yours* (BMG 1992)★★★, *The Music Never Ends - The Lyrics Of Alan And Marilyn Bergman* (1997)★★★.

McGuinn, Roger

b. James Joseph McGuinn, 13 July 1942, Chicago, Illinois, USA. After a period playing at various folk clubs in Chicago, lead guitarist Jim McGuinn briefly joined the Limeliters before accepting a job as an accompanist in the Chad Mitchell Trio in 1960. He played on two of their albums, *Mighty Day On Campus* and *Live At The Bitter End*, but after a couple of years became frustrated with his limited role in the ensemble. Bobby Darin, having switched from pop to folk, also recruited McGuinn for a spell, and the guitarist continued to learn his craft by appearing on sessions for artists such as Hoyt Axton, Judy Collins and Tom And Jerry (alias Simon And Garfunkel). By 1964, McGuinn was playing regularly as a soloist at the Troubadour in Hollywood, and it was there that he formed the Jet Set with Gene Clark and David Crosby. Following the recruitment of bassist Chris Hillman and drummer Michael Clarke, the quintet emerged as the chart-topping Byrds. McGuinn was a focal point in the group from the outset, thanks largely to his distinctive 12-string Rickenbacker guitar playing, Dylanesque vocal style and rectangular glasses. The only Byrd actually to play an instrument on 'Mr Tambourine Man', McGuinn was often nominated 'leader' at recording sessions - though his authority was largely illusory during the early stages of the group's career. Never a prolific songwriter, McGuinn's importance to the Byrds lay largely in his playing and arranging skills. Always professing an interest in religion, he became involved in the sect Subud and changed his name to Roger before recording the celebrated *The Notorious Byrd Brothers*.

By 1968, he was the sole surviving, original Byrd and kept the group going until as late as 1973. That same year, he launched his solo career with a self-titled album which ably displayed his musical versatility - combining folk, surf and even space rock. The Rickenbacker twang was even more evident on his second album, *Peace On You* (1974), but he lost critical ground with a hastily produced third album. A starring spot in Bob Dylan's Rolling Thunder Revue, in 1975, revitalized his career at a crucial time, laying the foundations for the excellent *Cardiff Rose* (1976), his most complete work as a soloist. The patchy *Thunderbyrd* (1977), which included McGuinn's version of Tom Petty's 'American Girl', coincided with a UK tour which brought together three ex-Byrds in different groups on the same bill. Within a year, the trio united as McGuinn, Clark And Hillman, re-enacting the Byrds' stormy career in microcosm when Gene Clark again left after the second album, *City*. Meanwhile, McGuinn had undergone another religious conversion, this time emerging as a born-again Christian. For virtually the whole of the 80s he performed solo without a recording contract, and avoided any ill-advised Byrds reunions. A legal dispute with his former colleague Michael Clarke briefly saw McGuinn re-establish the Byrds with Chris Hillman and David Crosby. After losing the Byrds name at the injunction stage, a proposed world tour and live album failed to materialize. Instead, McGuinn won a major contract with Arista Records and set about recording his first album in over a decade. McGuinn's 'legendary' reputation as an innovative guitarist has grown to the extent that, during the late 80s, Rickenbacker manufactured a 'Roger McGuinn' production model. This guitar is pre-set to give a replica of his trademark 12-string sound. In 1990, McGuinn returned to the recording scene with the release of his first album in over a decade, *Back From Rio*. Critically acclaimed, the album charted on both sides of the Atlantic. McGuinn concentrated on solo performances for much of the early 80s, performing over 200 dates each year in the USA. His first live album was issued in 1996, containing reworkings of old favourites together with two new studio recordings.

●ALBUMS: *Roger McGuinn* (Columbia 1973)★★★, *Peace On You* (Columbia 1974)★★★, *Roger McGuinn And Band* (Columbia 1975)★★★, *Cardiff Rose* (Columbia 1976)★★★★, *Thunderbyrd* (Columbia 1977)★★★, *Back From Rio* (Arista 1990)★★★, *Live From Mars* (Hollywood 1996)★★.

●COMPILATIONS: *Born To Rock 'n' Roll* (Columbia Legacy 1992)★★★★.

●FURTHER READING: *Timeless Flight: The Definitive Biography of the Byrds*, Johnny Rogan.

McGUINNESS FLINT

Formed in 1969 by Tom McGuinness (b. 2 December 1941, London, England; bass, ex-Manfred Mann) and Hughie Flint (b. 15 March 1942; drums, ex-John Mayall). Dennis Coulson (keyboards), Benny Gallagher (b. Largs, Scotland; guitar/vocals), Graham Lyle (b. Largs, Scotland; guitar/vocals) and Paul Rutherford (saxophone) completed the original line-up, although the latter dropped out the following year. The group enjoyed immediate success with 'When I'm Dead And Gone' and 'Malt And Barley Blues', both of which reached the UK Top 5 and established their brand of light, folksy pop. Two excellent albums confirmed their undoubted promise, although a succession of disastrous live performances undermined progress. Further problems occurred in 1971, when principle songwriters Gallagher And Lyle left to pursue a career as a duo, but although Dixie Dean (bass/harmonica), John Bailey (guitar) and Neil Innes (piano, ex-Bonzo Dog Doo-Dah Band) replaced them, the group broke up at the end of the year. A resurrection of sorts occurred in 1972, when Coulson, Dean, McGuinness and Flint recorded *Lo And Behold*, a selection of Bob Dylan songs unavailable commercially. Coulson was then replaced by Lou Stonebridge, and with the addition of guitarist Jim Evans, a revamped McGuinness Flint re-emerged the following year. Two more albums were completed, but the unit was unable to recapture that first flush of success and broke up in 1975. Flint, Stonebridge and McGuinness later enjoyed fruitful periods with the Blues Band, albeit at different times.

●ALBUMS: *McGuinness Flint* (Capitol 1971)★★★, *Happy Birthday Ruthie Baby* (Capitol 1971)★★★, *Lo And Behold* (Capitol 1972)★★★, *Rainbow* (Capitol 1973)★★, *C'est La Vie* (Capitol 1974)★★.

●COMPILATIONS: *The Capitol Years* (EMI 1996)★★★.

McLAUGHLIN, JOHN

b. 4 January 1942, Yorkshire, England. Born into a musical family - his mother played violin - McLaughlin studied piano from the age of nine. He then took up the guitar because, like so many of his generation, he was inspired by the blues. By the time he was 14 years old, he had developed an interest in flamenco - the technical guitarist's most testing genre - and later started listening to jazz. He moved to London and his first professional gigs were as part of the early 60s blues boom, playing with Alexis Korner, Georgie Fame and Graham Bond. As the 60s progressed, McLaughlin became interested in more abstract forms, working and recording with John Surman and Dave Holland. He also spent some time in Germany playing free jazz with Gunter Hampel. His *Extrapolation*, recorded in 1969, with Surman and drummer Tony Oxley, was a landmark in British music. McLaughlin's clean, razor-sharp delivery wowed a public for whom guitars had become an obsession. The rock music of the Beatles and the Rolling Stones seemed to be adding something to R&B that the Americans had not considered, so when Tony Williams - the drummer who had played on Eric Dolphy's *Out To Lunch* - formed his own band, Lifetime, it seemed natural to invite the young English guitarist aboard. McLaughlin flew to New York in 1969, but left the band the following year. His own *My Goal's Beyond* (1970) flanked his guitar with the bass of Charlie Haden and the percussion of Airto Moreira. Meanwhile, ever conscious of new directions, Miles Davis had used McLaughlin on *In A Silent Way*, music to a rock beat that loosened rhythmic integration (a nod towards what Dolphy and Ornette Coleman were doing). However, it was McLaughlin's playing on the seminal *Bitches Brew* (1970) that set the jazz world alight: it seemed to be the ideal mixture of jazz chops and rock excitement. Nearly everyone involved went off to form fusion outfits, and McLaughlin was no exception. His Mahavishnu Orchestra broke new boundaries in jazz in terms of volume, brash virtuosity and multi-faceted complexity. The colossal drums of Billy Cobham steered McLaughlin, ex-Flock violinist Jerry Goodman and keyboard player Jan Hammer into an explosive creativity bordering on chaos. The creation of rock superstars had found its equivalent for jazz instrumentalists. McLaughlin sported a custom-built electric guitar with two fretboards. By this time, too, his early interest in Theosophy had developed into a serious fascination with Eastern mysticism: McLaughlin announced his allegiance to guru Snr i Chinmoy and started wearing white clothes. When Cobham and Hammer left to form their own bands, a second Mahavishnu Orchestra formed, with ex-Frank Zappa violinist Jean-Luc Ponty and drummer Michael Walden. This group never quite recaptured the over-the-top glory of the first Orchestra, and compositional coherence proved a problem. In the mid-70s, McLaughlin renounced electricity and formed

Shakti with Indian violinist L. Shankar and tabla-player Zakir Hussain. This time McLaughlin's customized guitar had raised frets, allowing him to approximate sitar-like drone sounds. In 1978, McLaughlin made another foray into the world of electricity with the One Truth Band, but punk had made the excesses of jazz-rock seem old-fashioned and the band did not last long. In 1978, he teamed up with Larry Coryell and Paco De Lucia as a virtuosic guitar trio. Guitar experts were astonished, but critics noted a rather dry precision in his acoustic playing: McLaughlin seemed to need electricity and volume to really spark him. After two solo albums (*Belo Horizonte, Music Spoken Here*), he played on Miles Davis's *You're Under Arrest* in 1984. In November 1985, he performed a guitar concerto written for him and the LA Philharmonic by Mike Gibbs. The same year he joined forces with Cobham again to create a violin-less Mahavishnu that featured saxophonist Bill Evans as an alternate solo voice. In 1986, they were joined by keyboardist Jim Beard. Two years later, McLaughlin toured with Trilok Gurtu, a percussionist trained in Indian classical music, and was again playing acoustic guitar; a 1989 trio concert (with Gurtu) at London's Royal Festival Hall was later released on record. McLaughlin was back in the UK in 1990, premiering his *Mediterranean Concerto* with the Scottish National Orchestra at the Glasgow Jazz Festival. *After The Rain* proved to be his most successful album for many years in 1995.

●ALBUMS: *Extrapolation* (Polydor/Marmalade 1969)★★★★, *Devotion* (Douglas 1970)★★★★, *My Goal's Beyond* (Douglas 1971)★★★, *Where Fortune Smiles* (Dawn 1971)★★★★, with the Mahavishnu Orchestra *The Inner Mounting Flame* (Columbia 1972)★★★★, with the Mahavishnu Orchestra *Birds Of Fire* (Columbia 1973)★★★★, with the Mahavishnu Orchestra *Between Nothingness And Eternity* (Columbia 1973)★★★, with Devadip Carlos Santana *Love, Devotion, Surrender* (Columbia 1973)★★★, with the Mahavishnu Orchestra *Apocalypse* (Columiba 1974)★★, with the Mahavishnu Orchestra *Visions Of The Emerald Beyond* (Columbia 1975)★★★, *Shakti With John McLaughlin* (Columbia 1975)★★★, with the Mahavishnu Orchestra *Inner Worlds* (Columbia 1976)★★★, *A Handful Of Beauty* (Columbia 1976)★★★, with Shakti *Natural Elements* (Columbia 1977)★★★, *Johnny McLaughlin, Electric Guitarist* (Columbia 1978)★★★★, with Al Di Meola, Paco De Lucia *Friday Night In San Francisco* (Columbia 1978)★★★, *Electric Dreams Electric Sighs* (Columbia 1979)★★★, *Belo Horizonte* (Warners 1982), *Music Spoken Here* (Warners 1982)★★★, with DiMeola, De Lucia *Passion Grace And Fire* (Mercury 1983)★★★, *Mahavishnu* (Warners 1985)★★★, *Inner Worlds* (Columbia 1987)★★★, with the Mahavishnu Orchestra *Adventures In Radioland* (Polygram 1987)★★★, *Mediterranean Concert/Duos For Guitar And Piano* (Columbia 1990)★★★, *Live At The Royal Festival Hall* (Mercury 1990)★★★, *Que Alegria* (Verve 1992)★★★, *Time Remembered: John McLaughlin Plays Bill Evans* (1993)★★★, *Tokyo Live* (Verve 1994)★★★, *After The Rain* (Verve 1995)★★★, *The Promise* (Verve 1995), *Paco De Lucia, Al DiMeola, John McLaughlin* (Verve 1996)★★★.

●COMPILATIONS: *The Best Of* (Columbia 1981)★★★★, *Compact Jazz* (Verve 1989)★★★, *The Collection* (Castle 1991)★★★, *Greatest Hits* (Columbia 1991)★★★, *Where Fortune Smiles* (Beat Goes On 1993)★★★.

●FURTHER READING: *John McLaughlin And The Mahavishnu Orchestra*, John McLaughlin.

McLEAN, DON

b. 2 October 1945, New Rochelle, New York, USA. McLean began his recording career performing in New York clubs during the early 60s. A peripatetic singer for much of his career, he was singing at elementary schools in Massachusetts when he wrote a musical tribute to Van Gogh in 1970. After receiving rejection slips from countless labels, his debut *Tapestry* was issued by Mediarts that same year, but failed to sell. United Artists next picked up his contract and issued an eight-minutes plus version of 'American Pie'. A paean to Buddy Holly, full of symbolic references to other performers such as Elvis Presley and Bob Dylan, the song topped the US chart and reached number 2 in the UK. The album of the same name was also an enormous success. In the UK, 'Vincent' fared even better than in his home country, reaching number 1. By 1971, McLean was acclaimed as one of the most talented and commercial of the burgeoning singer-songwriter school emerging from the USA. According to music business legend, the song 'Killing Me Softly With His Song' was written as a tribute to McLean, and was subsequently recorded by Lori Lieberman and Roberta Flack. McLean's affection for Buddy Holly was reiterated in 1973, with a successful cover of 'Everyday'. Meanwhile, his song catalogue was attracting attention, and Perry Como registered a surprise international hit with a cover version of McLean's 'And I Love You So'. Despite his promising start, McLean's career foundered during the mid-70s, but his penchant as a strong cover artist held him in good stead. In 1980, he returned to the charts with a revival of Roy Orbison's 'Crying' (UK number 1/US number 2). Thereafter, his old hits were repackaged and he toured extensively. As the 80s progressed, he moved into the country market, but remained popular in the pop mainstream. In 1991, his 20-year-old version of 'American Pie' unexpectedly returned to the UK Top 20, once again reviving interest in his back catalogue.

●ALBUMS: *Tapestry* (Mediarts 1970)★★, *American Pie* (United Artists 1971)★★★★, *Don McLean* (United Artists 1972)★★★, *Playin' Favorites* (United Artists 1974)★★, *Homeless Brother* (United Artists 1974)★★, *Solo* (United Artists 1976)★★, *Prime Time* (Arista 1977)★★, *Chain Lightning* (Millenium 1981)★★, *Believers* (Millenium 1981)★★, *Love Tracks* (1987)★★.

●COMPILATIONS: *The Very Best Of Don McLean* (United

Artists 1980)★★, *Don McLean's Greatest Hits - Then And Now* (EMI 1987)★★★, *The Best Of Don McLean* (EMI 1991)★★★.

McTELL, RALPH

b. 3 December 1944, Farnborough, Kent, England. Having followed the requisite bohemian path, busking in Europe and living in Cornwall, McTell emerged in the late 60s as one of Britain's leading folk singers with his first two albums, *Eight Frames A Second* and *Spiral Staircase*. The latter collection was notable for the inclusion of 'Streets Of London', the artist's best-known composition. He re-recorded this simple, but evocative, song in 1974, and was rewarded with a surprise number 2 UK hit. Its popularity obscured McTell's artistic development from acoustic troubadour to thoughtful singer-songwriter, exemplified on *You Well-Meaning Brought Me Here*, in which the singer tackled militarism and its attendant political geography in an erudite, compulsive manner. During live performances McTell demonstrated considerable dexterity on acoustic guitar. He was particularly proficient when playing ragtime blues. Subsequent releases included the excellent *Not Until Tomorrow*, which featured the infamous 'Zimmerman Blues', and *Easy*. During the 80s he pursued a career in children's television, and his later releases have featured songs from such work, as well as interpretations of other artist's compositions. Touring occasionally, McTell is still able to comfortably fill concert halls.

●ALBUMS: *Eight Frames A Second* (Transatlantic 1968)★★★, *Spiral Staircase* (Transatlantic 1969)★★★, *My Side Of Your Window* (Transatlantic 1970)★★★, *You Well-Meaning Brought Me Here* (Famous 1971)★★★★, *Not Until Tomorrow* (Reprise 1972)★★★★, *Easy* (Reprise 1974)★★★, *Streets* (Warners 1975)★★★, *Right Side Up* (Warners 1976)★★★, *Ralph, Albert And Sydney* (Warners 1977)★★★, *Slide Away The Screen* (Warners 1979)★★★, *Love Grows* (Mays 1982)★★★, *Water Of Dreams* (Mays 1982)★★★, *Weather The Storm* (Mays 1982)★★★, *Songs From Alphabet Zoo* (Mays 1983)★★★, *The Best Of Alphabet Zoo* (MFP 1984)★★★, *At The End Of A Perfect Day* (Telstar 1985)★★★, *Tickle On The Tum* (Mays 1986)★★★, *Bridge Of Sighs* (Mays 1987)★★★, *The Ferryman* (Mays 1987)★★★, *Blue Skies, Black Heroes* (Leola 1988)★★★, *Stealin' Back.* (Essential 1990)★★★, *The Boy With The Note* (1992)★★★, *Alphabet Zoo* (The Road Goes On Forever 1994)★★★, *Sand In Your Shoes* (Transatlantic 1995)★★★.

●COMPILATIONS: *Ralph McTell Revisited* (1970)★★★, *The Ralph McTell Collection* (Pickwick 1978)★★★, *Streets Of London* (Transatlantic 1981)★★★, *71/72* (1982)★★, *At His Best* (Cambra 1985)★★★.

MEAT LOAF

b. Marvin Lee Aday, 27 September 1951, Dallas, Texas, USA. Meat Loaf strongly claims this date, but others think it is 1947. The name Meat Loaf originated at school, when aged 13, he was christened 'Meat Loaf' by his football coach, owing to his enormous size and ungainly manner. Two years later his mother died of cancer, and fights with his alcoholic father grew worse. He moved to Los Angeles in 1967 and formed Popcorn Blizzard, a psychedelic rock group that toured the club circuit, opening for acts including the Who, Ted Nugent and the Stooges. In 1969 Meat Loaf successfully auditioned for a role in *Hair*, where he met soul vocalist Stoney. Stoney and Meat Loaf recorded a self-titled album in 1971, which spawned the minor *Billboard* chart hit, 'What You See Is What You Get'. *Hair* closed in New York in 1974, and Meat Loaf found new work in *More Than You Deserve*, a musical written by Jim Steinman, then took the part of Eddie in the film version of *The Rocky Horror Picture Show*. In 1976, he was recruited by Ted Nugent to sing lead vocals on his *Free For All*, after which he joined up with Jim Steinman again in the famous US satirical comedy outfit, the National Lampoon Roadshow. Meat Loaf and Steinman struck up a working musical relationship and started composing a grandiose rock opera. After a long search, they found Epic Records and producer Todd Rundgren sympathetic to their ideas and demo tapes. Enlisting the services of Bruce Springsteen's E Street Band, they recorded *Bat Out Of Hell* in 1978. This was pieced together around the high camp of the title track, an operatic horror melodrama that saw Meat Loaf raging against nature, and 'Paradise By The Dashboard Lights', with Ellen Foley providing female accompaniment. The album was ignored for the first six months after release, although Meat Loaf toured extensively, supporting Cheap Trick, among others. Eventually the breakthrough came, and *Bat Out Of Hell* rocketed towards the top of the charts in country after country. It stayed in the UK and US album charts for 395 and 88 weeks, respectively, and sold in excess of thirty million copies worldwide, the third biggest-selling album release of all time. However, with success came misfortune. Meat Loaf split with his manager, David Sonenberg, causing all manner of litigation. He was drinking heavily to cope with his new-found but barely anticipated stardom, and lost his voice. He also lost his songwriter too, as Steinman split to release solo what had been mooted as a thematic follow-up to *Bat Out Of Hell* - *Bad For Good*: 'I spent seven months trying to make a follow-up with him, and it was an infernal nightmare. He had lost his voice, he had lost his house, and he was pretty much losing his mind'. After a three-year gap, during which Meat Loaf declared himself voluntarily bankrupt, the eagerly anticipated follow-up, *Dead Ringer*, was released. Again it used Steinman's compositions, this time in his absence, and continued where *Bat Out Of Hell* left off, comprising grandiose arrangements, anthemic choruses and spirited rock 'n' roll. The title song made the Top 5 in the UK and the album hit number 1, but it only dented the lower end of the Top 50 *Billboard* album chart. This was, seemingly, the last time Meat Loaf would be able to use Steinman's sympathetic songwriting skills, and the consequent weakening of standards undoubtedly handicapped the second phase of his career. Concentrating on Europe, relentless touring helped both *Midnight At The Lost And Found* and *Bad Attitude* to creep into the UK Top 10 album chart. Nevertheless, this represented a significant decline in popularity compared with his Steinman-penned albums. *Blind Before I Stop* saw Meat Loaf teaming up with John Parr for the single 'Rock'n'Roll Mercenaries', which, surprisingly, was not a hit. The album was, however, his strongest post-Steinman release and featured a fine selection of accessible, blues-based, hard rock numbers. With live performances, things had never been better; Meat Loaf's band included Bob Kulick (brother of Kiss guitarist Bruce Kulick, and now of Skull), and ex-Rainbow drummer Chuck Burgi. They delivered an electrifying show which ran for nearly three hours. Recorded at London's Wembley Stadium, *Meat Loaf Live* emerged in 1987, and featured raw and exciting versions of his finest songs. By now Meat Loaf was also a veteran of several films, including *Roadie*, *Americathon* and, in the 90s, *Wayne's World* and *Leap Of Faith*. Apart from re-releases and compilations, he maintained vinyl silence well into the 90s. However, he signed a new deal with Virgin Records in 1990, and as rumours grew that he was once again working with Steinman, the media bandwagon began to roll. *Bat Out Of Hell II - Back Into Hell*, from its title onwards, displayed a calculated, stylistic cloning of its precursor. The public greeted the familiarity with open arms, pushing lead-off single 'I'd Do Anything For Love (But I Won't Do That)' to number 1 in both the US and UK, its parent album performing the same feat. Though critics could point at the formulaic nature of their approach, Meat Loaf had no doubts that by working with Steinman again, he had recaptured the magic: 'Nobody writes like Jim Steinman. All these things - bombastic, over the top, self-indulgent. All these things are positives.' Steinman was noticably absent from *Welcome To The Neighbourhood*, apart from two old compositions. Instead, the album contains songs that sound exactly like Steinman songs. Deadringers (sic) for this award are 'I'd Lie For You' and 'If This Is The Last Kiss', both written by Diane Warren.

●ALBUMS: *Bat Out Of Hell* (Epic 1978)★★★, *Dead Ringer* (Epic 1981)★★★, *Midnight At The Lost And Found* (Epic 1983)★★★, *Bad Attitude* (Arista 1985)★★★, *Blind Before I Stop* (Arista 1986)★★★, *Meat Loaf Live* (Arista 1987)★★★, *Bat Out Of Hell II: Back Into Hell* (Virgin 1993)★★★, *Alive In Hell* (Pure Music 1994)★★★.

●COMPILATIONS: *Hits Out Of Hell* (Epic 1984)★★★, with Bonnie Tyler *Heaven & Hell* (1993)★★, *Rock'n'Roll Hero* (Pickwick 1994)★★.

●VIDEOS: *Live At Wembley* (Videoform 1984), *Bad Attitude Live* (Virgin Vision 1986), *Hits Out Of Hell* (Epic 1985), *Meat Loaf Live* (MIA 1991), *Bat Out Of Hell II - Picture Show* (1994).

●FURTHER READING: *Meatloaf: Jim Steinman And The Phenomenology Of Excess*, Sandy Robertson.

MEDICINE HEAD

John Fiddler (b. 25 September 1947, Darlaston, Staffordshire, England; guitar/vocals) and Peter Hope-Evans (b. 28 September 1947, Brecon, Powys, Wales; harmonica/jew's harp) were confined to the small clubs of England's Midlands, until a demo tape brought the duo to pioneering BBC disc jockey John Peel's Dandelion label. Their debut album, *Old Bottles New Medicine*, offered delicate, sparse, atmospheric songs, and crude, rumbustious R&B, a contrast maintained on a second set, *Heavy On The Drum*. The duo enjoyed a surprise hit single when '(And The) Pictures In The Sky' reached number 22 in 1971, but their progress faltered when Hope-Evans left the group. Ex-Yardbird Keith Relf, at this point Medicine Head's producer, joined Fiddler and drummer John Davies for the group's third album, *Dark Side Of The Moon*. Hope-Evans and Fiddler resumed their partnership in 1972, although session musicians were employed on their subsequent album, *One And One Is One*. The title track became a number 3 UK hit in 1973, while a second single, 'Rising Sun', reached number 11; as a result, the line-up was expanded to include Roger Saunders (b. 9 March 1947, Barking, Essex, England; guitar), Ian Sainty (bass) and ex-Family member Rob Townsend (b. 7 July 1947, Leicester, Leicestershire, England; drums). Further ructions followed the release of *Thru' A Five* and by 1976, Medicine Head was again reduced to the original duo. *Two Man Band* (1976) marked the end of their collaboration. Fiddler then joined British Lions, which otherwise comprised former members of Mott The Hoople, and recorded several solo singles before fronting 're-formed' Yardbirds, Box Of Frogs, in 1983. He currently works as a solo act. Hope-Evans assisted Pete Townshend on his *White City* soundtrack (1985), and later played in several part-time groups.

●ALBUMS: *Old Bottles New Medicine* (Dandelion 1970)★★★, *Heavy On The Drum* (Dandelion 1971)★★★, *Dark Side Of The Moon* (Dandelion 1972)★★★, *One And One Is One* (Polydor 1973)★★★, *Thru' A Five* (Polydor 1974)★★, *Two Man Band* (Polydor 1976)★★, *Timepeace, Live In London 1975* (Red Steel 1995)★★.

●COMPILATIONS: *Pop History Volume XXV* (1973)★★, *Medicine Head* (1976)★★★, *Best Of Medicine Head* (Polydor 1981)★★★.

MELANIE

b. Melanie Safka, 3 February 1947, New York, USA. One of the surprise discoveries of the 1969 Woodstock Festival with her moving rendition of 'Beautiful People', Melanie briefly emerged as a force during the singer-songwriter boom of the early 70s. Although often stereotyped as a winsome 'earth-mother', much of her work had a sharp edge with a raging vocal style very different from her peers. Her first US hit, the powerful 'Lay Down' (1970), benefitted from the glorious backing of the Edwin Hawkins Singers. In Britain, she broke through that same year with a passionate and strikingly original version of the Rolling Stones' 'Ruby Tuesday'. *Candles In The Rain* was a best seller on both sides of the Atlantic, with an effective mixture of originals and inspired cover versions. 'What Have They Done To My Song, Ma?' gave her another minor hit, narrowly outselling a rival version from the singalong New Seekers. Her last major success came in 1971 with 'Brand New Key', which reached number 1 in the USA and also proved her biggest hit in Britain. In 1972, Melanie founded Neighbourhood Records, and its parochial title seemed to define her career thereafter. Marginalized as a stylized singer-songwriter, she found it difficult to retrieve past glories. Sporadic releases continued, however, and she has often been seen playing charity shows and benefit concerts all over the world.

●ALBUMS: *Born To Me* (1969)★★, *Affectionately Melanie* (Buddah 1969)★★, *Candles In The Rain* (Buddah 1970)★★★, *Leftover Wine* (Buddah 1970)★★★, *The Good Book* (Buddah 1971)★★★, *Gather Me* (Neighbor 1971)★★★, *Garden In The City* (Buddah 1971)★★, *Stoneground Words* (Neighbor 1972)★★, *Melanie At Carnegie Hall* (Neighbour 1973)★★, *Madrugada* (Neighbour 1974)★★, *As I See It Now* (1975)★★, *From The Beginning* (ABC 1975)★★★, *Sunset And Other Beginnings* (1975)★★, *Phonogenic - Not Just Another Pretty Face* (RCA 1978)★★★, *Ballroom Streets* (RCA 1979)★★, *Arabesque* (RCA 1982)★★, *Seventh Wave* (Neighborhood 1983)★★, *Cowabonga - Never Turn Your Back On A Wave* (Food For Thought 1989)★★, *Old Bitch Warrior* (Creastars/BMG 1996)★★.

●COMPILATIONS: *The Four Sides Of* (Wooded Hill 1997)★★★.

MELODY MAKER

The oldest-established pop music newspaper in the world was founded as the house journal of London music publisher Lawrence Wright in 1926, but soon became an independent monthly aimed primarily at dance band musicians. On the cover of its first issue in January 1926 it's banner read: A Monthly Magazine For All Who Are Directly Or Indirectly Interested In The Production Of Popular Music. After founding editor Edgar Jackson (1895-1967) left in 1929 to manage Jack Hylton's band, *Melody Maker* increased its jazz coverage. Composer Spike Hughes took over as record reviewer, and the paper sponsored a 1933 concert tour by Duke Ellington. In that year, *Melody Maker* became a weekly with a newspaper format. Ray Sonin took over from P. Mathison Brooks as editor in 1940 and was succeeded in 1949 by Pat Brand. With Max Jones (b. 1917) as its top jazz writer, by 1955, *Melody Maker* was selling 97,000 copies. However, the hostility to rock 'n' roll of some columnists saw the paper lose ground to *New Musical Express* (founded 1952) and to the newly launched *Record Mirror*. In 1956, *Melody Maker* published its first Top 20 singles chart but it did not wholeheartedly embrace the new pop music until 1963. When Jack

Hutton replaced Brand, the paper was redesigned and Chris Welch was hired as its first pop journalist. One of the most important sections of *Melody Maker* was its classified advertisements, notably the 'musicians wanted' section. Wishbone Ash and Camel were among the numerous British rock bands that found drummers or guitarists through the *Melody Maker* small advertisements.

With the addition of other, younger writers, *Melody Maker* provided full coverage of the progressive rock and folk scenes of the 60s, until it was hit in 1970 by the defection of Hutton and most of the staff to set up a rival weekly, *Sounds*. Under Hutton's deputy, Ray Coleman, however, *Melody Maker* had its most successful period in the early 70s, with sales reaching a peak of 200,000. Although most of the staff were hostile to punk, Caroline Coon was brought in to sing its praises. The 80s were a period of falling sales for the paper and all its weekly rivals, as new teenybopper papers led by *Smash Hits* and monthlies for the older rock fan (*Q*, *Mojo*) siphoned off sections of its audience. Despite an injection of new writing talent, notably from *Monitor*, a new wave fanzine based at Oxford University, *Melody Maker* turned inwards, writing about the latest indie rock bands in a style peppered with in-jokes. By 1991, *Sounds* and *Record Mirror* had disappeared, while the *New Musical Express* led the market, reviewing mainstream rock as well as independent label favourites. *Melody Maker* followed and seem likely to remain second fiddle in a market that has become less relevant with the appearance of magazines such as *Q*, *Mojo* and *Select*. Allan Jones was editor when the magazine celebrated 70 years with a special issue in April 1996, although he must find it frustrating to watch its readership continue to decline down to a meagre 55,000 copies by mid-1996.

●FURTHER READING: *Meoldy Maker Classic Rock Interviews*, Allan Jones (ed.).

MELVIN, HAROLD, AND THE BLUE NOTES

Formed in Philadelphia in 1954, the Blue Notes - Harold Melvin (b. 25 June 1939, Philadelphia, Pennsylvania, USA, d. 24 March 1997), Bernard Wilson, Jesse Gillis Jnr., Franklin Peaker and Roosevelt Brodie - began life as a doo-wop group. In 1960, they scored a minor hit with a ballad, 'My Hero', but failed to make a significant breakthrough despite several excellent singles. By the end of the decade only Melvin and Wilson remained from that early group, with John Atkins and Lawrence Brown completing the line-up. Two crucial events then changed their fortunes. Theodore 'Teddy' Pendergrass, drummer in the Blue Notes backing band, was brought into the frontline as the featured vocalist in place of the departing Atkins. A fifth singer, Lloyd Parkes, also joined the group which was then signed by producers Gamble And Huff, whose sculpted arrangements and insistent rhythm tracks provided the perfect foil for the

Pendergrass voice. His imploring delivery was best heard on 'If You Don't Know Me By Now' (1972), an aching ballad which encapsulated the intimacy of a relationship. Further singles, including 'The Love I Lost (1973) and 'Where Are All My Friends' (1974), enhanced Teddy's reputation and led to his demand for equal billing in the group. Melvin's refusal resulted in the singer's departure. However, while Pendergrass remained contracted to Philadelphia International and enjoyed considerable solo success, Melvin And The Blue Notes, with new singer David Ebo, moved to ABC Records. Despite securing a UK Top 5 hit with 'Don't Leave Me This Way' and a US R&B Top 10 hit with 'Reaching For The World' in 1977, the group was unable to recapture its erstwhile success. By the early 80s, they were without a recording contract, but continued to enjoy an in-concert popularity.

●ALBUMS: *Harold Melvin And The Blue Notes* (Philadelphia International 1972)★★★, *Black And Blue* (Philadelphia International 1973)★★★★, *To Be True* (Philadelphia International 1975)★★★★, *Wake Up Everybody* (Philadelphia International 1975)★★★★, *Reaching For The World* (ABC 1977)★★★★, *Now Is The Time* (ABC 1977)★★, *Blue Album* (Source 1980)★★, *All Things Happen In Time* (1981)★★.

●COMPILATIONS: *All Their Greatest Hits!* (Philadelphia International 1976)★★★★, *Greatest Hits - Collector's Item* (Philadelphia International 1985)★★★★, *Golden Highlights Of Harold Melvin* (Columbia 1986)★★★, *Satisfaction Guaranteed - The Best Of* (K-Tel 1989)★★★, *Collection Gold* (1993)★★★, *If You Don't Know Me By Now* (Epic Legacy 1995)★★★★.

MEMBRANES

Formed in Preston, Lancashire, in 1977, this UK punk group was based in the seaside town of Blackpool, later immortalized as 'Tatty Seaside Town'. Founder member John Robb (b. 4 May, 1961; bass) was initially joined by Mark Tilton (guitar), Martin Kelly (drums) and Martin Critchley (vocals), the latter soon departing as Critchley sidestepped from drums to keyboards, with 'Goofy Sid' Coulthart taking over behind the drumstool. Robb was to prove himself nothing if not a trier, organizing compilation appearances and inaugurating the near-legendary, near-indecipherable *Blackpool Rox* fanzine. Their first vinyl single was the 3-track 'Muscles' in 1981, gaining single of the week awards for its defiant, brash optimism and gaining ascendancy on the turntable of Radio 1's John Peel. It remains one of the most memorable DIY efforts of the early 80s. Steve Farmery joined on guitar after its release, with Martin Kelly leaving the keyboard position vacant. They joined Rondolet Records for 'Pin Stripe Hype', watching the label close down shortly afterwards. This also saw off Farmery, leaving the band as a trio for much of the rest of their productive career. Missing out on the opportunity to be Creation Records' first featured artists because of finance sent them downmarket to Criminal Damage. It,

too, proved a less than satisfactory home, and ultimately saw the group relocate to Manchester in 1983 in typically eternal optimism. The single which should have broken them was the acclaimed 'Spike Milligan's Tape Recorder', which somewhat pre-dated the guitar barrage of Big Black and Sonic Youth. However, distribution problems killed off the enthusiasm reciprocated by the media. The same problems applied to the 'Death To Trad Rock' 12-inch, after which Tilton left to be replaced by bass player, Stan. Although they finally made their postponed mark on Creation with the disappointing *Gift Of Life*, the band's fortunes were now in decline. Stan was replaced by Wallas as the band concentrated on the European circuit. Nick Brown was added on second guitar in 1987, followed in short order by Keith Curtis. Meanwhile, Robb was becoming more active as a freelance journalist for *Sounds*, and eventually *Melody Maker* and a host of other magazines. Despite the production services of Steve Albini (Big Black) on 1988's *Kiss Ass Godhead*, Wallas was the next departure, to be replaced by Paul Morley (ex-Slum Turkeys). However, total disintegration was imminent as Robb concentrated on his writing career, and launched his new dance project Sensurround.

●ALBUMS: *Gift Of Life* (Creation 1985)★★, *Songs Of Love And Fury* (In Tape 1986)★★, *Kiss Ass Godhead* (Homestead 1988)★★, *To Slay The Rock Pig* (Vinyl Drip 1989)★★.

●COMPILATIONS: *The Virgin Mary Versus Peter Sellers* (Vinyl Drip 1988)★★★, *Wrong Place At The Wrong Time* (Vinyl Drip 1993)★★★.

●VIDEOS: *The Death To Trad Rock Special* (Jettisoundz 1988).

MERTON PARKAS

One of several late 70s mod revivalists to make the UK charts, the Merton Parkas began life as the Sneakers in south Merton, London around 1975, playing old Motown classics. The line-up comprised brothers Mick (b. 11 September 1958; keyboards) and Danny Talbot (vocals), Neil Wurrell (bass) and Simon Smith (drums), and they chose their new name from Merton (the area of south London from which they came) and Parka (the ubiquitous item of mod attire). The Merton Parkas were great live favourites at the Bridgehouse in Canning Town, London, but were unable to appear on the *Mods Mayday '79* live compilation because they were negotiating contracts with Beggars Banquet, after the label's first signing, the Lurkers, had recommended them. They were one of the first neo-mod bands to record, and their debut single, 'You Need Wheels' was a hit in August 1979. Unfortunately, the rather trite lyrics had the Mertons branded as a novelty act, and they were often unfairly dismissed as bandwagon jumpers. Subsequent singles such as 'Plastic Smile', 'Give It To Me Now' (produced by Dennis Bovell of Matumbi), and 'Put Me In The Picture' failed to match the success of their debut. Mick Talbot was meanwhile making his

name as an in-demand keyboard player on the Jam's *Setting Sons* and an album by the Chords. The Mertons soon disbanded and Talbot went on to join Dexys Midnight Runners and the Bureau and appeared in the Style Council. Smith, meanwhile, joined the psychedelic revivalists Mood Six, and spent a while with the Times, before returning to the re-formed Mood Six.
●ALBUMS: *Face In The Crowd* (Beggars Banquet 1979)★★.

MESSINA, JIM

b. 5 December 1947, Harlingen, Texas, USA, (see Loggins And Messina; Poco; Buffalo Springfield).
●ALBUMS: *Oasis* (Columbia 1979)★★★, *Messina* (Warner 1981)★★, *One More Mile* (Warner 1983)★★, with the Jesters *Jim Messina And The Jesters, The Dragsters* (Audio Fidelity 1966)★★, *Watching The River Run* (River North 1996)★★★.

METERS

This fundamental quartet, Art Neville (b. Arthur Lanon Neville; keyboards), Leo Mocentelli (guitar), George Porter (bass) and Joseph 'Zigaboo/Ziggy' Modeliste (drums) came together during informal sessions held in various New Orleans nightclubs. Initially known as Art Neville and the Neville Sounds, they were spotted by producers Allen Toussaint and Marshall Sehorn, who signed the unit to their Sansu label to work on sessions for the duo's other artists, including Lee Dorsey and Betty Harris. Redubbed the Meters, the group's first singles, 'Sophisticated Cissy' and 'Cissy Strut', reached the US R&B Top 10 in 1969. These tough instrumentals mixed the bare-boned approach of Booker T. And The MGs with the emergent funk of Sly Stone, a style consolidated on several further releases and the unit's three albums for the Josie label. This canvas was broadened on a move to Warner Brothers/Reprise in 1972, where a series of critically acclaimed albums, including *Cabbage Alley* and *Rejuvenation*, reinforced their distinctive, sinewy rhythms. Such expertise was also heard on many sessions, including those for Robert Palmer, Dr. John and Paul McCartney, while in 1975, the group supported the Rolling Stones on their North American tour. Cyril Neville (vocals/percussion) was added to the line-up at this time, but the Meters found it difficult to make further commercial progress. In 1976, Art and Cyril joined Charles and Aaron Neville on a project entitled the Wild Tchoupitoulas. Led by an uncle, George Landry (Big Chief Jolly), this was the first time the brothers had played together. When the Meters split the following year, the quartet embarked on a new career, firstly as the Neville Family Band, then as the Neville Brothers.
●ALBUMS: *The Meters* (Josie 1969)★★★, *Look-Ka Py Py* (Josie 1970)★★★★, *Struttin'* (Josie 1970)★★★★, *Cabbage Alley* (Reprise 1972)★★★★, *Rejuvenation* (Reprise 1974)★★★★, *Fire On The Bayou* (Reprise 1975)★★★, *Trick Bag* (Reprise 1976)★★, *New Directions*

(Warners 1977)★★★, *Good Old Funky Music* (Pye 1979)★★★, *Uptown Rulers! Live On The Queen Mary* rec. 1975 (1992)★★★.
●COMPILATIONS: *Cissy Strut* (Island 1974)★★★, *Second Line Strut* (Charly 1980)★★★, *Here Come The Meter Men* (Charly 1986)★★★★, *Original Funkmasters* (1992)★★★★.

MFSB

'Mother, Father, Sister, Brother' or MFSB (and there was a less flattering alternative), was the house band employed by producers Gamble And Huff. Jesse James, Bobby Martin, Norman Harris, Ronnie Baker, Earl Young, Roland Chambers and Karl Chambers came to prominence as the uncredited performers on 'The Horse', a hit for Cliff Nobles And Co. in 1968. As the James Boys, the septet replicated with a cash-in release, 'The Mule', and the unit also recorded under other names, including the Music Makers and Family. It was as the instrumental muscle behind the Philadelphia International stable and artists such as the O'Jays and Harold Melvin And The Blue Notes that the group garnered its reputation. 'TSOP (The Sound Of Philadelphia)', the theme from television's *Soul Train* show, was a million-selling single in 1974, but later releases failed to match its exuberance and purpose. Undeniably rhythmic and undoubtedly competent, MFSB nonetheless lacked the focal point that the Three Degrees' voices provided on those early successes.
●ALBUMS: *MFSB* (Philadelphia International 1973)★★, *Love Is The Message* (Philadelphia International 1974)★★, *Universal Love* (Philadelphia International 1975)★★, *Philadelphia Freedom!* (Philadelphia International 1975)★★★, *Summertime* (Philadelphia International 1976)★★, *The End Of Phase 1* (Philadelphia International 1977)★★, *The Gamble-Huff Orchestra* (Philadelphia International 1979)★★, *Mysteries Of The World* (Philadelphia International 1981)★★.
●COMPILATIONS: *Love Is The Message: The Best Of MSFB* (Sony Legacy 1996)★★★.

MIDDLE OF THE ROAD

Originally known as Los Caracas when they performed throughout Europe, this Scottish quartet featured singer Sally Carr, backed by Ian Lewis, Eric Lewis and Ken Andrew. An astute cover of a novelty Continental song 'Chirpy Chirpy Cheep Cheep' saw them outsell a rival version by Mac And Katie Kissoon and hog the UK number 1 spot for five weeks in 1971. The follow-up, 'Tweedle Dee, Tweedle Dum' had already reached the top in Sweden, Denmark and Norway prior to its UK release, where it climbed to number 2. Further lightweight hits in the early 70s included 'Soley Soley', 'Sacramento' and 'Samson And Delilah', paving the way for many successful seasons in cabaret.
●ALBUMS: *Chirpy Chirpy Cheep Cheep* (Victor/RCA 1971)★★, *Drive On* (Victor/RCA 1974)★★.

MIDLER, BETTE

b. 1 December 1945, Paterson, New Jersey, USA. As a singer, comedienne and actress, Midler rose to fame with an outrageous, raunchy stage act, and became known as 'The Divine Miss M', 'Trash With Flash' and 'Sleaze With Ease'. Her mother, a fan of the movies, named her after Bette Davis. Raised in Hawaii, as one of the few white students in her school, and the only Jew, she 'toughened up fast', and won an award in the first grade for singing 'Silent Night'. Encouraged by her mother, she studied theatre at the University of Hawaii, and worked in a pineapple factory and as a secretary in a radio station before gaining her first professional acting job in 1965 in the movie *Hawaii*, playing the minor role of a missionary wife who is constantly sick. Moving to New York, she held jobs as a glove saleswoman in Stern's Department Store, a hat-check girl, and a go-go dancer, before joining the chorus of the hit Broadway musical *Fiddler On The Roof* in 1966. In February 1967, Midler took over one of the leading roles, as Tzeitel, the eldest daughter, and played the part for the next three years. While singing late-night after the show at the Improvisation Club, a showcase for young performers, she was noticed by an executive from the David Frost television show, and subsequently appeared several times with Frost, and on the *Merv Griffin Show*. After leaving *Fiddler On The Roof*, she performed briefly in the off-Broadway musical *Salvation*, and worked again as a go-go dancer in a Broadway bar, before taking a $50-a-night job at the Continental Baths, New York, singing to male homosexuals dressed in bath towels. Clad in toreador pants, or sequin gowns, strapless tops and platform shoes - uniforms of a bygone age - she strutted her extravagant stuff, singing songs from the 40s, 50s, and 60s - rock, blues, novelties - even reaching back to 1929 for the Harry Akst/Grant Clarke ballad 'Am I Blue?', which had been a hit then for Ethel Waters. News of these bizarre happenings soon got round, and outside audiences of both sexes, including show people, were allowed to view the show. Offers of other work flooded in, including the opportunity to appear regularly on Johnny Carson's *Tonight* show.

In May 1971, she played the dual roles of the Acid Queen and Mrs Walker in the Seattle Opera Company's production of the rock opera *Tommy* and, later in the year, made her official New York nightclub debut at the Downstairs At The Upstairs, the original two-week engagement being extended to 10, to accommodate the crowds. During the following year, she appeared with Carson at the Sahara in Las Vegas, and in June played to standing room only at Carnegie Hall in New York. In November, her first album, *The Divine Miss M*, was released by Atlantic Records, and is said to have sold 100,000 copies in the first month. It contained several of the cover versions that she featured in her stage act, such as the Andrews Sisters' 'Boogie Woogie Bugle Boy', the Dixie Cups' 'The Chapel Of Love', the Shangri-Las'

'The Leader Of The Pack' and Bobby Freeman's 'Do You Want To Dance?'. The pianist on most of the tracks was Barry Manilow, who was Midler's accompanist and musical director for three years in the early 70s. The album bears the dedication: 'This is for Judith'. Judith was Midler's sister who was killed in a road accident on her way to meet Bette when she was appearing in *Fiddler On The Roof*. Midler's second album, *Bette Midler*, also made the US Top 10. In 1973, Midler received the *After Dark* Award for Performer Of The Year, and soon became a superstar, able to fill concert halls throughout the USA. In 1979, she had her first starring role in the movie *The Rose*, which was loosely based on the life of rock singer Janis Joplin. Midler was nominated for an Academy Award as 'Best Actress', and won two Golden Globe Awards for her performance. Two songs from the film, the title track (a million-seller), and 'When A Man Loves A Woman', and the soundtrack album, entered the US charts, as did the album from Midler's next film, *Divine Madness*, a celluloid version of her concert performance in Pasadena, California. After all the success of the past decade, things started to go wrong in the early 80s. In 1982, the aptly named black comedy, *Jinxed!*, was a disaster at the box office, amid rumours of violent disagreements between Midler and her co-star Ken Wahl and director Don Siegel. Midler became *persona non grata* in Hollywood, and suffered a nervous breakdown. She married Martin Von Haselberg, a former commodities broker, in 1984, and signed to a long-term contract to the Walt Disney Studios, making her comeback in the comedy *Down And Out In Beverly Hills* (1985), with Nick Nolte and Richard Dreyfuss.

During the rest of the decade she eschewed touring, and concentrated on her acting career in a series of raucous comedy movies such as *Ruthless People* (1986), co-starring Danny De Vito, *Outrageous Fortune* (1987) and *Big Business* (1988). In 1988, *Beaches*, the first film to be made by her own company, All Girls Productions (their motto is, 'We hold a grudge'), gave her one of her best roles, and the opportunity to sing songs within the context of the story. These included standards such as 'Ballin' The Jack', Cole Porter's 'I've Still Got My Health', 'The Glory Of Love', 'Under The Boardwalk', and 'Otto Titsling'. Also included was 'Wind Beneath My Wings', by Larry Henley and Jeff Silbar, which reached number 1 in the US charts. Midler's recording won Grammys in 1990 for 'Record Of The Year' and 'Song Of The Year'. In 1990, Midler appeared in *Stella*, a remake of the classic weepie, *Stella Dallas*, in which she performed a hilarious mock striptease among the bottles and glasses on top of a bar, and *Scenes From A Mall*, a comedy co-staring Woody Allen. Her appearance as a USO entertainer in World War II, alongside actor James Caan, in *For The Boys* (1991), which she also co-produced, earned her a Golden Globe award for Best Actress. The movie showed her at her best, and featured her very individual readings of 'Stuff Like That There' and 'P. S. I Love You'. In the same year, she released *Some People's Lives*, her first non-soundtrack album since the 1983 flop, *No Frills*. It entered the US Top 10, and one of the tracks, 'From A Distance', had an extended chart life in the USA and UK. By the early 90s she was planning to revive her musical career, and in 1993 brought a spectacular new stage show to Radio City Music Hall. The lavish three-hour concert, her first for 10 years, was called *Experience The Divine*, and seemed as 'gaudy and outrageously tasteless as ever'. In 1994 Midler won an Emmy Nomination, along with Golden Globe and National Board of Review Awards for her outstanding performance as Rose in a CBS television musical production of *Gypsy*. In 1995, she recorded her first studio album for five years, *Bette Of Roses*.

●ALBUMS: *The Divine Miss M* (Atlantic 1972)★★★★, *Bette Midler* (Atlantic 1973)★★★, *Songs For The New Depression* (Atlantic 1976)★★, *Live At Last* (Atlantic 1977)★★★, *Broken Blossom* (Atlantic 1977)★★, *Thighs And Whispers* (Atlantic 1979)★★, *The Rose* film soundtrack (Atlantic 1979)★★★, *Divine Madness* film soundtrack (Atlantic 1980)★★, *No Frills* (Atlantic 1983)★★, *Mud Will Be Flung Tonight* (Atlantic 1985)★★, *Beaches* film soundtrack (Atlantic 1989)★★, *Some People's Lives* (Atlantic 1990)★★, *For The Boys* (Atlantic 1991)★★, *Bette Of Roses* (Atlantic 1995)★★.

●COMPILATIONS: *Best Of* (Atlantic 1978)★★★.

●FURTHER READING: *Bette Midler*, Rob Baker. *A View From A Broad*, Bette Midler. *The Saga Of Baby Divine*, Bette Midler. *An Intimate Biography Of Bette Midler*, George Mair.

MILES, JOHN

b. 23 April 1949, Jarrow, Tyne And Wear, England. Miles achieved international fame in 1976 with the classic rock ballad 'Music' ('music was my first love and it will be my last/the music of tomorrow, the music of the past'). His beginnings in the music business found him manufacturing toilet signs by day, but by night performing in a semi-professional band called the Influences, which also included Paul Thompson (later in Roxy Music) and Vic Malcolm (later in Geordie). After this band split, Miles formed his own John Miles Band, who were successful in their native north east and also recorded for the group's own Orange label. In 1975, Miles and bassist Bob Marshall moved to London and were signed to Decca. Recruiting Barry Black (and later adding pianist Gary Moberly) they reached the UK Top 20 with the Alan Parson-produced 'Highfly'. The 1976 epic length follow-up 'Music' reached number 3 and earned the band an American tour with Elton John. The accompanying album portrayed Miles as a moody, James Dean figure and the artist came across as such when defending his composition from quarters of the music press who unfairly ridiculed the artist as pretentious. He had two further UK hits in 'Remember Yesterday' (Top 40, 1976) and 'Slow Down' (Top 10, 1977), but Miles was forever linked with his self-confessional epic. This ultimately proved to be a burden on

Miles' development and although he continued to record into the 80s, he was never able to brush off the memory of that song. On 1983's *Play On*, Miles was using a 40-piece orchestra and Elton John's old producer Gus Dudgeon. In the early 90s Miles took to the road with artists including Joe Cocker and Tina Turner.

●ALBUMS: *Rebel* (Decca 1976)★★★, *Stranger In The City* (Decca 1977)★★★, *Zaragon* (Decca 1978)★★, *More Miles Per Hour* (Decca 1979)★★, *Miles High* (EMI 1981)★★, *Play On* (EMI 1983)★★, *Transition* (Valentino 1985)★★, *BBC Radio 1 Live In Concert* (Windsong 1993)★★, *Upfront* (1993)★★.

MILLER, FRANKIE (UK)

b. 1950, Glasgow, Scotland. Miller commenced his singing career in the late 60s group, the Stoics. Along with Robin Trower, Jim Dewar and Clive Bunker, he formed the short-lived Jude, whose potential was never captured on vinyl. With Brinsley Schwarz as his backing group, Miller recorded his first solo album, *Once In A Blue Moon*, in 1972. The following year he moved to New Orleans to work with Allen Toussaint on the highly regarded *High Life*, which displayed Miller's throaty, blues-styled vocals to considerable effect. Although the album did not sell well, it provided hit singles for both Three Dog Night and Bette Wright. By 1975, Miller had formed a full-time band featuring Henry McCullough, Mick Weaver, Chrissie Stewart and Stu Perry. Their album, *The Rock*, was a solid effort, but met with middling sales. With a completely new band comprising Ray Minhinnit (guitar), Charlie Harrison (bass), James Hall (keyboards) and Graham Deacon (drums), Miller next recorded *Full House*. The band of the same name lasted a year before Miller reverted to a solo excursion for *Perfect Fit*. The latter provided a surprise Top 10 UK hit with 'Darlin'', but Miller could not build on that success. His frequent change of musicians and producers has resulted in an erratic career that has always remained tantalizingly short of a major leap into the top league of white blues performers. Nevertheless, his live performances are as popular as ever, while his back catalogue has grown substantially over the years.

●ALBUMS: *Once In A Blue Moon* (Chrysalis 1972)★★★, *High Life* (Chrysalis 1973)★★★, *The Rock* (Chrysalis 1975)★★★, *Full House* (Chrysalis 1977)★★★, *Double Trouble* (Chrysalis 1978)★★★, *Falling In Love* (Chrysalis 1979)★★★, *Perfect Fit* (1979)★★★, *Easy Money* (1980)★★★, *Standing On The Edge* (Capitol 1982)★★★, *Rockin' Rollin' Frankie Miller* (Bear Family 1983)★★★, *Hey, Where Ya Goin'* (1984)★★★, *Dancing In The Rain* (Vertigo 1986)★★★.

●COMPILATIONS: *Best Of* (1992)★★★, *BBC Radio One Live In Concert* rec. 1977/78/79 (Windsong 1994)★★★.

MILLER, STEVE

b. 5 October 1943, Milwaukee, Wisconsin, USA. The young Miller was set on his musical path by having Les Paul as a family friend, and a father who openly encouraged music in the home. His first band, the Marksmen, was with schoolfriend Boz Scaggs; also with Scaggs, he formed the college band, the Ardells, and at university they became the Fabulous Night Trains. He moved to Chicago in 1964, and became involved in the local blues scene with Barry Goldberg, resulting in the Goldberg Miller Blues Band. Miller eventually moved to San Francisco in 1966, after hearing about the growing hippie music scene, and formed the Miller Blues Band. Within a year he had built a considerable reputation and as the Steve Miller Band, he signed with Capitol Records for a then unprecedented $50,000, following his appearance at the 1967 Monterey Pop Festival. The band at that time included Boz Scaggs, Lonnie Turner, Jim Peterman and Tim Davis, and it was this line-up that was flown to London to record the Glyn Johns-produced *Children Of The Future*. The album was a critical success although sales were moderate, but it was *Sailor* later that same year that became his *pièce de résistance*. The clear production and memorable songs have lasted well and it remains a critics' favourite. Miller's silky-smooth voice and masterful guitar gave the album a touch of class that many of the other San Francisco rock albums lacked. The atmospheric instrumental 'Song For Our Ancestors' and well-crafted love songs like 'Dear Mary' and 'Quicksilver Girl' were just three of the many outstanding tracks. Scaggs and Peterman departed after this album, and Miller added the talented Nicky Hopkins on keyboards for *Brave New World*, which completed a trio of albums recorded in London with Johns. The blistering 'My Dark Hour' featured Paul McCartney (as Paul Ramon) on bass, while the epic 'Cow Cow' showed off Hopkins' sensitive piano.

The excellent *Your Saving Grace* maintained the quality of previous albums and repeated the success. Lonnie Turner and Hopkins left at the end of 1969, and Miller replaced Turner with Bobby Winkleman from local band Frumious Bandersnatch. *Number 5* completed a cycle of excellent albums that hovered around similar chart positions, indicating that while Miller was highly popular, he was not expanding his audience. He decided to change the format for *Rock Love*, by having half of the album live. Unfortunately, he chose to record a live set with arguably his weakest band; both Ros Valory and Jack King left within a year and the album sold poorly. Following a European tour, and in an attempt to reverse the trend of his last album, he released *Recall The Beginning ... A Journey From Eden*, a perplexing album which showed Miller in a melancholic and lethargic mood; once again, Miller's fortunes declined further with poor sales.

After a gap of 18 months, Miller returned with the US chart-topping single 'The Joker', an easily contrived song over a simple riff in which Miller mentioned all references to his various self-titled aliases used in songs over the past years: 'Some people call me the Space Cowboy (*Brave New World*), some call me the Gangster Of Love (*Sailor*), some call me Maurice (*Recall The*

Beginning) . . !' The accompanying album was a similar success, stalling at number 2. His future had never looked brighter, but Miller chose to buy a farm and build a recording studio and he effectively vanished. When he reappeared on record three years later, only his loyal fans rated his commercial chances; however, the stunning *Fly Like An Eagle* became his best-selling album of all time and was a major breakthrough in the UK. This record, with its then state-of-the-art recording, won him many new fans, and finally put him in the major league as one of America's biggest acts. Almost as successful was the sister album *Book Of Dreams* (1977); they both gave him a number of major singles including the simplistic 'Rock 'N' Me' and the uplifting 'Jet Airliner'. Miller had now mastered and targeted his audience, with exactly the kind of songs he knew they wanted. Once again, he disappeared from the scene and a new album was not released for almost four years. The return this time was less spectacular. Although *Circle Of Love* contained one side of typical Miller - short, sharp, punchy melodic rock songs - side two was an over-long and self-indulgent epic, 'Macho City'. He once again corrected the fault by responding only six months later, with another US number 1, the catchy 'Abracadabra'. This gave him his second major hit in the UK, almost reaching the coveted top spot in 1982. In the USA, the album climbed near to the top and Miller was left with another million-plus sale. The momentum was lost over the following years, as a live album and *Italian X-Rays* were comparative failures. *Living In The 20th Century* contained a segment consisting of a tribute to Jimmy Reed, with whom Steve had played as a teenager. He opted out of the commercial market with the excellent *Born 2B Blue* in 1989. Together with his old colleague Ben Sidran, Miller paid homage to jazz and blues standards with some exquisite arrangements from Sidran. Songs like Billie Holiday's 'God Bless The Child' and 'Zip-A-Dee-Doo-Dah', were given lazy treatments with Miller's effortless voice. The record was only a moderate success.

In the autumn of 1990, while Miller bided his time with the luxury of deciding what to do next, over in Britain Levi's jeans had used 'The Joker' for one of their television advertisements. Capitol quickly released it, and astonishingly, Maurice, the space cowboy, the gangster of love, found himself with his first UK number 1. *Wide River* in 1993 was a return to his basic rock formula but it was not one of his better efforts. In 1996 Seal had a major US hit with a version of 'Fly Like An Eagle' and k.d. lang recorded 'The Joker' in 1997. Miller's collaboration with Paul McCartney on *Flaming Pie* was highly publicized. He co-wrote 'Used To Be Bad' and played guitar on what many regard as McCartney's finest post-Beatles work.

●ALBUMS: *Children Of the Future* (Capitol 1968)★★★★, *Sailor* (Capitol 1968)★★★★★, *Brave New World* (Capitol 1969)★★★★, *Your Saving Grace* (Capitol 1969)★★★, *Revolution* soundtrack 3 tracks only (United Artists

1969)★★, *Number 5* (Capitol 1970)★★★, *Rock Love* (Capitol 1971)★★, *Recall The Beginning ... A Journey From Eden* (Capitol 1972)★★★, *The Joker* (Capitol 1973)★★★, *Fly Like An Eagle* (Capitol 1976)★★★★, *Book Of Dreams* (Capitol 1977)★★★★, *Circle Of Love* (Capitol 1981)★★★, *Abracadabra* (Capitol 1982)★★★, *Steve Miller Band - Live!* (Capitol 1983)★★, *Italian X Rays* (Capitol 1984)★★, *Living In The 20th Century* (Capitol 1986)★★, *Born 2B Blue* (Capitol 1988)★★★, *Wide River* (1993)★★.

●COMPILATIONS: *Anthology* (Capitol 1972)★★★★, *Greatest Hits (1974-1978)* (Capitol 1978)★★★★, *A Decade Of American Music: Greatest Hits 1976-1986* (1987)★★★★, *The Best Of 1968-1973* (1990)★★★★, *Box Set* (Capitol 1994)★★★★.

MITCHELL, JONI

b. Roberta Joan Anderson, 7 November 1943, Fort McLeod, Alberta, Canada. After studying art in Calgary, this singer-songwriter moved to Toronto in 1964, where she married Chuck Mitchell in 1965. The two performed together at coffeehouses and folk clubs, playing several Mitchell originals including 'The Circle Game'. The latter was a response to Canadian Neil Young who had recently written 'Sugar Mountain', a paean to lost innocence, which Mitchell herself included in her sets during this period. While in Detroit, the Mitchells met folk singer Tom Rush, who unsuccessfully attempted to persuade Judy Collins to cover Joni's 'Urge For Going'. He later recorded the song himself, along with the title track of his next album, *The Circle Game*. The previously reluctant Collins also brought Mitchell's name to prominence by covering 'Michael From Mountains' and 'Both Sides Now' on her 1967 album *Wildflowers*.

Following her divorce in 1967, Mitchell moved to New York and for a time planned a career in design and clothing, selling Art Nouveau work. Her success on the New York folk circuit paid her bills, however, and she became known as a strong songwriter and engaging live performer, backed only by her acoustic guitar and dulcimer. At this time the astute producer Joe Boyd took her to England, where she played some low-key venues and on her return she appeared at the Gaslight South folk club in Coconut Grove, Florida. Her trip produced several songs, including the comical tribute to 'London Bridge', based on the traditional nursery rhyme. The song included such lines as 'London Bridge is falling up/Save the tea leaves in my cup . . .' Other early material included the plaintive 'Eastern Rain', 'Just Like Me' and 'Brandy Eyes', which displayed Mitchell's love of sharp description and internal rhyme. Mitchell was initially discovered by budding manager Elliot Roberts at New York's Cafe Au Go-Go, and shortly afterwards in Coconut Grove by former Byrds member, David Crosby. She and Crosby became lovers, and he went on to produce her startling debut album *Joni Mitchell* aka *Songs To A Seagull*. Divided into two sections, 'I Came To The City' and 'Out Of The City And Down To The Seaside', the work showed her early folk influence which was equally strong on the 1969 follow-up *Clouds*, which featured several songs joyously proclaiming the possibilities offered by life, as well as its melancholic side. 'Chelsea Morning' presented a feeling of wonder in its almost childlike appreciation of everyday observations. The title of the album was borrowed from a line in 'Both Sides Now', which had since become a massive worldwide hit for Judy Collins. The chorus ('It's love's illusions I recall/I really don't know love at all') became something of a statement of policy from Mitchell, whose analyses of love - real or illusory - dominated her work. With *Clouds*, Mitchell paused for reflection, drawing material from her past ('Tin Angel', 'Both Sides Now', 'Chelsea Morning') and blending them with songs devoted to new-found perplexities. If 'I Don't Know Where I Stand' recreates the tentative expectancy of an embryonic relationship, 'The Gallery' chronicles its decline, with the artist as the injured party. The singer, however, was unsatisfied with the final collection, and later termed it her artistic nadir.

Apart from her skills as a writer, Mitchell was a fine singer and imaginative guitarist with a love of open tuning. Although some critics still chose to see her primarily as a songwriter rather than a vocalist, there were already signs of important development on her third album, *Ladies Of The Canyon*. Its title track, with visions of antique chintz and wampum beads, mirrored the era's innocent naïvety, a feature also prevailing on 'Willy', the gauche portrait of her relationship with singer Graham Nash. Mitchell is nonetheless aware of the period's fragility, and her rendition of 'Woodstock' (which she never visited), a celebration of the hippie dream in the hands of Crosby, Stills, Nash And Young, becomes a eulogy herein. With piano now in evidence, the music sounded less sparse and the lyrics more ambitious. portraying the hippie audience as searchers for some lost Edenic bliss ('We are stardust, we are golden . . . and we've got to get ourselves back to the garden'). With 'For Free' (later covered by the Byrds), Mitchell presented another one of her hobbyhorses - the clash between commercial acceptance and artistic integrity. Within the song, Mitchell contrasts her professional success with the uncomplicated pleasure that a street performer enjoys. The extent of Mitchell's commercial acceptance was demonstrated on the humorous 'Big Yellow Taxi', a sardonic comment on the urban disregard for ecology. The single was a surprise UK number 11 hit and was even more surprisingly covered by Bob Dylan.

Following a sabbatical, Mitchell returned with her most introspective work to date, *Blue*. Less melodic than her previous albums, the arrangements were also more challenging and the material self-analytical to an almost alarming degree. Void of sentimentality, the work also saw her commenting on the American Dream in 'California' ('That was a dream some of us had'). Austere and at times anti-romantic, *Blue* was an essential product of the singer-songwriter era. On *Blue*, the artist moved from a purely folk-based perspective to that of rock, as the piano, rather than guitar, became the natural outlet for her compositions. Stephen Stills (guitar/bass), James Taylor (guitar), 'Sneaky' Pete Kleinow (pedal steel) and Russ Kunkel (drums) embellished material inspired by an extended sojourn travelling in Europe, and if its sense of loss and longing echoed previous works, a new maturity instilled a lasting resonance to the stellar inclusions, 'Carey', 'River' and the desolate title track. Any lingering sense of musical restraint was thrown off with For The Roses, in which elaborate horn and woodwind sections buoyed material on which personal themes mixed with third-person narratives. The dilemmas attached to fame and performing, first aired on 'For Free', reappeared on the title song and 'Blonde In The Bleachers' while 'Woman Of Heart And Mind' charted the reasons for dispute within a relationship in hitherto unexplored depths. 'You Turn Me On, I'm A Radio' gave Mitchell a US Top 30 entry, but a fifteen month gap ensued before Court And Spark appeared. Supported by the subtle, jazz-based LA Express, Mitchell offered a rich, luxuriant collection, marked by an increased sophistication and dazzling use of melody. The sweeping 'Help Me' climbed to number 7 in the USA in 1974, bringing its creator a hitherto unparalleled commercial success. The emergence of Mitchell as a well-rounded rock artist was clearly underlined on Court And Spark with its familiar commentary on the trials and tribulations of stardom ('Free Man In Paris'). The strength of the album lay in the powerful arrangements courtesy of Tom Scott, and guitarist Robben Ford, plus Mitchell's own love of jazz rhythms, most notably on her amusing version of Annie Ross's 'Twisted'. The quality of Mitchell's live performances, which included stadium gigs during 1974, was captured on the live album Miles Of Aisles.

In 1975, Mitchell produced the startling The Hissing Of Summer Lawns, which not only displayed her increasing interest in jazz, but also world music. Her most sophisticated work to date, the album was less concerned with introspection than a more generalized commentary on American mores. In 'Harry's House', the obsessive envy of personal possessions is described against a swirling musical backdrop that captures an almost anomic feeling of derangement. The Burundi drummers feature on 'The Jungle Line' in which African primitivism is juxtaposed alongside the swimming pools of the Hollywood aristocracy. 'Edith And The Kingpin' offers a startling evocation of mutual dependency and the complex nature of such a relationship ('His right hand holds Edith, his left hand holds his right/what does that hand desire that he grips it so tight?'). Finally, there was the exuberance of the opening 'In France They Kiss On Main Street' and a return to the theme of 'For Free' on 'The Boho Dance'. The album deserved the highest acclaim, but was greeted with a mixed reception on its release, which emphasized how difficult it was for Mitchell to break

free from her 'acoustic folk singer' persona. The Hissing Of Summer Lawns confirmed this new-found means of expression. Bereft of an accustomed introspective tenor, its comments on suburban values were surprising, yet were the natural accompaniment to an ever-growing desire to expand stylistic perimeters. However, although Hejira was equally adventurous, it was noticeably less ornate, echoing the stark simplicity of early releases. The fretless bass of Jaco Pastorius wrought an ever-present poignancy to a series of confessional compositions reflecting the aching restlessness encapsulated in 'Song For Sharon', an open letter to a childhood friend. The same sense of ambition marked with Hejira, Mitchell produced another in-depth work which, though less melodic and texturous than its predecessor, was still a major work. The dark humour of 'Coyote', the sharp observation of 'Amelia' and the lovingly cynical portrait of Furry Lewis, 'Furry Sings The Blues', were all memorable. The move into jazz territory continued throughout 1978-79, first with the double album, Don Juan's Reckless Daughter, and culminating in her collaboration with Charlie Mingus. The latter was probably Mitchell's bravest work to date, although its invention was not rewarded with sales and was greeted with suspicion by the jazz community. On Mingus, she adapted several of the master musician's best-known compositions. It was an admirable, but flawed, ambition, as her often-reverential lyrics failed to convey the music's erstwhile sense of spontaneity. 'God Must Be A Boogie Man' and 'The Wolf That Lives In Lindsay', for which Joni wrote words and music, succeeded simply because they were better matched.

A live double album, Shadows And Light featured Pat Metheny and Jaco Pastorius among the guest musicians. Mitchell signed a long-term contract with Geffen Records and the first fruits of this deal were revealed on Wild Things Run Fast in 1982; following this she married bassist Larry Klein, and appeared to wind down her activities. A more accessible work than her recent efforts, Wild Things Run Fast lacked the depth and exploratory commitment of its predecessors. The opening song, 'Chinese Cafe', remains one of her finest compositions, blending nostalgia with shattered hopes, but the remainder of the set was musically ill-focused, relying on unadventurous, largely leaden arrangements. Its lighter moments were well-chosen, however, particularly on the humorous reading of Leiber And Stoller's 'Baby, I Don't Care'. The Thomas Dolby-produced Dog Eat Dog was critically underrated and represented the best of her 80s work. Despite such hi-tech trappings, the shape of the material remained constant with 'Impossible Dreamer' echoing the atmosphere of Court And Spark. Elsewhere, 'Good Friends', an up-tempo duet with Michael McDonald, and 'Lucky Girl', confirmed Mitchell's newfound satisfaction and contentment. In interviews, Mitchell indicated her intention to pursue a career in painting, a comment which some took as evidence of the loss of her musical muse.

Chalk Mark In A Rain Storm continued in a similar vein, while including two notable reworkings of popular tunes, 'Cool Water', which also featured Willie Nelson, and 'Corrina Corrina', herein retitled 'A Bird That Whistles'. Their appearance anticipated the change of perspective contained on *Night Flight Home*, issued in 1991 following a three-year gap. Largely stripped of contemporaneous clutter, this acoustic-based collection invoked the intimacy of *Hejira*, thus allowing full rein to Mitchell's vocal and lyrical flair. Its release coincided with the artist's avowed wish to pursue her painting talents - exhibitions of her 80s canvases were held in London and Edinburgh - and future musical directions remain, as always, open to question. Her remarkable body of work encompasses the changing emotions and concerns of a generation: from idealism to adult responsibilities, while bearing her soul on the traumas of already public relationships. That she does so with insight and melodic flair accounts for a deserved longevity. With *Chalk Mark In A Rainstorm* and *Night Ride Home*, Mitchell reiterated the old themes in a more relaxed style without ever threatening a new direction. The creatively quiet decade that followed did little to detract from her status, though many were pleased to witness her renaissance in the 90s. Rumours abounded that her addiction to cigarettes had caused a serious throat ailment (her voice had become progressively lower and huskier); although this was never confirmed she was told to quit smoking - which she ignored. After contributing a track, 'If I Could', to Seal's 1994 album, she embarked on her first live dates in 12 years on a tour of Canada, before settling in to the studio once more to record *Turbulent Indigo* with production support from ex-husband Larry Klein in Los Angeles. Although it was not a major hit she won a Grammy in 1995 for Best Pop Album. Mitchell is one artist that deserves a detailed biography; while we wait, Bill Ruhlmann's revealing 25,000 word interview for *Goldmine* magazine will have to suffice. Still regarded as one of the finest singer/songwriters of her generation, Mitchell has displayed more artistic depth and consistency than most of her illustrious contemporaries from the 70s.

●ALBUMS: *Songs To A Seagull* (Reprise 1968)★★★, *Clouds* (Reprise 1969)★★★, *Ladies Of The Canyon* (Reprise 1970)★★★★, *Blue* (Reprise 1971)★★★★★, *For The Roses* (Asylum 1972)★★★★, *Court And Spark* (Asylum 1974)★★★★★, *Miles Of Aisles* (Asylum 1974)★★★, *The Hissing Of Summer Lawns* (Asylum 1975)★★★★, *Hejira* (Asylum 1976)★★★★, *Don Juan's Reckless Daughter* (Asylum 1977)★★★, *Mingus* (Asylum 1979)★★★★, *Shadows And Light* (Asylum 1980)★★★★, *Wild Things Run Fast* (Geffen 1982)★★★, *Dog Eat Dog* (Geffen 1985)★★★, *Chalk Mark In A Rainstorm* (Geffen 1988)★★★, *Night Ride Home* (Geffen 1991)★★★, *Turbulent Indigo* (Warners 1994)★★★.

●COMPILATIONS: *Joni Mitchell Hits* (Reprise 1996)★★★, *Joni Mitchell Misses* (Reprise 1996)★★★.

●FURTHER READING: *Joni Mitchell*, Leonore Fleischer.

MONTROSE

After working with Van Morrison, Boz Scaggs and Edgar Winter, guitarist Ronnie Montrose (b. Colorado, USA) formed Montrose in San Francisco in the autumn of 1973. Comprising vocalist Sammy Hagar, bassist Bill Church and drummer Denny Carmassi, they signed to Warner Brothers Records and released their self-titled debut the following year. Produced by Ted Templeman, *Montrose* was an album that set new standards in heavy metal; the combination of Hagar's raucous vocals with the guitarist's abrasive guitar sound was to become a blueprint against which new bands judged themselves for years to come. Including the classic recordings 'Bad Motor Scooter', 'Space Station No. 5' and 'Rock The Nation', the album still ranks as one of the cornerstones of the hard rock genre. Alan Fitzgerald replaced Bill Church on bass before the recording of the follow-up, *Paper Money*. Hagar was fired shortly after the tour to support it was completed. Bob James and Jim Alcivar were drafted in on vocals and keyboards, but they never recaptured the magic of the debut release. Hagar and Ronnie Montrose, the principal protagonists, went on to solo careers, the latter joined by several ex-members of Montrose in Gamma. Carmassie, in addition, re-emerged in the 90s as drummer for the Coverdale/Page project.

●ALBUMS: *Montrose* (Warners 1974)★★★, *Paper Money* (Warners 1974)★★, *Warner Brothers Presents Montrose* (Warners 1975)★★, *Jump On It* (Warners 1976)★★, *Open Fire* (Warners 1978)★★.

MOODY BLUES

The lengthy career of the Moody Blues has come in two distinct phases. The first from 1963-67, when they were a tough R&B-influenced unit, and the second from 1967 to the present, where they are now regarded as rock dinosaurs performing a blend of melodic pop utilizing symphonic themes which has been given many labels, among them pomp-rock, classical-rock and art-rock. The original band was formed in 1964 by Denny Laine (b. Brian Hines, 29 October 1944, Jersey; vocals, harmonica, guitar), Mike Pinder (b. 12 December 1942, Birmingham, England; piano, keyboards), Ray Thomas (b. 29 December 1942, Stourport on Severn, England; flute, vocals, harmonica), Graeme Edge (b. 30 March 1941, Rochester, Staffordshire, England; drums) and Clint Warwick (b. 25 June 1940, Birmingham, England; bass). During their formative months they established a strong London club following, and soon received their big break, as so many others did, performing live on the influential UK television show *Ready Steady Go*. A few months later their Bessie Banks cover, 'Go Now' topped the UK charts, complete with its striking piano introduction and solo. Although the single made the US Top 10, their commercial fortunes were on an immediate decline, although their following releases were impeccable.

Their excellent debut *The Magnificent Moodies* was a mature effort combining traditional white R&B standards with originals. In addition to 'Go Now' they tackled James Brown's 'I'll Go Crazy' and delivered a frenetic version of Sonny Boy Williamson's 'Bye Bye Bird'. Laine and Pinder contributed among others 'Stop' and 'Let Me Go'. Warwick and Laine departed in 1966 to be replaced by Justin Hayward (b. 14 October 1946, Swindon, Wiltshire, England) and John Lodge (b. 20 July 1945, Birmingham, England). So began phase two, which debuted with Hayward's classic, 'Nights In White Satin'. The accompanying *Days Of Future Passed* was an ambitious orchestral project with Peter Knight conducting the London Festival Orchestra and Tony Clark producing. The album was a massive success and started a run that continued through a further five albums, all involving Knight and Clark. The increased use of the mellotron gave an orchestrated feel to much of their work, and while they became phenomenally popular, they also received a great deal of criticism. During this period they founded Threshold Records, their own record label based from their home territory in Cobham, Surrey. In 1973 the group reached the UK Top 10 with a re-entry for 'Nights In White Satin'. (A further reissue made it a hit again in 1979.)

The band parted company in 1974 to allow each member to indulge in spin-off projects. Hayward and Lodge became the Blue Jays, with great success, Thomas released *From Mighty Oaks* and Edge teamed with Adrian Gurvitz for *Kick Off Your Muddy Boots*. The group reunited for *Octave*, which became another huge hit, although shortly after its release Pinder decided to leave the music business; he had been the only band member not to release a solo project. Further discontent ensued when Clark resigned. Patrick Moraz from Yes and Refugee joined the band as Hayward's 'Forever Autumn' hit the charts. This track was taken from the Jeff Wayne epic, *The War Of The Worlds*. Each subsequent release has met with predictable glory both in Europe and America. The Moodies march on with the comforting knowledge that they have the ability to fill concert halls and continue with a back catalogue that will sell until the days of future have passed.

●ALBUMS: *The Magnificent Moodies* (Decca 1965)★★★★, *Days Of Future Past* (Deram 1967)★★★★, *In Search Of The Lost Chord* (Deram 1968)★★★★, *On The Threshold Of A Dream* (Deram 1969)★★★★, *To Our Children's Children's Children* (Threshold 1969)★★★, *A Question Of Balance* (Threshold 1970)★★★, *Every Good Boy Deserves Favour* (Threshold 1971)★★★, *Seventh Sojourn* (Threshold 1972)★★★, *Caught Live + 5* (Decca 1977)★★, *Octave* (Decca 1978)★★, *Long Distance Voyager* (Threshold 1981)★★★★, *The Present* (Threshold 1983)★★★, *The Other Side Of Life* (Polydor 1986)★★★, *Sur La Mer* (Polydor 1988)★★, *Keys Of The Kingdom* (Polydor 1991)★★, *A Night At Red Rocks With The Colorado Symphony Orchestra* (Polydor/Threshold 1993)★★. Solo: Justin Hayward and John Lodge *Blue Jays* (Threshold 1975)★★★. John Lodge *Natural Avenue* (Threshold 1977)★★. Ray Thomas *From Mighty Oaks* (Threshold 1975)★★, *Hope Wishes And Dreams* (Threshold 1976)★★. Mike Pinder *The Promise* (Threshold 1976)★★, *Among The Stars* (One Step 1995)★★. Graeme Edge Band *Kick Off Your Muddy Boots* (Threshold 1975)★★, *Paradise Ballroom* (Threshold 1977)★★. Denny Laine *Aah Laine* (1973)★★, with Paul McCartney *Holly Days* (EMI 1977)★★, *Japanese Tears* (Scratch 1980)★★, *Weep For Love* (President 1985)★★, *Hometown Girls* (President 1985)★★, *Wings On My Feet* (President 1987)★★, *Master Suite* (Thunderbolt 1988)★★, *Lonely Road* (President 1988)★★, *Blue Nights* (President 1993)★★, *The Rock Survivor* (WCP 1994)★★.
●COMPILATIONS: *This Is The Moody Blues* (Threshold 1974)★★★★, *Out Of This World* (K-Tel 1979)★★★, *Voices In The Sky - The Best Of The Moody Blues* (Threshold 1985)★★★, *Greatest Hits* (Threshold 1989)★★★, *Time Traveller* 5-CD set (Polydor 1994)★★★, *The Very Best Of* (Polygram 1996)★★★.
●VIDEOS: *Cover Story* (Stylus 1990), *Star Portrait* (Gemini Vision 1991), *Legend Of A Band* (Channel 5 1991), *Live At Red Rocks* (1993).

MARTIN, MOON

b. John Martin, 1950, Oklahoma, USA. Emerging in 1979 with a style somewhere between new wave and nouveau 50s rock 'n' roll, Martin was nicknamed 'Moon' because he frequently employed lunar imagery in his songs. He began playing lead guitar in a straight C&W band Cec Wilson And The Panhandlers, then joined a Beatles-imitation group followed by a rockabilly unit called the Disciples. After moving to Los Angeles in the late 60s, he undertook session work for Del Shannon and Jackie DeShannon. In the meantime, the Disciples changed their name to Southwind and recorded three albums, all in a country rock vein. Martin continued his extra-curricular work, contributing to Linda Ronstadt's *Silk Purse*, Jesse Ed Davis's *Ululu* and some unreleased tracks by Gram Parsons. In 1974 Martin teamed-up with producer/arranger Jack Nitzsche, who took one of his songs, 'Cadillac Walk' to Mink DeVille. The song was a minor hit and DeVille recorded Martin's 'Rolene' on their second album. Martin next made a surprise appearance on Michelle Phillips' *Victim Of Romance*, for which he wrote three songs including the title track. After contributing two songs to an album by Lisa Burns, Martin worked on his debut solo album. *Shots From A Cold Nightmare*, an unusual sythesis of 50s/80s musical styles, was widely praised. After reaching the US Top 30 with 'Rolene', Martin released his second album, *Escape From Domination*, which had a stronger band feel with the inclusion of backing ensemble, the Ravens. Martin's homogeneous style lost some of its charm and bite by the third album and his subsequent work proved anti-climactic. He ended his association with Capitol Records and returned to songwriting.
●ALBUMS: with Southwind *Southwind* (Harvest

1969)★★★, *Ready To Ride* (Capitol 1971)★★★, *What A Place To Land* (Capitol 1972)★★, *Shots From A Cold Nightmare* (Capitol 1978)★★, *Escape From Domination* (1979)★★, *Street Fever* (1980)★★, *Mystery Ticket* (1982)★★.

MOORE, GT, AND THE REGGAE GUITARS

A popular act in London's pub and club circuit during the early 70s, this quintet consisted of former Heron member Gerald 'GT' Moore (guitar/vocals), Martin Hayward (guitar), Tim Jones (keyboards), Tom Whyte (bass) and Malcolm Mortimer (drums). Their melodic blend of rock and reggae was partially captured on the unit's self-titled debut, released in 1974, but like many contemporaries, GT Moore were unable to commit a live excitement to record. Their musicanship, however, was never in question and Whyte, Hayward and Moore made telling contributions to contemporaneous releases by Shusha. Tony Redunzo replaced Mortimer for *Reggae Blue*, but by this point the group was losing impetus and it was dissolved soon afterwards.
●ALBUMS: *GT Moore And The Reggae Guitars* (Charisma 1974)★★, *Reggae Blue* (Charisma 1975)★★.

MOORE, MELBA

Based in New York City, Melba Moore first garnered attention in the Broadway production of *Hair*. Although she has continued her thespian inclinations, winning an award for her performance in the musical *Purlie*, Moore has also forged a successful singing career. 'This Is It', a minor US hit, reached the UK Top 10 in 1976, and although her pop chart placings have since been inconsistent, Melba remained a fixture on the R&B lists over the following decade.
●ALBUMS: *Look What You're Doing To The Man* (Mercury 1971)★★, *Peach Melba* (Buddah 1975)★★★, *This Is It* (Buddah 1976)★★, *Melba* (Buddah 1976)★★, *A Portrait Of Melba* (Buddah 1978)★★, *Melba* (Epic 1978)★★, *Burn* (Epic 1979)★★, *Dancin' With Melba Moore* (Buddah 1979)★★, *What A Woman Needs* (Capitol 1981)★★, *The Other Side Of The Rainbow* (Capitol 1982)★★, *Never Say Never* (Capitol 1983)★★, *Read My Lips* (Capitol 1985)★★, *A Lot Of Love* (Capitol 1987)★★, *I'm In Love* (Capitol 1988)★★.

MORRISON, VAN

b. George Ivan Morrison, 31 August 1945, Belfast, Northern Ireland. The son of a noted collector of jazz and blues records, Morrison quickly developed an interest in music. At the age of 12 he joined Deannie Sands And The Javelins, an aspiring skiffle group, but within two years was an integral part of the Monarchs, a showband which, by 1963, was embracing R&B and soul. Tours of Scotland and England were undertaken before the group travelled to Germany where they completed a lone single for CBS, 'Bozoo Hully Gully'/'Twingy Baby', before disbanding. The experi-

ence Morrison garnered - he took up vocals, saxophone and harmonica - proved invaluable upon his return to Belfast and a subsequent merger with members of local attraction the Gamblers in a new act, Them. This exciting group scored two notable hit singles with 'Baby Please Don't Go' and 'Here Comes The Night' (both 1965), while the former's b-side 'Gloria', a snarling Morrison original, is revered as a classic of the garage-band genre. The group's progress was hampered by instability and Morrison's reluctance to court the pop marketplace - a feature continued throughout his career - but their albums showed the early blossoming of an original stylist. His reading of Bob Dylan's 'It's All Over Now, Baby Blue' (*Them Again*) is rightly regarded as one of the finest interpretations in a much-covered catalogue. Them was dissolved in 1966 following an arduous US tour, but within months the singer had returned to New York at the prompting of producer Bert Berns. Their partnership resulted in 'Brown-Eyed Girl', an ebullient celebration of love in a style redolent of classic black harmony groups. The single deservedly reached the US Top 10, in turn inspiring the hurriedly issued *Blowin' Your Mind*. Morrison later claimed the set was culled from sessions for projected singles and, although inconsistent, contained the cathartic 'T.B. Sheets', on which Morrison first introduced the stream-of-consciousness imagery recurring in later work. Berns' premature death brought this period to a sudden end, and for the ensuing 12 months Morrison punctuated live performances by preparing his next release.
Astral Weeks showed the benefit of such seclusion, as here an ambition to create without pop's constraints was fully realized. Drawing support from a stellar backing group which included Miles Davis' bassist Richard Davis and Modern Jazz Quartet drummer Connie Kay, Morrison created an ever-shifting musical tapestry, inspired by blues, soul and gospel, yet without ever imitating their sound. His vocal performance was both assured and highly emotional and the resultant collection is justifiably lauded as one of rock's landmark releases. On *Moondance* the artist returned to a more conventional sense of discipline, on which tighter, punchier, jazzier arrangements formed the platform for the singer's still-soaring inflections. 'Caravan', 'Into The Mystic' and the title track itself (reminiscent of Kenny Burrell's 'Midnight Blue'), became a staple part of Van's subsequent career, offering an optimistic spirit prevalent in the artist's immediate recordings. Both *Van Morrison, His Band And The Street Choir* and *Tupelo Honey* suggested a newfound peace of mind, as a now-married Morrison celebrated the idyll of his sylvan surroundings. 'Domino' and 'Wild Night' were the album's respective US hit singles, both of which invoked the punch of classic Stax-era soul, and if the former set offered a greater debt to R&B, its counterpart showed an infatuation with country styles. Both preoccupations were maintained on *St. Dominic's Preview*, one of Morrison's most enigmatic releases. Having opened the

set with 'Jackie Wilson Said', an effervescent tribute to the great soul singer later covered by Dexys Midnight Runners. Morrison wove a path through rock and late-night jazz culminating in two lengthy compositions, both laced with chiming acoustic 12-string guitar, 'Listen To The Lion' and 'Almost Independence Day'. Here he resumed vocal improvisation and by alternately whispering, pleading, shouting and extolling, created two intoxicating and hypnotic performances. Morrison's next release, *Hard Nose The Highway*, proved disappointing as the artist enhanced an ever-widening palette with contributions by the Oakland Symphony Chamber Chorus and such disparate inclusions as 'Green', culled from the educational children's show, *Sesame Street*, and the folk standard 'Wild Mountain Thyme', herein retitled 'Purple Heather'. Despite the presence of 'Wild Love' and 'The Great Deception', the album is generally regarded as inconsistent. However, Morrison reclaimed his iconoclastic position with the enthralling *It's Too Late To Stop Now*, an in-concert selection on which he was backed by the Caledonia Soul Orchestra. Morrison not only re-stated his own impressive catalogue, but acknowledged his mentors with a series of tight and outstanding recreations, notably of Sonny Boy 'Rice Miller' Williamson ('Take Your Hand Out Of Your Pocket'), Ray Charles ('I Believe To My Soul') and Bobby Bland ('Ain't Nothing You Can Do'). The result was a seamless tribute to R&B and one of rock's definitive live albums. It was succeeded by the pastoral *Veedon Fleece*, a set inspired by a sabbatical in Ireland during 1973. Its sense of spirituality - a keynote of Morrison's later work - is best captured on 'You Don't Pull No Punches But You Don't Push The River', but 'The Streets Of Arklow' and 'County Fair' are equally evocative. The judicious use of uillean pipes and woodwind enhanced the rural atmosphere of a collection which, although received with mixed reviews, is, in retrospect, a linchpin in the artist's subsequent development. A three-year hiatus ended with the release of *A Period Of Transition*, a largely undistinguished set on which the singer collaborated actively with Dr. John. *Wavelength*, which featured former Them organist Peter Bardens, was welcomed as a marked improvement and if lacking the triumphs of earlier work, contained none of its pitfalls and instead offered a mature musical consistency. Similar qualities abounded on *Into The Music* which included the noticeably buoyant 'Bright Side Of The Road', Van's first solo, albeit minor, UK chart entry. It also featured 'And The Healing Has Begun', wherein Morrison celebrated his past in order to address his future, and the shamelessly nostalgic 'It's All In The Game', a cover version of Tommy Edward's 1957 hit single. Although a general penchant for punchy soul suggested part of a continuing affinity, it instead marked the end of a stylistic era. On *Common One* Morrison resumed his introspective path and, on the expansive 'Somewhere In England', referred to the works of Wordsworth, Coleridge and T.S. Eliot in a piece

whose gruff, improvisatory nature polarized critics proclaiming it either mesmerizing or self-indulgent. A greater sense of discipline on *Beautiful Vision* resulted in another much-lauded classic. Although noted for 'Cleaning Windows', a joyous celebration of the singer's formative Belfast years, the album contained several rich, meditative compositions, notably 'Dweller On The Threshold' and 'Across The Bridge Where Angels Dwell'. *Inarticulate Speech Of The Heart* and *A Sense Of Wonder* continued in a similar vein, the former boasting the compulsive 'Rave On John Donne', wherein Morrison again placed his work on a strictly literary pantheon, while the latter opened with the equally evocative 'Tore Down A La Rimbaud'. The title track of the latter set the style for many beautifully wandering and spiritually uplifting songs of the next fertile period. *Live At The Grand Opera House, Belfast* was an insubstantial resumé, failing to capture the sense of occasion demonstrably apparent in person, but Morrison confirmed his artistic rebirth with *No Guru, No Method, No Teacher*. Here he openly acknowledged his musical past - the set included the punningly titled 'Here Comes The Knight' - as well as offering a searing riposte to those perceived as imitators on 'A Town Called Paradise'. 'Tir Na Nog' and 'One Irish Rover' continued his long-running affair with Celtic themes, a feature equally relevant on *Poetic Champions Compose*. The wedding of love and religion, another integral part of the artist's 80s work, was enhanced by the sumptuous 'Sometimes I Feel Like A Motherless Child', on which the singer's contemplative delivery was truly inspirational. Morrison, many years into his career, was now producing an astonishingly high standard of work. His albums during this period were events, not mere releases.

Irish Heartbeat, a festive collaboration with traditional act the Chieftains, offered a joyous but less intensive perspective. Although the title song and 'Celtic Ray' were exhumed from Morrison's own catalogue, its highlights included moving renditions of 'She Moved Through The Fair' and 'Carrickfergus'. By this time (1988) Morrison was resettled in London and had invited R&B vocalist/organist Georgie Fame to join his touring revue. *Avalon Sunset* enhanced the singer's commercial ascendancy when 'Whenever God Shines His Light On Me', a duet with Cliff Richard, became a UK Top 20 single, Morrison's first since Them's halcyon days. The album had once again a strong spiritual feel combined with childhood memories. Morrison, however, was also able to compose and deliver quite immaculate love songs, including the stunning 'Have I Told You Lately That I Love You'. *Enlightenment* thus engendered considerable interest although Morrison, as oblivious to pop's trappings as always, simply maintained his peerless progress. The mixture was as before, from the pulsating opening track, 'Real Real Gone', itself once considered for *Common One*, through gospel and the biographical, where 'Days Before Rock 'N' Roll' recalls the singer's discovery, by radio, of Ray Charles and

Little Richard. 1991 witnessed another unlikely collaboration when Morrison recorded several songs with Tom Jones, one of which, 'Carrying A Torch', was remade for *Hymns To The Silence*. This expansive double set confirmed the artist's prolific nature, yet reviews lauding its sense of grandeur also queried its self-obsession. *Too Long In Exile*, visited his R&B roots and includes a reworked 'Gloria', featuring a duet with John Lee Hooker. In February 1994 he was honoured at the Brit Awards for his outstanding contribution to music. *Days Like This* was highly accessible, easy on the ear and probably the most 'contented' album he has made since *Tupelo Honey* 24 years previously. That year a tribute album *No Prima Donna* was issued by Morrison's Exile productions, featuring contributions from diverse names including Shana Morrison (his daughter), Lisa Stansfield, Elvis Costello and the Phil Coulter Orchestra; it was a grave disappoinment for Morrison's fans. Van Morrison With Georgie Fame And Friends *How Long Has This Been Going On* in 1995 was a comfortable jazz album revisiting the past. He continued in this vein with Fame, Ben Sidran and one of his idols, Mose Allison, with a tribute album to the latter in 1996. His 1997 offering was *The Healing Game*, more original songs using the same glorious chord changes which the converted loved, but is unlikely to break any new ground. Morrison, whose disdain for the press is legendary, will doubtlessly remain unmoved, yet the paradox of a man capable of sumptuous music and a barking temper is indeed intriguing. It is a tribute that such aberrations can be set aside in order to enjoy his enthralling catalogue. Taken as a whole, this body of work is one the most necessary, complete and important collections in rock music, and it is still growing. Morrison was awarded the OBE for his services to music in 1996.

●ALBUMS: *Blowin' Your Mind* (Bang 1967)★★, *Astral Weeks* (Warners 1968)★★★★★, *Moondance* (Warners 1970)★★★★, *Van Morrison, His Band And The Street Choir* (Warners 1970)★★, *Tupelo Honey* (Warners 1971)★★★, *St. Dominic's Preview* (Warners 1972)★★★★, *Hard Nose The Highway* (Warners 1973)★★, *It's Too Late To Stop Now* (Warners 1974)★★★★, *Veedon Fleece* (Warners 1974)★★★★, *A Period Of Transition* (Warners 1977)★★★, *Wavelength* (Warners 1978)★★★, *Into The Music* (Vertigo 1979)★★★, *Common One* (Mercury 1980)★★, *Beautiful Vision* (Mercury 1982)★★★, *Inarticulate Speech Of The Heart* (Mercury 1983)★★, *Live At The Grand Opera House, Belfast* (Mercury 1984)★★, *A Sense Of Wonder* (Mercury 1984)★★★, *No Guru, No Method, No Teacher* (Mercury 1986)★★★★, *Poetic Champions Compose* (Mercury 1987)★★★★, with the Chieftains *Irish Heartbeat* (Mercury 1988)★★★, *Avalon Sunset* (Mercury 1989)★★★★, *Enlightenment* (Mercury 1990)★★★, *Hymns To The Silence* (Polydor 1991)★★★, *Too Long In Exile* (Polydor 1993)★★★, *A Night In San Francisco* (Polydor 1994)★★, *Days Like This* (Polydor 1995)★★★, with Georgie Fame *How Long Has This Been*

Going On (Verve 1995)★★★, with Fame, Mose Allison, Ben Sidran *Tell Me Something: The Songs Of Mose Allison* (Verve 1996)★★, *The Healing Game* (Polydor 1997)★★★.
●COMPILATIONS: *The Best Of Van Morrison* (Bang 1971)★★, *T.B. Sheets* (Bang 1973)★★, *This Is Where I Came In* (Bang 1977)★★, *The Best Of Van Morrison* (Polydor 1990)★★★★★, *Bang Masters* (Legacy 1991)★★★, *The Best Of Vol. 2* (Polydor 1992)★★★★, *New York Sessions '67* (Burning Airlines 1997)★★.
●VIDEOS: *The Concert* (Channel 5 1990).
●FURTHER READING: *Van Morrison: Into The Music*, Ritchie Yorke. *Van Morrison: The Great Deception*, Johnny Rogan. *Van Morrison: The Mystic's Music*, Howard A.DeWitt. *Van Morrison: Too Late To Stop Now*, Steve Turner. *Van Morrison: Inarticulate Speech Of The Heart*, John Collis.

MOST, MICKIE

b. Michael Peter Hayes, June 1938, Aldershot, Hampshire, England. In the late 50s Most toured and recorded for Decca as the Most Brothers with Alex Wharton who later produced the Moody Blues' hit 'Go Now'. From 1959-63 he worked in South Africa, producing his own hit versions of songs such as Chuck Berry's 'Johnny B. Goode' and Ray Peterson's 'Corrina Corrina'. He returned to Britain aiming to develop a career in production and after scoring a minor hit with 'Mister Porter', he became producer of the Newcastle R&B group the Animals. Beginning with 'Baby Let Me Take You Home' in 1964, Most supervised seven hit singles by the group and was now in demand as a producer. Much of his skill at this time lay in his choice of songs for artists such as the Nashville Teens and Herman's Hermits, for whom he found 'Silhouettes', 'I'm Into Something Good' and 'Wonderful World'. After his earliest UK successes Most was given a five-year retainer production deal by CBS in America, under which he produced records by Lulu, Terry Reid, Jeff Beck and Donovan, for whom he created a new electric sound on 'Sunshine Superman' (1966). He had later successes with artists such as Mary Hopkin (the 1970 Eurovision Song Contest entry, 'Knock Knock Who's There') and Julie Felix ('El Condor Pasa') but after 1969 he concentrated on running the RAK label. For over a decade, RAK singles were regularly to be found in the UK Top 10. The roster included Hot Chocolate, Alexis Korner's CCS, Smokie, Chris Spedding, Kim Wilde, New World, Suzi Quatro and Mud. The last three acts were produced by Nicky Chinn and Mike Chapman for RAK. During the 70s Most was a member of the panel on the UK television talent show *New Faces* and with the arrival of punk, he presented *Revolver*, a short-lived show devoted to the new music. However, he was out of sympathy with much of punk and the subsequent New Romantic trend and after the RAK back catalogue was sold to EMI in 1983, Most was less active. Among his few later productions was 'Me And My Foolish Heart' an early record by Johnny Hates Jazz which included his son Calvin. After taking a brief sabbatical, Most returned in 1988 with a revived RAK label, producing Perfect Stranger which featured ex-Uriah Heep singer Peter Goalby. In 1995 Most appeared once more in the *Sunday Times* 'Britain's Richest 500', this time announcing a car collection worth over £1m and a new house costing £4m with claims that it is the largest private house in Britain.

MOTORS

The Motors were based around the partnership of Nick Garvey (b. 26 April 1951, Stoke-on-Trent, Staffordshire, England) and Andy McMaster (b. 27 July 1947, Glasgow, Scotland) who first met in the pub rock band Ducks Deluxe. McMaster had a long career in pop music, having played in several bands in the 60s including the Sabres, which also featured Frankie Miller. McMaster released a solo single, 'Can't Get Drunk Without You', on President, and joined Ducks Deluxe in November 1974. Garvey was educated at Kings College in Cambridge and was an accomplished pianist, oboeist and trumpeter. Before he joined Ducks Deluxe in December 1972 he had acted as a road manager for the Flamin' Groovies. The pair left the Ducks early in 1975, just a few months before the unit disbanded. Garvey joined a group called the Snakes (along with future Wire vocalist Rob Gotobed) and they released one single. McMaster, meanwhile, went to work for a music publisher. Garvey's friend and manager Richard Ogden suggested that Garvey form his own band in order to record the songs he had written. This led to him contacting McMaster and in January 1977 they recorded demos together. The following month they recruited Ricky Wernham (aka Ricky Slaughter) from the Snakes on drums - he is the cousin of Knox from the Vibrators. Guitarist Rob Hendry was quickly replaced by Bram Tchaikovsky and the Motors were up and running. They made their live debut at the Marquee Club, London, in March 1977 and signed to Virgin in May.

A tour with the Kursaal Flyers and the Heavy Metal Kids led to the release of their debut single, 'Dancing The Night Away', and first album, produced by Mutt Lange. However, it was their second single, 'Airport', which became a huge hit in the UK. It is widely used to this day as a stock soundtrack when television programmes show film clips of aeroplanes taking off or landing. Despite this success, the group were already burning out. After performing at Reading in August the Motors decided to concentrate on writing new material. Wernham took the opportunity to leave, while Tchaikovsky formed his own band with the intention of returning to the Motors, though he never did. Garvey and McMaster eventually re-emerged with some new material for *Tenement Steps*. It was recorded with the assistance of former Man bassist Martin Ace, and drummer Terry Williams (ex-Man and Rockpile; future Dire Straits). After *Tenement Steps* the Motors seized up,

but both Garvey and McMaster have since released solo singles.
● ALBUMS: *The Motors I* (Virgin 1977)★★★, *Approved By The Motors* (Virgin 1978)★★★★, *Tenement Steps* (Virgin 1980)★★★.
● COMPILATIONS: *Greatest Hits* (Virgin 1981)★★★.

MOTT THE HOOPLE

Having played in a number of different rock groups in Hereford, England, during the late 60s, the founding members of this ensemble comprised: Overend Watts (b. Peter Watts, 13 May 1947, Birmingham, England; vocals/bass), Mick Ralphs (b. 31 March 1944, Hereford, England; vocals/guitar), Verden Allen (b. 26 May 1944, Hereford, England; organ) and Dale Griffin (b. 24 October 1948, Ross-on-Wye, England; vocals/drums). After dispensing with their lead singer Stan Tippens, they were on the point of dissolving when Ralphs sent a demo tape to Island Records producer Guy Stevens. He responded enthusiastically, and after placing an advertisement in *Melody Maker* auditioned a promising singer named Ian Hunter (b. 3 June 1946, Shrewsbury, England; vocals/keyboards/guitar). In June 1969 Stevens christened the group Mott The Hoople, after the novel by Willard Manus. Their self-titled debut album revealed a very strong Bob Dylan influence, most notably in Hunter's nasal vocal inflexions and visual image. With his corkscrew hair and permanent shades Hunter bore a strong resemblance to vintage 1966 Dylan and retained that style for his entire career. Their first album, with its M.C. Escher cover illustration, included pleasing interpretations of the Kinks' 'You Really Got Me' and Sonny Bono's 'Laugh At Me', and convinced many that Mott would become a major band. Their next three albums trod water, however, and it was only their popularity and power as a live act that kept them together. Despite teaming up with backing vocalist Steve Marriott on the George 'Shadow' Morton-produced 'Midnight Lady', a breakthrough hit remained elusive. On 26 March 1972, following the departure of Allen, they quit in disillusionment. Fairy godfather David Bowie convinced them to carry on, offered his assistance as producer, placed them under the wing of his manager, Tony De Fries, and even presented them with a stylish UK hit, 'All The Young Dudes'. The catchy 'Honaloochie Boogie' maintained the momentum but there was still one minor setback when Ralphs quit to form Bad Company. With new members Morgan Fisher and Ariel Bender (Luther Grosvenor) Mott enjoyed a run of further UK hits including 'All The Way From Memphis' and 'Roll Away The Stone'. During their final phase, Bowie's sideman Mick Ronson joined the group in place of Grosvenor (who had departed to join Widowmaker). Preparations for a European tour in late 1974 were disrupted when Hunter was hospitalized suffering from physical exhaustion, culminating in the cancellation of the entire tour. When rumours circulated that Hunter had signed a deal instigating a solo career, with Ronson working alongside him, the upheaval led to an irrevocable rift within the group resulting in the stormy demise of Mott The Hoople. With the official departure of Hunter and Ronson, the remaining members, Watts, Griffin and Fisher, determined to carry on, working simply as Mott.

●ALBUMS: *Mott The Hoople* (Island 1969)★★★, *Mad Shadows* (Island 1970)★★★, *Wild Life* (Island 1971)★★, *Brain Capers* (Island 1971)★★★, *All The Young Dudes* (Columbia 1972)★★★, *Mott* (Columbia 1973)★★★★, *The Hoople* (Columbia 1974)★★★★, *Live* (Columbia 1974)★★★, *Original Mixed Up Kids: The BBC Recordings* (Windsong 1996)★★★.

●COMPILATIONS: *Rock And Roll Queen* (Island 1972)★★, *Greatest Hits* (Columbia 1975)★★★★, *Shades Of Ian Hunter - The Ballad Of Ian Hunter And Mott The Hoople* (Columbia 1979)★★★★, *Two Miles From Heaven* (Island 1981)★★★, *All The Way From Memphis* (Hallmark 1981)★★★, *Greatest Hits* (Columbia 1981)★★★★, *Backsliding Fearlessly* (Rhino 1994)★★★.

●FURTHER READING: *The Diary Of A Rock 'N' Roll Star*, Ian Hunter.

MOUNTAIN

Mountain were one of the first generation heavy metal bands, formed by ex-Vagrants guitarist Leslie West (b. Leslie Weinstein, 22 October 1945, Queens, New York, USA) and bassist Felix Pappalardi (b. 1939, Bronx, New York, USA, d. 17 April 1983) in New York in 1968. Augmented by drummer Corky Laing and Steve Knight on keyboards they played the Woodstock festival in 1970, releasing *Mountain Climbing* shortly afterwards. Featuring dense guitar lines from West and the delicate melodies of Pappalardi, they quickly established their own sound, although Cream influences were detectable in places. The album was an unqualified success, peaking at number 17 in the *Billboard* album chart in November 1970. Their next two albums built on this foundation, as the band refined their style into an amalgam of heavy riffs, blues-based rock and extended guitar and keyboard solos. *Nantucket Sleighride* (the title track of which was used as the theme tune to television programme *World In Action*) and *Flowers Of Evil* made the *Billboard* charts at numbers 16 and 35, respectively. A live album followed, which included interminably long solos and was poorly received. The group temporarily disbanded to follow separate projects. Pappalardi returned to producing, while West and Laing teamed up with Cream's Jack Bruce to record as West, Bruce And Laing. In 1974, Mountain rose again with Alan Schwartzberg and Bob Mann replacing Laing and Knight to record *Twin Peaks*, live in Japan. This line-up was short-lived as Laing rejoined for the recording of the disappointing studio album, *Avalanche*. The band collapsed once more and West concentrated on his solo career again. Pappalardi was shot and killed by his wife in 1983. Two years later, West and Laing resurrected the band with Mark Clarke (former Rainbow and Uriah

Heep bassist) and released *Go For Your Life*. They toured with Deep Purple throughout Europe in 1985, but split up again soon afterwards.

●ALBUMS: *Mountain Climbing* (Bell 1970)★★★, *Nantucket Sleighride* (Island 1971)★★★, *Flowers Of Evil* (Island 1971)★★★, *The Road Goes On Forever-Mountain Live* (Island 1972)★★, *Avalanche* (Epic 1974)★★★, *Twin Peaks* (Columbia 1974)★★, *Go For Your Life* (Scotti Brothers 1985)★★.

●COMPILATIONS: *The Best Of* (Island 1973)★★★, *Over The Top* (Legacy 1995)★★, *Blood Of The Sun 1969-75* (Raven 1996)★★★.

MOUSKOURI, NANA

b. 13 October 1934, Athens, Greece. This bespectacled vocalist was steeped in the classics and jazz but was sufficiently broadminded to embrace a native style of pop after a stint on Radio Athens in 1958, and an artistic (and marital) liaison with orchestra leader Manos Hadjidakis facilitated a debut single, 'Les Enfants Du Piree', which was aimed at foreign consumers. Well-received performances at several international song festivals were added incentives for her team to relocate to Germany, where 'Weiss Rosen Aus Athen' (derived from a Greek folk tune), a number from Wadjidakis' soundtrack to the 1961 film *Traumland Der Sehnsucht*, sold a million copies. Now one of her country's foremost musical ambassadors, Mouskouri undertook a US college tour which was followed by further record success, particularly in France with such songs as 'L'Enfant Au Tambour', 'Parapluies De Cherbourg' (a duet with Michel Legrand) and a 1967 arrangement of the evergreen 'Guantanamera'. From the late 60s in Britain, she scored almost exclusively with albums with *Over And Over* lingering longest on the lists. Sales were boosted by regular BBC television series on which her backing combo, the Athenians, were granted instrumental spots. A collection of Mouskouri favourites from a BBC season in the early 70s spent many weeks in the Top 30 but, other than a postscript Top 10 single ('Only Love') in 1986, her UK chart career climaxed with 1976's *Passport*. By then, however, she had mounted a plateau of showbusiness high enough to survive comfortably without more hits. Recently she has combined her music career with the post of Ambassador and world representative of the entertainment business at UNICEF, and the Greek deputy to the European parliament. Recording regularly in five languages (French, English, German, Spanish and Greek), her new English album *Return To Love* was released in 1997.

●ALBUMS: *Over And Over* (Fontana 1969)★★★, *The Exquisite Nana Mouskouri* (Fontana 1970)★★★, *Recital '70* (Fontana 1970)★★★, *Turn On The Sun* (Fontana 1971)★★★, *British Concert* (Fontana 1972)★★★, *Songs From Her TV Series* (Fontana 1973)★★★, *Spotlight On Nana Mouskouri* (Fontana 1974)★★★, *Songs Of The British Isles* (Philips 1976)★★★, *Passport* (Philips 1976)★★★, *Roses And Sunshine* (Philips 1979)★★★,

Come With Me (RCA 1981)★★★, Ballades (Philips 1983)★★★, Nana i (Mercury 1984)★★★, Farben (Fontana 1984)★★★, Athens (Virgin 1984)★★★, Nana Mouskouri (Philips 1984)★★★, Why Worry? (Philips 1986)★★★, Alone (Philips 1986)★★★, Live At The Herodes Hatticus Theatre (Philips 1986)★★★, Nana ii (Philips 1987)★★★, Love Me Tender (Philips 1987)★★★, Je Chante Avec Toi Liberte (Philips 1988)★★★, The Magic Of Nana Mouskouri (Philips 1988)★★★, The Classical Nana (Philips 1990)★★★, Gospel (Philips 1990)★★★, Oh Happy Day (Philips 1990)★★★, Return To Love (Mercury 1997)★★★.

MR. BLOE

'Groovin' With Mr. Bloe', an instrumental dominated by harmonica, was put together by pianist Zack Laurence and issued on DJM Records. It was prevented from topping the UK chart in the summer of 1970 by Mungo Jerry's 'In The Summertime'. The Mr. Bloe project was abandoned after efforts including 'Anyway You Want It', 'One More Time' fell on deaf ears, despite contributions of compositions by Elton John and other James associates. The influence of the hit single was felt, nevertheless, in 1977 on the overall sound of 'A New Career In A New Town' on David Bowie's Low.
●ALBUMS: Groovin' With Mr Bloe (DJM 1973)★★★.

MUD

Originally formed in 1966, this lightweight UK pop outfit comprised Les Gray (b. 9 April 1946, Carshalton, Surrey, England; vocals), Dave Mount (b. 3 March 1947, Carshalton, Surrey, England; drums/vocals), Ray Stiles (b. 20 November 1946, Carshalton, Surrey, England; bass guitar/vocals) and Rob Davis (b. 1 October 1947, Carshalton, Surrey; lead guitar/vocals). Their debut, 'Flower Power', was unsuccessful but they continued touring for several years. The group's easy-going pop style made them natural contenders for appearances on The Basil Brush Show, but still the hits were not forthcoming. Eventually, in early 1973, they succeeded in the UK with 'Crazy' and 'Hypnosis'. Their uncomplicated blend of pop and rockabilly brought them an impressive run of 12 more Top 20 hits during the next three years, including three UK number 1 hits: 'Tiger Feet', 'Lonely This Christmas' and 'Oh Boy'. The group continued in cabaret, but their membership atropied after the hits had ceased. Gray attempted a solo career with little success, while Stiles turned up in 1988 as a latter-day member of the Hollies at the time of their belatedly chart-topping 'He Ain't Heavy He's My Brother'.
●ALBUMS: Mud Rock (RAK 1974)★★★, Mud Rock Vol. 2 (RAK 1975)★★, Use Your Imagination (Private Stock 1975)★★, It's Better Than Working (Private Stock 1976)★★, Mudpack (Private Stock 1978)★★, Rock On (RCA 1979)★★, As You Like It (RCA 1980)★, Mud (Runaway 1983)★.
●COMPILATIONS: Mud's Greatest Hits (RAK 1975)★★★,

Let's Have A Party (EMI 1990)★★, L-L-Lucy (Spectrum 1995)★★, The Gold Collection (EMI 1996)★★.

MULDAUR, MARIA

b. Maria Grazia Rosa Domenica d'Amato, 12 September 1943, Greenwich Village, New York, USA. Her name was changed to Muldaur when she married Geoff Muldaur, with whom she performed in the Jim Kweskin Jug Band. Although her mother was fond of classical music, Muldaur grew up liking blues and big band sounds. The 60s scene in Greenwich Village thrived musically, and she first joined the Even Dozen Jug Band, playing alongside John Sebastian, Stefan Grossman, Joshua Rifkin and Steve Katz. After leaving them she teamed up with the Jim Kweskin Jug Band. After two albums together, they split up, and Geoff and Maria were divorced in 1972. Maria Muldaur, her first solo effort, went platinum in the USA. It contained the classic single 'Midnight At The Oasis', which featured an excellent guitar solo by Amos Garrett. The album reached number 3 in the US charts in 1974, with the single making the US Top 10. A follow-up, 'I'm A Woman', made the Top 20 in the US charts in 1975. Muldaur toured the USA in 1975, and shortly after played in Europe for the first time. The US Top 30 album, Waitress In A Donut Shop, featured the songs of contemporary writers such as Kate And Anna McGarrigle, and with the assistance of musicians including Amos Garrett and J.J.Cale, she created a stronger jazz influence on the album. With sales of her records in decline, she was dropped by WEA, and since then has concentrated on recording with smaller labels such as Takoma, Spindrift, Making Waves and the Christian label Myrhh with whom she released There Is A Love. Shortly after Live In London was released, the label, Making Waves, folded. On The Sunny Side appeared on the largely unknown Music For Little People label. She has never been able to match the success of 'Midnight At The Oasis', but her soulful style of blues, tinged with jazz is still in demand.
●ALBUMS: Maria Muldaur (Reprise 1973)★★★★, Waitress In A Donut Shop (Reprise 1974)★★★, Sweet Harmony (Reprise 1976)★★★★, Southern Winds (Warners 1978)★★, Open Your Eyes (Warners 1979)★★★, Gospel Nights (1980)★★, There Is A Love (Myrhh 1982)★★, Sweet And Slow (Spindrift 1984)★★★, Transblucency (1985)★★★, Live In London (Making Waves 1987)★★★, On The Sunny Side (Music For Little People 1991)★★★, Louisiana Love Call (1992)★★★, Meet Me At Midnite (Black Top 1994)★★★, Jazzabelle (Stony Plain 1995)★★★, Fanning The Flames (Telarc 1996)★★★.

MUNGO JERRY

Mungo Jerry - Ray Dorset (vocals, guitar), Colin Earl (piano, vocals), Paul King (banjo, jug, guitar, vocals) and Mike Cole (bass) - was a little-known skiffle-cum-jug band that achieved instant fame following a sensational appearance at 1970's Hollywood Pop Festival, in Staffordshire, England, wherein they proved more popular than headliners the Grateful Dead, Traffic and Free. The group's performance coincided with the release of their debut single, 'In The Summertime', and the attendant publicity, combined with the song's nagging commerciality, resulted in a runaway smash. It topped the UK chart and, by the end of that year alone, global sales had totalled six million. Despite an eight-month gap between releases, Mungo Jerry's second single, 'Baby Jump', also reached number 1. By this time Mike Cole had been replaced by John Godfrey and the group's jug band sound had grown appreciably heavier. A third hit, in 1971, 'Lady Rose', showed a continued grasp of melody (the maxi-single also included the controversial 'Have A Whiff On Me' which was banned by the BBC). This successful year concluded with another Top 20 release, 'You Don't Have To Be In The Army To Fight In The War'. Paul King and Colin Earl left the group in 1972 and together with bassist Joe Rush, an early member of Mungo Jerry, formed the King Earl Boogie Band. Dorset released a solo album, Cold Blue Excursions, prior to convening a new line-up with John Godfrey, Jon Pope (piano) and Tim Reeves (drums). The new line-up had another Top 3 hit in 1973 with 'Alright Alright Alright', but the following year the overtly sexist 'Longlegged Woman Dressed In Black' became the group's final chart entry. Dorset continued to work with various versions of his creation into the 80s, but was never able to regain the group's early profile. A short-lived collaboration with Peter Green and Vincent Crane under the name Katmundu resulted in the disappointing A Case For The Blues (1986), but Dorset did achieve further success when he produced 'Feels Like I'm In Love' for singer Kelly Marie. This former Mungo b-side became a UK number 1 in August 1980.

●ALBUMS: *Mungo Jerry* (Dawn 1970)★★★, *Electronically Tested* (Dawn 1971)★★★, *You Don't Have To Be In The Army To Fight In The War* (Dawn 1971)★★★, *Memories Of A Stockbroker* (Janus 1971)★★, *Baby Jump* (Pye 1971)★★★, *Boot Power* (Dawn 1972)★★, *Impala Saga* (Polydor 1976)★★, *Lovin' In The Alleys, Fightin' In The Streets* (Polydor 1977)★★, *Ray Dorset And Mungo Jerry* (Polydor 1978)★★★, *Vig* (Balkanton 1978)★★, *Six Aside* (Satellite 1979)★★, *Together Again* (CNR Capriccio 1981)★★, *Boogie Up* (Music Team 1984)★★, *Too Fast To Live And Too Young To Die* (PRT 1987)★★, *All The Hits Plus More* (Prestige 1987)★★★, *Snakebite* (Prestige 1990)★★. Solo: Ray Dorset *Cold Blue Excursion* (Dawn 1972)★★★. Paul King *Been In The Pen Too Long* (Dawn 1972)★★, *Houdini's Moon* (A New Day 1995)★★, the King Earl Boogie Band *Trouble At Mill* (Dawn 1972)★★★, *The Mill Has Gone* (A New Day 1995)★★.

●COMPILATIONS: *Greatest Hits* (Dawn 1973)★★★, *Long Legged Woman* (Dawn 1974)★★★, *Golden Hour Presents* (Golden Hour 1974)★★★, *The File Series* (Pye 1977)★★★, *Greatest Hits* (Astan 1981)★★★, *In The Summertime* (Flashback 1985)★★★, *Mungo Jerry Collection* (Castle 1991)★★★, *Some Hits And More* (Reference 1991)★★★, *The Early Years* (Dojo 1992)★★★, *Hits Collection* (Pickwick 1993)★★★, *Summertime* (Spectrum 1995)★★★.

NASH, GRAHAM

b. 2 February 1942, Blackpool, Lancashire, England. Guitarist and vocalist Nash embraced music during the skiffle boom. He formed the Two Teens with classmate Allan Clarke in 1955, but by the following decade the duo, now known as Ricky And Dane, had joined local revue Kirk Stephens And The Deltas. In 1961 they broke away to found the Hollies, which evolved from provincial status into one of Britain's most popular 60s attractions with Nash's shrill voice cutting through their glorious harmony vocals. Although their early hits were drawn from outside sources, Nash, Clarke and guitarist Tony Hicks subsequently forged a prolific songwriting team. However, Nash's growing introspection, as demonstrated by 'King Midas In Reverse' (1967), was at odds with his partners' pop-based preferences and the following year he left to join 'supergroup' Crosby, Stills And Nash. Nash's distinctive nasal tenor instilled a sense of identity to the trio's harmonies, and although his compositional talent was viewed as lightweight by many commentators, 'Marrakesh Express' (originally written for the Hollies), 'Teach Your Children' and 'Just A Song Before I Go', were all highly successful when issued as singles. *Songs For Beginners* confirmed the artist's unpretentious, if naïve style with material weaving political statements, notably 'Chicago', to personal confessions. Stellar support from his girlfriend Rita Coolidge, plus Jerry Garcia and Dave Mason brought precision to a set that silenced many of Nash's critics. However, the stark and dour *Wild Tales*, recorded following the murder of Nash's girlfriend Amy Gosage, proved less successful and not unnaturally lacked the buoyancy of its predecessor; nevertheless it contained some strong material, including 'Prison Song' and 'Another Sleep Song'. Nash then spent the remainder of the decade as half of Crosby And Nash, or participating in the parent group's innumerable reunions. He devoted considerable time and effort to charitable and political projects, including *No Nukes* and *M.U.S.E.*, but a regenerated solo career was undermined by the poor reception afforded *Earth And Sky*. Having completed a brief spell in a rejuvenated Hollies (1983), Nash resumed his on-off commitments to Crosby, Stills, Nash And Young and to date has only released one further solo effort. The perplexing *Innocent Eyes* matched Nash with modern technology: a surfeit of programmed drum machines. The record sounded synthesized and over-produced and was rejected by the critics and public. Nash's first love has always been CS&N, and history has shown that his best post-Hollies work has been unselfishly saved for group rather than solo activities. Nash's own stability has enabled him to help his colleagues through numerous problems; he takes much of the credit for David Crosby's recovery from drug addiction.

●ALBUMS: *Songs For Beginners* (Atlantic 1971)★★★, *Wild Tales* (Atlantic 1974)★★★, *Earth And Sky* (Capitol 1980)★★★, *Innocent Eyes* (Atlantic 1986)★★.
●FURTHER READING: *Crosby, Stills And Nash*, Dave Zimmer.

NASH, JOHNNY

b. 9 August 1940, Houston, Texas, USA. The story of Nash's association with Bob Marley has been well documented. His background is similar to that of many Jamaican performers in that he sang in the church choir although not the fiery gospel type. By his early teens he performed cover versions of popular R&B hits of the 50s in a television show called *Matinee*. He was to enjoy his first US chart entry in 1957 with a cover of Doris Day's, 'A Very Special Love'. ABC decided to market the young singer as another Johnny Mathis which did nothing to enhance his career. Disillusioned with the label he concentrated on a career in the movies. In 1958 he starred in *Take A Giant Step*, and in 1960 he appeared alongside Dennis Hopper in *Key Witness* which was critically acclaimed in Europe. Returning to the recording studio he persevered with middle-of-the-road material but was unable to generate a hit. A number of label and style changes did not embellish his chart potential. By 1965 he finally scored a Top 5 hit in the R&B chart with the ballad, 'Lets Move And Groove Together'. He was unable to keep up the winning formula but in 1967 his R&B hit was enjoying chart success in Jamaica. The good fortunes in Jamaica led Nash to the island to promote his hit. It was here that he was exposed to ska and arranged a return visit to the island to record at Federal Studios. Accompanied by Byron Lee and The Dragonaires the sessions resulted in 'Cupid', 'Hold Me Tight' and 'You Got Soul'. When he released 'Hold Me Tight' the song became an international hit including a Top 5 success in the UK as well as a return to the Jamaican chart. He formed a partnership with Danny Simms and a label, JAD (Johnny and Danny) releasing recordings by Bob Marley, Byron Lee, Lloyd Price and Kim Weston as well as his own material until the label folded in the early 70s. He returned to recording in Jamaica at Harry J's studio where he met Marley who wrote, 'Stir It Up' which revived Nash's career by peaking at number 13 on the UK chart in June 1972. He continued to enjoy popularity with, 'I Can See Clearly Now' a UK Top 5 hit which was successfully covered by Jimmy Cliff in 1994 for the film, *Cool Runnings*. Other hits followed 'Ooh What A Feeling' and 'There Are More Questions Than Answers' but the further he drifted from reggae the less successful the single. He covered other Bob Marley compositions including 'Nice Time' and 'Guava Jelly' but they were not picked up for single release although the latter was on the b-side to 'There Are More Questions'. His career subsequently took another downward turn and was again revived when he returned to Jamaica to record an Ernie Smith composition, 'Tears On My Pillow' which reached number 1 in the UK Top 10 in June 1975. He also reached the UK chart with 'Let's Be Friends' and '(What) A Wonderful World' before choosing to devote more energy to films and his West Indian recording complex.

●ALBUMS: *A Teenager Sings The Blues* (ABC 1957)★★★, *I Got Rhythm* (ABC 1959)★★★, *Hold Me Tight* (JAD 1968)★★★, *Let's Go Dancing* (Columbia 1969)★★★, *I Can See Clearly Now* (Columbia 1972)★★★, *My Merry Go Round* (Columbia 1973)★★, *Celebrate Life* (Columbia 1974)★★★, *Tears On My Pillow* (Columbia 1975)★★★, *What A Wonderful World* (Columbia 1977)★★, *Johnny Nash Album* (Columbia 1980)★★★, *Stir It Up* (Hallmark 1981)★★, *Here Again* (London 1986)★★.

●COMPILATIONS: *Greatest Hits* (Columbia 1975)★★★, *The Johnny Nash Collection* (Epic 1977)★★★, *The Best Of* (Columbia 1996)★★★.

NAZARETH

Formed in 1968 in Dunfermline, Fife, Scotland, Nazareth evolved out of local attractions the Shadettes. Dan McCafferty (vocals), Manny Charlton (guitar), Pete Agnew (bass) and Darrell Sweet (drums) took their new name from the opening line in 'The Weight', a contemporary hit for the Band. After completing a gruelling Scottish tour, Nazareth opted to move to London. *Nazareth* and *Exercises* showed undoubted promise, while a third set, *Razamanaz*, spawned two UK Top 10 singles in 'Broken Down Angel' and 'Bad Bad Boy' (both 1973). New producer Roger Glover helped focus the quartet's brand of melodic hard rock, and such skills were equally prevalent on *Loud 'N' Proud*. An unlikely rendition of Joni Mitchell's 'This Flight Tonight' gave the group another major chart entry, while the Charlton-produced *Hair Of The Dog* confirmed Nazareth as an international attraction. Another cover version, this time of Tomorrow's 'My White Bicycle', was a Top 20 entry and although *Rampant* did not yield a single, the custom-recorded 'Love Hurts', originally a hit for the Everly Brothers, proved highly successful in the US and Canada. Nazareth's popularity remained undiminished throughout the 70s but, having tired of a four-piece line-up, they added guitarist Zal Cleminson, formerly of the Sensational Alex Harvey Band, for *No Mean City*. Still desirous for change, the group invited Jeff 'Skunk' Baxter, late of Steely Dan and the Doobie Brothers, to produce *Malice In Wonderland*. While stylistically different from previous albums, the result was artistically satisfying. Contrasting ambitions then led to Cleminson's amicable departure, but the line-up was subsequently augmented by former Spirit keyboard

player, John Locke. Baxter also produced the experimental *The Fool Circle*, while the group's desire to capture their in-concert fire resulted in 'Snaz. Glasgow guitarist Billy Rankin had now joined the group, but dissatisfaction with touring led to Locke's departure following 2XS. Rankin then switched to keyboards, but although Nazareth continued to enjoy popularity in the US and Europe, their stature in the UK was receding. Bereft of a major recording deal, Nazareth suspended their career during the late 80s, leaving McCafferty free to pursue solo ambitions (he had already released a solo album in 1975). A comeback album in 1992 with the addition of Billy Rankin produced the impressive *No Jive*, yet Nazareth's recent low profile in the UK will demand further live work to capitalize on this success.

●ALBUMS: *Nazareth* (Mooncrest 1971)★★★, *Exercises* (Mooncrest 1972)★★★, *Razamanaz* (Mooncrest 1973)★★★★, *Loud 'N' Proud* (Mooncrest 1974)★★★, *Rampant* (Mooncrest 1974)★★★, *Hair Of The Dog* (Mooncrest 1975)★★★★, *Close Enough For Rock 'N' Roll* (Mountain 1976)★★★, *Play 'N' The Game* (Mountain 1976)★★, *Expect No Mercy* (Mountain 1977)★★, *No Mean City* (Mountain 1978)★★, *Malice In Wonderland* (Mountain 1980)★★, *The Fool Circle* (NEMS 1981)★★, *'Snaz* (NEMS 1981)★★, *2XS* (NEMS 1982)★★, *Sound Elixir* (Vertigo 1983)★★, *The Catch* (Vertigo 1984)★★, *Cinema* (Vertigo 1986)★★, *Snakes & Ladders* (Vertigo 1990)★★, *No Jive* (Mainstream 1992)★★. Solo: Dan McCafferty *Dan McCafferty* (1975)★★.

●COMPILATIONS: *Greatest Hits* (Mountain 1975)★★★, *20 Greatest Hits: Nazareth* (Sahara 1985)★★★, *Anthology: Nazareth* (Raw Power 1988)★★★.

●VIDEOS: *Razamanaz* (Hendring 1990).

NESMITH, MICHAEL

b. Robert Michael Nesmith, 30 December 1942, Houston, Texas, USA. Although best known as a member of the Monkees, Nesmith enjoyed a prolific career in music prior to this group's inception. During the mid-60s folk boom he performed with bassist John London as Mike And John, but later pursed work as a solo act. Two singles, credited to Michael Blessing, were completed under the aegis of New Christy Minstrels' mastermind Randy Sparks, while Nesmith's compositions, 'Different Drum' and 'Mary Mary' were recorded, respectively, by the Stone Poneys and Paul Butterfield. Such experience gave the artist confidence to demand the right to determine the Monkees' musical policy and his sterling country rock performances were the highlight of the group's varied catalogue. In 1968 he recorded *The Witchita Train Whistle Sings*, an instrumental set, but his independent aspirations did not fully flourish until 1970 when he formed the First National Band. Former colleague London joined Orville 'Red' Rhodes (pedal steel) and John Ware (drums) in a group completing three exceptional albums which initially combined Nashville-styled country with the leader's acerbic pop (*Magnetic South*), but later grew to encompass a grander, even eccentric interpretation of the genre (*Nevada Fighter*). The band disintegrated during the latter's recording and a Second National Band, on which Nesmith and Rhodes were accompanied by Johnny Meeks (bass; ex-Gene Vincent and Merle Haggard) and Jack Panelli (drums), completed the less impressive *Tantamount To Treason*. The group was disbanded entirely for the sarcastically entitled *And The Hits Just Keep On Comin'*, a haunting, largely acoustic set regarded by many as the artist's finest work. In 1972 he founded the Countryside label under the aegis of Elektra Records, but despite critically acclaimed sets by Iain Matthews, Garland Frady and the ever-present Rhodes, the project was axed in the wake of boardroom politics. The excellent *Pretty Much Your Standard Ranch Stash* ended the artist's tenure with RCA, following which he founded a second label, Pacific Arts. *The Prison*, an allegorical narrative which came replete with a book, was highly criticized upon release, although recent opinion has lauded its ambition. Nesmith reasserted his commercial status in 1977 when 'Rio', culled from *From A Radio Engine To The Photon Wing*, reached the UK Top 30. The attendant video signalled a growing interest in the visual arts which flourished following *Infinite Rider On The Big Dogma*, his biggest selling US release. In 1982 *Elephant Parts* won the first ever Grammy for a video, while considerable acclaim was engendered by a subsequent series, *Michael Nesmith In Television Parts*, and the film *Repo Man*, which the artist financed. Having refused entreaties to join the Monkees' 20th Anniversary Tour, this articulate entrepreneur continues to pursue his various diverse interests including a highly successful video production company (Pacific Arts).

●ALBUMS: *The Wichita Train Whistle Sings* (Dot 1968)★★, *Magnetic South* (RCA 1970)★★★, *Loose Salute* (RCA 1971)★★★★, *Nevada Fighter* (RCA 1971)★★★★, *Tantamount To Treason* (RCA 1972)★★, *And The Hits Just Keep On Comin'* (RCA 1972)★★★, *Pretty Much Your Standard Ranch Stash* (RCA 1973)★★★, *The Prison* (Pacific Arts 1975)★★, *From A Radio Engine To The Photon Wing* (Pacific Arts 1977)★★★, *Live At The Palais* (Pacific Arts 1978)★★, *Infinite Rider On The Big Dogma* (Pacific Arts 1979)★★★, *Tropical Campfires* (Pacific Arts 1992)★★★, *The Garden* (Rio 1995)★★.

●COMPILATIONS: *The Best Of* (RCA 1977)★★★, *The Newer Stuff* (Awareness 1989)★★★, *The Older Stuff* (Rhino 1992)★★★★, *Complete* (Pacific Arts 1993)★★★.

●VIDEOS: *Elephant Parts* (Awareness 1992).

●FILMS: *Head* (1968).

NEW RIDERS OF THE PURPLE SAGE

Formed in 1969 the New Riders was initially envisaged as a part-time spin-off from the Grateful Dead. Group members Jerry Garcia (pedal steel guitar), Phil Lesh (bass) and Mickey Hart (drums) joined John Dawson (b. 1945, San Francisco, California, USA; guitar/vocals) and David Nelson (b. San Francisco, California, USA; guitar), mutual associates from San Francisco's once-thriving traditional music circuit. Although early live appearances were viewed as an informal warm-up to the main attraction, the New Riders quickly established an independent identity through the strength of Dawson's original songs. They secured a recording contract in 1971, by which time Dave Torbert had replaced Lesh, and Spencer Dryden (b. 7 April 1938, New York, USA), formerly of Jefferson Airplane, was installed as the group's permanent drummer. *New Riders Of The Purple Sage* blended country rock with hippie idealism, yet emerged as a worthy companion to the parent act's lauded *American Beauty*. Sporting one of the era's finest cover's (from the renowned Kelley/Mouse studio), the stand-out track was 'Dirty Business'. This lengthy 'acid country' opus featured some memorable guitar feedback. The final link with the Dead was severed when an over-committed Garcia made way for newcomer Buddy Cage (b. Canada). *Powerglide* introduced the punchier, more assertive sound the group now pursued which brought commercial rewards with the highly popular *The Adventures Of Panama Red*. Torbert left the line-up following *Home, Home On The Road* and was replaced by Skip Battin, formerly of the Byrds. In 1978 Dryden relinquished his drumstool in order to manage the band; while sundry musicians then joined and left, Dawson and Nelson remained at the helm until 1981. The New Riders were dissolved following the disastrous *Feelin' Alright*, although the latter musician subsequently resurrected the name with Gary Vogenson (guitar) and Rusty Gautier (bass). Nelson meanwhile resumed his association with the Dead in the Jerry Garcia Acoustic Band, and supervised several archive New Riders sets for the specialist Relix label.

●ALBUMS: *New Riders Of The Purple Sage* (Columbia 1971)★★★★, *Powerglide* (Columbia 1972)★★★, *Gypsy Cowboy* (Columbia 1972)★★, *The Adventures Of Panama Red* (Columbia 1973)★★★, *Home, Home On The Road* (Columbia 1974)★★, *Brujo* (Columbia 1974)★★, *Oh, What A Mighty Time* (Columbia 1975)★★, *New Riders* (MCA 1976)★★, *Who Are These Guys* (MCA 1977)★★, *Marin County Line* (MCA 1978)★, *Feelin' Alright* (1981)★, *Friend Of The Devil* (1991)★★.

●COMPILATIONS: *The Best Of The New Riders Of The Purple Sage* (Columbia 1976)★★★, *Before Time Began* (1976)★★, *Vintage NRPS* (1988)★★.

NEW SEEKERS

The original New Seekers comprised ex-Nocturnes Eve Graham (b. 19 April 1943, Perth, Scotland; vocals), Sally Graham (vocals), Chris Barrington (bass/vocals), Laurie Heath (guitar/vocals), and Marty Kristian (b. 27 May 1947, Leipzig, Germany - a Latvian who had been raised in Australia; guitar/vocals). This line-up recorded only one album, *The New Seekers*, before Heath, Barrington and Sally Graham were replaced by Lyn Paul (b. 16 February 1949, Manchester, England; ex-Nocturnes),

Peter Doyle (b. 28 July 1949, Melbourne, Australia), and Paul Layton (b. 4 August 1947, Beaconsfield, England). Ex-Seeker Keith Potger was originally a member of the group, but retreated to the less public role of manager. The male contingent played guitars in concert, but the act's main strengths were its interweaving vocal harmonies and a clean, winsome image. Their entertainments also embraced dance and comedy routines. Initially they appealed to US consumers who thrust a cover of Melanie's 'Look What They've Done To My Song, Ma' and 'Beautiful People' - all unsuccessful in Britain - high up the *Billboard* Hot 100. A UK breakthrough came with 'Never Ending Song Of Love' which reached number 2, and, even better, a rewrite of a Coca-Cola commercial, 'I'd Like To Teach The World To Sing', topping foreign charts too, and overtaking the Hillside Singers' original version in the USA. Their Eurovision Song Contest entry, 'Beg Steal Or Borrow' and the title track of 1972's *Circles* were also hits, but revivals of the Fleetwoods' 'Come Softly To Me' and Eclection's 'Nevertheless' were among 1973 singles whose modest Top 40 placings were hard-won, though the year ended well with another UK number 1 in 'You Won't Find Another Fool Like Me'.

By 1974, Doyle had left the group and had been replaced by Peter Oliver (b. 15 January 1952, Southampton, England; guitar/vocals). He appeared on *Together* and *Farewell Album*. The next single, 'I Get A Little Sentimental Over You', hurtled up the charts in spring 1974, but the five disbanded with a farewell tour of Britain. Two years later, however, the lure of a CBS contract brought about a reformation - minus Lyn Paul who had had a minor solo hit in 1975 and Oliver had now been replaced by Danny Finn - but no subsequent single could reconjure a more glorious past and, not-so-New anymore, the group disbanded for the last time in 1978.

●ALBUMS: *The New Seekers* (Phillips 1969)★★★, *Keith Potger & The New Seekers* (Phillips 1970)★★, *New Colours* (Polydor 1971)★★★, *Beautiful People* (Phillips 1971)★★, *We'd Like To Teach The World To Sing* (Polydor 1972)★★, *Live At The Royal Albert Hall* (Polydor 1972)★★, *Never Ending Song Of Love* (Polydor 1972)★★, *Circles* (Polydor 1972)★★, *Now* (Polydor 1973)★★, *Pinball Wizards* (Polydor 1973)★★, *Together* (Polydor 1974)★★, *Farewell Album* (Polydor 1974)★★, *Together Again* (Columbia 1976)★★.

●COMPILATIONS: *Look What They've Done To My Song, Ma* (Contour 1972)★★, *15 Great Hits* (Orbit 1983)★★, *The Best Of The New Seekers* (Contour 1985)★★★, *Greatest Hits* (Object 1987)★★. By Marty Kristian, Paul Layton And Peter Oliver *Peter Paul & Marty* (1973)★★.

NEW YORK CITY

An R&B vocal group from New York, USA. New York City were one of the finest representatives of the renaissance of vocal harmony groups and the explosion of the Philadelphia recording scene during the early 70s.

Members were Tim McQueen, John Brown (earlier a member of the Five Satins), Ed Shell, and Claude Johnson. The group first recorded for Buddah as Triboro Exchange, but it was not until their name change in 1972 and their signing to Chelsea Records that the group became successful. Under the aegis of Philadelphia producer/arranger Thom Bell the group flourished on the charts with such hits as 'I'm Doin' Fine Now' (number 14 R&B, number 17 pop), 'Quick, Fast, In A Hurry' (number 19 R&B, number 79 pop), and 'Happiness Is' (number 20 R&B). Their last chart record was in 1975, a time when stand-up vocal groups were becoming less of a factor in R&B. Their legacy was recalled in 1992 when in the UK the Pasadenas had a number 1 hit with 'I'm Doing Fine Now'.

●ALBUMS: *I'm Doing Fine Now* (Chelsea 1973)★★★, *Soulful Road* (Chelsea 1974)★★★.

●COMPILATIONS: *Best of New York City* (Chelsea 1976)★★★, *I'm Doing Fine Now* (Collectables 1993)★★★.

NEW YORK DOLLS

One of the most influential rock bands of the last 20 years, the New York Dolls pre-dated the punk and sleaze metal movements that followed and offered both a crash course in rebellion with style. Formed in 1972, the line-up stabilized with David Johansen (b. 9 January 1950, Staten Island, New York, USA; vocals), Johnny Thunders (b. John Anthony Genzale Jnr., 15 July 1952, New York, USA, d. 23 April 1991, New Orleans, Louisiana, USA; guitar), Arthur Harold Kane (bass), Sylvain Sylvain (guitar/piano) and Jerry Nolan (d. 14 January 1992; drums), the last two having replaced Rick Rivets and Billy Murcia (d. 6 November 1972). The band revelled in an outrageous glam-rock image: lipstick, high-heels and tacky leather outfits providing their visual currency. Underneath they were a first rate rock 'n' roll band, dragged up on the music of the Stooges, Rolling Stones and MC5. Their self-titled debut, released in 1973, was a major landmark in rock history, oozing attitude, vitality and controversy from every note. It met with widespread critical acclaim, but this never transferred to commercial success. The follow-up, *Too Much Too Soon*, was an appropriate title - and indicated that alcohol and drugs were beginning to take their toll. The album remains a charismatic collection of punk/glam-rock anthems, typically delivered with 'wasted' cool. Given a unanimous thumbs down from the music press the band began to implode shortly afterwards. Johansen embarked on a solo career and Thunders formed the Heartbreakers. The Dolls continued for a short time before eventually grinding to a halt in 1975, despite the auspices of new manager Malcolm McLaren. The link to the Sex Pistols and the UK punk movement is stronger than that fact alone, with the Dolls remaining a constant reference point for teen rebels the world over. Sadly for the band, their rewards were fleeting. Jerry Nolan died as a result of a stroke on 14 January 1992 whilst undergoing treatment for pneumonia and meningitis. Thunders had departed from an overdose, in mysterious circumstances, less than a year previously. *Red Patent Leather* is a poor quality and posthumously released live recording from May 1975 - *Rock 'N' Roll* offers a much more representative collection.

●ALBUMS: *New York Dolls* (Mercury 1973)★★★★, *Too Much Too Soon* (Mercury 1974)★★★, *Red Patent Leather* (New Rose 1984)★★.

●COMPILATIONS: *Lipstick Killers* (ROIR 1983)★★★, *Rock 'N' Roll* (Mercury 1994)★★★★.

●FURTHER READING: *New York Dolls*, Steven Morrissey.

NEWBURY, MICKEY

b. Milton J. Newbury Jnr., 19 May 1940, Houston, Texas, USA. Newbury began by singing tenor in a harmony group, the Embers, who recorded for Mercury Records. He worked as an air traffic controller in the US Air Force and was stationed in England. He later wrote 'Swiss Cottage Place', which was recorded by Roger Miller. In 1963 he worked on shrimp boats in Galveston, Texas, and started songwriting in earnest. In 1964 he was signed to Acuff-Rose Music in Nashville. Among his early compositions are 'Here Comes The Rain, Baby' (Eddy Arnold and Roy Orbison), 'Funny Familiar Forgotten Feelings' (Don Gibson and Tom Jones), 'How I Love Them Old Songs' (Carl Smith) and 'Sweet Memories' (Willie Nelson). In 1968 Kenny Rogers And The First Edition had a US pop hit with the psychedelic 'Just Dropped In (To See What Condition My Condition Was In)'. Newbury recorded low-key albums of his own but his voice was so mournful that even his happier songs sounded sad. After two albums for RCA, he moved to Mercury and wrote and recorded such sombre songs as 'She Even Woke Me Up To Say Goodbye' (later recorded by Jerry Lee Lewis), 'San Francisco Mabel Joy' (recorded by John Denver, Joan Baez, David Allan Coe and Kenny Rogers) and 'I Don't Think About Her (Him) No More', which has been recorded by Don Williams and Tammy Wynette, and also by Bobby Bare, under the title of 'Poison Red Berries'. Newbury, who by now lived on a houseboat, was intrigued by the way his wind chimes mingled with the rain, thus leading to the sound effects he used to link tracks. This gave his albums of similar material a concept. His gentle and evocative 'American Trilogy' - in actuality a medley of three Civil War songs ('Dixie', 'The Battle Hymn Of The Republic' and 'All My Trials') - was a hit in a full-blooded version by Elvis Presley in 1972. Says Newbury, 'It was more a detriment than a help because it was not indicative of what I could do.' Nevertheless, his *Rusty Tracks* also features reworkings of American folk songs. Among his successful compositions are 'Makes Me Wonder If I Ever Said Goodbye' (Johnny Rodriguez) and 'Blue Sky Shinin'' (Marie Osmond). He has scarcely made a mark as a performer in the US country charts (his highest position is number 53 for 'Sunshine') but he was elected

to the Nashville Songwriters International Hall of Fame in 1980. Ironically, he has released few new songs since and his 'new age' album in 1988 featured re-recordings of old material. His 1996 *Lulled By The Moonlight* was dedicated to first American pop songwriter Stephen Foster.

●ALBUMS: *Harlequin Melodies* (1968)★★, *Mickey Newbury Sings His Own* (1968)★★★, *Looks Like Rain* (1969)★★★, *'Frisco Mabel Joy* (Elektra 1971)★★★★, *Heaven Help The Child* (Elektra 1973)★★★, *Live At Montezuma* also issued as a double album with *Looks Like Rain* (Elektra 1973)★★★, *I Came To Hear The Music* (Elektra 1974)★★★, *Lovers* (Elektra 1975)★★★, *Rusty Tracks* (1977)★★, *His Eye Is On The Sparrow* (Hickory 1978)★★★, *The Sailor* (Hickory 1979)★★★, *After All These Years* (Mercury 1981)★★★, *In A New Age* (Airborne 1988)★★★, *Nights When I Am Sane* (Winter Harvest 1994)★★★, *Lulled By The Moonlight* (Mountain Retreat 1996)★★★.

●COMPILATIONS: *Sweet Memories* (MCA 1986)★★★.

NEWMAN, RANDY

b. 28 November 1943, Los Angeles, California, USA. One of the great middle America songwriters, Newman is William Faulkner, Garrison Keillor, Edward Hopper and Norman Rockwell, all set to music. Newman's songs are uncompromising and humorous but are often misconceived as being cruel and trite. His early compositions were recorded by other people, as Newman was paid $50 a month as a staff songwriter for Liberty Records housed in the famous Brill Building, New York. Early hit songs included 'Nobody Needs Your Love' and 'Just One Smile' by Gene Pitney, 'I Don't Want To Hear It Anymore' recorded by Dusty Springfield and P.J. Proby, 'I Think It's Going To Rain Today', by Judy Collins, UB40 and again by Dusty, as was the superb 'I've Been Wrong Before' which was also a hit for Cilla Black. Alan Price found favour with 'Simon Smith And His Amazing Dancing Bear' and 'Tickle Me', Peggy Lee succeeded with 'Love Story', and Three Dog Night and Eric Burdon did well with 'Mama Told Me Not To Come'. In addition, Newman's songs have been recorded by dozens of artists including Manfred Mann, Harpers Bizarre, Irma Thomas, Billy Fury, O'Jays, Petula Clark, Melissa Manchester, Frankie Laine, the Walker Brothers, the Nashville Teens, Lulu, Eric Burdon, Van Dyke Parks, Sheena Easton, Blood Sweat And Tears, Jackie DeShannon, Nina Simone, H.P. Lovecraft, Liza Minelli, Vic Dana, Rick Nelson, Ian Matthews, Fleetwoods, Bryan Hyland, Ringo Starr and Ray Charles. Newman's debut album came as late as 1968 and was the subject of bizarre advertising from Reprise Records. In February 1969 they announced through a hefty campaign that the record was not selling; they changed the cover and added a lyric sheet. This bold but defeatist ploy failed to increase the meagre sales. In 1970 he contributed to the *Performance* soundtrack and that same year his work was celebrated by having

Harry Nilsson record an album of his songs. His introspective lyrics are never self-indulgent; he writes in a morose way but it all merely reflects the human condition. Songs like 'Old Kentucky Home' and 'Baltimore' have hidden warmth. 'Rednecks' and 'Short People' are genuine observations, but on these songs Newman's humour was too subtle for the general public and he received indignant protests and threats. In 1979's 'Story Of A Rock 'N' Roll Band' he castigated both Kiss and ELO. One of the first examples of his film music came in 1971, with *Cold Turkey*, and he was nominated for an Oscar in 1982 for his score to *Ragtime*, and again, in 1984, for *The Natural*. In 1983, his 'I Love Love L.A.' was used to promote the Los Angeles Olympic Games of the following year. In 1986 he wrote 'Blue Shadows', the theme for *The Three Amigos!*, which was performed in the hit movie by Steve Martin and Chevy Chase. More film scores followed, such as *Awakenings*, *Parenthood* (including the song, 'I Love To See You Smile'), *Avalon* (the last two films were nominated for Academy Awards), *The Paper*, and *Maverick* (1994). Among his most recent studio work was *Land Of Dreams*, ironically co-produced by one of the victims of his acerbic wit, Jeff Lynne. *Faust* was an ambitious project that enlisted Elton John, James Taylor, Bonnie Raitt and Don Henley among a gamut of west coast superstars. He scored the music for the Disney film *Toy Story* in 1995. Newman continues to brilliantly observe, infuriate and mock while his croaky voice turns out more masterpieces commenting on American society.

●ALBUMS: *Randy Newman* (Reprise 1968)★★★, *12 Songs* (Reprise 1970)★★★★, *Randy Newman/Live* (Reprise 1971)★★★, *Sail Away* (Reprise 1972)★★★★, *Good Old Boys* (Reprise 1974)★★★★, *Little Criminals* (Warners 1977)★★★, *Born Again* (Warners 1979)★★★, *Ragtime* film soundtrack (1982)★★, *Trouble In Paradise* (Warners 1983)★★, *The Natural* film soundtrack (1984)★★, *Land Of Dreams* (Reprise 1988)★★★, *Parenthood* film soundtrack (1990)★★, *Awakenings* film soundtrack (Warners 1991)★★, *The Paper* film soundtrack (Reprise 1994)★★, *Faust* (Reprise 1995)★★★.

●COMPILATIONS: *Randy Newman Retrospect* (Warners 1983)★★★, *Lonely At The Top - The Best Of Randy Newman* (Warners 1987)★★★★.

NEWTON-JOHN, OLIVIA

b. 26 September 1948, Cambridge, England. Her showbusiness career began when she won a local contest to find 'the girl who looked most like Hayley Mills' in 1960 after the Newton-Johns had emigrated to Australia. Later she formed the Sol Four with schoolfriends. Though this vocal group disbanded, the encouragement of customers who heard her sing solo in a café led her to enter - and win - a television talent show. The prize was a 1966 holiday in London during which she recorded her debut single, Jackie DeShannon's 'Till You Say You'll Be Mine' after a stint in a duo with Pat Carroll. Staying on in England, Olivia became part of Toomorrow, a group created by bubblegum-pop potentate Don Kirshner, to fill the gap in the market left by the disbanded Monkees (not to be confused with Tomorrow). As well as a science fiction movie and its soundtrack, Toomorrow was also responsible for 'I Could Never Live Without Your Love,' a 1970 single, produced by the Shadows' Bruce Welch - with whom Olivia was romantically linked. Although Toomorrow petered out, Newton-John's link with Cliff Richard and the Shadows was a source of enduring professional benefit. A role in a Richard movie, tours as special guest in *The Cliff Richard Show*, and a residency - as a comedienne as well as a singer - on BBC Television's *It's Cliff!* guaranteed steady sales of her first album, and the start of a patchy British chart career with a Top 10 arrangement of Bob Dylan's 'If Not For You' in 1971. More typical of her output were singles such as 'Take Me Home Country Roads', penned by John Denver, 'Banks Of The Ohio' and, from the late John Rostill of the Shadows, 1973's 'Let Me Be There'. This last release sparked off by an appearance on the USA's *The Dean Martin Show* and crossed from the US country charts to the Hot 100, winning her a controversial Grammy for Best Female Country Vocal. After an uneasy performance in 1974's Eurovision Song Contest, Newton-John became omnipresent in North America, first as its most popular country artist, though her standing in pop improved considerably after a chart-topper with 'I Honestly Love You,' produced by John Farrar, another latter-day Shadow (and husband of the earlier mentioned Pat Carroll), who had assumed the task after the estrangement of Newton-John and Welch.

Newton-John also became renowned for her duets with other artists, notably in the movie of the musical Grease in which she and co-star John Travolta featured 'You're The One That I Want'. This irresistibly effervescent song became one of the most successful UK hit singles in pop history, topping the charts for a stupendous nine weeks. The follow-up, 'Summer Nights', was also a UK number 1 in 1978. Her 'Xanadu', the film's title opus with the Electric Light Orchestra, was another global number 1. However, not such a money-spinner was a further cinema venture with Travolta (1983's 'Two Of A Kind'). Neither was 'After Dark,' a single with the late Andy Gibb in 1980 nor *Now Voyager*, a 1984 album with his brother Barry. With singles like 'Physical' (1981) and the 1986 album *Soul Kiss* on Mercury Records she adopted a more raunchy image in place of her original perky wholesomeness.

During the late 80s/early 90s much of her time was spent, along with Pat (Carroll) Farrar, running her Australian-styled clothing business, Blue Koala. Following *The Rumour*, Olivia signed to Geffen for the release of a collection of children's songs and rhymes, *Warm And Tender*. The award of an OBE preceded her marriage to actor and dancer Matt Lattanzi; she remains a showbusiness evergreen although her life was clouded in 1992 when her fashion empire crashed, and it was announced that she was undergoing treatment for cancer. She subsequently revealed that she had won her battle with the disease, and in 1994 released an album that she had written, produced and financed herself. At the same time, it was estimated that in a career spanning nearly 30 years, she has sold more than 50 million records worldwide.

●ALBUMS: *If Not For You* (Pye 1971)★★★, *Let Me Be There* (MCA 1973)★★★, *Olivia Newton-John* (1973)★★, *If You Love Me Let Me Know* (MCA 1974)★★★, *Music Makes My Day* (Pye 1974)★★, *Long Live Love* (1974)★★, *Have You Never Been Mellow?* (MCA 1975)★★★, *Clearly Love* (MCA 1975)★★, *Come On Over* (MCA 1976)★★, *Don't Stop Believin'* (MCA 1976)★★, *Making A Good Thing Better* (MCA 1977)★★, with various artists *Grease* film soundtrack (1978)★★★★, *Totally Hot* (MCA 1978)★★★, with the Electric Light Orchestra *Xanadu* film soundtrack (MCA 1980)★★, *Physical* (MCA 1981)★★★, with various artists *Two Of A Kind* film soundtrack (1983)★★, *Soul Kiss* (MCA 1986)★★, *The Rumour* (MCA 1988)★★, *Warm And Tender* (Geffen 1990)★★, *Gaia: One Woman's Journey* (1994)★★.

●COMPILATIONS: *Olivia Newton-John's Greatest Hits* (MCA 1977)★★★, *Greatest Hits* i, (EMI 1978)★★★, *Olivia's Greatest Hits, Volume 2* (MCA 1982)★★, *Greatest Hits* ii, (EMI 1982)★★, *Back To Basics: The Essential Collection 1971-1992* (Phonogram 1992)★★★.

●VIDEOS: *Physical* (PMI 1984), *Live: Olivia Newton-John* (Channel 5 1986), *Down Under* (Channel 5 1989), *Soul Kiss* (Spectrum 1989).

●FURTHER READING: *Olivia Newton-John: Sunshine Supergirl*, Linda Jacobs. *Olivia Newton-John*, Peter Ruff.

●FILMS: *Grease* (1978).

NICO

b. Christa Paffgen (Pavolsky), 16 October 1938, Cologne, Germany, d. 18 July 1988. Introduced to a European social set which included film director Federico Fellini, Nico began an acting career with a memorable appearance in *La Dolce Vita*. Briefly based in London, she became acquainted with Rolling Stones' guitarist Brian Jones, and made her recording debut with the folk-tinged 'I'm Not Saying'. Nico then moved to New York, where she was introduced to Andy Warhol. She starred in the director's controversial cinema-verité epic, *Chelsea Girls*, before joining his newfound protégés, the Velvet Underground. Nico made telling contributions to this seminal group's debut album, but her desire to sing lead on all of the songs brought a swift rebuttal. She resumed a solo career in 1967 with *Chelsea Girl* which included three compositions by a young Jackson Browne, who accompanied Nico on live performances, and 'I'll Keep It With Mine', which Bob Dylan reportedly wrote with her in mind. Lou Reed and John Cale, former colleagues in the Velvet Underground, also provided memorable contributions, while the latter retained his association with the singer by producing her subsequent three albums. Here Nico's baleful,

gothic intonation was given free rein, and the haunting, often sparse use of harmonium accentuated her impressionistic songs. In 1974 she appeared in a brief tour of the UK in the company of Kevin Ayers, John Cale and Brian Eno, collectively known as ACNE. A live album of the concert at the Rainbow Theatre in London was subsequently released. That same year, following the release of *The End*, the singer ceased recording, but re-emerged in the immediate post-punk era. Her Teutonic emphasis inspired several figures, including Siouxsie Sioux of Siouxsie And The Banshees, but Nico's own 80s releases were plagued by inconsistency. Signs of an artistic revival followed treatment for drug addiction, but this unique artist died in Ibiza in 1988, after suffering a cerebral haemorrhage while cycling in intense heat.

●ALBUMS: *Chelsea Girl* (Verve 1967)★★, *The Marble Index* (Elektra 1969)★★★, *Desertshore* (Reprise 1971)★★★, with ACNE *June 1, 1974* (Island 1974)★★, *The End* (Island 1974)★★★, *Drama Of Exile* (Aura 1981)★★★, *Do Or Die! Nico In Europe, 1982 Diary* (Reach Out 1983)★★★, *Camera Obscura* (Beggars Banquet 1985)★★, *The Blue Angel* (Aura 1986)★★, *Behind The Iron Curtain* (Dojo 1986)★★, *Live In Tokyo* (Dojo 1987)★★, *Live In Denmark* (Vu 1987)★★, *En Personne En Europe* (One Over Two 1988)★★★, *Live Heroes* (Performance 1989)★★, *Hanging Gardens* (Emergo 1990)★★, *Icon* (Cleopatra 1996)★★, *Janitor Of Lunacy* (Cherry Red 1996)★★, *Nico's Last Concert: Fato Morgana* (SPV 1996)★★★.

●VIDEOS: *An Underground Experience* (Wide Angle/Visionary 1993), *Nico - Heroine* (1994).

●FURTHER READING: *The Life And Lies Of An Icon*, Richard Witts. *Songs They Never Play On The Radio: Nico, The Last Bohemian*, James Young.

NIGHTINGALE, ANNIE

b. *c*.1947, England. Although most readily associated with the BBC Radio schedules of the 70s and for her presentation of UK television's *The Old Grey Whistle Test*, Nightingale has remained active within broadcasting through to the present. She began her career in journalism, writing as a columnist for the *Daily Express* among other publications, before spending 12 years hosting *The Request Show* on BBC Radio 1. Though her profile diminished in the intervening years, in the mid-90s she was still hosting a Sunday morning programme between 2 and 4 am. However, rather than the rock and new wave sounds with which she was formerly identified, her current playlist on *The Chill Out Zone* is dedicated to the 'after club' crowd - and features selections from techno, ambient and jungle artists. In 1996 samples from the programme were packaged together by Heavenly Records for release as a various artist's album entitled *Annie On One*. In 1997, during a visit to Haiti, Nightingale was attacked by a mugger and seriously injured.

●ALBUMS: *Annie On One* (Heavenly 1996)★★★★.

NILSSON

b. Harry Edward Nelson III, 15 June 1941, Brooklyn, New York, USA, d. 15 January 1994, Los Angeles, California, USA. Nelson moved to Los Angeles as an adolescent and later undertook a range of different jobs before accepting a supervisor's position at the Security First National Bank. He nonetheless pursued a concurrent interest in music, recording demos of his early compositions which were then touted around the city's publishing houses. Producer Phil Spector drew on this cache of material, recording 'Paradise' and 'Here I Sit' with the Ronettes and 'This Could Be The Night' with the Modern Folk Quartet. None of these songs was released contemporaneously, but such interest inspired the artist's own releases for the Tower label. These singles - credited to 'Nilsson' - included 'You Can't Take Your Love Away From Me' and 'Good Times' (both 1966). The following year the Yardbirds recorded his 'Ten Little Indians', and Nilsson finally gave up his bank job upon hearing the Monkees' version of another composition, 'Cuddly Toy', on the radio. He secured a contract with RCA Records and made his album debut with the impressive *Pandemonium Shadow Show*. The selection was not only notable for Nilsson's remarkable three-octave voice, it also featured 'You Can't Do That', an enthralling montage of Beatles' songs which drew considerable praise from John Lennon and inspired their subsequent friendship. The artist's own compositions continued to find favour with other acts; the Turtles recorded 'The Story Of Rock 'N' Roll', Herb Alpert and Blood, Sweat And Tears covered 'Without Her', while Three Dog Night enjoyed a US chart-topper and gold disc with 'One'. Nilsson's own version of the last-named song appeared on *Ariel Ballet* - a title derived from his grandparents' circus act - which also included the singer's rendition of Fred Neil's 'Everybody's Talking'. This haunting recording was later adopted as the theme to the film *Midnight Cowboy* and gave Nilsson his first US Top 10 hit. *Harry* included 'The Puppy Song', later a smash for David Cassidy, while *Nilsson Sings Newman* comprised solely Randy Newman material and featured the songwriter on piano. This project was followed by *The Point*, the soundtrack to a full-length animated television feature, but Nilsson's greatest success came with *Nilsson Schmilsson* and its attendant single, 'Without You'. His emotional rendition of this Badfinger-composed song sold in excess of 1 million copies, topping both the US and UK charts and garnering a 1972 Grammy for Best Male Pop and Rock Vocal Performance. Having completed the similarly styled *Son Of Schmilsson*, this idiosyncratic performer confounded expectations with *A Little Touch Of Schmilsson In The Night*, which comprised beautifully orchestrated standards including 'Makin' Whoopee' and 'As Time Goes By'. Nilsson's subsequent career was blighted by well-publicized drinking with acquaintances John Lennon, Keith Moon and Ringo Starr. Lennon produced

Nilsson's *Pussy Cats* (1974), an anarchic set fuelled by self-indulgence, which comprised largely pop classics, including 'Subterranean Homesick Blues', 'Save The Last Dance For Me' and 'Rock Around The Clock'. Starr meanwhile assisted the artist on his film soundtrack, *Son Of Dracula*. Ensuing releases proved inconsistent, although a 1976 adaptation of *The Point*, staged at London's Mermaid Theatre, was highly successful, and marked the reunion of former Monkees Davy Jones and Mickey Dolenz. By the 80s Nilsson had largely retired from music altogether, preferring to pursue business interests, the most notable of which was a film distribution company based in California's Studio City. However, in 1988 RCA released *A Touch More Schmilsson In The Night* which, in common with its 1973 predecessor, offered the singer's affectionate renditions of popular favourites, including two of E.Y. 'Yip' Harburg's classics, 'It's Only a Paper Moon' and 'Over The Rainbow'. The unyielding paradox of Nilsson's career is that despite achieving recognition as a superior songwriter, his best-known and most successful records were penned by other acts.

●ALBUMS: *Pandemonium Shadow Show* (RCA Victor 1967)★★★, *Ariel Ballet* (RCA 1968)★★★, *Harry* (RCA 1969)★★★, *Skidoo* film soundtrack (RCA 1969)★★, *Nilsson Sings Newman* (RCA 1970)★★★★, *The Point* (RCA 1971)★★★, *Nilsson Schmilsson* (RCA 1971)★★★★, *Son Of Schmilsson* (RCA 1972)★★, *A Little Touch Of Schmilsson In The Night* (RCA 1973)★★★★, *Son Of Dracula* (Rapple 1974)★★, *Pussy Cats* (RCA 1974)★★★, *Duit On Mon Dei* (RCA 1975)★★, *The Sandman* (RCA 1975)★★, *That's The Way It Is* (RCA 1976)★★★, *Knillssonn* (RCA 1977)★★, *Night After Night* (1979)★★, *Flash Harry* (Mercury 1980)★★, *A Touch More Schmilsson In The Night* (RCA 1988)★★.

●COMPILATIONS: *Early Years* (One Up 1972)★★, *Ariel Pandemonium Ballet* (RCA 1973)★★★, *Early Tymes* (DJM 1977)★, *Nilsson's Greatest Music* (RCA 1978)★★★, *Harry And ...* (1979)★★, *Diamond Series: Nilsson* (Diamond Series 1988)★★, *Nilsson '62 - The Debut Sessions* (Retro 1996)★★, *As Time Goes By ... The Complete Scmilsson In The Night* (Camden 1997)★★★.

NITTY GRITTY DIRT BAND

Formed in Long Beach, California, in 1965, this enduring attraction evolved from the region's traditional circuit. Founder-members Jeff Hanna (b. 11 July 1947; guitar/vocals) and Bruce Kunkel (guitar/vocals) had worked together as the New Coast Two, prior to joining the Illegitimate Jug Band. Glen Grosclose (drums), Dave Hanna (guitar/vocals), Ralph Barr (guitar) and Les Thompson (bass/vocals) completed the embryonic Dirt Band line-up, although Groslcose and Dave Hanna quickly made way for Jimmie Fadden (drums/guitar) and Jackson Browne (guitar/vocals). Although the last musician only remained for a matter of months - he was replaced by John McEuen - his songs remained in the group's repertoire throughout their early career. *Nitty Gritty Dirt Band* comprised of jugband, vaudeville and pop material, ranging from the quirky 'Candy Man' to the orchestrated folk/pop 'Buy For Me The Rain', a minor US hit. *Ricochet* maintained this balance, following which Chris Darrow, formerly of Kaleidoscope (US), replaced Kunkel. The Dirt Band completed two further albums, and enjoyed a brief role in the film *Paint Your Wagon*, before disbanding in 1969. The group reconvened the following year around Jeff Hanna, John McEuen, Jimmie Fadden, Les Thompson and newcomer Jim Ibbotson. Having abandoned the jokey elements of their earlier incarnation, they pursued a career as purveyors of superior country-rock. The acclaimed *Uncle Charlie And His Dog Teddy* included excellent versions of Mike Nesmith's 'Some Of Shelly's Blues', Kenny Loggins' 'House At Pooh Corner' and Jerry Jeff Walker's 'Mr. Bojangles', a US Top 10 hit in 1970. *Will The Circle Be Unbroken*, recorded in Nashville, was an expansive collaboration between the group and traditional music mentors Doc Watson, Roy Acuff, Merle Travis and Earl Scruggs. Its charming informality inspired several stellar performances and the set played an important role in breaking down mistrust between country's establishment and the emergent 'long hair' practitioners. Les Thompson left the line-up following the album's completion, but the remaining quartet, buoyed by an enhanced reputation, continued their eclectic ambitions on *Stars And Stripes Forever* and *Dreams*. In 1976 the group dropped its 'Nitty Gritty' prefix and, as the Dirt Band, undertook a pioneering USSR tour the following year. Both Hanna and Ibbotson enjoyed brief sabbaticals, during which time supplementary musicians were introduced. By 1982 the prodigals had rejoined Fadden, McEuen and newcomer Bob Carpenter (keyboards) for *Let's Go*. The Dirt Band were, by then, an American institution with an enduring international popularity. 'Long Hard Road (Sharecropper Dreams)' and 'Modern Day Romance' topped the country charts in 1984 and 1985, respectively, but the following year a now-weary McEuen retired from the line-up. Former Eagles guitarist Bernie Leadon augmented the group for *Working Band*, but left again on its completion. He was, however, featured on *Will The Circle Be Unbroken Volume Two*, on which the Dirt Band rekindled the style of their greatest artistic triumph with the aid of several starring names, including Emmylou Harris, Chet Atkins, Johnny Cash, Ricky Skaggs, Roger McGuinn and Chris Hillman. The set deservedly drew plaudits for a group about to enter the 90s with its enthusiasm still intact. *Acoustic* in 1994 was a credible and well-produced set.

●ALBUMS: *The Nitty Gritty Dirt Band* (Liberty 1967)★★★, *Ricochet* (Liberty 1967)★★★, *Rare Junk* (Liberty 1968)★★, *Alive* (Liberty 1968)★★, *Uncle Charlie And His Dog Teddy* (Liberty 1970)★★★, *All The Good Times* (United Artists 1972)★★★, *Will The Circle Be Unbroken* triple album (United Artists 1972)★★★★, *Live* (United Artists 1973)★★, *Stars And Stripes Forever* (United Artists 1974)★★, *Dreams* (United Artists 1975)★★★. As Dirt Band *Dirt Band* (United Artists 1978)★★, *An American Dream* (United Artists 1979)★★, *Make A Little Magic* (United Artists 1980)★★, *Jealousy* (United Artists 1981)★★. As Nitty Gritty Dirt Band *Let's Go* (United Artists 1983)★★, *Plain Dirt Fashion* (Warners. 1984)★★★, *Partners, Brothers And Friends* (Warners 1985)★★★, *Hold On* (Warners 1987)★★★, *Workin' Band* (Warners. 1988)★★★, *Will The Circle Be Unbroken Volume II* (Warners. 1989)★★★★, *Rest Of The Dream* (MCA 1990)★★★, *Not Fade Away* (Liberty 1992)★★, *Acoustic* (Liberty 1994)★★★.

●COMPILATIONS: *Pure Dirt* (Liberty UK 1968)★★, *Dead And Alive* (Liberty UK 1969)★★, *Dirt, Silver And Gold* (United Artists 1976)★★★, *Gold From Dirt* (United Artists UK 1980)★★★, *Early Dirt 1967-1970* (Decal UK 1986)★★, *Twenty Years Of Dirt* (Warners 1987)★★★, *Country Store: The Nitty Gritty Dirt Band* (Country Store UK 1987)★★, *The Best Of The Nitty Gritty Dirt Band Vol 2* (Atlantic 1988)★★, *More Great Dirt: The Best Of The Nitty Gritty Dirt Band, Volume 2* (Warners 1989)★★.

NOLANS

This highly popular Irish family group originally consisted of brothers and sisters Tommy, Anne (b. 12 November 1950), Denise (b. 1952), Maureen (b. 14 June 1954), Brian, Linda (b. 23 February 1959), Bernadette (b. 17 October 1961) and Coleen Nolan (b. 12 March 1965, Blackpool, England). The Nolans lived in Dublin until 1962 when they emigrated to Blackpool. Parents Tommy and Maureen Nolan were singers and gradually brought their offspring into the act. In 1963 the entire family debuted as the Singing Nolans. After moving to London, the group's personnel was Anne, Denise, Linda, Bernadette, and Maureen. Their act proved very popular on UK television and variety shows. After recording their second album in 1977, and touring America with Engelbert Humperdinck, Denise left a year later in order to pursue a solo career. The sisters signed to CBS and were widely tipped to represent the UK in the Eurovision Song Contest but lost out to Black Lace. After a minor hit single with 'Spirit Body And Soul', Anne married and left the group for two years. She was replaced by the youngest sister, Coleen, and the quartet changed their name from the Nolan Sisters to the Nolans. A massive hit with the catchy 'I'm In The Mood For Dancing' brought them worldwide renown and even topped the charts in Japan. The Nolans had further UK Top 10 hits with 'Gotta Pull Myself Together' and 'Attention To Me', and, with Anne's return, became a quintet for a while until Linda married former Harmony Grass drummer Brian Hudson and retired from the group. Linda is sometimes known as the 'Naughty Nolan' because she launched her solo career by posing near-naked for publicity shots. Phenomenal success for the Nolans in Japan and Eire coincided with further minor chart appearances in the UK, as well as best-selling albums. Coleen, Bernadette and Denise have each recorded solo singles, while Linda and Coleen enjoyed a minor hit as the Young And Moody Band with 'Don't Do That'. In 1994 Coleen left to have a baby, and a year later, Anne and Maureen became a Nolans duo when Bernadette, who had been the lead singer with the group since she was 13, decided to go solo. Coleen is married to Shane Ritchie, who took over the leading role from Craig McLachlan in the acclaimed 1993 London revival of the musical, *Grease*.

●ALBUMS: *The Singing Nolans* (Nevis 1972)★★★, *The Nolan Sisters* (Hanover Grand 1977)★★★, *Nolan Sisters* (Epic 1979)★★★, *Making Waves* (Epic 1980)★★★★, *Portrait* (Epic 1982)★★★★, *Altogether* (Epic 1982)★★★, *Harmony* (Premier 1983)★★★, *Girls Just Wanna Have Fun* (Towerbell 1984)★★, *Love Songs* (Hallmark 1985)★★, *Tenderly* (1986)★★.

●COMPILATIONS: *20 Giant Hits* (Target 1977)★★★, *Best Of The Nolan Sisters Vol. 1* (Hallmark 1979)★★★, *Best Of The Nolan Sisters Vol 2* (Hallmark 1979)★★★, *The Nolan Sisters Collection* (Pickwick 1980)★★★, *I'm In The Mood For Dancing* (Hallmark 1983)★★★, *Times Gone By* (Spartan 1985)★★★, *Best Of The Nolans* (Ditto 1988)★★★.

●FURTHER READING: *In The Mood For Stardom: The Nolans*, Kim Treasurer.

NOONE, PETER

b. Peter Blair Dennis Bernard Noone, 5 November 1947, Manchester, England. After studying singing at the Manchester School of Music and Drama, the teenage Noone won a part in the television series *Coronation Street*. After taking up piano and guitar he talked his way into the Heartbeats, which later became Herman's Hermits. In the Herman guise, Noone scored a series of million-selling singles in the 60s before finally launching a solo career in 1970. A cover of David Bowie's 'Oh You Pretty Things' made the UK Top 10, but subsequent releases were largely ignored. By 1980 he was fronting a more contemporary-sounding group, the Tremblers, but in spite of his change of image, no hits were forthcoming. Two years later he reverted to his original career, taking an acting role in *The Pirates Of Penzance*. He subsequently moved to the USA where he hosts a music television show

●FILMS: *Hold On* (1965).

NRBQ

Formed in Miami, Florida, USA, 1968, the origins of NRBQ (New Rhythm & Blues Quintet) were actually in Louisville, Kentucky, a few years earlier. There, Terry Adams (keyboards) and Steve Ferguson (guitar) were members of a group called Merseybeats USA. Moving to Miami, the pair joined with New York musicians Frank Gadler (vocals) and Jody St. Nicholas (b. Joseph (Joey) Spampinato; bass/vocals), then working with a group named the Seven Of Us. Tom Staley (drums) completed the line-up and the group relocated to New Jersey. They were signed by Columbia Records in New York

and released their self-titled debut album in 1969. From the start NRBQ's music was an eclectic mix incorporating rockabilly, *avant garde* jazz, pop-rock, country, blues and novelty songs - their first album included songs by both early rocker Eddie Cochran and spacy-jazz musician Sun Ra. From the beginning and into the 90s, the group's live show included a large range of covers in addition to their own material - they claim a repertoire of thousands of songs. Humour marked both their recordings and concerts, where they would often grant audience requests to perform unlikely cover songs. Their second album, *Boppin' The Blues*, was a collaboration with rockabilly legend Carl Perkins. Like their debut, it was praised by critics but the group was dropped from Columbia. In the 70s they recorded for numerous labels, including Kama Sutra and Mercury Records before launching their own Red Rooster label in the late 70s.

Personnel changes during the 70s resulted in the group being trimmed to a quartet: Adams and Spampinato (reverting to his true name) remained from the original band, while guitarist Al Anderson, formerly of Connecticut's Wildweeds, joined in 1971; Tom Ardolino (drums) joined in 1974, since when the group has retained that line-up into the 90s. A good-time spirit and down-to-earth attitude towards performing marked NRBQ's live show, which could be unpredictable. The band recorded an album backing country singer Skeeter Davis (who later married Spampinato) and also the ex-Lovin' Spoonful singer John Sebastian in concert a number of times. For a while they were managed by a wrestling star, Captain Lou Albano, with whom they recorded a single. Spampinato appeared as a member of the house band in the Chuck Berry concert film *Hail! Hail! Rock 'N' Roll* and Adams recorded with jazz artist Carla Bley. Anderson has released two solo albums. In 1989 NRBQ signed to Virgin Records and released *Wild Weekend*, their first album to chart since the 1969 debut.

●ALBUMS: *NRBQ* (Columbia 1969)★★★, with Carl Perkins *Boppin' The Blues* (Columbia 1970)★★★, *Scraps* (Kama Sutra 1972)★★, *Workshop* (Kama Sutra 1973)★★, *All Hopped Up* (Red Rooster 1977)★★★, *At Yankee Stadium* (Red Rooster 1978)★★★★, *Kick Me Hard* (Red Rooster 1979)★★★, *Tiddlywinks* (Red Rooster 1980)★★★, *Tapdancin' Bats* (Red Rooster 1983)★★, *Grooves In Orbit* (Red Rooster 1983)★★, with Skeeter Davis *She Sings, They Play* (1985)★★, *God Bless Us All* (Rounder 1988)★★, *Diggin' Uncle Q* (1988)★★, *Wild Weekend* (Virgin 1989)★★, *Honest Dollar* (Ryko 1992), *Message For The Mess Age Forward* (Rhino 1994)★★★.

●COMPILATIONS: *Peek-a-Boo: The Best Of NRBQ* (Rhino 1990)★★★★, *Stay With Me: The Best Of* (Columbia 1993)★★★.

NUCLEUS

The doyen of British jazz-rock groups, Nucleus was formed in 1969 by trumpeter Ian Carr. He was joined by Chris Spedding (guitar, ex-Battered Ornaments), John

Marshall (drums) and Karl Jenkins (keyboards). The quartet was signed to the distinctive progressive outlet, Vertigo, and their debut, *Elastic Rock*, is arguably their exemplary work. The same line-up completed *We'll Talk About It Later*, but Spedding's subsequent departure heralded a bewildering succession of changes which undermined the group's potential. Carr nonetheless remained its driving force, a factor reinforced when *Solar Plexus*, a collection the trumpeter had intended as a solo release, became the unit's third album. In 1972 both Jenkins and Marshall left the group to join fellow fusion act, Soft Machine, and Nucleus became an inadvertent nursery for this 'rival' ensemble. Later members Roy Babbington and Alan Holdsworth also defected, although Carr was able to maintain an individuality despite such damaging interruptions. Subsequent albums, however, lacked the innovatory purpose of those first releases and Nucleus was dissolved during the early 80s. Nucleus took the jazz/rock genre further into jazz territory with skill, melody and a tremendous standard of musicianship. Their first three albums are vital in any comprehensive rock or jazz collection.

●ALBUMS: *Elastic Rock* (Vertigo 1970)★★★, *We'll Talk About It later* (Vertigo 1970)★★★, *Solar Plexus* (Vertigo 1971)★★★★, *Belladonna* (Vertigo 1972)★★★, *Labyrinth* (Vertigo 1973)★★★, *Roots* (Vertigo 1973)★★★, *Under The Sun* (Vertigo 1974)★★★, *Snake Hips Etcetera* (Vertigo 1975)★★★, *Direct Hits* (Vertigo 1976)★★★, *In Flagrante Delicto* (1978)★★★, *Out Of The Long Dark* (1979)★★, *Awakening* (1980)★★, *Live At The Theaterhaus* (1985)★★★.

NUGENT, TED

b. 13 December 1949, Detroit, Michigan, USA. Excited by 50s rock 'n' roll, Nugent taught himself the rudiments of guitar playing at the age of eight. As a teenager he played in the Royal Highboys and Lourds, but this formative period ended in 1964 upon his family's move to Chicago. Here, Nugent assembled the Amboy Dukes, which evolved from garage band status into a popular, hard rock attraction. He led the group throughout its various permutations, assuming increasing control as original members dropped out of the line-up. In 1974 a revitalized unit - dubbed Ted Nugent And The Amboy Dukes - completed the first of two albums for Frank Zappa's DiscReet label, but in 1976 the guitarist abandoned the now-anachronistic suffix and embarked on a fully-fledged solo career. Derek St. Holmes (guitar), Rob Grange (bass) and Cliff Davies (drums) joined him for *Ted Nugent* and *Free For All*, both of which maintained the high-energy rock of previous incarnations. However, it was as a live attraction that Nugent made his mark - he often claimed to have played more gigs per annum than any other artist or group. Ear-piercing guitar work and vocals - 'If it's too loud you're too old' ran one tour motto - were accompanied by a cultivated 'wild man' image, where the

artist would appear in loin-cloth and headband, brandishing the bow and arrow with which he claimed to hunt food for his family. Trapeze stunts, genuine guitar wizardry and a scarcely self-deprecating image ('If there had been blind people at the show they would have walked away seeing') all added to the formidable Nugent persona. The aggression of a Nugent concert was captured on the platinum-selling *Double Live Gonzo*, which featured many of his best-loved stage numbers, including 'Cat Scratch Fever', 'Motor City Madness' and the enduring 'Baby Please Don't Go'. Charlie Huhn (guitar) and John Sauter (bass) replaced St. Holmes and Grange for *Weekend Warriors*, and the same line-up remained intact for *State Of Shock* and *Scream Dream*. In 1981 Nugent undertook a worldwide tour fronting a new backing group, previously known as the D.C. Hawks, comprising Mike Gardner (bass), Mark Gerhardt (drums) and three guitarists, Kurt, Rick and Verne Wagoner. The following year the artist left Epic for Atlantic Records, and in the process established a new unit which included erstwhile sidemen Derek St. Holmes (vocals) and Carmine Appice (drums, ex-Vanilla Fudge). Despite such changes, Nugent was either unwilling, or unable, to alter the formula which had served him so well in the 70s. Successive solo releases offered little new and the artist drew greater publicity for appearances on talk shows and celebrity events. In 1989 Nugent teamed up with Tommy Shaw (vocals/guitar, ex-Styx), Jack Blades (bass, ex-Night Ranger) and Michael Cartellone (drums) to form the successful 'supergroup', Damn Yankees. After the Damn Yankees were put on hold in 1994, Nugent resumed his solo career for his first studio album in seven years. Reunited with Derek St. Holmes, *Spirit Of The Wild* also saw Nugent return to his usual lyrical posturing, including the pro-firearms 'I Shoot Back' and 'Kiss My Ass', a hate list featuring Courtney Love (of Hole) and the cartoon characters *Beavis and Butthead* among its targets.

●ALBUMS: *Ted Nugent* (Epic 1975)★★★, *Free For All* (Epic 1976)★★★, *Cat Scratch Fever* (Epic 1977)★★★★, *Double Live Gonzo* (Epic 1978)★★★, *Weekend Warriors* (Epic 1978)★★★, *State Of Shock* (Epic 1979)★★★, *Scream Dream* (Epic 1980)★★★, *Intensities In Ten Cities* (Epic 1981)★★★, *Nugent* (Atlantic 1982)★★, *Penetrator* (Atlantic 1984)★★, *Little Miss Dangerous* (Atlantic 1986)★★, *If You Can't Lick 'Em ... Lick 'Em* (Atlantic 1988)★★, *Spirit Of The Wild* (Atlantic 1995)★★.

●COMPILATIONS: *Great Gonzos: The Best Of Ted Nugent* (Epic 1981)★★★★, *Anthology: Ted Nugent* (Raw Power 1986)★★★.

●VIDEOS: *Whiplash Bash* (Hendring 1990).

●FURTHER READING: *The Legendary Ted Nugent*, Robert Holland.

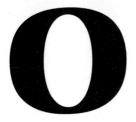

O'CONNOR, DES

b. January 1932. O'Connor served an apprenticeship on UK pop package tours - including that headlined by Buddy Holly - in the 50s before elevation to television as a smooth comedian-interlocutor. In the wake of Ken Dodd's mid-60s record success as a balladeer, EMI Records decided to try O'Connor's light baritone on a few exploratory singles in the same vein. He struck gold in 1967 when 'Careless Hands' reached the Top 10. The next year had him at the top with 'I Pretend', composed by Les Reed and Barry Mason. Further success followed with the excellent '1-2-3 O'Leary'. An up-tempo approach with 'Dick-A-Dum-Dum' (a paeon to London's fashionable King's Road) precipitated a gradual slip from the hit parade - though he retained a strong following in the UK. He was also the good-natured victim of derogatory *bon mots* from showbusiness peers about his singing but he enjoyed a measure of revenge in 1980 when his hosting of an ITV chat-show hoisted *Just For You* to number 17 - his highest position in the album chart since *I Pretend*. O'Connor has been at the sharp end of the critics' pens for many years, especially with regard to his musical ablity. He seems to have taken the sniping with remarkable good nature.
●ALBUMS: *I Pretend* (Columbia 1968)★★★, *With Love* (Columbia 1970)★★★, *Sing A Favourite Song* (Pye 1972)★★★, *Des O'Connor Collection* (Pickwick 1978)★★★, *With Feelings* (Hallmark 1979)★★★, *Christmas With...* (Pickwick 1979)★★★, *Careless Hands* (Ideal 1980)★★★, *Des O'Connor Remembers* (Warwick 1980)★★★, *This Is Des O'Connor* (EMI 1980)★★★, *Just For You* (Warwick 1980)★★★, *Golden Hits Des O'Connor* (MFP 1983)★★★, *Des O'Connor Now* (Telstar 1984)★★★, *The Great Songs* (Telstar 1985)★★★, *Anytime* (Hour Of Pleasure 1986)★★★, *True Love Ways* (Arista 1987)★★★, *Portrait* (1992)★★★.

O'JAYS

The core of this long-standing soul group, Eddie Levert (b. 16 June 1942) and Walter Williams (b. 25 August 1942) sang together as a gospel duo prior to forming the Triumphs in 1958. This doo-wop-influenced quintet was completed by William Powell, Bill Isles and Bobby Massey, and quickly grew popular around its hometown of Canton, Ohio, USA. The same line-up then recorded as the Mascots before taking the name the O'Jays after Cleveland disc jockey Eddie O'Jay, who had given them considerable help and advice. Having signed to Imperial Records in 1963, the O'Jays secured their first hit with 'Lonely Drifter', which was followed by an imaginative reworking of Benny Spellman's 'Lipstick Traces' (1965) and 'Stand In For Love' (1966). Despite gaining their first R&B Top 10 entry with 'I'll Be Sweeter Tomorrow (Than I Was Today)' (1967), the group found it difficult to maintain a constant profile, and were reduced to a four-piece following Isles' departure. However, they were in-demand session singers, backing artists including Nat 'King' Cole and the Ronettes. In 1968 the group met producers (Kenny) Gamble And (Leon) Huff with whom they recorded, unsuccessfully, on the duo's short-lived Neptune label. The line-up was reduced further in 1972 when Bobby Massey left. Paradoxically the O'Jays then began their most fertile period when Gamble And Huff signed them to Philadelphia International. The vibrant 'Back Stabbers', a US Top 3 hit, established the group's style, but the preachy 'Love Train', with its plea for world harmony, introduced the protest lyrics that were a feature of later releases 'Put Your Hands Together' (1973) and 'For The Love Of Money' (1974). *Back Stabbers*, meanwhile, rapidly achieved classic status and is regarded by many as Gamble And Huff's outstanding work. In 1975 Sammy Strain joined the line-up from Little Anthony And The Imperials when ill health forced William Powell to retire from live performances. This founder-member continued to record with the group until his death on 25 April 1976. 'Message In Our Music' (1976) and 'Use Ta Be My Girl' (1977) confirmed the O'Jays' continued popularity as they survived Philly soul's changing fortunes, with *So Full Of Love* (1978) achieving platinum sales. But as the genre felt the ravages of fashion so the group also suffered. The early 80s were commercially fallow, until *Love Fever* (1985) restated their direction with its blend of funk and rap. Two years later the O'Jays were unexpectedly back at the top of the soul chart with 'Lovin' You', confirming their status as one of soul music's most durable groups. The commercial resurrection was due in no small part to their renewed relationship with Gamble And Huff. Their output in the 90s has failed to achieve the success of their 70s releases, though Eddie's son, Gerald Levert, both as a member of LeVert and solo, has kept the family name alive. In 1995 Eddie, who had previously appeared alongside his son on several occasions, recorded an album of duets with Gerald for release as *Father And Son*. He is also the spokesperson for the social/business collective 100 Black Men, reaffirming the O'Jays' long-standing commitment to social change.
●ALBUMS: *Comin' Through* (Imperial 1965)★★★, *Soul Sounds* (Imperial 1967)★★★, *O'Jays* (Minit 1967)★★★, *Full Of Soul* (Minit 1968)★★★, *Back On Top* (Bell 1968)★★★, *The O'Jays In Philadelphia* (Neptune 1969)★★★, *Back Stabbers* (Philadelphia International 1972)★★★★, *Ship Ahoy* (Philadelphia International 1973)★★★★, *Live In London* (Philadelphia International 1974)★★, *Survival* (Philadelphia International

1975)★★★, *Family Reunion* (Philadelphia International 1975)★★, with the Moments *The O'Jays Meet The Moments* (Philadelphia International 1975)★★★, *Message In The Music* (Philadelphia International 1976)★★★, *Travelin' At The Speed Of Thought* (Philadelphia International 1977)★★, *So Full Of Love* (Philadelphia International 1978)★★★, *Identify Yourself* (Philadelphia International 1979)★★★, *Year 2000* (TSOP 1980)★★, *Peace* (Phoenix 1981)★★, *My Favourite Person* (Philadelphia International 1982)★★, *When I See You Again* (Epic 1983)★★, *Love And More* (Philadelphia International 1984)★★★, *Love Fever* (Philadelphia International 1985)★★★, *Close Company* (Philadelphia International 1985)★★★, *Let Me Touch You* (EMI 1987)★★★, *Seriously* (EMI 1989)★★, *Emotionally Yours* (EMI 1991)★★, *Heartbreaker* (EMI 1993)★★.

●COMPILATIONS: *Collectors' Items: Greatest Hits* (Philadelphia International 1977)★★★, *Greatest Hits* (Philadelphia International 1984)★★★★, *From The Beginning* (Chess 1984)★★★, *Working On Your Case* (Stateside 1985)★★★, *Reflections In Gold 1973-1982* (Charly 1988)★★★, *Love Train: The Best Of ...* (Columbia/Legacy 1995)★★★★.

O'SULLIVAN, GILBERT

b. Raymond O'Sullivan, 1 December 1946, Waterford, Eire. O'Sullivan's family moved to Swindon, England, during his childhood and after attending art college there, the singer was signed to CBS Records. Under the name Gilbert he issued the unsuccessful 'What Can I Do?' and soon moved on to Phil Solomon's Major Minor label, where 'Mr Moody's Garden' also failed. Seeking a new manager, Gilbert wrote to the starmaking Gordon Mills, who had already launched Tom Jones and Engelbert Humperdinck to international success. Mills was impressed by the demo tape enclosed and relaunched the artist on his new MAM label under the name Gilbert O'Sullivan. The debut 'Nothing Rhymed' had some clever lyrics and a strong melody. It reached the UK Top 10 in late 1970 and television audiences were amused or puzzled by the sight of O'Sullivan with his pudding basin haircut, short trousers and flat cap. The 'Bisto Kid' image was retained for the first few releases and the singer initially acted the part of an anti-star. At one point, he was living in the grounds of Mills' Weybridge house on a meagre £10-a-week allowance. His hit-making potential was undeniable and his ability to pen a memorable melody recalled the urbane charm of Paul McCartney. Early UK successes included 'We Will', 'No Matter How I Try' and 'Alone Again (Naturally)'. Any suspicions that O'Sullivan's charm was largely parochial were dashed when the latter single broke through in America, peaking at number 1 and selling over a million copies. The debut album, *Himself*, was also highly accomplished and included the radio favourite 'Matrimony', which would have provided a sizeable hit if released as a single. O'Sullivan went on to become one of the biggest-selling

artists of 1972. That year he enjoyed two consecutive UK number 1s with 'Clair' (written in honour of Mills's daughter) and 'Get Down'. These singles also reached the US Top 10. By this time, O'Sullivan's image had radically changed and he began to appreciate the superstar trappings enjoyed by Mills' other acts.

O'Sullivan's second album, *Back To Front*, reached number 1 in the UK and his appeal stretched across the board, embracing teen and adult audiences. For a time, he seemed likely to rival and even excel Elton John as Britain's most successful singer-songwriter export. Although further hits were forthcoming with 'Ooh Baby', 'Happiness Is Me And You' and 'Christmas Song', it was evident that his appeal had declined by the mid-70s. Following the UK Top 20 hit 'I Don't Love You But I Think I Like You' in the summer of 1975, his chart career ceased. After a spectacular falling out with Mills, he left MAM and returned to CBS, the label that had launched his career. Five years on, only one hit, 'What's In A Kiss?', emerged from the association. Minus Mills, it seemed that the superstar of the mid-70s was incapable of rekindling his once illustrious career. His disillusionment culminated in a High Court battle against his former manager and record company which came before Justice Mars Jones in the spring of 1982. The judge not only awarded O'Sullivan substantial damages and had all agreements with MAM set aside, but decreed that all the singer's master tapes and copyrights should be returned. The case made legal history and had enormous repercussions for the British music publishing world. Despite his court victory over the starmaking Mills, however, O'Sullivan has so far failed to re-establish his career as a major artist. A series of albums have appeared on the Park label and Sullivan now caters for a small but loyal following.

●ALBUMS: *Himself* (MAM 1971)★★★, *Back To Front* (MAM 1973)★★★★, *I'm A Writer Not A Fighter* (MAM 1973)★★★, *Stranger In My Own Backyard* (MAM 1974)★★, *Southpaw* (1977)★★, *Off Centre* (Columbia 1980)★★, *Life And Rhymes* (Columbia 1982)★★, *Frobisher Drive* (1988)★★, *In The Key Of G* (Chrysalis 1989)★★, *Sounds Of The Loop* (Park 1992)★★, *Live In Japan 1993* (Park 1993)★★, *By Larry* (Park 1994)★★, *Every Song Has It's Play* (Park 1995)★★.

●COMPILATIONS: *Greatest Hits* (MAM 1976)★★★, *20 Golden Greats* (K-Tel 1981)★★, *20 Of The Very Best* (Hallmark 1981)★★, *20 Golden Pieces Of Gilbert O' Sullivan* (Bulldog 1985)★★, *16 Golden Classics* (1986)★★, *Greatest Hits* (Big Time 1988)★★★.

OHIO PLAYERS

Formed in Dayton, Ohio, USA, in 1959, this multi-talented unit originated from three members of the Ohio Untouchables, Leroy 'Sugarfoot' Bonner, Clarence 'Satch' Satchell and Marshall Jones. They forged a reputation as a powerful instrumental group by providing the backing to the Falcons, whose R&B classic, 'I Found A Love' (1962), featured singer Wilson Pickett. The

Players began recording in their own right that same year, but did not achieve a notable success until the following decade when they embarked on a series of striking releases for the Westbound label after brief sessions for both Compass and Capitol Records. The group's experimental funk mirrored the work George Clinton had forged with Funkadelic for the same outlet and in 1973 the septet - Bonner, Satchell, Jones, Jimmy 'Diamond' Williams, Marvin 'Merv' Pierce, Billy Beck, Ralph 'Pee Wee' Middlebrook - had a massive R&B smash with the irrepressible 'Funky Worm'. The Players later switched to Mercury where their US hits included 'Fire' (1974) and 'Love Rollercoaster' (1975), both of which topped the soul and pop charts. 'Who'd She Coo?' became the group's last substantial hit the following year and although success did continue throughout the rest of the 70s, their releases grew increasingly predictable. The group had become renowned for their sexually explicit album covers, suggesting the possibilities of a jar of honey, or depicting macho males dominating scantily clad subservient females - and vice versa. However, their musical credibility was such that the unit's version of 'Over The Rainbow' was played at Judy Garland's funeral. Williams and Beck left the line-up in 1979 to form a new group, Shadow. A reshaped Ohio Players recorded throughout the 80s, and scored a minor soul hit in 1988 with 'Sweat'.

●ALBUMS: *First Impressions* (1968)★★, *Observations In Time* (1968)★★, *Pain* (Westbound 1972)★★★, *Pleasure* (Westbound 1973)★★★, *Ecstasy* (Westbound 1973)★★★, *Skin Tight* (Mercury 1974)★★, *Climax* a collection of out-takes (Westbound 1974)★★, *Fire* (Mercury 1974)★★★★, *Honey* (Mercury 1975)★★★★, *Contradiction* (Mercury 1976)★★★, *Angel* (Mercury 1977)★, *Mr. Mean* (Mercury 1977)★★, *Jass-Ay-Lay-Dee* (Mercury 1978)★★, *Everybody Up* (Arista 1979)★★, *Tenderness* (Boardwalk 1981)★★, *Ouch!* (Epic 1982)★★, *Graduation* (Air City 1985)★★, *Orgasm* (1993)★★.

●COMPILATIONS: *Greatest Hits* (Westbound 1975)★★★, *Rattlesnake* (Westbound 1975)★★, *Ohio Players Gold* (Mercury 1976)★★★★, *Ohio Players* (Capitol 1977)★★, *The Best Of The Westbound Years* (Westbound 1991)★★★, *Funk On Fire: The Mercury Anthology* (Mercury 1997)★★★.

OLD GREY WHISTLE TEST, THE

The name was coined after a BBC commissionaire/doorman (presumably grey-suited and senior in years) would whistle the latest pop hit: if he whistled it it had passed the test of acceptability. With *Top Of The Pops* enjoying consistently high viewing figures in 1969, the UK's BBC Television station decided its music coverage should be complemented by a less chart-orientated show reflecting the growth of the 'underground'. An initial attempt at fulfilling this need was made with *How It Is* (retitled *How Late It Is* when moved to a late night format), produced by Tony Palmer. It is nowadays remembered chiefly for hosting the only British television appearance of Led Zeppelin (a performance of 'Communication Breakdown' which has subsequently been erased). When BBC2 show *Colour Me Pop* was also axed, it left the field clear for the arrival of *The Old Grey Whistle Test*, first broadcast on 21 September 1971. America performed two songs live in the studio, accompanied by various filmed clips, with the show presented by journalist Richard Williams. It ran weekly until July 1972. The shows documented appearances by some of music's most enduring performers - including Jerry Lee Lewis, David Bowie, Stevie Wonder, the Beach Boys and Muddy Waters - all in its first series. However, it was the arrival of disc jockey 'Whispering' Bob Harris for the beginning of the second series in September 1972 that gave the show its identity. Harris's personal tastes informed the selection of many of the artists, including Rick Wakeman, who was the most regular early performer. Yet *The Old Grey Whistle Test* also offered a melting pot of 70s music unavailable elsewhere, with blues, folk, fusion, jazz and singer-songwriters all performing in the unique 'live studio' format. Harris remained as host until the end of the seventh series in June 1978. With the arrival of punk he finally took a back seat behind disc jockey Annie Nightingale, joined in the early 80s by journalist David Hepworth. From September 1982 Hepworth became the main presenter with assistance from Mark Ellen, though both later returned to publishing with *Q*, *Select* and *Mojo* magazines. The show was revamped in the autumn of 1983 with the arrival of Andy Kershaw (alongside Hepworth and Ellen), but it survived only a further three years as Janet Street Porter pushed the channel into 'yoof' music. A brave attempt to provide a broadcast outlet for adult fans of rock and pop, *The Old Grey Whistle Test*, in spite of its evident flaws, prospered for nearly a decade and a half, and provided some of the best surviving footage (recently unearthed by the Windsong reissue company) of artists as diverse as the Who, Tim Buckley, Lynyrd Skynyrd, Jack Bruce, Can, Captain Beefheart, Fairport Convention, Nico and Siouxsie And The Banshees in their prime.

OLDFIELD, MIKE

b. 15 May 1953, Reading, Berkshire, England. Multi-instrumentalist Oldfield will forever be remembered for a piece of symphonic length music he wrote before his 20th birthday. *Tubular Bells* sold 12 million copies worldwide and topped the charts in the USA and UK, staying in both for more than five years. He began his career providing acoustic guitar accompaniment to folk songs sung by his older sister, Sally Oldfield, who often appeared in Reading's pubs and clubs with Marianne Faithfull. Mike and Sally recorded *Sallyangie* together before he left to join Kevin Ayers And The Whole World, with whom he played bass and guitar for a short period. He continued working on his own material and produced a demo of instrumental music which later became *Tubular Bells*. Several record companies rejected the piece but entrepreneur Richard Branson, the head of Virgin stores, recognized its marketing potential. He asked Oldfield to re-record the demo in the recently acquired Manor Studios and it became one of Virgin's first releases. The 49-minute long piece was a series of basic melodies from folk, rock and classical sources which featured an array of different instruments, all played by Oldfield, and was introduced by guest master of ceremonies, Viv Stanshall. Excerpts from it were used in the horror film, *The Exorcist*, and a shortened version was released as a single in 1974.

On *Hergest Ridge* he attempted to capture Berkshire's pastoral beauty and largely succeeded, although matching the impact of *Tubular Bells* was clearly impossible and many critics dubbed the album 'Son of Tubular Bells' because of the similarity. It reached the top of the UK charts but, like all his subsequent album releases, it did not chart in the USA. Along with arranger, Dave Bedford, a former collaborator of Kevin Ayers, he scored *Tubular Bells* and a version recorded by the Royal Philharmonic Orchestra was released in 1975. *Ommadawn* featured the uillean pipes playing of the Chieftains' Paddy Moloney and a team of African drummers. It sold well but the critical response was that his introspective music had become over-formularized over the three albums. Virgin also saw the records as complementary works and packaged them together in 1976 as *Boxed*. Oldfield had two consecutive Christmas hits in 1975 and 1976 with the traditional 'In Dulci Jubilo' and 'Portsmouth'.

Around 1977-78, the shy, withdrawn Oldfield underwent a programme of self-assertiveness with the Exegesis method. The result was a complete reversal of personality and Oldfield took the opportunity in music press interviews to retaliate, almost to the point of parody, to accusations of limp, neo-hippie blandness and strongly defended himself against pillorying by the nascent punk movement. *Incantations* drew strongly on disco influences and *Exposed* was recorded at various concerts where Oldfield played with up to 50 other musicians. In 1979 Oldfield also recorded a version of the theme tune to the popular BBC television show, *Blue Peter*. Entitled 'Barnacle Bill', it was released as a charity single and was subsequently adopted by the programme as a revamped signature tune. It was retained as such up to the late 80s *Platinum*, *QE2* and *Five Miles Out* caught Oldfield slightly out of step with his contemporaries as he tried to hone his songwriting and avoid repeating himself. Hall And Oates recorded a version of 'Family Man', which had missed out as a single for Oldfield, and it became a Top 20 hit in the UK in 1983. Oldfield began working with soprano Maggie Reilly and she sang on the hit 'Moonlight Shadow' from *Crises*, where other guests included Roger Chapman (Family/Chapman Whitney). After *Discovery* he wrote the music for the award-winning film *The Killing Fields*. On *Islands* he was joined by further guest vocalists Bonnie Tyler and Kevin Ayers. Even though he was now

writing to a more standard pop structure, Oldfield found himself no longer in vogue and his music was largely portrayed in the music press as anachronistic. *Earth Moving*, with contributions from Maggie Reilly, Anita Hegerland and Chris Thompson (ex-Manfred Mann) failed to challenge the prevailing modern view. It appears that *Tubular Bells* will always ring rather too loudly and diminish most of Oldfield's other work, certainly in terms of commercial acceptance, but he continues releasing records welcomed by a large cult following which apparently cares little about his low profile and the scarcity of live appearances. In 1992 he worked with Trevor Horn on *Tubular Bells II* to mark the 20th anniversary of the original album. The album's success resulted in increased sales for the original *Tubular Bells* and led to a spectacular live concert of the new version.

● ALBUMS: with Sally Oldfield *Sallyangie* (Transatlantic 1968)★★, *Tubular Bells* (Virgin 1973)★★★★, *Hergest Ridge* (Virgin 1974)★★★, with the Royal Philharmonic Orchestra *The Orchestral Tubular Bells* (Virgin 1975)★★★, *Ommadawn* (Virgin 1975)★★★, *Incantations* (Virgin 1978)★★, *Exposed* (Virgin 1979)★★, *Platinum* (Virgin 1979)★★, *QE2* (Virgin 1980)★★, *Five Miles Out* (Virgin 1982)★★, *Crises* (Virgin 1983)★★, *Discovery* (Virgin 1984)★★, *The Killing Fields* film soundtrack (Virgin 1984)★★, *Islands* (Virgin 1987)★★, *Earth Moving* (Virgin 1989)★★, *Amarok* (Virgin 1990)★★, *Heaven's Open* (Virgin 1991)★★, *Tubular Bells II* (Warners 1992)★★★, *The Songs Of Distant Earth* (Warners 1994)★★, *Voyager* (Warners 1996)★★.

● COMPILATIONS: *Boxed* (Virgin 1976)★★★, *The Complete Mike Oldfield* (Virgin 1985)★★★.

● VIDEOS: *The Wind Chimes* (Virgin Vision 1988), *Essential Mike Oldfield* (Virgin Vision 1988), *Elements* (1993).

● FURTHER READING: *True Story Of The Making Of Tubular Bells*, Richard Newman. *Mike Oldfield: A Man And His Music*, Sean Moraghan.

101ERS

Formed in London in May 1974, the 101ers made their performing debut four months later at the Telegraph pub in Brixton. Led by guitarist/vocalist Joe Strummer, the group established itself on a fading pub-rock circuit about to be undermined by the advent of punk. Support slots by the Sex Pistols confirmed Strummer's growing agitation and he left to join the Clash in June 1976. The 101ers then broke up with Clive Timperley (guitar) later joining the Passions. Dan Kelleher (bass) moved on to the Derelicts and Richard Dudanski (drums) went on to work with the Raincoats and Public Image Limited. The group was commemorated by 'Keys To Your Heart', issued on the independent Chiswick label the following month. In 1981 Strummer sanctioned the release of *Elgin Avenue Breakdown*, a collection of live recordings, BBC sessions and studio out-takes. The material ranged from traditional R&B - 'Too Much Monkey Business',

'Route 66' - to ebullient originals which showed the singer's abrasive delivery already in place.
●ALBUMS: *Elgin Avenue Breakdown* (Andalucia 1981)★★.

ONLY ONES

The Only Ones were formed in 1976 with a line-up comprising: Peter Perrett (vocals/guitar), John Perry (guitar), Alan Mair (bass) and Mike Kellie (b. 24 March 1947, Birmingham, England; drums). Although touted as a new wave group, the unit included several old lags; Mair had previously worked with the Beatstalkers, while Kellie had drummed with Spooky Tooth, Peter Frampton and Balls. (Perrett's former band, England's Glory, had their demos released retrospectively after the Only Ones' demise.) After a promising independent single, 'Lovers Of Today', the group were signed by CBS Records and made their debut with the searing opus, 'Another Girl, Another Planet' - one of the new wave's most enduring songs. Front man Perrett, with his leopard-skin jacket and Lou Reed drawl, won considerable music press attention and the group's self-titled debut album was very well received. A second self-produced collection, *Even Serpents Shine,* was also distinctive, but internal group friction and disagreements with their record company hampered their progress. Producer Colin Thurston took control of *Baby's Got A Gun,* which included a guest appearance by Pauline Murray, but lacked the punch of their earlier work. With sales dwindling, CBS dropped the group from their roster and the Only Ones finally broke up in 1981, with Perrett by now in the throes of desperate drug addiction. Since that time the group, and in particular, Perrett, have frequently been hailed as influential figures. After over-coming his chemical dependencies, Perrett made known his intentions for a comeback in 1991. This eventually materialized when his new band, The One, took the stage at London's Underworld in January 1994. This coincided with reports that Perrett had now written over 40 new songs, and this was confirmed by the release of his debut solo album *Woke Up Sticky* in 1996.
●ALBUMS: *The Only Ones* (Columbia 1978)★★★, *Even Serpents Shine* (Columbia 1979)★★★, *Baby's Got A Gun* (Columbia 1980)★★, *Live At The BBC* (Strange Fruit 1995)★★★.
●COMPILATIONS: *Special View* (Columbia 1979)★★★★, *Remains* (Closer 1984)★★, *Alone In The Night* (Dojo 1986)★★, *The Only Ones Live In London* (Skyclad 1989)★★, *Only Ones Live* (Demon 1989)★★, *The Peel Sessions* (Strange Fruit 1989)★★★, *The Immortal Story* (Columbia 1992)★★★, *The Big Sleep* (Jungle 1993)★★★.

ORLANDO, TONY

b. 4 April 1944, New York, USA. An engaging, commercially minded singer, Orlando's early success came in 1961 when he achieved two US Top 40 entries with

'Halfway To Paradise' and 'Bless You'. The former, a superb Gerry Goffin/Carole King composition, was later successfully covered by Billy Fury, but Orlando enjoyed an emphatic UK hit when the latter reached number 5. Subsequent releases, including 'Happy Times' (1961) and 'Chills' (1962) were less impressive and Orlando began forging a backroom career in the music business, eventually rising to general manager of Columbia Records' April/Blackwood publishing division. In 1970 he was tempted back into recording when he formed the highly popular Dawn. A later solo album was recorded on the Elektra label. In 1986, Orlando celebrated 25 years in show business at Harrah's in Atlantic City, and, three years later, joined Dawn at the Hilton, Las Vegas, for a run through of most of their old hits, including 'Tie A Yellow Ribbon,' 'Candida', and 'Knock Three Times'.
●ALBUMS: *Bless You (And 11 Other Great Hits)* (Epic 1961)★★★, *Tony Orlando* (Elektra 1978)★★.
●COMPILATIONS: *Before Dawn* (Epic 1976)★★, *The Best Of Tony Orlando And Dawn* (Rhino 1995)★★★.
●FURTHER READING: *Tony Orlando,* Ann Morse.

ORLEANS

This mid-70s US group comprised John Hall (b. 1948, Baltimore, Maryland, USA guitar/vocal), Lance Hoppen (b. 1954, Bayshore, New York, USA bass), Wells Kelly (organ/vocal), Larry Hoppen (guitar/keyboards/vocal) and Jerry Marotta (drums). Drawing from a variety of sources - country, rock, soul and calypso - Orleans acquired a cult following as one of the more intelligent mainstream bands of their era. They signed with ABC in 1973, but were dropped after one album and were picked up by Elektra-Asylum. Success for their new label came immediately with 'Dance With Me' an American top 10 hit. They continued from strength to strength, until Hall left to pursue a solo career in 1977. Morotta departed soon afterwards. They were replaced by Bob Leinback and R.A. Martin, and although the new look Orleans were less well regarded, they enjoyed another US Top 10 hit in 1979 with 'Love Takes Time'.
●ALBUMS: *Orleans* later reissued as *Before The Dance* (ABC 1973)★★, *Let There Be Music* (Asylum 1975)★★★, *Walking And Dreaming* (Asylum 1976)★★★, *Forever* (Infinity 1979)★★, *Orleans* (1980)★★, *One Of A Kind* (1982)★★.

OSIBISA

Formed in London, England, in 1969 by three Ghanaian and three Caribbean musicians, Osibisa played a central role in developing an awareness of African music - in their case, specifically, West African highlife tinged with rock - among European and North American audiences in the 70s. Since then, Osibisa have suffered the fate of many once-celebrated 70s African-oriented performers. Their pioneering blend of rock and African rhythms has either been overlooked or downgraded for its lack of roots appeal. There is, in truth, some justification for this: Osibisa's style was too closely hitched to western rock, and too much of a fusion to survive the scrutiny of western audiences who, from the early 80s onwards, were looking for 'authentic' African music. But the group's towering achievements in the 70s should not be denigrated. The Ghanaian founder members of Osibisa - Teddy Osei (saxophone), Sol Amarfio (drums) and Mac Tontoh (trumpet, Osei's brother) - were seasoned members of the Accra highlife scene before they moved to London to launch their attack on the world stage. Osei and Amaflio had played in the Star Gazers, a top Ghanaian highlife band, before setting up the Comets, who scored a large West African hit with their 1958 single 'Pete Pete'. Tontoh was also a member of the Comets, before joining the Uhuru Dance Band, one of the first outfits to bring elements of jazz into Ghanaian highlife. The other founder members of Osibisa were Spartacus R, a Grenadian bass player, Robert Bailey (b. Trinidad; keyboards) and Wendel Richardson (b. Antigua; lead guitar). They were joined soon after their formation by the Ghanaian percussionist Darko Adams 'Potato' (b. 1932, d. 1 January 1995, Accra, Ghana). In 1962, Osei moved to London, where he was eventually given a scholarship by the Ghanaian government to study music. In 1964, he formed Cat's Paw, an early blueprint for Osibisa which blended highlife, rock and soul. In 1969, feeling the need for more accomplished African musicians within the line-up, he persuaded Tontoh and Amarfio to join him in London, where towards the end of the year Osibisa was born. The venture proved to be an immediate success, with the single 'Music For Gong Gong' a substantial hit in 1970 (three other singles later made the British Top 10: 'Sunshine Day', 'Dance The Body Music' and 'Coffee Song'). Osibisa's debut album displayed music whose rock references, especially in the guitar solos, combined with vibrant African cross rhythms. The band's true power only fully came across onstage, when African village scenarios and a mastery of rhythm and melody summoned up energy and spirit. *Woyaya* reached number 11 in the UK and its title track was later covered by Art Garfunkel. During the late 70s they spent much of their time on world tours, playing to particularly large audiences in Japan, India, Australia and Africa. In 1980 they performed a special concert at the Zimbabwean independence celebrations. By this time, however, Osibisa's star was in decline in Europe and America. The band continued touring and releasing records, but to steadily diminishing audiences. Business problems followed. After initially signing to MCA Records, Osibisa had changed labels several times, ending with Bronze Records. The moves reflected their growing frustration with British business, as each label in turn tried to persuade them to adapt their music to the disco style. Osibisa were prepared to make some concessions but only up to a point. In the mid-80s, the group directed their attention to the state of the music business in Ghana, planning a studio

and theatre complex which came to nothing following the withdrawal of state funding, and helping in the promotion of younger highlife artists. In 1984, Tontoh formed a London band to back three visiting Ghanaian musicians - A.B. Crentsil, Eric Agyeman and Thomas Frempong. An album, *Highlife Stars*, followed on Osibisa's own Flying Elephant label. Now effectively disbanded, Osibisa occasionally stage reunion concerts.
●ALBUMS: *Osibisa* (MCA 1971)★★★, *Woyaya* (MCA 1972)★★★★, *Heads* (MCA 1972)★★, *Happy Children* (Warners 1973)★★, *Superfly TNT* (1974)★★, *Osibirock* (Warners 1974)★★★, *Welcome Home* (1976)★★, *Ojah Awake* (1976)★★★, *Black Magic Night* (1977), *Mystic Energy* (Calibre 1981)★★, *Celebration* (Bronze 1983)★★, *Unleashed: Live In India 1981* (Magnet 1983)★★, *Live At The Marquee* (Premier 1984)★★★.
●COMPILATIONS: *The Best Of Osibisa* (MCA 1974)★★★, *The Best Of Osibisa* (BBC 1990)★★★★.
●VIDEOS: *Warrior* (Hendring 1990).

OSMOND, DONNY

b. Donald Clark Osmond, 9 December 1957, Ogden, Utah, USA. The most successful solo artist to emerge from family group the Osmonds, Donny was particularly successful at covering old hits. His first solo success came in the summer of 1971 with a version of Billy Sherrill's 'Sweet And Innocent', which reached the US Top 10. The follow-up, a revival of Gerry Goffin/Carole King's 'Go Away Little Girl' (previously a hit for both Steve Lawrence and Mark Wynter) took Osmond to the top of the US charts. 'Hey Girl', once a success for Freddie Scott, continued his US chart domination, which was now even more successful than that of the family group. By the summer of 1972, Osmondmania reached Britain, and a revival of Paul Anka's 'Puppy Love' gave Donny his first UK number 1. The singer's clean-cut good looks and perpetual smile brought him massive coverage in the pop press, while a back catalogue of hit songs from previous generations sustained his chart career. 'Too Young' and 'Why' both hit the UK Top 10, while 'The Twelfth Of Never' and 'Young Love' both reached number 1. His material appeared to concentrate on the pangs of adolescent love, which made him the perfect teenage idol for the period. In 1974, Donny began a series of duets with his sister Marie Osmond, which included more UK Top 10 hits with 'I'm Leaving It All Up To You' and 'Morning Side Of The Mountain'. It was clear that Donny's teen appeal was severely circumscribed by his youth and in 1977 he tried unsuccessfully to reach a more mature audience with *Donald Clark Osmond*. Although minor hits followed, the singer's appeal was waning alarmingly by the late 70s. After the break-up of the group in 1980, Donny went on to star in the 1982 revival of the musical *Little Johnny Jones*, which closed after only one night on Broadway, and ceased recording after the mid-70s. A decade later, a rugged Osmond returned with 'I'm In It For Love' and the more successful 'Soldier Of Love' which reached the US Top 30. Most agreed that his attempts at mainstream rock were much more impressive than anyone might have imagined. In the early 90s, Osmond proved his versatility once more when he played the lead in Canadian and North American productions of Andrew Lloyd Webber's musical *Joseph And The Amazing Technicolor Dreamcoat*.

●ALBUMS: *The Donny Osmond Album* (MGM 1971)★★, *To You With Love, Donny* (MGM 1971)★★, *Portrait Of Donny* (MGM 1972)★★, *Too Young* (MGM 1972)★★, *My Best Of You* (MGM 1972)★★, *Alone Together* (MGM 1973)★★, *A Time For Us* (MGM 1973)★★, *Donny* (MGM 1974)★★, *Discotrain* (Polydor 1976)★★, *Donald Clark Osmond* (Polydor 1977)★★, *Donny Osmond* (Virgin 1988)★★★, *Eyes Don't Lie* (Capitol 1990)★★. With Marie Osmond *I'm Leaving It All Up To You* (MGM 1974)★★, *Make The World Go Away* (MGM 1975)★★, *Donny And Marie - Featuring Songs From Their Television Show* (Polydor 1976)★★, *Deep Purple* (Polydor 1976)★★, *Donny And Marie - A New Season* (Polydor 1977)★★, *Winning Combination* (Polydor 1978)★★, *Goin' Coconuts* (Polydor 1978)★★.

OSMOND, LITTLE JIMMY

b. 16 April 1963, Canoga Park, California, USA. The youngest member of the Osmonds family, Jimmy unexpectedly emerged as a pre-teen idol in 1972. Overweight and cute, he was launched at the peak of Osmondmania and topped the Christmas charts in the UK with his singalong 'Long-Haired Lover From Liverpool'. In doing so, he became, at nine years of age, the youngest individual ever to reach number 1 in the UK up to that time. He returned to the charts during the next two years with Lavern Baker's old hit 'Tweedle Dee' and Eddie Hodges' 'I'm Gonna Knock On Your Door'. His brief popularity in Britain was eclipsed by fan mania in Japan where he was known as 'Jimmy Boy'. When the hits ceased and he grew up, he became successful as an entrepreneur and rock impresario.

●ALBUMS: *Killer Joe* (MGM 1972)★.

OSMOND, MARIE

b. 13 October 1959, Ogden, Utah, USA. Following the success of her elder siblings in the Osmonds, Marie launched her own singing career in late 1973. Her revival of Anita Bryant's 'Paper Roses' reached the US Top 5 and did even better in the UK, peaking at number 2. Following two solo albums, she successfully collaborated with her brother Donny Osmond on a series of duets. They enjoyed a transatlantic Top 10 hit with a version of Dale And Griffin's 'I'm Leaving It All Up To You' and repeated that achievement with a cover of Tommy Edwards' 'Morning Side Of The Mountain'. Marie simultaneously continued her solo career with a reworking of Connie Francis's 'Who's Sorry Now?' The brother and sister duo next moved into the country market with a version of Eddy Arnold's 'Make The World Go Away'. By early 1976, their popularity was still

strong and they featured in a one-hour variety television show titled *Donny And Marie*. The programme spawned a hit album and another UK/US hit with a revival of Nino Tempo And April Stevens' 'Deep Purple'. By 1977, the Mormon duo were covering Tamla/Motown material, duetting on Marvin Gaye And Tammi Terrell's 'Ain't Nothing Like The Real Thing'. The duets continued until 1978 and their last significant success was a cover of the Righteous Brothers' '(You're My) Soul And Inspiration'. That same year, Donny and Marie starred together in the movie *Goin' Coconuts*. Following the break-up of the Osmonds the sister continued with her own television series *Marie*. Thereafter, she moved successfully into country music and recorded several albums for the Curb label.

●ALBUMS: *Paper Roses* (MGM 1973)★★, *In My Little Corner Of The World* (MGM 1974)★★, *Who's Sorry Now?* (MGM 1975)★★, *This Is The Way That I Feel* (Polydor 1977)★★, *There's No Stopping Your Heart* (Capitol 1986)★★, *I Only Wanted You* (Capitol 1986)★★, *All In Love* (Capitol 1988)★★. With Donny Osmond *I'm Leaving It All Up To You* (MGM 1974)★★, *Make The World Go Away* (MGM 1975)★, *Donny And Marie - Featuring Songs From Their Television Show* (Polydor 1976)★★, *Deep Purple* (Polydor 1976)★★, *Donny And Marie - A New Season* (Polydor 1977)★★, *Winning Combination* (Polydor 1978)★★, *Goin' Coconuts* (Polydor 1978)★★.

OSMONDS

This famous family all-vocal group from Ogden, Utah, USA, comprised Alan Osmond (b. 22 June 1949), Wayne Osmond (b. 28 August 1951), Merrill Osmond (b. 30 April 1953), Jay Osmond (b. 2 March 1955) and Donny Osmond (b. 9 December 1957). The group first came to public notice following regular television appearances on the top-rated *Andy Williams Show*. From 1967-69, they also appeared on television's *Jerry Lewis Show*. Initially known as the Osmond Brothers they recorded for Andy Williams' record label Barnaby. By 1971, their potential was recognized by Mike Curb, who saw them as likely rivals to the star-studded Jackson 5. Signed to MGM Records, they recorded the catchy 'One Bad Apple', which topped the US charts for five weeks. Before long, they became a national institution, and various members of the family including Donny Osmond, Marie Osmond and Little Jimmy Osmond enjoyed hits in their own right. As a group, the primary members enjoyed a string of hits, including 'Double Lovin'', 'Yo Yo' and 'Down By The Lazy River'. By the time Osmondmania hit the UK in 1972, the group peaked with their ecologically-conscious 'Crazy Horses', complete with intriguing electric organ effects. Their clean-cut image and well-scrubbed good looks brought them immense popularity among teenagers and they even starred in their own cartoon series. Probably their most ambitious moment came with the evangelical concept album, *The Plan*, in which they attempted to express their Mormon beliefs. Released at the height of their success, the album reached number 6 in the UK. During the early to mid-70s, they continued to release successive hits, including 'Going Home', 'Let Me In' and 'I Can't Stop'. Their sole UK number 1 as a group was 'Love Me For A Reason', composed by Johnny Bristol. Their last major hit in the UK was 'The Proud One' in 1975, after which their popularity waned. The individual members continued to prosper in varying degrees, but the family group disbanded in 1980. Two years later, the older members of the group re-formed without Donny, and moved into the country market. During the mid-80s, they appeared regularly at the Country Music Festival in London, but their recorded output decreased.

●ALBUMS: *Osmonds* (MGM 1971)★★, *Homemade* (MGM 1971)★★, *Phase-III* (MGM 1972)★★, *The Osmonds 'Live'* (MGM 1972)★, *Crazy Horses* (MGM 1972)★★★, *The Plan* (MGM 1973)★★, *Our Best To You* (MGM 1974)★★, *Love Me For A Reason* (MGM 1974)★★, *I'm Still Gonna Need You* (MGM 1975)★★, *The Proud One* (MGM 1975)★★, *Around The World - Live In Concert* (MGM 1975)★, *Brainstorm* (Polydor 1976)★★, *The Osmonds Christmas Album* (Polydor 1976)★★, *Today* (1985)★★.

●COMPILATIONS: *The Osmonds Greatest Hits* (Polydor 1978)★★★, *The Very Best Of The Osmonds* (Polydor 1996)★★★.

●VIDEOS: *Very Best Of* (Wienerworld 1996).

●FURTHER READING: *At Last ... Donny!*, James Gregory. *The Osmond Brothers And The New Pop Scene*, Richard Robinson. *Donny And The Osmonds Backstage*, James Gregory. *The Osmond Story*, George Tremlett. *The Osmonds*, Monica Delaney. *On Tour With Donny & Marie And The Osmonds*, Lynn Roeder. *Donny And Marie Osmond: Breaking All The Rules*, Constance Van Brunt McMillan. *The Osmonds: The Official Story Of The Osmond Family*, Paul H. Dunn. *Donny And Marie*, Patricia Mulrooney Eldred.

OTWAY, JOHN

b. 2 October, 1952, Aylesbury, Buckinghamshire, England. The enigmatic madcap John Otway first came to prominence in the early 70s with his guitar/fiddle-playing partner Wild Willie Barrett. Otway's animated performances and unusual vocal style caught the attention of Pete Townshend, who produced the duo's first two Track label singles, 'Murder Man' and 'Louisa On A Horse'. Extensive gigging, highlighted by crazed and highly entertaining stage antics, won Otway and Barrett a loyal collegiate following and finally a minor hit with 'Really Free' in 1977. Its b-side, 'Beware Of The Flowers ('Cause I'm Sure They're Going To Get You Yeh)' was equally appealing and eccentric and augured well for further hits. Although Otway (with and without Barrett) soldiered on with syllable-stretching versions of Tom Jones's 'Green Green Grass Of Home' and quirky novelty workouts such as 'Headbutts', he remains a 70s curio, still locked into the UK college/club circuit.

●ALBUMS: *John Otway And Wild Willie Barrett* (Polydor 1977)★★★, *Deep And Meaningless* (Polydor 1978)★★★, *Where Did I Go Right* (Polydor 1979)★★★, *Way And Bar* (1980)★★, *All Balls And No Willy* (Empire 1982)★★, *The Wimp And The Wild* (1989)★★, *Under The Covers And Over The Top* (1992)★★, *Live!* (Amazing Feet 1994)★★★, *Premature Adulation* (Amazing Feet 1995)★★★.

●COMPILATIONS: *Gone With The Bin Or The Best Of Otway And Barrett* (Polydor 1981)★★★, *Greatest Hits* (Strike Back 1986)★★★.

●VIDEOS: *John Otway And Wild Willie Barrett* (ReVision 1990).

●FURTHER READING: *Cor Baby That's Really Me*, John Otway.

OUTLAWS (USA)

Formed in Tampa, Florida, USA in 1974, the Outlaws comprised Billy Jones (guitar), Henry Paul (guitar), Hugh Thomasson (guitar), Monty Yoho (drums) and Frank O'Keefe (bass) - who was superceded by Harvey Arnold in 1977. With Thomasson as main composer, they were respected by fans (if not critics) for a strong stage presentation and artistic consistency that hinged on an unreconstructed mixture of salient points from the Eagles, Allman Brothers and similarly guitar-dominated, denim-clad acts of the 70s. The first signing to Arista, their 1975 debut album - produced by Paul A. Rothchild - reached number 13 in *Billboard*'s chart. The set included the riveting lengthy guitar battle 'Green Grass And High Tides', which was the highlight of the group's live act. Singles success with 'There Goes Another Love Song' and 'Lady In Waiting' (the title track of their second album) was followed by regular touring. A coast-to-coast tour in 1976 and further less publicized work on the road necessitated the hire of a second drummer, David Dix, who was heard on 1978's in-concert *Bring It Back Alive* - the first without Paul (replaced by Freddy Salem) whose resignation was followed in 1979 by those of Yoho and Arnold. In 1981 the band was on the edge of the US Top 20 with the title track of *Ghost Riders* - a revival of Vaughn Monroe's much-covered ballad - but, when this proved their chart swansong, the outfit - with Thomasson the only remaining original member - disbanded shortly after *Les Hombres Malo*. Following modest success with two albums by the Henry Paul Band, its leader rejoined Thomasson in a re-formed Outlaws who issued *Soldiers Of Fortune* in 1986.

●ALBUMS: *The Outlaws* (Arista 1975)★★★★, *Lady In Waiting* (Arista 1976)★★★, *Hurry Sundown* (Arista 1977)★★, *Bring It Back Alive* (Arista 1978)★★★, *Playin' To Win* (Arista 1978)★★, *In The Eye Of The Storm* (Arista 1979)★★, *Ghost Riders* (Arista 1980)★★★, *Los Hombres Malo* (Arista 1982)★★, *Soldiers Of Fortune* (Pasha 1986)★★.

●COMPILATIONS: *Greatest Hits Of The Outlaws/High Tides Forever* (Arista 1982)★★★★, *On The Run Again* (Raw Power 1986)★★.

OZARK MOUNTAIN DAREDEVILS

One of country rock's more inventive exponents, the Ozark Mountain Daredevils featured the songwriting team of John Dillon (b. 6 February 1947, Stuttgart, Arkansas, USA; guitar, fiddle, vocals) and Steve Cash (b. 5 May 1946, Springfield, Missouri, USA; harmonica, vocals) with Randle Chowning (guitar, vocals), Buddy Brayfield (keyboards), Michael 'Supe' Granda (b. 24 December 1950, St. Louis, Missouri, USA; bass) and Larry Lee (b. 5 January 1947, Springfield, Missouri, USA; drums). The group were originally based in Springfield, Missouri. Their acclaimed debut album, recorded in London under the aegis of producer Glyn Johns, contained the US Top 30 single, 'If You Want To Get To Heaven', while a second success, 'Jackie Blue' which reached number 3, came from the group's follow-up collection, *It'll Shine When It Shines*. Recorded at Chowning's ranch, this excellent set showcased the Ozarks' strong harmonies and intuitive musicianship, factors maintained on subsequent releases, *The Car Over The Lake Album* and *Men From Earth*. A 1978 release, *It's Alive*, fulfilled the group's obligation to A&M Records and two years later they made their debut on CBS. Paradoxically the Ozarks' subsequent work lacked the purpose of those early releases although the unit continues to enjoy a cult popularity. The group was reactivated in the late 80s by Dillon and Cash with Granda, Steve Canaday (b. 12 September 1944, Springfield, Missouri, USA; drums) and D. Clinton Thompson (guitar) and the resulting album, *Modern History*, released on the UK independent Conifer label, found the Ozarks with a new lease of life.

●ALBUMS: *The Ozark Mountain Daredevils* (A&M 1974)★★★, *It'll Shine When It Shines* (A&M 1974)★★★★, *The Car Over The Lake Album* (A&M 1975)★★★★, *Men From Earth* (A&M 1976)★★★, *Don't Look Down* (A&M 1977)★★, *It's Alive* (A&M 1978)★★, *Ozark Mountain Daredevils* (Columbia 1980)★★, *Modern History* (Request/Conifer 1990)★★★.

●COMPILATIONS: *The Best Of The Ozark Mountain Daredevils* (A&M 1983)★★★.

PABLO CRUISE

Formed in 1973, this San Francisco-based group was founded when two ex-members of Stoneground, Cory Lerois (b. California, USA; keyboards) and Steve Price (b. California, USA; drums), were joined by Dave Jenkins (b. Florida, USA; guitar) and Bud Cockrell (b. Missouri, USA; bass) from It's A Beautiful Day. *Pablo Cruise* enjoyed critical acclaim for its astute blend of rich, jazz-influenced textures and accomplished instrumental work and while *Lifeline* enhanced this reputation, the quartet reaped commercial rewards when 'Whatcha Gonna Do?' from *A Place In The Sun* reached number 6 in the US singles chart. 'Love Will Find A Way' achieved the same position the following year, while promoting *Worlds Away* into the US Top 10, while 'Don't Want To Live Without It' also entered the Top 30 as the group adroitly added elements of disco to an already cosmopolitan approach. Former Santana bassist Bruce Day joined the group for *Part Of The Game*, replacing Cockrell, but he in turn was supplanted by John Pierce and second guitarist Angelo Rossi. Although *Reflector*, a collaboration with veteran R&B producer Tom Dowd, generated another hit in 'Cool Love', Pablo Cruise was increasingly viewed as moribund in the wake of the 'new wave'. Internal problems led to further wholesale changes and a period of inactivity followed the release of *Out Of Our Hands*, after which the line-up reverted to that of the original quartet.

●ALBUMS: *Pablo Cruise* (A&M 1975)★★, *Lifeline* (A&M 1976)★★★, *A Place In The Sun* (A&M 1977)★★, *Worlds Away* (A&M 1978)★★★, *Part Of The Game* (A&M 1979)★★, *Reflector* (A&M 1981)★★, *Out Of Our Hands* (A&M 1983)★★.

PALMER, ROBERT

b. Alan Palmer, 19 January 1949, Batley, Yorkshire, England. Britain's leading 'blue-eyed soul' singer has served a musical apprenticeship over four decades in which time he has participated in many different styles of music. In the UK progressive music boom of the late 60s, Palmer joined the interestingly named Mandrake Paddle Steamer part-time, so as not to interfere with his day job as a graphic designer. Shortly afterwards he left for the lure of London to join the highly respected but commercially unsuccessful Alan Bown Set, replacing the departed Jess Roden. The following year he joined the ambitious conglomeration Dada, an experimental jazz/rock unit featuring Elkie Brooks. Out of Dada came the much loved Vinegar Joe, with which he made three albums. Already having sights on a solo career, Robert had worked on what became his debut *Sneakin' Sally Through The Alley* in 1974. Backed by the Meters and Lowell George, the album was an artistic triumph. A long-term relationship with Chris Blackwell's Island Records began. Blackwell had faith in artists like Palmer and John Martyn and allowed their creativity to flow, over and above commercial considerations.

Little Feat appeared on his follow-up *Pressure Drop* after Palmer had relocated to New York. Still without significant sales, he moved to the luxury of the Bahamas, where he lived for many years. In 1976 he released *Some People Can Do What They Like* to mixed reaction. Palmer persevered, although he was better known in America for many years. His first major US hit single came in 1979 with the R&B Moon Martin rocker, 'Bad Case Of Loving You'. He collaborated with Gary Numan on *Clues* which became a bigger hit in the UK than in America. The infectious 'Johnny And Mary' sneaked into the UK charts and two years later 'Some Guys Have All The Luck' made the Top 20. Seeming to give up on his solo career, he joined the Duran Duran-based, Power Station in 1985. Continuing his own career, *Riptide*, released at the end of that year, gave him his biggest success. The album was a super-slick production of instantly appealing songs and it made the UK Top 5. In 1986, in addition to singing on John Martyn's *Sapphire*, he found himself at the top of the US charts with the beautifully produced 'Addicted To Love'. The record became a worldwide hit, making the UK Top 5. It was accompanied by a sexy (or sexist) video featuring a number of identical-looking girls playing instruments behind Palmer. He followed this with another catchy hit 'I Didn't Mean To Turn You On'. Following a move to Switzerland with his family he left Island after 14 years, and joined EMI. *Heavy Nova* was accompanied by the major hit 'She Makes My Day' in 1988. The next year a formidable compilation of his Island work was released, and found more success than *Heavy Nova*. He returned to the UK Top 10 with UB40 in 1990 with the Bob Dylan song 'I'll Be Your Baby Tonight' and in 1991, with a medley of Marvin Gaye songs, 'Mercy Mercy Me'/'I Want You'. *Honey* was another credible release with notable tracks such as 'Know By Now' and the title song. Palmer remains a respected artist, songwriter and the possessor of an excellent voice. He is also to be admired for his wardrobe of suits, having worn them when they were an anathema to most rock stars. Nowadays, Palmer finds himself praised for being a well-dressed man.

●ALBUMS: *Sneakin' Sally Through The Alley* (Island 1974)★★★, *Pressure Drop* (Island 1975)★★, *Some People Can Do What They Like* (Island 1976)★★, *Double Fun* (Island 1978)★★, *Secrets* (Island 1979)★★, *Clues* (Island 1980)★★, *Maybe It's Live* (Island 1982)★★, *Pride* (Island 1983)★★, *Riptide* (Island 1985)★★★, *Heavy Nova* (EMI 1988)★★★, *Don't Explain* (EMI 1990)★★, *Ridin' High* (EMI 1992)★★, *Honey* (EMI 1994)★★★.
●COMPILATIONS: *The Early Years* (C5 1987)★★, *Addictions, Volume 1* (Island 1989)★★★★, *Addictions, Volume 2* (Island 1992)★★★.
●VIDEOS: *Some Guys Have All The Luck* (Palace Video 1984), *Super Nova* (PMI 1989), *Video Addictions* (Polygram 1992), *Robert Palmer: The Very Best Of* (PMI 1995).

PAPER LACE

This UK pop group was formed in 1969, and comprised Michael Vaughan (b. 27 July 1950, Sheffield, England; guitar), Chris Morris (b. 1 November 1954, Nottingham, England), Carlo Santanna (b. 29 July 1947, nr. Rome, Italy; guitar), Philip Wright (b. 9 April 1950, Nottingham, England; drums/lead vocals) and Cliff Fish (b. 13 August 1949, Ripley, England; bass). All were residents of Nottingham, England, the lace manufacturing city that lent their mainstream pop group its name. A season at Tiffany's, a Rochdale club, led to television appearances, but a passport to the charts did not arrive until a 1974 victory in *Opportunity Knocks*, the ITV talent contest series, put their winning song, Mitch Murray and Peter Callender's 'Billy Don't Be A Hero', on the road to a UK number 1. Hopes of emulating this success in the USA were dashed by Bo Donaldson And The Heywoods' cover. The follow-up, 'The Night Chicago Died', set in the Prohibition era, was untroubled by any such competition and topped the US charts, narrowly missing out in the UK by peaking at number 3. 'The Black-Eyed Boys', a UK number 11 hit from Murray and Callender was the group's last taste of chart success - apart from a joint effort with local football heroes, Nottingham Forest FC, for the 1978 singalong, 'We've Got The Whole World In Our Hands'.
●ALBUMS: *Paper Lace And Other Bits Of Material* (1974)★★, *First Edition* (1975)★★.
●COMPILATIONS: *The Paper Lace Collection* (Pickwick 1976)★★.

PAPPALARDI, FELIX

b. 1939, New York, USA, d. April 17 1983. A highly respected bass player and arranger, Pappalardi was present at countless sessions, when folk musicians started to employ electric instruments on a regular basis. Ian And Sylvia, Fred Neil, Tom Rush, and Richard and Mimi Farina were among those benefiting from his measured contributions. He later worked with the Mugwumps, a seminal New York folk rock quartet which included Cass Elliot and Denny Doherty, later of the Mamas And The Papas, and future Lovin' Spoonful guitarist, Zalman Yanovsky. Pappalardi also oversaw sessions by the Vagrants and the Youngbloods, contributing several original songs, composed with his wife Gail Collins, to both groups' releases. An association with Cream established his international reputation. Felix produced the group's studio work from *Disraeli Gears* onwards, a position he maintained when bassist Jack Bruce embarked on a solo career in 1969. Cream's break-up left a vacuum which Pappalardi attempted to fill with Mountain, the brash rock group he formed with former Vagrant guitarist Leslie West. Partial deafness, attributed to exposure to the excessive volumes that Mountain performed at, ultimately forced the bassist to retire and subsequent work was confined to the recording studio. He recorded two albums in the late 70s, one of which, *Felix Pappalardi & Creation*, included the services of Paul Butterfield and Japanese musicians, Masayuki Higuchi (drums), Shigru Matsumoto (bass), Yoshiaki Iijima (guitar) and Kazuo Takeda (guitar). Pappalardi's life ended tragically in April 1983 when he was shot dead by his wife.

●ALBUMS: *Felix Pappalardi & Creation* (A&M 1976)★, *Don't Worry, Ma* (1979)★.

PARKER, ALAN

b. 1944, Matlock, Derbyshire, England. At one time a member of Blue Mink, Alan Parker decided early in his career that more fruitful rewards lay outside of the celebrity pop star circuit. As a session guitarist in the 60s, Parker played on material by Cat Stevens, Joe Cocker, Frank Sinatra, Ella Fitzgerald, Sonny And Cher, the Dave Clark Five and the Walker Brothers (including 'The Sun Ain't Gonna Shine Anymore') among many others. In 1969 he formed Blue Mink with fellow 'session élite' singers Roger Cook and Madeline Bell. They had their most notable success with 'Melting Pot', but the group soon broke up as the individual members returned to lucrative playing and writing projects. In the 70s Parker was one of the studio musicians supplying the Bay City Rollers with their chart fodder, and he was also a member of CCS, whose version of Led Zeppelin's 'Whole Lotta Love' became the theme tune to *Top Of The Pops*. He also had a Top 5 hit in 1972 as a member of the Congregation, with 'Softly Whispering I Love You'. Together with former Blue Mink colleague Herbie Flowers he worked on the sessions for David Bowie's *Diamond Dogs* in 1974. However, by now Parker was also spending much of his time working on television theme music, including that for *Take My Wife* and *Angels*, as well as commercials, notably the famed 'Beanz Meanz Heinz' jingle. He also wrote over 40 albums' worth of 'library music' for television. In the early 80s he began writing music for films, including *Jaws 3-D*. In the mid-90s he returned to television work, composing the theme music to the BBC Television series, *Rhodes*.

PARKER, GRAHAM

b. 18 November 1950, London, England. Having begun his career in aspiring soul groups the Black Rockers and Deep Cut Three, R&B vocalist Parker undertook menial employment while completing several demo tapes of his original songs. One such collection came to the attention of David Robinson, owner of a small recording studio within a building housing the north London, Hope & Anchor pub. Impressed, he pieced together a backing group - Brinsley Schwarz (guitar/vocals), Bob Andrews (keyboards/vocals), both ex-Brinsley Schwarz, Martin Belmont (guitar/vocals, ex-Ducks Deluxe), Andrew Bodnar (bass) and Steve Goulding (drums) - known collectively as the Rumour, and the new aggregation joined the dying embers of the 'pub rock' scene. The patronage of Radio London disc jockey Charlie Gillett helped engender a recording deal and both *Howlin' Wind* and *Heat Treatment* received almost universal acclaim. Parker's gritty delivery was both tough and passionate, placing the singer on a level with US contemporaries Bruce Springsteen and Southside Johnny And The Asbury Jukes. Although the artist also enjoyed two chart entries with *The Pink Parker* EP (1977) and 'Hold Back The Night' (1978), his momentum was effectively stalled by the divided critical opinion to the commercial *Stick To Me*, and a live double set, *The Parkerilla*. While the public gave them a UK Top 40 hit with 'Hey Lord, Don't Ask Me Questions', and despite both albums attaining UK Top 20 status, many felt Parker and the Rumour were losing their original fire, and bitter wrangles with his record company further undermined progress. *Squeezing Out Sparks*, his debut for Arista Records (in the USA), reclaimed former glories and was lauded in both *Rolling Stone* and *Village Voice*. Persistent contradictions between the critics and chart positions added fuel to the confusion in the group line-up. Their most successful UK chart album, 1980's *The Up Escalator* (released on Stiff Records in the UK), marked the end of Parker's partnership with the Rumour. With the break-up, any magic that had remained from the early days had truly gone. The remainder of the 80s was spent rebuilding his career and personal life in the USA. In 1988 *Mona Lisa's Sister* proved a dramatic return to form, rightly praised for its drive and sense of purpose. Ex-Rumour bassist Andrew Bodnar joined former Attractions Steve Nieve (keyboards) and Pete Thomas (drums) for *Human Soul*, an ambitious concept album split between sides labelled 'real' and 'surreal'. This surprising departure indicated Parker's increasing desire to expand the perimeters of his exhilarating style. Into the 90s, Parker proved fully capable, and confident, of performing to large audiences solo, with acoustic guitar or with full backing. In early 1992 he changed record labels once more by signing to Capitol Records in the USA.

●ALBUMS: *Howlin' Wind* (Vertigo 1976)★★★★, *Heat Treatment* (Vertigo 1976)★★★, *Stick To Me* (Vertigo 1977)★★★, *The Parkerilla* (Vertigo 1978)★, *Squeezing Out Sparks* (Vertigo 1979)★★★★, *The Up Escalator* (Stiff 1980)★★★, *Another Grey Area* (RCA 1982)★★★, *The Real Macaw* (RCA 1983)★★★, *Steady Nerves* (Elektra 1985)★★, *Mona Lisa's Sister* (Demon 1988)★★★★, *Human Soul* (Demon 1989)★★★, *Live! Alone In America* (Demon 1989)★★★, *Struck By Lightning* (Demon 1991)★★★, *Burning Questions* (1992)★★★, *Live Alone!*

Discovering Japan (1993)★★★, *12 Haunted Episodes* (Razor & Tie 1995)★★★, *Live From New York, NY* (Rock The House 1996)★★★, *Acid Bubblegum* (Razor & Tie 1996)★★★, *BBC Live In Concert* (Strange Fruit 1996)★★★.
●COMPILATIONS: *The Best Of Graham Parker And The Rumour* (Vertigo 1980)★★★★.

PARKER, RAY, JNR.

b. 1 May 1954, Detroit, Michigan, USA. This accomplished musician gained his reputation during the late 60s as a member of the house band at the 20 Grand Club. This Detroit nightspot often featured Tamla/Motown acts, one of which, the (Detroit) Spinners, was so impressed with the young guitarist's skills that they added him to their touring group. Parker was also employed as a studio musician for the emergent Invictus/Hot Wax stable and his choppy style was particularly prevalent on 'Want Ads', a number 1 single for Honey Cone. Parker also participated on two Stevie Wonder albums, *Talking Book* and *Innervisions*, an association that prompted a permanent move to Los Angeles. Here Parker continued his session work (Marvin Gaye, Boz Scaggs, Labelle, Barry White and Love Unlimited) until 1977 when he formed Raydio with other Detroit musicians Arnell Carmichael (synthesizer), Jerry Knight (bass), Vincent Bonham (piano), Larry Tolbert, Darren Carmichael and Charles Fearing. 'Jack And Jill', a pop/soul reading of the nursery rhyme, gave the group an international hit, while further releases consistently reached the R&B charts. 'A Woman Needs Love (Just Like You Do)', credited to Ray Parker Jnr. And Raydio, was a US Top 5 hit in 1981, while the following year the leader embarked on a solo path with 'The Other Woman'. In 1984 Parker secured a multi-million selling single with the theme song to the film *Ghostbusters*, although its lustre was somewhat tarnished by allegations that he had plagiarized a Huey Lewis composition, 'I Want A New Drug'. Nonetheless, Parker's success continued as the song secured him a 1984 Grammy Award for Best Pop Instrumental Performance.
●ALBUMS: as Raydio *Raydio* (Arista 1977)★★★, *Rock On* (Arista 1979)★★★. As Ray Parker Jnr. And Raydio *Two Places At The Same Time* (Arista 1980)★★★, *A Woman Needs Love* (Arista 1981)★★★. As Ray Parker *The Other Woman* (Arista 1982)★★, *Woman Out Of Control* (Arista 1983)★★, *Sex And The Single Man* (Arista 1985)★★, *After Dark* (Geffen 1987)★★, *I Love You Like You Are* (MCA 1991)★★.
●COMPILATIONS: *Greatest Hits* (Arista 1982)★★★★, *Chartbusters* (Arista 1984)★★★, *The Collection* (1993)★★★.

PARKS, VAN DYKE

b. 3 January 1941, Mississippi, USA. A former child actor, Parks had appeared in several Hollywood films prior to embarking on a musical career. Having studied classical piano, he joined MGM, but rather than follow this direction, began writing and recording pop songs. One of his early compositions, 'High Coin', was later covered by several disparate acts, including Jackie DeShannon, Bobby Vee, the West Coast Pop Art Experimental Band and the Charlatans, while 'Come To The Sunshine', an early Parks single, was later recorded by Harpers Bizarre, a group he also produced. Although Van Dyke fulfilled a similar role with the Mojo Men, whose cover version of Buffalo Springfield's 'Sit Down I Think I Love You' was a US hit in 1966, this period is better recalled for his work with Brian Wilson who was infatuated with Parks' intellectual air. The pair collaborated on Wilson's most ambitious compositions - 'Heroes And Villains' and 'Surf's Up' - but the full fruit of their labours, the doomed *Smile* project, was eventually scrapped when the remainder of Wilson's group, the Beach Boys, objected to the dense, obscure (although quite brilliant) lyricism Parks had brought to their leader's new compositions.

Van Dyke's first solo, *Song Cycle*, continued the direction this relationship had suggested with a complex array of sounds and ideas abounding with musical puns, Tin Pan Alley themes and exhaustive, elaborate arrangements. Commercial indifference to this ambitious project was such that Warner Brothers Records took out a series of adverts under the banner, 'The once-in-a-lifetime Van Dyke Parks 1 cent sale' offering purchasers the chance to trade a second-hand copy for two new albums, one of which was to be passed on to a 'poor, but open friend'. Undeterred, Parks still forged his idiosyncratic path, producing albums for Ry Cooder, Randy Newman, and Arlo Guthrie, as well as pursuing work as a session musician, first unveiled on the Byrds 'Fifth Dimension', with appearances on albums by Tim Buckley, Judy Collins and Little Feat. *Discover America*, Van Dyke's second album, showcased his love of Trinidadian music, and blended contemporary compositions with show tunes from an earlier era. *Clang Of The Yankee Reaper* continued this new-found, relaxed emphasis but Parks then withdrew from active recording and only re-emerged in 1984 with *Jump!*, a musical interpretation of the *Brer Rabbit* stories. This challenging performer still refused to be easily categorized and a fifth collection, *Tokyo Rose*, showed Parks continuing to sail his own course. His most significant move in recent years was to collaborate again with Brian Wilson. Their project *Orange Crate Art* was a celebration of old American values and although reviews were mostly favourable it failed to sell.
●ALBUMS: *Song Cycle* (Warners 1968)★★★, *Discover America* (Warners 1972)★★★, *Clang Of The Yankee Reaper* (Warners 1975)★★★, *Jump!* (Warners 1984)★★, *Tokyo Rose* (Warners 1989)★★★, with Brian Wilson *Orange Crate Art* (Warners 1995)★★.
●COMPILATIONS: *Idiosyncratic Path: The Best Of ...* (Diablo 1994)★★★.

PARLIAMENT

This exceptional US vocal quintet was formed in 1955 by George Clinton (b. 22 July 1941, Kannapolis, North Carolina, USA), Raymond Davis (b. 29 March 1940, Sumter, South Carolina, USA), Calvin Simon (b. 22 May 1942, Beckley, West Virginia, USA), Clarence 'Fuzzy' Haskins (b. 8 June 1941, Elkhorn, West Virginia, USA) and Grady Thomas (b. 5 January 1941, Newark, New Jersey, USA). George Clinton's interest in music did not fully emerge until his family moved to the urban setting of Plainfield, New Jersey. Here, he fashioned the Parliaments after the influential doo-wop group, Frankie Lymon And The Teenagers. Two singles, 'Poor Willie' and 'Lonely Island', mark this formative era, but it was not until 1967 that Clinton was able to secure a more defined direction with the release of '(I Wanna) Testify'. Recorded in Detroit, the single reached the US Top 20, but this promise was all but lost when Revilot, the label to which the band was signed, went out of business. All existing contracts were then sold to Atlantic, but Clinton preferred to abandon the Parliaments' name altogether in order to be free to sign elsewhere. Clinton took the existing line-up and its backing group to Westbound Records, where the entire collective recorded as Funkadelic. However, the outstanding problem over their erstwhile title was resolved in 1970, and the same musicians were signed to the Invictus label as Parliament. This group unleashed the experimental and eclectic Osmium (1970) before securing an R&B hit with the irrepressible 'Breakdown'. For the next three years the 'Parliafunkadelicament Thang' concentrated on Funkadelic releases, but disagreements with the Westbound hierarchy inspired Parliament's second revival. Signed to the Casablanca label in 1974, the group's first singles, 'Up For The Down Stroke', 'Chocolate City' and 'P. Funk (Wants To Get Funked Up)', were marginally more mainstream than the more radical material Clinton had already issued, but the distinctions became increasingly blurred. Some 40 musicians were now gathered together under the P. Funk banner, including several refugees from the James Brown camp including Bootsy Collins, Fred Wesley and Maceo Parker, while live shows offered elements of both camps. Parliament's success within the R&B chart continued with 'Give Up The Funk (Tear The Roof Off The Sucker)' (1976), and two 1978 best-sellers, 'Flashlight' and 'Aqua Boogie (A Psychoalphadiscobetabioaquadoloop)', where the group's hard-kicking funk was matched by the superlative horn charts and their leader's unorthodox vision. Their last chart entry was in 1980 with 'Agony Of Defeet', after which Clinton decided to shelve the Parliament name again when problems arose following Polygram's acquisition of the Casablanca catalogue.

●ALBUMS: as Parliament Osmium (Invictus 1970)★★★, Up For The Down Stroke (Casablanca 1974)★★★★, Chocolate City (Casablanca 1975)★★★, Mothership Connection (Casablanca 1976)★★★★, The Clones Of Doctor Funkenstein (Casablanca 1976)★★★★, Parliament Live - P. Funk Earth Tour (Casablanca 1977)★★★, Funkentelechy Vs The Placebo Syndrome (Casablanca 1977)★★★★, Motor-Booty Affair (Casablanca 1978)★★★★, Gloryhallastoopid (Or Pin The Tale On The Funky) (Casablanca 1979)★★★, Trombipulation (Casablanca 1980)★★★, Dope Dogs (Hot Hands 1995)★★★.

●COMPILATIONS: Parliament's Greatest Hits (Casablanca 1984)★★★★, The Best Of Parliament (Club 1986)★★★, Rhenium (Demon 1990)★★★, Tear The Roof Off 1974-80 (Casablanca 1993)★★★★, Live 1976-93 (Sequel 1994)★★★★.

PARSONS, ALAN

b. 20 December 1949. A staff engineer at EMI's recording studios, Parsons first attracted attention for his work on the final Beatles album, Abbey Road. Such skills were then employed on several of Wings' early releases, but the artist's reputation was established in the wake of his contributions to Pink Floyd's multi-million seller, Dark Side Of The Moon, and his productions for Pilot, Cockney Rebel and Al Stewart. Inspired by the 'concept' approach beloved by the latter act, Parsons forged a partnership with songwriter Eric Woolfson and created the Alan Parsons Project. The duo's debut Tales Of Mystery And Imagination, in which they adapted the work of Edgar Allen Poe, set the pattern for future releases whereby successive creations examined specific themes, including science fiction (I Robot) and mysticism (Pyramid). By calling on a circle of talented sessionmen and guest performers, including Arthur Brown, Gary Brooker, Graham Dye (ex-Scarlet Party) and Colin Blunstone, Parsons and Woolfson created a crafted, if rather sterile, body of work. However, despite enjoying a US Top 3 single in 1982 with 'Eye In The Sky', the Project's subsequent recordings have failed to repeat the commercial success of those early releases.

●ALBUMS: Tales Of Mystery And Imagination (Charisma 1975)★★★, I Robot (Arista 1977)★★★, Pyramid (Arista 1978)★★, Eve (Arista 1979)★★★, The Turn Of A Friendly Card (Arista 1980)★★★, Eye In The Sky (Arista 1982)★★★, Ammonia Avenue (Arista 1984)★★★, Vulture Culture (Arista 1985)★★, Stereotomy (Arista 1985)★★, Gaudi (Arista 1987)★★, Try Anything Once (Arista 1993)★★, On Air (Tot 1997)★★.

●COMPILATIONS: The Best Of The Alan Parsons Project (Arista 1983)★★★, Limelight - The Best Of The Alan Parsons Project Volume 2 (Arista 1988)★★, Instrumental Works (Arista 1988)★★★.

PARSONS, GRAM

b. Cecil Ingram Connor, 5 November 1946, Winter Haven, Florida, USA, d. 19 September 1973. Parsons' brief but influential career began in high school as a member of the Pacers. This rock 'n' roll act later gave way to the Legends which, at various points, featured country singer Jim Stafford as well as Kent Lavoie, later known as Lobo. By 1963 Parsons had joined the Shilos, a popular campus attraction modelled on clean-cut folk attraction the Journeymen. The quartet - Parsons, George Wrigley, Paul Surratt and Joe Kelly - later moved to New York's Greenwich Village, but Parsons left the line-up in 1965 upon enrolling at Harvard College. His studies ended almost immediately and, inspired by the concurrent folk rock boom, founded the International Submarine Band with John Nuese (guitar), Ian Dunlop (bass) and Mickey Gauvin (drums). Two excellent singles followed, but having relocated to Los Angeles, Parsons' vision of a contemporary country music found little favour amid the prevalent psychedelic trend. The group was nonetheless signed by producer Lee Hazelwood, but with Dunlop and Gauvin now absent from the line-up, Bob Buchanan (guitar) and Jon Corneal (drums) joined Gram and Nuese for *Safe At Home*. This excellent set is now rightly viewed as a landmark in the development of country rock, blending standards with several excellent Parsons originals, notably 'Luxury Liner'. However, by the time of its release (April 1968), the quartet had not only folded, but Parsons had accepted an offer to join the Byrds.

His induction resulted in *Sweetheart Of The Rodeo* on which the newcomer determined the group's musical direction. This synthesis of country and traditional styles followed the mould of *Safe At Home*, but was buoyed by the act's excellent harmony work. Although Parsons' role as vocalist was later diminished by Hazelwood's court injunction - the producer claimed it breached their early contract - his influence was undeniable, as exemplified on the stellar 'Hickory Wind'. However, within months Gram had left the Byrds in protest over a South African tour and instead spent several months within the Rolling Stones' circle. The following year he formed the Flying Burrito Brothers with another ex-Byrd, Chris Hillman, 'Sneaky' Pete Kleinow (pedal steel guitar) and bassist Chris Ethridge (bass). *The Gilded Palace Of Sin* drew inspiration from southern soul and urban country music and included one of Parsons' most poignant compositions, 'Hot Burrito #1'. *Burrito Deluxe* failed to scale the same heights as internal problems undermined the unit's potential. Gram's growing drug dependency exacerbated this estrangement and he was fired from the group in April 1970. Initial solo recordings with producer Terry Melcher were inconclusive, but in 1972 Parsons was introduced to singer Emmylou Harris and together they completed *G.P.* with the assistance of Elvis Presley's regular back-up band. An attendant tour leading the Fallen Angels - Jock Bartley (guitar), Neil Flanz (pedal steel), Kyle Tullis (bass) and N.D. Smart II (drums) - followed, but Parsons' appetite for self-destruction remained intact. Parsons lived the life of a true 'honky tonk hero' with all the excesses of Hank Williams, even down to his immaculate embroidered Nudie tailored suits. Sessions for a second album blended established

favourites with original songs, many of which had been written years beforehand. Despite its piecemeal content, the resultant set, *Grievous Angel*, was a triumph, in which plaintive duets ('Love Hurts', 'Hearts On Fire') underscored the quality of the Parsons/Harris partnership, while 'Brass Buttons' and 'In My Hour Of Darkness' revealed a gift for touching lyricism. Parson's death in 1973 as a result of 'drug toxicity' emphasized its air of poignancy, and the mysterious theft of his body after the funeral, whereupon his road manager, Philip Kaufman, cremated the body in the desert, carrying out Parsons' wishes, added to the singer's legend. Although his records were not a commercial success during his lifetime, Parsons' influence on a generation of performers, from the Eagles to Elvis Costello, is a fitting testament to his talent. Emmylou Harris adopted his mantle with a series of superior of country rock releases, while an excellent concept album, *Ballad Of Sally Rose* (1985), undoubtedly drew on her brief relationship with this star-struck singer. Parsons' catalogue is painfully small compared to his enormous importance in contemporary country rock, and his work is destined to stand alongside that of his hero Hank Williams.

● ALBUMS: *G.P.* (Reprise 1972)★★★, *Grievous Angel* (Reprise 1973)★★★★, *Sleepless Nights* (A&M 1976)★★★, *Gram Parsons And The Fallen Angels - Live 1973* (Sierra 1981)★★★.

● COMPILATIONS: *Gram Parsons* (Warners 1982)★★★, *The Early Years 1963-1965* (Sierra 1984)★★★.

● FURTHER READING: *Gram Parsons: A Music Biography*, Sid Griffin (ed.). *Hickory Wind: The Life And Times Of Gram Parsons*, Ben Fong-Torres.

PARTON, DOLLY

b. 19 January 1946, Locust Ridge, Tennessee, USA, Dolly Rebecca Parton's poor farming parents paid the doctor in corn meal for attending the birth of the fourth of their 12 offspring. After her appearances as a singing guitarist on local radio as a child, including the *Grand Ole Opry* in Nashville, Parton left school in 1964. Her recorded output had included a raucous rockabilly song called 'Puppy Love' for a small label as early as 1958, but a signing to Monument in 1966 - the time of her marriage to the reclusive Carl Dean - yielded a C&W hit with 'Dumb Blonde' as well as enlistment in the prestigious *Porter Wagoner Show* as its stetsoned leader's voluptuous female foil in duets and comedy sketches. While this post adulterated her more serious artistic worth, she notched up further country smashes, among them 'Joshua', the autobiographical 'Coat Of Many Colours' and, with Wagoner, 'Last Thing On My Mind' (the Tom Paxton folk standard), 'Better Move It On Home' and 1974's 'Please Don't Stop Loving Me'.

On the crest of another solo hit with 'Jolene' on RCA that same year, she resigned from the show to strike out on her own - though she continued to record periodically with Wagoner. Encompassing a generous portion of her own compositions, her post-1974 repertoire was less overtly country, even later embracing a lucrative stab at disco in 1979's 'Baby I'm Burning' and non-originals ranging from 'House Of The Rising Sun' to Jackie Wilson's 'Higher And Higher'. 'Jolene' became a 'sleeper' UK Top 10 entry in 1976 and she continued her run in the US country chart with such as 'Bargain Store' (banned from some radio stations for 'suggestive' lyrics), 'All I Can Do' and 'Light Of A Clear Blue Morning' (1977). That same year, 'Here You Come Again' crossed into the US pop Hot 100, and her siblings basked in reflected glory - mainly Randy who played bass in her backing band before landing an RCA contract himself, and Stella Parton who had already harried the country list with 1975's 'Ode To Olivia' and 'I Want To Hold You With My Dreams Tonight'.

Their famous sister next ventured into film acting, starring with Lily Tomlin and Jane Fonda in 1981's 9 To 5 (for which she provided the title theme), and with Burt Reynolds in the musical Best Little Whorehouse In Texas. Less impressive were Rhinestone and 1990's Steel Magnolias. She also hosted a 1987 television variety series which lost a ratings war. Nevertheless, her success as a recording artist, songwriter and big-breasted 'personality' remained unstoppable. As well as ploughing back royalties for 70s covers of Parton numbers by Emmylou Harris, Linda Ronstadt and Maria Muldaur into her Dollywood entertainment complex, she teamed up with Kenny Rogers in 1983 to reach the number 1 position in the USA and the UK Top 10 with a Bee Gees composition, 'Islands In The Stream'. With Rogers too, she managed another US country number 1 two years later with 'Real Love'. Although other 80s singles such as 'I Will Always Love You' and 'Tennessee Homesick Blues' were not major chart hits, they became as well-known as many that did. Trio with Ronstadt and Harris won a Grammy for best country album in 1987. Her CBS debut, Rainbow, represented her deepest plunge into mainstream pop - though 1989's White Limozeen (produced by Ricky Skaggs) retained the loyalty of her multi-national grassroots following. Her celebration of international womanhood, 'Eagle When She Flies', confirmed her return to the country market in 1991. In 1992, Whitney Houston had the biggest selling single of the year in the UK with Parton's composition, 'I Will Always Love You', which she sang in the film, The Bodyguard. Her excellent 1995 album reprised the latter song as a duet with Vince Gill.

●ALBUMS: Hello, I'm Dolly (Monument 1967)★★, Dolly Parton And George Jones (1968)★★, Just Because I'm A Woman (RCA 1968)★★★, with Porter Wagoner Just The Two Of Us (RCA 1969)★★★, with Wagoner Always, Always (RCA 1969)★★★, My Blue Ridge Mountain Boy (RCA 1969)★★★, with Wagoner Porter Wayne And Dolly Rebecca (RCA 1970)★★★, A Real Live Dolly (RCA 1970)★★★, with Wagoner Once More (RCA 1970)★★★, with Wagoner Two Of A Kind (RCA 1971)★★★, Coat Of Many Colours (RCA 1971)★★★★, with Wagoner We

Found It (RCA 1973)★★★, My Tennessee Mountain Home (RCA 1973)★★★★, Love Is Like A Butterfly (RCA 1974)★★★★, Jolene (RCA 1974)★★★★, The Bargain Store (RCA 1975)★★★★, Dolly (RCA 1976)★★★, All I Can Do (RCA 1976)★★★, New Harvest ... First Gathering (RCA 1977)★★★★, Here You Come Again (RCA 1977)★★, Heartbreaker (RCA 1978)★★, Dolly Parton And Friends At Goldband (1979)★★, Great Balls Of Fire (RCA 1979)★★, Dolly Dolly Dolly (RCA 1980)★★, 9 To 5 And Odd Jobs (RCA 1980)★★★, Heartbreak Express (RCA 1982)★★, The Best Little Whorehouse In Texas film soundtrack (MCA 1982)★★, with Kris Kristofferson, Brenda Lee, Willie Nelson The Winning Hand (Monument 1983)★★★, Burlap And Satin (RCA 1983)★★, The Great Pretender (RCA 1984)★★, Rhinestone film soundtrack (RCA 1984)★★, with Kenny Rogers Once Upon A Christmas (RCA 1984)★★, with Linda Ronstadt, Emmylou Harris Trio (Warners 1987)★★★, Rainbow (Columbia 1987)★★, White Limozeen (Columbia 1989)★★★, Eagle When She Flies (Columbia 1991)★★★, Straight Talk film soundtrack (Hollywood 1992,)★★, Slow Dancing With The Moon (1993)★★★, with Tammy Wynette, Loretta Lynn Honky Tonk Angels (1993)★★★, Heartsongs - Live From Home (Columbia 1994)★★★, Something Special (Columbia 1995)★★★, Treasures (Rising Tide 1996)★★★.

●COMPILATIONS: The Best Of Porter Wagoner And Dolly Parton (RCA 1972)★★★★, The Best Of Dolly Parton (RCA 1973)★★★★, The Best Of Dolly Parton Volume 2 (RCA 1975)★★★★, The Dolly Parton Collection (Pickwick 1979)★★★, The Very Best Of Dolly Parton (RCA 1981)★★★★, The Dolly Parton Collection (Monument 1982)★★★, Greatest Hits (RCA 1982)★★, Greatest Hits Volume 2 (RCA 1989)★★, Anthology (Connoisseur 1991)★★★, The Essential Dolly Parton - One (RCA 1995)★★★, The Greatest Hits (Telstar 1995)★★★, I Will Always Love You And Other Greatest Hits (Columbia 1996)★★★, The Essential Dolly Parton (RCA 1996)★★★★.

●VIDEOS: Dolly Parton In London (RCA/Columbia 1988), with Kenny Rogers Real Love (RCA/Columbia 1988).

●FURTHER READING: Dolly Parton: Country Goin' To Town, Susan Saunders. Dolly Parton, Otis James. The Official Dolly Parton Scrapbook, Connie Berman. Dolly, Alanna Nash. Dolly Parton (By Scott Keely), Scott Keely. Dolly Parton, Robert K. Krishef. Dolly, Here I Come Again, Leonore Fleischer. My Story, Dolly Parton.

PARTRIDGE FAMILY

David Cassidy (b. 12 April 1950, New York, USA), and his real life step-mother actress Shirley Jones (b. 31 March 1934, Smithton, Pennsylvania, USA), were the only members of the fictitious television family group to be heard on their records. Jones, who had starred in hit film musicals such as Oklahoma!, Carousel and The Music Man married David's father, actor Jack Cassidy, in 1956. The Partridge Family, a humorous series about a family pop group (based loosely on the Cowsills) started on US television on 25 September 1970. It was an instant hit and sent their debut single, 'I Think I Love You', to the top of the chart. In less than two years the fake family, whose records were produced by Wes Farrell, had put another six singles and albums into the US Top 40, including the Top 10 successes, 'Doesn't Somebody Want To Be Wanted' and 'I'll Meet You Halfway'. When their US popularity began to wane the series took off in the UK, giving them five UK Top 20 hits, most of which were less successful Stateside. The show made Cassidy a transatlantic teen-idol and he also had a run of solo hits. By the time the television series ended in 1974 the hits for both acts had dried up.

●ALBUMS: *The Partridge Family Album* (Bell 1970)★★, *Up To Date* (Bell 1971)★★, *A Partridge Family Christmas Card* (Bell 1971)★★, *The Partridge Family Sound Magazine* (Bell 1971)★★, *The Partridge Family Shopping Bag* (Bell 1972)★★, *The Partridge Family Notebook* (Bell 1972)★★, *Crossword Puzzle* (Bell 1973)★.

●COMPILATIONS: *The Partridge Family At Home With Their Hits* (Bell 1972)★★, *Greatest Hits* (Arista 1990)★★.

PASADENA ROOF ORCHESTRA

Britain's most commercially successful traditional jazz-based act of the 70s was formed in the mid-60s by baker John Arthey (bass) as a larger, slicker recreation of a 20s ragtime band than that of the Temperance Seven. Among its mainstays were John Parry (vocals), arranger Keith Nichols (piano), Mac White (clarinet) and trumpeters Clive Baker, Enrico Tomasino and Mike Henry. Transient members included Viv Stanshall (euphonium). Despite much interest from London's music press - especially the *Melody Maker* - the Orchestra had no major record hits, but their albums did brisk business in foyers on the European college circuit and at the more prestigious jazz festivals where they command high fees as a popular attraction of considerable longevity.

●ALBUMS: *The Show Must Go On* (1977)★★★, *A Talking Picture* (Columbia 1978)★★★, *Night Out* (Columbia 1979)★★★, *Puttin' On The Ritz* (Spot 1983)★★★★, *Fifteen Years On* (Pasadena Roof Orchestra 1985)★★★, *Good News* (Transatlantic 1987)★★★, *On Tour* (Transatlantic 1987)★★★, *Happy Feet* (Pasadena Roof Orchestra 1988)★★★★.

●COMPILATIONS: *Anthology* (Transatlantic 1978)★★★, *Everythin' Stops For Tea* (Cambra 1984)★★★, *C'mon Along And Listen To* (Conifer 1986)★★★, *Isn't It Romantic* (Transatlantic 1987)★★★, *Collection* (Castle 1987)★★★, *Top Hat, White Tie And Tails* (Ditto 1988)★★★, *16 Greatest Hits* (Fun 1988)★★★, *Sentimental Journey* (1993)★★★.

PASTORIUS, JACO

b. John Francis Pastorius, 1 December 1951, Norristown, Pennsylvania, USA, d. 12 September 1987, Fort Lauderdale, Florida, USA. Encouraged by his father, a drummer and vocalist, to pursue a career in music, Pastorius learned to play bass, drums, guitar,

piano and saxophone while in his teens. As a result of a football injury to his arm, his ambitions were mainly orientated towards the drums, but he soon found work playing bass for visiting pop and soul acts. After backing the Temptations and the Supremes, he developed a cult following, and his reputation spread. In 1975, Bobby Colomby, drummer with Blood, Sweat And Tears, was impressed enough to arrange the recording of Pastorius's first album, and a year later Pat Metheny asked him to play bass on his own first album for ECM Records, additionally he worked with Joni Mitchell. But the most important stage in Pastorius's career came in 1976: joining Weather Report to record the highly influential *Heavy Weather*, his astonishing technique on the fretless bass and his flamboyant behaviour onstage consolidated the band's popularity and boosted his own image to star status. He established his own band, Word Of Mouth, in 1980, and they enjoyed three years of successful tours, while Pastorius himself recorded intermittently with some of the top musicians in jazz. However, Pastorius suffered from alcoholism and manic depression. In 1987, after increasing bouts of inactivity, he suffered fatal injuries in a brawl outside the Midnight Club in his home town of Fort Lauderdale. Pastorius was one of the most influential bass players since Charles Mingus, and extended the possibilities of the electric bass as a melodic instrument in a way that has affected many bassists since.

●ALBUMS: *Jaco* (DIW 1974)★★★, *Jaco Pastorius* (Epic 1975)★★★★, with Weather Report *Heavy Weather* (Columbia 1976)★★★★, *Word Of Mouth* (Warners 1980)★★, *Invitation* (1982)★★, *PDB* (DIW 1987)★★, *Honestly* (Jazzpoint 1986)★★, *Heavy N' Jazz* (Jazzpoint 1987)★★, *Jazz Street* (Timeless 1987)★★★, *Live In Italy* rec. 1986 (Jazzpoint 1991)★★★, *Holiday For Pans* rec. 1980-82 (Sound Hills 1993)★★★, *The Birthday Concert* (Warners 1995)★★★.

●FURTHER READING: *Jaco: The Extraordinary And Tragic Life Of Jaco Pastorius*, Bill Milkowski.

PAUL, BILLY

b. Paul Williams 1 December 1934, Philadelphia, Pennsylvania, USA. Although Paul had been an active singer in the Philadelphia area since the 50s, singing in jazz clubs and briefly with Harold Melvin And The Blue Notes, it was not until he met producer Kenny Gamble that his career prospered. After signing to the Neptune label, he enjoyed a successful spell on the Philadelphia International label. His instinctive jazz-based delivery provided an unlikely foil for the label's highly structured, sweet-soul sound but Paul's impressive debut hit, 'Me And Mrs Jones', nonetheless encapsulated the genre. A classic confessional tale of infidelity, Billy's unorthodox style enhanced the ballad's sense of guilt. His later releases included 'Thanks For Saving My Life' (1974), 'Let's Make A Baby' (1976) and 'Let 'Em In' (1977), the last of which adapted the Paul McCartney hit to emphasize lyrical references to Dr. Martin Luther

King. Billy continued to make excellent records but his last chart entry, to date, came in 1980 with 'You're My Sweetness'.

●ALBUMS: *Ebony Woman* (Neptune 1970)★★, *Going East* (Philadelphia International 1971)★★★, *360 Degrees Of Billy Paul* (Philadelphia International 1972)★★★, *Feelin' Good At The Cadillac Club* (Philadelphia International 1973)★★★, *War Of The Gods* (Philadelphia International 1973)★★★, *Live In Europe* (Philadelphia International 1974)★★, *Got My Head On Straight* (Philadelphia International 1975)★★★, *When Love Is New* (Philadelphia International 1975)★★★, *Let 'Em In* (Philadelphia International 1977)★★, *Only The Strong Survive* (Philadelphia International 1978)★★, *First Class* (Philadelphia International 1979)★★, *Lately* (Total Experience 1985)★★★, *Wide Open* (Ichiban 1988)★★★.

●COMPILATIONS: *Best Of Billy Paul* (Philadelphia International 1980)★★★★, *Billy Paul's Greatest Hits* (Philadelphia International 1983)★★★.

PAYNE, FREDA

b. Freda Charcilia Payne, 19 September 1945, Detroit, Michigan, USA. Schooled in jazz and classical music, this urbane singer attended the Institute Of Musical Arts and worked with Pearl Bailey prior to recording her debut album in 1963 for MGM Records. Payne signed to Holland/Dozier/Holland's label Invictus and her first recording, 'The Unhooked Generation', introduced a new-found soul style, but it was the magnificent follow-up, 'Band Of Gold' (1970), that established Payne's reputation. This ambiguous wedding-night drama was a US number 3 and UK number 1 and prepared the way for several more excellent singles in 'Deeper And Deeper', 'You Brought The Joy' and 'Bring The Boys Home', an uncompromising anti-Vietnam anthem. Ensuing releases lacked that early purpose and were marred by Payne's increasingly unemotional delivery. The singer moved to ABC/Dunhill (1974), Capitol (1976) and Sutra (1982), but Payne was also drawn to television work and later hosted a syndicated talk show, 'For You Black Woman'.

●ALBUMS: *After The Lights Go Down And Much More* (MGM 1963)★★, *How Do You Say I Don't Love You Anymore* (1966)★★★, *Band Of Gold* (Invictus 1970)★★★, *Contact* (Invictus 1971)★★★, *Reaching Out* (Invictus 1973)★★★, *Payne And Pleasure* (Dunhill 1974)★★, *Out Of Payne Comes Love* (ABC 1975)★★, *Stares And Whispers* (Capitol 1977)★★, *Supernatural High* (Capitol 1978)★★, *Hot* (1979)★★.

●COMPILATIONS: *The Best Of Freda Payne* (Invictus 1972)★★★, *Bands Of Gold* (HDH/Demon 1984)★★★, *Deeper And Deeper* (HDH/Demon 1989)★★★.

PEEBLES, ANN

b. 27 April 1947, East St. Louis, Missouri, USA. An impromptu appearance at the Rosewood Club in Memphis led to Peebles' recording contract. Bandleader Gene Miller took the singer to producer Willie Mitchell whose skills fashioned an impressive debut single, 'Walk Away' (1969). Peebles' style was more fully shaped with 'Part Time Love' (1970), an irresistibly punchy reworking of the Clay Hammond-penned standard, while powerful original songs, including 'Slipped Tripped And Fell In Love' (1972) and 'I'm Gonna Tear Your Playhouse Down' (1973), later recorded by Paul Young and Graham Parker, confirmed her promise. Her work matured with the magnificent 'I Can't Stand The Rain', which defined the Hi Records sound and deservedly ensured the singer's immortality. Don Bryant, Peebles' husband and a songwriter of ability, wrote that classic as well as '99 lbs' (1971). Later releases, '(You Keep Me) Hangin' On' and 'Do I Need You', were also strong, but Peebles was latterly hampered by a now established formula and sales subsided. 'If You Got The Time (I've Got The Love)' (1979) was the singer's last R&B hit, but her work nonetheless remains among the finest in the 70s soul canon. After a return to the gospel fold in the mid-80s, Peebles bounced back in 1989 with *Call Me*. In 1992 the fine back-to-the-Memphis-sound, *Full Time Love*, was issued. She appeared that summer at the Porretta Terme Soul Festival in Italy and her rivetting performance was captured on a CD of the festival, *Sweet Soul Music - Live!*, released by Italian label 103.

●ALBUMS: *This Is Ann Peebles* (Hi 1969)★★★, *Part Time Love* (Hi 1971)★★★, *Straight From The Heart* (Hi 1972)★★★, *I Can't Stand The Rain* (Hi 1974)★★★★, *Tellin' It* (Hi 1976)★★★, *If This Is Heaven* (Hi 1978)★★★, *The Handwriting On The Wall* (Hi 1979)★★★, *Call Me* (Waylo 1990)★★★, *Full Time Love* (Rounder/Bullseye 1992)★★★, *Fill This World With Love* (Bullseye 1996)★★★.

●COMPILATIONS: *I'm Gonna Tear Your Playhouse Down* (Hi 1985)★★★★, *99 lbs* (Hi 1987)★★★, *Greatest Hits* (Hi 1988)★★★★, *Lookin' For A Lovin'* (Hi 1990)★★★, *Straight From The Heart/I Can't Stand The Rain* (1992)★★★, *Tellin' It/If This Is Heaven* (1992)★★★, *This Is Ann Peebles/The Handwriting On The Wall* (1993)★★★, *The Flipside Of ...* (1993), *U.S. R&B Hits* (1995)★★★.

PENDERGRASS, TEDDY

b. Theodore Pendergrass, 26 March 1950, Philadelphia, Pennsylvania, USA. Pendergrass joined Harold Melvin And The Blue Notes in 1969, when they invited his group, the Cadillacs, to work as backing musicians. Initially their drummer, Pendergrass became the featured vocalist within a year. His ragged, passionate interpretations brought distinction to such releases as 'I Miss You' and 'If You Don't Know Me By Now'. Clashes with Melvin led to an inevitable split and in 1976 Pendergrass embarked on a successful solo career, remaining with the Philadelphia International label. His skills were most apparent on slower material which proved ideal for the singer's uncompromisingly sensual approach, and earned him a huge following amongst women. 'The Whole Town's Laughing At Me' (1977),

'Close The Door' (1978) and 'Turn Off The Lights' (1979) stand among the best of his early work and if later releases were increasingly drawn towards a smoother, more polished direction, Pendergrass was still capable of creating excellent records, including a moving rendition of 'Love TKO', a haunting Womack And Womack composition. However, his life was inexorably changed in 1982, following a near-fatal car accident which left the singer confined to a wheelchair, although his voice was intact. Nonetheless, after months of physical and emotional therapy, he was able to begin recording again. 'Hold Me' (1984), Teddy's debut hit on his new outlet, Asylum Records, also featured Whitney Houston, while further success followed with 'Love 4/2' (1986) 'Joy' and '2 A.M.' (both 1988). In 1991 'It Should've Been You' did a lot to reinstate him in people's mind's as a major artist. He moved to a new label in 1996 after a lengthy gap in his career.

●ALBUMS: *Teddy Pendergrass* (Philadelphia International 1977)★★★, *Life Is A Song Worth Singing* (Philadelphia International 1978)★★★, *Teddy* (Philadelphia International 1979)★★★★, *Teddy Live! (Coast To Coast)* (Philadelphia International 1979)★★, *T.P.* (Philadelphia International 1980)★★★★, *It's Time For Love* (Philadelphia International 1981)★★★, *This One's For You* (Philadelphia International 1982)★★★, *Heaven Only Knows* (Philadelphia International 1983)★★★, *Love Language* (Asylum 1984)★★, *Workin' It Back* (Asylum 1985)★★★, *Joy* (Elektra 1988)★★★, *Truly Blessed* (Elektra 1991)★★★, *Little More Magic* (Elektra 1993)★★★, *You And I* (BMG/Surefire 1997)★★★.

●COMPILATIONS: *Greatest Hits* (Philadelphia International 1984)★★★★, *Teddy Pendergrass* (1989)★★★, *The Philly Years* (Repertoire 1995)★★★★.

●VIDEOS: *Teddy Pendergrass Live* (Columbia-Fox 1988).

PENDRAGON

Progressive rockers Pendragon took their name, like so many others working in the same genre in the mid-70s, from the Arthurian dynasty/mythos. Formed in Gloucestershire, England in 1978, the name was originally Zeus Pendragon, but this prefix was quickly abandoned, unlike the group's long-standing line-up of Nick Barrett (guitar/vocals), Nigel Harris (drums), Peter Gee (bass) and John Barnfield (keyboards). Numerous tours followed, but with the UK music industry now revolutionised by punk and new wave, no record company offered them a sympathetic hearing. That situation did not change until 1982, when Marillion's commercial breakthrough prepared the ground for more expansive rock songwriting. The group played at the 1983 Reading Festival and signed to Elusive Records, owned by Marillion's then manager. Two albums followed, *Fly High Fall Far* and *The Jewel*, both showcasing Pendragon's penchant for grand themes not restricted by the three minute compression of the traditional pop song. They also toured widely, including dates in France, Germany and Holland. Afterwards they started their own label, Toff Records, which continues to release all Pendragon material (sometimes in association with the group's vibrant fan club, the Mob). Arguably the group's best release proved to be *The World*, produced by Tony Taverner. The album's typically arresting and lavish artwork was conceived and executed by respected artist Simon Williams - strong visuals have always played their part in the group's presentation. 1993's *The Window Of Life* was also comparatively well-received (Pendragon have never totally overcome UK critical resistance to anything even remotely connected to the 'prog-rock' genre) and was promoted with the group's most extensive tour to date. They also signed their entire catalogue over to Pony Canyon for distribution in Japan, a nation that represents one of the most fertile sources of their popularity.

●ALBUMS: *Fly High Fall Far* mini-album (Elusive 1983)★★★, *The Jewel* (Elusive 1985)★★★, *9:15 Live* (Awareness 1986)★★, *Kowtow* (Toff 1988)★★★, *The World* (Toff 1991)★★★, *Live In Lille, The Very Very Bootleg Album* fan club only (Toff 1992)★★, *The Window Of Life* (Toff 1993)★★★, *Fall Dreams And Angels* mini-album (Fan Club 1994)★★, *Utretch ... The Final Frontier* (Fan Club 1995)★★★, *The Masquerade Overture* (Toff 1996)★★★.

●COMPILATIONS: *The Best Of* (Toff 1990)★★★.

PERE UBU

Formed in Cleveland, Ohio, USA, in 1975, and taking their name from Alfred Jarry's play, Pere Ubu evolved from several of the region's experimental groups, including Rocket From The Tombs and Foggy And The Shrimps. Their initial line-up, comprising David Thomas (vocals), Peter Laughner (guitar), Tom Herman (guitar/bass/organ), Tim Wright (guitar/bass), Allen Ravenstine (synthesizer/saxophone) and Scott Krauss (drums) completed the compulsive '30 Seconds Over Tokyo', while a second single, 'Final Solution', was recorded following Ravenstine's departure. Wright and Laughner then left the fold, but new bassist Tony Maimone augmented the nucleus of Thomas, Herman and Krauss before the prodigal Ravenstine returned to complete the most innovative version of the group. Two more singles, 'Street Waves' and 'The Modern Dance', were released before the quintet secured an international recording deal. Their debut album, also titled *The Modern Dance*, was an exceptional collection, blending new wave art-rock with early Roxy Music. Rhythmically, the group was reminiscent of Captain Beefheart's Magic Band while Thomas's vocal gymnastics were both distinctive and compelling. Two further albums, *Dub Housing* and *New Picnic Time*, maintained this sense of adventure although the demonstrable power of that debut set was gradually becoming diffuse. Nonetheless, the three albums displayed a purpose and invention that deservedly received considerable critical acclaim. In 1979 Tom Herman was replaced by former Red Crayola guitarist Mayo Thompson, who introduced a sculpted, measured approach to what had once seemed a propulsive, intuitive sound. The *Age Of Walking* was deemed obtuse, and the group became pigeonholed as both difficult and inconsequential. A dissatisfied Krauss left the line-up, and Anton Fier (ex-Feelies) joined Pere Ubu for the disappointing *Song Of The Bailing Man*. This lightweight selection appeared following the release of *The Sound Of The Sand*, David Thomas's first solo album, and reflected a general disinterest in the parent group's progress. Maimone then joined Krauss in Home And Garden, Herman surfaced with a new group, Tripod Jimmie, while Raventine and Thompson collaborated within a restructured Red Crayola. Thomas meanwhile enjoyed the highest profile with a further five solo albums. By 1985 both Maimone and Raventine were working with the singer's new group, the Wooden Birds. Scott Krauss set the seeds of a Pere Ubu reunion by appearing for an encore during a Cleveland concert. 'It walked like a duck, looked like a duck, quacked like a duck, so it was a duck,' Thomas later remarked, and by the end of 1987, the Ubu name had been officially reinstated. Jim Jones (guitar) and Chris Cutler (drums) completed the new line-up for the exceptional *The Tenement Year*, which coupled the charm of earlier work with a new-found accessibility. *Cloudland* emphasized this enchanting direction although the group's age-old instability still threatened their long-term ambitions. Both Cutler and Ravenstine left the line-up. The latter was replaced by Eric Drew Feldman, formerly of Captain Beefheart. 1995's *Ray Gun Suitcase* was the first album to be produced by Thomas himself, and was recorded in the open air in nearby woods. Stylistically it had been informed by the singer and his wife's stay in Memphis during 'Elvis' Death Week'. It featured new band members Michele Temple on bass, a musician who earns her living playing lute in a medieval group and also leads the Viviennes, and Robert Wheeler, apparently the last living relative of Thomas Alva Edison and proficient in the thereamins, an instrument he builds himself. Asked at this juncture why Pere Ubu were still around after more than two decades, Thomas responded, 'We're too dumb to quit and lack the imagination to see a better future.'

●ALBUMS: *The Modern Dance* (Blank 1977)★★★★, *Dub Housing* (Chrysalis 1978)★★★★, *New Picnic Time* (Rough Trade 1979)★★★, *The Art Of Walking* (Rough Trade 1980)★★★, *390 Degrees Of Simulated Stereo - Ubu Live: Volume 1* (Rough Trade 1981)★★★, *Song Of The Bailing Man* (Rough Trade 1982)★★, *The Tenement Year* (Enigma 1988)★★★, *One Man Drives While The Other Man Screams - Live Volume 2: Pere Ubu On Tour* (Rough Trade 1989)★★, *Cloudland* (Fontana 1989)★★★, *Worlds In Collision* (Fontana 1991)★★★, *Ray Gun Suitcase* (Cooking Vinyl 1995)★★★.

●COMPILATIONS: *Terminal Tower: An Archival Collection* (Twin/Tone 1985)★★★★, *Datapanik In The Year Zero* (Cooking Vinyl 1996)★★★★.

PERKINS, AL

Al Perkins was with Don Henley, later of the Eagles, in the late 60s band, Shiloh. He replaced 'Sneaky' Pete Kleinow in the Flying Burrito Brothers in 1971, a time when they were frustrated at their lack of progress. However, their final album, *The Last Of The Red Hot Burritos*, is regarded by many as their best work. Within six months, he and fellow Burrito Chris Hillman had joined Manassas with Stephen Stills. Perkins has played on numerous record dates and credits include Gene Clark, Bob Dylan, the Eagles, Roger McGuinn, Randy Newman, Dolly Parton, the Rolling Stones, Al Stewart and James Taylor.

PERRY, MARK

One of the first to spot the oncoming onslaught of UK punk, Mark Perry (b. *c*.1957, London, England) was a bank clerk who, inspired by the Ramones, started the *Sniffin' Glue (And Other Rock 'N' Roll Habits)* fanzine in mid-1976. After leaving his job and shortening his name to Mark P., he and south London pals like Danny Baker became the unofficial media messiahs of punk rock. *Sniffin' Glue* only lasted until August 1977 but by that time Perry was working on several labels and his new band, with Alex Ferguson; Alternative TV (signifying Alternative *to* TV). He had previously played in a trio called the New Beatles with Steve Walsh and Tyrone Thomas. Perry soon adapted the new band's name to ATV as everyone was either mispronouncing or misspelling it anyway. Their first release was a flexi-disc on the Sniffin' Glue label. This was later reissued on Deptford Fun City, a label set up by Perry (in conjunction with Miles Copeland). ATV released several albums on DFC before becoming the Good Missionaries in 1979. After one album, *Fire From Heaven*, Perry left and recorded as the Reflection, the Door And The Window, and as a solo artist. There were just two 1980 singles credited to him but he also cropped up on various compilations. ATV re-formed in 1981 for *Strange Kicks* only to break up again. Perry's album, *Snappy Turns*, also appeared in that year. ATV re-formed for a second time in 1984, initially for a gig at the Euston Tavern in Kings Cross and this reformation lasted about a year. They split up just long enough to give themselves time to re-form again and stayed together until 1987. More recently Perry has been involved in a band called Baby Ice Dog.

●ALBUMS: *Snappy Turns* (Deptford Fun City 1981)★★.

PERRY, RICHARD

b. 18 June 1942, Brooklyn, New York, USA. His work with artists ranging from Barbra Streisand and Carly Simon to Tiny Tim and Captain Beefheart made Perry the 'name' producer of the 70s. As a teenager he sang with New York group the Legends whose members included Goldie Zelkowicz (aka Genya Ravan). He began songwriting with Kenny Vance and produced singles for the Kama Sutra and Red Bird labels. In 1967 Perry moved to Los Angeles, producing the debut album of Captain Beefheart And The Magic Band before joining Warner Brothers Records as a staff producer. In two years with the label, Perry displayed his versatility by supervising recordings by Tiny Tim, Ella Fitzgerald, actor Theodore Bikel and all-female rock group, Fanny. Next, he undertook the project that catapulted him into the forefront of US producers. Columbia Records wished to bring Broadway musical star Barbra Streisand to a mass audience and Perry chose a selection of contemporary material for the *Stoney End* album. The title track became a US Top 10 hit. Harry Nilsson, Carly Simon ('You're So Vain'), Ringo Starr, Leo Sayer and Diana Ross were among the other artists with whom he worked before setting up his own label, Planet, in 1978. Its most successful signing was the Pointer Sisters, who recorded six albums for the label before moving to RCA in 1986. Perry's later work included *Rock, Rhythm And Blues* (1989), a various artists album including contributions from Chaka Khan, the Pointer Sisters and Rick James.

PERSUASIONS

Formed in the Bedford-Stuyvesant area in New York City, this talented group has continued the a cappella tradition despite prevalent trends elsewhere. Jerry Lawson (b. 23 January 1944, Fort Lauderdale, Florida, USA; lead), Joseph 'Jesse' Russell (b. 25 September 1939, Henderson, North Carolina, USA; tenor), Little Jayotis Washington (b. 12 May 1941, Detroit, Michigan, USA; tenor), Herbert 'Tubo' Rhoad (b. 1 October 1944, Bamberg, South Carolina, USA, d. 8 December 1988; baritone) and Jimmy 'Bro' Hayes (b. 12 November 1943, Hopewell, Virginia, USA; bass) began working together in 1966. Having recorded for Minit, the Persuasions gained prominence four years later with *Accapella*, a part live/part studio album released on Frank Zappa's Straight label. Their unadorned voices were later heard on several superb collections including *Street Corner Symphony* and *Chirpin'*, while the group also supplied harmonies on Joni Mitchell's *Shadows And Light* (1980). During 1973-74, Willie C. Daniel replaced Jayotis Washington in the group. On 8 December 1988 Rhoad died, leaving a four-man group. The Persuasions continue to pursue this peerless path, winding sinewy harmonies around such varied songs as 'Slip Sliding Away', Five Hundred Miles' and 'Under The Boardwalk'.
●ALBUMS: *Accapella* (Straight 1970)★★★, *We Came To Play* (Capitol 1971)★★★, *Street Corner Symphony* (Capitol 1972)★★★★, *Spread The Word* (Capitol 1972)★★★, *We Still Ain't Got No Band* (MCA 1973)★★★, *More Than Before* (A&M 1974)★★, *I Just Wanna Sing With My Friends* (A&M 1974)★★, *Chirpin'* (Elektra 1977)★★★★, *Comin' At Ya* (Flying Fish 1979)★★★, *Good News* (Rounder 1983)★★, *No Frills* (Rounder 1986)★★★, *Stardust* (Catamount 1987)★★★, *Right Around The Corner* (Bullseye 1994)★★★, *Sincerely* (Bullseye 1996)★★★.

PETERS AND LEE

After Lennie Peters (b. 1939, London, England, d. 10 October 1992, Enfield, North London, England) was blinded at the age of 16 in an accident that put paid to his ambitions to become a boxer, he began singing and playing piano in pubs around the Islington area of London. Dianne Lee (b. *c*.1950, Sheffield, Yorkshire, England) was a dancer with her cousin, working as the Hailey Twins, and after Peters and Lee met on a tour of clubs, they decided to form a duo. They achieved some popularity on the club and holiday camp circuit, and subsequently won Hughie Green's top-rated television talent show *Opportunity Knocks*. Their blend of Tony Bennett and Ray Charles numbers made them one of the most popular winners of the programme, and led to their releasing the country-flavoured 'Welcome Home' which topped the UK chart in 1973. The accompanying *We Can Make It* also reached number 1 - it was the first time since the Beatles that a single and album from the same act had simultaneously held the UK number 1 spots. As well as becoming regulars on various television variety shows, the duo had three Top 20 singles in the ensuing years, including the number 3 hit, 'Don't Stay Away Too Long' (1974). After splitting up in 1980, they re-formed six years later and toured holiday camps until 1992 when it was announced that Peters was suffering from cancer. After his death, Dianne Lee turned to acting, and also performed in cabaret. In 1994 she played the title role in *Sinderella*, comedian Jim Davidson's bawdy pantomime. In the following year Pickwick Records resissued Peters and Lee's last album, *Through All The Years*, after their biggest hit, 'Welcome Home', was featured in a television commercial for Walker's Crisps.
●ALBUMS: *By Your Side* (Philips 1973)★★, *We Can Make It* (Philips 1973)★★, *Rainbow* (Philips 1974)★★, *Favourites* (Philips 1975)★★, *Invitation* (Philips 1976)★★, *Serenade* (Philips 1976)★★, *Smile* (Philips 1977)★★, *Remember When* (Philips 1980)★★, *The Farewell Album* (Celebrity 1981)★★, *All I Ever Need Is You* (Spot 1985)★★, *Through All The Years* (Galaxy 1992)★★. Solo: Lennie Peters *Unforgettable* (Celebrity 1981)★.
●COMPILATIONS: *Spotlight On Peters And Lee* (Philips 1979)★★, *Yesterday And Today* (Cambra 1983)★★, *Best Of Peters & Lee* (Ditto 1988)★★.

PICKETTYWITCH

Naming their London-based outfit after a Cornish village, singers Polly Brown and Maggie Farran and their turnover of backing musicians came to public attention in 1969 via ITV's *Opportunity Knocks* television talent show with 'Solomon Grundy', composed and arranged by Tony Macauley and John McLeod. This filled the b-side of the outfit's debut single, 'You Got Me So I Don't Know', but it was their second Pye single, 'The Same Old Feeling' that took them into the UK Top 5 during the spring of 1970. With choreographed head move-

ments peculiar to themselves, Pickettywitch promoted '(It's Like A) Sad Old Kinda Movie' and 'Baby I Won't Let You Down' to lesser effect on *Top Of The Pops* and on the cabaret circuit. Polly Brown was also in the news for her publicized romance with disc jockey, Jimmy Saville. After further Macauley-McLeod creations like 'Bring A Little Light Into My World', 'Summertime Feeling' and 'Waldo P. Emerson Jones' plus an album, the group split up - though a new Pickettywitch containing neither Farran nor Brown tried again in the mid-70s. As a soloist, Brown re-entered the British charts in 1974 with 'Up In A Puff Of Smoke', and a later single, 'Honey Honey' was a US hit. Farran subsequently headed a successful London publicity agency.
●ALBUMS: *Pickettywitch* (Pye 1970)★★.

PILOT

Formed in Edinburgh, Scotland, in 1973, Pilot initially consisted of David Paton (b. 29 October 1951, Edinburgh; bass, vocals) and Billy Lyall (b. 26 March 1953, Edinburgh; synthesizer, piano, flute, vocals), two former members of the Bay City Rollers and Stuart Tosh (b. 26 September 1951, Aberdeen, Scotland; drums). The trio won a contract with EMI Records after recording a series of demos in London. Session guitarist Ian Bairnson (b. 3 August 1953, Shetland Isles, Scotland) was recruited in the autumn of 1974. Having secured a Top 20 hit with 'Magic', the group reached the number 1 spot in 1975 with 'January', a simple, but perfectly crafted pop song. The group enjoyed two minor chart entries with 'Call Me Round' and 'Just A Smile', but their increasingly lightweight style quickly palled. Tosh left to join 10cc, while Bairnson and Paton pursued studio careers, which included sessions for Kate Bush's debut *The Kick Inside* (1978) and several recordings for Alan Parsons and Chris DeBurgh. Billy Lyall recorded a solo album, which featured several former colleagues, and later joined Dollar. In December 1989, he died weighing less than five stone, a victim of an AIDS-related illness.
●ALBUMS: *From The Album Of The Same Name* (EMI 1974)★★★, *Second Flight* (EMI 1975)★★★, *Morin Heights* (EMI 1976)★★, *Two's A Crowd* (EMI 1977)★★.
●COMPILATIONS: *The Best Of Pilot* (EMI 1980)★★, *Very Best Of Pilot* (See For Miles 1991)★★★.

PINK FAIRIES

The name 'Pink Fairies' was initially applied to a fluid group of musicians later known as Shagrat. The original Tolkein-inspired appellation was resurrected in 1970 when one of their number, Twink (b. John Alder), erstwhile drummer in Tomorrow and the Pretty Things, joined former Deviants Paul Rudolph (b. USA; guitar/vocals), Duncan Sanderson (bass/vocals) and Russell Hunter (drums). The Fairies' debut album, *Never Neverland*, was a curious amalgam of primeval rabble-rousing ('Say You Love Me') and English psychedelia ('Heavenly Man'). It also featured 'Do It' and

'Uncle Harry's Last Freak Out', two songs that became fixtures of the group's live set as they became stalwarts of the free festival and biker circuits. Twink left the band in 1971 and the remaining trio completed the disappointing *What A Bunch Of Sweeties* with the help of Trevor Burton from the Move. Rudolph, later to join Hawkwind, was briefly replaced by Mick Wayne before Larry Wallis joined for *Kings Of Oblivion*, the group's most exciting and unified release. The trio broke up in 1974, but the following year joined Rudolph and Twink for a one-off appearance at London's Chalk Farm Roundhouse. A farewell tour, with Sanderson, Wallis and Hunter, extended into 1977, by which time Martin Stone (ex-Chilli Willi And The Red Hot Peppers) had joined the line-up. The Pink Fairies were then officially dissolved, but the original line-up, without Rudolph but including Wallis, were reunited in 1987 for *Kill 'Em 'N' Eat 'Em* before going their separate ways once more.
●ALBUMS: *Never Neverland* (Polydor 1971)★★★, *What A Bunch Of Sweeties* (Polydor 1972)★★, *Kings Of Oblivion* (Polydor 1973)★★★, *Live At The Roundhouse* (Big Beat 1982)★★, *Previously Unreleased* (Big Beat 1984)★★, *Kill 'Em 'N' Eat 'Em* (Demon 1987)★★.
●COMPILATIONS: *Flashback* (Polydor 1975)★★★, *Pink Fairies* (Polydor 1990)★★★.

PINK FLOYD

One of the most predominant and celebrated rock bands of all time, the origins of Pink Floyd developed at Cambridge High School. Roger Keith 'Syd' Barrett (b. 6 January 1946, Cambridge, England; guitar/vocals), Roger Waters (b. 9 September 1944, Cambridge, England; bass/vocals) and Dave Gilmour (b. 6 March 1944, Cambridge, England; guitar/vocals) were pupils and friends there. Mutually drawn to music, Barrett and Gilmour undertook a busking tour of Europe prior to the former's enrolment at the Camberwell School Of Art in London. Waters was meanwhile studying architecture at the city's Regent Street Polytechnic. He formed an R&B-based group, Sigma 6, with fellow students Nick Mason (b. 27 January 1945, Birmingham, England; drums) and Rick Wright (b. 28 July 1945, London, England; keyboards). The early line-up included bassist Clive Metcalfe - Waters favoured guitar at this point - and (briefly) Juliette Gale (who later married Wright) but underwent the first crucial change when Bob Close (lead guitar) replaced Metcalfe. With Waters now on bass, the group took a variety of names, including the T-Set and the (Screaming) Abdabs. Sensing a malaise, Waters invited Barrett to join but the latter's blend of blues, pop and mysticism was at odds with Close's traditional outlook and the Abdabs fell apart at the end of 1965. Almost immediately Barrett, Waters, Mason and Wright reconvened as the Pink Floyd Sound, a name Syd had suggested, inspired by an album by Georgia blues musicians Pink Anderson and Floyd Council.

Within weeks the quartet had repaired to the

Thompson Private Recording Company, sited in the basement of a house. Here they recorded two songs, 'Lucy Leave', a Barrett original playfully blending pop and R&B, and a version of Slim Harpo's 'I'm A King Bee'. Although rudimentary, both tracks indicate a defined sense of purpose. Ditching the now superfluous 'Sound' suffix, Pink Floyd attracted notoriety as part of the nascent counter-culture milieu centred on the London Free School. A focus for the emergent underground, this self-help organisation inspired the founding of Britain's first alternative publication, *International Times*. The paper was launched at the Roundhouse on 15 October 1966; it was here Pink Floyd made its major debut. By December the group was appearing regularly at the UFO Club, spearheading Britain's psychedelic movement with extended, improvised sets and a highly-visual lightshow. Further demos ensued, produced by UFO-co-founder Joe Boyd, which in turn engendered a recording contract with EMI. Surprisingly, the band's hit singles were different to their live sound, featuring Barrett's quirky melodies and lyrics. 'Arnold Layne', a tale of a transvestite who steals ladies' clothes from washing lines, escaped a BBC ban to rise into the UK Top 20. 'See Emily Play', originally entitled 'Games For May' in honour of an event the group hosted at Queen Elizabeth Hall, reached number 6 in June 1967. It was succeeded by *The Piper At The Gates Of Dawn* which encapsulated Britain's 'Summer of Love'. Largely Barrett-penned, the set deftly combined childlike fantasy with experimentation, where whimsical pop songs nestled beside riff-laden sorties, notably the powerful 'Interstellar Overdrive'. Chart success begat package tours - including a memorable bill alongside the Jimi Hendrix Experience - which, when combined with a disastrous US tour, wrought unbearable pressure on Barrett's fragile psyche. His indulgence in hallucinogenic drugs exacerbated such problems and he often proved near-comatose on-stage and incoherent with interviewers. A third single, 'Apples And Oranges', enthralled but jarred in equal measures, while further recordings, 'Vegetable Man' and 'Scream Thy Last Scream', were deemed unsuitable for release. His colleagues, fearful for their friend and sensing a possible end to the band, brought Dave Gilmour into the line-up in February 1968. Plans for Barrett to maintain a backroom role, writing for the group but not touring, came to naught and his departure was announced the following April. He subsequently followed a captivating, but short-lived, solo career.

Although bereft of their principle songwriter, the realigned Pink Floyd completed *A Saucerful Of Secrets*. It featured one Barrett original, the harrowing 'Jugband Blues', as well as two songs destined to become an integral part of their live concerts, the title track itself and 'Set The Controls For The Heart Of The Sun'. Excellent, but flop singles, 'It Would Be So Nice' (a rare Wright original) and 'Point Me At The Sky', were also issued;

their failure prompted the group to disavow the format for 11 years. A film soundtrack, *More*, allowed Waters to flex compositional muscles, while the part-live, part-studio *Ummagumma*, although dated and self-indulgent by today's standards, was at the vanguard of progressive space-rock in 1969. By this point Pink Floyd were a major attraction, drawing 100,000 to their free concert in London the following year. Another pivotal live appearance, in the volcanic crater in Pompeii, became the subject of a much-loved late-night film.

Atom Heart Mother was a brave, if flawed, experiment, partially written with avant-garde composer, Ron Geesin. It featured the first in a series of impressive album covers, designed by the Hipgnosis studio, none of which featured photographs of the band. The seemingly abstract image of *Meddle*, is in fact a macro lens shot of an ear. The music within contained some classic pieces, notably 'One Of These Days' and the epic 'Echoes', but was again marred by inconsistency. Pink Floyd's festering talent finally exploded in 1973 with *Dark Side Of The Moon*. It marked the arrival of Waters as an important lyricist and Gilmour as a guitar hero. Brilliantly produced - with a sharp awareness of stereo effects - the album became one of the biggest selling records of all time, currently in excess of 25 million copies. Its astonishing run on the *Billboard* chart spanned over a decade and at last the group had rid itself of the spectre of the Barrett era. Perhaps with this in mind, a moving eulogy to their former member, 'Shine On You Crazy Diamond', was one of the high-points of *Wish You Were Here*. Syd apparently appeared at Abbey Road studio during the sessions, prepared to contribute but incapable of doing so. 'Have A Cigar', however, did feature a cameo appearance; that of Roy Harper. Although dwarfed in sales terms by its predecessor, this 1975 release is now regarded by aficionados as the group's artistic zenith. *Animals* featured a scathing attack on the 'clean-up television' campaigner, Mary Whitehouse, while the cover photograph, an inflatable pig soaring over Battersea power station, has since passed into Pink Floyd folklore. However it was with this album that tension within the band leaked into the public arena. Two of its tracks, 'Sheep' and 'Dogs', were reworkings of older material and, as one of the world's most successful bands, Pink Floyd were criticized as an anathema to 1977's punk movement. At the end of the year, almost as a backlash, Nick Mason produced the Damned's *Music For Pleasure*. Wright and Gilmour both released solo albums in 1978 as rumours of a break-up abounded. In 1979, however, the group unleashed *The Wall*, a Waters-dominated epic which has now become second only to *Dark Side Of The Moon* in terms of sales. A subtly screened autobiographical journey, *The Wall* allowed the bassist to vent his spleen, pouring anger and scorn on a succession of establishment talismen. It contained the anti-educational system diatribe, 'Another Brick In The Wall', which not only restored the group to the British singles chart, but provided them with their sole number 1 hit. *The Wall* was also the subject of an imaginative stage show, during which the group was bricked up behind a titular edifice. A film followed in 1982, starring Bob Geldof and featuring ground-breaking animation by Gerald Scarfe, who designed the album jacket.

Such success did nothing to ease Pink Floyd's internal hostility. Longstanding enmity between Waters and Wright - the latter almost left the group with Barrett - resulted in the bassist demanding Wright's departure. He left in 1979. By the early 80s relations within the band had not improved. Friction over financial matters and composing credits - Gilmour argued his contributions to *The Wall* had not been acknowledged - tore at the heart of the band. 'Because we haven't finished with each other yet,' was Mason's caustic reply to a question as to why Pink Floyd were still together and, to the surprise of many, another album did appear in 1983. *The Final Cut* was a stark, humourless set which Waters totally dominated. It was comprised of songs written for *The Wall*, but rejected by the group. Mason's contributions were negligible, Gilmour showed little interest - eventually asking that his production credit be removed - and Pink Floyd's fragmentation was evident to all. One single, 'Not Now John', did reach the UK Top 30, but by the end of the year knives were drawn and an acrimonious parting ensued. The following year Waters began a high-profile but commercially moribund solo career. Mason and Gilmour also issued solo albums (Wright completed his in 1978), but none of these releases came close to the success of their former group. The guitarist retained a higher profile as a session musician, and appeared with Brian Ferry at the Live Aid concert in 1984.

In 1987 Mason and Gilmour decided to resume work together under the Pink Floyd banner; Rick Wright also returned, albeit as a salaried member. Waters instigated an injunction, which was overruled, allowing temporary use of the name. The cryptically titled *A Momentary Lapse Of Reason*, although tentative in places, sounded more like a Pink Floyd album than its sombre 'predecessor', despite the muted input of Wright and Mason. Instead Gilmour relied on session musicians, including Phil Manzanera of Roxy Music. A massive world tour began in September that year, culminating 12 months and 200 concerts later. A live set, *Delicate Sound Of Thunder* followed in its wake but, more importantly, the rigours of touring rekindled Wright and Mason's confidence. Galvanized, Waters led an all-star cast for an extravagant adaptation of *The Wall*, performed live on the remains of the Berlin Wall in 1990. Despite international television coverage, the show failed to reignite his fortunes. In 1994 his former colleagues released *The Division Bell*, an accomplished set which may yet enter the Pink Floyd lexicon as one of their finest achievements. 'It sounds more like a genuine Pink Floyd album than anything since *Wish You Were Here*', Gilmour later stated, much to the relief of fans, critics and the band themselves. With Wright a full-time member again and Mason on sparkling form, the group embarked on another lengthy tour, judiciously balancing old and new material. The band also showcased their most spectacular lightshow to date during these performances. Critical praise was effusive, confirming that the group had survived the loss of yet another nominally 'crucial' member. *Pulse* cashed in on the success of the tours and was a perfectly recorded live album. The packaging featured a flashing LED, which was supposed to last (in flashing mode) for 6 months. The legacy of those 'faceless' record sleeves is irrefutable; Pink Floyd's music is somehow greater than the individuals creating it.

●ALBUMS: *The Piper At The Gates Of Dawn* (EMI Columbia 1967)★★★, *Saucerful Of Secrets* (EMI Columbia 1968)★★★★, *More* soundtrack (EMI Columbia 1969)★★, *Ummagumma* (Harvest 1969)★★★, *Atom Heart Mother* (Harvest 1970)★★★, *Meddle* (Harvest 1971)★★★★, *Obscured By Clouds* soundtrack (Harvest 1972)★★, *Dark Side Of The Moon* (Harvest 1973)★★★★★, *Wish You Were Here* (Harvest 1975)★★★★, *Animals* (Harvest 1977)★★★★, *The Wall* (Harvest 1979)★★★★, *The Final Cut* (Harvest 1983)★★, *A Momentary Lapse Of Reason* (EMI 1987)★★★, *Delicate Sound Of Thunder* (EMI 1988)★★★, *The Division Bell* (EMI 1994)★★★, *Pulse* (EMI 1995)★★. Solo: Rick Wright *Wet Dream* Harvest 1978)★★, with Dave Harris *Zee* (Harvest 1984)★★, *Broken China* (EMI 1996)★★.

●COMPILATIONS: *Relics* Harvest 1971)★★★★, *A Nice Pair* (Harvest 1974)★★★★, *First Eleven* 11-LP box set (EMI 1977)★★★, *A Collection Of Great Dance Songs* (Harvest 1981)★★, *Works* (Capitol 1983)★★★, *Shine On* 8-CD box set (EMI 1992)★★★.

●VIDEOS: *Pink Floyd: London '66-'67* (See For Miles 1994), *Delicate Sound Of Thunder* (Columbia 1994), *Live At Pompeii* (4 Front 1995), *Pulse: 20,10,94* (PMI 1995).

●FURTHER READING: *The Pink Floyd*, Rick Sanders. *Pink Floyd*, Jean Marie Leduc. *Pink Floyd: The Illustrated Discography*, Miles. *The Wall*, Roger Waters and David Appleby. *Syd Barrett: The Making Of The Madcap Laughs*, Malcom Jones. *Pink Floyd: Another Brick*, Miles. *Pink Floyd: A Visual Documentary*, Miles and Andy Mabbett. *Pink Floyd: Bricks In The Wall*, Karl Dallas. *Sauceful Of Secrets: The Pink Floyd Odyssey*, Nicholas Schaffner. *Pink Floyd Back-Stage*, Bob Hassall. *Pink Floyd*, W. Ruhlmann. *Complete Guide To The Music Of*, Andy Mabbett. *Pink Floyd Through The Eyes Of ... The Band, Its Fans, Friends And Foes*, Bruno MacDonald (ed.).

PIPKINS

This clownish duo of Roger Cook and Tony Burrows had first sung together professionally in the Kestrels. They were reunited in 1969 to record and promote 'Gimme Dat Ding!', an infuriatingly insidious ditty composed by Mike Hazelwood and Albert Hammond for the UK children's television series, *Oliver And The Overlord*. A polished production, it jostled to number 6 in the domestic

hit parade in 1970 after several outsized trouser-dropping plugs by Burrows and Cook on *Top Of The Pops*. The single also made the US Top 10 and an accompanying album reached the lower regions of the US Top 200 lists. This was the last the world saw of the Pipkins - but their triumph was but one in a golden year for Burrows who, in his capacity as a session vocalist, also ministered to 1970 hits by Edison Lighthouse, White Plains and Brotherhood Of Man.
●ALBUMS: *Gimme Dat Ding* (Columbia 1970)★★.

PIRATES

The original Pirates - Alan Caddy (lead guitar), Tony Docherty (rhythm guitar), Johnny Gordon (bass), Ken McKay (drums), Mike West and Tom Brown (backing vocals) - formed in 1959 to back singer Johnny Kidd. The line-up later underwent extensive changes, but by 1962 had settled around Mick Green (guitar), Johnny Spence (bass) and Frank Farley (drums), each of whom were former members of the Redcaps. Their recording commitments to Kidd aside, the trio also completed an excellent 'solo' single in 1964 which coupled rousing versions of 'My Babe' and 'Casting My Spell'. John Weider, later of the New Animals and Family, joined the Pirates when Green left to join the Dakotas later that year, but he in turn was replaced by Jon Morshead. The newcomer accompanied Spence and Farley on a second single, 'Shades Of Blue', recorded in 1966 upon splitting permanently from Kidd. However, the trio was disbanded within weeks when the latter joined erstwhile colleague Green in the Dakotas, from where they subsequently moved into the Cliff Bennett Band. The pair then forged separate careers but revived the Pirates, with Spence, in 1976. Their inspired, uncluttered grasp of R&B proved highly popular and a series of powerful albums, although not major sellers, showed a group of undoubted purpose. They disbanded again in 1982, weary of incessant touring, but the Pirates remain one of British pop's most enduring acts. Green's distinctive, staccato, rhythm/lead style was later adopted by Wilko Johnson of Dr. Feelgood, and he remains one of the UK's most respected musicians.
●ALBUMS: *Out Of Their Skulls* (Warners 1977)★★★, *Skull Wars* (Warners 1978)★★★, *Happy Birthday Rock 'N' Roll* (Cube 1979)★★★, *A Fistful Of Dubloons* (Edsel 1981)★★★, *Still Shakin'* (Thunderbolt 1988)★★★.

PLASTIC ONO BAND

Formed in 1969, the Plastic Ono band initially served as an alternative outlet for John Lennon and his wife Yoko Ono during the fractious final days of the Beatles. The group's debut single, 'Give Peace A Chance', was recorded live in a Montreal hotel room during the much-publicized 'Bed-In' and featured an assortment of underground luminaries attending this unconventional anti-war protest. A more structured group - Lennon, Ono, Eric Clapton (guitar), Klaus Voorman (bass) and Alan White (drums) - was assembled for a Canadian

concert captured on *Live Peace In Toronto 1969*. This audio-verité release contrasted Ono's free-form and lengthy 'Don't Worry Kyoto' with several rock 'n' roll standards and a preview airing of 'Cold Turkey', the nerve-twitching composition which became the second Plastic Ono single when the Beatles spurned Lennon's initial offer. Bereft of the cosy sentiments of 'Give Peace A Chance', this tough rocker failed to emulate its predecessor's number 2 position, a fact noted by Lennon when he returned his MBE in protest at British passivity over conflicts in Biafra and Vietnam. An expanded version of the group performed at the Lyceum in London during a UNICEF benefit and the Plastic Ono name was also used in a supporting role on several ensuing John and Yoko releases, notably *John Lennon: The Plastic Ono Band*, the artist's first, and arguably finest, solo album. Inspired by Arthur Janov's Primal Scream Therapy, the album was a veritable exorcism of all Lennon's past demons, and a harrowing yet therapeutic glimpse into the abyss of his soul from the bleak atheism of 'God' to the Oedipal 'Mother', the self-mocking 'Working Class Hero', the elegiac child-like wonderment of 'Remember', the confrontation with the self in 'Isolation' and the spine-chilling, macabre nursery rhyme ending, 'My Mummy's Dead'. Voorman was the sole survivor from the earlier version of the Plastic Ono Band, which had included George Harrison and Ringo Starr. Although the epithet also appeared on *Imagine*, *Sometime In New York City* and *Walls And Bridges* (where it was dubbed the Plastic Ono Nuclear Band), it simply applied to whichever musicians had made contributions and had ceased to have any real meaning.
●ALBUMS: *Live Peace In Toronto 1969* (Apple 1970)★★★, *John Lennon: The Plastic Ono Band* (Apple 1970)★★★★★, *Sometime In New York City* also contains the group's live Lyceum concert recording (Apple 1972)★★★.

POCO

This US group formed as Pogo in the summer of 1968 from the ashes of the seminal Buffalo Springfield, who along with the Byrds were pivotal in the creation of country rock. The band comprised Richie Furay (b. 9 May 1944, Yellow Springs, Ohio, USA; vocals/guitar), Randy Meisner (b. 8 March, 1946, Scottsbluff, Nebraska, USA; vocal/bass), George Grantham (b. 20 November 1947, Cordell, Oklahoma, USA; drums/vocals), Jim Messina (b. 5 December 1947, Harlingen, Texas, USA; vocals/guitar) and Rusty Young (b. 23 February 1946, Long Beach, California, USA; vocals/pedal steel guitar). Following an objection from Walt Kelly, the copyright owner of the Pogo cartoon character, they adopted the infinitely superior name, Poco. Poco defined as a musical term means 'a little' or 'little by little'. Their debut *Pickin' Up The Pieces* was arguably more country than rock, but its critical success made Poco the leaders of the genre. Meisner departed (later to co-found the Eagles) following a disagreement and *Poco* was released by the remaining quartet, again to critical applause, and like its predecessor made a respectable showing midway in the US Top 100. The album's landmark was an entire side consisting of a Latin-styled, mainly instrumental suite, 'El Tonto De Nadie Regresa'. On this, Rusty Young pushed the capabilities of pedal steel to its limit with an outstanding performance, and justifiably became one of America's top players. The energetically live *Deliverin'* made the US Top 30, the band having added the vocal talent of Timothy B. Schmit (b. 30 October 1947, Sacramento, California, USA; bass/vocals) and from the Illinois Speed Press, Paul Cotton (b. 26 February 1943, Los Angeles, California, USA; vocal/guitar). The departing Jim Messina then formed a successful partnership, Loggins And Messina, with Kenny Loggins. The new line-up consolidated their position with *From The Inside*, but it was the superb *A Good Feelin' To Know* that became their most critically acclaimed work. Contained on this uplifting set are some of Furay's finest songs; there were no weak moments, although worthy of special mention are the title track and the sublime 'I Can See Everything'. Another strong collection, *Crazy Eyes*, included another Furay classic in the 10-minute title track. Furay was tempted away by a lucrative offer to join a planned supergroup with Chris Hillman and J.D. Souther. Poco, meanwhile, persevered, still producing fine albums, but with moderate sales. Looking over their shoulder, they could see their former support band the Eagles carrying away their mantle.

During the mid-70s the stable line-up of Cotton, Schmit, Grantham and Young released three excellent albums, *Head Over Heels*, *Rose Of Cimarron* and *Indian Summer*. Each well-produced record contained a palatable mix of styles with each member except Grantham, an accomplished writer, and as always their production standards were immaculate. Inexplicably the band were unable to broach the US Top 40, and like Furay, Schmit was tempted away to join the monstrously successful Eagles. Grantham left shortly afterwards and the future looked decidedly bleak. The recruitment from England of two new members, Charlie Harrison (bass/vocals) and Steve Chapman (drums/vocals), seemed like artistic suicide, but following the further addition of American Kim Bullard on keyboards, they released *Legend* in 1978. Justice was seen to be done; the album made the US Top 20, became a million-seller and dealt them two major hit singles, 'Crazy Love' and 'Heart Of The Night'. This new stable line-up made a further four albums with gradually declining success. Poco sounded particularly jaded on *Ghost Town* in 1982; the magic had evaporated. A contract-fulfilling *Inamorata* was made in 1984. Fans rejoiced to see Furay, Grantham and Schmit together again, and although it was a fine album it sold poorly. Poco then disappeared. Five years later rumours circulated of a new Poco, and lo, Furay, Messina, Meisner, Grantham and Young returned with the exhilarating *Legacy*. Ironically, after all the years of frustration, this was one of their biggest albums,

spawning further hit singles. Poco remain, along with the Eagles, the undefeated champions of country rock.
●ALBUMS: *Pickin' Up The Pieces* (Epic 1969)★★★, *Poco* (Epic 1970)★★★, *Deliverin'* (Epic 1971)★★★, *From The Inside* (Epic 1971)★★★, *A Good Feelin' To Know* (Epic 1972)★★★★, *Crazy Eyes* (Epic 1973)★★★, *Seven* (Epic 1974)★★★, *Cantamos* (Epic 1974)★★, *Head Over Heels* (ABC 1975)★★★★, *Live* (Epic 1976)★★, *Rose Of Cimarron* (ABC 1976)★★★★, *Indian Summer* (ABC 1977)★★★★, *Legend* (ABC 1978)★★★, *Under The Gun* (MCA 1980)★★, *Blue And Gray* (MCA 1981)★★, *Cowboys And Englishmen* (MCA 1982)★★, *Ghost Town* (Atlantic 1982)★★, *Inamorata* (Atlantic 1984)★★★, *Legacy* (RCA 1989)★★★.
●COMPILATIONS: *The Very Best Of Poco* (Epic 1975)★★★, *Songs Of Paul Cotton* (Epic 1980)★★★, *Songs Of Richie Furay* (Epic 1980)★★★, *Backtracks* (MCA 1983)★★★, *Crazy Loving: The Best Of Poco 1975-1982* (RCA 1989)★★★, *Poco: The Forgotten Trail 1969-1974* (Epic/Legacy 1990)★★★★.

POINTER SISTERS

These four sisters, Anita (b. 23 January 1948), Bonnie (b. 11 July 1950), Ruth (b. 1946) and June (b. 1954), were all born and raised in Oakland, California, USA, and first sang together in the West Oakland Church of God where their parents were ministers. Despite their family's reservations, Bonnie, June and Anita embarked on a secular path which culminated in work as backing singers with several of the region's acts including Cold Blood, Boz Scaggs, Elvin Bishop and Grace Slick. Ruth joined the group in 1972, a year before their self-named debut album was released. During this early period the quartet cultivated a nostalgic 40s image, where feather boas and floral dresses matched their close, Andrews Sisters-styled harmonies. Their repertoire, however, was remarkably varied and included versions of Allen Toussaint's 'Yes We Can Can' and Willie Dixon's 'Wang Dang Doodle', as well as original compositions. One such song, 'Fairytale', won a 1974 Grammy award for Best Country Vocal Performance. However, the sisters were uneasy with the typecast, nostalgia image restraining them as vocalists. They broke up briefly in 1977, but while Bonnie Pointer embarked on a solo career, the remaining trio regrouped and signed with producer Richard Perry's new label, Planet. 'Fire', a crafted Bruce Springsteen composition, was a million-selling single in 1979, and the group's rebirth was complete. The Pointers' progress continued with two further gold discs, 'He's So Shy' and the sensual 'Slow Hand', while two 1984 releases, 'Jump (For My Love)' and 'Automatic', won further Grammy awards. June and Anita also recorded contemporaneous solo releases, but although 'Dare Me' gave the group another major hit in 1985, subsequent work lacked the sparkle of their earlier achievements.
●ALBUMS: *The Pointer Sisters* (Blue Thumb 1973)★★★, *That's A Plenty* (Blue Thumb 1974)★★, *Live At The Opera*

House (Blue Thumb 1974)★★, *Steppin'* (Blue Thumb 1975)★★, *Havin' A Party* (Blue Thumb 1977)★★, *Energy* (Planet 1978)★★★, *Priority* (Planet 1979)★★★, *Special Things* (Planet 1980)★★★, *Black And White* (Planet 1981)★★★, *So Excited!* (Planet 1982)★★★, *Break Out* (Planet 1983)★★★, *Contact* (RCA 1985)★★★, *Hot Together* (RCA 1986)★★, *Serious Slammin'* (RCA 1988)★★, *Right Rhythm* (Motown 1990)★★, *Only Sisters Can Do That* (1993)★★. Solo: Anita Pointer *Love For What It Is* (RCA 1987)★★. June Pointer *Baby Sitter* (Planet 1983)★★.

●COMPILATIONS: *The Best Of The Pointer Sisters* (Blue Thumb 1976)★★★★, *Pointer Sister's Greatest Hits* (Planet 1982)★★★, *Jump - The Best Of The Pointer Sisters* (RCA 1989)★★★★, *The Collection* (1993)★★★.

PRELUDE

A light UK folk trio formed in 1970, when Irene Hume (b. Irene Marshall, 5 August 1948, Gateshead, Tyne And Wear, England; vocals/percussion) began singing with her husband Brian Hume (b. 21 June 1947, Gateshead, Tyne And Wear, England; guitar/vocals), and Ian Vardy (b. 21 March 1947, Gateshead, Tyne And Wear, England; guitar/vocals). They began to write their own material and built a following on the folk circuit. *How Long Is Forever?* was recorded at Rockfield studios in Wales, and it was from this release that the cover of Neil Young's 'After The Goldrush' was taken. This single reached number 21 in the UK charts in January 1974 - and when reissued eight years later got to number 28. Their first nationwide tour followed, with Michael Chapman. 'After The Goldrush' also charted in the US peaking at number 22, and the group subsequently toured the USA. They then toured the UK supporting artists such as Ralph McTell and Joan Armatrading. 'Platinum Blonde' reached number 45 in the UK charts in 1980, and in the same year the group made a comeback with *Prelude*. In 1981 they toured the UK with Don McLean. Apart from the release of 'Only The Lonely', which climbed to number 55 in the UK charts in 1982, the next few years were spent touring and recording, but nothing was released, and Vardy left the band in 1985. Irene and Brian continued as a duo until 1987, when they were joined by Jim Hornsby (guitar/dobro). By 1993, Hornsby had left and Prelude continued as a duo once more, still writing and performing on the folk circuit.

●ALBUMS: *How Long Is Forever?* (Dawn 1973)★★★, *Dutch Courage* (Dawn 1975)★★, *Owl Creek Incident* (Dawn 1975)★★, *Back Into The Light* (Pye 1976)★★, *Prelude* (1980)★★.

PRESTON, BILLY

b. 9 September 1946, Houston, Texas, USA. Preston's topsy-turvy musical career began in 1956 when he played organ with gospel singer, Mahalia Jackson and appeared in the film *St Louis Blues* as a young W.C. Handy. As a teenager he worked with Sam Cooke and Little Richard and it was during the latter's 1962 European tour that Billy first met the Beatles, with whom he later collaborated. Preston established himself as an adept instrumentalist recording in his own right, especially on the driving 'Billy's Bag'. He also appeared frequently as a backing musician on the US television show, *Shindig*. After relocating to Britain as part of the Ray Charles' revue he was signed to Apple in 1969. George Harrison produced his UK hit, 'That's The Way God Planned It', and Preston also contributed keyboards to the Beatles' 'Get Back' and *Let It Be*. The following year he made a guest appearance at the Concert For Bangla Desh. He subsequently moved to A&M Records where he had a successful run of hit singles, with 'Outa-Space' (1972), a US number 1 in 1973 with 'Will It Go Round In Circles', 'Space Race' (1973), and another US number 1 in 1974 with 'Nothing From Nothing'. His compositional talents were also in evidence on 'You Are So Beautiful', a US Top 10 hit for Joe Cocker. Preston meanwhile continued as a sideman, most notably with Sly And The Family Stone and on the Rolling Stones' 1975 US tour. A sentimental duet with Syreeta, 'With You I'm Born Again', was an international hit in 1980. In 1989 Preston toured with Ringo Starr's All Star Band and recorded for Ian Levine's Motor City label in 1990-91, including further collaborations with Syreeta. He was arrested on a morals charge in the USA in 1991.

●ALBUMS: *Gospel In My Soul* (1962)★★, *16 Year Old Soul* (Derby 1963)★★, *The Most Exciting Organ Ever* (VeeJay 1965)★★★, *Early Hits Of 1965* (Vee Jay 1965)★★, *The Apple Of Their Eye* (1965)★★, *The Wildest Organ In Town!* (VeeJay 1966)★★★, *That's The Way God Planned It* (Apple 1969)★★★, *Greazee Soul* (Apple 1969)★★★, *Encouraging Words* (Apple 1970)★★, *I Wrote A Simple Song* (A&M 1972)★★★, *Music Is My Life* (A&M 1972)★★★, *Everybody Likes Some Kind Of Music* (A&M 1973)★★, *The Kids & Me* (A&M 1974)★★★, *Live European Tour* (A&M 1974), *It's My Pleasure* (A&M 1975)★★★, *Do What You Want* (A&M 1976), *Billy Preston* (A&M 1976)★★, *A Whole New Thing* (A&M 1977)★★, *Soul'd Out* (A&M 1977)★★, with Syreeta *Fast Break* film soundtrack (Motown 1979)★★, *Late At Night* (Motown 1980)★★★, *Behold* (Myrrh 1980)★★, *Universal Love* (1980)★★, *The Way I Am* (Motown 1981)★★, *Billy Preston & Syreeta* (Motown 1981)★★, *Pressin' On* (Motown 1982)★★, *Billy's Back* (NuGroov 1995)★★.

●COMPILATIONS: *The Best Of Billy Preston* (A&M 1988)★★★, *Collection* (Castle 1989)★★★.

PREVIN, DORY

b. Dory Langdon, 27 October 1937, Woodbridge, New Jersey, USA, she was the daughter of a musician who became a child singer and dancer in New Jersey, graduating to musical theatre as a chorus line member. Her abilities as a songwriter next brought Langdon work composing music for television programmes. After moving to Hollywood, she met and married André

Previn in 1959, the year in which he composed the tune 'No Words For Dory'. Now a lyricist for movie sound-tracks, Dory Previn worked with Andre, Elmer Bernstein and others on songs for such films as *Pepe*, *Two For The Seesaw*, and *Valley Of The Dolls*, whose theme tune was a big hit for Dionne Warwick in 1967. By now the Previns had separated and in the late 60s Dory turned to more personal lyrics, publishing a book of poems before launching a recording career with United Artists. Produced by Nik Venet, her early albums were noted for angry, intimate and often despairing material like 'The Lady With The Braid' and 'Who Will Follow Norma Jean?'. The title track of *Mary C. Brown & The Hollywood Sign* was based on a true story of a suicide attempt and was turned by Previn into a stage musical. In 1974, she left U.A. for Warner Brothers Records where Joel Dorn produced her 1976 album.

●ALBUMS: *On My Way To Where* (United Artists 1970)★★, *Mythical Kings & Iguanas* (United Artists 1971)★★★, *Reflections In A Mud Puddle* (United Artists 1971)★★, *Mary C. Brown & The Hollywood Sign* (United Artists 1972)★★★, *Live At Carnegie Hall* (United Artists 1973)★★, *Dory Previn* (Warners 1975)★★★, *We Are Children Of Coincidence And Harpo Marx* (Warners 1976)★★, *1 AM Phone Calls* (1977)★★.

●FURTHER READING: *Midnight Baby: An Autobiography*, Dory Previn. *Bog-Trotter: An Autobiography With Lyrics*, Dory Previn.

PRICE, ALAN

b. 19 April 1941, Fatfield, Co. Durham, England. From the age of eight Price taught himself the piano, guitar and bass and lost no time in playing with local bands, usually containing various members of the as yet unformed Animals. His first major band was variously known as the Kansas City Five, (or Seven or Nine), the Kontours, the Pagans and finally the Alan Price Rhythm And Blues Combo. The late Graham Bond recommended the combo to his manager Ronan O'Rahilly and the name was changed as the band prepared to infiltrate the London R&B scene. As the most musically talented member of the Animals, Price eventually found the constant high profile and touring too much. Always an introvert and having a more sophisticated and broader musical palette than the rest of the band, it was only a matter of time before the mentally exhausted Price left the Animals. Fear of flying was given as the official reason in May 1965, although leaving the band at the peak of their success was seen as tantamount to professional suicide. That year he appeared in the D.A. Pennebaker movie *Don't Look Back* as one of Bob Dylan's entourage. Within a short time he had assembled the Alan Price Set, who debuted in August that year with 'Any Day Now'. Although not a hit, the record showed great promise. This was confirmed with their second release, a stirring version of Screamin' Jay Hawkins' 'I Put A Spell On You'. While the record featured Price's distinctive fast arpeggio organ sound, the public were happy to discover that he could also sing well.

He followed with further singles which showed an unashamedly pop bias. In 1967 he had two major hits written by Randy Newman; 'Simon Smith And His Amazing Dancing Bear' and 'The House That Jack Built'. In 1970 he teamed up with Georgie Fame as Fame And Price Together and had a hit with the MOR-sounding 'Rosetta'. That same year he wrote the score for two musicals, *Home*, written by Lindsay Anderson, and his own *The Brass Band Man*. Price was then commissioned to write the music for Anderson's film, *O Lucky Man!* in 1973, for which he won a BAFTA award. His apparent serious nature and 'straight' appearance kept him apart from the hipper music scene, of which his former colleague Eric Burdon was one of the leading lights. His vaudeville-tinged playing effectively allied him with an older audience. In 1974 Price once again went against the grain and hit the charts with 'Jarrow Song', having been brought up in the town famous for its workers' march of 1936. Price's social conscience was stirred, and he produced the excellent autobiographical album *Between Today And Yesterday*. The critical success of the album garnered him a BBC television documentary.

Price starred in *Alfie Darling* in 1975, winning the Most Promising New British Actor award. In 1978 and 1979 he dented the charts with 'Just For You', some copies of which were pressed in heart-shaped red vinyl. He enjoys a fruitful career, often appears on television and is always able to fill a concert hall, in addition to continuing to write stage musicals like *Andy Capp* and *Who's A Lucky Boy?* Price took part in two abortive Animals reunions in 1977 and 1983. He recorded a new album in 1996 with his Electric Blues Company which was a return to his R&B club days in Newcastle, albeit that he is now based in Barnes, south London.

●ALBUMS: *The Price To Play* (Decca 1966)★★★, *A Price On His Head* (Decca 1967)★★★, *The Price Is Right* (Parrot 1968)★★★, *Fame And Price, Price And Fame Together* (Columbia 1971)★★★, *O Lucky Man!* film soundtrack (Warners 1973)★★★, *Between Today And Yesterday* (Warners 1974)★★★★, *Metropolitan Man* (Polydor 1974)★★★, *Performing Price* (Polydor 1975)★★★, *Shouts Across The Street* (Polydor 1976)★★★, *Rainbows End* (Jet 1977)★★, *Alan Price* (Jet 1977)★★, *England My England* (Jet 1978)★★★, *Rising Sun* (Jet 1980)★★★, *A Rock And Roll Night At The Royal Court* (Key 1981)★★★, *Geordie Roots And Branches* (MWM 1983)★★★, *Travellin' Man* (Trojan 1986)★★★, *Liberty* (Ariola 1989)★★★, *Live In Concert* (1993)★★, with The Electric Blues Company *A Gigster's Life For Me* (Indigo 1995)★★.

●COMPILATIONS: *The World Of Alan Price* (Decca 1970)★★★, *Profile: Alan Price* (Teldec 1983)★★, *16 Golden Classics* (Unforgettable 1986)★★, *Greatest Hits* (K-Tel 1987)★★, *The Best Of Alan Price* (MFP 1987)★★★, *The Best Of And The Rest Of* (Action Replay 1989)★★★.

●FURTHER READING: *Wild Animals*, Andy Blackford.

PRIDE, CHARLEY

b. 18 March 1938, Sledge, Mississippi, USA. Charley Pride was born on a cotton farm, which, as a result of his success, he was later able to purchase. Pride says, 'My dad named me Charl Frank Pride, but I was born in the country and the midwife wrote it down as Charley'. Harold Dorman, who wrote and recorded 'Mountain of Love', also hails from Sledge and wrote 'Mississippi Cotton Pickin' Delta Town' about the area, for Pride. As an adolescent, Pride followed what he heard on the radio with a cheap guitar, breaking with stereotypes by preferring country music to the blues. He played baseball professionally but he reverted to music when the Los Angeles Angels told him that he didn't have a 'major league arm'. In 1965 producer Jack Clement brought Pride to Chet Atkins at RCA Records. They considered not disclosing that he was black until the records were established, but Atkins decided that it was unfair to all concerned. 'The Snakes Crawl at Night' sold on its own merit and it was followed by 'Just Between You And Me' which won a Grammy for the best country record by a male performer. On 7 January 1967 Ernest Tubb introduced him at the *Grand Ole Opry*, 42 years after the first black performer to appear there, DeFord Bailey in 1925. Prejudice ran high but the quality of Pride's music, particularly the atmospheric live album from Panther Hall, meant that he was accepted by the redneck community. At one momentous concert, Willie Nelson kissed him onstage. Pride has had 29 number 1 records on the US country charts including six consecutive chart-toppers between 1969 and 1971. An extraordinary feat.

His most significant recordings include 'Is Anybody Goin' to San Antone?', which he learned and recorded in 15 minutes, and 'Crystal Chandelier', which he took from a Carl Belew record and is still the most-requested song in UK country clubs. Strangely enough, 'Crystal Chandelier' was not a US hit, where his biggest single is 'Kiss An Angel Good Mornin''. Unfortunately, Pride fell into the same trap as Elvis Presley by recording songs that he published, so he did not always record the best material available. Nevertheless, over the years, Charley Pride has encouraged such new talents as Kris Kristofferson, Ronnie Milsap, Dave And Sugar (who were his back-up singers) and Gary Stewart (who was his opening act). In 1975 Pride hosted a live double-album from the *Opry*, *In Person*, which also featured Atkins, Milsap, Dolly Parton, Jerry Reed and Stewart. By the mid-80s, Pride was disappointed at the way RCA was promoting 'New Country' in preference to established performers so he left the label. He then recorded what is arguably his most interesting project, a tribute album to Brook Benton. Sadly, it was not released, as he signed with 16th Avenue Records who preferred new material. Records like 'I'm Gonna Love Her On The Radio' and 'Amy's Eyes' continue his brand of easy listening country, but he has yet to recapture his sales of

the late 60s. Pride has had a long and contented family life and his son, Dion, plays in his band ('We took the name from Dion And The Belmonts. We just liked it.'). Seeing him perform in concert underlines what a magnificent voice he has. Sadly, he does not test it in other, more demanding musical forms, although he argues that 'the most powerful songs are the simple ones.'

● ALBUMS: *Country Charley Pride* (RCA 1966)★★★, *Pride Of Country Music* (RCA 1967)★★★★, *The Country Way* (RCA 1968)★★★, *Make Mine Country* (RCA 1968)★★★, *Songs Of Pride ... Charley, That Is* (RCA 1968)★★★, *Charley Pride - In Person* (RCA 1968)★★★, *The Sensational Charley Pride* (RCA 1969)★★★★, *Just Plain Charley* (RCA 1970)★★★, *Charley Pride's Tenth Album* (RCA 1970)★★★, *Christmas In My Home Town* (RCA 1970)★★, *From Me To You (To All My Wonderful Fans)* (RCA 1971)★★★, *Did You Think To Pray?* (RCA 1971)★★, *I'm Just Me* (RCA 1971)★★★, *Charley Pride Sings Heart Songs* (RCA 1971)★★★, *A Sunshiny Day With Charley Pride* (RCA 1972)★★★, *Songs Of Love By Charley Pride* (RCA 1973)★★★, *Sweet Country* (RCA 1973)★★★, *Amazing Love* (RCA 1973)★★★, *Country Feelin'* (RCA 1974)★★★, *Pride Of America* (RCA 1974)★★, *Charley* (RCA 1975)★★★, *The Happiness Of Having You* (RCA 1975)★★★, *Sunday Morning With Charley Pride* (RCA 1976)★★★, *She's Just An Old Love Turned Memory* (RCA 1977)★★★, *Someone Loves You Honey* (RCA 1978)★★★, *Burgers And Fries* (RCA 1978)★★★, *You're My Jamaica* (RCA 1979)★★, *There's A Little Bit Of Hank In Me* (RCA 1980)★★★, *Roll On Mississippi* (RCA 1981)★★★, *Charley Sings Everybody's Choice* (RCA 1982)★★★, *Live* (1982)★★, *Night Games* (RCA 1983)★★★, *The Power Of Love* (RCA 1984)★★★, *After All This Time* (Ritz 1987)★★★, *I'm Gonna Love Her On The Radio* (Ritz 1988)★★★, *Moody Woman* (1989)★★★, *Amy's Eyes* (Ritz 1990)★★★, *Classics With Pride* (Ritz 1991)★★★★, *My 6 Latest & 6 Greatest* (1993)★★★.

● COMPILATIONS: *The Best Of Charley Pride* (RCA 1969)★★★★, *The Best Of Charley Pride, Volume 2* (RCA 1972)★★★★, *The Incomparable Charley Pride* (RCA 1973)★★★, *The Best Of Charley Pride, Volume 3* (RCA 1977)★★★, *Greatest Hits* (RCA 1981)★★★★, *The Very Best Of ...* (Ritz 1995)★★★★.

● VIDEOS: *Charley Pride-Live* (MSD 1988)★★★, *Charley Pride* (Telstar 1992).

● FURTHER READING: *Charley Pride*, Pamela Barclay. *Pride; The Charley Pride Story*, Charley Pride with Jim Henderson.

PRINE, JOHN

b. 10 October 1946, Maywood, Illinois, USA. Prine came from a musical background in that his Grandfather had played with Merle Travis. Prine started playing guitar at the age of 14. He then spent time in College, worked as a postman for five years, and spent two years in the Army. He began his musical career around 1970, by singing in clubs in the Chicago area. Prine signed to Atlantic in 1971, releasing the powerful *John Prine*. The album contained the excellent Vietnam veteran song 'Sam Stone' with the wonderfully evocative line, 'There's a hole in daddy's arm where all the money goes, and Jesus Christ died for nothing I suppose'. Over the years Prine achieved cult status, his songs being increasingly covered by other artists. 'Angel From Montgomery', 'Speed Of The Sound Of Loneliness', and 'Paradise' being three in particular. He was inevitably given the unenviable tag 'the new Dylan' at one stage. His last album for Atlantic, *Common Sense* (produced by Steve Cropper) was his only album to make the US Top 100. Whilst the quality and content of all his work has been quite excellant his other albums only scratched the US Top 200. His first release for Asylum, *Bruised Orange*, was well received, but the follow-up, *Pink Cadillac*, was not so well accommodated by the public or the critics. However, *The Missing Years* changed everything with massive sales at home, and a Grammy award for best Contemporary Folk Album, making Prine almost a household name. His outstanding songs had been covered by the likes of Bonnie Raitt and John Denver over the years, and he co-wrote the hit 'I Just Want To Dance With You' with Daniel O'Donnell. His career has now taken on taken on a new lease of life in the 90s. Prine presented *Town And Country* for UK's Channel Four Television in 1992, a series of music programmes featuring singers such as Nanci Griffith, and Rodney Crowell. In keeping with his career upswing *Lost Dogs And Mixed Blessings* is another strong work. Prine's songs are getting quirkier and only the author knows what some of them are about.

●ALBUMS: *John Prine* (Atlantic 1972)★★★★, *Diamonds In The Rough* (Atlantic 1972)★★★, *Sweet Revenge* (Atlantic 1973)★★★, *Common Sense* (Atlantic 1975)★★★, *Bruised Orange* (Asylum 1978)★★★, *Pink Cadillac* (Asylum 1979)★★★, *Storm Windows* (Asylum 1980)★★★, *Aimless Love* (Oh Boy 1985)★★★, *German Afternoons* (Demon 1987)★★★, *John Prine Live* (Oh Boy 1988)★★★, *The Missing Years* (Oh Boy 1992)★★★★, *Live* (1993)★★★, *Lost Dogs & Mixed Blessings* (Rykodisk 1995)★★★, *Live On Tour* (Oh Boy 1997)★★★.

●COMPILATIONS: *Prime Prine* (Atlantic 1977)★★, *Anthology: Great Days* (Rhino 1993)★★★★.

PROFESSOR LONGHAIR

b. Henry Roeland Byrd, 19 December 1918, Bogalusa, Louisiana, USA, d. 30 January 1980. Byrd grew up in New Orleans where he was part of a novelty dance team in the 30s. He also played piano, accompanying John Lee 'Sonny Boy' Williamson. After wartime service, Byrd gained a residency at the Caldonia club, whose owner christened him Professor Longhair. By now, he had developed a piano style that combined rumba and mambo element with more standard boogie-woogie and barrelhouse rhythms. Particularly with the help of his most ardent disciple, Dr John, Longhair has become recognized as the most influential New Orleans R&B pianist since Jelly Roll Morton. In 1949 he made

the first record of his most famous tune, 'Mardi Gras In New Orleans' for the Star Talent label, which credited the artist as Professor Longhair And His Shuffling Hungarians. He next recorded 'Baldhead' for Mercury as Roy Byrd and his Blues Jumpers and the song became a national R&B hit in 1950. Soon there were more singles on Atlantic (a new version of 'Mardi Gras' and the well-known 'Tipitina' in 1953) and Federal. A mild stroke interrupted his career in the mid-50s and for some years he performed infrequently apart from at Carnival season when a third version of his topical song, 'Go To The Mardi Gras' (1958) received extensive radio play. Despite recording Earl King's 'Big Chief' in 1964, Longhair was virtually inactive throughout the 60s. He returned to the limelight at the first New Orleans Jazz & Heritage Festival in 1971 when, accompanied by Snooks Eaglin, he received standing ovations. (A recording of the concert was finally issued in 1987). This led to European tours in 1973 and 1975 and to recordings with Gatemouth Brown and for Harvest. Longhair's final album, for Alligator, was completed shortly before he died of a heart attack in January 1980. In 1991 he was posthumously inducted into the Rock 'n' Roll Hall Of Fame.

●ALBUMS: *New Orleans Piano* reissue (Atco 1972)★★★★, *Rock 'N' Roll Gumbo* (1974)★★★★, *Live On The Queen Mary* (Harvest 1978)★★★, *Crawfish Fiesta* (Alligator 1980)★★★, *The London Concert* (1981)★★★, *The Last Mardi Gras* (Atlantic 1982)★★★★, *Houseparty New Orleans Style (The Lost Sessions 1971-1972)* (Rounder 1987)★★★, *Live In Germany* (1993)★★★.

●COMPILATIONS: *Fess: The Professor Longhair Anthology* (Rhino 1994)★★★★.

●FURTHER READING: *A Bio-discography*, John Crosby.

PUNK

While Punk's anti-authoritarian and rebellious imagery has its antecedents in both the 50s and 60s, the music itself was very much a product of its environment and decade - the 70s. Critics disagree as to its exact birthplace. New York's 'no-wave' movement of the mid-70s (Ramones, Television) set the historical precedent, building from a platform of raw native rock, originated by the Stooges and MC5. Significantly, the Sex Pistols were managed by Malcolm McClaren, who had worked with the New York Dolls as well as learning from the Situationist rhetoric of the Paris student revolts of the late 60s. Certainly the Ramones' sound, primal rock 'n' roll executed in minimalist fashion, has been the dominant thread in musical terms through to the 90s. However, the Sex Pistols achieved something more powerful in their brief career, with their 'no future' ideology capturing a massive following among Britain's disenfranchised urban youth. Others soon took the baton from them. The Clash built an ideological framework that dominated punk until their demise in the early 80s. The Buzzcocks were practically the only group to concentrate on romance - although 'Orgasm

Addict', an early ode to masturbation, revealed how the new agenda was being shaped. Siouxsie And The Banshees, former camp followers of the Pistols, added art school chic and in their lead singer had the most powerful female figurehead of the day. The Damned were rarely dignified with serious consideration because of their self-deprecating humour, an impression which does little justice to their inherent charisma and musical vitality. The Stranglers' contribution has been historically deconstructed and disposed of, but their engaging anti-charisma and petulance fitted the times perfectly. Along with the Clash's Joe Strummer, they offered the strongest link between punk and the musically sympathetic pub rock scene of the mid-70s. The Jam were the band most obviously rooted in conventional pop music, and this was both their downfall (they were widely attacked for their conservatism - wearing suits and adopting what author Jon Savage unkindly referred to as 'Little Englandisms') and triumph (Paul Weller was one of the most capable songwriters of his generation). Other bands of note included Alternative TV, formed by *Sniffin' Glue* editor Mark Perry, the Adverts (whose epithet 'One Chord Wonders' defined the punk ethos of enthusiasm over technical ability), X Ray Spex, the Slits and many more. What was unique to the punk movement was the space it allowed disparate ideas to form. From Jayne County's transexuality to the pre-teen punk of Eater, punk legitimized access to an art form previously reserved for career musicians - a reaction in part to the perceived studied, detached virtuosity of the rock groups of the early and mid-70s. Punk shook not only the music industry from its complacency but also deeply affected England's self-image. The Sex Pistols swearing on television provoked genuine moral outrage. More enduringly, the group's acidic 'God Save The Queen' was the most important social document of dissidence in an otherwise nationalistic period celebrating the reigning monarch's Jubilee year. The backlash was palpable - members of the Sex Pistols were attacked with knives in the street and with banner headlines ('The Filth And The Fury') in the mainstream press. The Sex Pistols' spark became global currency. In America many bands followed the Sex Pistols' lead, beginning with the Germs. Darby Crash of the Germs mirrored the nihilism of the Pistols' anarchic figurehead Sid Vicious and was soon dead from a drug overdose. Also in California the Dead Kennedys and Black Flag became popular, the former contributing articulate, ultra-liberal messages, the latter providing a blueprint for the punk derivation known as hardcore. Minor Threat, located in America's capital, had even greater influence with their puritanical beliefs (no meat, drugs, alcohol, casual sex). Formerly of the same state, Bad Brains relocated to New York as the first black punk group and wrote the enduring 'Pay To Cum'. Punk bands soon formed in every country and continent in the world, supported by an international network of DIY fanzines and self-promoted concerts. In the 80s,

with the Sex Pistols long gone and the Clash artistically redundant, the punk movement splintered irrevocably. The communal society of Crass and their ilk contrasted sharply with supporters of Oi!, where violent imagery betrayed a flirtation with extreme right-wing politics. Despite revival tours and a gaggle of groups less worthy of close attention (Vibrators, UK Subs) continuing to release records, punk had succumbed to messy partisanship. Ironically, the risible Exploited's cry of 'Punk's Not Dead', which spearheaded a third wave of punk (Chron Gen, Discharge, Anti-Pasti), was probably the final nail in its coffin. In America hardcore remained popular, and an underground scene propelled by magazines such as *Maximum Rock 'n' Roll* continued to thrive. The development of important groups such as Big Black and Sonic Youth can be definitively linked with the punk tradition, not least by the participants themselves. With Nirvana's arrival in the early 90s punk swung back into vogue. Though called grunge, the trio never claimed to be anything other than a punk band, citing influences such as the Wipers, Raincoats and Ramones. Nirvana's breakthrough opened the way for first Green Day, then the Offspring and Rancid, to become million-sellers. For the first time punk had found mainstream commercial acceptance in the world's biggest music market, prompting *Newsweek* to place the legend '1994 - The Year That Punk Broke' on its cover. Nearly twenty years since its inception punk had found commercial approbation, but its penetration into every strand of media, from broadcast journalism to fashion and art, had long since been cemented.

●VIDEOS: *Punk In London '77* (Studio K7 1991), *The Best Punk Compilation In The World Ever* (Virgin 1995).

●FURTHER READING: *England's Dreaming: Sex Pistols And Punk Rock*, Jon Savage. *Smash The State: A Discography Of Canadian Punk 1977-92*, Frank Manley. *Ranters And Crowd Pleasers: Punk In Pop Music 1977-92*, Greil Marcus. *Punk Diary 1970-1979*, George Gimarc. *Punk: An A-Z*, Barry Lazell. *Destroy: The Definitive History Of Punk*, Alvin Gibbs. *And God Created Punk*, Erica Echenberg and Mark P. *Please Kill Me: The Uncensored Oral History Of Punk*, Legs McNeil and Gillian McCain.

PURE PRAIRIE LEAGUE

Formed in 1971, this US country rock group comprised Craig Lee Fuller (vocals/guitar), George Powell (vocals/guitar), John Call (pedal steel guitar), Jim Lanham (bass) and Jim Caughlin (drums). Their self-titled debut album was a strong effort, which included the excellent 'Tears', 'You're Between Me' (a tribute to McKendree Spring) and 'It's All On Me'. The work also featured some novel sleeve artwork, using Norman Rockwell's portrait of an ageing cowboy as a symbol of the Old West. On *Pure Prairie League*, the figure was seen wistfully clutching a record titled 'Dreams Of Long Ago'. For successive albums, the cowboy was portrayed being ejected from a saloon, stranded in a desert and struggling with a pair of boots. The image effectively gave

Pure Prairie League a brand name, but by the time of their *Bustin' Out*, Fuller and Powell were left to run the group using session musicians. This album proved their masterpiece, one of the best and most underrated records produced in country rock. Its originality lay in the use of string arrangements, for which they recruited the services of former David Bowie acolyte Mick Ronson. His work was particularly effective on the expansive 'Boulder Skies' and 'Call Me Tell Me'. A single from the album, 'Amie', was a US hit and prompted the return of John Call, but when Fuller left in 1975 to form American Flyer, the group lost its major writing talent and inspiration. Powell continued with bassist Mike Reilly, lead guitarist Larry Goshorn and pianist Michael Connor. Several minor albums followed and the group achieved a surprise US Top 10 hit in 1980 with 'Let Me Love You Tonight'. Fuller is now with Little Feat, while latter-day guitarist Vince Gill, who joined Pure Prairie League in 1979, has become a superstar in the country market in the 90s.

●ALBUMS: *Pure Prairie League* (RCA 1972)★★★, *Bustin' Out* (RCA 1975)★★★★, *Two Lane Highway* (RCA 1975)★★★★, *If The Shoe Fits* (RCA 1976)★★★, *Dance* (RCA 1976)★★★, *Live!! Takin' The Stage* (RCA 1977)★★, *Just Fly* (RCA 1978)★★, *Can't Hold Back* (RCA 1979)★★, *Firin' Up* (Casablanca 1980)★★, *Something In The Night* (Casablanca 1981)★★.

●COMPILATIONS: *Pure Prairie Collection* (RCA 1981)★★★.

QUATRO, SUZI

b. 3 June 1950, Detroit, Michigan, USA. From patting bongos at the age of seven in her father's jazz band, she graduated to go-go dancing in a pop series on local television. With an older sister, Patti (later of Fanny) she formed the all-female Suzi Soul And The Pleasure Seekers in 1964 for engagements that included a tour of army bases in Vietnam. In 1971, her comeliness and skills as bass guitarist, singer and chief show-off in Cradle were noted by Mickie Most who persuaded her to record Nicky Chinn-Mike Chapman songs for his RAK label in England. Backed initially by Britons Alastair McKenzie (keyboards), Dave Neal (drums) and her future husband, ex-Nashville Teens member Len Tuckey (guitar), a second RAK single, 1973's 'Can The Can', topped hit parades throughout the world at the zenith of the glam-rock craze - of which rowdy Suzi, androgynous in her glistening biker leathers, became an icon. Her sound hinged mostly on a hard rock chug beneath lyrics in which scansion overruled meaning ('the 48 crash/is a silken sash bash'). The team's winning streak with releases such as '48 Crash', 'Daytona Demon' and 'Devil Gate Drive' - a second UK number 1 - faltered when 'Your Mama Won't Like Me' stuck outside the Top 30, signalling two virtually hitless years before a mellower policy brought a return to the Top 10 with 'If You Can't Give Me Love'. Quatro's chart fortunes in Britain have since lurched from 'She's In Love With You' at number 11 to 1982's 'Heart Of Stone' at a lowly 68. 'Stumblin' In' - duet with Smokie's Chris Norman - was her biggest US Hot 100 strike (number 8) but barely touched the UK Top 40. By the late 80s, her output had reduced to pot-shots like teaming up with Reg Presley of the Troggs for a disco revival of 'Wild Thing'. More satisfying than tilting for hit records, however, was her development as a singing actress - albeit in character as 'Leather Tuscadero' in *Happy Days*, a cameo in ITV's *Minder* and as the heroine of a 1986 London production of Irving Berlin's *Annie Get Your Gun*.

●ALBUMS: *Suzi Quatro* (RAK 1973)★★★, *Quatro* (RAK 1974)★★, *Your Mama Won't Like Me* (RAK 1975)★★, *Aggro-Phobia* (RAK 1977)★★, *Live 'N' Kickin'* (EMI Japan 1977)★★, *If You Knew Suzi* (RAK 1978)★★, *Suzi And Other Four Letter Words* (RAK 1979)★★, *Rock Hard* (Dreamland 1980)★★, *Main Attraction* (Polydor 1983)★★, *Saturday Night Special* (Biff 1987)★★, *Rock 'Til Ya Drop* (Biff 1988)★★.

●COMPILATIONS: *The Suzi Quatro Story* (RAK 1975)★★, *Suzi Quatro's Greatest Hits* (RAK 1980)★★★, *The Wild One (The Greatest Hits)* (EMI 1990)★★★, *The Gold Collection* (EMI 1996)★★★.
●FURTHER READING: *Suzi Quatro*, Margaret Mander.

QUEEN

Arguably Britain's most consistently successful group of the past two decades, Queen began life as a glam rock unit in 1972. Brian May (b. 19 July 1947, Twickenham, Middlesex, England; guitar) and Roger Taylor (b. Roger Meddows-Taylor, 26 July 1949, Kings Lynn, Norfolk, England; drums) had been playing in Johnny Quale And The Reactions, Beat Unlimited and a college group called Smile with bassist Tim Staffell. When the latter left to join Humpty Bong (featuring former Bee Gees drummer Colin Petersen), May and Taylor elected to form a new band with vocalist Freddie Mercury (b. Frederick Bulsara, 5 September 1946, Zanzibar, Africa, d. 24 November 1991). Early in 1971 bassist John Deacon (b. 19 August 1951, Leicester, England) completed the line-up. Queen were signed to EMI late in 1972 and launched the following spring with a gig at London's Marquee club. Soon after the failed single, 'Keep Yourself Alive', they issued a self-titled album, which was an interesting fusion of 70s glam and late 60s heavy rock (it had been preceded by a Mercury 'solo' single, credited to Larry Lurex). Queen toured extensively and recorded a second album which fulfilled their early promise by reaching the UK Top 5. Soon after, 'Seven Seas Of Rhye' gave them their first hit single, while *Sheer Heart Attack* consolidated their commercial standing. The title-track from the album was also the band's first US hit. The pomp and circumstance of Queen's recordings and live act were embodied in the outrageously camp theatrics of the satin-clad Mercury, who was swiftly emerging as one of rock's most notable showmen during the mid-70s. 1975 proved to be a watershed in the group's career. After touring the Far East, they entered the studio with producer Roy Thomas Baker and completed the epic 'Bohemian Rhapsody', in which Mercury succeeded in transforming a seven-minute single into a mini-opera. The track was both startling and unique in pop and dominated the Christmas charts in the UK, remaining at number 1 for an astonishing nine weeks. The power of the single was reinforced by an elaborate video production, highly innovative for its period and later much copied by other acts. An attendant album, *A Night At The Opera*, was one of the most expensive and expansive albums of its period and lodged at number 1 in the UK, as well as hitting the US Top 5. Queen were now aspiring to the superstar bracket. Their career thereafter was a carefully marketed succession of hit singles, annual albums and extravagantly produced stage shows. *A Day At The Races* continued the bombast, while the catchy 'Somebody To Love' and anthemic 'We Are The Champions' both reached number 2 in the UK.

Although Queen seemed in danger of being stereotyped as over-produced glam rock refugees, they successfully brought eclecticism to their singles output with the 50s rock 'n' roll panache of 'Crazy Little Thing Called Love' and the disco-influenced 'Another One Bites The Dust' (both US number 1s). Despite this stylistic diversity, each Queen single seemed destined to become an anthem, as evidenced by the continued use of much of their output on US sporting occasions. The group's soundtrack for the movie *Flash Gordon* was another success, but was cited by many critics as typical of their pretentious approach. By the close of 1981, Queen were back at number 1 in the UK for the first time since 'Bohemian Rhapsody' with 'Under Pressure' (a collaboration with David Bowie). After a flurry of solo ventures, the group returned in fine form in 1984 with the satirical 'Radio Gaga', followed by the histrionic 'I Want To Break Free' (and accompanying cross-dressing video). A performance at 1985's Live Aid displayed the group at their most professional and many acclaimed them the stars of the day, though there were others who accused them of hypocrisy for breaking the boycott of apartheid-locked South Africa. Coincidentally, their next single was 'One Vision', an idealistic song in keeping with the spirit of Live Aid. Queen's recorded output lessened during the late 80s as they concentrated on extra-curricular ventures. The space between releases did not affect the group's popularity, however, as was proven in 1991 when *Innuendo* entered the UK chart at number 1. By this time they had become an institution. Via faultless musicianship, held together by May's guitar virtuosity and the spectacular Mercury; Queen were one of the great theatrical rock acts. The career of the group effectively ended with the death of lead singer Freddie Mercury on 24 November 1991. 'Bohemian Rhapsody' was immediately reissued to raise money for AIDS research projects, and soared to the top of the British charts. A memorial concert for Mercury took place at London's Wembley Stadium in the spring of 1992, featuring an array of stars including Liza Minnelli, Elton John, Guns N'Roses, George Michael, David Bowie and Annie Lennox (Eurythmics). Of the remaining members Brian May's solo career enjoyed the highest profile, while Roger Taylor worked with the Cross. Queen never announced an official break-up, so it was with nervous anticipation that a new Queen album was welcomed in 1995. The Mercury vocals were recorded during his last year while at home in Switzerland and the rest of the band have worked hard on the remaining songs. While Mercury must be applauded for the way he carried his illness with great dignity it is fair to say that May, Taylor and Deacon have done wonders in crafting an album from slightly inferior material. It will never be known whether all the tracks on *Made In Heaven* would have found their way onto an album had Mercury been with us today.
●ALBUMS: *Queen* (EMI 1973)★★★, *Queen II* (EMI 1974)★★★, *Sheer Heart Attack* (EMI 1974)★★★, *A Night*

At The Opera (EMI 1975)★★★, *A Day At The Races* (EMI 1976)★★★, *News Of The World* (EMI 1977)★★, *Jazz* (EMI 1978)★★, *Live Killers* (EMI 1979)★★, *The Game* (EMI 1980)★★★, *Flash Gordon* (EMI 1980)★★, *Hot Space* (EMI 1982)★, *The Works* (EMI 1984)★★★, *A Kind Of Magic* (EMI 1986)★★★, *Live Magic* (EMI 1986)★★, *The Miracle* (EMI 1989)★★, *Queen At The Beeb* (Band Of Joy 1989)★, *Innuendo* (EMI 1991)★★★, *Made In Heaven* (EMI 1995)★★★.
●COMPILATIONS: *Greatest Hits* (EMI 1981)★★★★★, *The Complete Works* (EMI 1985)★★★, *Greatest Hits Vol. 2* (EMI 1991)★★★.
●VIDEOS: *Greatest Flix* (PMI 1984), *We Will Rock You* (Peppermint 1984), *Magic Years Vol. 1, 2 & 3* (PMI 1987), *Live In Budapest* (PMI 1987), *Rare Live* (PMI 1989), *The Miracle* (PMI 1989), *Greatest Flix 2* (Video Collection 1991), *Box Of Flix* (PMI 1991), *Queen At Wembley* (PMI 1992), *Live In Rio* (Music Club 1993), *Champions Of The World* (PMI 1995), *Rock You* (Music Club 1995).
●FURTHER READING: *Queen*, Larry Pryce. *The Queen Story*, George Tremlett. *Queen: The First Ten Years*, Mike West. *Queen's Greatest Pix*, Jacques Lowe. *Queen: An Illustrated Biography*, Judith Davis. *Queen: A Visual Documentary*, Ken Dean. *Freddie Mercury: This Is The Real Life*, David Evans and David Minns. *Queen: As It Began*, Jacky Gun and Jim Jenkins. *Queen Unseen*, Michael Putland. *Queen And I, The Brian May Story*, Laura Jackson. *Queen: A Concert Documentary*, Greg Brooks. *Queen: The Early Years*, Mark Hodkinson. *The Complete Guide To The Music Of ...*, Peter Hogan. *Queen Live*, Greg Brooks. *Freddie Mercury - More Of The Real Life*, David Evans and David Minns.

QUINTESSENCE

This briefly-popular act encapsulated the spiritual ambitions prevalent among sections of the 60s' British 'underground' movement. The original line-up - Raja Ram (b. Ron Rothfield; vocals/flute), Shiva Shankar (aka Shiva Jones; vocals/keyboards), Alan Mostert (lead guitar), Maha Dev (rhythm guitar), Sambhu Babaji (bass) and Jake Milton (drums) - was forged following rehearsals at London's Notting Hill's All Saints Hall and their ensuing debut, *In Blissful Company*, captured the sextet's rudimentary blend of jazz rock and Eastern philosophies. Mostert's powerful guitar style endeared the group to the progressive audience, but a commitment to religious themes was maintained on *Dive Deep* and *Self*. The departures of Shankar and Maha Dev - the former resurfaced in the similarly-styled Kala - robbed Quintessence of a sense of purpose and the group split up following the release of *Indweller*.
●ALBUMS: *In Blissful Company* (Island 1969)★★, *Quintessence* (Island 1970)★★★, *Dive Deep* (Island 1971)★★, *Self* (RCA 1972)★★, *Indweller* (RCA 1972)★★.

QUIVER

Essentially a melodic UK progressive rock band from the ruins of Junior's Eyes, who occasionally followed a country rock path and achieved more success following their merger with the Sutherland Brothers. The line-up was basically Tim Renwick (b. 7 August 1949, Cambridge, England; guitar/vocals/flute) and Cal Batchelor (guitar/vocals/keyboards). They had used a number of drummers at different times, including Timi Donald. Renwick had formerly been playing with Junior's Eyes, and he and Batchelor recruited John 'Willie' Wilson (b. John Wilson, 8 July 1947, Cambridge, England; drums/vocals/percussion), who was playing with Cochise at that time. Subsequently, the line-up of Wilson, Renwick, Batchelor, and ex-Village and future notable bassist of Elvis Costello And the Attractions, Bruce Thomas (b. 14 August 1948, Middlesbrough, Cleveland, England; bass/vocals), recorded *Quiver*, producing it themselves. For the recording, they were augmented by Dick Parry (saxophone). The same line-up recorded *Gone In The Morning*, but due to lack of commercial success, the group were dropped by Warner Brothers Records. Bereft of new ideas, the group decided to join together with the Sutherland Brothers. The two line-ups saw each other working, and merged in late 1972, also adding Pete Wood (b. Middlesex, England, d. 1994, New York, USA; keyboards). Shortly afterwards they were signed to Island Records, and with a number of personnel changes, achieved a degree of chart success. Renwick went on to form 747 and Kicks and is now a much in-demand session guitar player and has toured with bands such as Pink Floyd and Mike And The Mechanics, while Wilson is playing with the Coyotes. Quiver's greatest claim, however, is as the first ever band to play the legendary Rainbow Theatre in London.
●ALBUMS: *Quiver* (Warners 1971)★★, *Gone In The Morning* (Warners 1972)★★.

RABBITT, EDDIE

b. Edward Thomas Rabbitt, 27 November 1944, Brooklyn, New York City, USA. Rabbitt, whose name is Gaelic, was raised in East Orange, New Jersey. His father, Thomas Rabbitt, a refrigeration engineer, played fiddle and accordion and is featured alongside his son on the 1978 track, 'Song Of Ireland'. On a scouting holiday, Rabbitt was introduced to country music and he soon became immersed in the history of its performers. Rabbitt's first single was 'Six Nights And Seven Days' on 20th Century Fox in 1964, and he had further singles for Columbia, 'Bottles' and 'I Just Don't Care No More'. Rabbitt, who found he could make no headway singing country music in New York, decided to move to Nashville in 1968. Sitting in a bath in a cheap hotel, he had the idea for 'Working My Way Up From The Bottom', which was recorded by Roy Drusky. At first, he had difficulty in placing other songs although George Morgan recorded 'The Sounds Of Goodbye' and Bobby Lewis 'Love Me And Make It All Better'. He secured a recording contract and at the same time gave Lamar Fike a tape of songs for Elvis Presley. Presley chose the one he was planning to do himself, 'Kentucky Rain', and took it to number 16 in the US country charts and number 21 in th UK. Presley also recorded 'Patch It Up' and 'Inherit The Wind'. In 1974 Ronnie Milsap topped the US country charts with 'Pure Love', which Rabbitt had written for his future wife, Janine, the references in the song being to commercials for Ivory soap ('99 44/100th per cent'), and 'Cap'n Crunch'. Rabbitt also recorded 'Sweet Janine' on his first album. He had his first US country success as a performer with 'You Get To Me' in 1974, and, two years later, topped the US country charts with 'Drinkin' My Baby (Off My Mind)', a good time drinking song he had written with Even Stevens. He often wrote with Stevens and also with his producer, David Molloy. Rabbitt followed his success with the traditional-sounding 'Rocky Mountain Music' and two more drinking songs, 'Two Dollars In The Jukebox (Five In A Bottle)' and 'Pour Me Another Tequila'. Rabbitt was criticized by the Women's Christian Temperance Union for damaging their cause. Further number 1s came with 'I Just Want To Love You', which he had written during the session, 'Suspicions' and the theme for the Clint Eastwood film, *Every Which Way But Loose*, which also made number 41 in the UK. Rabbitt harmonized with himself on the 1980 country number 1, 'Gone Too Far'. Inspired by the rhythm of Bob Dylan's 'Subterranean

Homesick Blues', he wrote 'Drivin' My Life Away', a US Top 5 pop hit as well as a number 1 country hit, for the 1980 film *Roadie*. A fragment of a song he had written 12 years earlier gave him the concept for 'I Love A Rainy Night', which topped both the US pop and country charts. He had further number 1 country hits with 'Step By Step' (US pop 5) and the Eagles-styled 'Someone Could Lose A Heart Tonight' (US pop 15). He also had chart-topping country duets with Crystal Gayle ('You And I') and Juice Newton ('Both To Each Other (Friends And Lovers)'), the latter being the theme for the television soap opera, *Days Of Our Lives*. Rabbitt's son, Timmy, was born with a rare disease in 1983 and Rabbitt cut back on his commitments until Timmy's death in 1985. Another son, Tommy, was born in good health in 1986. Rabbitt topped the US country charts by reviving a pure rock 'n' roll song from his youth in New York, Dion's 'The Wanderer'. During his son's illness, he had found songwriting difficult but wrote his 1988 US country number 1, 'I Wanna Dance With You'. His ambition is to write 'a classic, one of those songs that will support me for the rest of my life'.

● ALBUMS: *Eddie Rabbitt* (1975)★★, *Rocky Mountain Music* (Elektra 1976)★★, *Variations* (Elektra 1978)★★, *Loveline* (Elektra 1979)★★, *Horizon* (Elektra 1980)★★, *Step By Step* (Elektra 1981)★★, *Radio Romance* (Elektra 1982)★★, *Rabbitt Trax* (RCA 1986)★★, *I Wanna Dance With You* (1988)★★, *Jersey Boy* (Capitol Nashville 1990)★★, *Ten Rounds* (Capitol Nashville 1991)★★.

● COMPILATIONS: *The Best Of Eddie Rabbitt* (Elektra 1979)★★★.

RACEY

One of Mickie Most's numerous UK successes on the RAK label in the 70s, this pop group originated from Weston Super Mare, Somerset, England. The line-up featured Phil Fursdon (vocals/guitar), Richard Gower (vocals/keyboards), Pete Miller (vocals/bass) and Clive Wilson (vocals/drums). After playing extensively round the pub circuits, an early supporter called Steve Matthews brought them to the attention of Most in London. He quickly signed them after hearing a demo, and they released their debut 'Baby It's You', written by Chris Norman and Pete Spencer of Smokie, which narrowly missed the charts. However, they got their hit with second single, 'Lay Your Love On Me', which rose to number 3 in the UK charts in 1979. 'Some Girls' went one place better in March, but after two more hits, including a cover of Dion's 'Runaround Sue', the race was over.

● ALBUMS: *Smash And Grab* (RAK 1979)★★.

RACING CARS

From his Manchester, England, audio shop, ex-Mindbenders Bob Land (bass) was persuaded to re-enter showbusiness in 1975 with Graham Headley Williams (guitar), Gareth Mortimer (guitar), Roy Edwards (keyboards) and Robert Wilding (drums).

Released by Chrysalis, their records included bit-parts for session pianist Geraint Watkins, American saxophonist Jerry Jumonville, the Bowles Brothers Band (on vocal harmonies) and Swinging Blue Jeans guitarist Ray Ennis. Reaching number 39 in the UK album list, the band's debut *Downtown Tonight* also produced an unexpected Top 20 entry with the ballad 'They Shoot Horses Don't They'. No more hits were forthcoming but the group were sufficiently established in the colleges to issue two further albums.

●ALBUMS: *Downtown Tonight* (Chrysalis 1977)★★, *Weekend Rendezvous* (Chrysalis 1977)★★, *Bring On The Night* (Chrysalis 1978)★★★.

RADIO STARS

This UK group was formed in 1977 by Andy Ellison (vocals), Ian McLeod (guitar) and Martin Gordon (bass), all of whom were previously members of Jet. Drummer Steve Parry completed the line-up of a group engendering considerable interest through its association with John's Children (Ellison) and Sparks (Gordon). A series of tongue-in-cheek singles, including 'Dirty Pictures' and 'Nervous Wreck', captured the quartet's brand of quirky pop/punk, but although the latter reached the fringes of the Top 40, the group was unable to achieve consistent success. Trevor White, also ex-Sparks, was later added to the line-up but Gordon's departure in December 1978 undermined any lingering potential and Radio Stars disbanded the following year. Ellison and White subsequently undertook several low-key projects and the singer later revived the group's name, but with little success.

●ALBUMS: *Songs For Swinging Lovers* (Chiswick 1977)★★★, *Radio Stars' Holiday Album* (Chiswick 1978)★★.

RAFFERTY, GERRY

b. 16 April 1947, Paisley, Scotland. The lengthy career of the reclusive Rafferty started as a member of the Humblebums with Billy Connolly and Tam Harvey in 1968. After its demise through commercial indifference, Transatlantic Records offered him a solo contract. The result was *Can I Have My Money Back?*, a superb blend of folk and gentle pop music, featuring one of the earliest cover paintings from the well-known Scottish artist 'Patrick' (playwright John Byrne). Rafferty showed great promise as a songwriter with the rolling 'Steamboat Row' and the plaintive and observant, 'Her Father Didn't Like Me Anyway', but the album was a commercial failure. Rafferty's next solo project came after an interruption of seven years, four as a member of the brilliant but turbulent Stealers Wheel, and three through litigation over managerial problems. Much of this is documented in his lyrics both with Stealers Wheel and as a soloist. *City To City* in 1978 raised his profile and gave him a hit single that created a classic song with probably the most famous saxophone introduction in pop music, performed by Raphael

Ravenscroft. 'Baker Street' became a multi-million seller and narrowly missed the top of the charts. The album sold similar numbers and Rafferty became a reluctant star. He declined to perform in the USA even though his album was number 1. The follow-up *Night Owl* was almost as successful, containing a similar batch of strong songs with intriguing lyrics and haunting melodies. Rafferty's output has been sparse during the 80s and none of his recent work has matched his earlier songs. He made a single contribution to the film *Local Hero* and produced the Top 3 hit for the Proclaimers with 'Letter From America' in 1987. *North And South* continued the themes of his previous albums, although the lengthy introductions to each track made it unsuitable for radio play. During the early 90s Rafferty's marriage broke up, and, as is often the case, this stimulated more songwriting creativity. *On A Wing And A Prayer* was certainly a return to form, but although the reviews were favourable it made little impression on the charts. *Over My Head* in 1995 was a lacklustre affair; interestingly, the only songs that offered something original were re-recorded Stealers Wheel tracks, written with his former songwritng partner Joe Egan. 'Over My Head' and 'Late Again' are the highpoints of an album on which Rafferty seems bereft of ideas. *One More Dream* was a good selection of songs but was marred by having some tracks re-recorded, actually detracting from the atmosphere and quality of the originals.

●ALBUMS: *Can I Have My Money Back?* (Transatlantic 1971)★★★★, *City To City* (United Artists 1978)★★★★, *Night Owl* (United Artists 1979)★★★★, *Snakes And Ladders* (United Artists 1980)★★★, *Sleepwalking* (Liberty 1982)★★, *North And South* (1988)★★, *On A Wing And A Prayer* (1992)★★, *Over My Head* (Polydor 1995)★★.

●COMPILATIONS: *Early Collection* (Transatlantic 1986)★★★, *Blood And Glory* (Transatlantic 1988)★★, *Right Down The Line: The Best Of Gerry Rafferty* (EMI 1991)★★★, *One More Dream - The Very Best Of* (Polygram 1995)★★★★.

RAINBOW

In 1975 guitarist Ritchie Blackmore (b. 14 April 1945, Weston-Super-Mare, England; guitar) left Deep Purple, forming Rainbow the following year. His earlier involvement with American band Elf led to his recruitment of the latter's Ronnie James Dio (vocals), Mickey Lee Soule, (keyboards), Craig Gruber on bass and Gary Driscoll as drummer. Their debut, *Ritchie Blackmore's Rainbow*, was released in 1975, and was undeservedly seen by some as a poor imitation of Deep Purple. The constant turnover of personnel was representative of Blackmore's quest for the ultimate line-up and sound. Dissatisfaction with the debut album led to new personnel being assembled. Jimmy Bain took over from Gruber, and Cozy Powell replaced Driscoll. With Tony Carey on keyboards, *Rainbow Rising* was released, an album far more confident than its predecessor. Shortly after this Bain and Carey left, being replaced by Bob

Daisley and David Stone respectively. It was when Rainbow moved to America that difficulties between Dio and Blackmore came to a head, resulting in Dio's departure from the band in 1978. His replacement was Graham Bonnet, whose only album with Rainbow, *Down To Earth*, saw the return as bassist of Roger Glover, the man Blackmore had forced out of Deep Purple in 1973. The album was a marked departure from the Dio days, and while it is often considered one of the weaker Rainbow collections, it did provide an enduring single, 'Since You've Been Gone', written and originally recorded by Russ Ballard. Bonnet and Powell soon became victims of another reorganization of Rainbow's line-up. Drummer Bobby Rondinelli and particularly new vocalist Joe Lynn Turner brought an American feel to the band, a commercial sound introduced on *Difficult To Cure*, the album that produced their biggest hit in 'I Surrender'. Thereafter the group went into decline as their increasingly middle-of-the-road albums were ignored by fans (former Brand X drummer Chuck Burgi replaced Rondinelli for 1983's *Bent Out Of Shape*). In 1984 the Rainbow project was ended following the highly popular Deep Purple reunion. The group played its last gig on 14 March 1984 in Japan, accompanied by a symphony orchestra as Blackmore, with a typical absence of modesty, adapted Beethoven's 'Ninth Symphony'. A compilation, *Finyl Vinyl*, appeared in 1986, and (necessarily) featured several different incarnations of Rainbow as well as unreleased recordings. Since then the name has been resurrected in a number of line-ups. A new studio recording was issued in 1995. The present vocalist is Dougie White.

● ALBUMS: *Ritchie Blackmore's Rainbow* (Oyster 1975)★★★, *Rainbow Rising* (Polydor 1976)★★★★, *Live On Stage* (Polydor 1977)★★, *Long Live Rock And Roll* (Polydor 1978)★★★, *Down To Earth* (Polydor 1979)★★★, *Difficult To Cure* (Polydor 1981)★★, *Straight Between The Eyes* (Polydor 1982)★★, *Bent Out Of Shape* (Polydor 1983)★★, *Stranger In Us All* (RCA 1995)★★.

● COMPILATIONS: *Best Of* (Polydor 1983)★★★, *Finyl Vinyl* (Polydor 1986)★★, *Live In Germany* (Connoisseur 1990)★★.

● VIDEOS: *The Final Cut* (Polygram 1986), *Live Between The Eyes* (Channel 5 1988).

● FURTHER READING: *Rainbow*, Peter Makowski.

RAITT, BONNIE

b. 8 November 1949, Burbank, California, USA. Born into a musical family, her father, John Raitt, starred in Broadway productions of *Oklahoma!* and *Carousel*. Having learned guitar as a child, Raitt became infatuated with traditional blues, although her talent for performing did not fully flourish until she attended college in Cambridge, Massachusetts. Raitt initially opened for John Hammond, before establishing her reputation with prolific live appearances throughout the east coast circuit on which she was accompanied by longtime

bassist, Dan 'Freebo' Friedberg. Raitt then acquired the management services of Dick Waterman, who guided the career of many of the singer's mentors, including Son House, Mississippi Fred McDowell and Sippie Wallace. She often travelled and appeared with these performers and *Bonnie Raitt* contained material drawn from their considerable lexicon. Chicago bluesmen Junior Wells and A.C. Reed also appeared on the album, but its somewhat reverential approach was replaced by the contemporary perspective unveiled on *Give It Up*. This excellent set included versions of Jackson Browne's 'Under The Falling Sky' and Eric Kaz's 'Love Has No Pride' and established the artist as an inventive and sympathetic interpreter. *Taking My Time* features assistance from Lowell George and Bill Payne from Little Feat and included an even greater diversity, ranging from the pulsating 'You've Been In Love Too Long' to the traditional 'Kokomo Blues'. Subsequent releases followed a similar pattern, and although *Streetlights* was a minor disappointment, *Home Plate*, produced by veteran Paul A. Rothchild, reasserted her talent. Nonetheless Raitt refused to embrace a conventional career, preferring to tour in more intimate surroundings. Thus the success engendered by *Sweet Forgiveness* came as a natural progression and reflected a genuine popularity. However, its follow-up, *The Glow*, although quite commercial, failed to capitalize on this newfound fortune and while offering a spirited reading of Mable John's 'Your Good Thing', much of the material was self-composed and lacked the breadth of style of its predecessors. Subsequent releases, *Green Light* and *Nine Lives*, proved less satisfying and Raitt was then dropped by Warner Brothers Records, her outlet of 15 years. Those sensing an artistic and personal decline were proved incorrect in 1989 when *Nick Of Time* became one of the year's most acclaimed and best-selling releases. Raitt herself confessed to slight amazement at winning a Grammy award. The album was a highly accomplished piece of work, smoothing some of her rough, trademark blues edges for an AOR market. The emotional title track became a US hit single while the album, produced by Don Was of Was (Not Was), also featured sterling material from John Hiatt and Bonnie Hayes. Raitt also garnered praise for her contributions to John Lee Hooker's superb 1990 release, *The Healer*, and that same year reached a wider audience with her appearance at the concert for Nelson Mandela at Wembley Stadium. She continued in the same musical vein with the excellent *Luck Of The Draw* featuring strong material from Paul Brady, Hiatt and Raitt herself. The album was another multi-million seller and demonstrated Raitt's new mastery in singing smooth emotional ballads, none better than the evocative 'I Can't Make You Love Me'. Her personal life also stabilized following her marriage in 1991 (to Irish actor/poet Michael O'Keefe), and after years of singing about broken hearts, faithless lovers and 'no good men', Raitt entered the 90s at the peak of her powers. She was also growing in stature as a songwriter: on her 1994 album she displayed the confidence to provide four of the songs herself, her first nine albums having yielded only eight of her own compositions. Although that album, *Longing In Their Hearts*, spawned further US hits and achieved 2 million sales it was a record that trod water. Even her US hit version of Roy Orbison's 'You Got It' from the film *Boys On The Side* sounded weak. On her first ever live album, *Road Tested*, Raitt was joined by Bruce Hornsby, Jackson Browne, Kim Wilson, Ruth Brown, Charles Brown and Bryan Adams.

●ALBUMS: *Bonnie Raitt* (Warners 1971)★★★, *Give It Up* (Warners 1972)★★★, *Takin' My Time* (Warners 1973)★★★★, *Streetlights* (Warners 1974)★★★, *Home Plate* (Warners 1975)★★, *Sweet Forgiveness* (Warners 1977)★★, *The Glow* (Warners 1979)★★★, *Green Light* (Warners 1982)★★★, *Nine Lives* (Warners 1986)★★, *Nick Of Time* (Capitol 1989)★★★★, *Luck Of The Draw* (Capitol 1991)★★★★, *Longing In Their Hearts* (Capitol 1994)★★★, *Road Tested* (Capitol 1995)★★.

●COMPILATIONS: *The Bonnie Raitt Collection* (Warners 1990)★★★★.

●VIDEOS: *The Video Collection* (PMI 1992), *Road Tested* (Capitol 1995).

●FURTHER READING: *Just In The Nick Of Time*, Mark Bego.

RAK RECORDS

Mickie Most (b. Michael Peter Hayes, June 1938, Aldershot, Surrey, England) started out in the music business as a performer who had a string of successes in South Africa in the 60s (with Mickie Most And The Playboys). He came home from constant touring of that country and became a producer, working with everyone from the Animals to Donovan. In the late 60s he decided to introduce the American selling style of rack-jobbing to the UK. This is where the salesman sets up a rack of albums for sale in places outside of record shops such as garages and supermarkets. To achieve this he formed Rak Records - the 'c' dropped from Rack as he thought it looked less harsh. Unfortunately supermarkets were not enthusiastic - although within a decade it was a commonplace outlet - but Most chose to keep the company name. In 1970 he decided to form a production company, but initially he had no artists signed as all the people with whom he was working were already on the books of other companies. However, this changed in 1970 when he released Rak's first single - Julie Felix singing the Paul Simon-penned 'If I Could (El Condor Pasa)'. This was followed by a release from Peter Noone whom Most knew from producing Herman's Hermits. Rak quickly became big business, picking up Hot Chocolate from Apple, Alexis Korner's CCS - Collective Consciousness Society (whose version of 'Whole Lotta Love' was the theme music to *Top Of The Pops* for the best part of a decade) - the Australian folk group New World (later implicated in the Janie Jones 'sex for airplay' scandal), and dozens of teenybop

groups such as Kenny, Suzi Quatro, Mud, the Arrows and Smokie. Songwriters and producers such as Nicky Chinn and Mike Chapman had many hits through Rak, and at one point the company was situated in Charles Street, Mayfair, next door to the equally successful Bell Records (Gary Glitter, Bay City Rollers, etc.) causing some people to dub it 'teen-pan alley'. At the same time as running Rak, Most also became famous as a panelist on the talent show *New Faces*. As the teeny bop era passed into punk, Rak became less prolific with the hits though they bounced back briefly in the 80s with Kim Wilde.

RAM JAM

Formed in the mid-70s, Ram Jam was an east coast of America group best known for its one Top 20 single, 'Black Betty', in 1977. That song was the focus of a boycott by several groups who considered it offensive to black women, even though it had originally been written by Huddie 'Lead Belly' Ledbetter, the legendary black folk and blues singer. The group consisted of guitarist Bill Bartlett (b. 1949), bassist Howie Blauvelt (formerly a member of Billy Joel's early group the Hassles), singer Myke Scavone and drummer Pete Charles. Bartlett had earlier been lead guitarist with the Lemon Pipers. After leaving that group, Bartlett retired from music for some time, before recording a demo of the Lead Belly song. Released on Epic Records, it reached number 18, but the group never had another hit. In the UK they succeeded twice, in 1977 (number 7) and in 1990 a remix version reached number 13, making them a quite extraordinary one-hit-wonder.

●ALBUMS: *Ram Jam* (Epic 1977)★★, *Portrait Of An Artist As A Young Ram* (Epic 1978)★.

RAMONES

The Ramones, comprising Johnny Ramone (b. John Cummings, 8 October 1951, Long Island, New York, USA; guitar), Dee Dee Ramone (b. Douglas Colvin, 18 September 1952, Vancouver, British Columbia, Canada; bass) and Joey Ramone (b. Jeffrey Hyman, 19 May 1952; drums) made their debut at New York's Performance Studio on 30 March 1974. Two months later manager Tommy Ramone (b. Tommy Erdelyi, 29 January 1952, Budapest, Hungary) replaced Joey on drums, who then switched to vocals. The quartet later secured a residency at the renowned CBGB's club where they became one of the city's leading proponents of punk rock. The fever-paced *Ramones* was a startling first album. Its high-octane assault drew from 50s kitsch and 60s garage bands, while leather jackets, ripped jeans and an affected dumbness enhanced their music's cartoon-like quality. The group's debut appearance in London in July 1976 influenced a generation of British punk musicians, while *The Ramones Leave Home*, which included 'Suzie Is A Headbanger' and 'Gimme Gimme Shock Treatment', confirmed the sonic attack of its predecessor. *Rocket To Russia* was marginally less frenetic as

the group's novelty appeal waned, although 'Sheena Is A Punk Rocker' gave the group their first UK Top 30 hit in 1977. In May 1978 Tommy Ramone left to pursue a career in production and former Richard Hell drummer Marc Bell, remodelled as Marky Ramone, replaced him for *Road To Ruin*, as the band sought to expand their appealing, but limited, style. They took a starring role in the trivial *Rock 'N' Roll High School* film, a participation which led to their collaboration with producer Phil Spector. The resultant release, *End Of The Century*, was a curious hybrid, and while Johnny balked at Spector's laborious recording technique, Joey, whose penchant for girl-group material gave the Ramones their sense of melody, was less noticeably critical. The album contained a sympathetic version of the Ronettes' 'Baby I Love You', which became the group's biggest UK hit single when it reached the Top 10. The Ramones entered the 80s looking increasingly anachronistic, unable or unwilling to change. *Pleasant Dreams*, produced by Graham Gouldman, revealed a group now outshone by the emergent hardcore acts they had inspired. However, *Subterranean Jungle* showed a renewed purpose which was maintained sporadically on *Animal Boy* and *Halfway To Sanity*, the former containing 'Bonzo Goes To Bitburg', a hilarious riposte to Ronald Reagan's ill-advised visit to a cemetery containing graves of Nazi SS personnel. Although increasingly confined to pop's fringes, a revitalized line-up - Joey, Johnny, Marky and newcomer C.J. - undertook a successful 1990 US tour alongside fellow CBGB's graduate Deborah Harry and Talking Heads' offshoot Tom Tom Club. 1992 brought *Mondo Bizarro*, from which 'Censorshit', an attack on Tipper Gore, head of the PMRC, was the most notable moment. By 1995 and *Adios Amigos*, rumours inferred that the two-minute buzzsaw guitar trail may have finally run cold, with the impression of a epitaph exacerbated by the album's title. As Johnny conceded: 'I know that you have to deal with a life without applause, and I'm looking forward to trying it. A lot of musicians are addicted to it and won't get out.' They announced their final gig in August 1996, a tearful event at The Palace club in Hollywood. Whatever their record sales acheived their contribution to name-dropping rock is monumental, history will show whether such fame was influential.
●ALBUMS: *Ramones* (Sire 1976)★★★★, *The Ramones Leave Home* (Sire 1977)★★★★, *Rocket To Russia* (Sire 1977)★★★★, *Road To Ruin* (Sire 1978)★★★★, *It's Alive* (Sire 1979)★★★, *End Of The Century* (Sire 1980)★★★, *Pleasant Dreams* (Sire 1981)★★★, *Subterranean Jungle* (Sire 1983)★★★, *Too Tough To Die* (Sire 1984)★★★★, *Animal Boy* (Sire 1986)★★★, *Halfway To Sanity* (Sire 1987)★★, *Brain Drain* (Sire 1989)★★, *Loco Live* (Chrysalis 1991)★★, *Mondo Bizarro* (Chrysalis 1992)★★, *Acid Eaters* (Chrysalis 1993)★★, *Adios Amigos* (Chrysalis 1995)★★★.
●COMPILATIONS: *Ramones Mania* (Sire 1988)★★★, *All The Stuff And More (Volume One)* (Sire 1990)★★★★, *End*

Of The Decade (Beggars Banquet 1990)★★★★, *All The Stuff And More* (Sire 1991)★★★★, *Greatest Hits Live* (Radioactive 1996)★★★.
●FURTHER READING: *The Ramones: An Illustrated Biography*, Miles. *Ramones: An American Band*, Jim Bessman.

RARE BIRD

Steve Gould (vocals/saxophone/bass) and Dave Kaffinette (keyboards) fronted this British group throughout its recording career. Graham Field (organ) and Mark Ashton (drums) completed the line-up featured on *Rare Bird*, which included their memorable 1970 hit single, 'Sympathy'. Although this atmospheric protest ballad only reached the lower reaches of the UK Top 30, it proved highly popular on the Continent and has since become a cult favourite. The group came under the wing of Tony Stratton-Smith, but failed to translate their European charm into further success at home. Gould and Kaffinette were joined by Andy Curtis (guitar) and Fred Kelly (percussion) for *Epic Forest*, but despite initial promise, this restructured line-up failed to revitalize Rare Bird's increasingly ailing fortunes.
●ALBUMS: *Rare Bird* (Probe 1970)★★★, *As Your Mind Flies By* (1970)★★, *Epic Forest* (Polydor 1972)★★★, *Somebody's Watching* (Polydor 1973)★★, *Born Again* (Polydor 1974)★★, *Rare Bird* (Polydorv1975)★★.
●COMPILATIONS: *Sympathy* (Charisma 1976)★★, *Rare Bird - Polydor Special* (Polydor 1977)★★★.

RARE EARTH

Saxophonist Gil Bridges and drummer Pete Rivera (Hoorelbeke) formed their first R&B band, the Sunliners, in Detroit in 1961. Bassist John Parrish joined in 1962; guitarist Rod Richards and keyboards player Kenny James followed in 1966. Other members included Ralph Terrana (keyboards), Russ Terrana (guitar) and Fred Saxon (saxophone). After years of playing in local clubs and releasing unspectacular records on MGM, Hercules and Golden World, they were signed to Verve Records and released *Dreams And Answers*. They signed to Motown Records in 1969, where they had the honour of having a newly formed progressive rock label named after them (following their hopeful suggestion to Motown executives). Rare Earth Records scored an immediate success with a rock-flavoured version of the Temptations' hit 'Get Ready', which reached the US Top 10. The single was edited down from a 20-minute recording that occupied one side of their debut Motown album: it showcased the band's instrumental prowess, but also typified their tendency towards artistic excess. A cover of another Temptations classic, '(I Know) I'm Losing You', brought them more success in 1970, as did original material like 'Born To Wander' and 'I Just Want To Celebrate'. The band had already suffered the first in a bewildering series of personnel changes that dogged their progress over the next decade, as Rod Richards and Kenny James were replaced by Ray Monette and Mark Olson respectively, and Ed Guzman (b. c.1944, d. 29 July 1993) was added on percussion. This line-up had several minor US hits in the early 70s, until internal upheavals in 1973 led to a complete revamp of the band's style. The Temptations' mentor, Norman Whitfield, produced the highly regarded *Ma* that year. By the release of *Back To Earth* in 1975, he in turn had been supplanted by Jerry La Croix. Subsequent releases proved commercially unsuccessful, though the band continued to record and tour into the 80s. Former members Pete Rivera (Hoorelbeke) and Michael Urso later combined with Motown writer/producer Tom Baird as Hub for two albums on Capitol Records *Hub* and *Cheeta*. At the turn of the decade the line-up comprised Gil Bridges, Ray Monette, Edward Guzman, Wayne Baraks, Rick Warner, Dean Boucher, Randy Burghdoff. They joined Ian Levine's Motor City label in 1990 and issued 'Playing To Win' and 'Love Is Here And Now You've Gone'. The band continue to be hugely successful in Germany. During the mid-90s Pete Hoorelbeke/Rivera was playing with the Classic Rock All Stars, a band that comprised Spencer Davis, Mike Pinera (ex-Blues Image and Iron Butterfly) and Jerry Corbetta (Sugarloaf). A live album was issued in 1994.

● ALBUMS: *Dreams And Answers* (Verve 1968)★★★, *Get Ready* (Rare Earth 1969)★★★, *Ecology* (Rare Earth 1970)★★★, *One World* (Rare Earth 1971)★★★, *In Concert* (Rare Earth 1971)★★, *Willie Remembers* (Rare Earth 1972)★★★, *Ma* (Rare Earth 1973)★★★, *Back To Earth* (Rare Earth 1975)★★★, *Midnight Lady* (Rare Earth 1976)★★, *Rare Earth* (Prodigal 1977)★★, *Band Together* (Prodigal 1978)★★, *Grand Slam* (Prodigal 1978)★★, *Made In Switzerland* (Line 1989)★★, *Different World* (Koch 1993)★★.

● COMPILATIONS: *The Best Of Rare Earth* (Rare Earth 1972)★★★, *Rare Earth: Superstars Series* (Motown 1981)★★★, *Greatest Hits And Rare Classics* (Motown 1991)★★★, *Earth Tones: The Essential Rare Earth* (Motown 1994)★★★, *Anthology* (Motown 1995)★★★.

RASPBERRIES

Formed in 1970, this popular 70s US group evolved from several aspiring Ohio-based bands. The original line-up included two former members of Cyrus Erie, Eric Carmen (b. 11 August 1949, Cleveland, Ohio, USA; vocals/guitar/keyboards) and Marty Murphy (guitar), as well as ex-Choir drummer Jim Bonfanti (b. 17 December 1948, Windber, Pennsylvania, USA). Murphy was quickly replaced by Wally Bryson (b. 18 July 1949, Gastonia, North Carolina, USA), a veteran of both groups, who in turn introduced John Alleksic. However, the latter was removed in favour of Dave Smalley (b. 10 July 1949, Oil City, Pennsylvania, USA; guitar/bass), another ex-Choir acolyte. The Raspberries' love of the Beatles was apparent on their debut 'Don't Wanna Say Goodbye'. Its melodic flair set the tone of 'Go All The Way', a gorgeous slice of Anglophilia which rose to

number 5 in the US chart. *Raspberries* confirmed the quartet's undoubted promise, but it was on *Fresh*, released a mere four months later, that their talent fully blossomed. Here the group's crafted harmonies recalled those of the Beach Boys and Hollies, while a buoyant *joie de vivre* was apparent on such memorable songs as 'Let's Pretend' and 'I Wanna Be With You'. This cohesion, sadly, did not last and while *Side 3* included wider influences drawn from the Who and Small Faces, it also reflected a growing split between Carmen and the Bonfanti/Smalley team who were summarily fired in 1973. Scott McCarl (guitar) and Michael McBride (drums, ex-Cyrus Erie) completed the new Raspberries line-up which debuted the following year with the gloriously ambitious 'Overnight Sensation (Hit Record)'. In that one song they packed hook after hook, change after change; it was for many the most perfect pop song written since 'Good Vibrations'. The attendant album, cheekily entitled *Starting Over*, contained several equally memorable songs, but it was clear that Carmen now required a broader canvas for his work. He disbanded the group in 1975 and embarked on an intermittently successful solo career, while Bryson resurfaced in two disappointing pop/rock bands, Tattoo and Fotomaker. In the 90s the Raspberries' contribution to power pop was freshly examined. Two reissued packages from the excellent UK collector's label RPM were released in 1996 with copious sleeve notes from Raspberryologist Ken Sharp.

● ALBUMS: *Raspberries* (Capitol 1972)★★, *Fresh* (Capitol 1972)★★★, *Side 3* (Capitol 1973)★★, *Starting Over* (Capitol 1974)★★★.

● COMPILATIONS: *Raspberries' Best Featuring Eric Carmen* (Capitol 1976)★★★, *Overnight Sensation - The Very Best Of The Raspberries* (Zap 1987)★★★, *Collectors Series* (Capitol 1991)★★★, *Power Pop: Volume One* (RPM 1996)★★★★, *Power Pop Volume Two* (RPM 1996)★★★.

● FURTHER READING: *Overnight Sensation: The Story Of The Raspberries*, Ken Sharp.

RAVAN, GENYA

b. Genya Zelkowitz, Poland. Ravan's family fled from the Nazis to New York. By the early 60s, she was leading Goldie And The Gingerbreads and although they did not chart in the US, they enjoyed a UK Top 30 entry with 'Can't You Hear My Heartbeat', and they were also appreciated for their exacting musical standards. After disbandment in 1969, Zelkowitz sang in various jazz combos before joining the otherwise all-male Ten Wheel Drive who combined jazz with progressive rock. She released three solo albums attributed to Goldie Zelkowitz before reverting to Goldie Ravan for two further recordings. From the late 70s to the present, the former name has been the one most used for sleeve credits for session work on albums by Gamma and Lou Reed among others, and for her duet with Ellen Foley, 'Mr. Music'. As a record producer she has been responsible for Dead Boys' *Young Loud And Snotty* and an attempt to relaunch Ronnie Spector as a punk star with 1980's *Siren*.

●ALBUMS: *With Baby* (1972)★★, *They Love Me/They Love Me Not* (Dunhill 1973)★★, *Goldie Zelkowitz* (Janus 1974)★★, *Urban Desire* (20th Century Fox 1978)★★★, *... And I Mean It!* (20th Century Fox 1979)★★★.

RAWLS, LOU

b. 1 December 1935, Chicago, Illinois, USA. Briefly a member of the acclaimed gospel group, the Pilgrim Travellers, this distinctive singer began forging a secular career following his move to California in 1958. An association with Sam Cooke culminated in 'Bring It On Home To Me', where Rawls' throaty counterpoint punctuated his colleague's sweet lead vocal. Rawls' own recordings showed him comfortable with either small jazz combos or cultured soul, while an earthier perspective was shown on his 1965 release, *Live!*. He had two Top 20 singles with 'Love Is A Hurtin' Thing' (1966) and 'Dead End Street' (1967), and enjoyed further success with a 1969 reading of Mable John's 'Your Good Thing (Is About To End)'. Several attempts were made to mould Rawls into an all-round entertainer, but while his early 70s work was generally less compulsive, the singer's arrival at Philadelphia International signalled a dramatic rebirth. 'You'll Never Find Another Love Like Mine', an international hit in 1976, matched the classic Philly sound with Rawl's almost plumby delivery and prepared the way for a series of exemplary releases including 'See You When I Git There' (1977) and 'Let Me Be Good To You' (1979). The singer maintained his association with producers Gamble And Huff into the next decade. His last chart entry, 'I Wish You Belonged to Me', came in 1987 on the duo's self-named label, since when he has recorded for the jazz outlet, Blue Note. Rawls has also pursued an acting career and provided the voice for several Budweiser beer commercials.

●ALBUMS: *Lou Rawls Sings, Les McCann Ltd Plays Stormy Monday* (1962)★★★, *Black And Blue* (Capitol 1963)★★★, *Tobacco Road* (Capitol 1963)★★★, *Nobody But Lou Rawls* (Capitol 1965)★★★, *Lou Rawls And Strings* (Capitol 1965)★★, *Lou Rawls Live!* (Capitol 1966)★★★, *Lou Rawls Soulin'* (Capitol 1966)★★★, *Lou Rawls Carryin' On!* (Capitol 1967)★★★, *Too Much!* (Capitol 1967)★★★, *That's Lou* (Capitol 1967)★★★, *Merry Christmas Ho! Ho! Ho!* (Capitol 1967)★, *Feeling Good* (Capitol 1968)★★★, *You're Good For Me* (Capitol 1968)★★★, *The Way It Was - The Way It Is* (Capitol 1969)★★★, *Your Good Thing* (Capitol 1969)★★★, *You've Made Me So Very Happy* (Capitol 1970)★★, *Bring It On Home To Me* (1970)★★★, *Natural Man* (MGM 1971)★★, *Silk And Soul* (MGM 1972)★★, *All Things In Time* (Philadelphia International 1976)★★★, *Unmistakably Lou* (Philadelphia International 1977)★★★★, *When You Hear Lou, You've Heard It All* (Philadelphia International 1977)★★★★, *Lou Rawls Live* (Philadelphia International 1978)★★★, *Let Me Be Good To You* (Philadelphia International 1979)★★★★, *Sit Down And Talk To Me* (Philadelphia

International 1980)★★★, *Shades Of Blue* (Philadelphia International 1981)★★★, *Now Is The Time* (Portrait 1982)★★★, *When The Night Comes* (Epic 1983)★★★, *Close Company* (Epic 1984)★★★, *Love All Your Blues Away* (Epic 1986)★★★, *At Last* (Blue Note 1989)★★★, *Portrait Of The Blues* (1992)★★★.

●COMPILATIONS: *The Best Of Lou Rawls: The Capitol/Blue Note Years* (Capitol 1968)★★★, *Soul Serenade* (Stateside 1985)★★★, *Stormy Monday* (See For Miles 1985)★★★, *Classic Soul* (Blue Moon 1986)★★★, *Greatest Hits In Concert* (1993)★★★, *For You My Love* (1994)★★★, *The Philly Years* (Repertoire 1995)★★★★.

REAL THING

This Liverpool-based group had its origins in the Mersey boom. Lead singer Eddie Amoo was a former member of the Chants, whose excellent beat singles garnered considerable praise. Although they failed to chart, the Chants continued to record for various labels until the name was ultimately dropped. The Real Thing emerged in 1976 with 'You To Me Are Everything' which reached number 1 in the UK. Their next release, 'Can't Get By Without You' continued their brand of commercial sweet soul, but later singles were less successful until a more forthright performance in 1979 with the *Star Wars*-influenced, 'Can You Feel The Force', took the group back into the Top 5 establishing their popularity with the British disco audience. Since then the Real Thing's new material has fared less well, although remixes of those first two hits charted 10 years after their initial release.

●ALBUMS: *The Real Thing* (Pye 1976)★★, *Four From Eight* (Pye 1977)★★, *Step Into Our World* (Pye 1978)★★, *Can You Feel The Force* (Pye 1979)★★.

●COMPILATIONS: *Greatest Hits* (K-Tel 1980)★★★, *100 Minutes Of The Real Thing* (PRT 1982)★★, *Best Of The Real Thing* (West 5 1986)★★, *Heart And Soul Of The Real Thing* (Heart And Soul 1990)★★, *A Golden Hour Of The Real Thing* (Knight 1991)★★.

REDBONE

A North American Indian band formed in 1968, Redbone included brothers Pat and Lolly Vegas (both b. Fresno, California, USA), who had already pursued minor performing careers. Lolly had recorded as early as 1961, while together the brothers completed *At The Haunted House*, as well as several singles. The duo were also successful songwriters, and a compulsive dance-based composition, 'Niki Hoeky', was interpreted by such diverse acts as P.J. Proby and Bobbie Gentry. Redbone, an Anglicized cajun epithet for half-breed, was completed by Tony Bellamy (b. Los Angeles, California, USA; rhythm guitar/vocals) and Peter DePoe (b. Neah Bay Reservation, Washington, USA; drums). DePoe, whose native name was 'Last Walking Bear', had been for some time a ceremonial drummer on his reservation. With Pat on bass and Lolly on guitar and vocals, the group initially backed several different artists, including Odetta and John Lee Hooker, before embarking on an independent direction. The quartet scored an international hit with 'Witch Queen Of New Orleans', which owed much to the then-popular southern, or Cajun, 'swamp-rock' style. In 1974 they enjoyed their sole million-seller, 'Come And Get Your Love', but the group was unable to transform their taut, but rhythmic, style into a consistent success.

●ALBUMS: *Redbone* (Epic 1970)★★, *Potlatch* (Epic 1970)★★, *Witch Queen Of New Orleans* (Epic 1971)★★, *Message From A Drum* (Epic 1972)★★, *Already Here* (Epic 1972)★★, *Wovoka* (Epic 1974)★★, *Beaded Dreams Through Turquoise Eyes* (Epic 1974)★★, *Cycles* (RCA 1978)★★.

●COMPILATIONS: *Come And Get Your Redbone (Best Of Redbone)* (Epic 1975)★★★, *Rock Giants* (1982)★★.

REDBONE, LEON

Believed to have been born in Canada, this enigmatic, gravelly voiced singer ('I am a performer, but only in the metaphysical sense') resolutely declines to divulge his origins. He was first heard of in Toronto during the early 70s, and achieved some popularity on the US television show *Saturday Night Live*. Even then he maintained an air of strict privacy, so much so that the contact number he gave to the legendary jazz and rock producer John Hammond Jnr. turned out to be a 'Dial-A-Joke' line. With his trademark fedora, dark glasses, and Groucho Marx moustache, Redbone celebrates a pre-World War II era of ragtime, jazz, blues, and minstrel shows, resurrecting the work of his heroes, who include 'Jelly Roll' Morton, Lonnie Johnson, Joe Venuti, the young Bing Crosby, and vaudeville performer Emmett Miller. Jazz violinist Venuti was featured on Redbone's *On The Track* in 1976, along with Don McLean, who played the banjo. The album is said to have sold more than 100,000 copies, and his next release, *Double Time*, made the US Top 40. Redbone is joined by well-known musical personalities on most of his albums, and for *Whistling In The Wind*, he duetted with Merle Haggard on 'Settin' By The Fire' and Ringo Starr on 'My Little Grass Shack'. Joe Venuti was present too, and the other tracks on this varied and entertaining set included 'Bouquet Of Roses', 'If I Could Be With You', 'Love Letters In The Sand', and 'I'm Crazy 'Bout My Baby'. Redbone's distinctive baritone became familiar to British television viewers in the late 80s/early 90s when he sang 'Relax', 'Sleepy Time', and 'Untwist Again' in a series of commercials with nostalgic themes for British Rail's Inter-City service.

●ALBUMS: *On The Track* (Warners 1976)★★★★, *Double Time* (Warners 1977)★★★, *Champagne Charlie* (Warners 1978)★★, *From Branch To Branch* (ATCO/Emerald 1981)★★★, *Red To Blue* (August 1986)★★★, *No Regrets* (Sugar Hill 1988)★★★, *Christmas Island* (Private Music 1990)★★★, *Sugar* (Private Music 1990)★★★, *Up A Lazy River* (Private Music 1992)★★★, *Whistling In The Wind* (Private Music 1994)★★★.

REDDY, HELEN

b. 25 October 1942, Melbourne, Victoria, Australia, A big-voiced interpreter of rock ballads, with a reputation as a high-profile feminist and campaigner on social issues, Helen Reddy came from a show business family. She was a child performer and had already starred in her own television show before winning a trip to New York in an Australian talent contest in 1966. There, an appearance on the influential *Tonight Show* led to a recording contract with Capitol, and a 1971 hit single with 'I Don't Know How To Love Him' from Andrew Lloyd Webber and Tim Rice's *Jesus Christ Superstar*. The following year, the powerful feminist anthem, 'I Am Woman', which she co-wrote with Peter Allen, went to number 1 in the USA, and sold over a million copies. It also gained Reddy a Grammy for best female vocal performance (part of her acceptance speech went: 'I want to thank God because she makes everything possible'), and was adopted by the United Nations as its theme for International Women's Year. Over the next five years, she had a dozen further hit singles, including 'Leave Me Alone (Ruby Red Dress), 'Keep On Singing', 'You And Me Against The World', 'Emotion', and two contrasting number 1s, Alex Harvey's modern country ballad 'Delta Dawn' (1973), and the chilling, dramatic 'Angie Baby' in 1974. Her 1976 hit, 'I Can't Hear You No More', was composed by Carole King and Gerry Goffin, while Reddy's final Top 20 record (to date) was a revival of Cilla Black's 1964 chart-topper, 'You're My World', co-produced by Kim Fowley. Reddy also became a well-known television personality, hosting the *Midnight Special* show for most of the 70s, taking a cameo role in *Airport 75* and starring in the 1978 film *Pete's Dragon*. She also sang 'Little Boys', the theme song for the film *The Man Who Loved Women* (1983). Disenchanted with life in general during the 80s, she performed infrequently, but made her first major showcase in years at the Westwood Playhouse, Los Angeles, in 1986. Since then she has appeared in concert and cabaret worldwide. In 1995 she performed at London's Café Royal in the evenings, while rehearsed during the day to take over from Carole King in the hit musical *Blood Brothers* on Broadway.

●ALBUMS: *I Don't Know How To Love Him* (Capitol 1971)★★★, *Helen Reddy* (Capitol 1971)★★★, *I Am Woman* (Capitol 1972)★★★, *Long Hard Climb* (Capitol 1973)★★, *Love Song For Jeffrey* (Capitol 1974)★★, *Free And Easy* (Capitol 1974)★★, *No Way To Treat A Lady* (Capitol 1975)★★, *Music Music* (Capitol 1976)★★, *Ear Candy* (Capitol 1977)★★★, *We'll Sing In The Sunshine* (Capitol 1978)★★, *Live In London* (Capitol 1979)★★, *Reddy* (Capitol 1979)★★, *Take What You Find* (Capitol 1980)★★, *Play Me Out* (MCA 1981)★★, *Imagination* (MCA 1983)★★, *Take It Home* (Columbia 1984)★★.

●COMPILATIONS: *Helen Reddy's Greatest Hits* (Capitol 1975)★★★, *Greatest Hits* (Capitol 1987)★★★, *Feel So Young (The Helen Reddy Collection)* (Pickwick 1991)★★★, *The Very Best Of ...* (1993)★★★.

REED, LOU

b. Lewis Allen Reed (also Firbank), 2 March 1942, Freeport, Long Island, New York, USA. A member of several high school bands, Reed made his recording debut with the Shades in 1957. Their 'So Blue' enjoyed brief notoriety when played by influential disc jockey Murray The K, but was lost in the plethora of independent singles released in this period. Having graduated from Syracuse University, Reed took a job as a contract songwriter with Pickwick Records which specialized in cash-in, exploitative recordings. His many compositions from this era included 'The Ostrich' (1965), a tongue-in-cheek dance song which so impressed the label hierarchy that Reed formed the Primitives to promote it as a single. The group also included a recent acquaintance, John Cale, thus sewing the early seeds of the Velvet Underground. Reed led this outstanding unit between 1966 and 1970, contributing almost all of the material and shaping its ultimate direction. His songs, for the most part, drew on the incisive discipline of R&B, while pointed lyrics displayed an acerbic view of contemporary urban life. Reed's departure left a creative vacuum within the group, yet he too seemed drained of inspiration following the break. He sought employment outside of music and two years passed before *Lou Reed* was released. Recorded in London with British musicians, including Steve Howe and Rick Wakeman, the set boasted some excellent songs - several of which were intended for the Velvet Underground - but was marred by an indistinct production. Nonetheless, an attendant UK tour with the Tots, a group of New York teenagers, was an artistic success. David Bowie, a long-time Velvets' aficionado, oversaw *Transformer*, which captured a prevailing mood of decadence. Although uneven, it included the classic 'Walk On The Wild Side', a homage to transsexuals and social misfits drawn to artist/film-maker Andy Warhol. This explicit song became a surprise hit, reaching the UK Top 10 and US Top 20 in 1973, but Reed refused to become trapped by the temporary nature of the genre and returned to the dark side of his talents with *Berlin*. By steering a course through sado-masochism, attempted suicide and nihilism, the artist expunged his newfound commerciality and challenged his audience in a way few contemporaries dared. Yet this period was blighted by self-parody and while a crack back-up band built around guitarists Dick Wagner and Steve Hunter provided undoubted muscle on the live *Rock 'N' Roll Animal*, *Sally Can't Dance* showed an artist bereft of direction and purpose. Having sanctioned a second in-concert set, Reed released the stark *Metal Machine Music*, an electronic, atonal work spaced over a double album. Savaged by critics upon release, its ill-synchronized oscillations have since been lauded by élitist sections of the *avant garde* fraternity, while others view its release as a work of mischief in which Reed displayed the ultimate riposte to careerist convention. It was followed by the sedate *Coney Island Baby*, Reed's softest, simplest collection to date, the inherent charm of which was diluted on *Rock 'N' Roll Heart*, a careless, inconsequential collection which marked an artistic nadir. However, its successor, *Street Hassle*, displayed a rejuvenated power, resuming the singer's empathy with New York's subcultures. The title track, later revived by Simple Minds, was undeniably impressive, while 'Dirt' and 'I Wanna Be Black' revealed a wryness missing from much of the artist's solo work. Although subsequent releases, *The Bells* and *Growing Up in Public*, failed to scale similar heights, they offered a newfound sense of maturity. Reed entered the 80s a stronger, more incisive performer, buoyed by a fruitful association with guitarist Robert Quine, formerly of Richard Hell's Void-Oids. *The Blue Mask* was another purposeful collection and set a pattern for the punchy, concise material found on *Legendary Hearts* and *Mistrial*.

However, despite the promise these selections offered, few commentators were prepared for the artistic rebirth found on *New York*. Here the sound was stripped to the bone, accentuating the rhythmic pulse of compositions focusing on the seedy low-life that Reed excels in chronicling. His lyrics reasserted the fire of his best work as the artist regained the power to paint moribund pictures which neither asked, nor received, pity. *New York* was a splendid return to form and created considerable interest in his back catalogue. *Songs For 'Drella* was a haunting epitaph for Andy Warhol on which Reed collaborated with John Cale. It showed another facet of the dramatic regeneration that places this immensely talented artist back at rock's cutting edge. In 1993 Reed joined together with his legendary colleagues for a high-profile Velvet Underground reunion. Although it was short-lived (rumours of old feuds with Cale) Reed has the benefit on being able to fall back on his solo work at any given time.

●ALBUMS: *Lou Reed* (RCA 1972)★★, *Transformer* (RCA 1972)★★★★, *Berlin* (RCA 1973)★★★, *Rock 'N' Roll Animal* (RCA 1974)★★★, *Sally Can't Dance* (RCA 1974)★★, *Metal Machine Music* (RCA 1975)★, *Lou Reed Live* (RCA 1975)★★, *Coney Island Baby* (RCA 1976)★★★★, *Rock 'N' Roll Heart* (Arista 1976)★★, *Street Hassle* (Arista 1978)★★★★, *Live - Take No Prisoners* (RCA 1978)★★, *The Bells* (Arista 1979)★★★, *Growing Up In Public* (Arista 1980)★★, *The Blue Mask* (RCA 1982)★★★, *Legendary Hearts* (RCA 1983)★★★, *New Sensations* (RCA 1984)★★★★, *Live In Italy* (RCA 1984)★★, *Mistrial* (RCA 1986)★★, *New York* (Sire 1989)★★★★, with John Cale *Songs For 'Drella* (Warners 1990)★★★★, *Magic And Loss* (Sire 1992)★★★★, *Set The Twilight Reeling* (Warners 1996)★★★.

●COMPILATIONS: *Walk On The Wild Side - The Best Of Lou Reed* (RCA 1977)★★★, *Rock 'N' Roll Diary 1967-1980* (Arista 1980)★★★, *I Can't Stand It* (RCA 1983)★★, *New York Superstar* (Fame 1986)★★, *Between Thought And Expression* 3-CD Box Set(RCA 1992)★★★★.

●VIDEOS: *The New York Album* (Warner Music 1990),

Songs For Drella (Warner Music 1991), *A Night With Lou Reed* (PNE 1996).
●FURTHER READING: *Lou Reed & The Velvets*, Nigel Trevena. *Rock And Roll Animal*, No author. *Lou Reed & The Velvet Underground*, Diana Clapton. *Lou Reed: Growing Up In Public*, Peter Doggett. *Between Thought And Expression: Selected Lyrics*, Lou Reed. *Waiting For the Man: A Biography Of Lou Reed*, Jeremy Reed. *Transformer: The Lou Reed Story*, Victor Bockris. *Between The Lines*, Michael Wrenn.

REEVES, MARTHA

b. Martha Reeves, 18 July 1941, Alabama, USA. Reeves was schooled in both gospel and classical music, but it was vocal group R&B that caught her imagination. She began performing in the late 50s under the name Martha Lavaille, briefly joining the Fascinations and then the Del-Phis. In 1961 she joined the fledgling Motown organization in Detroit, where she served as secretary to William Stevenson in the A&R department. Her other duties included supervising Little Stevie Wonder during office hours, and singing occasional backing vocals on recording sessions. Impressed by the power and flexibility of her voice, Berry Gordy offered her the chance to record for the label. She reassembled the Del-Phis quartet as the Vels for a single in 1962, and later that year she led the group on their debut release under a new name, Martha And The Vandellas. From 1963 onwards, they became one of Motown's most successful recording outfits, and Reeves' strident vocals were showcased on classic hits like 'Heat Wave', 'Dancing In The Street' and 'Nowhere To Run'. She was given individual credit in front of the group from 1967 onwards, but their career was interrupted the following year when she was taken seriously ill, and had to retire from performing. Fully recovered, Reeves emerged in 1970 with a new line-up of Vandellas. After two years of episodic success, she reacted bitterly to Motown's decision to relocate from Detroit to Hollywood, and fought a legal battle to be released from her contract. The eventual settlement entailed that she lost the use of the Vandellas' name, but left her free to sign a solo contract with MCA in 1973. Her debut album was the result of lengthy recording sessions with producer Richard Perry. It gained much critical acclaim but was commercially disappointing, failing to satisfy either rock or soul fans with its hybrid style. Moving to Arista Records in 1977, she was submerged by the late 70s disco boom on a series of albums that allowed her little room to display her talents. Since the early 80s she has found consistent work on package tours featuring former Motown artists. During the late 80s she toured with a 'fake' Vandellas before being reunited with the original group (Annette Sterling and Rosalind Holmes) on Ian Levine's Motor City label. They released 'Step Into My Shoes' in 1989 while ex-Vandella Lois Reeves also recorded for Levine's label.
●ALBUMS: *Martha Reeves* (MCA 1974)★★★, *The Rest Of My Life* (Arista 1977)★, *We Meet Again* (Milestone 1978)★, *Gotta Keep Moving* (1980)★.
●COMPILATIONS: *We Meet Again/Gotta Keep Moving* (1993)★, *Early Classics* (Spectrum 1996)★★.

REID, TERRY

b. 13 November 1949, Huntingdon, England. Reid first attracted attention in Peter Jay And The Jaywalkers where his ragged voice helped transform their *passé* beat-group image into something more contemporary. Reid's debut single, 'The Hand Don't Fit The Glove', was issued in 1967, but he achieved a greater recognition upon forming a trio with Pete Solley (keyboards) and Keith Webb (drums). Having turned down Jimmy Page's overtures to join the embryonic Led Zeppelin, Reid became a popular figure in the USA following a tour supporting Cream. His debut *Bang Bang You're Terry Reid* produced by Mickie Most, emphasized the artist's exceptional vocal talent and impassioned guitar style, while a second collection featured soaring versions of Donovan's 'Superlungs My Supergirl' and Lorraine Ellison's 'Stay With Me Baby'. Terry's own compositions included the excellent 'Speak Now Or Forever Hold Your Peace' and 'Friends', which later became a hit for Arrival. Much of Reid's *River*, was recorded in America, where the singer had settled. More introspective than his earlier work, its meandering tunes enraged some critics but enthralled others, who drew parallels with Van Morrison's *Astral Weeks*. However, the consensus viewed its follow-up, *Seed Of Memory*, a major disappointment while a fifth collection, *Rogue Waves*, which featured several undistinguished cover versions, was equally frustrating. Following a long period out of the limelight, Reid re-established his recording career with *The Driver*, which featured able support from Joe Walsh, Tim Schmidt and Howard Jones.
●ALBUMS: *Bang Bang You're Terry Reid* (Epic 1968)★★★★, *Terry Reid* (Epic 1969)★★★, *River* (Atlantic 1973)★★★, *Seed Of Memory* (ABC 1976)★★★, *Rogue Waves* (Capitol 1979)★★, *The Driver* (Warners 1991)★★.
●COMPILATIONS: *The Most Of Terry Reid* (1971)★★, *The Hand Don't Fit The Glove* (See For Miles 1985)★★★★.

RENAISSANCE

In 1968, former Yardbirds Jim McCarty (b. 25 July 1943, Liverpool, England; drums) and Keith Relf (b. 22 March 1943, Richmond, Surrey, England; vocals/acoustic guitar) reunited as Together for two self-composed singles that in their pastoral lyricism and acoustic emphasis anticipated the more lucrative Renaissance in which they were joined by ex-Nashville Teens John Hawken (keyboards), Louis Cennamo (bass/vocals) and Relf's sister Jane (vocals). Produced by Paul Samwell-Smith (another Yardbirds veteran), their promising debut album embraced folk, classical and *musique concrète* reference points. However, though McCarty played and co-wrote tracks on *Prologue*, he and the others had abandoned Renaissance who continued with Annie Haslam (vocals), Robert Hendry (guitar/vocals), John Tout (keyboards), Jonathan Camp (bass/vocals) and Terry Slade (drums). As the last was replaced by Terence Sullivan in 1975, so Hendry was two years earlier by Mike Dunford, who provided melodies to poet Betty Thatcher's lyrics for *Ashes Are Burning* and later records which met with greater commercial acclaim in North America than Europe - so much so that the group found it more convenient to take up US residency. Indeed, *Turn Of The Cards* was not available in Britain until a year after its release in the USA, and the group's only concert recording was from Carnegie Hall with the New York Philharmonic. An orchestra had also augmented a Renaissance interpretation of Rimsky-Korsakov's *Scheherazade* featuring the stunning vocal harmonies that enlivened *A Song For All Seasons*, which became their biggest UK seller in the wake of a Top 10 entry for its 'Northern Lights' (1978). Haslam recorded the solo *Annie In Wonderland* but 1979's *Azur D'Or* was the only other album by Renaissance or its associates to make even a minor impression in the UK. In 1980, the band weathered the departures of Sullivan and Tout as pragmatically as they had worse upheavals in the past - and, indeed, Renaissance's considerable cult following has since taken many years to dwindle. Independent prog specialists HTD Records reissued albums of new material in the mid-90s.

●ALBUMS: *Renaissance* (Elektra 1969)★★★, *Prologue* (Sovereign 1972)★★★, *Ashes Are Burning* (Sovereign 1973)★★, *Turn Of The Cards* (BTM 1974)★★★, *Scheherazade And Other Stories* (BTM 1975)★★★, *Live At Carnegie Hall* (BTM 1976)★★, *Novella* (Warners 1977)★★, *A Song For All Seasons* (Warners 1978)★★★, *Azur D'Or* (Warners 1979)★★, *Camera Camera* (IRS 1981)★★, *Time Line* (IRS 1983)★★, *The Other Woman* (HTD 1995)★★, *Blessing In Disguise* (One Way 1995)★★, *Ocean Gypsy* (HTD 1997)★★, *Songs Of Renaissance Days* (HTD 1997)★★.

●COMPILATIONS: *Da Capo* (Repertoire 1996)★★★.

RENBOURN, JOHN

Renbourn received his first guitar at the age of 13, insisting on the present because he wished to emulate the singing cowboys he had seen in American movies. After a brief dalliance with classical music he turned his attention to folk. Having flirted with various part-time electric bands (including the blues-inclined Hogsnort Rupert And His Famous Porkestra), Renbourn began his folk-singing career on London's club circuit. Startling guitarwork compensated for his less assured vocals and he quickly established a reputation as a leading traditionalist, whose interpretations of classic country blues and Elizabethan material provided a remarkable contrast to the freer styles of Davey Graham and Bert Jansch. Friendship with the latter resulted in Renbourn's debut album, but it was on the following collection, *Another Monday*, that the artist's talent truly flourished. The two guitarists were the inspiration behind the Pentangle, but Renbourn, like Jansch, continued to record as a solo act during the group's existence. When the individual musicians went their separate ways again in 1973, John maintained his unique, eclectic approach and further excursions into medieval music contrasted with the eastern styles or country blues prevalent on later albums. His 1988 album was recorded with the assistance of Maggie Boyle, Tony Roberts and Steve Tilston under the collective title of 'John Renbourn's Ship Of Fools'. Although his studio releases are now less frequent, the guitarist remains a popular figure on the British and international folk circuit, and is often to be found double-heading with fellow maestro Isaac Guillory.

●ALBUMS: *John Renbourn* (1965)★★★, with Bert Jansch *Bert And John* (1966)★★★, *Another Monday* (1967)★★★, *Sir John A Lot Of Merrie Englandes Musik Thynge And Ye Grene Knyghte* (Transatlantic 1968)★★★, *The Lady And The Unicorn* (Transatlantic 1970)★★★, *Faro Annie* (Transatlantic 1972)★★★★, *The Hermit* (Transatlantic 1977)★★★, *Maid In Bedlam* (Transatlantic 1977)★★★, with Stefan Grossman *John Renbourn And Stefan Grossman* (Kicking Mule 1978)★★★, *Black Balloon* (1979)★★★, *Enchanted Garden* (Transatlantic 1980)★★★, *Live In Concert* (Spindrift 1985)★★★, *Nine Maidens* (Spindrift 1986)★★★★, with Grossman *The Three Kingdoms* (Sonet 1987)★★★★, *Ship Of Fools* (In-Market 1989)★★★, with Robin Williamson *Wheel Of Fortune* (Demon Fiend 1994)★★★.

●COMPILATIONS: *The John Renbourn Sampler* (Transatlantic 1971)★★★, *Heads And Tails* (1973)★★★, *The Essential Collection Volume 1: The Solo Years* (Transatlantic 1987)★★★★, *The Essential Collection Volume 2: Moon Shines Bright* (Transatlantic 1987)★★★, *The Folk Blues Of John Renbourn* (Transatlantic 1988)★★★, *The Mediaeval Almanac* (Transatlantic 1989)★★★, *The Essential John Renbourn (A Best Of)* (1992)★★★, *Will The Circle Be Unbroken?* (1995)★★★.

REO SPEEDWAGON

Formed in Champaign, Illinois, USA, in 1970 when pianist Neal Doughty (b. 29 July 1946, Evanston, Illinois, USA) and drummer Alan Gratzer (b. 9 November 1948, Syracuse, New York, USA) were joined by guitarist and songwriter Gary Richrath (b. 10 October 1949, Peoria, Illinois, USA). Although still in its embryonic stage, the group already had its unusual name which was derived from an early American fire-engine, designed by one Ransom E. Olds. Barry Luttnell (vocals) and Greg Philbin (bass) completed the line-up featured on *REO Speedwagon*, but the former was quickly replaced by Kevin Cronin (b. 6 October 1951, Evanston, Illinois, USA). The quintet then began the perilous climb from local to national prominence, but despite their growing popularity, particularly in America's Midwest, the band was initially unable to complete a consistent album. Although *REO Two* and *Ridin' The Storm Out* eventually achieved gold status, disputes regarding direction culminated in the departure of their second vocalist. Michael Murphy took his place in 1974, but when ensuing albums failed to generate new interest, Cronin rejoined his former colleagues. Bassist Bruce Hall (b. 3 May 1953, Champaign, Illinois, USA) was also brought into a line-up acutely aware that previous releases had failed to reflect their in-concert prowess. The live summary, *You Get What You Play For*, overcame this problem to become the group's first platinum disc, a distinction shared by its successor, *You Can Tune A Piano, But You Can't Tuna Fish*. However, sales for *Nine Lives* proved disappointing, inspiring the misjudged view that the band had peaked. Such impressions were banished in 1980 with the release of *Hi Infidelity*, a crafted, self-confident collection which topped the US album charts and spawned a series of highly successful singles. An emotive ballad, 'Keep On Lovin' You', reached number 1 in the US and number 7 in the UK, while its follow-up, 'Take It On The Run', also hit the US Top 5. However, a lengthy tour in support of the album proved creatively draining and *Good Trouble* is generally accepted as one of REO's least worthy efforts. The quintet withdrew from the stadium circuit and, having rented a Los Angeles warehouse, enjoyed six months of informal rehearsals during which time they regained a creative empathy. *Wheels Are Turning* recaptured the zest apparent on *Hi Infidelity* and engendered a second US number 1 in 'Can't Fight This Feeling'. *Life As We Know It* and its successor, *The Earth, A Small Man, His Dog And A Chicken*, emphasized the group's now accustomed professionalism, by which time the line-up featured Cronin, Doughty, Hall, Dave Amato (b. 3 March 1953; lead guitar, ex-Ted Nugent), Bryan Hitt (b. 5 January 1954; drums, ex-Wang Chung) and Jesse Harms (b. 6 July 1952; keyboards). Too often lazily dubbed 'faceless', or conveniently bracketed with other in-concert 70s favourites Styx and Kansas, REO Speedwagon have proved the importance of a massive, secure, grass roots following.

●ALBUMS: *REO Speedwagon* (Epic 1971)★★★, *REO Two* (Epic 1972)★★★, *Ridin' The Storm Out* (Epic 1974)★★★, *Lost In A Dream* (Epic 1974)★★, *This Time We Mean It* (Epic 1975)★★, *REO* (Epic 1976)★★, *REO Speedwagon Live/You Get What You Play For* (Epic 1977)★★, *You Can Tune A Piano But You Can't Tuna Fish* (Epic 1978)★★, *Nine Lives* (Epic 1979)★★, *Hi Infidelity* (Epic 1980)★★, *Good Trouble* (Epic 1982)★★, *Wheels Are Turning* (Epic 1984)★★, *Life As We Know It* (Epic 1987)★★, *The Earth, A Small Man, His Dog And A Chicken* (Epic 1990)★★, *Building The Bridge* (Essential 1996)★★.

●COMPILATIONS: *A Decade Of Rock 'N' Roll 1970-1980* (Epic 1980)★★★, *Best Foot Forward* (Epic 1985)★★, *The Hits* (Epic 1988)★★★, *A Second Decade Of Rock 'N' Roll 1981-1991* (Epic 1991)★★.

●VIDEOS: *Wheels Are Turnin'* (Virgin Vision 1987), *REO Speedwagon* (Fox Video 1988).

RETURN TO FOREVER

This jazz group featured Chick Corea (b. 12 June 1941, Chelsea, Massachusetts, USA; keyboards), Joe Farrell (b. 16 December 1937, Chicago Heights, Illinois, USA, d. 10 January 1986; soprano saxophone/flute), Flora Purim (b. 6 March 1942, Rio de Janeiro, Brazil; vocals), Stanley Clarke (b. 30 June 1951, Philadelphia, USA; bass/electric bass), and Airto Moreira (b. 5 August 1941, Itaiopolis, Brazil; percussion). Formed by Chick Corea in 1971, Return To Forever began as a Latin-influenced fusion band, mixing the wild vocals of Purim with the tight, funk-edged slapping bass of Clarke to create a new sound. The group toured and made two commercially successful albums before disbanding in 1973. Keeping Clarke, Corea immediately put together the second of what was to be three successive Return To Forever bands. Hiring Bill Connors to play electric guitar (soon replaced by Earl Klugh and then Al DiMeola), and drummer Lenny White, the second band was much more of a rock-orientated group. Producing a harder overall sound, and aided by Corea's adoption of various electronic keyboard gadgetry, the new band achieved massive popularity, particularly with rock audiences, and its 1976 *Romantic Warrior* quickly became its best-selling album. The third and final Return To Forever was a huge but not altogether successful departure from what had come before. Corea put together a 13-piece band that included small string and brass sections, as well as Clarke and Farrell from the original band. A soft, unchallenging music resulted, and Return To Forever refined itself out of existence in 1980. Corea, Clarke, DiMeola, and White joined up for a single tour in 1983.

●ALBUMS: *Light As A Feather* (Polydor 1972)★★★★, *Return To Forever* (ECM 1973)★★★★, *Hymn Of The Seventh Galaxy* (Polydor 1973)★★★★, *Where Have I Known You Before?* (Polydor 1974)★★★, *No Mystery* (Polydor 1975)★★, *The Leprechaun* (Polydor 1976)★★★★, *Romantic Warrior* (Columbia 1976)★★★, *Live: The Complete Concert* (Columbia 1979)★★★.

●COMPILATIONS: *The Best Of Return To Forever* (Columbia 1980)★★★★, *Return To The 7th Galaxy: The Return To Forever Anthology Featuring Chick Corea* (Chronicles/Verve 1996)★★★★.

REZILLOS

Formed in Edinburgh, Scotland, in March 1976, the Rezillos were initially an informal aggregation consisting of Eugene Reynolds (b. Alan Forbes; vocals), Fay Fife (b. Sheila Hynde; vocals), Luke Warm aka Jo Callis (lead guitar), Hi Fi Harris (b. Mark Harris; guitar), Dr. D.K. Smythe (bass), Angel Patterson (b. Alan Patterson; drums) and Gale Warning (backing vocals). Their irreverent repertoire consisted of pre-beat favourites by Screaming Lord Sutch and the Piltdown Men, judicious material from the Dave Clark Five and glam-rock staples by the Sweet. Their image, part Marlon Brando, part Shangri-Las, allied them with the punk movement, although their love of pop heritage denied wholesale involvement. The Rezillos' debut single, 'I Can't Stand My Baby', encapsulated their crazed obsessions, but its success introduced a discipline at odds with their initial irreverence. Harris, Smythe and Warning left the line-up, while auxiliary member William Mysterious (b. William Donaldson; bass/saxophone) joined the group on a permanent basis. Now signed to a major label, Sire Records, the quintet undertook several tours and had a UK Top 20 hit with the satirical 'Top Of The Pops' in August 1978. The group's debut album, *Can't Stand The Rezillos*, also charted, before internal pressures began pulling them apart. Mysterious was replaced by Simon Templar, but in December 1978 the Rezillos folded following a brief farewell tour. Fife and Reynolds formed the Revillos, while the rest of the band became known as Shake. Callis later found fame in the Human League. In the 90s the Revillos/Rezillos re-formed for tours in Japan, from which a live album was culled to bookmark their fifteen year career.

●ALBUMS: *Can't Stand The Rezillos* (Sire 1978)★★★, *Mission Accomplished ... But The Beat Goes On* (Sire 1979)★★.

●COMPILATIONS: *Can't Stand The Rezillos, The (Almost) Complete Rezillos* (Sire 1995)★★★, *Live And On Fire In Japan* (Vinyl Japan 1995)★★.

RICHMAN, JONATHAN

b. 16 May 1951, Boston, Massachusetts, USA. Richman rose to prominence during the early 70s as leader of the Modern Lovers. Drawing inspiration from 50s pop and the Velvet Underground, the group initially offered a garage band sound, as evinced on their UK hit 'Roadrunner' and the infectious instrumental 'Egyptian Reggae' in 1977. However, Richman increasingly distanced himself from electric music and latterly embraced an acoustic-based direction. He disbanded the group in 1978 to pursue an idiosyncratic solo career in which his naïve style was deemed charming or irritating according to taste. His songs, including 'Ice Cream Man', 'My Love Is A Flower (Just Beginning To Bloom)', showed a childlike simplicity which seemed oblivious to changes in trends around him. Richman exhumed the Modern Lovers name during the 80s without any alteration to his style and the artist continues to enjoy considerable cult popularity. In the 90s he made a cameo appearance in the movie *Kingpin*. In 1996 he signed to Neil Young's imprint Vapor Records and released *Surrender To Jonathan*. The album was a departure from the past with a much denser sound (even a brass section). Included is a reworking of 'Egyptian Reggae' together with more quirks of his fertile mind such as 'I Was Dancing In The Lesbian Bar'.

●ALBUMS: *Jonathan Richman And The Modern Lovers* (Beserkley 1977)★★★, *Rock 'N' Roll With The Modern Lovers* (Beserkley 1977)★★, *Modern Lovers Live* (Beserkley 1977)★★, *Back In Your Life* (Beserkley

1979)★★★, *The Jonathan Richman Songbook* (Beserkley 1980)★★★, *Jonathan Sings!* (Rough Trade 1984)★★★, *Rockin' And Romance* (Rough Trade 1985)★★, *Its Time For Jonathan Richman And The Modern Lovers* (Rough Trade 1986)★★, with Barrence Whitfield *Jonathan Richman & Barence Whitfield* (Rounder 1988), *Modern Lovers 88* (Demon 1988)★★, *Jonathan Richman* (Special Delivery 1989)★★, *Jonathan Goes Country* (Special Delivery 1990)★★, *I, Jonathan* (Rounder 1992)★★★, *Jonathan Tu Vas A Emoncionar* (Rounder 1993)★★, *Plea For Tenderness* (Nectar Masters 1994)★★, *You Must Ask The Heart* (Rounder 1995)★★, *Surrender To Jonathan* (Vapor 1996)★★★.

●COMPILATIONS: *The Beserkley Years: The Best Of Jonathan Richman And The Modern Lovers* (Rhino 1987)★★★, *23 Great Recordings* (Castle/Beserkley 1990).

RIFKIN, JOSHUA

b. 22 April 1944, New York, USA. A pianist, musicologist, arranger and conductor, Rifkin was instrumental in reviving interest in the important composer of ragtime music, Scott Joplin. During the 60s, Rifkin studied at the Juilliard School of Music, New York University, Gottingen University and Princeton; and worked on composition with Karl-Heinz Stockhausen in Darmstadt. At the same time, he played ragtime and piano jazz, and recorded for Elektra as a member of the Even Dozen Jug Band. Also for Elektra, he conducted *The Baroque Beatles*, classical-style versions of John Lennon and Paul McCartney songs. He also arranged and conducted *Wildflowers*, and other recordings for Judy Collins. In 1970 he was appointed Professor of Music at Brandeis University in Massachusetts, and musical director of the Elektra ancillary, Nonesuch Records. The following year, the Lincoln Centre produced the highly successful *An Evening With Scott Joplin*, at which Rifkin was a featured artist. From 1970-74, he released a series of three *Piano Rags By Scott Joplin*, which won *Stereo Review* and *Billboard* awards as records of the year, and coincided with the release of the film, *The Sting* (1973), whose soundtrack featured 'The Entertainer' and several other Joplin tunes, arranged by another Juilliard 'old boy', Marvin Hamlisch. The film won seven Academy Awards, and, together with Rifkin's albums, sparked off a nationwide revival of Joplin's works. Subsequently, Rifkin worked a good deal in the classical field, conducting concerts and releasing several albums. He was also at the forefront of the move to revitalize vintage recordings of ragtime music by the digital process.

●ALBUMS: *The Baroque Beatles Book* (Elektra 1965)★★★★, *Piano Rags By Scott Joplin, Volumes 1 & 2* (Nonesuch 1974)★★★, *Piano Rags By Scott Joplin, Volume 3* (Nonesuch 1974)★★★, *Digital Ragtime* (EMI 1980)★★.

RIPERTON, MINNIE

b. 8 November 1947, Chicago, Illinois, USA, d. 12 July 1979. A former singer with the Gems, Riperton recorded under the name 'Andrea Davis' prior to joining the Rotary Connection. She remained with this adventurous, black pop/psychedelic group between 1967 and 1970, before embarking on a solo career. In 1973 the singer began working with Wonderlove, Stevie Wonder's backing group. Two years later he returned this compliment, producing Riperton's *Perfect Angel*, and contributing two original compositions to the selection. However, it was 'Loving You', a song written by Riperton and her husband,Richard Rudolph, that brought international success (US number 1/UK number 2) in 1975. This delicate performance featured the artist's soaring multi-octave voice, but set a standard later releases found hard to emulate. Riperton died from cancer in July 1979.

●ALBUMS: *Come To My Garden* (Janus 1969)★★, *Perfect Angel* (Epic 1974)★★★, *Adventures In Paradise* (Epic 1975)★★, *Stay In Love* (Epic 1977)★★, *Minnie* (Capitol 1979)★★, *Love Lives Forever* (Capitol 1980)★★.

●COMPILATIONS: *The Best Of Minnie Riperton* (1981)★★.

ROBERTSON, B.A.

b. Brian Robertson, Glasgow, Scotland. This gregarious vocalist achieved notoriety when, as Brian Alexander Robertson, his debut *Wringing Applause*, was accompanied by excessive hype. He nonetheless survived the ensuing backlash to secure an international deal with Asylum through which he enjoyed three UK Top 10 singles with 'Bang Bang', 'Knocked It Off' (both 1979) and 'To Be Or Not To Be' (1980). His tongue-in-cheek delivery was also apparent on 'Hold Me', a duet with Maggie Bell, and 'We Have A Dream', on which he fronted the 1982 Scotland World Cup Squad. The following year Robertson scored a minor hit with 'Time' a collaboration with former Abba member Frida, and although chart success has since proved elusive, the artist has pursued a successful and financially rewarding career as a songwriter. He composed the theme tune to *Wogan*, BBC Television's thrice-weekly chat show. His on-camera foolishness belies a considerable talent.

●ALBUMS: *Wringing Applause* (1973)★★, *Initial Success* (Asylum 1980)★★, *Bully For You* (Asylum 1981)★★, *B.A. Robertson* (Warners 1982)★★.

ROBINSON, TOM

b. 1 July 1950, Cambridge, England. Robinson's wayward youth included the study of oboe, clarinet and bass guitar, and a spell in Finchden Manor, a readjustment centre in Kent, where he met guitarist Danny Kurstow with whom he formed his first group, Davanq, in 1971. Two years later Robinson formed Café Society with Hereward Kaye and Ray Doyle and they signed to the Kinks' Konk label. In 1974, *Café Society* was recorded with help from Ray Davies and Mick Avory. During the taping of an intended second album, administrative discord was manifested in what was now the Tom Robinson Band's on-stage mocking of Davies, and, later, the Kinks' reciprocal dig at Robinson in a 1977 b-side, 'Prince Of The Punks' - with whom Robinson's band had been categorized (not entirely accurately) when contracted by EMI Records the previous year. Konk, nevertheless, retained publishing interests in 13 Robinson numbers. Some of these were selected for TRB's *Power In The Darkness* debut and attendant UK Top 40 singles - notably the catchy '2468 Motorway'. Backed by keyboardist Mark Ambler, drummer 'Dolphin' Taylor plus the faithful Kurstow, lead singer Robinson's active support of many radical causes riddled his lyrical output, but the gravity of 'Summer Of 79' and 'Up Against The Wall' was mitigated by grace-saving humour. The quartet's *Rising Free* EP, for example, contained the singalong 'Glad To Be Gay' anthem - which was also a highlight of both TRB's 1978 benefit concert for the Northern Ireland Gay Rights and One Parent Families Association, and Robinson's solo set during a Lesbian and Gay Rights March in Washington in 1979, shortly after parting with his band (Taylor going on to Stiff Little Fingers). This followed a disappointing critical and market reaction to *TRB2* (supervised by Todd Rundgren) - on which the sloganeering was overdone and the musical performance tepid. While Kurstow joined ex-Sex Pistol Glen Matlock in the Spectres, Robinson led the short-lived Section 27 and began songwriting collaborations with Elton John and Peter Gabriel. By 1981 he had relocated to Berlin to record the solo *North By Northwest* and work in alternative cabaret and fringe theatre. Professionally, this period proved fruitful - with 1982's strident 'War Baby' and evocative 'Atmospherics' in the UK Top 40, and a revival of Steely Dan's 'Ricki Don't Lose That Number', from *Hope And Glory*, which fared as well as the original in the same chart. However, when *Still Loving You* produced no equivalent of even this modest triumph Robinson, now a contented father, regrouped his original band. Subsequent engagements were viewed by many as akin to a nostalgia revue - and certainly several old favourites were evident on the Berlin concert set, *Last Tango*. However, Robinson's lyrical eloquence argues that further solid work may lie ahead now he has returned to recording with Cooking Vinyl Records.

●ALBUMS: *Power In The Darkness* (Harvest 1978)★★★★, *TRB2* (Harvest 1979)★★, with Sector 27 *Sector 27* (Fontana 1980)★★, *North By Northwest* (Fontana 1982)★★★, *Hope And Glory* (RCA 1984)★★★, *Still Loving You* (RCA 1986)★★★, *Last Tango* (Line 1989)★★, with Jakko M. Jakszuk *We Never Had It So Good* (Musidisc 1990)★★★, *Living In A Boom Time* (Cooking Vinyl 1992)★★★, *Love Over Rage* (Cooking Vinyl 1994)★★★, *Having It Both Ways* (Cooking Vinyl 1996)★★★.

●COMPILATIONS: *Tom Robinson Band* (EMI 1981)★★★, *Cabaret '79* (Panic 1982)★★★, *The Collection 1977-1987* (EMI 1987)★★★★.

ROCKPILE

The name Rockpile was derived from a 1972 album by founding vocalist/guitarist Dave Edmunds. In 1979 he suspended his solo career by officially joining forces with three musicians who had featured on several albums issued under his own name. Ex-Brinsley Schwarz frontman, Nick Lowe, bassist Billy Bremner (ex-Lulu And The Luvvers) and drummer Terry Williams (ex-Love Sculpture - with Edmunds - and Man), completed the founding line-up. *Seconds Of Pleasure* fused Edmunds' love of classic rock 'n' roll with Lowe's grasp of quirky pop, but although Rockpile members continued to guest on the pair's solo albums (*Twangin'*/Edmunds; *Nick The Knife*/Lowe), the quartet split up following internal disputes. The two vocalists subsequently pursued independent paths, while Williams eventually joined Dire Straits.

●ALBUMS: *Seconds Of Pleasure* (F-Beat 1980)★★★.

ROCKY HORROR SHOW, THE

One of the phenomenons of the UK musical theatre in the 70s and 80s, this rock musical opened at the Royal Court Theatre Upstairs on 19 June 1973. The book, music and lyrics were by Richard O'Brien who had played a minor role in the London production of *Jesus Christ Superstar*. The abolition of theatrical censorship in Britain nearly five years previously, provided the opportunity to present what turned out to be a jumble of 50s and 60s sexual deviation, drug abuse, horror and science fiction movies, rock 'n' roll music, and much else besides. The story followed a young all-American couple, Brad (Christopher Malcolm) and Janet (Julie Covington), who take refuge in a remote castle. It is the home of several weird characters, including Frank 'N' Furter (Tim Curry), a 'sweet transvestite from Transexual, Transylvania', Magenta (Patricia Quinn), an usherette, Columbia (Little Nell), who tap-danced a lot, and the satanic Riff Raff (Richard O'Brien). The outrageously charismatic Frank 'N' Furter, dressed in the obligatory black stockings and suspenders, creates his perfect man, Rocky Horror, when he is not ravishing both Brad and Janet, and the remainder of the plot has to be experienced to be believed. The mostly 50s-style songs included 'Science Fiction, Double Feature', 'Dammit, Janet', 'Over At The Frankenstein Place', 'Sweet Transvestite', 'Time Warp', 'Sword Of Damocles', 'Hot Patootie (Bless My Soul)', 'Touch-A-Touch-A-Touch-A-Touch Me', 'Once In A While', 'Rose Tint My World', 'I'm Going Home' and 'Superheroes'. This 'harmless indulgence of the most monstrous fantasies' caught on in a big way, especially when it moved in August 1973 to the ideal environment of a seedy cinema in the trendy King's Road, Chelsea. After an incredible period of five and a half years, Frank 'N' Furter and his pals finally made it to the West End's Comedy Theatre in April 1979, where they stayed until September of the following year. The total London run amounted to 2960

performances, but New York audiences demurred, and that production closed after only 45 performances at the Belasco theatre in 1975. In the following year, several of the original cast reassembled to film the *The Rocky Horror Picture Show* which proved to be a critical and financial disaster in the UK, but, ironically, in the USA where the original show had flopped, the movie became a hot cult item on university campuses. However, legend has it that the Waverly Theatre in New York was the scene of the first example of the audience participation craze which has since become the norm. Fanatical fans in America and many other countries in the world, including Britain, who return again and again to see the movie, now dress up in clothes similar to those worn on the screen, and join in with the dialogue and lyrics, as well as constantly heckling and introducing their own ad-lib material. The movie's success helped the stage show's survival in the UK, where, on various provincial tours, the audiences repeated the excesses of the cinema. One of the 'highspots' comes when Brad and Jane are married, and a barrage of rice and various other celebratory souvenirs are despatched from the auditorium, threatening the life and limbs of the participating thespians. It even happened when the show was revived briefly at the Piccadilly Theatre in London in 1990, where, when Frank 'N' Furter sang 'The chips are down, I needed a break', the audience tended to hurl bars of KitKat on to the stage. Two years later, in addition to *The Rocky Horror* fan clubs that have sprung up around the world, the first convention of the British version, snappily called 'Timewarp', was held in London. A 1991 Dublin production of the piece was halted when Frank 'N' Furter's costume fell foul of the Irish decency laws. The 21st Birthday Anniversary production of *The Rocky Horror Show* took place at the Duke of York's Theatre in 1994, with Jonathon Morris as Frank 'N' Furter, and the celebrations began all over again in the following year when the leading character was played by ex-ice skating champion Robin Cousins.

●FURTHER READING: *The Rocky Horror Show: Participation Guide*, Sal Piro and Michael Hess.

RODEN, JESS

This former member of the respected 60s band the Alan Bown Set formed Bronco in 1970. Their brand of US-influenced rock was too derivative and they folded after two albums for Island Records. He then joined former Doors members, John Densmore and Robby Krieger in the Butts Band. His solo debut *Jess Roden* in 1974 prompted him to form the Jess Roden Band, and he made the well-received *You Can Keep Your Hat On* in 1976. Roden returned in 1980 as part of the Rivets, who released an undistinguished album. Roden now lives in New York working as a graphic artist. In 1995 an album of live recordings made with Robert Palmer in the mid-70s was issued.

●ALBUMS: *Jess Roden* (1974)★★★, *You Can Keep Your Hat On* (Island 1976)★★★, *Stone Chaser* (Island

1979)★★, as Jess Roden And The Humans *Jess Roden And The Humans* (Arrangement 1995)★★★.

RODGERS, CLODAGH

b. 1947, County Down, Northern Ireland. After eight years in showbusiness, this Anglo-Irish singer unexpectedly climbed into the Top 10 with 'Come Back And Shake Me' in April 1969. With the backing of songwriter Kenny Young and husband Johnny Morris (a record plugger at Decca) Rodgers successfully followed up with 'Goodnight Midnight' and 'Biljo', and also walked off with the 'Best Legs In Show Business' trophy. She had the legs and her voice insured for £1 million. A veteran of continental song festivals, she was a natural choice as the British entrant for the Eurovision Song Contest in 1971, and although she failed to secure victory, the catchy 'Jack In The Box' brought her another Top 10 UK hit. In the same year her 'Lady Love Bug' made the Top 30, and since then she has toured in various productions and appeared in cabaret and pantomime. In 1985 she co-starred with Joe Brown, Lynsey de Paul, Jeremy Clyde, Peter Duncan and Chad Stewart in the West End musical *Pump Boys And Dinettes*.
●ALBUMS: *Clodagh Rodgers* (RCA 1969)★★★, *Midnight Clodagh* (RCA 1969)★★, *Clodagh Rodgers* (RCA 1969)★★, *Rodgers And Hart* (RCA 1971), *It's Different Now* (RCA 1972)★★, *You Are My Music* (RCA 1973)★★, *Save Me* (Polydor 1977)★★.

ROGERS, KENNY

b. Kenneth David Rogers, 21 August 1938, Houston, Texas, USA. Rogers was the fourth of eight children, born in a poor area, where his father worked in a shipyard and his mother in a hospital. By sheer perseverance, he became the first member of his family to graduate. By 1955 Rogers was part of a doo-wop group, the Scholars, who recorded 'Poor Little Doggie', 'Spin The Wheel' and 'Kangewah', which was written by gossip columnist, Louella Parsons. At 19, he recorded 'That Crazy Feeling' as Kenneth Rogers for a small Houston label. Rogers' brother, Lelan, who had worked for US Decca, promoted the record and its limited success prompted the brothers to form their own label, Ken-Lee, although Rogers' single 'Jole Blon' was unsuccessful. Rogers also recorded 'For You Alone' for the Carlton label as Kenny Rogers The First. When Lelan managed Mickey Gilley, Rogers played bass on his 1960 single, 'Is It Wrong?' and he played stand-up bass with the Bobby Doyle Three and appears on their 1962 album of standards, *In A Most Unusual Way*. After recording solo for Mercury, Rogers joined the New Christy Minstrels and he appears on their 1967 album of pop hits, *New Kicks!*, while forming a splinter group with other Minstrels - Mike Settle, Thelma Camacho and Terry Williams. They took their name, the First Edition, from the flyleaf of a book and developed a newsprint motif, dressing in black and white and appearing on black and white sets. They signed with

Reprise and Rogers sang lead on their first major hit, Mickey Newbury's song about the alleged pleasures of LSD, 'Just Dropped In (To See What Condition My Condition Was In)'. *The First Edition* was in the mould of the Association and Fifth Dimension, but they had developed their own style by *The First Edition's 2nd*. The album did not produce a hit single and was not released in the UK, but the First Edition returned to the US charts with Mike Settle's ballad, 'But You Know I Love You', which was also recorded by Buddy Knox and Nancy Sinatra.

The First Edition had heard Roger Miller's low-key arrangement of 'Ruby, Don't Take Your Love To Town' and they enhanced it with an urgent drumbeat. Mel Tillis' song was based on an incident following the Korean war but it had implications for Vietnam. The record, credited to Kenny Rogers And The First Edition, reached number 6 in the US charts and number 2 in the UK. Its follow-up, 'Reuben James', about a coloured man who was blamed for everything, was only moderately successful, but they bounced back with Mac Davis's sexually explicit 'Something's Burning' (US number 11, UK number 8). The b-side, Rogers' own 'Momma's Waitin'', incorporates the major themes of country music - mother, prison, death, God and coming home - in a single song. The group had further US success with 'Tell It All Brother' and 'Heed The Call', performed the music for the Jason Robards film, *Fools*, and hosted a popular television series. In 1972 all stops were pulled out for the beautifully packaged double album, *The Ballad Of Calico*, written by Michael Murphey and dealing with life in a silver mining town. After leaving Reprise, Rogers formed his own Jolly Rogers label which he has since described as 'a lesson in futility', and, when the group broke up in 1974, he owed $65,000. In 1975 Rogers signed with United Artists and his producer, Larry Butler, envisaged how he could satisfy both pop and country markets. Impotence was an extraordinary subject for a hit record, but 'Lucille' (US number 5, UK number 1) established Rogers as a country star. He wrote and recorded 'Sweet Music Man' but the song is more appropriate for female singers and has been recorded by Billie Jo Spears, Anne Murray, Tammy Wynette, Dolly Parton and Millie Jackson. Rogers, who had a second solo hit with 'Daytime Friends', toured the UK with Crystal Gayle, and, although plans to record with her did not materialize, he formed a successful partnership with Dottie West. Don Schlitz's story-song, 'The Gambler', was ideal for Rogers and inspired the television movies, *The Gambler*, *The Gambler II* and *The Gambler Returns* which featured Rogers. His love for poignant ballads about life on the road, such as 'She Believes In Me' (US number 5), is explained by his own life.

Rogers had the first of four marriages in 1958 and blames constant touring for the failure of his relationships. His fourth marriage was to Marianne Gorden, a presenter of the USA television series *Hee-Haw* and an actress who appeared in *Rosemary's Baby*. His stage show then promoted his happy family life and included home movies of their child, Christopher Cody. (Rogers says the worst aspect of touring is being bombarded with grey-bearded lookalikes!) 'You Decorated My Life' was another US hit and then came 'Coward Of The County' (US number 3, UK number 1). This song too became a successful television movie and the album *Kenny* sold five million copies. Rogers also made the documentary *Kenny Rogers And The American Cowboy*, and a concept album about a modern-day Texas cowboy, *Gideon*, led to a successful duet with one of its writers Kim Carnes, 'Don't Fall In Love With A Dreamer' (US number 4). Rogers' also had success with 'Love The World Away' from the soundtrack of the film, *Urban Cowboy*, and 'Love Will Turn You Around' from · *Six Pack*, a lighthearted television movie in which he starred. Rogers' voice was ideal for Lionel Richie's slow-paced love songs and 'Lady' topped the US charts for six weeks. This was followed by 'I Don't Need You' (US number 3) from the album Richie produced for Rogers, *Share Your Love*. Rogers and Sheena Easton revived the Bob Seger song, 'We've Got Tonight' (US number 6). Having sold 35 million albums for United Artists, Rogers moved to RCA and *Eyes That See In The Dark,* was produced by Barry Gibb and featured the Bee Gees. It included 'Islands In The Stream' (US number 1, UK number 7) with Dolly Parton, which was helped by her playful approach on the video. Further US hits include 'What About Me?' with James Ingram and Kim Carnes and 'Make No Mistake, She's Mine' with Ronnie Milsap. Surprisingly, Rogers has not recorded with his close friend Glen Campbell, although he took the cover photograph for his album, *Southern Nights*. Rogers was also featured on the most successful single ever made, USA For Africa's 'We Are The World'. George Martin was an inspired choice of producer for *The Heart Of The Matter* album, which led to two singles which topped the US country charts, 'Morning Desire' and 'Tomb Of The Unknown Love'. The title track from *They Don't Make Them Like They Used To* was the theme song for the Kirk Douglas and Burt Lancaster film, *Tough Guys*, but overall, Rogers' services on RCA may have disappointed its management who had spent $20 million to secure his success. Rogers returned to Reprise but the opening track of his first album, 'Planet Texas', sounded like a joke. His son, Kenny Rogers Jnr, sang background vocals on his father's records and launched his own career in 1989 with the single, 'Take Another Step Closer'. Now, Rogers breeds Arabian horses and cattle on his 1200-acre farm in Georgia and has homes in Malibu, Bel Air and Beverly Hills. He owns entertainment centres and recording studios and has 200 employees. This is impressive for someone who was described by *Rolling Stone* as an 'overweight lightweight'. He says, 'I've never taken my talent that seriously. At one time I had a three-and-a-half octave range and sang the high parts in a jazz group. Now I don't use it

because I don't have to. If Muhammad Ali can beat anyone without training, why train?'

●ALBUMS: by the First Edition *The First Edition* (Reprise 1967)★★, *The First Edition's 2nd* (Reprise 1968)★★, *The First Edition '69* (Reprise 1969). By Kenny Rogers And The First Edition *Ruby, Don't Take Your Love To Town* (Reprise 1969)★★★, *Something's Burning* (Reprise 1970)★★★★, *Fools* soundtrack (1970)★★★, *Tell It All Brother* (Reprise 1971)★★★, *Transition* (Reprise 1971)★★★, *The Ballad Of Calico* (Reprise 1972)★★★, *Backroads* (1972)★★★, *Monumental* (1973)★★★, *Rollin'* (1974)★★. By Kenny Rogers *Love Lifted Me* (United Artists 1976)★★★, *Kenny Rogers* (United Artists 1977)★★, *Daytime Friends* (United Artists 1977)★★★, *Love Or Something Like It* (United Artists 1978)★★★, *The Gambler* (United Artists 1978)★★★★, with Dottie West *Classics* (United Artists 1979)★★, *Kenny* (United Artists 1979)★★★★, with West *Every Time Two Fools Collide* (United Artists 1980)★★★, *Gideon* (United Artists 1980)★★★, *Share Your Love* (Liberty 1981)★★★, *Christmas* (Liberty 1981)★★, *Love Will Turn You Around* (Liberty 1982)★★★, *We've Got Tonight* (Liberty 1983)★★★★, *Eyes That See In The Dark* (RCA 1983)★★★★, *Duets* (Liberty 1984)★★★, *What About Me?* (RCA 1984)★★★, with Dolly Parton *Once Upon A Christmas* (RCA 1984)★★★, *Love Is What We Make It* (Liberty 1985)★★, *The Heart Of The Matter* (RCA 1985)★★, *Short Stories* (1986)★★, *They Don't Make Them Like They Used To* (RCA 1986)★★, *I Prefer The Moonlight* (RCA 1987)★★, *Something Inside So Strong* (Reprise 1989)★★, *Christmas In America* (Reprise 1989)★★, *You're My Kind Of People* (1991)★★★, *Some Prisons Don't Have Walls* (1991)★★, *Back Home Again* (1992)★★★, *If Only My Heart Had A Voice* (1993)★★★, *The Gift* (Magnatone 1996)★★★.

●COMPILATIONS: Kenny Rogers And The First Edition *Greatest Hits* (Reprise 1971)★★★. Kenny Rogers *Ten Years Of Gold* (United Artists 1978)★★★, *Kenny Rogers' Greatest Hits* (Liberty 1980)★★★★, *Twenty Greatest Hits* (Liberty 1983)★★★, *The Very Best Of Kenny Rogers* (Warners 1990)★★★,

●VIDEOS: with Dolly Parton *Real Love* (RCA/Columbia 1988).

●FURTHER READING: *Making It In Music*, Kenny Rogers and Len Epand. *Kenny Rogers - Gambler, Dreamer, Lover*, Martha Hume.

ROLLING STONES

Originally billed as the Rollin' Stones, the first line-up of this immemorial English 60s group was a nucleus of Mick Jagger (b. Michael Philip Jagger, 26 July 1943, Dartford, Kent, England; vocals), Keith Richard (b. Keith Richards, 18 December 1943, Dartford, Kent, England; guitar), Brian Jones (b. Lewis Brian Hopkin-Jones, 28 February 1942, Cheltenham, Gloucestershire, England, d. 3 July 1969; rhythm guitar) and Ian Stewart (b. 1938, d. 12 December 1985; piano). Jagger and Richard were primary school friends who resumed their camaraderie in their closing teenage years after finding they had a mutual love for R&B and particularly the music of Chuck Berry, Muddy Waters and Bo Diddley. Initially, they were teamed with bassist Dick Taylor (later of the Pretty Things) and before long their ranks extended to include Jones, Stewart and occasional drummer Tony Chapman. Their patron at this point was the renowned musician Alexis Korner, who had arranged their debut gig at London's Marquee club on 21 July 1962. In their first few months the group met some opposition from jazz and blues aficionados for their alleged lack of musical 'purity' and the line-up remained unsettled for several months.

In late 1962 bassist Bill Wyman (b. William Perks, 24 October 1936, Plumstead, London, England) replaced Dick Taylor while drummers came and went, including Carlo Little (from Screaming Lord Sutch's Savages) and Mick Avory (later of the Kinks, who was billed as appearing at their debut gig, but didn't play). It was not until as late as January 1963 that drummer Charlie Watts (b. 2 June 1941, London, England) reluctantly surrendered his day job and committed himself to the group. After securing a residency at Giorgio Gomelsky's Crawdaddy Club in Richmond, the Stones' live reputation spread rapidly through London's hip cognoscenti. One evening, the flamboyant Andrew Loog Oldham appeared at the club and was so entranced by the commercial prospects of Jagger's sexuality that he wrested them away from Gomelsky and, backed by the financial and business clout of agent Eric Easton, became their manager. Within weeks, Oldham had produced their first couple of official recordings at IBC Studios. By this time, record company scouts were on the prowl with Decca's Dick Rowe leading the march and successfully signing the group. After re-purchasing the IBC demos, Oldham selected Chuck Berry's 'Come On' as their debut. The record was promoted on the prestigious UK television pop programme *Thank Your Lucky Stars* and the Stones were featured sporting matching houndstooth jackets with velvet collars. This was one of Oldham's few concessions to propriety for he soon pushed the boys as unregenerate rebels. Unfortunately, pianist Ian Stewart was not deemed sufficiently pop star-like for Oldham's purpose and was unceremoniously removed from the line-up, although he remained road manager and occasional pianist. After supporting the Everly Brothers, Little Richard, Gene Vincent and Bo Diddley on a Don Arden UK package tour, the Stones released their second single, a gift from John Lennon and Paul McCartney entitled 'I Wanna Be Your Man'. The disc fared better than its predecessor climbing into the Top 10 in January 1964. That same month the group enjoyed their first bill-topping tour supported by the Ronettes.

The early months of 1964 saw the Stones catapulted to fame amid outrage and controversy about the surliness of their demeanour and the length of their hair. This was still a world in which the older members of the community were barely coming to terms with the Beatles' neatly groomed mop-tops. While newspapers asked 'Would you let your daughter marry a Rolling Stone?', the quintet engaged in a flurry of recording activity which saw the release of an EP and an album both titled *The Rolling Stones*. The discs consisted almost exclusively of extraneous material and captured the group at their most derivative stage. Already, however, there were strong signs of an ability to combine different styles. The third single, 'Not Fade Away', saw them fuse Buddy Holly's quaint original with a chunky Bo Diddley beat that highlighted Jagger's vocal to considerable effect. The presence of Phil Spector and Gene Pitney at these sessions underlined how hip the Stones had already become in the music business after such a short time. With the momentum increasing by the month, Oldham characteristically overreached himself by organizing a US tour which proved premature and disappointing. After returning to the UK, the Stones released a decisive cover of the Valentinos' 'It's All Over Now', which gave them their first number 1. A bestselling EP, *Five By Five*, cemented their growing reputation, while a national tour escalated into a series of near riots with scenes of hysteria wherever they played. There was an ugly strain to the Stones' appeal which easily translated into violence. At the Winter Gardens Blackpool the group hosted the most astonishing rock riot yet witnessed on British soil. Frenzied fans displayed their feelings for the group by smashing chandeliers and demolishing a Steinway grand piano. By the end of the evening over 50 people were escorted to hospital for treatment. Other concerts were terminated within minutes of the group appearing on stage and the hysteria continued throughout Europe. A return to the USA saw them disrupt the stagey *Ed Sullivan Show*, prompting the presenter to ban rock 'n' roll groups in temporary retaliation. In spite of all the chaos at home and abroad, America remained resistant to their appeal, although that situation changed dramatically in the New Year.

In November 1964, 'Little Red Rooster' was released and entered the *New Musical Express* chart at number 1, a feat more usually associated with the Beatles and, previously, Elvis Presley. The Stones now had a formidable fan base and their records were becoming more accomplished and ambitious with each successive release. Jagger's accentuated phrasing and posturing stage persona made 'Little Red Rooster' sound surprisingly fresh while Brian Jones' use of slide guitar was imperative to the single's success. Up until this point, the group had recorded cover versions as a-sides, but manager Andrew Oldham was determined that they should emulate the example of Lennon/McCartney and locked them in a room until they emerged with satisfactory material. Their early efforts, 'It Should Have Been You' and 'Will You Be My Lover Tonight?' (both recorded by the late George Bean) were bland, but Gene Pitney scored a hit with the emphatic 'That Girl Belongs To

Yesterday' and Jagger's girlfriend Marianne Faithfull became a teenage recording star with the moving 'As Tears Go By'. In 1965 the group achieved their international breakthrough and released three extraordinary self-penned number 1 singles. 'The Last Time' saw them emerge with their own distinctive rhythmic style and underlined an ability to fuse R&B and pop in an enticing fashion. America finally succumbed to their spell with '(I Can't Get No) Satisfaction', a quintessential pop lyric with the still youthful Jagger sounding like a jaundiced roué. Released in the UK during the 'summer of protest songs', the single encapsulated the restless weariness of a group already old before its time. The distinctive riff, which Keith Richard invented with almost casual dismissal, became one of the most famous hook lines in the entire glossary of pop and was picked up and imitated by a generation of garage groups thereafter. The 1965 trilogy of hits was completed with the engagingly surreal 'Get Off Of My Cloud' in which Jagger's surly persona seemed at its most pronounced to date. As well as the number 1 hits of 1965, there was also a celebrated live EP, *Got Live If You Want It* which reached the Top 10, and *The Rolling Stones No. 2*, which continued the innovative idea of not including the group's name on the front of the sleeve. There was also some well-documented bad boy controversy when Jagger, Jones and Wyman were arrested and charged with urinating on the wall of an East London petrol station. Such scandalous behaviour merely reinforced the public's already ingrained view of the Stones as juvenile degenerates.

With the notorious Allen Klein replacing Eric Easton as Oldham's co-manager, the Stones consolidated their success by renegotiating their Decca contract. Their single output in the USA simultaneously increased with the release of a couple of tracks unavailable in single form in the UK. The sardonic put-down of suburban valium abuse, 'Mother's Little Helper' and the Elizabethan-styled 'Lady Jane', complete with atmospheric dulcimer, displayed their contrasting styles to considerable effect. Both these songs were included on their fourth album, *Aftermath*. A breakthrough work in a crucial year, the recording revealed the Stones as accomplished rockers and balladeers, while their writing potential was emphasized by Chris Farlowe's chart-topping cover of 'Out Of Time'. There were also signs of the Stones' inveterate misogyny, particularly on the cocky 'Under My Thumb' and an acerbic 'Stupid Girl'. Back in the singles chart, the group's triumphant run continued with the startlingly chaotic '19th Nervous Breakdown' in which frustration, impatience and chauvinism were brilliantly mixed with scale-sliding descending guitar lines. 'Paint It Black' was even stronger, a raga-influenced piece with a lyric so doom-laden and defeatist in its imagery that it is a wonder that the angry performance sounded so passionate and urgent. The Stones' nihilism reached its peak on the extraordinary 'Have You Seen Your Mother Baby,

Standing In The Shadow?', a scabrous-sounding solicitation taken at breathtaking pace with Jagger spitting out a diatribe of barely coherent abuse. It was probably the group's most adventurous production to date, but its acerbic sound, lengthy title and obscure theme contributed to rob the song of sufficient commercial potential to continue the chart-topping run. Ever outrageous, the group promoted the record with a photo session in which they appeared in drag, thereby adding a clever, sexual ambivalence to their already iconoclastic public image.

In 1967 the Stones' anti-climactic escapades confronted an establishment crackdown. The year began with an accomplished double a-sided single, 'Let's Spend The Night Together'/'Ruby Tuesday' which, like the Beatles' 'Penny Lane'/'Strawberry Fields Forever', narrowly failed to reach number 1 in their home country. The accompanying album, *Between The Buttons*, trod water and also represented Oldham's final production. Increasingly alienated by the Stones' bohemianism, he moved further away from them in the ensuing months and surrendered the management reins to his partner Klein later in the year. On 12 February, Jagger and Richard were arrested at the latter's West Wittering home 'Redlands' and charged with drugs offences. Three months later, increasingly unstable Brian Jones was raided and charged with similar offences. The Jagger/Richard trial in June was a cause célèbre which culminated in the notorious duo receiving heavy fines and a salutary prison sentence. Judicial outrage was tempered by public clemency, most effectively voiced by *The Times*' editor William Rees-Mogg who, borrowing a phrase from Pope, offered an eloquent plea in their defence under the leader title, 'Who Breaks A Butterfly On A Wheel?' Another unexpected ally was rival group the Who, who rallied to the Stones' cause by releasing a single coupling 'Under My Thumb' and 'The Last Time'. The sentences were duly quashed on appeal in July, with Jagger receiving a conditional discharge for possession of amphetamines. Three months later, Brian Jones tasted judicial wrath with a nine-month sentence and suffered a nervous breakdown before seeing his imprisonment rescinded at the end of the year.

The flurry of drug busts, court cases, appeals and constant media attention had a marked effect on the Stones' recording career which was severely curtailed. During their summer of impending imprisonment, they released the fey 'We Love You', complete with slamming prison cell doors in the background. It was a weak, flaccid statement rather than a rebellious rallying cry. The image of the cultural anarchists cowering in defeat was not particularly palatable to their fans and even with all the publicity, the single barely scraped into the Top 10. The eventful year ended with the Stones' apparent answer to *Sgt Pepper's Lonely Hearts Club Band* - the extravagantly titled *Their Satanic Majesties Request*. Beneath the exotic 3-D cover was an album of psychedelic/cosmic experimentation bereft of the R&B grit that had previously been synonymous with the Stones' sound. Although the album had some strong moments, it had the same inexplicably placid inertia of 'We Love You', minus notable melodies or a convincing direction. The overall impression conveyed was that in trying to compete with the Beatles' experimentation, the Stones had somehow lost the plot. Their drug use had channelled them into laudable experimentation but simultaneously left them open to accusations of having 'gone soft'. The revitalization of the Stones was demonstrated in the early summer of 1968 with 'Jumpin' Jack Flash', a single that rivalled the best of their previous output. The succeeding album, *Beggars Banquet*, produced by Jimmy Miller, was also a return to strength and included the socio-political 'Street Fighting Man' and the brilliantly macabre 'Sympathy For The Devil', in which Jagger's seductive vocal was backed by hypnotic Afro-rhythms and dervish yelps.

While the Stones were re-establishing themselves, Brian Jones was falling deeper into drug abuse. A conviction in late 1968 prompted doubts about his availability for US tours and in the succeeding months he contributed less and less to recordings and became increasingly jealous of Jagger's leading role in the group. Richard's wooing and impregnation of Jones' girlfriend Anita Pallenberg merely increased the tension. Matters reached a crisis point in June 1969 when Jones officially left the group. The following month he was found dead in the swimming pool of the Sussex house that had once belonged to writer A.A. Milne. The official verdict was 'death by misadventure'. A free concert at London's Hyde Park two days after his death was attended by a crowd of 250,000 and became a symbolic wake for the tragic youth. Jagger released thousands of butterfly's and narrated a poem by Shelley for Brian. Three days later, Jagger's former love Marianne Faithfull attempted suicide. This was truly the end of the first era of the Rolling Stones.

The group played out the last months of the 60s with a mixture of vinyl triumph and further tragedy. The sublime 'Honky Tonk Women' kept them at number 1 for most of the summer and few would have guessed that this was to be their last UK chart topper. The new album, *Let It Bleed* (a parody of the Beatles' *Let It Be*) was an exceptional work spearheaded by the anthemic 'Gimme Shelter' and revealing strong country influences ('Country Honk'), startling orchestration ('You Can't Always Get What You Want') and menacing blues ('Midnight Rambler'). It was a promising debut from John Mayall's former guitarist Mick Taylor (b. 17 January 1948, Hertfordshire, England) who had replaced Jones only a matter of weeks before his death. Even while *Let It Bleed* was heading for the top of the album charts, however, the Stones were singing out the 60s to the backdrop of a Hells Angels killing of a black man at the Altamont Festival in California. The tragedy was captured on film in the grisly *Gimme Shelter* movie released the following year. After the events of 1969, it

was not surprising that the group had a relatively quiet 1970. Jagger's contrasting thespian outings reached the screen in the form of *Performance* and *Ned Kelly* while Jean-Luc Goddard's tedious portrait of the group in the studio was delivered on *One Plus One*. For a group who had once claimed to make more challenging and gripping films than the Beatles and yet combine artistic credibility with mass appeal, it all seemed a long time coming.

After concluding their Decca contract with a bootleg-deterring live album, *Get Yer Ya-Ya's Out*, the Stones established their own self-titled label. The first release was a three track single, 'Brown Sugar'/'Bitch'/'Let It Rock', which contained some of their best work, but narrowly failed to reach number 1 in the UK. The lead track contained a quintessential Stones riff: insistent, undemonstrative and stunning, with the emphatic brass work of Bobby Keyes embellishing Jagger's vocal power. The new album, *Sticky Fingers*, was as consistent as it was accomplished, encompassing the bluesy 'You Gotta Move', the thrilling 'Moonlight Mile', the wistful 'Wild Horses' and the chilling 'Sister Morphine', one the most despairing drug songs ever written. The entire album was permeated by images of sex and death, yet the tone of the work was neither self-indulgent nor maudlin. The group's playful fascination with sex was further demonstrated on the elaborately designed Andy Warhol sleeve which featured a waist-view shot of a figure clad in denim, with a real zip fastener which opened to display the lips and tongue motif that was shortly to become their corporate image. Within a year of *Sticky Fingers*, the group returned with a double album, *Exile On Main Street*. With Keith Richard firmly in control, the group were rocking out on a series of quick-fire songs. The album was severely criticized at the time of its release for its uneven quality but was subsequently re-evaluated favourably, particularly in contrast to their later work.

The Stones' soporific slide into the 70s mainstream probably began during 1973 when their jet-setting was threatening to upstage their musical endeavours. Jagger's marriage and Richard's confrontations with the law took centre stage while increasingly average albums came and went. *Goat's Head Soup* was decidedly patchy but offered some strong moments and brought a deserved US number 1 with the imploring 'Angie'. 1974's 'It's Only Rock 'n' Roll' proved a better song title than a single, while the undistinguished album of the same name saw the group reverting to Tamla/Motown for the Temptations' 'Ain't Too Proud To Beg'.

The departure of Mick Taylor at the end of 1974 was followed by a protracted period in which the group sought a suitable replacement. By the time of their next release, *Black And Blue*, former *Faces* guitarist Ron Wood (b. 1 June 1947, London, England) was confirmed as Taylor's successor. The album showed the group seeking a possible new direction playing variants on white reggae, but the results were less than impressive.

By the second half of the 70s the gaps in the Stones' recording and touring schedules were becoming wider. The days when they specially recorded for the singles market were long past and considerable impetus had been lost. Even big rallying points, such as the celebrated concert at Knebworth in 1976, lacked a major album to promote the show and served mainly as a greatest hits package.

By 1977, the British music press had taken punk to its heart and the Stones were dismissed as champagne-swilling old men, who had completely lost touch with their audience. The Clash effectively summed up the mood of the time with their slogan 'No Elvis, Beatles, Stones' in '1977'.

Against the odds, the Stones responded to the challenge of their younger critics with a comeback album of remarkable power. *Some Girls* was their most consistent work in years, with some exceptional high-energy workouts, not least the breathtaking 'Shattered'. The disco groove of 'Miss You' brought them another US number 1 and showed that they could invigorate their repertoire with new ideas that worked. Jagger's wonderful pastiche of an American preacher on the mock country 'Far Away Eyes' was another unexpected highlight. There was even an attendant controversy thanks to some multi-racist chauvinism on the title track, not to mention 'When The Whip Comes Down' and 'Beast Of Burden'. Even the cover jacket had to be re-shot because it featured unauthorized photos of the famous, most notably actresses Lucille Ball, Farrah Fawcett and Raquel Welch. To conclude a remarkable year, Keith Richard escaped what seemed an almost certain jail sentence in Toronto for drugs offences and was merely fined and ordered to play a couple of charity concerts. As if in celebration of his release and reconciliation with his father, he reverted to his original family name Richards. In the wake of Richards' reformation and Jagger's much-publicized and extremely expensive divorce from his model wife Bianca, the Stones reconvened in 1980 for *Emotional Rescue*, a rather lightweight album dominated by Jagger's falsetto and overuse of disco rhythms. Nevertheless, the album gave the Stones their first UK number 1 since 1973 and the title track was a Top 10 hit on both sides of the Atlantic. Early the following year a major US tour (highlights of which were included on *Still Life*) garnered enthusiastic reviews, while a host of repackaged albums reinforced the group's legacy. 1981's *Tattoo You* was essentially a crop of old out-takes but the material was anything but stale. On the contrary, the album was surprisingly strong and the concomitant single, 'Start Me Up', was a reminder of the Stones at their 60s best, a time when they were capable of producing classic singles at will. One of the Stones' cleverest devices throughout the 80s was their ability to compensate for average work by occasional flashes of excellence. The workmanlike *Undercover*, for example, not only boasted a brilliantly menacing title track ('Undercover Of The Night') but

one of the best promotional videos of the period. While critics continually questioned the group's relevance, the Stones were still releasing worthwhile work, albeit in smaller doses.

A three-year silence on record was broken by *Dirty Work* in 1986, which saw the Stones sign to CBS Records and team up with producer Steve Lillywhite. Surprisingly, it was not a Stones original that produced the expected offshoot single hit, but a cover of Bob And Earl's 'Harlem Shuffle'. A major record label signing often coincides with a flurry of new work, but the Stones were clearly moving away from each other creatively and concentrating more and more on individual projects. Wyman had already tasted some chart success in 1983 with the biggest solo success from a Stones' number, 'Je Suis Un Rock Star' and it came as little surprise when Jagger issued his own solo album, *She's The Boss*, in 1985. A much-publicized feud with Keith Richards led to speculation that the Rolling Stones story had come to an anti-climactic end, a view reinforced by the appearance of a second Jagger album, *Primitive Cool*, in 1987. When Richards himself released the first solo work of his career in 1988, the Stones' obituary had virtually been written. As if to confound the obituarists, however, the Stones reconvened in 1989 and announced that they would be working on a new album and commencing a world tour. Later that year the hastily recorded *Steel Wheels* appeared and the critical reception was generally good. 'Mixed Emotions' and 'Rock And A Hard Place' were radio hits while 'Continental Drift' included contributions from the master musicians of Joujouka, previously immortalized on vinyl by the late Brian Jones. After nearly 30 years in existence, the Rolling Stones began the 90s with the biggest grossing international tour of all time, and ended speculation about their future by reiterating their intention of playing on indefinitely. *Voodoo Lounge* in 1994 was one of their finest recordings: it was both lyrically daring and musically fresh. They sounded charged up and raring to go for the 1995 US tour. Monies taken at each gig could almost finance the national debt and provided confirmation (as if it were needed) that they are still the world's greatest rock band, a title that is likely to stick, even though Bill Wyman officially resigned in 1993. Riding a crest after an extraordinarily active 1995 *Stripped* was a dynamic semi-plugged album. Fresh-sounding and energetic acoustic versions of 'Street Fighting Man', 'Wild Horses' and 'Let It Bleed' among others, emphasized just how great the Jagger/Richards songwriting team is. The year was marred however by some outspoken comments by Keith Richards on R.E.M. and Nirvana. These clumsy comments are unlikely to endear the grand old man of rock to a younger audience. This was all the more surprising as the Stones had so far appeared in touch with today's rock music. Citing R.E.M. as 'wimpy cult stuff' and Kurt Cobain as 'some prissy little spoiled kid' were, at best, ill-chosen comments.

●ALBUMS: *The Rolling Stones* (London/Decca 1964)★★★★, *12X5* (London 1964)★★★★, *The Rolling Stones* (London/Decca 1965)★★★★, *The Rolling Stones Now!* (London 1965)★★★★, *December's Children (And Everybody's* (London 1965)★★★★, *Out Of Our Heads* (Decca/London 1965)★★★★, *Aftermath* (Decca/London 1966)★★★★, *Got Live If You Want It* (London 1966)★★★, *Between The Buttons* (London/Decca 1967)★★★, *Their Satanic Majesties Request* (Decca/London 1967)★★★, *Flowers* (London 1967)★★★, *Beggars Banquet* (London 1968)★★★★★, *Let It Bleed* (London/Decca 1969)★★★★★, *Get Yer Ya-Ya's Out!* (Decca/London1970)★★★★, *Sticky Fingers* (Rolling Stones 1971)★★★★, *Exile On Main Street* (Rolling Stones 1972)★★★★★, *Goat's Head Soup* (Rolling Stones 1973)★★★, *It's Only Rock 'N' Roll* (Rolling Stones 1974)★★★, *Black And Blue* (Rolling Stones 1976)★★★, *Love You Live* (Rolling Stones 1977)★★★, *Some Girls* (Rolling Stones 1978)★★★, *Emotional Rescue* (Rolling Stones 1980)★★, *Tattoo You* (Rolling Stones 1981)★★★, *Still Life (American Concerts 1981)* (Rolling Stones 1982)★★, *Undercover* (Rolling Stones 1983)★★, *Dirty Work* (Rolling Stones 1986)★★★, *Steel Wheels* (Rolling Stones 1989)★★★, *Flashpoint* (Rolling Stones 1991)★★★, *Voodoo Lounge* (Virgin 1994)★★★★, *Stripped* (Virgin 1995)★★★.
●COMPILATIONS: *Big Hits (High Tide And Green Grass* (London 1966)★★★★, *Through The Past, Darkly* (London 1969)★★★★, *Hot Rocks 1964-1971* (London 1972)★★★★, *More Hot Rocks (Big Hits And Fazed Cookies)* (London 1972)★★★★, *The Rolling Stones Singles Collection: The London Years* 3-CD box set (Abko/London 1989)★★★★★. Many other compilation and archive albums have also been issued.
CD Rom: *Voodoo Lounge* (Virgin 1995).
●VIDEOS: *The Stones In The Park* (BMG 1993), *Gimme Shelter* (1993), *Live At The Max* (Polygram 1994), *25 x 5 The Continuing Adventures Of The Rolling Stones* (1994), *Sympathy For The Devil* (BMG 1995), *Voodoo Lounge* (Game Entertainment 1995).
●FURTHER READING: *The Rolling Stones File*, Tim Hewat. *The Stones*, Philip Carmelo Luce. *Uptight With The Rolling Stones*, Richard Elman. *Rolling Stones: An Unauthorized Biography In Words, Photographs And Music*, David Dalton. *Mick Jagger: The Singer Not The Song*, J. Marks. *Mick Jagger: Everybody's Lucifer*, Anthony Scaduto. *STP: A Journey Through America With The Rolling Stones*, Robert Greenfield. *Les Rolling Stones*, Philippe Contantin. *The Rolling Stones Story*, George Tremlett. *The Rolling Stones*, Cindy Ehrlich. *The Rolling Stones: A Celebration*, Nik Cohn. *The Rolling Stones*, Tony Jasper. *The Rolling Stones: An Illustrated Record*, Roy Carr. *The Rolling Stones*, Jeremy Pascall. *The Rolling Stones On Tour*, Annie Leibowitz. *Up And Down With The Rolling Stones*, Tony Sanchez with John Blake. *The Rolling Stones: An Annotated Bibliography*, Mary Laverne Dimmick. *Keith Richards*, Barbara Charone. *Rolling Stones In Their Own Words*, Rolling Stones. *The Rolling Stones: An Illustrated Discography*, Miles. *The Rolling Stones In Their Own Words*, David Dalton and Mick Farren. *The Rolling Stones: The First Twenty Years*, David Dalton. *Mick Jagger In His Own Words*, Miles. *The Rolling Stones In Concert*, Linda Martin. *The Rolling Stones: Live In America*, Philip Kamin and Peter Goddard. *Death Of A Rolling Stone: The Brian Jones Story*, Mandy Aftel. *Jagger*, Carey Schofield. *The Rolling Stones A To Z*, Sue Weiner and Lisa Howard. *The Rolling Stones*, Robert Palmer. *The Stones*, Philip Norman. *Satisfaction: The Rolling Stones*, Gered Mankowitz. *The Rolling Stones*, Dezo Hoffman. *On The Road With The Rolling Stones*, Chet Flippo. *The True Adventures Of The Rolling Stones*, Stanley Booth. *Heart Of Stone: The Definitive Rolling Stones Discography*, Felix Aeppli. *Yesterday's Papers: The Rolling Stones In Print*, Jessica MacPhail. *The Life And Good Times Of The Rolling Stones*, Philip Norman. *Stone Alone*, Bill Wyman and Ray Coleman. *The Rolling Stones 25th Anniversary Tour*, Greg Quill. *Blown Away: The Rolling Stones And The Death Of The Sixties*, A.E. Hotchner. *The Rolling Stones: Complete Recording Sessions 1963-1989*, Martin Elliott. *The Rolling Stones Story*, Robert Draper. *The Rolling Stones Chronicle: The First Thirty Years*, Massimo Bonanno. *Rolling Stones: Images Of The World Tour 1989-1990*, David Fricke and Robert Sandall. *The Rolling Stones' Rock 'N' Roll Circus*, no author listed. *The Rolling Stones: Behind The Buttons (Limited Edition)*, Gered Mankowitz and Robert Whitaker (Photographers). *Golden Stone: The Untold Life And Mysterious Death Of Brian Jones*, Laura Jackson. *Rolling Stones: Das Weissbuch*, Dieter Hoffmann. *Not Fade Away: Rolling Stones Collection*, Geoffrey Giuliano. *Keith Richards: The Unauthorised Biography*, Victor Bockris. *The Rolling Stones: The Complete Works Vol.1 1962-75*, Nico Zentgraf. *Street Fighting Years*, Stephen Barnard. *Paint It Black: The Murder Of Brian Jones*, Geoffrey Giuliano. *Brian Jones: The Inside Story Of The Original Rolling Stone*, Nicholas Fitzgerald. *Who Killed Christopher Robin*, Terry Rawlings. *A Visual Documentary*, Miles. *Not Fade Away*, Chris Eborn. *Complete Guide To The Music Of*, James Hector. *The Rolling Stones Chronicle*, Massimo Bonanno.

ROMEO, MAX

b. Max Smith, c.1947, Jamaica, West Indies. It was Romeo who first introduced Britain to the concept of rude reggae with 'Wet Dream', which, despite a total radio ban, reached number 10 in the UK charts. He toured the UK several times in the space of a year and issued two albums: *A Dream* being the best selling. However, despite other similarly styled singles like 'Mini Skirt Vision', he did not enjoy chart success again. Romeo was, essentially, something of a gospel singer with the ability to convey a revivalist fervour on his records such as 'Let The Power Fall' (a Jamaican political anthem in 1972) and 'Pray For Me'. Furthermore, he had an ability to get the trials, tribulations and amusements of Jamaican life into a song, as evinced by 'Eating Competition', 'Sixpence' and 'Aily And Ailaloo'. In 1972 Romeo began a liaison with producers Lee

Perry and Winston 'Niney' Holness, and from this point on his records had a musical fire to match his apocalyptical vision and contrasting humour: 'Babylose Burning', 'Three Blind Mice', 'The Coming Of Jah' all maintained his star status in Jamaica between 1972 and 1975. *Revelation Time* was one of the best albums of 1975, and 1976's *War Ina Babylon* was hailed by the rock press as one of the all-time classic reggae albums. However, Perry had much to do with those records' artistic success, and following a much-publicized split between the pair - with Perry recording 'White Belly Rat' about Romeo, and scrawling 'Judas' over the singer's picture in Perry's studio - Romeo was cast adrift without musical roots. *I Love My Music*, recorded with the help of Keith Richards, was a flop, and the stronger *Reconstruction* fared no better. A move to New York's Wackies label in the early 80s did little to reverse his fortunes, and by the late 80s Max Romeo's name was forgotten in the mainstream reggae market. However, in the spring of 1992, London producer Jah Shaka recorded *Far I Captain Of My Ship* on Jah Shaka Records, an unabashed, Jamaican-recorded roots album generally reckoned to be Romeo's best for over 15 years.
●ALBUMS: *A Dream* (1970)★★★, *Let The Power Fall* (1972)★★★, *Revelation Time* (Tropical Sound Tracs 1975)★★★★, *War Ina Babylon* (Island 1976)★★★★, *Reconstruction* (1978)★★★, *I Love My Music* (1979)★★, *Rondos* (1980)★★, *Holding Out My Love For You* (Shanachie 1987)★★, *Far I Captain Of My Ship* (Jah Shaka 1992)★★★★, *On The Beach* (1993)★★★.

RONSTADT, LINDA

b. Linda Maria Ronstadt, 15 July 1946, Tucson, Arizona, USA. The daughter of a professional musician, Ronstadt's first singing experience was gained with her sisters in the Three Ronstadts. She met guitarist Bob Kimmel at Arizona's State University and together the two aspirants moved to Los Angeles where they were joined by songwriter Kenny Edwards. Taking the name the Stone Poneys, the trio became popular among the city's folk fraternity and had a US Top 20 hit with 'Different Drum'. Ronstadt embarked on a solo career in 1968. Her early solo albums, *Hand Sown, Home Grown* and *Silk Purse* signalled a move towards country-flavoured material, albeit of a more conservative nature. The singer's third album marked a major turning point and featured a core of excellent musicians, including Don Henley, Glen Frey, Bernie Leadon and Randy Meisner who subsequently formed the Eagles. The content emphasized a contemporary approach with songs by Neil Young, Jackson Browne and Eric Anderson, and the set established Ronstadt as a force in Californian rock. The artist's subsequent two albums showed the dichotomy prevalent in her music. *Don't Cry Now* was largely undistinguished, chiefly because the material was weaker, while *Heart Like A Wheel*, paradoxically given to Linda's former label to complete contractual obligations, was excellent.

This platinum-selling set included 'You're No Good', a US number 1 pop hit, and a dramatic version of Hank Williams' 'I Can't Help It', which won Ronstadt a Grammy award for best female country vocal. This highly successful release set the pattern for the singer's work throughout the rest of the decade. Her albums were now carefully constructed to appease both the rock and country audiences, mixing traditional material, singer-songwriter angst and a handful of rock 'n' roll/soul classics, be they from Tamla/Motown ('Heatwave'), Roy Orbison ('Blue Bayou') or Buddy Holly ('That'll Be The Day'). Despite effusive praise from the establishment media and a consistent popularity, this predictable approach resulted in lethargy, and although *Mad Love* showed a desire to break the mould, Ronstadt was increasingly trapped in an artistic cocoon.

The singer's work during the 80s has proved more divergent. Her performance in Joseph Papp's production of *Pirates Of Penzance* drew favourable reviews, although her subsequent role in the more demanding *La Boheme* was less impressive. Ronstadt also undertook a series of releases with veteran arranger/conductor Nelson Riddle, which resulted in three albums - *What's New*, *Lush Life* and *For Sentimental Reasons* - consisting of popular standards. In 1987 a duet with James Ingram produced 'Somewhere Out There', the title track to the film *An American Tail*, which gave her a number 2 US hit (UK Top 10) hit, while that same year her collaboration with Dolly Parton and Emmylou Harris, *Trio* and a selection of mariachi songs, *Canciones De Mi Padre*, showed an artist determined to challenge preconceptions. Her 1989 set, *Cry Like A Rainstorm*, revealed a crafted approach to mainstream recording and included 'Don't Know Much', a haunting duet with Aaron Neville, which gave Linda Ronstadt another number 2 hit in the USA (and the UK). The highly acclaimed *Winter Light* was produced by herself and George Massenburg, and came across as a personal and highly emotional album. Ronstadt, while hugely popular and successful, has never been truly recognized by the *cognoscenti*. Her change in styles may have been a contributing factor. She has courted (with great success), country rock, country, rock 'n' roll, Latin, standards, opera, light opera, AOR and white soul. In 1996 she was firmly in the middle-of-the-road with *Dedicated To The One I Love*, an album of lullabies and love songs 'for the baby you love ages 1 to 91'.
●ALBUMS: *Hand Sown, Home Grown* (Capitol 1969)★★, *Silk Purse* (Capitol 1970)★★, *Linda Ronstadt* (Capitol 1971)★★, *Don't Cry Now* (Asylum 1973)★★, *Heart Like A Wheel* (Capitol 1974)★★★★, *Prisoner In Disguise* (Asylum 1975)★★★, *Hasten Down The Wind* (Asylum 1976)★★★, *Simple Dreams* (Asylum 1977)★★★, *Living In The USA* (Asylum 1978)★★, *Mad Love* (Asylum 1980)★★, with Kevin Kline, Estelle Parsons, Rex Smith *Pirates Of Penzance* (1981), *Get Closer* (Asylum 1982)★★, *What's New* (Asylum 1983)★★★, *Lush Life* (Asylum

1984)★★★, *For Sentimental Reasons* (Asylum 1986)★★★, with Emmylou Harris, Dolly Parton *Trio* (Warners 1987)★★★, *Canciones De Mi Padre* (Elektra 1987)★★★, *Cry Like A Rainstorm - Howl Like The Wind* (Elektra 1989)★★★, *Mas Canciones* (Elektra 1991)★★★, *Frenesi* (Elektra 1992)★★★, *Winter Light* (Elektra 1993)★★★★, *Feels Like Home* (Warners 1995)★★★, *Dedicated To The One I Love* (Elektra 1996)★★★.

●COMPILATIONS: *Different Drum* includes five Stone Poney tracks (Capitol 1974)★★, *Greatest Hits: Linda Ronstadt* (Asylum 1976)★★★★, *A Retrospective* (Capitol 1977)★★★, *Greatest Hits: Linda Ronstadt Volume 2* (Asylum 1980)★★★.

●FURTHER READING: *Linda Ronstadt: A Portrait*, Richard Kanakaris. *The Linda Ronstadt Scrapbook*, Mary Ellen Moore. *Linda Ronstadt*, Vivian Claire. *Linda Ronstadt: An Illustrated Biography*, Connie Berman. *Linda Ronstadt: It's So Easy*, Mark Bego.

ROSS, DIANA

b. Diane Ernestine Ross, 26 March 1944, Detroit, USA. While still in high school Ross became the fourth and final member of the Primettes, who recorded for Lu-Pine in 1960, signed to Motown Records in 1961 and then changed their name to the Supremes. She was a backing vocalist on the group's early releases, until Motown supremo Berry Gordy insisted that she become their lead singer, a role she retained for the next six years. In recognition of her prominent position in the Supremes, she received individual billing on all their releases from 1967 onwards. Throughout her final years with the group, Ross was being groomed for a solo career under the close personal supervision of Gordy, with whom she was rumoured to have romantic links. In late 1969, he announced that Ross would be leaving the Supremes, and she played her final concert with the group in January 1970. Later that year Ross began a long series of successful solo releases, with the chart-topping 'Ain't No Mountain High Enough'. In April 1971, she married businessman Robert Silberstein, but they were divorced in 1976 after renewed speculation about her relationship with Gordy.

As she continued to enjoy success with lightweight love songs in the early 70s, Motown's plan to widen Ross's appeal led her to host a television special, *Diana!*, in 1971. In 1972, she starred in Motown's film biography of Billie Holiday, *Lady Sings The Blues*, winning an Oscar nomination for her stirring portrayal of the jazz singer's physical decline into drug addiction. However, subsequent starring roles in *Mahogany* (1975) and *The Wiz* (1978) drew a mixed critical response. In 1973, Ross released an album of duets with Marvin Gaye, though allegedly the pair did not meet during the recording of the project. She achieved another US number 1 with 'Touch Me In The Morning', and repeated that success with the theme song from *Mahogany* in 1975. 'Love Hangover' in 1976 saw her moving into the contemporary disco field, a shift of direction that was consoli-

dated on the 1980 album *Diana*, produced by Nile Rodgers and Bernard Edwards of Chic. Her choice of hit material continued to be inspired and the 80s started with a major hit, 'Upside Down', which rooted itself at the top of the US chart for a month; similar but lesser success followed with 'I'm Coming Out' and 'It's My Turn'. The following year a collaboration with Lionel Richie produced the title track to the film Endless Love; this tearjerker spent more than two months at the top of the US chart. By now, Ross was as much a media personality as a soul singer, winning column inches for her liaison with Gene Simmons of Kiss. There was also intense speculation about the nature of her relationship with Michael Jackson, whose career she had helped to guide since 1969.

After months of rumour about her future, Ross left Motown in 1981, and signed contracts with RCA for North America, and Capitol for the rest of the world. She formed her own production company and had further hits. A reworking of Frankie Lymon's 'Why Do Fools Fall In Love' and Michael Jackson's 'Muscles' confirmed her pre-eminence in the field of disco-pop. During the remainder of the 80s only 'Missing You', a tribute to the late Marvin Gaye, brought her the success to which she had become accustomed. In Britain, however, she achieved a number 1 hit in 1986 with 'Chain Reaction', an affectionate recreation of her days with the Supremes, written and produced by the Bee Gees. In 1986, Ross married a Norwegian shipping magnate, effectively quashing renewed rumours that she might wed Berry Gordy and return to Motown. Since then, she has won more publicity for her epic live performances, notably an open-air concert in New York's Central Park in a torrential storm, than for her sporadic releases of new material, which continue to occupy the lighter end of the black music market.

●ALBUMS: *Reach Out* (Motown 1970)★★★, *Everything Is Everything* (Motown 1970)★★★, *Diana!* (Motown 1971)★★★, *Surrender* (Motown 1971)★★★, *Lady Sings The Blues* (Motown 1972)★★★★, *Touch Me In The Morning* (Motown 1973)★★★, with Marvin Gaye *Diana And Marvin* (Motown 1973)★★★, *Live At Caesar's Palace* (Motown 1974)★★★, *Mahogany* (Motown 1975)★★, *Diana Ross* (Motown 1976)★★★, *An Evening With Diana Ross* (Motown 1977)★★★, *Baby It's Me* (Motown 1977)★★★, *Ross* (Motown 1978)★★★, *The Boss* (Motown 1979)★★★, *Diana* (Motown 1980)★★★, *To Love Again* (Motown 1981)★★★, *Why Do Fools Fall In Love* (RCA 1981)★★★, *Silk Electric* (RCA 1982)★★, *Ross* (RCA 1983)★★, *Swept Away* (RCA 1984)★★, *Eaten Alive* (RCA 1985)★★, *Red Hot Rhythm 'N' Blues* (RCA 1987)★★★, *Working Overtime* (Motown 1989)★★, *Greatest Hits Live* (Motown 1989)★★★, *Force Behind The Power* (Motown 1991)★★, *Live, Stolen Moments* (1993)★★, with Placido Domingo, José Carreras *Christmas In Vienna* (Sony 1993)★★, *Take Me Higher* (Motown 1995)★★.

●COMPILATIONS: *All The Great Hits* (Motown

1981)★★★★, *Diana Ross Anthology* (Motown 1983)★★★★, *One Woman, The Ultimate Collection* (EMI 1993)★★★★, *Voice Of Love* (EMI 1996)★★★★.
●VIDEOS: *The Visions Of Diana Ross* (PMI 1986), *One Woman - The Video Collection* (1993), *Stolen Moments* (1994).
●FURTHER READING: *Diana Ross*, Leonore K. Itzkowitz. *Diana Ross*, Patricia Mulrooney Eldred. *Diana Ross: Supreme Lady*, Connie Berman. *I'm Gonna Make You Love Me: The Story Of Diana Ross*, James Haskins. *Diana Ross: An Illustrated Biography*, Geoff Brown. *Dreamgirl: My Life As A Supreme*, Mary Wilson. *Call Her Miss Ross*, J. Randy Taraborrelli. *Supreme Faith: Someday We'll Be Together*, Mary Wilson with Patricia Romanowski. *Secrets Of The Sparrow*, Diana Ross.

ROUSSOS, DEMIS

b. 15 June 1947, Alexandria, Egypt. This multi-lingual Greek's father was a semi-professional classical guitarist, and his mother a singer. At music college in Athens, Roussos mastered trumpet, double bass, organ and bouzouki. These talents were put to commercial use with his founder membership of Aphrodite's Child in 1963. Following 1968's million-selling 'Rain And Tears', he began a career as a solo vocalist which, after a slow start, hit its stride with *Forever And Ever*, a chart success in Europe. 'Happy To Be On An Island In The Sun' climbed into the UK Top 5 but it seemed as if the new sensation had dwindled as both 'Can't Say How Much I Love You', the follow-up, and the second album struggled in their respective listings. However, Roussos was to return with a vengeance in 1976 with the self-produced *The Roussos Phenomenon*, the first EP to top the UK singles chart. That same year, 'When Forever Has Gone' peaked at number 2. Within months, he bade farewell to the Top 40 with the EP *Kyrila*. Although general consumer reaction to subsequent releases has been modest, the impact of their perpetrator on theatre box office takings has been immense. Roussos has lent a high euphonious tenor to essentially middle-of-the-road material. Style transcends content when, with dramatic *son et lumiere* effects and garbed in billowing robes, his Grand Entrance - like Zeus descending from Olympus - still leaves an indelible impression on every packed audience before he sings even a note.
●ALBUMS: *Forever And Ever* (Philips 1974)★★★, *Souvenirs* (Philips 1975)★★★, *Happy To Be* (Philips 1976)★★★, *My Only Fascination* (Philips 1976)★★, *Magic* (Philips 1977)★★, *Love And Life* (Philips 1978)★★, *Man Of The World* (Mercury 1980)★★, *Velvet Mornings* (Philips 1980)★★, *Demis* (Polydor 1982)★★, *Reflection* (Starblend 1984)★★, *Live!* (BR Music 1988)★★, *My Friend The Wind* (MFP 1989)★★, *Lost In Love* (1993)★★.
●COMPILATIONS: *25 World Hits* (Philips 1982)★★★, *Demis Roussos* (Philips 1984)★★★, *Greatest Hits* (Philips 1984)★★★, *The Golden Voice Of Demis Roussos* (Philips 1988)★★★.

ROXY MUSIC

This highly regarded and heavily influential UK group came together in January 1971 with a line-up comprising Bryan Ferry (b. 26 September 1945, Washington, Co. Durham, England; vocals, keyboards); Brian Eno (b. Brian Peter George St. Baptiste de la Salle Eno, 15 May 1948, Woodbridge, Suffolk, England; electronics, keyboards); Graham Simpson (bass) and Andy Mackay (b. 23 July 1946, England). Over the next year, several new members came and went, including drummer Dexter Lloyd, guitarist Roger Bunn and former Nice guitarist David O'List. By early 1972, a relatively settled line-up emerged with the recruitment of Paul Thompson (b. 13 May 1951, Jarrow, Northumberland, England; drums) and Phil Manzanera (b. Philip Targett Adams (b. 31 January 1951, London, England; guitar). Roxy's self-titled 1972 debut album for Island Records was a musical pot pourri, with Ferry's 50s-tinged vocals juxtaposed alongside distinctive 60s rhythms and 70s electronics. The novel sleeve concept underlined Roxy's art school background, while the group image (from 50s quiffs to futurist lurex jackets) emphasized their stylistic diversity. Reviews verged on the ecstatic, acclaiming the album as one of the finest debuts in living memory. Ferry's quirky love songs were often bleak in theme but strangely effervescent, fusing romanticism with bitter irony. On 'If There Was Something', for example, a quaint melody gradually descends into marvellous cliché ('I would do anything for you . . . I would climb the ocean blue') and bathos ('I would put roses round your door . . . growing potatoes by the score'). 'The Bob (Medley)' was another clever touch; a montage of wartime Britain presented in the form of a love song. As a follow-up to their first album, the group issued 'Virginia Plain', a classic single combining Ferry's cinematic interests and love of surrealistic art. During the same period, Simpson departed and thereafter Roxy went through a succession of bassists, including John Porter, John Gustafson, John Wetton, Rik Kenton, Sal Maida, Rick Wills and Gary Tibbs.

After failing to break into America, the group had a second UK Top 10 hit with 'Pyjamarama' and released *For Your Pleasure*, produced by Chris Thomas. Another arresting work, the album featured the stunning 'Do The Strand', arguably the group's most effective rock workout, with breathtaking saxophone work from Mackay. 'Beauty Queen' and 'Editions Of You' were contrastingly strong tracks and the album's centrepiece was 'In Every Dream Home A Heartache', Ferry's paean to an inflatable rubber doll and a chilling evocation of consumerist alienation. On 21 June 1973, Eno left, following a series of disagreements with Ferry over his role in the group. The replacement was former Curved Air violinist Eddie Jobson, who willingly accepted the role of hired musician rather than taking on full membership. After taking time off to record a solo album of cover versions, Ferry took Roxy on a nationwide tour to promote the excellent *Stranded*. 'Street Life', the first album track to be issued as a single, proved another Top 10 hit. The song neatly summed up his contradictory attitude to city life: 'You may be stranded if you stick around — and that's really something'. The epic 'A Song For Europe', with a melody borrowed from George Harrison's 'When My Guitar Gently Weeps', was another tour of alienation. The most complex and rewarding piece on the album, however, was 'Mother Of Pearl', a macrocosm of Ferry's lounge-lizard image, complete with plastic goddesses and lifeless parties. Following his second solo album, Ferry completed work on Roxy's fourth album, *Country Life*, another strong set ranging from the up-tempo single 'All I Want Is You' to the aggressive 'The Thrill Of It All' and the musically exotic 'Triptych'. In the USA, the album sleeve was withdrawn due to its risqué portrayal of two semi-naked women, and Roxy took advantage of the controversy by undertaking two consecutive US tours. Their hopes of capturing stadium-sized audiences ultimately remained unfulfilled. In spite of a challenging pilot single, 'Love Is The Drug', Roxy's next album, *Siren*, proved a major disappointment, lacking the charm and innovation of its predecessors. Only 'Both Ends Burning', which hinted at a disco direction, gave evidence of real vocal passion. The album was followed by a three-year gap during which the individual members pursued various solo projects. The 1979 comeback, *Manifesto*, received mixed reviews but included two excellent hit singles, 'Angel Eyes' and the fatalistic 'Dance Away'. The succeeding *Flesh And Blood* was a more accomplished work with some strong arrangements, including a reworking of Wilson Pickett's 'In The Midnight Hour' and an unusual interpretation of the Byrds' 'Eight Miles High'. Two UK hit singles were also in attendance: 'Over You' and 'Oh Yeah (On The Radio)'. In 1981 Roxy finally achieved their first number 1 single with 'Jealous Guy', an elegiac tribute to its recently assassinated composer John Lennon. The following year, they released their final album *Avalon*, which topped the album charts and was praised by most critics. Roxy Music left behind an inventive body of work that was diverse and highly influential in the 70s. Glam, techno, dance, ambient and electronic genres all owe a considerable debt to the Ferry/Eno days. It is a great pity that at the time of writing their standing is minimal, buried under the coat tails of Ferry's AOR solo success, although at some stage a major reappraisal must surely come.

●ALBUMS: *Roxy Music* (Island 1972)★★★★, *For Your Pleasure* (Island 1973)★★★★, *Stranded* (Island 1973)★★★★, *Country Life* (Island 1974)★★★, *Siren* (Island 1975)★★★, *Viva! Roxy Music* (Island 1976)★★★, *Manifesto* (Polydor 1979)★★★, *Flesh And Blood* (Polydor 1980)★★★, *Avalon* (EG 1981)★★★★, *The High Road* (EG 1983)★★★.

●COMPILATIONS: *Greatest Hits* (Polydor 1977)★★★, *The Atlantic Years 1973-1980* (EG 1983)★★★, *Street Life -*

20 Great Hits (1986)★★★★, *The Ultimate Collection* (1988)★★★★, *The Compact Collection* 3-CD box set (1992)★★★, *The Thrill Of It All* 4-CD box set (Virgin 1995)★★★. Bryan Ferry And Roxy Music *More Than This - The Best Of* (Virgin 1995)★★★.

●VIDEOS: *Total Recall* (Virgin 1990).

●FURTHER READING: *Roxy Music: Style With Substance - Roxy's First Ten Years*, Johnny Rogan. *The Bryan Ferry Story*, Rex Balfour. *Bryan Ferry & Roxy Music*, Barry Lazell and Dafydd Rees.

RUBETTES

Former songwriters of the Pete Best Four, Wayne Bickerton and Tony Waddington created the Rubettes from session musicians after their composition, 'Sugar Baby Love', was rejected by existing acts. A fusion of 50s revivalism and glam-rock, it gave the new group's career a flying start by topping the UK charts and climbing into the US Top 40 in 1974. The song was mimed on television and promoted in concert by Alan Williams (b. 22 December 1948, Welwyn Garden City, Hertfordshire, England; vocals/guitar), Tony Thorpe (b. 20 July 1947, London, England; guitar), Bill Hurd (b. 11 August 1948, London, England; keyboards), Mick Clarke (b. 10 August 1946, Grimsby, Humberside, England; bass) and John Richardson (b. 3 May 1948, Dagenham, Essex, England). Despite adverse publicity when it was revealed that a Paul Da Vinci had warbled the punishing falsetto lead vocal on 'Sugar Baby Love', the five stayed together and were able to continue as hit parade contenders and touring attractions - particularly in Britain and northern Europe - for another three years. 'Tonight', 'Juke Box Jive', 'I Can Do It' and lesser hits mixed mainly Waddington-Bickerton and band originals. Five years after their grand exit with 1977's countrified 'Baby I Know' in the domestic Top 10, Thorpe returned from obscurity to sing lead on the Firm's 'Arthur Daley (E's Alright)', a chartbusting paean to the main character in the television series *Minder*. This was followed in 1987 with the UK number 1, 'Star Trekkin''.

●ALBUMS: *We Can Do It*, (State 1975)★★★, *Still Unwinding* (Polydor 1979)★★, *Impact* (Impact 1982)★★.

●COMPILATIONS: *Best Of The Rubettes* (Polydor 1983)★★★, *The Singles Collection 1974 - 1979* (1992)★★★, *Juke Box Jive* (1993)★★.

●FURTHER READING: *The Rubettes Story*, Alan Rowett.

RUBINOOS

The Rubinoos carried on the great pop tradition of UK bands like the Hollies and the Beatles and that espoused by other American acts like the Raspberries. They were formed in the Bay Area of San Francisco, California, in 1973 by Tommy 'TV' Dunbar and Jon Rubin, who were thrown out of high school together and enrolled in a so-called Progressive School where they learned to smoke illegal substances. They called themselves the Rubinoos after Jon's surname, Rubin, acting as vocalist while Dunbar played guitar. They

were joined by Royse Ader on bass and Donn Spindit on drums. Their early set consisted of cover versions, including the Archies' 'Sugar Sugar'. The Rubinoos were often pelted with vegetables until the American new wave scene helped make 60s pop respectable again. Dunbar's brother Rob was in a band called Earthquake and their manager, Matthew Kaufman, helped get the Rubinoos gigs. He also added them to his impressive roster on Beserkley Records. Their debut single in 1977 (produced by Kaufman) was a version of Tommy James And The Shondells' 'I Think We're Alone Now'. Both this, and their self-penned but similarly styled 'I Wanna Be Your Boyfriend', were much vaunted but not hits. They became a popular live attraction particularly for their showstopping 'Rock And Roll Is Dead (And We Don't Care)'. Regardless of their lack of major success they ploughed on, though Ader left in 1980 and by the time of their 1983 mini-album, *Party Of Two*, they were just a duo of Rubin and Dunbar. However, the four original members re-formed in 1988.
●ALBUMS: *The Rubinoos* (Beserkley 1977)★★★, *Rubinoos In Wax* (Beserkley 1979)★★, *Back To The Drawing Board* (Beserkley 1979)★★, *Party Of Two* (1983)★★.

RUFFIN, DAVID

b. 18 January 1941, Meridian, Mississippi, USA, d. 1 June 1991. The younger brother of Jimmy Ruffin and the cousin of Melvin Franklin of the Temptations, David Ruffin was the son of a minister, and began his singing career with the gospel group the Dixie Nightingales. He combined the roles of vocalist and drummer in the doo-wop combo the Voice Masters from 1958, before signing to the Anna label in Detroit as a soloist in 1960. His releases there and on Check-Mate in 1961 proved unsuccessful, though they demonstrated the raw potential of his vocal skills. In 1963, Ruffin replaced Eldridge Bryant as tenor vocalist in the Temptations. At first he played a supporting role behind the falsetto leads of Eddie Kendricks. From 1965 onwards he was allowed to take the spotlight on hits like 'My Girl' and 'I Wish It Would Rain', which illustrated his commanding way with a ballad, and raunchier R&B material like 'I'm Losing You' and 'Ain't Too Proud To Beg'. Adopting the role of frontman, Ruffin was soon singled out by the media as the key member of the group, though his erratic behaviour caused some tension within the ranks. The Motown hierarchy slowly began to ease him out of the line-up, achieving their aim when they refused to give him solo billing in front of the group's name in 1968. Still under contract to the label, he embarked on an episodic solo career. 'My Whole World Ended', a Top 10 hit in 1969, re-established his credentials as a great soul singer, under the tutelage of producers Harvey Fuqua and Johnny Bristol. Subsequent releases failed to utilize his talents to the full, and an album of duets with his brother Jimmy also proved disappointing. After three years of comparative silence, Ruffin re-emerged in 1973 with the first of a series of workmanlike albums which spawned one Top 10 single, the Van McCoy-produced 'Walk Away From Love', and a batch of minor hits. In 1979, he left Motown for Warner Brothers Records, where his career fell into decline. In the early 80s he was briefly jailed for tax evasion, and his slide was only halted when a Temptations reunion in 1983 brought him back into contact with Eddie Kendricks. After the project was complete, Ruffin and Kendricks established a regular partnership, which was boosted when they were showcased on a prestigious concert at New York's Apollo by long-time Temptations fans, Hall And Oates. This event was captured on a 1985 live album, and Ruffin and Kendricks also joined the rock duo at the Live Aid concert in Philadelphia. They subsequently recorded a well-received album of duets for RCA, which revived memories of their vocal interplay with the Temptations two decades earlier. He recorded with Ian Levine's Motor City label in 1990 including 'Hurt The One You Love' and toured with Eddie Kendricks and Dennis Edwards as Tribute To The Temptations on a package tour in 1991. A few weeks after the last performance he died in tragic circumstances after an overdose of crack (cocaine).
●ALBUMS: *My Whole World Ended* (Motown 1969)★★★, *Feelin' Good* (Motown 1969)★★, with Jimmy Ruffin *I Am My Brother's Keeper* (1970)★★, *David Ruffin* (Motown 1973)★★, *Me'N'Rock'N'Roll Are Here To Stay* (Motown 1974)★★, *Who I Am* (Motown 1975)★★, *Everything's Coming Up Love* (Motown 1976)★★, *In My Stride* (Motown 1977)★★, *So Soon We Change* (Warners 1979)★, *Gentleman Ruffin* (Warners 1980)★★, with Kendrick *Ruffin And Kendrick* (RCA 1987)★★★.
●COMPILATIONS: *David Ruffin At His Best* (Motown 1978)★★★.

RUFFIN, JIMMY

b. 7 May 1939, Collinsville, Mississippi, USA. The son of a minister, Ruffin was born into a musical family: his brother, David Ruffin, and cousin, Melvin Franklin, both became mainstays of the Temptations. Ruffin abandoned his gospel background to become a session singer in the early 60s, joining the Motown stable in 1961 for a one-off single before he was drafted for national service. After leaving the US Army, he returned to Motown, turning down the opportunity to join the Temptations and instead recommending his brother for the job. His commercial breakthrough came in 1966 with the major US and UK hit 'What Becomes Of The Broken-Hearted', which displayed his emotional, if rather static, vocals. After three smaller hits, Ruffin found success in the USA hard to sustain, concentrating instead on the British market. 'I'll Say Forever My Love' and 'It's Wonderful' consolidated his position in the UK, and in 1970 he was voted the world's top singer in one British poll. Ruffin left Motown in the early 70s after an unsuccessful collaboration with his brother, and achieved minor success with singles on Polydor and Chess. Despite his popularity as a live performer in Britain, he enjoyed no significant hits until 1980, when 'Hold On To My Love', written and produced by Robin Gibb of the Bee Gees, brought him his first USA Top 30 hit for 14 years. A duet with Maxine Nightingale, 'Turn To Me', was a big seller in 1982, while Ruffin's only other success of note in the 80s was the British chart-contender 'There Will Never Be Another You' in 1985. He joined Ian Levine's Motor City label in 1988 and recorded two singles with Brenda Holloway.

● ALBUMS: *Top Ten* (Soul 1967)★★★, *Ruff'n'Ready* (Soul 1969)★★, *The Groove Governor* (1970)★★, with David Ruffin *I Am My Brother's Keeper* (1970)★★, *Jimmy Ruffin* (1973)★★, *Love Is All We Need* (1975)★★, *Sunrise* (RSO 1980)★★★.

● COMPILATIONS: *Greatest Hits* (Tamla Motown 1974)★★★, *20 Golden Classics* (Motown 1981)★★★, *Greatest Motown Hits* (Motown 1989)★★★, *Early Classics* (Spectrum 1996)★★.

RUFUS

This Chicago-based group evolved from the American Breed when three original members, Al Ciner (guitar), Charles Colbert (bass) and Lee Graziano (drums), were joined by Kevin Murphy (keyboards), Paulette McWilliams (vocals), Ron Stockard and Dennis Belfield. Initially known as Smoke, then Ask Rufus, it was several months before a stable unit evolved. Graziano made way for Andre Fisher, but the crucial change came when Chaka Khan (b. Yvette Marie Stevens, 23 March 1953, Great Lakes Naval Training Station, Illinois, USA) joined in place of McWilliams. The group, now known simply as Rufus, signed with the ABC label in 1973, but made little headway until a chance encounter with Stevie Wonder during sessions for a second album. Impressed by Khan's singing, he donated an original song, 'Tell Me Something Good' which, when issued as a single, became a gold disc. It began a run of exceptional releases, including 'You Got The Love' (1974), 'Sweet Thing' (1975) and 'At Midnight (My Love Will Lift You Up)' (1977), all of which topped the R&B chart. By this time Rufus had stabilized around Khan, Murphy, Tony Maiden (guitar), Dave Wolinski (keyboards), Bobby Watson (bass) and John Robinson (drums), but it was clear that the singer was the star attraction. She began recording as a solo act in 1978, but returned to the fold in 1980 for *Masterjam*, which contained 'Do You Love What You Feel', a further number 1 soul single. Khan continued to pursue her own career and perform with Rufus, who secured an international hit in 1983 with 'Ain't Nobody'. The song was written by Wolinski, by now an established figure in soul circles through his work on Michael Jackson's *Off The Wall*. The distinction between Chaka Khan's successful solo recordings and her work with Rufus has become blurred over the years, but it remains arguable whether or not she achieved the same empathy elsewhere.

● ALBUMS: *Rufus* (ABC 1973)★★, *Rags To Rufus* (ABC 1974)★★★★, *Rufusized* (ABC 1975)★★★★, *Rufus Featuring Chaka Khan* (ABC 1975)★★★, *Ask Rufus* (ABC 1977)★★★, *Street Player* (ABC 1978)★★★, *Numbers* (ABC 1979)★, *Masterjam* (MCA 1979)★★★, *Party 'Til You're Broke* (MCA 1981)★★, *Camouflage* (MCA 1981)★★, *Live - Stompin' At The Savoy* (Warners 1983)★★.

● FILMS: *Breakdance - The Movie* (1984).

RUNAWAYS

Formed in 1975, the Runaways were initially the product of producer/svengali Kim Fowley and teenage lyricist Kari Krome. Together they pieced together an adolescent female group following several auditions in the Los Angeles area. The original line-up consisted of Joan Jett (b. Joan Larkin, 22 September 1960, Philadelphia, Pennsylvania, USA; guitar/vocals), Micki Steele (bass - later of the Bangles) and Sandy West (drums), but was quickly bolstered by the addition of Lita Ford (b. 23 September 1959, London, England; guitar/vocals) and Cherie Currie (vocals). The departure of Steele prompted several replacements, the last of whom was Jackie Fox (b. Jacqueline Fuchs) who had failed her first audition. Although originally viewed as a vehicle for compositions by Fowley and associate Mars Bonfire (b. Dennis Edmonton), material by Jett and Krome helped assert the quintet's independence. *The Runaways* showed a group indebted to the 'glam-rock' of the Sweet and punchy pop of Suzi Quatro, and included the salutary 'Cherry Bomb'. *Queens Of Noise* repeated the pattern, but the strain of touring - the quintet were highly popular in Japan - took its toll on Jackie Fox, who left the line-up and abandoned music altogether, becoming an attorney practising in intellectual property law. Personality clashes resulted in the departure of Cherie Currie, whose solo career stalled following the failure of her debut, *Beauty's Only Skin Deep*. Guitarist/vocalist Vicki Blue and bassist Laurie McAllister completed a revitalized Runaways, but the latter was quickly dropped. The Runaways split in 1980 but both Jett and Ford later enjoyed solo careers, the former enjoying commercial success during the 80s. In 1985 Fowley resurrected the old group's name with all-new personnel. This opportunistic concoction split up on completing *Young And Fast*. In 1994 reports surfaced that Fowley was being sued by Jett, Ford, Currie and West over unpaid royalties. Fox was not involved in the action, presumably because she is now herself a practising lawyer.

● ALBUMS: *The Runaways* (Mercury 1976)★★★, *Queens Of Noise* (Mercury 1977)★★, *Live In Japan* (Mercury 1977)★★, *Waitin' For The Night* (Mercury 1977)★★, *And Now ... The Runaways* (Phonogram 1979)★★, *Young And Fast* (Allegiance 1987)★.

● COMPILATIONS: *Rock Heavies* (Mercury 1979)★★★, *Flamin' Schoolgirls* (Phonogram 1982)★★.

RUNDGREN, TODD

b. 22 June 1948, Philadelphia, Pennsylvania, USA. One of rock's eccentric talents, Rundgren began his career in local bar-band Woody's Truck Stop, before forming the Nazz in 1967. This acclaimed quartet completed three albums of anglophile pop/rock before disintegrating in 1970. Rundgren sought solace as an engineer - his credits included *Stage Fright* by the Band - before recording *Runt*, a name derived from his nickname. Brothers Hunt and Tony Sales (drums and bass respectively), later of Tin Machine, joined the artist on a set deftly combining technical expertise with his love of melody. This exceptionally accomplished album spawned a US Top 20 hit in 'We Got To Get You A Woman' and paved the way for the equally charming *The Ballad Of Todd Rundgren*. However, it was with *Something/Anything?* that this performer truly flourished. The first three sides were entirely his own creation - as writer, singer, musician and producer - and contained some of Rundgren's most popular songs, including 'I Saw The Light' and 'It Wouldn't Have Made Any Difference'. Although the final side was devoted to an indulgent 'pop opera', the set is rightly regarded as one of the landmark releases of the early 70s. *A Wizard, A True Star* offered a similarly dazzling array of styles, ranging from a suite of short song-snippets to a medley of soul ballads, including 'I'm So Proud' and 'Ooh Baby Baby'. *Todd*, a second double set, proved equally ambitious, although its erratic content suggested that Rundgren was temporarily bereft of direction. His riposte was Utopia, a progressive rock ensemble which initially featured three musicians on keyboards/synthesizers - Moogy Klingman, M. Frog Labat and Ralph Shuckett - John Segler, then Kasim Sulton, (bass) and John Wilcox (drums). Although Roger Powell latterly assumed all keyboard duties, the group's penchant for lengthy instrumental interludes and semi-mystical overtones remained intact.

A popular live attraction, Utopia taxed the loyalties of Rundgren aficionados, particularly when their unrepentant self-indulgence encroached into the artist's 'solo' work, notably on *Initiation*. *Faithful* did reflect a return to pop with 'Love Of The Common Man' and 'The Verb To Love', while acknowledging Rundgren's inspirational roots with note-for-note remakes of several 60s classics, including 'If Six Was Nine' (Jimi Hendrix), 'Good Vibrations' (the Beach Boys) and 'Strawberry Fields Forever' (the Beatles). In 1977 Utopia released *Ra* and *Oops! Wrong Planet*, the latter of which had Rundgren taking a less prominent role. He nonetheless maintained a frenetic workload and having already established his credentials as a producer with the New York Dolls, Grand Funk Railroad and Hall And Oates, commenced work on Meatloaf's *Bat Out Of Hell*, which has since become one of the best-selling albums of all time. The artist also recorded *Hermit Of Mink Hollow*, a superb set recalling the grasp of pop offered on *Something/Anything?* and deservedly lauded by critics. Rundgren entered the 80s determined to continue his eclectic path. Utopia's *Deface The Music* was a dazzling pastiche of Beatles music from 'I Wanna Hold Your Hand' to 'Tomorrow Never Knows' while another 'solo' set, *Healing*, flirted with ambient styles. His earlier profligacy lessened as the decade progressed but retained the capacity to surprise, most notably on the inventive *Acappella*. Production work for XTC joined later recordings in proving his many talents have remained as true as ever. In 1994 he scored the music for the film *Dumb And Dumber*.

●ALBUMS: *Runt* (Bearsville 1970)★★★, *The Ballad Of Todd Rundgren* (Bearsville 1971)★★★★, *Something/Anything?* (Bearsville 1972)★★★★, *A Wizard, A True Star* (Bearsville 1973)★★★, *Todd* (Bearsville 1974)★★, *Initiation* (Bearsville 1975)★, *Faithful* (Bearsville 1976)★★★, *Hermit Of Mink Hollow* (Bearsville 1978)★★★★, *Back To The Bars* (Bearsville 1978)★★, *Healing* (Bearsville 1981)★★★, *The Ever Popular Tortured Artist Effect* (Lamborghini 1983)★★, *A Cappella* (Warners 1985)★★, *Nearly Human* (Warners 1989)★★★, *Second Wind* (Warners 1991)★★, *No World Order* (Food For Thought 1993)★★, *The Individualist* (Navarre 1996)★★. With Utopia *Todd Rundgren's Utopia* (Bearsville 1974)★★, *Another Live* (Bearsville 1975)★★, *Ra* (Bearsville 1977)★★, *Oops! Wrong Planet* (Bearsville 1977)★★★, *Adventures In Utopia* (Bearsville 1980)★★★, *Deface The Music* (Bearsville 1980)★★★, *Swing To The Right* (Bearsville 1982)★★, *Utopia* (Network 1982)★★, *Oblivion* (Passport 1984)★★, *POV* (Passport 1985)★★, *Trivia* (Passport 1986)★★, *Redux 92 Live In Japan* (Rhino 1993)★★.

●COMPILATIONS: *The Collection* (Castle 1988)★★★★, *Anthology: Todd Rundgren* (Rhino 1989)★★★★, *Anthology 1974-1985* (Rhino/ Bearsville 1995)★★★.

RUSSELL, LEON

b. 2 April 1941, Lawton, Oklahoma, USA. The many talents of Russell include that of singer, songwriter, producer, arranger, entrepreneur, record company executive and multi-instrumentalist. While he tasted great honours as a solo star in the early 70s, it is his all-round contribution, much of it in the background, that has made him a vitally important figure in rock music for more than 30 years. His impressive career began, after having already mastered piano and trumpet as a child, when he played with Ronnie Hawkins and Jerry Lee Lewis in the late 50s. He became a regular session pianist for the pivotal US television show *Shindig* as well as being present on most of the classic Phil Spector singles, including the Ronettes, Crystals and the Righteous Brothers. James Burton is reputed to have taught him the guitar around this time. He has appeared on hundreds of major singles right across the music spectrum, playing with a huge number of artists, including Frank Sinatra, Bobby Darin, the Byrds, Herb Alpert and Paul Revere. He formed his own unit Asylum Choir in 1968 together with Marc Benno and formed a cultist duo that was a commercial disaster. He befriended Delaney And Bonnie and created the famous Mad Dogs And Englishmen tour, which included Joe Cocker. Cocker recorded Russell's 'Delta Lady' during this time, to great success. Russell founded his own label Shelter Records with UK producer Denny Cordell and released the self-titled debut which received unanimous critical approbation. His own session players included Steve Winwood, George Harrison, Eric Clapton, Charlie Watts, Bill Wyman and Ringo Starr. Following further session work including playing with Bob Dylan and Dave Mason, he appeared at the historic Concert for Bangladesh in 1971 and was forced to rest the following year when he suffered a nervous and physical breakdown.

He returned in 1972 with *Carney*. This US number 2, million-seller, was semi-autobiographical using the circus clown theme as an analogy to his own punishing career. The following year Russell delivered a superb country album, *Hank Wilson's Back*, acknowledging his debt to classic country singers. That year he released an album by his future wife, Mary McCreary, and in 1974 an excellent version of Tim Hardin's 'If I Were A Carpenter'. Russell concentrated on his own career and in 1977 was awarded a Grammy for his song 'This Masquerade', which made the US Top 10 the previous year for George Benson. A partnership with Willie Nelson produced a superb country album in 1979; it became one of his biggest albums. 'Heartbreak Hotel' topped the US country chart, endorsing Russell's acceptance as a country singer. An excursion into bluegrass resulted in the 1981 live set with the New Grass Revival. Following *Hank Wilson's Volume II* in 1984 Leon became involved with his own video production company. He returned in 1992 with the disappointing *Anything Will Happen*. Russell has already earned his retirement twice over and his place in the history books. If there were such a trophy he would be a contender for the 'most outstanding all-round contribution to rock' music award, yet sadly in recent years he has easily won the 'where on earth is he' nomination.

●ALBUMS: *Look Inside The Asylum Choir* (Shelter 1968)★★, *Leon Russell* (Shelter 1970)★★★★, *Leon Russell And The Shelter People* (Shelter 1971)★★★★, *Asylum Choir II* (Shelter 1971)★★, *Carney* (Shelter 1972)★★★★, *Leon Live* (Shelter 1973)★★★, *Hank Wilson's Back, Vol.1* (Shelter 1973)★★★, *Stop All That Jazz* (Shelter 1974)★★, *Will O' The Wisp* (Shelter 1975)★★, *Wedding Album* (Paradise 1976)★★, *Make Love To The Music* (Paradise 1977)★★, *Americana* (Paradise 1978)★★, with Willie Nelson *One For The Road* (Columbia 1979)★★★, *Live And Love* (1979)★★★, with the New Grass Revival *The Live Album* (Paradise 1981)★★★, *Hank Wilson Vol.II* (1984)★★, *Anything Can Happen* (Virgin 1992)★★.

●COMPILATIONS: *Best Of Leon* (Shelter 1976)★★★★.

●VIDEOS: with Edgar Winter *Main Street Cafe* (Hendring 1990).

RUTLES

The product of satirists Neil Innes (ex-Bonzo Dog Doo-Dah Band) and Eric Idle, formerly of the comedy team *Monty Python's Flying Circus*, the Rutles was an affectionate and perceptive parody of the Beatles' career, which emerged from the duo's *Rutland Weekend Television* BBC comedy series. Innes played Ron Nasty (Lennon), Idle played Dirk McQuickly (McCartney), while Rikki Fataar (ex-Beach Boys) and John Halsey (ex-Patto) completed the line-up as Stig O'Hara (Harrison) and Barry Wom (Starr), respectively. Ollie Halsall, who died in 1992, played the fourth member in the recording studio. The Rutles' film, *All You Need Is Cash*, and attendant album deftly combined elements drawn from both founder-members' past work. Innes' songs recreated the different, and indeed, contrasting, styles of music the Beatles offered, ranging from the Mersey pop of 'I Must Be In Love' and 'Ouch!' to the psychedelia of 'Piggy In The Middle'. Mick Jagger and Paul Simon made excellent cameo appearances while George Harrison enjoyed a small acting role. The project is now rightly regarded, alongside Spinal Tap, as one of rock's most lasting parodies and the Rutles were themselves lampooned in 1991 when maverick New York label Shimmy Disc produced *Rutles Highway Revisited* wherein its roster performed a unique interpretation of the original album. In the wake of the Beatles Anthology in the mid-90s, the prefab four also gave it another shot, this time as the prefab three, with the departure of McQuickly. The resulting *Archaeology* was once again an eerie reminder of how easy it is to copy the style, sound and lyrical flavour of the world's greatest ever group (the Beatles that is, not the Rutles!).

●ALBUMS: *The Rutles* (Warners 1978)★★★★, *Archaeology* (Virgin 1996)★★.

●VIDEOS: *All You Need Is Cash* (Palace Video 1988).

RUTS

This punk/reggae-influenced group comprised Malcolm Owen (vocals), Paul Fox (guitar/vocals), Dave Ruffy (drums) and John 'Segs' Jennings (bass). They first came to the fore in 1979 with the UK Top 10 single, 'Babylon's Burning'. Their gigs of that year were the most stunning of punk's second generation, with one in Bradford cited by Justin Sullivan of New Model Army as the biggest influence on his career. Their style resembled that of the Clash, but while Owen was occasionally compared to Joe Strummer, there was something just as original sparking the group's songwriting. The strident 'Something That I Said' gave them another hit and their debut album, *The Crack*, though not representing the band as well as their blistering singles, was well received. The rampaging 'Staring At The Rude Boys' neatly displayed their rock/dub talents, but their progress was arrested by Owen's drug-related death on 14 July 1980. On the run-out groove of their final single together the band scratched the legend 'Can I Use Your

Bathroom?' in tribute - Owen having died in the bath. The remaining members were joined by Gary Barnacle and elected to continue as Ruts DC. They recorded two further albums under that name, moving towards funk-influenced reggae. Without Owen, however, the spirit of the group was not the same and they faded from prominence, though their influence lives on in bands such as the Wildhearts and the Almighty. Fox went on to a successful production career.

●ALBUMS: *The Crack* (Virgin 1979)★★★, *Grin And Bear It* (Virgin 1980)★★★. As Ruts DC *Animal Now* (Virgin 1981)★★, *Rhythm Collision Vol 1* (Bohemian 1982)★★. As Ruts DC And The Mad Professor: *Rhythm Collision Dub Vol. 1* cassette only (ROIR 1987)★★.

●COMPILATIONS: *The Ruts Live* (Dojo 1987)★★, *The Peel Sessions* (Strange Fruit 1990)★★★, *Rhythm Collision Dub* (Roir Europe/Danceteria 1994)★★, *The Best Of The Ruts* (Virgin 1995)★★★.

SAD CAFE

Formed in 1976, Sad Cafe originally consisted of Paul Young (vocals), Ian Wilson (guitar), Mike Hehir (guitar), Lenni (saxophone), Vic Emerson (keyboards), John Stimpson (bass) and David Irving (drums). They evolved out of two Manchester groups, Gyro and Mandala, although Young had previously sung in an earlier beat group, the Toggery Five. Their debut *Fanx Ta Ra*, introduced the group's blend of hard-rock riffs and adult pop, but it was a second collection, *Misplaced Ideals*, which brought them international success when one of its tracks, 'Run Home Girl', became a US hit. *Facades*, produced by 10cc guitarist Eric Stewart, contained 'Every Day Hurts', a UK Top 3 single in 1979, and two further Top 40 entries the following year, 'Strange Little Girl' and 'My Oh My'. John Stimpson had became the group's manager in August 1980 and his place in the line-up was taken by Des Tong. However, despite enjoying a handful of minor hits, Sad Cafe were unable to sustain their early success although they continued to record, intermittently, throughout the 80s.

●ALBUMS: *Fanx Ta Ra* (RCA 1977)★★, *Misplaced Ideals* (RCA 1978)★★★, *Facades* (RCA 1979)★★, *Sad Cafe* (RCA 1980)★★, *Live* (RCA 1981)★★, *Ole* (Polydor 1981)★★, *The Politics Of Existing* (Legacy 1986)★★, *Whatever It Takes* (Legacy 1989)★★.

●COMPILATIONS: *The Best Of Sad Cafe* (RCA 1985)★★★.

SAHM, DOUG

b. 6 November 1941, San Antonio, Texas, USA. Born of Lebanese-American extraction, Sahm is highly knowledgeable and a superbly competent performer of Texas musical styles, whether they be blues, country, rock 'n' roll, western swing, cajun or polkas. He made his recording debut in 1955 with 'A Real American Joe', under the name of Little Doug Sahm and within three years was fronting the Pharoahs, the first of several rough-hewn backing groups. Sahm recorded a succession of singles for local labels, including his Little Richard pastiche 'Crazy Daisy' (1959), plus 'Sapphire' (1961) and 'If You Ever Need Me' (1964). For several years, Sahm had been pestering producer, Huey P. Meaux, to record him. Meaux, having success with Barbara Lynn and Dale And Grace, was not interested. However, the producer found himself without a market when Beatlemania hit America, and shut himself away in a hotel with the Beatles' records, determined to discover what made them sell. He then called Sahm, told him to grow his hair, form a group and write a tune with a Cajun two-step beat. Accordingly, Sahm assembled his friends, Augie Meyers (keyboards), Frank Morin (saxophone), Harvey Kagan (bass) and Johnny Perez (drums). Meaux gave them an English-sounding name, the Sir Douglas Quintet and subsequently achieved an international hit in 1965 with the catchy 'She's About A Mover'.

The group also had success in the US charts with 'The Rains Came', but, after being arrested for possession of drugs, the group disbanded and Sahm moved to California to avoid a heavy fine. He formed the Honkey Blues Band, but had difficulty in getting it on the road. He then gathered the rest of the Quintet in California for another classic single, 'Mendocino', its spoken introduction being indicative of the hippie-era. The album, also called *Mendocino*, is a forerunner of country rock. The Sir Douglas Quintet toured Europe and made the successful *Together After Five*, while Sahm made an excellent country single, 'Be Real', under the name of Wayne Douglas. He moved to Prunedale in northern California and befriended a Chicano band, Louie And The Lovers, producing their *Rise*. Sahm, having resolved his problems with the authorities, went back to Texas and released *The Return Of Doug Saldaña*, the name reflecting his affection for Chicanos. The album, co-produced with Meaux, included an affectionate tribute to Freddy Fender, 'Wasted Days And Wasted Nights', which prompted Meaux to resurrect Fender's career and turn him into a country superstar. Sahm appeared with Kris Kristofferson in the film, *Cisco Pike*, and told his record company that the song he performed, 'Michoacan', was about a state in Mexico. Disc jockeys, however, realized that he was actually praising marijuana and airplay was restricted. Atlantic Records' key producer, Jerry Wexler, decided that progressive country was becoming fashionable and signed both Willie Nelson and Doug Sahm. Sahm's high-spirited *Doug Sahm And Band*, was made in New York with Bob Dylan, Dr. John and accordionist Flaco Jiminez, and Sahm achieved minor success with 'Is Anybody Going To San Antone?'. The Sir Douglas Quintet were resurrected intermittently which resulted in two fine live albums, *Wanted Very Much Alive* and *Back To The 'Dillo*. Although it might seem strange that the band should tour with the new wave band the Pretenders, Sahm's voice and style were arguably an influence on Elvis Costello. Sahm himself says, 'I'm a part of Willie Nelson's world and at the same time I'm a part of the Grateful Dead's. I don't ever stay in one bag'. Among Sahm's finest albums are *Hell Of A Spell*, a blues album dedicated to Guitar Slim, and *The Return Of The Formerly Brothers*, with guitarist Amos Garrett and pianist Gene Taylor. In 1990, Doug re-used the name, the Texas Tornadoes, for an album with Meyers, Jiminez and Fender. The album, which included Sahm's witty 'Who Were You Thinkin' Of?' and Butch Hancock's 'She Never

Spoke Spanish To Me', showed that he has lost none of his powers. In the UK, the Sir Douglas Quintet may be regarded as one-hit-wonders, but in reality Sahm has recorded a remarkable catalogue of Texas music. *Day Dreaming At Midnight* was a prime example. It was produced by ex-Creedence Clearwater Revival member Doug Clifford and was a rousing collection notably for 'Too Little Too Late' and the blistering Bob Dylan pastiche 'Dylan Come Lately'.

●ALBUMS: *Doug Sahm And Band* (Atlantic 1973)★★, *Rough Edges* (Mercury 1973)★★, *Texas Tornado* (Atlantic 1973)★★★, *Groovers Paradise* (Warners 1974)★★★, *Texas Rock For Country Rollers* (ABC/Dot 1976)★★★, *Live Love* (1977)★★, *Hell Of A Spell* (Takoma 1979)★★★, *Texas Road Runner* (Moonshine 1986)★★★, *Live Doug Sahm* (Topline 1987)★★★, *Back To The 'Dillo* (Sonet 1988)★★★★, *Juke Box Music* (Ace 1989)★★★★, *The Texas Tornadoes* (Warners 1990)★★★, as Texas Tornados *Zone Of Our Own* (Warners 1991)★★★★, *Hangin' On By A Thread* (1992)★★★, with Amos Garrett, Gene Taylor *The Return Of The Formerly Brothers* (1992)★★★, *Day Dreaming At Midnight* (Elektra 1994)★★★★, *The Last Real Texas Blues Band* (Antone's 1995)★★★.

●COMPILATIONS: *Sir Douglas - Way Back When He Was Just Doug Sahm* (1979)★★★, *Sir Douglas - His First Recordings* (1981)★★★, *Sir Doug's Recording Trip* (Edsel 1989)★★★, *The Best Of Doug Sahm And The Sir Douglas Quintet* (1991)★★★★.

SAILOR

Sailor were formed in 1974 by songwriter and acoustic guitarist George Kajanus (b. Georg Hultgren, Norway) who, apart from claiming to be a Norwegian prince, was a member of the folk rock group Eclection. The remainder of Sailor comprised Phil Pickett (b. Germany; nickleodeon) and Grant Serpell (b. Maidenhead, England; drums). They released their debut 'Traffic Jam'on CBS/Epic Records. A projected 1975 tour with Mott was cancelled when Mott split. Subsequent tours with Kiki Dee and Cockney Rebel did have the desired effect. They reached number 2 in the UK charts with the sparkling 'A Glass Of Champagne'. They had two more hits with 'Girls Girls Girls' and 'One Drink Too Many' before the onset of punk overwhelmed them, but they continued gigging. The line-up underwent some changes but Marsh and Pickett were still on board by 1982. Kajanus formed the offshoot group Data in 1980 and they made three albums under that name. In 1983, Pickett acted as keyboard player and songwriter for Culture Club and his 'Karma Chameleon' was an international hit for them; though he was later sued by the writers of Jimmy Jones' 'Handy Man' for alleged plagiarism. In 1984 Pickett wrote and performed ITV's 'Olympic Games Theme' and also produced Thereze Bazaar's solo album. The group re-formed in 1991, releasing their first album in 13 years.

●ALBUMS: *Sailor* (Epic 1974)★★, *Trouble* (Epic

1975)★★, *The Third Step* (Epic 1976)★★, *Checkpoint* (Epic 1977)★★, *Hideaway* (Epic 1978)★★, *Dressed For Drowning* (Caribou 1980)★★, *Sailor* (1991)★★.
●COMPILATIONS: *Greatest Hits* (Epic 1978)★★★.

SAINTS

Formed in Brisbane, Australia in 1975, the Saints were the first Australian punk band to be recognized as being relevant by the UK media. The band comprised Chris Bailey (vocals/guitar), Kym Bradshaw (bass, replaced by Alisdair Ward in 1977), Ed Kuepper (guitar) and Ivor Hay (drums). They were plucked from obscurity via their single 'I'm Stranded' being reviewed as single of the week by the now defunct UK weekly music paper, *Sounds*. Following this, and encouraging sales for their debut album, the band based itself in the UK. Although labelled a punk band, the Saints did not strictly conform to the English perception of punk, as their roots were more R&B-based. A refusal to imitate the punk fashion was certainly instrumental in their rapid fall from favour, although they have since attained considerable cult status. Co-founder Kuepper left the group in 1978 to form the Laughing Clowns. The band stayed together long enough, with various personnel, to record two more albums, disbanding in 1979. Chris Bailey performed with a variety of musicians during the 80s, using the Saints' name, as well as touring solo, playing acoustic guitar. He re-formed the original line-up of the Saints in 1984 (minus Kuepper) and has recorded constantly over the ensuing decade. As a retaliation to Bailey's continued usage of Kuepper's songs in the latter-day Saints line-up, Kuepper formed the Aints in 1990.
●ALBUMS: *I'm Stranded* (1977)★★★, *Eternally Yours* (1978)★★★, *Prehistoric Sounds* (1978)★★★, *Monkey Puzzle* (New Rose 1981)★★, *Casablanca* (1982)★★, *A Little Madness To Be Free* (New Rose 1984)★★, *Live In A Mud Hut* (New Rose 1985)★★, *All Fool's Day* (Polydor 1986)★★★, *Prodigal Son* (Funhouse 1989)★★, *Howling* (Blue Rose 1996)★★.
●COMPILATIONS: *Best Of Saints* (Razor 1986)★★★, *Songs Of Salvation 1976-1988* (1991)★★★, *Know Your Product* (EMI 1996)★★★.

SANTANA

This US group were the pioneers of Afro-Latin rock and as such are head and shoulders above all pretenders to the throne. Santana emerged as part of the late 60s San Francisco new wave scene, which they rapidly transcended. Over the past 25 years the leader Carlos Santana (b. 20 July 1947, Autlan de Navarro, Jalisco, Mexico) has introduced jazz and funk into his unique blend of polyrhythmic music. Carlos owns the name, and has maintained his role as leader through a constant change of personnel, yet fully maintaining the Santana sound of 1967. The original line-up consisted of Gregg Rolie, Michael Shrieve, David Brown (b. 15 February 1947, New York, USA), Marcus Malone and Mike Carabello. Later important members were José Chepito Areas, Neal Schon, Tom Coster, Armando Peraza, Raul Rekow, Graham Lear, Orestes Vilato and Coke Escovedo. Santana was a regional favourite by 1969 and Carlos appeared on Al Kooper and Mike Bloomfield's *The Live Adventures Of. . .* The Woodstock Festival of 1969 was the band's major breakthrough; their performance gave rock fans a first taste of 'Cubano rock' and was one of the highlights.

The first three albums are outstanding examples of the genre. *Santana*, *Abraxas* and *Santana III* spent months high in the US charts, the latter two staying at number 1 for many weeks. These albums included numerous, memorable and fiery tracks including 'Jingo', Tito Puente's 'Oye Como Va', a definitive version of Peter Green's 'Black Magic Woman' and possibly the most sensual rock instrumental of all time; 'Samba Pa Ti'. On this Carlos plays a solo that oozes sexuality over an irresistible slow Latin beat that builds to the inevitable climax. *Caravanserai* marked a change of style as Rolie and Schon departed to form Journey. This important album is almost a single suite showing a move towards jazz in the mode of Miles Davis' *In A Silent Way*. At that time Carlos became a disciple of Sri Chimnoy and, after befriending fellow guitarist John McLaughlin, he released the glorious *Love Devotion And Surrender*. During that year he released a live album with soul/funk drummer Buddy Miles. All these albums were considerable hits. *Welcome* (featuring vocalist Leon Thomas and guest John McLaughlin) and *Borboletta* (with guests Flora Purim and Stanley Clarke) were lesser albums. He returned to hard Latin rock with the excellent *Amigos* in 1977. A version of the Zombies 'She's Not There' became a hit single from *Moonflower* in 1977. In his parallel world Carlos was maintaining a jazz-fusion path with a series of fine albums, the most notable of which was *The Swing Of Delight* with Herbie Hancock and Wayne Shorter. *Zebop!* in 1981 was a *tour de force*, and Santana's guitar playing was particularly impressive, with a clarity not heard since the earliest albums. The hit single from this collection was the admirable Russ Ballard song 'Winning'. The solo *Havana Moon* featured guests, Willie Nelson and Booker T. Jones, although the difference between what is solo Santana and band Santana has become almost irrelevant as Carlos is such an iconoclastic leader. *Beyond Appearances* in 1985 maintained his considerable recorded output. The same year he toured with Bob Dylan to ecstatic audiences. He scored the music for *La Bamba* in 1986 and reunited with Buddy Miles in 1987 to record *Freedom*. In 1989 Santana's contribution to the title track of John Lee Hooker's excellent album *The Healer* was arguably the highlight of the set. This featured one of his most sparse, yet breathtaking guitar solo's. During the summer of 1993 the band toured South America and a live album, *Sacred Fire*, was released. At the same time Carlos also put his own record company, Guts And Grace, on to the market,

beginning with a compilation of classic live performances from original artists such as Jimi Hendrix, Bob
Marley and Marvin Gaye. In 1994 Santana appeared at
Woodstock II with the knowledge that their performance at the original festival was one of the highlights
of that event. The line-up in 1995 featured Tony
Lindsay as vocalist. Any association with the name
Santana continues to be a positive one; whether as the
band or solo, Carlos Santana is an outstanding figure in
rock music and has influenced countless aspiring guitarists. Recent compilations such as *Dance Of The
Rainbow Serpent* and *Live At The Fillmore* emphasize his
steady influence and consistancy over four decades. He
received the *Billboard* lifetime achievment award in
1996.

●ALBUMS: *Santana* (Columbia 1969)★★★★, *Abraxas*
(Columbia 1970)★★★★, *Santana III* (Columbia
1971)★★★★, *Caravanserai* (Columbia 1972)★★★★,
Carlos Santana And Buddy Miles! Live! (Columbia
1972)★★, *Love Devotion Surrender* (Columbia
1973)★★★, *Welcome* (Columbia 1973)★★★, *Borboletta*
(Columbia 1974)★★★, *Illuminations* (Columbia
1974)★★, *Lotus* (Columbia 1975)★★★, *Amigos*
(Columbia 1976)★★★★, *Festival* (Columbia 1977)★★★,
Moonflower (Columbia 1977)★★★, *Inner Secrets*
(Columbia 1978)★★, *Marathon* (Columbia 1979)★★★,
Oneness: Silver Dreams, Golden Reality (Columbia
1979)★★, *The Swing Of Delight* (Columbia 1980)★★,
Zebop! (Columbia 1981)★★★★, *Shango* (Columbia
1982)★★★, *Havana Moon* (Columbia 1983)★★, *Beyond
Appearances* (Columbia 1985)★★, *La Bamba* (Columbia
1986)★★, *Freedom* (Columbia 1987)★★★, *Blues For
Salvador* (Columbia 1987)★★★, *Persuasion* (Thunderbolt
1989)★★, *Spirits Dancing In The Flesh* (Columbia
1990)★★, *Milagro* (Polydor 1992)★★, *Sacred Fire: Live In
South America* (Columbia 1993)★★, with the Santana
Brothers *Santana Brothers* (Island 1994)★★, *Live At The
Fillmore 1968* (Columbia/Legacy 1997)★★.

●COMPILATIONS: *Greatest Hits* (Columbia
1974)★★★★, *Viva Santana - The Very Best* (Columbia
1988)★★★★, *The Very Best Of Santana, Volumes 1 And 2*
(Arcade 1988)★★★★, *Dance Of The Rainbow Serpent* 3-
CD box set (Columbia/Legacy 1995)★★★★.

●VIDEOS: *Influences* (DCI 1995), *Viva Santana!*
(Columbia 1995), *Lightdance* (Miramar Images 1995).

SASSAFRAS

b. Michael Johnson, *c.*1963, Kingston, Jamaica, West
Indies. Prior to his career in music Sassafras was
employed at the riding stables at the Caymans Park
racecourse in Jamaica. A regular visitor to the course
was the entrepreneurial Jack Scorpio who built his own
popular sound system in the early 70s and ventured
into record production in the 80s. His first production
was Sassafras performing 'Pocomania Jump', a reference to the religious culture that has survived in
Jamaica since the days of slavery. The tune was an
instant hit leading to a deluge of Pocomania-themed

songs notably the DJ Gregory Peck's version, 'Poco Man
Jam'. Sassafras followed his hit with 'Calypso Jump',
which was equally as popular in the dancehall. As a reference to his origins at the racetrack he was referred to
as the Horseman. He recorded singles in combination
with Johnny Clarke 'Take Heed' and the Paragons
'Modelling Crowd'. The two performers were the main
DJs for the Black Scorpio sound based in the
Waterhouse area. In the mid-80s Sassafras ventured to
New York, USA, where he played on various sounds
establishing international eminence. He also toured the
UK where he performed at the Easter Reggae Festival
organised by the Greater London Council alongside,
Roy Shirley, Leroy Smart and Edi Fitzroy. By 1989 he
recorded in combination with Barrington Levy, a ver-
sion of Toots And The Maytals' 'Pomps And Pride' as
'Step Up In Life'. The song was produced by Sassafras
and Jah Screw.

●ALBUMS: *Pocomania Jump* (Scorpio 1982)★★★,
Horseman Connection (Starlight 1982)★★★.

SATURDAY NIGHT FEVER

One of the most popular films of the 1970s, *Saturday
Night Fever* (1977) launched John Travolta as a teen-idol.
He starred as a member of a Brooklyn street gang,
obsessed by dancing which provides a release from his
impoverished background. Travolta's routines were
remarkable - inspiring numerous pastiches - and his
portrayal of the inarticulate central character is highly
convincing. Sadly, several external factors have robbed
Saturday Night Fever of its undoubted strengths. An
expurgated version, undertaken to reach a younger
audience, has become the print through which many
encounter the film. This trimming robbed it of dramatic
purpose, editing 'bad' language, sex scenes and violence
integral to the plot. More crucially, disco music did not
enjoy critical popularity and many disparaged *Saturday
Night Fever* on this premise alone. This did not stop the
soundtrack becoming, for a while, the best-selling
album of all time, retaining the UK number 1 spot for
18 consecutive weeks. Despite contributions from
Tavares and the Trammps, it is chiefly remembered for
several excellent tracks by the Bee Gees. Four selections, 'How Deep Is Your Love', 'More Than A Woman',
'Staying Alive' and 'You Should Be Dancing' reached the
UK Top 10 in their own right as singles, while 'Night
Fever' held the top spot in 1978. Had *Saturday Night
Fever* charted punk, it would probably have enjoyed
greater approbation. As it stands, it remains a taut,
absorbing teen-orientated film.

SAVALAS, TELLY

d. January 1994. Although a successful actor in various
film and television roles, Savalas will always be most
closely identified with the title role of detective series
Kojak, his bald head, liking for lollipops (boosting sales
by 500% when the series was at its peak) and fondness
for phrases like 'Who Loves Ya Baby?' building some-

thing approaching a 70s icon. However, he also enjoyed a briefly successful singing career, sending a sentimental cover of David Gates' 'If' to number 1 in the UK charts in February 1975. His croaky, melodramatic version seemed to capture some of Kojak's charisma, but its follow-up, a version of the Righteous Brothers' 'You've Lost That Lovin' Feeling', had even less appeal. ●ALBUMS: *Telly* (MCA 1975)★.

SAVOY BROWN

Formed in 1966 as the Savoy Brown Blues Band, this institution continues to be led by founding guitarist Kim Simmonds. The original line-up comprising Simmonds (b. 6 December 1947), Brice Portius (vocals), Ray Chappell (bass), John O'Leary (harmonica), Bob Hall (piano) and Leo Mannings (drums), were featured on early sessions for producer Mike Vernon's Purdah label, before a second guitarist, Martin Stone, joined in place of O'Leary. The reshaped sextet then secured a recording deal with Decca. Their debut *Shake Down*, was a competent appraisal of blues favourites, featuring material by Freddie King, Albert King and Willie Dixon. Unhappy with this reverential approach, Simmonds pulled the group apart, retaining Hall on an auxiliary basis and adding Chris Youlden (vocals), Dave Peverett (guitar/vocals), Rivers Jobe (bass) and Roger Earl (drums). The new line-up completed *Getting To The Point* before Jobe was replaced by Tone Stevens. The restructured unit was an integral part of the British blues boom. In Youlden they possessed a striking frontman, resplendent in bowler hat and monocle, whose confident, mature delivery added panache to the group's repertoire. Their original songs matched those they chose to cover, while the Simmonds/Peverett interplay added fire to Savoy Brown's live performances. 'Train To Nowhere', from *Blue Matter*, has since become one of the genre's best-loved recordings. Youlden left the group following *Raw Sienna*, but the inner turbulence afflicting the group culminated at the end of 1970 when Peverett, Stevens and Earl walked out to form Foghat.

Simmonds meanwhile toured America with a restructured line-up - Dave Walker (vocals), Paul Raymond (keyboards), Andy Pyle (bass) and Dave Bidwell (drums) - setting a precedent for Savoy Brown's subsequent development. Having honed a simple, blues-boogie style, the guitarist now seemed content to repeat it and the group's ensuing releases are of decreasing interest. Simmonds later settled in America, undertaking gruelling tours with musicians who become available, his determination both undeterred and admirable. The reintroduction of Walker to the group in the late 80s marked a return to the group's original sound.

●ALBUMS: *Shake Down* (Deram 1967)★★★, *Getting To The Point* (Deram 1968)★★★, *Blue Matter* (Deram 1969)★★★★, *A Step Further* (Deram 1969)★★★, *Raw Sienna* (Deram 1970)★★★, *Looking In* (Deram 1970)★★, *Street Corner Talking* (Deram 1971)★★, *Hellbound Train* (Deram 1972)★★★, *Lion's Share* (Deram 1972)★★, *Jack The Toad* (Deram 1973)★★, *Boogie Brothers* (Deram 1974)★★, *Wire Fire* (Deram 1975)★★, *Skin 'N' Bone* (Deram 1976)★★, *Savage Return* (1978)★★, *Rock 'N' Roll Warriors* (1981)★★, *Just Live* (1981)★★★, *A Hard Way To Go* (1985)★★★, *Make Me Sweat* (GNP 1988)★★, *Kings Of Boogie* (GNP 1989)★★, *Live And Kickin'* (GNP 1990)★★, *Let It Ride* (1992)★★, *Bring It Home* (1995)★★★. Solo: Kim Simmonds*Solitaire* (1997)★★★, Chris Youlden *Chris Youlden And The Big Picture* (Matico 1993)★★.

●COMPILATIONS: *The Best Of Savoy Brown* (Deram 1977)★★★, *Blues Roots* (1978)★★★, *Highway Blues* (1985)★★★, *The Savoy Brown Collection* (Polygram 1994)★★★.

SAYER, LEO

b. 21 May 1948, Shoreham-on-Sea, Sussex, England. Sayer fronted the Terraplane Blues Band and Phydeaux while a Sussex art student before moving to London, where he supplemented his wages as a typographic designer (during this time he designed 3 of his own typefaces) by street busking and via floor spots in folk clubs. In 1971, he formed Patches in Brighton who were managed by Dave Courtney to whose melodies he provided lyrics. Speculating in artist management, Courtney's former employer, Adam Faith found the group ultimately unimpressive and chose only to promote its animated X-factor - Sayer. During initial sessions at Roger Daltrey's studio, the Who's vocalist was sufficiently impressed by the raw material to record some Courtney-Sayer numbers himself. These included 'Giving It All Away', Daltrey's biggest solo hit. After a miss with 'Why Is Everybody Going Home', Sayer reached the UK number 1 spot with 1973's exuberant 'The Show Must Go On' but immediate US success was thwarted by a chart-topping cover by Three Dog Night. Seeing him mime the song in a clown costume and pancaked face on BBC television's *Top Of The Pops*, some dismissed Sayer as a one-shot novelty, but he had the last laugh on such detractors when his popularity continued into the next decade. After 'One Man Band' and 'Long Tall Glasses' - the US Hot 100 breakthrough - came the severing of Sayer's partnership with Courtney in 1975 during the making of *Another Year*. With a new co-writer in Frank Furrell (ex-Supertramp) from his backing group, Sayer rallied with the clever 'Moonlighting'. Though the year ended on a sour note with an ill-advised version of the Beatles' 'Let It Be', 1976 brought a US million-seller in 'You Make Me Feel Like Dancing' just as disco sashayed near its *Saturday Night Fever* apogee. Sayer and Faith parted company shortly after the 'Let It Be' release. From 1977's *Endless Flight* (produced by fashionable Richard Perry), the non-original ballad, 'When I Need You', marked Sayer's commercial peak at home - where the BBC engaged him for two television series. However, with the title track of *Thunder In My Heart* halting just outside the UK Top 20, hits suddenly became harder to come by with 1978's 'I Can't Stop Lovin' You' and telling revivals of Buddy Holly's 'Raining In My Heart' and Bobby Vee's 'More Than I Can Say' the only unequivocal smashes as his 1983 chart swansong (with 'Till You Come Back To Me') loomed nearer. Nevertheless, even 1979's fallow period for singles was mitigated by huge returns for a compilation. By the late 80s Sayer was bereft of a recording contract, having severed his longstanding relationship with Chrysalis Records and was reduced to self-financing his UK tours. A legal wrangle with his former manager, Adam Faith, resulted in Sayer reportedly receiving £650,000 in lost royalties. Although a financial settlement was agreed, it was nowhere near the figure quoted, although Sayer did get back the ownership of his masters and song publishing. His recording career recommenced in 1990 after signing to EMI and he was reunited with producer Alan Tarney. Indications of a revival in his chart fortunes remain to be seen; however, this artist has been written off twice before, in 1973 and 1979, and critics should not be so quick to do so again.

●ALBUMS: *Silver Bird* (Chrysalis 1974)★★★, *Just A Boy* (Chrysalis 1974)★★★, *Another Year* (Chrysalis 1975)★★, *Endless Flight* (Chrysalis 1976)★★★, *Thunder In My Heart* (Chrysalis 1977)★★, *Leo Sayer* (Chrysalis 1978)★★, *Here* (Chrysalis 1979)★★, *Living In A Fantasy* (Chrysalis 1980)★★, *World Radio* (Chrysalis 1982)★★, *Have You Ever Been In Love* (Chrysalis 1983)★★, *Cool Touch* (EMI 1990)★★.
●COMPILATIONS: *The Very Best Of Leo Sayer* (Chrysalis 1979)★★★, *All The Best* (1993)★★★, *The Show Must Go On: The Anthology* (Rhino 1997)★★★.

SCAGGS, BOZ
b. William Royce Scaggs, 8 June 1944, Ohio, USA. Scaggs was raised in Dallas, Texas, where he joined fellow guitarist Steve Miller in a high school group, the Marksmen. The musicians maintained this partnership in the Ardells, a group they formed at the University of Wisconsin, but this early association ended when Scaggs returned to Texas. Boz then formed an R&B unit, the Wigs, whom he took to London in anticipation of a more receptive audience. The group broke up when this failed to materialize and the guitarist headed for mainland Europe where he forged a career as an itinerant folk-singer. Scaggs was particularly successful in Sweden, where he recorded a rudimentary solo album, *Boz*. This interlude in exile ended in 1967 when he received an invitation from his erstwhile colleague to join the fledgling Steve Miller Band. Scaggs recorded two albums with this pioneering unit but left for a solo career in 1968. *Boz Scaggs*, recorded at the renowned Fame studios in Muscle Shoals, was a magnificent offering and featured sterling contributions from Duane Allman, particularly on the extended reading of Fenton Robinson's 'Loan Me A Dime'. Over the next five years, Boz pursued an exemplary soul/rock direction

with several excellent albums, including *My Time* and *Slow Dancer*. Skilled production work from Glyn Johns and Johnny Bristol reinforced a high quality, but it was not until 1976, and the smooth *Silk Degrees*, that this was translated into commercial success. A slick session band, which later became Toto, enhanced some of Scaggs' finest compositions, including 'Lowdown' (a US chart number 3 hit), 'What Can I Say?' and 'Lido Shuffle', each of which reached the UK Top 30. The album also featured 'We're All Alone', which has since become a standard. Paradoxically the singer's career faltered in the wake of this exceptional album and despite enjoying several hit singles during 1980, Scaggs maintained a low profile during the subsequent decade. It was eight years before a new selection, *Other Roads*, appeared and a further six before *Some Change*. The latter was an uninspired collection. Scaggs took heed of the failings of that release and moved back to his roots with *Come On Home*, an earthy collection of R&B classics that went some way to remove the gloss of his recent work.
●ALBUMS: *Boz* (1966)★★, *Boz Scaggs* (Atlantic 1969)★★★, *Moments* (Columbia 1971)★★★, *Boz Scaggs And Band* (Columbia 1971)★★★, *My Time* (Columbia 1972)★★★, *Slow Dancer* (Columbia 1974)★★★, *Silk Degrees* (Columbia 1976)★★★★, *Two Down Then Left* (Columbia 1977)★★, *Middle Man* (Columbia 1980)★★★, *Other Roads* (Columbia 1988)★★★, *Some Change* (Virgin 1994)★★, *Come On Home* (Virgin 1997)★★★★.
●COMPILATIONS: *Hits!* (Columbia 1980)★★★.

SCHULZE, KLAUS
Born in Germany, Schulze is one of the fathers of modern electronic music. Originally a drummer, he was a founder-member of Tangerine Dream in 1967 and played on the group's debut. His debut solo album was on the Ohr subsidiary of Hansa Records but much of his later work appeared on his own Brain label. During the late 70s he recorded on synthesizer with Stomu Yamash'ta (*Go Two*) and was the first musician to perform live at the London Planetarium. He also toured with Arthur Brown, who sang on *Dune*, an album inspired by Frank Herbert's cult science fiction novel. In the 80s Schulze concentrated on recording albums whose titles and mesmeric synthesized compositions were the essence of 'new age' music. In 1987, he recorded the soundtrack for the film *Babel* with Andreas Grosser.
●ALBUMS: *Irrlicht* (Ohr 1972)★★★, *Cyborg* (1973)★★★, *Blackdance* (1974)★★★, *Picture Music* (1974)★★★, *Timewind* (1975)★★★, *Moondawn* (Brain 1976)★★★, *Body Love* (1977)★★★, *Mirage* (Brain 1977)★★★, *Body Love II* (1977)★★★, *X* (1978)★★★, *Blanche* (1979)★★★, *Dune* (Brain 1979)★★★, *Live* (1980)★★★, *Dig It* (Brain 1980)★★★, *Trancefer* (1981)★★★, *Rock On* (1981)★★★, *Audentity* (1983)★★★, *Drive Inn* (1984)★★, *Aphrica* (1984)★★, *Angst* (1985)★★★, *Dreams* (Thunderbolt 1987)★★, *Babel* film soundtrack (Venture 1987)★★★,

En = Trance (Thunderbolt 1988)★★★, *The Dresden Performance* (Venture 1991)★★★, *The Dome Event* (1993)★★★, with Bill Laswell, Pete Namlook *Dark Side Of The Moog IV* (Fax 1996)★★★.

SCORPIONS (GERMANY)

This German hard rock group was formed by guitarists Rudolf and Michael Schenker (b. 10 January 1955, Savstedt, Germany) in 1971. With Klaus Meine (b. 25 May 1948; vocals), Lothar Heinberg (bass) and Wolfgang Dziony (drums), they exploded onto the international heavy rock scene with *Lonesome Crow* in 1972. This tough and exciting record was characterized by Schenker's distinctive, fiery guitarwork on his Gibson 'Flying V' and Klaus Meine's dramatic vocals. Soon after the album was released, Heinberg, Dziony and Schenker left, the latter joining UFO. Francis Buchholz and Jurgen Rosenthal stepped in on bass and drums, respectively, for the recording of *Fly To The Rainbow*. Ulrich Roth was recruited as Schenker's replacement in 1974 and Rudy Lenners took over the drum stool from Rosenthal the following year. The following releases, *Trance* and *Virgin Killer*, epitomized the Scorpions new-found confidence and unique style; a fusion of intimidating power-riffs, wailing guitar solos and melodic vocal lines. Produced by Dieter Dierks, the improvements musically were now matched technically. Their reputation began to grow throughout Europe and the Far East, backed up by exhaustive touring. *Taken By Force* saw Herman Rarebell replace Lenners, with the band branching out into anthemic power-ballads, bolstered by emotive production, for the first time. Although commercially successful, Roth was not happy with this move, and he left to form Electric Sun following a major tour to support the album. *Tokyo Tapes* was recorded on this tour and marked the end of the first phase of the band's career. This was a live set featuring renditions of their strongest numbers. Mathias Jabs was recruited as Roth's replacement, but had to step down temporarily in favour of Michael Schenker, who had just left UFO under acrimonious circumstances. Schenker contributed guitar on three tracks of *Lovedrive* and toured with them afterwards. He was replaced by Jabs permanently after collapsing onstage during their European tour in 1979. The band had now achieved a stable line-up, and shared the mutual goal of breaking through in the USA. Relentless touring schedules ensued and their albums leaned more and more towards sophisticated hard-edged melodic rock. *Blackout* made the US *Billboard* Top 10, as did the following *Love At First Sting* which featured 'Still Loving You', an enduring hard rock ballad. *World Wide Live* was released in 1985, another double live set, but this time only featuring material from the second phase of the band's career. It captured the band at their melodic best, peaking at number 14 in a four-month stay on the US chart. The band took a well-earned break before releasing *Savage Amusement* in 1988, their first studio album for almost four years. This marked a slight change in emphasis again, adopting a more restrained approach. Nevertheless it proved a huge success, reaching number 5 in the USA and number 1 throughout Europe. The band switched to Phonogram Records in 1989 and ended their 20-year association with producer Dieter Dierks. *Crazy World* followed and became their most successful album to date. The politically poignant 'Wind Of Change', lifted as a single, became their first million-seller as it reached the number 1 position in country after country around the world. Produced by Keith Olsen, *Crazy World* transformed the band's sound, ensuring enormous crossover potential without radically compromising their identity or alienating their original fanbase. Buchholz was sacked in 1992, at which time investigators began to look into the band's accounts for alleged tax evasion. His replacement was classically trained musician Ralph Heickermann, who had previously provided computer programming for Kingdom Come, as well as varied soundtrack work. Heickermann made his debut on a perfunctory 1995 live album, their third such venture. Allied to a lack of new material, *Live Bites* only served to heighten suspicions about the long-term viability and vitality of the band.

●ALBUMS: *Action/Lonesome Crow* (Brain 1972)★★★, *Fly To The Rainbow* (RCA 1974)★★★, *In Trance* (RCA 1975)★★★, *Virgin Killers* (RCA 1976)★★, *Taken By Force* (RCA 1978)★★, *Tokyo Tapes* (RCA 1978)★★, *Lovedrive* (EMI 1979)★★, *Animal Magnetism* (EMI 1980)★★, *Blackout* (EMI 1982)★★, *Love At First Sting* (EMI 1984)★★, *World Wide Live* (EMI 1985)★★★, *Savage Amusement* (EMI 1988)★★, *Crazy World* (Vertigo 1990)★★, *Face The Heat* (Vertigo 1993)★★, *Live Bites* (Mercury 1995)★, *Pure Instincts* (East West 1996)★★. Solo: Herman Rarebell *Nip In The Bud* (Harvest 1981)★.
●COMPILATIONS: *The Best Of The Scorpions* (RCA 1979)★★★, *The Best Of The Scorpions, Volume 2* (RCA 1984)★★, *Gold Ballads* (Harvest 1987)★★, *CD Box Set* (EMI 1991)★★, *Deadly Sting* (EMI 1995)★★. ●VIDEOS: *First Sting* (PMI 1985), *World Wide Live* (1985), *Crazy World Tour* (1991).

SCOTT, TOM

b. 19 May 1948, Los Angeles, California, USA. Scott's mother - Margery Wright - was a pianist, his father - Nathan Scott - a film and television composer. Scott played clarinet in high school and won a teenage competition with his Neoteric Trio at the Hollywood Bowl in 1965. He learned all the saxophones and played in the studios for TV shows such as *Ironside*. He performed on Roger Kellaway's *Spirit Feel* in 1967, playing fluent alto and soprano over a proto-fusion encounter of hard bop and rock music. As a member of Spontaneous Combustion in 1969, he played on *Come And Stick Your Head In*, an experimental record in the jazz-rock idiom. His own records - *Honeysuckle Breeze* (1967) and *Rural Still Life* (1968) - presented a tight, forceful jazz funk.

From his early 20s he wrote prolifically for television and films (including *Conquest Of The Planet Of The Apes*), his sound becoming the blueprint for LA cop show soundtracks: urgent, funky, streamlined. His band, the LA Express, became one of the most successful fusion bands of the 70s. Joni Mitchell used them as her backing band on *Miles Of Aisles* (and guested on 1975's *Tom Cat*) and George Harrison played slide guitar on *New York Connection*. 1987's *Streamlines* showed that Scott had not lost his sound, but an interest in samples of ethnic instruments had given his music a more world music feel.

● ALBUMS: *Honeysuckle Breeze* (1967)★★★, *Rural Still Life* (1968)★★★, with Spontaneous Combustion *Come And Stick Your Head In* (1969)★★★, *Tom Scott & the LA Express* (Ode 1974)★★★, *Tom Cat* (Ode 1975)★★, *New York Connection* (Ode 1975)★★, *Blow It Out* (Epic 1977)★★, *Apple Juice* (1981), *Desire* (Elektra 1982), *Streamlines* (GRP 1987)★★★, *Target* (1993), *Night Creatures* (GRP 1994)★★★.

● FILMS: *Americation* (1979).

SCOTT-HERON, GIL

b. 1 April 1949, Chicago, Illinois, USA. Raised in Jackson, Tennessee, by his grandmother, Scott-Heron moved to New York at the age of 13 and had published two novels (*The Vulture* and *The Nigger Factory*) plus a book of poems by the time he was 12. His estranged father played football for Glasgow Celtic. He met musician Brian Jackson when both were students at Lincoln University, Pennsylvania, and in 1972 they formed the Midnight Band to play their original blend of jazz, soul and prototype rap music. *Small Talk At 125th And Lenox* was mostly an album of poems (from his book of the same name), but later albums showed Scott-Heron developing into a skilled songwriter whose work was soon covered by other artists: for example, Labelle recorded his 'The Revolution Will Not Be Televised' and Esther Phillips made a gripping version of 'Home Is Where The Hatred Is'. In 1973 he had a minor hit with 'The Bottle'. *Winter In America* and *The First Minute Of A New Day*, for new label Arista, were both heavily jazz-influenced, but later sets saw Scott-Heron exploring more pop-oriented formats, and in 1976 he had a hit with the disco-based protest single, 'Johannesburg'. One of his best records of the 80s, *Reflections*, featured a fine version of Marvin Gaye's 'Inner City Blues'; but his strongest songs were generally his own barbed political diatribes, in which he confronted issues such as nuclear power, apartheid and poverty and made a series of scathing attacks on American politicians. Richard Nixon, Gerald Ford, Barry Goldwater and Jimmy Carter were all targets of his trenchant satire and his anti-Reagan rap, 'B-Movie', gave him another small hit in 1982. An important precursor of today's rap artists, Scott-Heron once described Jackson (who left the band in 1980) and himself as 'interpreters of the black experience'. However, by the 90s his view of the develop-

ment of rap had become more jaundiced: 'They need to study music. I played in several bands before I began my career as a poet. There's a big difference between putting words over some music, and blending those same words into the music. There's not a lot of humour. They use a lot of slang and colloquialisms, and you don't really see inside the person. Instead, you just get a lot of posturing'. In 1994 he released his first album for ten years, *Spirits*, which began with 'Message To The Messenger', an address to today's rap artists: 'Young rappers, one more suggestion before I get out of your way, But I appreciate the respect you give me and what you got to say, I'm sayin' protect your community and spread that respect around, Tell brothers and sisters they got to calm that bullshit down, 'Cause we're terrorizin' our old folks and we brought fear into our homes'.

● ALBUMS: *Small Talk At 125th And Lenox* (Flying Dutchman 1972)★★★, *Free Will* (Flying Dutchman 1972)★★★, *Pieces Of A Man* (Flying Dutchman 1973)★★★, *Winter In America* (Strata East 1974)★★★, *The First Minute Of A New Day* (Arista 1975)★★★, *From South Africa To South Carolina* (Arista 1975)★★★, *It's Your World* (Arista 1976)★★★, *Bridges* (Arista 1977)★★★, *Secrets* (Arista 1978)★★★, *1980* (Arista 1980)★★★, *Real Eyes* (Arista 1980)★★★, *Reflections* (Arista 1981)★★★, *Moving Target* (Arista 1982)★★★, *Spirits* (TVT Records 1994)★★★.

● COMPILATIONS: *The Revolution Will Not Be Televised* (Flying Dutchman 1974)★★★★, *The Mind Of Gil Scott-Heron* (Arista 1979)★★★, *The Best Of Gil Scott-Heron* (Arista 1984)★★★★, *Tales Of Gil* double album (Essential 1990)★★★, *Glory: The Gil Scott-Heron Collection* (Arista 1990)★★★.

● VIDEOS: *Tales Of Gil* (1990).

SEALS AND CROFTS

A duo consisting of Jim Seals (b. 17 October 1941, Sidney, Texas, USA) and Dash Crofts (b. 14 August 1940, Cisco, Texas, USA), Seals And Crofts were one of the most popular soft rock-pop acts of the 70s. The pair first worked together in 1958 as guitarist (Seals) and drummer (Crofts) for Texan singer Dean Beard, with whom they recorded a number of singles that did not chart. When Beard was asked to join the Champs, of 'Tequila' fame, Seals and Crofts came along, relocating to Los Angeles. They stayed with the Champs until 1965, when Crofts returned to Texas. The following year, Seals joined a group called the Dawnbreakers, and Crofts returned to Los Angeles to join as well. Both Seals and Crofts converted to the Baha'i religion in 1969 (10 years later they left the music business to devote themselves to it full-time). Following the split of the Dawnbreakers, Seals and Crofts continued as an acoustic music duo (Seals played guitar, saxophone and violin, Crofts guitar and mandolin), recording their first album, which did not chart, for the Talent Associates label. Meanwhile, the pair performed live and built a following. In 1970 *Down Home*, made the charts and led to a label change to Warner Brothers Records. Their second album for that company, 1972's *Summer Breeze*, made number 7 on the US charts and the title single reached number 6. ('Summer Breeze' also provided the Isley Brothers with a UK Top 20 hit in 1974.) It was followed in 1973 by their best-selling *Diamond Girl*, which also yielded a number 6 title single. They maintained their popularity throughout the mid-70s, coming up with yet another number 6 single, 'Get Closer', in 1976. Following the release of the 1978 album *Takin' It Easy* and the same-titled single, which became their final chart entries, Seals And Crofts became less involved in music and devoted themselves to their faith.

●ALBUMS: *Seals And Crofts* (TA 1970)★★★, *Down Home* (TA 1970)★★★, *Year Of Sunday* (Warners 1972)★★★, *Summer Breeze* (Warners 1972)★★★, *Diamond Girl* (Warners 1973)★★★, *Unborn Child* (Warners 1974)★★, *I'll Play For You* (Warners 1975)★★, *Get Closer* (Warners 1976)★★, *Sudan Village* (Warners 1976)★★, *One On One* film soundtrack (Warners 1977)★★, *Takin' It Easy* (Warners 1978)★★, *The Longest Road* (1980)★★.
●COMPILATIONS: *Greatest Hits* (Warners 1975)★★★.

SEALS, TROY

b. 16 November 1938, Big Hill, Kentucky, USA. Seals, a cousin to Dan Seals, began playing guitar in his teens and formed his own rock 'n' roll band. In 1960, he was working in a club in Ohio with Lonnie Mack and Denny Rice, where he befriended a visiting performer, Conway Twitty. Twitty introduced him to Jo Ann Campbell, who had had a few successes on the US pop charts. Seals married Campbell and they worked as a duo, making the US R&B charts with 'I Found A Love, Oh What A Love' in 1964. After some time working as a construction worker, Seals moved to Nashville to sell his songs. 'There's A Honky Tonk Angel (Who'll Take Me Back In)', written by Seals and Rice, was a US country number 1 for Conway Twitty, while Cliff Richard's version for the UK market was withdrawn when he discovered what honky tonk angels were (!). Elvis Presley also recorded the song, along with Seals' 'Pieces Of My Life'. Seals' most recorded song is 'We Had It All', written with Donnie Fritts, which has been recorded by Rita Coolidge, Waylon Jennings, Brenda Lee, Stu Stevens and Scott Walker. His songwriting partners include Don Goodman and Will Jennings, a university professor in English literature, and together they all wrote 'Feelins'', a US country number 1 for Conway Twitty and Loretta Lynn; with Mentor Williams 'When We Make Love', a US country number 1 for Alabama; with Max D. Barnes 'Don't Take It Away' (another US country number 1 for Conway Twitty) and 'Storms Of Life' (Randy Travis). One of his best songs is the mysterious 'Seven Spanish Angels', written with Eddie Setser, a US country number 1 for Willie Nelson and Ray Charles. Seals has done much session work as a guitarist and has had a few minor country hits himself.

●ALBUMS: *Now Presenting Troy Seals* (1973)★★, *Troy Seals* (Columbia 1976)★★.

SEATRAIN

The original Seatrain line-up - John Gregory (guitar/vocals), Richard Greene (violin), Donald Kretmar (saxophone/bass), Andy Kulberg (bass/flute) and Roy Blumenfeld (drums) - evolved from the New York-based Blues Project and this particular quintet completed the previous group's contractual obligations with the *Planned Obsolescence* album. The unit's first official self-titled album was released in 1969. By this point the group had been augmented by lyricist James T. Roberts and this imaginative collection fused such seemingly disparate elements as rock, bluegrass and Elizabethan-styled folksiness. Internal problems sadly doomed this quirky line-up, and after approximately 25 members had passed through the band, a stable Seatrain line-up emerged with only Kulberg and Greene remaining from the initial band. The three newcomers were Lloyd Baskin (keyboards/vocals), Larry Atamanuk (drums) and former Earth Opera member Peter Rowan (guitar/vocals). A second album, also entitled *Seatrain*, was recorded in London under the aegis of George Martin, as was their third collection, *The Marblehead Messenger*. Both albums displayed an engaging, eclectic style, but were doomed to commercial indifference. The departure of Rowan and Greene to the critically acclaimed Muleskinner was a severe blow and although Kulberg and Baskin persevered by bringing Peter Walsh (guitar), Bill Elliott (keyboards) and Julio Coronado (drums) into the group, a fourth release, *Watch*, was a major disappointment. When Seatrain latterly disbanded, Kulberg pursued a career composing for numerous television shows.

●ALBUMS: *Seatrain* (A&M 1969)★★, *Seatrain* (Capitol 1970)★★, *The Marblehead Messenger* (Capitol 1971)★★★, *Watch* (1973)★★.

SEBASTIAN, JOHN

b. 17 March 1944, New York, USA. The son of the famous classical harmonica player John Sebastian. John Jnr. is best known for his seminal jug band/rock fusion with the much-loved Lovin' Spoonful in the 60s, which established him as one of the finest American songwriters of the era. When the Spoonful finally collapsed Sebastian started a solo career that was briefly threatened when he was asked to become the fourth member of Crosby, Stills And Nash, but he declined when it was found that Stephen Stills wanted him to play drums. In 1969 his performance was one of the highlights of the Woodstock Festival, singing his warm and friendly material to a deliriously happy audience. His tie-dye jacket and jeans appearance, warm rapport, and acoustic set (aided by copious amounts of LSD) elevated him to star status. Sebastian debuted in 1970 with an outstanding solo work *John B Sebastian*, containing much of the spirit of Woodstock. Notable tracks such as the autobiographical 'Red Eye Express' and the evocative 'How Have You Been', were bound together with one of his finest songs, the painfully short 'She's A Lady'. Less than two minutes long, this love song was perfect for the times, and was a lyrical triumph with lines like 'She's a lady, and I chance to see her in my shuffling daze, she's a lady, hypnotised me there that day, I came to play in my usual way, hey'. Simply accompanied by Stills' and Crosby's mellow guitars, it remains a modern classic. Sebastian faltered with the uneven *Four Of Us*, a travelogue of hippie ideology but followed a few months later with *Real Live*, an engaging record recorded at four gigs in California. At that time Sebastian was performing at a punishing rate throughout Europe and America. *Tarzana Kid* in 1974 sold poorly, but has latterly grown in stature with critics. At this time Sebastian was working with the late Lowell George, and a strong Little Feat influence is shown. The album's high point is a Sebastian/George classic, the beautiful 'Face Of Appalachia'. Two years later Sebastian was asked to write the theme song for a US comedy television series, *Welcome Back Kotter*. The result was a number 1 hit, 'Welcome Back'. Astonishingly, since then, no new album had appeared until 1992, when a Japanese label released his most recent songs. Throughout that time, however, Sebastian never stopped working. He accompanied Sha Na Na and NRBQ on many lengthy tours, appeared as a television presenter, wrote a children's book and among other commissions he composed the music for the *Care Bears* television series. Severe problems with his throat threatened his singing career at one point. He declined to be part of the 1992 re-formed Lovin' Spoonful. Sebastian was, is and always will be the heart and soul of that band. He returned with the delightful *Tar Beach* in 1993. Although long-term fans noted that his voice was slightly weaker, the album contained a varied mixture of rock, blues and country. Many songs he had written more than a decade earlier were included, the most notable being his uplifting tribute to Smokey Robinson; 'Smokey Don't Go'. Together with the J-Band, which featured Jimmy Vivino, Fritz Richmond and James Wormworth, he released *I Want My Roots* in 1996. Hardly prolific, Sebastian remains one of the best American songwriters of the 60s. It is a great pity that he is not more active in the recording studio.

●ALBUMS: *John B. Sebastian* (Reprise 1970)★★★★, *The Four Of Us* (Reprise 1971)★★, *Real Live* (Reprise 1971)★★★, *Tarzana Kid* (Reprise 1974)★★★, *Welcome Back* (Warners 1976)★★, *Tar Beach* (Shanachie 1993)★★, *I Want My Roots* (Music Masters 1996)★★, *King Biscuit Flower Hour: John Sebastian* (BMG 1996)★★★.

SEGER, BOB

b. 6 May 1945, Detroit, Michigan, USA. Seger began his long career in the early 60s as a member of the Decibels. He subsequently joined Doug Brown and the Omens as organist, but was installed as their vocalist and songwriter when such talents surfaced. The group made its recording debut as the Beach Bums, with 'The Ballad Of The Yellow Beret', but this pastiche of the contemporaneous Barry Sadler hit, 'The Ballad Of The Green Beret', was withdrawn in the face of a threatened lawsuit. The act then became known as Bob Seger and the Last Heard and as such completed several powerful singles, notably 'East Side Story' (1966) and 'Heavy Music' (1967). Seger was signed by Capitol Records in 1968 and the singer's new group, the Bob Seger System, enjoyed a US Top 20 hit that year with 'Ramblin' Gamblin' Man'. Numerous excellent hard-rock releases followed, including the impressive *Mongrel* album, but the artist was unable to repeat his early success and disbanded the group in 1971.

Having spent a period studying for a college degree, Seger returned to music with his own label, Palladium, and three unspectacular albums ensued. He garnered considerable acclaim for his 1974 single, 'Get Out Of Denver', which has since become a much-covered classic. However, Seger only achieved deserved commercial success upon returning to Capitol when *Beautiful Loser* reached the lower reaches of the US album charts (number 131). Now fronting the Silver Bullet Band - Drew Abbott (guitar), Robyn Robbins (keyboards), Alto Reed (saxophone), Chris Campbell (bass) and Charlie Allen Martin (drums) - Seger reinforced his in-concert popularity with the exciting *Live Bullet*, which was in turn followed by *Night Moves*, his first platinum disc. The title track reached the US Top 5 in 1977, a feat 'Still The Same' repeated the following year. The latter hit was culled from the triple-platinum album, *Stranger In Town*, which also included 'Hollywood Nights', 'Old Time Rock 'N' Roll' and 'We've Got Tonight'. By couching simple sentiments in traditional, R&B-based rock, the set confirmed Seger's ability to articulate the aspirations of blue-collar America, a feature enhanced by his punishing tour schedule. *Against The Wind* also topped the US album charts, while another live set, *Nine Tonight*, allowed the artist time to recharge creative energies.

He recruited Jimmy Iovine for *The Distance* which stalled at number 5. While Seger is rightly seen as a major artist in the USA he has been unable to appeal to anything more than a cult audience in the UK. Among his later hit singles were the Rodney Crowell song 'Shame On The Moon' (1983), 'Old Time Rock 'n' Roll' (from the film *Risky Business*), 'Understanding' (from the film *Teachers*) and the number 1 hit 'Shakedown', taken from the soundtrack of *Beverly Hills Cop II*. Seger released his first studio album for five years in 1991. Co-produced by Don Was, it was a Top 10 hit in the USA, clearly showing his massive following had remained. A highly successful greatest hits collection issued in 1994 (with copious sleevenotes from Seger) also demonstrated just what a huge following he still has. *It's A Mystery* came after a long gap, presumably buoyed by recent success. It ploughed typical Segar territory with regular riff rockers such as 'Lock And Load' alongside acoustic forays such as 'By The River'. The most interesting track on the album was the title track, a great mantric rocker sounding less like Segar and more like Hüsker Dü. He followed the success of the album with a box-office breaking tour of America in 1996. Ticketmaster claimed that the concert in his hometown sold 100,000 tickets in 57 minutes.

●ALBUMS: *Ramblin' Gamblin' Man* (Capitol 1969)★★★, *Noah* (Capitol 1969)★★★, *Mongrel* (Capitol 1970)★★★, *Brand New Morning* (Capitol 1971)★★★, *Back In '72* (Palladium 1973)★★★, *Smokin' O.P.'s* (Palladium 1973)★★★, *Seven* (Palladium 1974)★★★, *Beautiful Loser* (Capitol 1975)★★★, *Live Bullet* (Capitol 1976)★★★★, *Night Moves* (Capitol 1976)★★★★, *Stranger In Town* (Capitol 1978)★★★★, *Against The Wind* (Capitol 1980)★★★, *Nine Tonight* (Capitol 1981)★★★, *The Distance* (Capitol 1982)★★★, *Like A Rock* (Capitol 1986)★★★, *The Fire Inside* (Capitol 1991)★★★, *It's A Mystery* (Capitol 1995)★★★.

●COMPILATIONS: *Bob Seger And The Silver Bullet Band Greatest Hits* (Capitol 1994)★★★★.

●FILMS: *American Pop* (1981).

SENSATIONAL ALEX HARVEY BAND

Formed in 1972 when veteran vocalist Alex Harvey (b. 5 February 1935, Glasgow, Scotland, d. 4 February 1981) teamed with struggling Glasgow group, Tear Gas. Zal Cleminson (b. 4 May 1949; guitar), Hugh McKenna (b. 28 November 1949; keyboards), Chris Glen (b. 6 November 1950, Paisley, Renfrewshire, Scotland; bass) and Ted McKenna (b. 10 March 1950; drums) gave the singer the uncultured power his uncompromising rasp required and were the perfect foil to the sense of drama he created. Armed with a musical and cultural heritage, Harvey embarked on a unique direction combining elements of rock, R&B and the British music hall. He created the slum-kid Vambo, celebrated pulp fiction with 'Sergeant Fury' and extolled a passion for 'b-movie' lore in 'Don't Worry About The Lights Mother, They're Burning Big Louie Tonight'. *Framed*, SAHB's debut, was accompanied by a period of frenetic live activity. *Next* reflected a consequent confidence which was especially apparent on the title track, a harrowing, atmospheric rendition of a Jacques Brel composition. The quintet continued their commercial ascendancy with *The Impossible Dream* and *Tomorrow Belongs To Me*, while enhancing their in-concert reputation with a series of excellent and increasingly ambitious stage shows. Harvey's presence was a determining factor in their visual appeal, but Cleminson's intelligent use of clown make-up and mime brought yet another factor to the unit's creative think-tank. *Live* encapsulated this era, while SAHB's irreverence was made clear in their exaggerated reading of Tom Jones' hit 'Delilah', which gave the group a UK Top 10 single. Its success inspired The

Penthouse Tapes, which featured such disparate favourites as 'Crazy Horses' (the Osmonds) 'School's Out' (Alice Cooper) and 'Goodnight Irene' (Lead Belly). The group enjoyed another hit single with 'Boston Tea Party' (1976), but the rigorous schedule extracted a toll on their vocalist. He entered hospital to attend to a recurring liver problem, during which time the remaining members recorded *Fourplay* as SAHB (without Harvey). Hugh McKenna was then replaced by Tommy Eyre and in August 1977 Harvey rejoined the group to complete *Rock Drill*. However, three months later he walked out on his colleagues during a rehearsal for BBC's *Sight And Sound* programme and despite the ill-feeling this caused, it was later accepted that his return had been premature given the extent of his illness. Despite pursuing a solo career at a more measured pace, Harvey died as a result of a heart attack on 4 February 1981. Ted McKenna, Cleminson and Glen had meanwhile formed the short-lived Zal, with Billy Rankin (guitar) and Leroi Jones (vocals), but this illstarred ensemble struggled in the face of punk and split up in April 1978. McKenna later joined Rory Gallagher and MSG, while Cleminson was briefly a member of Nazareth. In 1992 members of the original band were reunited as the Sensational Party Boys. The band became very popular once more, in their native Glasgow and surrounding areas. They officially changed their name in August 1993 back to the Sensational Alex Harvey Band with the original line-up (less Harvey). Their credible front man is ex-Zero Zero and Strangeways vocalist Stevie Doherty (b. 17 July 1959, Coatbridge, Scotland). He is able to perform the catalogue with great presence and power, without attempting to emulate Harvey.

●ALBUMS: *Framed* (Vertigo 1972)★★, *Next* (Vertigo 1973)★★★, *The Impossible Dream* (Vertigo 1974)★★★, *Tomorrow Belongs To Me* (Vertigo 1975)★★★, *Live* (Vertigo 1975)★★★, *The Penthouse Tapes* (Vertigo 1976)★★★, *SAHB Stories* (Mountain 1976)★★★, *Rock Drill* (Mountain 1978)★★, *Live In Concert* (Windsong 1991)★★★, *Live On The Test* (Windsong 1994)★★★.

●COMPILATIONS: *Big Hits And Close Shaves* (Vertigo 1977)★★★, *Collectors Items* (Mountain 1980)★★★, *The Best Of The Sensational Alex Harvey Band* (RCA 1982)★★★★, *The Legend* (Sahara 1985)★★★, *Anthology - Alex Harvey* (1986)★★★, *Collection - Alex Harvey* (Castle 1986)★★★. SAHB (without Alex) *Fourplay* (Mountain 1977)★★.

●VIDEOS: *Live On The Test* (Windsong 1994).

SESSIONS, RONNIE

b. 7 December 1948, Henrietta, Oklahoma, USA. Sessions grew up in Bakersfield, California. His first record, in 1957, was a novelty version of Little Richard's 'Keep A-Knockin'' made with Richard's band. Through a schoolboy friend he knew the host, Herb Henson, of a television series, *Trading Post*, and he became a regular performer. He studied to be a vet but also recorded for local labels and, joining Gene Autry's Republic label in 1968, he had regional hits with 'The Life Of Riley' and 'More Than Satisfied'. He moved to Nashville and his songwriting talent was recognized by Hank Cochran. However, his first country hits were with revivals of pop songs, 'Never Been To Spain' and 'Tossin' And Turnin''. Over at MCA, he had major country hits in 1977 with 'Wiggle, Wiggle' and Bobby Goldsboro's 'Me And Millie (Stompin' Grapes And Gettin' Silly)'. He failed to consolidate his success and, after being dropped by MCA in 1980, he has hardly recorded since. His last US country chart entry was in 1986 with 'I Bought The Shoes That Just Walked Out On Me'.

●ALBUMS: *Ronnie Sessions* (MCA 1977)★★.

SEX PISTOLS

This incandescent UK punk group came together under the aegis of entrepreneur Malcolm McLaren during the summer of 1975. Periodically known as the Swankers, with lead vocalist Wally Nightingale, they soon metamorphosized into the Sex Pistols with a line up comprising: Steve Jones (b. 3 May 1955, London, England; guitar), Paul Cook (b. 20 July 1956, London, England; drums), Glen Matlock (b. 27 August 1956, Paddington, London, England; bass) and Johnny Rotten (b. John Lydon, 31 January 1956, Finsbury Park, London, England; vocals). By 1976 the group was playing irregularly around London and boasted a small following of teenagers, whose spiked hair, torn clothes and safety pins echoed the new fashion that McLaren was transforming into commodity. The group's gigs became synonymous with violence, which reached a peak during the 100 Club's Punk Rock Festival when a girl was blinded in a glass-smashing incident involving the group's most fearful follower, Sid Vicious. The adverse publicity did not prevent the group from signing to EMI Records later that year when they also released their first single, 'Anarchy In The UK'. From Rotten's sneering laugh at the opening of the song to the final seconds of feedback, it was a riveting debut. The Pistols promoted the work on London Weekend Television's *Today* programme, which ended in a stream of four-letter abuse that brought the group banner headlines in the following morning's tabloid press. More controversy ensued when the group's 'Anarchy' tour was decimated and the single suffered distribution problems and bans from shops. Eventually, it peaked at number 38 in the UK charts. Soon afterwards, the group was dropped from EMI in a blaze of publicity. By February 1977, Matlock was replaced by punk caricature Sid Vicious (b. John Simon Ritchie, 10 May 1957, London, England, d. 2 February 1979). The following month, the group was signed to A&M Records outside the gates of Buckingham Palace. One week later, A&M cancelled the contract, with McLaren picking up another parting cheque of £40,000. After reluctantly signing to the small label Virgin Records, the group issued 'God Save The Queen'. The single tore into the heart of British nation-

alism at a time when the populace was celebrating the Queen's Jubilee. Despite a daytime radio ban the single rose to number 1 in the *New Musical Express* chart (number 2 in the 'official' charts, though some commentators detected skulduggery at play to prevent it from reaching the top spot). The Pistols suffered for their art as outraged royalists attacked them whenever they appeared on the streets. A third single, the melodic 'Pretty Vacant' (largely the work of the departed Matlock), proved their most accessible single to date and restored them to the Top 10. By the winter the group hit again with 'Holidays In The Sun' and issued their controversially titled album, *Never Mind The Bollocks - Here's The Sex Pistols*. The work rocketed to number 1 in the UK album charts amid partisan claims that it was a milestone in rock. In truth, it was a more patchy affair, containing a preponderance of previously released material which merely underlined that the group was running short of ideas. An ill-fated attempt to capture the group's story on film wasted much time and revenue, while a poorly received tour of America fractured the Pistols' already strained relationship. In early 1978, Rotten announced that he was leaving the group after a gig in San Francisco. According to the manager Malcolm McLaren he was fired. McLaren, meanwhile, was intent on taking the group to Brazil in order that they could be filmed playing with the train robber, Ronnie Biggs. Vicious, incapacitated by heroin addiction, could not make the trip, but Jones and Cook were happy to indulge in the publicity stunt. McLaren mischievously promoted Biggs as the group's new lead singer and another controversial single emerged: 'Cosh The Driver'. It was later retitled 'No One Is Innocent (A Punk Prayer)' and issued as a double a-side with Vicious's somehow charming rendition of the Frank Sinatra standard, 'My Way'. McLaren's movie was finally completed by director Julien Temple under the title *The Great Rock 'N' Roll Swindle*. A self-conscious rewriting of history, it callously wrote Matlock out of the script and saw the unavailable Rotten relegated to old footage. While the film was being completed, the Pistols' disintegration was completed. Vicious, now the centre of the group, recorded a lame version of Eddie Cochran's 'C'mon Everybody' before returning to New York. On 12 October 1978, his girlfriend Nancy Spungen was found stabbed in his hotel room and Vicious was charged with murder. While released on bail, he suffered a fatal overdose of heroin and died peacefully in his sleep on the morning of 2 February 1979. Virgin Records continued to issue the desultory fragments of Pistols work that they had on catalogue, including the appropriately titled compilation, *Flogging A Dead Horse*. The group's impact as the grand symbol of UK punk rock has ensured their longevity. The unholy saga appropriately ended in the High Court a decade later in 1986, when Rotten and his fellow ex-Pistols won substantial damages against their former manager. After years of rumour and sigh it was confirmed that the original band would re-form for one lucrative tour in 1996. The press conference to launch their rebirth was at the 100 Club in London. The usual abuse was dished out, giving rise to the fact that nothing has changed except the lines on their faces and rising hairlines. They think Green Day and Oasis are too 'poppy'. The tour was awaited with eagerness as this was really one case of putting their mouths where the money is. Their debut at Finsbury Park was nostalgic rather than groundbreaking. Rotten was still obnoxious and they still hate Matlock. What they did prove, however, was that they still can play and sweat, just like the hundreds of pretenders that followed in their wake over the past two decades.

●ALBUMS: *Never Mind The Bollocks - Here's The Sex Pistols* (Virgin 1977)★★★★★, *Filthy Lucre Live* (Virgin 1996)★★★.

●COMPILATIONS: *The Great Rock 'N' Roll Swindle* (Virgin 1979)★★★, *Some Product - Carri On Sex Pistols* (Virgin 1979)★★, *Flogging A Dead Horse* (Virgin 1980)★★, *Kiss This* (Virgin 1992)★★, *Alive* (Essential 1996)★★, *This Is Crap* double CD reissue with *Never Mind The Bollocks* (Virgin 1996)★★★.

●VIDEOS: *The Great Rock 'N' Roll Swindle* (Virgin Video 1982), *Live At Longhorns* (Pearson New Entertainment 1996), *Live In Winterland* (Pearson New Emtertainment 1996).

●FURTHER READING: *Sex Pistols Scrap Book*, Ray Stevenson. *Sex Pistols: The Inside Story*, Fred and Judy Vermorel. *Sex Pistols File*, Ray Stevenson. *The Great Rock 'N' Roll Swindle: A Novel*, Michael Moorcock. *The Sid Vicious Family Album*, Anne Beverley. *The Sex Pistols Diary*, Lee Wood. *I Was A Teenage Sex Pistol*, Glen Matlock. *12 Days On The Road: The Sex Pistols And America*, Neil Monk and Jimmy Guterman. *Chaos: The Sex Pistols*, Bob Gruen. *England's Dreaming: Sex Pistols And Punk Rock*, Jon Savage. *Never Mind The B*ll*cks: A Photographed Record Of The Sex Pistols*, Dennis Morris. *Sex Pistols: Agents Of Anarchy*, Tony Scrivener. *Sid's Way: The Life And Death Of Sid Vicious*, Keith Bateson and Alan Parker. *Rotten: No Irish, No Blacks, No Dogs*, Johnny Rotten. *Sex Pistols Retrospective*, no author listed. *Sid Vicious Rock 'N' Roll Star,* Malcom Butt. *Sid Vicious: They Died Too Young*, Tom Stockdale.

●FILMS: *The Great Rock 'N' Roll Swindle.*

SHA NA NA

Spearheading the US rock 'n' roll revivalism that began in the late 60s, the group emerged from Columbia University in 1968 with a repertoire derived exclusively from the 50s, and a choreographed stage act that embraced a jiving contest for audience participants. Looking the anachronistic part - gold lamé, brilliantine cockades, drainpiped hosiery, *et al* - the initial line-up consisted of vocalists Scott Powell, Johnny Contardo, Frederick Greene, Don York and Richard Joffe; guitarists Chris Donald, Elliot Cahn and Henry Gross; pianists Scott Symon and John Bauman, plus Bruce Clarke (bass), Jocko Marcellino (drums) and - the only

musician with a revered past - saxophonist Leonard Baker (ex-Danny And The Juniors). Surprisingly, there were few personnel changes until a streamlining to a less cumbersome 10-piece in 1973. The band were launched internationally by a show-stealing appearance at 1969's Woodstock Festival (which was included in the subsequent film and album spin-offs), but their onstage recreations of old sounds did not easily translate onto disc - especially if the original versions had emotional significance for the listener. From 1972's *The Night Is Still Young*, 'Bounce In Your Buggy' - one of few self-composed numbers - was the closest the outfit ever came to a hit (though Gross enjoyed a solo US smash in 1976 with 'Shannon'). Nevertheless, the approbation of the famous was manifest in Keith Moon's compering of a Sha Na Na bash in 1971 and John Lennon's choice of the band to open his One-For-One charity concert in New York a year later. By 1974, however, their act had degenerated to a dreary repetition that took its toll in discord, nervous breakdowns and more unresolvable internal problems culminating in a fatal heroin overdose by Vincent Taylor, a latter-day member. Yet Sha Na Na's early example enabled archivist-performers such as Darts, Shakin' Stevens and the Stray Cats to further the cause of a seemingly outmoded musical form.

●ALBUMS: *Rock & Roll Is Here To Stay* (Kama Sutra 1969)★★★, *The Night Is Still Young* (Kama Sutra 1972)★★★, *The Golden Age Of Rock & Roll* (Kama Sutra 1973)★★, *Sha Na Na Is Here To Stay* (Buddah 1975)★★, *Rock And Roll Revival* (1977)★★.

●COMPILATIONS: *20 Greatest Hits* (Black Tulip 1989)★★★.

●FILMS: *Grease* (1978).

STEVENS, SHAKIN'

b. Michael Barrett, 4 March 1948, Ely, South Glamorgan, Wales. A rock 'n' roll singer in the style of the early Elvis Presley, Stevens brought this 50s spirit to a long series of pop hits during the 80s. In the late 60s he was lead singer with a Welsh rock revival group, the Backbeats which became Shakin' Stevens And The Sunsets. During 1970-73 the band recorded unsuccessful albums for EMI, CBS and Dureco in Holland, where the Sunsets had a large following. In 1976, they recorded a cover version of the Hank Mizell hit 'Jungle Rock' before disbanding. Shakin' Stevens then began a solo career appearing on stage in Jack Good's West End musical *Elvis* and on UK television in a new series of *Oh Boy!*, Good's 50s live music show. His recording career still faltered, however, when a 1977 album for Track was followed by commercially unsuccessful revivals of such 50s hits as Roy Head's 'Treat Her Right' and Jody Reynolds' death song 'Endless Sleep', produced by ex-Springfields member Mike Hurst at CBS. A change of producer to Stuart Colman in 1980 brought Stevens' first Top 20 hit, 'Marie Marie', first recorded by the Blasters and the following year Colman's infectious rockabilly arrangement of the 1954 Rosemary Clooney number 1

'This Ole House' topped the UK chart. The backing group was revival band Matchbox.

Over the next seven years, Stevens had over 20 Top 20 hits in the UK, although he made almost no impact in the USA. Among his hits were three number 1s - a revival of Jim Lowe's 1956 song 'Green Door' (1981), Stevens' own 'Oh Julie' (1982) and 'Merry Christmas Everyone' (1985). With an audience equally divided between young children and the middle-aged, his other recordings included brief excursions into soul (the Supremes' 'Come See About Me' in 1987) and ballads (the Bing Crosby/Grace Kelly film theme 'True Love', 1988), while he duetted with fellow Welsh artist Bonnie Tyler on 'A Rockin' Good Way (To Mess Around And Fall In Love)' (1984), which was first recorded in 1960 by Dinah Washington and Brook Benton.

At the dawn of the 90s, there were signs that Stevens' hold over his British audiences was faltering. For while the Pete Hammond-produced 'I Might' reached the Top 20, his subsequent records in 1990/1 made little impact. A major promotion for the compilation *The Epic Years* (billed as Shaky) failed to dent the UK top 50. 1993 started badly for Stevens as litigation with his former band the Sunsets was resolved, both Dave Edmunds and Shaky having to pay out £500,000 in back royalties.

●ALBUMS: *A Legend* (Parlophone 1970)★★, *I'm No J.D.* (CBS 1971)★★, *Rockin' And Shakin'* (Contour 1972)★, *Shakin' Stevens And The Sunsets* (Emerald 1973)★, *Shakin' Stevens* (Track 1977)★, *Take One!* (Epic 1979)★★, *This Ole House* (Epic 1981)★★, *Shaky* (Epic 1981)★★, *Give Me Your Heart Tonight* (Epic 1982)★★, *The Bop Won't Stop* (Epic 1983)★★, *Lipstick, Powder And Paint* (Epic 1985)★★, *Manhattan Melodrama* (CJS 1985)★★, *Let's Boogie* (Epic 1987)★★, *A Whole Lotta Shaky* (Epic 1988)★★, *Rock 'N' Roll* (Telstar 1990)★★, *Merry Christmas Everyone* (1991)★.

●COMPILATIONS: *Greatest Hits* (Epic 1984)★★, *The Track Years* (MFP 1986)★★, *The Epic Years* (Epic 1992)★★, *Greatest Hits* (Rhino 1995)★★★.

●VIDEOS: *Shakin' Stevens Video Show Volumes 1&2* (CMV 1989).

SHAKTI

Formed in the mid-70s, Shakti, defined on the sleeve notes of its debut album to be Sanskrit for 'creative intelligence, beauty and power', was a brave and innovative attempt to fuse music from the east and west. The first line-up featured Zakir Hussain (tabla, percussion, vocals), R. Raghavan (mridangam, a south Indian cylindrical drum), Lakshminarayana Shankar (violin, viola, vocals), V.H. 'Vikku' Vinayakram (ghatam, a south Indian clay drum) and John McLaughlin (guitar/vocals). Raghavan appeared only on the group's debut album. McLaughlin had previosly worked with Graham Bond and then with Miles Davis in New York during the late 60s, but began to experiment with Indian textures on his 1971 solo album, *My Goal's Beyond*, also forming the Mahavishnu Orchestra. The idea for Shakti was to explore more deeply elements of Hindustani (north Indian) and Karnatic (south Indian) classical styles, allied to western improvised jazz. Shakti's three mid-70s albums were recorded in New York in two years alongside extensive touring. The first of these, *Shakti With John McLaughlin*, was recorded live at Southampton College in Long Island in July 1975, capturing the group in its most effective setting. Both *A Handful Of Beauty* and *Natural Elements* saw the group's musicianship progress as they learnt the secrets of each member's tradition, but the group's rise was forestalled by CBS Records' reluctance to offer further sponsorship. The group did re-form for a tour of India in 1985, but, although all the members were keen to resurrect the project, their various commitments precluded it.

●ALBUMS: *Shakti With John McLaughlin* (Columbia 1976)★★★, *A Handful Of Beauty* (Columbia 1976)★★★, *Natural Elements* (Columbia 1977)★★★.

●COMPILATIONS: *Shakti With John McLaughlan* (Sony 1991)★★★, *The Best Of Shakti* (Sony 1994)★★★.

SHALAMAR

This group was created by Dick Griffey, booking agent for US television's *Soul Train* show, and Simon Soussan, a veteran of Britain's 'northern soul' scene. The latter produced 'Uptown Festival', a medley of popular Tamla/Motown favourites, which was issued on Griffey's Solar label. Although credited to 'Shalamar', the track featured session musicians, but its success inspired Griffey to create a performing group. Jody Watley (b. 30 January 1959, Chicago, Illinois, USA), Jeffrey Daniels and Gerald Brown were recruited via *Soul Train* in 1977, although Brown was replaced the following year by Howard Hewitt (b. Akron, Ohio, USA). 'The Second Time Around' gave the trio an R&B chart topper in 1979, but subsequent releases were better received in the UK where lightweight soul/disco offerings, including 'I Can Make You Feel Good', 'A Night To Remember' and 'There It Is', provided three Top 10 entries in 1982. Daniels and Watley then left the group to pursue solo careers. Their replacements, Delisa Davis and Micki Free, joined in 1984. The group won a Grammy award for 'Don't Get Stopped In Beverly Hills', a track from *Heartbeat* used in the Eddie Murphy film *Beverly Hills Cop*, but Hewitt's departure in 1976 eroded any newfound confidence. Justin restored the group to a trio, continuing to attain further, albeit minor, hit singles. By now Shalamar's golden, if brief period had ended; nevertheless the Shalamar name survived into the late 80s when Justin, along with newcomers Free and Davis, recorded *Circumstantial Evidence*.

●ALBUMS: *Uptown Festival* (Soul Train 1977)★★, *Disco Gardens* (Solar 1978)★★, *Big Fun* (Solar 1979)★★★, *Three For Love* (Solar 1981)★★★, *Go For It* (Solar 1981)★★★, *Friends* (Solar 1982)★★★, *The Look* (Solar 1982)★★★, *Heartbreak* (Solar 1984)★★, *Circumstantial Evidence* (Solar 1987)★★, *Wake Up* (Solar 1990)★★.

●COMPILATIONS: *Greatest Hits* (Solar 1982)★★★, *The*

Greatest Hits (Stylus 1986)★★★, *Here It Is - The Best Of* (MCA 1992)★★★ *A Night To Remember* (Spectrum 1995)★★.
●FILMS: *Footloose* (1984).

SHAM 69

Originally formed in London, England, in 1976, this five-piece skinhead/punk-influenced group comprised Jimmy Pursey (vocals), Albie Slider (bass), Neil Harris (lead guitar), Johnny Goodfornothing (rhythm guitar) and Billy Bostik (drums). Pursey was a fierce, working-class idealist, an avenging angel of the unemployed, who ironically sacked most of the above line-up within a year due to their lack of commitment. A streamlined aggregation featuring Dave Parsons (guitar), Dave Treganna (bass) and Mark Cain (drums) helped Pursey reach the UK charts with a series of anthemic hits including 'Angels With Dirty Faces', 'If The Kids Are United', 'Hurry Up Harry' and 'Hersham Boys'. Although Pursey championed proletarian solidarity, his rabble-rousing all too often brought violence and disruption from a small right-wing faction causing wary promoters to shun the group. After a troubled couple of years attempting to reconcile his ideals and their results, Pursey elected to go solo, but his time had passed. The group re-formed in the early 90s and performed at punk nostalgia/revival concerts.
●ALBUMS: *Tell Us The Truth* (Polydor 1978)★★★, *That's Life* (Polydor 1978)★★, *Adventures Of The Hersham Boys* (Polydor 1979)★★, *The Game* (Polydor 1980)★★, *Volunteer* (Legacy 1988)★, *Kings & Queens* (CMP 1993)★, *Soapy Water And Mr Marmalde* (A Plus Eye 1995)★.
●COMPILATIONS: *The First, The Best And The Last* (Polydor 1980)★★, *Angels With Dirty Faces - The Best Of* (Receiver 1986)★★★, *Live And Loud* (Link 1987)★★, *Live And Loud Vol. 2* (Link 1988)★, *The Best Of The Rest Of Sham 69* (Receiver 1989)★★, *Complete Live* (Castle 1989)★★, *Live At The Roxy* rec. 1977 (Receiver 1990)★★, *BBC Radio 1 Live In Concert* (Windsong 1993)★★, *The Best Of ...* (Essential 1995)★★★.
●VIDEOS: *Live In Japan* (Visionary 1993).

SHEAR, JULES

b. 7 March 1952, Pittsburgh, Pennsylvania, USA. Singer-songwriter Jules Shear recorded numerous albums both solo and with groups beginning in the late 70s, and wrote for such artists as Cyndi Lauper, the Bangles, Art Garfunkel and Olivia Newton-John. Shear moved from Pittsburgh to Los Angeles in the 70s. His first recorded work was with the band Funky Kings in 1976, also featuring singer-songwriter Jack Tempchin, who had written previously with the Eagles. Two years later Shear fronted Jules And The Polar Bears, a pop group that critics lumped in with the emerging new wave movement. The group debuted with the excellent *Got No Breeding*, which featured some of Shear's finest work, most notably 'Lovers By Rote'. After one more album, however, they disbanded in 1980. Shear next surfaced with the solo *Watch Dog* in 1983 and released three further albums under his own name. He briefly fronted the band Reckless Sleepers in 1988, which released one album, but Shear has yet to make a major commercial impact. In 1988, Iain Matthews recorded an entire album of Shear compositions, *Walking A Changing Line*, for Windham Hill Records. It was alleged that many of the lyrics of Aimee Mann's *Whatever* in 1994 were directed towards Shear, following the break-up of their relationship.
●ALBUMS: *Funky Kings* (1976)★★, *Got No Breeding* (1978)★★★, *Fenetiks* (1979)★★, *Watch Dog* (EMI 1983)★★★, *The Eternal Return* (EMI America 1985)★★★, *Demo-itis* (Enigma 1986)★★★, *Big Boss Sounds* (1988)★★★, *The Third Party* (IRS 1989)★★, *The Great Puzzle* (Polydor 1992)★★★, *Healing Bones* (Polygram 1994)★★.
●COMPILATIONS: *Horse Of A Different Color 1976-1989* (Razor And Tie 1994)★★★.

SHERBET

Formed in Sydney, Australia, in 1969, Sherbet became an Antipodean pop phenomenon, Sherbet dominated the Australian charts throughout the 70s achieving massive success with the teenage and pre-teen audience. The band became so well known that it seemed they could not put a foot wrong. The group was comprised of musicians with experience in various 'second division' Sydney bands and utilized the UK influence of Slade and the Sweet. The band performed an impressive stage show, with a more than adequate vocalist in Daryl Braithwaite (b. 11 January 1949, Melbourne, Australia) and a strong writing team in Garth Porter (keyboards/vocals) and Clive Shakespeare (b. 3 June 1957, Australia; guitar/vocals). The initial line-up was completed with Alan Sandow (b. 28 February 1958, Australia; drums) and Bruce Worrall (bass). The band's management also worked overtime courting the media, arranging tours to every far-flung population centre in Australia, including many that had never had a pop or rock band visit before. The band achieved 10 Australian Top 10 hit singles with 10 making the Top 40, and enjoyed similar success with their albums. Tony Mitchell (b. 21 October 1951, Australia) replaced Worrall in 1972. An attempt at the UK market was successful with the 'Howzat' single reaching number 4 in 1976, but they were unable to capitalize further on this success. In 1976 Clive Shakespeare departed and was briefly replaced by ex-Daddy Cool member Gunther Gorman, who in turn was supplanted by Harvey James. A favourite amongst the fans was 'You've Got The Gun' (1976) which had been a minor hit before they made the big time, a song that displayed their English influences. They also attempted to break into the US market with their 1979 album going under the name 'Highway'. Making little progress they returned to Australia, renamed themselves the Sherbs and changed direction to a more mature, heavier AOR sound. This alienated them from their teen following and also failed to attract the older audience which now regarded them with suspicion. In the 1980-84 period they released 10 singles and three albums to good critical reviews but few sales, although *The Skill* did reach the US Top 100. Shakespeare and Porter are now involved in production work, while Braithwaite has had two very successful solo albums, demonstrating his expressive vocals and songwriting.

●ALBUMS: *Time Change Natural Progression* (1972)★★★, *On With The Show* (1973)★★★, *Slipstream* (1974)★★★, *In Concert* (1975)★★★, *Life* (1975)★★★, *Howzat!* (Epic 1976)★★★, *Photoplay* (Epic 1977)★★★, *Caught In The Act* (1978)★★★, *Sherbet/Highway* (1979)★★★. As the Sherbs *The Skill* (Atco 1980)★★★, *Defying Gravity* (1981)★★★, *Shaping Up* (1982)★★★.

SHOCKING BLUE

Formed in 1967 by ex-Motions guitarist Robbie van Leeuwen (b. 1944), this Dutch quartet originally featured lead vocalist Fred de Wilde, bassist Klassje van der Wal and drummer Cornelius van der Beek. After one minor hit in their homeland, 'Lucy Brown Is Back In Town', there was a major line-up change when the group's management replaced De Wilde with Mariska Veres (b. 1949). With her solid vocals, long dark hair, heavy make-up and low-cut garments Veres brought the group a sexy image and another Netherlands hit 'Send Me A Postcard Darling'. Next came 'Venus', a massive European hit, which went on to top the US charts in February 1970 after Jerry Ross had signed the group to his Colossus label. With the talented Van Leeuwen dominating the composing and production credits, Shocking Blue attempted to bridge the gap between the pop and progressive markets. Their *Shocking Blue At Home* contained such lengthy songs as 'California Here I Come', 'The Butterfly And I' and featured a sitar on the innovative 'Acka Raga'. They remained largely a pop unit in the UK market however, where they enjoyed another minor hit with 'Mighty Joe', which had reached number 1 in Holland. Thereafter, the transatlantic hits evaporated although they managed another Dutch chart topper with 'Never Marry A Railroad Man'. Within four years of their international fame, they broke up in 1974, with Van Leeuwen later resurfacing in the folk/jazz group, Galaxy Inc. His most famous song, 'Venus', was frequently covered and was back at number 1 in the USA in 1981 and 1986 by Stars On 45 and Bananarama, respectively.

●ALBUMS: *The Shocking Blue* (Colossus 1970)★★★, *Shocking Blue At Home* (Penny Farthing 1970)★★, *Scorpio's Dance* (Penny Farthing 1970)★★, *Beat With Us* (1972)★★.

SHOES

Formed in Zion, Illinois, USA, this group comprised Jeff Murphy (vocal/guitar), brother John Murphy (bass/vocal), Gary Klebe (guitar/vocal) and Skip Meyer (drums). They preferred composing and recording on a TEAC four-track machine in the Murphy's living room to concert performances. When an architecture scholarship took Klebe to France in 1974, the others taped *One In Versailles* and pressed 300 copies to surprise him. On his return, this privatized policy continued with *Bazooka*, a tape circulated among immediate fans. Containing 15 original compositions, *Black Vinyl Shoes* reached a wider public that included Greg Shaw, who signed them to his Bomp label for a one-shot double a-side, 'Tomorrow Night'/'Okay'. The former was remade in 1979 in England during sessions for *Present Tense*, the group's debut on Elektra Records. Subsequent product did not, however, include the hits needed to walk the Shoes into the pop mainstream.

●ALBUMS: *Black Vinyl Shoes* (Sire 1977)★★★★, *Present Tense* (Elektra 1979)★★★, *Tongue Twister* (Elektra 1980)★★★, *Boomerang* (Fan Club 1982)★★★, *Silhouette* (Demon 1984)★★, *Stolen Wishes* (Black Vinyl 1989)★★.

SHOWADDYWADDY

When two promising Leicestershire groups fused their talents in 1973, the result was an octet comprising Dave Bartram (vocals), Billy Gask (vocals), Russ Fields (guitar), Trevor Oakes (guitar), Al James (bass), Rod Teas (bass), Malcolm Allured (drums) and Romeo Challenger (drums). Showaddywaddy personified the easy-listening dilution of rock 'n' roll and rockabilly and their visual appeal and showmanship won them talent contests and, more importantly, a contract with Bell Records. Initially penning their own hits, they charted steadily, but after reaching number 2 with Eddie Cochran's 'Three Steps To Heaven', the cover version game was begun in earnest. Fifteen of their singles reached the UK Top 20 during the late 70s but the seemingly foolproof hit formula ran dry in the following decade when the rock 'n' roll revival had passed. They have been constantly working although there is now some dispute as to the ownership of the name. Many members have passed through their ranks over the years. In March 1996 Bartram, Geoffrey Betts and Roderick Sinclair sued Allured, Gask and Ray Martinez.

●ALBUMS: *Showaddywaddy* (Bell 1974)★★★, *Step Two* (Bell 1975)★★★, *Trocadero* (Bell 1976)★★, *Red Star* (Arista 1977)★★, *Crepes And Drapes* (Arista 1979)★★, *Bright Lights* (Arista 1980)★★, *Good Times* (1981)★★, *Jump Boogie And Jive* (President 1991)★★.

●COMPILATIONS: *Greatest Hits* (Arista 1976)★★, *The Very Best Of* (Arista 1981)★★★, *Living Legends* (RCA 1983)★★, *The Best Steps To Heaven* (Tiger 1987)★★, *20 Steps To The Top* (Repertoire 1991)★★, *20 Greatest Hits* (IMD 1992)★★★, *The Very Best Of ...* (Summit 1996)★★★.

SIFFRE, LABI

Siffre was born and brought up in Bayswater, London, England, to an English mother and Nigerian father. He first took employment as a mini-cab driver and delivery man but practised guitar whenever he could, going on to study music harmonics. He played his first gigs as one of a trio of like-minded youngsters, before taking up a nine-month residency at Annie's Rooms. His tenure completed, he travelled to Cannes, France, and played with a variety of soul musicians and bands. He returned to the UK in the late 60s and had solo hits in 1971 with 'It Must Be Love' (later covered by Madness) and 'Crying, Laughing, Loving, Lying'. Although 'Watch Me' in 1972 was his last hit of the 70s, he made a spectacular comeback in 1987 with the anthemic '(Something Inside) So Strong'. In recent years Siffre has devoted most of his time to his poetry and has shown a sensitive and intelligent grasp of world issues. His relaxed nature and engaging personality has made his poetry readings more popular than his songs.

●ALBUMS: *Labi Siffre* (1970)★★★, *Singer And The Song* (Pye 1971)★★★, *Crying, Laughing, Loving, Lying* (Pye 1972)★★★, *So Strong* (Polydor 1988)★★★, *Make My Day* (Connoisseur 1989)★★★.

●COMPILATIONS: *The Labi Siffre Collection* (Conifer 1986)★★★.

SILL, JUDEE

b. c.1949, Los Angeles, USA, d. 1974. This Los Angeles-based artist first attracted attention for her work with the city's folk rock fraternity. An early composition, 'Dead Time Bummer Blues', was recorded by the Leaves, whose bassist, Jim Pons, later joined the Turtles. He introduced Sill to Blimp, the group's publishing company, the fruit of which was 'Lady O', their finest late-period performance. The song also appeared on *Judee Sill*, the artist's poignant debut, which was largely produced by Pons in partnership with another ex-Leave, John Beck. Graham Nash supervised the sole exception, 'Jesus Was A Crossmaker', which drew considerable comment over its lyrical content and was one of the songs Sill featured on a rare UK television appearance. *Heart Food* continued this uncompromising individual's quest for excellence and deftly balanced upbeat, country-tinged compositions with dramatic emotional ballads. A gift for melody suggested a long, successful career, but Judee Sill subsequently abandoned full-time music and died in mysterious circumstances in 1974.

●ALBUMS: *Judee Sill* (Asylum 1971)★★★, *Heart Food* (Asylum 1973)★★★.

SILVER CONVENTION

This studio group was created by Munich-based producers Silvester Levay and Michael Kunze. After enjoying a UK hit in 1975 with 'Save Me', they went on to reach number 1 in the USA with 'Fly, Robin, Fly'. The international fame persuaded the duo to audition some female singers to adopt the Silver Convention name and the lucky trio were Linda Thompson (ex-Les Humphries Singers), Ramona Wulf (formerly a solo artist) and Penny McLean. This 'second generation'

Silver Convention proved more than a match for their anonymous studio counterparts and achieved transatlantic Top 10 success with the infectious 'Get Up And Boogie (That's Right)', one of the most distinctive disco numbers of the period. A significant line-up change followed with the departure of Thompson, replaced by Rhonda Heath. Further minor hits followed until the group quietly disbanded in the late 70s.

●ALBUMS: *Save Me* (Magnet 1975)★★, *Silver Convention* (Magnet 1976)★★, *Madhouse* (Magnet 1976)★★, *Golden Girls* (Magnet 1977)★★.

●COMPILATIONS: *Silver Convention: Greatest Hits* (Magnet 1977)★★★.

SIMON AND GARFUNKEL

This highly successful vocal duo first played together during their early years in New York. Paul Simon (b. 13 October 1941, Newark, New Jersey, USA) and Art Garfunkel (b. Arthur Garfunkel, 5 November 1941, Queens, New York, USA) were initially inspired by the Everly Brothers and under the name Tom And Jerry enjoyed a US hit with the rock 'n' roll-styled 'Hey Schoolgirl'. They also completed an album which was later reissued after their rise to international prominence in the 60s. Garfunkel subsequently returned to college and Simon pursued a solo career before the duo reunited in 1964 for *Wednesday Morning 3AM*. A strong, harmonic work, which included an acoustic reading of 'The Sound Of Silence', the album did not sell well enough to encourage the group to stay together. While Simon was in England the folk rock-boom was in the ascendant and producer Tom Wilson made the presumptuous but prescient decision to overdub 'Sound Of Silence' with electric instrumentation. Within weeks, the song was number 1 in the US charts, and Simon and Garfunkel were hastily reunited. An album titled after their million-selling single was rush-released early in 1966 and proved a commendable work. Among its major achievements was 'Homeward Bound', an evocative and moving portrayal of life on the road, which went on to become a transatlantic hit. The solipsistic 'I Am A Rock' was another international success with such angst-ridden lines as, 'I have no need of friendship, friendship causes pain'. In keeping with the social commentary that permeated their mid-60s work, the group included two songs whose theme was suicide: 'A Most Peculiar Man' and 'Richard Cory'. Embraced by a vast following, especially among the student population, the duo certainly looked the part with their college scarves, duffle coats and cerebral demeanour. Their next single, 'The Dangling Conversation', was their most ambitious lyric to date and far too esoteric for the Top 20. Nevertheless, the work testified to their artistic courage and boded well for the release of a second album within a year: *Parsley, Sage, Rosemary And Thyme*. The album took its title from a repeated line in 'Scarborough Fair', which was their excellent harmonic weaving of that traditional song and another, 'Canticle'.

An accomplished work, the album had a varied mood from the grandly serious 'For Emily, Whenever I May Find Her' to the bouncy '59th Street Bridge Song (Feelin' Groovy)' (subsequently a hit for Harpers Bizarre). After two strong but uncommercial singles, 'At The Zoo' and 'Fakin' It', the duo contributed to the soundtrack of the 1968 film, *The Graduate*. The key song in the film was 'Mrs Robinson' which provided the group with one of their biggest international sellers. That same year saw the release of *Bookends*, a superbly crafted work, ranging from the serene 'Save The Life Of My Child' to the personal odyssey 'America' and the vivid imagery of 'Old Friends'. *Bookends* is still felt by many to be their finest work.

In 1969 the duo released 'The Boxer', a long single that nevertheless found commercial success on both sides of the Atlantic. This classic single reappeared on the group's next album, the celebrated *Bridge Over Troubled Water*. One of the best-selling albums of all time (303 weeks on the UK chart), the work's title track became a standard with its lush, orchestral arrangement and contrasting tempo. Heavily gospel-influenced, the album included several well-covered songs such as 'Keep The Customer Satisfied', 'Cecilia' and 'El Condor Pasa'. While at the peak of their commercial success, with an album that dominated the top of the chart listings for months, the duo became irascible and their partnership abruptly ceased. The release of a *Greatest Hits* package in 1972 included four previously unissued live tracks and during the same year the duo performed together at a benefit concert for Senator George McGovern. In 1981 they again reunited. The results were captured in 1981 on *The Concert In Central Park*. After a long break, a further duet occurred on the hit single 'My Little Town' in 1975. Although another studio album was undertaken, the sessions broke down and Simon transferred the planned material to his 1983 solo *Hearts And Bones*. In 1993 Simon and Garfunkel settled their differences long enough to complete 21 sell-out dates in New York.

●ALBUMS: *Wednesday Morning 3AM* (Columbia 1968)★★, *The Sound Of Silence* (Columbia 1966)★★★★, *Parsley, Sage, Rosemary And Thyme* (Columbia 1966)★★★★, *The Graduate* film soundtrack (Columbia 1968)★★, *Bookends* (Columbia 1968)★★★★, *Bridge Over Troubled Water* (Columbia 1970)★★★★, *The Concert In Central Park* (Geffen 1981)★★★.

●COMPILATIONS: *Simon And Garfunkel's Greatest Hits* (Columbia 1972)★★★★, *The Simon And Garfunkel Collection* (Columbia 1981)★★★★, *The Definitive Simon And Garfunkel* (Columbia 1992)★★★★.

●FURTHER READING: *Simon & Garfunkel: A Biography In Words & Pictures*, Michael S. Cohen. *Paul Simon: Now And Then*, Spencer Leigh. *Paul Simon*, Dave Marsh. *Simon And Garfunkel*, Robert Matthew-Walker. *Bookends: The Simon And Garfunkel Story*, Patrick Humphries. *The Boy In The Bubble: A Biography Of Paul Simon*, Patrick Humphries. *Simon And Garfunkel: Old Friends*, Joseph Morella and Patricia Barey.

SIMON, CARLY

b. 25 June 1945, New York, USA. Simon became one of the most popular singer-songwriters of the 70s and achieved equal success with film music in the 80s. In the early 60s she played Greenwich Village clubs with her sister Lucy. As the Simon Sisters they had one minor hit with 'Winkin' Blinkin And Nod' (Kapp Records 1964) and recorded two albums of soft folk and children's material. After the duo split up, Carly Simon made an unsuccessful attempt to launch a solo career through Albert Grossman (then Bob Dylan's manager) before concentrating on songwriting with film critic Jacob Brackman. In 1971, two of their songs, the wistful 'That's The Way I've Always Heard It Should Be' and the Paul Samwell-Smith-produced 'Anticipation' were US hits for Simon. Her voice was given a rock accompaniment by Richard Perry on her third album which included her most famous song, 'You're So Vain', whose target was variously supposed to be Warren Beatty and/or Mick Jagger, who provided backing vocals. The song was a million-seller in 1972 and nearly two decades later was reissued in Britain after it had been used in a television commercial. *No Secrets* remains her most applauded work, and featured among numerous gems, 'The Right Thing To Do'.

Simon's next Top 10 hit was an insipid revival of the Charlie And Inez Foxx song 'Mockingbird' on which she duetted with James Taylor to whom she was married from 1972-83. Their marriage was given enormous coverage in the US media, rivalling that of Richard Burton and Elizabeth Taylor. Their divorce received similar treatment as Simon found solace with Taylor's drummer Russell Kunkel. *Hotcakes* became a US Top 3 album in 1972. During the latter part of the 70s, Simon was less prolific as a writer and recording artist although she played benefit concerts for anti-nuclear causes. Her most successful records were the James Bond film theme. 'Nobody Does It Better', written by Carole Bayer Sager and Marvin Hamlisch, and 'You Belong To Me', a collaboration with Michael McDonald, both in 1977. During the 80s, Simon's worked moved away from the singer-songwriter field and towards the pop mainstream. She released two albums of pre-war Broadway standards (*Torch* and *My Romance*) and increased her involvement with films. Her UK hit 'Why' (1982) was written by Chic and used in the movie *Soup For One*, while she appeared in *Perfect* with John Travolta. However, her biggest achievement of the decade was to compose and perform two of its memorable film themes. Both 'Coming Around Again' (from *Heartburn*, 1986) and the Oscar-winning 'Let The River Run' (from *Working Girl*, 1989) demonstrated the continuing depth of Simon's songwriting talent while the quality of her previous work was showcased on a 1988 live album and video recorded in the open air at Martha's Vineyard, Massachusetts. In 1990, her career came full circle when Lucy Simon was a guest artist on

Have You Seen Me Lately? After a lengthy gap in recording *Letters Never Sent* was released in 1995. This was a perplexing album, lyrically nostalgic and sad with lush arrangements, which peaked outside the Top 100 in the USA.

●ALBUMS: as the Simon Sisters *The Simon Sisters* (Kapp 1964)★★, as the Simon Sisters *Cuddlebug* (Kapp 1965)★★, *Carly Simon* (Elektra 1971)★★, *Anticipation* (Elektra 1971)★★★★, *No Secrets* (Elektra 1972)★★★★, *Hotcakes* (Elektra 1974)★★★, *Playing Possum* (Elektra 1975)★★★, *Another Passenger* (Elektra 1976)★★★, *Boys In The Trees* (Elektra 1978)★★★, *Spy* (Elektra 1979)★★★, *Come Upstairs* (Warners 1980)★★, *Torch* (Warners 1981)★★, *Hello Big Man* (Warners 1983)★★★, *Spoiled Girl* (Epic 1985)★★, *Coming Around Again* (Arista 1987)★★, *Greatest Hits Live* (Arista 1988)★★★, *My Romance* (Arista 1990)★★, *Have You Seen Me Lately?* (Arista 1990)★★★, *Letters Never Sent* (Arista 1994)★★★.
●COMPILATIONS: *The Best Of Carly Simon* (Elektra 1975)★★★, *Clouds In My Coffee* 3-CD box set (Arista 1995)★★★.
●VIDEOS: *Live At Grand Central* (Polygram 1996).
●FURTHER READING: *Carly Simon*, Charles Morse.

SIMON, JOE

b. 2 September 1943, Simmesport, Louisiana, USA. Simon's professional career began following his move to Oakland, California, where a 1962 release, 'My Adorable One', was a minor hit. In 1964, Joe met John Richbourg, a Nashville-based disc jockey who began guiding the singer's musical path, initially on the Sound Stage 7 label. 'Let's Do It Over' (1965), Simon's first R&B hit, emphasized Richbourg's preference for a blend of gentle soul and country, and the singer's smooth delivery found its niche on such poignant songs as 'Teenager's Prayer', 'Nine Pound Steel' (both 1967) and 'The Chokin' Kind', a US R&B number 1 in 1969. The following year Simon moved to the Polydor subsidiary, Spring. He maintained his ties with Richbourg until 1971, when a Gamble And Huff production, 'Drowning In The Sea Of Love' was an R&B Number 3. Further success came with 'The Power Of Love' (1972), 'Step By Step' (1973 - his only UK hit), 'Theme From Cleopatra Jones' (1973) and 'Get Down Get Down (Get On The Floor)' (1975), but the artist increasingly sacrificed his craft in favour of the dancefloor. His late 70s releases were less well received and in 1980 he returned to Nashville. Since then Joe's work has been restricted to local labels.

●ALBUMS: *Simon Pure Soul* (Sound Stage 1967)★★★, *No Sad Songs* (Sound Stage 1968)★★★, *Simon Sings* (Sound Stage 1969)★★★, *The Chokin' Kind* (Sound Stage 1969)★★★, *Joe Simon - Better Than Ever* (Sound Stage 1969)★★★, *Sounds Of Simon* (Spring 1971)★★★, *Drowning In The Sea Of Love* (Spring 1972)★★★, *Power Of Love* (Spring 1973)★★★, *Mood, Heart And Soul* (Spring 1974)★★★, *Simon Country* (Spring 1974)★★★, *Get Down* (Spring 1975)★★★, *Joe Simon Today* (Spring 1976)★★★,

Easy To Love (Spring 1977)★★★, *Bad Case Of Love* (Spring 1978)★★, *Love Vibration* (Spring 1979)★★, *Happy Birthday Baby* (Spring 1979)★★, *Soul Neighbors* (1984)★★, *Mr. Right* (1985)★★★.
●COMPILATIONS: *Joe Simon 1962/3 Hush/Vee Jay* recordings (c.1969), *Joe Simon's Greatest Hits* (1972)★★★, *The Best Of Joe Simon* (Sound Stage 1972)★★★, *The World Of ...* double album (Sound Stage 1973)★★★★, *The Best Of ...* (1977)★★★, *Lookin' Back - The Best Of Joe Simon 1966-70* (Charly 1988)★★★.

SIMON, PAUL

b. Paul Frederic Simon, 13 October 1941, Newark, New Jersey, USA. Simon first entered the music business with partner Art Garfunkel in the duo Tom And Jerry. In 1957, they had a US hit with the rock 'n' roll-influenced 'Hey Schoolgirl'. After one album, they broke up in order to return to college. Although Simon briefly worked with Carole King recording demonstration discs for minor acts, he did not record again until the early 60s. Employing various pseudonyms, Simon enjoyed a couple of minor US hits during 1962-63 as Tico And The Triumphs ('Motorcycle') and Jerry Landis ('The Lone Teen-Ranger'). After moving to Europe in 1964, Simon busked in Paris and appeared at various folk clubs in London. Upon returning to New York, he was signed to CBS Records by producer Tom Wilson and reunited with his erstwhile partner Garfunkel. Their 1964 recording *Wednesday Morning 3 AM*, which included 'The Sound Of Silence' initially failed to sell, prompting Simon to return to London. While there, he made *The Paul Simon Songbook*, a solo work, recorded on one microphone with the astonishingly low budget of £60. Among its contents were several of Simon's most well-known compositions, including 'I Am A Rock', 'A Most Peculiar Man' and 'Kathy's Song'. The album was virtually ignored until Tom Wilson altered Simon's artistic stature overnight. Back in the USA, the producer grafted electric instrumentation on to Simon And Garfunkel's acoustic recording of 'Sound Of Silence' and created a folk rock classic that soared to the top of the US charts. Between 1965 and 1970, Simon And Garfunkel became one of the most successful recording duos in the history of popular music. The partnership ended amid musical disagreements and a realization that they had grown apart.

After the break-up, Simon took songwriting classes in New York and prepared a stylistically diverse solo album, *Paul Simon* (1972). The work incorporated elements of Latin, reggae and jazz and spawned the hit singles 'Mother And Child Reunion' and 'Me And Julio Down By The Schoolyard'. One year later, Simon returned with the much more commercial *There Goes Rhymin' Simon* which enjoyed massive chart success and included two major hits, 'Kodachrome' and 'Take Me To The Mardi Gras'. A highly successful tour resulted in *Live Rhymin'*, which featured several Simon And Garfunkel standards. This flurry of creativity in

1975 culminated in the chart-topping *Still Crazy After All These Years* which won several Grammy awards. The wry '50 Ways To Leave Your Lover', taken from the album, provided Simon with his first number 1 single as a soloist, while the hit 'My Little Town' featured a tantalizing duet with Garfunkel. A five-year hiatus followed during which Simon took stock of his career. He appeared briefly in Woody Allen's movie *Annie Hall*, recorded a hit single with Garfunkel and James Taylor ('Wonderful World'), released a *Greatest Hits* package featuring the catchy 'Slip Slidin' Away' and switched labels from CBS to Warner Brothers Records. In 1980, he released the ambitious *One Trick Pony*, from his film of the same name. The movie included cameo appearances by the Lovin' Spoonful and Tiny Tim but was not particularly well received even though it was far more literate than most 'rock-related' films. In the wake of that project, Simon suffered a long period of writer's block, which delayed the recording of his next album. Meanwhile, a double album live reunion of Simon And Garfunkel recorded in Central Park was issued and sold extremely well. It was intended to preview a studio reunion, but the sessions were subsequently scrapped. Instead, Simon concentrated on his next album, which finally emerged in 1983 as *Hearts And Bones*. An intense and underrated effort, it sold poorly despite its evocative hit single 'The Late Great Johnny Ace' (dedicated to both the doomed 50s star and the assassinated John Lennon). Simon was dismayed by the album's lack of commercial success and critics felt that he was in a creative rut. That situation altered during 1984 when Simon was introduced to the enlivening music of the South African black townships. After an appearance at the celebrated USA For Africa recording of 'We Are The World', Simon immersed himself in the music of the Dark Continent. *Graceland* (1986) was one of the most intriguing and commercially successful albums of the decade with Simon utilizing musical contributions from Ladysmith Black Mambazo, Los Lobos, Linda Ronstadt and Rockie Dopsie And The Twisters. The project and subsequent tour was bathed in controversy due to accusations (misconceived according to the United Nations Anti-Apartheid Committee) that Simon had broken the cultural boycott against South Africa. The success of the album in combining contrasting cross-cultural musical heritages was typical of a performer who had already incorporated folk, R&B, calypso and blues into his earlier repertoire. The album spawned several notable hits, 'The Boy In The Bubble' (with its technological imagery), 'You Can Call Me Al' (inspired by an amusing case of mistaken identity) and 'Graceland' (an oblique homage to Elvis Presley's Memphis home). Although *Graceland* seemed a near impossible work to follow, Simon continued his pan-cultural investigations with *The Rhythm Of The Saints*, which incorporated African and Brazilian musical elements. He married Edie Brickell in 1994.

● ALBUMS: *The Paul Simon Songbook* (Columbia 1965)★★★, *Paul Simon* (Columbia 1972)★★★★, *There Goes Rhymin' Simon* (Columbia 1973)★★★★, *Live Rhymin'* (Columbia 1974)★★, *Still Crazy After All These Years* (Columbia 1975)★★★★, *One Trick Pony* film soundtrack (Warners 1980)★★, *Hearts And Bones* (Warners 1983)★★, *Graceland* (Warners 1986)★★★★, *The Rhythm Of The Saints* (Warners 1990)★★★, Paul Simon's *Concert In The Park* (Warners 1991)★★★.

● COMPILATIONS: *Greatest Hits, Etc.* (Columbia 1977)★★★★, *Negotiations And Love Songs* , *Paul Simon (1964/1993)* 3-CD box set (Warners 1993)★★★.

● VIDEOS: *Concert In The Park* (Warners 1991), *Paul Simon: Born At The Right Time* (1993).

● FURTHER READING: *The Boy In The Bubble*, Patrick Humphries

● FILMS: *One Trick Pony* (1980).

SISTER SLEDGE

Debra (b. 1955), Joan (1957), Kim (1958) and Kathie Sledge (1959) were all born and raised in Philadelphia, Pennsylvania, USA. They started their recording career in 1971 and spent a short time working as backing singers before enjoying a series of minor R&B hits between 1974 and 1977. Two years later they entered a fruitful relationship with Chic masterminds Nile Rodgers and Bernard Edwards which resulted in several sparkling singles including 'He's The Greatest Dancer', 'We Are Family' and 'Lost In Music', each of which reached the the UK Top 20 in 1979. The Sisters then left the Chic organization and began to produce their own material in 1981. Although success in the USA waned, the quartet retained their UK popularity and two remixes of former hits served as a prelude to 'Frankie', a simple but irrepressible song which reached number 1 in 1985. Since then however, Sister Sledge have been unable to maintain this status.

● ALBUMS: *Circle Of Love* (Atco 1975)★★, *Together* (Atlantic 1977)★★, *We Are Family* (Atlantic 1979)★★★, *Love Somebody Today* (Atlantic 1980)★★, *All American Girls* (Atlantic 1981)★★, *The Sisters* (Atlantic 1982)★★, *Bet Cha Say That To All The Girls* (Atlantic 1983)★★, *When The Boys Meet The Girls* (Atlantic 1985)★★.

● COMPILATIONS: *Greatest Hits* (Atlantic 1986)★★★, *The Best Of. ..* (Rhino 1992)★★★★.

SKELLERN, PETER

b. 14 March 1947, Bury, Lancashire, England. A composer, singer and musician, Skellern played trombone in a school band and served as organist and choirmaster in a local church before attending the Guildhall School of Music, from which he graduated with honours in 1968. Because he 'didn't want to spend the next 50 years playing Chopin', he joined March Hare which, as Harlan County, recorded a country pop album before disbanding in 1971. Married with two children, Skellern worked as a hotel porter in Shaftesbury, Dorset, before striking lucky with a self-composed UK number 3 hit, 'You're A Lady'. *Peter Skellern, Not Without A Friend* was all original, bar Hoagy Carmichael's 'Rockin' Chair', and another hit single with the title track to 1975's *Hold On To Love* established Skellern as a purveyor of wittily observed, if homely, love songs of similar stamp to Gilbert O'Sullivan. He earned the approbation of the ex-Beatles coterie which, already manifested in Derek Taylor's production of *Not Without A Friend*, was further demonstrated when George Harrison assisted on *Hard Times*; the title number was later recorded by Starr. A minor hit in 1978 with 'Love Is The Sweetest Thing' (featuring Grimethorpe Colliery Band) was part of a tribute to Fred Astaire that won a Music Trades Association award for Best MOR Album of 1979. Skellern subsequently wrote and performed six autobiographical programmes for BBC television, followed by a series of musical plays (*Happy Endings*) and also hosted the chat show *Private Lives* in 1983. A year later he formed Oasis with Julian Lloyd Webber, Mary Hopkin and guitarist Bill Lovelady in an attempt to fuse mutual classical and pop interests, but the group's recordings failed to make a major impact. In 1985 he joined Richard Stilgoe for *Stilgoe And Skellern Stompin' At The Savoy*, a show in aid of The Lords Taverners charity organization. This led to the two entertainers working together on several successful tours, and in their two-man revue, *Who Plays Wins*, which was presented in the West End and New York. After becoming disenchanted with the record business for a time, in 1995 Skellern issued his first album for nearly eight years. Originally conceived as a tribute to the Ink Spots, it eventually consisted of a number of songs associated with that legendary group, and a few Hoagy Carmichael compositions 'just to break it up'.

●ALBUMS: *Peter Skellern With Harlan County* (1971)★★, *Peter Skellern* (Decca 1972)★★★, *Not Without A Friend* (Decca 1973)★★★, *Holding My Own* (1974)★★, *Hold On To Love* (Decca 1975)★★★, *Hard Times* (1976)★★, *Skellern* (Mercury 1978)★★★, *Astaire* (Mercury 1979)★★★, *Still Magic* (Mercury 1980)★★, *Happy Endings* (BBC 1981)★★★, *A String Of Pearls* (Mercury 1982)★★★, *Lovelight* (Sonet 1987)★★★, *Stardust Memories* (Warners 1995)★★★.

●COMPILATIONS: *Introducing ... Right From The Start* (Elite 1981)★★★, *Best Of Peter Skellern* (Decca 1985)★★★, *The Singer And The Song* (1993)★★★.

SKID ROW (EIRE)

This blues-based rock band was put together by Gary Moore in Dublin, Eire, in 1968, when the guitarist was only 16 years old. Recruiting Phil Lynott (vocals/bass), Eric Bell (guitar) and Brian Downey (drums) the initial line-up only survived 12 months. Lynott, Bell and Downey left to form Thin Lizzy, with Brendan Shiels (bass/vocals) and Noel Bridgeman (drums) joining Moore as replacements in a new power trio. The group completed two singles, 'New Places, Old Faces' and 'Saturday Morning Man' - only released in Ireland - before securing a UK contract via CBS Records. Skid Row was a popular live attraction and tours of the US and Europe, supporting Canned Heat and Savoy Brown, augured well for the future. Their albums were also well received, but Moore's growing reputation as an inventive and versatile guitarist outstripped the group's musical confines. He left in 1971 to work with the folk rock band Dr. Strangely Strange and later on to the Gary Moore Band. Although Paul Chapman proved an able replacement, Skid Row's momentum now faltered and the trio was disbanded the following year. Sheils has, on occasion, revived the name for various endeavours, while Chapman later found fame with UFO.

●ALBUMS: *Skid Row* (Columbia 1970)★★★, *34 Hours* (Columbia 1971)★★★, *Alive And Kicking* (Columbia 1978)★★.

●COMPILATIONS: *Skid Row* (Columbia 1987)★★★.

SKIDS

A Scottish new wave band founded in Dunfermline in 1977 by Stuart Adamson (b. 11 April 1958, Manchester, UK; guitar/vocals), Richard Jobson (vocals), Tom Kellichan (drums) and Willie Simpson (bass). After issuing 'Reasons' on their own No Bad label, the group were signed by Virgin. David Batchelor produced 'Sweet Suburbia' and 'The Saints Are Coming' before 'Into The Valley' reached the UK Top 10 in 1979. Despite criticism of Jobson's lyrics as pretentious, the Skids enjoyed a further year of chart success as 'Masquerade' and 'Working For The Yankee Dollar' reached the Top 20. Both came from the second album, which was produced by Bill Nelson of Be-Bop Deluxe. Soon afterwards the band was hit by personnel changes. Russell Webb and Mike Baillie replaced Simpson and Kellichan and more crucially, the Skids' songwriting team was split when Adamson left after the release of the third album, which proved to be the group's most commercial, reaching the Top 10 and containing the minor hit 'Circus Games'. Without Adamson, *Joy*, an exploration of Celtic culture, was more or less a Jobson solo effort. The Skids dissolved in 1982, with *Fanfare* issued by Virgin as a mixture of greatest hits and unreleased tracks. In 1983, Stuart Adamson launched the career of his new band, Big Country. Richard Jobson recorded one album with a new band, the Armoury Show before pursuing a solo career as poet, songwriter and broadcaster. He released albums on Belgian label Les Disques Crepuscules and Parlophone Records.

●ALBUMS: *Scared To Dance* (Virgin 1979)★★★, *Days In Europa* (Virgin 1979)★★★, *Absolute Game* (Virgin 1980)★★★, *Joy* (Virgin 1981)★★, *Fanfare* (Virgin 1982)★★.

●COMPILATIONS: *Dumferline* (Virgin 1993)★★★, *The Best Of ...* (Virgin 1995)★★★.

SKIN ALLEY

This UK rock quartet - Bob James (guitar, saxophone), Krzysztof Henryk Juskiewicz (keyboards), Thomas Crimble (bass, vocals) and Alvin Pope (drums) -

released their debut album in 1969. The set was produced by Dick Taylor, formerly of the Pretty Things, however, the group's workmanlike approach undermined any potential this pairing offered. Nick Graham (vocals, keyboards, bass, flute) joined the line-up for their second album, *To Pagham And Beyond*. Crimble subsequently left the group, as did Pope, who was replaced by Tony Knight. However, despite securing a lucrative agreement with the American label, Stax, Skin Alley broke up following the release of a fourth collection, *Skintight*.

●ALBUMS: *Skin Alley* (CBS 1969)★★, *To Pagham And Beyond* (CBS 1970)★★, *Two Quid Deal* (Transatlantic 1972)★★, *Skintight* (Transatlantic 1973)★★.

SLADE

Originally recording as the 'N Betweens, this UK quartet comprised Noddy Holder (b. Neville Holder, 15 June 1950, Walsall, West Midlands, England; vocals/guitar), Dave Hill (b. 4 April 1952, Fleet Castle, Devon, England; guitar), Jimmy Lea (b. 14 June 1952, Wolverhampton, West Midlands, England; bass) and Don Powell (b. 10 September 1950, Bilston, West Midlands, England; drums). During the spring of 1966 they performed regularly in the Midlands, playing an unusual mixture of soul standards, juxtaposed with a sprinkling of hard rock items. A chance meeting with producer Kim Fowley led to a one-off single, 'You Better Run', released in August 1966. Two further years of obscurity followed until their agent secured them an audition with Fontana Records' A&R head Jack Baverstock. He insisted that they change their name to Ambrose Slade and it was under that moniker that they recorded *Beginnings*. Chaff on the winds of opportunity, they next fell into the hands of former Animals bassist turned manager, Chas Chandler. He abbreviated their name to Slade and oversaw their new incarnation as a skinhead group for the stomping 'Wild Winds Are Blowing'. Their image as 'bovver boys', complete with cropped hair and Dr Marten boots, provoked some scathing press from a media sensitive to youth culture violence. Slade persevered with their skinhead phase until 1970 when it was clear that their notoriety was *passé*. While growing their hair and cultivating a more colourful image, they retained their aggressive musicianship and screaming vocals for the bluesy 'Get Down Get With It', which reached number 20 in the UK. Under Chandler's guidance, Holder and Lea commenced composing their own material, relying on distinctive riffs, a boot-stomping beat and sloganeering lyrics, usually topped off by a deliberately misspelt title. 'Coz I Luv You' took them to number 1 in the UK in late 1971, precipitating an incredible run of chart success that continued uninterrupted for the next three years. After the average 'Look Wot You Dun' (which still hit number 4), they served up a veritable beer barrel of frothy chart-toppers including 'Take Me Bak 'Ome', 'Mama Weer Al Crazee Now', 'Cum On Feel The Noize'

and 'Skweeze Me Pleeze Me'. Their finest moment was 1977's 'Merry Xmas Everybody', one of the great festive rock songs. Unpretentious and proudly working class, the group appealed to teenage audiences who cheered their larynx-wrenching singles and gloried in their garish yet peculiarly masculine forays into glam rock. Holder, clearly no sex symbol, offered a solid, cheery image, with Dickensian side whiskers and a hat covered in mirrors, while Hill took tasteless dressing to marvellous new extremes. Largely dependent upon a young, fickle audience, and seemingly incapable of spreading their parochial charm to the USA, Slade's supremacy proved ephemeral. They participated in a movie, *Slade In Flame*, which was surprisingly impressive, and undertook extensive tours, yet by the mid-70s they were yesterday's teen heroes. The ensuing punk explosion made them virtually redundant and prompted in 1977 the appropriately titled, *Whatever Happened To Slade*. Undeterred, they carried on just as they had done in the late 60s, awaiting a new break. An appearance at the 1980 Reading Festival brought them credibility anew. This performance was captured on the *Slade Alive At Reading '80* EP which pushed the group into the UK singles chart for the first time in three years. The festive 'Merry Xmas Everybody' was re-recorded and charted that same year (the first in a run of seven consecutive years, subsequently in its original form). Slade returned to the Top 10 in January 1981 with 'We'll Bring The House Down' and they have continued to gig extensively, being rewarded in 1983 with the number 2 hit, 'My Oh My', followed the next year with 'Run Run Away', a UK number 7 and their first US Top 20 hit, and the anthemic 'All Join Hands' (number 15). Slade were one of the few groups to have survived the heady days of glitter and glam with their reputation intact and were regarded with endearing affection by a wide spectrum of age groups, which makes it seem churlish to point out that their creative peak is way behind them, as highlighted by the derivative Slade II (minus Holder and Lea). Holder meanwhile has become a popular all-round television personality and hosts a regular 70s rock programme on radio. The compilation *Feel The Noize - The Very Best Of* in 1996 received outstanding reviews in the UK heralding a mini glam rock revival.

●ALBUMS: as Ambrose Slade *Ambrose Slade - Beginnings* (Fontana 1969)★★, *Play It Loud* (Polydor 1970)★★, *Slade Alive* (Polydor 1972)★★★, *Slayed* (Polydor 1972)★★★, *Old, New, Borrowed And Blue* (Polydor 1974)★★★, *Stomp Your Hands, Clap Your Feet* (Warners 1974)★★★, *Slade In Flame* (Polydor 1974)★★★, *Nobody's Fools* (Polydor 1976)★★★, *Whatever Happened To Slade?* (Barn 1977)★★★, *Slade Alive Vol. 2* (Barn 1978)★★, *Return To Base* (Barn 1979)★★, *We'll Bring The House Down* (Cheapskate 1981)★★, *Till Deaf Us Do Part* (RCA 1981)★★, *Slade On Stage* (RCA 1982)★★, *Slade Alive* (Polydor 1983)★★, *The Amazing Kamikaze Syndrome* (RCA 1983)★★, *On Stage* (RCA 1984)★★, *Rogues Gallery* (RCA 1985)★★, *Crackers - The Slade Christmas Party*

Album (Telstar 1985)★★, *You Boyz Make Big Noize* (RCA 1987)★★, as Slade II *Keep On Rockin'* (Total 1996)★★.
●COMPILATIONS: *Sladest* (Polydor 1973)★★, *Slade Smashes* (Barn 1980)★★★, *Story Of* (Polydor 1981)★★★, *Slade's Greats* (Polydor 1984)★★★, *Keep Your Hands Off My Power Supply* (Columbia 1984)★★★, *Wall Of Hits* (Polydor 1991)★★★, *Slade Collection 81-87* (RCA 1991)★★, *Feel The Noize - The Very Best Of* (Polydor 1996)★★★★.
●VIDEOS: *Slade In Flame* (Hendring 1990), *Wall Of Hits* (Polygram 1991).
●FURTHER READING: *The Slade Story*, George Tremlett. *Slade In Flame*, John Pidgeon. *Slade: Feel The Noize*, Chris Charlesworth.
●FILMS: *Slade In Flame* (1974)

SLICK, GRACE

b. Grace Wing, 30 October 1939, Evanston, Illinois, USA. A former fashion model, Grace Slick began a career in music by contributing recorder and piano soundtracks to husband Jerry's films. This experience was later enhanced by an interest in the nascent San Francisco rock scene and in August 1965 the couple formed the Great Society. This short-lived group combined melodic and experimental styles, but Slick quickly tired of their endearing amateurism, and joined Jefferson Airplane the following year, taking two renowned songs, 'Somebody To Love' and 'White Rabbit', with her. Slick's powerful, distinctive voice established her as the unit's focal point, as well as one of the era's best-known figures. Now separated from her husband, Slick began a personal and professional relationship with band guitarist Paul Kantner. Together they recorded *Blows Against The Empire* (1970 - credited to Kantner), *Sunfighter* (1971) and *Baron Von Tollbooth And The Chrome Nun* (1973), which many commentators feel superior to concurrent Airplane releases. Indeed commitment to such projects may have undermined the parent group, although *Manhole*, Slick's experimental solo debut, boasted a largely idiosyncratic content. Dour and self-indulgent, the set's disappointments were deflected by the formation of Jefferson Starship whom Slick fronted until 1978 when alcohol-related problems resulted in her departure. *Dreams* nonetheless displayed a rekindled creativity and its success resulted in the singer rejoining her former colleagues in 1981. Slick maintained her own career with *Welcome To The Wrecking Ball*, but this heavy-handed collection merely reflected Jefferson Starship's slide towards AOR rock, rather than asserting an independence. Despite the release of *Software*, Slick became increasingly committed to the parent group, now known simply as Starship. They enjoyed a series of highly successful releases, including three US chart toppers, 'We Built This City (On Rock 'N' Roll)', 'Sara' and 'Nothing's Gonna Stop Us Now', the latter of which also reached number 1 in Britain. However, internal dissent culminated in 1989 with Grace leaving the line-up for a

second time; she has since maintained a relatively low profile. Slick nonetheless remains one of the most charismatic artists to emerge from San Francisco's 'golden era'.
●ALBUMS: with Paul Kantner *Sunfighter* (Grunt 1971)★★★, with Kantner, David Freiberg *Baron Von Tollbooth And The Chrome Nun* (Grunt 1973)★★★, *Manhole* (Grunt 1974)★★★, *Dreams* (RCA 1980)★★★, *Welcome To The Wrecking Ball* (RCA 1981)★★, *Software* (RCA 1984)★★.
●FURTHER READING: *Grace Slick - The Biography*, Barbara Rowe.

SLITS

This UK feminist punk group formed in 1976 with a line-up featuring Ari-Up (b. Arianna Foster; vocals), Kate Korus (guitar), Palmolive (drums; ex-Raincoats) and Suzi Gutsy (bass). Korus soon left to form the Modettes and Gutsy quit to team up with the Flicks. They were replaced by guitarist Viv Albertine and bass player Tessa Pollitt and it was this line-up that supported the Clash during the spring of 1977. The group were known for their uncompromising attitude and professed lack of technique, but their music was as aggressive and confrontational as the best of the punk fraternity. Their failure to secure a record contract during the first wave of the punk explosion was surprising. By the time they made their recording debut, Palmolive had been ousted and replaced by Big In Japan percussionist, Budgie (b. Peter Clark, 21 August 1957). Signed to Island Records, they worked with reggae producer Dennis Bovell on the dub-influenced *Cut*. The album attracted considerable press interest for its sleeve, which featured the group naked, after rolling in the mud. The departure of Budgie to Siouxsie And The Banshees (replaced by the Pop Group's Bruce Smith) coincided with the arrival of reggae musician Prince Hammer and trumpeter Don Cherry (father of Neneh Cherry). A series of singles followed, including a memorable version of John Holt's 'Man Next Door'. By 1981, the Slits had lost much of their original cutting edge and it came as little surprise when they disbanded at the end of the year.
●ALBUMS: *Cut* (Island 1979)★★★, *Bootleg Retrospective* (Rough Trade 1980)★★★, *Return Of The Giant Slits* (Columbia 1981)★★.
●COMPILATIONS: *The Peel Sessions* (Strange Fruit 1988)★★.

SMITH, LONNIE LISTON

b. 28 December 1940, Richmond, Virginia, USA. Not to be confused with the soul/jazz organist Lonnie Smith. Born into a very musical family, Smith seemed destined from a very early age to make music his career. His father and two brothers were all vocalists, but it was the keyboard that attracted Lonnie. After studying at Morgan State University, he moved to New York and immersed himself in the city's thriving jazz scene. Accompanying Betty Carter for a year in 1963, Smith soon became a highly sought-after pianist, working with successive jazz stars, from Roland Kirk (1964-65), Art Blakey (1966-67), and Joe Williams (1967-68), through to Pharoah Sanders (1969-71), Gato Barbieri (1971-73), and finally Miles Davis (1972-73). In 1974, Smith formed the Cosmic Echoes with his brother Donald as vocalist. Playing a very popular soft fusion, they recorded a highly successful album in 1975, and remained popular throughout the decade. In 1991, after some time out of the spotlight, Smith recorded a high quality album, *Magic Lady*, and embarked on a European tour (including the UK).

●ALBUMS: with Pharoah Sanders *Karma* (Impulse 1969)★★★, *Astral Traveling* (Flying Dutchman 1973), with Miles Davis *Big Fun* (Columbia 1974)★★★, with the Cosmic Echoes *Expansions* (Flying Dutchman 1975)★★, with the Cosmic Echoes *Visions Of A New World* (Flying Dutchman 1975)★★★, with the Cosmic Echoes *Reflections Of A Golden Dream* (Flying Dutchman 1976)★★★★, with the Cosmic Echoes *Renaissance* (RCA 1976)★★★, *Live!* (RCA 1977)★★★, *Loveland* (Columbia 1978)★★★, *Exotic Myteries* (Columbia 1979)★★★, *Dreams Of Tomorrow* (Doctor Jazz 1983)★★★, *Silhouettes* (Doctor Jazz 1984)★★★, *Rejuvenation* (Doctor Jazz 1986), *Magic Lady* (1991)★★★.

●COMPILATIONS: *The Best Of Lonnie Liston Smith* (Columbia 1981)★★★★.

SMITH, PATTI

b. 31 December 1946, Chicago, Illinois, USA. Smith was raised in New Jersey and became infatuated by music, principally the Rolling Stones, the Velvet Underground, Jimi Hendrix and James Brown. Her initial talent focused on poetry and art, while her first major label recording was a version of a Jim Morrison poem on Ray Manzarek's (both Doors) solo album. Her early writing, captured on three anthologies, *Seventh Heaven* (1971), *Kodak* (1972) and *Witt* (1973), was inspired by Arthur Rimbaud and William Burroughs, but as the 70s progressed she was increasingly drawn towards fusing such work with rock. In 1971, Smith was accompanied by guitarist Lenny Kaye for a reading in St Mark's Church, and this informal liaison continued for three years until the duo was joined by Richard Sohl (piano) in the first Patti Smith Group. Their debut recording, 'Hey Joe'/'Piss Factory', was in part financed by photographer Robert Mapplethorpe, later responsible for many of the artist's striking album portraits. By 1974 the unit had become one of the most popular acts at New York's pivotal CBGB's club. Ivan Kral (bass) and J.D. Daugherty (drums) were then added to the line-up featured on *Horses*. This highly lauded set, produced by John Cale, skilfully invoked Smith's 60s mentors but in a celebratory manner. By simultaneously capturing the fire of punk, Smith completed a collection welcomed by both old and new audiences. However, *Radio Ethiopia* was perceived as self-indulgent and the artist's career was further undermined when she incurred a broken neck upon falling off a stage early in 1977. A lengthy recuperation ensued but Smith re-emerged in July with a series of excellent concerts and the following year enjoyed considerable commercial success with *Easter*. This powerful set included 'Because The Night', co-written with Bruce Springsteen, which deservedly reached the UK Top 5, but *Wave* failed to sustain such acclaim. She had previously collaborated on three Blue Öyster Cult albums, with her then partner Allen Lanier. Patti then married former MC5 guitarist Fred 'Sonic' Smith, and retired from active performing for much of the 80s to raise a family. She resumed recording in 1988 with *Dream Of Life*, which contained the artist's customary call-to-arms idealism ('People Have The Power') and respect for rock and poetic tradition. Following a series of tragic events in her life, triggered by the death of her husband she embarked on what was seen as an exhortation album, *Gone Again*. It was intense and melancholic; in time it may well be seen as her best work.

●ALBUMS: *Horses* (Arista 1975)★★★★, *Radio Ethiopia* (Arista 1976)★★★, *Easter* (Arista 1978)★★★, *Wave* (Arista 1979)★★, *Dream Of Life* (Arista 1988)★★, *Gone Again* (Arista 1996)★★★.

●FURTHER READING: *A Useless Death*, Patti Smith. *The Tongue Of Love*, Patti Smith. *Seventh Heaven*, Patti Smith. *Witt*, Patti Smith. *Babel*, Patti Smith. *The Night*, Patti Smith and Tom Verlaine. *Ha! Ha! Houdini!*, Patti Smith. *Patti Smith: Rock & Roll Madonna*, Dusty Roach. *Patti Smith: High On Rebellion*, Muir. *Early Work: 1970-1979*, Patti Smith.

SMOKIE

This UK pop band from Bradford, Yorkshire, featured Chris Norman (vocals), Terry Utley (guitar), and Alan Silson (bass). The three were previously together in 1966 with a band titled the Elizabethans. Pete Spencer replaced their original drummer shortly afterwards. Turning professional in 1968, they changed their name to Kindness, performing at holiday camps and ballrooms. A variety of record company contracts failed to ignite any hit singles, however. Along the way they changed their name to Smokey, but it was not until they joined Rak Records, where Mickie Most introduced them to songwriters Chinn And Chapman, that they saw any success. They then had frequent successes with 'If You Think You Know How To Love Me' and 'Don't Play Your Rock 'n' Roll To Me' in 1975, after which they changed the spelling of their name to Smokie. Their 1976 version of the Chinn/Chapman composition 'Living Next Door To Alice', originally recorded by New World, became a hit in the face of opposition from the burgeoning punk scene. Norman, meanwhile, joined fellow Rak artist Suzi Quatro on the 1978 hit duet 'Stumblin' In'. By 1978 and *The Montreux Album*, the band, through Norman and Spencer, were taking a greater share of writing credits, but this coincided with a drop in their fortunes. They bounced back briefly in 1980 with a cover of Bobby Vee's 'Take Good Care Of My Baby', but this proved to be their last hit. Norman and Spencer moved on to writing for other artists including fellow Rak teenybop groups, and both Kevin Keegan's 'Head Over Heels' and the England World Cup Squad's 'This Time We'll Get It Right'.

●ALBUMS: *Smokie/Changing All The Time* (RAK 1975)★★, *Bright Lights And Back Alleys* (RAK 1977)★★, *The Montreux Album* (RAK 1978)★★.

●COMPILATIONS: *Greatest Hits* (RAK 1977)★★★, *Smokie's Hits* (RAK 1980)★★★, *Best Of Smokie* (Telstar 1980)★★, *Greatest Hits Live* (1993)★★.

SNIFF 'N' THE TEARS

This London group was formed from the Ashes of Moon in 1974 only to disband within months after thwarted attempts to gain a recording contract. Its principal composer, Paul Roberts (vocals), returned to the world of art where his paintings had been exhibited in many European capitals. However, with the advent of the late 70s new wave, drummer Luigi Salvoni listened again to the 1974 demos and persuaded Roberts (then resident in France) to try again with Mick Dyche (guitar), Laurence Netto (guitar), Keith Miller (keyboards) and Nick South (bass). After another self-financed studio session, they were signed to Chiswick Records in the summer of 1978. One of Roberts' magnificent paintings graced the sleeve of *Fickle Heart* (produced by Salvoni) from which the catchy 'Driver's Seat' was a hit in the USA and Australasia while faltering just outside the UK Top 40. 1980's *The Game's Up* compounded *Billboard*'s comparison of them to Dire Straits. They began a downward spiral with *Ride Blue Divide* (with Lew Lewis on harmonica) the last album to make a moderate commercial impact.

●ALBUMS: *Fickle Heart* (Chiswick 1978)★★★, *The Game's Up* (Chiswick 1980)★★★, *Love Action* (Chiswick 1981)★★, *Ride Blue Divide* (Chiswick 1982)★★.

●COMPILATIONS: *Retrospective* (Chiswick 1988)★★★, *A Best Of Sniff 'N' The Tears* (Chiswick 1991)★★★.

SNOW, PHOEBE

b. Phoebe Laub, 17 July 1952, New York, USA. Phoebe Snow was a singer with jazz and folk influences who released a string of popular albums in the 70s that showcased her versatile, elastic contralto vocals. Snow and her family moved to Teaneck, New Jersey, where she studied piano during her childhood. She switched to guitar while in her teens. She wrote poetry and fashioned songs around her poems, which led her into performing at New York clubs in the early 70s. She was signed to Leon Russell's Shelter Records label in 1974 and released her self-titled debut album, which reached the US Top 5, as did the single 'Poetry Man'. The album included jazz greats Stan Getz and Teddy Wilson guesting. Snow duetted with Paul Simon on his song 'Gone At Last' in 1975 and also toured with him. She switched to Columbia Records for *Second Childhood* in

1976, and stayed with that company throughout the decade, although her album sales decreased with each new release. In 1981 she switched to Mirage Records, distributed by Atlantic Records, and rebounded with *Rock Away*, which reached number 51 in the USA. In 1989 she reappeared on Elektra Records and in 1990-91 made numerous club appearances in the New York area, performing with a makeshift band that also included ex-Steely Dan member Donald Fagen and former Doobie Brothers singer Michael McDonald.

●ALBUMS: *Phoebe Snow* (Shelter 1974)★★★★, *Second Childhood* (Columbia 1976)★★★, *It Looks Like Snow* (Columbia 1976)★★★, *Never Letting Go* (Columbia 1977)★★★, *Against The Grain* (Columbia 1978)★★★, *Rock Away* (Mirage 1981)★★★, *Something Real* (Elektra 1989)★★★.

●COMPILATIONS: *Best Of* (Columbia 1981)★★★★.

SONDHEIM, STEPHEN

b. Stephen Joshua Sondheim, 22 March 1930, New York, USA. Sondheim is generally regarded as the most important theatrical composer of the 70s and 80s - his introduction of the concept musical (some say, anti-musical) or 'unified show', has made him a cult figure. Born into an affluent family, his father was a prominent New York dress manufacturer; Sondheim studied piano and organ sporadically from the age of seven. When he was 10 his parents divorced, and he spent some time at military school. His mother's friendship with the Oscar Hammerstein II family in Philadelphia enabled Sondheim to meet the lyricist, who took him under his wing and educated him in the art of writing for the musical theatre. After majoring in music at Williams College, Sondheim graduated in 1950 with the Hutchinson Prize For Musical Composition, a two-year fellowship, which enabled him to study with the innovative composer Milton Babbitt. During the early 50s, he contributed material to television shows such as *Topper*, and wrote the songs for a proposed Broadway musical, *Saturday Night* (1955), which was never staged due to the death of producer Lemuel Ayres. Sondheim also wrote the incidental music for the play *Girls Of Summer* (1956). His first major success was as a lyric writer, with Leonard Bernstein's music, for the 1957 Broadway hit musical *West Side Story*. Initially, Bernstein was billed as co-lyricist, but had his name removed before the New York opening, giving Sondheim full credit. The show ran for 734 performances on Broadway, and 1,039 in London. The songs included 'Jet Song', 'Maria', 'Something's Coming', 'Tonight', 'America', 'One Hand, One Heart', 'I Feel Pretty', 'Somewhere' and 'A Boy Like That'. A film version was released in 1961 and there were New York revivals in 1968 and 1980. Productions in London in 1974 and 1984 were also significant in that they marked the first of many collaborations between Sondheim and producer Harold Prince.

It was another powerful theatrical personality, David Merrick, who mounted *Gypsy* (1959), based on stripper

Gypsy Rose Lee's book, *Gypsy: A Memoir*, and considered by some to be the pinnacle achievement of the Broadway musical stage. Sondheim was set to write both music and lyrics before the show's star Ethel Merman demanded a more experienced composer. Jule Styne proved to be acceptable, and Sondheim concentrated on the lyrics, which have been called his best work in the musical theatre, despite the critical acclaim accorded his later shows. *Gypsy's* memorable score included 'Let Me Entertain You', 'Some People', 'Small World', 'You'll Never Get Away From Me', 'If Momma Was Married', 'All I Need Is The Girl', 'Everything's Coming Up Roses', 'Together, Wherever We Go', 'You Gotta Have A Gimmick' and 'Rose's Turn'. Merman apparently refused to embark on a long London run, so the show was not mounted there until 1973. Angela Lansbury enjoyed a personal triumph then as the domineering mother, Rose, and repeated her success in the Broadway revival in 1974. In 1989, both the show and its star, Tyne Daly (well known for television's *Cagney and Lacey*), won Tony Awards in the 30th anniversary revival, which ran through until 1991. Rosalind Russell played Rose in the 1962 movie version, which received lukewarm reviews. For *Gypsy*, Sondheim had interrupted work on *A Funny Thing Happened On The Way To The Forum* (1962), to which he contributed both music and lyrics. Based on the plays of Plautus, it has been variously called 'a fast moving farce', 'a vaudeville-based Roman spoof' and 'a musical madhouse'. Sondheim's songs, which included the prologue, 'Comedy Tonight' ('Something appealing, something appalling/Something for everyone, a comedy tonight!') and 'Everybody Ought To Have A Maid', celebrated moments of joy or desire and punctuated the thematic action. The show won several Tony Awards, including 'Best Musical' and 'Best Producer', but nothing for Sondheim's score. The show was revived on Broadway in 1972 with Phil Silvers in the leading role, and had two London productions (1963 and 1986), both starring British comedian Frankie Howerd. A film version, starring Zero Mostel and Silvers, dropped several of the original songs. *Anyone Can Whistle* (1964), 'a daft moral fable about corrupt city officials', with an original book by Laurents and songs by Sondheim, lasted just a week. The critics were unanimous in their condemnation of the musical with a theme that 'madness is the only hope for world sanity'. The original cast recording, which included 'Simple', 'I've Got You To Lean On', 'A Parade In Town', 'Me And My Town' and the appealing title song, was recorded after the show closed, and became a cult item.

Sondheim was back to 'lyrics only' for *Do I Hear A Waltz?* (1965). The durable Broadway composer Richard Rodgers supplied the music for the show, which he described as 'not a satisfying experience'. In retrospect, it was perhaps underrated. Adapted by Arthur Laurents from his play, *The Time Of The Cuckoo*, the show revolved around an American tourist in Venice, and

included 'Moon In My Window', 'This Week's Americans', 'Perfectly Lovely Couple', 'We're Gonna Be All Right', and 'Here We Are Again'. Broadway had to wait until 1970 for the next Sondheim musical, the first to be directed by Harold Prince. *Company* had no plot, but concerned 'the lives of five Manhattan couples held together by their rather excessively protective feelings about a 'bachelor friend'. Its ironic, acerbic score included 'The Little Things You Do Together' ('The concerts you enjoy together/Neighbours you annoy together/Children you destroy together...'), 'Sorry-Grateful', 'You Could Drive A Person Crazy', 'Have I Got A Girl For You?', 'Someone Is Waiting', 'Another Hundred People', 'Getting Married Today', 'Side By Side By Side', 'What Would We Do Without You?', 'Poor Baby', 'Tick Tock', 'Barcelona', 'The Ladies Who Lunch' ('Another chance to disapprove, another brilliant zinger/Another reason not to move, another vodka stinger/I'll drink to that!') and 'Being Alive'. With a book by George Furth, produced and directed by Prince, the musical numbers staged by Michael Bennett, and starring Elaine Stritch and Larry Kert (for most of the run), *Company* ran for 690 performances. It gained the New York Drama Critics' Circle Award for Best Musical, and six Tony Awards, including Best Musical, and Best Music and Lyrics for Sondheim, the first awards of his Broadway career. The marathon recording session for the original cast album, produced by Thomas Z. Shepard, was the subject of a highly acclaimed television documentary.

The next Prince-Bennett-Sondheim project, with a book by James Goldman, was the mammoth *Follies* (1971), 'the story of four people in their early 50s: two ex-show girls from the *Weismann Follies*, and two stage-door-Johnnies whom they married 30 years ago, who attend a reunion, and start looking backwards...'. It was a lavish, spectacular production, with a cast of 50, and a Sondheim score which contained 22 'book' songs, including 'Who's That Woman?' (sometimes referred to as the 'the mirror number'), 'Ah Paris!', 'Could I Leave You?', 'I'm Still Here' ('Then you career from career, to career/I'm almost through my memoirs/And I'm here!'); and several 'pastiche' numbers in the style of the 'great' songwriters such as George Gershwin and Dorothy Fields ('Losing My Mind'); Cole Porter ('The Story Of Lucy and Jessie'); Sigmund Romberg and Rudolph Friml ('One More Kiss'); Jerome Kern ('Loveland'); Irving Berlin (the prologue, 'Beautiful Girls') and De Sylva, Brown, And Henderson ('Broadway Baby'). Although the show received a great deal of publicity and gained the Drama Critics Circle Award for Best Musical, plus seven Tony awards, it closed after 522 performances with the loss of its entire $800,000 investment. A spokesperson commented: 'We sold more posters than tickets'. *Follies In Concert*, with the New York Philharmonic, played two performances in September 1985 at the Lincoln Center, and featured several legendary Broadway names such as Carol

Burnett, Betty Comden, Adolph Green, Lee Remick, and Barbara Cook. The show was taped for television, and generated a much-acclaimed RCA album, which compensated for the disappointingly truncated recording of the original show. The show did not reach London until 1987, when the young Cameron Mackintosh produced a 'new conception' with Goldman's revised book, and several new songs replacing some of the originals. It closed after 600 performances, because of high running costs. *A Little Night Music* (1973) was the first Sondheim-Prince project to be based on an earlier source; in this instance, Ingmar Bergman's film *Smiles Of A Summer Night*. Set at the turn of the century, in Sweden it was an operetta, with all the music in three quarter time, or multiples thereof. The critics saw in it echoes of Mahler, Ravel, Rachmaninoff, Brahms, and even Johann Strauss. The score contained Sondheims's first song hit for which he wrote both words and music, 'Send In The Clowns'. Other songs included 'Liaisons', 'A Weekend In The Country', 'The Glamorous Life', 'In Praise Of Women', 'Remember' and 'Night Waltz'. The show ran for 601 performances, and was a healthy financial success. It gained the New York Drama Critics Award for Best Musical, and five Tony awards, including Sondheim's music and lyrics for a record third time in a row. The London run starred Jean Simmons, while Elizabeth Taylor played Desiree in the 1978 movie version.

On the back of the show's 1973 Broadway success, and the composer's increasing popularity, a benefit concert, *Sondheim: A Musical Tribute*, was mounted at the Shubert Theatre, featuring every available performer who had been associated with his shows, singing familiar, and not so familiar, material. *Pacific Overtures* (1976) was, perhaps, Sondheim's most daring and ambitious musical to date. John Weidman's book purported to relate the entire 120 years history of Japan, from Commodore Perry's arrival in 1856, to its emergence as the powerful industrial force of the 20th century. The production was heavily influenced by the Japanese Kabuki Theatre. The entire cast were Asian, and Sondheim used many Oriental instruments to obtain his effects. Musical numbers included 'Chrysanthemum Tea', 'Please Hello', 'Welcome To Kanagawa', 'Next', 'Someone In A Tree' and 'The Advantages Of Floating In The Middle Of The Sea'. The show closed after 193 performances, losing its entire budget of over half-a-million dollars, but it still won the Drama Critics Circle Award for Best Musical. It was revived off-Broadway in 1984.

The next Broadway project bearing Sondheim's name was much more successful, and far more conventional. *Side By Side By Sondheim* (1977), an anthology of some of his songs, started out at London's Mermaid Theatre the year before. Starring the original London cast of Millicent Martin, Julia McKenzie, David Kernan and Ned Sherrin, the New York production received almost unanimously favourable notices, and proved that many of Sondheim's songs, when presented in this revue form and removed from the sometimes bewildering librettos, could be popular items in their own right. In complete contrast was *Sweeney Todd, The Demon Barber Of Fleet Street* (1979), Hugh Wheeler's version of the grisly tale of a 19th century barber who slits the throats of his clients, and turns the bodies over to Mrs Lovett (Angela Lansbury), who bakes them into pies. Sondheim's 'endlessly inventive, highly expressive score', considered to be near-opera, included the gruesome, 'Not While I'm Around', 'Epiphany', 'A Little Priest', the more gentle 'Pretty Women' and 'My Friends'. Generally accepted as one of the most ambitious Broadway musicals ever staged ('a staggering theatrical spectacle'; 'one giant step forward for vegetarianism'), *Sweeney Todd* ran for over 500 performances, and gained eight Tony Awards, including Best Musical, Score and Book. In 1980, it played in London for four months, and starred Denis Quilley and Sheila Hancock, and was successfully revived by the Royal National Theatre in 1993.

According to Sondheim himself, *Merrily We Roll Along* (1981), with a book by George Furth, was deliberately written in 'a consistent musical comedy style'. It was based on the 1934 play by George S. Kaufman and Moss Hart, and despite a run of only 16 performances, the pastiche score contained some 'insinuatingly catchy numbers'. It also marked the end, for the time being, of Sondheim's association with Harold Prince, who had produced and directed nearly all of his shows. Depressed and dejected, Sondheim threatened to give up writing for the theatre. However, in 1982, he began working with James Lapine, who had attracted some attention for his direction of the off-Broadway musical, *March Of The Falsettos* (1981).

The first fruits of the Sondheim-Lapine association, *Sunday In The Park With George* also started off-Broadway, as a Playwrights Horizon workshop production, before opening on Broadway in 1984. Inspired by George Seurat's 19th century painting, *Sunday Afternoon On The Island Of La Grande Jatte*, with book and direction by Lapine, the two-act show starred Mandy Patinkin and Bernadette Peters, and an 'intriguingly intricate' Sondheim score that included 'Finishing The Hat', 'Lesson No.8', and 'Move On'. The run of a year-and-a-half was due in no small part to energetic promotion by the *New York Times*, which caused the theatrical competition to dub the show, *Sunday In The Times With George*. In 1985, it was awarded the coveted Pulitzer Prize for Drama, and in 1990 became one of the rare musicals to be staged at London's Royal National Theatre. In 1987, Sondheim again received a Tony award for *Into the Woods*, a musical fairy tale of a baker and his wife, who live under the curse of a wicked witch, played by Bernadette Peters. The critics called it Sondheim's most accessible show for many years, with a score that included 'Cinderella At The Grave', 'Hello, Little Girl' and 'Children Will Listen'. It won the New

York Drama Critics Circle, and Drama Desk Awards, for Best Musical, and a Grammy for Best Original Cast album. 'Angry', rather than accessible, was the critics' verdict of *Assassins*, with a book by John Weidman, which opened for a limited run off Broadway early in 1991, and played the Donmar Warehouse in London a year later. Dubbed by *Newsweek*: 'Sondheim's most audacious, far out and grotesque work of his career', it 'attempted to examine the common thread of killers and would-be killers from John Wilkes Booth, the murderer of Lincoln, through Lee Harvey Oswald to John Hinckley Jnr, who shot Ronald Reagan'. The pastiche score included 'Everybody's Got The Right', 'The Ballad Of Booth' and 'The Ballad Of Czolgosz'. In 1993, a one-night tribute *Sondheim: A Celebration At Carnegie Hall*, was transmitted on US network television in the 'Great Performers' series, and, on a rather smaller scale, the off Broadway revue *Putting It Together*, which was packed with Sondheim songs, brought Julie Andrews back to the New York musical stage for the first time since *Camelot*. In May 1994, *Passion*, the result of Sondheim's third collaboration with James Lapine, opened on Broadway and ran for 280 performances.

Besides his main Broadway works over the years, Sondheim provided material for many other stage projects, such as the music and lyrics for *The Frogs* (1974), songs for the revue *Marry Me A Little* and a song for the play *A Mighty Man Is He*. He also contributed the incidental music to *The Girls Of Summer*, 'Come Over Here' and 'Home Is the Place' for Tony Bennett. In addition, Sondheim wrote the incidental music for the play *Invitation To A March*, the score for the mini-musical *Passionella*, the lyrics (with Mary Rodgers' music) for *The Mad Show* and new lyrics for composer Leonard Bernstein's 1974 revival of *Candide*. Sondheim's film work has included the music for *Stravinsky*, *Reds*, and *Dick Tracy*. He received an Oscar for his 'Sooner Or Later (I Always Get My Man)', from the latter film. Sondheim also wrote the screenplay, with Anthony Perkins, for *The Last Of Sheila*, a film 'full of impossible situations, demented logic and indecipherable clues', inspired by his penchant for board games and puzzles of every description. For television, Sondheim wrote the music and lyrics for *Evening Primrose*, which starred Perkins, and made his own acting debut in 1974, with Jack Cassidy, in a revival of the George S. Kaufman-Ring Lardner play *June Moon*. While never pretending to write 'hit songs' (apparently the term 'hummable' makes him bristle), Sondheim has nevertheless had his moments in the charts with songs such as 'Small World' (Johnny Mathis); 'Tonight' (Ferrante And Teicher); 'Maria' and 'Somewhere' (P.J. Proby); 'Send In The Clowns' (Judy Collins), and 'Losing My Mind' (Liza Minnelli). Probably Sondheim's greatest impact on records, apart from the Original Cast albums which to date have won seven Grammys, was Barbra Streisand's *The Broadway Album* in 1985. Seven tracks, involving eight songs, were Sondheim's (two in collaboration with

Bernstein), and he rewrote three of them for Streisand, including 'Send In The Clowns'. *The Broadway Album* stayed at number 1 in the US charts for three weeks, and sold over three million copies. Other gratifying moments for Sondheim occurred in 1983 when he was voted a member of the American Academy and the Institute of Arts and Letters, and again in 1990, when he became Oxford University's first Professor of Drama. As for his contribution to the musical theatre, opinions are sharply divided. John Podhoretz in the *Washington Times* said that 'with *West Side Story*, the musical took a crucial, and in retrospect, suicidal step into the realm of social commentary, and created a self-destructive form in which characters were taken to task and made fun of, for doing things like bursting into song'. Others, like Harold Prince, have said that Stephen Sondheim is simply the best in the world.

●ALBUMS: various artists *Sondheim: A Celebration At Carnegie Hall* (RCA Victor 1994)★★★, various artists *Putting It Together* original cast recording (RCA Victor 1994)★★★.

●FURTHER READING: *Sondheim & Co.*, Craig Zadan. *Sondheim And The American Musical*, Paul Sheran and Tom Sutcliffe. *Song By Song By Sondheim (The Stephen Sondheim Songbook)*, edited by Sheridan Morley. *Sunday In the Park With George*, Stephen Sondheim and James Lapine. *Sondheim*, Martin Gottfried. *Art Isn't Easy: Theatre Of Stephen Sondheim*, Joanne Gordon. *Sondheim's Broadway Musicals*, Stephen Banfield.

SOUL CHILDREN

This group was formed as a vehicle for the songwriting talents of Isaac Hayes and David Porter in Memphis, Tennessee, USA. Comprising of Anita Louis (b. 24 November 1949, Memphis, Tennessee, USA), Shelbra Bennett (b. Memphis, Tennessee, USA), John 'Blackfoot' Colbert (b. 20 November 1946, Greenville, Mississippi, USA) and Norman West (b. 30 October 1939, Monroe, Louisiana, USA), they first surfaced in 1968 with 'Give 'Em Love'. This excellent Hayes/Porter composition established their startling vocal interplay which, at times, suggested a male/female Sam And Dave. Although artistically consistent, only three of the group's singles, 'The Sweeter He Is' (1969), 'Hearsay' (1970) and 'I'll Be The Other Woman' (1973), reached the US R&B Top 10. The Soul Children were later reduced to a trio and moved to Epic when their former outlet, Stax, went into liquidation. Colbert later found fame under the name J. Blackfoot when one of his releases, 'Taxi', was a 1983 hit in both the US and UK.

●ALBUMS: *Soul Children* (Stax 1969)★★★, *Best Of Two Worlds* (Stax 1971)★★★, *Genesis* (Stax 1972)★★★, *Friction* (1974)★★★, *The Soul Years* (1974)★★★, *Finders Keepers* (Epic 1976)★★★, *Where Is Your Woman Tonight* (Epic 1977)★★★, *Open Door Policy* (1978)★★★.

●COMPILATIONS: *Soul Children/Genesis* (1990)★★★, *Friction/Best Of Two Worlds* (1992)★★★, *The Singles Plus Open Door Policy* (1993)★★★★.

SOUTH, JOE

b. Joe Souter, 28 February 1940, Atlanta, Georgia, USA. South was obsessed with technology and, as a child, he developed his own radio station with a transmission area of a mile. A novelty song, 'The Purple People Eater Meets The Witch Doctor', sold well in 1958, and he became a session guitarist in both Nashville and Muscle Shoals. South backed Eddy Arnold, Aretha Franklin, Wilson Pickett, Marty Robbins and, in particular, Bob Dylan (*Blonde On Blonde*) and Simon And Garfunkel (most of *The Sounds Of Silence* LP). His 1962 single, 'Masquerade', was released in the UK, but his first writing/producing successes came with the Tams' 'Untie Me' and various Billy Joe Royal singles including 'Down In The Boondocks' and 'I Knew You When'. In 1968, he sang and played several instruments on Royal's *Introspect*. One track, 'Games People Play', reached number 12 in the US charts and number 6 in the UK, and he also played guitar and sang harmony on Boots Randolph's cover version. The song's title was taken from Eric Berne's best-selling book about the psychology of human relationships. Another song title, '(I Never Promised You A) Rose Garden', came from a novel by Hannah Green, and was a transatlantic hit for country singer, Lynn Anderson. 'These Are Not My People' was a US country hit for Freddie Weller, 'Birds Of A Feather' was made popular by Paul Revere And The Raiders, but, more significantly, 'Hush' became Deep Purple's first US Top 10 hit in 1968. South himself made number 12 in the US with 'Walk A Mile In My Shoes', which was also featured by Elvis Presley in concert, but his own career was not helped by a drugs bust, a pretentious single 'I'm A Star', and a poor stage presence. He told one audience to 'start dancing around the hall, then when you come in front of the stage, each one of you can kiss my ass.' South's songs reflect southern life but they also reflect his own insecurities and it is not surprising that he stopped performing. He had heeded his own words, 'Don't It Make You Want To Go Home'.

●ALBUMS: *Introspect* released in the UK as *Games People Play* (Capitol 1969)★★★★, *Don't It Make You Want To Go Home* (Capitol 1970)★★★, *Walkin' Shoes* (1970)★★★, *So The Seeds Are Growing* (1971)★★★, *Midnight Rainbows* (1975)★★, *Joe South, You're The Reason, To Have, To Hold And To Let Go* (1976)★★, *Look Inside* (1976)★★★.

●COMPILATIONS: *Joe South's Greatest Hits* (Capitol 1970)★★★, *The Joe South Story* (1971)★★, *Introspect* (See For Miles 1986)★★★, *The Best Of Joe South* (Rhino 1990)★★★.

SOUTHER HILLMAN FURAY BAND

Formed in September 1973 and based in Los Angeles, California, USA, the Souther Hillman Furay Band was a west coast supergroup that failed to jell. J.D. Souther (vocals, guitar) had been a former member of Longbranch Pennywhistle with future Eagles guitarist and vocalist, Glen Frey. It was through this association that Souther was signed to Asylum Records, for whom he recorded an excellent solo album in 1972. Chris Hillman (vocals, bass, guitar, mandolin), famed for his spells in the Byrds and Flying Burrito Brothers had recently left Manassas, a group led by ex-Buffalo Springfield founder, Stephen Stills. Richie Furay (vocals, guitar), had also been a member of Buffalo Springfield, before founding country rock act, Poco. Despite this impressive pedigree, *The Souther Hillman Furay Band* was a marked disappointment. Hopes to emulate Crosby, Stills And Nash foundered on weak material and unimaginative arrangements. *Trouble In Paradise* was even poorer, Souther's moody introspection at odds with his partners' more buoyant perspectives. The group was disbanded in 1975, after which Souther resumed his solo career. Hillman and Furay meanwhile formed bands bearing their respective names.

●ALBUMS: *The Souther Hillman Furay Band* (Asylum 1974)★★★, *Trouble In Paradise* (Asylum 1975)★★.

SOUTHER, J.D.

b. John David Souther, 2 November 1945, Detroit, Michigan, USA. Souther's family migrated to Amarillo, Texas, where he was courted by local bands for his precocious talent as a singing guitarist. However, he committed himself to Longbranch Pennywhistle, a duo with future Eagles guitarist, Glenn Frey who shared his admiration for Hank Williams, Ray Charles and Buddy Holly. While sharing a Los Angeles apartment with Jackson Browne, the pair recorded an album before going their separate ways in 1970 - although Souther later collaborated on songs for the Eagles. His compositions were also recorded by Bonnie Raitt and Linda Ronstadt. After *John David Souther* for Asylum Records, he became a linchpin of the Souther Hillman Furay Band with ex-members of the Byrds, Buffalo Springfield, the Flying Burrito Brothers and Manassas for two albums prior to his discontent over the group's musical direction. A subsequent excellent second solo offering, *Black Rose*, was produced by Peter Asher and included performances by Joe Walsh, Lowell George and other country rock luminaries. Souther's promotional tour drew encouraging responses, but it failed to live up to market expectations. Disappointed, Souther withdrew into session work. In 1979, Souther tried again with *You're Only Lonely* which contained the expected quota of guest stars, among them Jackson Browne, John Sebastian and Phil Everly. Following critically acclaimed concerts in New York and California, his tenacity was rewarded when the tie-in single of the album's title track climbed into the US pop Top 10, selling even better in the country chart. Two years later a Souther/James Taylor composition, 'Her Town Too', almost reached the US Top 10. Since then, Souther's output as a songwriter has been considerable.

●ALBUMS: *John David Souther* (Asylum 1971)★★, *Black*

Rose (Asylum 1976)★★★, *You're Only Lonely* (Columbia 1979)★★, *Home By Dawn* (1984)★★.

SOUTHSIDE JOHNNY AND THE ASBURY JUKES

R&B fanatic Southside Johnny (b. John Lyons, 4 December 1948, New Jersey, USA) sang with the Blackberry Booze Band in the late 60s before teaming up with the Asbury Jukes with school friends Billy Rush (guitar), Kevin Kavanaugh (keyboards), Kenneth Pentifallo (bass) and Alan 'Doc' Berger (drums), plus transient members of a horn section. Popular in Upstage, Stone Poney and other parochial clubs, they sought a wider audience via a 1976 promotional album, *Live At The Bottom Line*, which helped facilitate a contract with Epic. Like another local lad, Bruce Springsteen, the group bolstered their reputation with practical demonstrations of credible influences by enlisting Ronnie Spector, Lee Dorsey, and black vocal groups of the 50s on *I Wanna Go Home* and its follow-up, *This Time It's For Real*. Both were weighted further with Springsteen sleevenotes and songs as well as production supervision by his guitarist (and ex-Juke) Steven Van Zandt. After *Hearts Of Stone* failed to reach a mass public, Epic dropped the band with the valedictory *Having A Party* - essentially a 'best of' compilation.

Mitigating this setback were increasing touring fees, which permitted sensational augmentation with saxophonists Carlo Novi and Stan Harrison, trumpeters Ricki Gazda and Tony Palligrosi, and ex-Diana Ross trombonist Richard Rosenberg, as well as an additional guitarist in Joel Gramolini and replacement drummer Steve Becker. A debut on Mercury, 1979's *The Jukes*, sold well as did *Love Is A Sacrifice* in 1980 but, for all the polished production by Barry Beckett many felt that much nascent passion had been dissipated. This was possibly traceable to the borrowing of the horns by Van Zandt for his Disciples Of Soul, and the exits of Pentifallo - and Berger, writer (with Lyons and Rush) of the band's original material. The in-concert *Reach Out And Touch The Sky* (with its fiery Sam Cooke medley) halted a commercial decline that resumed with later studio efforts - though radio interest in a revival of Left Banke's 'Walk Away Renee' (from *At Least We Got Shoes*) and a Jersey Artists For Mankind charity single (organized by Lyons) suggests that all might not yet be lost. They halted the decline in 1991 with *Better Days*. This lyrically nostalgic album contained a Springsteen song, 'Walk You All The Way Home', in addition to Van Zandt's numerous contributions.

●ALBUMS: *I Don't Wanna Go Home* (Epic 1976)★★★★, *This Time It's For Real* (Epic 1977)★★★, *Hearts Of Stone* (Epic 1978)★★★★, *The Jukes* (Mercury 1979)★★, *Love Is A Sacrifice* (Mercury 1980)★★, *Reach Out And Touch The Sky: Southside Johnny And The Asbury Jukes Live!)* (Mercury 1981)★★★★, *Trash It Up! Live* (Mirage 1983)★★★, *In The Heat* (Mirage 1984)★★, *At Least We Got Shoes* (Atlantic 1986)★★, *Better Days* (Impact

1991)★★★, *Spittin' Fire* (Grapevine 1997)★★★. Solo: Southside Johnny *Slow Dance* (Cypress 1988)★★★.
●COMPILATIONS: *Having A Party* (Epic 1980)★★★★, *The Best Of* (1993)★★★★.
●VIDEOS: *Having A Party* (Channel 5 1989).

SPARKS

Ex-child actors and veterans of Los Angeles' Urban Renewal Project, vocalist Russell Mael and his elder brother Ron (keyboards) led Halfnelson in 1968 (with renowned rock critic John Mendelssohn on drums). By 1971, this had evolved into Sparks in which the Maels were joined by Earle Mankay (guitar), Jim Mankay (bass) and Harley Fernstein (drums). At the urging of Todd Rundgren - their eventual producer - Albert Grossman signed them to Bearsville. While it emitted a regional US hit in 'Wonder Girl,' Sparks' debut album sold poorly - as did the subsequent *A Woofer In Tweeter's Clothing*. A stressful club tour of Europe - during which they were often heckled - amassed, nonetheless, a cult following in glam-rock England where the Maels emigrated in 1973 to gain an Island recording contract and enlist a new Sparks from native players. Drummer 'Dinky' Diamond from Aldershot's Sound Of Time was a mainstay during this period but among many others passing through the ranks were guitarist Adrian Fisher from Toby and Jook's bass player Ian Hampton. Overseen by Muff Winwood, this Anglo-American edition of Sparks notched up eight UK chart entries, starting with 1974's unprecedented and startling 'This Town Ain't Big Enough For Both Of Us' from *Kimono My House*. With eccentric arrangements in the Roxy Music vein, 'Amateur Hour' and later singles were also notable for Ron's lyrical idiosyncracies as well as wide stereo separation between the bass guitar section and Russell's twittering falsetto. Their appeal hinged visually on the disparity between creepy Ron's conservative garb and 'Hitler' moustache, and Russell's bubbly androgyny. *Propaganda* was a stylistic departure but the basic formula was unaltered. Sparks' over-dependence on this combined with an unsteady stage act to provoke fading interest in further merchandise - despite strategies like hiring Tony Visconti to supervise 1975's *Indiscreet*, and the Maels' return to California to make *Big Beat* with expensive LA session musicians.

Sparks engineered a transient comeback to the British Top 20 in 1977 with two singles from *Number One In Heaven*, produced by Giorgio Moroder - and 1981's 'When I'm With You' (from *Terminal Jive*) sold well in France. Later, the brothers succeeded in the US Hot 100 - particularly with 1983's 'Cool Places,' a tie-up with the Go-Go's' guitarist Jane Wiedlin - which intimates that their future may hold more surprises. They were still active and receiving plenty of media attention in the 90s and their recent work has been well received, especially *Gratuitous Sax And Senseless Violins*.

●ALBUMS: *Sparks* (Bearsville 1971)★★, *A Woofer In Tweeter's Clothing* (Bearsville 1972)★★★, *Kimono My*

House (Island 1974)★★★, *Propaganda* (Island 1974)★★, *Indiscreet* (Island 1975)★★, *Big Beat* (Columbia 1978)★★, *Number One In Heaven* (Virgin 1979)★★, *Terminal Jive* (Virgin 1980)★★, *Whoop That Sucker* (Why-Fi 1981)★★, *Angst In My Pants* (Atlantic 1982)★★, *Sparks In Outer Space* (Atlantic 1983)★★, *Interior Design* (Carrere 1989)★★, *Half Nelson* (1993)★★★, *Gratuitous Sax And Senseless Violins* (Arista 1994)★★★.

●COMPILATIONS: *Mael Intuition-The Best Of Sparks 1974-1976* (Island 1979)★★★.

SPEARS, BILLIE JO

b. 14 January 1937, Beaumont, Texas, USA. Discovered by songwriter Jack Rhodes, Spears' first record, as Billie Jo Moore, 'Too Old For Toys, Too Young For Boys', earned her $4200 at the age of 15. Despite appearances on *Louisiana Hayride*, she did not record regularly until she signed with United Artists in 1964. Following her producer, Kelso Herston, to Capitol Records, she had country hits with 'He's Got More Love In His Little Finger' and 'Mr. Walker, It's All Over'. After time off, following the removal of a nodule on her vocal cords, she recorded briefly for Brite Star and Cutlass. In 1974, Spears returned to United Artists where producer Larry Butler was developing a successful country roster. Her trans-Atlantic smash, 'Blanket on the Ground', was controversial in America. 'It sounded like a cheating song,' says Spears, 'and the public don't think girls should sing cheating songs!' In actuality, it was about adding romance to a marriage and its success prompted other records with a similar theme and tempo - 'What I've Got In Mind' (which had originally been a rhumba) and ''57 Chevrolet'. The traditional 'Sing Me An Old-Fashioned Song' sold well in the UK, while her cover of Dorothy Moore's ballad 'Misty Blue' was successful in the USA. She is also known for her cover of Gloria Gaynor's 'I Will Survive'. She maintains, 'It is still a country record. I am country. I could never go pop with my mouthful of firecrackers.' A duet album with Del Reeves, *By Request*, and a tribute to her producer, *Larry Butler And Friends*, with Crystal Gayle and Dottie West were not released in the UK. A single of her blues-soaked cover of 'Heartbreak Hotel' was cancelled in 1977 because she did not want to exploit Elvis Presley's death. Billie Jo Spears has performed prolifically, including over 300 concerts in the UK, and her ambition is to make a live album at the Pavillion, Glasgow. Among her UK recordings are a duet with Carey Duncan of 'I Can Hear Kentucky Calling Me' and an album *B.J. - Billie Jo Spears Today* with her stage band, Owlkatraz. Of late, she has recorded husky-voiced versions of familiar songs for mass-marketed albums. A true ambassador of country music, she signs autographs and talks to fans after every appearance. She buys all her stage clothes in the UK and refuses to wear anything casual. 'If I didn't wear gowns,' she says, 'they'd throw rotten tomatoes.'

●ALBUMS: *The Voice Of Billie Jo Spears* (Capitol 1968)★★★, *Mr.Walker, It's All Over* (Capitol 1969)★★★, *Miss Sincerity* (Capitol 1969)★★★, *With Love* (Capitol 1970)★★★, *Country Girl* (Capitol 1970)★★★, *Just Singin'* (Capitol 1972)★★★, *Blanket On The Ground* (United Artists 1974)★★★, *Billie Jo* (United Artists 1975)★★★, *What I've Got In Mind* (United Artists 1976)★★★, with Del Reeves *By Request* (United Artists 1976)★★, *If You Want Me* (United Artists 1977)★★★, *Everytime I Sing A Love Song* (United Artists 1977)★★★, *Lonely Hearts Club* (United Artists 1978)★★★, *Love Ain't Gonna Wait For Us* (United Artists 1978)★★★, *I Will Survive* (1979)★★★, *Standing Tall* (1980)★★★, *Special Songs* (Liberty 1981)★★★, with Reeves *Del And Billie Jo* (1982)★★, *B.J. - Billie Jo Spears Today* (1983)★★★, *We Just Came Apart At The Dreams* (1984)★★, *Misty Blue* (1992)★★, *Unmistakably* (1992)★★.

●COMPILATIONS: *Singles - Billie Jo Spears* (United Artists 1979)★★★, *17 Golden Pieces Of Billie Jo Spears* (Bulldog 1983)★★★, *20 Country Greats* (Warwick 1986)★★★, *50 Original Tracks* (1993)★★★, *Stand By Your Man* (1993)★★★, *The Queen Of Country Music* (MFP 1994).

SPECIALS

This Coventry, England, ska-influenced group was formed in the summer of 1977 as the Special AKA, with a line-up comprising Jerry Dammers (b. Gerald Dankin, 22 May 1954, India; keyboards), Terry Hall (b. 19 March 1959, Coventry, England; vocals), Neville Staples (vocals/percussion), Lynval Golding (b. 24 July 1951, Coventy, England; guitar), Roddy Radiation (b. Rodney Byers; guitar), Sir Horace Gentleman (b. Horace Panter; bass) and John Bradbury (drums). Following touring with the Clash, they set up their own multi-racial 2-Tone label and issued the Prince Buster-inspired 'Gangsters', which reached the UK Top 10. After signing their label to Chrysalis Records, the group abbreviated their name to the Specials. Their Elvis Costello-produced debut album was a refreshing, exuberant effort which included the Top 10 single 'A Message To You, Rudi'. The group spearheaded what became the 2-Tone movement and their label enjoyed an array of sparkling hits from Madness, the Beat and the Selecter. In January 1980 the Specials were at their peak following the release of their live EP, *The Special AKA Live*. The pro-contraceptive title track, 'Too Much Too Young', propelled them to number 1 in the UK charts. Further Top 10 hits with 'Rat Race', 'Stereotype' and 'Do Nothing' followed. The Specials' ability to 'capture the moment' in pop was most persuasively felt with 'Ghost Town', which topped the charts during the summer of 1981 while Britain was suffering inner-city riots. At this new peak of success, the group fragmented. Staples, Hall and Golding went on to form the intriguing Fun Boy Three, leaving Dammers to continue with a new line-up, which reverted to the old name, the Special AKA. After the minor success of 'Racist Friend' and the anthemic Top 10 hit, 'Nelson Mandela', Dammers became more politically active with Artists Against

Apartheid. He was also a major force behind the Nelson Mandela 70th Birthday Party concert at London's Wembley Stadium on 11 June 1988. The retitled 'Free Nelson Mandela (70th Birthday Remake)' was issued to coincide with the show. However, Dammers was reluctant to record again due to outstanding debts over the *In The Studio* album, which had to be cleared before he was free of contract. In 1993 Desmond Dekker joined Staples, Golding, Radiation and Gentleman on *King Of Kings*. Dammers, meanwhile, had a new band, Jazz Odyssey, but he soon retired to DJing and studio projects after he developed tinnitus.

●ALBUMS: *The Specials* (2-Tone/Chrysalis 1979)★★★, *More Specials* (2-Tone/Chrysalis 1980)★★★, as the Special AKA *In The Studio* (2-Tone/Chrysalis 1984)★★★, with Desmond Dekker *King Of Kings* (Trojan 1993)★★★.
●COMPILATIONS: *The Singles Collection* (Chrysalis 1991)★★★★, *The Selecter & The Specials: Live In Concert* (Windsong 1993)★★.

SPEDDING, CHRIS
b. 17 June 1944, Sheffield, Yorkshire, England. An underestimated talent, this inventive guitarist began his career in a beat group, the Vulcans, prior to following a haphazard path touring in country bands and supporting cabaret attractions on the cruise ship *Himalaya*. Spells backing Alan Price and Paul Jones preceded Spedding's involvement in the Battered Ornaments where he established a reputation for technique and imagination. The guitarist was subsequently heard on Jack Bruce's *Songs For A Tailor*, and on early releases by Nucleus, a leading jazz-rock ensemble. Session work for Lulu, John Cale, Dusty Springfield and others was interspersed by two low-key solo albums, *Backward Progression* and *The Only Lick I Know*. Spedding also formed the much-touted Sharks with former Free bassist Andy Fraser, but internal ructions undermined the group's potential. The guitarist resumed studio work in 1975, but also joined Roy Harper in Trigger, the singer's short-lived backing band. Spedding's clinical approach resulted in several career-based anomalies. He donned the requisite costume to perform with the Wombles and contrived an ill-fitting leather-boy image for a series of pop punk singles under the guidance of producer Mickie Most. 'Motor-Biking', in 1975, provided the UK Top 20 single the guitarist doubtlessly deserved, but these unusual interludes have discoloured perception of his other work.

●ALBUMS: *Backward Progression* (Harvest 1971)★★★, *The Only Lick I Know* (Harvest 1972)★★★, *Chris Spedding* (RAK 1976)★★★, *Hurt* (RAK 1977)★★★, *Guitar Graffiti* (RAK 1978)★★★, *I'm Not Like Everybody Else* (RAK 1980)★★★, *Friday The 13th* (RAK 1981)★★★, *Enemy Within* (New Rose 1986)★★, *Cafe Days* (New Rose 1990)★★★, *Guitar Jamboree* (Fan Club 1994)★★, *Just Plug Him In!* (Fan Club 1994)★★, *Gesundheit!* (Versailles 1995)★★★.
●COMPILATIONS: *Mean And Moody* (See For Miles 1985)★★★, *Motorbikin': The Best Of Chris Spedding* (EMI 1991)★★★.
●FILMS: *Give My Regards To Broad Street* (1985).

SPLINTER
Splinter were a duo of Beatles fanatics from north-east England, comprising Bob Purvis (b. *c*.1950, Newcastle-upon-Tyne, Tyne And Wear, England), Bill Elliot (b. *c*.1950, Newcastle-upon-Tyne, Tyne And Wear, England), who played in a variety of Tyneside groups. Purvis had also worked with producer Tony Visconti, and Elliot sang on the John Lennon-produced 'God Save Oz' record, in defence of *Oz* magazine when it was faced with obscenity charges in the early 70s. Fellow Beatle George Harrison became the duo's mentor and signed them to his Dark Horse label, where they had their sole hit, 'Costafine Town', in 1974. In 1979 they released a single, 'Danger Zone', on Chas Chandler's Barn label, but otherwise have remained silent.

●ALBUMS: *Splinter* (Dark Horse 1974)★★.

SPLIT ENZ
Originally formed in Auckland, New Zealand, in 1972 as Split Ends, this expansive group evolved around the duo of Tim Finn (b. 25 June 1952, Te Awamuta, New Zealand; vocals/piano) and Jonathan 'Mike' Chunn (b. New Zealand; bass/keyboards) with Geoff Chunn (b. New Zealand; drums - later replaced by Paul Emlyn Crowther), Paul 'Wally' Wilkinson (b. New Zealand; guitar), Miles Golding (b. New Zealand; violin), Rob Gillies (b. New Zealand; saxophone), Michael Howard (b. New Zealand; flute) and Phil Judd (b. New Zealand; vocals/guitar/mandolin). Their reluctance to perform on the traditional bar circuit left only the college and university venues, as well as the occasional open-air park concert, to enact their brand of theatrical pop. They featured an eclectic set, wore unusual costumes, facial make-up (which drew comparisons in their homeland to Skyhooks), and even featured a spoons player (percussionist/costume designer Noel Crombie). After three singles released in New Zealand, the band were well established in their homeland, particularly after reaching the final of a national television talent show. After moving to Australia in early 1975, and altering their name, the group recorded their first album for the Mushroom label. At the invitation of Phil Manzanera, who had seen the band when they supported Roxy Music on tour in Australia, the band flew to the UK. Signed to the Chrysalis label in Europe, Manzanera recorded the band's second album which included some reworking of their earlier material. Unfortunately, the band's arrival in England coincided with the punk movement and they found acceptance difficult. Returning to Australia in 1977, Split Enz recruited Tim Finn's brother Neil (b. 27 May 1958, Te Awamutu, New Zealand) to replace Judd. The departure of Wilkinson, Crowther and Chunn also made way for Nigel Griggs (b. 18 August 1949, New Zealand; bass)

and Malcolm Green (b. 25 January 1953, England; drums). The 1980 album *True Colours*, on A&M Records, contained their most successful single, Neil Finn's glorious 'I Got You' with reached number 12 in the UK. Follow-up releases saw the band reach modest positions in the US album charts, but they ran into trouble in the UK when their 'Six Months In A Leaky Boat' was banned by the BBC as its title was considered too provocative at a time when the British were fighting the Falklands war. While Tim Finn recorded a solo album, the group lost their momentum, eventually dissolving in 1985 after the release of *Conflicting Emotions* Tim Finn continued his solo career, while Neil went on to form Crowded House (also with Tim until 1992) with latter years' group member Paul Hester (drums). Griggs, Judd and Crombie formed Schnell Fenster. Phil Judd released a solo album in 1983, *Private Lives*, on the Mushroom label.

●ALBUMS: *Mental Notes* (Mushroom 1975)★★, *Second Thoughts* (Chrysalis 1976)★★, *Dizrhythmia* (1977)★★★★, *Frenzy* (1979)★★★, *True Colours* (A&M 1980)★★★★, *Waiata* (A&M 1981)★★★, *Time And Tide* (A&M 1982)★★★, *Conflicting Emotions* (A&M 1984)★★, *See Ya Round* (1984)★★, *Livin' Enz* (1985)★★.
●COMPILATIONS: *The Beginning Of The Enz* (1980)★★★, *Anniversary* (Mushroom 1995)★★★★.

SPRINGFIELD, RICK

b. Richard Springthorpe, 23 August 1949, Sydney, Australia. The son of an army officer, Springfield's musical interests developed while living in England in the early 60s; on his return to Australia he played guitar and piano in the house band of a Melbourne club. At the end of the 60s, Springfield played with the Jordy Boys, Rock House and the MPD Band before joining Zoot. The group had several hits with Springfield compositions before he turned solo with the number 1 single 'Speak To The Sky'. He moved to the USA in 1972 where he was groomed to become a new teenybop idol and a new version of 'Speak To The Sky' was a Top 20 US hit. After contractual disputes kept him inactive for two years, he joined Wes Farrell's Chelsea label where Elton John's rhythm section, Dee Murray (bass) and Nigel Olsson (drums), backed him on *Wait For The Night*. Soon afterwards the label collapsed and Springfield began a new career as a television actor. After guest appearances in *The Rockford Files*, *Wonder Woman* and *The Six Million Dollar Man*, he landed a leading role in the soap opera *General Hospital*. This exposure helped to give him a series of big hits on RCA Records in 1981-82 including 'Jessie's Girl' which reached number 1 and the Top 10 records 'I've Done Everything For You', and 'Don't Talk To Strangers'. The later hit 'Love Somebody' came from the 1984 film *Hard To Hold* in which Springfield played a rock singer. The next year a reissue of one 1978 track ('Bruce'; a tale about being mistaken for Bruce Springsteen) was a Top 30 hit and later Springfield albums were equally popular in America.

●ALBUMS: *Beginnings* (Capitol 1972)★★, *Comic Book* (1974)★★★, *Heroes* (1974)★★★, *Wait For The Night* (Chelsea 1976)★★★, *Working Class Dog* (RCA 1981)★★★, *Success Hasn't Spoiled Me Yet* (RCA 1982)★★, *Living In Oz* (RCA 1983)★★, *Beautiful Feelings* (Mercury 1985)★★, *Tao* (RCA 1985)★★, *Rock Of Life* (RCA 1988)★★.
●COMPILATIONS: *Rick Springfield's Greatest Hits* (RCA 1989)★★★.

SPRINGSTEEN, BRUCE

b. 23 September 1949, Freehold, New Jersey, USA. As the world's greatest living rock 'n' roll star, Springsteen has unconsciously proved former *Rolling Stone* critic Jon Landau totally correct. Landau appeared smug and brave when he made the arrogant statement in 1974, 'I saw rock 'n' roll future, and its name is Bruce Springsteen'. Prior to that, Springsteen had paid his dues, playing in local bands around New Jersey, notably with the Castiles, Earth, Steel Mill and Dr Zoom And The Sonic Boom, before he settled as the Bruce Springsteen Band with David Sancious (keyboards), Gary Tallent (bass,) Clarence Clemmons (saxophone,) Steven Van Zandt (guitar), Danny Federici (keyboards) and Vini Lopez (drums). Following an introduction to CBS A&R legend John Hammond, Springsteen was signed as a solo artist; the company sensed a future Bob Dylan. Springsteen ignored their plans and set about recording his debut with the band *Greetings From Asbury Park*. The album sold poorly, although critics in the USA and UK saw its potential. The follow-up only 10 months later was a much stronger collection, *The Wild, The Innocent And The E. Street Shuffle*. Future classics were on this similarly low-selling album, including 'Rosalita' and 'Incident On 57th Street'. It also contains the beautiful 'Asbury Park Fourth Of July (Sandy)', later recorded by the Hollies. His musicians were renamed the E. Street Band after its release and during the following May, Landau saw the band and made his now famous statement. He eventually became Springsteen's record producer and manager.

During this time, the first two albums began to sell steadily, following a heavy schedule of concerts, as word got out to the public that here was something special. Springsteen wrote directly to his fans in a language they understood. Here was a working-class American, writing about his job, his car/bike, his girlfriend and his hometown. *Born To Run* came in 1975 and immediately put him into rock's first division. This superb album contained a wealth of lyrical frustration, anger and hope. The playing was faultless and the high-quality songs are among his best. Critics and fans loved it, and the album was a significant hit on both sides of the Atlantic. During the accompanying tour Springsteen collected rave reviews and appeared as cover feature in both *Newsweek* and *Time*. Throughout his European tour the UK press were similar in their praise and exhaustive coverage, which led to a backlash of Bruce Springsteen jokes. Springsteen's recording career was then held up for three years as he and Landau entered into litigation with Mike Appel, with whom Springsteen had struck a management agreement in 1972. Other artists kept the torch burning brightly, with Manfred Mann's Earth Band releasing a sparkling version of his song 'Blinded By The Light' and Patti Smith recording a definitive cover of his 'Because The Night'. Other artists like ex-Hollie Allan Clarke, Robert Gordon, and the Pointer Sisters recorded his material. With the lawsuits successfully completed, the anti-climactic *Darkness On The Edge Of Town* arrived in 1978. The album reflected the problems of the past years and is a moody album, yet 15 years later it still stands as a great work. The show-stopping 'Badlands' and 'The Promised Land' were two of the album's masterpieces. From the moment the record was released in June, Bruce and the band embarked on a gruelling tour which took them into 1979.

On his 30th birthday he played at the historic MUSE concert; the subsequent *No Nukes* album and video captured a vintage Springsteen performance of high energy and humour. After feigning collapse onstage, he cheekily persuaded the audience to beg for an encore having previously pointed out to them that he could not carry on like this as he was 30 years old! The audience loved the banter and together with the great Clarence Clemmons, he roared into an encore of 'Rosalita'. The next months were spent recording the double set *The River*, which received almost as much praise as *Born To Run*. All shades of Springsteen are shown; it is brooding, depressing, pensive, uplifting, exciting and celebratory. In 20 songs, he covers every aspect of his life, and more importantly he covers aspects of the listener's life. It is hard to pick out any single tracks, but 'Hungry Heart', 'The River' and 'Fade Away' were all released and became hit singles. The following year he toured Europe again, and helped to resurrect Gary 'U.S.' Bonds' career by producing and writing some of his comeback *Dedication*. 'This Little Girl' is one of Springsteen's finest songs and Bonds found himself back in the charts after almost 20 years' absence.

In September 1982 *Nebraska* arrived. This stark acoustic set was recorded solo, directly onto a cassette recorder. It is raw Springsteen, uncompromising and sometimes painful; Bruce without his clothes on. At one point on the album he imitates a wolf cry, but to many it was a genuine howl, that struck terror when turned up loudly. *Nebraska* was yet another major achievement. After a further lengthy wait for a new album, *Born In The USA* arrived in 1984. As is often the case, the album that is the most commercially accessible, best selling and longest resident in the charts, is not always the artist's best work. *Born In The USA* was a prime example. Selling over 12 million copies, it stayed in the UK charts for two-and-a-half years; in the country of origin it stayed even longer. Numerous hit singles were released including the title anthem, 'Cover Me' and 'I'm On Fire'.

During one bout of Springsteen-mania on his 1985 European tour, all seven albums to date were in the UK charts. That year also saw him marry Julianne Phillips, and support political and social issues. He participated in the USA For Africa's 'We Are The World' and joined former E. Street Band member Steven Van Zandt on the Artists United Against Apartheid song 'Sun City'. In festive style his perennial 'Santa Claus Is Coming To Town' made the UK Top 10 in December. Along with Bob Dylan, Springsteen is the most bootlegged artist in history. In order to stem the flow he released a five-album boxed set at the end of 1986. The superbly recorded *Live 1975-1985* entered the US charts at number 1.

The following year *Tunnel Of Love* was released; the advance orders took it to number 1 on the day of release in the UK and USA. It was another exceptionally strong work. Springsteen followed it with another major tour and visited the UK that summer. After months of speculation and paparazzi lens' intrusions, Springsteen's affair with his backing singer Patti Scialfa was confirmed, with his wife filing for divorce. Springsteen continued to be political by supporting the Human Rights Now tour for Amnesty International in 1988, although from that time on he has maintained a lower profile. During the late 80s he performed numerous low-key gigs in bars and clubs and occasional worthy causes as well as his own *Tunnel Of Love* tour. Springsteen's successful European tour was clouded by the press's continuing obsession with his divorce. In 1989 he recorded 'Viva Las Vegas' as part of a benefit album, and reached the age of 40. During the inactivity of that year the E. Street Band disintegrated upon Springsteen's suggestion. During the early 90s the press followed his every move, anxiously awaiting signs of action as Springsteen continued to enjoy life, occasionally appearing with other famous musicians. It is a testament to Springsteen's standing that he can maintain his position, having released only eight albums of new material in almost 20 years. In 1992, he issued two albums simultaneously: *Human Touch* and *Lucky Town*, both scaled the charts in predictable fashion and both fans and critics welcomed him back, although not quite with the fervour of the past. He composed 'Streets Of Philadelphia', the emotionally charged title track for the film *Philadelphia* in 1994. In 1995 he was working with the E. Street Band (including Clemmons) once more. His *Greatest Hits* collection also included two new tracks and two previously unreleased oldies. As a complete about turn, *The Ghost Of Tom Joad* at the end of 1995 was a solo acoustic album. This was in direct contrast to the stark and hollow power of Nebraska; *Tom Joad* was warm, mellow and sad. Sounding a lot like Dylan, Springsteen had become ol' grandpappy, telling stories of Vietnam, prison life and lost love. He no longer sounded angry or energetic; merely philosophical. It was, however, one of his strongest albums in years, yet one of his least successful.

●ALBUMS: *Greetings From Asbury Park* (Columbia

1973)★★★, *The Wild, The Innocent And The E. Street Shuffle* (Columbia 1973)★★★★, *Born To Run* (Columbia 1975)★★★★★, *Darkness On The Edge Of Town* (Columbia 1978)★★★★, *The River* (Columbia 1980)★★★★, *Nebraska* (Columbia 1982)★★★★, *Born In The USA* (Columbia 1984)★★★, *Live 1975-85* (Columbia 1986)★★★, *Tunnel Of Love* (Columbia 1987)★★★★, *Human Touch* (Columbia 1992)★★★, *Lucky Town* (Columbia 1992)★★★, *In Concert - MTV Plugged* (Columbia 1993)★★★, *The Ghost Of Tom Joad* (Columbia 1995)★★★★.
●COMPILATIONS: *Greatest Hits* (Columbia 1995)★★★★.
●FURTHER READING: *Springsteen: Born To Run*, Dave March. *Bruce Springsteen*, Peter Gambaccini. *Springsteen: Blinded By The Light*, Patrick Humphries and Chris Hunt. *Springsteen: No Surrender*, Kate Lynch. *Bruce Springsteen Here & Now*, Craig MacInnis. *The E. Street Shuffle*, Clinton Heylin and Simon Gee. *Glory Days*, Dave Marsh. *Backstreets: Springsteen - The Man And His Music*, Ed. Charles R. Cross. *Down Thunder Road*, Mark Eliot. *Bruce Springsteen In His Own Words*, John Duffy.

STACKWADDY

This group was formed in Manchester, England, in 1969 by Mick Stott (lead guitar) and Stuart Banham (bass), previously of the New Religion. John Knail (vocals/harmonica) and Steve Revell (drums) completed the new act's line-up which first drew attention with an impressive appearance at Buxton's 1969 Progressive Blues Festival. Stackwaddy were later signed to UK disc jockey John Peel's Dandelion label. Both *Stackwaddy* and *Bugger Off* revealed aspirations similar to British 60s R&B groups, played in an uncluttered, irreverent, but exciting style. Included were versions of the Pretty Things' 'Rosalyn', Frank Zappa's 'Willie The Pimp' and the wryly titled 'Meat Pies Have Come But The Band's Not Here Yet', but Stackwaddy's guttural music proved unfashionable and the original group split up. However, between 1973 and 1976 Barnham led a revamped line-up comprising Mike Sweeny (vocals), Wayne Jackson (bass) and Kevin Wilkinson (drums).
●ALBUMS: *Stackwaddy* (Dandelion 1971)★★★, *Bugger Off* (Dandelion 1972)★★★.

STAFFORD, JIM

b. 16 January c.1946, Florida, USA. Stafford had a series of novelty hits in the mid-70s, but his career began as a member of the Legends which also included Gram Parsons and Lobo (Kent Lavoie). Working with Miami producer Phil Gernhard, Stafford signed to MGM as a solo singer, releasing 'Swamp Witch' in 1973. A minor hit, it was followed by the million-selling 'Spiders And Snakes', which used a swamp-rock sound reminiscent of Tony Joe White to tell a humorous tale. The song was composed by David Bellamy of the Bellamy Brothers. In 1974, Stafford tried a soft ballad with a twist, 'My Girl Bill' (his biggest UK hit) and another zany number,

'Wildwood Weed', which reached the US Top 10. Both were co-produced by Lobo. The same strand of humour ran through Stafford's 1975 singles 'Your Bulldog Drinks Champagne' and 'I Got Drunk And Missed It'. By now a minor celebrity, Stafford hosted a networked summer variety show from Los Angeles, where he met and married Bobbie Gentry. Such later records as 'Jasper' (Polydor 1976), co-written with Dave Loggins, and 'Turns Loose Of My Leg' (Curb/Warner Brothers Records 1977) were only minor hits but Stafford continued to record into the 80s for labels such as Elektra, Town House and CBS.
●ALBUMS: *Jim Stafford* (MGM 1974)★★, *Spiders And Snakes* (MGM 1974)★★, *Not Just Another Pretty Fool* (MGM 1975)★★.

STANSHALL, VIVIAN

b. 21 March 1943, Shillingford, Oxfordshire, England, d. 5 March 1995. Stanshall's love of pre-war ephemera, traditional jazz and an art school prankishness was instrumental in shaping the original tenor of the Bonzo Dog Doo-Dah Band. This satirical unit was one of the most humourous and inventive groups to emerge from the 60s, but fell foul of the eclectic pursuits of its divergent members. Stanshall's first offering following the Bonzo's collapse was 'Labio Dental Fricative', a single credited to the Sean Head Showband, an impromptu unit that included guitarist Eric Clapton. A second release, a brazenly tongue-in-cheek rendition of Terry Stafford's 'Suspicion', featured Vivian Stanshall And His Gargantuan Chums, and was coupled to 'Blind Date', the singer's only recording with biG GRunt, the group he had formed with Roger Ruskin Spear, Dennis Cowan and 'Borneo' Fred Munt, three refugees from the immediate Bonzo Dog circle. Each band member, bar Munt, appeared on *Let's Make Up And Be Friendly*, the album the Bonzos belatedly completed to fulfil contractual obligations. Despite a handful of excellent live appearances, biG GRunt's undoubted potential withered to a premature end when Stanshall entered hospital following a nervous breakdown.
Men Opening Umbrellas, Stanshall's debut album, was released in 1974. Steve Winwood was one of the many musicians featured on the record, inaugurating a working relationship which continued with the excellent 'Vacant Chair' on Winwood's solo debut *Steve Winwood* and major lyrical contributions to *Arc Of A Diver*, his 1980 release. Indeed, despite recording a punk-inspired version of Cliff Richard's 'The Young Ones', Stanshall achieved notoriety for his contributions to other outside projects, narrating Mike Oldfield's *Tubular Bells* and as a contributor to the BBC Radio 4 programme, *Start The Week*. It was while deputizing for the Radio 1 disc jockey John Peel that Stanshall developed his infamous monologue, *Rawlinson End*. This later formed the basis for the artist's 1978 release, *Sir Henry At Rawlinson End*, which later inspired a film of the same title and starred Trevor Howard. Stanshall con-

tinued to tread his idiosyncratic path throughout the 80s. An album of songs, *Teddy Bears Don't Knit*, was followed by another spoken-word release, *Henry At Ndidis Kraal*. In 1991, he continued the Rawlinson saga by staging at London's Bloomsbury Theatre, *Rawlinson Dogends*, which included in the show's backing band former Bonzo colleagues, Roger Ruskin-Spear and Rodney Slater. In the 90s Stanshall carved out a separate career using his voice in advertising, making full use of his luxurious, stately tones. Until his tragic death, caused by a fire at his home, Stanshall was one of England's most cherished eccentrics. At his memorial service which was attended by a host of professional admirers, Steve Winwood sang an impassioned 'Arc Of A Diver' accompanied by his acoustic guitar. Neil Innes made a moving speech which contained the poignant line 'did he (Stanshall) fear that nobody would love him if he allowed himself to be ordinary?'
●ALBUMS: *Men Opening Umbrellas Ahead* (Warners 1974)★★★, *Sir Henry At Rawlinson End* (Charisma 1978)★★★, *Teddy Bears Don't Knit* (Charisma 1981)★★★, *Henry At Ndidi's Kraal* (Demon 1984)★★.
●FURTHER READING: *Mojo* magazine, May 1995.

STARDUST, ALVIN

b. Bernard William Jewry, 27 September 1942, London, England. Jewry first enjoyed pop fame during the early 60s under the name Shane Fenton. When the arrival of the Beatles and the subsequent Mersey beat explosion occurred, Fenton effectively retired from singing. In one of the more unlikely comebacks in British pop history, he re-emerged in 1973 as hit singer Alvin Stardust. Bedecked in menacingly black leather, with an image that fused Gene Vincent with Dave Berry, Stardust returned to the charts with the UK number 2 hit 'My Coo-Ca-Choo'. It was followed by the chart-topping 'Jealous Mind' which, like its predecessor, was composed by songwriter Peter Shelley. Two further UK Top 10 hits followed, with 'Red Dress' and 'You You You' before his chart career petered out with 'Tell Me Why' and 'Good Love Can Never Die'. The indomitable Stardust revitalized his career once more during the early 80s with the Top 10 successes 'Pretend' and the commemorative ballad 'I Feel Like Buddy Holly', which also mentioned Paul McCartney. Stardust ended 1984 with two further hits 'I Won't Run Away' and 'So Near Christmas'. He remains a popular star on the British showbusiness scene and in recent years, as a born-again Christian, presented and performed on BBC television with Christian pop and rock acts.
●ALBUMS: *The Untouchable* (Magnet 1974)★★★, *Alvin Stardust* (Magnet 1974)★★, *Rock With Alvin* (Magnet 1975)★★, *I'm A Moody Guy* (Magnet 1982)★★, *I Feel Like ... Alvin Stardust* (Chrysalis 1984)★★.
●COMPILATIONS: *Greatest Hits: Alvin Stardust* (Magnet 1977)★★★, *20 Of The Best* (Object 1987)★★★.
●FURTHER READING: *The Alvin Stardust Story*, George Tremlett .

STARR, RINGO

b. Richard Starkey, 7 July 1940, Dingle, Liverpool, England. Starkey established his reputation on the nascent Merseybeat circuit as drummer with Rory Storm And The Hurricanes. He later became acquainted with the Beatles, and having established a lively rapport with three of the group, became the natural successor to the taciturn Pete Best upon his firing in 1962. Ringo - a name derived from his many finger adornments - offered a simple, uncluttered playing style which formed the ideal bedrock for his partners' sense of melody. Although overshadowed musically, a deadpan sense of humour helped establish his individuality and each album also contained an obligatory Starr vocal. The most notable of these was 'Yellow Submarine', a million-selling single in 1966. Starr's success in the group's attendant films, *A Hard Day's Night* and *Help!*, inspired an acting career and comedy roles in *Candy* and *The Magic Christian* ensued. His solo recording career started with *Sentimental Journey*, a collection of standards, and *Beaucoups Of Blues*, a country selection recorded in Nashville, both predated the Beatles' demise. Fears that his career would then falter proved unfounded. Starr's debut single, 'It Don't Come Easy', co-written with George Harrison, topped the US charts and sold in excess of 1 million copies while the same pair also created 'Back Off Boogaloo' (UK number 2) and 'Photograph'. *Ringo* featured songs and contributions from each of his former colleagues, although none were recorded together. Buoyed by strong original material and judicious rock 'n' roll favourites, the album later achieved platinum status and was rightly lauded as one of the strongest ex-Beatles' collections. 'You're Sixteen' topped the US chart in 1974, but despite further success with 'Oh My My', 'Snookeroo' (penned by Elton John and Bernie Taupin) and 'Only You', Starr's momentum then waned. A highly praised role in the film *That'll Be The Day* (1973) was followed by the poorly received movie *Caveman*, while the albums *Ringo The 4th* and *Bad Boy* showed an artist bereft of direction.

A 1983 album, *Old Wave*, was denied a release in both the US and UK, while the period was also marred by alcoholism and chronic ill health. During this nadir, Starr reached a completely new audience as narrator of the award-winning children's television series, *Thomas The Tank Engine*, but signalled his return to active performing with a guest appearance on Carl Perkins' tribute show. However, an album recorded with US producer Chips Moman in 1987 was abandoned when sessions were blighted by excessive imbibing. Starr then underwent highly publicized treatment at an alcohol rehabilitation clinic with his wife, actress Barbara Bach, before reasserting his musical career with the All-Starr Band. Levon Helm, Billy Preston, Joe Walsh and Dr. John were among those joining the drummer for a successful 1989 US tour, later the subject of an album and video. The stellar cast Starr was able to assemble confirmed the respect he is still afforded. Starr received a high profile in 1992 with a new album and tour. The record coincided with the 25th anniversary of *Sgt. Pepper's* which was a timely reminder that Starr's playing on that album was quite superb, and, in addition to his equally fine performance on *Abbey Road*, begs for a reappraisal of his standing as a drummer, which appears grossly underrated.

●ALBUMS: *Sentimental Journey* (Apple 1969)★★, *Beaucoups Of Blues* (Apple 1970)★★, *Ringo* (Apple 1973)★★★, *Goodnight Vienna* (Apple 1974)★★, *Ringo's Rotogravure* (Polydor 1976)★★, *Ringo The 4th* (Polydor 1977)★★, *Bad Boy* (Polydor 1977)★★, *Stop And Smell The Roses* (RCA 1981)★★, *Old Wave* (Bellaphon 1983)★, *Ringo Starr And His All-Starr Band* (EMI 1990)★★★, *Time Takes Time* (Arista 1992)★★, *Live From Montreux* (1993)★★.

●COMPILATIONS: *Blast From Your Past* (Apple 1975)★★★, *StarrStruck: Ringo's Best (1976-1983)* (Rhino 1989)★★★.

●FURTHER READING: *Ringo Starr Straightman Or Joker*, Alan Clayson.

●FILMS: *A Hard Day's Night* (1964), *Help* (1965), *Give My Regards To Broad Street* (1985).

STARRY EYED AND LAUGHING

This promising UK group formed in May 1973 as a duo: Tony Poole (b. 28 July 1952, Northampton, England; vocals/12-string guitar) and Ross McGeeney (b. 22 December 1950, Northamptonshire, England; vocals/lead guitar). Taking their name from a line in Bob Dylan's song 'Chimes Of Freedom', the group were initially hugely influenced by the Byrds, with Roger McGuinn-style jingle-jangle Rickenbacker guitarwork and vocals. After briefly performing with bassist Steve Hall and drummer Nick Brown, the group found more suitable replacements in the form of Iain Whitmore (b. 5 October 1953, Shoreham, Sussex, England) and Mike Wackford (b. 6 February 1953, Worthing, Sussex, England). After securing a contract with CBS Records in April 1974, the quartet issued a self-titled debut album the following September. The work was dominated by Poole/McGeeney compositions and critics duly noted the striking Byrds flavouring. After a year on the road, the group completed *Thought Talk*, which was issued in October 1975. Although the title was taken from the Byrds' song 'I See You', the album was a less derivative, more mature, work, with Poole showing his melodic excellence on 'One Foot In The Boat' and Whitmore emerging as a highly talented writer on the orchestrated 'Fools Gold'. Following a promotional tour of the USA that autumn, the group suddenly fragmented. McGeeney was replaced by Roger Kelly, and Whitmore quit in the spring of 1976. A valedictory gig for the German television show *Rockpalast* saw McGeeney return, playing alongside Kelly. Later that year, Poole briefly shortened the group title to Starry Eyed and recorded a couple of commercial singles produced by Flo And Eddie, but the anticipated radio hits were not forthcoming and so the story ended.

●ALBUMS: *Starry Eyed And Laughing* (Columbia 1974)★★★, *Thought Talk* (Columbia 1975)★★★.

STATLER BROTHERS

The Statler Brothers originated in Staunton, a town on the edge of Shenandoah Valley, Virginia, USA. In 1955 Harold W. Reid (b. 21 August 1939, Augusta County, Virginia, USA; bass), Philip E. Balsley (b. 8 August 1939, Augusta County, Virginia, USA; baritone), Lew C. DeWitt (b. 8 March 1939, Roanoke County, Virginia, USA; tenor) and Joe McDorman formed a gospel quartet. Although McDorman never became a Statler, he has worked with them occasionally. In 1960 he was replaced by Harold's brother, Donald S. Reid (b. 5 June 1945, Staunton, Virginia, USA), who is now the group's lead singer. Originally the quartet was called The Kingsmen, but they changed it to avoid confusion with a US pop group. The Statler Brothers was chosen from the manufacturer's name on a box of tissues, and the group point out that they might have been the Kleenex Brothers. In 1963, they auditioned for Johnny Cash, who invited them to be part of his road show. He also secured a record contract with Columbia, but the label was disappointed with the poor sales of their first records. Having been refused further studio time, they recorded Lew DeWitt's song, 'Flowers On The Wall', during a break in one of Cash's sessions. The infectious novelty made number 4 on the US pop charts (number 2, country) and, despite the American references, also entered the UK Top 40. The Statler Brothers continued with Cash's roadshow and recorded both with him ('Daddy Sang Bass') and on their own ('Ruthless', 'You Can't Have Your Kate And Edith Too'). Dissatisfied by the promotion of their records and by the lukewarm material they were given, they switched to Mercury Records in 1970 and their records have been produced by Jerry Kennedy since then.

With such US country hits as 'Bed Of Roses', 'Do You Remember These?', 'I'll Go To My Grave Loving You' and the number 1 'Do You Know You Are My Sunshine?', they established themselves as the number 1 country vocal group. They left Cash's roadshow in 1972, but they recorded a tribute to him, 'We Got Paid By Cash', as well as tributes to their favourite gospel group ('The Blackwood Brothers By The Statler Brothers') and their favourite guitarist ('Chet Atkins' Hand'). DeWitt was incapacitated through Crohn's disease and left in 1982. He released the solo *On My Own* in 1985, but died in Waynesboro, Virginia, on 15 August 1990. Many of their songs relate to their love of the cinema - 'The Movies', 'Whatever Happened To Randolph Scott?' and 'Elizabeth', a country number 1 written, inspired by watching the film *Giant*, by Jimmy Fortune, who replaced DeWitt. Fortune also wrote two other number 1 US country records for them, 'My Only

Love' and 'Too Much On My Heart'. They also had considerable success with a spirited revival of 'Hello Mary Lou', which was praised by its composer, Gene Pitney. Their stage act includes the homespun humour of their alter egos, Lester 'Roadhog' Moran And The Cadillac Cowboys, and they gave themselves a plywood disc when the first 1250 of the resulting album were sold. On the other hand, The Statler Brothers' Old-Fashioned Fourth Of July Celebration in Staunton attracts 70,000 a year. The Statler Brothers are managed from office buildings that used to be the school that Dewitt and The Reids attended.

●ALBUMS: *Flowers On The Wall* (Columbia 1966)★★★, *Big Hits* (Columbia 1967)★★★, *Oh Happy Day* (Columbia 1969)★★, *Bed Of Roses* (Mercury 1971)★★★, *Pictures Of Moments To Remember* (Mercury 1971)★★★, *Interview* (Mercury 1972)★★, *Country Music Then And Now* (Mercury 1972)★★★, *Symphonies In E Major* (Mercury 1973)★★, *Thank You World* (Mercury 1974)★★★, as Lester 'Roadhog' Moran And His Cadillac Cowboys *Alive At Johnny Mack Brown High School* (Mercury 1973)★★★, *Carry Me Back* (Mercury 1973)★★★, *Sons Of The Motherland* (Mercury 1975)★★★, *The Holy Bible - Old Testament* (Mercury 1975)★★, *The Holy Bible - New Testament* (Mercury 1975)★★, *Harold, Lew, Phil And Don* (Mercury 1976)★★★, *The Country America Loves* (Mercury 1977)★★★, *Short Stories* (Mercury 1977)★★★, *Entertainers ... On And Off The Record* (Mercury 1978)★★★, *Christmas Card* (Mercury 1979)★★, *The Originals* (Mercury 1979)★★★, *Tenth Anniversary* (Mercury 1980)★★★, *Years Ago* (Mercury 1981)★★★, *The Legend Goes On* (Mercury 1982)★★★, *Country Gospel* (Mercury 1982)★★★, *Today* (Mercury 1983)★★★, *Atlanta Blue* (Mercury 1984)★★★, *Partners In Rhyme* (Mercury 1985)★★★, *Christmas Present* (Mercury 1985)★★, *Four For The Show* (Mercury 1986)★★★, *Radio Gospel Favourites* (Mercury 1986)★★★, *Maple Street Memories* (Mercury 1987)★★★, *Live* (1990)★★★, *Music, Memories And You* (1990)★★★, *All American Cowboy* (1991)★★★, *Words And Music* (1992)★★★, *Home* (1993)★★★.

●VIDEOS: *Brothers In Song* (Polygram 1986).

STATON, CANDI

b. Hanceville, Alabama, USA. A former member of the Jewel Gospel Trio, Staton left the group, and her first husband, for a secular career. She was then discovered performing at a club by Clarence Carter, who took the singer to the Fame label. Carter wrote her debut hit, the uncompromising 'I'd Rather Be An Old Man's Sweetheart (Than A Young Man's Fool)', and helped guide the singer's early releases. She later began pursuing a country-influenced path, especially in the wake of her successful version of Tammy Wynette's 'Stand By Your Man'. Staton and Carter were, by now, married, although this relationship subsequently ended in divorce. Staton left Fame for Warner Brothers Records

in 1974 but it was two years before 'Young Hearts Run Free', an excellent pop-styled hit, consolidated this new phase. 'Nights On Broadway', written by the Bee Gees, then became a UK Top 10 single, although it unaccountably flopped in America. The singer has continued to enjoy intermittent UK success but US hits have been restricted to the R&B chart. 'You Lost The Love' a collaboration with the Force was a popular dancefloor track and a UK Top 40 hit in 1991. In the 90s Staton has been recording in the gospel field.

●ALBUMS: *I'm Just A Prisoner* (Fame 1969)★★★, *Stand By Your Man* (Fame 1971)★★★, *Candi Staton* (Fame 1972)★★★, *Candi* (Fame 1974)★★★, *Young Hearts Run Free* (Warners 1976)★★★, *Music Speaks Louder Than Words* (Warners 1977)★★, *House Of Love* (Warners 1978)★★, *Chance* (Warners 1979)★★, *Candi Staton* (Warners 1980)★★, *Make Me An Instrument* (Myrrh 1985)★★★, *Sing A Song* (1986)★★★, *Love Lifted Me* (1988)★★★, *Stand Up And Be A Witness* (Blue Moon 1990)★★★, *It's Time* (Intersound 1995)★★★.

●COMPILATIONS: shared with Bettye Swann *Tell It Like It Is* (1986)★★★, *Nightlites* (1992), *Candy* (1992), *Young Hearts Run Free* (1992)★★★.

STATUS QUO

The origins of this durable and now legendary attraction lie in the Spectres, a London-based beat group. Founder members Mike (later Francis) Rossi (b. 29 May 1949, Peckham, London, England; guitar/vocals) and Alan Lancaster (b. 7 February 1949, Peckham, London, England; bass) led the act from its inception in 1962 until 1967, by which time Roy Lynes (organ) and John Coughlan (b. 19 September 1946, Dulwich, London, England; drums) completed its line-up. The Spectres' three singles encompassed several styles of music, ranging from pop to brash R&B, but the quartet took a new name, Traffic Jam, when such releases proved commercially unsuccessful. A similar failure beset 'Almost But Not Quite There', but the group was nonetheless buoyed by the arrival of Rick Parfitt aka Rick Harrison (b. 12 October 1948, Woking, Surrey, England; guitar/vocals), lately of cabaret attraction the Highlights. The revamped unit assumed their 'Status Quo' appellation in August 1967 and initially sought work backing various solo artists, including Madeline Bell and Tommy Quickly. Such employment came to an abrupt end the following year when the quintet's debut single, 'Pictures Of Matchstick Men', soared to number 7. One of the era's most distinctive performances, the song's ringing guitar pattern and *de rigueur* phasing courted pop and psychedelic affectations. A follow-up release, 'Black Veils Of Melancholy', exaggerated latter trappings at the expense of melody, but the group enjoyed another UK Top 10 hit with the jaunty 'Ice In The Sun', co-written by former 50s singer, Marty Wilde. Subsequent recordings in a similar vein struggled to emulate such success, and despite reaching number 12 with 'Down The Dustpipe', Status Quo was increasingly viewed as a *passé* novelty. However, the song itself, which featured a simple riff and wailing harmonica, indicated the musical direction unveiled more fully on *Ma Kelly's Greasy Spoon*. The album included Quo's version of Steamhammer's 'Junior's Wailing', which had inspired this conversion to a simpler, 'boogie' style. Gone too were the satin shirts, frock coats and kipper ties, replaced by long hair, denim jeans and plimsolls. The departure of Lynes *en route* to Scotland - 'He just got off the train and that was the last we ever saw of him' (Rossi) - brought the unit's guitar work to the fore, although indifference from their record company blighted progress. Assiduous live appearances built up a grass roots following and impressive slots at the Reading and Great Western Festivals (both 1972) signalled a commercial turning point. Now signed to the renowned Vertigo label, Status Quo scored a UK Top 10 hit that year with 'Paper Plane' but more importantly, reached number 5 in the album charts with *Piledriver*. A subsequent release, *Hello*, entered at number 1, confirming the group's emergence as a major attraction. Since that point their style has basically remained unchanged, fusing simple, 12-bar riffs to catchy melodies, while an unpretentious 'lads' image has proved equally enduring. Each of their 70s albums reached the Top 5, while a consistent presence in the singles chart included such notable entries as 'Caroline' (1973), 'Down Down' (a chart topper in 1974), 'Whatever You Want' (1979) and 'Lies'/'Don't Drive My Car' (1980). An uncharacteristic ballad, 'Living On An Island' (1979), showed a softer perspective while Quo also proved adept at adapting outside material, as evinced by their version of John Fogerty's 'Rockin' All Over The World' (1977). That song was later re-recorded as 'Running All Over The World' to promote the charitable *Race Against Time* in 1988. The quartet undertook a lengthy break during 1980, but answered rumours of a permanent split with *Just Supposin'*. However, a dissatisfied Coughlan left the group in 1981 in order to form his own act, Diesel. Pete Kircher (ex-Original Mirrors) took his place, but Quo was then undermined by the growing estrangement between Lancaster and Rossi and Parfitt. The bassist moved to Australia in 1983 - a cardboard cut-out substituted on several television slots - but he remained a member for the next two years. Lancaster's final appearance with the group was at *Live Aid*, following which he unsuccessfully took out a High Court injunction to prevent the group performing without him. Rossi and Parfitt secured the rights to the name 'Status Quo' and re-formed the act around John Edwards (bass), Jeff Rich (drums) and keyboard player Andy Bown. The last-named musician, formerly of the Herd and Judas Jump, had begun his association with the group in 1973, but only now became an official member. Despite such traumas Quo continued to enjoy commercial approbation with Top 10 entries 'Dear John' (1982), 'Marguerita Time' (1983), 'In The Army Now' (1986) and 'Burning Bridges (On And Off And On

Again)' (1988), while *1+9+8+2* was their fourth chart-topping album. Status Quo celebrated its silver anniversary in October 1991 by entering *The Guinness Book Of Records*, having completed four charity concerts in four UK cities in the space of 12 hours. This ambitious undertaking, the subject of a television documentary, was succeeded by a national tour which confirmed the group's continued mass-market popularity. 1994 brought another number 1 single with 'Come On You Reds', a musically dubious project recorded with the league football champions, Manchester United. The much-loved Status Quo have carved a large niche in music history by producing uncomplicated, unpretentious and infectious rock music. An ill-chosen version of 'Fun Fun Fun' in 1996 had the Beach Boys relegated to harmony backing vocals and did little for either Quo's or the Beach Boys' reputation. At the same time the group sued BBC's Radio 1 for not playlisting the single or their latest album (*Don't Stop*). Francis Rossi released a solo single 'Give Myself To Love' in July 1996 followed by an album *King Of The Doghouse*. As expected, they lost the case against Radio 1; that incident aside, their track record is incredible - just two statistics worthy of consideration are: worldwide sales of over 100 million, and even with the dubious 'Fun Fun Fun', they have racked up 50 UK hit singles (more than any other band).

●ALBUMS: *Picturesque Matchstickable Messages* (Pye 1968)★★★, *Spare Parts* (Pye 1969)★★, *Ma Kelly's Greasy Spoon* (Pye 1970)★★, *Dog Of Two Head* (Pye 1971)★★★, *Piledriver* (Vertigo 1972)★★★★, *Hello* (Vertigo 1973)★★★, *Quo* (Vertigo 1974)★★★, *On The Level* (Vertigo 1975)★★★, *Blue For You* (Vertigo 1976)★★, *Status Quo Live!* double album (Vertigo 1977)★★, *Rockin' All Over The World* (Vertigo 1977)★★★, *If You Can't Stand The Heat* (Vertigo 1978)★★★, *Whatever You Want* (Vertigo 1979)★★★, *Just Supposin'* (Vertigo 1980)★★★, *Never Too Late* (Vertigo 1982)★★, *1+9+8+2* (Vertigo 1982)★★, *Back To Back* (Vertigo 1983)★★, *In The Army Now* (Vertigo 1986)★★★, *Ain't Complaining* (Vertigo 1988)★★★, *Perfect Remedy* (Vertigo 1989)★★, *Rock 'Til You Drop* (Vertigo 1991)★★, *Live Alive Quo* (Vertigo 1992)★★, *Thirsty Work* (Polydor 1994)★★, *Don't Stop* (Polygram 1996)★★.

●COMPILATIONS: *Status Quo-tations* (Marble Arch 1969)★★★, *The Best Of Status Quo* (Pye 1973)★★★, *The Golden Hour Of Status Quo* (Golden Hour 1973)★★★, *Down The Dustpipe* (Golden Hour 1975)★★★, *The Rest Of Status Quo* (Pye 1976)★★, *The Status Quo File* (Pye 1977)★★★, *The Status Quo Collection* (Pickwick 1978)★★★, *Twelve Gold Bars* (Vertigo 1980)★★★, *Spotlight On Status Quo Volume 1* double album (PRT 1980)★★★, *Fresh Quota* (PRT 1981)★★★, *100 Minutes Of Status Quo* (PRT 1982)★★★, *Spotlight On Status Quo Volume 2* (PRT 1982)★★★, *From The Makers Of...*(Phonogram 1983)★★★, *Works* (PRT 1983)★★★, *To Be Or Not To Be* (Contour 1983)★★★, *Twelve Gold Bars Volume 1 & 2* (Vertigo 1984)★★★, *Na Na Na* (Flashback

1985)★★★, *Collection: Status Quo* (Castle 1985)★★★, *Quotations, Volume 1* (PRT 1987)★★★, *Quotations, Volume 2* (PRT 1987)★★★, *From The Beginning* (PRT 1988)★★★, *C.90 Collector* (Legacy 1989)★★★, *B-Sides And Rarities* (Castle 1990)★★★, *The Early Works 1968 - '73* CD box set (Essential 1990)★★★, *The Other Side Of ...* (Connoisseur 1995)★★★.

●VIDEOS: *Live At The NEC* (Polygram 1984), *Best Of Status Quo, Preserved* (Channel 5 1986), *End Of The Road 1984* (Channel 51986), *Rocking All Over The Years* (Channel 5 1987), *The Anniversary Waltz* (Castle 1991), *Rock Til You Drop* (Polygram 1991), *Don't Stop* (Polygram 1996).

●FURTHER READING: *Status Quo: The Authorized Biography*, John Shearlaw. *Status Quo*, Tom Hibbert. *Status Quo: Rockin' All Over The World*, Neil Jeffries. *25th Anniversary Edition*, John Shearlaw. *Just For The Record: The Autobioography Of Status Quo*, Francis Rossi and Rick Parfitt.

STEALERS WHEEL

The turbulent, acrimonious and comparatively brief career of Stealers Wheel enabled the two main members Gerry Rafferty and Joe Egan to produce some memorable and inventive, relaxed pop music. During the early 70s, Rafferty (b. 16 April 1946, Paisley, Scotland) and long-time friend Joe Egan (b. *c.*1946 Scotland) assembled in London to form a British Crosby, Stills And Nash, together with Rab Noakes, Ian Campbell and Roger Brown. After rehearsing and negotiating a record contract with A&M Records, the band had already fragmented before they entered the studio to meet with legendary producers Leiber And Stoller. Paul Pilnick (guitar), Tony Williams (bass) and ex-Juicy Lucy member Rod Coombes (drums) bailed out Rafferty and Egan; the result was a surprising success, achieved by the sheer quality of their songs and the blend of the two leaders' voices. 'Stuck In The Middle With You' is an enduring song reminiscent of mid-period Beatles, and it found favour by reaching the Top 10 on both sides of the Atlantic. While the song was high on the charts Rafferty departed and was replaced by former Spooky Tooth lead guitarist Luther Grosvenor (aka Ariel Bender). Rafferty had returned by the time the second album was due to be recorded, but the musical chairs continued as all the remaining members left the band, leaving Rafferty and Egan holding the baby. Various session players completed *Ferguslie Park*, astonishingly another superb, melodic and cohesive album. The album was a failure commercially and the two leaders set about completing their contractual obligations and recording their final work *Right Or Wrong*. Even with similarly strong material, notably the evocative 'Benidictus' and the arresting 'Found My Way To You', the album failed. Rafferty and Egan, disillusioned, buried the name forever. Management problems plagued their career and lyrics of these troubled times continued to appear on both Egan and Rafferty's

subsequent solo work. 'Stuck In The Middle' was used prominently in the film *Reservoir Dogs* in 1993.

●ALBUMS: *Stealers Wheel* (A&M 1972)★★★★, *Ferguslie Park* (A&M 1973)★★★★, *Right Or Wrong* (A&M 1975)★★★.

●COMPILATIONS: *The Best Of Stealers Wheel* (A&M 1978)★★★.

STEAM

Formed in 1969 in Bridgeport, Connecticut, USA, Steam recorded a single, 'Na Na Hey Hey Kiss Him Goodbye', that went to number 1 in the USA during 1969. The group had roots in an early 60s band called the Chateaus, which recorded a number of singles for Coral Records and Warner Brothers Records that were unsuccessful. Two of the members of that band, pianist Paul Leka and drummer Gary DeCarlo, met up again in 1969, the year after Leka had co-written the hit 'Green Tambourine' for the Lemon Pipers. Leka then went to work for Mercury Records; he and DeCarlo teamed up with another ex-Chateau, Dale Frashuer, to update the song that became 'Na Na Hey Hey Kiss Him Goodbye', which they had written in 1961. They had not intended to let the finished version with the 'na na hey hey' chorus go out as a finished product, but Mercury released it on its Fontana subsidiary. The group quickly adapted the name Steam and watched as the single went to the top. Leka assembled a touring version of Steam which did not include the other two originators of their hit. A second single, 'I've Gotta Make You Love Me', was issued but missed the Top 40, while the sole Steam album fizzled at number 84, causing a quick end to this one-hit group. The popularity of their sole transatlantic hit was emphasized when Bananarama took 'Na Na Hey Hey Kiss Him Goodbye' back into the UK Top 10 in 1983.

●ALBUMS: *Steam* (Mercury 1970)★★.

STEEL PULSE

Probably the UK's most highly regarded roots reggae outfit, Steel Pulse originally formed at Handsworth School, Birmingham, and comprised David Hinds (lead vocals, guitar), Basil Gabbidon (lead guitar, vocals) and Ronnie McQueen (bass). However, it is Hinds who, as songwriter, has always been the engine behind Steel Pulse, from their early days establishing themselves in the Birmingham club scene onwards. Formed in 1975, their debut release, 'Kibudu, Mansetta And Abuku', arrived on the small independent label Dip, and linked the plight of urban black youth with the image of a greater African homeland. They followed it with 'Nyah Love' for Anchor. Surprisingly, they were initially refused live dates in Caribbean venues in the Midlands because of their Rastafarian beliefs. Aligning themselves closely with the Rock Against Racism organisation, they chose to tour instead with sympathetic elements of the punk movement, including the Stranglers, XTC, etc.: 'Punks had a way of enjoying themselves -

throw bottles at you, beer, spit at you, that kind of thing'. Eventually they found a more natural home in support slots for Burning Spear, which brought them to the attention of Island Records.

Their first release for Island was the 'Ku Klux Klan' single, a considered tilt at the evils of racism, and one often accompanied by a visual parody of the sect onstage. By this time their ranks had swelled to include Selwyn 'Bumbo' Brown (keyboards), Steve 'Grizzly' Nesbitt (drums), Fonso Martin (vocals, percussion) and Michael Riley (vocals). *Handsworth Revolution* was an accomplished long-playing debut and one of the major landmarks in the evolution of British reggae. However, despite critical and moderate commercial success over three albums, the relationship with Island was soured by the advent of *Caught You* (released in the US as *Reggae Fever*). They switched to Elektra, and unveiled their most consistent collection of songs since their debut with *True Democracy*, distinguished by the Garvey-eulogizing 'Rally Around' cut. A further definitive set arrived in *Earth Crisis*. Unfortunately, Elektra chose to take a leaf out of Island's book in trying to coerce Steel Pulse into a more mainstream vein, asking them to emulate the pop-reggae stance of Eddy Grant. *Babylon Bandit* was consequently weakened, but did contain the anthemic 'Not King James Version', which was a powerful indictment on the omission of black people and history from certain versions of the Bible. Their next move was to MCA for *State Of Emergency*, which retained some of the synthesized dance elements of its predecessor. Though it was a significantly happier compromise, it still paled before any of their earlier albums. *Centennial* was recorded live at the Elysee Montmarte in Paris, and dedicated to the hundred year anniversary of the birth of Haile Selassie. It was the first recording since the defection of Fonso Martin, leaving the trio of Hinds, Nesbitt and Selwyn. While they still faced inverted snobbery at the hands of British reggae fans, in America their reputation was growing, becoming the first ever reggae band to appear on the *Tonight* television show. Their profile was raised further when, in 1992, Hinds challenged the New York Taxi and Limousine Commission in the Supreme High Court, asserting that their cab drivers discriminated against black people in general and Rastas in particular.

●ALBUMS: *Handsworth Revolution* (Island 1978)★★★★, *Tribute To The Martyrs* (Island 1979)★★★, *Caught You/Reggae Fever* (Mango/Island 1980)★★★, *True Democracy* (Elektra 1982)★★★, *Earth Crisis* (Elektra 1984)★★★, *Babylon Bandit* (Elektra 1985)★★, *State Of Emergency* (MCA 1988)★★, *Victims* (MCA 1992)★★, *Rastafari Centennial* (MCA 1992)★★★.
●COMPILATIONS: *Reggae Greats* (Mango/Island 1985)★★★★.

STEELEYE SPAN

The roots of this pivotal English folk rock group lay in several ill-fated rehearsals between Ashley 'Tyger'

Hutchings (b. January 1945, London, England; bass, ex-Fairport Convention), Irish trio Sweeny's Men - Terry Woods (vocals, guitar, mandolin), Johnny Moynihan (vocals, fiddle) and Andy Irvine (vocals, mandolin) - and Woods' wife Gay (vocals, concertina, autoharp). When Moynihan and Irvine subsequently retracted, the remaining musicians were joined by Tim Hart (vocals, guitar, dulcimer, harmonium) and Maddy Prior (vocals), two well-known figures in folk circles. Taking their name from a Lincolnshire waggoner celebrated in song, Steeleye Span began extensive rehearsals before recording the excellent *Hark, The Village Wait*. The set comprised traditional material, expertly arranged and performed to encompass the rock-based perspective Hutchings helped create on the Fairport's *Liege And Lief*, while retaining the purity of the songs. The Woods then left to pursue their own career and were replaced by Martin Carthy (vocals, guitar) and Peter Knight (vocals, fiddle) for *Please To See The King* and *Ten Man Mop*. This particular line-up toured extensively, but the departure of Hutchings for the purist Albion Country Band signalled a dramatic realignment in the Steeleye camp. Carthy resumed his solo career when conflict arose over the extent of change and two musicians of a rock-based persuasion - Bob Johnson (guitar) and Rick Kemp (bass) - were brought in. The quintet also left manager/producer Sandy Robertson for the higher-profile of Jo Lustig, who secured the group's new recording contract with Chrysalis Records. Both *Below The Salt* and *Parcel Of Rogues*, displayed an electric content and tight dynamics, while the punningly entitled *Now We Are Six*, which was produced by Jethro Tull's Ian Anderson and had David Bowie playing saxophone on 'Thomas The Rhymer', emphasized the terse drumming of newcomer Nigel Pegrum. The group enjoyed two hit singles with 'Gaudete' (1973) and 'All Around My Hat' (1975), the latter of which reached the UK Top 5 and was produced by Mike Batt. On *Commoners Crown* the group recruited actor/comedian Peter Sellers to play ukelele on 'New York Girls'. However, the charm of Steeleye's early work was gradually eroding and although their soaring harmonies remained as strong as ever, experiments with reggae and heavier rock rhythms alienated rather than attracted prospective audiences. The group was 'rested' following the disappointing *Rocket Cottage* (1976), but reconvened the following year for *Storm Force Ten*. However, Knight and Johnson were otherwise employed and this line-up was completed by John Kirkpatrick (accordion) and the prodigal Martin Carthy. Although their formal disbanding was announced in March 1978, Steeleye Span has been resurrected on subsequent occasions. Hart, Prior and Carthy have also pursued successful solo careers. The most recent recording *Time* featured Prior, Kemp, Johnson, Knight, Liam Gonockey, Tim Harries and from the very beginning, Gay Woods.

●ALBUMS: *Hark, The Village Wait* (Chrysalis 1970)★★★★, *Please To See The King* (Chrysalis

1971)★★★, *Ten Man Mop (Or Mr. Reservoir Strikes Again)* (Chrysalis 1971)★★★, *Below The Salt* (Chrysalis 1972)★★★, *Parcel Of Rogues* (Chrysalis 1973)★★★, *Now We Are Six* (Chrysalis 1974)★★★, *Commoners Crown* (Chrysalis 1975)★★★, *All Around My Hat* (Chrysalis 1975)★★★, *Rocket Cottage* (Chrysalis 1976)★★, *Storm Force Ten* (Chrysalis 1977)★★★, *Live At Last* (Chrysalis 1978)★★, *Sails Of Silver* (Chrysalis 1980)★★★, *Back In Line* (Flutterby 1986)★★★, *Tempted And Tried* (Chrysalis 1989)★★★, *In Concert* (Park 1995)★★★, *Time* (Park 1996)★★★.

●COMPILATIONS: *Individually And Collectively* (1972)★★★, *Steeleye Span Almanac* (1973)★★★, *Original Masters* (Chrysalis 1977)★★★, *Time Span* (1978)★★, *Best Of Steeleye Span* (Chrysalis 1984)★★★★, *Steeleye Span* (Cambra 1985)★★★, *Portfolio* (Chrysalis 1988)★★★, *The Early Years* (Connoisseur 1989)★★.

STEELY DAN

The seeds of this much-respected rock group were sewn at New York's Bard College where founder members Donald Fagen (b. 10 January 1948, Passaic, New Jersey, USA; keyboards/vocals) and Walter Becker (b. 20 February 1950, Queens, New York, USA; bass/vocals) were students. They subsequently forged a songwriting team and their many demos were later collected on several exploitative compilations. Formative versions of 'Brooklyn', 'Berry Town' and 'Parker's Band' - each of which were re-recorded on official Steely Dan releases - were recorded during this period. The duo also enjoyed a contemporaneous association with pop/harmony act Jay And The Americans, for which they adopted the pseudonyms Gus Marker and Tristan Fabriani. Becker and Fagen appeared on the group's last US Top 20 hit, 'Walkin' In The Rain' (1969), the albums *Wax Museum* and *Capture The Moment*, and accompanied the unit on tour. Group vocalist Jerry Vance and drummer John Discepolo joined the pair for *You Gotta Walk It Like You Talk It (Or You'll Lose That Beat)*, the soundtrack to a low-key movie. Denny Dias (guitar) also contributed to these sessions and he joined Fagen and Becker on their next project which evolved following an alliance with producer Gary Katz. Taking the name 'Steely Dan' from the steam-powered dildo in William Burroughs' novel *The Naked Lunch*, the trio was quickly expanded by the arrival of David Palmer (b. Plainfield, New Jersey, USA; vocals, ex-Myddle Class), Jeff 'Skunk' Baxter (b. 13 December 1948, Washington, DC, USA; guitar, ex-Ultimate Spinach) and Jim Hodder (b. Boston, Massachusetts, USA, d. 5 June 1992; drums). The accomplished *Can't Buy A Thrill* was completed within weeks, but drew considerable critical praise for its deft melodies and immaculate musicianship. The title track and 'Do It Again' reached the US Top 20 when issued as singles and this newfound fame inspired the sarcasm of 'Show Biz Kids' on *Countdown To Ecstacy*.

Their second album was another undoubted classic of the 70s, and featured such bittersweet celebrations as 'The Boston Rag' and 'My Old School'. By this point Palmer had left the line-up following an uncomfortable US tour, but although Baxter declared the set superior to its predecessor, the same commercial approbation did not follow. This was reversed with the release of *Pretzel Logic*, Steely Dan's first US Top 10 album. Here Fagen and Becker drew more fully on their love of jazz, acquiring the riff of 'Rikki Don't Lose That Number' from Horace Silver's 'Song Of My Father' and recreating Duke Ellington's 'East St. Louis Toodle-O'. The former reached number 4 in the US charts. The group's clarity of purpose and enthralling dexterity was never so apparent, but internal conflicts simmered over a reluctance to tour, shown by Becker and, especially, Fagen who was unhappy with the in-concert role of frontman. Steely Dan's final live appearance was on 4 July 1974 and ensuing strife resulted in the departures of both Baxter and Hodder. The guitarist resurfaced in the Doobie Brothers, with whom he was already guesting, while the drummer reverted to session work. The faithful Dias joined newcomers Michael McDonald (keyboards/vocals) and Jeff Porcaro (drums) for *Katy Lied* which also featured cameos by guitarist Rick Derringer and saxophonist Phil Woods. At the time of issue the set was, however, greeted with disquiet as the transformation from active unit to purely studio creation resulted in crafted anonymity. In recent years the album has shown its strengths and is now highly rated. *The Royal Scam* redressed the commercial balance and in its title track offered one of the group's most impressive tracks to date. Becker and Fagen were, by now, the sole arbiters of Steely Dan, McDonald having followed Baxter into the Doobie Brothers and Dias and Porcaro opting for studio employment. The new collection boasted another series of sumptuous tunes and included 'Haitian Divorce', the group's lone Top 20 hit in Britain. *Aja* continued in a similar vein where an array of quality musicians - including Wayne Shorter, Jim Horn and Tom Scott - brought meticulousness to a set notable for the seemingly effortless, jazz/disco sweep evinced on 'Peg'. A similar pattern was unveiled on the immaculately recorded *Gaucho*, the release of which was marred by conflict between the group and record label over escalating recording costs. The latter's nervousness was assuaged when the album achieved platinum sales and an attendant single, 'Hey Nineteen', reached the US Top 10. However, Becker and Fagen had now tired of their creation and in June 1981 they announced the break-up of their partnership. The following year Fagen released *The Nightfly*, a superb collection which continued where his erstwhile group had ended. Producer Katz supervised the accustomed cabal of Los Angeles session musicians to create a sound and texture emphasizing the latter's dominant role in later Steely Dan releases. Becker, meanwhile, produced albums for China Crisis and Rickie Lee Jones, but in May 1990 the pair were reunited in New York's Hit Factory studio to collaborate on material for a forthcoming Fagen project. 'We're not working as Steely Dan,' stated Becker, but aficionados were undoubtedly heartened by news of their rekindled partnership. Although it took a further three years, the partnership worked together on Donald Fagen's impressive *Kamakiriad* and played together as Steely Dan to delighted fans. Becker released his solo effort, the largely ignored *11 Tracks Of Whack*. Nothing jells quite like the two working together as Steely Dan. The world awaits any sign of new material.

●ALBUMS: *Can't Buy A Thrill* (Probe 1972)★★★★, *Countdown To Ecstacy* (Probe 1973)★★★★, *Pretzel Logic* (Probe 1974)★★★★, *Katy Lied* (ABC 1975)★★★★, *The Royal Scam* (ABC 1976)★★★★, *Aja* (ABC 1977)★★★★, *Gaucho* (MCA 1980)★★★, *Alive In America* rec. 1993, 1994 (Giant/BMG 1995)★★. Solo: Walter Becker *11 Tracks Of Whack* (Giant 1994)★★★.

●COMPILATIONS: *You Gotta Walk It Like You Talk It (Or You'll Lose That Beat)* early recordings (Spark 1974)★★, *Greatest Hits* (ABC 1979)★★★, *Gold* (MCA 1982)★★, *A Decade Of Steely Dan* (MCA 1985)★★★★, *Reelin' In The Years* (MCA 1985)★★★, *Berry Town* early Becker/Fagen material (Bellaphon 1986)★★, *Sun Mountain* early Becker/Fagen material (Showcase 1986)★★, *Old Regime* early Becker/Fagen material (Thunderbolt 1987)★★, *Stone Piano* early Becker/Fagen material (Thunderbolt 1988)★★, *Gold (Expanded Edition)* (MCA 1991)★★★, *Citizen Steely Dan, 1972-80* 4-CD box set (1993)★★★★, *Remastered: The Best Of* (MCA 1994)★★★★.

●FURTHER READING: *Steely Dan: Reelin' In The Years*, Brian Sweet.

STEVENS, CAT

b. Steven Georgiou, 21 July 1947, London, England. For Yusuf Islam, the constant search for the meaning of life that littered his lyrics and arose in interviews, seems to have arrived. Those who criticized his sometimes trite espousal now accept that his conversion to the Islamic faith and his retirement from a music world of 'sin and greed' was a committed move that will not be reversed. His legacy as Cat Stevens is a considerable catalogue of timeless songs, many destined to become classics. In 1966, producer Mike Hurst spotted Cat performing at the Hammersmith College, London; he was so impressed that he arranged to record him and his song, 'I Love My Dog'. Tony Hall at Decca Records was similarly impressed and Stevens became the first artist on the new Deram label. The record and its b-side 'Portobello Road' showed great promise and over the next two years Stevens delivered many perfect pop songs. Some were recorded by himself but many other artists queued up for material from this precociously talented teenager. His own hits; 'Matthew And Son', 'I'm Gonna Get Me A Gun' and 'Bad Night' were equalled by the quality of his songs for others; the soulful 'First Cut Is The Deepest' by P.P. Arnold and the addictive 'Here Comes My Baby' by the Tremeloes. His two Decca albums were packed full of short, infectious

songs, although they suffered from dated accompaniments. Stevens contracted tuberculosis and was absent for some time. During his convalescence he took stock of his life. Over the next eight years and 11 albums, the astute listener can detect a troubled soul.

Mona Bone Jakon was the first in the series of albums known as bedsitter music. It was followed by two hugely successful works: *Tea For The Tillerman* and *Teaser And The Firecat*. These revealed the solitary songwriter, letting the listener into his private thoughts, aspirations and desires. Stevens was the master of this genre and produced a wealth of simplistic, yet beautiful songs. Anthems like 'Wild World', 'Peace Train' and 'Moon Shadow', love songs including 'Lady D'Arbanville', 'Hard Headed Woman' and 'Can't Keep It In', are all faultless and memorable compositions. Stevens was at his sharpest with his posing numbers that hinted of dubiety, religion and scepticism. Two of his finest songs are 'Father And Son' and 'Sitting'. The first is a dialogue between father and son, and gives the listener an insight into his lonely childhood in Soho. The line, 'How can I try to explain, when I do he turns away again, its always been the same, same old story' the child continues with 'from the moment I could talk, I was ordered to listen, now there's a way that I know, that I have to go, away, I know I have to go'. The song is astonishingly powerful in relating Stevens' own turmoil to virtually every person that has ever heard the song. 'Sitting' is similarly powerful, although it is a song of great hope. It opens confidently, 'Ooh I'm on my way I know I am, somewhere not so far from here, all I know is all I feel right now, I feel the power growing in my hair'. Few were unmoved by these two songs. In his time Stevens had eight consecutive gold albums and 10 hit singles in the UK and 14 in the USA. In recent years he has been very active teaching and spreading the word of Islam; in 1991 prior to the Gulf War he travelled to Baghdad to seek the freedom of hostages. Reports in 1994 suggested that he was ready to return to the world of the recording studio, albeit only to offer a spoken word narrative on *Mohammed - The Life Of The Prophet*.

●ALBUMS: *Matthew & Son* (Deram 1967)★★★, *New Masters* (Deram 1968)★★★, *Mona Bone Jakon* (Island 1970)★★★, *Tea For The Tillerman* (Island 1970)★★★★, *Teaser & The Firecat* (Island 1971)★★★★, *Very Young And Early Songs* (Deram 1972)★★, *Catch Bull At Four* (Island 1972)★★★★, *Foreigner* (Island 1973)★★, *Buddah And The Chocolate Box* (Island 1974)★★, *View From The Top* (Deram 1974)★★, *Numbers* (Island 1975)★, *Izitso* (Island 1977)★, *Back To Earth* (Island 1978)★★, as Yusuf Islam *The Life Of The Last Prophet* (1995)★.

●COMPILATIONS: *Greatest Hits* (Island 1975)★★★★, *The Very Best Of Cat Stevens* (Island 1990)★★★★. Videos *Tea For The Tillerman Live - The Best Of* (1993).

●FURTHER READING: *Cat Stevens*, Chris Charlesworth.

STEWART, AL

b. 5 September 1945, Glasgow, Scotland. Stewart first came to prominence during the folk boom of the mid-60s. His musical career began in Bournemouth, where he played guitar, backing Tony Blackburn in the Sabres. In 1965, he moved to London, played at various folk clubs and shared lodgings with Jackson C. Frank, Sandy Denny and Paul Simon. Stewart was signed to Decca in 1966 and released one unsuccessful single, 'The Elf', featuring Jimmy Page on lead guitar. The following year, he joined CBS and released the acoustic, string-accompanied, introspective *Bedsitter Images*. The succeeding *Love Chronicles*, a diary of Stewart's romantic life, was most notable for the lengthy title track and the fact that it used a contentious word ('fucking') in an allegedly artistic context. The singer's interest in acoustic folk continued on *Zero She Flies*, which featured the historical narrative 'Manuscript'. Stewart's interest in the confessional love song reached its conclusion on *Orange*, with the impressive 'Night Of The 4th Of May'. This was followed by his most ambitious work to date, *Past, Present And Future*. Pursuing his interest in historical themes, Stewart presented some of his best acoustic workouts in the impressive 'Roads To Moscow' and epic 'Nostradamus'. A considerable gap ensued before the release of *Modern Times*, which saw Stewart making inroads into the American market for the first time.

After leaving CBS and signing to RCA, he relocated to California and surprised many by the commercial power of his celebrated *Year Of The Cat*, which reached the US Top 10. The title track also gave Stewart his first US hit. Another switch of label to Arista preceded *Time Passages*, which suffered by comparison with its predecessor. The underrated *24 P Carrots* was succeeded by a part studio/part live album, which merely consolidated his position. With *Russians And Americans*, Stewart embraced a more noticeable political stance, but the sales were disappointing. Legal and contractual problems effectively deterred him from recording for four years until the welcome, if portentous, *The Last Days Of The Century*. During that time he had relocated to France and set about expanding his impressive cellar of vintage wines. Stewart remains one of the more underrated performers, despite his commercial breakthrough in the 70s.

●ALBUMS: *Bedsitter Images* (Columbia 1967)★★, *Love Chronicles* (Columbia 1969)★★★, *Zero She Flies* (Columbia 1970)★★★, *The First Album (Bedsitter Images)* (Columbia 1970)★★, *Orange* (Columbia 1972)★★★, *Past, Present And Future* (Columbia 1973)★★★, *Modern Times* (Columbia 1975)★★★, *Year Of The Cat* (RCA 1976)★★★★, *Time Passages* (RCA 1978)★★, *24 P Carrots* (RCA 1980)★★★, *Indian Summer/Live* (RCA 1981)★★★, *Russians And Americans* (RCA 1984)★★★, *Last Days Of The Century* (Enigma 1988)★★★, *Rhymes In Rooms - Al Stewart Live Featuring Peter White* (EMI 1991)★★★, *Famous Last Words* (Permanent 1993)★★★, with

Laurence Juber *Between The Wars* (EMI 1995)★★★.
●COMPILATIONS: *The Early Years* (RCA 1978)★★, *Best Of Al Stewart* (RCA 1985)★★, *Chronicles ... The Best Of Al Stewart* (EMI 1991)★★★, *To Whom It May Concern 1966-70* (EMI 1994)★★★, *The Best Of ...* (EMI 1997)★★★.

STEWART, JOHN

b. 5 September 1939, San Diego, California, USA. Stewart's musical career began in the 50s when, as frontman of the Furies, he recorded 'Rocking Anna' for a tiny independent label. Having discovered folk music, Stewart began performing with college friend John Montgomery, but achieved wider success as a songwriter when several of his compositions, including 'Molly Dee' and 'Green Grasses', were recorded by the Kingston Trio. Indeed, the artist joined this prestigious group in 1961, following his spell in the similar sounding Cumberland Three. Stewart left the Kingston trio in 1967. His reputation was enhanced when a new composition, 'Daydream Believer', became a number 1 hit for the Monkees and this dalliance with pop continued when the artist contributed 'Never Goin' Back' to a disintegrating Lovin' Spoonful on their final album.

In 1968 Stewart was joined by singer Buffy Ford, whom he married in 1975. Together they completed *Signals Through The Glass*, before the former resumed his solo path with the excellent *California Bloodlines*. This country-inspired collection established Stewart's sonorous delivery and displayed a view of America which, if sometimes sentimental, was both optimistic and refreshing. It was a style the performer continued over a series of albums which, despite critical approval, achieved only moderate success. Stewart's fortunes were upturned in 1979 when a duet with Stevie Nicks, 'Gold', became a US hit. The attendant *Bombs Away Dream Babies*, featured assistance from Fleetwood Mac guitarist, Lindsay Buckingham and although markedly different in tone to its predecessors, the set augured well for the future. However, despite contributions from Linda Ronstadt and Phil Everly, the follow-up, *Dream Babies Go To Hollywood*, proved an anti-climax. Stewart subsequently turned from commercial pursuits and resumed a more specialist direction with a series of low-key recordings for independent companies.

●ALBUMS: *Signals Through The Glass* (1968)★★, *California Bloodlines* (Capitol 1969)★★★, *Willard* (Capitol 1970)★★, *The Lonesome Picker Rides Again* (Warners 1972)★★★, *Sunstorm* (1972)★★★, *Cannons In The Rain* (RCA 1973)★★, *The Phoenix Concerts - Live* (RCA 1974)★★★, *Wingless Angels* (RCA 1975)★★, *Fire In The Wind* (RSO 1977)★★, *Bombs Away Dream Babies* (RSO 1979)★★★★, *Dream Babies Go Hollywood* (RSO 1980)★★, *Blondes* (1982)★★, *Trancas* (Sunstorm 1984)★★, *Centennial* (1984)★★, *The Last Campaign* (1985)★★, *Neon Beach* (1991)★★★, *Bullets In The Hour Glass* (1993)★★★, *Greetings From John Stewart* (1993)★★, *Airdream Believer* (Shanachie 1995)★★.
●COMPILATIONS: *Forgotten Songs Of Some Old Yesterday*

(RCA 1980)★★★, *California Bloodlines Plus...* (See For Miles 1987)★★★.

STEWART, ROD

b. Roderick David Stewart, 10 January 1945, Highgate, London, England. The leading British rock star of the 70s started his career as an apprentice professional with Brentford Football Club (over the years Stewart has made it known that football is his second love). Following a spell roaming Europe with folk artist Wizz Jones in the early 60s he returned to join Jimmy Powell And The Five Dimensions in 1963. This frantic R&B band featured Rod playing furious harmonica, reminiscent of James Cotton and Little Walter. As word got out, he was attracted to London and was hired by Long John Baldry in his band the Hoochie Coochie Men (formerly Cyril Davies' All Stars). Without significant success outside the club scene, the band disintegrated and evolved into the Steampacket, with Baldry, Stewart, Brian Auger, Julie Driscoll, Mickey Waller and Rick Brown. Following a television documentary on the swinging mod scene, featuring Stewart, he earned his moniker, 'Rod the Mod'. In 1965, he joined the blues-based Shotgun Express as joint lead vocalist with Beryl Marsden. The impressive line-up included Peter Green, Mick Fleetwood and Peter Bardens. By the following year, Stewart was well-known in R&B and blues circles, but it was joining the Jeff Beck Group that gave him national exposure. During his tenure with Beck he recorded two important albums, *Truth* and *Cosa Nostra-Beck Ola* and made a number of gruelling tours of America.

When the group broke up (partly through exhaustion) Stewart and Ron Wood joined the Faces, now having lost their smallest face, Steve Marriot. Simultaneously, Stewart had been signed as a solo artist to Phonogram, and he managed to juggle both careers expertly over the next six years. Though critically well received, his first album sold only moderately; it was *Gasoline Alley* that made the breakthrough. In addition to the superb title track it contained the glorious 'Lady Day'. This album marked the beginning of the 'mandolin' sound supplied by the talented guitarist Martin Quittenton. Stewart became a superstar on the strength of his next two albums, *Every Picture Tells A Story* and *Never A Dull Moment*. Taken as one body of work, they represent Stewart at his best. His choice and exemplary execution of non-originals gave him numerous hits from these albums including; 'Reason To Believe' (Tim Hardin), 'I'm Losing You' (Temptations), 'Angel' (Jimi Hendrix). His own classics were the irresistible chart-topping magnum opus 'Maggie May' and the wonderful 'You Wear It Well', all sung in his now familiar frail, hoarse voice. In the mid-70s, following the release of the below average *Smiler*, Stewart embarked on a relationship with the actress Britt Ekland. Besotted with her, he allowed her to dictate his sense of dress, and for a while appeared in faintly ludicrous dungarees made out of

silk and ridiculous jump suits. At the same time he became the darling of the magazine and gutter press, a reputation he has unwillingly maintained through his succession of affairs with women. *Atlantic Crossing* was his last critical success for many years; it included the future football crowd anthem and number 1 hit, 'Sailing' (written by Gavin Sutherland), and a fine reading of Dobie Gray's 'Drift Away'. His albums throughout the second half of the 70s were patchy affairs, although they became phenomenally successful, selling millions, and in many cases topping the charts worldwide. The high spots during this glitzy phase, which saw him readily embrace the prevalent disco era, were 'The Killing Of Georgie', Cat Stevens' 'First Cut Is The Deepest', 'Tonight's The Night' and 'You're In My Heart'. Other hits included 'Hot Legs' and the superbly immodest but irresistible number 1, 'D'Ya Think I'm Sexy'. His 'Ole Ola', meanwhile, was adopted by the Scottish World Cup football team, an area in which his popularity has always endured.

He entered the 80s newly married, to George Hamilton IV's ex-wife, Alana, and maintained his momentum of regular hits and successful albums; his large body of fans ensured a chart placing irrespective of the quality. The 80s saw Stewart spending his time jet-setting all over the world, with the press rarely far from his heels (covering his marriage break-up, his long relationship with Kelly Emberg, and the unceasing round of parties). Behind the jack-the-lad persona was an artist who still had a good ear for a quality song, a talent which surfaced throughout the decade with numbers like 'How Long' (Paul Carrick), 'Some Guys Have All The Luck' (Robert Palmer) and, reunited with Jeff Beck, a superb performance of Curtis Mayfield's 'People Get Ready'. His biggest hits of the 80s were 'What Am I Gonna Do', 'Every Beat Of My Heart' and his best of the decade, 'Baby Jane'. As the 90s got under way Stewart, now remarried, indicated that he had settled down, and found an enduring love at last. His new guise has not affected his record sales; in April 1991 he was high on the UK chart with 'Rhythm Of My Heart' and had the best-selling *Vagabond Heart*. *Unplugged And Seated* in 1993 boosted his credibility with an exciting performance of familiar songs. A new album in 1995 was his best for some years and during the launch Stewart undertook some interviews which were both revealing and hilarious. The once seemingly pompous rock star, dressed to the nines in baggy silks is really 'Rod the Mod' after all. Rod Stewart, one of the biggest 'superstars' of the century, has now turned 50 without his audience diminishing in any way. Rarely has his credibility been higher than now.

●ALBUMS: *An Old Raincoat Won't Ever Let You Down* (Vertigo 1970)★★★★, *Gasoline Alley* (Vertigo 1970)★★★★, *Every Picture Tells A Story* (Mercury 1971)★★★★, *Never A Dull Moment* (Mercury 1972)★★★★, *Smiler* (Mercury 1974)★★, *Atlantic Crossing* (Warners 1975)★★★, *A Night On The Town*

(Riva 1976)★★★, *Foot Loose And Fancy Free* (Riva 1977)★★, *Blondes Have More Fun* (Riva 1978)★★, *Foolish Behaviour* (Riva 1980)★, *Tonight I'm Yours* (Riva 1981)★★, *Absolutely Live* (Riva 1982)★, *Body Wishes* (Warners 1983)★, *Camouflage* (Warners 1984)★, *Out Of Order* (Warners 1988)★★, *Vagabond Heart* (Warners 1991)★★★, *Unplugged And Seated* (Warners 1993)★★★★, *A Spanner In The Works* (Warners 1995)★★★, *If We Fall In Love Tonight* (Warners 1996)★★★.

●COMPILATIONS: *Sing It Again Rod* (Mercury 1973)★★★★, *The Vintage Years* (Mercury 1976)★★★, *Recorded Highlights And Action Replays* (Phillips 1976)★★★, *The Best Of Rod Stewart* (Mercury 1977)★★★★, *The Best Of Rod Stewart Volume 2* (Mercury 1977)★★★, *Rod Stewart's Greatest Hits Volume 1* (Riva 1979)★★★, *Hot Rods* (Mercury 1980)★★, *Maggie May* (Pickwick 1981)★★, *Rod Stewart* (Pickwick 1982)★★, *Jukebox Heaven* (Pickwick 1987)★★, *The Best Of Rod Stewart* (Warners 1989)★★★★, *Storyteller* (Warners 1989)★★★★, *The Early Years* (1992)★★★, *Lead Vocalist* (1993)★★★.

●FURTHER READING: *The Rod Stewart Story*, George Tremlett. *Rod Stewart And The Faces*, John Pidgeon. *Rod Stewart: A Biography In Words & Pictures*, Richard Cromelin. *Rod Stewart*, Tony Jasper. *Rod Stewart: A Life On The Town*, Peter Burton. *Rod Stewart*, Gerd Rockl and Paul Sahner. *Rod Stewart*, Paul Nelson and Lester Bangs. *Rod Stewart: A Biography*, Tim Ewbank and Stafford Hildred. *Rod Stewart: Vagabond Heart*, Geoffrey Guiliano.

STIFF LITTLE FINGERS

This Irish punk band were formed from the ashes of cover group Highway Star. Taking their new name from a track on the Vibrators' *Pure Mania* debut, Stiff Little Fingers soon attracted one of the most fervent fan bases of the era. Present at the Clash's Belfast gig in 1977, Jake Burns (vocals/lead guitar) led Henry Cluney (rhythm guitar), Ali McMordie (bass) and Brian Falloon (drums) as Ireland's first new wave cover band. The original drummer, Gordon Blair, had gone on to play with Rudi. When journalist Gordon Ogilvie saw the band live he urged them to concentrate on their own material, quickly becoming their manager and co-lyricist. They recorded their first two original songs, 'Suspect Device'/'Wasted Life' soon after, on their own Rigid Digits label. The first pressing of 350 copies sold out almost as soon as BBC disc jockey John Peel span it. Rough Trade quickly picked up the distribution, and released the band's second single, 'Alternative Ulster', in conjunction with Rigid Digits. After a major tour supporting the Tom Robinson Band, the group were almost signed to Island, but remained on Rough Trade for their long playing debut, *Inflammable Material*. With songs concentrating on personal experiences in the politically charged climate of Northern Ireland, the album still managed to surprise many with its inclusion of diverse rock patterns and a flawed love song. The release

marked the departure of Falloon who was replaced by Jim Reilly. The follow-up, *Nobodys Heroes*, revealed great strides in technique and sophistication with the band branching out into dub, reggae and pop. The dialogue with the audience was still direct, however, urging tolerance, self-respect and unity, and rejecting the trappings of rock stardom. They came in for criticism, however, for Ogilvie's patronage. After a disappointing live album, the impressive *Go For It!* saw the band at the peak of their abilities and popularity. Reilly left for the USA, joining Red Rockers shortly afterwards, with Brian 'Dolphin' Taylor (ex-Tom Robinson Band) drafted in as his replacement. 1982's *Now Then* embraced songs of a more pop-rock nature, though in many ways the compromise was an unhappy one. Burns left at the beginning of the following year, forming The Big Wheel. However, live and on record he was unable to shake off comparisons to Stiff Little Fingers, and he soon opted instead for a career as trainee producer at BBC Radio 1. McMordie formed Fiction Groove and contributed to Sinead O'Conner's *The Lion And The Cobra*, while Cluney taught guitar back in Ireland. Taylor returned for a brief stint of drumming with TRB, but the spectre of Stiff Little Fingers remained. One reunion gig gave birth to further events, until 1990 when they re-formed on a permanent basis. McMordie had grown tired of the rock circuit, however, and his replacement was the group's old friend Bruce Foxton (ex-Jam). In the early 90s they embarked on further major tours and recorded two respectable albums, *Flags And Emblems* and *Fly The Flag*, but lost the long-serving Henry Cluney amid much acrimony.

●ALBUMS: *Inflammable Material* (Rough Trade 1979)★★★, *Nobody's Heroes* (Chrysalis 1980)★★★, *Hanx!* (Chrysalis 1980)★★, *Go For It!* (Chrysalis 1981)★★★, *Now Then* (Chrysalis 1982)★★, *Flags And Emblems* (Essential! 1991)★★, *Fly The Flag* (Essential! 1993)★★, *Get A Life* (Castle Communications 1994)★★, *Pure Fingers Live - St. Patrix 1993* (Dojo 1995)★★.

●COMPILATIONS: *All The Best* (Chrysalis 1983)★★★, *Live And Loud* (Link 1988)★★, *No Sleep Till Belfast* (Kaz 1988)★★, *See You Up There* (Virgin 1989)★★, *Live In Sweden* (Limited Edition 1989)★★, *The Peel Sessions* (Strange Fruit 1989)★★, *Greatest Hits Live* (Link 1991)★★, *Alternative Chartbusters* (Link 1991)★★.

STIFF RECORDS

Britain's premier 'new wave' label of the 70s was founded in 1976 by pub-rock producer and promoter, Dave Robinson, and Andrew Jakeman, tour manager of Dr Feelgood. The first release, 'Heart Of The City' by Nick Lowe, was financed by a £400 loan from Dr Feelgood's singer, Lee Brilleaux. From 1976-77, the label released material by a range of London-based pub and punk rock bands such as Roogalator, Lew Lewis, the Adverts and the Damned. Stiff also signed Elvis Costello whose fourth single, 'Watching The Detectives', was the label's first hit. Costello had achieved prominence as a member of Stiff's first package tour of numerous British cities. Like its 1978 successor, the tour served to publicize and popularize the label and its artists. During the early days it was extremely hip to be seen wearing a Stiff T-shirt bearing its uncompromising slogan, 'If it ain't Stiff it ain't worth a fuck'. Towards the end of 1977, Stiff suffered a setback when Jakeman, Costello and Nick Lowe left to join the Radar label. However, Stiff's fortunes were transformed by the success of Ian Dury whose anthem, 'Sex And Drugs And Rock 'N' Roll', had made little impact when first issued in 1977. A year later, however, 'What A Waste' inaugurated a run of four hit singles. Lene Lovich, Jona Lewie and Madness also provided Top 20 records for the label in 1978-80, when Robinson switched distribution from EMI to CBS Records. In the early 80s Stiff flirted with reggae (Desmond Dekker) and soul (various productions by Eddy Grant), but the bulk of its releases still came from artists on the eccentric fringe of the new wave such as Tenpole Tudor and Wreckless Eric. The company also issued one album from Graham Parker before he moved to the larger RCA Records label. There were also hits from the Belle Stars and Dave Stewart with Barbara Gaskin. From the outset, Robinson had been interested in new wave developments in America and over the years Stiff licensed material by such artists as Rachel Sweet, Devo, the Plasmatics and Jane Aire. In 1984 Stiff was merged with Island Records and Robinson became managing director of both companies. This coincided with the departure of Madness to start their own label (Zarjazz), although Stiff's new signing, the Pogues, provided hits throughout the mid-80s. The merger was not a success, however, and in 1986 Robinson resumed control of an independent Stiff, only to see it suffer an immediate cash-crisis. The assets of the company, which had a turnover of £4m at its peak, were sold to ZTT Records for a reputed £300,000. Under the new ownership there were initial releases from the Pogues, hard bop drummer Tommy Chase and female vocal group the Mint Juleps. But by the 90s the pioneering Stiff had become simply a reissue label.

●FURTHER READING: *Stiff, The Story Of a Record Label, 1976-1982*, Bert Muirhead.

STILLS, STEPHEN

b. 3 January 1945, Dallas, Texas, USA. The often dubbed 'musical genius' is better known for his work with the pivotal Buffalo Springfield, and for many years his association with David Crosby, Graham Nash and Neil Young. After the Springfield's break-up, Stills, at a loose end, joined with Al Kooper and Mike Bloomfield for the million-selling *Super Session*. His contributions included Donovan's 'Season Of The Witch', on which he played one of the decade's most famous wah-wah guitar solos. His solo career began during one of Crosby, Stills And Nash's many hiatuses. Then living in England at Ringo Starr's former home, Stills enlisted a team of musical heavyweights to play on his self-titled debut which reached the US Top 3 in 1970. This outstanding album remains his best work, and is justifiably still available. In addition to the irresistible hit single 'Love The One You're With' the album contains a healthy mixture of styles, all demonstrating his considerable dexterity as a songwriter, guitarist and singer. The solo acoustic 'Black Queen' for example, was reputedly recorded while Stills was completely drunk, and yet his mastery of the (C.F.) Martin acoustic guitar still prevails. All tracks reach the listener, from the infectious 'Old Times Good Times', featuring Jimi Hendrix to 'Go Back Home', featuring Eric Clapton; it is unfair to single out any track for they are all exemplary. On this one album, Stills demonstrated the extent of his powers. *Stephen Stills 2* was a similar success containing the innocently profound 'Change Partners', a brass reworking of the Springfield's 'Bluebird' and the brilliant yet oddly timed blues number 'Nothing To Do But Today'. For a while it appeared that Stills' solo career would eclipse that of his CSNY involvement. His superbly eclectic double album with Manassas and its consolidating follow-up made Stills an immensely important figure during these years. Ultimately Stephen was unable to match his opening pair of albums. While *Stills* was an admirable effort, the subsequent live album and *Illegal Stills* were patchy. His nadir came in 1978 when, following the break up of his marriage to French chanteuse Veronique Sanson he produced *Thoroughfare Gap*, a collection riddled with uninspired songs of self pity. Only the title track was worthy of his name. No official solo release came until 1984, when Ahmet Ertegun reluctantly allowed Stills to put out *Right By You*. While the slick production did not appeal to all Stills aficionados, it proved to be his most cohesive work since *Stephen Stills 2*, although appealing more to the AOR market. The moderate hit 'Can't Let Go' featured both Stills and Michael Finnigan, exercising their fine voices to great effect. Since then the brilliant but erratic Stills has continued his stop-go career with Crosby, Nash, and occasionally Young. Stills released a solo acoustic self-financed work in 1991. *Stills Alone* was a return to his folk and blues roots and featured hoarse-voiced versions of the Beatles 'In My Life' and Bob Dylan's 'Ballad Of Hollis Brown'. As a guitarist, his work in 1992 with a rejuvenated Crosby, Stills And Nash was quite breathtaking, demonstrating that those early accolades were not misjudged. It is a great pity that his songwriting which was so prolific in the early 70s has seemingly deserted him.

●ALBUMS: with Al Kooper, Mike Bloomfield *Super Session* (Columbia 1968)★★★, *Stephen Stills* (Atlantic 1970)★★★★★, *Stephen Stills 2* (Atlantic 1971)★★★★, *Stills* (Columbia 1975)★★★★, *Stephen Stills Live* (Atlantic 1975)★★★, *Illegal Stills* (Columbia 1976)★★, *Thoroughfare Gap* (Columbia 1978)★, *Right By You* (Atlantic 1984)★★★, *Stills Alone.* (1991)★★★.

●COMPILATIONS: *Still Stills* (Atlantic 1976)★★★.

STILLS-YOUNG BAND

Former cohorts in both Buffalo Springfield and Crosby, Stills, Nash And Young, Stephen Stills (guitar/vocals) and Neil Young (guitar/vocals) began this brief association in 1975 when the latter made several impromptu appearances during one of the former's promotional tours. An album followed on which the duo was joined by Stills' regular band - Jerry Aeillo (keyboards), George Perry (bass), Joe Vitale (drums/flute) and Joe Lala (percussion) - and although initial sessions also featured David Crosby and Graham Nash, their contributions were latterly wiped, causing friction between the four former colleagues. A proposed reunion was scuppered and Crosby And Nash returned to their duet recordings. *Long May You Run* did contain several worthwhile songs, including the title track and 'Black Coral', but it was generally viewed as a disappointment. A promotional tour ended in disarray when Young abandoned the group after a handful of dates, leaving the enigmatic note: 'Dear Stephen, funny how some things that start spontaneously end that way. Eat a peach, Neil'.
●ALBUMS: *Long May You Run* (Reprise 1976)★★★.

STONE THE CROWS

Singer Maggie Bell and guitarist Leslie Harvey (younger brother of Alex Harvey), served their musical apprenticeships in Glasgow's Palais dancebands. In 1967 they toured American bases in Germany with a group which also included Bill and Bobby Patrick. The following year Bell and Harvey formed Power, house band at the Burns Howff bar, which included Jimmy Dewar (bass) and John McGuinness (organ). Harvey subsequently toured USA, augmenting another Glasgow-based group, Cartoone. This newly formed quartet was managed by Peter Grant, whom the guitarist then brought to Scotland to view Power. Grant signed the group, who were renamed Stone The Crows on the addition of former John Mayall drummer, Colin Allen. The quintet's early blues-based albums were notable for both Bell and Dewar's expressive vocals and Harvey's textured, economic guitar work. However, an inability to match their live popularity with record sales led to disaffection and both McGuinness and Dewar left on completing *Ode To John Law*. Steve Thompson (bass) and Ronnie Leahy (keyboards) joined the band for *Teenage Licks*, their most successful album to date and Bell was awarded the first of several top vocalist awards. On 3 May 1972, Harvey died after being electrocuted onstage at the Swanage Top Rank Ballroom. Although the group completed a fourth album with Jimmy McCulloch from Thunderclap Newman, they lacked the heart to continue and broke up the following year.
●ALBUMS: *Stone The Crows* (Polydor 1970)★★★, *Ode To John Law* (Polydor 1970)★★★, *Teenage Licks* (Polydor 1971)★★★, *'Ontinuous Performance* (1972)★★.
●COMPILATIONS: *Flashback - Stone The Crows* (1976)★★★.

STOOGES

Purveyors, with the MC5, of classic, high-energy American rock, the Stooges' influence on successive generations is considerable. They were led by the enigmatic James Jewel Osterberg (aka Iggy Stooge and Iggy Pop, b. 21 April 1947, Ann Arbor, Michigan, USA) who assumed his unusual sobriquet in deference to the Iguanas, a high school band in which he drummed. Iggy formed the Psychedelic Stooges with guitarist Ron Asheton. Scott Asheton (drums) and Dave Alexander (bass) completed the line-up which quickly became a fixture of Detroit's thriving underground circuit. By September 1967, the group had dropped its adjectival prefix and had achieved a notoriety through the onstage behaviour of its uninhibited frontman. The Stooges' first album was produced by John Cale although the group's initial choice was veteran soul svengali, Jerry Ragovoy. This exciting debut matched its malevolent, garage band sneer with the air of nihilism prevalent in the immediate post-summer of love era. Iggy's exaggerated, Mick Jagger-influenced swagger swept over the group's three-chord maelstrom to create an enthralling and compulsive sound. The band were augmented by saxophonist Steven Mackay for *Funhouse*. This exceptional release documented a contemporary live set, opening with the forthright 'Down On The Street' and closing with the anarchic, almost free-form, 'LA Blues'. This uncompromising collection proved uncommercial and the Stooges were then dropped by their record label. A second guitarist, Bill Cheatham joined in August 1970, while over the next few months two bassists, Zeke Zettner and Jimmy Recca, passed through the ranks as replacements for Dave Alexander. Cheatham was then ousted in favour of James Williamson, who made a significant contribution to the ensuing Stooges period. Long-time Iggy fan, David Bowie, brought the group to the Mainman management stable and the singer was also responsible for mixing *Raw Power*. Although it lacked the purpose of its predecessors, the set became the Stooges' most successful release and contained two of their best-known performances, 'Gimme Danger' and 'Search And Destroy'. However, the quartet - Iggy, Williamson and the Asheton brothers - were dropped from Mainman for alleged drug dependence. In 1973, Scott Thurston (keyboards) was added to the line-up, but their impetus was waning. The Stooges made their final live appearance on 9 February, 1974 at Detroit's Michigan Palace. This tawdry performance ended with a battle between the group and a local biker gang, the results of which were captured on *Metallic KO*. Within days a drained Iggy Pop announced the formal end of the Stooges. *Rubber Legs* and *Open Up And Bleed* are both collections of rough mixes and live recordings, for collectors and serious fans only.
●ALBUMS: *The Stooges* (Elektra 1969)★★★★, *Funhouse* (Elektra 1970)★★★★, as Iggy And The Stooges *Raw*

Power (Columbia 1973)★★★★, *Metallic KO* (Skydog 1976)★★, *Rubber Legs* rare recordings from 1973/4 (Fan Club 1988)★★, *Open Up And Bleed* (Bomp 1996)★★.
●COMPILATIONS: as Iggy Pop And James Williamson *Kill City* (Bomp 1977)★★, *No Fun* (Elektra 1980)★★, as Iggy And The Stooges *I'm Sick Of You* (Line 1981)★★, *I Gotta Right* (Invasion 1983)★★.

STRANGLERS

One of the longest-surviving groups from the British new wave explosion of the late 70s, the Stranglers first rehearsed in Guildford as early as 1974. Two years later, the full line-up emerged comprising: Hugh Cornwell (b. 28 August 1949, London, England; vocals/guitar), Jean Jacques Burnel (b. 21 February 1952, London, England; vocals/bass), Jet Black (b. Brian Duffy, 26 August 1943; drums) and Dave Greenfield (keyboards). Following a tour supporting Patti Smith during 1976 and some favourable press reports (the first to bring comparisons to the Doors), the group were signed by United Artists Records. Courting controversy from the outset, they caused a sensation and saw their date at London's Roundhouse cut short when Cornwell wore an allegedly obscene T-shirt. In February 1977 the Stranglers' debut single, '(Get A) Grip (On Yourself)', reached number 44 in the UK charts and inexplicably dropped out after only one week. According to the chart compilers, the sales were inadvertently assigned to another record, but it was too late to rectify the damage. 'Grip' saw the group at their early best. Bathed in swirling organ and backed by a throbbing beat, the single displayed Cornwell's gruff vocal to strong effect. The b-side, 'London Lady', was taken at a faster pace and revealed the first signs of an overbearing misogynism that would later see them fall foul of critics. Initially bracketed with punk, the Stranglers owed as much to their pub rock background and it soon emerged that they were older and more knowing than their teenage contemporaries. Nevertheless, their first album, *Rattus Norvegicus*, was greeted with enthusiasm by the rock press and sold extremely well. The blasphemous lyrics of 'Hanging Around' and the gruesome imagery of 'Down In The Sewer' seemingly proved less acceptable than the women-baiting subject matter of their next single, 'Peaches'. Banned by BBC Radio, the song still charted thanks to airplay offering up the b-side, 'Go Buddy Go'. Rather than bowing to the feminist criticisms levelled against them, the group subsequently compounded the felony by introducing strippers at a Battersea Park, London concert (though male strippers were also present). Journalists were treated in an even more cavalier fashion and the group were renowned for their violent antics against those who opposed them (karate black belt Burnel attacked writer Jon Savage after one unhelpful review). Having initially alienated the press, their work was almost universally derided thereafter. The public kept faith, however, and ensured that the Stranglers enjoyed a formi-

dable run of hits over the next few years. The lugubrious protest, 'Something Better Change', and faster paced 'No More Heroes' both reached the UK Top 10, while 'Five Minutes' and 'Nice 'N Sleazy' each entered the Top 20. In the background there were the usual slices of bad publicity. Burnel and Black were arrested for being drunk and disorderly before charges were dropped. Cornwell was not so fortunate and found himself sentenced to three months' imprisonment on drugs charges in January 1980. Within two months of his release, the group found themselves under arrest in Nice, France, after allegedly inciting a riot. Later that year they received a heavy fine in a French court. The group's uncompromising outlaw image tended to distract from subtle changes that had been occurring in their musical repertoire. Their brave cover of the Burt Bacharach/Hal David standard, 'Walk On By', reached number 21 in spite of the fact that 100,000 copies of the record had already been issued *gratis* with *Black And White*. Equally effective and contrasting was the melodic 'Duchess', which displayed the Stranglers' plaintive edge to surprising effect. Their albums also revealed a new diversity from *The Raven* (with its elaborate 3-D cover) to the genuinely strange *The Meninblack*. The latter was primarily Cornwell's concept, and introduced the idea of extra-terrestrial hitmen who silence individuals that have witnessed UFO landings - an ever vengeful music press delighted in pulling it to pieces. For their next album, *La Folie*, the group were accompanied on tour by a ballet company. The album spawned the group's biggest hit, the evocative 'Golden Brown', with its startling, classical-influenced harpsichord arrangement. It reached the UK number 2 spot, resting just behind Buck Fizz's 'Land Of Make Believe'. Even at their most melodic the Stranglers ran into a minor furore when it was alleged that the song was concerned with heroin consumption. Fortunately, the theme was so lyrically obscure that the accusations failed to prove convincing enough to provoke a ban. Another single from *La Folie* was the sentimental 'Strange Little Girl', which also climbed into the UK Top 10. The melodic influence continued on 'European Female', but in spite of the hits, the group's subsequent albums failed to attract serious critical attention. As unremittingly ambitious as ever, the Stranglers' 1986 album, *Dreamtime*, was inspired by Aboriginal culture and complemented their outsider image. Just as it seemed that their appeal was becoming merely cultish, they returned to their old style with a cover of the Kinks' 'All Day And All Of The Night'. It was enough to provide them with their first Top 10 hit for five years. Increasingly unpredictable, the group re-recorded their first single, 'Grip', which ironically fared better than the original, reaching the Top 40 in January 1989. Despite their small handful of collaborative ventures, it seemed unlikely that either Cornwell or Burnel would ever consider abandoning the group for solo careers. Perpetual derision by the press finally took its cumulative toll on the lead singer, however, and in the summer of 1990 Cornwell announced that he was quitting the group. The lacklustre *10* was written specifically for the American market, but failed to sell, in light of which Cornwell called time on his involvement. Burnel, Black and Greenfield were left with the unenviable problem of finding an experienced replacement and deciding whether to retain the name Stranglers. The band recruited vocalist Paul Roberts (b. England, 31 December 1959) and guitarist John Ellis (formerly of the Vibrators and a veteran of Burnel's Purple Helmets side project). *Stranglers In The Night* was arguably a return to form, but still failed to recapture old glories. A second set with the band's new line-up then emerged in 1995, with strong performances on tracks such as 'Golden Boy', but with Cornwell's absence felt most acutely in the unadventurous songwriting. *Written In Red* was a stronger effort in 1997.

●ALBUMS: *Rattus Norvegicus* (United Artists 1977)★★★★, *No More Heroes* (United Artists 1977)★★★★, *Black And White* (United Artists 1978)★★★, *Live (X Cert)* (United Artists 1979)★★★, *The Raven* (United Artists 1979)★★★, *The Meninblack* (Liberty 1981)★★★, *La Folie* (Liberty 1981)★★★★, *Feline* (Epic 1983)★★★, *Aural Sculpture* (Epic 1984)★★★, *Dreamtime* (Epic 1986)★★, *All Live And All Of The Night* (Epic 1988)★★, *10* (Epic 1990)★★, *Stranglers In The Night* (China 1992)★★, *About Time* (When?/Castle 1995)★★, *Written In Red* (When?/Castle 1997)★★.

●COMPILATIONS: *The Collection* (Liberty 1982)★★★, *Off The Beaten Track* (Liberty 1986)★★, *The Singles* (EMI 1989)★★★★, *Greatest Hits: 1977-1990* (Epic 1990)★★★★, *The Old Testament (The UA Recordings 1977- 1982)* (EMI 1992)★★★, *The Early Years 74/75/76 Rare, Live And Unreleased* (Newspeak 1992)★, *Saturday Night Sunday Morning* (Castle 1993)★★, *Strangled - From Birth And Beyond* (SIS 1994)★★, *The Stranglers And Friends: Live In Concert* rec. 1980 (Receiver 1995)★★, *The Hit Men* (EMI 1997)★★★★.

●VIDEOS: *Saturday Night Sunday Morning* (PNE 1996).

●FURTHER READING: *Inside Information*, Hugh Cornwell. *Much Ado About Nothing*, Jet Black.

STRAWBS

This versatile unit was formed in 1967 by guitarists Dave Cousins (b. 7 January 1945; guitar/banjo/piano/recorder) and Tony Hooper. They initially worked as a bluegrass group, the Strawberry Hill Boys, with mandolinist Arthur Phillips, but later pursued a folk-based direction. Truncating their name to the Strawbs, the founding duo added Ron Chesterman on bass prior to the arrival of singer Sandy Denny whose short spell in the line-up is documented in *All Our Own Work*. This endearing collection, released in the wake of Denny's success with Fairport Convention, features an early version of her exemplary composition, 'Who Knows Where The Time Goes'. Cousins, Hooper and Chesterman released their official debut, *Strawbs*, in 1968. This excellent selection featured several of the group's finest compositions, including 'Oh How She Changed' and 'The Battle', and was acclaimed by both folk and rock audiences. *Dragonfly*, was less well-received, prompting a realignment in the band. The original duo was joined by former Velvet Opera members John Ford (b. 1 July 1948, Fulham, London, England; bass/acoustic guitar) and Richard Hudson (b. Richard William Stafford Hudson, 9 May 1948, London, England; drums/guitar/sitar), plus Rick Wakeman (keyboards), a graduate of the Royal Academy of Music. The Strawbs embraced electric rock with *Just A Collection Of Antiques And Curios*, although critical analysis concentrated on Wakeman's contribution.

Such plaudits continued on *From The Witchwood* but the pianist grew frustrated within the group's framework and left to join Yes. He was replaced by Blue Weaver (b. 11 March 1947, Cardiff, South Glamorgan, Wales; guitar/autoharp/piano) from Amen Corner. Despite the commercial success generated by the outstanding *Grave New World* (1972), tension within the Strawbs mounted, and in 1972, Hooper was replaced by Dave Lambert (b. 8 March 1949, Hounslow, Middlesex, England). Relations between Cousins and Hudson and Ford were also deteriorating and although 'Lay Down' gave the band its first UK Top 20 single, the jocular 'Part Of The Union', written by the bassist and drummer, became the Strawbs' most successful release. The group split following an acrimonious US tour. The departing rhythm section formed their own unit, Hudson-Ford while Cousins and Lambert brought in pianist John Hawken (ex-Nashville Teens; Renaissance), Chas Cronk (bass) and Rod Coombes (drums, ex-Steelers Wheel). However, a series of poorly received albums suggested the Strawbs had lost both direction and inspiration. Cousins nonetheless presided over several fluctuating line-ups and continued to record into the 80s. In 1987, the group reunited, including the trio of Cousins, Hooper And Hudson, for the *Don't Say Goodbye*. album.

●ALBUMS: *Strawbs* (A&M 1969)★★★★, *Dragonfly* (A&M 1970)★★★, *Just A Collection Of Antiques And Curios* (A&M 1970)★★★, *From The Witchwood* (A&M 1971)★★★, *Grave New World* (A&M 1972)★★★★, as Sandy Denny And The Strawbs *All Our Own Work* (A&M 1973)★★★, *Bursting At The Seams* (A&M 1973)★★★, *Hero And Heroine* (A&M 1974)★★★, *Ghosts* (A&M 1975)★★★, *Nomadness* (A&M 1976)★★★, *Deep Cuts* (Oyster 1976)★★★, *Burning For You* (Oyster 1977)★★★, *Dead Lines* (Arista 1978)★★★, *Don't Say Goodbye* (Toots 1987)★★★.

●COMPILATIONS: *Strawbs By Choice* (A&M 1974)★★★, *Best Of The Strawbs* (A&M 1978)★★★, *A Choice Collection* (1992)★★★, *Uncanned Preserves* (Road Goes On Forever 1992)★★★, *Greatest Hits Live* (Road Goes On Forever 1994)★★, *Heartbreak Hill* (Road Goes On Forever 1995)★★★, *In Concert* (Windsong 1995)★★★, *Halcyon Days: The Very Best Of ...* (A&M 1997)★★★.

STREETWALKERS

After Family's farewell tour in autumn 1973, vocalist Roger Chapman and guitarist Charles Whitney, collaborated on *Streetwalkers* with help from guitarist Bob Tench (from the Jeff Beck Group) and members of King Crimson. These were among the *ad hoc* UK aggregation that backed Chapman and Whitney for a brief promotional tour - and Tench became the nucleus of a more fixed set-up when the pair recommenced operations as 'Streetwalkers'. With Jon Plotel (bass, ex-Casablanca) and Nicko McBain (drums), the group recorded *Downtown Flyers* which, like its predecessor, was far less self-consciously 'weird' than Family's output had been and, with Chapman's vibrato moderated, drew much inspiration from R&B and soul stylings. A popular attraction on the college circuit - especially in Germany - the quartet's *Red Card* reached the UK Top 20 but this triumph was dampened by internal difficulties. In July 1976, Plotel and Nicko were replaced by Michael Feat and David Dowie. Augmented by Brian Johnson on keyboards, Streetwalkers released the undistinguished *Vicious But Fair* before bowing out with a concert album in late 1977. However, the group survived in spirit via Chapman's subsequent stage performances with a new band, his three solo albums and his characteristically agonized singing in a television commercial for Brutus jeans.

●ALBUMS: *Streetwalkers* (Vertigo 1974)★★★, *Downtown Flyers* (Vertigo 1975)★★★, *Red Card* (Vertigo 1976)★★★, *Vicious But Fair* (Vertigo 1977)★★, *Live* (Vertigo 1977)★★★.
●COMPILATIONS: *Best Of The Streetwalkers* (Vertigo 1991)★★★.

STRING-DRIVEN THING

With animated, shock-headed violinist Graham Smith their visual selling-point, Pauline Adams (vocals), her husband Chris (guitar/vocals) and Colin Wilson (guitar/bass) trod an idiosyncratically British rock path in the early 70s. Like acts of similar stamp, they were later augmented by a drummer, when Billy Fairley toughened up the sound on their second album featuring new recruits Clare Sealey (cello) and Bill Hatje (who took over Wilson's bass duties). The band's performances on children's television proved surprisingly popular, and a wider fame was predicted. The departure of the Adamses and Hatje in 1974 was seen as unfortunate but by no means disastrous as the group were able to continue in recognizable form with, respectively, Kimberley Beacon, Graham White and James Exell for *Please Mind Your Head*, on which Henry McDonald (keyboards) and jazz saxophonist Alan Skidmore (then one of Georgie Fame's Blue Flames) were heard too. Even more iconoclastic was the appearance of *Oh Boy* regular Cuddley Dudley on mouth organ for their final album before Smith's defection to Van Der Graaf Generator in 1976 and String-Driven Thing's correlated break-up.

●ALBUMS: *String-Driven Thing* (Charisma 1972)★★★, *Machine That Cried* (Charisma 1973)★★★, *Please Mind Your Head* (Charisma 1974)★★★, *Keep Yer 'And On It* (Charisma 1975)★★★.

STYLISTICS

The Stylistics were formed in 1968 from the fragments of two Philadelphia groups, the Monarchs and the Percussions, by Russell Thompkins Jnr (b. 21 March 1951, Philadelphia, Pennsylvania, USA), Airrion Love (b. 8 August 1949, Philadelphia, Pennsylvania, USA), James Smith (b. 16 June 1950, New York, USA), Herbie Murrell (b. 27 April 1949, Lane, South Carolina, USA) and James Dunn (b. 4 February 1950, Philadelphia, Pennsylvania, USA). The quintet's debut single, 'You're A Big Girl Now' was initially issued on a local independent, but became a national hit following its acquisition by the Avco label. The Stylistics were then signed to this outlet directly and teamed with producer/composer Thom Bell. This skillful musician had already worked successfully with the Delfonics and his sculpted, sweet soul arrangements proved ideal for his new charges. In partnership with lyricist Linda Creed, Bell fashioned a series of immaculate singles, including 'You Are Everything' (1971), 'Betcha By Golly Wow' and 'I'm Stone In Love With You' (both 1972), where Simpkins' aching voice soared against the group's sumptuous harmonies and a cool, yet inventive accompaniment. The style reached its apogee in 1974 with 'You Make Me Feel Brand New', a number 2 single in both the US and UK. This release marked the end of Bell's collaboration with the group who were now pushed towards the easy listening market. With arranger Van McCoy turning sweet into saccharine, the material grew increasingly bland, while Thompkins' falsetto, once heartfelt, now seemed contrived. Although their American fortune waned, the Stylistics continued to enjoy success in Britain with 'Sing Baby Sing', 'Can't Give You Anything (But My Love)' (both 1975) and '16 Bars' (1976), while a compilation album that same year, *The Best Of The Stylistics*, became one of the UK's best-selling albums. Despite this remarkable popularity, purists labelled the group a parody of its former self. Ill-health forced Dunn to retire in 1978, whereupon the remaining quartet left Avco for a brief spell with Mercury. Two years later they were signed to the TSOP/Philadelphia International stable, which resulted in some crafted recordings reminiscent of their heyday, but problems within the company undermined the group's progress. Subsequent singles for Streetwise took the Stylistics into the lower reaches of the R&B chart, but their halcyon days now seem to be over even though they released new material in the mid-90s.

●ALBUMS: *The Stylistics* (Avco 1971)★★★, *Round 2: The Stylistics* (Avco 1972)★★★, *Rockin' Roll Baby* (Avco 1973)★★★★, *Let's Put It All Together* (Avco 1974)★★★★, *Heavy* UK title:*From The Mountain* (Avco 1974)★★★, *Thank You Baby* (Avco 1975)★★★, *You Are Beautiful*

(Avco 1975)★★★, *Fabulous* (H&L 1976)★★★, *Once Upon A Juke Box* (H&L 1976)★★★, *Sun And Soul* (H&L 1977)★★★, *Wonder Woman* (H&L 1978)★★★, *In Fashion* (H&L 1978)★★★, *Black Satin* (H&L 1979)★★★, *Love Spell* (1979)★★★, *Live In Japan* (1979)★★, *The Lion Sleeps Tonight* (1979)★★★, *Hurry Up This Way Again* (TSOP/Phil. Int. 1980)★★★, *Closer Than Close* (TSOP/Phil. Int. 1981)★★★, *1982* (TSOP/Phil. Int. 1982)★★★, *Some Things Never Change* (Virgin 1985)★★, *Love Talks* (1993)★★, *Love Is Back In Style* (Marathon 1996)★★.

●COMPILATIONS: *The Best Of The Stylistics* (Avco 1975)★★★★, *Spotlight On The Stylistics* (1977)★★★, *Very Best Of The Stylistics* (H&L 1983)★★★★.

STYX

This Chicago-based quintet are widely believed to be responsible for the development of the term pomp-rock (pompous, overblown arrangements, with perfect-pitch harmonies and a very full production). Styx evolved from the bands Tradewinds and T.W.4, but renamed themselves after the fabled river of Greek mythology, when they signed to Wooden Nickel, a subsidiary of RCA Records, in 1972. The line-up comprised Dennis De Young (vocals/keyboards), James Young (guitar/vocals), Chuck Panozzo (bass), John Panozzo (b. 20 September 1947, USA, d. 16 July 1996, Chicago, Illinois, USA; drums) and John Curulewski (guitar). Combining symphonic and progressive influences they released a series of varied and highly melodic albums during the early 70s. Success was slow to catch up with them; *Styx II*, originally released in 1973, spawned the Top Ten *Billboard* hit 'Lady' in 1975. The album then made similar progress, eventually peaking at number 20. After signing to A&M Records in 1975, John Curulewski departed with the release of *Equinox*, to be replaced by Tommy Shaw. This was a real turning point in the band's career as Shaw took over lead vocals and contributed significantly on the writing side. From here on Styx albums had an added degree of accessibility and moved towards a more commercial approach. *The Grand Illusion*, released in 1977, was Shaw's first major success, peaking at number 6 during its nine-month stay on the *Billboard* album chart. It also featured the number 8-peaking single, 'Sail Away'. *Pieces Of Eight* and *Cornerstone* consolidated their success, with the latter containing 'Babe', the band's first number 1 single in the USA. *Paradise Theater* was the Styx's *tour de force*, a complex, laser-etched concept album, complete with elaborate and expensive packaging. It generated two further US Top 10 hits in 'The Best Of Times' and 'Too Much Time On My Hands'. The album became their most successful ever, and also stayed at number 1 for three weeks on the album chart. *Kilroy Was Here* followed, yet another concept album, which brought them close to repetition. A watered down pop-rock album with a big-budget production, its success came on the back of their previous album rather than on its own

merits. *Caught In The Act* was an uninspired live offering. They disbanded shortly after its release. Styx re-formed in 1990 with the original line-up, except for pop-rock funkster Glenn Burtnick, who replaced Tommy Shaw (who had joined Damn Yankees). *Edge Of The Century* indicated that the band still had something to offer, with a diverse and classy selection of contemporary AOR. As one of the tracks on the album stated, the group were self-evidently 'Not Dead Yet'.

●ALBUMS: *Styx* (Wooden Nickel 1972)★★, *Styx II* (Wooden Nickel 1973)★★★, *The Serpent Is Rising* (Wooden Nickel 1973)★★★, *Man Of Miracles* (Wooden Nickel 1974)★★★, *Equinox* (A&M 1975)★★★, *Crystal Ball* (A&M 1976)★★★, *The Grand Illusion* (A&M 1977)★★★, *Pieces Of Eight* (A&M 1978)★★★, *Cornerstone* (A&M 1979)★★★, *Paradise Theater* (A&M 1980)★★★★, *Kilroy Was Here* (A&M 1983)★★★, *Caught In The Act/Live* (A&M 1984)★★, *Edge Of The Century* (A&M 1990)★★★.

●COMPILATIONS: *The Best Of Styx* (A&M 1979)★★★, *Classics Volume 15* (A&M 1987)★★★.

●VIDEOS: *Caught In The Act* (1984).

SUMMER, DONNA

b. Ladonna Gaines, 31 December 1948, Boston, Massachusetts, USA, Summer's 'Love To Love You Baby' made her the best-known of all 70s disco divas. Having sung with rock bands in Boston, Summer moved to Europe in 1968 and appeared in German versions of *Hair* and *Porgy And Bess* and married Austrian actor Helmut Sommer, from whom she took her stage name. Summer's first records were 'Hostage' and 'Lady Of The Night' for Giorgio Moroder's Oasis label in Munich. They were local hits but it was 'Love To Love You Baby' (1975) which made her an international star. The track featured Summer's erotic sighs and moans above Moroder's hypnotic disco beats and it sold a million copies in the US on Neil Bogart's Casablanca label. In 1977, a similar formula took 'I Feel Love' to the top of the UK chart and 'Down Deep Inside', Summer's theme song for the film *The Deep* was a big international success. Her own film debut came the next year in *Thank God It's Friday* in which she sang another million-seller 'Last Dance'. This was the peak period of Summer's career as she scored three more US number 1s in 1978-79 with a revival of Jim Webb's 'MacArthur Park', 'Hot Stuff', 'Bad Girls' and 'No More Tears (Enough Is Enough)' a duet with Barbra Streisand. The demise of disco coincided with a legal dispute between Summer and Bogart and in 1980 she signed to David Geffen's new company.

Her work now took on a more pronounced soul and gospel flavour - she had become a born-again Christian. Some of her major US hits during the early 80s were 'On The Radio', 'The Wanderer', 'She Works Hard For The Money' and 'Love Is In Control (Finger On The Trigger)' in 1982, produced by Quincy Jones. After a three-year absence from music, Summer returned in

1987 with a US and European tour and another hit with the catchy 'Dinner With Gershwin'. Other major US and UK hits include 'This Time I Know It's For Real' and 'I Don't Wanna Get Hurt'. Her best-selling 1989 album for Warner Brothers Records was written and produced by Stock Aitken And Waterman while Clivilles And Cole worked on *Love Is Gonna Change*. The 90s have proved only moderately successful for her.

●ALBUMS: *Love To Love You Baby* (Oasis 1975)★★★, *A Love Trilogy* (Oasis 1976)★★, *Four Seasons Of Love* (Casablanca 1976)★★, *I Remember Yesterday* (Casablanca 1977)★★★, *Once Upon A Time* (Casblanca 1977)★★★, *Live And More* (Casablanca 1978)★★, *Bad Girls* (Casablanca 1979)★★★★, *The Wanderer* (Geffen 1980)★★★★, *Donna Summer* (Geffen 1982)★★★, *She Works Hard For The Money* (Mercury 1983)★★★★, *Cats Without Claws* (Geffen 1984)★★, *All Systems Go* (Geffen 1987)★★, *Another Place And Time* (Warners 1989)★★, *Love Is Gonna Change* (Warners 1990)★★, *Mistaken Identity* (Warners 1991)★★, *This Time I Know It's For Real* (1993)★★.

●COMPILATIONS: *On The Radio - Greatest Hits, Volumes 1 And 2* (Casablanca 1979)★★★★, *Walk Away - Collector's Edition (The Best Of 1977-1980)* (Casablanca 1980)★★★, *The Best Of Donna Summer* (East West 1990)★★★★.

●FURTHER READING: *Donna Summer: An Unauthorized Biography*, James Haskins.

SUPERFLY

This 1972 release was one of several films starring African-American actors in a genre dubbed 'blaxpolitation'. The first, and best, of these was *Shaft*, which featured a taut score by Isaac Hayes. *Superfly* featured the less-feted Jeff Alexander as its musical director, but he proved astute in signing former Impressions leader Curtis Mayfield to contribute several excellent compositions. Two powerful songs, 'Freddy's Dead' and the title track itself, reached the US Top 10, providing a boost to their creator's solo career. Their success helped promote *Superfly* and gave it a prominence the one-dimensional plot did not deserve. Ron O'Neal starred as a drugs pusher looking for the one big deal that would enable him to retire, but the ambivalent script suggested that violent New York cocaine dealers possess the air of noble outlaws. Indeed, several black self-help groups picketed several cinemas showing the film. Mayfield himself later expressed disquiet about the theme, preferring the cautionary 'Freddy's Dead' than other, more celebratory, inclusions. The singer later scored *Claudine* and *Short Eyes*, neither of which enjoyed the commercial approbation of *Superfly*. The film itself inspired an even more lacklustre follow-up, *Superfly TNT*.

SUPERTRAMP

Many aspiring musicians would have envied the opportunity that was given to Supertramp in 1969. They were financed by the Dutch millionaire Stanley August Miesegaes, which enabled Richard Davies (b. 22 July 1944, Swindon, Wiltshire, England; vocals/keyboards) to recruit, through the *Melody Maker*, the band of his choice. He enlisted Roger Hodgson (b. 21 March 1950, Portsmouth, Hampshire, England; guitar), Dave Winthrop (b. 27 November 1948, New Jersey, USA; saxophone), Richard Palmer (guitar) and Bob Miller (drums). The debut *Supertramp* was an unspectacular affair of lengthy self-indulgent solos. The follow-up, *Indelibly Stamped* was similarly unsuccessful and meandering; the controversial cover created most interest, depicting a busty, naked tattooed female. The band were in dire straits when their fairy godfather departed, along with Winthrop and Palmer. They recruited ex-Alan Bown band members, John Helliwell (b. 15 February 1945, Todmorden, Yorkshire, England) and Dougie Thompson (b. 24 March 1951, Glasgow, Scotland) and from Bees Make Honey, Bob Benberg. They had a remarkable change in fortune as *Crime Of The Century* became one of the top-selling albums of 1974. The band had refined their keyboard-dominated sound and produced an album that was well reviewed. Their debut hit 'Dreamer' was taken from the album, while 'Bloody Well Right' was a Top 40 hit in the USA, going on to become one of their classic live numbers. The subsequent *Crisis? What Crisis?* and *Even In The Quietest Moments* were lesser works, being erratic in content. The choral 'Give A Little Bit', with its infectious acoustic guitar introduction was a minor transatlantic hit in 1977. Supertramp were elevated to rock's first division with the faultless *Breakfast In America*. Four of the tracks became hits, 'The Logical Song', 'Take The Long Way Home', 'Goodbye Stranger' and the title track. The album stayed on top of the US charts for six weeks and became their biggest seller, with over 18 million copies to date. The obligatory live album came in 1980 and was followed by the R&B-influenced *Famous Last Words*. Hodgson left shortly afterwards, unhappy with the bluesier direction the band were taking and made two respectable solo albums, *In The Eye Of A Storm* and *Hai Hai*. Supertramp continued with occasional tours and infrequent albums. Their recent releases, however, have only found minor success.

●ALBUMS: *Supertramp* (A&M 1970)★★, *Indelibly Stamped* (A&M 1971)★★, *Crime Of The Century* (A&M 1974)★★★, *Crisis? What Crisis?* (A&M 1975)★★★, *Even In The Quietest Moments* (A&M 1977)★★★, *Breakfast In America* (A&M 1979)★★★★, *Paris* (A&M 1980)★★★, *Famous Last Words* (A&M 1982)★★★, *Brother Where You Bound* (A&M 1985)★★, *Free As A Bird* (A&M 1987)★★, *Supertramp Live 88* (A&M 1988)★★, *Some Things Never Change* (Chrysalis 1997)★★★.

●COMPILATIONS: *The Autobiography Of Supertramp* (A&M 1986)★★★, *The Very Best Of* (A&M 1992)★★★.

●FURTHER READING: *The Supertramp Book*, Martin Melhuish.

SURMAN, JOHN

b. John Douglas Surman, 30 August 1944, Tavistock, Devon, England. Surman, a remarkable player on soprano and baritone saxophones, bass clarinet, bamboo flutes and sometimes tenor saxophone and synthesizers. He was a member of the Jazz Workshop at Plymouth Arts Centre with Mike Westbrook whilst still at school, and came to London with Westbrook's band in 1962. He studied at London College of Music (1962-65) and London University Institute of Education (1966). By the time he ceased to be a regular member of Westbrook's band in 1968 he was also working in Ronnie Scott's nine-piece outfit (the Band) with Humphrey Lyttelton and had twice been voted the world's best baritone saxophone player by *Melody Maker* readers as well as top instrumentalist at the 1968 Montreux International Jazz Festival. Since then various of his albums have collected awards from all over the world. From 1968-69 he led a group, varying from a quartet to an octet, centring around Mike Osborne, Harry Miller and Alan Jackson. During the 60s and 70s he also played with Alexis Korner's New Church, Mike Gibbs, Graham Collier, Chris McGregor, Dave Holland, John McLaughlin (on the guitarist's acclaimed *Extrapolation*), John Warren and Harry Beckett. Owing to lack of work in the UK, he emigrated to Europe where he formed the Trio with Barre Phillips and Stu Martin. Surman next worked with Terje Rypdal (*Morning Glory*), before the Trio briefly re-formed, augmented by Albert Mangelsdorff to become MUMPS. At this time he first met Jack DeJohnette with whom he was to work regularly in the 80s and 90s. In 1973 he formed another highly impressive and influential trio, S.O.S., with Osborne and Alan Skidmore. He began experimenting with electronics during this period, a facet of his work explored in depth on his albums of the late 70s and 80s. He formed duos with Stan Tracey and Karin Krog, in 1978 (the latter becoming a regular musical associate), and from 1979-82 worked with Miroslav Vitous. Surman also composes for all sizes of jazz groups, as well as writing pieces for choirs and for dance companies, notably the Carolyn Carlson Dance Theatre at the Paris Opera, with whom he worked from 1974-79. In 1981, Surman's pivotal album *The Amazing Adventures Of Simon Simon* was released. This was the springboard for a number of beautiful recordings that started with *Upon Reflection* and redefined the word sparseness. Working solo, save for the contribution of Jack DeJohnette (drums, congas, electric piano) *Simon Simon* arguably remains Surman's finest work. That year he also formed the Brass Project, working with the noted arranger John Warren and during the 80s he was a member of Gil Evans' British band and later of his New York band. He also worked with Paul Bley and Bill Frisell and, in 1986, toured with Elvin Jones, Holland and Mangelsdorff. In 1990 the conceptual *Road To St Ives* explored themes of Simon Simon. This was another

brilliant and evocative solo excursion travelling through Cornwall from 'Polperro' to 'Bedruthan Steps'. In the early 90s he recorded some memorable albums working with John Abercrombie, Marc Johnson, Krog, Rypdal and Mangelsdorf although it is his solo work in recent years that has been particularly inspired, notably *Stranger Than Fiction* in 1994 and another conceptual project *A Biography Of The Rev. Absolom Dave*. A powerful and resourceful improviser who leaves out more than he puts in, he is without doubt one of the key figures in contemporary jazz over the past three decades.
●ALBUMS: *Release* (1968)★★★, *John Surman* (1968)★★★★, *How Many Clouds Can You See* (1969)★★★, with John McLaughlin *Extrapolation* (1969)★★★, *Marching Song* (1969)★★★, *Where Fortune Smiles* (1970)★★★, *The Trio* (1970)★★★, *Conflagration* (1971)★★★, with John Warren *Tales Of The Algonquin* (1971)★★★, *Westering Home* (1972)★★★, *Morning Glory* (1973)★★★, *S.O.S.* (1975)★★★, *Live At Woodstock Town Hall* (1975)★★★, *Live At Moers Festival* (1975)★★★, *Surman For All Saints* (Ogun 1979)★★★, *Upon Reflection* (ECM 1979)★★★, *The Amazing Adventures Of Simon Simon* (ECM 1981)★★★★, with Karin Krog *Such Winters Of Memory* (ECM 1982)★★★, with Barry Altschul *Irina* (1983)★★★, *Withholding Pattern* (ECM 1984)★★★, with Paul Bley *Fragments* (1986)★★★, with Alexis Korner *Alexis Korner And ... 1961-72* (1986)★★★, with the Trio *By Contact* rec. 1971 (1987)★★★★, *Private City* (ECM 1987)★★★, *The Paul Bley Quartet* (1988)★★★, *The Road To St. Ives* (ECM 1990)★★★★, *Adventure Playground* (ECM 1991)★★★, with John Taylor *Ambleside Days* (1992)★★★, with Warren *The Brass Project* (ECM 1992) with Albert Mangelsdorff *Room 1220* (1993)★★★, with John Abercrombie, Marc Johnson, Peter Erskine *November* (ECM 1994)★★★, *Stranger Than Fiction* (ECM 1994)★★★★, with Krog, Terje Rypdal, Vigleik Storaas *Nordic Quartet* (ECM 1995)★★★, *A Biography Of The Rev. Absolom Dave* (ECM 1995)★★★★.

SUTHERLAND BROTHERS (AND QUIVER)

Basically a duo from the outset, comprising brothers Iain Sutherland (b. 17 November 1948, Ellon, Aberdeenshire, Scotland; vocals/guitar/keyboards) and Gavin Sutherland (b. 6 October 1951, Peterhead, Aberdeenshire, Scotland; bass/guitar/vocals). The two had been signed to Island Records, releasing *The Sutherland Brothers Band*. It was during this period that they wrote and recorded the song 'Sailing', later a UK number 1 for Rod Stewart. Having completed their second album with the use of session musicians, they began seeking a permanent backing group. A meeting between their manager Wayne Bordell, and Quiver showed a mutual need for each others talents. The Sutherland Brothers needed a band, and Quiver needed new songs, so the Sutherland Brothers And Quiver were born, comprising Iain and Gavin, Tim Renwick (b. 7 August 1949, Cambridge, England; guitar/vocals/flute),

Willie Wilson (b. John Wilson, 8 July 1947, Cambridge, England; drums, vocals, percussion), Bruce Thomas (b. 14 August 1948, Middlesbrough, Cleveland, England; bass), Cal Batchelor (vocals/guitar/keyboards), and Pete Wood (b. Middlesex, England, d. 1994, New York, USA; keyboards). Within a few months they released *Lifeboat*. In the USA, the release was credited as the Sutherland Brothers And Quiver, but in the UK as the Sutherland Brothers. There were also variations in the track listing between the UK and American releases. The band recorded three tracks, 'I Don't Want To Love You But You Got Me Anyway', 'Have You Had A Vision', and 'Not Fade Away', prior to playing a support tour, of the USA, to Elton John, in 1973. After recording, Cal Batchelor announced that he was going to leave the band as he could no longer see a future for him in it. The subsequent tour of the USA went ahead without him. *Dream Kid*, produced by Muff Winwood, saw bassist Bruce Thomas leave shortly afterwards. (He later joined Elvis Costello And The Attractions.) Terry 'Tex' Comer from Ace, took over the role of bass player to play on half the recordings for *Beat Of The Street*. In fact, the song 'How Long', often thought to be a love song, was actually written about how the group had been trying to persuade Comer to join them for some time. Taking on Mick Blackburn as manager, they secured a contract with CBS, and *Reach For The Sky* was released on 7 November 1975. Produced by Ron and Howie Albert, it featured Dave Gilmour on pedal steel guitar on one track. Gilmour had produced 'We Get Along', the b-side of 'Arms Of Mary'. Wood left to become Al Stewart's keyboard player. By the time *Slipstream* was released, the line-up was Wilson, Renwick, Gavin, and Iain., although shortly afterwards Renwick left. Produced by Bruce Welch, the recording of *Down To Earth* was augmented by a number of respected session musicians, including Ray Flacke (guitar), and Brian Bennett (percussion). By the time of *When The Night Comes Down*, Wilson had left. More recently Gavin has spent time writing and editing books, as well as continuing to write songs, and playing with local musicians in Scotland. Iain has also been composing, but with only occasional performances.

●ALBUMS: *The Sutherland Brothers Band* (Island 1972)★★★. With Quiver *Lifeboat* (Island 1972)★★★, *Dream Kid* (Island 1974)★★★★, *Beat Of The Street* (Island 1974)★★★, *Reach For The Sky* (Columbia 1975)★★★, *Slipstream* (Columbia 1976)★★★, *Down To Earth* (Columbia 1977)★★★, *When The Night Comes Down* (Columbia 1978)★★.

●COMPILATIONS: *Sailing* (Island 1976)★★★.

●FURTHER READING: *The Whaling Years, Peterhead 1788-1893*, Gavin Sutherland.

SWAN, BILLY

b. Billy Lance Swan, 12 May 1942, in Cape Giradeau, Missouri, USA. Swan grew up listening to country stars like Hank Williams and Lefty Frizzell and then fell under the spell of 50s rock 'n' rollers. At the age of 16, he wrote 'Lover Please', which was recorded by a local plumber who also had an early morning television show (!), *Mirt Mirley And The Rhythm Steppers*. Elvis Presley's bass player, Bill Black, approved and recorded it with his Combo in 1960 before passing it to Clyde McPhatter. McPhatter's version went to number 7 on the US charts, but was overshadowed in the UK by the Vernons Girls, whose version made number 16. Swan, who had insurance money as a result of losing an eye in an accident, moved to Memphis, primarily to write for Bill Black's Combo. He befriended Elvis Presley's uncle, Travis Smith, who was a gate guard at Graceland. Soon, Swan was also minding the gate and attending Elvis's late night visits to cinemas and funfairs. Swan decided that he would be more likely to find work as a musician in Nashville, but the only employment he found was as a janitor at Columbia's studios. He quit while Bob Dylan was recording *Blonde On Blonde*, offering his job to Kris Kristofferson who had entered the building looking for work. Billy swanned around for some time, mainly working as a roadie for Mel Tillis, before meeting Tony Joe White and producing demos of his 'swamp rock'. Swan was invited to produce White officially and their work included *Black And White* with its million-selling single, 'Polk Salad Annie'.

By now Kristofferson had his own record contract and he invited Swan to play bass with his band. They appeared at the Isle of Wight Festival in 1970 where Kristofferson's song 'Blame It On The Stones' was taken at face value. While Kristofferson was being jeered, Swan leaned over and said, 'They love you, Kris.' Swan then joined Kinky Friedman in his band, the Texas Jewboys: he appears on his albums and Friedman recorded 'Lover Please'. Kristofferson invited him to join his band again and producer Chip Young, noticing that Swan's voice was similar to Ringo Starr's, invited him to record for Monument. The first single was a revival of Hank Williams' 'Wedding Bells'. Swan was given an electric organ as a wedding present by Kristofferson and Rita Coolidge. He was fooling around and the chords to 'I Can Help' appeared. Within a few minutes, he also had the lyrics. On the record, Chip Young's guitar effectively balances Billy's swirling organ and, with its heavy echo, the production was very 50s. The tune was so infectious that it topped the US charts for two weeks and made number 6 in the UK.

The subsequent album was a cheerful, good-time affair, almost as though Sun Records had decided to modernize their sound. Billy had a similar song prepared for the follow-up single, 'Everything's The Same (Ain't Nothin' Changed)', but Monument preferred to take something from the album to promote its sales. 'I'm Her Fool', with its humorous barking ending was released but it was banned by several radio stations because of the line, 'She pets me when I bury my bone'. A slow version of 'Don't Be Cruel' made number 42 in the UK. Elvis Presley recorded a full-blooded version of

'I Can Help' in 1975, which became a UK Top 30 hit in 1983. Apparently, Presley was amused by the line, 'If your child needs a daddy, I can help', and he sent Swan the socks he wore on the session as a souvenir. Elvis died before he could record Swan's 'No Way Around It (It's Love)'. One of the many asides on Jerry Lee Lewis' version of 'I Can Help' is 'Think about it, Elvis'. Billy Swan released three more albums for Monument and then one each for A&M and Epic, but he failed to recapture the overall quality of his first. Amongst his guest musicians were Carl Perkins, who joined him on remakes of 'Blue Suede Shoes' and 'Your True Love' and an unreleased 'Matchbox', and Scotty Moore and Otis Blackwell. The Kristoffersons recorded 'Lover Please', also a song by Swan and his wife, Marlu, 'Number One'. Swan and Kristofferson co-wrote 'Nobody Loves Anybody Anymore' on Kristofferson's *To The Bone*. Swan has also played on albums by Barefoot Jerry, Harry Chapin, Fred Frith and Dennis Linde. He has worked with T-Bone Burnett on several of his albums and they co-wrote 'Drivin' Wheel' (later recorded by Emmylou Harris), 'The Bird That I Held In My Hand'. Swan briefly worked with Randy Meisner of the Eagles in a country rock band, Black Tie, who released *When The Night Falls* in 1986. The album includes a tribute to rock 'n' roll's wildman, 'Jerry Lee', as well as familiar songs like 'If You Gotta Make a Fool of Somebody' and 'Chain Gang'. Since then, Swan has preferred the security of touring with Kris Kristofferson.

●ALBUMS: *I Can Help* (Monument 1975)★★★★, *Billy Swan* (Monument 1975)★★★★, *Rock 'N' Roll Moon* (Monument 1976)★★★, *Billy Swan - Four* (Monument 1977)★★★, *You're OK, I'm OK* (A&M 1978)★★, *I'm Into Lovin' You* (Epic 1981)★★, *Bop To Be* (Elite 1995)★★★.

SWARBRICK, DAVE

b. 5 April 1941, New Malden, Surrey, England. Violinist and vocalist Swarbrick has played with many well-known groups and performers both in the folk and other areas of music. He is usually best remembered for his time with Fairport Convention, whom he first joined in 1969. In his earlier days he played fiddle and mandola for the Ian Campbell Folk Group. Additionally, Swarbrick has recorded and toured with Simon Nicol and Martin Carthy. Swarbrick first teamed up with Carthy in 1966 and when he played on Carthy's debut album for Fontana in 1968, was fined by his own record company Transatlantic for performing without their permission. Continual playing of the electric violin had a detrimental effect on Swarbrick's hearing; leaving him virtually deaf in one ear. This, however, has not stopped him working. Swarbrick left Fairport Convention in 1984, and shortly after formed Whippersnapper with Martin Jenkins, Chris Leslie and Kevin Dempsey. After two accomplished albums, Swarbrick left the band in the middle of a tour. In 1990, he once more teamed up with Martin Carthy to record the excellent *Life And Limb*. Swarbrick is now a member of the Keith Hancock Band, which includes long-time associate Martin Carthy and Rauri McFarlane.

●ALBUMS: with Martin Carthy, Diz Disley *Rags, Reels And Airs* (1967)★★★, with Carthy *Byker Hill* (Fontana 1967)★★★★, with Carthy *But Two Came By* (1968)★★★, with Carthy *Prince Heathen* (1969)★★★, *Selections* (1971)★★★, *Swarbrick* (Transatlantic 1976)★★★, *Swarbrick 2* (Transatlantic 1977)★★★, *Dave Swarbrick And Friends* (1978)★★★, *Lift The Lid And Listen* (Sonet 1978)★★★, *The Ceilidh Album* (Sonet 1979)★★★, *Smiddyburn* (Logo 1981)★★★, with Simon Nicol *Live At The White Bear* (White Bear 1982)★★★, *Flittin'* (Spindrift 1983)★★★, with Nicol *In The Club* (1983)★★★, with Nicol *Close To The Wind* (Woodworm 1984)★★★, with Carthy *Life And Limb* (Special Delivery 1990)★★★, *Live At Jackson's Lane* (1991)★★★, with Carthy *Skin & Bone* (1992)★★★★.

SWEET

The nucleus of the Sweet came together in 1966, when drummer Mick Tucker (b. 17 July 1949, Harlesden, London, England) and vocalist Brian Connolly (b. 5 October 1945, Hamilton, Scotland, d. 10 February 1997; other dates of birth vary between 1944 and 1949) played together in Wainwright's Gentlemen, a small-time club circuit band whose repertoire comprised a mixture of Motown, R&B and psychedelia. The pair broke away to form Sweetshop, later shortened to Sweet, with Steve Priest (b. 23 February 1950, Hayes, Middlesex) on bass and Frank Torpey on guitar. After releasing four unsuccessful singles on Fontana and EMI, Torpey was replaced by Andy Scott (b. 30 June 1951, Wrexham, Wales) and the new line-up signed to RCA. The band were introduced to the writing partnership of Chinn And Chapman, who provided the band with a string of hit singles. Their initial success was down to bubblegum pop anthems such as 'Funny, Funny', 'Co-Co', 'Poppa Joe' and 'Little Willy'. However, the band were writing their own hard-rock numbers on the b-sides of these hits. This resulted in Chinn/Chapman coming up with heavier pop-rock numbers, most notably the powerful 'Blockbuster', which reached number 1 in the UK at the beginning of 1973. The group's determinedly effete, glam-rock image was reinforced by a succession of Top 10 hits, including 'Hell Raiser', 'Ballroom Blitz', 'Teenage Rampage' and 'The Six Teens'.

Sweet decided to take greater control of their own destiny in 1974 and recorded the album *Sweet Fanny Adams* without the assistance of Chinn and Chapman. The album charted at number 27, but disappeared again after just two weeks. The work marked a significant departure from their commercially minded singles on which they had built their reputation. 'Set Me Free', 'Restless' and 'Sweet F.A.' epitomized their no-frills hard-rock style. *Desolation Boulevard* included the self-penned 'Fox On The Run' which reached number 2 in the UK singles chart. This gave the band confidence and renewed RCA's faith in the band as a commercial proposition. However, as Sweet became more of an albums band, the hit singles began to dry up, with 1978's 'Love Is Like Oxygen' being their last Top 10 hit. Following a move to Polydor, they recorded four albums with each release making less impact than its predecessor. Their brand of melodic rock, infused with infectious hooks and brutal riffs, now failed to satisfy both the teeny-bopper and the more mature rock fan. Since 1982, various incarnations of the band have appeared from time to time, with any number from one to three of the original members in the line-up. The most recent of these was in 1989, when they recorded a live album at London's Marquee Club, with Paul Mario Day (ex-More) handling the vocals. Brian Connolly suffered from a muscular disorder, and experienced numerous heart attacks. His grim situation was warmed in 1992 with the incredible success of the film *Ballroom Blitz* and the subsequent renewed interest in the Sweet, but he died in 1997.

●ALBUMS: *Funny How Sweet Co Co Can Be* (RCA 1971)★★, *Sweet* (1973)★★, *Sweet Fanny Adams* (RCA 1974)★★★, *Desolation Boulevard* (RCA 1974)★★★, *Strung Up* (RCA 1975)★★★, *Give Us A Wink* (RCA 1976)★★, *Off The Record* (RCA 1977)★★, *Level Headed* (Polydor 1978)★★, *Cut Above The Rest* (Polydor 1979)★★, *Water's Edge* (Polydor 1980)★★, *Identity Crisis* (Polydor 1982)★★, *Live At The Marquee* (SPV 1989)★, *Blockbusters* (RCA 1989)★★.

●COMPILATIONS: *Biggest Hits* (RCA 1972)★★, *Sweet's Golden Greats* (RCA 1977)★★★, *Sweet 16 - It's, It's The Sweet's Hits* (Anagram 1984)★★, *Hard Centres - The Rock Years* (Zebra 1987)★★, *The Collection* (Castle 1989)★★★, *Ballroom Blitz - Live 1973* (Dojo 1993)★★, *Love Is Like Oxygen - The Singles Collection 1978-1982* (Pseudonym 1993)★★, *Platinum Rare* (Repertoire 1995)★★, *Hit Singles: The Complete A And B Sides* (Repertoire 1996)★★, *Ballroom Blitz: The Very Best Of ...* (Polygram 1996)★★★.

T. REX

Although initially a six-piece group, formed by Marc Bolan (b. Mark Feld, 30 September 1947, Hackney, London, England, d. 16 September 1977; vocals/guitar) in 1967 on leaving John's Children, the new venture was reduced to an acoustic duo when a finance company repossessed their instruments and amplifiers. Steve 'Peregrine' Took (b. 28 July, 1949, Eltham, South London, England, d. 27 October 1980; percussion) completed the original line-up which was originally known as Tyrannosaurus Rex. Nurtured by disc jockey John Peel, the group quickly became an established act on the UK 'underground' circuit through numerous live appearances. Bolan's quivering voice and rhythmic guitar-playing were ably supported by Took's frenetic bongos and the sound created was one of the most distinctive of the era. 'Debora', their debut single, broached the UK Top 40, while a follow-up, 'One Inch Rock', reached number 28, but Tyrannosaurus Rex found a wider audience with their albums. *My People Were Fair...* and *Prophets, Seers & Sages* encapsulated Bolan's quirky talent and while his lyrics, made obtuse by a sometimes impenetrable delivery, invoked pixies, fawns, the work of J.R.R. Tolkien and the trappings of 'flower-power', his affection for pop's tradition resulted in many memorable melodies. Bolan also published *The Warlock Of Love*, a collection of poems which entered the best-selling book lists.

Unicorn (1969) introduced a much fuller sound as Tyrannosaurus Rex began to court a wider popularity. Long-time producer Tony Visconti (b. 24 April 1944, Brooklyn, New York, USA) emphasized the supporting instruments - organ, harmonium, bass guitar and drumkit - while adding piano on 'Catblack', one of the more popular selections. However, tension between Bolan and Took led to the latter's departure and Mickey Finn (b. 3 June 1947, Thornton Heath, Surrey), formerly with Hapshash And The Coloured Coat, took his place in 1970. The ensuing *A Beard Of Stars* completed the transformation into a fully fledged electric group and while the lyrical content and shape of the songs remained the same, the overall sound was noticeably punchier and more direct. The most obvious example, 'Elemental Child', featured Bolan's long, almost frantic, guitar solo. The duo's name was truncated to T. Rex in October 1970. The attendant single, 'Ride A White Swan', rose to number 2, a success that confirmed an irrevocable change in Bolan's music. Steve Currie (b. 20

May 1947, Grimsby, England, d. 28 April 1981; bass) and ex-commercial artist Bill (Fifield) Legend (b. 8 May 1944, Dagenham, Essex, England; drums, ex-Legend, the Epics and Bateson And Stott), were added to the line-up for 'Hot Love' and 'Get It On', both of which topped the UK charts, and *Electric Warrior*, a number 1 album. *T. Rextacy* became the watchword for pop's new phenomenon which continued unabated when 'Jeepster' reached number 2. However, the track was issued without Bolan's permission and in retort the singer left the Fly label to found his own T. Rex outlet. The pattern of hits continued throughout 1972 with two polished chart-toppers, 'Telegram Sam' and 'Metal Guru', and two number 2 hits, 'Children Of The Revolution' and 'Solid Gold Easy Action', while the now-anachronistic 'Debora' reached the Top 10 upon re-release. A documentary, *Born To Boogie*, filmed by Ringo Starr, captured this frenetic period, but although '20th Century Boy' and 'The Groover' (both 1973) were also substantial hits, they were the group's last UK Top 10 entries. Bolan's relationship with Visconti was severed following 'Truck On (Tyke)' and a tired predictability crept into the singer's work. Astringent touring of Britain, America, Japan and Australia undermined his creativity, reflected in the disappointing *Zinc Alloy...* and *Bolan's Zip Gun* albums.

American soul singer Gloria Jones (b. 19 September 1947, Ohio, USA), now Bolan's girlfriend, was added to the group, but a series of departures, including those of Currie, Legend and Finn, emphasized an internal dissent. Although 'New York City' bore a 'T. Rex' credit, the group had been officially declared defunct with session musicians completing future recordings. A series of minor hits - 'Dreamy Lady', 'London Boys' and 'Laser Love' - was punctuated by 'I Love To Boogie', which reached the UK Top 20, but its lustre was removed by charges of plagiarism. However, unlike many contemporaries, Bolan welcomed the punk explosion, championing the Damned and booking Generation X on his short-lived television show, *Marc*. The series featured poignant reunions with David Bowie and John's Children singer Andy Ellison and helped halt Bolan's sliding fortunes. A working unit of Herbie Flowers (bass) and Tony Newman (drums) was formed in the wake of a new recording contract with RCA, but on 16 September 1977, Marc Bolan was killed when the car in which he was a passenger struck a tree. The first of several T. Rex-related deaths, it was followed by those of Took (October 1980) and Currie (April 1981). A vociferous fan club has kept Bolan's name alive through multiple reissues and repackages and the singer has retained a cult popularity. Although his spell as a top-selling act was brief, he was instrumental in restating pop values in the face of prevailing progressive trends. When 70s pop is discussed, Bolan and his merry Hobbits are one of the main contenders.

●ALBUMS: as Tyrannosaurus Rex *My People Were Fair And Had Sky In Their Hair But Now They're Content To Wear Stars On Their Brows* (Regal Zonophone 1968)★★★, *Prophets Seers & Sages, The Angels Of The Ages* (Regal Zonophone 1968)★★★, *Unicorn* (Regal Zonophone 1969)★★★, *A Beard Of Stars* (Regal Zonophone 1970)★★★; as T. Rex *T. Rex* (Fly 1970)★★★, *Electric Warrior* (Fly 1971)★★★★, *The Slider* (EMI 1972)★★★, *Tanx* (EMI 1973)★★★, *Zinc Alloy And The Hidden Riders Of Tomorrow Or A Creamed Cage In August* (EMI 1974)★★, *Bolan's Zip Gun* (EMI 1975)★★★, *Futuristic Dragon* (EMI 1976)★★, *Dandy In The Underworld* (EMI 1977)★★, *T. Rex In Concert - The Electric Warrior Tour 1971* (Marc 1981)★★★, *Rabbit Fighter* alternate *The Slider* (Edsel 1994)★★★, *Left Hand Luke* alternate *Tanx* (Edsel 1994)★★★, *Change (The Alternate Zinc Alloy)* (Edsel 1995)★★, *Precious Star* alternate *Bolan's Zip Gun* (Edsel 1996)★★★, *Dazzling Raiment* alternate *Futuristic Dragon* (Edsel 1997)★★.

●COMPILATIONS: *The Best Of T. Rex* contains Tyrannosaurus Rex material (Fly 1971)★★★, *Bolan Boogie* (Fly 1972)★★★, *Great Hits* (EMI 1973)★★★★, *Light Of Love* (Casablanca 1974)★★, *Marc - The Words And Music 1947-1977* (Cube 1978), *Solid Gold T. Rex* (EMI 1979)★★★, *The Unobtainable T. Rex* (EMI 1980)★★, *Children Of Rarn Suite* (Marc On Wax 1982)★★, *Across The Airwaves* (Cube 1982)★★, *Billy Super Duper* (Marc 1982)★★, *Dance In The Midnight* (Marc On Wax 1983)★★, *Beyond The Rising Sun* (Cambra 1984)★★, *The Best Of The 20th Century Boy* (K-Tel 1985)★★★, *Till Dawn* (Marc On Wax 1985)★★, *The T. Rex Collection* (Castle 1986)★★★★, *A Crown Of Jewels* (Dojo 1986)★★, *The Singles Collection* (Marc On Wax 1987)★★★, *The Marc Shows* (Marc On Wax 1989)★★★, *Great Hits 1972-1977: The A-Sides* (Edsel 1994)★★★★, *Great Hits 1972-1977: The B-Sides* (Edsel 1994)★★, *Unchained: Unreleased Recordings Vols. 1-4* (Edsel 1995)★★, *A BBC History* (Band Of Joy 1996)★★★★, *Unchained Volumes 5 & 6* (Edsel 1996)★★, *Unchained Volume 7* (Edsel 1997)★★.

●FURTHER READING: *Tyrannosaurus Rex*, Ray Stevenson.

TAJ MAHAL

b. Henry Saint Clair Fredericks, 17 May 1940, New York, USA. The son of a jazz arranger, Mahal developed his early interest in black music by studying its origins at university. After graduating, he began performing in Boston clubs, before moving to the west coast in 1965. The artist was a founder-member of the legendary Rising Sons, a respected folk rock group that also included Ry Cooder and Spirit drummer Ed Cassidy. Mahal resumed his solo career when the group's projected debut album was shelved. His first solo album, *Taj Mahal*, released in 1968, was a powerful, yet intimate compendium of electrified country blues which introduced an early backing band of Jesse Davis (guitar), Gary Gilmore (bass) and Chuck Blakwell (drums). A second album, *The Natch'l Blues*, offered similarly excellent fare while extending his palette to include interpretations of two soul songs. This early period reached its apogee with *Giant Steps/The Ole Folks At Home*, a double album comprising a traditional-styled acoustic album and a vibrant rock selection. Mahal continued to broaden his remarkable canvas. *The Real Thing*, recorded in concert, featured support from a tuba section, while the singer's pursuit of ethnic styles resulted in the African-American persuasion of *Happy Just To Be Like I Am* and the West Indian influence of *Mo Roots*. He has maintained his chameleon-like quality over a succession of cultured releases, during which the singer has remained a popular live attraction at the head of a fluctuating backing group, known initially as the Intergalactic Soul Messengers, then as the International Rhythm Band. In the 90s Taj veered closer to soul and R&B. His interpretations of Doc Pomus' 'Lonely Avenue' and Dave Bartholomew/Fats Domino's 'Let The Four Winds Blow' were particularly noteworthy on *Phantom Blues*, as was the work of sessionmen Jon Cleary (piano) and Mick Weaver (organ).

● ALBUMS: *Taj Mahal* (Columbia 1968)★★★★, *Giant Steps/De Ole Folks At Home* (Columbia 1969)★★★★, *The Natch'l Blues* (Columbia 1969)★★★★, *The Real Thing* (Columbia 1971)★★★, *Happy Just To Be Like I Am* (Columbia 1972)★★, *Recycling The Blues And Other Related Stuff* (Columbia 1972)★★★, *The Sounder* (1973)★★, *Oooh So Good 'N' Blues* (Columbia 1973)★★★, *Mo' Roots* (Columbia 1974)★★★, *Music Keeps Me Together* (Columbia 1975)★★, *Satisfied 'N Tickled Too* (Columbia 1976)★★, *Music Fuh Ya'* (Warners 1977)★★, *Brothers* (Warners 1977)★★, *Evolution* (Warners 1977)★★, *Taj Mahal And The International Rhythm Band Live* (1979)★★★, *Live* (1981)★★, *Take A Giant Step* (Magnet 1983)★★★, *Taj* (Sonet 1987)★★★, *Live And Direct* (Teldec 1987)★★★, *Big Blues-Live At Ronnie Scott's* (Essential 1990)★★★, *Mule Bone* (Gramavision 1991)★★★, *Like Never Before* (Private Music 1991)★★★, *Dancing The Blues* (Private Music/BMG 1994)★★★, *An Evening Of Acoustic Music* (Tradition & Moderne/Topic 1995)★★★, *Phantom Blues* (Private 1996)★★★★, *An Evening Of Acoustic Music* (Ruf 1997)★★★.

● COMPILATIONS: *Going Home* (Columbia 1980)★★★★, *The Taj Mahal Collection* (Castle 1987)★★★.

● VIDEOS: *At Ronnie Scott's 1988* (Hendring 1989).

TANGERINE DREAM

Like Amon Duul and Can, Tangerine Dream were German-based purveyors of imaginative electronic music. There have been numerous line-ups since the band's formation in 1968, although Edgar Froese (b. 6 June 1944, Tilsit, East Prussia) has remained at the head of affairs throughout. After playing with college band the Ones, who released a single and performed for Salvador Dali at his villa, Froese put together Tangerine Dream with himself on guitar, Voker Hombach (flute/violin), Kirt Herkenber (bass) and Lanse Hapshash (drums). Heavily influenced by US bands like the Doors, Jefferson Airplane and the Grateful

Dead, they performed live at various student counter-culture events. By 1969 they had split and remained inactive until Froese recruited Steve Jollife (electric flute). He departed soon afterwards, although he later returned to the fold. A debut album was recorded, for which Froese brought in Konrad Schnitzler and Klaus Schulze, who later embarked on a solo career for Virgin Records. Jazz drummer Christoph Franke (ex-Agitation Free) joined in 1971, as did organist Steve Schroyder. This line-up recorded *Alpha Centauri*, which combined space age rock in the style of Pink Floyd with classical structures. Peter Baumann (ex-Ants) replaced Schroyder, and this became the band's first stable line-up, staying together until 1977.

Zeit saw the band's instrumentation incorporate new synthesizer technology, while *Atem* focused on atmospheric, restrained passages. Influential BBC disc jockey John Peel named it the best album of 1973. *Phaedra* established their biggest foothold in the UK market when it reached number 15 in the album charts in 1974. Their attentions turned, however, to a series of film soundtracks, while Froese released his first solo, *Aqua*. At the height of punk, and as one of the named targets of the insurrection, *Stratosfear* emerged. It was their most commercial album so far. Guitar, piano and harpsichord were all incorporated, taking the edge off the harsh electronics. After the hectic touring schedule of the following year, Baumann left to pursue his solo career. He went on to form his own Private Music label, and, ironically, signed Tangerine Dream for releases in the USA. He was replaced by former member and multi-instrumentalist Jollife, as well as drummer Klaus Kreiger. The ensuing *Cyclone* featured vocals and lyrics for the first time, although they returned to instrumental work with *Force Majeure*. As the new decade dawned, the band became the first western group to play in East Berlin. *Tangram* and *Exit* relied on melody more than their precursors, the latter featuring the emotive 'Kiev Mission', which included a message from the Russian Peace Movement. *Le Parc* used advanced sampling technology, which seemed to be a little at odds with the band's natural abilities. Schmoelling became the next to depart for a solo career in 1985, replaced by classically trained Paul Haslinger. Three years later Chris Franke, after 17 years service, followed Schmoelling's example. Computer programmer Ralf Wadephal took his place but when he left the band elected to continue as a duo. Although often criticized, the band was pivotal in refining a sound that effectively pioneered the new-age ambient electronic music more than a decade later. Their importance in this field should not be underestimated.

● ALBUMS: *Electronic Meditation* (Ohr 1970)★★★, *Alpha Centauri* (Ohr 1971)★★★, *Zeit (Largo In Four Movements)* (Ohr 1972)★★★, *Atem* (Ohr 1973)★★★, *Phaedra* (Virgin 1974)★★★★, *Rubycon* (Virgin 1975)★★★, *Ricochet* (Virgin 1975)★★★, *Stratosfear* (Virgin 1976)★★★★, *Encore-Live* (Virgin 1977)★★, *Sorcerer* soundtrack (MCA

1977)★★, *Cyclone* (Virgin 1978)★★★, *Force Majeure* (Virgin 1979)★★★, *Thief* soundtrack (Virgin 1980)★★, *Tangram* (Virgin 1980)★★★, *Quichotte* (Amiga 1980) reissued as *Pergamon* (Virgin 1986)★★★, *Exit* (Virgin 1981)★★★, *White Eagle* (Virgin 1982)★★★, *Logos-Live At The Dominion* (Virgin 1983)★★, *Wavelength* soundtrack (Varese Sarabande 1983)★★, *Risky Business* soundtrack (Virgin 1983)★★, *Hyperborea* (Virgin 1983)★★, *Firestarter* soundtrack (MCA 1984)★★, *Flashpoint* soundtrack (EMI 1984)★★, *Poland-The Warsaw Concert* (Jive Electro 1984)★★, *Heartbreakers* soundtrack (Virgin 1985)★★, *Le Parc* (Jive Electro 1985)★★, *Legend* soundtrack (MCA 1986)★★, *Underwater Sunlight* (Jive Electro 1986)★★, *Near Dark* soundtrack (Silva Screen 1987)★★, *Tyger* (Jive Electro 1987)★★, *Three O'Clock High* soundtrack (Varese Sarabande 1987)★★, *Shy People* soundtrack (Varese Sarabande 1987)★★, *Live Miles* (Jive Electro 1988)★★, *Optical Race* (Private Race 1988)★★★, *Lily On The Beach* (1989)★★, *Melrose* (1990)★★, *Rockoon* (1992)★★, *Canyon Dreams* (1993)★★, *Turn Of The Tides* (Miramar 1994)★★, *Goblin's Club* (Sequel 1996)★★★.
●COMPILATIONS: *Dream Sequence* (Virgin 1985)★★★, *The Collection* (Castle 1987)★★★, *Book Of Dreams* (Essential 1996)★★★, *The Dream Mixes* (TDI 1996)★★★, *The Dream Roots Collection* (Essential 1997)★★★.
●VIDEOS: *Three Phase* (1993).

TASTE

A popular blues-rock attraction, Taste was formed in Cork, Eire, in 1966 when Eric Kittringham (bass) and Norman Damery (drums) joined Rory Gallagher (b. 2 March 1949, Ballyshannon, Co. Donegal, Eire, d. 14 June 1995), erstwhile guitarist with the Impact Showband. The new group became a leading attraction in Ireland and in Germany, but in 1968 Gallagher replaced the original rhythm section with Charlie McCracken (bass) and John Wilson (ex-Them) on drums. The new line-up then became a part of London's burgeoning blues and progressive circuit. Their debut, *Taste*, was one of the era's most popular releases, and featured several in-concert favourites, including 'Same Old Story' and 'Sugar Mama'. *On The Boards* was another commercial success, and the group seemed poised to inherit the power-trio mantle vacated by Cream. However, the unit broke up in October 1970 following a rancorous split between Gallagher and his colleagues. The guitarist then began a fruitful solo career until his untimely death in 1995.
●ALBUMS: *Taste* (Polydor 1969)★★★, *On The Boards* (Polydor 1970)★★★★, *Live Taste* (Polydor 1971)★★, *Live At The Isle Of Wight* (Polydor 1972)★★.
●COMPILATIONS: *The Greatest Rock Sensation* (Polydor 1985)★★★.

TAVARES

This US group was formed in 1964 in New Bedford, Massachusetts, USA. The line-up consisted of five brothers, Ralph, Antone 'Chubby', Feliciano 'Butch', Arthur 'Pooch' and Perry Lee 'Tiny' Tavares. Originally known as Chubby And The Turnpikes, the group assumed its family's surname in 1969. Although they lacked a distinctive lead voice or a characteristic sound, the Tavares' undemanding blend of light soul and pop resulted in several commercial successes. The brothers' early run of R&B hits culminated in 1975 with 'It Only Takes A Minute', a soul chart-topper and a US pop Top 10 entry. The following year the group scored their sole million-seller in 'Heaven Must Be Missing An Angel' before enjoying further success with one of their strongest songs, 'Don't Take Away The Music'. Both of these singles reached number 4 in the UK where Tavares enjoyed an enduring popularity. 'Whodunit' (1977) was another major release, while 'More Than A Woman' (1978), a song from that year's box-office smash, *Saturday Night Fever*, gave the group their last significant hit. Tavares continued to reach the R&B lists until 1984, but their safe, almost old-fashioned style gradually fell from favour.
●ALBUMS: *Check It Out* (Capitol 1974)★★★★, *Hard Core Poetry* (Capitol 1974)★★★, *In The City* (Capitol 1975)★★★, *Sky High!* (Capitol 1976)★★★, *Love Storm* (Capitol 1977)★★★★, *Future Bound* (Capitol 1978)★★★, *Madam Butterfly* (Capitol 1979)★★★, *Supercharged* (Capitol 1980)★★★, *New Directions* (RCA 1982)★★★.
●COMPILATIONS: *The Best Of The Tavares* (Capitol 1977)★★★★.

TAYLOR, JAMES

b. 12 March 1948, Boston, Massachusetts, USA. The embodiment of the American singer-songwriter from the late 60s and early 70s was the frail and troubled James Taylor. He was born into a wealthy family. His mother was a classically trained soprano and encouraged James and his siblings to become musical. As a child he wanted for nothing and divided his time between two substantial homes. He befriended Danny 'Kootch' Kortchmar at the age of 15 and won a local talent contest. As is often the case, boarding school education suited the parents more than the child, and Taylor rebelled at Milton Academy at the age of 16, joining his brother Alex in a rock band, the Fabulous Corsairs. At only 17 he committed himself to the McLean Mental Institution in Massachusetts. Following his nine-month stay he reunited with 'Kootch' and together they formed the commercially disastrous Flying Machine. At 18, now being supported by his parents in his own apartment, the seemingly affluent James drew the predictable crowd of hangers-on and emotional parasites. He experimented with drugs and was soon addicted to heroin. He had the drive to move out, and after several months of travelling he arrived in London and found a flat in Notting Hill (which in 1968 was hardly the place for someone trying to kick a drug habit!). Once again 'Kootch' came to the rescue, and suggested Taylor take a demo tape to Peter Asher.

'Kootch' had supported Peter And Gordon on an American tour, and Asher was now looking for talent as head of the new Apple Records. Both Asher and Paul McCartney liked the work and the thin, weak and by now world-weary teenager was given the opportunity to record. *James Taylor* was not a success when released, even though classic songs like 'Carolina On My Mind' and 'Something In The Way She Moves' appeared on it. Depressed and still addicted to heroin, Taylor returned to America, this time to the Austin Riggs Mental Institution. Meanwhile, Asher, frustrated at the disorganized Apple, moved to America, and persevering with Taylor, he secured a contract with Warner Brothers Records and rounded up a team of supportive musician friends; 'Kootch', Leland Sklar, Russ Kunkel and Carole King. Many of the songs written in the institution appeared on the superlative *Sweet Baby James*. The album eventually spent two years in the US charts and contained a jewel of a song: 'Fire And Rain'. In this, he encapsulated his entire life, problems and fears; it stands as one of the finest songs of the era. Taylor received rave notices from critics and he was quickly elevated to superstardom. The follow-up *Mud Slide Slim And The Blue Horizon* consolidated the previous success and contained the definitive reading of Carole King's 'You've Got A Friend'. In 1972, now free of drugs, Taylor worked with the Beach Boys' Dennis Wilson on the cult drag-race film *Two Lane Blacktop* and released *One Man Dog* which contained another hit, 'Don't Let Me Be Lonely Tonight'. Fortunately Taylor was not lonely for long; he married Carly Simon in the biggest showbusiness wedding since Burton and Taylor. They duetted on a version of the Charlie And Inez Foxx hit, 'Mockingbird' which made the US Top 5 in 1974.

Taylor's albums began to form a pattern of mostly original compositions, mixed with an immaculately chosen blend of R&B, soul and rock 'n' roll classics. Ironically most of his subsequent hits were non-originals: Holland Dozier And Holland's 'How Sweet It Is', Otis Blackwell's 'Handy Man', and Goffin And King's 'Up On The Roof'. Taylor was also displaying confidence and sparkling onstage wit, having a superb rapport with his audiences, where once his shyness was excruciating. Simon filed for divorce a decade after their marriage, but Taylor accepted the breakdown and carried on with his profession. The assured Taylor is instrumentally captured by Pat Metheny's joyous composition 'James' recorded on Metheny's *Offramp* album in 1982. In 1985 Taylor released the immaculate *That's Why I'm Here*. The reason he is here, as the lyric explains is: 'fortune and fame is such a curious game, perfect strangers can call you by name, pay good money to hear "Fire And Rain"', again and again and again'. This one song says as much about James Taylor today as 'Fire And Rain' did many years ago. He has survived, he is happy, he is still creative and above all, his concerts exude a warmth that demonstrates he is genuinely grateful to be able to perform. In recent years Taylor continues to add guest har-mony vocals to all and sundry in addition to regularly touring. *Hourglass* in 1997 was well received by the critics and became one of his highest charting records for many years. Quite why is a mystery, because it was no better or worse that his most recent studio recordings. Perhaps the critical wind of change has once again blown in his favour. The double live album that was issued in 1993 is a necessary purchase for those who stopped buying his records when they moved out of their bedsitters in 1971. One autobiography crying to be written is this man's.

●ALBUMS: *James Taylor* (Apple 1968)★★★, *Sweet Baby James* (Warners 1970)★★★★, *James Taylor And The Original Flying Machine - 1967* (Euphoria 1970)★★, *Mud Slide Slim And The Blue Horizon* (Warners 1971)★★★★, *One Man Dog* (Warners 1972)★★★, *Walking Man* (Warners 1974)★★★, *Gorilla* (Warners 1975)★★★, *In The Pocket* (Warners 1976)★★, *JT* (Columbia 1977)★★★★, *Flag* (Columbia 1979)★★, *Dad Loves His Work* (Columbia 1981)★★, *That's Why I'm Here* (Columbia 1985)★★★★, *Never Die Young* (Columbia 1988)★★★, *New Moon Shine* (Columbia 1991)★★★, *Live In Rio* rec. 1985 (Columbia 1992)★★★, *Live* (1993)★★★, *Hourglass* (Columbia 1997)★★★.
●COMPILATIONS: *Greatest Hits* (Warners 1976)★★★★, *Classic Songs* (Warners 1987)★★★★★, *The Best Of James Taylor - The Classic Years* (1990)★★★★.
●VIDEOS: *James Taylor In Concert* (1991), *Squibnocket* (1993).

TAYLOR, R. DEAN

Toronto-born R. Dean Taylor remains the most successful white artist to emerge from the Motown Records stable. The protégé of writer/producer Brian Holland, he worked on many of the mid-60s hits produced by the Holland/Dozier/Holland partnership, and later claimed to have helped compose several songs credited to them. He began his recording career in 1965 with 'Let's Go Somewhere', but found more success with two of his compositions for the Supremes, 'Love Child' and 'I'm Living In Shame', both of which brought a new realism into the group's work. In 1967, he recorded the classic soul number 'There's A Ghost In My House', which enjoyed cult status in Britain. A year later he released the evocative 'Gotta See Jane', which also charted in the UK that summer. His most memorable single was 'Indiana Wants Me', an effect-laden melodrama which climbed high in both the UK and US charts in 1970. Despite his popularity in Britain, where a revival of 'There's A Ghost In My House' reached the Top 3 in 1974, Taylor was unable to repeat this success with his subsequent recordings, either on his own Jane label in 1973, or with Polydor from 1974.
●ALBUMS: *I Think Therefore I Am* (Rare Earth 1971)★★, *Indiana Wants Me* (Tamla Motown 1971)★★, *LA Sunset* (Polydor 1975)★★.

TEAR GAS

A Glasgow, Scotland, progressive rock band formed in the late 60s, Tear Gas initially comprised Eddie Campbell (keyboards), Zal Cleminson (guitar), Chris Glen (bass/vocals), Gilson Lavis (drums) and Andy Mulvey (vocals). Mulvey had previously sung with local beat group the Poets. After changing from their original name, Mustard, they chose Tear Gas as a variation on the same theme. However, Mulvey was soon replaced by keyboardist/vocalist David Batchelor, and Lavis (who later played with Squeeze) by Richard Monro from Ritchie Blackmore's Mandrake Root. It was this line-up who made their recorded debut with 1970's *Piggy Go Getter*, an album typical of the time with its extended guitar and keyboard passages. However, they were more playful than some - 'We were a really loud band. In fact we used to open with Jethro Tull's 'Love Story', which started very softly and the crowd would drift towards the front. Then we'd turn the volume up and blow everyone out of the hall.' Later in 1970 Hugh McKenna replaced Batchelor while his cousin Ted McKenna (ex-Dream Police) took over from Monro on drums. Itinerant musician Ronnie Leahy also contributed keyboards in Batchelor's absence, though the group were by now living in penury six to a room in Shepherd's Bush, London. A second album was recorded for release on Regal Zonophone Records but again met with a lacklustre response from the critics. Despite regular touring in an effort to establish themselves, it was not until they teamed up with Alex Harvey in August 1972 to become the Sensational Alex Harvey Band that they saw any real success.
●ALBUMS: *Piggy Go Getter* (Famous 1970)★★, *Tear Gas* (Regal Zonophone 1971)★★.

TEENAGE JESUS AND THE JERKS

The 17-year-old Lydia Lunch formed Teenage Jesus And The Jerks in the UK during 1976 to channel her feelings of contempt towards a complacent music industry, but almost immediately clashed with founder members James Chance (b. James Siegfried) and Reck, both of whom left before any recordings were completed. Chance later formed the Contortions, Reck going on to front one of Japan's most successful punk acts, Friction. Lunch's distraught singing and atonal guitar cut against drummer Bradley Field and bassist Jim Sclavunos (later replaced by filmmaker Gordon Stevenson) to create an uncompromising, unholy noise labelled 'no wave', which was first heard on their single, 'Orphans', in 1978. 'Baby Doll' reared its ugly head nearly a year later, followed by a mini-album and 12-inch EP. *Pink* boasted seven excellent tracks, while *Pre*, on the Ze label, collected several early recordings. They disbanded in 1980 when Lydia Lunch progressed to the less violent, murkier sound of Beirut Slump. Field moved on to rejoin Chance as one of his Contortions. However, the discordant, tortuous racket they exuded from Teenage Jesus And The Jerks has influenced a variety of distinguished names since then, from the Birthday Party to Sonic Youth. It is no coincidence that Lunch has worked with them both.
●ALBUMS: *Pink* (Lust Unlust 1979)★★★, *Pre* (Ze 1980)★★.

TELEVISION

Lead guitarist/vocalist Tom Verlaine (b. Thomas Miller, 13 December 1949, Mount Morris, New Jersey, USA) first worked with bassist Richard Hell (b. Richard Myers, 2 October 1949, Lexington, Kentucky, USA) and drummer Billy Ficca in the early 70s as the Neon Boys. By the end of 1973, with the addition of rhythm guitarist Richard Lloyd, they reunited as Television. Early the following year they secured a residency at the Bowery club, CBGB's, and found themselves at the forefront of the New York new wave explosion. Conflicts between Verlaine and Hell led to the departure of the latter who later re-emerged with the Heartbreakers. Meanwhile, Television found a replacement bassist in Fred Smith from Blondie. The new line-up recorded the raw but arresting 'Little Johnny Jewel', a tribute to Iggy Pop, for their own label, Ork Records. This led to their signing with Elektra Records for whom they recorded their debut album in 1977. *Marquee Moon* was largely ignored in their homeland, but elicited astonished, ecstatic reviews in the UK. where it was applauded as one of rock's most accomplished debut albums. Verlaine's sneering, nasal vocal and searing, jagged twin guitar interplay with Lloyd were the hallmarks of Television's work, particularly on such stand-out tracks as 'Torn Curtain', 'Venus' and 'Prove It'. Although the group looked set for a long and distinguished career, the follow-up, *Adventure*, was a lesser work and the group broke up in 1978. Since then both Verlaine and Lloyd pursued solo careers with mixed results. In November 1991, Verlaine, Lloyd, Smith and Ficca revived Television and spent the ensuing time rehearsing for a comeback album for Capitol Records. They returned to Britain and made an appearance at the 1992 Glastonbury Festival.
●ALBUMS: *Marquee Moon* (Elektra 1978)★★★★, *Adventure* (Elektra 1979)★★★, *The Blow Up* rec. live 1978, cassette only (ROIR 1983)★★, *Television* (Capitol 1993)★★.

TEMPEST

Initially comprising Mark Clarke (bass), Jon Hiseman (drums), Allan Holdsworth (guitar) and Paul Williams (vocals), the Tempest were formed after Clarke and Hiseman's departure from Colosseum, though on this occasion they favoured a more conventional rock sound than the jazz-rock experimentation of their former band. They recruited Williams, already an established vocalist through his work with Zoot Money, John Mayall and Juicy Lucy. Holdsworth had previously made his recorded debut with 'Igginbottom. In 1973

they recorded their debut album for Bronze Records, *Jon Hiseman's Tempest*, and began the first of numerous continental tours. Despite a receptive European market, the group lost the services of Williams in June 1973. Holdsworth also left a month later, subsequently joining Soft Machine then Level 42. The remaining members recruited Ollie Halsall as guitarist. This line-up played at the Reading Festival in August 1973 and recorded *Living In Fear*. However, by the following year the group had broken up permanently. Halsall subsequently worked with John Otway, while Hiseman put together a new version of his former group known as Colosseum II. Clarke later worked with Uriah Heep, among others. This Tempest should not be confused with an early 80s UK group of the same name.
●ALBUMS: *Jon Hiseman's Tempest* (Bronze 1973)★★★, *Living In Fear* (Bronze 1974)★★★.

10CC

The formation of 10cc in 1970 represented the birth of a Manchester supergroup. The line-up - Eric Stewart (b. 20 January 1945, Manchester, England; vocals/guitar), Lol Creme (b. Lawrence Creme, 19 September 1947, Manchester, England; vocals/guitar), Kevin Godley (b. 7 October 1945, Manchester, England; vocals/drums) and Graham Gouldman (b. 10 May 1945, Manchester, England; vocals/guitar) - boasted years of musical experience stretching back to the mid-60s. Stewart was a former member of both Wayne Fontana And The Mindbenders and the Mindbenders; Gouldman had played in the Mockingbirds and written many hits for artists such as Herman's Hermits, the Yardbirds, the Hollies and Jeff Beck; Godley And Creme had worked in various session groups, including Hotlegs, which spawned 10cc. After working with Neil Sedaka, the 10cc ensemble launched their own recording career on Jonathan King's UK label with the 50s doo-wop pastiche 'Donna'. The song reached number 2 in the UK chart, spearheading a run which continued almost uninterrupted until the end of the decade. 10cc specialized in reinterpreting pop's great tradition by affectionately adopting old styles and introducing them to new teenage audiences. At the same time, their wit, wordplay and subtle satire appealed to an older audience, who appreciated mild irony, strong musicianship and first rate production. The chart-topping 'Rubber Bullets', the high school romp 'The Dean And I', the sardonic 'Wall Street Shuffle', zestful 'Silly Love' and mock-philosophical 'Life Is A Minestrone' were all delightful slices of 70s pop and among the best singles of their time. In 1975, the group achieved their most memorable hit with the tragi-comic UK chart-topper 'I'm Not In Love', a song that also brought them success in the USA. The group continued its peak period with the mischievous 'Art For Art Sake' and bizarre travelogue 'I'm Mandy Fly Me' before internal strife undermined their progress. In 1976, the group split in half as Godley And Creme pursued work in video production and as a

recording duo. Stewart and Gouldman retained the 10cc tag and toured with a line-up comprising Tony O'Malley (keyboards), Rick Fenn (guitar) and Stuart Tosh (drums). The streamlined 10cc continued to chart with the over-sweetened 'The Things We Do For Love' and the mock-reggae chart topper 'Dreadlock Holiday'. Nevertheless, it was generally agreed that their recordings lacked the depth, invention, humour and charm of the original line-up. The hits ceased after 1982 and Stewart and Gouldman went on to pursue other ventures. The former produced Sad Cafe and collaborated with Paul McCartney, while the more industrious Gouldman produced Gilbert O'Sullivan and the Ramones before forming the duo Wax, with Andrew Gold. 10cc issued a new album in 1992 after Gouldman and Stewart began writing songs with each other after a long break. Godley and Creme joined in during the recording, although they did not participate in any writing. The moderate reception the album received seemed to indicate that a full-scale reunion would not take place. Their back catalogue of quality pop songs will continue to be highly respected, although the 1994 live album was a reunion that sounded as though they were doing it as a penance.
●ALBUMS: *10cc* (UK 1973)★★★, *Sheet Music* (UK 1974)★★★, *The Original Soundtrack* (Mercury 1975)★★★, *How Dare You* (Mercury 1976)★★, *Deceptive Bends* (Mercury 1977)★★, *Live And Let Live* (Mercury 1977)★★, *Bloody Tourists* (Mercury 1978)★★, *Look Hear!* (Mercury 1980)★★, *Ten Out Of 10* (Mercury 1981)★★, *10cc In Concert* (Pickwick 1982)★★, *Window In The Jungle* (Mercury 1983)★★, *Meanwhile* (Polydor 1992)★★, *10cc Live* (Creative Man 1994)★.
●COMPILATIONS: *10cc - The Greatest Hits* (UK 1975)★★, *Greatest Hits 1972-1978* (Mercury 1979)★★★★, *The Early Years* (1993)★★, *Food For Thought* (1993), *The Very Best Of* (Mercury 1997)★★★★.
●VIDEOS: *Live In Concert* (VCL 1986), *Live At The International Music Show* (Video Collection 1987), *Changing Faces, The Very Best Of* (Channel 5 1988).
●FURTHER READING: *The 10cc Story*, George Tremlett.

TERRY AND THE PIRATES

This US rock band's complex history began in 1970 when the group's driving force, Terry Dolan, a former veteran of San Francisco's folk circuit, embarked on a recording career. Several local musicians, including John Cipollina and Nicky Hopkins from Quicksilver Messenger Service, and future Steve Miller Band guitarist Greg Douglas assisted a project which, although never released, established the idea of a part-time group. Terry And The Pirates never boasted a settled line-up, but its fluid concept, free from commercial restraints, evoked the spirit of the 'classic' San Franciscan era, particularly with respect to Cipollina's inventive, improvisational guitar work. During their constantly changing line-up they included Lonnie Turner (Steve Miller Band), David Weber, Jim

McPherson and Hutch Hutchinson (Copperhead and Raven) and Jeff Myer (Savage Resurrection and Jesse Colin Young's band). Their albums feature material compiled from various sources, but it is for an in-concert prowess that the Pirates will be remembered. Cipollina's death in 1989 has robbed Dolan of his surest lieutenant; *Silverado Trail* was a fitting tribute to this excellent musician's talent.

●ALBUMS: *Too Close For Comfort* (Wild Bunch 1979)★★★, *The Doubtful Handshake* (Line 1980)★★★, *Wind Dancer* (Rag baby 1981)★★★, *Rising Of The Moon* (1982)★★★, *Acoustic Rangers* (1988)★★★, *Silverado Trail* (1990)★★★.

TERRY DACTYL AND THE DINOSAURS

This UK jugband-cum-skiffle group enjoyed a concurrent career as Brett Marvin And The Thunderbolts. Little effort was spared to hide this fact, even though each 'act' was signed to different recording companies. The Dinosaurs enjoyed the patronage of producer/entrepreneur Jonathan King, who signed them to his UK label. Their debut single, 'Seaside Shuffle', reached number 2 in 1972, while the following year the group scored a minor chart entry with 'On A Saturday Night'. The 'Brett Marvin' appellation was fully resurrected when further releases proved unsuccessful, while vocalist/keyboard player Jona Lewie later embarked on a solo career.

THIN LIZZY

Formed in Dublin, Eire, in 1969, this fondly remembered hard-rocking group comprised Phil Lynott (b. 20 August 1951, Dublin, Eire, d. 4 January 1986; vocals/bass), Eric Bell (b. 3 September 1947, Belfast, Northern Ireland; guitar) and Brian Downey (b. 27 January 1951, Dublin, Eire; drums). After signing to Decca Records, they issued two albums, neither of which charted. A change of fortune occurred after they recorded a novelty rock version of the traditional 'Whiskey In The Jar'. The single reached the UK Top 10 and popularized the group's blend of Irish folk and strident guitar work. The group then underwent a series of line-up changes during early 1974. Bell was replaced by Gary Moore and two more temporary guitarists were recruited, Andy Gee and John Cann. The arrival of guitarists Brian Robertson (b. 12 September 1956, Glasgow, Scotland) and Scott Gorham (b. 17 March 1951, Santa Monica, California, USA) stabilized the group as they entered their most productive phase. A series of UK concerts throughout 1975 saw the group make considerable headway. 1976 was the breakthrough year with the acclaimed *Jailbreak* hitting the charts. The driving macho celebration of 'The Boys Are Back In Town' reached the UK Top 10 and US Top 20 and was voted single of the year by the influential *New Musical Express*. In early 1977 Robertson was forced to leave the group due to a hand injury following a fight and was replaced by the returning Moore. Another UK Top 20 hit followed with the scathing 'Don't Believe A Word', drawn from *Johnny The Fox*. Moore then returned to Colosseum and the recovered Robertson took his place. Both 'Dancin' In The Moonlight' and *Bad Reputation* were UK Top 10 hits and were soon followed by the excellent double album, *Live And Dangerous*. In 1979 the group scaled new commercial heights with such Top 20 singles as 'Waiting For An Alibi' and 'Do Anything You Want To', plus the best-selling *Black Rose*. The torturous line-up changes continued apace. Robertson again left and joined Wild Horses. Moore returned, but within a year was replaced by Midge Ure (formerly of Slik and the Rich Kids). By late 1979, the peripatetic Ure had moved on to Ultravox and was replaced by Snowy White. In early 1980, Lynott married Caroline Crowther, daughter of the television personality Leslie Crowther. After recording some solo work, Lynott reunited with Thin Lizzy for *Chinatown*, which included the controversial Top 10 single, 'Killer On The Loose'. The heavily promoted *Adventures Of Thin Lizzy* maintained their standing, before White bowed out on *Renegade*. He was replaced by John Sykes, formerly of the Tygers Of Pan Tang. One more album, *Thunder And Lightning*, followed before Lynott split up the group in the summer of 1984. A posthumous live album, *Life-Live*, was issued at the end of that year. Its title took on an ironically macabre significance two years later when Lynott died of heart failure and pneumonia after a drugs overdose. Four months later, in May 1986, Thin Lizzy re-formed for the Self Aid concert organized in Eire by Bob Geldof, who replaced Lynott on vocals for the day. The 90s found Brian Robertson touring with tribute band, Ain't Lizzy, while the original group's name remained on the lips of many young groups as a primary influence.

●ALBUMS: *Thin Lizzy* (Decca 1971)★★, *Shades Of A Blue Orphanage* (Decca 1972)★★, *Vagabonds Of The Western World* (Decca 1973)★★★, *Night Life* (Vertigo 1974)★★★, *Fighting* (Vertigo 1975)★★★, *Jailbreak* (Vertigo 1976)★★★★, *Johnny The Fox* (Vertigo 1976)★★★, *Bad Reputation* (Vertigo 1977)★★★, *Live And Dangerous* (Vertigo 1978)★★★★, *Black Rose* (Vertigo 1979)★★★, *Renegade* (Vertigo 1981)★★, *Thunder And Lightning* (Vertigo 1983)★★, *Life-Live* double album (Vertigo 1983)★★, *BBC Radio 1 Live In Concert* rec. 1983 (Windsong 1992)★★★.

●COMPILATIONS: *Remembering - Part One* (Decca 1976)★★, *The Continuing Saga Of The Ageing Orphans* (Decca 1979)★★, *Rockers* (Decca 1981)★★, *Adventures Of Thin Lizzy* (Vertigo 1981)★★★, *Lizzy Killers* (Vertigo 1983)★★★, *The Collection* double album (Castle 1985)★★★, *The Best Of Phil Lynott And Thin Lizzy* (Telstar 1987)★★★, *Dedication - The Best Of Thin Lizzy* (Vertigo 1991)★★★★, *The Peel Sessions* (Strange Fruit 1994)★★, *Wild One - The Very Best Of ...* (Mercury 1995)★★★★.

●VIDEOS: *Live And Dangerous* (1986), *Dedication* (1991).

●FURTHER READING: *Songs For While I'm Away*, Philip

Lynott. *Thin Lizzy*, Larry Pryce. *Philip*, Philip Lynott. *Thin Lizzy: The Approved Biography*, Chris Salewicz. *My Boy: The Philip Lynott Story*, Philomena Lynott with Jackie Hayden.

THOMPSON, DANNY

b. April 1939, London, England. An expressive, inventive double bass player, Thompson became established in British jazz circles through his work with Tubby Hayes. In 1964 he joined Alexis Korner's Blues Incorporated where he forged an intuitive partnership with drummer Terry Cox following John Marshall's departure. Three years later the duo formed the rhythm section in Pentangle, a folk 'supergroup' which featured singer Jacquie McShee and guitarists John Renbourn and Bert Jansch. Thompson remained with this seminal quintet until their demise in 1972 but forged a concurrent career as a leading session musician. He appeared on releases by Donovan, Cliff Richard ('Congratulations') and Rod Stewart ('Maggie May'), but was acclaimed for peerless contributions to albums by folk singers Nick Drake and John Martyn. The bassist's collaborations with the latter were particularly of note (and their legendary drinking sessions) and their working relationship spanned several excellent albums, including *Solid Air*, *Inside Out* and *Live At Leeds*. A notorious imbiber, Thompson then found his workload and confidence diminishing. He successfully conquered his alcohol problem and resumed session work with typically excellent contributions to releases by Kate Bush, David Sylvian and Talk Talk. In 1987 the bassist formed his own group, Whatever, and recorded new age and world music collections. In the 90s his remarkable dexterity was heard on regular tours with Richard Thompson, the only criticism received was that Thompson (Danny) should have been given a microphone in addition to Thompson (Richard), as the inter-song banter was hilarious. In the mid-90s he was the regular bassist with Everything But The Girl, but continued with his other solo projects and recorded with Richard Thompson. He remains a leading instrumentalist, respected for his sympathetic and emotional style on the stand-up bass. Thompson is a giant, both in stature and in his contribution to jazz and rock or whatever. Should the music ever desert him, Thompson could carve a career as a stand-up comic.
●ALBUMS: *Whatever* (Hannibal 1987)★★★, *Whatever Next* (Antilles/New Direction 1989)★★★, with Toumani Diabate, Ketama *Songhai* (Hannibal 1989)★★★, *Elemental* (Antilles/New Direction 1990)★★★, with Richard Thompson *Live At Crawley 1993* (What Disc 1995)★★★, *Singing The Storm* (Cooking Vinyl 1996)★★★, with Richard Thompson *Industry* (Parlophone 1997)★★★.

THREE DEGREES

Protégées of producer/songwriter Richard Barrett, Fayette Pickney, Linda Turner and Shirley Porter had a

US hit with their first single, 'Gee Baby (I'm Sorry)', in 1965. This Philadelphia-based trio, sponsored by Kenny Gamble and Leon Huff, secured further pop success the next year with 'Look In My Eyes', but struggled to sustain this momentum until 1970, when their emphatic reworking of the Chantels' standard, 'Maybe', returned them to the chart. By this point Sheila Ferguson and Valerie Holiday had joined the line-up in place of Turner and Porter. The Three Degrees' golden period came on signing with Philadelphia International. They shared vocals with MFSB on 'TSOP', the theme song to television's successful *Soul Train* show. This US pop and R&B number 1 preceded the trio's international hits, 'Year Of Decision' and 'When Will I See You Again?' (both 1974). These glossy performances were particularly popular in the UK, where the group continued to chart, notably with the Top 10 hits, 'Take Good Care Of Yourself' (1975), 'Woman In Love' and 'My Simple Heart' (both 1979). Helen Scott appeared on the 1976 album *Standing Up For Love*. Now signed to Ariola Records, the Three Degrees' releases grew increasingly bland as they emphasized the cabaret element suppressed in their early work. Fêted by royalty - Prince Charles stated they were his favourite group after booking them for his 30th birthday party - in the 80s the group were resident in the UK where they were a fixture on the variety and supper-club circuit. Ferguson entered the 90s as a solo artist, heralded by the release of a remix of 'When Will I See You Again?'. As to their proud heritage as 70s hit-makers of stunning visual appearance, Valerie Holiday has this to add: 'They were wigs. You think anyone would really do that to their hair?'
●ALBUMS: *Maybe* (Roulette 1970)★★★, *Three Degrees* (Philadelphia International 1974)★★★, *International* (Philadelphia International 1975)★★★, *So Much In Love* (1975)★★, *Take Good Care Of Yourself* (1975)★★, *The Three Degrees Live* (Philadelphia International 1975)★★, *Three Degrees Live In Japan* (Columbia 1975)★★, *Standing Up For Love* (1977)★★, *The Three Degrees* (Ariola 1978)★★, *New Dimensions* (Ariola 1978)★★, *3D* (1979)★★, *Three Degrees And Holding* (1989)★★, *Woman In Love* (1993)★★. Solo: Fayette Pickney *One Degree* (1979)★.
●COMPILATIONS: *Gold* (K-Tel 1980)★★, *Hits Hits Hits* (Hallmark 1981)★★, *20 Golden Greats* (1984)★★★, *The Complete Swan Recordings* (1992)★★, *The Roulette Years* (Sequel 1995)★★, *A Collection Of Their 20 Greatest Hits* (Columbia 1996)★★★.

THREE DOG NIGHT

This highly successful US harmony rock trio formed in 1968 with a line-up comprising Danny Hutton (b. Daniel Anthony Hutton 10 September 1942, Buncrana, Eire), Cory Wells (b. 5 February 1942, Buffalo, New York, USA) and Chuck Negron (b. Charles Negron, 8 June 1942, New York, USA). The three lead singers were backed by Jim Greenspoon (b. 7 February 1948,

Los Angeles, California, USA; organ), Joe Schermie (b. 12 February 1948, Madison, Wisconsin, USA; bass), Mike Allsup (b. 8 March 1947, Modesto, California, USA; guitar) and Floyd Sneed (b. 22 November 1943, Calgary, Alberta, USA; drums). With their distinctive and some-times extraordinary harmonic blend, the group regis-tered an impressive 21 *Billboard* Top 40 hits between 1969 and 1975. Their startling version of Lennon/McCartney's 'It's For You' typified the group at their best, but it was their original arrangements of the work of less well-known writers that brought welcome exposure and considerable royalties to fresh talent. Both Nilsson and Laura Nyro first glimpsed the Top 10 courtesy of Three Dog Night's covers of 'One' and 'Eli's Coming', respectively. The risqué 'Mama Told Me Not To Come' provided the same service for Randy Newman while also giving the group their first number 1 in 1970. During the next two years they registered two further US chart toppers, 'Joy To The World' (composed by Hoyt Axton) and 'Black And White' (a UK hit for reggae group Greyhound). Always ready to record promising material and adapt it to their distinctive harmonic blend, they brought vicarious US chart success to Russ Ballard's 'Liar' and Leo Sayer's UK number 1 'The Show Must Go On'. By the early 70s, there were gradual changes in the trio's back-up musicians, with several members of Rufus joining during 1976. The departure of Danny Hutton (replaced by Jay Gruska) proved a body blow, however, and precipitated the group's decline and disbandment. During 1981, they reunited briefly with Hutton but failed to retrieve past chart glo-ries. The strength of Three Dog Night lay in the power of their harmonies and the strength of the material they adapted. In the age of the singer-songwriter, they were seldom applauded by critics but their inventive arrangements struck a chord with the public to the tune of 10 million-selling records and total sales of over 90 million. Three Dog Night brought a fresh approach to the art of covering seemingly uncommercial material and demonstrated how a strong song can be translated into something approaching a standard.

●ALBUMS: *Three Dog Night* (Dunhill 1969)★★★, *Suitable For Framing* (Dunhill 1969)★★, *Captured Live At The Forum* (Dunhill 1969)★★, *It Ain't Easy* (Dunhill 1970)★★★★, *Naturally* (Dunhill 1970)★★, *Golden Bisquits* (Dunhill 1971)★★★★, *Harmony* (Dunhill 1971)★★★, *Seven Separate Fools* (Dunhill 1972)★★★, *Around The World With Three Dog Night* (Dunhill 1973)★★, *Cyan* (Dunhill 1973)★★, *Hard Labor* (Dunhill 1974)★★, *Coming Down Your Way* (ABC 1975)★★, *American Pastime* (ABC 1976)★★, *It's A Jungle* (Lamborghini 1983)★.

●COMPILATIONS: *Joy To The World - Their Greatest Hits* (Dunhill 1975)★★★, *The Best Of* (Dunhill 1989)★★★, *Celebrate: The Three Dog Night Story* (1993)★★, *That Ain't The Way To Have Fun: Greatest Hits* (Connoisseur Collection 1995)★★★.

TITELMAN, RUSS

b. 16 August 1944, Los Angeles, California, USA. Titelman grew up in the hot musical environment that was 50s Los Angeles, and quickly made contacts that aided him throughout his long career in the entertain-ment business. The most important of these was Phil Spector. After making his debut as a guitarist on the Paris Sisters' 'Be My Boy' in 1961, Titelman became a full-time member of the Spectors Three Vocal Trio. By the following year he had graduated from high school and started studying drama at Los Angeles City College. However, he soon elected to return to the music industry, and entered the studio with friends to record a song entitled 'Just A Little Touch Of Your Love'. Songwriter Barry Mann then took Titelman to New York, where he wrote songs for the Cinderellas - 'Baby, Baby (I Still Love You)' - among others. He also worked with Carole King as his arranger, and provided the Chiffons and Lesley Gore with songs. Brian Wilson of the Beach Boys was his co-writer on two songs, 'Sheri, She Needs Me' and 'Guess I'm Dumb', the latter recorded by Glen Campbell. In 1964 he joined the *Shindig* television house band, at which time he also appeared on Righteous Brothers and Phil Ochs sessions. Moving into film work, he collaborated with Jack Nitzsche on *Village Of The Giants* and a rejected score for *Candy*, before recording 'Memo From Turner' with Ry Cooder and Randy Newman for the Mick Jagger film, *Performance*. That soundtrack started Titelman's 25 year association with Warner Brothers Records. Through his friendship with Lowell George he produced Little Feat's debut album, but he did not become a full-time staff member at Warners until July 1971, 'because I was like a hippie and I didn't want a full-time job.' He became friend and producer to Randy Newman, and through the 70s worked on projects with James Taylor, Graham Central Station, Rickie Lee Jones and George Harrison. In the early 80s he produced for Chaka Khan, and was co-producer on Paul Simon's *Hearts And Bones*. Outside of mainstream rock and pop, his work with jazz and R&B artists has paired him with George Benson, David Sanborn, Womack And Womack and Patti Austin. From 1989-94 he worked extensively with Eric Clapton, and many cite his contributions to *Journeyman*, *24 Nights*, *Unplugged* and *From The Cradle* as crucial to Clapton's renaissance.

TITUS GROAN

Comprising Stuart Cowell (keyboards, guitar, vocals), John Lee (bass), Tony Priestland (saxophone, flute, oboe) and Jim Toomey (drums), this UK progressive rock group took their name from the central character of Mervyn Peake's gothic novel - in a variation on the Tolkien/*Lord Of The Rings* fixation expressed by many similar groups of the time. Otherwise there were few distinctive qualities immediately apparent to the lis-tener on hearing their two 1970 releases for Dawn

Records. The single, 'Open The Door Homer', shared a lack of conviction with the attendant self-titled debut album. Though the use of wind instruments offered fresh possibilities, the group's lack of cohesive song-writing ability ensured that these were not utilized. The group broke up shortly after the release of the album, which was eventually reissued on CD by See For Miles Records in 1989. Toomey later joined the Tourists.

●ALBUMS: *Titus Groan* (Dawn 1970)★★.

TOSH, PETER

b. Winston Hubert McIntosh, 19 October 1944, Westmoreland, Jamaica, West Indies, d. 11 September 1987, Kingston, Jamaica. Of all the reggae singers from the mid-60s, none 'came on strong' like Peter Tosh, which he declared in his anthem, 'I'm The Toughest'. It was he who provided the bite to Bob Marley's bark in the original Wailers, and it was he who appeared most true to the rude boy image that the group fostered during the ska era. Tosh was the first to emerge from the morass of doo-wop wails and chants that constituted the Wailers' early records, recording as Peter Tosh or Peter Touch And The Wailers on 'Hoot Nanny Hoot', 'Shame And Scandal', and 'Maga Dog', the latter another theme for the singer. He also made records without the Wailers and with Rita Anderson, later to become Rita Marley. The Wailers were a loose band by 1966; Bob Marley went to America to look for work, and Tosh and Neville 'Bunny Wailer' Livingstone either recorded together or separately. At some point Tosh ran into trouble with the law and spent a brief period in prison, probably on marijuana charges. When he was not working with the Wailers, he recorded solo material ('Maga Dog' again, or 'Leave My Business') with producer Joe Gibbs, once more retaining his ferocious vocal style.

When the Wailers worked with Leslie Kong in 1969 Tosh was at the forefront with 'Soon Come' and 'Stop The Train', but at Lee Perry's Wailers sessions (1970-71) he was often reduced to harmonizing, save for three mighty tracks: '400 Years', an attack on slavery, 'No Sympathy', where Tosh equated rejection in love with the lot of the black ghetto resident, and 'Downpresser', another anti-oppression statement and perhaps his best ever record. When the Wailers split from Perry and joined Island Records, the writing was on the wall for Tosh; Island apparently preferred Marley's cooler, more sympathetic style, and despite contributing 'Get Up Stand Up' to *Burnin'*, the band's second album for the label, both Tosh and Bunny Wailer quit the group in 1973. Tosh concentrated on work for his own label, Intel Diplo HIM (meaning: Intelligent Diplomat for His Imperial Majesty), and signed to Virgin in 1976. The patronage of Mick Jagger at Rolling Stones Records, which he joined in 1978, nearly gave him a chart hit with a cover of the Temptations' 'Don't Look Back'. Reggae fans complained that Jagger's voice was louder than Tosh's in the mix. *Bush Doctor*, his first album for

the label, sold well, but *Mystic Man* and *Wanted, Dread & Alive* did not. He also released three albums with EMI, the last, *No Nuclear War*, his best since *Legalize It*. The record won the first best reggae album Grammy award in March 1988, but by then Tosh was dead, shot in a robbery at his home in Kingston in September 1987. The 'tuffest' reggae singer of all had finally succumbed to the gun.

●ALBUMS: *Legalize It* (Virgin 1976)★★★★, *Equal Rights* (Virgin 1977)★★★★, *Bush Doctor* (Rolling Stones 1978)★★★★, *Mystic Man* (Rolling Stones/EMI 1979)★★★, *Wanted, Dread & Alive* (Rolling Stones/Dynamic 1981)★★★, *Mama Africa* (Intel Diplo/EMI 1983)★★★, *Captured Live* (EMI 1984)★★★, *No Nuclear War* (EMI 1987)★★★.

●COMPILATIONS: *The Toughest* (Parlophone 1988)★★★, *The Gold Collection* (EMI 1996)★★★.

●VIDEOS: *Live* (1986), *Downpresser Man* (1988), *Red X* (1993).

TOTO

The experienced Los Angeles session team of Bobby Kimball (b. Robert Toteaux, 29 March 1947; vocals), Steve Lukather (b. 4 October 1957, Los Angeles, USA; guitar), David Paitch (b. 25 June 1954, Los Angeles, USA; keyboards/vocals, son of Marty Paitch), Steve Porcaro (b. 2 September 1957, Los Angeles; keyboards/vocals), David Hungate (b. Los Angeles, USA; bass) and Jeff Porcaro (b. 1 April 1954, Los Angeles, USA; d. September 1992; drums) decided in 1978 to begin functioning in their own right after years of blithe dedication to the music of others on tour and disc. A couple of Toto albums found over a million buyers each but, overall, this rather faceless group met moderate success with moderate records - penned mainly by Paitch - on which polished, close-miked vocal harmonies floated effortlessly over layers of treated sound. 1979's *Toto* was attended by a smash hit in 'Hold The Line' but the band's most commercial period was 1982-3 when the Grammy award-winning *Toto IV* spawned two international hits with the stunningly atmospheric 'Africa' and 'Rosanna', as well as the US Top 10 single, 'I Won't Hold You Back'. The following year, Kimball and Hungate were replaced by, respectively, Dave Fergie Frederikson (b. 15 May 1951, Louisiana, Missouri) and Mike, another Porcaro sibling (b. 29 May 1955, Los Angeles, USA). Sales of *Isolation* and the group's soundtrack to the science fiction film *Dune* were poor, but some lost ground was regained when it became known that Toto were responsible for the backing track of USA For Africa's single 'We Are The World'. With a new lead singer in Joseph Williams, the group made the big time again with 'I'll Be Over You', a composition by Lukather and Randy Goodrun from 1986's *Fahrenheit*. Two years later, Toto re-entered the US Top 40, with 'Pamela' (from *The Seventh One*), produced to the expected slick standard by Earth, Wind And Fire's George Massenburg and Little Feat's Bill Payne. By then, Steve Porcaro had returned to employment in the studios from which he and the rest had emerged. Jeff Porcaro died in 1992 after a heart attack caused by an allergic reaction to pesticide. His replacement on subsequent British dates was session drummer Simon Phillips.

●ALBUMS: *Toto* (Columbia 1978)★★★, *Hydra* (Columbia 1979)★★, *Turn Back* (Columbia 1981)★★, *Toto IV* (Columbia 1982)★★★★, *Isolation* (Columbia 1984)★★, *Dune* (Polydor 1984)★, *Fahrenheit* (Columbia 1986)★★, *The Seventh One* (Columbia 1988)★★★, *Kingdom Of Desire* (Columbia 1992)★★, *Absolutely Live* (1993)★, *Tambu* (Columbia 1995)★★.

●COMPILATIONS: *Past To Present 1977-1990* (Columbia 1990)★★★.

TOURISTS

A UK power-pop group of the late 70s, the Tourists were notable as the first setting in which the David A. Stewart-Annie Lennox partnership came into the spotlight. The band grew out of an earlier duo formed by ex-Longdancer guitarist Stewart (b. 9 September 1952, Sunderland, Tyne And Wear, England) with fellow Sunderland singer-songwriter Pete Coombes who had been a member of Peculiar Star. The pair played folk clubs and cabaret around Europe in 1974-76. Returning to London, they met Lennox (b 25 December 1954, Aberdeen, Scotland) a former Royal Academy of Music student who had toured with jazz-rock big band Red Brass. As Catch they made one single, 'Black Blood' (Logo 1977), before re-forming as the five-strong Tourists with Jim Toomey (drums) and Eddie Chin (bass). The first album appeared on Logo Records in 1979, recorded with German producer Conny Plank. All the songs, including two minor hit singles, were by Coombes, but the band's first real success came with a revival of the 1963 Dusty Springfield hit 'I Only Want To Be With You' and 'So Good To Be Back Home Again', which both reached the Top 10. After a contractual dispute with Logo, the Tourists made *Luminous Basement* for RCA, produced by Tom Allom at George Martin's studio in Montserrat. It sold poorly and after a final UK tour The band split in 1980. Coombes and Chin formed Acid Drops while Lennox and Stewart re-emerged the next year as the Eurythmics.

●ALBUMS: *The Tourists* (Logo 1979)★★, *Reality Effect* (Logo 1979)★★★★, *Luminous Basement* (RCA 1980)★★★.

TOWER OF POWER

Formed in 1967 in Oakland, California, USA, this durable group - Rufus Miller (vocals), Greg Adams (trumpet), Emilio 'Mimi' Castillo (b. Detroit, Michigan; saxophone), Steve Kupka (saxophone), Lenny Pickett (saxophone), Mic Gillette (horns), Willie Fulton (guitar), Francis Prestia (bass), Brent Byer (percussion) and David Garibaldi (drums) - was originally known as the Motowns/Motown Soul Band. One of several Bay Area groups preferring soul to the prevalent acid-rock

sound, Tower Of Power's debut album, *East Bay Grease* (1969), followed several popular appearances at San Francisco's Fillmore auditorium. Having now signed to the Warner Brothers Records label, the group's next two albums, *Bump City* and *Tower Of Power* each produced a hit single in 'You're Still A Young Man' and 'So Very Hard To Go', respectively, but their progress was hampered by a recurring vocalist problem. Miller was replaced, first by Rick Stevens and then Lenny Williams (b. 1945, San Francisco, California, USA), while the rhythm section also proved unstable. Curiously, the horn section stayed intact and was much in demand for session work, a factor that doubtlessly kept the parent group intact despite dwindling commercial fortunes. 'Don't Change Horses (In The Middle Of A Stream)' (1974) was the group's last US Top 30 single, but although they switched to Columbia in 1976, the Power returned to Warners after three lacklustre albums. Still bedevilled by personnel changes, recordings under their own name are now infrequent, but the brass players remain part of the west coast backroom circle for their work with, among others, Huey Lewis and Phil Collins.

●ALBUMS: *East Bay Grease* (San Fransisco 1969)★★★, *Bump City* (Warners 1971)★★★, *Tower Of Power* (Warners 1973)★★★★, *Back To Oakland* (Warners 1974)★★★★, *Urban Renewal* (Warners 1975)★★★★, *In The Slot* (Warners 1975)★★★, *Live And In Living Colour* (Warners 1976)★★★★, *Ain't Nothin' Stoppin' Us Now* (Columbia 1976)★★★, *We Came To Play!* (Columbia 1978)★★★, *Back On The Streets* (Columbia 1979)★★★, *Tower Of Power* (1982)★★★, *Power* (1988)★★★, *Direct* (1988)★★★, *Monster On A Leash* (Epic 1991)★★★, *Souled Out* (Epic 1995)★★★.

●COMPILATIONS: *What Is Hip?* (Edsel 1986)★★★★.

TRACTOR

One of the classic progressive rock bands, Tractor have enjoyed a heightened profile over recent years which has as much to do with the former members' vociferous self-publicity as any enduring quality of music. A trio of Steve Clayton (keyboards, bass, drums, flute), Dave Addison (bass) and Jim Milne (guitar, vocals, bass), Tractor were formed in Rochdale, Yorkshire, England, originally as the Way We Live. Their self-titled debut album for John Peel's Dandelion Records in 1972 (for whom the Way We Live had also recorded) was accompanied by a single, 'Stony Glory'. Neither set the charts alight, but the album demonstrated a greater degree of songwriting fluency than many of their peers. At times the material was palpably heavy rock, akin to early Black Sabbath, while at others the group wove more intricate, psychedelic rock ballads. With strange sound effects and impenetrable lyrics, the result was not altogether unpleasing. The album even included a track, 'Ravenscroft 13 Bar Boogie', written in obvious dedication to Peel. However, as with many of the Dandelion acts, it proved to be their sole original album. The group

did reunite in the late 70s as Jim Milne And Tractor, recording singles such as 'Roll The Dice' (1975). Milne then joined punk band the Sneaks before returning to teaching. Clayton took up painting while Addison retrained in computers. In the 90s a series of rather less interesting compilation albums of studio out-takes and demos appeared.
● ALBUMS: *Tractor* (Dandelion 1972)★★★.
● COMPILATIONS: *Worst Enemies* (Sunflower 1991)★★, *Original Masters* (World Wide 1992)★★.

TRAMMPS

This Philadelphia-based group was formed by Earl Young and Jimmy Ellis, two former members of the Volcanoes, who had a local R&B hit with their 'Storm Warning' single. The duo was joined by Dennis Harris (guitar), Ron Kersey (keyboards), John Hart (organ), Stanley Wade (bass) and Michael Thompson (drums), taking their name from a jibe that 'all (they would) ever be is tramps.' Initially the group won its reputation updating 'standards' of which 'Zing Went The Strings Of My Heart' (1972) was a minor hit. They then followed a more individual direction on their own label, Golden Fleece, before enjoying a major UK hit with the excellent 'Hold Back The Night' (1975). Two years later the Trammps completed their *tour de force*, 'Disco Inferno', which featured in the film *Saturday Night Fever*, and irrevocably linked their name to the dancefloor. By this point the line-up had undergone several changes. The group's instigators, Young and Ellis, remained at the helm, alongside Stan and Harold Wade and baritone Robert Upchurch. There changes could not, however, halt the Trammps' commercial slide when the disco bubble burst and their 80s releases made little impression on either the soul or pop charts.
● ALBUMS: *The Legendary Zing Album* (Golden Fleece 1975)★★★, *Trammps* (Golden Fleece 1975)★★★, *Where The Happy People Go* (Atlantic 1976)★★★, *Disco Inferno* (Atlantic 1977)★★, *Trammps III* (Atlantic 1977)★★, *The Whole World's Dancing* (Atlantic 1979)★★, *Mixin' It Up* (Atlantic 1980)★★, *Slipping Out* (Atlantic 1981)★★.
● COMPILATIONS: *The Best Of The Trammps* (Atlantic 1978)★★★★.

TRAMP

A classic example of the whole not matching the component parts, Tramp featured several high-profile veterans of the British blues boom including Mick Fleetwood (drums), Bob Brunning (bass), Danny Kirwan (guitar), Dave Kelly (vocals), Jo Ann Kelly (vocals) and Bob Hall (keyboards). Hall, like Brunning, had earlier been co-leader of the Brunning-Hall Sunflower Blues Band. Tramp made their debut for Music Man Records in 1969 with a self-titled collection that lacked direction or convincing songwriting. Far better were the group's singles, 'Each Day' (1969) and 'Vietnam Rose' (1970). A further album was issued in 1974, by which time the group featured an expanded line-up with Dave Brooks (saxophone) and Ian Morton (percussion) joining the original sextet. Again, however, *Put A Record On* featured nothing towards which an average bar room blues band might not have aspired, and sold poorly. With such high-profile names involved, both Tramp albums have subsequently been reissued on CD.
● ALBUMS: *Tramp* (Music Man 1969)★★, *Put A Record On* (Spark 1974)★★.

TRAVERS, PAT, BAND

Canadian guitarist Pat Travers began his career playing in his brother's band. Having moved to London, he set up a group of his own consisting of Peter 'Mars' Cowling (bass) and drummer Roy Dyke (of Ashton, Gardner And Dyke). In 1976 they played at the Reading Rock Festival, and this led to greater recognition of their debut, *Pat Travers*. In 1977 Nicko McBrain, who subsequently joined Iron Maiden, replaced Roy Dyke. Travers himself turned his talents to songwriting, his music taking a more experimental turn, and being aided by other artists, including Scott Gorham. During their 1977 tour, Clive Edwards replaced McBrain, and Michael Dycke added another guitar. Guitarist Pat Thrall, who had been a member of Automatic Man, and Tommy Aldridge (drums), formerly of Black Oak Arkansas, were recruited to work on *Heat In The Street*, an extremely powerful album. Their relationship with the band was short-lived, however. After the tour to support *Crash And Burn*, Thrall and Aldridge departed in order to work with Ozzy Osbourne. Subsequent recordings featured Sandy Gennaro (drums) and Michael Shrieve (ex-Santana), and were notable for their solid, blues-like sound. In 1984 the line-up of Pat Marchino (drums), Barry Dunaway (bass), Jerry Riggs (guitar) and Travers released *Hot Shot*, an album which was not a commercial success. There was then a lengthy break in Travers' recording career until 1990 when he released *School Of Hard Knocks*. The following year Travers worked again with Thrall, Aldridge and Cowling, touring Japan along with Jerry Riggs and Scott Zymowski, and planning a reunion album, after which came a series of blues-orientated albums, including the well-received *Blues Tracks* and *Blues Magnet*.
● ALBUMS: *Pat Travers* (Polydor 1976)★★★, *Makin' Magic* (Polydor 1977)★★★, *Putting It Straight* (Polydor 1977)★★★, *Heat In The Street* (Polydor 1978)★★★, *Go For What You Know* (Polydor 1979)★★★, *Crash And Burn* (Polydor 1980)★★★, *Radio Active* (Polydor 1981)★★★, *Black Pearl* (Polydor 1982)★★★, *Hot Shot* (Polydor 1984)★★★, *School Of Hard Knocks* (Razor 1990)★★★, *Boom Boom* (Essential 1991)★★★, *Just A Touch* (1993)★★★, *Blues Tracks* (1993)★★★, *Blues Magnet* (Provogue 1994)★★★, *Halfway To Somewhere* (Provogue 1995)★★★, *Lookin' Up* (Provogue 1996)★★★.
● COMPILATIONS: *Anthology Volume 1* (Polydor 1990)★★★★, *Anthology Volume 2* (Polydor 1990)★★★★.
● VIDEOS: *Boom Boom* (1991).

TROWER, ROBIN

b. 9 March 1947, London, England. Guitarist Trower spent his early career in the Paramounts, a popular Southend, Essex-based R&B/beat group which completed five singles between 1963 and 1965. Having briefly worked with a trio dubbed the Jam, he joined several colleagues from his earlier act in Procol Harum. Trower remained in this much-praised unit until 1971, when his desire to pursue a tougher musical style proved incompatible with their well-established grandiose inflections. He initially formed the short-lived Jude with Frankie Miller (vocals), Jim Dewar (bass/vocals) and Clive Bunker (drums, ex-Jethro Tull), but having retained Dewar (formerly with Lulu and Stone The Crows), founded the Robin Trower Band with drummer Reg Isidore. *Twice Removed From Yesterday* and *Bridge Of Sighs* explored a melodic, guitar-based path, redolent of the late-period Jimi Hendrix, whom Robin was often criticized for merely aping. His lyrical technique, offset by Dewar's gritty delivery, nonetheless proved highly popular and the trio achieved considerable success in the USA. Although ex-Sly And Family Stone drummer Bill Lordan replaced Isidore in 1974, *For Earth Below* and *Long Misty Days* maintained the same musical balance. However, Trower's desire for a purer version of R&B resulted in his inviting black producer Don Davis to collaborate on *In City Dreams* and *Caravan To Midnight*. The new style alienated the guitarist's rock audience, while the rock-based *Victims Of The Fury* was bedevilled by weaker material. In 1981 he and Lordan formed BLT with bassist Jack Bruce, but within two years Trower had reconvened the Robin Trower Band with Dewar, David Bronze (bass), Alan Clarke and Bobby Clouter (both drums). *Back It Up* failed to repeat former glories and the artist was then dropped by longtime label, Chrysalis Records. The well-received *Passion*, released independently, engendered a new contract with Atlantic Records, for whom a new line-up of Trower, Bronze, Davey Pattison (vocals) and Pete Thompson (drums) completed *Take What You Need*. Trower is also heavily involved in record production.

●ALBUMS: *Twice Removed From Yesterday* (Chrysalis 1973)★★★, *Bridge Of Sighs* (Chrysalis 1974)★★★★, *For Earth Below* (Chrysalis 1975)★★★, *Robin Trower Live* (Chrysalis 1976)★★★★, *Long Misty Days* (Chrysalis 1976)★★★, *In City Dreams* (Chrysalis 1977)★★, *Caravan To Midnight* (Chrysalis 1978)★★, *Victims Of The Fury* (Chrysalis 1980)★★, *Back It Up* (Chrysalis 1983)★★★, *Beyond The Mist* (Music For Nations 1985)★★★, *Passion* (Gryp 1987)★★★, *Take What You Need* (Atlantic 1988)★★★, *In The Line Of Fire* (Atlantic 1990)★★.

●COMPILATIONS: *Portfolio* (Chrysalis 1987)★★★.

TUBES

Never short of personnel, the Tubes comprised Rick Anderson (b. 1 August 1947, Saint Paul, Minnesota, USA; bass), Michael Cotten (b. 25 January 1950, Kansas City, Missouri, USA; keyboards), Prairie Prince (b. 7 May 1950, Charlotte, North Carolina, USA; drums), Bill Spooner (b. 16 April 1949, Phoenix, Arizona, USA; guitar). Roger Steen (b. 13 November 1949, Pipestone, Minnesota, USA; guitar), Re Styles (b. 3 March 1950, USA; vocals), Fee Waybill (b. John Waldo, 17 September 1950, Omaha, Nebraska, USA; vocals) and Vince Welnick (b. 21 February 1951, Phoenix, Arizona, USA; keyboards). Founder-members Anderson, Spooner and Welmick teamed up in Phoenix in the late 60s, but it was in San Francisco in 1972 that the Tubes were born. Fronted by Waybill, the band's stage act became wilder and crazier, a manic mixture of loud rock music, outrageous theatrics and burlesque. The videos were risqué with scantily clad women, a 'drugged-out superstar' Quay Lude and 'a crippled Nazi', Dr. Strangekiss. The group were signed to A&M Records in 1975 and their debut album, produced by Al Kooper, included the bombastic UK Top 30 hit 'White Punks On Dope'. Their alleged sexism was tempered somewhat during the late 70s. Their fourth album, *Remote Control*, was produced by Todd Rundgren, after which they left A&M for Capitol Records. *The Completion Backward Principle* was regarded as a compromise, despite its AOR potency with flashes of humour. The group's satirical thrust declined due to over-familiarity but prior to their demise, they enjoyed their greatest commercial success with the US Top 10 hit 'She's A Beauty' in 1983.

●ALBUMS: *The Tubes* (A&M 1975)★★, *Young And Rich* (A&M 1976)★★★, *Now* (A&M 1977)★★, *What Do You Want From Your Life* (A&M 1978)★★, *Remote Control* (A&M 1979)★★, *The Completion Backward Principle* (Capitol 1981)★★, *Outside Inside* (Capitol 1983)★★, *Love Bomb* (Capitol 1985)★★.

●COMPILATIONS: *T.R.A.S.H. (Tubes Rarities And Smash Hits)* (A&M 1981)★★★, *The Best Of* (1993)★★★.

TUCKY BUZZARD

A UK hard rock band of the early 70s, Tucky Buzzard comprised David Brown (bass), Paul Francis (drums), Nick Graham (keyboards, ex-End), Tim Henderson (vocals) and Terry Taylor (guitar, ex-End). The group made their debut for Capitol Records with *Warm Slash*, a modestly entertaining hybrid of progressive and hard rock. However, neither that collection nor their 1971 single, 'She's A Striker', managed to push them into the charts, and they were dropped by Capitol shortly afterwards. They signed instead to Deep Purple's Purple Records, making their debut for their new label with *Alright On The Night* and their best single, 'Gold Medallions'. By this time the line-up had shifted with Francis replaced on drums by Chris Johnson while Graham made way for additional guitarist Paul Kendrick. However, none of this was enough to propel them into the mainstream. Their final album included some excellent blues-rock compositions such as 'Bo-Bo's Hampton' but proved to be their final release.

●ALBUMS: *Warm Slash* (Capitol 1969)★★, *Coming On*

Again (Capitol 1971)★★, *Alright On The Night* (Purple 1973)★★★, *Buzzard* (Purple 1973)★★★.

TWILLEY, DWIGHT

b. 6 June 1951, Tulsa, Oklahoma, USA. A crafted performer, renowned for high quality pop, Dwight Twilley scored an impressive US Top 20 hit with his debut release, 'I'm On Fire'. This 1975 single combined elements of rock 'n' roll, the Beatles and Lou Christie, yet its compulsive charm remained contemporary. An attendant album, recorded with long-time associate Phil Seymour (b. 15 May 1952, Tulsa, Oklahoma, USA, d. 17 August 1993, Los Angeles, California, USA), took a year to complete. This delay, incurred when initial recordings proved unsatisfactory, undermined the duo's momentum and, despite critical acclaim, the collection failed to emulate its opening track. Twilley's subsequent releases were equally meritorious, but the singer's love of pop tradition was proving out of step. Seymour later embarked on a solo career and although his former colleague was hampered by record company indecision, the singer did achieve a further US Top 20 entry, 'Girls', in 1984.

●ALBUMS: *Sincerely* (Shelter 1976)★★★, *Twilley Don't Mind* (Arista 1977)★★★, *Twilley* (Arista 1979)★★★, *Blueprint* (1980)★★★, *Scuba Divers* (EMI 1982)★★★, *Jungle* (EMI 1984)★★★, *Wild Dogs* (1986)★★.
●FILMS: *Body Rock* (1984).

TWINK

b. John Alder, 1944, Colchester, Essex, England. As a child influenced by the native rock 'n' roll boom pioneered by Bill Haley and the skiffle of Lonnie Donegan, journeyman drummer John Alder/Twink formed his first group. The Airliners consisted of Alder and several fellow members of the Air Scouts. That group's main claim to fame was an appearance at a talent show hosted by Jim Dale. Alder played the washboard in that group but soon graduated to vocals and rhythm guitar for his next band, the Angels. His third and final skiffle group were the Black Zillions. Then came the Planets, his first rock 'n' roll group and the first time he had drummed, a group moulded in tribute to Gene Vincent's Bluecaps. Further low-key groups included Eddie Lee Cooper And The Trappers and Jimmy Pilgrim And The Strangers. In 1963 he joined the East Anglian group Dane Stevens And The Deepbeats, who played covers of R&B standards by Chuck Berry and Bo Diddley. That group became the subject of interest by Decca Records after the Rolling Stones had confirmed the commercial viability of such energetic music. The Deepbeats eventually became the Fairies. They and Alder made their debut recording in 1964 with a version of Bob Dylan's 'Don't Think Twice It's Alright'. Some argue that this was the first electric rendition of a Dylan song, who at this time had not reached the UK charts. The sessions for the single also featured a young Jimmy Page on guitar, and the record was produced by future Gary Glitter musical director Mike Leander. The Fairies were then booked for a Scottish tour, at which time they were sent gifts by admiring adolescent fans. Alder regularly received bottles of Twink home perm lotion, due to his long curly hair, and this sobriquet was soon adopted as his stage name. However, the Fairies' upward mobility was severely dented when singer Dane Stevens was sentenced to one year in jail after an automobile crash left two dead. The Fairies signed with HMV Records but no further success ensued and Twink then accepted an invitation to join Steve Howe and Keith West in the In Crowd. However, despite a move to psychedelia, that group never added to its existing tally of hit singles and, realizing their name was not in keeping with new developments, renamed themselves Tomorrow. However, the success of Keith West's solo recording of 'Excerpt From A Teenage Opera' led to the dissolution of that group. Junior Wood and Twink later bitterly attacked West in their one-off single as Aquarian Age, '10,000 Words In A Cardboard Box'. Twink then replaced Skip Allen in the Pretty Things. During his time with the Pretty Things Twink joined them in their appearance in the Norman Wisdom film *What's Good For The Goose*, but this was otherwise a lean period for a once great group. He then recorded his first solo album, *Think Pink*, assisted by backing band the Deviants/Social Deviants (which included Mick Farren, who also produced the album, as well as Steve 'Peregrine' Took and old colleague Junior Wood). With the commercial failure of the album Twink relocated to Portugal, but soon returned to form the Pink Fairies with former members of the Deviants. However, he left that group in 1971 and after a spell in Morocco, settled in Cambridge. There he played with a number of underachieving groups including the Last Minute Put Together Boogie Band, which included US singer Bruce Payne who had formerly played the lead in the original American version of *Hair*. That group also jammed with Syd Barrett, with whom Twink formed his next group, Stars. When that venture failed due to a hostile media response, he relocated to London, occasionally playing live with Hawkwind before rejoining the Pink Fairies for a brief six months. Following a serious automobile injury Twink then worked with the Rings, a group who attempted to jump the punk bandwagon. He returned to solo status in 1986 with the release of 'Apocalipstic', a single which also inaugurated his new, self-titled record label. He also acted widely at this time, appearing in television series *Allo Allo*, *David Copperfield* and *Chocky's Challenge*. He rejoined the Pink Fairies for their 1987 reunion tour, where he met members of Plasticland. This resulted in the collaboration *You Need A Fairy Godmother*, released in 1989 on Midnight Records. His second solo album proper, *Mr Rainbow*, came a year later, featuring new interpretations of songs from his extensive back catalogue.

●ALBUMS: *Think Pink* (Polydor 1970)★★, *Mr Rainbow* (Twink 1990)★★.

TWISTED SISTER

Formed in 1976, this New York quintet's original purpose was to provide the antidote to the disco music that was saturating the airwaves during the mid-70s. Featuring Dee Snider (vocals), Eddie Ojeda (guitar), Mark 'The Animal' Mendoza (bass, ex-Dictators), Jay Jay French (guitar) and Tony Petri (drums) they had a bizarre image that borrowed ideas from Kiss, Alice Cooper and the New York Dolls. Musically they combined sexually provocative lyrics and dumb choruses with heavy-duty, metallic rock 'n' roll. A.J. Pero (ex-Cities) took over on drums before the recording of their debut, *Under The Blade*. This was picked up from the independent Secret label by Atlantic Records, following a successful UK appearance at the Reading Festival and a controversial performance on *The Tube* television show in 1982. They never lived up to their initial promise, with successive albums simply regurgitating earlier ideas. Their greatest success was *Stay Hungry*, which cracked the Top 20 album charts on both sides of the Atlantic. It also included the hit single 'I Am, I'm Me', which peaked at number 18 in the UK. Their audience had become bored with them by the time *Come Out And Play* was released and the tour to support it was also a flop. Pero quit and returned to his former group, Cities; Joey 'Seven' Franco (ex-Good Rats) was drafted in as replacement. Snider steered the band in a more melodic direction on *Love Is For Suckers*. The album was stillborn; Atlantic terminated their contract, and the band imploded in 1987. Snider went on to form Desperado, with ex-Gillan guitarist Bernie Torme (subsequently evolving, more permanently, into Widowmaker). Looking back on his days dressing up with his old band, Snider would conclude: 'All that flash and shit wears thin. There's gotta be something beyond it. And there wasn't with Twisted Sister'.
● ALBUMS: *Under The Blade* (Secret 1982)★★, *You Can't Stop Rock 'N' Roll* (Atlantic 1983)★★, *Stay Hungry* (Atlantic 1984)★★★, *Come Out And Play* (Atlantic 1985)★★, *Love Is For Suckers* (Atlantic 1987)★★, *Live* (Music For Nations 1994)★★.

TYMES

Formed in Philadelphia during the 50s, George Williams, George Hilliard, Donald Banks, Albert Berry and Norman Burnett first came together in the Latineers. As the Tymes they secured a major hit with the evocative 'So Much In Love' (1962), a gorgeously simple performance that recalled the bygone doo-wop era while anticipating the sweet harmonies of 70s Philly soul. Further less successful singles then followed as the group entered a somewhat lean patch before a version of 'People' restored them to the charts. The Tymes scored international hits with two 1974 releases, 'You Little Trustmaker' and 'Ms. Grace' (a UK number 1), which pitched the group's harmonies into a modern context. Although the original line-up stayed intact for several years, Hilliard, then Berry, eventually left the group, while two later additions, Terri Gonzalez and Melanie Moore, suggested yet a further shake-up of their image. Such changes, however, failed to sustain the Tymes' chart career beyond 1976.
● ALBUMS: *So Much In Love* (Parkway 1963)★★★★, *The Sound Of The Wonderful Tymes* (Parkway 1963)★★★, *Somewhere* (Parkway 1964)★★, *People* (Direction 1968)★★★, *Trustmaker* (RCA 1974)★★★, *Tymes Up* (RCA 1976)★★, *Turning Point* (RCA 1976)★★, *Digging Their Roots* (RCA 1977)★★.
● COMPILATIONS: *Soul Gems* (Prestige 1990)★★★.

TZUKE, JUDIE

b 1955, London, England, Tzuke is a singer and songwriter whose small degree of commercial success contrasts with the quality of her recorded output. Of Polish extraction, she studied drama as a child and by the age of 15 was setting her poems to music. In 1975 she began writing with Mike Paxman and as Tzuke and Paxo they recorded 'These Are The Laws' for Tony Visconti's Good Earth company. In 1978, she joined Elton John's Rocket label and released the choral 'For You', followed by the epic ballad 'Stay With Me Till Dawn'. Produced by John Punter, it was a big UK hit. Her debut *Welcome To The Cruise* was a slick production and deservedly made the UK Top 20 album chart (number 13). Her most successful Rocket album was *Sports Car*, a lesser work which reached the Top 10. Tzuke also composed with Elton John, sharing credits on 'Give Me The Love' on *21 At 33*. For *Shoot The Moon*, she moved to Chrysalis Records, retaining the same production team of Paxman and keyboards player Paul Muggleton. Subtitled 'The Official Bootleg', *Road Noise* was recorded live. In the mid-80s she made two albums for the independent Legacy label before releasing 'We'll Go Dreaming' in 1989 on Polydor. In 1990 she unsuccessfully released a version of the Beach Boys' 'God Only Knows' on CBS Records and her 1991 album included a remake of her most famous song, 'Stay With Me Till Dawn', which had attained the status of a rock standard, having been anthologized on several compilations of romantic ballads during the 80s. Making guest appearances on *Wonderland* were Brian May and violinist Nigel Kennedy. Tzuke retains a solid following and continues to record excellent albums to limited response. She set up her own label Big Moon with Paxman and Paul Muggleton in 1996.
● ALBUMS: *Welcome To The Cruise* (Rocket 1979)★★★★, *Sports Car* (Rocket 1980)★★★, *I Am Phoenix* (Rocket 1981)★★, *Road Noise* (Chrysalis 1982)★★, *Shoot The Moon* (Chrysalis 1983)★★★, *Ritmo* (Chrysalis 1983)★★, *Judie Tzuke* (Legacy 1985)★★, *The Cat Is Out* (Legacy 1985)★★, *Turning Stones* (Polydor 1989)★★, *Left Hand Talking* (Columbia 1991)★★★, *Wonderland* (1992)★★★, *BBC In Concert* (Windsong 1995)★★★, *Under The Angels* (Big Moon 1996)★★★.
● COMPILATIONS: *The Best Of* (1993)★★★.

U

U-ROY

b. Ewart Beckford, 1942, Kingston, Jamaica, West
Indies. U-Roy began as a sound system DJ in 1961, spinning records for the Doctor Dickies set, later known as
Dickies Dynamic, in such well-known Jamaican venues
as Victoria Pier, Foresters Hall and Emmett Park. His
inspiration was the DJ Winston 'Count' Machuki, who
worked for Coxsone Dodd and subsequently on Prince
Buster's Voice Of The People sound system. By the mid-
60s he was DJ for Sir George The Atomic, based around
Maxfield Avenue in Kingston. Around 1967 he began to
work with King Tubby as DJ for his Home Town Hi-Fi.
From this association developed the whole modern DJ
style; Tubby's work at Duke Reid's studio, where he was
disc-cutter, led U-Roy to discover dub. He found that by
dropping out the vocal track and remixing the
remaining rhythm tracks he created new 'versions' of
much-loved tunes. He began to record a series of special acetate recordings, or dub plates, for exclusive use
on his sound system. The space left by the absent vocal
tracks enabled U-Roy to improvise his own jive-talk raps
or toasts when the sound system played dances. The
effect in the dancehall was immediate and electrifying.
In 1969 U-Roy was invited to play for Dodd's Down Beat
sound system, playing the number 2 set; the number 1
set had King Stitt as DJ. U-Roy became dissatisfied with
playing the latest Dodd music only after Stitt had first
exposed it to dance patrons, and returned to Tubby's.
He then began his recording career in full, recording
two discs for Lee Perry, 'Earth's Rightful Ruler' and 'OK
Corral', before moving to producer Keith Hudson, for
whom he made the outstanding 'Dynamic Fashion Way'.
U-Roy then began recording for Duke Reid, using as
backing tracks Reid's rocksteady hits from 1966-67;
their success was unprecedented. His first record for
Reid, 'Wake The Town', which used Alton Ellis's 'Girl
I've Got A Date' as backing, immediately soared to the
top of both Jamaican radio charts. His next two
releases, 'Rule The Nation' and 'Wear You To The Ball',
soon joined it. These three releases held the top three
positions in the Jamaican charts for 12 weeks during
early 1970. Other sound system DJs were quick to
follow U-Roy, including Dennis Alcapone and Scotty.
The radio stations refused to play DJ music just to give
singers a chance, so big was the demand. U-Roy
recorded 32 tracks for Reid, in the process versioning
almost every rocksteady hit issued on the label and
releasing two albums. By 1973 he was recording for

other producers, including Alvin Ranglin, Bunny Lee,
Glen Brown and Lloyd Charmers as well as self-produc-
tions. However, the rise of the next DJ generation
including Big Youth signalled the partial eclipse of U-
Roy. In 1975 he made a series of albums for producer
Prince Tony Robinson which were leased to Virgin
Records in the UK, wherein the DJ revisited Reid's earlier hits in the then prevalent rockers style. He
appeared at the London Lyceum in August 1976, backed
by a band featuring Channel One stalwarts Sly Dunbar
(bass) and Ansell Collins (organ). He operated his own
sound system, Stur-Gav, featuring Ranking Joe and
selector Jah Screw. When they left after the sound
system was broken up during the turbulent 1980
Jamaican election, it was rebuilt with new DJs Charlie
Chaplin and Josey Wales, and Inspector Willie as
selector. U-Roy continued to record sporadically
throughout the 80s, recording 'Hustling', a single for
Gussie Clarke, in 1984, and two excellent albums for
DJs turned producers Tapper Zukie and Prince Jazzbo,
in 1986 and 1987, respectively. In 1991 he played a successful 'revival' concert at the Hammersmith Palais,
London. U-Roy is the man who is responsible for
putting the DJ on the map, both as recording artist in
Jamaica and as a major indirect influence on the US
rappers. As such his contribution is immense.

● ALBUMS: *Version Galore* (Trojan 1971)★★★★, *U-Roy*
(Attack/Trojan 1974)★★★★, *Dread Inna Babylon* (Virgin
1975)★★★★, *Natty Rebel* (Virgin 1976)★★★, *Dread In A
Africa* (1976)★★★, *U-Roy Meet King Attorney*
(1977)★★★, *Rasta Ambassador* (Virgin 1977)★★★, *Jah
Son Of Africa* (Front Line 1978)★★★, *With Words Of
Wisdom* (Front Line 1979)★★★, *Love Is Not A Gamble*
(Stateline 1980)★★★, *Crucial Cuts* (Virgin 1983)★★★,
Line Up And Come (Tappa 1987)★★★, *Music Addict* (RAS
1987)★★★, as U-Roy And Friends *With A Flick Of My
Musical Wrist* rec. 1970-73 (Trojan 1988)★★★, *True Born
African* (Ariwa 1991)★★★, with Josey Wales *Teacher
Meets The Student* (Sonic Sounds 1992)★★★, *Original DJ*
(Frontline/Virgin 1995)★★★.

● COMPILATIONS: *The Best Of U-Roy* (Live & Love
1977)★★★, *Version Of Wisdom* (Front Line 1990)★★★,
Natty Rebel - Extra Version (Virgin 1991)★★★, *U-Roy CD
Box Set* (Virgin 1991)★★★★, *Super Boss*
(Esoldun/Treasure Isle 1992)★★★.

UFO

This well-regarded UK rock band formed in 1969 when
Andy Parker (drums) joined Phil Mogg (b. 1951,
London, England; vocals), Pete Way (bass) and Mick
Bolton (guitar) in Hocus Pocus. With a name change to
UFO and a musical style that fused progressive space-
rock and good-time boogie, they released three albums
that were successful only in Germany and Japan. In
1974 Bolton quit, to be replaced by Larry Wallis (ex-Pink
Fairies), followed by Bernie Marsden (later of
Whitesnake) and finally Michael Schenker. Securing a
contract with Chrysalis Records they recorded

Phenomenon, a powerful hard rock album which featured the classics 'Rock Bottom' and 'Doctor, Doctor'. Schenker's presence helped to forge their new sound, as he strangled the hard-edged metallic riffs out of his Flying V. A series of strong albums followed, and the band expanded to a five-piece in 1976, with the addition of a keyboardist, initially Danny Peyronel (ex-Heavy Metal Kids) and later Paul Raymond (formerly of Savoy Brown). *Lights Out* and *Strangers In The Night* consolidated the band's success, the latter a superb double live album recorded on their sell-out US tour of 1977. After long-running internal disagreements, Schenker quit in 1978 to rejoin the Scorpions and later form MSG. Paul Chapman (ex-Lone Star) was offered the guitarist's vacancy, having played with the band for short periods on two previous occasions. From this point on, they never recaptured the level of success and recognition they had attained with Schenker. A string of uninspiring albums followed, which lacked both aggression and the departed guitarist's riffs. Paul Raymond joined MSG in 1980, with Neil Carter (ex-Wild Horses) taking his place. Pete Way left after the release of *Mechanix*, eventually forming Waysted and ex-Eddie And The Hot Rods/Damned bassist Paul Gray took over his position. *Making Contact* represented the nadir of the band's creativity, being dated and devoid of the old energy. A farewell UK tour was undertaken in 1983, but it was a sad end for what was originally a fine band. Two years later Mogg resurrected the name with Raymond and Gray, plus ex-Magnum drummer Jim Simpson and the Japanese guitarist Atomic Tommy M. They recorded *Misdemeanor*, which unsuccessfully rekindled the old flame, with forceful guitars and hard and insistent melodies. Success eluded them and they disbanded again. In 1991, UFO were reborn once more. This time the line-up featured the nucleus of Mogg and Way, plus guitarist Laurence Archer (ex-Grand Slam) and drummer Clive Edwards (ex-Wild Horses). *High Stakes And Desperate Men* attempted to recapture the halcyon days of 1974-78, with limited success, but talk in 1993 of a full-scale reunion, including Schenker, was what really fueled fan interest. In 1995 the speculation was finally ended when the band's 'classic line-up' reformed to record *Walk On Water*, initially released in Japan only.
●ALBUMS: *UFO 1* (Beacon 1971)★★, *UFO 2 - Flying* (Beacon 1971)★★, *UFO Lands In Tokyo - Live* (1972)★★★, *Phenomenon* (Chrysalis 1974)★★★, *Force It* (Chrysalis 1975)★★★, *No Heavy Pettin'* (Chrysalis 1976)★★★★, *Lights Out* (Chrysalis 1977)★★★★, *Obsession* (Chrysalis 1978)★★, *Strangers In The Night* (Chrysalis 1979)★★★, *No Place To Run* (Chrysalis 1980)★★, *The Wild, The Willing And The Innocent* (Chrysalis 1981)★★, *Mechanix* (Chrysalis 1982)★★, *Making Contact* (Chrysalis 1983)★★, *Misdemeanor* (Chrysalis 1985)★★★, *Ain't Misbehavin'* (FM Revolver 1988)★★★, *High Stakes And Desperate Men* (Essential 1992)★★★, *BBC Live In Concert* (Windsong 1992)★★★,

Lights Out In Tokyo: Live (Castle 1993)★★★, *Walk On Water* (Zero 1995)★★★.
●COMPILATIONS: *Headstone - The Best Of UFO* (Chrysalis 1983)★★★, *The Collection* (Castle 1985)★★★, *The Decca Years* (Decca 1993)★★, *Doctor, Doctor* (Spectrum/Polydor 1995)★★★.
●VIDEOS: *Misdemeanor Live* (1985).

UK SUBS

This London band was formed in 1976 by veteran R&B singer Charlie Harper. Recruiting Nicky Garratt (guitar), Paul Slack (bass) and Pete Davies (drums), they specialized in shambolic sub-three minute bursts of alcohol-driven rock 'n' roll, but lacked the image and songs of peers such as the Damned, Clash and Sex Pistols. They did, however, attain a string of minor classic singles during the late 70s, including 'I Live In A Car', 'Stranglehold' and 'Tomorrow's Girls'. The latter two dented the lower reaches of the UK Top 40 singles chart. Both *Another Kind Of Blues* and *Brand New Age* were vintage Subs collections, but arguably the definitive statement came with *Crash Course*, which captured the band in all its chaotic glory in front of a live audience. It became their most successful chart album and biggest seller. The band's line-up had rarely been stable, with only Harper surviving each new incarnation. The arrival of Alvin Gibbs (bass) and Steve Roberts (drums) marked a change in emphasis, with the band including metal elements in their songs for the first time. Harper also had a sideline project between 1983 and 1985, Urban Dogs, who were a Stooges/MC5 influenced garage outfit. He had earlier released a solo album. The UK Subs are still active today, but their audience continues to diminish. *Mad Cow Fever*, released in 1991, was a sad testimony to the band's longevity, featuring an even mixture of rock 'n' roll standards and originals, without the drive and spontaneity of old. At least Harper had the compensation of a large royalty cheque on which to retire following Guns N'Roses' version of his 'Down On The Farm'.
●ALBUMS: *Another Kind Of Blues* (Gem 1979)★★, *Brand New Age* (Gem 1980)★★, *Crash Course* (Gem 1980)★★★, *Diminished Responsibility* (Gem 1981)★★, *Endangered Species* (NEMS 1982)★★, *Flood Of Lies* (Scarlet/Fall Out 1983)★, *Gross Out USA* (Fall Out 1984)★, *Huntington Beach* (Revolver 1986)★, *Killing Time* (Fall Out 1987)★, *Japan Today* (Fall Out 1990)★, *In Action* (Red Flame 1990)★, *Mad Cow Fever* (Jungle 1991)★, *Normal Service Resumed* (Jungle 1993)★, *The Punk Is Back* (Cannon 1995)★, *Occupied* (Fall Out 1996)★, *Peel Sessions 1978-79* (Jungle 1997)★★.
●COMPILATIONS: *Live At Gossips* cassette only (Chaos 1982)★, *Demonstration Tapes* (Konexion 1984)★, *Subs Standards* (Dojo 1986)★, *Raw Material* (Killerwatt 1986)★, *Left For Dead* cassette only (ROIR 1986)★, *Recorded 1979-81* (Abstract 1989)★, *Greatest Hits (Live In Paris* (Released Emotions 1990)★, *Down On The Farm (A Collection Of The Less Obvious)* (Streetlink 1991)★★, *The*

Singles 1979-81 (Abstract 1991)★★, *Europe Calling* (Released Emotions 1992)★, *Scum Of The Earth - The Best Of* (Music Club 1993)★★.

●VIDEOS: *Live At Peterless Leisure Centre Friday 10th June 1994* (Barn End 1994).

●FURTHER READING: *Neighbourhood Threat*, Alvin Gibbs.

URIAH HEEP

The critics have scoffed and generally poured derision on Uriah Heep over the years, but the band has sold millions of records and has had five US Top 40 albums. A technically brilliant heavy rock band, they deserve most credit for continuing despite almost 30 personnel changes and two deaths along the way. David Byron (b. 29 January 1947, Epping, Essex, England, d. 28 February 1985; vocals) formed the group with Mick Box (b. 8 June 1947, Walthamstow, London, England; lead guitar/vocals). The pair had teamed up in the Stalkers during the mid-60s, and after the group split they assembled another called Spice. This then evolved into Uriah Heep when the duo were joined by Ken Hensley (b. 24 August 1945, London, England; guitar/keyboards/vocals) and Paul Newton (b. 1946, Andover, England; bass). Hensley, a talented musician, had previously played guitar with Kit And The Saracens and the soul group, Jimmy Brown Sound. Before Uriah Heep were bonded under the experienced management of Gerry Bron, Hensley had played alongside Mick Taylor (later to become a member of the Rolling Stones) in the Gods. He had also played on an album by Toe Fat which included Cliff Bennett. The rota of drummers started with former Spice man Alex Napier, followed by Nigel Olsson (later with Elton John). Finding a permanent drummer was to remain one of the band's problems throughout their early years. Their debut, *Very 'eavy, Very 'umble* in 1970, was a simplistic, bass-driven passage from electric folk to a direct, harder sound. They auditioned numerous drummers before offering the job to Keith Baker, who recorded *Salisbury* before deciding that the tour schedule was too rigorous for his liking. *Salisbury* was a drastic development from the debut, with many lengthy, meandering solos and a 16-minute title track embellished by a 26-piece orchestra. The group were near the forefront of a richly embossed, fastidious style of music later dubbed 'progressive rock'. During 1971 the line-up was altered again when Lee Kerslake, another former member of the Gods and Toe Fat, replaced Ian Clarke. An ex-member of the Downbeats and Colosseum, Mark Clarke, superseded Paul Newton on bass guitar but lasted just three months before Gary Thain (b. 15 May 1948, Wellington, New Zealand, d. 19 March 1976; ex-Keef Hartley Band) took over. Gerry Bron had formed Bronze Records by 1971 and *Look At Yourself* became the group's first entry into the UK charts when it reached number 39 in November. The stability of the new line-up enabled the band to enter their most successful period during the early 70s when the fantastical, eccentric nature of their lyrics was supported by a grandiose musical approach. The quintet recorded five albums, beginning with *Demons And Wizards*, their first to enter the US charts. The musical and lyrical themes continued on *Magician's Birthday*, the double set *Uriah Heep Live*, *Sweet Freedom*, *Wonderworld* (their last Top 40 entry in the US chart) and *Return To Fantasy* as the band revealed a rare thirst for tough recording and performance schedules. Gary Thain was asked to leave in February 1975 after becoming too unreliable. He died of a drug overdose on 19 March 1976. John Wetton, formerly of King Crimson, Family and Roxy Music was expected to provide the impetus needed when he took over the bass guitar in March 1975. However, many observers considered that he had taken a retrogressive step in joining a group that was quickly becoming an anachronism. The union, celebrated on *Return To Fantasy*, failed on a creative level although it marked their first and last appearance in the UK Top 10. Wetton left after just over a year to back Bryan Ferry. Early in 1976, Uriah Heep were set to disintegrate when internal arguments broke out and they found the previously winning formula had become archaic and undeniably staid. In Ken Hensley's own words, they were 'a bunch of machines plummeting to a death'. There had been an earlier, brooding row when Thain suffered a near-fatal electric shock in Dallas and said he had not been shown enough regard for his injuries. Hensley walked out during a tour of the USA in the summer of 1976 and in a subsequent power-struggle, Byron was forced to leave. Byron soon afterwards joined Rough Diamond and after their brief lifespan released a series of solo albums before his death in 1985. Hensley had already embarked upon a short, parallel solo career, releasing two albums in 1973 and 1975. John Lawton, previously the singer with Lucifer's Friend, debuted on *Firefly*. The new bassist was David Bowie's former backing musician, Trevor Bolder. The singer's position underwent further changes during the late 70s and early 80s as the group found themselves playing to a cult following that was ever decreasing. Ex-Lone Star singer John Sloman performed on *Conquest* after which Hensley left the group, leaving original member Mick Box to pick up the pieces. A brief hiatus resulted and a new Uriah Heep that included Box, Kerslake, John Sinclair (keyboards), Bob Daisley (bass) and Peter Goalby (vocals, ex-Trapeze) was formed. Daisley later quit in 1983 and was replaced by the returning Bolder. Bronze Records collapsed in 1984 and the band signed with Portrait Records in the USA. Their earlier extensive touring allowed them to continue appearing at reasonably sized venues, especially across the USA, and in 1987 they had the distinction of becoming the first western heavy metal group to perform in Moscow. Inevitably, there were more personnel changes with the new additions of Bernie Shaw (vocals) and Phil Lanzon (keyboards), both formerly of Grand Prix. Despite seeming out of time with all other developments in hard rock, 1995's *Sea Of Light* offered another evocative slice of the band's trademark melodic rock, maintaining their high standards in fashioning superior AOR. Their European tour of the same year saw them reunite with former vocalist John Lawton as a temporary measure, with Bernie Shaw suffering from a throat problem.

●ALBUMS: *Very 'eavy, Very 'umble* aka *Uriah Heep* (USA) (Bronze 1970)★★, *Salisbury* (Bronze 1971)★★, *Look At Yourself* (Bronze 1971)★★★, *Demons And Wizards* (Bronze 1972)★★★, *The Magician's Birthday* (Bronze 1972)★★, *Uriah Heep Live* (Bronze 1973)★★, *Sweet Freedom* (Bronze 1973)★★★, *Wonderworld* (Bronze 1974)★★★, *Return To Fantasy* (Bronze 1975)★★★, *High And Mighty* (Bronze 1976)★★★, *Firefly* (Bronze 1977)★★★, *Innocent Victim* (Bronze 1978)★★, *Fallen Angel* (Bronze 1978)★★, *Conquest* (Bronze 1980)★★, *Abnominog* (Bronze 1982)★★, *Head First* (Bronze 1983)★★, *Equator* (Bronze 1985)★★, *Live In Europe* (Raw Power 1987)★★, *Live At Shepperton '74* (Castle 1988)★★, *Live In Moscow* (Bronze 1988)★★, *Raging Silence* (Legacy 1989)★★, *Still 'eavy, Still Proud* (Legacy 1990)★★, *Different World* (Legacy 1991)★★, *Sea Of Light* (SPV 1995)★★.

●COMPILATIONS: *The Best Of Uriah Heep* (Bronze 1976)★★★★, *Anthology* (Raw Power 1986)★★★, *The Collection* (Castle 1988)★★★, *The Uriah Heep Story* (EMI 1990)★★★★, *Rarities From The Bronze Age* (Sequel 1991)★★★, *CD Box Set* (Castle 1992)★★★, *The Lansdowne Tapes* (RPM 1993)★★, *Free Me* (Spectrum/Polygram 1995)★★, *Lady In Black* (Spectrum/Polygram 1995)★★, *A Time Of Revelation: 25 Years On* 4-CD box set (Essential 1996)★★★★.

●VIDEOS: *Easy Livin'* (1988), *Live Legends* (1990), *Gypsy* (1990), *Raging Through The Silence - Live At The Astoria* (1990).

UWAIFO, VICTOR

b. 3 January 1941, Benin City, Nigeria. Vocalist, guitarist and bandleader Uwaifo emerged in the mid-60s as one of Nigeria's most individual performers, with a style grounded in but not limited to the highlife of Ghana and western Nigeria. Like fellow Nigerian Fela Kuti, he also recorded extensively in 'broken' (or 'pidgin') English, and so was able to transcend tribal and linguistic barriers to develop an audience throughout Anglophone West Africa. Arriving in Lagos, the capital of Nigeria, in 1958 to complete his secondary education, he led a number of school bands before joining Victor Olaiya's All Stars on a part-time basis. In 1962, by then studying at the College of Technology in Yaba, he joined E.C. Arinze's Highlife Band. On completing his studies, he worked as an engineer for Nigerian television and in 1965, having saved enough money to buy instruments and amplification, formed his first band, the 15-piece Melody Maestros (whose line-up later included the young Sonny Okosun). Signing to Phonogram West Africa in 1966, the Melody Maestros enjoyed three hit singles the same year - 'Sirri Sirri', 'Guitar Boy' and 'Joromi' - with the latter selling in vast quantities not just in Nigeria but throughout Anglophone West Africa. Based on the story of a legendary hero of Benin City, 'Joromi' was so popular that it earned Africa's first Gold Disc Award in 1969. Later that year, Uwaifo and the Melody Maestros were one of Nigeria's representatives at the Black Arts Festival in Algeria, from where they went on to tour the USA and Japan. These tours were followed by visits to the USSR and Europe. In 1971, Uwaifo opened the Joromi Hotel in Benin City, and 10 years later established his own television studio, from where he produced a weekly music and culture programme which was transmitted throughout Nigeria. Continuing to record throughout the 80s, Uwaifo today spends the majority of his time administering his various business interests.

●ALBUMS: *Sir Victor Uwaifo: Sahara All Stars Band* (MEO 1967)★★★★, *Laugh And Cry* (BR 1977)★★★, *At The Crossroads* (Polydor Nigeria 1978)★★★, *Roots* (RT 1979)★★★, *Uwaifo 84* (Polydor Nigeria 1984)★★★, *No Palava* (Polydor Nigeria 1985)★★★.

VALLI, FRANKIE

b Frank Castelluccio, 3 May 1937, Newark, New Jersey, USA. Originally a solo singer, he joined the Variatones in 1954. They made their first records as the Four Lovers but achieved lasting success when they became the Four Seasons in 1962. Although he was lead singer with the group, Valli also had a solo recording career, starting with '(You're Gonna) Hurt Yourself') in late 1965. He scored a million-seller in 1967 with 'Can't Take My Eyes Off You'. From the same album came further US hits, 'I Make A Fool Of Myself' and 'To Give (The Reason I Live)' while 'You're Ready Now' was a reissued success in Britain in 1971. Valli and producer Bob Gaudio now set up a dual career, with Valli recording for Private Stock and a new Four Seasons group for Warner Brothers Records. Valli had his first solo number 1 with the high-pitched vocals on 'My Eyes Adored You' in 1975, followed by 'Swearin' To God' and a revival of Ruby And The Romantics' 'Our Day Will Come'. In 1978 he sold two million copies of the Barry Gibb-composed theme song from *Grease*. The follow-ups, 'Fancy Dancer' and 'Where Did We Go Wrong' (a duet with Chris Forde) sold poorly and in 1980 Valli had a series of ear operations to cure his increasing deafness. He subsequently rejoined the Four Seasons and enjoyed further success when 'Big Girls Don't Cry' was included in the film *Dirty Dancing*. In the 90s, Valli, with the Four Seasons, gained good reviews on his UK tour, and, in 1992, after not releasing any new material for 10 years, started work with Maurice Starr, the man behind New Kids On the Block.

●ALBUMS: *Solo* (Philips 1967)★★★, *Timeless* (Philips 1968)★★★, *Inside You* (1975)★★★, *Close Up* (Private St. 1975)★★★, *Story* (1976)★★, *Frankie Valli Is The Word* (Warners 1978)★★, *Heaven Above Me* (MCA 1980)★★★.
●COMPILATIONS: *The Best Of Frankie Valli* (1980)★★★.
●FILMS: *Grease* (1978).

VAN DER GRAAF GENERATOR

This UK band's name was suggested by its first drummer Chris Judge-Smith who, with Nick Peame (keyboards) and singer lyricist Peter Hammill (b. 1948, London, England) teamed up at Manchester University, England, in 1967. With the enlistment of Keith Ellis (ex-Koobas) on bass, and the substitution of Smith for Guy Evans, and Peame by electronics boffin and ex-church organist Hugh Banton, the band recorded a single, 'People You Were Going To', before breaking up.

However, as Hammill was not yet ready to function outside the context of a group, his intended album, *The Aerosol Grey Machine*, evolved into a band effort. By then Hammill had developed a manic, but clear vocal style and a fatalistic line as a wordsmith that demonstrated both his BSc. studies and a liking for artists such as Leonard Cohen and David Ackles. This self-expression was framed in 'progressive' fashion replete with much extrapolation, dynamic shifts and tempo refinements.

In 1969 Ellis was replaced by Nic Potter - ex-Misunderstood (like Evans) - and David Jackson (woodwinds), who were added as a second album tiptoed into the UK charts. However, the band remained more popular in Europe. At home, the next offering was promoted via a tour (minus Potter) with Lindisfarne, and a well-received set at 70s Plumpton Blues Festival, in which Hammill was almost upstaged by the inventive Jackson, who was also conspicuous in the epic 'A Plague Of Lighthouse Keepers' on *Pawn Hearts*. With another disbandment imminent by 1971, Hammill inaugurated a solo career that continued over five albums until the group re-formed, initially for a French tour in 1975. A more raw sound pervaded their albums, thanks to the recruitment of String-Driven Thing's violinist Graham Smith when Banton and Jackson departed in 1976. With Potter and Evans, the two embarked on a series of instrumental projects (*The Long Hello Volumes 1-4*) while Hammill continued as a soloist when, unable to expand commercially beyond a loyal cult market, they finally broke up after 1978's *Vital*.

●ALBUMS: *The Aerosol Grey Machine* (Mercury 1969)★★★, *The Least We Can Do Is Wave To Each Other* (Charisma 1970)★★★★, *H to He Who Am The Only One* (Charisma 1970)★★★, *Pawn Hearts* (Charisma 1971)★★★, *Godbluff* (Charisma 1975)★★★, *Still Life* (Charisma 1976)★★★, *World Record* (Charisma 1976)★★★, *The Quiet Zone /The Pleasure Dome* (Charisma 1977)★★★, *Vital* (Charisma 1978)★★.
●COMPILATIONS: *Repeat Performance* (Charisma 1980)★★★, *Time Vaults* (Demi-Monde 1985)★★★.
●FURTHER READING: *The Lemming Chronicles*, David Shaw-Parker.

VAN ZANDT, TOWNES

b. 7 March 1944, Fort Worth, Texas, USA, d. 1 January 1997. A country and folk-blues singer and guitarist, Van Zandt was a native Texan and great grandson of one of the original settlers who founded Fort Worth in the mid-19th Century. The son of a prominent oil family, Townes turned his back on financial security to pursue the beatnik life in Houston. First thumbing his way through cover versions, his acoustic sets later graced the Jester Lounge and other venues where his 'bawdy bar-room ballads' were first performed. Although little-known outside of a cult country rock following, many of his songs are better publicized by the cover versions afforded them by Merle Haggard, Emmylou Harris, Don Gibson and Willie Nelson. This gave songs such as

'Pancho And Lefty' and 'If I Needed You' the chance to rise to the top of the country charts. Much of Van Zandt's material was not released in the UK until the late 70s, though his recording career actually began with *For The Sake Of A Song*, released in the US in 1968. His media awareness belied the debt many artists, including the Cowboy Junkies and Go-Betweens, profess to owing him. Steve Earle went further: 'Townes Van Zandt is the best songwriter in the whole world, and I'll stand on Bob Dylan's coffee table in my cowboy boots and say that'. Interest is still alive as the recent reissue of the *Live And Obscure* (albeit retitled *Pancho And Lefty*) on Edsel proves. Van Zandt continued to live a reclusive life in a cabin in Tennessee up to his untimely death, recording occasionally purely for the chance to 'get the songs down for posterity'.

●ALBUMS: *For The Sake Of A Song* (1968)★★★, *Our Mother The Mountain* (Tomato 1969)★★★★, *Townes Van Zandt* (Tomato 1969)★★★, *Delta Momma Blues* (Tomato 1971)★★★, *High And Low And In Between* (Tomato 1972)★★★, *The Late Great Townes Van Zandt* (Tomato 1972)★★★, *Live At The Old Quarter* (Tomato 1977)★★★, *Flyin' Shoes* (Tomato 1978)★★★, *At My Window* (Heartland 1987)★★★, *Live And Obscure* (Heartland 1987)★★★, *Rain On A Conga Drum* (Exile 1991)★★★, *Pancho And Lefty* (Demon 1992)★★★, *Roadsongs* (Sugar Hill 1994)★★★, *No Deeper Blue* (Veracity 1995)★★★.

VERA, BILLY, AND THE BEATERS

Formed in 1979 around songwriter Billy Vera (b. William McCord, 28 May 1944, Riverside, California, USA; vocalist/guitarist). Billy and the Beaters was an aggregation that comprised Los Angeles studio musicians. A 10-piece group, whose best-known member other than Vera was Steely Dan/Doobie Brothers guitarist Jeff 'Skunk' Baxter. Other members at various times comprised: Barry Beckett (keyboards), Gene Chrisman (drums), Tommy Cogbill (bass), Ron Viola (saxophones), Pete Carr (guitar), Jim Ehinger (piano), Jimmy Johnson(guitar), Lon Price (saxophone), Beau Segal (drums), Jerry Peterson (saxophone). The band initially came together to work a club date at LA's Troubadour nightclub. They banded together officially following that engagement and solidified their act during a six-week residency there. In 1981 they signed with the small Alfa Records and recorded a live album at LA's Roxy club. Two singles, 'I Can Take Care Of Myself' and 'At This Moment', became moderate chart successes, but the latter made a comeback in 1986 after being used as the theme of the US television programme *Family Ties*, and ultimately reached number 1 in the USA. 'Here Comes The Dawn Again' was their live showstopper, which featured a biting saxophone solo. The group disbanded in the early 80s and Vera has become a highly respected songwriter and record producer in addition to working as a vintage soul and R&B album compiler.

●ALBUMS: *With Pen In Hand* (Atlantic 1968)★★, 1977 recordings *Out Of The Darkness* (Unidisc 1993)★★, *Billy Vera And The Beaters* (Alfa 1981)★★, *Retro Nuevo* (Capitol 1988)★★.

●COMPILATIONS: *By Request* (Rhino 1986)★★★.

VERLAINE, TOM

b. Thomas Miller, 13 December 1949, Mount Morris, New Jersey, USA. Trained as a classical pianist, guitarist/vocalist Verlaine became interested in rock music upon hearing the Rolling Stones' '19th Nervous Breakdown'. In 1968 he gravitated to New York's lower east side, and formed the Neon Boys with bassist Richard Hell and drummer Billy Ficca. Although collapsing within weeks, the band inspired the founding of Television, which made its debut in March 1974. Verlaine's desire for a regular venue transformed CBGB's from a struggling bar into New York's premier punk haven. Although his own group did not secure a major contract until 1976, his flourishing guitar work appeared on early releases by the Patti Smith Group. Television's debut, *Marquee Moon*, was acclaimed a classic, although a lukewarm reception for the ensuing *Adventure* exacerbated inner tensions. The group was disbanded in 1978, and Verlaine began a solo career. *Tom Verlaine* and *Dreamtime* continued the themes of the artist's former outlet, but failed to reap due commercial reward. *Words From The Front*, which featured the lengthy 'Days On The Mountain', attracted considerable UK interest and when *Cover* was issued to fulsome reviews, Verlaine took up temporary residence in London. *Flash Light* and *The Wonder* revealed an undiminished talent, with the latter his most consistent release to date. Verlaine's gifted lyricism and brittle, shimmering guitar work has ensured a reputation as one of rock's most innovative and respected talents. In 1991 a decision was made to re-form the original Television line-up and the following year was spent in rehearsals and recording. Meanwhile, Verlaine continued with his solo career, releasing the instrumental set, *Warm And Cool* early in 1992.

●ALBUMS: *Tom Verlaine* (Elektra 1979)★★★★, *Dreamtime* (Warners 1981)★★★, *Words From The Front* (Warners 1983)★★★, *Cover* (Warners 1984)★★★★, *Flash Light* (Fontana 1987)★★★★, *The Wonder* (Fontana 1990)★★★★, *Warm And Cool* (Rough Trade 1992)★★★.

●COMPILATIONS: *The Miller's Tale: A Tom Verlaine Anthology* (Virgin 1996)★★★★.

VIBRATORS

This first wave UK punk band were formed in February 1976 by Knox Ian Carnochan (b. 4 April 1945; vocals/guitar), John Ellis (b. 1 June 1952; guitar), Pat Collier (b. October 1951; bass), and Eddie (b. 1 April 1951; drums). Their first gig came as support to the Stranglers at Hornsey College of Art, before joining the Sex Pistols at the 100 Club during the summer of 1976. By September they were at the same venue supporting guitarist Chris Spedding (ex-Grease Band, and solo hitmaker for Rak). He helped get the band signed to Rak and in November 1976 they released their debut 45, 'We Vibrate', which earned a *New Musical Express* Single Of The Week plaudit. At the same time they also released a single with Spedding called 'Pogo Dancing', a cash-in on the new dance craze. They left Rak for Epic Records in 1977 to release their debut album, *Pure Mania.* Contained therein were the seminal Vibrator tracks 'Whips And Furs' and 'Stiff Little Fingers' (whence the Northern Irish band took their name). Collier left after a tour with Ian Hunter and formed the Boyfriends, later enjoying a significant production career. His replacement was Gary Tibbs, whose CV later included Adam And The Ants, Roxy Music, Mick Farren's Good Guys and many more. In 1978 they scored their first UK hit with 'Automatic Lover'. It was followed by *V2,* produced by Vic Maille. Ellis left soon afterwards to play for Peter Gabriel, the Purple Helmets and the Stranglers. He was replaced by Dave Birch on guitar and the band's sound was augmented with Don Snow on keyboards. Snow had formerly appeared with the Rezillos and Squeeze. The new single, 'Judy Says (Knock You In The Head)', became their second hit. Birch, Snow and Tibbs were the next departures and were replaced by Ben Brierly on bass and American Greg Van Cook on guitar. This line-up was short lived, however, as Know embarked on a solo career (it produced two good singles in a cover of Syd Barrett's 'Gigolo Aunt' and the poppy 'She's So Good Looking'). This signalled the end of the first phase of the Vibrators' career, with Eddie going on to drum for PiL and the Inmates. In 1980 a new Vibrators was formed with Kip (vocals), Jimmy V and the Birdman (guitars), Ian Woodcock (bass), and the only constant - Eddie (drums). They released two singles before, once again, splitting up. In 1982 the original line-up reformed. Since then the band have continued to tour and record. There have been a few further line-up changes. Most significant was the departure of Pat Collier. His replacements were Noel Thompson, then Marc Duncan (b. 9 May 1960) from Doll By Doll. Ellis also departed to become a Strangler. Mickie Owen (b. 3 March 1956) took over initially but was then replaced by ex-Members guitarist Nigel Bennett. *Unpunked* in 1996 was a surprisingly good album, showing that acoustic versions of their punk catalogue allows the quality of the original songs to show through.

●ALBUMS: *Pure Mania* (Columbia 1977)★★★★, *V2* (Epic 1978)★★★, *Batteries Not Included* (Columbia 1980)★★, *Guilty* (Anagram 1982)★★★, *Alaska 127* (Ram 1984)★★★, *Fifth Amendment* (Ram 1985)★★★, *Vibrators Live* (FM-Revolver 1986)★★, *Recharged* (FM-Revolver 1988)★★, *Meltdown* (FM-Revolver 1988)★★, *Vicious Circle* (FM-Revolver 1989)★★, *Volume 10* (FM-Revolver 1990)★★, *Power Of Money* (Anagram 1992)★★, *Live Marquee '77* (Released Emotions 1992)★★, *Hunting For You* (FM-Revolver 1994)★★, *Unpunked* (Vibes 1996)★★★.

●COMPILATIONS: *Yeah Yeah Yeah* (Repertoire 1988)★★★, *The Best Of The Vibrators* (1992)★★★, *The Independent Singles Collection* (Anagram 1992)★★★.

VICIOUS, SID

b. John Ritchie, 10 May 1957, London, England, d. 2 February 1979, New York, USA. One of the biggest icons of the 70s, Sid Vicious crystallized the 'live fast die young' creed. He was initially best known for being the friend of Johnny Rotten of the Sex Pistols, as well as being that group's most notorious and violent follower. However, he had also played drums at Siouxsie And The Banshees' first live appearance before answering the call to replace Glen Matlock on bass in the Sex Pistols in February 1977. His recruitment indicated much about the state of the band - his musical skills were non-existent and Pistols guitarist Steve Jones would simply play his parts in the studio and switch off his amplifier for live appearances - but he had the perfect leather-clad, doomed youth visual appeal. He became the toast of the tabloids through his relationship with American Nancy Spungen - a notorious junkie/groupie - with whose murder he was subsequently charged. He died of a heroin overdose after being released on bail. A posthumous solo album was released by Virgin Records. *Sid Sings* was a short collection of cover versions such as 'C'Mon Everybody' and 'Stepping Stone' (also included on Sex Pistols' albums of the time) and material by Iggy Pop and Johnny Thunders. The highlight was Vicious's one enduring rock 'n' roll moment - a rendition of Paul Anka/Frank Sinatra's 'My Way'. This had been immortalized in *The Great Rock 'n' Roll Swindle* film in a sequence which featured Vicious mowing down his audience with a pistol, and a performance that was later acknowledged even by a member of Take That (Robbie) as 'bang on!'. It was also the clear inspiration behind Shane MacGowan's version of the song released in 1996.

●ALBUMS: *Sid Sings* (Virgin 1979)★★, *Sid Dead Live* (Anagram 1997)★.

●FURTHER READING: *Sid's Way,* Alan Parker and Keith Bateson. *Sid Vicious Rock 'N' Roll Star,* Malcom Butt. *Sid Vicious: They Died Too Young,* Tom Stockdale.

VILLAGE PEOPLE

The Village People from New York City, USA, were a concept before they were a group. The brainchild of record producer Jacques Morali, the troupe was assembled in 1977 . His intention was to create a camp rock 'n' roll/dance act that would flaunt homosexual stereotypes yet appeal to gays. Before even constructing his dream group, Morali secured a recording contract with Casablanca Records, then riding high with a string of smash disco hits by Donna Summer. Morali's first recruit was Felipe Rose, a go-go dancer who was dressed in an American Indian costume when spotted by the entrepreneur. Morali then hired songwriters Phil Hurtt and Peter Whitehead to compose songs hinting at gay themes before filling out the group with Alexander

Briley, Randy Jones, David Hodo, Glenn Hughes and Victor Willis (later replaced by Ray Simpson). Each member of the group was outfitted to cash in on the homosexual 'macho' stereotyping; in addition to the American Indian there was a cowboy, a policeman, a hard-hat construction worker, a biker and a soldier. The group first charted in the UK with the Top 50 single, 'San Francisco (You Got Me)' in 1977, but the group's first major US hit was the Top 30 'Macho Man' in 1978, followed by two international hits, 'Y.M.C.A.' (UK number 1/US number 2) and 'In The Navy' (UK number 3/US number 2). Although gays did embrace the group at first, they tired of it as the mainstream audience picked up on the Village People. In the UK their success continued with the Top 20 singles 'Go West' (1979) and 'Can't Stop The Music' (1980). The latter was the theme-song to an ill-timed film excursion. With anti-disco fever prevalent in the USA, sales plummeted; the group's starring role in the universally panned film, *Can't Stop The Music*, virtually killed off their career. Attempts to resurface with new personnel and new styles (including a stint as Spandau Ballet-like 'New Romantics') did not aid their sagging fortunes. Miles Jaye, who had replaced Ray Simpson in the later years of the group, was signed to Teddy Pendergrass's Top Priority label as a solo artist, achieving some success in the US R&B singles chart. He subsequently signed to the Island outlet 4th & Broadway and released *Miles* (1987) and *Irresistible* (1989). Jacques Morali later died of an AIDS related-illness, aged 44, in December 1991.

●ALBUMS: *Village People* (DJM 1977)★★, *Macho Man* (DJM 1978)★★, *Cruisin'* (Mercury 1978)★★, *Go West* (Mercury 1979)★★, *Live And Sleazy* (Mercury 1979)★, *Can't Stop The Music* film soundtrack (Mercury 1980)★, *Renaissance* (Mercury 1981)★.

●COMPILATIONS: *Greatest Hits* (Groove & Move 1988)★★★, *The Hits* (Music Club 1991)★★★.

●VIDEOS: *The Best Of ...* (1994).

●FILMS: *Can't Stop The Music* (1980).

VINEGAR JOE

This powerful, R&B-based group was formed in 1971 at the suggestion of Island Records boss, Chris Blackwell. The main core of the group comprised Elkie Brooks (b. 25 February 1948, Salford, Lancashire, England; vocals), Robert Palmer (b. 19 January 1949, Batley, Yorkshire, England; vocals) and Peter Gage (b. 31 August 1947, Lewisham, London, England; guitar/piano/pedal steel guitar). It evolved from the remnants of Dada (formed 1970), an ambitious 12-piece jazz-rock outfit. The three members had enjoyed limited success previously during the 60s: Brooks had recorded as a solo act, Palmer had sung with Alan Bown, while Gage was a former member of the Zephyrs and later with Geno Washington And The Ram Jam Band. Additionally the line-up comprised Steve York (b. 24 April 1948, London; bass), while early members Tim Hinckley and later John Hawken were supplanted in June 1972 by Mike Deacon (b. 30 April 1945, Surrey, England; keyboards), while Bob Tait and later John Woods were replaced in January 1973 by Pete Gavin (b. 9 August 1946, Lewisham, London, England; drums). Jim Mullen was an additional guitarist from September 1972 to April 1973. Renowned for a forthright, gutsy approach, Vinegar Joe was quickly established as a popular in-concert attraction, but despite recording three solid and respectable albums, the unit was unable to capture its live appeal on record and broke up late in 1973. Palmer and Brooks then embarked on contrasting, but highly successful, individual careers.

●ALBUMS: *Vinegar Joe* (Island 1972)★★★, *Rock 'N' Roll Gypsies* (Island 1972)★★★, *Six Star General* (Island 1973)★★★.

WACKERS

This US group was formed in Eureka, North California, USA, in 1970. The line-up featured Bob Segarini (vocals/guitar), Randy Bishop (vocals/guitar), Michael Stull (vocals/guitar), Bill Kootch Troachim (bass/vocals) and Spencer Earnshaw (drums). Segarini was a veteran of a multitude of Bay Area groups, including the Family Tree and Roxy. Troachim was a member of the former, Bishop the latter, and the Wackers drew on this experience to create a sound which blended 'Beatlesque' melody lines with classic Californian sunshine harmonies. Their second album, *Hot Wacks*, showcased the group at its best, a feature enhanced by Gary Usher's exemplary production. Doomed to commercial indifference in the USA, the Wackers settled in Montreal, Canada, where they had been recording. J.P. Lauzon replaced Stull, prior to the release of a disappointing third album, but the reconstituted group received a major blow when their label refused to release the next collection, *Wack 'N' Roll*. Although two singles were latterly issued, this impasse prompted Bishop to depart for a solo career. Segarini, Troachim and Wayne Cullen, a late-period drummer, then abandoned the Wackers' name and formed a new group, the Dudes, with various Canadian musicians.

●ALBUMS: *Wackering Heights* (Elektra 1971)★★, *Hot Wacks* (Elektra 1972)★★★, *Shredder* (Elektra 1973)★★. Solo: Bob Segarini *Gotta Have Pop* (Epic 1978)★★, *Goodbye LA* (1980)★★.

WAINWRIGHT, LOUDON, III

b. 5 September 1946, Chapel Hill, North Carolina, USA. Loudon Wainwright I was in insurance while his son, Loudon Wainwright II, became a journalist for *Life* magazine. Wainwright's parents settled in Westchester Country, 60 miles outside of New York City although he went to a boarding school in Delaware ('School Days') and he was friends with an adolescent Liza Minnelli ('Liza'). He studied acting in Pittsburgh where singer George Gerdes encouraged his songwriting. By 1968, after a brief spell in an Oklahoma jail for a marijuana offence, Wainwright was playing folk clubs in New York and Boston and was signed to Atlantic Records. His first albums featured his high-pitched voice and guitar with few additions, and his intense, sardonic songs, described by him as 'reality with exaggeration', were about himself. He was hailed as the 'new Bob Dylan' for such songs as 'Glad To See You've Got Religion', 'Motel

Blues' and 'Be Careful, There's A Baby In The House'. He later said: 'I wasn't the new anyone. Media people call you the new-something because it's the only way they know to describe what you do'. His UK debut, opening for the Everly Brothers, was disastrous as Teddy Boys barracked him, but he found his *métier* at the 1972 Cambridge Folk Festival.

Wainwright's third album, for Columbia Records, included a surprise US Top 20 pop hit in 'Dead Skunk'. 'I had run over a skunk that had been run over a few times already. It took 15 minutes to write. I remember being bowled over at how much people liked it when I had put so little into it. It's about a dead skunk but people thought it was about Nixon and that's all right by me.' Wainwright wrote 'A.M. World' about his success and, almost defiantly, he followed it with *Attempted Moustache*, which had indistinct vocals and was uncommercial even by his standards, although it did include the whimsical 'Swimming Song'. *Unrequited*, partly recorded live, was a return to form and included the hilarious, but controversial, 'Rufus Is A Tit Man' (which Wainwright described as 'a love song, not a dirty song'), one of many songs he recorded about his children ('Pretty Little Martha' and 'Five Years Old'). His marriage to Kate McGarrigle (see Kate And Annie McGarrigle) ended in 1977 and Wainwright then had a child with Suzzy Roche of the Roches. His album, *A Live One*, actually recorded in 1976, demonstrates his wit but this gawky, lanky, square-jawed singer with enormous tongue, grimaces and contortions needs to be seen in person to be fully appreciated.

Wainwright has appeared in a few episodes of the television series *M*A*S*H*, appeared on stage in *The Birthday Party* and *Pump Boys And Dinettes*, and he is most recently best known in the UK for his topical songs on the Jasper Carrott television series. His wit and neuroses surfaced in such songs as 'Fear Of Flying' and 'Watch Me Rock, I'm Over 30' (both from *T-Shirt*), but he reached top form on three albums for Demon - *Fame And Wealth*, *I'm Alright* and *More Love Songs*. The albums, sometimes co-produced with Richard Thompson, have included 'I Don't Think Your Wife Likes Me', 'Hard Day On The Planet' (written while watching Live Aid), 'Unhappy Anniversary', 'Not John' (a tribute to John Lennon) and 'This Song Don't Have A Video'. Many of his later compositions are about the music industry of which he later claimed, 'I wanna be in showbiz one way or another until I die, so it's a mixed blessing not to be a huge success. I've been successful on my own terms - by failing'.

●ALBUMS: *Loudon Wainwright III* (Atlantic 1969)★★★, *Album II* (Atlantic 1971)★★★, *Album III* (Columbia 1973)★★★, *Attempted Moustache* (Columbia 1974)★★, *Unrequited* (Columbia 1975)★★, *T-Shirt* (Arista 1976)★★, *Final Exam* (Arista 1978)★★, *A Live One* (Radar 1979)★★★, *Fame And Wealth* (Demon 1983)★★★, *I'm Alright* (Demon 1984)★★★, *More Love Songs* (Demon 1986)★★★, *Therapy* (Silvertone 1989)★★★, *History*

(1992)★★★, *Career Moves* (1993)★★★, *Grown Man* (Virgin 1995)★★★.

WAKEMAN, RICK

b. 18 May 1949, London, England. The spectacular extravaganzas undertaken in the mid-70s by the former Yes and Strawbs keyboardist, masked the talent of one of rock's premier musicians. In the early 70s he and Keith Emerson regularly battled it out in the annual music press reader's poll for the prestige of the world's top keyboard player. Wakeman made a series of conceptual classical rock albums that were overblown with ambition; *The Six Wives Of Henry VIII* and *Journey To The Centre Of The Earth* briefly made him a superstar. He took his success to extremes by staging *The Myths And Legends Of King Arthur And The Knights Of The Round Table* using a full orchestra and 50-strong choir at Wembley's Empire Pool, on ice! All three albums were hugely successful and Rick attempted more of the same, but he was hampered with a mild heart attack and a serious drink problem. In 1981 he contributed to Sky's Kevin Peeks' *Awakening*. That year he co-wrote a musical version of George Orwell's *1984* with Tim Rice, and followed with sensitive film scores for *Lisztomania*, *The Burning*, *G'Ole*, *Crimes Of Passion*, and *Creepshow 2*. In 1982 he started his own record label Moon Records. Having overcome his alcoholism he became a born-again Christian and offered his new faith in the shape of *The Gospels*. Wakeman has been a first class pianist for many years, and stripped of all the pomp and grandeur he demonstrates a superb style, perfectly shown on the new-age *Country Airs*. At the end of the 80s he was back with his former superstar friends as Yes re-formed for a new tour. In 1991 he formed yet another label, Ambient Records, and worked with Norman Wisdom on a series of relaxation cassettes. By 1992, his son Adam was performing with his father and has subsequently released a number of albums with him. Wakeman's life is never dull: he is constantly working, either as a chat show guest, a showbusiness personality or as a highly accomplished pianist.
●ALBUMS: with the John Schroeder Orchestra *Piano Vibrations* (Polydor 1971)★★★, *The Six Wives Of Henry VIII* (A&M 1973)★★★, *Journey To The Centre Of The Earth* (A&M 1974)★★, *The Myths And Legends Of King Arthur And The Knights Of The Round Table* (A&M 1975)★★★, *Lisztomania* film soundtrack (A&M 1975)★★★, *No Earthly Connection* (A&M 1976)★★, *White Rock* soundtrack (A&M 1977)★★, *Rick Wakeman's Criminal Record* (A&M 1977)★★, *Rhapsodies* (A&M 1979)★★, *1984* (Charisma 1981)★★, *The Burning* soundtrack (Charisma 1982)★★, *Rock 'N' Roll Prophet* (Moon 1982)★★, *G'Ole* soundtrack (Charisma 1983)★★, *The Cost Of Living* (Charisma 1987)★★, *Live At Hammersmith* (President 1985)★★, *Silent Nights* (President 1985)★★, *Country Airs* (Coda 1986)★★★, *Crimes Of Passion* soundtrack (President 1986)★★, *The Family Album* (President 1987)★★, *The Gospels* (Stylus 1987)★★, *A Suite Of Gods*

(President 1988)★★, *Time Machine* (President 1988)★★, *Zodiaque* (President 1988)★★, *Sea Airs* (President 1989)★★, *Night Airs* (President 1990)★★, *In The Beginning* (Asaph 1990)★★, *Aspirent Sunrise* (Ambient 1990)★★, *Aspirent Sunset* (President 1990)★★, *Black Knights In The Court Of Ferdinand* (Ambient 1991)★★, *The Sun Trilogy* (Badger 1991)★★, *Phantom Power* soundtrack (Ambient 1991)★★, *Softsword: King John And The Magna Charter* (Ambient 1991)★★, with Norman Wisdom *A World Of Wisdom* (Ambient 1991)★★, *The Private Collection* (Ambient 1991)★★, *The Classical Connection* (Ambient 1991)★★, *The Classical Connection II* (Ambient 1991)★★, *2000 AD, Into The Future* (Ambient 1991)★★, with Adam Wakeman *Wakeman With Wakeman* (Rio Digital 1992)★★, *Ambient Sunshadows* (Rio Digital 1992)★★, *Heritage Suite* (President 1993)★★, *African Bach* (President 1993)★★, with Adam Wakeman *No Expense Spared* (President 1993)★★, *The Classic Tracks* (Prestige 1994)★★, with Adam Wakeman *The Official Bootleg* (Cyclops 1994)★★, *Romance Of The Victorian Age* (President 1994)★★, *Live On The Test* (Windsong 1994)★★★, *The Seven Wonders Of The World* (President 1995)★★, *Cirque Surreal - State Circus Of Imagination* (D-Sharp 1995)★★, *Visions* (President 1995)★★.
●COMPILATIONS: *Best Known Works* (1978)★★, *20th Anniversary Limited Edition* (A&M 1989)★★, *Greatest Hits* (1994)★★★, *Rock And Pop Legends* (Disky 1995)★★, *Voyage* (A&M 1997)★★★.
●VIDEOS: *The World* (Central 1988), *Rick Wakeman Live In Concert* (Castle 1991), *The World And Gospels* (Beckmann 1991), *The Classical Connection* (Beckmann 1991), *The Very Best Of Rick Wakeman - Chronicles* (Icon 1992), *Chronicles Live 1975* (Fragile 1994), *The Making Of Surreal* (Dan Ace 1995).
●FURTHER READING: *Rick Wakeman: The Caped Crusader*, Dan Wooding. *Say Yes!*, Rick Wakeman.

WALKER, JERRY JEFF

b. 16 March 1942, Oneonta, New York, USA. Although he initially pursued a career as a folk singer in New York's Greenwich Village, Walker first forged his reputation as a member of Circus Maximus. He left this promising group following their debut album when a jazz-based initiative proved incompatible with his own ambitions. Having moved to Key West in Florida, Walker resumed work as a solo artist with *Drifting Way Of Life*, before signing with the Atco label when his former outlet showed little interest in his country/folk material. He enjoyed a minor hit with 'Mr. Bojangles', a tale of a street dancer Walker reputedly met in a drunk tank. Although the singer's own rendition stalled in the chart's lower reaches, it became a US Top 10 entry by the Nitty Gritty Dirt Band and has since been the subject of numerous cover versions including a lethargic one by Bob Dylan. By the early 70s Walker was based in Austin, Texas, where he became a kindred spirit to the city's 'outlaw' fraternity, including Willie Nelson and

Waylon Jennings. He also built one of the region's most accomplished backing groups, later to follow its own career as the Lost Gonzo Band. A low-key approach denied the artist the same commercial success, but Jerry Jeff has enjoyed the approbation of colleagues and a committed cult following.

●ALBUMS: *Mr. Bojangles* (1968)★★★, *Drifting Way Of Life* (1969)★★★, *Jerry Jeff Walker* (1969)★★★, *Five Years Gone* (1969)★★★, *Bein' Free* (1970)★★★, *Jerry Jeff Walker* (MCA 1972)★★★, *Viva Terlingua!* (MCA 1973)★★★, *Walker's Collectables* (MCA 1975), *Ridin' High* (MCA 1975)★★★, *It's A Good Night For Singin'* (MCA 1976)★★★★, *A Man Must Carry On* (MCA 1977)★★★, *Contrary To Ordinary* (MCA 1978)★★★, *Jerry Jeff* (Elektra 1978)★★★, *Too Old To Change* (1979), *Reunion* (SouthCoast 1981), *Cowjazz* (1982), *Navajo Rug* (Rykodisc 1987)★★, *Gypsy Songman* (Temple Music 1988)★★, *Live At Guene Hall* (Rykodisc 1989)★★★, *Hill Country Rain* (1992)★★, *Viva Luckenbach!* (Rykodisc 1994)★★, *Christmas Gonzo Style* (Rykodisc 1994)★, *Night After Night* (Tried And True 1995)★★.

●COMPILATIONS: *The Best Of Jerry Jeff Walker* (MCA 1980)★★★★.

WALSH, JOE

b. 20 November 1947, New Jersey, USA. Guitar hero Walsh started his long and varied career in 1965 with the G-Clefs. Following a spell with local band the Measles, he found major success when he joined the James Gang in 1969. Walsh's growling, early heavy metal guitar technique was not unlike that of Jeff Beck, and the Walsh sound had much to do with the achievements of the James Gang. He left in 1972 and formed Barnstorm with Joe Vitale (drums) and Kenny Passarelli (bass). The self-titled album promised much and made a respectable showing in the US charts. Despite the follow-up being credited to Joe Walsh, *The Smoker You Drink The Player You Get* was still Barnstorm, although the band broke up that same year. *Smoker* became his first gold album and featured some of his classic songs such as 'Meadows' and 'Rocky Mountain Way'. On the latter he featured the voice bag, from which his distorted voice was emitted after being sung into a plastic tube. Walsh, along with Peter Frampton and Jeff Beck, popularized this effect in the early 70s. In 1974 he produced Dan Fogelberg's classic album *Souvenirs* and guested on albums by Stephen Stills, the Eagles and B.B. King. *So What* in 1975 was another gold album and featured the Walsh classic, 'Turn To Stone'. During the summer he performed at London's Wembley Stadium with the Beach Boys, Elton John and the Eagles. Five months later Walsh joined the Eagles when he replaced Bernie Leaden and became full-time joint lead guitarist with Glen Frey. His distinctive tone contributed greatly to their milestone *Hotel California*; his solo on the title track is one of the highlights. Additionally he retained his autonomy by continuing his highly successful career and released further solo

albums including the excellent *But Seriously Folks . . .* which featured the humorous autobiographical 'Life's Been Good'. The song dealt with his fortune and fame in a light-hearted manner, although there is a degree of smugness attached; for example, 'I have a mansion, forget the price, ain't never been there, they tell me its nice'. Such was Walsh's confidence that at one point he announced he would stand for President at the next election. He was wise to have maintained his solo career, as the Eagles only made one further album. Walsh shrewdly kept his best work for his own albums. In 1980 Walsh contributed to the best-selling soundtrack *Urban Cowboy* and was rewarded with a US Top 20 hit 'All Night Long'. Both *There Goes The Neighborhood* and *You Bought It - You Name It* maintained his profile and although his 1987 album *Got Any Gum?* was uninspiring, his career continues to prosper as a solo and session player. In 1992 he was playing with Ringo Starr on the latter's comeback tour. By 1995 a rakish and fit-looking Walsh was once again playing in front of vast audiences as a member of the reunited Eagles.

●ALBUMS: *Barnstorm* (ABC 1972)★★★, *The Smoker You Drink, The Player You Get* (ABC 1973)★★★★, *So What?* (ABC 1975)★★★★, *You Can't Argue With A Sick Mind* (ABC 1976)★★, *But Seriously Folks ...* (Asylum 1978)★★★, *There Goes The Neighborhood* (Asylum 1981)★★, *You Bought It - You Name It* (Warners 1983)★★, *The Confessor* (Warners 1985)★★, *Got Any Gum?* (Warners 1987)★★, *Ordinary Average Guy* (Epic 1991)★★, *Robocop - The Series Soundtrack* (Essential 1995)★★.

●COMPILATIONS: *The Best Of Joe Walsh* (ABC 1978)★★★, *All The Best* (Pickwick 1994)★★, *Look What I Did! - The Joe Walsh Anthology* 2-CD (MCA 1995)★★★.

WAMMACK, TRAVIS

b. 1946, Walnut, Mississippi, USA. Travis Wammack was one of the great unheralded rock 'n' roll session guitarists of the 60s and 70s, and also charted with a number of singles under his own name. He started playing guitar during his childhood after his family moved to Memphis, Tennessee. Influenced by country music and blues, his professional career began when he was in his teens, opening for rockabilly artists such as Warren Smith and Carl Perkins. Wammack had already made his first record by then, having recorded some of his own songs at the age of 12 for the small Fernwood label, with top Memphis musicians backing him. One single, 'Rock And Roll Blues', attracted some local attention but did not chart nationally. In 1961 Wammack began playing on sessions for guitarist Roland Janes, who had worked with Jerry Lee Lewis on the latter's Sun Records classics. Wammack recorded another of his own compositions, the guitar instrumental 'Scratchy', which was not released until 1964, on the ARA label, when it attained minor chart success. Unable to produce a follow-up chart record, Wammack continued to work for Janes until 1966, when he moved to Muscle

Shoals, Alabama, and began playing on sessions there at Rick Hall's Fame Studios. His guitar can be heard on recordings recorded there by Clarence Carter, Wilson Pickett, Aretha Franklin and the Osmonds, whose hit 'One Bad Apple' features Wammack's guitar. During 1972-73, Wammack finally reached the charts again under his own name, with two minor Fame Records singles. He switched to Capricorn Records in 1975 and scored his biggest hit, '(Shu-Doo-Pa-Poo-Poop) Love Being Your Fool', which reached number 38. There was one final chart single later that year, 'Easy Evil', also on Capricorn. Since then, Wammack has performed with the Allman Brothers Band, Percy Sledge, Tony Joe White and Little Richard, among others.

●ALBUMS: *Travis Wammack* (Fame 1972)★★, *Not For Sale* (Capricorn 1975)★★.

●COMPILATIONS: *That Scratchy Guitar From Memphis* (Bear Family 1987)★★★, *Scr-Scr-Scratchy* (Zu-Zazz 1989)★★★.

WAR

Veterans of the Californian west coast circuit, the core of War's line-up - Leroy 'Lonnie' Jordan (b. 21 November 1948, San Diego, California, USA; keyboards), Howard Scott (b. 15 March 1946, San Pedro, California, USA; guitar), Charles Miller (b. 2 June 1939, Olathe, Kansas, USA; flute/saxophone), Morris 'B.B.' Dickerson (b. 3 August 1949, Torrence, California, USA; bass) and Harold Brown (b. 17 March 1946, Long Beach, California, USA; drums) - had made several records under different names including the Creators, the Romeos and Senor Soul. In 1969, the quintet was working as Nightshift, an instrumental group, when ex-Animals lead singer, Eric Burdon, adopted them as his backing band. Renamed War, the ensemble was completed by Lee Oskar (b. Oskar Levetin Hansen 24 March 1948, Copenhagen, Denmark; harmonica) and 'Papa' Dee Allen (b. 18 July 1931, Wilmington, Delaware, USA, d. 29 August 1988; percussion).

Their debut, *Eric Burdon Declares War*, included the rhythmic 'Spill The Wine', but the group broke away from the UK vocalist following a second collection. War's potent fusion of funk, R&B, rock and Latin styles produced a progressive soul sound best heard on *All Day Music* and *The World Is A Ghetto*. They also enjoyed a significant success in the US singles charts with 'The Cisco Kid' (1973), 'Why Can't We Be Friends?' (1975) and 'Summer' (1976), each of which earned a gold disc, while in the UK they earned two Top 20 hits with 'Low Rider' (1976) and 'Galaxy' (1978). War's subsequent progress proved less fortunate. Despite an early promise, a move to MCA Records was largely unproductive as the group's record sales dipped. Lee Oskar embarked on an intermittent solo career and further changes undermined their original fire and purpose. Two 1982 singles, 'You Got The Power' and 'Outlaw', suggested a renaissance but the band was later obliged to finance its own releases. However, a 1987 remake of 'Low Rider', a previous smash hit, did reach the minor places in the R&B chart. Into the 90s the band struggle on, still performing although most of the original members have long since departed.

●ALBUMS: with Eric Burdon *Eric Burdon Declares War* (MGM 1970)★★★, with Burdon *The Black Man's Burdon* (MGM 1970)★★, *War* (United Artists 1971)★★★, *All Day Music* (United Artists 1971)★★★, *The World Is A Ghetto* (United Artists 1972)★★★★, *Deliver The Word* (United Artists 1973)★★★, *War Live!* (United Artists 1974)★★, *Why Can't We Be Friends?* (United Artists 1975)★★★★, *Galaxy* (MCA 1977)★★★, *Youngblood* (United Artists 1978)★★★, *The Music Band* (MCA 1979)★★, *The Music Band 2* (MCA 1979)★★, *The Music Band - Live* (1980)★★, *Outlaw* (RCA 1982)★★, *Life (Is So Strange)* (RCA 1983)★★, *Where Theres Smoke* (Coco Plum 1984)★★, *Peace Sign* (RCA/Avenue 1994)★★.

●COMPILATIONS: with Burdon *Love Is All Around* (ABC 1976)★★, *Greatest Hits* (United Artists 1976)★★★★, *Platinum Jazz* (Blue Note 1977)★★, *Best Of The Music Band* (MCA 1994)★★★, *Anthology 1970-1994* (Avenue/Rhino 1995)★★★★, *The Best Of War And More: Vol. 2* (Avenue/Rhino 1997)★★★.

WARD, CLIFFORD T.

b. 10 February 1946, Kidderminster, Worcestershire, England. Ward typified the early 70s bedsitter singer-songwriter with a series of albums that were at best delightful and at worst mawkish. His debut album appeared on disc jockey John Peel's brave-but-doomed Dandelion label in 1972. *Home Thoughts* proved to be his finest work and gave him wider recognition. Schoolteacher Ward constructed each song as a complete story, sometimes with great success. The beautiful 'Gaye' became a UK hit but surprisingly the stronger 'Home Thoughts From Abroad' and the infectious and lyrically excellent 'Wherewithal' failed to chart. *Mantlepieces* and *Escalator* contained a similar recipe of more harmless tales like the minor hit 'Scullery' with naïvely sexist lyrics like; 'You're my picture, my Picasso, you brighten up any scullery'. In later years although still recording the occasional album and still reluctant to perform live, Ward has received more kudos as a songwriter with his material being recorded by artists such as Cliff Richard and Justin Hayward. At the time of writing Ward was seriously ill after being struck down with multiple sclerosis. In 1992, friends and colleagues pieced together an album of out-takes and demos to give the ailing Ward some financial assistance.

●ALBUMS: *Singer Songwriter* (Dandelion 1972)★★, *Home Thoughts* (Charisma 1973)★★★, *Mantlepieces* (Charisma 1973)★★, *Escalator* (Charisma 1975)★★, *No More Rock And Roll* (Charisma 1975)★★, *Both Of Us* (Phillips 1984)★★, *Sometime Next Year* (Tembo 1986)★★, *Laugh It Off* (Ameless 1992)★★, *Julia And Other New Stories* (Graduate 1994)★★.

●COMPILATIONS: *Gaye And Other Stories* (1987)★★★.

WATERS, ROGER

b. 9 September 1944, Great Bookham, Cambridge, England. Waters' career as co-founder of Pink Floyd enabled him to be part of one of the most successful rock bands of all time. His astonishing peaks during a career of 17 years were *Dark Side Of The Moon* (1973) and *The Wall* (1979). Waters' lyrics often attempted to exorcise his personal anguish at the death of his father during World War II. They also addressed his increasing conflict with the pressures of rock stardom and his alienation from the audience. The introspective nature of these lyrics often led to accusations of indulgence, which in part led to the break-up of Pink Floyd in 1983. His first official solo album (he had previously recorded an album in 1970 with Ron Geesin as a soundtrack to the film *The Body*), was the crudely packaged *The Pros And Cons Of Hitchhiking*, which showed a departure from the bitter lyrics he had recently produced with Pink Floyd. Eric Clapton guested on the album. Waters wrote and performed the soundtrack to the Raymond Briggs animated anti-nuclear film, *When The Wind Blows* in 1986. *Radio K.A.O.S.* followed in 1987 together with the excellent single 'The Tide Is Turning (After Live Aid)'. During this time Waters was in bitter litigation with other members of his former group as he unsuccessfully tried to stop them using the Pink Floyd name. In 1990, as part of a project in aid of the Leonard Cheshire Memorial Fund For Disaster Relief, Waters masterminded a massive performance of *The Wall* by the remains of the Berlin Wall. This ambitious event was televised around the world and featured a host of star guests including performances by Van Morrison, Cyndi Lauper, Sinead O'Connor and Joni Mitchell, plus actors Albert Finney and Tim Curry. Time, if nothing else, has still to find a way of healing the rift between Waters and the remaining members of Pink Floyd.
●ALBUMS: with Ron Geesin *Music From The Body* soundtrack (Harvest 1970)★, *The Pros And Cons Of Hitch Hiking* (Harvest 1984)★★★, *When The Wind Blows* soundtrack (Virgin 1986)★★, *Radio K.A.O.S* (Harvest 1987)★★, *The Wall: Live In Berlin* (Mercury 1990)★★, *Amused To Death* (1993)★★.

WAYNE, JEFF

Born and raised in New York, and a graduate in journalism, Jeff Wayne studied at the famous Juilliard School of Music in New York. In the early 60s he was a member of the group the Sandpipers, although not at the time they had their worldwide hit with 'Guantanamera'. Wayne also worked as an arranger for the Righteous Brothers before coming to London in 1966. He studied at Trinity College of Music, after which his ambition was to write and stage a musical based on Charles Dickens' *A Tale Of Two Cities* (the lyrics were written by his father, Jerry Wayne). Starring Edward Woodward, the project finally made the stage in 1969, by which time Wayne had started to establish himself as a jingle writer. In the late 60s and early 70s he was responsible for some of the best known television advertising slogans and tunes such as 'McDougal's Flour - so fine it flows through the fingers'. He then became involved with the career of the singer and actor David Essex and produced most of his early hits as well as acting as his musical director on tour. Wayne sprang to the public's attention with his concept album based on H.G. Wells' *War Of The Worlds*. Written by Wayne and featuring the spoken or singing talents of Essex, actor Richard Burton, Justin Hayward, Phil Lynott, Chris Thompson and Julie Covington, the album was a huge success. Living off its royalties, Wayne kept a low profile for a time although in 1984 he performed on the Kevin Peek and Rick Wakeman album *Beyond The Planets*. In 1991 he announced that he was set to release his next project - *Spartacus*, featuring Anthony Hopkins, Jimmy Helms, and Ladysmith Black Mambazo amongst others.
●ALBUMS: *War Of The Worlds* (Columbia 1978)★★★, *War Of The Worlds - Highlights* (Columbia 1981)★★★.

WEATHER REPORT

Founded by Joe Zawinul (keyboards) and Wayne Shorter (reeds). The highly accomplished Weather Report was one of the groups credited with inventing jazz-rock fusion music in the 70s. The two founders had worked together as members of Miles Davis's band in 1969-71, playing on *Bitches' Brew*. The first line-up of Weather Report included Airto Moreira (percussion) and Miroslav Vitous (bass). Signing to CBS Records, the group's first album included compositions by Shorter and Zawinul and the line-up was strengthened by Eric Gravatt (drums) and Um Romao (percussion) on the best-selling *I Sing The Body Electric*. Among the tracks was Zawinul's ambitious 'Unknown Soldier', evoking the experience of war. During the mid-70s, the group adopted more elements of rock rhythms and electronic technology, a process that reached its peak on *Black Market*, where Zawinul played synthesizer and the brilliant electric bassist Jaco Pastorius made his first appearance with the group. Pastorius left the group in 1980.

Weather Report's popularity was at its peak in the late 70s and early 80s, when the group was a four-piece, with drummer Peter Erskine joining Pastorius and the two founder members. He was replaced by Omar Hakim from George Benson's band in 1982, and for the first time Weather Report included vocals on *Procession*. The singer was Janis Siegel from Manhattan Transfer. During the mid-80s, Zawinul and Shorter made solo albums before dissolving Weather Report in 1986. Shorter led his own small group while Zawinul formed Weather Update with guitarist Steve Khan and Erskine. Hakim went on to become a touring drummer, highly acclaimed for his work with Sting and Eric Clapton. Plans were afoot in 1996 to re-form the band around the nucleus of Shorter and Zawinul.

●ALBUMS: *Weather Report* i (Columbia 1971)★★★, *I Sing The Body Electric* (Columbia 1972)★★★★, *Sweetnighter* (Columbia 1973)★★★, *Mysterious Traveller* (Columbia 1974)★★★★, *Tail Spinnin'* (Columbia 1975)★★★, *Black Market* (Columbia 1976)★★★★, *Heavy Weather* (Columbia 1977)★★★★, *Mr. Gone* (Columbia 1978), *8:30* (Columbia 1979)★★★, *Night Passages* (Columbia 1980)★★★, *Weather Report* ii (Columbia 1982)★★★, *Procession* (Columbia 1983)★★★, *Domino Theory* (Columbia 1984)★★★, *Sportin' Life* (Columbia 1985)★★★, *This Is This* (Columbia 1986)★★★, *New Album* (Columbia 1988)★★★.

●COMPILATIONS: *Heavy Weather: The Collection* (Columbia 1990)★★★★, *The Weather Report Selection* 3-CD box set (Columbia 1992)★★★.

WEBB, JIMMY

b. James Layne Webb, 15 August 1946, Elk City, Oklahoma, USA. A music major at California's San Bernadino Valley College, Webb arranged a single for girl group the Contessas while still a student. Inspired, he moved to Hollywood where he secured work with Jobete Music, the publishing wing of Tamla/Motown Records. He wrote 'This Time Last Summer' for Brenda Holloway and 'My Christmas Tree' for the Supremes, before recording demo tapes of other compositions at a local recording studio. These reached singer Johnny Rivers, who recorded the original version of Webb's 'By The Time I Get To Phoenix' in October 1966. Rivers appointed Webb as in-house composer/arranger for his newly launched Soul City Records where he worked with the fledgling Fifth Dimension. Having completed the intriguing 'Rosecrans Blvd', the partnership flourished with 'Up, Up And Away', a breezy recording indebted to west coast harmony groups and uptown soul, which sold over one million copies and was later adopted by the TWA corporation for a series of commercials. More impressive still, it was the song the Apollo XI astronauts played in their locker room as they journeyed to the moon. Links with the Fifth Dimension were maintained on two attendant albums, *Up, Up And Away* and *Magic Garden* - which included the exquisite 'Carpet Man' - while Webb also worked extensively on Rivers' own *Rewind*.

The artist's relationship with the Fifth Dimension subsequently waned. By that point Webb had issued a single, 'Love Years Coming', credited to the Strawberry Children. More importantly, Glen Campbell exhumed 'By The Time I Get To Phoenix', which won a Grammy as the Best Vocal Performance of 1967. The following year Richard Harris scored a major international smash with 'MacArthur Park', a melodramatic epic marked by lyrical extravagance and a sumptuous melody. Although less commercially successful, the follow-up single, 'Didn't We', is arguably Webb's finest composition. He arranged and composed material for Harris's albums *A Tramp Shining* and *The Yard Went On Forever* (both 1968), but was dismayed when his own solo debut, *Jimmy Webb Sings Jimmy Webb*, was issued as it featured his early demo recordings, overdubbed and orchestrated without the artist's consent. Further success for Campbell with 'Wichita Lineman' (1968) and 'Galveston' (1969) demonstrated Webb's songwriting ability as its zenith. These moving stories expressed the writer's immense feeling for traditional, rural America and are rightly regarded as standards. Webb also composed/arranged material for Thelma Houston's impressive *Sunshower* (1969). The sole cover version on the album - a version of 'Jumping Jack Flash' - mischievously features a string passage based on Stravinsky. The same year Webb completed the film score for *Tell Them Willie Boy Is Here*, but grew impatient with a public perception of him merely as a songwriter.

A 1970 tour revealed his inexperience as a performer, although *Words And Music* showed the episode had engendered a tighter, rock-based style. 'I wanted to scale things down,' Webb later commented, '(and) find a role outside the "Jimmy Webb sound", whatever that was.' Guitarist Fred Tackett, later an associate of Little Feat, provided much of the accompaniment on a set including 'P.F. Sloan', a heartfelt tribute to a much neglected songwriter. *And So: On* proved even more impressive, with superb contributions by jazz musician Larry Coryell. The excellent *Letters*, which included a superb rendition of 'Galveston', was succeeded by *Land's End*, arguably Webb's finest creation. 'Just This One Time', a conscious recreation of the Righteous Brothers' sound and 'Crying In My Sleep' are breathtaking compositions while the title track is an inspired, orchestrated *tour de force*. The album featured a cameo appearance by Joni Mitchell, whose confessional style had a marked influence on Webb's subsequent work. Her own song, 'All I Want' was a highlight on *The Supremes Produced And Arranged By Jimmy Webb* (1973), one of several similarly styled projects the artist undertook at this time. On *Reunion* (1974) Webb rekindled his partnership with Glen Campbell; *Earthbound* (1975) saw him recreating a partnership with the Fifth Dimension. His own albums were released to critical acclaim, but when sales proved negligible, Webb undertook other outside projects. He wrote and/or produced material for Cher, Joan Baez, Joe Cocker and Frank Sinatra, although Art Garfunkel proved his main supporter and best interpreter from this period. *Watermark* (1978) contains what many regard as the definitive interpretations of several Webb songs.

The artist resumed his recording career with *El Mirage*, which was produced, conducted and arranged by George Martin. The set included 'The Highwayman', a title popularized by the country 'supergroup' featuring Johnny Cash, Kris Kristofferson, Willie Nelson and Waylon Jennings. Webb also continued to score film soundtracks, including *Voices* and *Hanoi Hilton* and by the end of the 80s was completing work on two musicals, *The Children's Crusade* and *Dandelion Wine*. Tiring of public indifference to his own releases, Webb ceased recording following the release of *Angel Heart*. However, he undertook several live shows in 1988 - the first in over a decade - and released his first studio album proper in 11 years with *Suspending Disbelief*. Sympathetically produced by Linda Ronstadt, it included Webb's own version of 'Too Young To Die', previously recorded by David Crosby. The set possessed all Webb's familiar strengths, but it is as a gifted composer, rather than performer, that he will be remembered.

●ALBUMS: *Jimmy Webb Sings Jimmy Webb* (Epic 1968)★★, *Words And Music* (Reprise 1970)★★★, *And So: On* (Reprise 1971)★★★, *Letters* (Reprise 1972)★★★★, *Land's End* (Asylum 1974)★★★★, *El Mirage* (Asylum 1977)★★★, *Voices* soundtrack (Planet 1979)★★, *Angel Heart* (Columbia/Lorimar 1982)★★★, *Hanoi Hilton* soundtrack (1987)★★, *Suspending Disbelief* (Warners 1993)★★★, *Ten Easy Pieces* (Guardian 1996)★★★.

●COMPILATIONS: *Archive* (Warners 1993)★★★★.

WEBB, MARTI

b. 1944, Cricklewood, London, England. In 1963, at the age of 19, singer Marti Webb was 'plucked from the chorus' of the London production of Leslie Bricusse and Anthony Newley's hit musical *Stop the World - I Want To Get Off*, to star opposite Tommy Steele in the even more successful *Half A Sixpence*. Although she was not chosen to recreate her role in the subsequent 1967 film version, she did dub the singing voice of her replacement, actress Julia Foster. Webb played Nancy in a national tour of Lionel Bart's *Oliver!* in 1965, and again two years later in the major West End revival. In the early 70s she appeared in one of the in-vogue 'biblical' musicals, *Godspell*, with a superior cast that included Jeremy Irons, David Essex and Julie Covington. She also featured in a musical adaptation of J.B. Priestley's *The Good Companions*, which had a score by André Previn and Johnny Mercer. Much better all round was *The Card*, with songs by Tony Hatch and Jackie Trent, in which Webb impressed with her duet with Jim Dale on 'Opposite Your Smile', and the solo 'I Could Be The One'. It was in the 80s, however, that she came to prominence after successfully replacing Elaine Page in *Evita*. In 1980 she appeared in an invited concert and a television broadcast of the 'song cycle' *Tell Me On A Sunday*, with a score by Andrew Lloyd Webber and lyricist Don Black. This spawned both a studio and television soundtrack album, and Webb took one of the show's songs, 'Take That Look Off Your Face', into the UK Top 10. Two years later, when an expanded version of *Tell Me On A Sunday* was joined with *Variations* to form the two-part 'theatrical concert', *Song And Dance*, Webb's 50 minute solo performance was hailed as a 'remarkable *tour de force*'. She also took over various roles in other Lloyd Webber productions, including his longest-running British musical, *Cats*. Webb's singles include 'Didn't Mean To Fall In Love', 'Ready For Roses Now', 'Ben' (UK Top 5), and three popular television themes: 'Always There' from *Howard's Way* (UK Top 20), 'Someday Soon'

from *The Onedin Line*, and a duet with Paul Jones on 'I Could Be So Good For You', from *Minder*. In the early 90s Webb toured the UK and the Channel Islands with *The Magic Of The Musicals*, co-starring with television's *Opportunity Knocks* winner, Mark Rattray. She also appeared with broadcaster David Jacobs in an evening of Gershwin songs at London's Café Royal, and presented *The Don Black Story* on BBC Radio 2. In 1995 Webb toured the UK in a major revival of *Evita*.

●ALBUMS: *Tell Me On A Sunday* (Polydor 1980)★★, *Won't Change Places* (Polydor 1981)★★, *I'm Not That Kind Of Girl* (Polydor 1983)★★, *Encore* (Starblend 1985)★★, *Always There* (BBC 1986)★★, *Sings Gershwin* (BBC 1987)★★, *Marti Webb - The Album* (1993)★★, *Performance* (Ronco 1993)★★, with Dave Willetts, Carl Wayne *Songs From Evita* (1994)★★.

WEBER, EBERHARD

b. 22 January 1940, Stuttgart, Germany. Weber's father taught him the cello from the age of six and he only turned to the bass in 1956. He liked the sound of Bill Haley's records, saw an old stand-up bass hanging on the wall in the school gym and tried it out. He played jazz in his spare time from making television commercials and working as a theatre director and only turned professional in 1972. With Wolfgang Dauner (keyboards) he played in a trio inspired by the Bill Evans Trio and in Dauner's psychedelic jazz-rock band, Etcetera. He worked with the Dave Pike Set and then joined Volker Kriegel's Spectrum, but did not share Kriegel's fascination with rock rhythms and left in 1974. Weber had already recorded *The Colours Of Chloë* for ECM Records and had developed the five-string bass, which gives him his individual sound, from an old Italian bass with a long neck and a small rectangular soundbox he had seen in an antique shop. His composition style seemed to owe something to minimalist writing but had developed when he realized that he only liked bits and pieces of other people's music and he had concluded 'that when I came to compose I would only use chords and phrases I really liked - and use them over and over'. *The Colours Of Chloë* brought him international recognition and he then worked with guitarist Ralph Towner (1974) and Gary Burton (1974-76). Meanwhile he formed his own band Colours with Rainer Bruninghaus, Charlie Mariano, and first Jon Christensen, and then John Marshall. He wanted a band that played in an absolutely European way with understated rhythm, spacey, impressionistic keyboard sounds and flowing melody. This European tradition provides 'the feeling for group empathy that I am drawn to' while the jazz tradition gives 'the whole feeling for improvisation . . . knowing when to stretch out or lay out'. He disbanded Colours when he could no longer hold these two traditions in balance and has since played with the United Jazz And Rock Ensemble and as a regular member of saxophonist Jan Garbarek's bands. Since 1985 he has also performed solo bass concerts, where his prodigious technique is evident. He is able to conjure from his electric instrument and a limited array of equipment, some glorious sounds.

●ALBUMS: *The Colours Of Chloë* (ECM 1974)★★★, *Yellow Fields* (ECM 1975)★★★, *The Following Morning* (ECM 1976)★★★, *Silent Feet* (ECM 1977)★★★, *Fluid Rustle* (ECM 1979)★★★, *Little Movements* (ECM 1980)★★★, *Later That Evening* (ECM 1982)★★★, *Chorus* (ECM 1984)★★★, *Orchestra* (ECM 1988)★★★, *Pendulum* (ECM 1994)★★★.

●COMPILATIONS: *Works* (ECM 1989)★★★★.

WELCH, BOB

b. 31 July 1946, Los Angeles, California, USA. Guitarist/vocalist Welch was working in a Parisian R&B club prior to joining Fleetwood Mac in 1971. He remained a member until December 1974 when the pressures of keeping the group afloat during its most turbulent era proved too great. During his stay he was quite prolific as a songwriter and wrote, among others, the excellent 'Sentimental Lady' for their *Bare Trees* and was credited with most of the material for *Heroes Are Hard To Find*. Welch then formed Paris with Hunt Sales and Glenn Cornick (ex-Jethro Tull), but left in 1977 to begin a solo career. Mick Fleetwood helped his former colleague secure a record contract and the resultant *French Kiss* spawned a US Top 10 hit in a reworking of 'Sentimental Lady' and two further chart entries in 'Ebony Eyes' and 'Hot Love Cold World'. 'Precious Love' from *Three Hearts* reached the US Top 20 in 1979, but Welch then proved unable to repeat such success. He subsequently moved base to Phoenix, Arizona, where he worked on film soundtracks and now resides in Nashville working on some new projects, still involved in music.

●ALBUMS: *French Kiss* (Capitol 1977)★★★, *Three Hearts* (Capitol 1979)★★, *The Other One* (Capitol 1980)★★, *Man Overboard* (Capitol 1980)★★, *Bob Welch* (RCA 1981)★★, *Eye Contact* (1983)★★.

●COMPILATIONS: *Collection: Bob Welch* (EMI 1983)★★★.

●FURTHER READING: *Fleetwood*, Mick Fleetwood. *Fleetwood Mac*, Roy Carr.

WETTON, JOHN

b. 12 June 1949, Willingdon, Derbyshire, England. This bass guitarist was first noted by British 'progressive' rock enthusiasts as one of Mogul Thrash, a short-lived rock band featuring ex-Colosseum member James Litherland. From 1971-72, he was employed in Family while also surfacing as an in-demand session player. He blossomed from pot-boiling stints with comparative unknowns such as Edward's Hand and Jack Knife to proudly assisting Rare Bird, Uriah Heep, Eno and Pete Sinfield. In 1973, he replaced Boz Burrell in King Crimson for whom his bass lines were more impressive than his lead vocals. There followed a stint with Roxy Music - immortalized on a 1976 concert album - and

work on solo recordings by individual members. A better offer persuaded him to join Uriah Heep in 1975 before a year off the road preceded his co-founding of UK in 1978. After three albums with the band, he embarked on his only solo effort, *Caught In The Crossfire*, on which his skills on guitar and keyboards were heard - along with contributions by Phil Manzanera and other associates from his professional past. Seduced again by the more dynamic versatility of a group, he accompanied Asia for a couple of albums and attendant tours while remaining available for hire in the studio by artists such as Philip Rambow and Wishbone Ash.

●ALBUMS: *Caught In The Crossfire* (EG 1980)★★, *Battle Lines* (Cromwell (1995)★★, *Akustika - Live In Amerika* (Pinnacle 1996)★★.

●COMPILATIONS: *Kings Road 1972 - 1980* (EG 1987)★★★. As Wetton Manzanera *Wetton Manzanera* (Geffen 1987)★★★, *Chasing The Dragon* (Mesa 1995)★★★.

WHITE, BARRY

b. 12 September 1944, Galveston, Texas, USA. Raised in Los Angeles, White immersed himself in the local music fraternity while still very young, playing piano on Jesse Belvin's hit, 'Goodnight My Love', at the age of 11. White made several records during the early 60s, under his own name, as 'Barry Lee', and as a member of the Upfronts, the Atlantics and the Majestics. However, he found a greater success as a backroom figure, guiding the careers of, among others, Felice Taylor and Viola Wills. In 1969 White put together Love Unlimited, a female vocal trio made up of Diana Taylor, Glodean James (his future wife) and her sister Linda. He also founded the Love Unlimited Orchestra, a 40-piece ensemble to accompany himself and the singing trio, for which he conducted, composed and arranged. Love Unlimited's success in 1972 with 'Walkin' In The Rain With The One I Love', featuring his gravelly, passion-soaked voice on the telephone, rejuvenated White's own career, during which he enjoyed major US hits with 'I'm Gonna Love You Just A Little More Baby', 'Never, Never Gonna Give Ya Up' (both 1973), 'Can't Get Enough Of Your Love, Babe' and 'You're The First, The Last, My Everything' (both 1974), all of which proved just as popular in the UK. With these, the artist established a well-wrought formula where catchy pop/soul melodies were fused to sweeping arrangements and the singer's husky growl. The style quickly verged on self-parody as the sexual content of the lyrics grew more explicit, but although his pop hits lessened towards the end of the 70s, he remained the idolatry subject of live performances. The singer's last major hit was in 1978 with Billy Joel's 'Just The Way You Are'. He later undertook several recordings with Glodean White before returning to the UK Top 20 in 1987 with 'Sho' You Right'. The subject of critical approbation, particularly with reference to his large frame. White's achievements during the peak of his career, in securing gold and platinum discs for worldwide sales, should not be underestimated. Lisa Stansfield has often voiced her approval of White's work and in 1992, she and White re-recorded a version of Stansfield's hit, 'All Around The World' but it was not as successful as the original.

●ALBUMS: *I've Got So Much To Give* (20th Century 1973)★★★, *Stone Gon'* (20th Century 1973)★★★, *Can't Get Enough* (20th Century 1974)★★★, *Just Another Way To Say I Love You* (20th Century 1975)★★★, *Let The Music Play* (20th Century 1976)★★★, *Is This Whatcha Wont?* (20th Century 1976)★★★, *Barry White Sings For Someone You Love* (20th Century 1977)★★★, *Barry White The Man* (20th Century 1978)★★★, *The Message Is Love* (Unlimited Gold 1979)★★★, *I Love To Sing The Songs I Sing* (20th Century 1979)★★, *Barry White's Sheet Music* (Unlimited Gold 1980)★★, *The Best Of Our Love* (Unlimited Gold 1981)★★, with Glodean James *Barry And Glodean* (Unlimited Gold 1981)★★★, *Beware!* (1981)★★, *Change* (Unlimited Gold 1982)★★, *Dedicated* (Unlimited Gold 1983)★★, *The Right Night And Barry White* (A&M 1987)★★, *The Man Is Back!* (A&M 1990)★★, *In Your Mix* (A&M 1991)★★★, *The Icon Is Love* (A&M 1994)★★.

●COMPILATIONS: *Barry White's Greatest Hits* (20th Century 1975)★★★★, *Barry White's Greatest Hits Vol.2* (20th Century 1977)★★★, *Heart And Soul* · (K-Tel 1985)★★, *Satin & Soul* (Connoisseur 1987)★★★, *The Collection* (Polydor 1988)★★★★, *Satin & Soul Vol. 2* (Connoisseur 1990)★★, *Just For You* (1993)★★★.

WHITE, TONY JOE

b. 23 July 1943, Oak Grove, Louisiana, USA. A country singer and songwriter, White was also tagged with the label 'swamp rock', a musical genre he helped to create. Originally he was a member of Tony And The Mojos before defecting to Texas to start Tony And The Twilights. He started recording in 1968 and many people presumed he was black after hearing his layered vocals. He had his first hit on Monument with 'Polk Salad Annie' in 1969, later covered by Elvis Presley. Also contained on his debut *Black And White* was 'Willie And Laura Mae Jones', which was covered by Dusty Springfield. After hitting once more with 'Groupie Girl' he wrote 'Rainy Night In Georgia' which became a standard. His first three albums were produced by Billy Swan, and Cozy Powell drummed for him at the 1970 Isle Of Wight festival. He moved to Warner Brothers Records in 1971 and had a hit in 1979 with 'Mamas Don't Let Your Cowboys Grow Up To Be Babies', an answer record to Ed Bruce's country chart-topper of the previous year, 'Mamas Don't Let Your Babies Grow Up To Be Cowboys'. White co-wrote 'Steamy Windows' with Tina Turner, which gave her a Top 20 UK hit in 1990. White is an artist who refuses to compromise and like J.J. Cale, he hits a groove and he sticks with it. His most recent albums (*Decent Groove* and *Lake Placid Blues*) indicate a man totally at peace with himself.

●ALBUMS: *Black And White* (Monument 1969)★★★, *Continued* (Monument 1969)★★★, *Tony Joe* (Monument 1970)★★★, *Tony Joe White* (Warners 1971)★★★, *The Train I'm On* (Warners 1972)★★★, *Home Made Ice Cream* (Warners 1973)★★★, *Eyes* (1977)★★, *Real Thing* (1980)★★, *Dangerous* (1983)★★★, *Roosevelt And Ira Lee* (Astan 1984)★★★, *Live!* (Dixie Frog 1990)★★★, *Closer To The Truth* (1992)★★★, *The Path Of A Decent Groove* (1993)★★★, *Lake Placid Blues* (Remark 1995)★★★.

●COMPILATIONS: *The Best Of Tony Joe White* (Warners 1979)★★★.

●FILMS: *Catch My Soul* (1974).

WHITESNAKE

This UK-based heavy rock band was led by David Coverdale (b. 21 September 1951, Saltburn, Tyne And Wear, England). The lead vocalist with Deep Purple since 1973, Coverdale left the group in 1976 and recorded two solo albums, *Whitesnake* and *Northwinds*. Shortly afterwards, he formed a touring band from musicians who had played on those records. Entitled David Coverdale's Whitesnake, the group included Micky Moody (guitar), Bernie Marsden (guitar), Brian Johnston (keyboards), Neil Murray (bass) and John Dowle (drums). For much of the late 70s the group toured in the UK, Europe and Japan (the first US tour was in 1980). During this period there were several personnel changes with ex-Deep Purple members Jon Lord and Ian Paice joining on keyboards and drums. Whitesnake's first British hit was 'Fool For Your Loving' (1980), composed by Coverdale, Marsden and Moody, and the double album, *Live in The Heart Of The City* (named after the Bobby Bland song featured onstage by Coverdale) reached the Top 10 the following year. At this point, the illness of Coverdale's daughter caused a hiatus in the group's career and when Whitesnake re-formed in 1982 only Lord and Moody remained from the earlier line-up. The new members were Mel Galley (guitar), ex-Back Door and Alexis Korner bassist Colin Hodgkinson and Cozy Powell (drums). However, this configuration lasted only briefly and by 1984 the long-serving Moody and Lord had left, the latter to join a regenerated Deep Purple. While Coverdale remained the focus of Whitesnake, there were numerous personnel changes in the following years. These had little effect on the band's growing reputation as one of the leading exponents of heavy rock, with unambiguously sexist record sleeves marking out their lyrical and aesthetic territory. Frequent tours finally brought a million-selling album in the USA with 1987's *Whitesnake* and Coverdale's bluesy ballad style brought Top 10 hits with 'Is This Love' and 'Here I Go Again'. They were co-written with ex-Thin Lizzy guitarist John Sykes, a member of Whitesnake from 1983-86. His replacement, Dutch-born Adrian Vandenburg, was co-writer with Coverdale on the band's 1989 album, co-produced by Keith Olsen and Mike Clink. Ex-Dio guitarist Vivian Campbell was also a member of the band in the early

90s. Coverdale joined forces with Jimmy Page for the release of *Coverdale/Page* in early 1993, but when Whitesnake's contract with Geffen Records in the USA expired in 1994, it was not renewed. Coverdale returned with a new album in 1997 with Vandenberg, Guy 'Starka' Pratt (bass), Brett Tuggle (keyboards) and Denny Carmassi (drums). *Restless Heart* was a mellow (by Whitesnake standards) recording which emphasized just what a terrific voice and range Coverdale has.

●ALBUMS: *Trouble* (United Artists 1978)★★★, *Love Hunter* (United Artists 1979)★★★, *Live At Hammersmith* (United Artists 1980)★★, *Ready An' Willing* (United Artists 1980)★★★, *Live In The Heart Of The City* (Sunburst 1980)★★★, *Come And Get It* (Liberty 1981)★★★, *Saints 'N Sinners* (Liberty 1982)★★, *Slide It In* (Liberty 1984)★★★, *Whitesnake* (Liberty 1987)★★★★, *1987* (Liberty 1992)★★★, *Slip Of The Tongue* (EMI 1989)★★★, *Restless Heart* (EMI 1997)★★★.

●COMPILATIONS: *Best Of* (EMI 1988)★★★★, *Greatest Hits* (MCA 1994)★★★★.

●VIDEOS: *Fourplay* (1984), *Whitesnake Live* (1984), *Trilogy* (1988).

●FURTHER READING: *Illustrated Biography*, Simon Robinson. *Whitesnake*, Tom Hibbert.

WHITTAKER, ROGER

b. 22 March 1936, Nairobi, Kenya. Born of English parents originally from Staffordshire, Whittaker spent his younger years living in Africa. It was here that he acquired his first musical instrument in the shape of a guitar made by an Italian prisoner-of-war. In 1956 he moved to South Africa to what was to be an ill-fated attempt at studying medicine in Cape Town. After a period of teaching, he arrived in Wales in 1959 to study marine biology and bio-chemistry. Until then, Whittaker had treated his musical career purely as a part-time occupation, entertaining small groups of friends and the occasional folk club date. By 1961, while still continuing his studies, he had played many cabaret slots and after recording an independently funded single for charity, he secured a contract with Fontana Records. His second single, 'Steel Man' (as Rog Whittaker), reached the lower regions of the UK charts. Roger decided to eschew a promising career in science in favour of one in entertainment. His brand of romantic folk ballads made him a favourite with audiences all around Britain, particularly in Northern Ireland, where he enjoyed a resident spot on the Ulster television show *This And That*.

His steady rise in popularity was bolstered by a successful appearance at the Knokke music festival in Belgium in 1967. Among his prize winning performances was the self-penned, 'Mexican Whistler', which was recorded in Paris soon after the festival and became a chart number 1 around the continent. Whittaker's easy-going, relaxed style made him a star performer on the European television and concert circuit. By learning the translations of his songs phonetically, he has taken the trouble to record especially for his German audience. This growing band of admirers spread in time to the Antipodes and Canada, yet he had still to crack the UK market. This was achieved in 1969 with 'The Leavin' (Durham Town)' and the follow-up, 'I Don't Believe In If Anymore'. Along with 'New World In The Morning', 'Why' (co-written with Joan Stanton) and 'The Last Farewell' (co-written with Ron Webster), these songs established Whittaker as a successful MOR performer and finally made him a star in his adopted home country, giving him his own BBC television series.

It was the 'Last Farewell' that eventually broke the singer in the USA, bringing him a Top 20 hit in 1975 and finally selling over 11,000,000 copies worldwide. During the ensuing round of coast-to-coast tours and talk shows, Roger launched a songwriting competition on behalf of UNESCO, earning him the B'nai B'rith Humanitarian Award. In 1986, after a gap of 11 years, Whittaker made a reappearance on the UK Top 10 singles chart with the standard 'The Skye Boat Song' in a duo performance with fellow light entertainer, Des O'Connor. He has never lost contact with his African roots and his concern for the diminishing numbers of rhinos in his native Kenya led to a campaign to fight the poachers, including the fund-raising song, 'Rescue The Rhinos'. As a prodigious recording and performing artist, Roger Whittaker's global record sales have reached in excess of 40,000,000, a glowing testimony of this singer's phenomenal success. In 1992, Roger Whittaker undertook a major UK concert tour with his 'outstandingly acclaimed American show', and continued to appear regularly in many other countries around the world.

●ALBUMS: *Butterfly* (1965)★★★, *Dynamic* (1967)★★★, *Mexican Whistler* (1967)★★★, *This Is Roger Whittaker* (Columbia 1968)★★★, *Settle Down With Roger Whittaker* (1969)★★★, *C'Est Ma Vie* (1969)★★★, *I Don't Believe In If Anymore* (Columbia 1970)★★★, *New World In The Morning* (Columbia 1971)★★★, *A Special Kind Of Man* (1971)★★★, *Whistling Round The World* (Starline 1971)★★★, *For My Friends* (Columbia 1972)★★★, *Head On Down The Road* (Columbia 1973)★★★, *The Last Farewell* (1974)★★★, *In Orbit* (Columbia 1974)★★★, *Travelling With Roger Whittaker* (1974)★★★, *Live In Canada* (1975)★★★, *Ride A Country Road* (1975)★★★, *The Magical World Of Roger Whittaker* (1975)★★★, *Live - With Saffron* (1975)★★★, *Reflections Of Love* (EMI 1976)★★★, *Folk Songs Of Our Time* (EMI 1977)★★★, *Roger Whittaker Sings The Hits* (Columbia 1978)★★★, *Imagine* (1978)★★★, *From The People To The People* (1979)★★★, *When I Need You* (1979)★★★, *Mirrors Of My Mind* (1979)★★★, *Wishes* (1979)★★★, *Voyager* (1980)★★★, *With Love* (1980)★★★, *Changes* (EMI 1981)★★★, *The Roger Whittaker Album* (1981)★★★, *Live In Concert* (Polydor 1981)★★★, *Roger Whittaker In Kenya* (1982)★★★, *The Wind Beneath My Wings* (1982)★★★, *Roger's Canadian Favourites* (1983)★★★, *Take A Little,*

Give A Little (1984)★★★, *Songs Of Love And Life* (1984)★★★, *Tidings Of Comfort And Joy* (1984)★★★, *The Country Feel* (Tembo 1985)★★★, *The Romantic Side* (1985)★★★, *Singing The Hits* (1985)★★★, *The Songwriter* (1985)★★★, *Skye Boat Song And Other Great Songs* (1986)★★★, *Easy Riding* (Easyriding 1988)★★★, *Living And Loving* (1988)★★★, *Love Will Be Our Home* (1989)★★★, *Maritime Memories* (1989)★★★, *A Time For Peace* (1989)★★★, *Live From The Tivoli* (1989)★★★, *Home Lovin' Man* (Tembo 1989)★★★★, *World's Most Beautiful Christmas Songs* (Tembo 1989)★★, *I'd Fall In Love Tonight* (1989)★★★, *You Deserve The Best* (RCA 1990)★★★, *The Country Collection* (1991)★★★, *Sincerely Yours* (1991)★★★, *You Deserve The Best* US release, different track listing from UK album (1991)★★★, *A Perfect Day* (RCA 1996)★★★.

●COMPILATIONS: *The Very Best Of Roger Whittaker* (Columbia 1975)★★★, *The Second Album Of The Very Best Of Roger Whittaker* (EMI 1976)★★★, *20 All Time Greats* (Polydor 1979)★★★, *The Best Of Roger Whittaker 1967-1975* (Polydor 1984)★★★, *Collection* (Castle 1986)★★★, *His Finest Collection* (Polydor 1987)★★★, *The Best Of Roger Whittaker* (Polydor 1991)★★★, *20 All-Time Greatest Hits* (1993)★★★.

●VIDEOS: *An Evening With Roger Whittaker* (MSD 1987).

●FURTHER READING: *So Far, So Good*, Roger and Natalie Whittaker.

WIDOWMAKER (UK)

A minor 'supergroup' formed in 1975 by ex-Love Affair vocalist Steve Ellis, ex-Spooky Tooth/Mott The Hoople guitarist Luther Grosvenor, aka Ariel Bender (b. 23 December, Worcester, England), ex-Chicken Shack/Broken Glass bassist Bob Daisley, ex-Skip Bifferty/Lindisfarne drummer Paul Nicholls and ex-Hawkwind/Leo Sayer guitarist Huw Lloyd Langton. With such experience and high credentials behind them they had little trouble getting a record contact. They signed to Jet Records, and soon set up a tour in America where their debut album was a Top 40 hit in 1976. Popular also in the UK, although records failed to chart, they appeared on the *Old Grey Whistle Test*, soon after which Ellis left to be replaced by John Butler, who was at that time fronting his own band. Together they recorded their second and slightly heavier album, *Too Late To Cry*, released in April 1977. It suffered from the media preoccupation with punk, and in July they split up. Daisley went on to work with Ozzy Osbourne, Rainbow and Uriah Heep, while Langton rejoined Hawkwind in November 1979, where he stayed until 1989 when he went solo.

●ALBUMS: *Widowmaker* (Jet 1976)★★, *Too Late To Cry* (Jet 1977)★★.

WIGAN'S CHOSEN FEW

The obscure Canadian group Chosen Few had a single on Canadian-American in 1967 and originally released the surf-styled song 'Footsee' in 1968 in the USA on Roulette. It vanished without trace, but then at the height of Britain's northern soul craze, it reappeared when entrepreneur Simon Soussan discovered that its instrumental b-side, when sped up, made a wonderful northern soul record, and he pressed some copies under the cover-up name the Sounds Of Soul. Dave McAleer's Disco Demand label picked up the rights to the track, added sounds from the 1966 FA Cup Final and the sound of a steam hammer and sped it up to match Soussan's version. Island Records insisted the act's name be changed (as they represented reggae group the Chosen Few) and McAleer added the prefix Wigan's as a tribute to the area where the record was already popular. It shot into the UK Top 10 and exuberant northern soul dancing (a forerunner of break-dancing) was seen for the first time nationwide when a group of selected club-goers danced to it on BBC Television's *Top Of The Pops*. Roulette knew nothing about the group or how to tell them of their success. Since they had recorded no more tracks for them a follow-up was never released.

●ALBUMS: as Wigan's Ovation *Northern Soul Dancer* (1993)★★.

WILD CHERRY

Wild Cherry's claim to fame was the US number 1 and UK Top 10 funky dance single, 'Play That Funky Music', in 1976, which has probably outlived the name of its creators in the minds of most fans. Wild Cherry was a white quintet formed that year in Steubenville, Ohio, USA. Its original membership consisted of Bob Parissi (guitar/vocals) and other musicians although they never recorded; Parissi re-formed the group with new recruits Bryan Bassett (guitar), Allen Wentz (bass), Mark Avsec (keyboards) and Ron Beitle (drums). The group took its name when Parissi, an accident victim laid up in hospital, looked at a box of cherry-flavoured cough drops and liked what he saw. They recorded for a small record label owned by Terry Knight. The second line-up had the famous hit; signed to Epic Records, the group preferred hard rock but often played in discos where patrons would shout, 'Play that funky music, white boy'. Writing a song around that phrase, they took it to Cleveland record producer Carl Maduri and concert promoter Mike Belkin, who secured them a record contract. The group charted with four subsequent singles but never came close to repeating the success of their 'funky' hit although the famous chant was used by white rapper, Vanilla Ice for his hit follow-up to 'Ice Ice Baby'.

●ALBUMS: *Wild Cherry* (Sweet City 1976)★★, *Electrified Funk* (Sweet City 1977)★, *I Love My Music* (Sweet City 1978)★, *Only The Wild Survive* (1979)★, *Don't Wait Too Long* (1979)★.

WILLIAMS, DENIECE

b. Deniece Chandler, 3 June 1951, Gary, Indiana, USA. Williams is a gospel/soul singer whose successes span the 70s and 80s. As a child she sang in a gospel choir and made her first recordings in the late 60s for the Chicago-based Toddlin' Town label. After training as a nurse, she was hired by Stevie Wonder to join his Wonderlove vocal backing group. She contributed to four of his albums before leaving Wonder to pursue a solo career. Produced by Maurice White of Earth, Wind And Fire, her first album included the UK hits 'That's What Friends Are For' and the number 1 'Free' which was revived in 1990 by British group BEF for their *Music Of Quality & Distinction Vol II* album of cover versions. In 1978, Williams joined Johnny Mathis for the immensely popular ballad 'Too Much Too Little Too Late' This was followed by an album of duets by the couple, *That's What Friends Are For*. Returning to a solo career, Williams moved to Maurice White's own label, ARC, but her next two albums made little impact. However, a revival of the 1965 song 'It's Gonna Take A Miracle', produced by Thom Bell, returned her to the US Top 10 in 1982. This was a prelude to the release of Williams' most well-known song, 'Let's Hear It For The Boy'. Originally made for the soundtrack of the 1984 film *Footloose*, it was issued as a single the following year and headed the US charts. Later records had no pop success although Deniece remained popular in the R&B audience and in 1988 she made her first gospel album for Sparrow. Williams is a prolific songwriter and her songs have been recorded by artists including Merry Clayton, the Emotions and Frankie Valli.

●ALBUMS: *This Is Niecy* (Columbia 1976)★★★★, *Songbird* (Columiba 1977)★★★, with Johnny Mathis *That's What Friends Are For* (Columbia 1978)★★★, *When Love Comes Calling* (Columbia 1979)★★★, *My Melody* (Columbia 1981)★★★★, *Niecy* (Columbia 1982)★★★★, *I'm So Proud* (Columbia 1983)★★★, *Let's Hear It For The Boy* (Columbia 1984)★★★, *Hot On The Trail* (Columbia 1986)★★★, *Water Under The Bridge* (Columbia 1987), *So Glad I Know* (Birdwing 1988)★★★, *As Good As It Gets* (Columbia 1989)★★★.

●FILMS: *Footloose* (1984).

WILLIAMS, DON

b. 27 May 1939, Floydada, Texas, USA. Through his father's work, Williams spent much of his childhood in Corpus Christi, Texas. Williams' mother played guitar and he grew up listening to country music. He and Lofton Kline formed a semi-professional folk group called the Strangers Two, and then, with the addition of Susan Taylor, they became the Pozo-Seco Singers, the phrase being a geological one to denote a dry well. Handled by Bob Dylan's manager Albert Grossman, they had US pop hits with 'Time', 'I Can Make It With You' and 'Look What You've Done'. Following Lofton Kline's departure, they had several replacements, resulting in a group lacking direction and were as likely to record 'Green Green Grass Of Home' as 'Strawberry Fields Forever'. After Williams had failed to switch the trio to country music, they disbanded in 1971.

He then worked for his father-in-law but also wrote for Susan Taylor's solo album via Jack Clement's music publishing company. Clement asked Williams to record albums of his company's best songs, mainly with a view to attracting other performers. In 1973 *Don Williams, Volume 1* was released on the fledgling JMI label and included such memorable songs as Bob McDill's apologia for growing old, 'Amanda', and Williams' own 'The Shelter Of Your Eyes'. Both became US country hits and JMI could hardly complain when Tommy Cash and then Waylon Jennings released 'I Recall A Gypsy Woman', thus depriving Williams of a certain winner. (In the UK, Williams' version made number 13, his biggest success.) Williams' work was reissued by ABC/Dot and *Don Williams, Volume 2* included 'Atta Way To Go' and 'We Should Be Together'. Williams then had a country number 1 with Wayland Holyfield's 'You're My Best Friend', which has become a standard and is the perennial singalong anthem at his concerts. By now, the Williams style had developed: gently paced love songs with straightforward arrangements, lyrics and sentiments. Williams was mining the same vein as Jim Reeves but he eschewed Reeves' smartness by dressing like a ranch-hand. At concerts, he'd put his hand to his battered stetson and say, 'You want me to remove my what?'.

Besides having a huge contingent of female fans, Williams counted Eric Clapton and Pete Townshend among his admirers. Clapton recorded his country hit 'Tulsa Time', written by Danny Flowers from Williams' Scratch Band. The Scratch Band released their own album, produced by Williams, in 1982. Williams played a band member himself in the Burt Reynolds film *W.W. And The Dixie Dancekings* and also appeared in *Smokey And The Bandit 2*. Williams' other successes include 'Till The Rivers All Run Dry', 'Some Broken Hearts Never Mend', 'Lay Down Beside Me' and his only US Top 30 pop hit 'I Believe In You'. Unlike most established country artists, he has not sought duet partners, although he and Emmylou Harris found success with an easy-paced version of Townes Van Zandt's 'If I Needed You'. Williams' best record is with Bob McDill's homage to his southern roots, 'Good Ol' Boys Like Me'. Moving to Capitol Records in the mid-80s Williams released such singles as 'Heartbeat In the Darkness' and 'Senorita', but the material was not as impressive. He took a sabbatical in 1988 and his recent RCA recordings, which include 'I've Been Loved By The Best', show that nothing has changed. Williams continues to be a major concert attraction maintaining his stress-free style. When interviewed, Williams gives the impression of being a contented man who takes life as he finds it. He is a rare being - a country star who is free of controversy.

●ALBUMS: with the Pozo-Seco Singers *Time* (1966)★★★, with the Pozo-Seco Singers *I Can Make It With You* (1967)★★★, with the Pozo-Seco Singers *Shades Of Time* (1968)★★★, *Don Williams, Volume 1* (ABC 1973)★★★, *Don Williams, Volume 2* (ABC 1974)★★★,

Don Williams, Volume 3 (ABC 1974)★★★, *You're My Best Friend* (ABC 1975)★★★, *Harmony* (ABC 1976)★★★, *Visions* (ABC 1977)★★★, *Country Boy* (ABC 1977)★★★, *Expressions* (ABC 1978)★★★, *Portrait* (1979)★★★, *I Believe In You* (MCA 1980)★★★, *Especially For You* (MCA 1981)★★★, *Listen To The Radio* (MCA 1982)★★★, *Yellow Moon* (MCA 1983)★★★, *Cafe Carolina* (MCA 1984)★★★, *New Moves* (Capitol 1986)★★, *Traces* (Capitol 1987)★★, *One Good Well* (1989)★★★, *As Long As I Have You* (RCA 1989)★★★, *True Love* (RCA 1990)★★★, *Currents* (RCA 1992)★★★, *Borrowed Tales* (Carlton/American Harvest 1995)★★★, *Flatlands* (Carlton 1996)★★★.
●COMPILATIONS: *Very Best Of Don Williams* (MCA 1980)★★★★, *Golden Greats* (MCA 1985)★★★★, *Best Of Don Williams, Volumes 2, 3 & 4* (MCA 1988)★★★.
●VIDEOS: *Live*.

WILLIAMS, HANK, JNR.

b. Randall Hank Williams Jnr., 26 May 1949, Shreveport, Louisiana, USA. The son of the most famous man in country music Hank Williams, he was nicknamed Bocephus after a puppet on the *Grand Ole Opry*. Being the son of a country legend has brought financial security, but it was difficult for him firmly to establish his own individuality. His mother Audrey was determined that he would follow in his father's footsteps. When only eight years old, he was touring, performing with his father's songs and even appeared on the *Grand Ole Opry*. He also had a high school band, Rockin' Randall And The Rockets. He signed for the same label as his father, MGM Records, as soon as his voice broke. In the 60s, Williams had country hits with 'Long Gone Lonesome Blues', 'Cajun Baby', a revival of 'Endless Sleep', and the only version of 'Nobody's Child' ever to make the country charts. He also recorded an embarrassing narration about his relationship with his father, 'Standing In The Shadows'. Even worse was his maudlin dialogue as Luke the Drifter Jnr., 'I Was With Red Foley (The Night He Passed Away)'. He copied his father's style for the soundtrack of the film biography of his father, *Your Cheatin' Heart* (1964), and starred in the inferior *A Time To Sing*. He was just 15 years old and Connie Francis was 26 when they released a duet about adultery, 'Walk On By'.

In 1974, Williams Jnr. moved to Alabama where he recorded a hard-hitting album *Hank Williams Jnr. And Friends* with Charlie Daniels and other top-class southern country rockers. Like his father, he has had arguments with Audrey, gone through an unhappy marriage and over-indulged in alcohol and drugs. 'Getting Over You' relates to his life, and in another song, he explains that it is the 'Family Tradition'. On 8 August 1975, Hank Williams Jnr. fell 500 feet down a Montana mountain face. Although close to death, he made a remarkable recovery, needing extensive medical and cosmetic surgery. Half of his face was reconstructed and he had to learn to speak (and sing) all over again. It was two years until he could perform once

more. Since 1977, Williams Jnr., who is managed by his opening act Merle Kilgore, has been associated with the 'outlaw country music' genre. Waylon Jennings, for example, wrote Hank Jnr.'s country hit, 'Are You Sure Hank Done It This Way?' and produced his album, *The New South*. In 1983, he had eight albums on the US country charts simultaneously, yet was not chosen as Entertainer of the Year in the Country Music Awards. In 1985, Williams released his fiftieth album, 'Five-O'. Williams' songs often lack distinctive melodies, while the lyrics concentrate on his macho, defiant persona. His best compositions include 'Montana Cafe', 'OD'd In Denver', the jazzy 'Women I've Never Had' and his account of a visit to a gay disco, 'Dinosaur'. 'If The South Woulda Won' was criticized for being racist but, possibly, he was being sardonic. However, there was no mistaking his tone to Saddam Hussein in 'Don't Give Us A Reason'. Among his other successes are 'I Fought The Law', 'Tennessee Stud', 'Ain't Misbehavin'' and his *cri de coeur*, 'If Heaven Ain't A Lot Like Dixie'. Although Williams has shown determination to move away from his father's shadow, he still sings about him. Many tribute songs by others - 'If You Don't Like Hank Williams' and 'Are You Sure Hank Done It This Way?' - have an added dimension through his interpretations. Williams himself was the subject of a tribute from David Allan Coe, who insisted that a man of six feet four inches and 15 stone should not be called 'Jnr.'

Williams' rowdy image did not fit in well with the clean-cut 'hat acts' of the early 90s, and his record sales and airplay faltered. He remains a sell-out concert draw, although a well-publicized incident during 1992 where he arrived onstage drunk, and spent most of the 20-minute performance insulting his audience, did little for his status in the Nashville community, although his father would have been mighty proud.

●ALBUMS: *Hank Williams Jnr. Sings The Songs Of Hank Williams* (MGM 1963)★★★, *Connie Francis And Hank Williams Jnr. Sing Great Country Favorites* (MGM 1964)★★★, *Father And Son - Hank Williams Sr And Hank Williams Jnr.* (MGM 1964)★★★, *Your Cheatin' Heart* film soundtrack (MGM 1965)★★, *Ballad Of The Hills And Plains* (MGM 1965)★★★, *Father And Son - Hank Williams Sr And Hank Williams Jnr. Again* (MGM 1965)★★★, *Blue's My Name* (MGM 1966)★★★, *Country Shadows* (MGM 1966)★★★, *My Own Way* (MGM 1967)★★★, *My Songs* (MGM 1968)★★★, *A Time To Sing* film soundtrack (MGM 1968)★★, *Luke The Drifter Jnr.* (MGM 1969)★★★, *Songs My Father Left Me* (MGM 1969)★★★, *Live At Cobo Hall, Detroit* (MGM 1969)★★★★, *Luke The Drifter Jnr., Volume 2* (1969)★★★, *Sunday Morning* (1970)★★★, *Singing My Songs* (1970)★★★, *Luke The Drifter Jnr., Volume 3* (1970)★★★, with Louis Johnson *Removing The Shadow* (1970)★★, *All For The Love Of Sunshine* (1970)★★★, *I've Got A Right To Cry/They All Used To Belong To Me* (1971) *Sweet Dreams* (1971)★★★, *Eleven Roses* (Polydor 1972)★★, with Johnson *Send Me Some Lovin'/Whole Lotta Lovin'* (1972)★★★, *After You/Pride's*

Not Hard To Swallow (1973)★★★, *Hank Williams: The Legend In Story And Song* a double album in which Hank Jnr. narrates his father's life (1973)★★★, *Just Pickin' - No Singing* (1973)★★★, *The Last Love Song* (1973)★★★, *Living Proof* (1974)★★★, *Bocephus* (1975)★★★, *Hank Williams Jnr. And Friends* (MGM 1975)★★★★, *One Night Stands* (Warners 1977)★★★, *The New South* (Warners 1977)★★★★, *Family Tradition* (Elektra 1979)★★★★, *Whiskey Bent And Hell Bound* (Elektra 1979)★★★★, *Habits Old And New* (Elektra 1980)★★★, *Rowdy* (Elektra 1980)★★★, *The Pressure Is On* (Elektra 1981)★★★, *High Notes* (Elektra 1982)★★★, *Strong Stuff* (Elektra 1983)★★★, *Man Of Steel* (Warners 1983)★★★, *Major Moves* (Warners 1984)★★★, *Five-O* (Warners 1985)★★★, *Montana Cafe* (Warners 1986)★★★★, *Live* (Warners 1987)★★★, *Born To Boogie* (Warners 1987)★★★★, *Wild Streak* (Warners 1988)★★★★, *Lone Wolf* (Warners/Curb 1990)★★, *America - The Way I See It* (Warners/Curb 1990)★, *Pure Hank* (Warners/Curb 1992)★★★, *Maverick* (Curb 1992)★★★, *Out Of Left Field* (1993)★★★, *Chronicles - Health And Happiness* (1993)★★★, *Hog Wild* (Curb 1995)★★★, *AKA Wham Bam Sam* (Curb 1996)★★★, *Three Hanks, Men With Broken Hearts* (Curb 1996).

●COMPILATIONS: *Hank Williams Jnr.'s Greatest Hits* (Elektra 1982)★★★, *The Magic Guitar Of Hank Williams Jnr.* (1986)★★★, *Country Store* (Country Store 1988)★★★, *The Best Of* (1993).

●VIDEOS: *Live In Concert* (1993).

●FURTHER READING: *Living Proof*, Hank Williams Jnr. with Michael Bane.

WILLIAMS, JOHN (COMPOSER)

b. John Towner Williams, 8 February 1932, Flushing, Long Island, New York, USA. A composer, arranger, and conductor for film background music from the early 60s to the present. As a boy, Williams learned to play several instruments, and studied composition and arranging in Los Angeles after moving there with his family in 1948. Later, he studied piano at the Juilliard School Of Music, before composing his first score for the film *I Passed For White* in 1960. it was followed by others, such as *Because They're Young*, *The Secret Ways*, *Bachelor Flat*, *Diamond Head*, *Gidget Goes To Rome*, and *None But The Brave*, directed by, and starring Frank Sinatra. Williams scored Ronald Reagan's last film, *The Killers*, in 1964, and continued with *Please Come Home*, *How To Steal A Million*, *The Rare Breed* and *A Guide For The Married Man*. In 1967 Williams gained the first of more than 25 Oscar nominations for his adaptation of the score to *Valley Of The Dolls*, and after writing original scores for other movies such as *Sergeant Ryker*, *Daddy's Gone A-Hunting*, and *The Reivers*, he won the Academy Award in 1971 for 'best adaptation' for *Fiddler On The Roof*. In the early 70s, Williams seemed to be primarily concerned with 'disaster' movies, such as *The Poseidon Adventure*, *The Towering Inferno*, *Earthquake* and *Jaws*, for which he won his second Oscar in 1975. He then pro-

ceeded to score some of the most commercially successful films in the history of the cinema, including the epic *Star Wars*, *Close Encounters Of The Third Kind*, *Superman*, *The Empire Strikes Back*, *Raiders Of The Lost Ark*, *E.T. The Extra Terrestrial* - another Academy Award winner for Williams. On and on Williams marched with *The Return Of The Jedi*, *Indiana Jones And The Temple Of Doom*, *Indiana Jones And The Last Crusade*, *The River*, *The Accidental Tourist*, *Born On The Fourth Of July* and *Presumed Innocent* (1990). As for recordings, he had US singles hits with orchestral versions of several of his films' themes and main titles, and a number of his soundtracks entered the album charts. Real pop prestige came to Williams in 1977, when record producer Meco Monardo conceived a disco treatment of his themes for *Star Wars*, which included music played in the film by the Cantina Band. 'Star Wars/Cantina Band' by Meco, spent two weeks at number 1 in the USA. For his work in the early 90s, Williams received Oscar nominations for the highly successful *Home Alone* (the score, and 'Somewhere In My Memory', lyric by Leslie Bricusse), the score for Oliver Stone's highly controversial *JFK*, and 'When You're Alone' (again with Bricusse) for Steven Spielberg's *Hook*. After contributing the music to *Far And Away* and *Home Alone 2: Lost In New York* (1992), Williams returned to Spielberg in 1993 to score the director's dinosaur drama, *Jurassic Park*, and another multi-Oscar winner, *Schindler's List*. Williams himself won an Academy Award for his sensitive music for the latter picture. As well as his highly impressive feature film credits, Williams has written for television productions such as *Heidi*, *Jane Eyre* and *The Screaming Woman*. In 1985, he was commissioned by NBC Television to construct themes for news stories, which resulted in pieces such as 'The Sound Of The News', and featured a fanfare for the main bulletin, a scherzo for the breakfast show, and several others, including 'The Pulse Of Events', and 'Fugue For Changing Times'. Williams' impressive list of blockbuster movies is unlikely ever to be beaten.

WILLIAMS, JOHN (GUITAR)

b. 24 April 1941, Melbourne, Australia. This renowned exponent of the Spanish guitar took flamenco unexpectedly into the pop charts with *John Williams Plays Spanish Music*. In the later 70s, a more calculated assault on this market saw his reading of Rodrigo's Concerto de Aranjuez (with the English Chamber Orchestra conducted by Daniel Barenboim) as well as the less focused *Travelling* and *Bridges* in the UK Top 20. With the comparative failure of *Cavatina*, Williams was faced with a choice of either a cosy career of hushed recitals for a substantial intellectual minority or transporting himself even nearer to the borders of cultured 'contemporary' pop. Adopting the latter course, he formed Sky with Kevin Peek (guitar), Herbie Flowers (bass), Francis Monkman (keyboards) and Tristan Fry (percussion). While this instrumental group went from strength to commercial strength, he issued solo albums and *Let The Music Take You*, an adventurous 1983 collaboration with Cleo Laine. Both these offerings and those of Sky were criticized in some professional quarters for an over-emphasis on technique, but many such sneers were rooted in green-eyed wonderment at Sky's million-selling records and sell-out world tours, including a concert in Williams' native Australia which was taped for release as *Sky Five Live* in 1983. The treadmill of the road was, nonetheless, among the reasons why Williams left Sky the following year. Rather than back-sliding to the easy option of bringing known serious music to the masses, his output since has tended to extend his stylistic range even further - as exemplified by a prominent hand in composer Paul Hart's *Concerto For Guitar and Jazz Orchestra*, and an album with Chilean folk group, Inti-Illimani.

●ALBUMS: *John Williams Plays Spanish Music* (Columbia 1970)★★★, *The Height Below* (Cube 1975)★★★, *Concerto De Aranjuez* (1976)★★★, with Cleo Laine *Best Friends* (1978)★★★★, *Travelling* (Cube 1978)★★★, *Bridges* (Lotus 1979)★★★, *Julian Bream And John Williams* (1979)★★★, *Cavatina* (Cube 1979)★★★★, *Portrait* (Columbia 1982)★★★, *The Guitar Is The Song* (Columbia 1983)★★★, *Let The Music Take You* (Columbia 1983)★★★, *Concerto For Guitar And Jazz Orchestra* (Columbia 1987)★★★, *John Williams/Paco Pena/Inti-Illimani* (Columbia 1987)★★★, *The Seville Concert: From The Royal Alcázar Palace* (1993)★★★.

●COMPILATIONS: *Spotlight On John Williams* (Castle 1980)★★★, *Platinum Collection* (Cube 1981)★★★, *Masterpieces* (1983)★★★, *Changes* (Sierra 1985)★★★, *Images* (Knight 1989)★★★.

WILLIAMS, PAUL

b 19 September 1940, Omaha, Nebraska, USA. Popular composer Paul Williams entered show business as a stuntman and film actor, appearing as a child in *The Loved One* (1964) and *The Chase* (1965). He turned to songwriting, and in the 70s composed many appealing and commercially successful numbers, such as We've Only Just Begun', 'Rainy Days And Mondays', and 'I Won't Last A Day Without You' (written with Roger Nichols), all three of which were popular for the Carpenters; 'Out In The Country' (Nicholls), 'Cried Like A Baby' (with Craig Doerge), 'Family Of Man' (Jack S. Conrad), 'Love Boat Theme' and 'My Fair Share' (both Charles Fox), 'You And Me Against The World', 'Inspiration', and 'Loneliness' (all with Ken Ascher), 'Nice To be Around (with Johnny Williams), and 'An Old Fashioned Song', 'That's Enough For Me', and 'Waking Up Alone' (words and music by Paul Williams). Williams recorded his first solo album for Reprise in 1970 before moving to A&M Records the following year. None of these albums sold well, but Williams developed a highly praised nightclub act in the early 70s. His first film score was for *Phantom Of The Paradise*, Brian de Palma's update of the *Phantom Of The Opera* story, in which Williams starred. This was followed by songs for *A Star Is Born* (1976), another modern version of an old movie, which starred Kris Kristofferson and Barbra Streisand, and included the Oscar-winning song 'Evergreen' (with Barbra Streisand). However, Williams' most impressive score was for the 30s pastiche *Bugsy Malone*, a gangster spoof with a cast consisting entirely of children. His later scores included *The End* (1977) and *The Muppet Movie* (1979), including 'Rainbow Connection', with Kenny Ascher. In 1988, Williams appeared at Michael's Pub in New York. His varied programme included some numbers intended for a future Broadway musical, as well as details of his recovery from the ravages of drugs and alcohol. In 1992, he contributed music and lyrics for the songs in the feature film *The Muppet Christmas Carol*, which starred Michael Caine.

●ALBUMS: *Someday Man* (Reprise 1970)★★, *Just An Old Fashioned Love Song* (A&M 1971)★★, *Life Goes On* (A&M 1972)★★, *Here Comes Inspiration* (A&M 1974)★★, *A Little Bit Of Love* (A&M 1974)★★, *Phantom Of The Paradise* film soundtrack (A&M 1975)★★, *Ordinary Fool* (A&M 1975)★★, *Bugsy Malone* film soundtrack (A&M 1975)★★.

●COMPILATIONS: *Best Of* (A&M 1975)★★, *Classics* (A&M 1977)★★.

WILSON, DENNIS

b. 4 December 1944, Hawthorne, California, USA, d. 28 December 1983. The former drummer with the Beach Boys started to develop as a notable songwriter during the late 60s when his elder brother, Brian, became less prolific. Wilson blossomed, showing a hitherto unseen sensitivity which had always been clouded by his wild nature and legendary womanizing. On *Smiley Smile* he composed 'Little Bird' and the hymn-like 'Be Still' and although both songs were painfully short, the talent was unfolding. Wilson showed his class on *Sunflower* in 1970 and again in 1972 with *Carl And The Passions-So Tough*. On the former he delivered four songs but the jewel in the crown was 'Forever', one of the finest Beach Boys songs of all time. Wilson displayed lyrics as the true romantic of the group with simple yet effective lines such as 'If every word I said could make you laugh, I'd talk forever'. His 'Cuddle Up' from *So Tough* was originally criticized for its lush orchestral arrangement, but 20 years on, it stands up as a highly individual song. Wilson continued writing similar songs although plagued by a growing drug habit. *Pacific Ocean Blue* in 1977 was a *tour de force* and must have left the other members of the band pleasantly aghast. This was a mature collection of songs, lyrically strong, melodic and expertly produced. Further rich textured orchestrations on tracks like 'Moonshine' and 'River Song' were breathtaking. The album was only a critical success and barely made the US Hot 100. Wilson, sadly became a tragic figure, his voice so badly wrecked through drug and alcohol abuse ended as merely a painful croak.

During a break from recording his unreleased *Bamboo* in 1983, Wilson drowned after diving from his yacht in the harbour at Marina Del Ray, California. As the only Beach Boy to have actually surfed, special dispensation was given by the US President to the Wilson family to bury Dennis at sea.

●ALBUMS: *Pacific Ocean Blue* (Caribou 1977)★★★★.

WINCHESTER, JESSE

b. 17 May 1944, Shreveport, Louisiana, USA. After receiving his draft papers from the US Forces, Winchester moved to Canada where he settled. His self-titled debut album, produced by Robbie Robertson, was thematically reminiscent of the work of the Band with its evocation of life in the deep south of the USA. The moving, bittersweet memories described in 'Brand New Tennessee Waltz', plus its haunting melody line, per-suaded a number of artists to cover the song, including the Everly Brothers. Winchester's *Third Down, 110 To Go* was produced by Todd Rundgren, but in spite of its solid quality failed to sell. On *Learn To Love* (1974), he com-mented on the Vietnam War in 'Pharoah's Army' and was assisted by several members of the Amazing Rhythm Aces. By 1976, Winchester was touring the USA, having received an amnesty from President Carter for his draft-dodging. He played low-key gigs abroad and continued to release albums, which veered slightly towards the burgeoning country rock market. His nar-rative love songs are effective and the quality of his writing is evinced by the number of important artists who have covered his songs, a list that includes Elvis Costello, Tim Hardin and Joan Baez. Stoney Plain Records began a CD reissue programme in 1995.

●ALBUMS: *Jesse Winchester* (Ampex 1970)★★★★, *Third Down, 110 To Go* (Bearsville 1972)★★★, *Learn To Love It* (Bearsville 1974)★★★, *Let The Rough Side Drag* (Bearsville 1976)★★★, *Nothin' But A Breeze* (Bearsville 1977)★★★, *A Touch On The Rainy Side* (Bearsville 1978)★★★, *Talk Memphis* (Bearsville 1981)★★★, *Humour Me* (Sugar Hill 1988)★★★.

●COMPILATIONS: *The Best Of Jesse Winchester* (See For Miles 1988)★★★★.

WINGFIELD, PETE

b. 7 May 1948, Kiphook, Hampshire, England. Wingfield was a pianist who previously led Pete's Disciples and played sessions with Top Topham, Graham Bond, and Memphis Slim. He was also an acknowledged soul music expert who started the *Soul Beat* fanzine in the late 60s, and in the 70s wrote for *Let It Rock* magazine. While at Sussex University he met fellow students Paul Butler (guitar), John Best (bass), and local teacher Chris Waters (drums) and formed the band Jellybread. With Wingfield doing most of the singing they made an album for their own Liphook label which they used as a demo and secured a contract with Blue Horizon Records. Although they gained some plaudits from the media they were generally unsuccessful and Wingfield

left in the summer of 1971. He next played in Keef Hartley's band but that liaison ended when Hartley was invited to drum for John Mayall. Wingfield did further sessions for Freddie King, then joined Colin Blunstone's band, and also backed Van Morrison for a time. With Joe Jammer, he became the core of the session band the Olympic Runners, who were the brainchild of Blue Horizon boss Mike Vernon. The Runners also included DeLisle Harper (bass) and Glen LeFleur (drums) who acted as the rhythm section on Wingfield's own 1975 album *Breakfast Special* which included the hit single '18 With A Bullet'. The Olympic Runners had some success in their own right in the late 70s. Wingfield still does sessions and various studio projects, putting out the occasional single. However, he is now better known for his production credits (such as Dexys Midnight Runners' *Searching For The Young Soul Rebels*, plus Blue Rondo A La Turk and the Kane Gang). He continues to be a regular member of the Everly Brothers' backing band for their UK tours.

●ALBUMS: *Breakfast Special* (Island 1975)★★★.

WINGS

Wings was Paul McCartney's first post-Beatles music venture. They achieved eight Top 10 albums in both the UK and USA (two and five, respectively, reaching number 1) and 'Mull Of Kintyre' is one of the biggest-selling singles of all time. Wings was formed during the summer of 1971, Paul and Linda being augmented by Denny Laine (ex-Moody Blues, who, as Denny And The Diplomats, had supported the Beatles at the Plaza Ballroom, Dudley, on 5 July 1963) on guitar/vocals, and Denny Seiwell on drums. That year's *Wild Life*, intended as an 'uncomplicated' offering, was indifferently received and is regarded by McCartney himself as a dis-appointment. Guitarist Henry McCullough (ex-Grease Band) joined at the end of 1971, and the early part of 1972 was taken up by the famous 'surprise' college gigs around the UK. Notoriety was achieved at about the same time by the BBC's banning of 'Give Ireland Back To The Irish' (which nevertheless reached number 16 in the UK and 21 in the USA). Later that year 'Hi Hi Hi' (doubled with 'C-Moon') also offended the censors for its 'overt sexual references', though it penetrated the Top 10 on both sides of the Atlantic. Early in 1973 Wings enjoyed a double number 1 in the USA with *Red Rose Speedway* and 'My Love', taken from the album. (Both were credited to Paul McCartney and Wings.) Shortly before they were due to travel to Lagos to work on the next album, McCullough and Seiwell quit, officially over 'musical policy differences'. There is much to sug-gest, however, that McCartney's single-mindedness and overbearing behaviour were the real reasons, and that 'physical contact' may have taken place. Ironically, the result was Paul McCartney And Wings' most acclaimed album, *Band On The Run*, with McCartney taking a multi-instrumental role. *Band On The Run* topped the album charts in the UK and USA, and kicked off 1974 by yielding two transatlantic Top 10 singles in 'Jet' and 'Band On The Run'. Towards the end of 1974, under the name the Country Hams they released 'Walking In The Park With Eloise', a song written 20 years earlier by McCartney's father. At the end of the year Jimmy McCulloch (Thunderclap Newman, Stone The Crows) was added on guitar and vocals, and Joe English on drums (the latter following a brief stint by ex-East Of Eden drummer Geoff Britton). Subsequent recordings were credited simply to Wings.

The new line-up got off to a strong start with *Venus And Mars*, another number one in the UK and USA, the single 'Listen To What The Man Said' also topping the US charts and reaching number 6 in the UK. Wings had become a major world act, and, riding on this success and 1975's *Wings At The Speed Of Sound* (UK number 2, US number 1) they embarked on a massive US tour. The resulting live triple *Wings Over America* was huge, becoming Wings' fifth consecutive US number 1 album and the biggest-selling triple of all time.

Success did not bring stability, McCulloch and English both leaving during 1977. In a repeat of the *Band On The Run* phenomenon, the remaining Wings recorded 'Mull Of Kintyre', which stayed at number 1 in the UK for 9 weeks. *London Town* broke Wings' run at the top of the US album charts and was poorly received. Laurence Juber and Steve Holly were added to the band, but 1979's *Back To The Egg* failed to impress anyone in particular, 'Getting Closer' not even hitting the UK singles chart. McCartney was arrested for drug possession in Tokyo at the start of their tour of Japan. This was the last straw for the loyal and resilient Denny Laine, who quit in exasperation. By this time McCartney had also started recording under his own name again, and Wings were effectively no more. McCartney was knighted in January 1997.

●ALBUMS: *Wild Life* (Apple 1971)★★, as Paul McCartney And Wings *Red Rose Speedway* (Apple 1973)★★★, as Paul McCartney And Wings *Band On The Run* (Apple 1973)★★★★,*Venus And Mars* (Apple 1975)★★★★, *Wings At The Speed Of Sound* (Apple 1976)★★★, *Wings Over America* (Parlophone 1976)★★★, *London Town* (Parlophone 1978)★★★, *Back To The Egg* (Parlophone 1979)★★★.

●COMPILATIONS: *Wings' Greatest Hits* (Parlophone 1978)★★★.

●FURTHER READING: *The Facts About A Rock Group, Featuring Wings*, David Gelly.

WINKIES

This 'pub rock' attraction made its debut in the Lord Nelson in London in 1973. Touted as one of the genre's most promising practitioners, it revolved around vocalist and guitarist Philip Rambow. Guy Humphries (guitar, vocals), Brian Turrington (bass, keyboards, vocals) and Michael Desmarias (drums) completed the line-up. The last-named pair were already respected session musicians. Both had appeared on John Cale's

Fear, while Turrington guested on three albums by Brian Eno, who in turn invited the Winkies to support him on his 1974 tour. The quartet's self-titled debut was produced by Guy Stevens (Mott The Hoople/the Clash, but it sadly failed to capture their in-concert fire. The Winkies disbanded in 1975 after which Rambow moved to New York. Upon his return to London he embraced punk/new wave in a solo career that engendered cult status.

●ALBUMS: *The Winkies* (Chrysalis 1975)★★.

WINTER, EDGAR

b. 28 December 1946, Beaumont, Texas, USA. Although at times overshadowed by his brother, Johnny Winter, Edgar has enjoyed an intermittently successful career. The siblings began performing together as teenagers, and were members of several itinerant groups performing in southern-state clubs and bars. Winter later forsook music for college, before accepting an offer to play saxophone in a local jazz band. He rejoined his brother in 1969, but the following year released *Entrance*. He then formed an R&B revue, Edgar Winter's White Trash, whose live set *Roadwork*, was an exciting testament to this talented ensemble. Winter then fronted a slimmer group - Dan Hartman (vocals), Ronnie Montrose (guitar) and Chuck Ruff (drums) - which appeared on the artist's only million-selling album, *They Only Come Out At Night*. This highly successful selection included the rousing instrumental, 'Frankenstein', which became a hit single in its own right. Guitarist Rick Derringer, who had produced Winter's previous two albums, replaced Montrose for *Shock Treatment*, but this and subsequent releases failed to maintain the singer's commercial ascendancy. He rejoined his brother in 1976 for the *Together* album, since which Edgar Winter's professional profile has been considerably lean. Together with his brother Johnny, he sued DC Comics for depicting them in a comic book as half-human, half-worm characters. The figures were illustrated by the creator of Jonah Hex. The Winter brothers were shown as 'Johnny And Edgar Autumn'.

●ALBUMS: *Entrance* (Epic 1970)★★, *Edgar Winter's White Trash* (Epic 1971)★★★, *Roadwork* (Epic 1972)★★★★, *They Only Come Out At Night* (Epic 1972)★★★★, *Shock Treatment* (Epic 1974)★★★, *Jasmine Nightdreams* (Blue Sky 1975)★★★, *Edgar Winter Group With Rick Derringer* (Blue Sky 1975)★★★, with Johnny Winter *Together* (Blue Sky 1976)★★★★, *Recycled* (Blue Sky 1977)★★★, *The Edgar Winter Album* (Blue Sky 1979)★★, *Standing On The Rock* (1981)★★, *Mission Earth* (1993)★★, *I'm Not A Kid Anymore* (L+R 1994)★★★.

●COMPILATIONS: *Rock Giants* (1982)★★★.

WINTER, JOHNNY

b. 23 February 1944, Leland, Mississippi, USA. Raised in Beaumont, Texas, with younger brother Edgar Winter, Johnny was a child prodigy prior to forging a career as a blues guitarist. He made his recording debut in 1960, fronting Johnny and the Jammers, and over the next eight years completed scores of masters, many of which remained unreleased until his success prompted their rediscovery. By 1968 the guitarist was leading Tommy Shannon (bass) and John Turner (drums) in a trio entitled Winter. The group recorded a single for the Austin-based Sonobeat label, consigning extra tracks from the same session to a demonstration disc. This was subsequently issued by United Artists as *The Progressive Blues Experiment*. An article in *Rolling Stone* magazine heaped effusive praise on the guitarist's talent and led to lucrative recording and management agreements. *Johnny Winter* ably demonstrated his exceptional dexterity while *Second Winter*, which included rousing versions of 'Johnny B. Goode' and 'Highway 61 Revisited', suggested a newfound emphasis on rock. This direction was confirmed in 1970 when Winter was joined by the McCoys, a group struggling to shed a teeny-bop image. Billed as Johnny Winter And - with guitarist Rick Derringer acting as a foil - the new line-up proclaimed itself with a self-titled studio collection and a fiery live set. These excellent releases brought Winter a much-deserved commercial success. Chronic heroin addiction forced him into partial retirement and it was two years before he re-emerged with *Still Alive And Well*. Subsequent work was bedevilled by indecision until the artist returned to his roots with *Nothing But The Blues* and *White Hot And Blue*. At the same time Winter assisted Muddy Waters by producing and arranging a series of acclaimed albums which recaptured the spirit of the veteran blues artist's classic recordings. Winter's recent work has proved equally vibrant and three releases for Alligator, a Chicago-based independent label, included the rousing *Guitar Slinger*, which displayed all the passion apparent on those early, seminal recordings. His career may have failed to match initial, extravagant expectations, but his contribution to the blues should not be underestimated; he remains an exceptional talent. Together with his brother Edgar, he sued DC Comics for depicting them in a comic book as half-human, half-worm characters. The figures were illustrated by the creator of Jonah Hex. The Winter brothers were shown as 'Johnny And Edgar Autumn'.

●ALBUMS: *Johnny Winter* (Columbia 1969)★★★★, *The Progressive Blues Experiment* (Sonobeat/Imperial 1969)★★, *Second Winter* (Columbia 1969)★★★, *Johnny Winter And* (Columbia 1970)★★★★, *Johnny Winter And Live* (Columbia 1971)★★★, *Still Alive And Well* (Columbia 1973)★★★, *Saints And Sinners* (Columbia 1974)★★★, *John Dawson Winter III* (Blue Sky 1974)★★★, *Captured Live!* (Blue Sky 1976)★★★, with Edgar Winter *Together* (Blue Sky 1976)★★★★, *Nothin' But The Blues* (Blue Sky 1977)★★★, *White Hot And Blue* (Blue Sky 1978)★★, *Raisin' Cain* (Blue Sky 1980)★★, *Raised On Rock* (Blue Sky 1981)★★, *Guitar Slinger* (Alligator 1984)★★★, *Serious Business* (Alligator 1985)★★★, *Third Degree* (Alligator 1986)★★★, *Winter Of '88* (MCA 1988)★★, *Let Me In* (Virgin/Pointblank 1991)★★★, *Jack Daniels Kind Of Day* (1992)★★★, *Hey, Where's Your Brother?* (Virgin/Pointblank 1992)★★★, with Jimmy Reed *Live At Liberty Hall, Houston* (1993)★★★.

●COMPILATIONS: *The Johnny Winter Story* (GRT 1969)★★★, *First Winter* (1970)★★★, *Early Times* (1971)★★, *About Blues* (1972)★★, *Before The Storm* (Janus 1972)★★★, *Austin Texas* (United Artists 1972)★★★, *The Johnny Winter Story* (1980)★★★, *The Johnny Winter Collection* (Castle 1986)★★★★, *Birds Can't Row Boats* (1988)★★★, *Scorchin' Blues* (Epic/Legacy 1992)★★★, *A Rock N'Roll Collection* (Columbia/Legacy 1994)★★★.

WIRE

This inventive UK group was formed in October 1976 by Colin Newman (b. 16 September 1954, Salisbury, Wiltshire, England; vocals/guitar), Bruce Gilbert (b. 18 May 1946, Watford, Hertfordshire, England; guitar), Graham Lewis (b. 22 February 1953, Grantham, Lincolnshire, England; bass/vocals) and Robert Gotobed (b. Mark Field, 1951, Leicester, England; drums) along with lead guitarist George Gill - the latter member had previously been a member of the Snakes, releasing a single on the Skydog label, while the rest of Wire all had art school backgrounds. Their early work was clearly influenced by punk and this incipient era was captured on a various artists live selection, *The Roxy, London, WC2*, their first recording as a four-piece following Gill's dismissal. Although not out of place among equally virulent company, the group was clearly more ambitious than many contemporaries. Wire was signed to the Harvest Records label in September 1977. Their impressive debut, *Pink Flag*, comprised 21 tracks, and ranged from the furious assault of 'Field Day For The Sundays' and 'Mr Suit' to the more brittle, almost melodic, interlude provided by 'Mannequin', which became the group's first single. Producer Mike Thorne, who acted as an unofficial fifth member, enhanced the set's sense of tension with a raw, stripped-to-basics sound. *Chairs Missing* offered elements found in its predecessor, but couched them in a newfound maturity. Gilbert's buzzsaw guitar became more measured, allowing space for Thorne's keyboards and synthesizers to provide an implicit anger. A spirit of adventure also marked *154* which contained several exceptional individual moments, including 'A Touching Display', a lengthy excursion into wall-of-sound feedback, and the haunting 'A Mutual Friend', scored for a delicate *cor anglais* passage and a striking contrast to the former's unfettered power. However, the album marked the end of Wire's Harvest contract and the divergent aims of the musicians became impossible to hold under one banner. The quartet was disbanded in the summer of 1980, leaving Newman free to pursue a solo career, while Gilbert and Lewis completed a myriad of projects under various identities including Dome, Duet Emmo and P'o, plus a number of solo works. Gotobed meanwhile concentrated on session work for Colin Newman, Fad Gadget and later organic farming. A posthumous release, *Document And Eyewitness*, chronicled Wire's final concert at London's Electric Ballroom in February 1980, but it was viewed as a disappointment in the wake of the preceding studio collections. It was not until 1985 that the group was resurrected and it was a further two years before they began recording again. *The Ideal Copy* revealed a continued desire to challenge, albeit in a less impulsive manner, and the set quickly topped the independent chart. *A Bell Is A Cup (Until It Is Struck)* maintained the newfound balance between art and commercial pop, including the impressive 'Kidney Bingos'. In 1990 the group abandoned the 'beat combo' concept adopted in 1985 and took on board the advantages and uses of computer and sequencer technology. The resulting *Manscape* showed that the group's sound had changed dramatically, but not with altogether satisfactory results. Following the album's release Gotobed announced his departure. The remaining trio ironically changed their name to Wir, but not before *The Drill* had been released. It contained a collection of variations on 'Drill', a track that had appeared on the EP *Snakedrill* in 1987. The new group's first release 'The First Letter', showed a harder edge than their more recent work, amusingly containing some reworked samples of *Pink Flag*. Wire subsequently became the subject of renewed interest in the mid-90s when indie darlings Elastica not only name-checked but also borrowed liberally from their back-catalogue.

●ALBUMS: *Pink Flag* (Harvest 1977)★★★★, *Chairs Missing* (Harvest 1978)★★★★, *154* (Harvest 1979)★★★★, *Document And Eyewitness* (Rough Trade 1981)★★, *The Ideal Copy* (Mute 1987)★★★★, *A Bell Is A Cup Until It Is Struck* (Mute 1988)★★, *It's Beginning To And Back Again* (Mute 1989)★★★, *Manscape* (Mute 1990)★★, *The Peel Sessions* (Strange Fruit 1990)★★★, *The Drill* (Mute 1991)★★. As Wir *The First Letter* (Mute 1991)★★★.

●COMPILATIONS: *Wire Play Pop* (Pink 1986)★★★, *On Returning* (Harvest 1989)★★★.

●FURTHER READING: *Wire ... Everybody Loves A History*, Kevin S. Eden.

WISHBONE ASH

In 1966 Steve Upton (b. 24 May 1946, Wrexham, Wales; drums), who had previously played with the Scimitars, joined Martin Turner (b. 1 October 1947, Torquay, Devon, England; bass/vocals) and Glen Turner (guitar) in the Torquay band, Empty Vessels. This trio then moved to London where they took the name Tanglewood. Glen Turner departed, before the similarly titled Ted Turner (b. David Alan Turner, 2 August 1950; guitar) joined the band. He had previously played in a Birmingham band, King Biscuit. Wishbone Ash was formed when Andy Powell (b. 8 February 1950; guitar) of the Sugarband joined Upton, Turner and Turner.

Heavily influenced by the music of the Yardbirds and the Allman Brothers, Wishbone Ash's hallmark was the powerful sound of twin lead guitars. Their biggest commercial success was *Argus*, released in 1973. This was a prime example of the band's preoccupation with historical themes, complex instrumentals, and folk rock. Ted Turner departed in 1974, and was replaced by Laurie Wisefield, formerly of Home. Wishbone Ash continued successfully, becoming tax exiles in the USA, returning to England in 1975 to play at the Reading Rock festival. In 1980 Martin Turner left. John Wetton, formerly of Uriah Heep and Roxy Music, served as his replacement, and singer Claire Hammill joined the band, along with Trevor Bolder. This line-up released only one album before disbanding in 1982, and it was the recruitment of Mervyn Spence to replace Bolder that seemed to give some of its former vitality back to Wishbone Ash. In 1987 the original quartet began working together again, recording *Nouveau Calls*. This project involved the renewal of their relationship with former Police manager Miles Copeland, who had looked after Wishbone Ash's affairs for a brief spell in the 60s. They continue to perform to a loyal and devoted following.

●ALBUMS: *Wishbone Ash* (MCA 1970)★★★, *Pilgrimage* (MCA 1972)★★, *Argus* (MCA 1973)★★★, *Wishbone 4* (MCA 1973)★★★, *Live Dates* (MCA 1974)★★★, *There's The Rub* (MCA 1974)★★, *Locked In* (MCA 1976)★★, *New England* (MCA 1977)★★, *Frontpage News* (MCA 1977)★★, *No Smoke Without Fire* (MCA 1978)★★, *Live In Tokyo* (MCA 1978)★★, *Just Testing* (MCA 1979)★★, *Live Dates Vol. II* (MCA 1979)★★, *Number The Brave* (MCA 1981)★★, *Twin Barrels Burning* (MCA 1982)★★, *Raw To The Bone* (Neat 1985)★★, *Nouveau Calls* (IRS 1987)★★, *Here To Hear* (IRS 1989)★★, *Strange Affair* (IRS 1991)★★, *BBC Radio 1 Live In Concert* (Windsong 1991)★★★, *The Ash Live In Chicago* (Permanent 1992)★★, *Illuminations* (1996)★★.

●COMPILATIONS: *Hot Ash* (MCA 1981)★★, *Classic Ash* (MCA 1981)★★★, *The Best Of Wishbone Ash* (MCA 1982)★★★.

●VIDEOS: *Phoenix* (1990), *Wishbone Ash Live* (1990).

WITHERS, BILL

b. 4 July 1938, Slab Fork, West Virginia, USA. Having moved to California in 1967 after nine years in the US Navy, Withers began hawking his original songs around several west coast companies. He signed to Sussex Records in 1971 and secured an immediate hit with his debut single, 'Ain't No Sunshine'. Produced by Booker T. Jones, with Stephen Stills amongst the guest musicians, this sparse but compulsive performance was a million-seller, a feat emulated in 1972 by two more excellent releases, 'Lean On Me' and 'Use Me'. Withers' light, folksy/soul continued to attain further success with 'Make Love To Your Mind' (1975), the sublime 'Lovely Day' (1977), (a single revamped by a remix in 1988) and 'Just The Two Of Us' (1981), his exhilarating duet with saxophonist Grover Washington Jnr., which earned the two artists a Grammy in 1982 for the Best R&B performance. 'Lovely Day' re-entered the UK pop charts in 1988 after exposure from a UK television commercial, reaching the Top 5. A professional rather than charismatic performer, Withers remains a skilled songwriter.

●ALBUMS: *Just As I Am* (Sussex 1971)★★★★, *Still Bill* (Sussex 1972)★★★★, *Live At Carnegie Hall* (Sussex 1973)★★, *+ʹJustments* (Sussex 1974)★★★, *Making Music* (Columbia 1975)★★★, *Naked And Warm* (Columbia 1976)★★★, *Menagerie* (Columbia 1977)★★★, *ʹBout Love* (Columbia 1979)★★★, *Watching You Watching Me* (Columbia 1985)★★★, *Still Bill* (1993)★★★.

●COMPILATIONS: *The Best Of Bill Withers* (Sussex 1975)★★★★, *Bill Withers' Greatest Hits* (Columbia 1981)★★★, *Lean On Me: The Best Of...* (Columbia/Legacy 1995)★★★.

WIZZARD

Having already achieved success with the Move and the Electric Light Orchestra, the ever-experimental Roy Wood put together Wizzard in 1972 with a line up comprising Rick Price (vocals/bass), Hugh McDowell (cello), Bill Hunt (keyboards), Mike Burney (saxophone), Nick Pentelow (saxophone), Keith Smart (drums) and Charlie Grima (drums). The octet made their debut at the 1972 Wembley Rock 'n' Roll Festival and hit the charts later that year with the chaotic but intriguing 'Ball Park Incident'. Wood was at his peak as a producer during this period and his Phil Spector-like 'wall of sound' pop experiments produced two memorable UK number 1 hits ('See My Baby Jive', 'Angel Fingers') and a perennial festive hit, 'I Wish It Could Be Christmas Every Day'. There was even a playful stab at rivals ELO on the cheeky b-side 'Bend Over Beethoven'. Much of Wizzard's charm came from the complementary pop theatricalism of Wood, who covered himself with war paint, painted stars on his forehead and sported an unruly mane of multi-coloured hair. Although less impressive on their album excursions, Wizzard's *Introducing Eddy And The Falcons* was a clever and affectionate rock 'n' roll pastiche with tributes to artists including Del Shannon, Gene Vincent, Dion, Duane Eddy and Cliff Richard. By 1975, the group was making in-roads into the US market where manager Don Arden was increasingly involved with lucrative stadia rock. Wizzard failed to persuade the management to increase their financial input, however, and swiftly folded. Wood, Rick Price and Mike Burney abbreviated the group name for the short-lived Wizzo Band, whose unusual brand of jazz funk proved too esoteric for commercial tastes. After less than a year in operation, this offshoot group self-destructed in March 1978, following which Wood concentrated on solo work and production.

●ALBUMS: *Wizzard Brew* (Harvest 1973)★★★, *Introducing Eddy And The Falcons* (Warners 1974)★★★, *Super Active Wizzo* (1977)★★★.

●COMPILATIONS: *See My Baby Jive* (Harvest 1974)★★★.

WOMACK, BOBBY

b. 4 March 1944, Cleveland, Ohio, USA. A founder-member of the Valentinos, this accomplished musician also worked as a guitarist in Sam Cooke's touring band. He scandalized the music fraternity by marrying Barbara Campbell, Cooke's widow, barely three months after the ill-fated singer's death. Womack's early solo singles, 'Nothing You Can Do' and the superb 'I Found A True Love', were all but shunned and, with the Valentinos now in disarray, he reverted to session work. Womack became a fixture at Chips Moman's American Recording Studio, but although he appeared on many recordings, this period is best recalled for his work with Wilson Pickett. 'I'm In Love' and 'I'm A Midnight Mover' are two of the 17 Womack songs that particular artist recorded. Womack, meanwhile, resurrected his solo career with singles on Keymen and Atlantic Records. Signing with Minit, he began a string of R&B hits, including 'It's Gonna Rain', 'How I Miss You Baby' (both 1969) and 'More Than I Can Stand (1970). His authoritative early album, *The Womack Live*, then introduced the freer, more personal direction he undertook in the 70s. The final catalyst for change was *There's A Riot Going On*, Sly Stone's 1971 collection on which Womack played guitar. Its influence was most clearly heard on 'Communication', the title track to Womack's first album for United Artists.

Part of a prolific period, the follow-up album, *Understanding*, was equally strong, and both yielded impressive singles that achieved high positions in the R&B charts. 'That's The Way I Feel About Cha' (number 2), 'Woman's Gotta Have It' (number 1) and 'Harry Hippie' (number 8) confirmed his new-found status. Successive albums from *Facts Of Life*, *Looking For A Love Again* to *I Don't Know What The World Is Coming To*, consolidated the accustomed mixture of original songs, slow raps and cover versions. *BW Goes C&W* (1976), a self-explanatory experiment, completed his United Artists contract, but subsequent work for CBS and Arista was undistinguished. In 1981 Womack signed with Beverly Glen, a small Los Angeles independent, where he recorded *The Poet*. This powerful set re-established his career while a single, 'If You Think You're Lonely Now', reached number 3 on the R&B chart. *The Poet II* (1984) featured three duets with Patti LaBelle, one of which, 'Love Has Finally Come At Last', was another hit single. Womack moved to MCA Records in 1985, debuting with *So Many Rivers*. A longstanding friendship with the Rolling Stones was emphasized that year when he sang backing vocals on their version of 'Harlem Shuffle'. Womack's more recent work proclaims himself 'the last soul singer'. An expressive, emotional singer, his best work stands among black music's finest moments.

●ALBUMS: *Fly Me To The Moon* (Minit 1968)★★★, *My Prescription* (Minit 1969)★★★, *The Womack Live* (United Artists 1970)★★★, *Communication* (United Artists

1971)★★★, *Understanding* (United Artists 1972)★★★, *Across 110th Street* film soundtrack (United Artists 1972)★★, *Facts Of Life* (United Artists 1973)★★★, *Looking For A Love Again* (United Artists 1974)★★, *I Don't Know What The World Is Coming To* (United Artists 1975)★★★, *Safety Zone* (United Artists 1976)★★★, *BW Goes C&W* (United Artists 1976)★★, *Home Is Where The Heart Is* (Columbia 1976)★★, *Pieces* (Columbia 1977)★★, *Roads Of Life* (Arista 1979)★★, *The Poet* (Beverly Glen 1981)★★★, *The Poet II* (Beverly Glen 1984)★★, *Someday We'll All Be Free* (Beverly Glen 1985)★★, *So Many Rivers* (MCA 1985)★★, *Womagic* (MCA 1986)★★, *The Last Soul Man* (MCA 1987)★★.
●COMPILATIONS: *Bobby Womack's Greatest Hits* (United Artists 1974)★★★★, *Somebody Special* (Liberty 1984)★★★, *Check It Out* (Stateside 1986)★★★, *Womack Winners 1968-75* (Charly 1989, 1993)★★★, *Midnight Mover: The Bobby Womack Collection* double CD (1993)★★★★, *The Poet Trilogy* 3-CD (1994)★★★, *I Feel A Groove Comin' On* (Charly 1995)★★★, *The Soul Of Bobby Womack: Stop On By* (EMI 1997)★★★.

WOMBLES

The brainchild of producer, arranger and songwriter, Mike Batt, the anthropomorphic Wombles emerged from a children's television series to take the charts by storm in 1974. They enjoyed a series of hits based loosely on their Wimbledon Common lifestyle (an early attempt at ecological education for children, the Wombles recycled the rubbish found on the Common). 'The Wombling Song', 'Remember You're A Womble', 'Banana Rock' and 'Wombling Merry Christmas' were all Top 10 hits, making the group the most successful and consistent chart act of the year. By the end of 1975, however, the novelty had worn thin and Batt's solo outing 'Summertime City' was outselling his puppet counterparts.
●ALBUMS: *Wombling Songs* (Columbia 1973)★★, *Remember You're A Womble* (Columbia 1974)★★, *Christmas Package* (Columbia 1974)★★, *Superwombling* (Columbia 1975)★★, *Wombling Free* film soundtrack (Columbia 1978)★★.
●COMPILATIONS: *20 Wombling Greats* (Warwick 1977)★★★.

WOOD, RON

b. 1 June 1947, Hillingdon, Middlesex, England. This younger brother of the Artwoods' leader formed the Birds with other students at his Middlesex art school. Although they had a minor hit with 'Leaving Here' in 1965, they are better remembered for the publicity-earning writ they served on the Byrds for breach of copyright. Next, Wood joined the latter-day Creation before entering Jeff Beck's employ as second guitarist and then bass player. Ructions with Beck led to Wood's dismissal in 1969. After a brief reinstatement, he and Beck's vocalist, Rod Stewart, amalgamated with three former Small Faces. As the Faces, they became a major

international act in the early 70s. To a lesser degree than Stewart, Wood inaugurated a parallel solo career - beginning with 1974's *I've Got My Own Album To Do*. Although mainly self-composed, a highlight was a revival of James Ray's 'If You Gotta Make A Fool Of Somebody', a Merseybeat standard recalled by George Harrison who, with Wood, wrote 'Far East Man' for the album, and was among the famous friends mentioned on its sleeve. The most prominent of these was Keith Richards who likewise served Wood on 1975's *Now Look*, and invited him to be a temporary member of the Rolling Stones while the group searched for a replacement for guitarist Mick Taylor. However, after the Faces' final tour, Wood enlisted in December 1975 as a full-time member while continuing to release solo records such as 1979's *Gimme Some Neck* and its 'Seven Days' single. This had been penned by Bob Dylan, whom the new Stone assisted on a 1981 album. Also helping Dylan then was Ringo Starr, whose subsequent *Stop And Smell The Roses* included a Wood-Starr opus, 'Dead Giveaway'. Incurably addicted to jam sessions, Wood was a familiar sight in the 'impromptu' all-star performances that concluded prestigious music industry award ceremonies. He was also noticed performing during televised spectaculars, starring old idols like Fats Domino, Chuck Berry and Jerry Lee Lewis. Included among Wood's other extra-mural activities was an exhibition of his portrait paintings.
●ALBUMS: *I've Got My Own Album To Do* (Warners 1974)★★★, *Now Look* (Warners 1975)★★★, with Ronnie Lane *Mahoney's Last Stand* (Atlantic 1976)★★★, *Gimme Some Neck* (Columbia 1979)★★, *1, 2, 3, 4* (Columbia 1981)★★★, *Cancel Everything* (Thunderbolt 1985)★★, with Bo Diddley *Live At The Ritz* (1988)★★, *Slide On This* (Continuum 1992)★★, *Slide On Live ... Plugged In & Standing* (Continuum 1993)★★★.
●FURTHER READING: *Ron Wood: The Works*, Ron Wood with Bill German.

WOOD, ROY

b. Ulysses Adrian Wood, 8 November 1946, Birmingham, England. Having been named after Homer's Greek mythological hero, Wood abandoned this eminently suitable pop star sobriquet in favour of the more prosaic Roy. As a teenager, he was a itinerant guitarist, moving steadily through a succession of minor Birmingham groups including the Falcons, the Lawmen, Gerry Levene and the Avengers and Mike Sheridan and the Nightriders. After a failed career at art school, he pooled his talents with some of the best musicians on the Birmingham beat scene to form the Move. Under the guidance of Tony Secunda, they established themselves as one of the best pop groups of their time, with Wood emerging as their leading songwriter. By the time of 'Fire Brigade' (1967), Wood was instilled as lead singer and it was his fertile pop imagination that took the group through a plethora of musical styles, ranging from psychedelia to rock 'n' roll revivalism, classical rock and heavy metal. Never content to be bracketed to one musical area, Wood decided to supplement the Move's pop work by launching the grandly named Electric Light Orchestra, whose aim was to produce more experimental album-orientated rock with a classical influence. Wood survived as ELO's frontman for only one single and album before a personality clash with fellow member Jeff Lynne prompted his departure in June 1972. He returned soon after with Wizzard, one of the most inventive and appealing pop groups of the early 70s. During this period, he also enjoyed a parallel solo career and although his two albums were uneven, they revealed his surplus creative energies as a multi-instrumentalist, engineer, producer and even sleeve designer. Back in the singles chart, Wood the soloist enjoyed several UK hits including the majestic 'Forever', an inspired and affectionate tribute to Neil Sedaka and the Beach Boys, with the composer playing the part of an English Phil Spector. Wood's eccentric ingenuity continued on various singles and b-sides, not least the confusing 'Bengal Jig', which fused bagpipes and sitar!

By the late 70s, Wood was ploughing less commercial ground with the Wizzo Band, Rock Brigade and the Helicopters, while his former group ELO produced million-selling albums. The chart absence of Wood since 1975 remains one of pop's great mysteries especially in view of his previous track record as producer, songwriter and brilliant manipulator of contrasting pop genres.

●ALBUMS: *Boulders* (Harvest 1973)★★★, *Mustard* (Jet 1975)★★★, *On The Road Again* (Warners 1979)★★, *Starting Up* (Legacy 1987)★★.

●COMPILATIONS: *The Roy Wood Story* (Harvest 1976)★★, *The Singles* (Speed 1982)★★★, *The Best Of Roy Wood 1970-1974* (MFP 1985)★★★.

WOODS, GAY AND TERRY

Playing together in a duo during the late 60s, Gay and Terry Woods became pivotal figures in the Irish folk scene through their involvement with Sweeney's Men, Steeleye Span and Dr. Strangely Strange, whom they left at the end of 1970. Husband and wife Gay and Terry were ambitious mavericks at the adventurous end of folk rock. As the Woods Band, their debut album mixed traditional ballads and their own songs. They worked extensively in England and Europe, before disbanding and retiring to Eire. Subsequently, they signed with Polydor, and, with a familiar set of folk/rock musicians, recorded a series of increasingly experimental singer-songwriter albums. Gay's soft, tender vocal contrasted with Terry's lazy drawl and hypnotic Irish melodies. The finest of these is *The Time Is Right*, an appealing blend of acoustic/electric elements and intuitive compositions. *Tenderhooks* was cut for the small Mulligan label in Dublin, and was a much more upbeat piece of warm, rolling roots rock. Previously used to touring as an acoustic duo, The Woods once again assembled an electric band to promote it, and, although at the height of their creativity, decided to separate. Gay moved into progressive ballad rock with Auto De Fe, and Terry temporarily revived the Woods Band before giving up music altogether. Some years later he emerged from retirement and joined the Pogues, where this enduring, rebellious musician continues to be influential.

●ALBUMS: *The Woods Band* (Greenwich 1970)★★★, *Backwoods* (Polydor 1975)★★★, *The Time Is Right* (Polydor 1976)★★★, *Renowned* (Polydor 1976)★★★, *Tenderhooks* (Rockburgh 1978)★★★.

WOOLLEY, SHEP

b. 15 October 1944, Birmingham, England. From an early age, Shep loved music, and played ukelele. His mother bought him a guitar in 1958 and he joined 15 others in a local skiffle group. In 1960, Woolley entered the Royal Navy, taking his guitar with him, and continued to play all over the world, at the same time organizing shows and groups. Woolley's first venture into a folk club came in 1969, when he was inspired by Bob Dylan and the songs of the American Depression. Writing his own songs, Shep found that he had a natural flair for humorous material, and jokes and monologues began to appear in his act. By 1973, he had essentially become a folk comedian, but he was also still a naval gunnery instructor, so, in 1975, Shep left the forces to concentrate on performing. In 1974, he appeared on *New Faces*, the television talent show. From 1975-85, Woolley presented the folk show on Radio Victory in Portsmouth, England. He has played all over the world and is regularly in demand for festivals. Woolley tends to play fewer folk clubs these days, concentrating on summer seasons and concerts. A naturally funny man, he deserves to become as widely known as others of the genre.

●ALBUMS: *Pipe Down* (Sweet Folk All 1972)★★★, *Songs Of Oars And Scrubbers And Other Dirty Habits* (Sweet Folk All 1973)★★★, *Goodbye Sailor* (Sweet Folk All 1976)★★, *First Take* (1980)★★, with various artists *Reunion* (1984)★★, *On The Button* (1986)★★, *Delivering The Goods* (1990)★★.

WORLD

Vocalist/guitarist/songwriter Neil Innes and bassist Dennis Cowan formed the World in 1970 upon the break-up of their former group, the Bonzo Dog Doo-Dah Band. Roger McKew (guitar) and Ian Wallace (drums) joined them in this short-lived act. *Lucky Planet*, although somewhat low-key, confirmed Innes's grasp of pop melody, but the group's potential did not have time to flourish. Cowan was concurrently involved in Viv Stanshall's solo recordings and in 1971 Innes opted to join McGuinness Flint, albeit briefly. Following this, and having completed outstanding Bonzo Dog Doo-Dah Band contractual obligations, he helped form Grimms before embarking on a solo career.

●ALBUMS: *Lucky Planet* (Liberty 1970)★★★.

WRIGHT, BETTY

b. 21 December 1953, Miami, Florida, USA. A former member of her family gospel group, the Echoes Of Joy, Wright's first recordings were as a backing singer. She later embarked on a solo career and enjoyed a minor hit with 'Girls Can't Do What The Guys Do' in 1968. 'Clean Up Woman' (1972), a US R&B number 2/pop number 6 hit, established a punchier, less passive style which later releases, 'Baby Sitter' (1972) and 'Let Me Be Your Lovemaker' (1973), consolidated. Although 'Shoorah Shoorah' and 'Where Is The Love?' reached the UK Top 30 in 1975, the singer was unable to sustain a wider success. Wright nonetheless continued recording into the 80s and has also forged a career as a US television talk show hostess.

● ALBUMS: *My First Time Around* (1968)★★★, *I Love The Way You Love* (Alston 1972)★★★, *Hard To Stop* (Atlantic 1973)★★★, *Danger: High Voltage* (Victor 1975)★★★, *Explosion* (RCA 1976)★★★, *This Time For Real* (Alston 1977)★★, *Betty Wright Live* (Alston 1978)★★★, *Betty Travellin' In The Wright Circle* (Alston 1979)★★, *Betty Wright* (Epic 1981)★★, *Wright Back At You* (Epic 1983)★★, *Sevens* (Fantasy 1987)★★, *Mother Wit* (Ms B 1988)★★, *4U2 Njoy* (Ms B 1989)★★.

● COMPILATIONS: *Golden Classics* (Collectables 1988)★★★, *Betty Wright Live* (1991)★★, *The Best Of ... The T.K. Years* (Sequel 1994)★★★★.

WRIGHT, GARY

b. 26 April 1945, New Jersey, USA. Wright attracted the attention of Island label owner Chris Blackwell when his rock group, the New York Times, supported Traffic on a 1967 tour of Scandinavia. An accomplished singer, composer and keyboard player, Wright was invited to join UK signing Art, whose career was bereft of direction. The revitalized unit, renamed Spooky Tooth, enjoyed considerable acclaim before Wright, who drew an increasing share of the spotlight, left for a solo career in 1970. Having contributed to sessions by George Harrison, Ringo Starr and Badfinger, the artist formed Wonderwheel around Jerry Donahue (guitar), Archie Legget (bass) and Bryson Graham (drums). Mick Jones, Legget's one-time colleague with French singer Johnny Hallyday, replaced Donahue prior to recording, but the ensuing releases failed to generate public interest. The group was disbanded in 1972 and while the bassist joined Kevin Ayers, the remaining trio became the core of a re-formed Spooky Tooth. Wright led the group for another two years before the name was finally put to rest. He resumed solo work with *The Dream Weaver*, a platinum-selling album which reached number 7 in the US chart, but this runaway success was not sustained. Despite an in-concert popularity, *Light Of Smiles* failed to reach the Top 20 while *Touch And Gone* and *Heading Home* missed the Top 100 altogether. *The Right Place* in 1981 was a much more satisfying and successful record

although Wright seemed to disappear for a while. He devoted the next few years to bringing up his children as a single parent. During this time of semi-retirement he worked on a number of film music scores including *Endangered Species* but received a bigger profile when 'Dream Weaver' was used to great effect in *Wayne's World*. He continues to record and has never ruled out the possibility of a Spooky Tooth reunion.

● ALBUMS: with Wonderwheel *Extraction* (A&M 1971)★★, *Footprint* (A&M 1972)★★, *Ring Of Changes* (A&M 1972)★★; Gary Wright solo *The Dream Weaver* (Warners 1975)★★★★, *The Light Of Smiles* (Warners 1977)★★, *Touch And Gone* (Warners 1977)★★, *Headin' Home* (Warners 1979)★★★, *The Right Place* (Warners 1981)★★, *Who Am I* (Cypress 1987)★★, *First Signs Of Life* (1995)★★.

● COMPILATIONS: *That Was Only Yesterday* (A&M 1976)★★★.

WURZELS

Originally Adge Cutler And The Wurzels, this English West Country group first scored a minor hit in 1967 with the comic 'Drink Up Thy Zider'. Following Cutler's tragic death in a car crash on 5 May 1974, Tommy Banner, Tony Baylis and Pete Budd soldiered on as the Wurzels. Producer Bob Barrett was impressed by their country yokel parodies of well-known hits and persuaded them to provide comic lyrics to Melanie's 'Brand New Key', which emerged as 'Combine Harvester', a surprise UK number 1 in the summer of 1976. The trio almost repeated that feat with their reworking of the continental hit 'Uno Paloma Blanca' retitled ' I Am A Cider Drinker'. Although they only achieved one more success with 'Farmer Bill's Cowman' (based on Whistling Jack Smith's 'I Was Kaiser Bill's Batman') they continued to appear occasionally on British television shows and maintain their popularity on the UK club circuit.

● ALBUMS: *Adge Cutler And The Wurzels* (Columbia 1967)★★, *Adge Cutler's Family Album* (Columbia 1967)★★, *Cutler Of The West* (Columbia 1968)★★, *The Wurzels Are Scrumptious* (One Up 1975)★★, *The Combine Harvester* (One Up 1976)★★, *Golden Delicious* (Note 1977)★★, *Give Me England* (Note 1977)★★, *I'll Never Get A Scrumpy Here* (Note 1978)★★, *I'm A Cider Drinker* (Encore 1979)★★.

● COMPILATIONS: *The Very Best Of Adge Cutler And The Wurzels* (EMI 1977)★★, *Greatest Hits* (Note 1979)★★, *Wurzels* (Ideal 1981)★★.

WYNETTE, TAMMY

b. Virginia Wynette Pugh, 5 May 1942, Itawamba County, near Tupelo, Mississippi, USA. Wynette is primarily known for two songs, 'Stand By Your Man' and 'D.I.V.O.R.C.E.', but her huge catalogue includes 20 US country number 1 hits, mostly about standing by your man or getting divorced. After her father died when she was 10 months old, she was raised by her mother and grandparents and she picked cotton from an early age. When 17 years old, she married construction worker, Euple Byrd, and trained as a hairdresser. She subsequently made an album with their third child, Tina - *George, Tammy And Tina* in 1975. Byrd did not share her ambition of being a country singer, so she left and moved to Nashville. She impressed producer Billy Sherrill and had her first success in 1966 with a Johnny Paycheck song, 'Apartment No. 9'. She almost topped the US country charts with 'I Don't Want To Play House', in which a child shuns his friends' game because he senses his parents' unhappiness. It was the template for numerous songs including 'Bedtime Story' in which Wynette attempts to explain divorce to a three-year-old and 'D.I.V.O.R.C.E.', in which she does not.

Her next marriage to guitarist Don Chapel disintegrated after he traded nude photographs of her and, after witnessing an argument, country star George Jones eloped with her. Not knowing the turmoil of her own life, American feminists in 1968 condemned Wynette for supporting her husband, right or wrong, in 'Stand By Your Man', but she maintains, 'Sherrill and I didn't have women's lib in mind. All we wanted to do was to write a pretty love song'. The way Wynette chokes on 'After all, he's just a man' indicates pity rather than than support. Having previously recorded a country chart-topper with David Houston ('My Elusive Dreams'), an artistic collaboration with George Jones was inevitable. Their albums scaled new heights in over-the-top romantic duets, particularly 'The Ceremony', which narrates the marriage vows set to music. In an effort to separate Jones from alcohol, she confiscated his car-keys, only to find him riding their electric lawn-mower to the nearest bar. 'The Bottle' was aimed at Jones as accurately as the real thing. 'Stand By Your Man' was used to good effect in *Five Easy Pieces* (which starred Jack Nicholson), and the record became a UK number 1 on its sixth reissue in 1975. It was followed by a UK Top 20 placing for 'D.I.V.O.R.C.E.', but it was Billy Connolly's cover-parody about his D.O.G. that went to the UK number 1 slot.

Wynette also had two best-selling compilations in the UK album charts. By now her marriage to Jones was over and 'Dear Daughters' explains the position to them. Jones, in more dramatic fashion, retaliated with 'The Battle'. Even more difficult to explain to her daughters was her 44-day marriage to estate agent, Michael Tomlin. After torrid affairs with Rudy Gatlin (of Larry Gatlin And The Gatlin Brothers) and Burt Reynolds (she saved the actor's life when he passed out in the bath), she married record producer George Richey, whose own stormy marriage had just ended. In 1978, she was kidnapped outside a Nashville car-park and was subjected to a brutal beating. She has also experienced many health problems including several stomach operations. Throughout the traumas, she continued to record songs about married life, 'That's The Way It Could Have Been', 'Til I Can Make It On My Own', '(You Make Me Want To Be) A Mother' and 'Love Doesn't Always Come (On The Night That It's Needed)'. None of these songs have found acceptance outside the country market, but 'Stand By Your Man' has become a standard with versions ranging from Loretta Lynn (who also took an opposing view in 'The Pill'), Billie Jo Spears and Tina Turner, to two male performers, David Allan Coe and Lyle Lovett.

Her autobiography was made into a television movie in 1981. In 1986, Wynette entered the Betty Ford clinic for drug dependency and, true to form, followed it with a single, 'Alive And Well'. She acted in a daytime soap, *Capital*, in 1987, although its drama was light relief when compared to her own life. Her stage show includes a lengthy walkabout to sing 'Stand By Your Man' to individual members of the audience. Her standing in the rock world increased when she was co-opted with the KLF on 'Justified And Ancient' which became a Top 3 UK hit in 1991. Her duet album, *Higher Ground*, is more imaginatively produced than her other recent albums and, although she undoubtedly has many more dramas to come, she says, 'All I really want to do is stay country and keep going 'til I'm older than Roy Acuff. Wynette's turbulent time with Jones has been well-documented, so much so that they were the most famous couple in the history of country music. The announcement that they were working together again came as a pleasant surprise to their many followers. Their previous reconciliation at the end of 1979 was an attempt to help Jones save his washed-up career. *One*, released in 1995, is felt by many to be the best of their career. The good feeling that is conveyed by tracks such as 'Solid As A Rock', is the result of their having chosen to sing together for purely musical reasons. There is no longer any emotional baggage, nor any resurrection needed - perhaps for the first time in their lives, they were motivated purely by the enjoyment of making music together.

●ALBUMS: *Your Good Girl's Gonna Go Bad* (Epic 1967)★★★, *Take Me To Your World* (Epic 1967)★★★, *D.I.V.O.R.C.E.* (Epic 1967)★★★★, *Stand By Your Man* (Epic 1968)★★★★, *Inspiration* (Epic 1969)★★★, *The Ways To Love A Man* (Epic 1969)★★★, *Run Angel Run* (1969)★★★, *Tammy's Touch* (Epic 1970)★★★, *The First Lady* (Epic 1970)★★★, *Christmas With Tammy Wynette* (Epic 1970)★★★, *We Sure Can Love Each Other* (Epic 1971)★★★, with George Jones *We Go Together* (Epic 1971)★★★, *Bedtime Story* (Epic 1972)★★★, with Jones *Me And The First Lady* (Epic 1972)★★★, *My Man* (Epic 1972)★★, with Jones *We Love To Sing About Jesus* (Epic 1972)★★, *Kids Say The Darndest Things* (Epic 1973)★★, with Jones *Let's Build A World Together* (Epic 1973)★★★, with Jones *We're Gonna Hold On* (Epic 1973)★★★, *Another Lonely Song* (Epic 1974)★★★, *Woman To Woman* (Epic 1974)★★, *George, Tammy And Tina* (Epic 1975)★★, *I Still Believe In Fairy Tales* (Epic 1975)★★★, *Til I Can*

Make It On My Own (Epic 1976)★★★, with Jones *Golden Ring* (Epic 1976)★★★, *You And Me* (Epic 1976)★★★, *Let's Get Together* (Epic 1977)★★, *One Of A Kind* (Epic 1977)★★★, *Womanhood* (Epic 1978)★★★, *Just Tammy* (Epic 1979)★★★, *Only Lonely Sometimes* (Epic 1980)★★★, with Jones *Together Again* (Epic 1980)★★★, *You Brought Me Back* (Epic 1981)★★★, *Good Love And Heartbreak* (Epic 1982)★★★, *Soft Touch* (Epic 1982)★★★, *Even The Strong Get Lonely* (Epic 1983)★★★, *Sometimes When We Touch* (Epic 1985)★★★, *Higher Ground* (Epic 1987)★★★, *Next To You* (Epic 1989)★★, *Heart Over Mind* (Epic 1990)★★★, with Dolly Parton, Loretta Lynn *Honky Tonk Angels* (1993)★★★, *Without Walls* (Epic 1994), with Jones *One* (MCA 1995)★★.
●COMPILATIONS: *Tammy's Greatest Hits* (Epic 1969)★★★★, *Tammy's Greatest Hits, Volume II* (Epic 1971)★★★★, *Tammy's Greatest Hits, Volume III* (Epic 1975)★★★, *Tammy's Greatest Hits, Volume IV* (Epic 1978)★★★, *Classic Collection* (Epic 1982)★★★, *Biggest Hits* (Epic 1983)★★★★, *Anniversary: 20 Years Of Hits* (Epic 1988)★★★★, *Tears Of Fire - The 25th Anniversary Collection* 3-CD set (Epic 1992)★★★, *Encore* (1993)★★★.
●VIDEOS: *Live In Nashville, Tammy Wynette In Concert* (1987), with George Jones, *Country Stars Live* (1990), *First Lady Of Country Music* (1991), *25th Anniversary Collection* (1991).
●FURTHER READING: *Stand By Your Man*, Tammy Wynette.

X

Formed in Los Angeles, California, USA, in 1977, X originally comprised Exene Cervenka (b. Christine Cervenka, 1 February 1956, Chicago, Illinois, USA; vocals), Billy Zoom (b. Tyson Kindale, Savannah, Illinois, USA; guitar), John Doe (b. John Nommensen, Decatur, Illinois, USA; bass) and Mick Basher (drums), although the last-named was quickly replaced by D.J. (Don) Bonebrake (b. North Hollywood, California, USA). The quartet made its debut with 'Adult Books'/'We're Desperate' (1978), and achieved a considerable live reputation for their imaginative blend of punk, rockabilly and blues. Major labels were initially wary of the group, but Slash, a leading independent, signed them in 1979. Former Doors' organist, Ray Manzarek, produced *Los Angeles* and *Wild Gift*, the latter of which established X as a major talent. Both the *New York Times* and the *Los Angeles Times* voted it Album Of The Year and such acclaim inspired a recording contract with Elektra Records. *Under The Big Black Sun* was another fine selection, although reception for *More Fun In The New World* was more muted, with several commentators deeming it 'over-commercial'. In the meantime X members were pursuing outside projects. *Adulterers Anonymous*, a poetry collection by Cervenka and Lydia Lunch, was published in 1982, while the singer joined Doe, Henry Rollins (Black Flag), Dave Alvin (the Blasters) and Jonny Ray Bartel in a part-time country outfit, the Knitters, releasing *Poor Little Critter On The Road* on the Slash label in 1985. Alvin replaced Billy Zoom following the release of *Ain't Love Grand* and X was subsequently augmented by ex-Lone Justice guitarist Tony Gilkyson. However, Alvin left for a solo career on the completion of *See How We Are*. Despite the release of *Live At The Whiskey A Go-Go*, X were clearly losing momentum and the group was dissolved. Doe and Cervenka have both since recorded as solo acts. They reunited in 1993 with a new recording contract for *Hey Zeus!*
●ALBUMS: *Los Angeles* (Slash 1980)★★★, *Wild Gift* (Slash 1981)★★★★, *The Decline...Of Western Civilization* soundtrack (Slash 1981)★★★, *Under The Big Black Sun* (Elektra 1982)★★★, *More Fun In The New World* (Elektra 1983)★★, *Ain't Love Grand* (Elektra 1985)★★★, *See How We Are* (Elektra 1987)★★, *Live At The Whiskey A Go-Go On The Fabulous Sunset Strip* (Elektra 1988)★★★, *Major League* soundtrack (Curb 1989)★★, *Hey Zeus!* (Big Life/Mercury 1993)★★, *Unclogged* (Infidelity 1995)★★.

Solo: John Doe *Meet John Doe* (DGC/Geffen 1990)★★★.
Exene Cervenka: with Wanda Coleman *Twin Sisters: Live At McCabe's* (Freeway 1985)★, *Old Wives' Tales* (Rhino 1989)★, *Running Scared* (RNA 1990)★.

X-RAY SPEX

One of the most inventive, original and genuinely exciting groups to appear during the punk era, X-Ray Spex were the brainchild of the colourful Poly Styrene (Marion Elliot), whose exotic clothes and tooth brace established her as an instant punk icon. With a line-up completed by Lora Logic, later replaced by Glyn Johns (saxophone), Jak Stafford (guitar), Paul Dean (bass) and B.P. Hurding (drums), the group began performing in 1977 and part of their second gig was captured for posterity on the seminal *Live At The Roxy WC2*. A series of extraordinary singles including 'Germ Free Adolescents', 'Oh Bondage Up Yours', 'The Day The World Turned Dayglo' and 'Identity' were not only riveting examples of high energy punk, but contained provocative, thoughtful lyrics berating the urban synthetic fashions of the 70s and urging individual expression. Always ambivalent about her pop-star status, Poly dismantled the group in 1979 and joined the Krishna Consciousness Movement. X-Ray Spex's final single, 'Highly Inflammable' was coupled with the pulsating 'Warrior In Woolworths', a parting reminder of Poly's early days as a shop assistant. Although she reactivated her recording career with the album *Translucence* (1980) and a 1986 EP *Gods And Goddesses*, no further commercial success was forthcoming. In 1996 the band reformed for the release of *Conscious Consumer*, with Elliot joined by founding members Lora Logic and Paul Dean.
●ALBUMS: *Germ Free Adolescents* (EMI 1978)★★★, *Conscious Consumer* (Receiver 1996)★★.

YABBY YOU

b. Vivian Jackson, Kingston, Jamaica, West Indies. Yabby acquired his nickname from the drawn out, chanting refrain on his 1972 debut single, 'Conquering Lion': 'Be You, Yabby Yabby You'. Despite courting controversy in his repudiation of Rastafarian godhead Haile Selassie, in favour of a personalized form of Christianity, his output throughout the 70s and early 80s has nonetheless rarely deviated far from the orthodox Rastafarianism typically expressed at the time. As leader of the Prophets (additional personnel at various times included Alrick Forbes, Dada Smith, Bobby Melody and the Ralph Brothers) Yabby recorded a remarkable series of roots reggae classics, including 'Jah Vengeance', 'Run Come Rally', 'Love Thy Neighbours', 'Valley Of Jehosaphat', 'Judgement On The Land', 'Fire In Kingston', 'Chant Down Babylon' and many others, mostly appearing on his own Vivian Jackson and Prophets labels in Jamaica. With the release of *Ramadam* in 1975, the UK variation of the Jamaican-issued *Conquering Lion* (some tracks were different), Yabby swiftly acquired cult status in the UK, his name synonymous with reggae music of a particularly deep, spiritual nature. He also gained a reputation as a producer of other artists, including DJs Trinity, Jah Stitch, Dillinger, Prince Pompado, Tapper Zukie and Clint Eastwood, and singers Wayne Wade, Junior Brown, Willie Williams, Patrick Andy, Tony Tuff, and Michael Prophet. In the 80s he retreated from the music business as his health deteriorated, though he made a comeback in the early 90s with some new productions and the reappearance of many of his classic singles and albums, re-pressed off the original stampers to cater for the large European collector's market.
●ALBUMS: *Conquering Lion/Ramadam* (Prophet 1975)★★★★, *Ram A Dam* (Eve 1976)★★★★, *King Tubby's Prophecy Of Dub* (Prophet 1976)★★★, *Deliver Me From My Enemies* (Prophet 1977)★★★, *Chant Down Babylon* (Ital 1978)★★★, *Beware Dub* (Grove Music 1978)★★★, *Jah Jah Way* (Island 1980)★★★, *One Love, One Heart* (Shanachie 1983)★★★, *Fleeing From The City* (Shanachie 1988)★★★.
●COMPILATIONS: *Yabby You Collection* (Greensleeves 1984)★★★.

YAMASH'TA, STOMU

b. Tsutomu Yamashita, 15 March 1947, Kyoto, Japan. A percussionist and composer, Yamash'ta attempted to combine *avant garde* and rock music in the 70s. He studied at the Kyoto Academy of Music, making his concert debut as a soloist at the age of 16. From 1964-69 he studied and performed in the USA with both classical and jazz musicians. During the 70s, such modern composers as Hans Werne Henze and Peter Maxwell Davies created works for him which were recorded in 1972 for L'Oiseau-Lyre. From 1973, Yamash'ta created what he called 'floating music', a fusion of classical, rock and Eastern styles with his own European group, Come To The Edge. Among his shows were Red Buddha Theatre and The Man From The East, which included elements of Japanese kabuki theatre and were highly praised by British and French critics. He recorded six albums for Island with collaborators Steve Winwood, Klaus Schulze, Gary Boyle and Murray Head. *Go Too* was released by *Arista* with Dennis Mackay producing. During the 80s, Yamash'ta returned to the classical concert halls but also recorded instrumental works for new age company Celestial Harmonies.

●ALBUMS: *Contemporary* (L'Oiseau 1972)★★★, *Red Buddha* (Egg 1972)★★★, *Come To The Edge* (Island 1973)★★★, *The Man From The East* (Island 1973)★★★, *Freedom Is Frightening* (Island 1974)★★★, *One By One* (Island 1974)★★★, *Raindog* (Island 1975)★★★, *Go* (Island 1976)★★★★, *Go Live From Paris* (Island 1976)★★★, *Go Too* (Arista 1977)★★★, *Sea And Sky* (Kuckuck 1987)★★★.

YELLOW DOG

This 70s act revolved around the talents of Kenny Young and Herbie Armstrong. American-born Young was already an established songwriter, having penned 'Under The Boardwalk' for the Drifters and 'Captain Of Your Ship' for Reparta And The Delrons. The latter proved highly popular in the UK, inspiring the composer to move his base to London where he met his future partner. Guitarist Armstrong was a former member of the Wheels, a Belfast group contemporaneous with Them, before founding a duo with bassist Rod Demick. The duo met up when they both joined Fox and enjoyed a period of UK chart success. On the break-up of Fox in 1977, Yellow Dog was formed and their self-titled album was issued in 1977. However, its brand of sweet pop clashed with the year's endemic punk explosion. Andy Roberts (guitar, ex-Liverpool Scene and Plainsong), Gary Taylor (bass, ex-Herd) and Gerry Conway (drums, ex-Fairport Convention) augmented the duo on this promising debut, which spawned a UK Top 10 single in 'Just One More Night'. A second album, in part completed with the assistance of Demick and keyboard player Peter Bardens, proved less successful and the group's name was dropped soon afterwards.

●ALBUMS: *Yellow Dog* (Virgin 1977)★★★, *Beware Of The Dog* (Virgin 1978)★★.

YES

During the progressive music boom of the early 70s, Yes were rivalled only by Emerson Lake And Palmer and Genesis for their brand of classical-laced rock which was initially refreshing and innovative. They evolved into a huge stadium attraction and enjoyed phenomenal success until the new wave came in 1977 and swept them aside. Yes were formed in 1968 by vocalist Jon Anderson (b. 25 October 1944, Accrington, Lancashire, England) and bassist Chris Squire (b. 4 March 1948, Wembley, London, England). Both had been experienced with 60s beat groups, notably the Warriors and the Syn, respectively. They were completed by Bill Bruford (b. 17 May 1948, London, England; drums), Pete Banks (b. 7 July 1947, Barnet, Hertfordshire, England) and Tony Kaye (b. 11 January 1946, Leicester, England). One of their early gigs was opening for Cream at their historic farewell concert at London's Royal Albert Hall, but it was pioneering disc jockey John Peel who gave them nationwide exposure, performing live on his BBC radio programme *Top Gear*. Their inventive versions of Buffalo Springfield's 'Everydays' and the Beatles' 'Every Little Thing' combined with their own admirable debut 'Sweetness', made them club favourites. Banks was replaced in 1970 by guitar virtuoso Steve Howe (b. 8 April 1947, London, England; ex-Tomorrow) who added further complexity to their highly creative instrumental passages. Neither their debut *Yes* nor *Time And A Word* made much of an impression beyond their growing following. Banks subsequently reunited with Kaye in Flash.

It was with *The Yes Album* that the band created major interest and sales. Kaye then departed and was replaced by the highly accomplished keyboard wizard, Rick Wakeman (b. 18 May 1949, London, England; ex-Strawbs). Wakeman's improvisational skill, like Howe's, took the band into realms of classical influence, and their solos became longer, although often they sounded self-indulgent. *Fragile* was a major success and the band found considerable support from the UK music press, especially *Melody Maker*. *Fragile* was a landmark in that it began a series of Roger Dean's Tolkien-inspired fantasy covers, integrated with his custom-calligraphed Yes colophon. The album spawned a surprise US hit single, 'Roundabout', which almost reached the Top 10 in 1972. Shortly afterwards Bruford departed and was replaced by ex-Plastic Ono Band drummer Alan White. Later that year Yes released *Close To The Edge*. Much of the four suites are instrumental, and allow the musicianship to dominate Anderson's often abstract lyrics. Squire's bass playing was formidable on this album, and he quickly became a regular winner of musicians' magazine polls. Now a major band, they confidently issued a triple live album *Yessongs*, followed by a double, *Tales From Topographic Oceans*. Both were huge successes, with the latter reaching number 1 in the UK.

Artistically, the band now started to decline; Wakeman

left to pursue a triumphant solo career. His replacement was ex-Refugee Patrick Moraz, who maintained the classical influence that Wakeman had instigated. Following *Relayer* the band fragmented to undertake solo projects, although none emulated Wakeman, who was having greater success than Yes at this time. When the band reconvened, Wakeman rejoined in place of Moraz, and continued a dual career. *Going For The One* was a less 'cosmic' album and moved the band back into the realms of rock music. Another hit single, 'Wonderous Stories', made the UK Top 10 in 1977, at the height of the punk era. Yes was the type of band that was an anathema to the new wave, and while their vast following bought *Tormato*, their credibility plummeted. Internal problems were also rife, resulting in the second departure of Wakeman, immediately followed by Anderson. Astonishingly, their replacements were Trevor Horn and Geoff Downes, who, as Buggles had topped the UK charts the previous year with 'Video Killed The Radio Star'. This bizarre marriage lasted a year before Yes finally said 'no' and broke up in 1981. All members enjoyed successful solo careers and it came as a surprise in 1983 to find a re-formed Yes topping the UK singles chart with the excellent Trevor Horn-produced 'Owner Of A Lonely Heart'. The subsequent *90125* showed a rejuvenated band with short contemporary dance/rock songs that fitted with 80s fashion. No new Yes output came until four years later with *Big Generator*, and in 1989 *Anderson, Bruford, Wakeman And Howe* was released during a lengthy legal dispute. Yes could not use the name, so instead they resorted to the Affirmative; Anderson, Howe etc. plays an 'Evening Of Yes Music' (cleverly using the famous logo). With the ownership problem solved, Yes announced a major tour in 1991, and were once again in the US Top 10 with *Union*. *Talk* was a sparkling album full of energy with two outstanding tracks, 'The Calling' and 'I Am Waiting', both destined to become part of their stage shows should they decide to perform regularly.

- ALBUMS: *Yes* (Atlantic 1969)★★★, *Time And A Word* (Atlantic 1970)★★★, *The Yes Album* (Atlantic 1971)★★★★, *Fragile* (Atlantic 1971)★★★★, *Close To The Edge* (Atlantic 1972)★★★★, *Yessongs* (Atlantic 1973)★★★, *Tales From The Topographic Oceans* (Atlantic 1973)★, *Relayer* (Atlantic 1974)★★, *Going For The One* (Atlantic 1977)★★, *Tormato* (Atlantic 1978)★★, *Drama* (Atlantic 1980)★, *Yesshows* (Atlantic 1980)★, *90125* (Atco 1983)★★★, *90125 Live-The Solos* (Atco 1986)★, *The Big Generator* (Atlantic 1987)★★, *Union* (Arista 1991)★★, *Talk* (Victory 1994)★★★, *Keys To Ascension* (BMG 1996)★★.
- COMPILATIONS: *Yesterdays* (Atlantic 1975)★★★, *Classic Yes* (Atlantic 1981)★★★.
- VIDEOS: *Anderson Bruford Wakeman Howe: An Evening Of Yes Music Plus* (1995).
- FURTHER READING: *Yes: The Authorized Biography*, Dan Hedges.

YETNIKOFF, WALTER

b. 11 August 1933, New York, USA. A legend in the music industry, Walter Yetnikoff made his reputation in the 70s and 80s as the high-flying, high-spending business courtier to artists including Billy Joel, Bruce Springsteen and Michael Jackson. His rise began in 1961 when he moved from entertainment law to become assistant to Clive Davis, the CBS Records general attorney. By 1972 he had become head of CBS International, then became president of the group in 1975. At this time he signed multi-million dollar agreements with James Taylor and the Beach Boys - who promptly refused to record for four years. By 1977 Yetnikoff's bizarre behaviour was the subject of regular gossip column inches, particularly his hard-drinking approach to artist negotiations, tactics about which several artists objected. Paul Simon, for one, departed to rivals Warner Brothers Records. However, by the end of the decade Yetnikoff had secured the signatures of both Paul McCartney and Michael Jackson. By 1983, with Jackson's *Thriller* a multi-million seller and artists including Culture Club and the Rolling Stones on board, the executive was able to boast of soaring company profits. This allowed him to re-negotiate his own contract, with an annual salary of nearly half a million by 1984. When Sony Records acquired CBS in 1987, Yetnikoff was rumoured to have received a bonus in the region of 20 million dollars, on the condition he took over as CEO of CBS Records. However, Yetnikoff remained a controversial figure - his public disagreement with Bruce Springsteen over the artist's sponsorship of Amnesty International notwithstanding. By the end of the decade he had become head of Sony's US film and record division, with responsibility for Columbia Pictures. However, his relationships with Springsteen, former executive Tommy Mottola and Michael Jackson all conspired to bring about his downfall from Sony at the beginning of the 90s. His severance pay was reputedly 25 million dollars. The rest of the 90s were taken up with the launch of Velvel Records - an umbrella organization promoting independent labels including Razor & Tie, Hybrid and Bottom Line Records, and the UK's Fire Records. Evidently, the music industry has not heard the last of Walter Yetnikoff.

YETTIES

The Yetties' original line-up comprised Bonny Sartin (b. Maurice John Sartin, 22 October 1943, near Sherborne, Dorset, England; percussion), Mac McCulloch (b. Malcolm McCulloch, 12 December 1945, London, England; guitar), Pete Shutler (b. Peter Cecil Shutler, 6 October 1945, Mudford, near Yeovil, Somerset, England; accordion/penny whistle/concertina/bowed psaltery) and Bob Common (b. 26 December 1940; vocals). The four eventually formed the Yetminster and Ryme Intrinseca Junior Folk Dance Display Team to play for dance evenings. Such was the problem with the name of the group, that one evening, for simplicity, they were introduced as the Yetties, and it stuck. They first performed in 1961 and shortly after this the group began Morris dancing with the Wessex Men, based in Yeovil, Somerset, and made their first appearance at the Sidmouth Folk Festival. The group also made subsequent regular appearances at the Yeovil Folk Dance club. They appeared on record in 1968, on an album recorded live at the Towersey Festival, along with other artists, but *Fifty Stones Of Loveliness* was their first proper release as a group. This was followed a year later by *Who's A-Fear'd*. On some of the early Yetties recordings, a fiddle player, Oscar Burridge played, though he was essentially part-time. The group appeared on a Cyril Tawney album in 1972, *Cyril Tawney In Port,* providing background music and vocals. Another 1972 release, *Bob Arnold, Mornin' All* featured the group providing background music and vocals for Bob Arnold. The same year, the group's version of *The Archers* theme tune, 'Barwick Green', was first used for the Sunday omnibus editions of the series on BBC radio. Bob Common left the group in 1979 and the Yetties continued as a trio.

Roger Trim (fiddle), had played in various duos and trios before joining the Yetties. He joined as a full-time member of the group in 1984, but departed in 1991, leaving the group to continue once more as a trio. In 1988 the group began its own project, *The Musical Heritage Of Thomas Hardy*, incorporating the Hardy family manuscripts, and at one time using Hardy's own violin in the work. Originally recorded in 1985 as an album, the project continues to be performed at festivals and concerts and on radio and television, and as a result, a 1988 release materialized. Despite having played worldwide, the Yetties have never lost the almost boyish enthusiasm that pervades their music, and still retain a loyal following.

●ALBUMS: *Fifty Stones Of Loveliness* (1969)★★★, *Who's A-Fear'd* (1970)★★★, *Keep A-Runnin'* (Argo 1970)★★★, *What The Yetties Did Next* (Argo 1971)★★★, *Our Friends* (Argo 1971)★★★, *Dorset Is Beautiful* (Argo 1972)★★★, *All At Sea* (Argo 1973)★★★, *Up In Arms* (Argo 1974)★★★, *The Yetties Of Yetminster* (Argo 1975)★★★, *The World Of The Yetties* (Argo 1975)★★★, *Let's Have A Party* (Argo 1975)★★★, *The Village Band* (Decca 1976)★★★, *Up Market* (Decca 1977)★★★, *Dorset Style* (Argo 1978)★★★, *Focus On The Yetties* (Argo 1978)★★★, *In Concert* (Decca 1979)★★★, *A Little Bit Of Dorset* (ASV 1981)★★★, *A Proper Job* (ASV 1981)★★★, *Roger Trim On The Fiddle* (1982)★★★, *Cider And Song* (1983)★★★, with John Arlott *The Sound Of Cricket* (1984)★★★, *The Banks Of Newfoundland* (1984)★★★, *Top Of The Crops* (1985)★★★, *The Yetties* (ASV 1986)★★★, *The Musical Heritage Of Thomas Hardy* (ASV 1988)★★★, *Rolling Home* (1991)★★★, *Looking For The Sunshine* (1992)★★★.

●COMPILATIONS: *Play It Again* (1989)★★★, *Singing All The Way* (ASV 1989)★★★.

YOUNG & CO

This funky sextet revolved around a nucleus of brothers Billy, Mike and Kenneth Young from West Virginia, USA. After moving to East Orange, New Jersey, in 1970 they formed the Young Movement with Buddy 'Hank' Hankerson, an ex-member of Aurra (bass/keyboards/guitar) and Dave Reyes (drums). The group changed their name to Flashflood in 1974 and recorded with Slave and Aurra. When vocalist and sole distaff member Jackie Thomas joined in 1979 they first recorded as Young & Co. Among the first three tracks they demoed was 'I Like What You're Doing', which helped secure a contract with Brunswick Records. When released, this single reputedly sold over 250,000 in the USA alone, yet never made the R&B or pop chart there. It did, however, reach the UK Top 20 in 1980 when picked up by the newly formed Excalibur label. The group later recorded for Sounds Of London and Atlantic Records but never tasted success again.

YOUNG, JESSE COLIN

b. Perry Miller, 11 November 1944, Manhattan, New York, USA. One of several optimistic performers frequenting the Greenwich Village folk circuit, Young was discovered in 1963 at the renowned Gerde's Folk City club. His debut *Soul Of A City Boy*, was recorded in one four-hour session, but despite its rudimentary quality, the collection showcased the singer's haunting tenor voice and compositional skills. A second set was equally enthralling, and featured excellent assistance from John Sebastian (harmonica) and Pete Childs (dobro). Its title, *Young Blood*, also provided a name for the rock group Young subsequently founded. The Youngbloods' career spanned six years but ended in 1972 when the members' interests became too diverse to remain in one ensemble. Jesse had already resumed his solo career with *Together*, a selection of new material and traditional songs, but his independence was more fully asserted on 1974's *Song For Juli*. The light, intimate style of these early releases was continued on subsequent recordings. Young rekindled memories of his erstwhile companions by re-recording two Youngbloods favourites, 'Sugar Babe' and 'Josianne', on his 1975 album, *Songbird*, but maintained a contemporary edge with two excellent selections, *American Dreams* and *Perfect Stranger*. The latter set included 'Fight For It', a notable duet with Carly Simon. Angered at what he perceived as mismanagement, Young later purchased the album's master tape for re-release on an independent label, and has since avoided recording for major companies.

●ALBUMS: *The Soul Of A City Boy* (Capitol 1964)★★, *Young Blood* (Mercury 1965)★★, *Together* (Raccoon 1972)★★, *Song For Juli* (Warners 1973)★★, *Lightshine* (Warners 1974)★★, *Songbird* (Warners 1975)★★, *On The Road* (Warners 1976)★★, *Love On The Wing* (Warners 1977)★★, *American Dreams* (Elektra 1978)★★, *Perfect*

Stranger (Elektra 1982)★★, *The Highway Is For Heroes* (Cypress 1988)★★.
●COMPILATIONS: *The Best Of Jesse Colin Young: The Solo Years* (Rhino 1991)★★★.

YOUNG, JOHN PAUL

b. 21 June 1950, Glasgow, Scotland. After fronting early 70s Sydney band, Elm Tree, former sheet metal worker Young spent the next two years in the Australian version of the stage show *Jesus Christ Superstar*. He had a hit with Vanda And Young's 'Pasadena' in 1972. Two unsuccessful singles followed and then he teamed up with Vanda And Young again in 1975 for 'Yesterday's Hero' which started a run of eight Australian Top 20 singles and two Top 20 albums, mostly songs written by Vanda And Young. Some of Young's singles also charted in Europe and South Africa, where he performed a number of times. He formed a touring band called the All Stars. The name was appropriate as members included Kevin Borich, Ray Goodwin (ex-Dragon), Johnny Dick and Warren Morgan (ex-Aztecs), Ian Winter (ex-Daddy Cool), Phil Manning, Tony Mitchell (ex-Sherbet), Ray Arnott (ex-Dingoes) and Vince Maloney (ex-Bee Gees). A happy-go-lucky artist, Young was seen to be somewhat apathetic about furthering his career. A last album recorded on a German label IC with new writers and producers ended his career, but Young retired gracefully and now works as a disc jockey.
●ALBUMS: *Hero* (1975)★★★, *JPY* (Midsong International 1976)★★★, *Green* (1977)★★, *Love Is In The Air* (Scotti Bros 1978)★★, *Heaven Sent* (1979)★★, *The Singer* (1981)★★, *One Foot In Front* (IC 1983)★★.
●COMPILATIONS: *All The Best* (1977)★★★, *1974-1979* (1979)★★★.

YOUNG, KENNY

Young first drew attention in New York's song publishing fraternity as the co-author of 'Under The Boardwalk', a 1964 hit for the Drifters, later popularized by the Rolling Stones. His next major success was 'Captain Of Your Ship', recorded in 1968 by Reparata And The Delrons. Although unsuccessful in the USA, the song reached number 13 in the UK. In keeping with several contemporaries, including Carole King and Chip Taylor, Young subsequently began a recording career, but his engaging singer-songwriter releases were commercially unsuccessful. He moved to London during the 70s and later formed a partnership with Herbie Armstrong. The pair formed Fox, who scored a Top 5 hit with 'Only You Can' (1975), and Yellow Dog, which reached number 8 with 'Just One More Night' (1978). However, Young's unashamedly commercial style later fell from favour and he later withdrew from performing.
●ALBUMS: *Clever Dogs Chase The Sun* (Warners 1972)★★★, *Last Stage For Silverwood* (Warners 197 3)★★★.

YOUNG, NEIL

b. 12 November 1945, Toronto, Canada. Having moved to Winnepeg as a child, Young began his enigmatic career as a member of several high school bands, including the Jades and Classics. He later joined the Squires, whose indebtedness to the UK instramental group the Shadows was captured on the Young composition 'Aurora'/'The Sultan'. In 1965 he embarked on a folk-based musical direction with appearances in Toronto's bohemian Yorkville enclave. A demonstration tape from this era contains early versions of 'Sugar Mountain', a paean to lost childhood later placed on 10 different single releases, and 'Don't Pity Me', revived a decade later as 'Don't Cry No Tears'. Young then joined the Mynah Birds, a pop-soul attraction which also featured Rick James, but this act folded prematurely upon the latter's arrest for draft evasion. Group bassist Bruce Palmer accompanied Young on a subsequent move to California where they teamed with Stephen Stills and Richie Furay to form the Buffalo Springfield. The now legendary tale results in Young and Palmer driving through a main street in LA in Young's distinctive black hearse. While halted at the traffic lights they were espied by Stephen Stills and Richie Furay, who knew there was only one person owning such a wagon. A joyous meeting took place and the rest is part of musical history. Young's tenure in this seminal 'west coast' act was tempered by several 'sabbaticals', but two luxurious, atmospheric compositions, 'Broken Arrow' and 'Expecting To Fly', recorded by the Springfield, established the highly sculptured orchestral-tinged sound prevalent on his debut solo record *Neil Young*. Although originally blighted by a selfless mix that buried the artist's vocals, the album contained several excellent compositions, notably 'The Loner', 'The Old Laughing Lady', 'I've Been Waiting For You' and 'Here We Are In The Years'. The set also featured two highly effective instrumentals, Young's evocative 'Emperor Of Wyoming' and 'String Quartet From Whiskey Boot Hill', a sublime arrangement and composition by Jack Nitzsche. The closing track, 'The Last Trip To Tulsa', was unique in Young's canon, an overlong surreal narrative whose performance betrayed the strong influence of Bob Dylan. Following his first album, Young was joined by Danny Whitten (guitar), Billy Talbot (bass) and Ralph Molina (drums) - three former members of the Rockets - in a new backing group dubbed Crazy Horse.

The now classic *Everybody Knows This Is Nowhere* captured a performer liberated from a previous self-consciousness with the extended 'Down By The River' and 'Cowgirl In The Sand' allowing space for his stutteringly simple, yet enthralling, guitar style. While the epic guitar pieces dominated the set, there were other highlights including the zestful 'Cinnamon Girl' and the haunting 'Running Dry', a mournful requiem featuring Bobby Notkoff on violin. The album underlined the intense relationship between Young and Crazy Horse. An attendant tour confirmed the strength of this new-found partnership, while Young also secured acclaim as a member of Crosby, Stills, Nash And Young. His relationship with Crazy Horse soured as Whitten grew increasingly dependent on heroin and the group was dropped following the recording of *After The Goldrush*. The set provided a commercial breakthough and included several of Young's best-known compositions, including the haunting title track, 'Only Love Can Break Your Heart', a US Top 40 hit, and the fiery 'Southern Man'. The highly commercial *Harvest* confirmed this newfound ascendancy and spawned a US chart-topper in 'Heart Of Gold' and remains his best-selling album. This commercial peak ended abruptly with *Journey Through The Past*, a highly indulgent soundtrack to a rarely screened autobiographical film. A disastrous tour with new backing group the Stray Gators exacerbated the gap between the artist and his potential audience, although *Time Fades Away*, a collection of new songs culled from the concerts, reclaimed the ragged feistiness of the Crazy Horse era. The set included the passionate 'Last Dance' and the superb 'Don't Be Denied', an unflinching autobiographical account of Young's early life in Canada.

The deaths of Whitten and road crew member Bruce Berry inspired the harrowing *Tonight's The Night*, on which Young's bare-nerved emotions were expounded over his bleakest songs to date. 'I'm singing this borrowed tune, I took from the Rolling Stones, alone in this empty room, too wasted to write my own', he intoned in world-weary fashion on 'Borrowed Tune', while in-concert Young offered multiple versions of the grief-stricken title song. This is now referred to as Young's dark period. However, the final set was rejected by the record company in favour of *On The Beach*, released to coincide with a Crosby, Stills, Nash And Young reunion tour. The work was initially greeted coolly and *Rolling Stone* described it as one of the 'most despairing albums of the decade'. This was a severe misinterpretation since *On The Beach* was actually a therapeutic work, enacting Young's shift to a more positive state of mind. In common with John Lennon's Plastic Ono Band, *On The Beach* saw Young stripping away his personality in a series of intense songs. The undoubted highlight of the set was the closing 'Ambulance Blues', arguably one of the most accomplished works of Young's career. In analyzing his place in the rock music world, Young offered a sardonic riposte to his detractors: 'So all you critics sit alone/You're no better than me for what you've shown/With your stomach pump and your hook and ladder dreams/We could get together for some scenes'. *On The Beach* was a consummate album and a crucial turning point in Young's career. The belatedly issued *Tonight's The Night* was no longer a shock, but testified to Young's absolute conviction. The album sold poorly but was retrospectively acclaimed as one of the bravest and most moving albums of the decade.

Young next chose to team up Crazy Horse again - Talbot, Molina and new guitarist Frank Stampedro - for *Zuma*. The set's highlight was provided by a guitar strewn 'Cortez The Killer' but, despite often ecstatic reviews, the overall performance was generally stronger than the material it supported. Another gripping recording, 'Like A Hurricane', was the pivotal feature of *American Stars 'N' Bars*, an otherwise piecemeal collection drawn from extant masters and newer, country-orientated recordings. The latter direction was maintained on *Comes A Time*, Young's most accessible set since *Harvest*, on which female vocalist Nicolette Larson acted as foil. The album's use of acoustic settings enhanced Young's pastoral intentions and the singer was moved to include a rare cover version; Ian Tyson's folk standard 'Four Strong Winds'. Characteristically, Young chose to follow up this by rejoining Crazy Horse for *Rust Never Sleeps*. The album rightly stands as one of Young's greatest and most consistent works. The acoustic 'My My, Hey Hey (Out Of The Blue)' and its electric counterpart 'Hey Hey, My My (Into The Black)' explained the central theme of the work - the transience of rock stardom. 'The Thrasher', one of Young's most complex and rewarding songs, reiterated the motif. 'Ride My Llama', 'Pocahontas' and 'Powderfinger' were all worthy additions to Young's classic catalogue. The album was preceded by a Young film of the same name and followed by a double live album.

During the 80s the artist became increasingly unpredictable as each new release denied the musical directions offered by its predecessor. Young clearly thrives on this unpredictability. The understated and under-rated *Hawks And Doves* was followed by excursions through electric R&B (*Re-Ac-Tor*), electro-techno-pop (*Trans*) and rockabilly (*Everybody's Rockin'*), before embracing ol' timey country (*Old Ways*), hard rock (*Landing On Water*) and R&B (*This Note's For You*). The last-named achieved notoriety when a video for the title song, which attacked the intertwining of rock with corporate sponsorship, was banned by MTV. The R&B experiment using brass (Neil And The Blue Notes) also saw Young regain some critical acclaim. Young's next project was culled from an aborted release, tentatively entitled *Times Square*. *Eldorado* invoked the raw abandonment of *Tonight's The Night*, but the five-song set was only issued in Japan and Australia. Three of its songs were latterly placed on *Freedom*, an artistic and commercial triumph which garnered positive reviews and assuaged those viewing its creator as merely eccentric. The set was generally acclaimed as Young's finest work in a decade and included some of his most intriguing lyrics, most notably the lengthy 'Crime In The City', itself an extract from an even longer piece, 'Sixty To Zero'. Young affirmed this regeneration with *Ragged Glory*, a collaboration with Crazy Horse marked by blistering guitar lines, snarled lyrics and a sense of urgency and excitement few from Neil's generation could hope to muster. Contemporary new wave band Sonic Youth supported the revitalized partnership on the US *Spook The Horse* tour, cementing Young's affection for pioneers.

An ensuing in-concert set, *Weld* (accompanied by an album of feedback experimentation, *Arc*), was rightly applauded as another milestone in Young's often contrary oeuvre. Following this, Young informed the media that he was making a return to *Harvest*-type-album, and the result was, for many, another one of his best albums. *Harvest Moon* captured the essence of what is now rightly seen as a great 70s album (*Harvest*) and yet it sounded perfect for the 90s. 'From Hank To Hendrix' and the title track are but two of a collection of Young songs destined to become classics. As if this were not enough, less than a year later he produced *Unplugged*, which was a confident live set recorded for MTV. *Sleeps With Angels* mixed some of his dirtiest guitar with some frail and winsome offerings. His ability to contrast is extraordinary: 'Piece of Crap' finds Young in punkish and vitriolic form, whilst the gentle 'My Heart' would not be out of place in a school church hall. In similar mood was his ethereal 'Philadelphia', perfectly suited for the film *Philadelphia*, for which it was composed.

A collaboration with Pearl Jam produced a good album in 1995, and once again this man thrilled, excited, baffled and amazed us; *Mirror Ball* is a gripping rock album which brought him many new (younger) fans. *Dead Man* was a challenging and rambling soundtrack of 'guitar', and neither a commercial or listenable excursion. *Broken Arrow* received a less than positive reception from the critics, although many fans saw little difference in quality, except for the ramshackle bar-room version of 'Baby What You Want Me To Do'. *Year Of The Horse* was yet another live album, tolerated by his fans but leaving an appetite for some new material. Even with a less than perfect discography, at the time of writing his artistic standing remains at an all-time high. However, he retains the right to surprise, infuriate, and even baffle, while his reluctance to court easy popularity must be applauded. More than any other artist working in the rock field over the past 20 or so years, Young is the greatest chameleon. His many admirers never know what to expect, but the reaction whenever a new project or direction arrives is almost universally favourable from all quarters. He transcends generations and stays hip and in touch with laconic ease, indifference and incredible style. In appraising 'grunge', let it be said that it was Young who first wore check workshirts outside torn jeans, and played blistering distorted guitar (with Crazy Horse). And he did it all more than 25 years ago.

●ALBUMS: *Neil Young* (Reprise 1969)★★★★, *Everybody Knows This Is Nowhere* (Reprise 1969)★★★★★, *After The Goldrush* (Reprise 1970)★★★★, *Harvest* (Reprise 1972)★★★, *Journey Through The Past* (Reprise 1972)★, *Time Fades Away* (Reprise 1973)★★★, *On The Beach* (Reprise 1974)★★★★★, *Tonight's The Night* (Reprise 1975)★★★★, *Zuma* (Reprise 1975)★★★★, *American* *Stars 'N' Bars* (Reprise 1977)★★, *Comes A Time* (Reprise 1978)★★★, *Rust Never Sleeps* (Reprise 1979)★★★★★, *Live Rust* (Reprise 1979)★★★, *Hawks And Doves* (Reprise 1980)★★★, *Re-Ac-Tor* (Reprise 1981)★★★, *Trans* (Geffen 1983)★★★, *Everybody's Rockin'* (Geffen 1983)★★, *Old Ways* (Geffen 1985)★★★, *Landing On Water* (Geffen 1986)★, *Life* (Geffen 1987)★★, *This Note's For You* (Reprise 1988)★★★★, *Eldorado* mini-album (Reprise 1989)★★★, *Freedom* (Reprise 1989)★★★★, *Ragged Glory* (Reprise 1990)★★★, *Weld* (Reprise 1991)★★★, *Arc/Weld* (Reprise 1991)★★, *Harvest Moon* (Reprise 1992)★★★, *Unplugged* (Reprise 1993)★★★, *Sleeps With Angels* (Reprise 1994)★★★★, *Mirror Ball* (Reprise 1995)★★★, *Dead Man* soundtrack (Vapor 1996)★★, *Broken Arrow* (Reprise/Vapour 1996)★★, *The Year Of The Horse* (Reprise 1997)★★★.

●COMPILATIONS: *Decade* (Reprise 1977)★★★★, *Greatest Hits* (Reprise 1985)★★, *Lucky Thirteen* (Geffen 1992)★★★.

●VIDEOS: *Neil Young & Crazy Horse: Rust Never Sleeps* (1984), *Berlin* (1988), *Freedom* (1990), *Weld* (Warners 1991), *Unplugged* (1993), *The Complex Sessions* (1994), *Human Highway* (Warners 1995).

●FURTHER READING: *Neil Young*, Carole Dufrechou. *Neil Young: The Definitive Story Of His Musical Career*, Johnny Rogan. *Neil And Me*, Scott Young. *Neil Young: Een Portret*, Herman Verbeke and Lucien van Diggelen. *Neil Young: Complete Illustrated Bootleg Discography*, Bruno Fisson and Alan Jenkins. *Aurora: The Story Of Neil Young And The Squires*, John Einarson. *Don't Be Denied: The Canadian Years*, John Einarson. *The Visual Documentary*, John Robertson. *His Life And Music*, Michael Heatley. *A Dreamer Of Pictures: Neil Young - The Man And His Music*, David Downing. *Neil Young And Broken Arrow: On A Journey Through The Past*, Alan Jenkins. *Neil Young: The Rolling Stone Files*, Holly George-Warren, (ed.), *Ghosts On The Road: Neil Young In Concert*, Pete Long.

●FILMS: *Journey Through The Past* (1973), *Human Highway* (1982).

Z

ZAP POW

Zap Pow were formed in the early 70s. The group consisted of some of the finest musicians in Jamaica and included Max Edwards (drums/vocals), Mike Williams (bass/vocals), Dwight Pinkney (guitar/vocals), Beres Hammond (lead vocals), Glen DaCosta (tenor saxophone), Joe McCormack (trombone) and David Madden (trumpet/vocals). In 1971 they recorded their debut, 'Mystic Mood', followed by the popular 'Breaking Down The Barriers', 'Nice Nice Time' and the internationally successful 'This Is Reggae Music'. An album released only in Jamaica that featured the hits assured their local popularity. In 1976 the group recorded at Harry J.'s and Dynamic studios, 'Jungle Beat' and 'Sweet Loving Love'. The release of *Zap Pow Now* featured unusual packaging, as the outer sleeve resembled a book of matches. The album secured healthy sales within the reggae market and topped the UK chart. The success inspired Trojan Records to re-release their debut with the addition of 'Money', 'Crazy Woman', 'Wild Honey' and a version of Harold Melvin And The Bluenotes' 'If You Don't Know Me By Now'. The label released the latter as a single which was a minor hit. By 1980 Hammond left the group to pursue a successful solo career. Pinkney's guitar skills were utilized in numerous sessions including Roots Radics and at Penthouse Studios for producer Donovan Germain. Edwards pursued a solo career, almost crossing over into pop territory with the release of 'Rockers Arena'. Williams became known as Mikey Zap Pow and enjoyed a hit with 'Sunshine People' and pursued a career in journalism specializing in reggae. The horn section was featured on many sessions including Bob Marley And The Wailers. They also toured individually supporting Sly And Robbie's Taxi Gang and Lloyd Parkes' We The People Band. Madden released a solo album, *David ... Going Bananas*, which featured both his vocals and trumpet playing on tracks including 'Musical Message' and a return to 'Mystic Mood'. The album was followed with *The Reggae Trumpetaa*, while fellow horn player DaCosta released *Mind Blowing Melody*.
●ALBUMS: *Zap Pow Now* (Vulcan 1976)★★★, *Revolution* (Trojan 1976)★★★.

ZAPPA, FRANK

b. Frank Vincent Zappa, 21 December 1940, Baltimore, Maryland, USA, d. 4 December 1993, Los Angeles, California, USA. Zappa's parents were second-generation Sicilian Greeks; his father played 'strolling crooner' guitar. At the age of 12 Frank became interested in drums, learning orchestral percussion at summer school in Monterey. By 1956 he was playing drums in a local R&B band called the Ramblers. Early exposure to a record of *Ionisation* by *avant garde* classical composer Edgard Varese instilled an interest in advanced rhythmic experimentation that never left him. The electric guitar also became a fascination, and he began collecting R&B records that featured guitar solos: Howlin' Wolf with Hubert Sumlin, Muddy Waters, Johnny 'Guitar' Watson and Clarence 'Gatemouth' Brown were special favourites. A school-friend, Don Van Vliet (later to become Captain Beefheart), shared his interest. In 1964 Zappa joined a local R&B outfit, the Soul Giants (Roy Collins; vocals, Roy Estrada; bass, Jimmy Carl Black; drums), and started writing songs for them. They changed their name to the Mothers ('Of Invention' was added at record company insistence). Produced by Tom Wilson in 1966 - the late black producer whose credits included Cecil Taylor, John Coltrane and Bob Dylan - *Freak Out!* was a stunning debut, a two-record set complete with a whole side of wild percussion, a vitriolic protest song, 'Trouble Every Day', and the kind of minute detail (sleevenotes, in-jokes, parodies) that generate instant cult appeal. They made great play of their hair and ugliness, becoming the perfect counter-cultural icon. Unlike the east coast band the Fugs, the Mothers were also musically skilled, a refined instrument for Zappa's eclectic and imaginative ideas. Tours and releases followed, including *We're Only In It For The Money*, (with its brilliant parody of the *Sgt Pepper* record cover) a scathing satire on hippiedom and the reactions to it in the USA, and a notable appearance at the Royal Albert Hall in London (documented in the compulsive *Uncle Meat*). *Cruising With Ruben & The Jets* was an excellent homage to the doo-wop era. British fans were particularly impressed with *Hot Rats*, a record that ditched the sociological commentary for barnstorming jazz-rock, blistering guitar solos, the extravagant 'Peaches En Regalia' and a cameo appearance by Captain Beefheart on 'Willie The Pimp'. The original band broke up (subsequently to resurface as the Grandmothers). Both the previous two albums appeared on Zappa's own Bizarre record label and together with his other outlet Straight Records he released a number of highly regarded albums (although commercial flops), including those by the GTO's, Larry Wild Man Fischer, Alice Cooper, Tim Buckley and the indispensible Zappa-produced classic *Trout Mask Replica* by Captain Beefheart.

Eager to gain a 'heavier' image than the band that had brought them fame, the Turtles' singers Flo And Eddie joined up with Zappa for the film *200 Motels* and three further albums. *Fillmore East June '71* included some intentionally outrageous subject matter prompting inevitable criticism from conservative observers. 1971 was not a happy year: on 4 December fire destroyed the band's equipment while they were playing at Montreux (an event commemorated in Deep Purple's 'Smoke On The Water') and soon afterwards Zappa was pushed off-stage at London's Rainbow theatre, crushing his larynx (lowering his voice a third), damaging his spine and keeping him wheelchair-bound for the best part of a year. He spent 1972 developing an extraordinary new species of big band fusion (*Waka/Jawaka* and *The Grand Wazoo*), working with top west coast session musicians. However, he found these excellent players dull touring companions, and decided to dump the 'jazztette' for an electric band. 1973's *Overnite Sensation* announced fusion-chops, salacious lyrics and driving rhythms. The live band featured an extraordinary combination of jazz-based swing and a rich, sonorous rock that probably only Zappa (with his interest in modern classical music) could achieve. Percussion virtuoso Ruth Underwood, violinist Jean-Luc Ponty, featured in the *King Kong* project, and keyboardist George Duke shone in this context. *Apostrophe (')* showcased Zappa's talents as a story-teller in the Lord Buckley tradition, and also (in the title track) featured a jam with bassist Jack Bruce: it reached number 10 in the *Billboard* chart in June 1974. *Roxy & Elsewhere* caught the band live, negotiating diabolically hard musical notation - 'Echidna's Arf' and 'The Bebop Tango' - with infectious good humour. *One Size Fits All*, an under-acknowledged masterpiece, built up extraordinary multi-tracked textures. 'Andy' was a song about b-movie cowboys, while 'Florentine Pogen' and 'Inca Roads' were complex extended pieces.

In 1975 Captain Beefheart joined Zappa for a tour and despite an earlier rift, sang on *Bongo Fury*, both re-uniting in disgust over the USA's bicentennial complacency. *Zoot Allures* in 1976 was principally a collaboration between Zappa and drummer Terry Bozzio, with Zappa over-dubbing most of the instruments himself. He was experimenting with what he termed 'xenochronicity' (combining unrelated tracks to create a piece of non-synchronous music) and produced intriguing results on 'Friendly Little Finger'. The title track took the concept of sleaze guitar onto a new level (as did the orgasmic moaning of 'The Torture Never Stops'), while 'Black Napkins' was an incomparable vehicle for guitar. If *Zoot Allures* now reads like a response to punk, Zappa was not to forsake large-scale rock showbiz. A series of concerts in New York at Halloween in 1976 had a wildly excited crowd applauding tales of singles bars, devil encounters and stunning Brecker Brothers virtuosity (recorded as *Live In New York*). This album was part of the fall-out from Zappa's break-up with Warner Brothers Records, who put out three excellent instrumental albums with 'non-authorized covers' (adopted, strangely enough, by Zappa for his CD re-releases): *Studio Tan*, *Sleep Dirt* and *Orchestral Favourites*. The punk-obsessed rock press did not know what to make of music that parodied Miklos Rosza, crossed jazz with cartoon scores, guyed rock 'n'

roll hysteria and stretched fusion into the 21st century. Undaunted by still being perceived as a hippie, which he clearly was not (*We're Only In It For The Money* had said the last word on the Summer Of Love while it was happening!), Zappa continued to tour.

His guitar-playing seemed to expand into a new dimension: 'Yo' Mama' on *Sheik Yerbouti* (1979) was a taste of the extravaganzas to come. In Ike Willis, Zappa found a vocalist who understood his required combination of emotional detachment and intimacy, and featured him extensively on *Joe's Garage*. After the mid-70s interest in philosophical concepts and band in-jokes, the music became more political. *Tinseltown Rebellion* and *You Are What You Is* commented on the growth of the fundamentalist Right.

In 1982 Zappa had a hit with 'Valley Girl', with his daughter Moon Unit satirizing the accents of young moneyed Hollywood people. That same year saw him produce and introduce a New York concert of music by Edgar Varese. *Ship Arriving Too Late To Save A Drowning Witch* had a title track which indicated that Zappa's interest in extended composition was not waning; this was confirmed by the release of a serious orchestral album in 1983. In 1984 he was quite outrageously prolific: he unearthed an 18th century composer named Francesco Zappa and recorded his work on a synclavier; he released a rock album *Them Or Us*, which widened still further the impact of his scurrilously inventive guitar; and renowned French composer Pierre Boulez conducted Zappa's work on *The Perfect Stranger*. Two releases, *Shut Up 'N Play Yer Guitar* and *Guitar* proved that Zappa's guitar playing was unique; *Jazz From Hell* presented wordless compositions for synclavier that drew inspiration from Conlon Nancarrow; *Thing-Fish* was a 'Broadway musical' about Aids, homophobia and racism. The next big project materialized in 1988: a 12-piece band playing covers, instrumentals and a brace of new political songs (collected respectively as *The Best Band You Never Heard In Your Life*, *Make A Jazz Noise Here* and *Broadway The Hard Way*). They rehearsed for three months and the power and precision of the band were breathtaking, but they broke up during their first tour. As well as the retrospective series *You Can't Do That On Stage Anymore*, Zappa released eight of his most popular bootlegs in a 'beat the boots' campaign. In Czechoslovakia, where he had long been a hero of the cultural underground, he was appointed their Cultural Liaison Officer with the West and in 1991 he announced he would be standing as an independent candidate in the 1992 US presidential election (almost immediately he received several death threats!). The man never ceased to astonish, both as a musician and composer: on the way he produced a towering body of work that is probably rock music's closest equivalent to the legacy of Duke Ellington. In November 1991 his daughter confirmed reports that Zappa was suffering from cancer of the prostate and in May 1993 Zappa, clearly weak from intensive chemotherapy, announced that he was fast losing the battle as it had spread into his bones. He lost the fight against the disease seven months later.

In 1995 a remarkable reissue programme was undertaken by Rykodisk in conjunction with Gail Zappa. The entire catalogue of over 50 albums were remastered, repackaged and released with loving care. Ryko deserve the highest praise for this bold move. Zappa's career in perspective shows a musical perfectionist using only the highest standards of musicianship and the finest recording quality. The reissued CD's highlight the both the extraordinary quality of the original master tapes and his idealism.

Frank Zappa's often brilliant combination of irreverent humour and 'serious' music', has and will, continue to baffle many. This musical bisexuality has made him misunderstood and hard to market. Why does somebody who has the gift of satire and comedy waste his time composing orchestral pieces? Why does a highly literate composer and outstanding musician choose to trivialise his work with pornographic humour? Because he is Frank Zappa. At some stage in the future FZ will be widely recognized as a musical genius and one of the greatest contributors to music of the 20th century.

●ALBUMS: *Freak Out!* (Verve 1966)★★★★, *Absolutely Free* (Verve 1967)★★★★, *We're Only In It For The Money* (Verve 1967)★★★★, *Lumpy Gravy* (Verve 1967)★★★, *Crusing With Ruben & The Jets* (Verve 1968)★★★, *Uncle Meat* (Bizarre 1969)★★★★, *Hot Rats* (Bizarre 1969)★★★★, *Burnt Weeny Sandwich* (Bizarre 1969)★★★, with Jean-Luc Ponty *King Kong* (1970)★★, *Weasels Ripped My Flesh* (Bizarre 1970)★★★★, *Chunga's Revenge* (Bizarre 1970)★★★★, *Live At The Fillmore East June '71* (Bizarre 1971)★★★, *200 Motels* (United Artists 1971)★★ *Just Another Band From LA* (Bizarre 1972)★★★, *Waka/Jawaka* (Bizarre 1972)★★★, *The Grand Wazoo* (Bizarre 1972)★★★, *Overnite Sensation* (DiscReet 1973)★★★, *Apostrophe (')* (DiscReet 1974)★★★★, *Roxy & Elsewhere* (DiscReet 1974)★★★, *One Size Fits All* (DiscReet 1975)★★★, *Bongo Fury* (DiscReet 1975)★★★, *Zoot Allures* (DiscReet 1976)★★★, *Zappa In New York* (DiscReet 1977)★★★, *Studio Tan* (DiscReet 1978)★★★, *Sleep Dirt* (DiscReet 1979)★★, *Orchestral Favourites* (DiscReet 1979)★★★, *Sheik Yerbouti* (Zappa 1979)★★★, *Joe's Garage Act 1* (Zappa 1980)★★★★, *Joe's Garage Acts 2 & 3* (Zappa 1980)★★★, *Tinseltown Rebellion* (Barking Pumpkin 1981)★★★, *You Are What You Is* (Barking Pumpkin 1981)★★★, *Ship Arriving Too Late To Save A Drowning Witch* (Barking Pumpkin 1982)★★★, *Baby Snakes* (Barking Pumpkin 1982)★★★, *Man From Utopia* (Barking Pumpkin 1983)★★★, *London Symphony Orchestra Vol I* (Barking Pumpkin 1983)★★★★, *Francesco Zappa* (Barking Pumpkin 1984)★★★, *Does Humor Belong In Music?* (EMI 1984)★★★, *Them Or Us* (EMI 1984)★★★, *The Perfect Stranger* (EMI 1984)★★★, *Shut Up 'N Play Yer Guitar* (Rykodisc 1984)★★★★, *Guitar* (Rykodisc 1984)★★★★, *Jazz From Hell* (Rykodisc 1984)★★★★, *Thing-Fish* (Rykodisc 1984)★★★★, *Meets The Mothers Of Prevention* (Rykodisc 1985)★★★, *London Symphony Orchestra Vol II* (Rykodisc 1987)★★★, *Broadway The Hard Way* (Rykodisc 1988)★★★, *The Best Band You Never Heard In Your Life* (Barking Pumpkin 1991)★★★★, *Make A Jazz Noise Here* (Barking Pumpkin 1991)★★★. Beating The Bootleggers: (all released 'officially' in 1991) *'Tis The Season To Be Jelly* (Foo-Eee 1967)★★★, *The Ark* (Foo-Eee 1968)★★★, *Freaks And Motherfuckers* (Foo-Eee 1970)★★★, *Piquantique* (Foo-Eee 1973)★★★, *Unmitigated Audacity* (Foo-Eee 1974)★★★, *Saarbrucken 1978* (Foo-Eee 1978)★★★, *Any Way The Wind Blows* (Foo-Eee 1979)★★★, *As An Am Zappa* (Foo-Eee 1981)★★★. With the Ensemble Modern *Yellow Shark* (Barking Pumpkin 1993)★★★, *Civilization Phaze III* (Barking Pumpkin 1995)★★★, *The Lost Episodes* (Ryko 1996)★★★, *Läther* (Rykodisc 1996)★★★★.

●COMPILATIONS: *Mothermania* (Verve 1969)★★★, *Rare Meat* (Ryko 1962-63)★★★, *You Can't Do That On Stage Any More Vol 1* (Ryko 1969-88)★★★★, *You Can't Do That On Stage Any More Vol 2* (Ryko 1974)★★★★, *You Can't Do That On Stage Any More Vol 3* (Ryko 1971-88)★★★★, *You Can't Do That On Stage Any More Vol 4* (Ryko 1969-88)★★★★, *You Can't Do That On Stage Any More Vol 5* (Ryko 1992)★★★★, *You Can't Do That On Stage Any More Vol 6* (Ryko 1992)★★★★, *Strictly Commercial: The Best Of* (Ryko 1995)★★★, *Have I Offended Someone?* (Ryko 1997)★★★. The entire catalogue is currently available on Ryko.

●VIDEOS: *Does Humor Belong In Music?* (1985), *200 Motels* (1988), *The True Story Of 200 Motels* (1992), *The Amazing Mr. Bickford* (1992), *Uncle Meat* (1993).

●FURTHER READING: *Frank Zappa, Plastic People Songbuch*, Carl Weissner. *Frank Zappa: Over Het Begin En Het Einde Van De Progressieve Popmuziek*, Rolf-Ulrich Kaiser. *No Commercial Potential: The Saga Of Frank Zappa: Then And Now*, David Walley. *Frank Zappa Et Les Mothers Of Invention*, Alain Dister. *The Lives & Times Of Zappa And The Mothers*, no editor listed. *Get Zapped: Zappalog The First Step To Zappology*, Norbert Obermanns. *Zappalog: The First Step Of Zappalogy (2nd Edition)*, Norbert Obermanns. *Viva Zappa*, Dominique Chevalier. *The Real Frank Zappa Book*, Frank Zappa, with Peter Occhiogrosso. *Frank Zappa: A Visual Documentary*, Miles (ed.). *Frank Zappa In His Own Words*, Miles. *Mother! The Frank Zappa Story*, Michael Gray. *Frank Zappa: The Negative Dialectics Of Poodle Play*, Ben Watson. *Electric Don Quixote*, Neil Slaven. *Electric Don Quixote: The Story Of Frank Zappa*, Neil Slaven.

●FILMS: *Head* (1968).

ZEVON, WARREN

b. 24 January 1947, Chicago, USA. After moving to the west coast, where he sought work as a songwriter in the mid-60s, Zevon wrote songs for the Turtles and Nino Tempo And April Stevens. He recorded several singles for the Turtles' label White Whale, including a version of Bob Dylan's 'If You Gotta Go', as Lyme And Cybelle. By the late 60s, he was signed to Imperial and recorded an inauspicious debut, *Zevon: Wanted Dead Or Alive*, produced by Kim Fowley. One track from the album, 'She Quit Me', was featured in the movie *Midnight Cowboy*. When the album failed to sell, Zevon took a job on the road as musical director to the Everly Brothers. He subsequently appeared uncredited on their album *Stories We Could Tell* and also guested on Phil Everly's three solo albums. By the early 70s, Zevon was signed as a songwriter by entrepreneur David Geffen, and finally released his long-awaited second album in 1976. *Warren Zevon* was a highly accomplished work, which revealed its creator's songwriting power to an exceptional degree. Produced by Jackson Browne, the work featured the cream of LA's session musicians and included guest appearances from Lindsey Buckingham, Stevie Nicks and Bonnie Raitt. The material ranged from the piano-accompanied 'Frank And Jesse James' to the self-mocking singalong 'Poor Poor Pitiful Me', the bittersweet 'Carmelita' and the majestic sweep of 'Desperados Under The Eaves' with superb harmonies arranged by Carl Wilson. Linda Ronstadt's cover of 'Hasten Down The Wind' also brought Zevon to the attention of a wider audience.

The follow-up *Excitable Boy* was released two years later and revealed another astonishing leap in Zevon's musical development. The production was confident and accomplished and the range of material even more fascinating. Zevon tackled American politics and history on 'Roland The Thompson Gunner' and 'Veracruz', wrote one of his finest and most devastating love songs in 'Accidentally Like A Martyr' and employed his satiric thrust to the heart on 'Excitable Boy' and 'Werewolves Of London'. A superb trilogy of Zevon albums was completed with *Bad Luck Streak In Dancing School* which was most notable for its inventive use of orchestration. Again, it was the sheer diversity of material and mood that impressed. The classical overtones of the title track, 'Interlude No. 2' and 'Wild Age' were complemented by Zevon's biting satire which was by now unmatched by any American artist, bar Randy Newman. 'Gorilla You're A Desperado' was a humorous attack on LA consumerism, while 'Play It All Night Long' was an anti-romantic portrait of rural life that contrasted markedly with the prevailing idyllic country rock mentality. Zevon's vision was permeated with images of incest and disease: 'Daddy's doing sister Sally/Grandma's dying of cancer now/The cattle all have brucellosis/We'll get through somehow'.

Zevon's ability to attract the interest and respect of his songwriting contemporaries was once more emphasized by the presence of Bruce Springsteen, with whom he co-wrote 'Jeannie Needs A Shooter'. Although Zevon seemed likely to establish himself as one of the prominent singer-songwriters of the 80s, personal problems would soon undo his progress. A promising live album was followed by the much neglected *The Envoy*. This concept album sold poorly and was the last major work from Zevon for five years. During the interim, he became an alcoholic and underwent counselling and therapy. He returned in 1987 with *Sentimental Hygiene*, a welcome return to top form, which featured a new array of guest stars including Neil Young, Michael Stipe and Peter Buck (from R.E.M.), Bob Dylan, Don Henley (formerly of the Eagles), Jennifer Warnes and Brian Setzer (ex-Stray Cats). Zevon also formed a band with Peter Buck, Mike Mills and Bill Berry under the name Hindu Love Gods, and issued an album in 1990 entitled *Hindu Love Gods*. Zevon's power was not lost among the star credits and shone through on a powerful set of songs, several of which brutally detailed his fight back from alcoholism. Never self-pitying, Zevon could afford a satiric glimpse at his own situation in 'Detox Mansion': 'Well it's tough to be somebody/And it's hard to fall apart/Up here on Rehab Mountain/We gonna learn these things by heart'. Zevon promoted the album extensively and has since built upon his reputation with the finely produced *Transverse City* and well-received *Mr Bad Example*. Those in any doubt should seek out the excellent anthology released in 1996 by Rhino Records.

●ALBUMS: *Zevon: Wanted Dead Or Alive* (Imperial 1969)★★, *Warren Zevon* (Asylum 1976)★★★★, *Excitable Boy* (Asylum 1978)★★★, *Bad Luck Streak In Dancing School* (Asylum 1980)★★★, *Stand In The Fire* (Asylum 1980)★★★★, *The Envoy* (Asylum 1982)★★★, *Sentimental Hygiene* (Virgin 1987)★★★★, *Transverse City* (Virgin 1989)★★★, *Mr Bad Example* (Giant 1991)★★★, *Learning To Flinch* (Giant 1993)★★★★, *Mutineer* (Giant 1995)★★★.

●COMPILATIONS: *A Quiet Normal Life - The Best Of Warren Zevon* (Asylum 1986)★★★, *I'll Sleep When I'm Dead (An Anthology)* (Rhino 1996)★★★★.

INDEX